D0924800

# The Liar, The Witch,
# & The Wormhole

### Book Four in The Crisanta Knight Series

# GEANNA CULBERTSON

BQB

Virginia

Published in the United States by BQB Publishing
(an imprint of Boutique of Quality Books Publishing Company, Inc.)
www.bqbpublishing.com

978-1-945448-10-2 (p)
978-1-945448-11-9 (e)

Library of Congress Control Number: 2018934014

Book design by Robin Krauss, www.bookformatters.com
Cover concept by Geanna Culbertson
Cover design by Ellis Dixon, www.ellisdixon.com

First editor: Pearlie Tan
Second editor: Olivia Swenson

## Books in The Crisanta Knight Series

*Crisanta Knight: Protagonist Bound*
Book One

*Crisanta Knight: The Severance Game*
Book Two

*Crisanta Knight: Inherent Fate*
Book Three

*Crisanta Knight: The Liar, The Witch, & The Wormhole*
Book Four

*Crisanta Knight: To Death & Back*
Book Five (2019)

# Dedication

This book, like everything I shall ever accomplish, is dedicated to my mom and dad. You are my heroes, my coaches, and my best friends. I am thankful for you every day for more reasons than there are words in this book.

# Special Thanks

### Terri Leidich & BQB Publishing

We're halfway there, Terri! We started this journey together in 2015 and I can't believe how far we've come. I appreciate you and all that you do for me. Here's to another three epic years!

### Pearlie Tan

This was a big book. I don't have to tell you that. What I do feel I have to tell you is that you helped me turn this book into something extraordinary. I look forward to you pushing me to be the best writer I can be for the next four books ahead!

### Olivia Swenson

Thank you for keeping me sharp and helping Book Four be the best that it can be. You make me a better writer, and for that I am truly grateful!

### Alexa Carter

Because you're awesome.

### Kathie Bennett, Susan Zurenda, & Magic Time Literary Agency

For helping me get to the next level and believing in me so fiercely.

*I also want to thank my awesome brother/advisor Gallien Culbertson, Ian Culbertson, Ellis Dixon, the Fine Family, Girls on the Run Los Angeles, and everyone else out there who has supported me on this journey thus far!*

# Bonus Dedication

Since this is going to be an eight-book series, each book will include a bonus dedication to individuals who have significantly impacted my life or this series in some way.

I want to dedicate this fourth book to a friend I have lost. Anyone who has ever had a dog knows that the love between you and your furry companion is pure and wonderful. Anyone who has ever lost a pet knows there is a hole left in your heart when they are gone. Gennie Marie Culbertson was the world's greatest Labrador and a good friend. She was an angel, a weirdo, and a loveable jerk. She definitely made an impact on my life and this series. In the dark hours before dawn, she would sleep by my side as I worked on these books. She kept me company and was a warm, sweet presence that filled my mornings with light, even when the world outside was dark and cold. Not a morning goes by that I don't look over my shoulder and wish she were there. Not a day will go by that my family and I will not remember her and smile about how hilarious and awesome she was.

# PROLOGUE

Potential. Identity. Future.

In the past, I believed these things were out of my control. Nowadays I wake with contentment and calm at the truth; I define all three for myself.

This was an understanding that was as treasured as it had been hard won.

For as long as anyone can remember, the Author has held the highest power in our land, the magical realm of Book. She selected which citizens were protagonists. If you were picked as a protagonist you attended one of the two private schools in our realm—Lady Agnue's School for Princesses & Other Female Protagonists or Lord Channing's School for Princes & Other Young Heroes—to train for the lead role in your future fairytale. If you were not selected you lived your life as a common character—a member of the ensemble class designed to form the masses that make the exceptional few stand out.

You knew you were chosen as a protagonist if the Author created a protagonist book with your name on it (i.e., *Cinderella*, *Hansel & Gretel*, and so forth). Typically, these books would begin blank and the Author would later fill in the pages with the stories of her main characters. While these stories differed, one thing every protagonist book had in common was the eventual emergence of a prologue prophecy that laid out the basis of each main character's destiny.

Main characters often waited years for their prophecies to be written. All royal children were supposed to have protagonist books, so as the daughter of Cinderella I always expected to receive one. In the twilight of my sixteenth year, it finally appeared. This triggered a series of events that would lead my friends and me on a collision course with the higher powers of our realm and to worlds beyond our imagination.

I hated my prophecy the instant I heard it. It prescribed a destiny where I would become the subservient wife of the annoying —though admittedly handsome—Prince Chance Darling. My best friend Blue (younger sister of Little Red Riding Hood) loathed the prophecy she'd been given too. Hers unfavorably tied her to our good friend Jason Sharp (the younger brother of Jack from *Jack & the Beanstalk*). Meanwhile, our best friend SJ (daughter of Snow White) hadn't received her prophecy yet, but she longed to prevent the Author from turning her fate into something unsavory as well.

Across the forest that separated our schools, our friends who attended Lord Channing's, the aforementioned Jason and his new roommate Daniel, had also received their prophecies. While Blue, SJ, and I may not have known the details, the boys were equally adamant about taking back their lives and challenging the Author for control of their fates. Hence our great plan to run away from school to find the Author and have her rewrite our destinies.

*Sigh.* How quickly great plans go out the window when you find out everything you know is a lie and people start trying to kill you.

After a long and arduous journey, we found the Author and learned that she didn't actually control our fates. She was a former Fairy Godmother called Liza who was enchanted to live forever under the thumb of our realm's Godmother Supreme, her older sister, Lena Lenore. Because of an illness she suffered from called Pure Magic Disease, Liza had the rare ability to see the future. Lena Lenore and the twenty-six ambassadors of our realm took advantage of this ability, using it to control the population by dividing it into commons and protagonists.

This revelation was only the tip of the iceberg. Along the way to finding the Author, my friends and I uncovered a much darker story arc in the works. The antagonists of our realm—who were mostly confined to their own barred-off kingdom called Alderon— were planning to overthrow Book and kill all its protagonists.

There were several important factors they needed to take care of on their road to achieving this goal and, lo and behold, one of them was me. As it turned out, the prophecy I'd been shown regarding Chance Darling was a fake planted by the antagonists to keep me from learning the truth. And that truth was that Liza had foreseen me as the game changer in the antagonists' plans. I was meant to either be the key force responsible for stopping them or helping them succeed.

Thanks to this prophecy the antagonists had hunted me like an animal throughout our Author quest. It was some nasty business, and I was certain that I would have died many times if it weren't for the bravery and strength of my friends, as well as my own combative skill and cunning.

I had always been looked down on at Lady Agnue's for my fighting talent and feistiness. After all, princesses were supposed to be damsels who mastered grace, beauty, and traditional feminine charm, not kicking, punching, and weapons training. But I was grateful I'd never succumbed to the princess stereotype. It had saved me more than once. And even if it hadn't, I was proud of the person I'd chosen to be in this life, and I was going to work hard to become an even better version of this hero-princess as time went on.

Unfortunately, if I was to survive the trials ahead, I had much less time than I'd like.

During the course of our antagonist dealings, my friends and I learned that the villains had other targets. Their main priority was a former Fairy Godmother named Paige Tomkins who had gone missing many years ago.

We didn't know why the antagonists wanted her, but we knew she was pivotal to their plan and was hiding in one of the Wonderlands—a collection of magical worlds that included Book and many other enchanted realms like Oz, Cloud Nine, and Neverland. More importantly, we knew that we had to find her before our enemies did.

Since becoming entangled in the antagonists' plans, Blue, SJ, Daniel, Jason, and I had accepted our roles as the few people who not only knew about the evil brewing in our realm, but who also had the ability to stop it. As such, we were going to do everything in our power to track down Paige Tomkins. Which brings us to the here and now.

After our Author quest, my friends and I returned to the safety of our schools for a much-needed intermission from the larger-than-life story arcs and homicidal characters pursuing us. Winter break provided the perfect time to catch up on missed assignments and get a bit of rest—but more notably it marked the beginning of our Wonderlands research.

Based on what we'd learned at school, information gleaned from a White Rabbit named Harry during our last mission, and a few conversations with Liza, we'd concluded that there were at least nine Wonderlands, including Book. Maps of other Wonderlands simply did not exist, and if we were going to have any chance at finding Paige Tomkins—and not get killed traversing these magical, unknown settings in the process—we needed to be prepared. Accordingly, our current mission was to map out the realms on our own.

Regrettably, the type of information we needed about the Wonderlands was stored in the restricted sections of our schools' libraries, making regular access tricky. However, over the last few weeks we'd managed just fine because most of the students at Lady Agnue's and Lord Channing's had gone home for winter break.

I didn't mind staying at school during vacation. Our research was vital, but more than that I was comfortable here. Aside from the close relationship I had with my older brother Alex, my castle in Midveil could be as rigid and cold as the very glass it was made from. Between what I'd just gone through last semester and the many responsibilities weighing on my shoulders, I absolutely did not want to spend my time off in a place that made me feel like an ant under a microscope.

Even though I'd always been a black sheep at school, Lady Agnue's was the place where I felt most at home because it was the place where my friends were. While we were not connected by blood, our many years together at Lady Agnue's and Lord

Channing's—as well as our recent adventures—had bonded us into our own version of family.

Alas, that sense of family and home were about to be disrupted once more.

While things like schoolwork and winter break may have been normal for other students, they were no longer normal for us. Our normal was antagonists trying to capture us, monsters and magic hunters trying to kill us, and quests that tested our hearts, minds, and resolve. That normalcy was about to resume without warning, and most certainly without mercy.

# CHAPTER I

# Fun with Friends & People Trying to Kill You

lue, SJ, and I were locked in a tower.

We weren't in mortal peril or anything. We were simply serving our punishment for having ditched school for a few weeks last semester to find the Author.

Upon our return, our headmistress Lady Agnue had sentenced the three of us to detention every day after school for basically an eternity. At an institution for princesses and other female protagonists, that meant spending several hours each day locked in one of the campus's tallest towers, *à la* Rapunzel.

Spring semester had begun this past week, which meant so had our punishment. The first couple of days were rough. With nothing but stone walls and a dead rat in the corner of the room, the situation looked pretty bleak . . . until I came up with a solution.

"Crisa, I realize anything is preferable to being trapped in this tower," SJ said with a sigh. "But I still do not feel comfortable with you using your magic for this. For one, you have only been training your powers for a few weeks. And two, what if someone should catch us?"

"You worry too much, SJ," Blue said as she confidently strode to stand beside me at the window. She popped the hood of her trusty powder-blue cloak, as if posing a challenge to SJ.

"I have to compensate for the both of you," SJ replied, crossing her arms. "Neither of you worry enough, so it falls to me to balance out the ratio."

Blue's intense blue eyes sparkled mischievously. "Sorry SJ, all I heard was blah blah blah, unnecessary panic, blah blah, anxiety attack, blah blah, Debbie Downer."

SJ furrowed her eyebrows in annoyance. I smirked slightly, but directed most of my attention to the vines that grew outside the window of our tower.

One little discovery my friends and I had made during our Author quest was that I had magic. When I was very young, my mother's Fairy Godmother, Emma (who was also my regular godmother), had gifted me with her magic wand. It was useless without a Fairy Godmother to operate it, as wands did not hold power; they merely conducted it. But she had enchanted it with the ability to transform into any weapon I willed it into. The only catch was that she also had to implant a spark of her magic into me because wands only responded to the magic of their designated Godmothers.

I smiled as gold sparks danced around my fingertips. When Emma gave me the magic to operate my wand she could never have anticipated that it would manifest into an ability that was so powerful and so cool.

*Come to life*, I mentally commanded the vines as I touched the green stems. *Then take us down.*

The gold sparks changed into an aura of energy that transferred from me into the vines. As the energy moved through them, they began to writhe against the stone walls of the tower.

Emma's spark of magic had manifested into the ability of life, meaning that I could bring anything to life, and whatever I poured my power into was bound by my bidding.

Since discovering this, I'd been training my magic and learning to harness it more actively and with more control. Enchanting these vines was just one example of the incredible things I was realizing I was capable of. It was good practice. In this particular case, it was also a convenient way for Blue, SJ, and me to escape our prison sentence.

Blue loved the idea. SJ had some misgivings. I understood both perspectives and paid no mind to their bickering. This kind of good-natured ribbing was normal for them. It would be normal in any circumstance for two girls who were such opposites.

Blue—my adventurous, mischievous, dear friend—liked to act on instinct and impulse. Fear rarely affected her and she loved a good fight. SJ—my equally dear, perfectly poised, levelheaded friend—preferred to act on logic and reason. Kindness came out of her as easily as breathing, and she was one of the most reliable people you would ever meet.

Aside from these conflicting personality traits, there were also major differences in where the girls came from. Blue was formerly a common character known only as the younger sister of Little Red Riding Hood. When her protagonist book appeared in early adolescence she was designated as a common female protagonist. Since then she'd dedicated herself to becoming a hero, despite our realm's traditional gender roles for female main characters that dictated she couldn't. Over the years, Blue had proven herself to be incomparably strong. She was the most masterful fighter at Lady Agnue's and could definitely give most heroes at Lord Channing's a run for their money with her trusty hunting knife.

SJ, on the other hand, was a princess like me. She'd known since birth that she was headed for protagonist school because all royals were supposed to be main characters. Unlike me, however, SJ had always embodied her traditional princess role perfectly. Top of our class at Lady Agnue's, she was the epitome of grace and beauty, a master at communicating with animals through song, and the ideal model for what a conventional fairytale princess should be.

In short, my friends were different. And as a main character who wanted to be both a hero and a princess, and a girl who valued strength and instinct as much as she valued kindness and logic, my role in our group was as the bridge between their often-opposing perspectives.

The vines I'd enchanted began to crawl inside the tower, slowly wrapping themselves around my waist, and then SJ's and Blue's. SJ made a sour face and her gray eyes narrowed with disapproval. The vines securely lifted us off the ground and took us through the window.

The fresh evening air engulfed me. There was still daylight left, but the sky was tinted with the pink of dusk. We had ninety minutes to make it to our rendezvous and get back before the school guards came to unlock the tower and set us free.

"I still say this is too risky," SJ continued even as the plants lowered us several hundred feet to the ground.

"That's what makes it fun," Blue countered. "Crisa knows what she's doing." Blue tilted her head toward me, dark blonde waves spilling out of her hood. "You know what you're doing, right?"

I glanced at the golden light still emanating from my hand. I may have been new to the whole magic thing, but I never felt more powerful and in control than when I was utilizing it.

"Absolutely," I said.

A minute later we touched down on the grass near the practice fields. This was a large area at the back of the campus with various obstacle courses, a track, stables that connected to the barn, and expansive fields used for horse races, archery practice, and various other combat training purposes. The practice fields had always been Blue's and my favorite place at Lady Agnue's. At the moment it was also the most deserted part of school, as all other students were inside getting ready for dinner.

Quickly but cautiously, my friends and I journeyed to the barn. The guards didn't begin their patrol of the practice fields until seven o'clock, but we still wanted to be careful. I grabbed the heavy handle of the barn door and yanked it slightly, allowing it to open a few inches. I peeked my head inside and glanced around.

All the lanterns were illuminated inside and bales of hay formed labyrinth-like walls that cut across the barn. "Guys?" I whispered. A figure stepped into the light and I smiled.

"It's about time you got here," Daniel said. His long, broad-shouldered shadow spilled across the floor as he approached us. I opened the barn door enough to let SJ and Blue through, then followed them in.

Daniel and Jason had gotten used to keeping hidden at our school. It wasn't hard for them; heroes at Lord Channing's were pros at stealth. I think they even offered a class in the subject.

Since we'd discovered a way to break out of the detention tower a few days ago, they'd been meeting us in the barn in the late aftenoons.

Jason was particularly well versed in sneaking onto our campus. Both boys had done it a few times prior to winter break. But Jason had continued the practice almost every day during vacation to meet up with us. Daniel hadn't; he was the only one in our group who had gone home for the three-week break. Still, even without the extra practice, Daniel was naturally suited to the shadows. He'd always reminded me of a lone wolf in that way—a brooding, withdrawn, and dangerous creature who watched from a distance. Until he met us, anyway.

He had changed a bit since then. While he still gave off an intimidating aura, he'd been a lot less withdrawn lately. I guess that was because he was no longer alone. Now he had a pack. Now he had us.

"Where's Jason?" Blue asked, noticing our other friend wasn't with him.

"He's getting the horses saddled up," Daniel responded, nodding toward the stables, which could be accessed on the other side of the barn.

"I'll go help him," I said as I closed and latched the barn door behind us.

"Nah, you did it yesterday. I'll go," Blue replied. "SJ, you wanna come?"

SJ glanced at Daniel and me then at Blue, weighing her options. "All right, but I do not know how much help I will be."

My friends disappeared around the haystacks. Daniel drew his gleaming sword from its sheath. "So I believe the score is three to two?"

I drew my wandpin from where I kept it clipped to my bra strap. The sparkly silver object may have looked like a hair accessory, but it was really my wand in disguise. I could transform it into this state by concentrating on the word *Lapellium*. And I could change it back into a wand with the word *Lapellius*, as I did now. The weapon elongated into my wand and then into my weapon of choice as I focused on that next.

*Spear.*

"You better enjoy that lead while it lasts," I told Daniel as he and I began to walk across the barn. "I'm not going to show you any mercy today."

"I'm not sure you falling on your butt after I sweep you off your feet qualifies as mercy," Daniel commented. "Comedy maybe. But not mercy."

I shot Daniel an annoyed look. His oak-colored eyes, which set off his dark brown hair, danced with mischief. He knew I could never refuse a challenge.

Putting it mildly, Daniel and I had a complex relationship. I'd disliked him when we'd first met and had spent a lot of time distrusting him in the months that followed. However, over the course of our mission to find the Author, we'd become friends.

I was glad for this. We fought well together and pushed each other to be sharper in everything from wit to weaponry. Nevertheless, there was an unspoken awkwardness between us over how close we really were and how close we actually wanted to be.

The breaking point that shifted our relationship last semester was when we were trapped in a genie lamp and had to be completely honest and vulnerable with each other. That event had resulted in us coming to know one another on a deeply personal level. Much as it made me cringe to admit, it had led to Daniel getting to know me better than anyone.

SJ, Blue, Jason, my parents, my two brothers—they were all close to me. But even with the people I was closest to, I tended to avoid talking about my deepest fears and insecurities if I could help it. Not Daniel though; I had no secrets from him. Not anymore.

I wasn't sure if this was a relief or a problem. While it was nice to know there was someone out there who knew my vulnerabilities, it also made me feel uncomfortable. I imagined Daniel felt the same way about me knowing his deepest secrets. But we both seemed to be content not addressing it for now, masking the depth of our relationship with casual banter and a mostly friendly rivalry. Speaking of which . . .

I jolted my spear left to block Daniel's sword then flipped it right to stop a second strike. Daniel's elbow shot up. I hinged and barely avoided getting smacked in the face. I swept my spear down and tried to catch his feet, but he leapt over the blow. Rapidly, I rotated to clash my staff against his sword as it headed toward my face. I stopped it inches from my nose.

He and I squared off, locked in the clash. My boots slipped slightly on the dark blue sparring mat that we'd laid down for our combat practice in the barn. My arms started to quiver under his strength, which I both admired and resented.

"Knight, if you're gonna have any shot at making the Twenty-Three Skidd team, you're going to have to up your strength training," Daniel provoked. "If you don't, the guys you're up against will tear you to shreds."

I broke our clash and leapt out of his range.

Twenty-Three Skidd was the most popular sport in our realm. It was a cross between lacrosse and jousting and was played on flying Pegasi over a large arena. I'd always been a big fan, but never had the chance to play because it was a boys-only sport. However, during a school field trip last semester, Blue and I had entered a Lord Channing's tournament in disguise and totally owned it. In the immediate aftermath of the event, most of our classmates had shunned us for it. But while we were away on our Author quest, many of the common protagonists at Lady Agnue's who were inspired by our defiance had petitioned for their right to participate in the sport alongside the boys. Eventually our schools reached a compromise. When Lord Channing's held tryouts for the open spots on its Twenty-Three Skidd teams this semester, the opportunity would be open to both male and female students.

Excited by the prospect, my friends and I had been concentrating on preparing ourselves for the tryouts. Ever the lady, SJ had no interest in the violent sport. But Blue and I had every intention of making one of the teams and knew perfectly well this would require a lot of training, especially since there were only eight available spots.

Jason and Daniel were helping us with the endeavor. Jason

was captain of one of the Twenty-Three Skidd teams. Daniel was also trying out, but he had gotten plenty of practice in with the guys at Lord Channing's. The two boys made excellent coaches. Unfortunately, whereas Jason was always supportive and encouraging, Daniel had a more direct approach that seemed unconcerned with insulting me.

He gave me a cocky, relaxed look as he beckoned me forward again. I spun my spear in my hand and accepted the invitation. We engaged each other relentlessly—his strikes and parries timed perfectly with mine. He rotated low and his sword came at my ankles. I jumped and landed on a bale of hay.

*Shield.*

My wand transformed; the part of the staff I held turned into a grip and a metal shield spiraled out. I clashed it against Daniel's sword. Daniel hopped onto an adjacent bale of hay and pursued me. He was too close now for me to use my spear.

*Sword.*

I parried several of his strikes, but had to change tactics quickly. Daniel was remarkable with a sword while I was just mediocre. Plus, he was backing me up higher onto the haystack wall and I couldn't see where I was going. Stealing a swift glance, I discovered we were eight feet above the sparring mat. The hay felt unstable and I was losing my balance. Daniel took a swing at my head. Instead of blocking, I lunged out of the way and leapt for the ground.

*Wand.*

*Lapellium.*

My wand morphed in midair. I landed on the mat and fell into a roll that allowed me to rise back to my feet with natural momentum. Daniel followed. Clearly showing off, he jumped off the haystack wall with a graceful flip, landing perfectly on the mat a mere few seconds after I did.

*Lapellius.*

*Spear.*

I evaded Daniel's sword and whirled my staff to bring it down upon him. He seemed to expect that and turned in time to grab the staff with his free hand, yanking it firmly. Instead of jerking forward along with it, which would have brought my neck to the mercy of his waiting blade, I let go of the spear.

This put me at a disadvantage. I was a much better fighter with a weapon than I was without one. I was decent at hand-to-hand combat (nearly being killed a half dozen times will do that to you). But I didn't get a lot of practice as most of my training partners—Blue, Daniel, and my brothers back home in Midveil—preferred fighting with weapons.

Daniel sliced at me and I hinged back. He swung and I bounded to the side. The boy may have been stronger, but I was faster. He took one strike after another, but I bobbed and weaved and ducked his every effort until I had a clear opening. When his sword hand was low from having taken a shot at my legs, I spun and kicked him in the hand. His grip faltered and the blade flew out of his grasp. Seeing him defenseless, I rushed in.

I took a swing with my right arm, but Daniel grabbed my wrist before I could make contact. "You're getting predictable," he said as he continued to hold my arm, twisting it a bit.

I smiled slyly. "Am I now?"

I glanced at the floor, indicating for him to do the same. When he did, he realized I'd snuck my leg behind his. In the next instant I jerked the arm he was holding back against his chest and swept his leg out from under him. He landed flat on his back on the sparring mat.

"Now who's getting swept off of his feet, hero?" I said.

I got to be smug for about two seconds before Daniel retaliated. Still on the ground, he abruptly stuck out his leg and swept me off *my* feet. I collapsed on my back with a thud.

*Ow.*

I stared up at cobwebs on the ceiling of the barn. "Truce?" I asked.

"Truce," Daniel replied. He got to his feet and then extended his hand. I gladly took it.

I was brushing some hay off my leggings and the long-sleeved, royal-blue-and-orange dress I was wearing when I heard a sound. Jason, Blue, and SJ rounded the corner of a haystack wall on the left, the aged wooden floors of the barn creaking under their feet.

"Hey, Crisa," Jason said, his bright blue eyes gleaming. There was some straw stuck in his blond hair that Blue seemed to suddenly notice. She gave him a curt dusting off.

"The horses are all saddled up. You guys ready?" Jason asked.

"Yep, let's do it," I responded.

Daniel and I collected our respective weapons from where we'd dropped them. I twirled my spear and transformed it back into a wandpin as I followed my friends through the barn and eventually into the stables.

The corridors were about ten feet wide here, but they twisted erratically with many sharp turns. Beams of wood stretched across the high ceiling. A gas lantern with an iron frame and a glass shell hung outside each individual stable. My friends and I always ended practice with plenty of time to come back and extinguish all the lanterns, lest we create a fire hazard.

"You know, I still don't see why we can't practice with the Pegasi from Lord Channing's," Blue commented as we passed the section of the stables that housed the palominos, her dark blonde waves bouncing around her shoulders. "Give me one good reason why we have to ride these guys instead of their awesome flying counterparts."

"Um, because after last semester when we took five of Lord Channing's Pegasi and came back with three, the school put us on quest-supply probation," Daniel said.

"That's a little harsh," Blue scoffed. "Three out of five is still a sixty percent return rate. Doesn't that count for something?"

"It counts as a strike on each of our permanent records is what it counts for," Daniel responded. "So does losing a carriage."

"Oh boo-hoo," Blue mocked. "So your files have some red ink in them. The three of us got detention for five months. Perspective, Daniel."

"Right, I can see you guys are really suffering," Daniel scoffed. "You were in detention for, what, three days before you started breaking out?"

"We're getting away from the point," Blue said, waving him off as we turned a corner. "If you can't check out Pegasi from Lord Channing's then we should be coming to you guys for these training sessions, not the other way around. I mean, Twenty-Three Skidd is played in the *air*. It's stupid to practice on regular horses when flying ones are an option. Plus, Channing's has a regulation-sized Twenty-Three Skidd arena. That sure beats the heck out of the field we've been using over here. Why don't the three of us meet you there tomorrow?"

"We've been over this, Blue," I said. "That wouldn't be fair to the other female protagonists. Lord Channing's only has eight open spots, the majority of which are probably going to its own students. With those kinds of odds, it wouldn't be right for us to have an advantage over the other girls at Lady Agnue's who want to try out."

Blue glanced at SJ for some kind of back up, but much to her annoyance our princess friend shrugged. "You know she is right," SJ said.

Blue huffed then looked back at me. "I hate how noble you are sometimes, you know that?"

"Yes, I know. Now focus. There's a time for mischief and there's a time for practice. And if any of us actually want to have a chance at making a team, now is definitely the time for the latter."

When we emerged from the stables Daniel, Blue, Jason, and I proceeded to armor up. I hopped onto one of the horses and transformed my wandpin into a lacrosse sword—the traditional weapon of Twenty-Three Skidd. It was a lot like a spear, which made me naturally adept with it. The only differences were that the blade end was much larger and resembled the tip of a jousting lance, the bottom end had a basket for catching and lobbing balls, and there was a grip function built in that allowed the staff to extend an extra two feet when you needed additional reach.

The boys and Blue swiftly saddled up, grabbing real lacrosse swords out of holsters attached to their saddles. We only had a little over an hour before SJ, Blue, and I had to be back in the tower, so we needed to make this snappy.

The only person who didn't grab armor was SJ. Although my dear friend packed a punch in her own way, she wasn't the sporty type. She didn't share our love of combat and we were fine with that. She had her own unique strengths that were too numerous to count.

I expected SJ to find a seat under one of the trees nearby and continue with her reading or study, which she usually did while we practiced. But that's when I noticed that she didn't have her book bag with her. Also, SJ was attempting to mount a horse. It didn't have a lacrosse sword in its saddle and it was significantly smaller than ours. Even so, the act was still pretty bold for her.

"SJ, what are you doing?" Jason asked. "I thought you weren't a fan of riding."

"I am not," SJ responded as she struggled to get situated atop the saddle. "However, I want to get over that. I had to steer Pegasi and horses several times over the course of our last adventure, so while you four go about your training, I am going to do a bit of practice of my own."

I eyed her skeptically. Despite her exceptionally strong bond with most animals, SJ and horses had never quite seen eye to eye. As a result, while she knew how to ride, she always opted against it if given the opportunity.

"All right." Blue shrugged. "Just don't get yourself killed."

"Thanks for the encouragement," SJ said as she almost slipped off her horse.

"You *sure* you're okay?" Jason asked.

"I am fine. I am just trying to . . . improve myself is all," she replied, a tad frustrated. "Now go on and practice. Do not worry about me. I shall be fine."

With some reluctance we conceded and did as she suggested. For forty-five minutes the four of us trained hard. Practicing Twenty-Three Skidd drills was a blast, but also exhausting—forcing me to realize that Daniel had been right. If I wanted to make one of the teams, I really did need to amp up my strength training. Working the lacrosse sword became increasingly arduous as time ticked by. It involved using one hand to rapidly rotate between blade and basket while your other hand maneuvered the reins of your steed.

I began to grow tired. It was bitterly cold, the fading light made it hard to see, and the boys were pushing us to our absolute limits.

The sky had turned gray and heather purple. Night was falling and so was the temperature. Daniel and Jason needed to return to their school and Blue, SJ, and I had a tower to sneak back into.

Distracted by this thought, and the exhaustion, I lobbed the ball in the wrong direction. Instead of passing it to Blue, I hurled it into the forest that separated our campus from Lord Channing's.

"Nice going, Knight," Daniel said as he took off his helmet. "Those aren't tennis balls, you know. They're special Twenty-Three Skidd stock that we'll get nailed for losing if we don't bring them back. You want us to lose training equipment privileges too?"

I took off my helmet and shook free my newly shortened, shoulder-length hair. I'd always had long hair, but I'd made the bold move to cut it over winter break. It felt more like me.

"No need to freak out, Daniel. I'll go get the ball," I said, dismounting.

"We'll pack things up here," Blue said as she slid off her own steed. "Wouldn't want to run late for our date with detention, would we?"

"So true," I responded as I unstrapped my armor.

"Crisa," SJ called abruptly. "Can I borrow your lacrosse sword while you are gone?"

I stopped short. "Why?"

"You all are very fond of this sport, so I was thinking I might take it up as well. Not competitively like the rest of you, but more so that I may participate when we are hanging out rather than be left on the sidelines."

"Sure. Go for it," I replied, handing her my wand in its lacrosse sword form. "Just be careful."

I kicked off my last piece of armor and wrapped my scarf around my neck. "I'll be right back," I said to the others.

I headed to the forest. When I reached the river I leapt out over the water and landed on a half-submerged stone. I felt a slight sensation against my skin like a bedsheet being pulled off my body. I turned around and watched the air behind me shimmer with pink and purple bursts of magic. My grin widened at my new ability.

Lady Agnue's was protected by an enchantment called an In and Out Spell. The spell was a type of magic barrier that prevented people from going in or out of the location it protected. There were four active In and Out Spells in Book. The first was around my school and it kept people and detrimental weather or atmosphere fluctuations from passing through. The second was around the antagonist kingdom of Alderon, but it only functioned at half capacity—allowing captured antagonists to be thrown in, but stopping them from getting out. The third was a very powerful version of the spell that isolated the Author's domain, the Indexlands. And the fourth, and most formidable of them all, was the grand In and Out spell that covered our entire realm and separated it from other worlds.

In and Out Spells could only be lowered by the Fairy Godmothers who'd cast them in the first place. They were also supposed to be unbreakable. Until last semester, that is.

In order to reach the Author, who we now knew as Liza, my friends and I had to break the In and Out Spell around the Indexlands. When we'd succeeded the five of us had become immune to that In and Out Spell, as well as any other existing lesser versions of the spell, including the ones around Alderon and Lady Agnue's.

That's how Daniel and Jason had been able to visit us recently. Normally the boys from Lord Channing's only saw us for our monthly balls, field trips, and springtime Twenty-Three Skidd finals matches when the Godmothers officially lowered the In and Out Spell. But now our friends could phase through the barrier with as much ease as I just had.

The pink and purple snaps of magic began to fade before me. In and Out Spells were normally invisible unless disturbed by someone or something trying to cross them. I let out a satisfied sigh and continued on my journey across the river.

I loved being able to do that. If I'd attempted to cross this river without being immune to the In and Out Spell, I would have been electrocuted to death. Feeling no repercussions from the spell made me feel stronger than ever.

As the barrier sealed itself up, I hopped from one half-submerged stone to the next until my royal-blue suede boots touched the grass on the other side. From there I began to wade through the dense collection of trees, searching for the ball.

The forest between Lady Agnue's and Lord Channing's extended over several hills for several acres. I hoped I hadn't lobbed the ball too far, but I didn't exactly have a light touch. The ball could have very well sailed for hundreds of feet.

I proceeded with care through the thriving roots that covered the forest floor. With sundown upon us, the forest was not well lit. I hurried along to outrun the fading light and keep from freezing. It was only the beginning of winter, but there were already small patches of snow on the ground, as well as on branches higher up. It was a fair sign of colder times to come.

We'd had our first snowfall earlier in the week, but alas, the In and Out Spell around Lady Agnue's prevented that kind of detrimental weather from penetrating the school. Snow and rain just slid off the side of the protective magic dome whenever there was a storm, so it never really looked like winter within the campus. Out here was a different story.

I breathed in the icy air. I'd always been a fan of winter. One of the only things I'd missed about going home to Midveil during winter break was the frosty seasonal change that hit every December. I had fond memories of frolicking in the snow, building snow people, battling my brother Alex with long icicles as if they were swords, and plopping down on a couch between him and my other brother Pietro as we drank hot chocolate.

I may have missed out on spending time with them this winter, but I was glad to at least have some exposure to the ice out here. I relished the beautiful contradictions of the season. The snow was one example. It was intensely cold and hard, though powdery soft and fluffy. When winter fell it always felt like everything was calmer than normal, but also sharper—more relaxed, yet more alive. Lately I'd been feeling the same way.

Despite my love of the weather, as twilight came and the

temperature continued to plummet, I hastened my pace. Turning into a more densely wooded part of the forest, I finally spotted the lime green Twenty-Three Skidd ball—still glowing brightly. I trotted over and picked it up. Stowing it in my pocket, I began to make my way back when suddenly I heard a snap. I turned in the direction of the noise and looked through the trees as best I could.

"Is someone there?" I called.

No one responded, but the hairs on the back of my neck stood erect. Most people would've written off a miscellaneous sound in the forest as a woodland animal or bird. Goodness knows there were plenty of them out here. But I knew better. If a situation had even the slightest possibility for something to go wrong, it was best for me to assume that it would.

I heard the noise again. It was like the snap of a twig, though muffled as if suppressed by the snow. Slowly I rounded a giant pine and peered through the frosted tips of a meaty curtain of branches. There was nothing—just silence, stillness, and isolation . . .

*Awgh!*

A hand appeared around the tree, grabbed my throat, and slammed me against the trunk. My body shook from the impact and my vision rattled, but instinct kicked in and I swung my arm out and jabbed an elbow into my attacker's forearm. The strike broke his hold. I smashed my fist against the man's temple and kicked him in the leg, causing his kneecap to buckle.

I bolted in the opposite direction before spinning back around to properly look at the person who'd assaulted me. He wore earth-toned clothing and a tattered fedora. His dark, shoulder-length hair was pulled into a ponytail and his eyes were foggy. Recognition sparked. I knew those eyes.

*A girl doesn't easily forget the man who tried to slice her open and steal her magic.*

*Parker.*

I should have probably kept running. But coming face-to-face with the magic hunter whose clutches I'd narrowly escaped a month and a half ago threw me for a loop. Like the rest of his kind, Parker sought magical objects and creatures with the intention of taking their powers. I knew from experience there was no non-violent approach to this. He needed to kill me to get what he wanted.

He rose to his feet.

I took a few steps back.

"You're a hard one to find," Parker said as he dusted some snow off his jacket.

"I didn't realize anyone was looking," I responded sharply.

"Oh, come on. A kid walking around the realm with Fairy Godmother magic? Did you really think that every magic hunter in Book wasn't going to sit up and take notice? You weren't so easy to detect before, but I gather you've figured out how your powers work and have been using them a lot. Over the last month, your scent has become much easier to track. Honestly, I'm surprised my friends and I are your first visitors."

*Friends.*

I whirled around and noticed another magic hunter approaching us from my right side while two more drew closer on my left. Automatically I reached my hand up to my shoulder, but I stopped short when I realized that I'd left my wand with SJ.

*Right. Four armed magic hunters and no weapon of my own. I guess I'll have to go with Plan B.*

I began to carefully step back toward the nearest tree.

"Pretty bold move coming to my school, though," I said in an attempt to stall a bit longer. "Or didn't you know that Lady Agnue's guards are trained to take down any unauthorized people who approach the grounds?"

"Which is why we didn't approach the grounds," Parker replied. "We heard from our allies in Alderon that you and your little friends have broken the curse of In and Out Spells and can now travel through them. That's a tempting power, girl. We knew it was only a matter of time before you left the protection of your school for one reason or another. We've been camping out in this forest for about a week, waiting for you to wander out here."

My palms touched bark as I backed up against one of the trees.

"Fascinating," I said. "But tell me, Parker, did any of your buddies in Alderon happen to mention what this magical power of mine you're after *is*?"

Parker and his friends hesitated.

"No? Well, allow me to enlighten you." I pressed my hands firmly against the tree trunk, took a quick breath, and channeled my focus.

*Wake up*, I thought as I felt the magic beginning to flow through my fingers. *Wake up. Rise. Defend.*

My life-giving powers pulsed from me into the tree I was touching. And just like that the mighty pine turned animate. Glowing gold for a moment, it pulled itself out of the ground and began to defend me. The tree flung itself in the direction of Parker and the two magic hunters on my left—rolling over them. I made a break for it.

I ducked beneath branches and darted around trees, trying to keep from slipping on patches of ice and tripping over the root-laden floor. I could hear the shouts of the hunters behind me. My feet picked up speed and my heart did the same.

I stole a glance back.

*Oh, crud.*

A magic hunter had gotten away from the tree and was in my pursuit. He'd drawn a bow and was taking aim. I barely jumped out of the way to avoid his arrow. It stabbed into a branch three inches to my right. I spun around and continued my dash.

Every few seconds I heard the distinct sound of another shot whizzing through the air and plunging into a nearby tree. I zigzagged to throw off the hunter's aim. As an arrow pierced some bark a few centimeters from my face, I turned my head to take another look back. I regretted it immediately, as it caused me to miss seeing a large root.

I tripped. There was nothing but a rough patch of ice to cushion my fall. I started to get up, but another arrow plunged into the ice an inch from my hand. I whipped my head around to see an additional arrow incoming. I dodged out of the way and it barely missed my cheek.

The arrow pinned my scarf to the ground at my side. As I was about to dislodge it, the archer approached with Parker next to him.

"Thanks for the demonstration," Parker said. "I look forward to trying out the power for myself."

The archer had his bow at the ready. Parker began to pull a dagger from the holster on his belt. My blood, or possibly my magic, throbbed inside me with dread. There was nothing within grasping distance for me to touch and enchant. I knew what I had to do.

*Ugh, Liza's going to be so mad.*

I extended my hand with a sharp, short breath and focused on the tree roots that both magic hunters were standing on.

*Trap*, I telepathically commanded.

My hand was enveloped by a bright golden glow and the roots I'd been concentrating on instantly came to life. They sprung up like enraged, squid-like monsters and entangled themselves around the bodies of Parker and the archer before he could fire. As the roots mercilessly wrapped themselves around my attackers' frames, I ripped out the arrow nailing my scarf to the ground and jumped to my feet. With fear and magic in my veins, I sprinted through the forest and plunged back through my school's In and Out Spell.

I collapsed on the grass on the other side of the river. My heart was practically in my throat from the adrenaline, and I felt powerful magic surging inside me. As I tried to breathe, I watched my crossing spot in the barrier seal itself up.

I looked down at my palm. The glow had not yet faded. I shook my hand to try and return it to normal. After a few seconds the golden light subsided and I took a deep breath. Once I felt recentered, my attention drifted to the trees.

The magic hunters would get free eventually. When they did they'd go back to hiding in the forest, waiting for me. I wondered how long they would bide their time out there and how many more were on the way.

I should have expected the onslaught. Emma had warned me

that once I discovered what my power was and figured out how to use it, my magical scent would go up like a flare to hunters across the realm.

Since making the decision to improve and enhance my abilities, I had been continuously channeling magic. Now that choice had caught up with me. Which meant that a lot of other things were about to catch up with me too.

# CHAPTER 2

# The Choice of Wickedness

 thought being chased and nearly killed by a handful of magic hunters was a lot to deal with. As it turns out, it was nothing in comparison to the freaked-out reactions I got from my friends.

We were in the barn and I had just told them what had happened in the forest. All but the lantern closest to the door had been extinguished, casting us in shadow.

I thought SJ's gray eyes were going to pop out of their sockets when I explained how Parker and his men had been camped out in the forest for a week, waiting for me to stray out there like a lost fawn.

"You could have been killed!" she exclaimed.

"Yeah, I got that," I said, exasperated. "But since it's hardly the first time, can we focus on something else please?"

"Okay, how about the fact that those hunters are still in the forest," Blue said. "While your magic may have slowed them down, I hardly think it'll stop them from coming after you. If anything, you probably encouraged them to keep up their mission by giving them an up-close-and-personal demonstration of what your powers can do. Not smart, Crisa."

"It wasn't like I was flaunting my abilities, Blue," I argued. "It was self-defense."

"*Careless* self-defense," SJ added.

"Well, what would *you* have had me do, SJ? I didn't exactly have my wand with me."

SJ fell silent. A bit of dismay set in and I realized what I'd said.

"I'm sorry. I didn't mean that it was your fault."

She nodded, but didn't respond.

"What do you want us to do now, Crisa?" Jason cut in. "It's your call."

"If they're still out there then I think we should give them a reason to leave," Daniel answered on my behalf. "Come on, Jason. What do you say we go knock a few magic hunter heads on our way back to campus?"

He made to move past us, but I put my hand on his arm. "Hold up there, hero. I appreciate the offer and the sentiment behind it, but that forest is huge. And if they've really been hiding out there for a week, then I think you're overestimating how easy it'll be to find them. Magic hunters are master trackers. Even if you get close, they'll sense you coming."

"Jason's a master tracker too, Knight. I'm sure we'll manage," Daniel said. "Besides, don't you want them taken care of?"

"Of course I do," I replied. "But I also want to make sure they don't get the jump on you or any of us. Parker said he and his friends weren't the only magic hunters following me. So it would be stupid for us to go charging through the forest when we don't have a clear understanding of how big a threat is out there."

"So, you want to just wait?" Blue asked, puzzled.

"For now, yes."

"But your safety, Crisa," SJ insisted.

"I'm safe *here*. The In and Out Spell will protect me, so you guys don't have to worry. Until we have a better idea of what we're dealing with, I think not engaging is the smartest plan. It's better to make a thought-out, strategic move than an immediate one rooted in vengeance and aggression. Right?"

SJ pouted. Usually she was the logical, reasonable one. I don't think she was very fond of me taking that stance away from her and then using it against her.

"All right," she said eventually. "Point taken. But you are not going back into the forest until these matters are sorted."

"That goes for you guys too," Blue interjected, pivoting toward the boys. "For today you can sneak out the main gate when the guards are changing shifts." She looked at her watch. "That's going to happen in seventeen minutes. You can get past them and then phase through that part of the In and Out Spell. After that . . ." She sighed sadly. "No more of these secret meet-and-greets. You guys can't go through the forest to get to and from Lord Channing's anymore. Until we figure out what to do about those hunters, we're *all* grounded."

"Blue, come on," Jason complained.

"No buts, Jason. SJ and I have enough to worry about with this one's safety constantly hanging in the balance," Blue said, gesturing at me. "I don't want to spend my time freaking out about your safety too. Both of you, that is," she added quickly.

Daniel and Jason were not happy, but they agreed. With our detention deadline rapidly approaching, we extinguished the last lantern in the barn and the five of us slipped out and parted ways. Blue, SJ, and I headed back to the tower while the boys proceeded to the front of the school, careful to remain unseen.

"You realize that you can't spend time on the far side of the practice fields anymore, right?" Blue said to me as we approached the tower.

"How do you mean?"

Blue and SJ exchanged a look.

"The In and Out Spell prevents human beings from passing through, not objects," SJ said. "If you get close enough to the river that separates the school from the forest and the hunters are there at the right moment, they could easily hit you with an arrow."

"But they wouldn't," I countered. "I read something about that last week in the library." I closed my eyes, trying to remember one of the many texts I'd scanned recently. I snapped my fingers and opened my eyes. "It was in *The Magic Hunter Code*. It said that when a magical creature is killed, its magic goes into the closest living thing. If the magic hunters want to take my magic, it would be stupid of them to shoot me while I'm on campus and they're in the forest. They wouldn't be able to collect my body so the magic would go into someone else, like one of the other students."

"They could use a grappling hook," Blue suggested a bit too casually. "You know, reel you in like a fish."

At first the notion seemed funny, but when it sunk in and I visualized it, my expression soured. "Fine. I'll keep to the barn and the stables for training."

Both SJ and Blue looked relieved with my decision. I summoned the vines to magically transport us up to the tower with only minutes to spare.

As the vines lifted us to our prison anew, I felt exhausted. That was a lot for one afternoon. Normally I handled the whole "people trying to kill me" thing in stride. You had to when it was such a regular occurrence. Unfortunately, my friends' worries made it harder. They made me remember that I wasn't invincible; I was just one girl with *a lot* of enemies and my odds against them were only getting smaller.

If I'd thought I'd gotten an earful from my friends, it barely compared to the lecture I received from Liza.

My magical mentor and I spoke three times a day. Liza had originally wanted us to train five times a day, but with my school schedule we'd been forced to compromise. I had to work my extracurricular magical lessons around my regular princess ones.

I supposed Liza didn't grasp the concept of time constraints.

It wasn't her fault. She was the Author. Which meant that outside of her time with me, her only other commitment was transcribing her vivid dreams into protagonist books, which the Fairy Godmothers and our realm's ambassadors used to maintain order over the land.

Furthermore, Liza was trapped in the Indexlands. She had been infinitely secluded from the rest of the world so that no one would find out the truth about how little control her predictions actually had over our fates.

My friends and I had been shocked to learn that the Author didn't decide our choices for us like we'd always been taught. Rather, they reflected what our futures would be based on our own decisions. That's why her prologue prophecies tended to be so vague; they could have several interpretations. The exact ways in which they'd eventually be realized were fully dependent on our actions. In other words, whatever happened to us was on *us*, not *her*. Not that our realm's leaders—much less Liza's Godmother Supreme sister, Lena Lenore—would ever let anyone know that.

Adding to her skewed conception of time, Liza was under an anti-aging spell that prolonged her life. Between that and being isolated with her eternal job, it was no wonder she had tons of room in her calendar for teaching me how to control my powers.

I communicated with Liza using my Mark Two magic compact mirror. Mark Twos were a new piece of magic tech. They were adaptations of the original magic mirrors, like the one used in *Beauty & the Beast*. These small, portable mirrors allowed for two-way interaction so long as both parties had a compact. The Mark Twos were being introduced realm-wide this spring, but Liza had sent me one in advance last month so that we could keep in touch. Right now, though, I wished I could block her calls. Her nagging was going on forever.

"For the hundredth time, Liza, I'm sorry," I said. "I know I'm not supposed to use the telepathy trick with my powers until I get better at controlling them, but I had no choice. It was either project the magic or get killed by hunters."

Liza sighed. Even in the tiny image of her that reflected in my magic compact mirror I could see the exasperation in her expression.

"I realize you didn't have a choice, Crisa. But you do understand why I am upset, don't you?"

"Yes, yes. Pure Magic: dangerous. Control over powers: good. I got it."

I knew I should have spoken to her with less sass. Pure Magic was not something to be taken lightly. And it definitely shouldn't be something I took lightly given that, just like Liza, I had Pure Magic Disease.

Magic was supposed to be easily removed and transferred from one person or object to the next, but in some unique cases it fused permanently to its host. When that happened the magic became classified as "pure" and the carrier took on the burdens of Pure Magic Disease. The benefits included developing a very powerful ability—in Liza's case it was teleportation; in my case it was giving life—and seeing the future in your dreams. The downside was that the power would eventually turn your heart dark and you would become an evil witch or warlock.

*So there was that.*

Just as Emma had had no idea the spark of magic she gave me would develop into such a powerful ability, she never could have predicted that this gift meant to protect me could lead to my destruction.

That's why I seriously appreciated Liza training me to control my magic. She was the only person out there who might save me from a dark fate.

Many years ago Liza had been a Godmother with our realm's Fairy Godmother Agency, but her magic had mutated into Pure Magic. Remarkably though, unlike every other carrier of Pure Magic Disease that'd come before her, Liza's heart had never turned dark. She'd taught herself to control her powers and keep them from consuming her. This gave me hope that maybe I could do the same thing.

I knew the odds were against me, but I had to believe I could do it. Because if I didn't, then what? I would end up like the other wicked witches and warlocks who suffered from the disease—will overtaken by power, heart turned black, and soul shriveled up like a dead flower. I definitely didn't want that to happen.

Aside from my own self-preservation, I couldn't fail because I had the weight of an entire realm riding on my success. If I was prophesized to be the key to either the antagonists' downfall or their triumph over Book, it wasn't hard to imagine that this fate was tied to whether or not my magic corrupted me.

I shuddered at the thought.

"Look, I really am sorry, Liza," I said, trying to sound more respectful. "I understand the gravity of the situation. Pushing my magic before I'm ready is dangerous, and the only means we really have for keeping it in check is the control I maintain."

"Exactly, Crisa," Liza responded. "Using large amounts of your magic is risky, especially in short periods of time. Until you are stronger and have had more practice, it is ten times more dangerous to project your powers telepathically than in the controlled manner of touch we've been practicing because—"

"It could cause me to exhaust my powers faster or even burn me out and kill me on the spot. I know, Liza."

That was another pair of gems that came with Pure Magic—Magic Exhaustion and Magic Burn Out. Powerful as my ability was, I could only use so much of it at a time before I temporarily ran out. That was Magic Exhaustion. I'd only experienced it once before, but it made me feel like a sponge that had all the water wrung out of it or a hamster that had overexerted itself on a running wheel.

The more I trained and mastered my abilities, the higher my magic limit. But there would always be a limit. I was only able to utilize so much magic before I exhausted it and my powers shut off. After that I was on my own. The magic required about a day to fully reboot.

Magic Burn Out, on the other hand, was a consequence that was not quite as forgiving. The gist was that if I ever pushed myself past the amount of magic I could handle, there was a risk that I could exhaust myself beyond repair. And by that I mean I would burn up and die. *Lovely, right?*

"That's one reason," Liza agreed. "And the other?"

I grimaced. "Telepathic magic runs too freely, which makes it harder for me to control."

Liza nodded. "Quite. Need I remind you what happened in Alderon last month?"

It had been about a month and a half since Arian (the leader of the antagonist hunting party that'd been pursuing me) had captured my friends and I and delivered us to the capital of Alderon to meet their wicked queen, Nadia. We'd escaped of course, but a lot of that had to do with me discovering my powers at just the right time. I'd used them during our escape and when I came face-to-face with Arian, I had inadvertently used my magic telepathically to get him to reveal information I needed. In doing so, I'd given in to the impulsive, easily corruptible nature of my Pure Magic.

My desire to hurt Arian had clouded my mind and I'd

temporarily lost control. It'd felt like I was another person—a shadow of myself driven by hatred and bloodlust. I'd been able to regain control over my powers, but another few seconds and I probably would have torn Arian to shreds.

Never again did I want to feel like my power was in control of me and not the other way around. If not using my magic telepathically until I was stronger and more skilled was the best way to prevent that, then I fully intended on keeping myself from going down that road until I was ready. Today had just been an exception.

"I remember, Liza," I said, swallowing down the unpleasant memories. "Now can we move on, *please*?"

"Not entirely, I'm afraid. Today's lesson is actually related to this subject." Liza cleared her throat. Her nagging tone was replaced with her teaching one. "As we've discussed, using your powers telepathically and overusing your powers are both triggers for losing control of your Pure Magic. But there is also one other very important trigger you must understand. Emotion."

"Emotion?" I repeated.

"Yes," Liza said. "Crisa, there is a reason I've spent the last few weeks teaching you about centering your breathing, clearing your mind, and focusing solely on the task at hand when employing the use of your magic. It is at this level of clarity that you can keep a hold of your powers. However, if you allow emotion to seep in when using your ability, it can easily become that extra oomph the magic needs to corrupt you. Emotion is the most dangerous trigger for losing control of Pure Magic.

"That incident in Alderon is the perfect example. When you used your powers telepathically on Arian, what pushed you over the edge was allowing your emotions toward him to cloud your judgment. You probably felt hatred, anger, and desperation. Those emotions are strong, which makes your magic strong too. But they are also overwhelming and can drown your conscience under instinct. Thus, it was a combination of the dark emotions inside you and your inherent powers that made you vulnerable to the manipulation of Pure Magic that day."

I couldn't help but fidget uncomfortably. Up til now I'd

blamed losing control of my magic in Alderon on the strength of the magic itself. The fact that this was only part of the problem and that it was mostly my own fault made me unsettled.

It had been my naturally dark emotions that caused me to succumb to the powers. Which meant that those feelings and wicked intentions had been inside me all along. They weren't the result of my magic taking over. The situation was actually the opposite.

"Crisa."

I turned my focus back to Liza's reflection.

"I can see the gears working in your head," she began slowly. "And I want you to know that it is okay. There is no need to feel shame over what happened. Everyone has those types of feelings now and then; they're inevitable even in the kindest of people. Having them doesn't make you wicked."

I twiddled with the golden fringe on the edge of one of my pillows. "How can you be so sure?" I asked, not meeting her gaze.

"Because wickedness is not something you fall into, Crisanta. It is a choice you make. If you do not let it in, even momentary slips will not force you to change. We all have things we regret—wicked thoughts or actions we're ashamed of. But isolated events do not define the heart. What does is how you handle the dark emotions that attempt to influence your decisions. With proper understanding of this, and the right training, I have faith that you will be able to handle them beautifully."

My body sunk into the deep purple comforter as I thought about this. I wasn't totally convinced, but I believed in Liza. Moreover, I believed in myself. I knew I could master my magic, keep darkness in check, *and* keep myself in check. No matter what kind of malevolence this disease tried to ignite inside me, I would fight it with all my soul. I would choose light and not wickedness.

After all, there were bigger things than my own fate depending on it.

# CHAPTER 3

## *Imminent*

f all the people who had an influence on my fate, Natalie Poole was arguably the most impactful. And I had never even met her.

Natalie lived in my dreamscape in a world called Earth. I had been dreaming about her for a long time, but it was only recently that I'd discovered that these scenes I witnessed while I slept were actually visions of the future.

Tonight, my dreams opened on the maple-haired young woman sitting in a classroom. All the kids looked about fifteen. The chalkboard behind the teacher had the words "Art History" written on it. Natalie had her nose buried in a textbook as kids piled in and took their seats. A boy with gray-blue eyes and dark curly hair was among them. When he walked in, Natalie raised her eyes ever so slightly. He gave her a smile that would've made any girl's heart melt. Then he sat down next to her.

"Hey," he said, sliding his backpack off his shoulder.

"Hey, Ryan," she replied, closing her book. She glanced toward the back of the room at the other boys he'd come in with. "You're not going to sit with your friends?"

"I thought I already was."

The pair of them dissolved into a dark blur as the scene faded. My dream was changing. My subconscious took on a physical form and I began to migrate through the haze. I was not surprised by the change. Sometimes I was an observer in my dreams, like I had been with Natalie a minute ago. Other times I walked through my dreamscape like an explorer or even a player.

As I moved, I saw silhouettes of pillars and archways. I started to feel warm. The heat was increasing and it felt like the air was getting thicker. I clutched at my throat. It was becoming difficult to breathe. Clouds of smoke and flashes of orange began to appear in the blackness. Wherever I was, it was on fire.

I was moving through a maze of debris—fallen pillars, shattered roof tiles, collapsed walls made of glass and metal. The heat and smoke escalated. A beam came crashing down. I barely saw it in my peripheral vision and flung myself to the ash-laden floor to avoid it. I started to get up but stopped short when I saw something familiar lying beneath a pile of rubble.

In a panic, I grabbed the object and held it up. It was a flag, or at least a portion of it anyway. My kingdom's flag.

I had grown up seeing these flags all over my home kingdom of Midveil. There was no mistaking it for what it was. It was powder blue with a gold crest and a sleeping lion at the center. The words "*Aut viam inveniam aut faciam*" were written around the image like a border.

Looking about frantically, I tried to figure out where I was. Most of the architecture in Midveil was composed of metal and glass. And since most of my kingdom's commercial buildings had flags on display, I couldn't narrow down the location. I could be anywhere in Midveil.

Suddenly I heard a distinct cracking; the ceiling was giving way. I looked up and leapt aside to dodge a falling column. It smashed into the floor next to me. I tried to get up again, but it felt like I was being held down.

The smoke and heat were becoming unbearable. The room was quaking. I knew the section of roof above my head was probably going to give out soon and I'd be squashed like a bug.

I was scared, not just of the imminent doom, but of how I felt. For reasons I could not explain, my entire core burned with heartache. It flared inside me—a combination of rage and sadness so powerful I had no past experiences to compare it to.

I was on my feet then. My vision was going in and out. Black to flame; debris to ash; columns to glass. The ceiling exploded. The whole room shook and the fury of the quake caused an enormous nearby mirror to shatter. Shards scattered everywhere.

Then I was abruptly thrust against a wall. Not as a result of the explosion, but because someone slammed me there. My eyes darted up to see Parker and the glint of his dagger heading toward my throat.

My hand jutted out to block him. It was successful, but he kept coming at me. I perceived that I was fighting back, but our struggle only came in curt flashes as the world grew hazier. I didn't believe we were in the same setting as before. There was no glass or crumbling columns or mirrors. However, I still felt the heat of fire against my cheeks and smoke clogging my lungs.

Parker grabbed my hair and yanked it back, exposing my throat. Our arms were entangled. I pushed whatever leverage I had to keep his blade away from me, but he was stronger than I was. I had no wand. I had no weapon. I had no backup of any kind. All I had was my fleeting strength and the haunting look of Parker's eyes staring into mine as his dagger inched closer.

Then, as briskly as the torment began, the smoke, fire, and magic hunter were swept away as if by a powerful wind. I found myself looking up at a maroon and purple canopy. I was awake again.

I exhaled deeply, as if the smoke in my nightmares had some-how manifested into my real-life lungs. I lay with my eyes closed for a few moments. Then I rolled to the edge of my bed, sat up, and picked up a journal and quill from my mahogany nightstand. With another deep breath, I began to scribble down the details of the dreams I'd woken from.

I'd suffered the wrath of vivid nightmares for years. Sometimes they featured people I knew, sometimes they didn't. No matter what they were about, I now knew that my dreams would all inevitably come true. Just like Liza's.

*Pure Magic. The gift that keeps on giving.*

Usually my dreams of the future took place in Book, but I also dreamt about Earth once in a while, specifically about Natalie Poole.

While all my visions were of keen interest to me, my dreams about Natalie tended to occupy my attention a lot more than the others. She had been a recurring presence in my subconscious for as long as I could remember. As my visions about her had gotten stronger, so had my understanding of her situation.

Natalie Poole wasn't just a normal girl. According to the prologue prophecy Liza had written about her, she had a destiny that intertwined our realms. Among other things, she was fated to open something called "The Eternity Gate," which would give Nadia, Arian, and all of the antagonists in Alderon the magical edge they'd need in order to vanquish the protagonists and overthrow Book.

Eternity was a mystical place between worlds that was responsible for controlling the balance of all realms. If any realm's good-to-dark magic ratio ever fell out of balance, Eternity's guardians would open an entrance to that realm (its Eternity Gate) to judge whether or not the world was worth saving or if it should be eliminated from the universe before it infected other realms.

During this judgment period ordinary magic across all realms was supposed to shut down. Thus, if Natalie opened the Eternity Gate, even if she was on Earth, the In and Out Spell around Alderon would evaporate, freeing the antagonists. Worse still? The Fairy Godmothers wouldn't have the magic to stop them. The only magic that would not be affected during that time would be Pure Magic, and aside from me and Liza, the only people with Pure Magic were all evil and presently locked up in Alderon.

Cue Natalie's importance.

My foes intended to trigger the opening of the Eternity Gate by destroying Natalie's life and tipping her aural magic (Earth's version of magic) in the direction of darkness. The more dreams I had of Natalie, the more I understood the details involved with this plot. For example, I'd learned that a girl who worked for Arian named Tara was on Earth making Natalie miserable. I also knew that the antagonists planned to ultimately destroy Natalie by killing her one true love, Ryan Jackson, on her twenty-first birthday.

Because of this, I didn't have long to save Natalie. There was a big time difference between Earth and Book. A month here was equal to over a year and a half there. So I really only had about one Book year to help her and stop the antagonists. Hence my accelerated magic training with Liza.

In addition to wanting to keep my Pure Magic from corrupting me, my hope was that if I gained enough control over my powers I would be able to communicate with Natalie through my dreams and warn her of what was coming.

Liza had been able to perform this type of communication with me before because she had vast control over her powers and dreamt about me frequently, making our connection strong enough for her Pure Magic to allow it. Since I dreamed about Natalie constantly, with enough training I hoped I would be able to do the same with her.

Noting down the last details in my dream journal, I closed the book and placed it on my nightstand.

I glanced over at my friends. They were both sound asleep. SJ lay perfectly undisturbed on her back as she breathed slowly and gracefully—her smooth sheets and perfectly braided black hair suggesting that she hadn't moved an inch since falling asleep. Blue, meanwhile, was buried beneath a mound of comforter. The only parts of her that were visible were a few dark blonde waves and her left arm, which was hanging off the mattress.

I envied them. While their states of sleeping may have been quite different, the one thing they shared was the one thing that would forever elude me—they both were at rest.

Deciding not to wake them, I slipped out of bed and out the doors to our balcony. They were always kept open, so I stepped through without making any noise.

The outside air was crisp and the sun rising over the forest was bright and cheerful. I stared at the distant, snow-encrusted pines. I wondered how many magic hunters were out there waiting for me. And I wondered how long I had before they got tired of waiting and came up with a Plan B. I knew it would happen eventually. My vision of Parker just now had verified this in a way that was beyond argument. He was coming for me. I didn't know when or where or how. But he was.

For the meantime, I was safe behind the protective shield of the In and Out Spell—so long as I didn't get too close to the outer parts of the campus and the hunters didn't have lucky timing and grappling hooks like Blue suggested. But this notion of safety filled me with as much comfort as it did resentment. I hated hiding and loathed the idea of cowering in fear. It would give me a great sense of satisfaction to go charging through the forest with the full force of my Pure Magic as I weeded out the hunters who had followed me here. This was my home and they were invading it.

Sadly, I'd been forced to conceal these impulses yesterday from SJ, Blue, Jason, and Daniel. If I let my true feelings on the matter show, my friends would go charging out there with me. And while I welcomed their help because I trusted them completely, I didn't want them diving into that forest when there were so many unknown variables at play. The five of us already lived in a world full of risk and danger. I didn't want to court more if I could help it.

In the silence and solitude I sighed. And for a moment, I let my brave face go.

I was scared. Not of anything specific, but of the general threats following me like a cursed mosquito. Much more than that, I was scared for what this meant for the people closest to me. Strong and capable as they were, I could never let go of the possibility that the trouble the universe kept sending my way might hurt my friends. This concern plagued the back of my mind constantly, but I was intent on keeping it hidden from everyone except myself, and maybe Daniel.

He was the only person I didn't have to conceal my true worries from. He already knew so much about me that there was no point in hiding anything from him. Everyone needed a sounding board, and he'd accidentally become mine. I hadn't really tested this out since we'd returned from our Author quest, but I hoped that if my worries ever got too big, I could still turn to him for support.

# CHAPTER 4

# My New Role

**W**hen my friends and I arrived at breakfast, I was met by two things: all-you-can-eat oatmeal and a bouquet of two-dozen red roses.

The latter is what gave me a stomachache.

It was not so much the flowers that inspired the nausea, but their sender. Chance Darling—the most handsome and persistent prince at Lord Channing's—had been attempting to win my affections for far too long. Last semester he'd declared that I was his "heart's desire" and had focused his attention on me like a hunter stalking a deer.

I was as fond of him as I was of going to the dentist. Actually, less so. At least when you visited the dentist you got a prize at the end, like a sticker or a colorful eraser. The only prize that came with Chance was his colorful sense of self-importance.

*Ugh. If only I could erase that.*

Naturally, because of my strong dislike for the boy, I shot him down at every possible opportunity. But he just would not give up. I'd sort of hoped that when I returned to school after our adventures he might've moved on to someone else. Alas, it was the opposite. He'd kicked it up a notch.

I had been bombarded with gifts at school every day since coming back. Being Monday, today's token was a grandiose flower arrangement on my breakfast table in the banquet hall. Had it been Tuesday, I would have received chocolates. On Thursdays, the prince (who was the grandson of King Midas) typically sent me something subtle like a five-pound gold necklace.

I rolled my eyes at the floral arrangement and got up to get more food from the buffet with SJ. There were three lowerclassmen ahead of us in line. Despite the fact that they were keeping their gossip to whispers, it was obvious that they were talking about me.

"Did you see the flowers Prince Darling sent Crisanta Knight this morning?" the blonde, perky one said.

"I know, right?" commented a tiny redhead. "I bet it's her on-point style that's bewitching him. Have you seen her rebellious new hair cut? And the way she dresses—half princess, half hero? I wrote to my parents in Middlebrook to send me combat boots as soon as possible so I could start dressing like her."

"Me too," agreed a second blonde. "And I'm going to start using my free period to go down to the practice fields for weapons' study. Crisanta Knight goes there every day and has become just as good in combat as she has in ballroom dancing."

The first blonde sighed. "I don't know how she does it. I mean, how does a girl go from being last in her class at this school to being the most heroic, coolest princess in the whole—"

SJ cleared her throat. Evidently, she'd had enough.

The three girls glanced back in surprise to see me standing behind them. Their faces turned red and they scuttled out of the banquet hall as fast as possible, too embarrassed to even look me in the eye.

"This stupid hero-princess worship has gone on for weeks now," I groaned. "How much longer do you think it's going to last?" I pushed my breakfast tray down the buffet line and finally got hold of the strawberry croissant I'd been after. Oatmeal may have been the special of the day, but I much preferred the baked treats from our school's kitchen.

After I secured the croissant, I reached for a handful of bacon. I glanced left and right to make sure no one was watching and then put the bacon in a small plastic baggie in my pocket.

"I do not know," SJ responded, a hint of irritation in her tone. "Hopefully it will be over soon." She turned to fill her bowl of oatmeal with a scoop of fresh berries before motioning toward our table with a wistful smile. "Shall we? Before those girls get the nerve to come back and ask you for an autograph?"

I huffed in amusement as we headed back to the table.

The girls at Lady Agnue's used to regard me like an undesirable outlier. Ever since we'd returned from our Author quest though, they'd been treating me differently, even if the truth about our adventures remained a secret due to a deal we'd made with our headmistress.

In the eyes of my peers I'd led a team of protagonists (including two boys) on a secret mission. The most handsome prince at our neighboring school was deeply infatuated with me. Alongside Blue, I was the key inspiration that led to our female classmates being allowed to try out for Twenty-Three Skidd teams. I'd brought a pet dragon back to school (though he currently resided at Lord Channing's). And word had spread of my newly improved combative skill.

Thanks to so many near-death experiences last semester, I was now a better fighter than all the common protagonists in school, aside from Blue. This fact had been noticed over winter break when I volunteered to spar with the girls who'd remained on campus.

It seemed I had inadvertently become a character that mystified and fascinated my classmates. It was strange to say the least. While I appreciated the newfound respect, I hadn't been trying to impress anyone. I was just doing what needed to be done. That and some twists of fate had transformed me into a minor celebrity.

I really didn't think I was worthy of my classmates' idolization. Blue and SJ had done just as much cool stuff, and their individual skills made them way more impressive than I was. But I guess the other girls had focused on me because I was unusual. Blue had always naturally fit in with the feisty common protagonists at school and SJ had always naturally fit in with the elegant princesses. I had never fit in anywhere. So maybe defying the stereotypes and settling into a hybrid archetype of my own is what got their attention.

I don't know. I suppose I preferred being looked up to versus being looked down upon, but in general I really just preferred being left alone. Which was pretty hard to accomplish when younger students kept whispering about me and following me around.

SJ and I sat at our table again as Princess Marie Sinclaire (daughter of the princess from *The Princess & the Pea*) came over and joined us. She brushed aside her white-blonde hair then checked her seat like she always did before sitting.

"My, what beautiful flowers," she commented, beholding the bouquet Chance had sent.

I pushed them across the table. "Here, you can have them. In fact, if you want more, feel free to stop by our room sometime and help yourself. Chance has sent me so many arrangements, it's like a dang florist lives there."

Marie gazed at the flowers longingly. "Must be nice," she said dreamily, "having a prince be so interested in you and being thought of so highly by the other girls."

"Yeah, nice." I sighed to myself. "Not the adjective I would have chosen."

"I can't do this," I said as I looked up from my Damsels in Distress textbook.

Madame Lisbon—our robust and rosy-cheeked D.I.D. professor—was having us "popcorn read" the chapter about the history of the Damsels of Camelot. I was finding the task rather difficult.

"Miss Knight," said Madame Lisbon, agitation filling her normally sparkling blue eyes. "Simply read the text as written."

I glanced down at the words, shook my head, and looked at my teacher defiantly. "Nope. Not happening."

"Miss Knight," the professor's voice rose sharply. "The passages in this text are from one of the oldest transcriptions of 'The Legend of King Arthur' known to any of our realms. And this excerpt, 'The Knight of Two Swords,' is a core piece of that story. So whether you agree with Sir Malory's portrayal of the situation or not, you *will* read it as written."

"No."

Madame Lisbon's shoulders tensed up to her ears. "Crisanta . . ."

SJ suddenly cleared her throat and began to read from the book at her own desk.

"The young noblewoman stood before Arthur and drew aside her gown—revealing a handsome sword and scabbard, hung from her girdle. 'My Lady,' said Arthur, 'a sword is hardly becoming to one of your sex. Please tell me why you wear something so ill-suited . . .'"

SJ looked up from her text and met Madame Lisbon's surprised stare. "There," she said innocently. "Passage read. May we move on, please?"

Madame Lisbon opened her mouth to respond when the bell rang through the room, freeing us. I swept my textbook off my desk and into my new book bag before making a break for the door. My professor shot me a glare on my way out, but I shrugged off her disapproval the second I stepped into the hall.

"Thanks for the save," I said to SJ as she and Blue followed me out. "I think Madame Lisbon was about to blow a gasket."

"You are welcome," SJ replied. "But, Crisa, do you really have to provoke *all* of our professors? I mean, I realize that King Arthur's words do not portray him as someone we would readily get along with—"

"He sounds like a total jerk," I interjected. "And for the record, I do not enjoy provoking anyone. It just sort of happens."

Blue and SJ both gave me a skeptical look.

"Okay, okay, I enjoy provoking *some* people," I admitted. "But that was an accident."

"You do realize Madame Lisbon is probably going to assign you extra homework tomorrow for openly defying her in front of the whole class, right?" Blue asked.

I shrugged. "No regrets. A girl's gotta have principles."

"Speaking of principals . . ." Blue tilted her chin slightly, directing my attention to Ms. Mammers, the assistant to our headmistress, who was charging down the corridor toward our group. I could spot her blue knit suit from fifty feet away.

*Oh, this can't be good.*

Ms. Mammers automatically straightened her jacket when she reached us and brushed a wisp of her short, bronze hair out of her face. She'd gotten it cut since I'd last seen her and it was hugging her head like a helmet. It did not look good.

"Miss Knight," the assistant said. "Lady Agnue requests your presence in her office immediately."

"Request denied," I replied bluntly.

Ms. Mammers blinked hard like a circuit had gotten fried in her brain. "You cannot deny this request, Crisanta Knight."

"Then don't dress it up *like* a request," I responded. "Call it what it really is. Lady Agnue is ordering me to her office for another one of her 'keep me in line' threat sessions."

Ms. Mammers gestured for me to follow. "Just come along. If you know the drill so well, then you know not to keep the headmistress waiting."

The flustered assistant began her journey back up the hall, her feathers adequately ruffled. Before following, I leaned back to my friends. "See, *her* I enjoy provoking."

Ms. Mammers was already halfway down the hall by that point so I sped after her. It always surprised me how a woman with such stumpy legs could move with the speed of an alley cat. I practically had to use my battle reflexes to bob and weave around the students to keep up with her.

I wished we could have walked slowly, or even in slow motion. I was not looking forward to another chat with Lady Agnue.

On our return to school, my friends and I had been fully intent on telling everyone what we'd learned about the Author. We also wanted to reveal the antagonists' plot to overtake the realm and destroy all main characters, and divulge the dirty secret of our realm's ambassadors—that they were forging protagonist books for royals who didn't have them and destroying the books of other, common protagonists when there were too many.

Regrettably, the headmistress made it clear that we were not to share any of this information, leveraging my Pure Magic to force us into silence.

The thing about Pure Magic Disease is that carriers were feared. As mentioned, aside from Liza (who no one knew about), every person who'd ever been a victim of the sickness had succumbed to its power and gone all magic crazy. As such, all carriers of Pure

Magic—no matter what stage of the disease they were in—were sentenced to Alderon immediately upon being discovered. Our realm's higher-ups figured it was best to separate them from the general, vulnerable public as soon as possible because it was only a matter of time before their hearts turned dark.

I hadn't even heard of Pure Magic Disease before all this, but some of the off-limits books in the school library confirmed that sentencing Pure Magic carriers to Alderon wasn't just a practice, it was a law put into place by the realm's leaders long ago.

That decision may have seemed like a good idea to the government at the time, but when you were an unlucky duck infected with the disease like me, the relocation was not ideal. Especially since Arian, Nadia, and every other antagonist in Alderon wanted me dead.

For the meantime, thankfully, I was safe from being shipped off.

While the Godmother Supreme, Lena Lenore, had discovered my magical abilities and suspected their pure nature, she was currently missing the evidence to prove it. Pure Magic could be identified by two tells—it could not be removed from its host and it gave its host dreams of the future. Last month Lenore had attained the first bit of evidence when she failed to take my magic away with a magic-sucking creature called a Stiltdegarth. But until she knew for a fact that I could dream of the future, she couldn't convince the rest of the realm's higher-ups that I had Pure Magic. That's where Lady Agnue came into play.

My headmistress told me that she had proof that I dreamed of the future. She threatened to share this evidence with Lenore if my friends and I breathed a word about all the things we'd learned on our Author quest.

We hated going along with the threat, but we agreed that my getting sent to—and promptly executed in—Alderon was definitely not a favorable next move. So, for the last several weeks we'd played along with Lady Agnue's terms while secretly working on our own plans for how to proceed on our mission to find Paige Tomkins before the antagonists.

Ms. Mammers and I came upon the final hallway leading up

to Lady Agnue's office. I was not a fan of this particular corridor. The walls were lined with oil paintings of all my headmistress's predecessors—the former Lady Agnues. Running this school was a family business, passed from one daughter to the next. It gave me a chill to see all those sharp-chinned brunettes looking down on me.

My escort held the door open. It was between a pair of paintings of the school and beneath a gold-gilded sign that read "Headmistress."

There was a velvety, forest-green couch in the waiting area that Ms. Mammers gestured for me to sit on. I obliged as Ms. Mammers placed herself behind the desk across from me. The desk was so tidy it made me wonder if the woman actually did any work when she was not running around fulfilling the headmistress's errands.

She pretended to ignore me as she stared at the calendar on her desk and circled things with a bronze quill, which matched her choppy, boyish haircut. Suddenly there was a knock on the door we'd just come through. Ms. Mammers glanced up as the door opened. It was one of the school guards.

"I need to speak to you about the security measures you want placed on those dangerous potion supplies Madame Alexanders ordered," he said.

"Can it wait?" Ms. Mammers asked.

"No."

Ms. Mammers' round face scrunched with annoyance. "Fine." She strode across the room and glowered at me like I was a pet learning to be housebroken. "Behave."

I was left alone in the waiting area. I stared at the closed door that connected to Lady Agnue's office. The headmistress had been calling me into her office every week to remind me to keep in line and keep my mouth shut. However, we'd already spoken a few days ago, so I was a bit surprised that she was ready for another round so soon. Did she spend all weekend lying in wait, thinking of fresh ways to tear me a new one?

Lady Agnue's door opened abruptly. My headmistress—

dressed in warm shades of gold—stood in the doorway. Beside her was Lena Lenore. My blood froze at the sight of her.

"Lovely to see you again, Crisanta," Lenore said.

My fingers clenched the velvet cushions on the couch. Lenore's voice was so simultaneously saccharine and wicked that it put me on edge.

Nearly six feet tall with dark flowing hair, hazel eyes, and surprisingly toned arms, she was a beautiful and regal woman who emanated power. Standing close to her felt like standing next to a steel skyscraper while looking up. It put you off balance and made you feel small.

Today, the Godmother Supreme wore a pastel pink pantsuit with light pink pumps. The sparkly silver straps of her shoes perfectly matched the contour shades of her eye makeup. I recalled the outfit. I'd dreamed of this moment before.

I flicked my eyes to Lenore, then Lady Agnue, then back to Lenore. Why was she here? Had Lady Agnue gone back on our deal? Did Lenore know about my Pure Magic? Was I about to get sent to Alderon? And exactly how many glitzy suits did Lenore own?

Lady Agnue gestured for me to enter her office. I got up slowly and made my way over. As the door closed behind me, I felt my pulse start to quicken.

Make no mistake; I was not afraid of Lady Agnue. And I didn't think I was afraid of Lenore either. She may have been Godmother Supreme, a pillar in our realm's upper-government, and the wielder of some pretty powerful magic, but I knew she could not hurt me outright. It was one of the restrictions of her Fairy Godmother magic. She couldn't use it to seriously harm another human being, let alone take a life.

Even so, I still treated her with caution. I understood that Lenore wouldn't hesitate to get rid of me if given the right opportunity. Any misstep or misspoken word on my part might give it to her.

Lady Agnue directed me to a vanilla-colored chair facing her desk, but I declined. I much preferred to stand during face-offs; they were not to be taken sitting down (both literally and figuratively).

"I have it on good authority that you've been talking with my sister," Lenore began.

"I don't know what you mean," I responded.

"Oh, come now, there's no need to deny it," Lenore said. "I know all about your visit to the Indexlands last month. It was impressive. But I saw no need to warn you of the consequences of sharing the discoveries you made there with anyone else. Cornwallace here told me that she secured your silence."

My eyes widened and I turned to my headmistress. "Your first name is *Cornwallace*?" I asked in disbelief. "Your name is Cornwallace Agnue?"

Lady Agnue glared at me fiercely; her copper eyes filled with dislike and condemnation. "Do you have something to comment on the matter, Miss Knight?"

It took every ounce of self-control I had not to make one of the thousand comments on the tip of my tongue.

I bit my lip to suppress a smile. "Nope. Nothing at all." I looked back at Lenore. "You were saying?"

"You and I have our own standing arrangement in regards to your discretion, Crisanta. So with Cornwallace's assurance, I saw no need to further highlight the terms of our agreement after your visit with Liza."

"By terms, do you mean forcing me to keep my mouth shut so that you won't use your magic or influence to destroy my friends and family?"

Lenore couldn't use her Fairy Godmother magic to physically harm or kill others. But if any of us revealed what we knew about the Godmothers' secrets, like their conspiracy with the ambassadors to forge and destroy protagonist books, Lenore had promised to find a way to hurt us. She'd said as much the last time we'd met. I remembered her exact words: "While I may not employ the most conventional method for keeping people silent, if you get in my way I will find other, more creative ways to fill your friends' and family's lives with misery."

*Comforting stuff, right?*

Lenore waved her hand as if I was an annoying fly. "The reason I am here," she continued, "is not because you found the Author. I came to campus because it has come to my attention that you have kept in contact with Liza since your return.

"As I'm sure you're aware, Mark Two magic compact mirrors will be hitting the market soon. However, what you may not know is that each of these mirrors gives off a slight, magical communication signal that a department within my agency is responsible for monitoring. With the compacts set to be released realm-wide in a few months, imagine my surprise when our sensors started picking up a series of pings on our magic signal tower. Then imagine my even *greater* surprise when we were able to trace the signal to regular communications between the Indexlands and this school. Needless to say, I knew there could only be one protagonist responsible."

"Lenore, you flatter me."

"It was unintentional," Lenore replied. "Tell me, Crisanta, what have you and my sister been chatting about so regularly? Could it have anything to do with, say . . . your *Pure Magic*?"

I had gotten quite good at a putting on a front; my poker face was practically a force of nature. Statues could take tips from me.

"Sorry to disappoint, Lenore, but no. Truth is, we just hit it off and she hooked me up with a Mark Two so we could keep in touch." I shrugged. "We have a lot in common, you know—hobbies, favorite foods, *enemies* . . ."

My normally composed headmistress appeared a bit unsettled as Lenore and I glowered at each other. After a moment, Lady Agnue cleared her throat. "Lena, I believe there was something you wanted to ask Crisanta. About her magic?"

"What about it?" I asked sharply.

Lenore straightened her blazer and meandered over to the window. "Be a dear and show us what you can do, will you?" Lenore said.

"Excuse me?"

"Your magic," Lenore clarified. "While I am without proof

that you wield Pure Magic, we know perfectly well that you possess magical abilities. I have heard that your power allows you to bring things to life. Your headmistress has similar suspicions."

"One of your classmates nearly had a heart attack this morning when she was on her way to the practice fields," Lady Agnue explained. "She noticed that the vines growing around Detention Tower Three were moving of their own volition. As that is the tower I sentenced you and your friends to, it is not a great leap to assume you had something to do with it."

I tensed. My powers could give life to things, but until recently I hadn't put much thought into what happened to them after I was done. So far it seemed that they just stayed alive and did whatever they wanted.

"We told the student who made the discovery that the vines had been affected by residue magic from the In and Out Spell," Lady Agnue went on. "I called the Godmother Supreme here to see if she could remedy the situation, but she was unable to reverse the vines' magic. They had to be torn down from the tower about an hour ago."

"Hence my interest in the magic behind the problem," Lenore said. "Come now, Crisanta. Be a good little princess and give us a demonstration of your abilities."

"Forget it," I huffed.

"Miss Knight," Lady Agnue interceded, her shoulders tensed tighter than the bun in her brown hair. "If you want this meeting to be over, show Lena your powers. She just wants to see them for herself. I assure you, this is not a trap."

*Said the cat to the mouse*, I thought.

"Fine," I groaned after a moment. *If it'll get Lenore out of here, then I might as well. The woman already knows. What harm could it do?*

My gaze fell upon a copy of the school newsletter laying open on Lady Agnue's desk. The sunlight from the window coated it in a radiant gleam. The window was open a touch, allowing fresh air to breeze through. I walked over to the desk and placed my hand on the newsletter, taking a deep breath to gather my focus.

*Wake up*, I commanded the thing. *Then fly out of here and be free of this office like I wish I could be.*

My hand became consumed by golden light, which transferred into the newsletter. The thing shook for a second then jerked itself off the desk. Using its open pages like wings, it fluttered into the air then flew out Lady Agnue's open window.

I took another deep breath to re-center myself, causing the glow around my hand to subside as the periodical vanished from view.

Lady Agnue's mouth hung agape. "That was . . ."

I could honestly say I had never seen my headmistress so stunned. Lenore, too, seemed amazed.

"Extraordinary," she said, finishing my headmistress's comment. "I haven't seen magic of this variety in some time."

"How do you mean?" I asked, assuming that she was once again trying to imply that I had Pure Magic.

"I mean that bringing things to life is a very special ability," Lenore explained. "Even the most powerful magical beings, like Fairy Godmothers and genies—before they disappeared—do not possess that gift. Just as we cannot use our magic to take life, we cannot use it to give life either. It is a restriction that our powers cannot bypass no matter how strong they are. Seeing someone, *anyone*, with that ability is . . . something to take note of."

"Um, all right," I replied awkwardly. I was genuinely unsure of what to say in response to that.

"On that note I shall be off," Lenore announced, checking her watch. "I have a staff meeting at noon and a disciplinary hearing to oversee before then." Lenore turned to Lady Agnue. "Always a pleasure to see you, Cornwallace. Do let me know if you acquire that information I asked for." She and Lady Agnue exchanged air kisses.

The Godmother Supreme pulled a ring with a ruby spiral from her finger. It transformed into a sleek, iridescent magic wand that shone as she waved it. Her body was enveloped within a ring of shimmering red sparks. They encircled her feet then rose up like the geyser of a fountain. The effect was almost to her chin when she gave me a final glance and smiled coldly. "I'll see you again soon, Crisanta. Do be careful. And watch out for that Malice Line."

I frowned. "What's a Malice Line?"

My question came too late. Lenore evaporated into a giant ball of glittering energy, which shot out the window and into the sky. She easily phased through the In and Out Spell (which she could do since she'd been one of the Godmothers who'd cast it) and disappeared out of sight.

"You should have at least tried to show some restraint, Miss Knight," Lady Agnue said. "I realize that you have a fondness for acting like an impertinent child in the presence of superiors, but it would be wise to resist the urge as much as possible when it comes to those who are more powerful than you."

"Didn't you hear?" I asked sarcastically. "Lenore seems to think I'm pretty powerful."

"And modest too," Lady Agnue countered. "Do not misunderstand, Miss Knight. I would love to have Lena find out about your Pure Magic and give you the sentence you deserve. However, the problem remains that if she did, I would have no leverage to secure your friends' silence on matters that would affect my student body. Thus, I am doing my part by not telling her what I know about your ability to see the future. But you, young lady, must do your part too. In addition to holding up your end of our bargain, you also need to hold that sharp tongue of yours when it comes to provoking the Godmother Supreme. It is clear you are not fond of her, but you must not give her any more reasons to want to destroy you. Knowing how you generally come across to people, I imagine she already has quite a few."

"And the flattery never ends." I rolled my eyes. "Can I go now? Or do you want another piece of me?"

"Go." Lady Agnue waved her hand. "After talking with you and being visited by Lena Lenore, I need a few minutes to myself. Between the two of you, it has been a rather stressful morning."

I looked at my headmistress with curiosity. "I thought Lenore was your friend."

"She is," Lady Agnue replied, "and a very dear one at that. We have been through a lot together. But trust and reluctance are not mutually exclusive, Miss Knight. People can still be wary of those closest to them. In fact, it is a duality of feeling that someone in my position has had to get used to."

"Yeah," I replied with a huff as I headed for the door. "Join the club."

## CHAPTER 5

# The Job

H it the deck!" I pushed Blue out of the way as the concoction in our cauldron boiled over. Magenta foam spewed all over our desk and toward a couple of nearby classmates.

In retrospect, letting novice brewers attempt a sleeping potion this complicated was probably a bad idea. In fact, as Marie Sinclaire and Lili Jane Watson (Princess of Salinas) hit the floor—completely unconscious—I was sure that it was.

*Oh, great.*

Marie was my friend and she'd forgive me, but I doubted Lili would. Unlike most of my classmates, Lili was not fond of the "New Crisanta Knight." Marie told me that it was because Lili had had a crush on Chance Darling for the last couple of years and resented that when he finally became available, he'd turned all his attention to me.

*Oh well. You can't please everyone.* And if I was honest, I generally preferred not to.

I felt bad that Lili and Marie had been knocked out, but it wasn't entirely my fault. Our potions professor, Madame Alexanders, should have been paying more attention, particularly when we were making something so dangerous, and particularly around students like me who weren't that skilled.

Potions class was not my thing. Well, most subjects at this school were not my thing. But lack of skill was much more evident in a class where mistakes could lead to combustion.

Thankfully, SJ was the most talented potionist in our year

and probably the whole school. Usually she was able to give Blue and me enough help so that our lab exercises ran smoothly. But she'd been assisting some other students when our magenta foam started erupting. Upon the aforementioned explosion though, she and Madame Alexanders rushed over.

The two worked in sync to calm the reactive materials in our mini cauldron so they'd stop boiling over. Once that was taken care of, they wheeled on us with their arms crossed.

"I thought my instructions were clear," SJ said sternly, gesturing to her notebook on our desk. "My notes highlight the step-by-step procedure for what to do."

"We followed them," Blue protested.

"*Really?*" SJ asked. She picked up a chunk of yucca root the size of a large finger and then pointed to her notes. "It says right here to *julienne* the yucca before adding them to the pot. That means to cut them into thin strips or match-like pieces. This yucca is not julienned."

"Well, maybe you shouldn't use so many fancy words in your notebook," Blue argued. "Who exactly are you trying to impress?"

"Ladies," Madame Alexanders interrupted. "That is enough. SJ, go fetch the nurse. Miss Sinclaire and Miss Watson can sleep off the effects of the potion in the infirmary. Crisa, Blue, clean this mess up immediately. Use the enchantment-absorbent sponges in the cupboard. And for the love of Book, *please* do not touch any of the Poppy petals in the process. As for the rest of you . . ." Madame Alexanders turned to our eavesdropping classmates. "There are only ten minutes left in the period and rest assured that if you have not completed the lab exercise by then, I *will* assign it as homework."

Blue and I proceeded to clean our lab desk, which took forever to scrub down. Heeding our professor's warning, we were careful not to touch any of the toxic Poppy petals in the process.

Madame Alexanders had informed us that Poppies were going to be an important part of our potions studies this semester. As we'd learned in an earlier lecture, the root of all sleeping potions was the Poppy. In Book, this sleep-inducing flower grew only in Tunderly, where my archenemy Mauvrey Weatherall (daughter of Sleeping Beauty) was from. According to our fairytale history texts, the flowers were also native to the lands of Oz and Camelot.

Personally, I wasn't so sure working with Poppy Potions was a smart idea. SJ could handle that level of brewing, but far less talented students like Blue and myself working with such a dangerous substance was not great. I'd already taken out two of my classmates. At this rate who knew how many more would drop in the months to come.

Luckily, this was a mild sleeping potion that was engineered to induce only thirty-minute naps, so Marie and Lili would be fine.

Although every sleeping potion required Poppy petals, the other ingredients varied depending on the type and strength of the potion. There were *a lot* of types and strengths of Poppy Potions out there. And Madame Alexanders seemed more than willing to have us delve into each and every one this semester.

*Who else feels like this is not going to end well?*

*Maybe I should book a bed in the infirmary now.*

The bell rang and students began to file out of the room. Several school nurses had come to collect Marie and Lili, and SJ had gone with them to escort the princesses to the infirmary. She probably felt partially responsible for their current state since I'd screwed up the potion on her watch.

Blue and I were nearly done cleaning. We kept scrubbing our desk until Jade and Big Girtha approached us.

Princess Jade (the least likeable of Aladdin's children) and Big Girtha Bobunk (the younger, larger sibling to the title characters of *Hansel & Gretel*) were far from my favorite classmates. Until recently, they had been friends with the aforementioned Mauvrey.

Since my nemesis disappeared a month ago, Big Girtha and Jade had been looking a bit lost. They still stuck together, but without their leader they'd sort of been drifting. Every day since Mauvrey's departure I'd seen them in classes, walking through the corridors, and sitting in the banquet hall, going through the motions of normalcy. But it was obvious to anyone who watched them for more than a second that they were feeling anything but normal. They were depressed and on edge.

If Big Girtha hadn't tried to squash me under Mauvrey's

orders on more than one occasion, and if Jade hadn't been so annoyingly prissy to me since our pre-teens, I might have felt sorry for them. The sight of the pair these last few weeks had been quite sad. Lackeys without leaders were a lot like cookies without milk. Incomplete.

As the two neared Blue and me, I varied between feeling aloof and having pity for them.

"How's it going?" Big Girtha asked.

Blue and I exchanged a look.

"Um, fine I guess," I said. "Did you guys need something?"

Jade glanced away for a moment, tucking a strand of her long, lush black hair behind an ear. Big Girtha elbowed her friend in the arm and the princess made a slight squeak.

Jade sighed and looked me in the eyes again. "Crisa," she began, "I realize that Girtha and I have not always been amiable to you, Blue, and SJ—"

"Amiable?" Blue interrupted. "You and your former ring-master have taken shots at us for years. Supersized over here went as far as breaking my arm last spring." Blue nodded to Big Girtha. "Isn't that right, Gigantore?"

"That was an accident," Big Girtha said defensively. "You know the risks of jousting. I rammed you off your horse fair and square in our final exam. If you didn't want to take the risk, you shouldn't have taken the elective."

Blue stepped in front of me and got in Big Girtha's face. "I know you greased my saddle before the match because Mauvrey didn't like me showing her up in Ballroom Dance class the day before. That's the only reason I slipped and the only reason you got the top mark in that elective instead of me."

Big Girtha—massive like a gargoyle crossbred with a bell tower—stared down at Blue. Her furry eyebrows narrowed beneath her choppy broomstick bangs. "Are you calling me a cheater?"

"I'm calling you a lot of things, you loggerheaded, clapper-clawed, she-bear," Blue replied. "But sure, let's start with cheater."

Feeling that this disagreement was about to move beyond

words, Jade and I put our hands on our respective friends' shoulders to hold them back.

"Look, what's done is done," I interceded. "What do you want? Out with it fast so we can go our separate ways."

"That is just it," Jade said carefully. "Girtha and I have been talking, Crisa, and we think it might be in all of our best interests *not* to go our separate ways."

"What's that?"

"Your tiny, cloaked friend here is right, Crisa," Big Girtha said, shooting Blue a glare. "Jade and I have spent a lot of time messing with you and your friends over the years because of Mauvrey. But as a result you, Blue, and SJ are the three people we know best at school. And now that Mauvrey's gone, well, your group seemed like the most obvious choice to . . ." Girtha's voice trailed off.

"To what?" I urged.

"To merge with," Jade finished.

"Let me get this straight," Blue clarified. "Because you two spent your free time finding ways to mess with us over the years, you think that qualifies you to hang out with us?"

"Actually, with Crisa," Jade replied. "She was Mauvrey's mortal nemesis after all, so we spent most of our time helping Mauvrey figure out ways to torment her. You and SJ kind of just came along for the ride. As such, now that Mauvrey is gone, it would seem that the person we are most compatible to support would be Crisa. We already know so much about her. She would be the most plausible person to take over as our group leader."

I was so surprised I literally had nothing to say. Luckily, Blue made up for it.

"Forget it," she snapped. "For all we know you're in cahoots with that witch who used to give you orders and are just waiting to get close enough to Crisa to finish what the she-demon started before she left campus."

"That's a lie," Big Girtha said. "I know there's been a lot of rumors floating around about what really happened to Mauvrey and what our headmistress isn't telling us, but we know as little about what went down with her as the rest of the school does. And now that she's gone we've had a lot of time to think and we've decided we want to change."

I scrunched my eyebrows together, perplexed and suspicious. The expression made Big Girtha rub the back of her head self-consciously, bristling her mud-colored hair.

"We've always known how the rest of the school sees us," Big Girtha said. "Like we're bullies and jerks. Only when Mauvrey was here to guide us, to be our friend, we didn't really care. We had each other; we were a crew and Mauvrey's presence was enough to intimidate other people from ever looking at us sideways. Without her though . . . well, we just don't want to be hated anymore, Crisa. We don't want to seem like antagonists in the making; we want people to see us in a different light. Which is all the more reason why we'd like to hang with you. Not only because we already know you pretty well from doing Mauvrey's bidding like Jade said, but because what better way to show the rest of the school that we've changed than by supporting the person we've always come after the most?"

"No way." Blue shook her head even more adamantly. "As if we'd believe any of this 'we want to change' malarkey. Your group merger is rejected. You get me? There is no chance the two of you are allowed anywhere near Crisa."

"But we are telling the truth," Jade insisted. "We *do* want to change, and in order to do that it is vital that people see that Crisa sees us as friends, not enemies. She has become one of the most popular girls in school. If she accepts us, then others will surely follow. If she does not, then we have no hope of changing our image."

"Tough," Blue huffed. "You and the Gargantuan made your beds a long time ago, Jade, and now you have to lie in them. You're all our enemies, including Crisa's. So why don't you and Big Girtha just take your change of heart and . . ."

"Whoa, whoa, whoa," I interjected, finally finding my voice and pushing my way between Blue, Jade, and Big Girtha.

"First of all, *Crisa* can decide for herself who she can and can't hang out with," I said, glancing at my well-meaning but overprotective friend. "And second . . ."

I looked back at Jade and Big Girtha. "I appreciate that you guys want to change, but Blue is right. You can't flip a switch like that and expect me to take you as new friends on face value. It's too weird. And no offense, but while you may not truly know everything that went down between me and Mauvrey before she disappeared, that doesn't change the fact that I don't trust you.

"The two of you have *literally* antagonized me, my friends, and a lot of other girls at school for years. If you ever want any of us to forget that, it's going to require a bit more than a plea for forgiveness. The bottom line: if both of you actually want to change, that's great. But you have to put in the effort that it requires. Change is not the sort of thing that I—or anyone—can just hand you like a pardon for a past transgression. It's something you have to earn through a lot of hard work. Trust me, I know. So that being said, I'm sorry, but for the time being I agree with Blue. Your offer to be our friends is rejected. And I really would prefer it if you stayed away from us."

Big Girtha and Jade looked at me sadly and I wondered for a moment if they were going to protest. I also wondered if my words had ticked Big Girtha off enough to cause her to lash out (as was her tendency) and use her freakish strength and massive hands to throttle me then and there. Probably not, as our professor was still at the front of the classroom, but I kept my guard up just in case.

Thankfully, Big Girtha and Jade walked away and out of the room without another word. The pair of them seemed so defeated that I almost felt bad for them. Then Blue smacked me on the back and I was jolted out of my misgivings.

"Way to tell them off," she said. "They got what they deserved."

"I wasn't trying to tell them off," I responded as I went to pack my books. "I was trying to tell them the truth. If they want to change they have to put in the hours. Becoming someone different is possible, but it's something you have to invest in completely. It's more than a decision; it's a commitment that requires work every day as you forge your way toward seeing it through."

Blue raised an eyebrow. "Wait, you mean you actually buy what they were selling? You believe they can change?"

"I mean I believe that *anybody* can change. Whether they will is up to them."

Blue studied me curiously and then shrugged. "Whatever. That happened. It was weird. Let's move on. We're gonna be late for our next class if we don't hustle." She grabbed her books and bag and headed for the door at the front of the room.

"We don't have a next class. It's lunchtime," I replied as I tossed my bag over my shoulder and followed.

"All the more reason not to be late," Blue responded, smiling.

I was trailing her out the door when Madame Alexanders called to me from her desk. "Miss Knight. Before you go, a word please?"

I signaled Blue to go ahead and approached Madame Alexanders's desk. It was the same as the student lab desks—thick like a brick, black like tar, and sturdy from end to end. Bunsen burners were spaced across it along with a collection of vials, beakers, and forceps.

My professor's auburn hair was in a loose bun held together by two chocolate brown clips. I couldn't tell if she was angry with me—her green eyes were still focused on her papers—but whenever a professor asked me to stay after class, I generally assumed it wasn't a social call.

"If this is about the explosion," I started, "it was a total, careless mistake, but I swear it will never happen again. I'll pay closer attention to the lecture next time. I promise."

"This is not about your lab exercise mishap, Crisanta. Accidents happen. This is about a job."

"A job?"

"Yes, one I would like to offer you," my professor went on. "With all the added kerfuffle that comes with basing a semester's worth of study on an ingredient as temperamental as the Poppy, there comes a great deal of prep work for our lessons. So much work, in fact, that I requested permission from Lady Agnue to select a student teaching assistant to aid me with the endeavor for the next several months."

I blinked at her, not quite processing what she was saying. Not because I was dense—it was obvious what she was getting at—but because it was too ridiculous a notion for me to comprehend.

"Are you saying you want *me* to be your TA?" I asked in disbelief.

"Exactly," Madame Alexanders confirmed. "You would help me set up equipment and grade papers on occasion, but most importantly you would work with me after school to do runthroughs of the following week's experiments."

"Professor, you've got to be joking," I said. "I'm barely mediocre at brewing. SJ's your best potionist, not only in this class, but in the whole school. You even trusted her enough to lend her that special potions book last semester. Shouldn't you be asking her to be your TA?"

"SJ is very gifted, and it is true that I have put a great deal of faith in her as a potionist in the past. But you have a lot of untapped potential that I'm afraid won't be tapped unless I show you how to tap it. Moreover, you have creativity and an adherence to instinct that SJ often suppresses in favor of a more rational approach."

I shook my head. "No way. I'm telling you, professor, SJ's your girl. Yeah, she's rational, but she's got talent coming out of her ears. She's brewed circles around the rest of this class for years and has worked hard to not only help us, but help you. She deserves this job. She's earned it."

"I am sorry, Crisanta, but my mind is made up. I don't want SJ. I want you."

"Well, I'm going to have to pass. I can't do that to SJ. And anyway, even if I wanted the job, I couldn't take it. I'm sure when you put through your request to Lady Agnue, she told you that the three of us are obliged to attend detention every day after school for the next five months."

"She mentioned that," Madame Alexanders responded. "But after I expressed my need of your specific assistance, I worked out a deal with her. If you agree to be my TA and work with me every day after school for an hour, you and your friends will be excused from detention."

"Are you serious? For how long?"

"Permanently," she replied. "Think of it as serving out your sentence by means of community service. Lady Agnue understands how much care is required for handling the Poppy. And when I explained how invaluable you would be to that work, but how reluctant you might be about accepting it, she agreed to the arrangement. Take the position as my teaching assistant, Crisanta, and you, Blue, and SJ are off the hook."

I thought about the offer. Our detention sentence hadn't been so terrible after I'd figured out how we could escape from the tower and hang out with the boys. But we couldn't do that anymore. The magic hunters were still out there. And now that Lady Agnue had discovered and destroyed the vines that grew on Detention Tower Three, we no longer had a means of escape. As it stood, SJ, Blue, and I were going to be stuck serving our full sentence unless something changed.

Madame Alexanders was offering a way out for all of us. I had the opportunity to free us from our punishment by doing a few extra hours of schoolwork each week. After everything SJ and Blue had done for me in recent months, I reasoned that I owed it to them to take that offer.

"Fine, professor," I eventually said. "I'll be your TA. But just for the record, I still say you're making a mistake by going with me instead of SJ."

"Don't sell yourself short, Miss Knight," Madame Alexanders responded. "You bring a lot more to the table than you realize. Now then, we shall begin our sessions next Monday. Four o'clock sharp, all right?"

"Um, yeah. Okay." I shrugged.

"Good," my professor said as she began to pack up her things with renewed enthusiasm. "Bring your textbook and a can-do attitude. With that and some faith, trust, and anti-rust lab equipment, I know we will do great things together."

"Uh-huh. Sure, professor," I said.

On that unconfident note, I rapidly made my way to the exit. When I slipped into the hallway and closed the door behind me,

I was met by the perplexed expressions of Blue and SJ. Evidently, SJ had come back from the infirmary just in time to overhear the exchange between the professor and me.

"Tell me I have really bad eavesdropping skills and Madame Alexanders didn't just ask you to be her TA for the semester," Blue said.

I glanced over at SJ. Whether she admitted it or not, this had to hurt. She was already in a fragile emotional state over recent turns of events in her life.

When we met Liza last semester we learned that SJ didn't have a protagonist book. She hadn't been chosen as a protagonist like the rest of us. The ambassadors had forged a book for her, as they did for any royal not naturally selected by the Author. Since then, SJ had been sort of adrift. She denied this, of course, and had gone about her days without displaying any obvious signs of internal conflict. But Blue and I knew better than to believe the misdirect. The truth was obvious. When SJ discovered she hadn't been chosen as a protagonist, she'd been totally shaken.

We'd supported her since the realization and hadn't brought up the matter. After all, SJ didn't need some book to prove she was special. She was SJ; being special was ingrained in her nature. She was one of the smartest kids in school, one of the kindest and most compassionate people in our realm, and had a prodigious talent for brewing potions that—when combined with her scientific curiosity and inventiveness—made her a rival to even the most renowned potionists in the world.

Even so, I understood from my own experiences that one's great strengths could be easily forgotten when self-doubt was introduced. And it seemed that when Madame Alexanders offered me that TA job instead of her, I had inadvertently helped self-doubt settle more firmly into my friend's mind-scape.

"SJ, I'm so sorry," I said hastily. "I tried to tell her that I was the wrong choice, that she was crazy not to pick you, but she wouldn't listen. She told me that if I agreed to do it we wouldn't have to serve any more detention. I thought taking the job would be best for all of us. But I swear, I'll go back inside right now and refuse it if you want me to; I'll insist that you're the one for the job."

SJ's expression was blank. "No need," she said calmly. "I heard everything, Crisa. I know what our teacher has to say about the matter, and about me."

"SJ, you can't listen to her. She doesn't know what she's talking about. She—"

"Crisa." SJ held up a hand. "I appreciate you defending my skills, but if I had been the right person for the position, Madame Alexanders would have asked me outright. She did not; ergo, I am not the person she wants. Which means that you made the proper choice in taking her up on the offer. Anything else would have been illogical."

"So . . . you're okay then?" Blue asked carefully. She tried to put a hand on SJ's shoulder, but SJ moved slightly out of reach.

"Of course," SJ replied. "Now come. It is Panini Day; we should get to the banquet hall before all of the good sandwiches are taken."

Blue and I began to follow her down the hallway. As we walked I marveled at the invisible walls I could sense SJ putting up with every passing step. I knew what doubt did to people. The memories of how it almost tore me apart were fresh. While the tone and small smile that came with SJ's reply had been intended to suggest otherwise, I knew that she was anything but okay. Her eyes had given her away.

Make no mistake, I had no plans to become an antagonist. But the way SJ looked at me for a moment before averting her gaze—a look of sadness, maybe a little jealousy, and the incunabula of internal struggle burning inside—made me feel like a villain, and worse than I had in a long time.

# CHAPTER 6

# Unexpected Chance

ell, don't you look poppin'!"

I spun around to see Blue standing in the bathroom doorway. She was dressed and ready for tonight's ball, but she had this excited, surprised expression on her face that I didn't quite understand.

"What's that?" I asked as I finished fastening a clasp on the back of my dress.

"I said you look poppin'!" she repeated, crossing her arms. "Like, seriously Crisa. Wow."

I blushed from the compliment. "Thanks," I said. "You look nice too."

"Wait, hold on. I don't think you're fully appreciating what I'm trying to say here," Blue asserted as she walked over to me. "SJ, come out the bathroom for a sec, will ya?"

"Blue, what is it?" SJ said as she emerged from the door. "We must depart for the ball at exactly seven o'clock or I will be late to help Madame Lisbon set up. We do not have time for any of your shenanigans."

Blue rolled her eyes. "Yeah, yeah, you've only mentioned that like fifty times in the last five minutes. Now will you please take a look at Crisa and tell her what you think."

SJ turned toward me, stopped short, and stared. The same stunned expression that had appeared on Blue's face now crossed hers.

"Crisa, you look . . . absolutely wonderful. That is not to say that you do not always look nice. I only mean that this dress is utterly amazing on you. You look like . . . Well, there is no contest. Tonight, you will be the most stunning princess at the ball."

"Um, thank you?" I replied awkwardly.

I didn't understand why they were being so weird. Blue had on a strappy, rose gold dress with a swirly pattern that shone when it caught the light. Her dark blonde waves—which she'd grown out since last semester—accentuated the look in a natural but polished way.

SJ, meanwhile, wore a royal blue lace dress that had long, see-through sleeves and a slit up the skirt. Her suede stilettos were the same deep black shade as her hair, which was neatly done up in an elegant ballerina bun. Her dangling diamond earrings were understated but sparkled like runaway stars. Overall, she radiated pure elegance.

In other words, *SJ and Blue* both looked utterly amazing. I never appeared anywhere near as put together as they did. I usually just looked like me, which was a seven out of ten on the reg and maybe an eight out of ten on a good day.

I shrugged off their compliments as I made my way into the bathroom to run a brush through my hair. I made direct eye contact with the girl in the mirror and took in the dress that had set my friends agape.

The satin number was graceful, simple, and a formfitting mermaid style. The top was a dark shade of rosewood that grew lighter and brighter in color until it erupted into a kind of electric crimson at the skirt.

It was an intriguing design, and I liked it. What I was less sure about was the actual cut of the dress. It was a halter-top with a much lower back than I was used to, which was highlighted by my newly shortened hair.

At least the gown didn't have a corset. I'd always hated those things, but after Mauvrey nearly killed me with a poisoned one last month, it was safe to say that my distaste for them had grown substantially.

*Mauvrey* . . .

While I tried not to think about her, looking at this dress—

about to go to a ball like I had been the night she'd tried to kill me—I couldn't help it.

Although I knew my school nemesis was a vicious, malice-driven girl, it was still hard to accept that she was *genuinely* wicked. Not only was she working with Nadia and the antagonists, she had a Shadow living inside of her like Arian did. Thinking about it gave me the shivers.

She, Arian, and other Shadow-compatible antagonists in Alderon were surrendering their souls so their bodies could serve as vessels for members of this dark species. In doing so—in becoming Shadow Guardians—they'd made themselves immune to certain types of magic. For example, they could easily pass through the weaker versions of In and Out Spells around Alderon and Lady Agnue's. As a trade-off, the Shadows continuously fed off their hosts' life energies—slowly consuming them by sucking them dry like leeches from the inside.

I shuddered again.

I wasn't worried about Mauvrey. I was pretty sure it was impossible to muster concern for someone who'd spent months secretly plotting to eliminate you. What bothered me was that I couldn't imagine what had possibly possessed her to choose such a fate. For years she had been a princess at the top of our class at Lady Agnue's—totally set to become a great protagonist one day. Why in the realm would she have thrown all that away in favor of becoming a villain?

I had known her for most of my life. Our families (both being royal) had gotten together for events long before she and I started attending Lady Agnue's. The saddest part was that we actually got on quite well when we were younger. She had been nice once. It wasn't until we were about nine or ten that her personality had taken a curt turn for the toxic. And now, for whatever reason, she'd gone all antagonist.

Not that anyone at school outside of my immediate circle of friends and our headmistress knew any of this. When Mauvrey fled the grounds after attempting homicide with the poisoned corset, Lady Agnue did not tell the student body the truth about her disappearance. She couldn't exactly explain anything accurate about Mauvrey's fate without also revealing many of the other tightly concealed secrets she was keeping.

The headmistress simply resigned to telling everyone that Mauvrey had become ill and returned home—as big a lie as you could possibly put together.

Wherever Mauvrey had vanished to, it definitely wasn't back to her own kingdom. For one, her newfound occupation as a Shadow-hosting super villainess wasn't exactly the type of work you could do from home. And two, I seriously doubted Lady Agnue had told Mauvrey's parents that their daughter was missing. Even now they probably thought she was here at school with the rest of us—blissfully unaware that their daughter had turned dark.

Geez, that was gonna be a rough conversation to have one day when they inevitably learned the truth. I could just imagine it:

*"Sorry, your highnesses. We know you already suffered a lot in your day, but turns out you don't get that happily ever after you thought you'd earned. Your only offspring has decided to turn evil and help a bunch of other crazy people overthrow the realm's protagonists."*

Sheesh, I felt bad for them already.

On second thought, for now maybe it *was* for their own good that Lady Agnue hadn't told Mauvrey's parents the truth. It's not like she would've been able to provide them with much information. Like I said, none of us knew where Mauvrey had run off to.

Hopefully this wouldn't be the case for much longer. Before I'd blacked out from the poison of Mauvrey's corset dress, I'd used my magic to activate a contingency plan. I'd given life to one of SJ's glass figurines—a small Pegasus—and ordered it to follow Mauvrey until she reached her hideout, then report back to me once it could lead me there. The tiny winged creature had yet to return, but I had faith that it was only a matter of time before the Pegasus came back and took us right to my nemesis.

I blinked. Lost in thought, I'd been inadvertently staring at my reflection in the mirror for some time now. I swiftly abandoned the looking glass to join my friends. If we were gonna make it all the way across the school to the grand ballroom by seven o'clock, we had to get going.

*Thank goodness for the combat boots I'm wearing beneath my dress. At least there are some things that never change.*

It was nearly nine and I felt uncharacteristically at peace.

My friends and I had made it with plenty of time to the grand ballroom to help Madame Lisbon finish setting up the festivities. Blue and I weren't exactly thrilled about arriving so early or partaking in mundane tasks like candelabra lighting or ice-sculpture monitoring. But when your best friend was head of the ball planning committee and you wanted to be supportive, this was part of the deal.

Almost an hour into the dance, SJ was still scurrying about making sure everything was running smoothly. Meanwhile, Blue, Jason, Daniel, and I were hanging out at my favorite spot in the room—the fancy appetizer table—waiting for her to get off duty.

The two boys—gentlemen that they were—had complimented us on our appearances when we'd arrived. We, in turn, had flattered them about theirs. They really were dressed quite dapper. Jason's suit was charcoal gray, and his tie was a bold shade of teal. Daniel wore a more classic look. His suit was pure black and was accented with a sharp black tie over his crisp white shirt.

It didn't escape my notice that both boys paused for a second when they saw me. Even if it was for just an instant, they displayed the same surprised reaction that Blue and SJ had shown when they'd first seen my ensemble. I couldn't help but think that this was either the greatest dress ever, or I had spinach in my teeth.

Regardless, I soon found myself enjoying the ball. The four of us (sometimes five if SJ could steal away from her responsibilities) hung out by the appetizer table having a perfectly pleasant time. We snacked on fancy finger food, talked about our classes, complained about homework, and laughed like we were a group of regular fairytale teenagers.

I closed my eyes for a moment, listening to the whir of the

orchestra and the sounds of chatter and clinking glasses that filled the room.

Balls used to annoy me a bit. In a lot of ways, they were unnecessary gatherings of pomp and circumstance with far too many rules to be fully enjoyed. However, after everything my friends and I had been through recently, I found myself relishing the normalcy. Even if it was only for a few hours, it was an escape from the real world. No magic training with Liza, no stares from teachers, no whispers from students, no hunters trying to kill me. For this brief intermission I was simply a girl in a dress in a room of small talk and tiny appetizers. That was something to be appreciated.

My sense of peace was interrupted when someone elbowed me in the arm. I opened my eyes and found Blue leaning against the table beside me.

"Whatcha thinking about?" she asked as she picked up a bacon-wrapped shrimp from one of the platters.

"Nothing." I shrugged. "I'm just happy I guess."

Blue munched on her snack and gazed around the ballroom. She swallowed and then tilted her head toward something. "Well, hold on to that thought."

I turned to see what she was alluding to. From the opposite end of the ballroom Chance Darling was headed my way.

Prince Chance Darling—charming by birth and vocation— looked strapping in his perfectly fitted designer suit and deep burgundy tie.

I understood why so many girls at Lady Agnue's went weak at the knees for him. His hypnotic sea foam green eyes shone with flecks of bronze. His expression always appeared determined. You could probably cut glass with that hard, chiseled jawline. And his hair had that naturally tousled look—although I highly suspected a fair amount of unnatural product went into making it appear that way.

Yet I was not taken with the prince like so many of my classmates were.

*Why?*

In a word, he was annoying. In a bunch of other words, he was also narcissistic, shallow, self-absorbed, self-entitled, and stuffier than the feta-stuffed grape leaves on the appetizer table.

Unfortunately, the prince was not as averse to me as I was to him.

I'd tried to make my feelings very clear, but his highness was relentless in his infatuation with me. Instead of simply picking a different girl to invest his time and energy in, he remained persistent, as demonstrated by the flowers and other gifts I'd received since my return to school.

I had a feeling that it was only a matter of time before he sought me out at the ball tonight. I'd hoped it would be later rather than sooner though.

"Crisa," Jason leaned over the snack table, "do you want me to ask you to dance—help you dodge this one?"

I considered his tempting offer. Dancing with Jason would keep Chance from asking me. It was sort of a gentlemen-caller loophole within the mandatory statutes of conduct at a ball. Still, that would only buy me a ten-minute window of safety before those same rules dictated Chance could cut in.

My not-so-secret admirer would not give up easily, and eventually I would have to dance with him. I figured might as well get it over with. Aside from that, I'd decided earlier in the week to think of Chance's advances as more exasperating than upsetting. I was craving normalcy, or at least something to take my mind off my multitude of actual problems. While I was quite fond of several changes that had occurred since last semester, sometimes I felt nostalgic for the types of benign, insignificant things that used to swirl around my mind before I had to trade my normal teenage worries for those of a person destined for far more responsibility.

"Thanks, Jason," I said. "But I'm okay. I think I'll throw him a bone."

I looked over at Chance, who was closing in on twenty feet.

"But one of you boys better come and get me in ten minutes," I added quickly, pointing to Jason and Daniel. "I'm charitable, but I'm not deaf. Even in my most tolerant state I don't think I can listen to him blather on for more than that. Got it?"

The boys nodded in agreement and not a moment too soon. The pompous prince in question gallivanted over to our group. He bowed formally before me. "Crisanta."

"Hi Chance," I responded blandly. "Running a bit behind, aren't you?"

"What do you mean?"

"It's nearly nine and this is the first I've seen of you all night. Based on the constant flood of flowers and gold jewelry you keep sending, I'd have thought you would have sought me out the second the ball started. Don't tell me your tardiness is due to the fact that you finally wised up and picked another girl?"

"Not exactly," Chance replied. "It occurred to me that I might have been coming on too strong lately. Since you have yet to respond to any of my gifts of courtship, I thought it might be best to give you some space."

"Smart boy," I said. "But I take it your definition of 'some space' has an expiration of about fifty-five minutes, otherwise you wouldn't be here bothering me now."

Chance looked frustrated, and a tad embarrassed that my friends were witnessing our exchange. He stole a glance at their smirking expressions and his cheeks flushed slightly. He leaned closer to me, lowering his voice to try and make our conversation less public.

"Why must you always be so curt with me, Crisanta? You make my advances sound so unwarranted."

I leaned in and lowered my voice to match his. "That's because they *are*, Chance. When are you going to realize that?"

The prince and I locked eyes. It was the same kind of look Daniel and I gave each other when caught in a combative stalemate.

Chance took a step back and extended his hand. "Dance with me, Crisanta?"

*Funny how he asks as if I had a choice.*

I was enjoying our exchange and was about to respond with another cutting comment when Chance said something that completely surprised me.

"Crisanta, contrary to what you might believe, you should know that I *am* actually asking here. If you do not wish to dance, then I shall respect your decision and bid you adieu for the evening—no strings attached and no reporting you to your headmistress for breaking the rules. Honest."

*Hold up. Did he really just say that? Was his highness seriously offering me a choice? Ugh, what is going on with this week?*

Big Girtha and Jade wanted to be my friends. Madame Alexanders asked me to be her TA. And now Chance—the fairest and most annoying of them all—was giving me a choice in whether or not I wanted to spend time with him.

*So much for normalcy.*

Too stunned to seize the opportunity I'd been given, I decided to stay the course. I'd already wrapped my mind around being forced to dance with Chance, so I might as well go through with it. Past that . . . I kind of wanted to see where this new behavior of his was coming from. And where it was going.

"All right. I'll dance with you, Chance. But don't get any ideas. This doesn't change anything between us."

Chance gave me a smile. Not his usual smug, pearly white one—a smile of relief. I placed my hand in his (as was the custom) and allowed him to lead me onto the dance floor. As we made our way, I quickly turned back to my friends.

"*Ten minutes,*" I mouthed.

I tensed a bit as I heard voices whispering my name as we passed. Chance and I entered the dance circle. He placed his hand upon my waist and I put mine on his shoulder.

The two of us smoothly migrated into the waltz. We box-stepped and swayed in silence for a minute, our movements so light and effortless we might as well have been dancing on air. This both pleased and surprised me.

Much to the shock of my classmates, my professors, and even myself, my dancing abilities had drastically improved this semester. I attributed the turnaround to the inadvertent high-stakes practice I'd received while fending for my life. My agility, footwork, and reflexes had sharpened immensely from frequent combat in so many unorthodox settings. Combined with my many years of dance training, I now moved with the princess-like grace that my mother had always hoped for.

*Who would have thought violent fights could improve one's dancing? Go figure.*

"I surprised you, didn't I?" Chance asked, interrupting my thoughts.

I looked up at him, confused.

"When I gave you a choice as to whether or not you wanted to dance with me," he clarified. "I surprised you."

"Well, yeah," I admitted. "You're known for a lot of things, Chance, but caring about someone else's needs before your own isn't one of them."

A hurt look flashed across his face, and I wondered if maybe that comment had been too mean. Ordinarily Chance would have deserved the remark. Every conversation we'd ever exchanged had been tinged with his narcissism. Since he'd started trying to "win my heart" or whatever, he'd only further highlighted his obnoxious qualities. But right at this particular moment, I had to acknowledge that he was acting differently. And as long as he was being far less loathsome than usual, maybe my brash comebacks were not as warranted.

"Can I ask you something?" Chance said.

"I'm already dancing with you," I responded. "What more do you want?"

"Specifically," he cleared his throat, "I would genuinely like to know why you are so set against me, Crisanta. Why are you so adamantly invested in rejecting me at every possible turn?"

"Is that a serious question, Chance? First, you are the exact opposite of the type of person I care to spend time with. Second, you don't even know me. So I have to assume that your reasons for chasing after me are purely superficial, right?"

"Maybe initially . . ." Chance replied slowly. "But what if I told you that while I did originally pursue you because of more . . . *external* factors, those are no longer the ones motivating me? That the reasons for my continued interest are actually based in something quite real. What would you say then, Crisanta Knight?"

"I would say that I don't believe you," I stated flatly.

"Why not?"

"Because you're *you*."

"Yes, but perhaps the version of me you are picturing is not an accurate representation of the truth."

"Oh, yeah?" I countered. "Prove it."

"All right, I shall." Chance kept his gaze locked with mine with every step. As he talked, his sea foam eyes were so adamantly fixed on me that the room around us seemed to blur.

"One of the reasons you gave for your continuous spurning of my affections is that you claim my advances must all be superficial because I don't know you," Chance said. "Well, maybe I do not know you *completely*. But here is what I have come to know about you.

"In addition to being beautiful, you are also shrewdly intelligent and unafraid to speak your mind. You exude a confidence that most girls would try to bury beneath conformity. You do not back down, no matter the circumstance or opponent. Despite what some of the more traditional school staff members refuse to admit, you have the moral grace and compassion of true royalty. And moreover, you were brave enough to leave school and all that was familiar in order to pursue a mission of your very own. That, Crisanta Knight, is what I know about you. Given that, you must understand why I am so interested in learning more, why I am desperately trying to convince you to give me the opportunity."

His seemingly thoughtful response swirled around my mind like a tornado that didn't know which way to go. It was a lot to take in, and frankly I wasn't sure if I believed him.

"Chance," I responded with a sigh. "It's no secret that you're charming." A small spark of satisfaction shone in Chance's eyes until I flattened it. "That wasn't intended to be a compliment. Charm is very different than sincerity, and the latter is not a quality I typically associate with you. How do I know that you're not just saying what you think you should in order to get me to even *consider* not writing you off like I have been for the last few months?"

"Because I have changed," he asserted. "Honestly, Crisanta, I am not the same person you knew before."

He sighed, not in an overly dramatic kind of way, but in a genuine, pensive way that made his words sink in that much deeper.

"During your absence last semester and throughout our winter break, I found myself thinking a lot about you—more than I'd anticipated, and in a different way than I'd expected. I not only wanted to see you again, I wanted to talk to you. I wanted to hear you lecture me about my irritating levels of gallant behavior, or shrug off my advances, or counter something I said with your bold and cutting wit. It may sound foolish, but in not seeing you for so long I came to realize that maybe I had never really seen you at all. That I'd been so focused on the superficial aspects of you as a person that I never noticed that the substance beneath was infinitely more intriguing. Which brings us to the prince you see here and now—a changed man trying to fight for you. If you'll let me, that is."

I was speechless. All this talk about Chance changing, and thinking of me, and wanting to get to know me better—it was unfathomable, ridiculous, and totally bizarre.

"I don't know, Chance," I said.

"If you'd be willing to let me?" he asked.

"If I can really believe that you've changed," I replied. "Like I said before, sincerity has never been one of your strong suits."

"Then let me plea my case in another way—perhaps one that pertains to you more personally."

I tilted my head at him. "All right."

"If there is one general consensus going around our schools right now, it's that you've changed. I'm not just talking about all the things you've done to make a name for yourself. Your demeanor is different. You're more confident, calmer, and comfortable in who you are. The transformation is noticeable even in the way you carry yourself."

"So what's your point?"

"My point is the following: do you or do you not believe you have changed?"

"I do," I agreed. "A lot more than I ever thought possible, to be honest. And I hope to continue changing for the better."

Chance nodded. "Okay, well if you believe you can change, why do you have such trouble believing that I am capable of the same thing? Do we not all deserve the opportunity to try and better ourselves if we truly want to?"

"Yes, but Chance—"

"A chance," he interrupted. "That is all I am asking for, Crisanta—a chance to prove to you that I, too, have changed, that my intentions are true, and that I am worthy of your time."

I stared at him, shock and uncertainty all over my face.

"Look, I shall make you a deal," he said. "From now on, no more flowers, no more jewelry, no more overt advances of any sort. Instead, I promise to leave you alone until I can think of some true way to show you that my feelings are genuine. All I ask in return is that you agree to keep an open mind about me until then. What do you say, Crisanta? Can you find it in your heart to find those terms acceptable?"

It was strange. I practically always had a plan. Whether I was facing magic hunters, antagonists, monsters, or hybrid actor-wolves, I consistently relied on my quick thinking and creativity to come up with an appropriate course of action. But as I studied Chance Darling with his apparent change of motivation and his heart on his sleeve, I truly didn't know what to do.

I had asserted to Blue this week that I believed anyone could change, even Jade and Big Girtha. So why not Chance? Unlike my former lackey tormentors, he actually seemed to be willing to put in the work it required. Would it really be the worse thing in the world to give him the opportunity to rise to his best intentions?

"You know," I said after a long pause, "even if I agree to this, and even if you have really changed, the odds that anything will ever happen between us are a million to one."

Chance smiled. "I shall take those odds, Crisanta Knight. For you, I will gladly—"

"Move along?" Daniel said, suddenly appearing at my side. He gave my dance partner a stony but slightly amused expression. "Nice of you to offer. Makes my job easier."

*Had it really been ten minutes? It felt like the world had stopped.*

Daniel looked at the prince. "Chance."

Chance met his gaze. "Daniel," he responded coldly.

"You don't mind if I cut in, do you?"

I felt Chance's grip tighten ever so slightly.

"Not at all," he replied.

Chance glanced at me again and the ice in his irises softened with warmth and affection. "I shall speak with you again when the time is right, Crisanta. Until then, know my thoughts are with you."

I nodded, but that was it. There were no more words exchanged between us. Chance bowed gracefully, kissed my hand (which I wasn't sure how I felt about), and left.

Daniel proceeded to take his position in front of me and the two of us moved to the music. As we stepped along, I glanced over his shoulder and caught another sight of Chance as he headed back across the ballroom.

*Hmm, curiouser and curiouser.*

"You okay?" Daniel asked. "You look confused."

"What? No," I said, snapping back to the present. "I was just . . . caught off guard."

"That's a rare thing for you," Daniel replied. "Something Chance said?"

"Sort of. I don't know; he was acting different. And it was good different, but when you've come to expect a certain type of behavior from someone and they do the opposite, it sort of throws you, you know?"

Daniel nodded. "Yeah, I felt the same way about your reaction to the magic hunter incident."

I raised an eyebrow. "Care to expand on that?"

Daniel hesitated and gave me a pained look, which I readily recognized. He was trying to figure out the easiest way to tell me something without ticking me off.

"Do you remember the first time we danced together?" he asked.

"How could I not?" I replied. "We'd only just met and you'd

already earned a top three spot on the list of people I'd like to throttle."

Daniel rolled his eyes. "Right, and you were just the pinnacle of friendliness to me—not even the slightest hint of hostility if I remember correctly."

"Okay, so neither of us would've won any awards for congeniality that day," I admitted. "What's your point?"

"I accused you of being weak, but you know I don't see you that way now—that I think you're the opposite."

"*But . . .*" I prompted. I knew him well enough to sense when he was holding something back, especially when it was in regards to something that he knew might offend me.

"*But,*" Daniel responded, "what happened to you the other day? Between your magic and all our combined skills, the five of us would have had no problem taking care of a half dozen magic hunters, and we could've sent a message to any others who might've had the bright idea to come after you in the process. But you were too scared to go back into the forest and face them. You didn't want any of us to go either. What was the deal with that? What happened to the girl who never backed down from a fight?'"

"She's pacing herself," I replied. "It's kind of necessary when the actual number of fights headed toward her multiplies each day."

My throat tightened a bit. Much as opening up to Daniel could be helpful, I felt a little hesitant. He and I hadn't discussed anything about what happened between us during our quest to find the Author. We hadn't cemented the strength of our bond since coming back, and that allowed the doubting gnats that lived in the corners of my mind to flit anxiously. Talking about personal stuff and being vulnerable with him now was a test. We were crossing into delicate territory for the first time since the genie lamp.

I shook my head and pushed away my old misgivings. This was a good thing. This was territory that had served us both well in the past. Daniel and I trusted each other. Whether or not we said it out loud, it truly did bring me great comfort to have someone to open up to, and I believed he felt the same way.

"I worry about you guys," I admitted. "I know how strong we are as a team, but every person out there who wants to kill me would kill any of you to do it. So in regards to the hunters, I meant what I said about us being smart and not taking them on until we knew how big the threat is. But I'd be lying if I said that my old inclination to protect you guys didn't play a part in the decision."

Daniel nodded. "That's fair. I think any of us would feel the same way if the situation were reversed. Just remember one thing."

"What?"

"While your reasoning for staying out of the forest was smart, your friends are not stupid. We know how to protect ourselves. You have to trust that we'll be able to keep from getting killed just as we trust that you can keep yourself alive."

"Yeah. I know you're right." I sighed. Relief flooded over me. Like I said, being able to talk to Daniel was a good thing. I was glad we'd passed this initial test.

Apparently seeing the peace return to my face, Daniel changed the subject. "I have some big news. Jason and I wanted to make the announcement to the lot of you at the same time, but while you were with Chance we told SJ and Blue, and I figured I could just tell you now. Jason and I found another Wonderland."

My eyes widened. "Shut up! You did not."

Between Liza, Harry the White Rabbit, and our own reading, my friends and I knew about nine Wonderlands: Oz, Neverland, Camelot, Cloud Nine, Limbo, The Giants' Keep, Toyland, the actual Wonderland from *Alice in Wonderland*, and, of course, Book. We were familiar with most of these in some way. Through our classes at school, we were exposed to a lot of other realm fairytale lore—case in point *Le Morte d'Arthur* was a book about Camelot. But the books we read were generally about protagonists. They were very limiting in terms of teaching us about the geography and dynamics of other realms. Furthermore, none of our lessons had ever taught us what Harry did, that all these places were connected like some magical club. All the Wonderlands were linked and accessible through wormholes that periodically appeared in the enchanted dimensional barriers that separated us. I didn't think anyone beyond some of our realm's higher-ups knew that.

Since we figured the antagonists and the Fairy Godmothers would have found Paige Tomkins at some point in the last ten years if she was still in our realm, and because Arian wasn't searching for her in Book, we were planning on starting our quest for the woman in one of the other Wonderlands. The problem remained that there were now *ten* Wonderlands that we knew of—if Jason and Daniel's discovery was true—and maps of these worlds did not exist. Again, the only information our schools provided on these places revolved around the adventures of specific protagonists.

As such, my friends and I were steadfastly investigating every old and obscure text we could find in the restricted section of our school libraries for any descriptive, geographical, or otherwise important information that could help us create our own maps from scratch. It was slow, difficult work, but it was our best plan for moving forward.

We'd divvied up the Wonderlands we knew about, making the most of Lord Channing's and Lady Agnue's unique collections. As we researched, we noted which books contained information about multiple worlds so that when we traded assignments toward the end of February, we'd have a place to start. SJ, Blue, and I were currently mapping Neverland, Camelot, Limbo, and Wonderland—though with my magic training taking up so much time, SJ and Blue were only letting me work on Neverland. The boys were researching Oz, Cloud Nine, The Giants' Keep, and Toyland. When we eventually switched assignments, we'd work on the next group of realms for two months; then it would be early April and we'd leave to find Paige Tomkins with our completed maps at the start of spring break.

It was a risk to put off our search for so many months. Arian had likely already begun his exploration of the Wonderlands in search of the missing Fairy Godmother. But we needed more time. If we threw ourselves into unknown worlds without any idea of what to expect, let alone how to navigate them, our hope for locating Paige would be so low it might as well be a negative number. Plus, with Wonderlands being magical, unpredictable settings, who knew how many unexpected, enchanted things could and *would* kill us if we wandered out there like lost bunnies.

The fact that Jason and Daniel had discovered another Wonderland was both exciting and overwhelming. We were still so far from discovering where Paige was, and time was short.

"What is it?" I asked once I got over my shock. "The Wonderland you discovered?"

"It's called the North Pole," Daniel replied. "I was flipping through a book about holidays celebrated in other realms, and I found a reference to this thing called Christmas. It's a holiday in December with a lot of different meanings and traditions. There are turtle doves and light-up trees, flying reindeer, this dude called Jesus plays a part, and apparently some guy named Saint Nicholas rules the wintery world and has an elf workforce dedicated solely to creating presents for the occasion."

"Sounds awesome," I said.

"Yeah, and Jason volunteered to map it. He got so stoked after we found it that he adjusted his research focus for the week and actually dug up a handful of other references to the realm in some of our library's other sections."

"More holiday books?"

"And books about elf culture."

"Well, that is big news. And great news. Maybe for once we'll have an edge on Arian when we embark on this quest."

"Maybe we'll get lucky and Arian will get murdered by an elf. They may be small, but I read that they're great with tools and have big tempers."

I smiled at the idea. Though I suspected Arian getting stabbed by an elf with a screwdriver was pretty unlikely, we could use every advantage we could get. He and his team of antagonists were good. We'd slowed them down last semester by destroying the enchanted objects they were going to use to aid their mission, but Arian was nothing if not persistent. He was also skilled, ruthless, and motivated—qualities that only emphasized the notion that if my friends and I were going to find Paige first, our clock was ticking.

Unfortunately, with winter break having ended two weeks ago, our mapmaking mission had gotten significantly more challenging. Clandestinely sneaking into the restricted section of our libraries was way easier when so many staff and students were away. Now that they were all back, we'd had to kick our covertness up a notch.

My eyes wandered to a grand clock on the far end of the ballroom. It was huge—the size of a large decorative fountain one might find at a shopping mall. The twisted, elegant construction was made of gold and rubies. The tick of the second hand seemed to momentarily drown out the noise of the ball.

We had a few months left to prep what we needed to find Paige. That may have seemed like a long time, but I knew it would pass quickly and that scared me. A lot was coming, and I couldn't help but feel overwhelmed.

While I, by no means, intended to "pull a Paige" and run away and hide, I'd been slightly anxious about this next part of our adventure since I'd decided it was our group's best course of action. After being hunted, captured, and nearly killed a half dozen ways the last time we'd left school, I wasn't itching to reprise the experience.

*History does tend to repeat itself, right?*

I swallowed the inhibition. We *had* to find Paige. Though we didn't know exactly what we would do once we found her, we knew that the five of us protecting her from Arian was better than leaving her out there on her own. Whatever he and the antagonists wanted her for could not be good. She was an important part of their plan; somehow she was meant to aid their mission of freeing the antagonists, killing the protagonists, and overthrowing the realm. My friends and I needed to do everything in our power to prevent our enemies from getting to her first.

As I thought on this, my heart blazed with a reminder. The world and the future were full of unknowns, but I knew one thing with absolute certainty, one thing that I'd known since the second I'd met Arian and learned of Nadia's cruel intentions for the realm.

Stopping them was as much my responsibility as it would be my pleasure.

Arian, Nadia, Mauvrey, and the magic hunters could try to deter us. But like Daniel said, I was far from the type of girl who backed down from a fight. So, fight I would. Even if doing so might eventually be my downfall.

"You have that look on your face again." Daniel's voice drew me back. "You're nervous about what's coming."

"Can you blame me?" I asked. "Getting shot at is good exercise, but it's hardly a relaxing pastime. As determined as I am about facing what's out there, thinking about how many people are going to be after us is a lot to digest."

"Which is why you won't be digesting it alone," Daniel responded. "If it makes you feel any better, I'm nervous about what's coming too. We all are. But knowing we're in it together helps."

I held his gaze and nodded. "Yeah," I said. "It does."

It seemed that my hesitance about us embracing the depth of our relationship had been for nothing. Trusting and talking to Daniel made me feel strong. I hoped that I could offer him the same type of support in return.

"You know, Daniel, I appreciate that I can talk to you like this. I don't open up easily, but I'm glad I have a friend like you to bounce this stuff off of. So I want you to know that if you ever wanted to talk about *your* stuff, I'm here too."

I hadn't meant for it to—I thought we were on the same page—but my statement threw Daniel for such a loop that he tripped on the hem of my dress. A shadow of discomfort settled over his face.

I studied the wariness in his eyes, trying to size up how he was feeling. A touch of horror sunk in as I formed a conclusion. I had been wrong. I thought the way we'd been talking these last few minutes was an indicator that he finally accepted how close we'd become, just as I had. But it wasn't so. It was clear from his reaction that we were not in a place where he felt comfortable acknowledging the depth of our friendship.

It was true that I'd had some reservations about it as well, but I'd gone out on a limb to try and cross that bridge. One look in his hard eyes and I immediately regretted the choice. Maybe we were better off avoiding the topic.

To save face for the both of us, I fell back on a tried-and-true failsafe—I dodged the subject. "Ooh, look. They're putting out a fresh plate of bacon-wrapped shrimp. Come on, Daniel Daniels, let's hit it."

# CHAPTER 7

# The Experiment

 ell me again, how do I cut the radishes, professor?"

It was about half past four o'clock on Friday afternoon and I was finishing up my very first week of Potions TA sessions with Madame Alexanders. She had been very patient with me thus far, despite my ineptitude.

On Monday I made our first batch of potions combust by accidentally touching the concoction when I was testing its heat. On Tuesday I'd come through on collecting the ingredients Madame Alexanders had asked me to gather, but I cut them incorrectly, which caused our brew to boil over like violent soup. Wednesday proved to be disastrous when almost everything I touched exploded. And Thursday simply defied explanation.

But today was Friday, and I was adamant about not screwing up our experiments at least once this week.

"The radishes should be cut into equilateral rhombuses," Madame Alexanders said in response to my question.

I picked up my knife to follow her instruction, but stopped short. "Wait, isn't that just a square?"

"Miss Knight, do I have to do everything for you?" my professor sighed.

"No, no; I got it. One set of equilateral rhombuses coming up."

I went back to work completing the tasks that Madame Alexanders had assigned. After finishing with the radishes, I also prepared the chamomile, lavender dust, broiled snake heart, and siren scales for today's brew.

Our goal this week was to create a sleeping potion that triggered terrible nightmares. Madame Alexanders wanted to teach the rest of the class how to concoct it next Tuesday, so this was our last chance to get it right in the testing stage. I wasn't entirely sure how we would know whether or not we'd been successful. I assumed, for now, that so long as nothing was exploding, we were on the right track.

"All right," Madame Alexanders said as she turned up the heat of the Bunsen burner. "Now for the next step."

Using a ladle, Madame Alexanders scooped a serving of the potion into two beakers. She pulled a spindle from one of her lab cases and pricked her finger over one of the beakers. A single drop of blood fell into the mixture—turning the contents a violent shade of orange. My professor produced another spindle and held it out, gesturing for me to do the same.

"You've got to be kidding," I said. "I'm not stabbing myself for the sake of some lab assignment."

"Crisanta, one of the reasons for having a TA is so that we can have more than one test subject per experiment. It's scientific inquiry, my dear. In order to prove a hypothesis is valid you cannot simply take the first result as the golden rule; there must be multiple tests with consistent results."

"But I—"

"Crisanta, you agreed to be my TA, did you not?"

"Yes."

"Are you afraid of a prick of pain?"

"Well, no."

"Then please, proceed."

"Fine," I huffed, snatching the spindle. "Because princesses pricking themselves on spindles always works out *so* well," I muttered under my breath.

A droplet of my blood fell into the second beaker. Its contents took on the new orange shade as well. Madame Alexanders promptly reached into a lab case and removed a jar that contained the very flower I'd been dreading working with. This was the first time we were actually going to try incorporating the Poppy into our designated *Poppy* Potion.

My professor unscrewed the lid and used a pair of forceps to carefully lift the red-and-black polka-dotted flower out of the jar and place it on a silver dish.

As Madame Alexanders had emphasized again and again in class, we were never supposed to directly touch Poppies. While their effects varied when mixed into different potions, direct skin contact with the flowers was dangerous on all counts.

When people touched Poppy flowers they were catapulted into a deep, stone-like sleep that drained the victims' strength so that by the time they woke up they were vastly weakened. The duration of the sleep and the conjunctive weakening varied from person to person. But whether you grazed a single Poppy petal or a ton of them were dumped on top of you, the sleep and energy-draining process began instantaneously. Accordingly, my professor could not overemphasize the importance of *not touching them*.

Madame Alexanders held the Poppy with her forceps and used a pair of tweezers to pluck six petals from its full blossom. She deposited three petals into each of our beakers. The moment the petals sunk into the orange liquid, the concoction fizzled, making loud, snapping sounds that reminded me of popping bubble wrap and breaking breadsticks in half.

As the noise continued, the potion within each beaker began to change color again. Dark purple lines streaked and pulsed through the liquid like irritated synapses in the nervous system. Eventually these streaks blended in with the mixture, the entire concoction turning a sickly shade of mauve. After the contents of the beakers settled, my professor took a syringe out from another lab case and filled it with the new liquid.

"For my records," she explained as she injected the potion into a vial before corking it.

Once the vial was stored, my professor abruptly grasped the beaker in front of her and took a sip of the liquid. After she'd swallowed it, she checked her pulse by placing two fingers to her neck. Then she held up both arms—underside up.

For a second, nothing happened. Then the veins in her arms started to darken. From her fingertips to her shoulders, her veins turned a deep purple. I would have freaked out had it not been for the calm, almost content look on my professor's face and the reassuring nod she gave me.

When all the veins in her arms had been affected, Madame Alexanders smiled. "Well, I would say that we have our very first successful Poppy Potion on our hands, Crisanta. But I suppose we shall not know for certain until the morning."

"Why then?"

"If we have nightmares while we are asleep tonight, then the Poppy Potion will have done its job. That is what we were engineering this potion for, after all—to affect the quality of one's sleep, not to *cause* sleep."

I paused for a second, registering something. "Wait, did you say *we*?"

Madame Alexanders glanced down at the other beaker sitting on the table between us. "As I said, dear, we cannot be certain of our success without holding multiple tests."

I stared with revulsion at Madame Alexanders's violet veins.

"Do I have to?"

"Yes."

I grimaced, causing Madame Alexanders to put her hand on my shoulder. "Come now, I know it looks frightening, but the vein coloration will only last a few hours, and beyond the bad dreams there will be no other side effects."

My eyes fell to the floor.

"You are not afraid of a few nightmares are you?" my professor asked, noticing my aversion.

I was not sure how to respond without divulging anything too proprietary, so I went for a vague truth. "I already get a lot of nightmares, professor. So if I drink this, what do you suppose will happen?"

"I believe that means your nightmares will be even worse."

"Great," I huffed. "Just what I need." I stalled for a moment and shifted uncomfortably as another thought occurred to me. "Professor, I also have Twenty-Three Skidd tryouts tomorrow. If there was ever a reason to get a good night's sleep . . ."

"Crisanta, we had a deal. If you want to keep yourself, and your friends, from being returned to detention, you need to commit to this job completely. And, dear . . . if I may speak so boldly, you are a very fierce young lady. I was present when you and Blue entered the Twenty-Three Skidd tournament in Adelaide last semester. A few nightmares will not slow you down tomorrow, I assure you."

Though I appreciated the compliment, I was still reluctant. My trepidation seemed to strike a chord of sympathy with my professor. "I realize it is a lot to ask, Crisanta. TA positions are rarely associated with being a guinea pig."

I grimaced. "Is this going to be a regular thing, drinking gross potions and such for the sake of science?"

"I'm afraid so."

I thought on this and made a strategic decision. "Then let's make a new deal that takes into account the previously unforeseen dangers of this TA position."

My professor looked at me skeptically. "I'm listening."

"If I do make a Twenty-Three Skidd team, there are going to be practices. According to my friends at Lord Channing's, most teams practice twice during the week and once on weekends. The deal is that I'll drink whatever concoction you give me, but I'll only do these TA sessions three days a week so that if I'm chosen, it won't interfere with my schedule."

Madame Alexanders studied me for a long moment. I knew I was pushing my luck. This job had already got my friends and me out of detention, but the problem of practice schedules had been on my mind for about a week now. While the odds of making a Twenty-Three Skidd team were slim, I needed assurance I'd be able to make practice sessions if I did.

"Very well," Madame Alexanders replied.

"Really?" I perked up.

My professor nodded and gestured toward my designated beaker. "Yes. Now drink up."

I gripped the beaker then flicked my eyes to my professor one more time. "You're sure there are no other side effects?"

"One hundred percent."

I still didn't think drinking nightmare potions was a good idea, but I gulped down my hestitation at the promise of eventual freedom twice a week should my tryouts go well.

I shut my eyes tight and took a sip of the potion. Immediately after I swallowed, my stomach felt like it had been frosted over by some malicious, ice-based enchantment. Conversely, my throat felt warm, like I'd just chugged a bowl of chicken soup.

I noticed the veins in my own arms changing color. As I watched the deep purple creep its way up my arms, Madame Alexanders put two fingers to my neck and took my pulse. A pulse, by the way, that was speeding like a hummingbird's heartbeat.

Once she'd taken it, my professor removed a notebook from her lab case and scribbled down a few private thoughts. Thankfully, once the discoloration in my veins had finished its course, the weird sensations in my stomach and throat subsided. Hastily, I snatched my jacket off a lab stool and put it on to hide the freakishness that now *literally* pulsed through me.

Madame Alexanders closed her notebook and grinned triumphantly. "Well done, Crisanta. You are now free to go. We are done for the day."

"I should hope so," I said as I grabbed my book bag and headed for the door. "See you Monday, professor. Have a good night."

"Oh, I am not planning on it, dear," my professor responded all too excitedly. "In fact, if we've done our jobs right, neither of us will."

"Hurry up, SJ. You're gonna get us caught," Blue urged.

We were in the restricted section of our school's library. It was sixteen minutes past nine o'clock and, being Friday, the library had closed a little over an hour ago. Accessing the restricted section involved walking to the back of the library and going through a set of doors under a marble arch between two rows of bookshelves. Because this would have been impossible with the librarian, Mrs. Fofferman, or the guards around, we went after-hours. The doors beneath the archway were locked—only

Mrs. Fofferman had an actual key—but Blue was our key on these clandestine missions. Her lock-picking skills were exemplary.

"Borrowing" books from the restricted section involved breaking in when the guards had their nine o'clock debriefing sessions on Mondays, Wednesdays, and Fridays, taking a few texts out for us to investigate, and then returning the books in secret and repeating the process when we had the next opportunity. The guards were only away for twenty minutes, so we had to get in and out quickly.

I glanced around anxiously. Moonlight streaming in from some of the high windows offered the only illumination. The windows were interned within decorative metal cages that resembled the thorny greenery of rosebushes. This cast weird shadows across the mauve, fluffy carpeting. It also made the twenty-foot cherry wood bookshelves seem like larger-than-life monsters. I cautiously eyed the streams of semi-sparkling dust particles that floated through the air and clung to the shelves.

Blue and I had gathered the books we wanted for the night, but SJ was taking too long. She was currently trying to map Alice's Wonderland and mentioned that she needed a book on the King and Queen of Hearts, which she'd spotted on a previous night. What she had not mentioned, however, was that the particular book was twelve shelves up.

I squeezed the two texts in my hand apprehensively as I watched SJ lean out to try and grab the book. She was standing on a rolling ladder attached to the bookshelf two feet short of her goal. The problem was that she couldn't move the ladder any closer because of the burning dust cloud floating beside her.

These texts were off-limits for a reason. In addition to the fact that the information contained within could be proprietary, the books were old and one of a kind. Thus, our school's staff relied on more than just a lock at the door and a scary librarian to keep unwanted readers out. Lady Agnue had an arrangement with our realm's transportation department that gave her access to small quantities of magic dust.

Magic dust powered our realm's magic trains. Mined in the

mountains, it was a fuel source beyond compare. While only approved transportation authority workers were allowed to gather it, they sold small quantities of magic dust to Lady Agnue so that Madame Alexanders could further enhance it for security applications.

Yup, those dust particles I'd described a minute ago were not simply the result of dirty airspace and shelving. These clouds were purposefully enhanced via potion and placed in the library to pose problems for people who entered the restricted section without permission.

Burning dust particles were like floating particles of acid that affected anything biological. So the books were fine, but intruders wouldn't be. The particles floated about the restricted section like innocent bubbles caught in a breeze, ready to scorch the skin of wayward students.

There was currently a large cloud of the stuff floating between SJ and her book. Another smaller cloud was wafting steadily closer to her from above.

Blue was so distracted keeping an eye on SJ that she didn't notice a cluster of dust hovering toward us. I stretched my hand across her chest and directed her to take a step back. The dust drifted by us and continued on its way.

I heard a slight yelp and my attention darted back to SJ. A small particle of dust had touched her hand. Even in the dim light, I could see the red burn on her skin. It was like she'd touched a hot cast iron pan.

"SJ, are you—"

"Forget the ladder," Blue interrupted before I could get out my concern. "SJ, just climb up the shelves and get that dang book yourself."

"Blue, my elective this semester is Advanced Embroidery, not acrobatics. I am trying my best," she responded.

Blue sighed and shook her head. "Honestly," she said to me. Then she pulled the book bag off her shoulder and shoved it in my arms. "Hold this a minute."

Blue rubbed her hands together, released a few quick breaths, and then bent into a runner's lunge. I saw her analyze the space between SJ and where we were standing, taking note of every cloud of burning dust clinging to the shelves and rolling through the air. Then she popped the hood of her classic blue cloak, which she always did in major moments of mischief, and took off. She bolted along the corridor between the shelves, leaping and ducking to avoid the burning dust. Then she bounded off the ground and scaled the bookshelf like an alley cat crossbred with a mountain climber. In less than six seconds she reached the book SJ wanted and snatched it off the shelf.

Clinging deftly to her position, Blue twisted around and regarded me. "Catch," she said, and she sent the book sailing through the air. I caught it in my arms. Blue gave SJ a cocky look. "See, was that so hard?"

SJ huffed with indignation and descended the ladder while Blue came down in a manner as athletically impressive as her ascent.

"Now let's get out of here," Blue said, taking her book bag back from me. She checked her watch. "We only have three minutes until the guards finish their meeting."

Gathering up our things, we left the restricted section. Blue locked the doors and we scurried to the main exit.

The library was huge—maybe a third the size of the ballroom. Dozens of wooden tables, shining from being so well polished, reflected the unlit gold lamps with lavender glass shells that were spaced along each one.

When I was here to study—not break rules and steal books—I much preferred the less conventional seating. Tucked away in the corners were fifteen-foot tall structures made to look like enormous, multi-armed golden candelabras. Only instead of candles, each arm held a comfy purple seat like a laidback birdcage chair.

Every candelabra's stem had a thin staircase spiraling up it, which was used to reach the tallest arms. I rather liked to recline into these chairs for long hours of reading when I felt too cramped in my room. Even during midterms I could count on these seats to be empty. Most girls at Lady Agnue's weren't as fond of precarious positions as I was. But then, there were a lot of things most girls at Lady Agnue's didn't do that I did.

Such as feed bacon to statues.

Outside of the library main doors, two granite pillars provided seating for Guardgoyles. They were supposed to serve as an alarm system, but they were quite chatty. In fact, I'd never seen them do anything *but* talk. Given that one had to be silent inside the library, I found this to be an odd contradiction.

Guardgoyles were stationed in other areas of the school too, but students—myself included—rarely saw them. They were mainly placed in the parts of campus where the staff members had their living quarters and in some of our school's watchtowers.

The two outside the library were named Russell and Nick and they were super chill. They were tasked with sounding the alarm if students tried to sneak food into the library, borrow more books than permitted at a time, or (in our case) gain access when it was closed. However, unbeknownst to the school's staff, the Guardgoyles could be bribed with bacon.

I pulled the plastic baggie from my jacket pocket as the three of us slipped out of the library doors. While Blue relocked them, I approached the Guardgoyle on the left.

"We're back, Nick."

"Crisanta Knight," the Guardgoyle said. "I see your visit inside was productive." He tilted his chin at my stack of books, which I had just placed on the floor while he stretched his wings.

Made of stone, Guardgoyles had the bodies and tails of lions, but their heads were more like Doberman Pinschers—ears erect for listening. They also had wings like dragons protruding from their bodies. They could move these wings, as well as their necks, heads, and tails, but no more than that. They were permanently glued to their designated positions.

I scaled the uneven brick wall à la Blue to reach Nick. I held out my hand and gave him two strips of bacon. "Here's your second helping," I said.

Every Monday, Wednesday, and Friday morning I took a few strips of bacon from the banquet hall in preparation for our evening activities. We'd made an arrangement with the Guardgoyles over winter break. In exchange for four pieces of bacon each, three times a week, Nick and Russell didn't sound the alarm when we went into the library after-hours. We gave them two pieces when we entered, and two pieces when we left.

Personally, I thought we got the better end of that deal, considering if we'd gotten caught we would be in a world of trouble.

"Hmm. Hickory smoked bacon isn't my favorite," Nick commented through his mouthful of meat. "You know I prefer applewood."

I leapt off the wall and landed silently on the cold tile. "Sorry," I said, walking past an anxious SJ to reach the other Guardgoyle. "That's all they had today. I'll bring you extra on Monday."

Nick harrumphed, but continued chewing. I climbed the right wall just as easily and presented the second serving to Russell. He greedily snatched up the bacon, his stone incisors scraping my palm.

"Hey, watch the teeth," I said.

"Watch your sass," Russell replied. "We may be dogs, but we own you in this situation."

I raised my eyebrows. Then Russell grinned and licked his chops before stretching out his neck toward my hand. "Just kidding," he said. "Now give me a pat."

I matched his grin, patted his rough, stone head, and then leapt down right as Blue finished locking up. "One minute to spare," she said. "We better skedaddle."

"Good night, girls," Nick and Russell said in unison.

I turned back and *shhhed* them, but waved goodnight all the same then scooped up my books.

"I hate this, you know," SJ said, as my friends and I hurried down the corridor. "Thievery is stressful and exhausting."

"At least you don't have to battle boys on Pegasi tomorrow," Blue grumbled. "Why did the night before tryouts have to be our only shot at borrowing books for the weekend? We need to get to bed fast. It's vital that Crisa and I get some rest before tomorrow."

*Right, rest,* I thought as we dashed around a corner and

entered the final hall before the stairs. *I'm sure that'll be easy with the adrenaline of a break-in, a stomach full of nightmare potion, and my usual dreams of the future weighing me down . . .*

Hm. Pirates. That's new.

A ship swayed beneath my boots. Boards creaked with my every step. Scraggly, intimidating men stood menacingly around me and gas lanterns across the deck began to glow as the gray skies of my dreamscape turned into night.

There were two pirates waiting for me ahead. One had a crooked posture and nose. He had a stereotypical parrot perched on his shoulder, wore striped knee socks, and held a lantern that illuminated the gold in his teeth. The other man was handsome in a malicious sort of way. His black hair was tied in a ponytail, and the polished buttons on his jacket made him stand out compared to the dirty rags worn by the other men on board. Suddenly this man grabbed me by the collar and thrust me forward. I tumbled onto a plank, barely able to keep myself from falling over.

On my hands and knees, I looked down at the otherwise black water to see a pair of giant yellow eyes peering up at me. I was hypnotized by those eyes, paralyzed as I watched a great, scaly body circle in the waves beneath me. Waiting.

The scene swirled—colors distorting and putting me more off balance than the shaking plank. I was standing now, and staring at the water until a voice drew me back. The man with the ponytail was taunting me.

"You're but a passing ship in the night that cannot possibly hope to hold water in the long run. And speaking of holding water, I do hope you're a fast swimmer, because my old friend gets antsy when I tease him with fresh meat."

I flicked my eyes toward the monster below. In the distance I thought I heard ticking. I tried to sharpen my focus on the creature, but my vision swelled with haziness. By the time clarity returned, all traces of the sea were gone. They'd been replaced by stone.

My mind drifted through rocky passageways. It was blurry

and the terrain was constantly changing. I saw plummeting drops, wide caverns, and stalactites and stalagmites. Was I inside a mountain? It was cold but not dark. Patches of white, clinging to the rocks, emitted a shimmering light

My consciousness veered out of the tunnel, which continued farther ahead, onto a bright rocky platform. The light was coming from the left where the platform dropped off. I drifted to the ledge and stared down. Eight feet beneath me, a black transparent dome covered a great chasm like a force field. This chasm had so much of the white stuff seeping through the stone that I was completely dazzled.

My vision grew clearer and I realized what the white substance was—magic dust. I'd been seeing deposits of it throughout the mountain, but within the chasm the veins were deeply concentrated.

My consciousness hovered over the force field before passing through it, diving into the mountain's depths. I descended for a hundred feet. The chasm widened on the way down. The magic dust deposits also grew until at the bottom of the chasm every surface seemed covered in the glowing material. There I came upon a work camp abundant in hovels and mining machinery. At first I didn't notice the people operating the equipment. Their rags and slow movement camouflaged them against the dull gray of the machines. But on further inspection there were at least three or four dozen men, women, and children down here.

Suddenly my attention diverted to a very distinct sound coming from up top.

The sound of high heels began to echo through the mountain, and it had the effect of an electrical current on the miners—supercharging them into high gear. The people began to work faster, moving like lightning where they had been barely trudging along before.

My consciousness was suddenly at the top of the chasm again, above the black dome. With a screech like a banshee on a sugar high, a monkey with giant bat wings came flying out of the tunnel across from me. It flew over the force field, baring its fangs and clawing at the airspace above the barrier—careful not to touch it. As the sound of high heels drew closer, the force field rapidly dissipated.

The cries and shouts of people wafted up from the work camp below. The flying monkey dove into the chasm with its claws outstretched, reappearing with a terrified man in its clutches. With a scream, the monster took off the way it'd come, the man in its grasp crying and pleading for mercy.

In the moment of silence after the barbaric attack, I couldn't catch my breath. But the terror was not over. As the cries of the first flying monkey faded down the tunnel, a half dozen of its winged brethren emerged. They began diving into the crater after more people.

Shouts filled the cavern. Agonized, mangled silhouettes and shadows reflected against the walls as the monkeys disappeared with their catch. All the while, the steady beat of approaching high heels grew louder.

My subconscious did not stick around to meet the person who owned the footwear. It began to glide like a ghost through different parts of the mountain again, darting from cavern to cavern like it was searching for something, until it arrived in a massive room, about the size of the school library.

The ceiling was terribly high. Magic dust clung to the tips of stalactites, making them look like daggers dipped in powdered sugar. But the feature that caught my attention was the floor. Reefs of rock zigzagged along the ground. The different heights made the place feel like a labyrinth. In the middle of the cavern was an open area split by a river.

My consciousness swooped to the ground of the enormous room, and I found myself wandering through the maze of rock, my hands tracing the rough barriers. An icy draft touched my skin. Wherever this mountain was, it was somewhere up north. I kept moving. The river came from a runoff that started at the back of the cavern, and wormed through the floor in many avenues carved from years of its passing.

On the other side of the river, opposite where it began, something glimmered profoundly. A giant crystal, large enough to be a dining room table for six people, sat in the middle of a pool where the water collected. The crystal appeared opaque white, but as I moved closer, I began to see purple and green lights buzzing inside. There was water within the crystal as well, and the lights zoomed through it like fireflies desperate to break free of a jar.

It was mystifying. I was ten feet away when a swirl of icy shadows and wind whisked me away. My dreamscape changed— the warmth from the sun and the smell of spring melted away the cavern's chilly grasp. Alas, as calming as this atmosphere was, the situation I was dropped into was gruesome.

I stood on a grassy plain surrounded by hills and severed by a churning river. Both hills and plain were an odd shade of pale blue, as if the terrain had absorbed color from the sky. A fierce battle was underway by the gray sands of the riverbank. Blue, Jason, and SJ were up against an enormous company of knights wearing armor that was black, gold, or blood red.

SJ used her slingshot to fire portable potions (a highly concentrated weapon of her own invention that released different potions she'd brewed upon impact). Jason and Blue moved like hurricanes through their assailants—him with his trusty axe and her with her equally trusty hunting knife.

The threesome was outnumbered. The ratio could not have been kinder than ten to one and before long the odds began to overwhelm them.

My perspective shifted to focus on SJ and the knights she was fighting. The knights were coming at her from all angles. She did well at first, but while she was fending off two attackers from the front, one approached her from behind that she didn't see. He raised his sword.

Abruptly my perspective shifted to Blue. A knight struck a blow so hard that she was thrust to the ground as she deflected it. She rolled down the riverbank, gray sand sticking to her hair and clothes. She attempted to get up, but another knight slammed his shield into the side of her head. Blood formed at a gash on the edge of her hairline, but she continued to fight ferociously. She launched herself up in the form of a spinning kick that knocked her assailant away. When she whirled back around, another knight was already throwing a spear at her chest.

The world seemed to move in slow motion as the weapon moved toward her. Blue had no time to deflect or defend. She was without hope. And in that horrible split-second before the spear hit, she knew it.

Mortality screamed for mercy, but she didn't. The spear's point reflected in her eyes and then . . .

Jason threw himself in front of Blue. The spear penetrated him instead of her.

"Jason!" she screamed.

The scene stood motionless, as if time was holding its breath. Then everything sped up so quickly it felt like a sensory explosion. Jason fell to the ground by the river. The knight yanked out his bloodied spear. He attempted another strike at Blue, but she shouted in fury and tackled him to the sand. She unleashed a downpour of fists to his face. Other knights tried to attack her, but she brandished the knight's spear—the very one that had struck Jason—and obliterated anyone who came close in a cyclone of rage.

The ground started to rumble. Panicked cries of knights began to echo around the plain as a golden glow blinded the company.

I did not see what was coming after them; my dream perspective remained with Blue, who had run back to Jason's side.

She fell to her knees beside him in the sand. Jason's face was expressionless, his body motionless, his shirt stained in dark red. Blue grabbed him by the shoulders and shook him, shouting his name once more. He remained still and her face turned ghostly white. She put her hands to his stomach where the wound was, and blood coated her skin.

The ground quivered, the river sloshing in the confines of its banks. The glow in the background became brighter and the scene shook and shone with increasing intensity. Then, just as the world threatened to tear itself apart, I woke up. My heart felt as though it had all but burst from my chest. The top and sweatpants I wore were soaked with sweat. I panted like I'd run ten thousand laps.

The term "bad dream" by no means described what I'd just experienced. That was the worst nightmare I'd ever had. Madame Alexanders would be thrilled. I, however, could not have been more devastated.

I did not write down the vision in my journal like I typically did. I would never be able to forget this dream even if I tried.

I looked over at Blue and SJ. Sometimes I woke them up by talking in my sleep when I had particularly vivid dreams, but I could see both their faces at the moment, and each was still lost in slumber.

Before I even fully realized, I was out on the balcony. I had grabbed a jacket, slid on my boots, and was now leaning over the railing, trying to rid myself of the grisly images I'd seen.

I placed a hand on the vines that surrounded our balcony and brought them to life like the ones outside our detention tower. I didn't care if Lady Agnue got mad. I didn't care if she had to call Lenore back here and the vines got torn down. I had to get away.

The vines awakened and lowered me to the ground six floors below. I proceeded to wander across the campus, keeping to the shadows so as not to be spotted by any guards. My mind was blank, as lost as the stars behind the charcoal clouds.

I found myself heading toward the practice fields. Their pull was comforting to me like a homing beacon. I made my way to the back of the barn. There was a tree there that I was partial to when I felt the need for some space. It was a deciduous one with a particularly smooth, thick trunk, and a cradle of roots at its base. Angled away from the school, it was a great place to seek solitude. There, in the silence, I leaned against the trunk and gazed out at the grounds. My body shuddered violently, trying to shake the darkness of my latest vision.

Before starting our training, Liza had warned me that the more I used magic, and the stronger my powers became, the more intense and revealing my visions of the future would be. Despite this warning, I feared that I had underestimated how brutal a consequence this could be. I mean, what I'd just seen . . .

I clutched my head in my hands.

Jason was going to die.

I swallowed hard, sunk to the ground, and hugged my knees to my chest to keep from crying. My eyes shut tightly as my mind whirred.

*When? Where? Why?* And most importantly, *how?* Not how was it going to happen. *How* was I going to tell him? And how was I going to tell Blue?

Jason was a good friend to all of us, so seeing him get killed was hard enough. But Jason was more than a friend to Blue, even if he didn't know it yet. At the end of last semester Blue had revealed to me (and later SJ) that she had feelings for him. She claimed that she wasn't sure how deep those feelings ran, and was not sure what those feelings would progress into, but she did not want Jason, or Daniel, or anyone else, to know they existed. Yet.

In all honesty it made perfect sense. Blue and Jason were really good friends. They had tons in common, were always on the same page, and fit like a sandwich with a side of chips. I didn't know how Blue—or Jason for that matter—hadn't seen the signs sooner. But I supposed this kind of clarity was usually more obvious to people on the outside of a situation.

I could understand why Blue may have denied her feelings for a while. Crushing on a friend could be complicated. I was happy she'd come to terms with how she felt, but clearly her timing was not great.

*No girl wants to learn that the boy she's into is doomed after finally fessing up to liking him.*

It was true that Blue was already on notice that Jason's fate may not be so savory. Her prologue prophecy had revealed that he was going to "die twice" and that it was going to be her fault on both counts. However, we knew from our time with Liza that such predictions could be interpreted to have different meanings. Ergo, the whole "die twice" bit, along with Liza's assurances, actually calmed our worries. Since a person could not physically die *twice* we assumed the prologue alluded to something more figurative.

Unfortunately, unlike prologue prophecies, my visions had no such wiggle room. My dreams of the future were never wrong. Sometimes they showed incomplete images—fragments of what was to come—and not always in the proper order. So there were some gray areas. But such zones of uncertainty were opportunities to influence the before and after, not change what had been foreseen. Which meant that one way or another, what I'd dreamt tonight would come to pass. Jason would be killed by that riverbank. In sacrificing himself to save Blue, his death would inadvertently be her fault.

It was unavoidable. The future had been set.

I thumped my head against the tree in frustration. A couple of leaves drifted to the ground. My burst of anger returned to sadness as I watched them fall.

My heart didn't simply hurt from the realization about Jason's future. For lack of a better word, it felt like my heart had been julienned. Jason—my friend, my dear friend—was going to be killed, and I didn't know what to do. Worse, I knew there was nothing I *could* do.

I got up from the grass slowly as thoughts raced through my mind. Whether I wanted to or not, I knew I had to tell him and Blue. They deserved to know, and I was past keeping secrets from people, especially when the knowledge I held pertained directly to them.

As this vision was about him, I'd have to start with Jason. Although, I had no idea when a good time was to tell someone— let alone one of your closest friends—that they were going to die.

I wasn't one to break down easily, but it was all I could do not to scream.

With too much weighing on my mind to head back to bed, and the dark cold eating away at me in my nest of roots, I decided to go into the barn. Beating up hay dummies always helped ease my tensions. Plus, the Twenty-Three Skidd tryouts were tomorrow. If I was going to be up all night, I might as well get some last-minute practice. It would be a shallow distraction given what I'd just learned, but I had to fight these terrible feelings in light of several factors.

One, I didn't know when this dream would come to fruition. It might happen in a week; it might happen in three years. Two, I couldn't let on that something was wrong until I'd had the chance to talk with Jason and Blue. And three, I still had dozens of other Book-destroying, protagonist-murdering, antagonist-plotting problems to worry about. Those ongoing plot lines would inevitably determine the future of the entire realm, so I had to put them first. Just like I knew Jason would.

I pushed open the barn doors and was surprised to find it flooded with light. A good number of gas lanterns within the barn were lit—their vibrant flames crackling away like miniature suns behind their glass barriers.

*What moron left the lights on?* I wondered as I stepped inside. *If the wind knocked over a single one of these lanterns without anyone here, it could set the whole place on fire.*

I closed the doors behind me and made my way deeper into the barn, drawing my wandpin from the jacket pocket I'd popped it into before leaving my room.

*Lapellius.*

The wand extended itself.

*Lacrosse sword.*

The handle thickened in my grip as my wand extended. The spear of a jousting lance sprouted at one end and the basket of a lacrosse stick emerged simultaneously on the other.

Eager to forget my terrible dreams, I made my way to where the hay dummies were kept. I set up a few and began laying into them. With one swift strike-twirl-twist-strike combo after another, my mind eventually went blank as my body moved in a state of autopilot. At least, it did until I was startled by a sudden voice.

"Hey."

I spun around with the blade of my lacrosse sword at the ready. I pulled it back when I saw the person to whom the voice belonged—Big Girtha.

"Geez!" I said as I relaxed the weapon. "You almost gave me a heart attack!"

"Sorry, sorry." she responded. "I heard something and came

to check it out. Figured a raccoon got inside the barn. Didn't expect to find a person. What're you doin' out here?"

"Trouble sleeping," I replied. "And you?"

"Same. It gets old sometimes, so I come down here and try to tire myself out. That way maybe I'll sleep better, or at least clear my head. I have a sparring mat and a few hay dummies set up over there." Big Girtha gestured somewhere beyond the haystack walls surrounding my area. "I came back here to get a few more because I destroyed the ones I was working with."

These hay dummies were normally super durable. I wondered what she could've been doing that had caused so much damage.

"What's your weapon of choice?" I asked curiously.

"These," Big Girtha said, holding up two balled fists. She nodded to her right bicep then her left bicep. "I call this one Kraken, and this one Kraken."

"Aren't people who name their arm muscles supposed to give them different names?"

"Ordinarily," Big Girtha agreed. "But this way, when I'm about to throw down with someone, my battle cry can be: 'Release the Krakens!' A singular version of that word doesn't sound anywhere near as cool."

I couldn't help but smile. "Not bad," I said. "I once considered having a battle cry myself. But then I realized that when someone is trying to kill you, it's not wise to waste time on something trivial like yelling 'Whablamo!'"

Big Girtha stared at me. "When did someone try to kill you?"

I stopped and fully comprehended the severity of what I'd let slip.

No one outside of my group of friends, Liza, Lady Agnue, and of course my enemies, knew the whole story behind my exploits last semester. All the alternative versions of the truth gossiped up by my classmates until now had been far off base. Regrettably, I'd just given one of my classmates a shred of *actual* truth that I had not intended to divulge. And the classmate in question was a former nemesis!

"What? Never mind. Forget I said anything," I responded vaguely, trying to avoid her gaze and the subject.

Alas, Big Girtha was not as dense as her physique. I'd given her a palatable clue, and she was connecting the dots.

"While you were gone last semester, people tried to kill you," Big Girtha repeated, thinking out loud. "I know your fighting has gotten a lot better, and you practice all the time. I saw you and Blue come down here all through winter break. But you train differently than you used to. Not just because you use a spear instead of a sword, but because of your aggression. The look on your face when you train . . . it's so angry and serious. And then there's Mauvrey . . ."

I grimaced, but Big Girtha continued.

"When Jade and I brought her up the other day, your eyes went totally dead. Blue got so defensive too, like she was worried about something big, something more than how we used to mess around with each other."

Big Girtha exhaled as she began to pace. "Mauvrey started acting weird when you left school last semester, Crisa, like she was preoccupied with something. And there were a lot of times when I noticed her doing strange things. She'd sneak out of our room late at night when she thought Jade and I were asleep and wouldn't come back until right before dawn. She began studying potions and researching magic. She seemed uninterested in anything normal. The paranoia she's always had about stupid things like coins on the floor became more extreme. And one day I found a corset in her closet that had been dyed black. I thought it looked familiar—a lot like the missing, poisonous one from the Treasure Archives—but I didn't say anything.

"Next thing I know you're back at school. I see Mauvrey working on something in our sewing classroom after-hours. On the night of the Ball of the First Frost you're sent to the infirmary. Then Mauvrey goes missing, and when I go dumpster diving for my Looting & Shooting final exam later that week I find a black ball gown in a garment bag with your name sewn into the tag. It was like someone had stolen the dress the school seamstresses made you for the ball and thrown it out."

Big Girtha shook her head. "I guess I just didn't want to believe it . . ."

"Believe what?" I was almost too afraid to ask.

"That Mauvrey tried to kill you," Big Girtha said grimly. "She was the one who broke into the Treasure Archives and stole that corset. She has to be. She got rid of your actual dress and disguised that poisoned corset to look like a gown for the ball, which you wore and almost died from. When she failed to kill you, she ran away from school. Didn't she?"

I refused to meet Big Girtha's eyes.

She hadn't been completely spot-on. Mauvrey hadn't left school because she'd failed in her attempt to kill me. She'd left because she genuinely thought she'd succeeded and—believing that her job was done—went to rejoin Arian and the rest of her antagonist buddies.

Also, while I figured the late-night ventures Big Girtha was referring to were cases of Mauvrey meeting up with Arian, and that her magic research had to do with defeating me and breaking into the Archives, I had no idea what had prompted an escalation of her irrational fear of coins. She'd had that peculiar tick for years. I'd discovered it during our first year at Lady Agnue's when we were roommates.

Once, during one of our arguments, Mauvrey had said she wished I would just get expelled already so that she wouldn't have to share a room with me. In response, I had rolled my eyes and picked up a bronze coin lying on the floor by my nightstand.

"Here," I said. "Maybe your wish will come true."

I tossed the coin onto her comforter as a form of harmless snark, but she totally freaked out. She flung herself backward so fast she fell off the other side of the bed.

It was an odd reaction. And over the years I discovered that it was not an isolated incident. For whatever reason, Mauvrey was super weird about coins. She never picked them up from the floor. She never even flipped one to settle a bet.

Strange as it may have sounded, part of me had sort of liked this about Mauvrey. The quirk was the most interesting, unorthodox thing about the girl. Now, of course, she had the whole "evil and homicidal" thing going for her.

I'd always assumed I was the only person to have noticed

Mauvrey's distaste for pocket change. But it seemed Big Girtha knew about it too. The bulky girl was a lot more perceptive than I'd given her credit for.

Big Girtha was now far too close to the truth, *my truth*, for comfort. When I finally got the nerve to face her, I knew by the look in her eyes there was nothing I could say that would convince her otherwise. I would've been wasting my time denying it. So I decided not to. Instead I took a different approach—first a warning, then a forced leap of faith.

"Look, Big Girtha," I said, "there's a lot more happening right now that you don't understand. Dangerous, unpleasant stuff, not just to do with me, but the whole realm. Which is why my advice to you is to let the matter go. Stop digging. If you don't, you might not like what you find."

"I'm not making any promises, Crisa," she responded. "I mean, would you stop digging if the situation was reversed?"

"Admittedly not," I replied. "Which brings me to the following. I can't stop you from asking questions, but there is one promise I am going to have to ask you to make. Big Girtha, you can't tell anyone about Mauvrey. It's part of a deal I have going with Lady Agnue. If she finds out that I let even a little piece of the truth slip, what she'll do to me is way worse than anything Mauvrey ever did."

Big Girtha nodded. "Don't worry, Crisa. I'll keep your secret. I just have one condition."

I looked at her suspiciously. "What?"

"Stop calling me Big Girtha," she said. "I know that's what everyone in school has always called me, but the fact is I seriously hate it. I'm plus-sized and sturdy like an ox-herder, but I have feelings. And whether you're seventeen or seventy, no girl likes having a nickname that revolves around her massive build."

Her honesty threw me and I felt an unexpected tinge of guilt. "I'm sorry, uh, *Girtha*. I had no idea."

"It's cool," she replied. "You're not the only one who can put up a front, you know. But if you and your friends could lose the nickname, maybe the other girls will follow. Oh, and it would also help if Blue stopped with her more colorful nicknames for me too. I mean, Gigantore? Really? How's that *not* supposed to hurt my feelings?"

"I'll talk to her," I promised. "And, um, thanks. For keeping my secret."

"I should be thanking you for trusting me enough to keep it. I guess this means we really can be friends, huh?"

"Girtha, I'm trusting you because I have to, not because I want to," I responded bluntly. "It's a step in the right direction. But make no mistake, the faith I just placed in you is out of necessity, not camaraderie. If you ever want me to trust you fully, you're gonna have to prove to me that you can be trusted first."

# CHAPTER 8

# Drawing the Line

ey boy! I missed you!" I called out. Blue, SJ, and I approached the spot where Jason and Daniel were waiting.

"I don't blame you," Daniel responded. "I'm pretty charming, even by our schools' standards."

I punched him in the arm. "Duh, I wasn't talking to you. I was talking to the big, beautiful guy behind you!"

My pet dragon Lucky was busy rolling around on the grass in the distance. He didn't appear to have heard me, so I brought my fingers to my lips and whistled. When Lucky heard the familiar pitch he immediately stomped over—crushing the pristine lawn and wildflowers beneath his massive feet.

He flopped onto the ground in front of me and huffed affectionately as I patted his enormous, scaly snout. It was just past dawn and the orange color of the sky made his silvery scales shimmer.

Lucky had been one of the creatures I'd accidentally brought to life last semester before I understood what my magic was capable of. Previously, he'd been an impressive stone statue of a dragon residing in our realm's capital, Century City. When I brought him to life he became an impressive *real* dragon with silvery skin and glowing golden eyes.

After flying all around the realm in his attempt to reunite with me, his apparent master, he had saved my friends and me from the antagonists in the citadel of Alderon. Since then I'd developed a great fondness for him. Sadly, I rarely got to see Lucky. While Lady Agnue had been forced to accept a lot of the baggage we'd come back with from our adventures, she'd drawn the line at a dragon.

This brought us to an interesting stalemate, especially since Lucky didn't seem to want to leave. Personally, I didn't get it. If I was a flying, fire-breathing beast, the world would be my oyster, and I'd get away from this school as fast as possible. But Lucky had grown to like us and also liked having a home. Although he went out for the occasional flight, he always came back. So we had to adjust.

Refusing to let the creature live at our school, the headmistress made arrangements for Lucky to reside over at Lord Channing's. It had a much bigger campus and a lot more outdoor space for Lucky to roam free.

The boys were happy to accept their new boarder, as he brought an exciting new realm of possibilities to their training. With my permission (which I gave so long as they showed him proper respect) they used Lucky to sharpen their battle reflexes. Naturally they weren't allowed to physically hurt Lucky in any way. But they'd come up with a wide range of fighting drills that involved avoiding his tail, claws, and firepower.

Lucky certainly didn't seem to mind. In fact, from what I'd heard from Daniel and Jason, he actually enjoyed the drills. It kept his mind off missing me, which he expressed from time to time by flying over the main campus of Lord Channing's and roaring loudly.

Under Lady Agnue's insistence, I'd had to order Lucky to stay away from our campus and listen to Jason and Daniel. I didn't use magic to enforce the order; I just told him. He'd listened, but clearly wasn't happy about it.

Today, much to his delight and mine, we were reunited. It was the day of the Twenty-Three Skidd tryouts, and while I would have preferred to be a bit more well-rested, I was thrilled to be making the trip over to Lord Channing's for the main event. That's why Lucky was here—to transport us.

My friends and I had realized something earlier in the week: how exactly was I going to get to tryouts? The magic hunters in the forest between our campuses ruled out any regular methods of getting to the boys' school. My classmates were going to take the main road to Lord Channing's when the In and Out Spell was lowered later, but that wasn't an option for me. The hunters could track my scent and would sense me coming. Even flying there on Pegasi could be risky, as it left me vulnerable to hunters with bows and arrows.

As a result, we'd decided to level with Lady Agnue. While my headmistress highly doubted that the threat of the magic hunters was as great as we'd described, she had agreed that she was liable to at least *try* and ensure my safety. Thus, she'd granted permission for Daniel and Jason to bring Lucky over to fly us. She'd told the guards patrolling our campus not to be alarmed when he landed this morning. The only catch was that we had to go at this ghastly hour so our classmates wouldn't see Daniel and Jason.

The girls at school—like the boys at Lord Channing's—already knew about Lucky, so seeing my dear dragon on campus wouldn't freak them out. But Lady Agnue didn't want anyone to know that Daniel and Jason could phase through the In and Out Spell. Hence our dawn departure. We needed to be in the air and in the clear before the other students woke up. Given that it was five o'clock on a Saturday, and no sane teenager would ever willingly wake up that early, I felt safe that we were in the clear.

As we prepared to take off, I was grateful for our headmistress's uncharacteristic, begrudging help. In addition to allowing Lucky to transport us, Lady Agnue had made a few other provisions to minimize the threats we claimed existed beyond the school. When the In and Out Spell was lowered for other students to cross through later today, it was only going to go down for three minutes to reduce any risk of hunters coming through the forest. It would then rise back up until the end of tryouts. Meanwhile, when the force field was lowered, guards were going to be positioned at all vantage points—watching vigilantly in case anyone unauthorized tried to sneak on campus.

I appreciated that. While Lady Agnue seemed perfectly content with the idea of having me shipped off to Alderon if I crossed her, as long as I maintained my good behavior she was committed to living up to her responsibility as headmistress to protect the school against any possible threats, even if that meant protecting *me* in the process.

Eager to get going, Blue, SJ, and I hopped on Lucky with Jason and Daniel, and we took off into the sky.

Dawn's cold beauty rushed against my face, and I grinned ear to ear. It was peaceful to be surrounded by nothing but crisp air and clean clouds. I glanced over my shoulder at Lady Agnue's. The school's towers and turrets looked remarkable from a distance. The practice fields, too, were quite a sight. It was only at this great height that you could truly appreciate the expanse of pure green grass stretched out like a fine rug, the assortment of trees everywhere, the track and obstacle courses that gleamed in the soft light, and the barn and massive stables.

Their glorious display faded from view as Lucky bridged the area above the forest separating our two academies. Instinctively my hand tightened around the ridge of Lucky's back that I held onto. We were hundreds of feet above the ground, and I couldn't see much of anything beyond the tops of the trees. Still, I couldn't shake the feeling that I was being watched.

I took a glimpse back at Daniel. He was scanning the forest below but his expression was far away, lost in thought. There was a hard solemnness in his eyes that I hadn't seen in some time. The look troubled me.

He noticed me staring and I quickly averted my eyes. It was just in time too. Beyond the forest was Lord Channing's campus. Seeing it caused my good mood to return.

While SJ refused to look at much of anything up here (she'd never been a big fan of heights), Blue and I gazed ahead with intrigue. Our monthly balls and other inter-school functions were always held at Lady Agnue's. The only events that we were invited to at Lord Channing's were Twenty-Three Skidd finals matches in the spring, and we'd always been taken there through a back entrance because it was the fastest route. Peering over Lucky's huge head, I caught my first full sight of the school.

The main structure and subsidiary buildings were built from sharp gray stone with chrome finishes. Towers jettisoned into the sky. Some were rectangular, windows checker-boarding their exterior. Others were rounded and topped with dark blue turrets. At the center of the school was a tall building that curved into a blue steel cupola. A navy flag with the school's silver crest flew from the top.

Farther to the right was the boys' training campus. There were seven separate forums for combat practice accompanied by four immense fields, each with its own barn and stable, and two gigantic swimming pools.

At the far end of the training campus (adjacent to an obstacle-laden course) was a colossal arena. It was regulation size for Twenty-Three Skidd, but also had the capacity to host a myriad of other sporting and athletic events. The scale of it took my breath away.

Although I may not have known what it felt like to fall in love, I assumed that it had to feel something like this. My heart was so inflated with excitement at the sight of the training campus that I thought it might leap out of my chest. My arms tingled as if touched by butterflies. No adjective in my vernacular could provide me with the right word to adequately describe the joyful speechlessness I was experiencing.

We landed right outside the arena. After I patted him goodbye on the nose, Lucky trotted away to continue rolling around in the early morning sunshine while my friends and I approached our final destination on foot. We entered through a tunnel on the southeast side. Gravel crunched beneath my boots like the anticipation building in my gut.

Soon enough, the tunnel deposited us inside the stadium. I simply stood there for a moment, marveling at its magnificence. The tryouts weren't set to begin for a while. We presently had the place to ourselves—all the better to fully appreciate the venue for the first time.

The bleachers were navy and dark gray as per the school's colors. Freshly lacquered lacrosse swords and leather saddles hung in dugouts at the lowest level of the stadium. The goal posts stretched high into the sky, nearly touching the clouds.

I yawned a bit, then mentally kicked myself for not getting more sleep. To yawn in this place of wonder was an insult. I regretted drinking Madame Alexander's potion. I regretted spending time I didn't have in the barn releasing stress through combat last night. I regretted a lot of things. But I was not going to let that stop me. Madame Alexanders was right. I was fierce. More than that, I was relentless. And I was not going to let a little sleepiness stop me from acing tryouts today.

Jason and Daniel left us for a few minutes to go wrangle a few Pegasi from the stables. Blue, SJ, and I were left to explore the facilities. As we did, I tried to behave as nonchalantly as possible. The joy of today's agenda should have provided me with sufficient distraction from the terrible thoughts in my brain, but in moments of relative solitude like this, they were harder to ignore.

I'd been doing my best to act normally around Blue this morning, silently dreading the talk we'd have to have. I knew I could only put off telling her about my dream about Jason for so long. Just like I could only put off telling *Jason* about Jason for so long. But I recognized that today was not a good day for it.

Blue was excited about the tryouts and was fully invested in acing them. Jason, on the other hand, was excited to help *run* tryouts. Being captain of one of the teams meant he would need to keep his eyes open in order to select his newest players.

Now was not the time to burst his—or Blue's—bubbles with such awful news. I didn't want them to feel the emotions I was currently suppressing.

Before leaving Girtha and returning to my room last night, I made the decision to keep the dark truth about Jason's fate to myself a little longer. I had no other choice. While I knew he and Blue would be devastated by what I'd seen, the least I could do was give them a few more days. A few more days of relatively normal existence before their worlds were shattered.

"Duck!"

I leaned forward on the neck of my Pegasus to avoid being nailed by an opposing player's lacrosse sword. When I was clear, I rammed the player in the chest with my own weapon, knocking him off his steed. As he went tumbling through the clouds, I patted my Pegasus (the ever-trusty Sadie).

"Thanks!" I called to Daniel, who'd shouted the warning. He saluted and sped away—the silvery, holographic wings of his black Pegasus cutting through the sky.

For the Twenty-Three Skidd tryouts we had been divided into teams to compete in scrimmage matches. Normal Twenty-Three Skidd teams had nine players. For this particular round Daniel, Blue, Girtha, and I were on the same team, along with five boys from Lord Channing's that I did not know.

The tryouts were open to everyone, no matter their age or year in school. The team I'd been assigned to was performing really well. Daniel and I were totally in sync today. We were able to showcase both our teamwork and individual prowess for the captains judging from below. Even so, we still had work to do. We were fifty minutes in with the score at twenty-two to twenty-one. Our team was one point down. Unlike normal games that played until a team made twenty-three points, this trial was only an hour long, and I wanted to win, not lose or tie.

Throughout the sky were various projection orbs the size of cantaloupes. These flying, magical spheres captured real-time images of what was going on and projected them onto floating, holographic screens over the arena.

I wasn't going to lie. Hearing all those cheers while seeing my face on a fifty-foot screen was awesome. I felt like a rock star.

The air rushed against my face as I went after the player currently in possession of the ball. I grinned at the feel of the open sky. All of my worries dissipated. There were no magic hunters, antagonists, or visions of the future—just me in my element. I was in a state of profound peace that I sometimes forgot existed.

In recognition of this precious feeling, I vowed to myself that no matter what was to come, or wherever life took me, I had to keep going. Because moments like this (as well as the promise of moments like this) were worth fighting for.

I changed course, evading an oncoming attacker.

As I flew, I marveled at the colors around me. Pegasi wings

were holographic—made of shimmering light, not feathers like many fairytale books depicted—and came in all colors. My steed Sadie had gorgeous purple and green wings that glittered from every angle. Additionally, the eyes of Pegasi glowed either bright silver or vivid cobalt and their noses exuded colorful puffs of blue and orange smoke when they got excited.

A rush of black and silver appeared at my side again. Daniel flew up next to me as the player we'd both been chasing came into view.

The player had a pretty solid protective formation around him. His teammates—one on each side, one below, and one overhead—were doing everything in their power to defend him as he made his way to the goal.

We couldn't allow them to reach it. Our opponents were only one point away from beating us. Luckily, with Twenty-Three Skidd, our defense and offense could be as aggressive and violent as we liked. All players were geared up in heavy-duty protective armor, and there was an enormous net draped across the bottom of the arena to catch players knocked off their Pegasi.

If anything got too serious, judges flying on their own Pegasi could also intervene. It was their responsibility to referee/announce the matches. Though they tended to do a lot more of the latter since Twenty-Three Skidd had an "anything-goes" attitude.

The judges called the matches with the aid of projection orbs, which also picked up sound. One orb always remained at the side of each judge so his narration could be amplified alongside the orb's real-time imagery.

Daniel and I had to make a defensive move on our opponents. The rest of our teammates were occupied elsewhere, fighting opposing players and trying to defend the goal. Daniel gestured toward our shared target. "Together?" he asked.

"Definitely," I called back. "You take high and right. I'll take low and left."

Daniel nodded. The two of us bumped fists, like we'd grown accustomed to doing whenever we ran a play as a pair.

He swooped toward one side; I went around the other. His

Pegasus rammed the body of the higher opponent's steed while mine slammed the body of the lower one. The impacts were fast and forceful like freight trains—knocking the players out of their protective formation and giving us a chance to move in and attack the others.

As Daniel fought the player flying to the right of our main target, I challenged the one on the left. In that same instant, Blue dove in to lend us a hand. She charged straight at the player I was fighting—her lacrosse sword driving directly toward him. It was a distraction. At the last second she swerved out of the way while I powerfully jabbed my staff into the player's gut and smacked him off his saddle. He tumbled off his steed to the giant net below.

The unmanned Pegasus he'd left behind brought an unforeseen problem. It refused to move out of the way—preventing me from getting closer to the player I was after. Having defeated his own target, Daniel noticed this issue and rose overhead. He swung his leg over his Pegasus and jumped, landing on the saddle of the rogue Pegasus. He then drove his new ride toward the now-unprotected lead player.

Out of the corner of my eye I saw Blue defending us. She dealt with an opposing team member speeding for Daniel by flying up, swinging her lacrosse sword, catching the enemy's head in her basket, then heaving him backward like *he* was the ball caught in play.

He went tumbling while I charged.

Daniel and I fought the remaining player in perfect synchronicity. When our opponent was properly distracted, I secured my lacrosse sword in its holster, Daniel veered left, and I swung my leg over Sadie and tackled the player clean off his horse. His lacrosse sword and the ball it held plummeted. Midair, I twisted my body around to give Daniel a thumbs-up, signaling that I was okay. He dove after the ball, caught it, and took off after the goal.

Unlike the player I'd body-slammed, I was not worried about the fall to the net below. I had a contingency plan. And her name was Sadie.

Sadie had gotten used to my reckless maneuvers. So as I

plunged through the sky, she did not hesitate to come after me. Just like the first time I'd accidentally gotten unsaddled during a Twenty-Three Skidd tournament, Sadie swooped down in my pursuit. By the time she closed the gap between us, I was easily able to grab onto her mane.

Back in the saddle, the two of us flew into the clouds to wild cheers. The observers in the arena were thrilled by my move and the goal Daniel had just scored, which tied the game a mere three minutes before the end of the match. It was a victory, but not enough. If we didn't score soon, the game would end in a tie.

Sadie leveled off, and we flew in search of our next target. A moment later, Blue and her own silvery steed pulled up next to us. She lifted her visor.

"Now you're just showing off!" she shouted, commenting on my latest maneuver.

I raised my own visor and grinned. "And what do you call those moves *you* just pulled?"

"I call it style!" Blue winked.

She looked below us. There was a new chase underway. Blue made a gesture with her hands to signal which defensive play she wanted to try.

The two of us parted ways. She dove right. I dove left. We simultaneously arrived on either side of the enemy player in possession of the ball. Blue swung her lacrosse sword at his head. He blocked then rotated the weapon to stop my incoming strike on his left. Blue attacked again; he reacted. I lunged; he responded. We sparred like this briefly, exchanging rapid strikes one after another.

Strike, block, strike, spin, swing, dodge, block, evade, strike. Then our enemy made a mistake. Blue and I had been taking turns back and forth, aiming at the exact same spots and getting him used to a pattern. I abruptly broke the sequence. After I struck and he spun his attention back to Blue, I went in a second time at a much lower angle.

With a spin of my wrist, the basket of my lacrosse sword abruptly caught the player's foot. I thrust it upward—flipping him off his Pegasus. He spun off the steed's back and dropped his lacrosse sword. Blue was ready and dove after the falling ball the moment it shook free. She made for the goal post with me after her, watching her back from higher up.

I glanced at the holographic clock overhead to check the time we had left.

Thirty seconds before the end of the match.

We were gonna make it. Or so I thought.

When I turned my attention forward again, I saw three players charging directly at Blue. Two more were coming from underneath. The rest of the players on our team moved to defend her, but she knew she couldn't make it through the obstacle in time. She looked over her shoulder and gave me a wave of her hand. With one massive heave she launched the ball back and up forty feet into my waiting basket.

I stretched out my arm, activated the grip function on my lacrosse sword to elongate the staff, and caught the pass.

"Go, girl, go!" I shouted to Sadie.

The two of us took off at the speed of light. The opponents who'd been chasing Blue came after me, but I felt confident I could outfly them.

*Twenty seconds.*

I signaled Sadie to veer right—steering her away from an opponent who was trying to close in. A second opponent started flying very close to my other side. In a few seconds he was within striking range. I let go of Sadie's reins and thrust the staff of my weapon out—gripping it with both hands and carefully keeping the basket side up so the ball wouldn't fall. Grasping Sadie's mane in my left hand, I leaned to the side and sent a sudden, powerful kick to the attacker's ribcage. It knocked him clean off his steed. I grabbed my reins again, and Sadie and I charged toward the incoming goal with everything we had.

*Ten seconds.*

The goal post came into my line of sight. I could do this. We were closing in. Fifty feet. Forty feet. Thirty feet. Twent—

*Eep, look out!*

Out of nowhere, an opponent suddenly swooped in front of me. Disaster and a serious crash were imminent, but then Big Girtha—I mean *Girtha*—intervened.

A split second after the enemy player penetrated my flight path, Girtha knocked him right out of it. She and her Pegasus came barreling in from the side and rammed the opponent clean out of the way, clearing my path.

Sadie and I rushed within scoring distance. I swung my staff and hurled the ball through the goal just before the clock struck zero. Score!

The crowd went ballistic. And so did I. Sadie and I shot back into the sky and circled around for a victory lap before landing on the field. The net and the other players were still coming down as the audience continued cheering.

When everyone was on the ground again and my team had officially been declared the winner, I pulled off my helmet and shook my hair free. I was happy. *So happy*. And then I saw Jason smiling and giving me a thumbs up from the dugout where he and the other team captains were judging from. My heart sank and I felt terrible guilt. How could I allow myself to be this happy when I knew such a terrible secret?

I proceeded to walk off the field with everyone else. The Pegasi needed to be prepared for the next round of players while we, the players of the most recent match, were meant to take our seats in the audience. As I neared the stands, clusters of my classmates on the lower levels bolted down the steps and swarmed me—offering congratulations and words of admiration. Even after several weeks of this, I still hadn't gotten used to how the other girls treated me like a queen amongst princesses. Being fawned over to this degree made me feel claustrophobic.

While trying to be gracious about the attention, I spotted SJ watching me from the stands a few rows above the nearest dugout. I gave her an awkward shrug and a smile, then a wave. She returned the wave, but I thought her smile seemed a little forced.

I thanked my fans and excused myself from their throng as

soon as possible. I did not feel like making my way to the bleachers; instead I elected to head for a quieter spot at the base of the arena near the tunnels. I was exhausted in more ways than one and needed a few minutes to clear my head. I placed my hand against the cold, cement wall to catch my breath. Alas, my moment of solitude lasted only a few seconds. Someone cast a large shadow on the wall beside me.

"Hey, good job out there," Girtha said as she took off her helmet. "You were on fire."

"Thanks," I responded, a bit surprised that I was returning her grin, if only modestly. "You did great too. And I appreciate the save at the end. It helped."

"*Helped?* Crisa, you would've been a goner without me. We wouldn't have won and you probably would have gotten a concussion."

"All right, fair point," I conceded.

"What's going on here?" Blue asked, appearing on my other side with her helmet under her arm and aggression furrowing her brow. "Humpty Dumpty bothering you, Crisa?"

Girtha gave me a hurt look. "I thought you said you'd talk to her about this."

"I did," I replied.

I turned toward Blue and elbowed my friend in the shoulder. "Blue, we went over this like, three hours ago. You've gotta stop calling Girtha those awful names. They're mean."

"Ugh, do I really have to? I mean, if the massive shoe fits, right?"

"Blue."

"Oh, fine," Blue huffed. She placed her helmet down then turned to face Girtha. "I'm sorry," she muttered.

"Apology reluctantly accepted," Girtha said.

"Well, the apology was reluctantly *given*, so I should hope so," Blue responded.

Girtha narrowed her eyes—her forehead crinkling beneath her choppy bangs. She gave Blue a glare, which Blue mirrored.

"I'll see you later, Crisa," Girtha said. "If you're up late again and need someone to spar with, you know where to find me."

At that, Girtha trudged away to the bleachers. Blue shifted her attention back to me. "What did she mean by that?" she asked.

"Oh, nothing," I said. "Last night I had a lot of visions that were bugging me so I went down to the practice fields and ran into Girtha. Evidently she's also fond of releasing angst through combat."

Blue punched me in the arm, which hurt even through my armor. Girlfriend was strong.

"Ow, what was that for?"

"Crisa, you're the one who said we should stay away from the forest separating our schools with those magic hunters on the loose. Sneaking all the way out to the practice fields in the middle of the night is a bonehead move."

"Blue, I was way too far from the In and Out Spell border for them to see me even if they were watching at that late hour. You're overreacting."

The hard expression on Blue's face softened, but she crossed her arms with a tinge of bitterness. "Yeah maybe," she conceded. "But still, this whole thing is setting me on edge—waiting and doing nothing when those hunters could strike in other ways."

I tilted my head. "What do you mean?"

Blue bit her lip. Her bitterness faded to something else. *Embarrassment?*

"I know you don't need more on your plate, Crisa," Blue began. "But those hunters have been waiting for you a while. And we hang out in the practice fields *a lot*. Which means they could have been spying on you all this time and learnt that you have friends. Friends who are *not* protected by the In and Out Spell and who they could try to . . ."

She cut herself off and stared at the grass. Then she sighed. "I sound paranoid, don't I?"

"No more than I usually do," I said, putting a hand on her shoulder.

"Yeah, but you've got *actual* reasons to worry," Blue said. "My freaking out is just dumb. I mean, yes, Lord Channing's isn't protected by an In and Out Spell like Lady Agnue's. But a bunch of magic hunters, no matter how formidable, wouldn't attack an entire school of heroes, right?"

"Exactly," I agreed. "They'll be fine, Blue. The magic hunters pose no threat to the boys." Then I gave her a knowing look and lowered my voice to a whisper. "Or to Jason."

"Who said anything about Jason?" Blue asked defensively.

"Blue."

She groaned. "You think it's stupid, don't you?"

"Of course not. You like him; it's understandable that you'd worry."

"Is it?"

I blinked—not sure how to respond.

"I'm genuinely asking here," Blue clarified. "Other than my hot-burning love for Bruce Willis that I developed when we visited Earth last semester, I've never really liked a boy before. I'm not sure if my freaking out is normal or completely off base."

"You're asking me?" I said. "I've never felt that way about a guy either. Aside from our friends, I barely tolerate the species."

Blue shook her head. "Well, you're lucky. I don't like this. This whole *feeling your feelings* business is murky territory. You're better off trying to avoid it for as long as possible."

"Noted," I said.

The judge on the field blew his whistle and all the new players began mounting their Pegasi. Blue glanced in their direction. "Come on. Let's go find SJ and take our seats. Wouldn't want to miss any of the action."

"You go ahead," I responded. "I'm pretty tired from not getting enough sleep last night. I think I'm gonna head to the locker room."

"Suit yourself," Blue said. "But you'll miss checking out your handsome prince charming in action." Blue nodded to the field.

Chance Darling was among the new wave of players getting ready to take off. He was already on a Twenty-Three Skidd team, but like several other veterans, he was participating in the tryouts to help fill the gaps in the competing teams.

He saw me looking at him. For a second I worried he might

pull another one of his public declaration of affection moves. Thankfully, all he did was give me a slight smile and a wave before turning away.

I guess he meant it when he said he was going to leave me be for a while.

"I'll live," I finally replied to Blue. "I've had enough ups and downs for twenty-four hours."

"Okay, I'll see you later then," Blue said.

I pivoted, but before I had the chance to take my leave, Blue's voice stopped me. "Oh hey, did you want to talk about your visions? The ones you said were bugging you last night? I know you've had some bad ones in the past, but they've never literally driven you from our room."

I felt panic rising, but kept my expression neutral. "It can wait. I'll tell you later."

"Promise?"

"Yeah," I said, holding back the sudden urge to fall apart. "Promise."

Blue patted me on the shoulder. She went to join the other spectators just as the judge blew his whistle a second time and the mounted riders shot into the sky to cheers around the stadium. Finally alone, I exhaled deeply as I turned into the tunnel. I began to meander down it, thinking about my dreams.

*I had to tell Blue; I had to tell Jason, but . . .*

"Hey, you heading out?" Daniel's voice interrupted my thoughts.

I rotated toward him as he caught up with me.

"Yup," I responded. "You?"

"Same," Daniel answered.

We walked in silence for a minute.

"You did good today, Knight," he said after a lull.

I gave him a look. "Why, Daniel, is that an actual compliment I'm detecting?"

"What can I say?" he shrugged. "Sometimes even you deserve them."

"Well, thank you," I said. "You were great too, in case you didn't already know."

"I did."

"Yeah, I figured." I smirked.

The gravel crunched beneath our feet as we continued to walk. Light streamed into the tunnel, causing our shadows to elongate across the ground with every step. I pensively listened to the applause from the audience before turning to glance at Daniel.

I noticed something about him, something I had picked up on earlier. There was a sadness in his eyes today. I knew from personal experience what a person looked like when they were in pain and trying to hide it. I'd practically lived with that expression on my face during our mission to find the Author.

I resisted the urge to ask him about it, though. As proven by the conversation at our last ball, much as I wanted him to feel like he could open up to me, he had to do it himself. I couldn't force him.

"Do you think we'll make it?" I asked him, picking a different topic. "Onto the teams, I mean."

He gave the question a moment of thought before responding.

"I don't know," he said. "There's a lot of competition. Jason might be one of the captains, but he takes his job seriously and isn't going to show any favoritism. He and the other captains only want the best for their teams. And while you, me, and Blue are good, none of us have had a lot of experience—you guys because your school doesn't have teams, and me because I've only been here for a semester. So honestly, this could go either way."

I huffed. "And here I thought the one thing I could always count on from you was your confidence."

"The one thing you can always count on from me is to be straight with you, Knight. Whether that's reassuring or disconcerting is more on you."

"I guess it's reassuring," I replied after a pause. "Everyone needs somebody to tell them how things are even when they don't want to see it. And I do appreciate you being that person for me. Sometimes I need it."

"Sometimes?"

"Okay, a lot."

"But not always?"

"Hey, even my pride goes on holiday every once in a while," I said.

"Just not today," Daniel responded.

We'd reached the end of the tunnel. There were two locker rooms—a doorway on either side of us. Daniel was headed to the left one. My destination was the door on the right, which the girls had been temporarily using for tryouts today.

"Why do you say that?" I asked.

"Something's wrong," Daniel said steadily. "There's something you're not telling us."

I sighed and shook my head. I didn't know how he always knew what I was thinking, but I had learned not to fight it. "I had a bad vision," I admitted. "A *really* bad vision."

"You want to talk about it?"

A wave of darkness flooded over me as I recalled the images of my latest dream. "No," I said firmly. "Not this time."

"Knight, don't go all cryptic on me again. You already know you can trust me."

"Yeah, and I do. But this is different. Can't you respect that there are some things a person has to keep to herself? I've certainly been respecting your space, giving you time to come to me on your own."

Now it was Daniel's turn to look turned off. Our ability to read each other was a two-way street. Sometimes I think he forgot how easy it was for me to sense when he was hiding something too.

"There's nothing to tell," he lied.

"Daniel, please." I crossed my arms.

We exchanged a glare.

"All right, fine," he said begrudgingly. "You want the truth? When I went home to Century City over winter break I saw some bad signs. Rumors have been spreading about a mounting common character rebellion. While I was there, capital guards found burning flags of Book kingdoms hanging throughout the city every morning. There is also a growing list of missing persons. Yesterday I got a letter from Kai saying that some Capitol Building clerks were found murdered in their homes. The unrest is growing and officials haven't gotten any leads on the commons responsible. I'm worried. Something is coming and I wish I was there with her." Daniel shot me another glower as he finished his story. "There. You poked your nose into my business and got what you were looking for. Happy?"

I wasn't.

A commons rebellion did not sound good. And yet, as I stood in Daniel's cold gaze, I understood that I'd crossed a line in making him talk to me about Kai.

It'd been ages since Daniel brought up his girlfriend. He'd confided in me about her when the two of us had been trapped in Aladdin's genie lamp. Since then, though, he hadn't raised the subject again, despite my attempts to get him to share more about himself.

I understood why he avoided talking about her. Kai was a sensitive topic for us. Daniel's prologue prophecy had foretold that I was going to be a key ally for them both, but that I also had the potential to bring her to an end.

Since speaking with Liza—when we realized that our prophecies had more than one interpretation—a lot of the tension had been alleviated. Even before that, Daniel had told me he didn't hold his prophecy against me. He knew its outcome relied on his choices, and he wasn't going to blame me for what Liza had predicted.

Despite this, he still got a bit weird even saying Kai's name in front of me. I wished I could change that. He didn't need to feel so awkward about sharing with me. We knew each other better than that. Yes, we were avoiding acknowledging this, but as of late I was willing to be open with him about most things. I was trying anyway.

As such, he shouldn't have gotten so defensive over me inciting the same from him. His response just now felt uncalled for. I'd let it go the other night at the ball, but now I was annoyed. I had been letting him in on the things that were hardest for me to talk about—my fears, my doubts, etc. He should've felt comfortable doing the same with me. He certainly shouldn't have been acting so nasty about it.

"Sorry," Daniel said coldly. He'd noticed I was upset and was trying to remedy the situation, but I could tell by his tone that he felt no remorse. "You know I'm not that fond of sharing personal stuff. It's not in my nature."

"Nice try, Daniel," I replied. "But you can't use that as an excuse anymore."

"Why not?"

"Because you already let me in," I replied bluntly.

"Yes, and *you* let *me* in. But are either of us sure that was such a good idea?"

"What do you mean?"

"Oh, come on, Knight, you know exactly what I mean. I'm not the only one here conflicted over what happened between us last semester—how we confided in each other so deeply. I can see it in your eyes whenever we talk about the personal stuff. You may be leaning into it more than I am, but you think our relationship is weird too."

I shifted awkwardly. He wasn't wrong, but I didn't know how to say it out loud.

"I've been trying to be a good friend and be there for you," Daniel continued, "but tell me that you don't feel it too, that there isn't some part of you that's uncomfortable with how well we know each other."

Our conversation had reached a delicate point. I didn't respond, but the uncertainty on my face was all the confirmation Daniel needed. What he didn't realize though, was that my reaction was only one part uncertainty. The other part was wariness over what I feared he was about to do. He saw what he wanted to see, not the full picture.

"Yeah. That's what I thought," he said. "The same goes for me. While letting each other in allowed us to build the trust we needed to get through our last mission, it feels strange talking about deep stuff with you on a regular basis."

I swallowed the hurt. The guardedness I'd been trying so hard to push away began to seep back into me. "So what are you saying?" I asked. "You don't want to be friends anymore?"

"No," Daniel replied. "I'm saying we classify here and now

what kind of friends we are. There's a line, Knight, and ever since we got back to school we've been dancing around it. But we can't do that forever. We either deal with what went down between us and come to terms with knowing each other this personally, or we pretend like the whole thing never happened and move on. We stay friends, but the non-close kind."

Daniel's eyes locked with mine for a long, hard beat.

"Is that what you want?" I asked.

He crossed his arms. "I think it'd be easier. We get along fine now. Eliminating the deep stuff wouldn't change that. It'd only make things run smoother."

I wanted to tell him I didn't think that was true. I wanted to tell him that this was a mistake and I didn't want to go backward. I'd spent a long time building up the strength and courage to place this kind of trust in him. If he threw it back in my face, then what had been the point of it all?

I opened my mouth to express some of these sentiments, but my lips tightened when I saw Daniel's expression. He was sure of his decision. It had already been made without my input. He no longer wanted my trust and there was nothing I could do about it.

"Yeah," I said, lying to hide my hurt. "I guess so."

"Then we're in agreement," he said. "You and I stay exactly as we are. We keep it simple. We talk about nothing relating to what we said in the lamp, nothing personal, and nothing—"

"Nothing that matters," I finished.

"Yeah," he said. "Nothing that matters."

# CHAPTER 9

# Aury

ou're not focusing."

"I am too."

"Really? Because if you were focusing you would be glowing, not arguing."

I opened my eyes and glared at Liza's reflection in my Mark Two. I'd been sitting on my bed in the same meditation pose for half an hour and felt no closer to accomplishing the task at hand—bringing something to life *temporarily*. Liza and I had been stuck on this lesson for two weeks now and I was having trouble progressing. Maybe it was because my mind wasn't clear. Until a couple days ago, the crevices in my brain not occupied with thoughts of schoolwork and antagonists had dwelled on upcoming Twenty-Three Skidd tryouts and TA potions sessions. Now that headspace was churning over my vision of Jason's death, my reluctance about telling him and Blue, and Daniel's decision to push me away.

"Can we take a break?" I asked, frustrated. "I know I need to learn how to do this, but is it really so urgent?"

"I don't know," Liza said. "Why don't you ask the vines Lady Agnue tore down? Or that piece of wood that almost decapitated SJ a few weeks ago?"

I huffed, knowing she was right.

When Mauvrey had almost killed me with the poisoned corset, I'd been too weak to get help. Doing the only thing I could think of at the time, I'd brought a portion of our bedroom's wooden floor to life to fly me to the infirmary.

Since then the chunk of floorboard had stayed alive like

everything else I enchanted. However, unlike Lucky who I kept as a pet, the vines that Lady Agnue had removed, or other objects like that tree in the forest, which I never saw again, this wooden slab had been giving us a bit of trouble.

After rescuing me, I stowed the wooden slab in our room for a while. It slept under my bed at first, but unless I kept giving it commands it went a little wild, flying around the room like an out of control Frisbee. When it started getting out of our room and zipping across the grounds at night—smacking into towers and trees and turrets—Lady Agnue intervened. She locked the wooden slab in the school's old dungeons, which hadn't been used since the concept of tower detention was thought up.

None of the other students or teachers would ever find the wooden slab in the dungeons, and it would not damage any more school property. But I felt bad that it was trapped down there. I had given it life, so it was my responsibility. Shoving it away seemed like a cop out.

I sighed and tried to fight my tiredness. Liza was right to insist I learn this lesson and I was wrong to complain about it. There were clearly repercussions to my bringing things to life.

"Come on, try again," Liza encouraged. "When you focus on that alarm clock, concentrate solely on the action you want it to take. Picture the clock doing just that and then going inactive immediately after. Your magic responds to your will—your train of thought. If you give that train a sole track with a set destination, it will run its course and then stop."

I tucked my hair behind my ears, sat up straighter, and focused. Closing my eyes, I clasped the clock that normally sat on Blue's nightstand. I felt its cool, metallic surface on my fingertips as I summoned my magic.

"Walk across the room and go back to where you belong," I commanded aloud. As I said this, I visualized the action. I pictured the little red clock using its four silver legs to journey to the other side of the room. Then I imagined the clock using the open drawers on Blue's nightstand to hop to the top before reverting back to an inanimate state.

I felt the magic energy pulse through me, but this time more gently. Suddenly the clock leaped from my hand. I opened my eyes and watched in amazement as it replicated the exact path I'd seen in my head. It waddled across the floor to Blue's bedside, jumped from drawer to drawer up her nightstand, settled itself on top, and then it just stopped. It wasn't alive anymore; it had finished its duty and was an ordinary clock once more.

I'd done it! After many hours of fruitless practice, I'd finally been able to give life to something temporarily! An immense sense of satisfaction rushed through me.

"Excellent work," Liza declared. "You finally got it, Crisa. You should be proud. This is a very important part of learning to control your powers. When my Pure Magic first developed into the power of teleportation, every time I tried to teleport something or someone they would go where I wanted, but then they would continue teleporting uncontrollably based on whatever I was thinking next.

"Once I learned to control the connection I had to my powers, the problem was resolved and managing my abilities became easier. Just like it will be for you. With a lot more practice, this level of control will eventually help you handle your magic telepathically, allowing you to bring things to life to a much greater degree without burning yourself out or exhausting yourself so quickly. That will still require a great deal of training, mind you. But for now, at least this means you won't have to worry about leaving so many miscellaneous objects alive in your wake, like that wooden slab. From now on, whenever you enchant *anything* be sure to employ this new skill. All right, Crisa?"

"Hold on," I said, getting an idea. "If I can project my magic into something temporarily—essentially giving it life and then taking it away—why not just do the latter part to resolve the problem of the wooden slab altogether? Couldn't I directly focus my powers on that set destination you were talking about and bring an end to the life I originally gave it?"

In my mind this was a brilliant, natural notion. However, the expression that appeared on Liza's face was sour and stern, making me feel like I'd made a terrible suggestion.

"No, Crisa," she replied. "You couldn't do that."

"Why not?" I asked. "It makes perfect sense. If I can do that trick on the clock—provide life and take it back—why couldn't I do the second half of the process and—"

"Crisa," Liza interrupted. "Who here has had Pure Magic for longer?"

I exhaled in frustration. "You."

"And who has managed to avoid having that Pure Magic turn them dark for over a hundred and fifty years?"

"You."

"So then," Liza replied. "Wouldn't you say that I might know a bit more about the situation than you?"

I thought about the wooden slab flying around downstairs. "Yeah, I guess. But I still don't see why I—"

"Crisa."

"All right, all right," I said, holding up my hands in surrender. "I trust you. I'll leave Woody be. Happy?"

"The word is relieved," Liza replied. "If you want me to be happy, keep listening to me and fighting your rebellious instinct to do otherwise, and we'll see if we can't work up to that."

I looked at the very clock I'd enchanted and disenchanted a minute ago. Lunch period was nearly up. "I have to head to Princess First Aid class," I told Liza as I grabbed my book bag. "Any final words of wisdom before I go, oh great magical mentor?"

"For you?" she replied. "Just the same ones as always: try and stay out of trouble."

I winked at her before closing my Mark Two. "I'll do my best."

After an extensive morning of class, training with Liza, and more class, I eventually made it to the end of the school day. Alas, my reward was not a Monday afternoon nap, or a plate of cookies, or any other form of peace I so desperately craved: it was, as always, more work.

I headed to my potions classroom to meet Madame Alexanders. As I approached, I heard yelling. Hurriedly I opened the door to see what was the matter.

"You hooligans! Go and practice somewhere else! There are dangerous substances in here!"

Madame Alexanders had her pudgy face pressed against one of the two large, floor-to-ceiling windows next to her desk. She was staring down at the grounds below, rapping a fist against the glass.

"Professor?"

Madame Alexanders whirled around. "Crisanta, dear, come in."

"What was all that about?" I asked, nodding toward the window.

"Oh, some of your classmates are running Twenty-Three Skidd drills on the lawn. Their ball has hit my windows three times now and I am terribly worried that it is only a matter of time before they break one."

"They're five floors down, professor," I said, reassuringly. "I think we're safe."

"Very well," she said. "But we must keep an eye on them and those lacrosse swords they're wielding. I sense mischief afoot."

I turned to put my bag down. A second later, I was startled to discover Madame Alexanders hovering over me—*way* too close to my personal space.

"So?" she prodded.

I sighed, well aware of what she wanted. "Congratulations, professor. The potion was a total success. I had the worst nightmares of my life on Friday night. And *that's* saying something."

"Really? Oh, that is wonderful news!" She clapped her hands together and opened up her notebook to scribble something down. Then she went over to her trusty lab cases and began unpacking ingredients.

I tried to distract myself from the awful memories of my nightmare about Jason and strode over to her desk. "What kind of sleeping potion is on the agenda today?" I asked.

"For a change of pace, today we are making a sweet dreams sleeping potion," she responded. "We'll need lavender, ginger root, eucalyptus, sand, and . . . oh, fiddlewotts!"

"What's wrong?"

"I forgot to get the fresh honeycomb from the beehives on the roof this morning."

"We have beehives on the roof?" I asked. "Is that allowed?"

"Would you think less of me if I told you it wasn't?"

I smirked. "Actually, I think it would promote you to being my favorite teacher."

"Very good then," Madame Alexanders responded. "I must go and collect the honeycomb if we are to proceed with today's experiment. Be a dear and please prepare the other ingredients while I am gone. The instructions are on the table." She pointed to a piece of purple parchment with a hastily written list of bullet points then gathered her keys from her desk.

"Wait, what if I have questions?" I asked.

"Then I suppose you'll have to find answers," my professor said as she headed for the door. "I have faith in you, Crisanta," she called back. "Just try not to blow up the laboratory before I return." Madame Alexanders exited the room and I reluctantly picked up the instructions.

*All right, Crisa. You can do this.*

I began by taking out the lavender oil and pouring it into one of the beakers over the burner, slowly bringing it to a boil. I thinly grated the ginger root into a small cauldron and added sand. Next I dropped twelve eucalyptus leaves into the lavender oil every thirty-seven seconds on the dot like the directions indicated.

With those tasks complete, I poured the contents of the beaker into the cauldron. A light pink cloud exuded from the brew. It smelled sweet, but not overbearing. I breathed it in and discovered the brew emanated a happy sort of feeling, like a cross between how you felt when you took a hot bath and ate ice cream with hot fudge.

I picked up the parchment to read the next instruction. All that was left before the honeycomb was adding an entire Poppy.

Carefully, I removed the jar containing the flowers from one of Madame Alexanders's lab cases. I held it up to the light. The jar was fogged up, but I could see six Poppies crammed inside. They were bright red with black spots. The flowers seemed so small and docile-looking that I had trouble believing that even the slightest touch would cause a person to fall into a long, deep slumber that sucked out their life force like a Stiltdegarth or a Shadow.

*Hmm. Why does our realm have so many things that can do that?*

I uncorked the jar. A light mist came out of it when I did. It seemed like the Poppies were producing it. I used a pair of forceps to pluck out a flower then closed the jar. Holding the forceps slightly away from my body, I moved slowly toward the cauldron.

*Almost there . . . almost there . . . Just hold it steady.*

*CRASH!*

A Twenty-Three Skidd ball came spiraling through one of the windows. It smacked into the cauldron, causing its boiling contents to splash onto my arm. The burn was so intense that I tossed the forceps, along with the Poppy, into the air.

My reflexes worked involuntarily then. I didn't mean to reach out for the Poppy; it just happened. My hand caught the blossom in midair before my brain could prevent me from doing so. And then . . .

Then nothing.

I expected to hit the floor and fall unconscious immediately due to the flower's potent, sleep-inducing powers. But I didn't. Somehow, I remained awake. I remained unharmed.

*What in the—?*

Hesitantly, I held up the Poppy. A glowing purple color was spreading up the veins in my hands and arms, but I didn't feel any different.

I swiftly put the Poppy back in the jar and examined my arm more carefully. The instant I stopped touching the flower the purple discoloration ceased its progression. A faint golden glow began to emanate from my veins—outshining the purple hue. The glow increased in brightness for a moment like a flash, then my arms returned to normal.

I took a step back and took stock of my vitals. My pulse was regular, my stomach and throat seemed unaffected, and my head was clear. Overall I felt unchanged, which was rather disconcerting.

I stared at the jar of Poppies. I didn't understand. Simply touching the flower should have knocked me out. My veins should still be that awful shade of purple. And the energy should have been sucked out of me. This didn't make any sense.

"Yoo-hoo!"

I spun around.

"Sorry it took me so long, the bees were a bit perturbed," Madame Alexanders said as she came through the door—arms wrapped around a big, white bucket of honeycomb, which partially blocked her view.

She was all smiles at first, but when she caught a glance at the panicked expression on my face, she stopped short. "Are you all right, dear?"

My eyes darted to the jar of Poppies. "Um, yeah, I just . . ." Then I pointed to the broken window. "Those darn hooligans busted your window."

Madame Alexanders set her bucket onto a lab desk and her eyebrows shot up. "Good gracious! They did!"

She hustled over to the shattered window and started yelling, but I severely doubted that the kids who'd broken it were still in the vicinity. They'd probably gotten the heck out of there as soon as they realized what they'd done.

After Madame Alexanders finished with her rant and the school janitor had come to clean up the broken glass, she and I completed the day's experiment. I let her add the Poppy to the concoction this time. And I kept my mouth shut about what had transpired in her absence.

We successfully brewed the sweet dreams potion and each chugged it down to test its outcome like we had with the nightmare potion.

On drinking the potion, I experienced the same symptoms as Friday: icy stomach, a hot throat, hastened pulse, and purple veins. However, I wasn't sure what to expect as a result of the potion's effects. Would they actually work on my dreams the way they were supposed to?

I thought the nightmare Poppy Potion had worked just fine. I'd certainly had nightmares last Friday night. But what if those dreams hadn't been the result of the potion? I mean, technically I already had nightmares with relative frequency. So what if my visions of the pirate ship, and the flying monkeys, and Jason were only normal visions—completely unrelated to the Poppy Potion that Madame Alexanders and I had consumed?

It was an outlandish theory, but given what had just gone down in the potions lab, not an implausible one. Touching the Poppy barely had any effect on me. I'd held the toxic flower in my hand and nothing drastic had happened.

I didn't know how that was possible. But it was grounds to believe that the first potion, and possibly this new one too, might not affect me.

When Madame Alexanders and I finally finished, I couldn't make it to my room fast enough. I collapsed on my bed with a sigh. In an effort to keep my thoughts from running away with me, I reached beneath my mattress and pulled out the book I kept hidden there: *Shadow Guardians—Origins, Dangers, & Weaknesses* by Aimee Durant.

Ever since Daniel had procured the text for me last semester from the Capitol Building's library, I'd tried to read it whenever I had a spare minute. Unfortunately, I didn't have a lot of those, so my progress through the thick book had been extremely slow. Especially since the font was an ant-sized, single-spaced, non-indented print formatted on old, weathered pages. Oh, and it was written in Mountain Troll.

SJ and Blue had helped me figure that out. But since none of us spoke the language—I'd studied Nymph for my language course last year and the pair of them had taken Spanish—I'd been borrowing books from the school library to translate the text line by line.

The work was exhausting, but I kept at it nonetheless. It was my hope that the book would eventually provide me with some information I could use to get an edge on Arian, Mauvrey, and any of the other antagonists who wielded Shadows. So no matter how long it took, I was not giving up. The answers were here. I felt sure of it.

My translated notes were sandwiched inside the book's front cover. I grabbed the Mountain Troll dictionary I'd found most useful—*Mountain Troll Words and Phrases* by Dennis McWorth—

which I'd checked out of the library in the normal way, hopped back on my bed, and got to work, continuing from the page where I'd left off.

I actually seemed to be getting somewhere today. After about thirty minutes I finished translating a full page and read it from the start.

"As Shadows draw their power from darkness (both the literal kind and figurative kind associated with human nature), they can be weakened by light in the same sense. Some circumstances such as aversion to literal light are easily overcome when the Shadows exist within a host. However, the more figurative interpretations of this law are harder to compensate for. Their essence is more complex.

"What research has proven is that Shadows and Shadow Guardians stay away from items that embody human symbols of light, such as selflessness, kindness, hope, and faith. Some examples include family mementos and items of deep sentimental value to the human host. More commonplace examples include four-leaf clovers and spare coins. Such objects are commonly associated with wishing—a sentiment of light which embodies true, vulnerable moments of hope and faith. As a result, they are toxic to both Shadows and their Guardians."

I put the book down as I processed the information.

*Holy bananas! That makes total sense!*

It explained Mauvrey's weird phobia of coins. She'd been scared of them this whole time because the Shadow inside her made them toxic to touch. But geez, she'd had that fear for as long as we'd been at Lady Agnue's. How many years had one of those things been living inside of her?

I lay back on my bed, my head full and my body tired from such an odd afternoon. As I exhaled with exhaustion, SJ came in.

"Long day?" she asked.

"The longest," I responded without sitting up. "I think I just learned something pretty important from the Shadow Guardians book, but that was far from the most of it. During our TA session, Madame Alexanders left me alone to brew a potion and there were some . . . issues."

"Hmm, shocking."

That made me sit up. SJ seemed to be looking for something on her desk so she didn't notice that I was staring at her in surprise.

"What's that supposed to mean?" I asked, lifting an eyebrow.

SJ shrugged. "Nothing. Just, what did you expect when you accepted the position? You are not talented at potions, Crisa."

"Yeah, I know. But you don't have to point it out. I get it. I suck."

"Well, take comfort in the fact that you at least suck less than I do." SJ stopped rummaging around her desk. She stood frozen with her back to me so I couldn't see her face.

Oh, crud. This is what I'd been afraid of since I accepted the TA position.

"SJ," I said, watching her steadily. "You know what happened with Madame Alexanders is not something you should stress out about, right? I can't explain why she didn't pick you. You're a natural and it *should* have been you. I don't know how many times I have to tell you that. The fact that you weren't selected doesn't make any sense."

"No," she sighed. "But I suppose it would not be the first time."

"First time for what?"

"First time that my not being selected for something did not make any sense."

*Oh boy.* I had a feeling this conversation was coming. Logical, sensible, and rational as SJ was, I knew not having a protagonist book had to be getting to her. I'd long suspected that it was only a matter of time before her insecurity about the matter reared its ugly head.

"SJ," I responded slowly as I made my way over to her. "You know the Author's protagonist selection isn't what we thought it was. You can't let not having a book get to you. It doesn't mean anything."

"That is easy for you to say. *You* were chosen," SJ replied.

"Yes, and look what it's gotten me. Because of that stupid book Liza wrote, I have my own personal war to wage against a kingdom full of antagonists who've made it a point to hunt me down because my prologue prophecy told them they have to. The rest of us—Blue, Jason, Daniel—aren't any better off for having books and being 'selected' as protagonists. You should be thankful that you—"

"That I what?" SJ interrupted, finally turning to face me. "That I am not important enough to be considered a threat to the antagonists? Not special enough to be considered *anything* to anyone?"

"SJ, you're plenty important and plenty special, book or no book. You know that."

"I am sorry, Crisa, but I do not. At least not anymore. I am not like you or Blue or Jason or Daniel. I am not strong, or brave, or bold. I am not a naturally formidable fighter. And I am not a hero. But the thing is, I have always accepted that. Those were attributes that I saw in the four of you, and I had things of my own that I was proud of, being an exemplary princess and potionist most of all. But now I do not even have those to call mine."

She took a deep breath and gave me a vulnerable look. "Do you know why the friendship between you, me, and Blue has worked so well over the years, Crisa? It was not because we were the same; it was because we were different. Blue was our scrappy, fearless hero with a talent for combat. I was the model princess with an affinity for potions. And you had a bit of each archetype, but not enough to overstep your place."

"I'm sorry, *my place?*" I repeated in surprise. "What are you talking about? What happened to the girl who used to tell me that she was just as unhappy living in a world with assigned roles as I was? The girl who fought her way across the realm with the rest of us to reach the Author to change that? Now you're acting like places and roles still matter."

"I was all for trying to achieve more with my life than what I was assigned when I thought that I had a role in my own book," SJ countered. "But meeting the Author was a wake-up call and now I know the truth. I cannot hope to be more because I was never intended to be anything at all. Not like you."

"Me?"

"Yes, you. Book or no book, as you say, Crisa, you are changing.

Every day you are finding your own as a hero, as a princess, and as this girl that everyone in school is suddenly looking up to. It is ridiculous and unfair. You are moving into the light while I am moving into the shadows because some Fairy Godmother with a magic disease wrote your name down in a book. You have become this annoyingly special, magical 'chosen one' and, as if you were not already the constant center of attention, you had to take away the only two things that were mine—being a perfect princess and my potions."

I had never felt this angry toward SJ before. We'd had our disagreements, but they never ran so deep. This was something new. I couldn't believe what she was accusing me of. The spite and condemnation in her tone offended me even more. Her words sent a tremor of ire up my spine.

"I haven't taken anything from you, SJ," I responded sternly. "You're blowing this whole thing out of proportion. The reality is that me getting a bit more respect from the other protagonists has nothing to do with you. It's probably just a fluke that will be over with soon. But even if it isn't, it shouldn't matter to you because *you* are a great protagonist. As to the potions, I asked you if you wanted me to turn the job down and you told me not to. Blue and I have assured you a hundred times over that our professor was off her rocker in not picking you. Any sane person in this school knows that you're the best. For goodness' sake, look at the portable potions you invented. That's brilliance, SJ, and creativity, and resourcefulness, and protagonist potential at its finest. If you don't see that, then I don't know what to tell you except that you can't blame me for stealing your thunder. Because if anyone is taking away your spot in the light, it's not me; it's you in your own stupid refusal to step into it."

SJ and I had a silent staring stand-off. After a tense moment, she seized her bag off her desk and headed for the exit to our room without saying another word. She didn't even look back. She just left with a loud slam of the door—leaving me feeling a whirlwind of rage and disappointment, all directed at her.

# CHAPTER 10

# Connections Lost & Found

hat's with you two?" Blue asked as we were putting back our borrowed books in the library's restricted section.

SJ and I hadn't spoken a word to each other during dinner. We just sipped soup and chewed chicken in silence. Now, back in the library for our book borrowing session, it seemed Blue finally decided to say something.

SJ appeared deeply absorbed in a large, withered text and didn't reply.

"Nothing," I said, sliding my current book about Neverland back on the shelf in exchange for two new ones—a text focusing on famous mermaid lagoons and another on ancient jungle temples. Unfortunately, I'd been so distracted by the task and Blue's question that I didn't see the small cloud of burning dust floating my way. I sidestepped, but a few specks grazed my shoulder. Since the dust only affected biological things, it easily passed through the cloth of my dress and burned the skin underneath.

"Argh." I cringed.

SJ gave me a once over, but didn't ask if I was okay.

"Yeah, sure," Blue said in disbelief as she slid down her ladder. "Well, whenever you're ready to talk about it, I'm here." She looked at each of us. "For both of you."

She had two new texts in her possession—one entitled *Monsters of Camelot* and another called *Enchanted Woodland Creatures— Squirrels, Beavers, Armadillo Edition*. I decided to change the subject from the awkward topic at hand and pointed at the latter text. "What Wonderland map is the woodland creatures book for?"

Blue scooped up another book she'd already set aside on a nearby shelf and ducked under a cloud of incoming dust. "It's for Limbo," she responded with a huff. "I hope the boys have better luck with it when we switch map assignments at next week's ball. I have had zero. The only thing I've been able to find is a bunch of references to some beaver. If it weren't for your White Rabbit friend's assertion that it's a Wonderland, Crisa, I would have trouble believing it even exists."

SJ gave her watch a glance. "Five minutes," she said. She snatched one more book off a shelf then nodded at the exit. "Shall we go?"

Blue and I checked that we had everything then followed her out. As Blue worked on relocking the doors to the restricted section, I decided to take a moment to swallow my pride and give forgiveness a go. I pivoted and leaned in closer to SJ.

"Hey," I whispered. "About our fight earlier—"

"Crisa," she whispered back, cutting me off. "I do not want to talk about it, or talk to you. Let us just do our jobs and carry on."

I withdrew. I had been mad at SJ for what she'd said earlier. In fact, I'd been steaming at her for all the things she'd accused me of. But given our history, and the compassion I felt for her insecurity, I'd decided to be the bigger person and try to give her an out. Maybe we could just pretend like it never happened and let it go. I ground my teeth. Clearly she didn't want that. She was being as curt with me as ever, and that ticked me off even more.

Blue finished locking the doors and we hurried through the library. Once we were outside, I put down my books and scaled the brick wall while Blue secured the main doors.

"You look bummed," Nick the Guardgoyle commented as I reached out to give him his bacon. I glanced back at SJ, who was staring off into the distance with a thin frown on her face.

"Rough day," I responded.

"Want a piece of my bacon?" Nick offered. "I can share today if it helps."

I managed a smile. "Thanks, but I'm good."

I clambered down the wall and made my way toward Russell.

"I'm not going to offer to share my bacon," he told me as I ascended. "I don't know you like that."

"Aw, and here I thought we'd been growing closer these past few weeks," I said with fake sadness.

"I'm still upset about that night you brought us vegan bacon."

"Hey, don't blame me," I said with a shrug. "I'm the one who had to carry it around all day. My book bag still smells like tofu and broken dreams."

I leapt off the wall right as Blue finished with the doors. I picked up my books. SJ gave me a sour look, and I mirrored it, but we both stopped glowering at each other when Blue turned around.

"Night, boys," I waved to Nick and Russell.

"Good night," Russell said.

"Hope you handle your issues," Nick added.

I stole another glance at SJ.

*Yeah, don't we all.*

The rest of the week passed in a blur.

Every day, I went to class, skipped lunch to train with Liza, went to class, trained in the practice fields, went to class again, worked with Madame Alexanders, then finished off the day with Wonderland mapmaking in my room, with a bit of actual homework thrown in. If I was feeling particularly ambitious, I got out my Mountain Troll dictionary and Shadow Guardians book. But I rarely had time for that anymore.

The most colorful parts of my day were the frosty run-ins I had with SJ. The two of us had barely spoken since our argument.

In addition to all this, I was increasingly worried about my potions TA sessions with Madame Alexanders. More specifically, I was perplexed about what was wrong with me. Poppies did not seem to affect me the same way they affected others.

After the flower-touching incident, I'd paid special attention to the effect of the sweet dreams potion. Lo and behold, my dreams had been nightmarish as usual, which meant something was amiss.

Initially I assumed the potion was flawed, but when Madame Alexanders reported how well it had worked on her and a few other students she'd allowed to sample the brew for extra credit, I realized that the problem was me. I needed to investigate further. Just not now.

SJ, Blue, and I had been working intensely on finishing our Wonderland map assignments. We'd be trading tasks with the boys at the February ball next week. But as soon as that was over, I intended to look into why Poppies had a different effect on me. Maybe Blue could help me find answers in the library.

With my days jam-packed and my nocturnal consciousness more tormented than usual, I felt exhausted all the time. Ironically, the only thing that brought me peace was sneaking off to the barn for some combat drills when the rest of the school was asleep.

While the loss of z's made me yawn during the day, I welcomed the change of pace at night. It was a distraction, and a productive one at that. Every night I'd gone down to the barn this week I'd crossed paths with Girtha. Evidently she was stressed too; she claimed she couldn't sleep because she was anxious about the results of the Twenty-Three Skidd tryouts, which would be posted this Sunday. I didn't share with her my multiple stressors, and I was glad she knew well enough not to ask.

The two of us ended up training together. I showed her some moves with the spear and helped her improve her agility. In exchange, she aided me with my unarmed combat.

After what went down with the magic hunters a few weeks ago (and the chilling dream I'd had of Parker nearly killing me with a dagger), I'd been wanting to work on my hand-to-hand fighting skills. I wanted to be able to rely on more than just my magic and my wand to save me. If for some reason I didn't have access to either, I still needed to be able to defend myself. Girtha was the perfect person to help me with this endeavor.

She was one of the few protagonists at school who preferred things the old-fashioned way—no weapons, just fists. Between growing up in a forest, being picked on as child for her larger size, and having a pair of much older, extremely scrappy siblings,

Girtha had learned from an early age how to fend for herself with nothing but her two hands. She was a force to contend with *au naturel*, and she made for a good sparring partner late into the night when I had a lot of pent-up frustration that needed releasing.

Of course, I didn't know how much of a challenge I posed to her in return. Attacking Girtha was like attacking a stone wall— there were very few weak spots. Moreover, she was incredibly strong and fully capable of tossing me around like a rag doll.

*Ooof!*

I smacked into one of the haystack walls hard, the wind knocked out of me.

"Why don't we try something else," Girtha proposed as I caught my breath.

"What's the matter?" I asked, getting up with a painful grunt. "Getting bored of throwing me across the room?"

Girtha scoffed. "No, it's good weight training actually. But even with the sparring mats we've laid down and the walls of hay, I'm assuming you've had enough."

"Not even close," I scoffed in return. "Besides, I think I'm finally starting to get the hang of this." I stood upright and stretched. "Ready for round six?"

"You know it," she replied. She cracked her neck and then her knuckles.

We took our positions. Girtha lunged at me and I ducked under her arm. I spun and threw a reverse, spinning kick. She turned in time to block it, grabbed my foot out of the air, then used it to slam me to the ground.

*Ooof!*

"Can I make a suggestion?" Girtha asked as I heaved myself off the sparring mat.

"Please," I said, rubbing my leg.

"Look, you're fast, your reflexes are good, and you're great with improvisation. Combining that with a weapon makes you pretty formidable. But one thing you're not accounting for is space. You're used to distancing yourself from your opponent because your spear relies on that type of fighting style. But hand-to-hand combat is different, even more so for an offensive fighter like you. When you put too much space between you and your opponent, you leave yourself vulnerable. Weaponless fights are *always* won at close range, Crisa. Got it?

I nodded.

"Round seven?" she asked.

"You're on," I said. "And this time I'm comin' for ya."

"Take it down a notch, princess. Just try not to tap out before ten seconds."

I frowned, provoked. "Yeah, I'll keep that in mind."

Girtha lunged at me again, but this time I didn't duck and dive out of the way like my instincts urged me to do. Instead, I met her head on. My left arm thrust to the side, blocking her strike. Meanwhile I lifted my right hand to punch her in the solar plexus.

She swatted my hand away and moved to nail me with a left hook. I raised my arm just in time to stop it. She struck right. I blocked left. She kneed me in the side of the leg, but instead of buckling from the blow, I moved with it—spinning and hitting her in the temple with the back of my fist.

Girtha's balance wavered for a second, but not long enough for me to make any kind of strike. She shoved me back with her massive arms. I staggered a few feet then ducked her next blow. Rapidly I leapt in and kicked her knee outward. She stumbled a bit, but still managed to seize my arm and flip me over.

I landed on the mat with a thud. It stunned me, but my adrenaline compensated. Girtha was leaning over me, still balanced on one knee. As she lunged down to strike, I grabbed her arm and the back of her shirt collar and flipped her forward.

She fell and I twisted myself to dodge her incoming body. She landed beside me. I tried to roll away and get up before she could beat me to the punch, but halfway to my feet she snatched me by the neck and tackled me down.

Girtha had the superior position now—bearing over me and pinning me to the floor with her meaty hand. I struggled to push back, but her strength and size were choking me.

"Come on, Crisa," she said. "You don't need to be stronger than me; just find a way out."

"That's . . . sort of hard to do . . . without . . . oxygen," I gasped as Girtha's hand crushed my throat. "Can't . . . think straight."

"You don't need to think; just act. Do what you did before. Use my advantage against me."

She was bigger, heavier, and had the better position. Fighting against her was like fighting an avalanche. So I let her do what avalanches do best—tumble.

I hinged my leg and kicked out Girtha's knee. She lost her balance. I released her arm and hit her square in the jaw. My fingers wrapped behind her neck and—striking her underarm with my other hand—I pulled her down.

She rolled sideways, releasing my neck. The moment she crashed I let go and shoved her away. From there I jumped to my feet and stood over her.

"*Whablamo!* Totally lasted more than ten seconds!" I declared triumphantly as I stared down at my defeated sparring partner.

"Crisa," Girtha said.

"Yeah?"

"Putting aside everything I've told you about hand-to-hand combat, when it comes to fighting in general, do you know what rule number one is?"

"What?"

"Don't get cocky." Girtha suddenly swung her massive arm and swept my leg out from under me.

*Ooof!*

My head throbbed for a second from having hit the mat so hard, but I supposed I was getting used to it. I totally should have seen that move coming. It served me right for getting smug. The same move had taken me down when I was fighting Daniel just a few weeks ago in this very barn. Lesson learned; no more cockiness.

After the oxygen had fully returned to my diaphragm, I stood back up.

"Good job. That was way better," Girtha said. "You even got a battle scar out of it." She pointed to my face.

I wiped the side of my hand over my lips and discovered a tinge of blood.

*Oh, crud.*

I made my way to an area at the back of the barn where a dusty mirror hung. The glow of the nearest flaming gas lantern illuminated my reflection. Despite the cobwebs and the dirt clinging to the mirror, I could make out a decent-sized cut on my bottom lip.

"SJ's gonna judge me so hard tomorrow when she sees this," I huffed.

"So?" Girtha replied. "Tell her it's an occupational hazard of being awesome."

"Somehow I don't think that's gonna fly."

I sighed, thinking on my sadness over what had gone down with SJ this week. I hadn't vented to anyone about my fight with her. Blue obviously noticed something was wrong, but I didn't want to drag her into it. It wouldn't be fair to make her take sides. Meanwhile, my other usual go-to friends, Jason and Daniel, were at Lord Channing's. Even if they were here, I couldn't talk to either of them about this. Jason would probably try to force SJ and me into some kind of reconciliation. And Daniel . . . well, he wasn't an option. He'd made it very clear that I wasn't to share anything personal with him ever again.

Irritation grew inside me. The disagreement with SJ had cut me deep. The thing was, I didn't just feel sad over our sudden estrangement; I resented it. I had enough problems to worry about. I shouldn't have to waste headspace or heartspace concerned with someone who was supposed to be my best friend and was suddenly acting like my rival. I'd been using my magic training with Liza as an excuse these last few days to avoid SJ at lunch, and it was easy to keep to myself in classes and just focus on our teachers. But dinners, our late-night library ventures, and even just being in our room together had grown unbelievably awkward.

I scowled in exasperation. Then the frustration got the better of me and I abruptly spun and punched a hay dummy so hard it nearly teetered over. When I turned around I saw Girtha eyeing me.

"Something wrong?" she asked.

"No," I lied. "Let's go again. I feel like hitting something."

Girtha smirked. "Good luck with that."

She cracked her knuckles and lunged at me. I braced myself, reconsidered my life choices, then bobbed and weaved to avoid getting hit in the face.

*Sigh. If only all problems were this easy to dodge.*

Girtha took advantage of my lack of focus and smacked me in the side. I rolled to the ground. My stomach hurt from the impact, but it was nothing compared to the blow SJ's spurn had delivered. Not to mention Daniel's.

*And if only they were this easy to recover from.*

I launched myself up and rushed in anew—fire, ire, strain, and pain fueling me forward, and making me both stronger and weaker for the challenge ahead. Like they always did.

# CHAPTER 11

# Waffles & Wonderful News

 y heart pounded with trepidation at the sight of Arian. I hadn't laid eyes on the intimidating antagonist since Alderon. Both my real life and nocturnal visions had been free of his presence since returning to school. But all good things had to come to an end.

I saw him at the center of my dreamscape, proud and strong as ever. He was taller than I remembered, with black eyes and equally dark hair, a hard chin, and a scar on the side of his face that I'd put there. He and a small man in a gray hood were in a room with stone walls and navy curtains. An oak table stood between them with maps spread across it.

"They got away, my lord," the small man said to him meekly. "They lost the citadel knights in the Forest of Mists. The Gwenivere Brigade helped them."

"I know that, you dolt," Arian responded. "What I don't know is how they managed to align themselves with the Brigade so quickly. Rampart should've been able to keep them here." Arian pounded the table in annoyance. The force of his strike was so strong I thought it might split the wood in half.

"Why is it so hard for people to hold on to one princess?" Arian scowled.

"In fairness, sir, hasn't she escaped *you* several times?"

Arian looked like he might split the man in half. I think the man knew it too, because he took a step back.

Arian directed his gaze to the maps in front of him. "As much as it would please me to slit her throat myself, I cannot waste time hunting Crisanta Knight right now. Mauvrey and I have to get our own Knight to the isle. I know Rampart already put a bounty on her head, but use the Mark Twos to contact every hunter we've employed and make them aware of where the princess and her friends are headed. With enough of them searching for her, there is no chance she will make it through the Passage Perelous alive."

"With respect, my lord," the man interceded, "as proven by the events in the citadel, the girl's allies make it more difficult. Their presence greatly reduces her vulnerability."

"Then remove them from the playing field."

Arian mulled over a thought. An idea shone in his irises and he readdressed his underling.

"*Silva In Motu*," he said. "Tell the hunters to be waiting for her there. Then let's see how strong Crisanta Knight is when her precious friends aren't around to protect her."

I woke from the dream when the bird that SJ employed to act as our alarm clock began its high-pitched song.

For once, Blue was the first person out of bed. On most school days we had to work as a team to get her up. And ordinarily she refused to rise before noon on weekends. Today, though, she couldn't get ready fast enough.

I didn't blame her. It was Sunday. The Twenty-Three Skidd tryout results were being posted this morning. She and I rapidly got dressed. I barely had a chance to tie up the laces on my boots before she grabbed my arm and yanked me out the door.

SJ didn't even get up. She waved our alarm bird away, rolled over in bed, and didn't wish us any kind of luck on our way out. The bird was hurt that she'd disregarded him. And so was I.

Blue didn't notice, though. She was too excited. We raced down the hall to the staircase. There were others girls descending the fuchsia carpeted steps. By the time we got to the second floor there was a mass of slow-moving students in front of us. Thinking quickly, Blue heaved herself onto the smooth silver bannister and pushed off. I followed, and we slid down the rest of the way—the speed of the winding descent making our hair flap.

We reached the bottom and landed on the checkered tile of

the ground floor like it was no big deal. Blue grasped my wrist and pulled me forward without another second lost.

"Move out the way!" she said as she shoved through the crowd gathered in the foyer.

The tryout results were posted on the bulletin board that usually held memos about school clubs and special events. The area around the board was packed. Today may have been a Sunday, but girls of all ages had woken up early to take a gander at the outcome. There were several dozen of us who'd tried out, and countless more were curious about the turnout. Realm-wide, Twenty-Three Skidd was an all-boys sport. For even one of us to make a team would be an incredible win for our gender.

"Can you see anything?" I asked as we got closer.

"Um . . ." Blue jumped up and down. "Not yet."

She and I continued to push our way forward. A task, it seemed, that may have been more difficult than fighting fire-breathing chipmunks.

I began to feel nervous as we edged closer to the board. Lady Agnue's and Lord Channing's had classes that went from fifth grade to senior year of high school, and the majority of the student body (maybe 80%) was made up of common female protagonists like Blue and common male heroes like Daniel. So many of those common protagonists had tried out last week and there were only eight spots available. The odds were not in our favor. It was highly unlikely that—

"Holy cow!" Blue exclaimed, moving to the front of the throng.

I was right beside her. I stared at the sheet and blinked. My name and Blue's name were both written on the roster. We'd made it onto two separate teams, but we'd made it nonetheless.

"We did it!" Blue shouted.

It felt like my heart did a backflip. A huge grin spread across my face. Blue and I hugged and jumped with excitement. This was the greatest news! I was so happy I could hardly stand it.

The two of us made our way back through the crowd and headed toward the banquet hall. "I can't believe we both made it," I said as I passed her a plate in the buffet line.

"I can," she replied. "We were both awesome at tryouts."

"Yeah, I know. It's just . . . things aren't usually that easy."

"Oh, calm yourself, Miss Gloom and Doom." Blue rolled her eyes as she began to help herself to breakfast. "I swear, you almost die four or five times and suddenly it's like you've forgotten what it feels like to have things go your way. Trust me, girl; there's no need to panic. Sometimes this is real life."

"You're right," I said, letting myself feel happy again. I raised my eyebrows when I noticed that Blue had gone to town on the waffle station. Her plate now held three waffles, a pile of whipped cream the size of a sandcastle, and an assortment of syrups that ran over the whole tower like an overflowing volcano.

"What?" Blue said in response to my shocked expression. "We're on the team now. I have to carbo load."

I shrugged and helped myself to a monstrous plate of waffles as well.

Blue and I took our plates and sat down at our favorite table. More protagonists were starting to pour into the banquet hall now. A number of them were coming in with melancholy expressions on their faces from not making a team. However, a select few protagonists entered the banquet hall beaming.

Along with Blue and me, three other Lady Agnue's students had made the cut—Girtha, Jacqueline Day Ripley (who was one year our senior), and Divya Patel (who was four years our junior). They strutted into the banquet hall triumphantly. Girtha gave me a smile and a nod from across the room. I returned the gesture. Jacqueline and Divya did the same.

I didn't know either of these girls well since we were not in the same year, but I assumed we'd get to know each other in the future. I looked forward to it, even if we would be on competing teams.

"It's really cool that five girls made it onto the teams and only three boys got chosen," I commented as I dug into my waffles. "I wonder if any of the guys at Lord Channing's are upset about the way things turned out."

"Who cares." Blue shrugged. "Those haters can suck it. The five of us were clearly better, despite all their hero training. We'll have to keep proving ourselves, though. Even if the five of us are on different teams, we need to work together to show the boys, and the teachers, that we are just as capable and shouldn't be underestimated."

I nodded in agreement. Blue was right; we did share that common goal in spite of being on separate teams.

Girtha and Divya had both made it onto the team known as the Lyons; that was Chance Darling's team. Jacqueline obtained the only open spot on the Jacklebees. A prince at Lord Channing's named Andrew secured a slot on the Tenants. Meanwhile, Blue and a boy called Christopher had gotten the two available positions on Jason's team—the Crusaders.

Making Jason's team was clearly filling her with more elation than she wanted to let on, but there was no denying the joy dancing in her eyes.

I had claimed the seventh available spot and had ended up on a team known as the Seven Suns. I had made this team alongside the final newly selected Twenty-Three Skidd player for the season—Daniel.

*Of course.*

He and I could just not shake each other. The universe kept forcing us together no matter how much we both would have preferred otherwise.

I was annoyed and also anxious about what this might mean for our performance. Daniel had really hurt me when he threw my trust back in my face. And while we may have decided that we could be casual friends, I didn't know if I could get over this betrayal enough for us to work on a team like we had before. Being selected together led me to believe that the captains of the Seven Suns saw our dynamic teamwork in action during the tryouts and thought we'd make a great duo. But now . . . I didn't know.

"You excited to be on the same team as Daniel?" Blue asked in between forkfuls.

"Excited isn't the word," I responded. "A better one would probably be amused. I'm sure you're over the moon about *your* team assignment though."

Blue glanced down at her waffles—trying to bury her lack of

a poker face—but I saw her blush the same shade of raspberry as the syrup on her plate.

"I don't think he sees me that way," she eventually said. "We're buds, but he didn't put me on his team for that reason. If he had, he would've given the other spot on the Crusaders to either you or Daniel, not that Christopher kid. Which means that Jason actually believes in me as a player. Which *also* means I can't let him down. We're the first girls to ever play on Twenty-Three Skidd teams, Crisa. The captains took a huge risk in picking us. I have to focus and deliver. I won't let Jason's reputation get hurt because of me."

I nodded and went on eating my waffles, stifling the horrible urge to tell her that it wasn't Jason's *reputation* she had to worry about.

I looked up and saw SJ had come into the banquet hall . . . with Jade. The two had their heads together and were talking like old friends. SJ's eyes caught mine for a split second before she and Jade continued toward the waffle station.

"What's that about?" I asked, tilting my chin in their direction.

Blue glanced over her shoulder then shrugged. "SJ's been hanging out with Jade recently."

That caught my attention. I lowered my fork despite the fact that it was already loaded with waffles. "Why?"

"I think SJ felt sorry for her. Gossip runs fast and opinions change quickly around here, and you, Miss Popular, caused a shift. Since you started your late-night sparring sessions with Girtha, you've been treating her differently. You're nicer to her in classes and stuff; you even let her sit with us for dinner a couple times this week. I was not a fan, but I digress. The point is that the other girls have noticed. Between you accepting her and her awesome performance in the Twenty-Three Skidd tryouts, she's started to make new friends. That left Jade even more alone than before, and SJ sort of came to the rescue. The two of them have been spending their free time together lately—studying in the library, riding horses out in the practice fields, potions lab stuff. I'm surprised you haven't noticed."

*I haven't noticed because SJ and I have been so adamantly avoiding each other*, I thought.

"I spend my free time in my room practicing magic with Liza," I responded curtly.

Blue shrugged again. Her non-committal gesture was annoying me. I lifted the waffle-laden fork to my mouth.

"You don't like Girtha *or* Jade," I reminded her around a mouthful. "At least with Girtha we have Twenty-Three Skidd in common, and lately she's given me reason to think she's coming around. Hence the trial run invite to sit with us the other day. But Jade's the worst and has made no effort to change. You're not at all weirded out by SJ latching onto her?"

"Maybe she needs it," Blue said, not noticing my irritation.

"Who? SJ or Jade?"

"Both of them. Jade needs a friend and a good role model and SJ . . ." Blue frowned like the matter gave her a slight headache. "Well, maybe she needs the attention. Jade is so grateful to finally have someone be nice to her that she treats SJ like she's queen of awesomeness."

I watched SJ and Jade move away from the waffle station and start to make their way toward us. I sighed and conceded to try and be a bigger person. I had let Girtha sit with us the other night, after all. If SJ wanted to bring in someone new I needed to deal with that. "I guess we should invite them to sit with us," I conceded.

*Maybe this will actually be a nice change of pace,* I thought to myself as they headed over. Our meals together since the fight had been awkward. That was part of the reason why I'd let Girtha join us a couple times. SJ barely talked anymore. Blue made up for it—girl loved to gab—but it was hardly the same. Perhaps Jade's enthusiasm would bridge the silence and we could move forward.

I gave SJ a wave to signal her over. She clearly saw me but changed course. She and Jade headed to a table where Marie Sinclaire and Lili Jane Watson were seated.

"Jade is mad at you," Blue said, seeing my stunned expression.

"She kind of blames you for Girtha branching out and outgrowing her. It's no big deal."

I put my fork down altogether. "It's a huge deal," I asserted. "You're saying Jade blames me for costing her one of her best friends. And Lili already hates my guts because of the whole jealousy over Chance thing. Don't you think it's bad for our friendship if SJ is connecting with people who don't like me?"

"What's bad for our friendship is SJ having an identity crisis," Blue said. "She's going through some stuff right now, Crisa. And while it is totally not your fault, lately you've been bringing it out in her. Maybe she needs some space to get her head on straight. If she has to make some new friends to get a little extra self-worth, it's not the end of the world. She'll come back to us when she's ready."

I stared at my friend. I couldn't believe a few minutes ago I had been on figurative Cloud Nine with the most wonderful news ever, and now I was consumed with twisted, pained emotions about SJ.

Blue was smart, and she was observant. But while she had noticed the tension between SJ and me, she wasn't fully aware of the extent I was bringing out SJ's insecurities or the degree to which SJ hated me for it. Without understanding that, how could she get how much it hurt me to see SJ intentionally befriending people who didn't like me and replacing us with new friends because it was easier than looking me in the eye?

After a moment of solemn reflection, a thought occurred to me. "Blue, doesn't SJ's behavior bother you?"

Blue furrowed her eyebrows then sighed. "Crisa, obviously it makes me sad to see SJ like this, but I don't blame her for it. The moment we found out she didn't have a protagonist book, I think you and I both knew it was a ticking time bomb. The foundation on which she built her identity was shattered. Now she has to rebuild. I am not going to side with either of you in this tiff you have going—not because I don't care, but because life's too short. You of all people should know that. I have a best friend with a prophecy and magic that people are trying to kill her for, a crush on one of my other best friends that's making me dizzy, involvement in an ongoing plot with antagonists and the fate of several realms, schoolwork, and my own prophecy to worry about. *You* have way more than that. So I think we should avoid any extra drama when we can and enjoy the victories the universe gives us."

Blue grabbed her glass of orange juice "We made Twenty-Three Skidd teams today, Crisa. In a sea of shadows, it's a bright spot. How about we let it keep us above water for a little while before bigger things pull us back under?"

She raised her glass of juice high in a toast and eyed me expectantly. I hesitated at first, glancing over at SJ, but then picked up my glass and took a long, deep breath.

"Okay," I said.

We clinked glasses. Blue took an easy swig. Mine was a bit harder, but I swallowed down my gulp along with my regrets.

CHAPTER 12

# Time-Crack

o do you have, like, reserved seating in the headmistress's office? I feel like you get called in there
so much you should be a part of some rewards program."

I gave Blue an annoyed look. "*Ha ha,*" I said
dryly. "Ms. Mammers's note said for both of us to come. So maybe
I'm not the only one in trouble for a change."

"Aw, but there is a difference," Blue countered good-
naturedly as we entered the hallway with all the paintings of past
Lady Agnue's. "Other girls get into trouble. You, my friend, are
trouble."

The message summoning Blue and me to the headmistress's
office had been delivered to our room via sparrow three hours
after we'd finished breakfast. We'd been hard at work on our
Wonderlands maps at the time; SJ was nowhere to be found and
probably off with her new friends.

The note said to come at noon, so here we were. I wasn't
really sure why. I usually dealt with Lady Agnue on my own, and
stranger still, the note hadn't seemed hostile.

I opened the door to the office and was surprised to find
Girtha, Jacqueline Day Ripley, and Divya Patel on the velvet
forest-green couch across from Ms. Mammers's desk. The assistant
was nowhere in sight.

"Hey," I said, surprised.

"Hey, Crisa," Girtha said. She nodded cordially to Blue.
"Blue."

"Girtha." Blue swallowed her discomfort and forced out a

vague attempt at friendliness. "Congratulations on making the team."

"Thanks, you too," Girtha responded.

There was a slight lull before I cleared my throat and stepped forward with my hand outstretched. "Hi, I'm not sure if we've officially met." I said to Jacqueline and Divya.

Young Divya was small-framed and four-foot-ten at best—pretty short, even for someone in the neighborhood of thirteen. Her skin was light brown and her dark hair was long and braided to the side. Despite her size, her eyes and smile were huge.

Meanwhile, Jacqueline was a bit taller than me. She wore glasses and had short hair with choppy layers. She also had clearly defined arm muscles; however hers were lean whereas Girtha's and mine were thicker, making us look undeniably sturdy if not slightly less feminine.

"Hi there," Divya said, shaking my hand. "Divya Patel. I'm a third year here. Common protagonist."

"Jacqueline Day Ripley, but you can call me Jackie. I'm a common protagonist too," Jackie said as she shook my hand next. "I'm actually graduating in the spring, but am super stoked that I get to compete in Twenty-Three Skidd before then."

I smiled. "Same," I replied. Then I gestured to my friend. "This is Blue Dieda and I'm—"

"Crisanta Knight," Divya interrupted. "Yeah, we know."

I must've blushed because Jackie smirked. "Still not used to everyone knowing your name?"

"I'm not sure I'll ever get used to it," I replied. "It's kind of weird."

"Stop being awesome and maybe people will forget you," Jackie said amiably.

My embarrassment faded as my grin turned sassy. "Easier said than done."

The two of us exchanged a smirk.

"So do any of you know why we're here?" I asked, changing the subject.

"It must have something to do with Twenty-Three Skidd," Blue said. "It's the only thing we all have in common."

"That is correct, Miss Dieda," Lady Agnue said.

I hadn't even heard her open the door. Our headmistress—wearing a floral pencil skirt and high-collared silk blouse—was standing in the doorway of her office. She didn't look mad, but I was on guard right away. It was a precaution I'd gotten used to taking.

"Ladies, Crisanta, please come in," she said, gesturing to her inner office.

Blue led our group into the office, followed by me, Jackie, Divya, and Girtha. My eyes widened with joy as I recognized a familiar face inside. "Debbie!"

My own Fairy Godmother—trainee Debbie Nightengale—stood by the window chatting with three Fairy Godmothers I didn't recognize and one who I did. The woman beside Debbie was named Sonya July. Daniel and I had met her briefly last semester when we broke into Fairy Godmother headquarters.

Debbie's face lit up when she saw me. She rushed forward and gave me a big hug, which I gladly returned. I didn't even care that the other girls were staring. The light from the window behind Debbie made her brilliant red locks look like fire. She had her hair pulled back as usual; a handful of crystal bobby pins decorated the updo, one of which was her magic wand in disguise.

Debbie was majoring in fashion design and weather manipulation for her Fairy Godmother Training. She always wore the craziest outfits, and today was no exception. Her dress was patterned after a beautiful forest. Light and lime green from the tips of trees crawled along the top of the bodice and neckline, while dark forest made up the majority of the skirt. The trees in this design moved slightly—leaves rustling magically in the wind. The occasional bird migrated within the pattern, flying from one tree to the next. Also, the whole ensemble smelled vaguely like pine.

"Congratulations on making the team!" she said. "I knew you would!"

"Debbie," another Godmother said, stepping forward. "Decorum, please. Fairy Godmothers are not supposed to treat Godkids like friends. They are our charges."

My Fairy Godmother rolled her eyes then turned around and put her hands on her hips. "Tami, as *top of our class*, and Lena Lenore's personally selected leader for this mission, I will decide what decorum is appropriate. Crisanta Knight is *my* Godkid, and I will treat her as I see fit."

My eyebrows raised, surprised by the animosity between the two. Then I remembered when Debbie and I first met she mentioned her desire to beat out some "trick" named Tami Robinswood for Godmother Trainee of the Year. This tall, thin, dark-haired Godmother must've been her.

Lady Agnue shut the door behind Girtha. She didn't bother offering us a seat; there were only two spare ones anyway. She did position herself in the chair behind her desk though. Then she folded her hands and addressed us all.

"We have an interesting problem on our hands," she said. "The five of you making Twenty-Three Skidd teams means that you will need to attend practice at Lord Channing's. The teams share the stadium. Each team practices three times a week—twice during the week and once on weekends. As you well know, it takes a group of powerful Fairy Godmothers to lower the In and Out Spell, and the ones who do it must be the same ones that cast it in the first place, including Lena Lenore. However, the Fairy Godmother Supreme and her high ranking Godmothers have better things to do than tend to the extracurricular activities of five young protagonists. They are not going to come here every afternoon and lower the spell then return every evening to activate it again. That would be ridiculous."

"Then how are we going to get to practice?" Blue interrupted.

"I am getting to that, Miss Dieda," Lady Agnue said, raising her hand in annoyance. "These women here are Fairy Godmother Trainees. They do not have the power nor the permission to lower the spell entirely, but their magic is still strong. So together they have created a time-crack."

"A what?" Divya said.

"A time-crack," Sonya July repeated. "Strong enchantments like your school's In and Out Spell are almost impossible to break without action from the people who enacted them. However, with the right combination of magic and power, little loopholes or cracks can form temporarily."

"Each of us has a different Fairy Godmother Training emphasis," Debbie continued. "Sonya is focusing on healing magic. Gale and Stephanie—" she pointed at the two other Fairy Godmother Trainees, "are specializing in time magic—freezing it, speeding it up, etc. I have a flare for weather manipulation. And *Tami* is surprisingly good at making small In and Out Spells. Together, the five of us have created a temporary time-crack in the In and Out Spell around your school."

Lady Agnue nodded in agreement and picked up the explanation from there. "When Lord Channing and I agreed to let girls try out for Twenty-Three Skidd teams, we developed a contingency plan should any of you make it. The Godmothers have been collaborating since then on creating this time-crack as a solution."

"It was our Trainee Final Project," Sonya interjected. "We're entering our last few months of training before we're promoted to full Godmothers and all of us have been working in teams to complete special tasks."

"Yes, yes," Lady Agnue went on, not seeming to care. "Returning to the point, a week ago these women finally found the right combination of magic to create the time-crack, and on hearing the news that you five made teams, it was enacted this morning."

"Hold on," I said. "I still don't get what a time-crack is."

"*Crisanta*, I am getting to that," Lady Agnue replied. "A time-crack is a dent in an otherwise powerful spell. It allows a crack to form in an enchantment for a certain amount of time. These Godmothers have crafted a time-crack that will cause the very top of the In and Out Spell—the pinnacle of the dome—to open every day at exactly 3:15 p.m. for five minutes. Then it will reseal itself until the process repeats at 5:40 p.m. for another five minutes. If you have practice that day, those will be your opportunities to get to and from school. Lord Channing has gifted us with a—

selection of Pegasi that now belong to our school, so you ladies can use them to fly through the opening for Twenty-Three Skidd practice. Crisanta, you may use your dragon if you wish."

"Why did you put the time-crack at the top of the dome?" Jackie asked curiously. "Why not just put it on ground level, like at the school main gate?"

*For the same reason she's letting me use my dragon*, I realized. *She really does believe me about the magic hunters and doesn't want to risk any of them sneaking on campus.*

"Security reasons," Lady Agnue responded swiftly. "Now that is all. The five of you are free to go. Just be on time when those time-cracks open. If you miss them, that is your problem and you will miss practice."

We all nodded vigorously.

"And be sure to thank these Godmothers for what they have done for you," the headmistress added.

The five of us took turns thanking each Godmother profusely and exited Lady Agnue's office. I hung back for a second and made direct eye contact with Lady Agnue. "Thank you," I said, meaning it. Despite the contempt I held for the woman, and her ongoing preference for my doom, I appreciated what she was doing for me—and us—here.

Lady Agnue didn't respond. She simply waved me away and started talking to the Godmothers about magic dust ratios or something like that. I entered Ms. Mammers's office. The other girls weren't there; they must've gone into the hall. I was halfway to the door when Debbie abruptly emerged from Lady Agnue's office and caught up with me.

"Hey wait," she said. She closed the door behind her and gave me another hug. Then she gripped my head in her hands like I was a good dog who'd just recovered a ball. "I am *so* proud of you. I promise I'll be at your first Twenty-Three Skidd match cheering you on."

"Thanks, Deb." I smiled. "Oh, and congrats on being top of your class. Does that mean you won that Godmother Trainee of the Year competition?"

"Sure did. Tami can rub her nose in it."

"You were pretty harsh on her," I commented.

"Trust me; she deserves it," Debbie said. "She's a lot meaner than you might think, and honestly, even a little cruel."

"Well, I'm glad you beat her butt," I said. "And I'm holding you to that promise. See you at my first match."

"Miss Nightengale," I heard Lady Agnue call.

"Gotta go," Debbie said. She gave me another affectionate squeeze before dashing back. I left the office and went into the hall where Blue and the others were waiting for me. I was about to say something when Ms. Mammers brusquely sped around the corner, a manila folder in her hand. I wondered where she'd been this whole time.

"Oh good. I am glad I caught you before you departed." The assistant reached into her folder and withdrew five pieces of parchment. She handed one to each of us. "These are your team schedules. I was waiting for a messenger falcon to bring them over from Lord Channing's. Good luck with your new athletic endeavors. I hope none of you get seriously injured, embarrass our school, or die."

The way she said it made me doubt if she meant it.

Ms. Mammers scurried past our group and entered her office, slamming the door in her wake. The five of us studied our practice schedules intensely.

"Tuesdays, Thursdays, and Saturdays from 3:30 to 4:30," I read.

"Girtha and I have those days too, but from 4:30 to 5:30," Divya said.

We all traded to look at one another's schedules. Blue and Jackie had practice on Mondays, Wednesdays, and Sundays, but at different times.

"I guess on the days we're over there and aren't practicing we just hang out on the Lord Channing's grounds," Girtha commented. "Maybe we can make use of their sweet training areas."

"Oh man, that'd be awesome," Jackie said. "I can't wait. Practice is going to be so fun. You all better watch out. My team is going to smoke yours."

"Yeah, good luck with that," Blue said. "Anyway, nice to meet you Jackie and Divya. Crisa and I gotta get going. We have plans. Jackie, I'll see you Monday."

We said our goodbyes and parted ways. As I followed Blue down the hall I gave her a puzzled look. "We have plans?"

"Crisa, with Twenty-Three Skidd we're about to add another layer of responsibility to our lives. We have to get those Wonderland maps finished this week so we can trade with the boys at the ball next Saturday."

"Oh, right," I said. "That."

"Yes. That. Did you forget that you're our designated chosen one and we've got a death match coming with a bunch of antagonists?"

I furrowed my eyebrows. "Blue, I'm not—"

"I'm kidding," Blue said. "Well, kind of. Anyway, come on. Mapmaking first, break gender stereotypes with our athletic prowess later."

"Can we get a snack in between?" I asked.

"Do you even need to ask?" Blue countered with a smile.

# CHAPTER 13

## The New Norm

I t was a quarter past three on Tuesday. As part of my deal with Madame Alexanders, I was free from my TA work and it was time for my first Twenty-Three Skidd practice.

I should have been over the moon. Divya and Girtha certainly were a minute ago when they took off on their Pegasi for the magical time-crack that had opened at the peak of the In and Out Spell. It was a beautiful, incredible thing to watch— the top of the force field had become visible before peeling back like a blooming flower. Now the edges sparkled so brilliantly that I could see their every line even from way down here.

Alas, my mind was atwitter with anxiety as my pet dragon Lucky plunged through the time-crack driven by Daniel. They landed on the grass in front of me.

I hadn't seen Daniel since tryouts. I imagined he must've been weirded out with us being placed on the same team. I wasn't thrilled about the idea either, but what could we do?

"Let's go," he said, waving me over.

I decided not talking about it was the best plan. Daniel may have been uncomfortable with us being on the same team, but I didn't just feel uncomfortable. I felt angry, disappointed, and sad. He'd made me open my heart to a world of trust and then slammed the door shut. I would've been lying if I said I didn't hate him a little for it.

"Move back," I said. "I'm driving."

He didn't protest. And we didn't speak the whole way to Lord Channing's. After we landed and dismounted, we walked to the arena side by side, but miles apart. When the entrance tunnel opened up onto the field, a sense of deep, overwhelming satisfaction filled my chest and replaced the bitterness I held there. I was going to concentrate on Blue's advice to avoid extra drama and take joy in the victories the universe gave me. I was a good Twenty-Three Skidd player on my own. I didn't need Daniel. I would rock this either way and have a great time doing it.

I didn't know where Divya and Girtha had gone off to, but there were nine other boys waiting for us on the green. I recognized maybe two or three from having seen them at balls. But outside of Jason, Daniel, and Jason's former roommate Mark, I didn't socialize with guys much. This was going to be something new.

Two of the older guys separated themselves from the pack and extended their hands. One was about my height. He had a solid tan, curly hair, and a mischievous spark in his coffee eyes. The other guy was taller than Daniel, just over six feet. His hair was blond, but lighter than Jason's. It was kind of white-ish like Marie Sinclaire's. Actually, he looked a lot like Marie now that I thought about it.

"Hey, I'm Javier Marcos," coffee eyes said to me, shaking my hand. "This is Gordon Sinclaire. We're your team captains. Welcome to the Seven Suns."

I remembered Marie mentioning she had a brother at Lord Channing's. I guess this was him. I looked him up and down. The prince was pretty cute in a pale kind of way, but Javier was definitely more rugged.

I shook hands with both of them and Daniel did the same. We were then introduced to the rest of the guys on the team. Daniel already seemed to know a few, but for me, it was a blur of handshakes and heroes. Some of the guys seemed genuinely enthusiastic and welcoming. Four of them definitely didn't. I sensed coldness, almost a kind of disapproval when they were forced to shake my hand.

I guess I should have expected that. The boys I usually hung out with were civilized; they respected and understood that girls could be just as powerful and strong as guys. But I would've been a fool to believe this was a universal acceptance. Just like a lot of people at Lady Agnue's were old-school and traditional, I imagined plenty of the Lord Channing's community was the same. There were probably a good number of boys who didn't believe princesses (or girls) could hack it playing in the same physical arena. I was here to prove them wrong. I had to develop a thick skin and let my skills do the talking.

"Dillain Bardó," the last boy in the lineup said. He smiled, but his hazel eyes were patronizing. His grip was also a little too tight. I dealt with that by squeezing harder and locking my intense green eyes with his.

"Crisanta Knight," I replied. "Pleasure."

"Okay," Javier said, getting our attention. "Now that everyone knows everyone, let's go over some of the basics for our new teammates. Every Twenty-Three Skidd team has eleven players— nine first stringers who play in the matches and two alternates. Rosters for who will be starting a match will be decided the week prior to each game. Our first match is in less than three weeks and it will be against the Crusaders. We're going to start with some warm-up drills, so everybody get armored up, grab a lacrosse sword, and then pick up a Pegasus from Redwood over there." Javier gestured to the other side of the field where an extremely large, thick-built man was leading a herd of Pegasi onto the green.

"Our groundskeeper," Daniel whispered to me.

"Javi," Dillain said. "Are we doing the light warm-up drills or the advanced set?"

"Advanced," Javier replied.

"Maybe some of us should start with the light drills." Dillain shot me a look.

A couple of the other guys snickered.

"I can handle anything you throw at me," I replied, pivoting toward Javier and Gordon. "Just the same as the other guys here. You wouldn't have picked me if that wasn't true, right?"

"Right," Gordon agreed. He wheeled around to the rest of the guys. "Listen up. Let's get this out in the open now. I know some of you aren't a fan of Javi and my decision to put a girl, let alone a princess, on the team instead of some of the other guys that tried out. Well, suck it up. She's here because she deserves to be and she'll only stay on this team if she *keeps* deserving to be. So treat her no differently." He addressed me and Daniel then. "We train hard here. Right now you two are marked as our alternates since these guys are all returning players. If you want that to change, you have to prove yourselves. There'll be no going slow or special treatment. We clear?"

"Clear," Daniel and I said in unison.

"Good. Now let's get started."

It was one of the most difficult hours I'd ever endured.

The boys on the team were at the peak of athleticism. They were fast, strong, and aggressive. After some intensive warm-ups that involved trying to get past team blockades and swerving our Pegasi to evade arrows launched from mechanisms that rose from beneath the field, the rest of our training was freestyle fighting. What that meant was every man (or woman) for themselves. There was one ball and we had to try and get possession of it and score in either goal to earn points. Regrettably, you also earned points for every player you dismounted from a Pegasus.

With no judges to intervene and no one on your side to swoop in and help you, it was almost scary. I hadn't feared for my life like that in some time. The net that came out of the ground did not comfort the situation much. Especially since I got sent toward it three times.

In all of my past experiences with Twenty-Three Skidd, I had never hit the net before. I'd never been truly injured in the sport either. Today was a first for both, and I was not happy about it.

The first time I went down was when a boy named Ambrose jabbed me in the side with his lacrosse sword, rammed his steed into mine, and then elbowed me so hard in the head that my skull rattled in my helmet. I plunged two hundred feet and plopped into the net, which promptly bounced me back up several times before settling. It throbbed like the humiliation inside me, and the bruise forming on my head.

A while later a kid called Bailie, who was a Half-Legacy (the nephew to the Frog Prince, I think) was flying over me when he activated the grip function on his lacrosse sword. The staff extended. I saw it happen in my peripheral vision, but couldn't avoid what I knew was coming. Dillain and another jerk named Mirosavich boxed me in and kept me from flying away. They ganged up on me, and while I was defending myself against their various strikes, Bailie reached down, caught my head in his lacrosse sword's basket, and sent me flying.

By the time I re-saddled, we only had five minutes left of practice. I kicked my aggression up a notch to move past my bruised ego, and my bruised pride, and somehow managed the ferocity to capture the ball for the first time since we'd started. I darted around one boy after another and headed for the goal, but I never made it. Dillain dove in and slammed his lacrosse sword at my head. The blow caused me to let go of my lacrosse sword and slip off my Pegasus, but grabbed the horn of the saddle at the last second. I didn't want to go down a third time. Alas, that's just what Dillain had in mind. He hadn't gone after the ball when I'd dropped my lacrosse sword. He wanted to earn his point another way. He dove down, reached up, and gripped my foot in the basket of his lacrosse sword. Then he yanked me off forcefully and sent me plummeting.

I crashed into the net a third time and stared up at the sky.

The rest of the week didn't get any better.

I thought I was great at Twenty-Three Skidd. But I'd never been tested so extremely, nor had I ever played with four guys who clearly wanted to humiliate me. It also didn't help that it felt like I was completely alone. Whenever I'd played before I'd had Blue, or Daniel, or even Girtha on my side. I didn't have them now. Blue and Girtha had their own teams. And Daniel may have been on mine, but we weren't like we once were. Even when we had group exercises that required teamwork, our flow was off. We weren't in sync and our captains clearly picked up on it.

When practice was over on Saturday, they asked us to stay after for a few minutes. I agreed; I didn't have anywhere to go. I had another hour before the time-crack in the In and Out Spell opened. I waited while Javier and Gordon finished talking with groundskeeper Redwood. Our other teammates milled around putting away their armor and equipment.

"I'd have that shoulder checked before you accept any dance requests at the ball tonight," Dillain said snarkily, coming to stand next to me.

I stopped rubbing my shoulder, which ached since Dillain and Bailie had double-teamed me earlier and I'd gotten smacked and dismounted. "Thanks for the concern," I replied dryly.

"What with you being so popular you probably get dance requests all the time," Dillain continued. "A pretty, fiery girl like you must be beating them off with a stick. Though you certainly can't beat anybody off with a stick here, so maybe you're easier to ensnare than you'd like people to think."

I felt my fist ball up, but then a hand was brusquely on my arm.

"Knight, he's baiting you," Daniel said.

"Obviously," I said, shaking him off. I readdressed Dillain. "By all means ask me to dance tonight, Dillain. In fact, I dare you. By the end of it I promise your shoulder will be no better off than mine."

Dillain smirked and sauntered off, ramming into me as he passed. I cocked my head toward Daniel when he'd gone. "I wasn't going to hit him," I said.

"Are you sure?"

I didn't answer. Gordon and Javier called us over at that point. They didn't seem happy.

"Look," Javier said. "You guys are decent as individual players, but Gordon and I have been really underwhelmed with your performance this first week. You're not the same players we saw in tryouts. What happened to the teamwork, the accountability, the way you moved together?"

"Daniel, you wanna take this one?" I said, shooting him a look.

"Knight and I aren't a set," Daniel responded. "We did well together at the tryouts, but we want to be seen as standalone players."

"If that's the case, then you're going to have to work a lot harder," Gordon said. "You guys are still alternates. Unless a miracle occurs, you'll stay that way for the rest of the season and won't see a single game. And if that happens, Javier and I will probably have to kick you off the team. It's nothing personal, but we want to win and only the best heroes—boy *or* girl—are going to cut it. You got it?"

It was like being punched in the stomach. I would know. I'd been punched in the stomach several times over the course of my various antagonist face-offs.

"Got it," I said.

The captains left Daniel and me standing there in sullen quietude.

*This is your fault*, my eyes said to him.

*Maybe, but I'm not sorry*, his eyes told me in return.

"Come on, we have a trade to make," I said. He and I made our way to the storage closet near the dugout where our team stowed our various things during practice. We went inside and I grabbed a backpack that Blue had packed for me earlier while Daniel picked up a black duffel bag. Originally our group had planned to trade Wonderland maps at tonight's ball, but with us having practice today, we thought this would be a lot easier.

"FYI, I had zero luck mapping Cloud Nine," Daniel said, holding up his duffel bag. "I searched our whole library and couldn't find anything other than some references to magic Ravens."

"Well, I guess we're even then," I replied. "Blue was unsuccessful with her attempts at mapping Limbo other than some info about a beaver."

We exchanged bags. I clutched the duffel. A long silence passed.

"I'll see you tonight?" Daniel asked.

"Yeah, see you."

We parted ways. I shouldered the duffel bag and headed out of the arena just as Girtha, Divya, and the rest of their teammates on the Lyons were entering. I spotted Chance Darling at the front of the pack. He gave me a conservative smile. I tried my best to return it, but was too preoccupied by Daniel to give him more than a second thought or glance. Despite the look on his face that said he wanted to maybe say hi to me, I hurried past him before he could speak. I didn't manage to escape Girtha and Divya, though.

"Hey, you doing all right?" Girtha asked as we intersected near the tunnel.

"Yeah, fine," I said brusquely. "You guys okay?"

"We're excellent," Divya replied. "We actually spoke with Redwood when we got here and he had some great news. Lord Channing finally gave us clearance to use the rest of the boys' training areas in the hour that we're here and not practicing."

"That's fantastic," I exclaimed. And it was. The boy heroes had so many more advantages for training than we did. This could make a difference.

The news picked up my mood significantly. I bid goodbye to Divya and Girtha as they went to join their team and then trotted outside. I spent the next hour exploring the different sectors of the Lord Channing's training campus—the combat forums, the fields, the obstacle course and so on. I wanted to familiarize myself with my options. The gears in my brain turned and turned.

When the hour of the time-crack eventually rolled around, I whistled for Lucky. He flew me back to Lady Agnue's before returning to Lord Channing's. He was a smart dragon and had gotten used to our routine. I no longer needed Daniel to pick me up or drop me off.

The gears in my brain continued to churn from there. They went on like that for the rest of the weekend—through the ball, which was a blur, through late into the night when I was staring at the ceiling before and in between nightmares, and all day Sunday until the evening when I was in the library sitting in my favorite high-up, candelabra chair. As I perched above the ground, sunk into the squish of the seat with required class reading strewn over my lap, I came to a decision in regards to my spot on the Seven Suns. I was going to fight for it.

I couldn't control a lot of things that were happening right now—SJ's problem with me, Jason's eventual fate, Daniel's betrayal of my trust. But I could control this. I had a lot of bad eating away at me and I was going to fight for this bright spot.

Everyone needed a light in their tunnel, and I was going to protect this one. Because at the moment, it was my only saving grace in a world I was becoming a stranger to.

# CHAPTER 14

# Number 17

he next two weeks were a series of great digressions and progressions.

On the less savory side of my school routine was SJ. This was the longest we'd ever gone being mad at each other. With every day that passed, I felt her drifting further from me. Aside from when we were in our room or secretly borrowing restricted books from the library, she and I never shared words or space anymore. She was always with Lili and Jade. And when we were together, I felt her regard me with an aura of condemnation.

It really put me off. If I wanted to feel this cold and looked down upon I would go back to Midveil and walk the halls of my own castle. My school had always been more like a home than my kingdom, but SJ was making Lady Agnue's feel like anything but. I suddenly felt very alone and my resentment over the matter grew every day.

Another part of my routine that provided ongoing vexation was my TA sessions with Madame Alexanders. I hated having to consume whatever potion she and I brewed for the day. They didn't always taste that gross, but knowing that you were drinking mixtures made with bat spit and almond milk made them hard to swallow, regardless of flavor.

Past the icky additions to my diet, I felt bad about lying to Madame Alexanders on a regular basis. I liked and respected her as a teacher, and as a person she was pretty cool too. But I needed to mislead her. The potions we were brewing clearly did not have the same effect on me as they did on her and everyone else.

Ever since the incident with the Poppy, and the sweet dreams potion failing to impact me, I'd been fudging the truth about how our brews affected me. Whenever Madame Alexanders and I tested a potion, the next day I simply made up the outcome on my end to encourage my teacher to move forward with the experiment for the rest of the class.

Did I feel bad about this? Sure. But did that matter? Evidently not, because the Poppy Potions we made in class had the same effects on the students as they did on Madame Alexanders during our trial runs. Since my professor never caught on to my deception, I didn't see any reason why I should tell her. Why raise a red flag?

I had checked out a couple books on Poppies from the library to investigate the situation and found nothing to explain it. Besides that, being immune to Poppies was strange and I didn't want to call any more attention to myself. SJ's spiteful words about me being a spotlight-stealing "chosen one" had gotten under my skin.

I was grateful that at least I didn't have to lie to my professor every day. After a few TA sessions I discovered that the potions worked on me about a third of the time. I was so excited not to have to fake the results on those occasions that I probably overemphasized how strong an effect they had on me when my professor and I discussed them the next day. It cemented my understanding that it wasn't the potions, but the Poppies that weren't affecting me. Combined with different ingredients, I could still feel something.

While the SJ and TA session aspects of my life felt unstable, even deteriorative at times, other parts of my norm were flourishing. Our Wonderland map progress was constant. I was working on Toyland right now and moving along nicely. My magic training with Liza was going well. I was getting much better at the whole "bring things to life temporarily" thing. And most of all, I was improving with Twenty-Three Skidd.

Since getting lectured by Javier and Gordon, my fire had been ignited to a new degree. I trained passionately every chance I got—in the practice fields whenever I had free time, with Girtha several nights a week in the barn, and during the extra hour I had at Lord Channing's every other day after practice. I felt myself getting stronger by the day, and it started to show.

During Seven Suns practice I was knocked to the net less and less. I scored more points. I even began knocking other players off their Pegasi. I paid no mind to the aloof Daniel or condescending Dillain and his friends anymore. I was all focus. And on that Thursday before our first Twenty-Three Skidd match, that focus finally bore fruit.

Only minutes remained in practice. Our team was split in two for a scrimmage. I was feeling confident. I was riding Sadie today. Last week I'd spoken to Redwood about always making sure she was present at practice. I was fine on all Pegasi, but I trusted her the most with my riskier maneuvers. And as my ferocity grew, so did they.

I'd already scored four points and had the ball yet again. Bailie and Dillain zoomed after me. They came at me from both sides, but I was ready. I lunged by body back to evade Dillain's swinging lacrosse sword. Then I activated the grip function on my weapon to smack Bailie. With a kick and a reign pull I yanked my Pegasus to the right abruptly and rammed Bailie's steed then hinged and kicked him straight in the ribcage. He was off balance, and I brought my weapon down upon him with no mercy to sweep him off his saddle.

As he went tumbling through the clouds, I locked my lacrosse sword in its holster just as Dillain darted in. Speedily my feet left the stirrups and I climbed on top my saddle so that I was standing upon it. I had faith that Sadie would remain steady. Dillain swung his weapon and I leapt up to avoid it once then leapt to dodge it again. I met his cocky eyes and then I jumped. I tackled him clean off his ride.

Moments later Sadie was coming after me. The only problem was that Dillain and I were still entangled. He knew what I wanted to do, but wasn't going to allow me to remount Sadie. He had me tight by the arms so we'd fall together. I struggled, but when he would not let go I used my helmet to head-butt him. It was enough of jolt to get him to release one of my arms. From there, I swiftly punched him in the face and I was free.

I kicked his lower back for good measure—bounding off it like a boost—just as Sadie came into range. I remounted her and zipped between Ambrose and a kid named Ricky straight to the goal and scored. There was no cheering like there had been at tryouts, but I felt a surge of satisfaction swell through me nonetheless. I descended to the field; practice was over and all the boys were coming down.

"Good job, everyone," Gordon said once he'd taken off his helmet. "You're all dismissed. Except you, Bailie." Gordon and Javier exchanged a look. "Javi and I need to have a word with you. Crisa, you stay too. We'll need to talk to you after."

I said okay and went to put away my armor and weaponry in the dugout with the rest of the guys. Dillain wouldn't look me in the eye, which I took as a compliment. It required all of my restraint not to rub my triumph in his face.

After his stuff had been stowed, Daniel gave me a slight nod before departing. I waited on a bench until Javier, Gordon, and Bailie emerged a couple minutes later from the captains' communal office, which could be accessed through a door underneath a portion of bleachers. Javier and Gordon signaled me to come inside and join them while Bailie stomped away. He was all rage and he unapologetically rammed me as he passed.

I entered the captains' office for the first time. It wasn't anything spectacular. There were trophies and other accolades on the walls, equipment in the corner, and a desk at the back with two chairs behind and two in front. There was also another door cracked open a smidge. Beyond it I could see a sort of locker room set up crossed with a lounge.

"Do you know what this is about?" Gordon asked as he leaned against the desk.

"Not really," I admitted. "I know I got a little aggressive in practice today, but I thought that's what you wanted."

"It is," Javier said. "And now in return you get something that you wanted." He went around the desk and pulled a key from a drawer. Then he gestured for me to follow him and Gordon into the room beyond.

"This is the locker room that the captains use," he explained. "We get ready in here while the other two locker rooms are assigned to the competing teams on the day of a match. Now that some of the teams have girls, we've had to adjust. The captains voted, and we've decided that whenever teams with girls are playing, the captains will give up their locker room and lounge for Lady Agnue's use while we get ready with the rest of our teams."

We'd stopped at a row of lockers. It took me a minute to absorb what was happening. The locker in front of us had my name on it: "C. Knight."

Javier handed me the key in his hand and gestured to the locker. I carefully unlocked it and discovered armor inside, my armor.

During practice we all used the communal armor and lacrosse swords stored in the dugouts. But during matches every person had special armor—decked in colors that represented the appropriate team with the player's name and a number engraved on the back of the plating. Within that wonderful locker I saw a set made just for me, along with a matching helmet and a new lacrosse sword. "Knight" gleamed on the back of the armor above the number "17."

"You're starting in the match on Sunday," Gordon said. "You've earned it. Daniel and Bailie will be the alternates, in that order."

I had to stop myself from hugging them both. Instead I just grinned ear-to-ear and thanked them the normal way.

I felt like I was floating while I wandered around the Lord Channing's training campus and as I flew Lucky back to school.

Once I'd returned to my room, I had a speedy shower and changed. Dinners at Lady Agnue's were always formal, but when I put on my dress for the evening I realized that the outfit was incomplete. It called for a jacket. A specific jacket.

After the locker presentation, Gordon and Javier had given me my official Seven Suns team jacket. It was a casual white zip-up with navy accents on the cuffs, arms, and collar, and our team insignia emblazoned on the right chest area. They told me that they'd given Daniel one earlier in the day too. All team members got jackets, even if they weren't first-string players. But as I put my arms through the sleeves and gazed at the way it looked over my glittery scarlet dress, I felt like Gordon was completely right. I had truly earned this.

Not caring that it was informal, I elected to wear it to dinner tonight. It definitely got me some stares, more than usual I should say. Many girls came over and asked me about it, then gushed with awe when I told them I was starting in the game this weekend. I normally was not keen on my classmates' attention, but today I didn't mind. I was proud of what I'd done and how I'd improved in the last two weeks.

Blue approved of my outfit choice wholeheartedly, and asserted she would wear her jacket all day to classes tomorrow. Apparently her team captains (Jason and a boy named Hector) had decided that she would start in the match on Sunday too. My team would be playing hers—the Seven Suns vs. the Crusaders. I'd never been so excited to be competing against a friend before.

SJ sat at a different table to have her meal, as she had been doing quite often lately. There was a moment when I thought she might join us. When she entered and spotted Jade and Lili, she realized they were already sharing a table with Girtha, Marie Sinclaire, and Divya Patel. SJ's expression wavered when she looked at Girtha. I guess she hadn't decided if Girtha's presence was less desirable than my own. Blue had been making progress on that front, what with having Twenty-Three Skidd in common, but I don't think SJ and Girtha had ever shared a non-antagonistic conversation. I saw SJ's eyes ever so slightly fall upon our table where I sat with Blue and several other classmates giving us attention and showering us with questions.

When SJ met my gaze, her eyes narrowed and she stayed true to her original course and slid beside Jade. It wasn't until later that evening that I understood what had been going through her mind at the time.

I had just finished changing out of my dress when SJ returned to our room. I had been intending to meet Blue in the library.

Midterms were coming up and since I spent a lot of my spare time reading books I wasn't supposed to, I garnered I should spend some time catching up on those I was. I wished I'd left sooner.

SJ gave me a snide look. "Where are you going?"

"Library," I replied.

"I assume you are taking your special jacket?" she said as she moved for the bathroom. "If you do not, how will you be the center of attention?"

My teeth clenched, but I didn't offer a retort, despite the fact that I had several shrewd ones at the ready. I did, however, grab my team jacket off my bed and put it on just to spite her. That must've been what had irritated her when she saw me at dinner. SJ leaned against the bathroom door with a dramatic sigh and then moved inside, still talking to me.

"You cannot help it, can you?" she continued. "Despite the airs you put on about not wanting this 'chosen one' status, you like it."

She emerged from the bathroom and went to fetch the hairbrush from her desk. "I understand. It must be exhausting though, pretending to be humble and aloof when you cannot go one day without showing off the fact that you are—"

"SJ," I said suddenly—so abruptly and fiercely that she halted in her tracks. "Just stop, okay. If you don't want to be my friend right now, fine. But could you not be my enemy? I've got plenty as it is. Keep this up and you might as well just move to Alderon and join their cause."

SJ blinked, utterly startled. I did not stay in the room a minute longer. I grabbed my book bag and left for the library in a huff.

"Girl, you look like you're steamin'," Nick the Guardgoyle said as I approached the main doors.

"Rough night," I replied.

"Heard you're starting in the big game on Sunday, though," Russell commented. "That's gotta boost your spirits."

*It did until SJ came along.*

"Yeah," I said quickly. "Anyway, see you guys later. I have some studying to do."

I entered the library and scanned the floor for Blue. It looked like she'd saved me a seat, but the table was packed with students. When she spotted me, I pointed to the back of the library. She got what I was saying and returned to her book. I made my way to the giant candelabra I had my eye on and clambered to the top. Once seated, I took a couple of texts out of my book bag, but before I cracked them open I released a huge sigh.

*Why do people have to constantly disappoint you?*

Lower left block. Uppercut. Right hook. Spin. Rear elbow. Back kick. Roundhouse.

Girtha hit a haystack wall with a thud. I'd been improving dramatically in our combat practices, and tonight I was a bit more charged than usual. My glee over Twenty-Three Skidd crossed with my anger about SJ made for a deadly cyclone of powerful emotions. If this kept up I might even have to cancel my training sessions with Liza tomorrow. I was supposed to stay away from magic when I couldn't clear my head. Since everything with Daniel and SJ, there'd been good days and bad days. I was able to focus most of the time, but every once in a while when I was feeling particularly ragey, both Liza and I agreed to take a step back. It was vital that I never let my magical side and emotional side get together.

"You've gotten so much better," Girtha commented. It was stating the obvious, but I still appreciated it.

She took a beat to wipe a bead of sweat from her forehead with a towel. "Hey, can I ask you something?" she said after a moment.

"Yeah, what is it?"

"What's going on with you and SJ?"

I felt my blood pressure go up and had to stifle a wave of resentment that went with it. "Nothing," I said. "Stuff between her and me has been weird recently. We got into a fight a few weeks back and the state of things has kind of been going downhill since then."

"Well, that's not right," Girtha replied. "You guys are the closest. Why don't you talk to her?"

"Pass," I said sharply. "If she wants to talk she can come to me.

For once I'm not at fault, and I'm not going to do her ego any favors by pretending that I am." I kicked the nearest bale of hay. "She needs to get over her issues for herself."

"That's pretty cold," Girtha said, crossing her arms.

"Well, *she's* being pretty cold. You should hear some of the things she's said to me."

"Crisa . . ." Girtha started slowly. "I know it's probably not my place to say so, but—"

"Then don't," I interrupted, my feelings welling up inside.

"Don't what?"

"You're right. It's not your place to say so. So *don't* say anything," I snapped.

My frustration was justifiable, but when I saw the hurt look on Girtha's face, I knew that lashing out at her wasn't. Just because Girtha and I didn't have the best history or closest bond didn't give me an excuse to lose my temper. I wasn't sure if I felt comfortable calling her "my friend" yet—a few weeks of good behavior and camaraderie didn't erase years of animosity and torment—but that didn't mean she hadn't been trying her best to act like it. And I owed her the common courtesy of respecting that.

"I'm sorry," I said. "Snapping at you was uncalled for."

Girtha looked at me straight on. "No. It wasn't. I shouldn't be sticking my nose in your business. It's like you said before, we're not friends, right?"

## CHAPTER 15

# *Hunted*

 could not concentrate on pumpkin juice and pixie dust.

It was Friday and I was tired. I'd been tired every day this week. But today I felt like I'd hit a wall. The extra energy I'd been putting into workouts and Twenty-Three Skidd practice had been exacerbated by nightmares. It was true those never stopped, but last night's had been insufferable—a replay of Jason's death.

As I absentmindedly stirred the beaker in my hand, I thought back to the morning. I'd woken with a start, calling out Jason's name. My body ached from the pain the vision had caused, and my head throbbed. Blue had rushed out of the bathroom wielding her toothbrush as if it was a weapon.

"Hey, what happened? You okay?" she'd asked.

The sheets were still knotted between my fists and I was at a loss for what to say. I still hadn't told Jason or Blue about the vision. I needed more time. *They* needed more time.

"I had a dream about Jason," I'd admitted reluctantly. "But before you say anything, don't ask me what it was. I think it'd be best if I told him what I saw first—respect his privacy and all that, you know? I mean, you would want me to do the same thing if I had a dream about you and happened to run into someone else first, right?"

"Yeah, I guess."

"Well there you go."

Blue seemed a bit miffed, but she accepted my explanation.

"I've said it before and I'll say it again. I hate how noble you are sometimes."

"Trust me," I'd responded. "It's not that fun for me either."

"Crisanta!" Madame Alexanders's voice startled me out of my daydream. The shout was so unexpected that I dropped the beaker in my hand. The glass splintered on the floor, orange liquid everywhere. I dove to clean it up with one of the enchantment absorption sponges, but my professor stopped me.

"Leave it," she said as she went over to her desk and set her lab cases upon it. "There is another matter that requires our attention."

"Professor, what is it?" I asked.

"I'm afraid we've had a bit of a break-in, my dear," she said, looking devastated. "I was down in the storage cellar beneath the school to collect the Poppies for today's experiments when I discovered that a whole shipment of the flowers is missing." She put her hand to her head like SJ so often did when she felt a headache coming on.

"Missing? You mean somebody stole them?"

"Keep it down," my professor said. She went to close the door. "Crisanta, those flowers are toxic to the touch. Can you imagine the panic that would ensue if this situation were to become public? Good gracious, I might even lose my teaching position."

"Professor, I hardly think you're going to get fired because a few ingredients went missing. It's not your fault they were taken. That's on the school's security. Just look at what went down with the Treasure Archives last semester. Junk happens."

"Yes, Crisanta; junk does indeed happen. But that is no excuse. Professors at this school have been dismissed for far lesser transgressions. Didn't you ever wonder what became of Madame Lin?"

"Our school's old Color Coordination instructor? Yeah, she was cool. She taught me how to coordinate my combat boots with my accessories. Whatever happened to her?"

"She tried to introduce a lesson plan about mixing and matching stripes with polka dot patterns, which she called 'Command Clashing.' It did not go over well with the headmistress."

Madame Alexanders laid her head against the table in defeat. It was weird; adults were supposed to be the ones consoling kids when something bad happened. I wasn't quite sure what to do here.

I awkwardly patted my professor on the shoulder. "Don't worry, Madame Alexanders, we'll find whoever is responsible. And in the meantime we'll keep it quiet. You have more Poppies, right? No one has to be the wiser."

My professor was hesitant but calmed down enough to finish our session. However, she didn't say much for the rest of the afternoon.

In my room later, I toiled away with Liza, my body breaking a sweat as I channeled my magic into my latest goal.

So far today's session was going surprisingly well. I hadn't ended up needing to cancel, despite my spat with SJ and Girtha last night. I was getting better at blocking my emotions when it mattered. Or maybe I just had so many right now they were canceling each other out.

*All right, concentrate,* I told myself.

I placed my hand on the stack of wooden blocks from Blue's Fort Architecture class. The glow emanated from my hand into the top block—the only block I was touching.

I focused harder.

Slowly the glow began to spread from the top block into the two dozen others piled beneath it. They all floated off the ground, flew across the room, and re-stacked themselves in the form of a perfect pyramid, exactly as I'd commanded.

"Not bad, Crisa," Liza said through my Mark Two. "If you keep practicing like you have been, this ability to transfer your magic into multiple connected objects by merely touching one will serve you well."

"It'll certainly help with cleaning my room," I said as I marveled at the sturdy pyramid of blocks I'd assembled. "I think Mary Poppins would be proud."

"Yes, well, she lives in a retirement community in Middlebrook, if I remember correctly. So maybe one day you can visit her and compare housekeeping tricks. For now, though, can we focus more on training and less on your jokes?"

"Geez, snippy much?" I commented.

"Sorry," Liza sighed. "I'm a bit on edge. I have my weekly call with my sister in about an hour and it's not my favorite pastime, especially since she keeps asking me about what you and I are always talking about."

"What do you tell her?"

"Not the truth, obviously. But I don't believe she has ever bought for one second what I've told her in its place." Liza groaned. "Are all sisters this obnoxious and persistent, or do you think it's just her?"

"I couldn't say; I only have brothers," I replied. "But even so, I think the great Lena Lenore is in a category of irritating all her own. I'd offer to bug her with a few prank calls in the middle of the night in retaliation if I didn't think she'd turn me into a duck for it."

"That, and I doubt you'd be able to reach her," Liza said. "She probably blocked you from calling her the moment she learned you had a Mark Two."

The news didn't offend or surprise me. Blocking a caller seemed like a good way to avoid talking to someone you were at odds with. I wished I had a similarly simple way to avoid SJ. I flicked my eyes to her empty desk. Our estrangement was getting old.

I tore my eyes away from my book and lifted my head to the sound of laughter.

The door to our suite opened. SJ was with Jade and Lili. They were all carrying books; they must've come from the library. With midterms next week, we'd all been cramming.

The moment they saw me sitting on my bed, the giggling stopped. Jade and Lili shot me a disapproving look, which I met with a confident glare and an eyebrow raise, as if challenging them to say something.

"I shall see you both tomorrow," SJ told her new friends.

They wished her goodnight and left. SJ shut the door behind them. I resumed studying and didn't say a word. My attention went back to the copy of *Le Morte d'Arthur*, which I'd been reading as a double-dipping homework assignment. I was not a fan of the book, but it provided me with the research I needed for my Damsels in Distress term paper and a diorama I was building for Fairytale History class.

SJ started to shiver—the wind coming in from our balcony was particularly strong tonight. She went to retrieve a robe from the closet. When she returned, she spoke.

"You were not at dinner."

I glanced up from *Le Morte d'Arthur*. I was surprised she noticed or cared. Aside from our ugly conversation last night, being in the room with SJ lately was like having a snowman for a roommate. It was bearable when Blue was around as SJ might engage in some small talk to emulate normalcy, but Blue was still in the library studying with friends from her Homemade Explosives class, so I didn't know what had compelled SJ to start a conversation with me, especially after yesterday's fight.

"I was training," I replied.

"With Liza or in the practice fields?" SJ asked.

"Does it matter?" I said as I tossed the text aside in favor of some less morbid reading.

The next two books on my nightstand included the textbook for my Princess First Aid class (the complement to the Animal First Aid course I'd taken last semester) and a copy of *Peter Pan*. I'd already mastered most of the techniques in the former—from setting a broken ankle to performing CPR—so I picked up *Peter Pan*. We had a test on pirate ship structural design the following week. Studying boat parts was by no means a thrilling way to spend a Friday night, but it sure beat having to interact with SJ. I flipped the book open to a diagram of masts and rigging.

Out of the corner of my eye I saw SJ wander about the room,

fidgeting. I could sense the anger and frustration in her body language. At the same time, her conflicted expression indicated that she didn't quite know what to do now that I'd ceased to engage.

While one eye remained on my book, I watched her out of the other with curiosity. If I had to fathom a guess, I think she felt bad, or even a tad guilty. Had my comments last night about acting like an enemy gotten to her? Or was that too much to hope for?

Blue came bursting through the door.

"Guess what! I know how to build a bomb out of six different kinds of flowers!" she announced triumphantly as she kicked the door shut behind her.

I smiled—pretending the feud between me and SJ did not exist. "Congratulations," I said. "You'll have to teach me some time. The most interesting thing I learned this week was how to make homemade facial masks from produce found in the orchard."

Blue punched the air with enthusiasm. "Excellent. Then we'll have clear skin when we eventually blow up Nadia's castle in Alderon."

SJ and I both looked at Blue, taken aback by the citation of our mortal enemy's name in such casual context.

"Sorry," Blue said, sensing she'd overstepped. "Just a joke."

"A poor one," SJ huffed. "That humor is not appropriate when we are swiftly approaching our designated departure date for pursuing Paige Tomkins."

The mere mention of Paige's name distracted me from my feelings about SJ. We'd been progressing steadily in our Wonderlands mapmaking. We had just over a month left before the deadline we'd given ourselves was reached. Soon enough it would be spring break and we would take what we had and set off on our much-anticipated quest to find the missing Fairy Godmother.

It was weird, and I felt slightly guilty if not foolish. I'd gotten so caught up in the tensions and goals related to my school world lately that the greater storyline of my life had not been at the forefront. In a matter of weeks, schoolwork, TA sessions, and even Twenty-Three Skidd wouldn't matter. We would be off to face larger-than-life threats in worlds far beyond this place.

"Maybe we should touch base with the boys after the game on Sunday to see how they're coming along with their maps," Blue suggested.

"Good idea," I replied.

Blue smiled at me widely. "I seriously cannot wait. Our very first match is going to be legendary." She was almost squealing with excitement—very un-Blue behavior, but I knew how she felt. Not even SJ's cold expression, which rivaled the chilly gusts outside, could bring me down in that regard.

"Me too," I said.

SJ didn't comment and strode across the room to tightly latch the balcony doors. She was getting really good at shutting things out.

In my dream, I walked across the white, endless void. I felt calm at first, like when I'd wandered into the snowy forest outside of Lady Agnue's before the magic hunters attacked. Then faces began appearing. They flickered around me like the large holographic images of the projection orbs at Twenty-Three Skidd matches.

Each face lasted for only a few seconds before dissipating back into the void. Some were familiar—Lenore, Madame Alexanders, my brother Alex. But there were other faces that I didn't recognize. A girl in her early twenties with brown hair and eyes, a thin face, and strong features. A woman with long black hair and flawless skin that would've given SJ a run for her money. A middle-aged man with blond hair, glinting blue eyes, and regal eyebrows arched with wisdom and sadness.

Something in the distance started to come into focus—a patch of dark green. No sooner had I spotted it, did it zoom toward me.

I found myself immersed in the deep throat of a forest cloaked in nighttime. After a minute, I began to hear shouting. I forged deeper into the forest and saw a group of young children fighting fully grown adults. A congregation of colorful fairies zipped about shooting magic dust and helping the kids. There were dozens of people in the chaos, but one face captured my attention—Mauvrey's.

She darted through the trees. I chased after her, but everything around me was starting to blur. A strange purple smog bled into the edges of my dreamscape. It rapidly blanketed the dream and made it hard to see and breathe.

Mauvrey's blonde locks were fading from view. The sounds of fighting grew fainter. The purple smoke became thicker.

My dream changed. It shifted through images of an enormous cornfield, a plate of nachos, and pumpkins coated in green, glowing energy. Each flash was swiftly swallowed by the purple smoke.

With an abrupt flash I stood in the void again, but this time in my physical form. The white emptiness had been almost totally enveloped by smoke. I buckled to my hands and knees as the strange pollution seeped into my lungs. My eyes started to close as my body felt heavier. Just when I thought I could not resist it any longer, my hands began to glow, followed by my arms, followed by my everything else.

I stood up and my entire body shined powerfully—golden energy radiating from me like a comet. I let the magic inside of me build and build until the power could no longer be contained. With one large pulse, I blasted the magic outward—blasting the smoke away with it.

Everything went black instantly.

I began to hear voices muttering. Reality. I could feel it. I was no longer dreaming.

"What was that glow?"

"I don't know, her magic acting up I guess."

"We'd better hurry and get her out of here before one of the guards find us. That flash was big. Someone could've seen it from across the grounds."

"Through here. We'll cut through the barn and stables. The lights are already on in there, so if it happens again, at least it'll be concealed."

I tried to open my eyes. The lids felt like steel curtains. When

I managed to get them at a half squint, I saw arms, wooden floors, and shoes.

*Where am I?*

The smell of hay permeated my nose. A heavy pressure on my stomach made it hard to breathe. My eyes opened completely and I discovered that the arms I'd been seeing were my own, dangling below me. My veins had traces of purple in them, but the hue was being chased away by the golden glow of my magic.

All of a sudden it felt like someone injected me with a shot of adrenaline. My senses snapped back, and I fully comprehended what was happening and where I was. I had been tossed over someone's shoulder and was being carried through the barn in the practice fields!

I lifted my head and saw three faces looking back at me. I instantly recognized them as magic hunters. Including Parker.

"She's awake!"

*Crud.*

I hammered my fist into the spine of the man carrying me. He dropped me to the floor and I landed with a thud on one of the sparring mats. There was no time to process. With the speed of a wild dog, I rolled to my side, jumped up, and ran.

"Get her!" Parker shouted.

I bolted through the barn's labyrinthine hay walls in my attempt to outrun the hunters. It was not easy. The hazy state I'd been in a moment ago seemed to be attempting a comeback. Adrenaline and fear had chased it away partially, but grogginess was encroaching on my normal speed and sharp focus. My vision kept going in and out—one second it was clear, the next it was foggy, stained purple, and shifting like a kaleidoscope.

My strength was faltering too. My steps were uneven and unsteady, causing me to stumble. An arrow suddenly flew by my face and hit one of the larger gas lanterns illuminating the barn. The barn and stables had many smaller lanterns, but a few core fixtures were massive and fat like pregnant cattle, their flames tall as grandfather clocks. The lantern crashed to the floor behind me, its bountiful fire catching onto the hay around it instantly and viciously.

I ran faster and skidded into the corridors of the stable. The wind banged the open windows back and forth in rhythm with my erratic canter. A second arrow sailed overhead and caused another lantern to drop and release its flames. The third and fourth arrows burrowed into stable walls.

The fire was spreading. I could smell the burning hay and wood. My bare feet pounded against the hard floor. My heart throbbed against my weakened chest. I turned a corner, but not fast enough.

The fifth arrow fired and it did not miss its mark. It pierced my shoulder and the pain and momentum of the impact brought me down. I fell to my side. Through my purple-clotted vision, the shadows of four hunters were cast over me.

"Hold her down," Parker ordered.

As I got to my knees, two hunters rushed in. They pinned my hands behind my back then slammed me to the ground face first, twisting my shoulder in the process. I cried out from the sting of my arrow wound, but I doubted anyone outside of our confrontation could hear me. The school was too far away. Two hunters crouched beside me and one dropped his knee into my back for good measure so I'd stay down.

I tried to channel my magic, but I had neither the state of mind nor the power. Whatever the hunters had dosed me with was clouding the control I had over my abilities as well as diminishing my strength and filling my head with fog.

"I don't know how you managed to overcome the Poppy Potion we hit you and your friends with," Parker sneered as he approached. "But I hope you've enjoyed your last few minutes of consciousness."

Parker drew a dagger from his side. He was five feet from me. My face half-smushed against the floor, I glared up at him with malice. His form was darkened from the shadows and his back illuminated by the fire, which had all but consumed the corridor we'd come from.

I hadn't felt true fear in a long time. I'd arguably never felt it to this degree. No weapon, no friends, head too foggy to channel magic let alone think properly. Even if the haziness hadn't been an issue I was so scared I probably would've been frozen still.

The heat of the flames was getting uncomfortable; orange hues streaked every surface I could see. The smell of burning hay and wood was nauseating. Parker and the hunters seemed to pay no mind to the encroaching flames. Their focus was solely on me.

Panic rose in my chest and helplessness weighed me down like shackles. I tried to channel myself—the girl who always had a plan, who could always escape—but she wasn't there. She was suffocating under the influence of the Poppy Potion and stifling fear.

"I'm going to enjoy this," Parker said as he eyed me.

My heart stopped. Then I heard a voice.

"Funny, I was thinking the same thing!"

A bucket suddenly flew through the air and crashed into Parker's head—knocking him to the ground. A couple more buckets and a brick came hurling immediately after and impacted the skulls of my other captors. I felt the pressure of the hunter's knee leave my back. He and the rest had been knocked away, if only for a second.

I closed my eyes for a moment and channeled everything inside of me. This was my only chance. The clarity had come when I needed to wake up and free myself from the hunter carrying me. I needed to will the same adrenaline boost once again.

*Focus*, I urged myself, burying my feelings of panic beneath a wave of aggression. *Please focus*.

I felt a sensation going up my arms. I hastily got to my hands and knees and saw my gold glow pulsing through my veins—chasing away the last of the purple hue. In tune with it, my vision cleared and my strength returned. No time for fear, just action. My body was forcing its way into fight mode.

With at least two-thirds of my faculties returned, I gritted my teeth and ripped out the arrow lodged in my shoulder. With a twist, I stabbed the closest hunter in the arm with it. I tried to get to my feet, but the second hunter who'd been holding me seized my ankle and pulled me down. I rolled to my side, prepared to defend myself, but he was curtly kicked in the head by a massive boot. Looking up, I couldn't have been more relieved to see the owner of that boot. Girtha.

She kicked the diaphragm of the downed hunter before punching him in the face. He lay motionless on the floor. The other two hunters came at her and she tackled them both to the ground.

I got up to help her, but Parker leapt in my path. He raised his dagger and I blocked his strike, forcing him away with a powerful kick. He came at me again. I ducked as he swung. He tossed the dagger into his other hand. When I jumped to evade his blade, his right fist hammered into my shoulder wound.

I slammed against the stable wall, pain radiating from where Parker had made contact. He lunged at me. I staggered to the side, shaking my head to clear the fuzziness of pain. At his next lunge, I wrapped my arm around his to keep him from stabbing me. He twisted my arm, grabbed my hair, and pulled my head back—exposing my throat. His arm was still entangled with mine, but his dagger was so close to my face that my breath fogged up the blade.

We struggled, just like we had in my vision. I wished I had my wand, but I'd left it on my nightstand in my room before going to sleep. I mentally smacked myself.

*Note to self: Always attach wand to sleeping clothes.*

Panic pulsed through me anew. The encroaching fire swirled around us and my temporary clarity wavered. The smoke I was choking on made matters worse, but I refused to be crippled by fear again. Like a burst of instinct, Girtha's advice from earlier in the semester came rushing back to me.

*Don't think. Use his advantage against him.*

My eyes darted to Parker, then his blade.

*Let's see how he likes it.*

I turned my head and bit into Parker's dagger-wielding forearm. When my teeth pierced his skin, he shouted and pulled away, giving me the opportunity and momentum to stab him in the side with his own blade.

I released a back-fist against Parker's face, followed by a left hook, a hammer strike, and an angry kick that sent him tumbling to the floor.

"Crisa!" Girtha was at my side, having defeated the other three hunters. "We have to get out of here! This whole place is burning down!"

I nodded, still too shocked to speak, and followed her through the burning building. Debris fell as the barn burned. I ignored all of it, just as I ignored the burning in my shoulder from the arrow wound and the stinging in my chest from the Poppy Potion. My vision was starting to blotch purple again, but I willed past it. Apparently, I could only hold the Poppy's power at bay for so long.

By the time Girtha and I bolted out of the stables, the fire had spread to the practice fields. With the help of the powerful winds sweeping over the campus, the trees, grass, and obstacle courses had become caught in the mess of flames.

Before the two of us could decide what to do, the school's alarms began to ring. We usually only heard them during our yearly emergency drills. The sound filled me with relief.

School guards came racing down the campus—some with hoses, some with bullhorns, others driving a Fire Department Carriage equipped with tankards of water, a ladder, and a surprisingly alert Dalmatian with a crystal collar.

They immediately started to contain the inferno. I glanced back toward the stables as I heard panicked whinnies.

*Oh no! The horses!*

Without thinking, I dashed back toward the flaming building. "Crisa!" Girtha called after me. "Don't!"

I didn't stop. I thrust open the doors to the stable and bolted inside. The three dozen horses were frantic as the flames coursed through their dwelling. I fought through smoke and fire, along with my own returning haziness, to reach and unlock the latches to their stalls.

The scene was a blur and I couldn't tell if that was more from the smoke inhalation or the Poppy Potion seizing my insides. It was like one of my choppier dreams—everything came in short, sharp flashes. The horses were bucking and whinnying. I could see the whites in their eyes. Burning beams fell from the ceiling. My vision tunneled and then widened like a broken strobe light. Somehow my hands worked on their own and the next thing I knew I was unlatching the final stall. The last mare cantered toward the exit in the wake of all the others I'd set free. I went stumbling out after it—gasping and choking. The roof of the stable came crashing down immediately behind me.

I tumbled onto the dirt and grass. When I lifted my head, I saw the pure devastation around me—flames, school guards desperately trying to combat the fires from spreading to the forest, panicked students and staff members flooding onto the lawn.

Ash had begun to fall like malevolent snow. Squinting through the night, I realized that the smoke from the vast fires was accumulating overhead—the In and Out Spell was keeping it from escaping. The magic of the spell must have thought it was some kind of detrimental weather and was not letting it pass through—like a reverse of when storms tried to penetrate from the outside. As a result, the magical dome that was intended to protect us was creating a quick-filling carbon monoxide prison.

I pulled myself together enough to reach for my pants pocket. *Yes!*

Prior to falling asleep, I'd been talking with Liza and had stashed my Mark Two in my pocket. I flipped it open.

"Lena Lenore!" I shouted desperately to the thing. The compact buzzed for a moment as it tried to call the Godmother Supreme, but soon a message flashed that read, "*Caller Blocked.*"

"Are you kidding me?" I groaned in frustration. "Ugh, fine. *Liza* Lenore!"

The compact buzzed again as wind slapped my face and ash rained down on my bare arms and sweatpants. Many of my assembled classmates in the distance were starting to cough from exposure to the fumes.

*Come on, come on!*

Liza's face suddenly appeared in the tiny looking glass. "Hello?" she yawned.

"Liza! Call your sister!" I shouted.

"Crisa!" My mentor's eyebrows shot up. "What's wrong?"

"The practice fields are on fire and the smoke is choking us to death. The Godmothers need to lower the In and Out Spell." I coughed violently as smoke rasped against my lungs. "You were right; Lenore blocked my compact. You have to call her and tell her to drop the spell before everyone at Lady Agnue's suffocates!"

"I will! Hold on, Crisa!" Liza hung up to call her sister.

The practice fields, my most treasured space at Lady Agnue's, were in ruin. I watched the place I loved most in the world burn. The searing pain from my injuries and the building smoke were nothing compared to the guilt of knowing that this disaster was my fault.

Thankfully, a moment later our school's enchanted force field flashed indigo and silver and pink and purple, and then lowered into the ground. Smoke rushed into the sky. I saw Lenore and a number of other Godmothers flying overhead. They'd brought the spell down. Together the seven of them cast another kind of spell right after it descended, which caused rain clouds to rush in and pour over the entire area, extinguishing the flames.

People across the grounds cheered as they got soaked; others clapped with relief and hugged. We were saved. Before long, all the fires were drowned out and the chaos was put to an end.

As the last of the rain came down and the adrenaline left me completely, I inevitably sank back to the earth. The mud against my skin was cold and wet. My breath was shallow and sharp. As leftover Poppy Potion toxins continued to course through my body and the injuries I'd sustained throbbed harder, I closed my eyes and wished that this had all just been another nightmare.

# CHAPTER 16

## Choice & Consequence

y dreams had never been more indiscernible. Every neuron in my mind must've been churning, for the only vision I could recall once I woke up was of a pair of feminine hands wringing out a glistening sponge in a river. A purple energy oozed out of the sponge. The energy condensed slightly and then went with the current. My subconscious found enough clarity, and widened enough to reveal that the water actually belonged to the narrow river in the mountains I'd envisioned before, which led up to the large stone filled with purple and green lights.

The purple energy flowed downstream and when it reached the pool around the rock, the mystical stone glowed bright purple too. I think it was absorbing the energy. This thought hung in my head as I drifted back to the world of the awake.

According to the infirmary clock it was late afternoon. My injured shoulder was bandaged, and it hurt terribly. I sat up slowly. When I saw the people lying in the cots beside me, I leapt from my bed with the speed of a jackrabbit. SJ and Blue were both asleep. It didn't look like normal sleep, though. Their breathing was too thin, their bodies too still, and their arm veins too sickeningly violet.

As I rushed to their bedsides, the doors of the infirmary creaked open.

"Crisanta, thank goodness you are awake!" Madame Alexanders gushed.

Like a cross between a worried parent and a curious scientist, she put her hand to my forehead to check for a fever, then to my neck to take its pulse. Finally, she took my good arm into her hands and studied it.

I pulled away. "Professor, what happened to Blue and SJ?"

"The same thing that happened to you, my dear," my professor admitted, shaking her head. "When those magic hunters broke into the school, they released a very potent Poppy Potion in your bedroom to keep you and your friends unconscious so that you wouldn't fight back."

Madame Alexanders removed a sealed plastic bag from the pocket of her lab coat. Inside the bag, beneath the "Hazardous Waste" label, were shreds of red flower petals that, even now, still emanated a light fog.

"The school's guards and I completed a sweep of your room this morning. We found a canister that suggests the hunters deployed the potion through some kind of silent grenade device, which filled the room with the concoction. Your suite is safe now. It seems all the potion's gases seeped into your skin the moment they became airborne."

Madame Alexanders gestured to the plastic bag. "Based on these trace particles we were able to scrape up, and the tests I've run on them thus far, this was a very powerful potion with high toxicity levels that could have done some very serious harm." There was a smile on her lips as she spoke.

"You say that like it's a good a thing," I commented, surprised at her reaction.

"Well, it is," she replied. "I mean the fact that the three of you are okay despite the poisonous nature of this potion is an extremely good thing. Blue and SJ will be fine. When the staff took roll after the fire, we discovered they were missing. They were found in your room like this shortly thereafter. Had they been left there untreated, the Poppy Potion could have done permanent nerve, respiratory, or even brain damage. Since we caught it in time, I was able to whip up an antidote that will allow them to sleep off the effects. They will wake up in a few hours feeling as if they have come out of a very deep sleep. As for you . . ."

"As for me?"

"Considering the outcome if you hadn't overcome the Poppy Potion on your own, I would say that it is also a very good thing that you have been lying to me about the results of our experiments together. Wouldn't you?"

I grimaced. "How long have you known?"

"Just since this morning when I was treating you and your friends," Madame Alexanders replied. "I thought I'd need to give you the same antidote as them, but discovered that you had none of the same symptoms. When the guards told me that they found you by the stables and your friend Girtha explained to me and Lady Agnue what happened, I figured it out. A potion of this magnitude should have knocked you out as surely as it did Blue and SJ. Based on the work we've been doing together, there was no outlier to suggest otherwise. Which leads me to believe that you have not always been truthful with your results. Am I right?"

"Sort of," I replied begrudgingly. "I mean, it wasn't *all* a lie. Some of the potions really did affect me, but others didn't. I know I should've told you, but I felt weird admitting it."

"Crisanta, different potions affect different people in different ways; that is nothing to feel weird about."

"But it wasn't just the potions," I said slowly.

I took a breath before letting the truth pour out of me.

"Honestly, I don't think it was the potions we were making that I was immune to at all; it was the Poppies themselves. A few weeks ago, I accidentally touched one and nothing happened. I held one of those stupid flowers in my hand for a solid minute and was basically fine. *That* is what I was hesitant to admit. I didn't want to call more attention to the matter, or to me. People around here already treat me differently. I didn't want to add more fuel to the fire." I met my professor's eyes. "Are you mad?"

"Yes and no," she said. "I am angry that you lied to me, and that you have skewed our experiments' findings over the last few weeks. However—whatever the reason you are immune to Poppies is—I am glad it is so. Otherwise . . ." My professor swallowed hard and put her hand on my shoulder affectionately. "Well, let's just be thankful that we don't have to discuss the otherwise."

I nodded and went back to stand between Blue and SJ's beds. I studied my friends with concern.

"Really, Crisanta. They will be all right," my professor assured me. "And you will be too. I've given the nurses a special antidote to apply to your shoulder that will heal you good as new over the next few days while you stay in the infirmary."

"Thanks," I replied, "but I'll take it to go. I've spent more than enough of my days in this place."

"I'm sorry, my dear, but that was not a request. Those are the headmistress's orders. She says you are to stay here for at least the next three days."

"I thought you said I was fine. If that's true, why do I have to stay?"

"For one, bed rest. You were dosed with some pretty powerful toxins and took a shot in the shoulder, Crisanta. You have been through a trauma."

*That's putting it mildly.*

"Maybe so," I said. "But I'm fine now. I don't need to be isolated in here."

"Perhaps not. Nevertheless, this is not only for your benefit. It is also so that Lady Agnue can try and diffuse the situation outside these walls."

"I don't understand."

"Crisanta, *magic hunters* broke into the school. While the rest of the students and staff do not know the specifics that Girtha shared with me and the headmistress, they are aware that it had something to do with you."

"How much do they know?" I asked.

"Nothing for certain," Madame Alexanders replied. "They can only guess at wild theories. So for now, your secret is safe. Despite that, I think you can appreciate why Lady Agnue and I believe it is for the best that you keep your distance from your classmates for a few days until this simmers down. We wouldn't want to call any more unwanted attention to your situation by, as you say, 'adding more fuel to the fire'."

I rubbed my arm anxiously. "I guess so. But I don't know how much of a difference three days will make. The other girls aren't stupid. They're bound to put two and two together with or without our confirmation. Magic hunters hunt magic. If they were hunting me, then it's kind of obvious that I have—"

The infirmary door creaked open again. Madame Lisbon stuck her head into the room. She gave me a slight nod, then looked at Madame Alexanders.

"Patricia, Cornwallace would like to see you in her office."

"I'll be there in a minute," Madame Alexanders replied.

She turned back to me briefly. "Don't worry, my dear, we shall figure something out. In the meantime, stay here where you are safe. There are guards at the door. The other students have been asked not to bother you."

"Um, thanks," I said. I dropped my gaze to the floor, but Madame Alexanders lifted my chin up with the ridge of her hand.

"Take heart, Crisanta," she said. "While things may look bleak, if the events of last night proved anything, it is that you are not so easily defeated."

With that, my professor departed the room with Madame Lisbon—leaving me alone to worry over my friends. Their faces were as pale as the infirmary's linen. As I watched the Poppy's purple glow pulsate steadily in the veins of their arms, guilt rose in my throat, forcing me to turn away.

The door opened once more. Much to my surprise, Jason and Daniel entered. Before I could open my mouth, they dashed over to where I stood. Jason threw his arms around me. I stifled the pain in my shoulder and felt heartened by his embrace.

"Lady Agnue told us what happened!" he said. He drew back quickly and rushed over to Blue and SJ, concern weighing down his expression. "Are they okay?"

"Yeah," I responded. "They will be. The effects are supposed to wear off in a few hours."

"And what about you?" Daniel asked.

"What about me?"

"Oh, you know, how's studying for midterms going?" Daniel rolled his eyes. "What do you think, Knight? I mean, are *you* okay?"

"I'm fine," I said as I nodded toward the bandaged wound on

my shoulder. "A little worse for wear, but I'll get over it. Madame Alexanders hooked me up with some quick-healing potion that'll have me back to fighting shape in no time."

"Good," he said steadily.

A moment passed.

"But besides the shot," he continued, "are you actually okay? We talked to Girtha. She said you were almost taken, that those hunters almost—"

"Daniel," I said, cutting him off. "Remember that line we discussed?"

I didn't care what kind of trauma had just happened. Daniel couldn't talk to me like this, as if he was genuinely worried about my feelings. He was the one that set boundaries and pushed me away. I wasn't going to pretend like he didn't. Not even for a second.

Jason looked up suddenly. "What are you guys talking about?"

"Nothing," I replied, glancing at Daniel. "In fact, it's nothing that matters at all. Isn't that what we agreed on, Daniel?"

"Yeah," Daniel responded, shooting me a glare. "That's what we said, all right."

The infirmary door screeched for a fourth time. One of the school's nurses came in and almost blew a gasket.

"What are you doing out of bed?" she cried. "Young lady, if you want to get better you need rest. As for you two heroes, I understand that the headmistress has given you permission to be on the grounds while the In and Out Spell is lowered, but visiting hours are over for the day. You don't have to go back to Lord Channing's, but you do have to get the heck out of here."

Jason looked pained as he left. Daniel appeared slightly angry. I was simply relieved. There were bound to be a lot of unpleasant, awkward conversations regarding this incident over the next few days and I was in no hurry to get started. Maybe Madame Alexanders and this bossy nurse were right. Maybe I did need rest.

I spent the remainder of the day anxiously waiting for SJ and Blue to wake up.

The nurses had closed all the windows. When I attempted to open one, I instantly understood why they had been shut. The air outside smelled of smoke and burnt wood, making me cough and feel sick from the memory of the destruction of my most beloved part of campus.

By the time SJ and Blue woke up, I still hadn't found the words to express how sorry I was for having put them in harm's way. All I could do was hug them both fiercely, even SJ. The fighting between us and the hurt she'd inspired didn't change the fact that I loved her. She was one of my best friends and she'd almost died. I couldn't feel any anger toward her today. I was only relieved she was alive.

When they were clearheaded enough, I went straight into recap mode. I explained what happened—how the magic hunters drugged us, how Girtha saved me, how my immunity to Poppies allowed me to overcome the potion's effects, and how the practice fields had burned down in the process.

"Crisa, you could have been killed," SJ said.

"It's hardly the first time," I sighed in response, feeling a sense of déjà vu.

"It is the first time that anyone has gotten past the In and Out Spell around the grounds," SJ replied. "Excluding us, of course. Does anyone even know how the hunters gained access?"

"So far, no," I said. "But I think they may have gotten in before last night."

"Why do you say that?"

"Earlier in the week a shipment of Poppies went missing from the school storage," I explained. "Madame Alexanders told me yesterday afternoon. She goes down there on Mondays, Wednesdays, and Fridays before our sessions. Since the hunters used a Poppy Potion to knock us out, I think it stands to reason that they broke in at some point between Wednesday and Friday and have been biding their time waiting for the right moment."

"It's a good thing you're immune then," Blue commented.

"To the flowers, not the potions mixed with them," I corrected.

"It's like I was telling Madame Alexanders; some of the brews she and I made did affect me, just in different ways than the other students. While the Poppy itself might not affect my system, depending on what it's combined with, a potion could still drop me. That's why the hunters were able to get me as far as the practice fields before I woke up. The stuff they brewed the flower with was strong enough to knock me out, but not strong enough to *keep* me out."

"That was lucky, Crisa," SJ said. "You do realize how close you came to—"

"I do." A shiver went up my spine, setting me on edge. "And I'd rather not relive it."

"I never thought I'd say this," Blue said then, "but thank goodness for Big Girtha."

"It's just Girtha," I said. "And yeah; you're absolutely right. I feel like I owe her my life. But for starters, I *know* I owe her a thank you."

Even as I slept I could feel my body tossing and turning from the angst my nightmares wrought.

Again I was plagued by visions of fire and crumbling buildings. Given my most recent trauma, these images were incredibly unpleasant to endure.

I was sprinting through a structure with long columns and glass raining down. Roof and wall gave way to the flames of explosions. Before I knew it, I was crouching on rubble and pulling out a Midveil flag. I looked up as the column came crashing like it did before. Then I was running again. A mirror burst. Debris crunched beneath my boots. My heart beat hard. Every ounce of me wished I could understand where I was or what was happening.

I shut my eyes as I faltered. When I opened them anew, I was no longer trapped in the place of destruction. I should have been thankful. However, what I saw next was five times more terrifying. I was looking up at Mauvrey.

It felt like I was lying in something small and boxy. I couldn't move or speak. The blonde hair of the homicidal princess spilled around her face as she smiled down at me.

"Sweet dreams, Crisa," she said.

With a sarcastic blow of a kiss and a small wave, she slammed a lid overhead—sealing me in confined darkness.

I woke with a start, grateful as my eyes took in the infirmary.

Arian's and Nadia's faces filled me with hatred and dread whenever they crept into my dreamscape. But my loathing of Mauvrey was far more visceral. Having known her my whole life, her betrayal and subsequent antagonism felt so much more personal.

As I stared up at the ceiling, I registered it was a new day. I rolled onto my side and saw Daniel. He was sitting in one of the infirmary chairs reading a leather-bound book with *Peter Pan* written across the cover—an exact replica of the book currently on my nightstand.

He noticed I was awake but didn't look up. "Bad vision?" he asked as he turned another page.

"I've had worse," I replied.

I glanced around and realized the two of us were alone.

After they'd woken from the Poppy Potion last night, the nurses had asserted that SJ and Blue return to our room. As they bore no other side effects from the poisoning, there was no reason for them to stay.

Of course, my friends had immediately cited *my* still being in the infirmary as a reason to stay. But the nurses disagreed. They insisted that it'd be best if I had some space to recover and get my head right. As it stood, it seemed neither part of that plan was working out so well. Nightmares clogged my mind, my shoulder continued to sear, and the boy sitting across from me only aggravated both.

"What are you doing here?" I asked Daniel as I scooched myself up to a seated position.

"Keeping an eye on you," he responded evenly.

I rolled my eyes. "Seriously? Contrary to popular opinion, Daniel, I'm not in constant danger and do not need someone to constantly watch over me."

"That's debatable," Daniel scoffed. "But it's also irrelevant. I'm not the one to pick that bone with, Knight. Me being here wasn't exactly my idea; it was Blue's. Her take on the subject has been pretty clear. Guards posted outside or not, so long as the In and Out Spell is down while guards search the forest, we should each take turns watching you. No exceptions unless we want to see how she reacts when people cross her, which, based on the throwing knives she's always carrying, involves the direct approach. I just picked the morning shift because I know you're not a fan of getting up early so I figured if I was lucky you might be unconscious for the duration."

"How considerate," I mused.

"More like preemptive," he replied. "Given . . . everything, I thought it'd be better if we didn't hang out one-on-one more than necessary."

"Yeah." I nodded. "I suppose that'd be for the—"

"Ah, good, you are awake," Lady Agnue said as she abruptly came strolling into the infirmary. My headmistress turned to Daniel—her scary badger eyes contradicting her cordial smile. "Mr. Daniels, I would like a word with Crisanta in private. Be a dear and go familiarize yourself with the hallway, will you?"

Daniel shrugged, closed his book, and left without giving me another glance. The door shut behind him with a thump, and I felt myself instinctively sit up straighter as my headmistress stalked over to me. She reached out and handed me the crisp, white envelope she was holding.

I started to open it, but I inadvertently ripped the seal at an odd angle and the top of the envelope began to tear. I'd always had trouble opening envelopes properly. It was an embarrassing quirk I was not proud of.

"Oh for goodness' sake." Lady Agnue snatched the envelope away and opened it herself before handing it back to me. I took out the letter and read.

*Your Royal Highnesses King Jeremiah Knight and Queen Cinderella Knight,*

*This past week, an incident occurred on our campus that involved magic hunters attempting to kidnap your daughter, Crisanta Katherine Knight.*

*The kidnapping was foiled but, regrettably, Lady Agnue's School for Princesses & Other Female Protagonists is no longer able to provide adequate care for Crisanta under these circumstances.*

*Steps are being taken to improve campus security. However, until they are completed, we believe that it is in the best interest of your daughter, and the rest of the student body, to send her home.*

*She will be arriving by week's end via a secure method of transportation. Please direct any and all questions to me through my assistant, Linda Mammers. Thank you, and my condolences.*

*Sincerely Yours,*
*Lady Cornwallace Agnue*

"You've got to be joking," I said. "You can't send this!"

"I can and I have," Lady Agnue replied. "A messenger departed this morning. The letter should reach your parents by tomorrow evening. This is merely a copy for my records."

"You're expelling me! Just like that?"

"Alas, no," Lady Agnue said. "You can calm down, Miss Knight. I am not expelling you. I am simply ordering a temporary but mandatory leave of absence while this business of the threats pursuing you is sorted. What I said in that letter is true. For now, while we attempt to wrangle any hunters and make the campus safer, it is in your best interest to go home where your own castle and security can protect you properly. Furthermore, while those hunters may have been looking for you, their presence put the whole of my student body at risk. Until our security is tightened and the danger is completely eliminated, you being here *continues* to put them at risk. And I cannot allow that."

I wanted to argue but couldn't. I actually agreed with Lady Agnue—a realization that made me nauseous.

The hunters, the fire, the near asphyxiation of the entire student body—they may not have been my doing, but they were definitely my fault. So long as I had this target painted on my back, every person in proximity to me was in danger. Which meant that I had to leave.

My castle in Midveil had huge walls and a small army of King's Guard soldiers to keep me safe. But just as importantly, those resources would protect anyone I was close to from external harm as well.

"So what happens now?" I asked.

"Now you write to your parents and tell them the truth," Lady Agnue responded. "I thought I would at least give you that. Tell them what really happened and why you are coming home. I shall have your letter sent so that it reaches them just after mine does. This way, they shall be fully informed and can understand that your return is not so much a punishment as it is a preventative measure. On another note . . ." Lady Agnue sighed. "You should know that I informed the student body about your magic."

My eyes nearly bugged out of my head. Lady Agnue raised her hand to silence me before the questions burst out. "Before you say anything, I did not share any information that was included in our initial deal of silence—the Author, the antagonists, the ambassadors' influence on protagonist selection. However, because magic hunters broke into the school, I recognized there would be no way to lie our way out of this. I decided it would be simpler to address the issue head on so none of the security, staff, or students will question why I sent you home. They can accept what happened at face value."

Past the initial shock, I genuinely didn't know how I felt about everyone being aware of my magic. I wasn't upset about it, but I hadn't been prepared either. Everything was going to be different now. Magic was rare and special. The only non-antagonists who typically possessed it were Fairy Godmothers.

The other students already treated me like I was an admirable outlier; I could only imagine how they would react to this. A princess with magical powers . . . If SJ was annoyed about people giving me extra attention before, she was in for an unpleasant escalation of the problem.

"How did they take it?" I asked.

"I did not exactly hold office hours to discuss feelings on the matter, Crisanta, but the general consensus is that the students are amazed and curious. I did not tell them your specific power, but I assume you will do that at some point. It is all everyone is talking about. It seems the mystique your classmates have been regarding you with has reached a new level."

*Yup. SJ is going to love that.*

"This is another reason why I have forbidden anyone you do not approve of from visiting you here in the infirmary," Lady Agnue added. "If I had not, this room would emulate a rave right now."

My headmistress rolled her eyes like she found the whole thing ridiculous and then turned to leave. "I will have Ms. Mammers come for your letter later today. Rest well, Miss Knight."

"Lady Agnue . . ." I said.

"Yes?"

"How long until I can come back?"

Lady Agnue thought for a moment before responding. "Two months," she finally said.

"Two months! You really think it'll take that much time to catch a few magic hunters?"

"Not exactly," my headmistress replied. "Two months because that is when the next Vicennalia Aurora is scheduled to strike."

"The Vicen-what?"

"The Vicennalia Aurora," she repeated. "It is an event that sweeps the land every twenty-five years. I realize you were not born yet when the last one occurred—why, I was just a girl myself. But as it approaches, I am sure you will become quite familiar with it. Kingdoms across the realm will be participating in the festivities."

"Great. But what does that have to do with *me*?" I asked.

"Simple," Lady Agnue said. "The main hullaballoo with the Vicennalia Aurora is that it causes a massive flux in magical energy—destabilizing all forms of enchantment and making some forms of magic weaker while others get stronger. Even if we catch the hunters from last night, on the day of the Vicennalia Aurora there is a chance that the In and Out Spell around the grounds will not be capable of keeping others out.

"Since we have no way of .elling in advance how the Aurora fluctuation will affect different magical entities, most Fairy God-mothers will be assigned to watch over the In and Out Spells surrounding Alderon and the Indexlands. That way, even if the spells' magic is destabilized, the Godmothers can compensate by using their powers to keep the force fields up. With this task being so important, the Godmothers' attention cannot be devoted to anything else during the Vicennalia Aurora, not even the In and Out Spell around our school. Ergo, if something were to go wrong on campus, we would not be able to call on them for help. Meaning—"

"Meaning unless I want to put myself and the other students in even greater harm's way, I need to be as far away from here as possible when this thing happens."

"Precisely," Lady Agnue responded. "After that you can return to school. Or not. If you decide against coming back or something unspeakable happens to you before then, I would not call it a loss."

"Thanks," I scoffed. "But ill-willed well-wishes aside, Lady Agnue, I'll be back here in two months on the dot. You can count on it."

Lady Agnue smiled like a Cheshire Cat, which made my toes tingle with unease.

Just as she was exiting the infirmary, SJ entered. She had her beige leather book bag slung over her shoulder and was carrying the same *Peter Pan* book Daniel had been reading.

"How are you feeling?" she asked.

It was a general question, but I was glad we were talking.

"Fine," I replied. "A bit claustrophobic due to all the unwanted visitors I've been getting, but fine nonetheless. What happened to Daniel? I thought it was his turn to watch me?"

"He had to go."

"And so you volunteered to take his place?"

"All the others were busy."

"Doing what?"

"Crisa. Today is Sunday," SJ said.

*Sunday? Where would Daniel, Blue, and Jason all be on a Sunday? The only thing the four us do together that SJ doesn't partake in is . . .*

*Oh, crud.*

"The Twenty-Three Skidd match!"

I reached out to throw off the cot's covers, forgetting my shoulder wound.

"Awgh," I grimaced when the pain caught up with me.

SJ came over to my bedside and stopped me from getting up. "Crisa, I am sorry but you are in no shape to participate in the match today. Even if Lady Agnue had not grounded you to the infirmary, your shoulder has yet to properly heal. If you do not rest and let the antidote do its work, you could permanently damage it."

My heart sank to a level so subterranean I felt like it would turn into a fossil before I completely dug it out again. All that hard work, all that drive, all that love for something I was genuinely good at. None of it mattered. The bright spot in my life had been blotted out.

"The match . . ." I said in a whisper.

"There will be other matches," SJ replied.

"No," I sighed. "There won't be. Not for me anyway. Lady Agnue is sending me home."

I told SJ what had transpired before her arrival. She seemed sad to hear the news, but I wasn't sure how much of her reaction was genuine.

"I cannot believe you will not be here for two months," she said.

"Yeah. Bad news for me, but good news for you," I said carefully, testing for her reaction. "Two months without me here should give you a chance to recover some of that protagonist limelight you claim I stole from you."

"Crisa, I would never wish for you to be removed from the school," SJ said defensively.

"Right." I rolled my eyes. "You just wish I had never stepped out of my place and out of your perfect princess shadow."

SJ narrowed her expression. "You see, this is why I tried so long to keep from saying anything to you all those weeks during and after winter break. I did not think you would understand."

A bit of the anger I'd been suppressing since the hunter incident came through. "Well, your intuition was spot on with that one, because I definitely don't understand."

"All right. Fine. We shall let it be then," SJ responded bluntly. "To paraphrase what you once told me, there are bigger things happening right now than you and me. We still need to find Paige Tomkins before Arian and the antagonists. We still need to decide what to do about the kingdoms' ambassadors and their manipulation of protagonist selection. And we still must figure out how to stop Nadia and keep you from getting killed or magically corrupted.

"Therefore I think it would be best if we leave this matter between us alone. For while I may not be like you, Crisa—the *mighty, magical chosen one*—or as heroic as any of our true protagonist friends, I am committed to doing everything within my power to see all three of the aforementioned missions through. And I have the good sense to know that continuing to bicker like this will only get in the way."

"So, what then?" I asked. "You want to pretend like everything's okay between us? That nothing's wrong?"

"I see no other way that does not damage our group's objectives."

"Fine. I can do that." I shrugged. "But just to be clear, your stance on everything that was said between us . . ."

"It remains the same."

SJ sat down and opened her book, effectively ending our conversation. I watched her for a moment.

I hated what she'd done to us. We'd been the closest of friends for years. We were practically like sisters. Last semester I'd damaged our friendship for a time by pushing her away. I was grateful that I had come to my senses so we could return to the way we were before. But it seemed we couldn't. I was not the only one who'd come back to school a different person. She had too. Only while my character had changed because I'd found myself along the way, hers had changed because she'd lost herself. This was not the girl I once knew.

I could pretend like everything was fine between us. I'd done it before. And SJ was right; if we wanted to go on with our plans (and not cut our friendship to further ruin) this was the best option. I just loathed that this was what we'd come to.

*Sigh. Let the feigned friendliness begin, I guess.*

"Did you borrow that book from Daniel?" I asked, trying my best to extend the fake olive branch and show her that I accepted her terms.

SJ glanced up. "No. This is my copy. Poppy poisoning, massive fire damage, and near kidnapping or not, we still have our midterm on pirate ship structural design coming up. In fact . . ." She reached into her book bag and pulled out my own copy of *Peter Pan.* "Here. I brought this so you could get some studying in while you are just lying there."

"Hey, I thought I was supposed to be recovering. And anyway, I'm leaving school. Why should I have to prepare for a test?"

"Because you are leaving at the *end* of the week and midterms begin tomorrow. What about your relationship with Lady Agnue or any of our professors would lead you to believe that they would allow you to skip midterms?"

Again, I knew she was right. I groaned in protest as she handed me the text.

"See," SJ nagged. "This is where *not* provoking all of our teachers would come in handy."

"Yeah, yeah. I got it," I huffed as I opened the book.

# CHAPTER 17

# Pre-Deportation Blues

t five o'clock Blue came to visit me fresh from the Twenty-Three Skidd match. At first she was reluctant to share any of the specifics, but on my insistence she eventually divulged how extraordinary it had been.

The Crusaders won with a final score of twenty-three to nineteen. As first alternate, Daniel had taken my place on the Seven Suns. Jason and Blue had apparently been absolutely dynamic, and with her assist he'd scored the winning goal. A horde of my classmates, I was told, carried her off the field on their shoulders.

It was everyone's opinion that Lady Agnue and Lord Channing had made the right decision in not canceling the game. After the attack and the fire, the student bodies needed a morale boost and something to distract them from scarier prospects. I only wished I'd had that kind of distraction.

I ached with sadness as Blue spoke. I was happy for her and supported her 100 percent. But knowing that she would get to live out this dream while I had been forced to surrender mine was not something a girl could get over in an afternoon.

I think she picked up on that. The details soon ceased and we moved on to other, less emotionally searing topics.

At six o'clock one of the nurses brought me dinner—a piece of plain grilled chicken without the skin and a side of steamed cauliflower. Madame Alexanders had advised the infirmary staff only feed me gluten-free, dairy-free, fat-free foods (i.e., cardboard) for the next few days, as it was supposed to help the antidote on my shoulder work faster.

I didn't know how much this diet was contributing to my recovery but felt certain that it wasn't worth the sacrifice. Furthermore, I was annoyed that the infirmary staff kept bringing me pots of hot tea and didn't seem to take my request for a substitute, like hot chocolate, seriously.

At seven o'clock Daniel returned and he and I quizzed each other on the masts, rigging, and architectural designs of the *Jolly Roger*, Captain Hook's infamous pirate vessel. He and Jason had a similar midterm at Lord Channing's and he was in as dire need of exam prep as I was.

I was thankful for this distraction as it provided a totally acceptable, non-awkward way for us to spend time together. Staring at Hook's red-and-black boat in our textbooks was a lot more comfortable than staring at each other. The shift in our relationship had made things weird, but I could tell Daniel was also being sensitive about the Twenty-Three Skidd match today. He never brought it up, for which I was grateful.

Whenever there was a lull in conversation, I concentrated on the illustrations of the *Jolly Roger*'s enormous sails, bronze mast, and skull and crossbones flag. I still wasn't used to Daniel and I being like this—shallow friends. Keeping our conversation from wandering was the only thing I could do to control the situation. If I didn't, the anger and resentment I still felt toward him would prevent us from being productive.

Oddly, our friendship was a lot like my relationship with SJ at the moment. It was a mug that had fallen to the floor and broken its handle. It still worked and served a purpose, but you just couldn't rely on it the way you used to.

I sighed to myself. I guess I would have to get used to broken things and shallow friendships.

In retrospect, maybe it shouldn't have bothered me so much that I was being sent back to Midveil. I hadn't returned to my kingdom over winter break because I wanted to be where I felt most at home, which used to be at Lady Agnue's. As the saying went, "Home is where the heart is." But after two of the people I was closest to in the world had pushed me away, it didn't feel like my heart was here anymore. I had to go.

At eight o'clock the rest of our friends joined Daniel and me, and we touched base on our plan for finding Paige Tomkins. Now that I was leaving, Blue offered to take over my Toyland mapmaking. I felt bad about giving her extra work but I knew Blue loved fairytale history and research so much that the task was right up her alley. She promised that as soon as midterms were over, she would finish what I'd started.

The boys updated us on the progress of their Wonderland mapmaking after we gave them details about ours.

"It's been a bit slow lately," Jason said. "With midterms, library schedules have shifted. We've had to be even more careful to cover our tracks. It's annoying, but doing this the right way is essential. If we get caught, it's all over. Channing's does not show mercy to guys who mess with the rules. A kid in our Bladesmith class got caught mixing Tungsten metal into his final project last semester and got sentenced to a full year of Gryphon hunting duty off campus."

"Tungsten metal?"

"Our final projects were supposed to be made with a steel alloy mixture," Daniel explained.

"Uh-huh. Sure," I said, pretending to understand. "Anyway, I see your concern. Our library schedules have shifted slightly for midterms too, but our security measures aren't as intense as yours. We just have a couple locks, burning dust, and hungry Guardgoyles to worry about. Didn't you say your library has spike pits beneath the carpet and retractable shelves?"

"And a giant guard snake and ghost librarians," Jason replied.

"I'd love to see that someday," Blue commented, dreamy-eyed.

"Trust me, no you wouldn't."

"Back to the point," I said. "Other than the usual obstacles, it seems we're pretty much on track for our spring break deadline. We just have to keep working hard to be ready to leave on the day classes let out."

"One problem," Daniel pointed out. "*You're* not going to be here. So by *we*, I take it you mean *us*."

*Oh. Right.*

*Like it's not bad enough I'm being sent home like a toddler with a tummy ache. Now I have to look like a total jerk-wad leader for talking about work assignments that I'm not even going to be a part of.*

"We don't need Crisa to do this," Blue interceded on my behalf. "She was only handling one Wonderland anyway. Her being gone won't make a difference."

"I agree," said SJ. "We can do just fine without her."

I tried not to take offense to the phrasing.

"Then it's settled," Jason announced. "Crisa, don't worry. We'll finish the maps and in five weeks when spring break arrives, we'll come get you and embark on the mission. Just tell your parents we're coming for a visit."

"Right. I'll just be waiting helplessly at home," I said, a bit annoyed by my friends' readiness to go on without me. Daniel clearly sensed my frustration, but was having none of it.

"Knight, stop complaining. You're going home to your *castle*; not some prison in Alderon. It's not the end of the world. Frankly, it's probably for the best given that once you're gone we can get our work done in peace without having to worry about whether or not someone's trying to kill you."

"Great," I huffed. "So glad my expulsion could lighten your load."

"Crisa, you're being overdramatic," Blue said. "You're not being expelled. You're taking a leave of absence."

"There doesn't seem to be much difference between taking a leave of absence and being sent home in shame," I replied curtly. "But it's fine. In five weeks, the four of you can come to Midveil and 'get me.' I'll have extra place settings waiting for you at dinner. I warn you now, though, the dress code will be formal."

I insisted that my friends leave me alone for the night.

My attempt at solace lasted twelve minutes before a whoosh of red sparkles assailed the infirmary. It crashed into the outside of the window closest to my cot and, realizing it couldn't get through, started banging against it. Having an inkling about who this might be, I eased my way to the window and let her in.

The red, shimmering blur rushed inside, and I swiftly shut the window against the frigid air. Hovering in front of me, the sparkling blob expanded, thickened, and contorted until it formed the shape of a woman. Debbie materialized from the energy. She held her wand in one hand and looked a tad flustered, but she got over it when she saw my face. She zipped in for a quick hug.

"How are you feeling?" she asked. "I was so worried. The Godmother Supreme briefed us all on what happened, but she forbade any of us from coming here. She didn't want me to see you."

"Then why are you here?"

"Because *I* wanted to see you."

I couldn't help but smile a little. Then I got serious again, all business. "Does Lenore know how the magic hunters got in?"

"I'm afraid not."

"What about Tami? You said she's good with In and Out Spells. Any chance she was involved?"

Debbie shook her head. "Tami can produce and control her own miniature versions of In and Out Spells. But only the Godmothers who originally cast the spell can lower it again. And with a spell this strong, they'd almost always have to work as a team. Only a few Godmothers out there might have the power to do something that grand on their own."

I crossed my arms and huffed, frustrated and feeling a bit more vulnerable than usual.

"What is it?" Debbie asked.

"Death is getting closer," I replied plainly. "This is the first close call that's really hit home. SJ's always been stressed out about me being almost killed but I'm not sure it's really resonated until now. My story could very well end with me dying, couldn't it?"

A knock suddenly came at the door, sending Debbie into a panic.

"I can't let anyone know I was here," she whispered hurriedly.

"Go," I replied. "Thanks for coming by. And if I don't see you again for a while . . ."

Another knock at the door.

"Just a second!" I called.

Debbie patted my head affectionately, a small, sad smile on her face. "No one is going to kill you, Crisa. I may not be the Author, but I know you'll be all right."

I didn't say anything more. I just hoped her words would not fall on a universe of deaf ears. Debbie waved her wand and turned back into a red ball of energy. I opened the window to let her out, hopped back into bed, and picked up a book as a third knock came. I rolled my eyes and shouted "come in" to whoever was on the other side.

I had been so bombarded with stress today that the very sound of the infirmary doors groaning open again made me want to hurl a pillow at whoever came in. I was glad I restrained myself from doing so, for the girl who arrived was one person I actually wanted to see.

"Hey, you up?" Girtha asked as she stepped in.

"I was just studying," I said, gesturing to the pile of textbooks beside me. The lavender one I currently held in my hand was particularly heavy and came from my elective for the semester—*A Lady & Her Environment: A Creative Crafting Course*. I was glad to put it down as Girtha approached.

Girtha shifted a bit as she stood before me. "I hope you don't mind me coming by. I know you've been through a heap of trauma this weekend. Lady Agnue put my name on your approved list of visitors since I was the one who helped bring you in."

"I don't mind," I said. "But as long as you're not here to keep an eye on me too."

"Please." Girtha shrugged. She stomped over to the cot next to mine and sat down. "You're the last person that needs someone to keep an eye on them."

"The greater majority would disagree with you after what happened with the magic hunters."

"Well I think it's true *especially* because of what happened with the magic hunters," Girtha argued. "You were in a rough situation. You were outnumbered and taken by surprise. But how many people could overcome the effects of a Poppy Potion, get shot in the shoulder, and win a knife fight against a hunter twice their size while half-drugged? Everyone has bad days, Crisa. If that's what one of yours looks like, then I think it's safe to say that if it was a fair fight you would've been beyond capable of taking care of yourself."

A feeling of relief filled my body like a deep breath. "Thanks," I said. "After the day I've had you don't know how badly I needed to hear that. I owe you a massive thank you for your save though. I may be capable of taking care of myself ordinarily, but I needed help that night. And you provided it."

"Forget about it," Girtha said. "I saw you in trouble and I stepped in."

"Girtha, you put yourself in harm's way for me. Most people don't do that. *Friends* do. I was lucky you were there."

Girtha smiled. Then she smacked me in the leg playfully, the way Blue amiably punched me in the arm from time to time. The only difference was that Girtha's fist was double the size and weight of Blue's, so her smack ricocheted through my entire body.

A buzzing noise interrupted our moment of camaraderie. It was a familiar pitch and made me reach for my pocket out of instinct. Alas, my Mark Two wasn't there. Girtha pulled my magic compact mirror out of her jacket pocket and handed it to me just as it stopped buzzing.

"When they were doing inspections of the grounds after the fire, I found this by the stables near where you passed out," she explained. "I figured you must've dropped it, so I held on to it. I didn't want Lady Agnue or one of the guards to take it while you were sleeping. It doesn't exactly look like something our headmistress would approve of."

"Thanks," I said. "That was a good call. Lady Agnue is definitely not a fan of me having this. It's a Mark Two magic compact mirror for communication. They should be coming out on the market soon. I'll pick one up for you if I ever see them for sale when I'm back in Midveil."

I paused as the reminder of Midveil sunk in like a mental anchor. I still couldn't believe I was headed back there. I'd sent my letter to my family as Lady Agnue had instructed. Now I simmered in angst as I wondered what my parents would think when they read it. I wondered what my dad would think. Just imagining his reaction made my blood pressure go up.

"Yeah, I heard you were leaving school for a while," Girtha said. "Bummer. But hey, look on the bright side. At least you get to see your family, right?"

"You don't know my family," I replied. "This school may pose a lot of challenges, but my family is a whole other minefield."

"Tell me about it," Girtha said. "My dad didn't have the money to take care of three kids single-handedly when we were little. So—future protagonists or not—one summer he abandoned my siblings, Hansel and Gretel, but chose to keep me since I was a baby. After they killed that witch at the Valley of Edible Enchantments and came back rich and famous, Dad obviously welcomed my brother and sister home. Still, even after all these years there's a weird, unspoken tension between the four of us over what went down. Makes family dinners pretty awkward."

"Rough," I commented. "I guess it's a good thing the versions of *Hansel & Gretel* we're taught in school don't come with an epilogue."

Abruptly my Mark Two began buzzing again.

"It's been doing that every so often since yesterday. Whenever I open it a lady's face appears, but instantly vanishes when she sees me," Girtha said.

"Yeah, that's my . . . friend. Liza. I guess she's kind of paranoid about strangers considering that I'm one of only a few people she regularly talks to."

The compact kept buzzing.

"I hate to cut our talk short, but if she's been trying to call me since yesterday, I should probably answer this."

"No worries," Girtha replied as she moved for the door. "Rest up. And if I don't see you before you leave, good luck with the homecoming. Try not to have too much fun while you're away. I want my sparring partner to come back."

I smiled. "Fight you later."

"Fight you later," Girtha agreed with a grin.

When she shut the door, I flipped open the compact. Liza's

freaked-out face filled the looking glass. Upon seeing that it was me answering the call, she let out a huge sigh of relief.

"Crisa, thank goodness," she said. "I've been worried sick!"

"I know, sorry. I would have called sooner, but a lot has happened. I took a shot in the shoulder, got drugged with some Poppy Potion, and was almost killed by a few magic hunters. First off though, thank you for always taking my calls no matter how crazy the hour. You really saved us, Liza. If you hadn't contacted Lenore and told her to lower the In and Out Spell around the school, I don't know what would've happened."

"Crisa, that's just it though," Liza said earnestly. "I've been calling you nonstop because I failed. And since you never called me back, I didn't know what happened with you and the school."

"What do you mean you failed?"

"Lena never answered my call," Liza explained. "I tried for hours, but was never able to reach her on her Mark Two. She must not have had it with her."

"That doesn't make any sense. She and a whole team of Fairy Godmothers showed up not two minutes after I spoke to you," I protested. "How would Lenore have known to be at Lady Agnue's if no one told her what was going on?"

"I don't know," Liza responded.

The wheels turned in my head.

Why had Lenore been so close to the campus? Why had she been so ready to lower the In and Out Spell on a chance Saturday at three o'clock in the morning? And how did the magic hunters even get into the school in the first place?

There was no way to break an In and Out Spell unless you fractured the enchantment the way my friends and I had last semester, which was not something a few hunters could do on a whim. The only way to get into this school other than that was by being a Shadow Guardian or if the In and Out Spell was lowered, and the hunters clearly weren't Shadow Guardians or else they would've come after me earlier. Which meant that the spell *had* to have been lowered. But the only people who could do that were powerful Fairy Godmothers—specifically the team who'd enacted the spell in the first place.

Wait, no. That was wrong. Debbie just told me such Godmothers would *almost always* have to work as a team. But she said that a few Godmothers out there might have the power to drop the spell on their own. I didn't have a list of all such women, but I did know of one.

Realization hit me like a large rock.

"Oh, I'm gonna waste her!" I said angrily, squeezing the compact so tight it nearly cracked.

"Waste who?" Liza asked.

"Your sister," I responded. "Lenore's the one who lowered the In and Out Spell and allowed the magic hunters to sneak onto campus. She must've done it alone earlier this week when we were all asleep so they could steal the Poppies, and again the night of the attack. That's how she knew to come to the school when we were in trouble. It wasn't luck she was nearby; she was already in the area to re-lower the spell once the hunters had me and needed to escape. She probably just called those other Godmothers to her aid after the fact to make it look less suspicious."

"Crisa, I know my sister is . . . well, my sister. But do you really think she'd plot with magic hunters to try and have you killed?"

"Honestly? I do," I replied. "She can't send me to Alderon without proof of my Pure Magic. She can't flat out eliminate me herself since the restrictions of Fairy Godmother magic won't let her kill anyone. And she's knows that she can't threaten me into keeping my mouth shut forever. I'm a problem for her, a bump in her perfect little world order that she can't smooth out. She's been looking for a way to get rid of me and must've thought she finally found a creative way to do it without getting her hands dirty. Only she didn't expect the grounds to catch fire and was forced to intervene and abandon her plans."

"But would she truly stoop so low to try and keep order over the realm?" Liza asked, more sadness than doubt in her voice.

I raised my eyebrows. "I don't know. How long has she had you trapped in the Indexlands writing protagonist books? A hundred and fifty years?"

"Point taken," Liza sighed. "But what are you going to do,

Crisa? Contrary to how you're feeling, you cannot exactly 'waste' my sister."

"Yes, I got that. I just need to think."

"Well, think carefully. Whether or not Lena was responsible for this weekend's events, she has been playing her hand with you with relative subtlety. I wouldn't want you to do anything that might provoke her into changing that—into coming after you with no mercy."

"Right," I said. "Cuz no one's ever done *that* before."

CHAPTER 18

# Goodbyes

I t was my final day in the infirmary and I was itching to get out of there like my shoulder was itching to get out of its bandage.

Tomorrow I would return to my relatively normal activities and begin my farewell tour of the school—finishing my midterms, packing my stuff, and trying my best to fend off the hordes of girls who all had a thousand questions to ask me.

I hoped that with midterms this week and my classmates busy studying, I might be able to scurry in and out of the halls without being bothered as I went from test to test. But I suspected this was a hollow dream. Lately I could not get away from people.

Since I wasn't supposed to go back to regular class until tomorrow, my test on pirate ship design was being presented to me in the form of a "take home exam." One of the school's administrative assistants had delivered it to me an hour ago and was supervising my progress.

Hastily I worked through my last diagram—filling in the blanks on a visual representation of the *Jolly Roger*.

Suddenly the timer went off. I barely managed to complete the last question before the exam was yanked away and stuffed into a folder. The assistant who'd been monitoring me nodded cordially, then took her leave without another word.

As she exited, Jason came in carrying a bunch of textbooks.

"Hey!" he said as he set the books on the table across from me.

"Hey!" I responded. "What are you doing here? Don't you have class?"

"Yeah, but I'm on lunch right now. And since the school's In and Out Spell is down again as the magic hunter hunt continues, I thought I'd come visit."

Concern flashed in my eyes and I opened my mouth to speak, but Jason held up a hand. "Before you say anything, yes, I used the school's main road and entrance like Daniel and I have been doing since Saturday."

"Good." I nodded. "And thanks for coming. It's nice of you to visit. What's with all the books, though?"

"I ran into SJ on my way here and she told me to get these to you. She gave me a message as well." Jason cleared his throat and spoke in a voice six octaves higher than his own in order to imitate SJ. "She said, 'Crisa, you cannot avoid studying for your Damsels in Distress midterm forever. It is tomorrow afternoon and you have a semester's worth of procrastination to overcome if you want to pass.'"

I smiled at Jason's imitation, but the thought of that much studying on a subject I actively despised and had been dodging made my stomach turn. Maybe this truce with SJ was a mistake. Us talking again meant her nagging me again, which she was as prone to doing as I was prone to ignoring.

"Too bad our mission this semester couldn't have caused us to miss midterms like it did last fall," I commented. "I think I prefer fighting monsters to studying. At least with the former you always have the option of stabbing out your frustration."

Jason glanced at the pile of books he'd brought then rubbed his arm sheepishly. "Sorry. Maybe I shouldn't have brought them?"

"No, SJ's right," I admitted begrudgingly. "I just finished a test is all, so I need a minute before I can dive back into studying."

"Pirate ship design?" he asked.

"Yeah."

"Daniel and I have our test on that tomorrow. Any tips?"

"Well, ordinarily I would say play sick, but looks like these days even a trip to the infirmary doesn't qualify as a get-out-of-jail-free card."

"Bummer, and I know a wicked way to fake Liptoid Fever too,"

Jason said, grinning. "But hey, forget midterms for a sec. I brought you a present. Thought it might cheer you up."

He pulled something out of his backpack. I leaned over to see what it was.

*Cookies!*

"I noticed what you've been eating in here and know you well enough to guess that you could really use this," he explained as he tossed me one of the two giant chocolate chip cookies he had sealed within a plastic bag.

"You have no idea!" I said as I took the treat gratefully. I bit into it and instantly felt some of my stress melt away like the chocolate chips that melted in my mouth.

"Thanks, Jason. You're my savior."

"No problem," he said.

He sat in the chair across from me and chewed on his own cookie. It'd been a while since the two of us had hung out on our own. In that peaceful lull, I regrettably remembered the thing I'd promised myself I would do the next time we were alone. I'd been putting off telling Jason about my vision of his death. Since I was leaving soon, my window for doing so was about to close. This was probably my last opportunity.

"Jason . . ." I began. "There's something I've been meaning to talk to you about. I had a vision about you a little over a month ago. I've had the same vision again a few times now and, well, I've been going back and forth about whether or not I should tell you about it."

"Is it important?" he asked.

"Yeah," I said. "But it's also pretty messed up. I'm totally willing to tell you if you want; it is your right to know. But honestly— I'm warning you—once you know, there's no going back. And I promise you that the second I finish, you'll wish there was."

"Ominous build up there, Crisa. You trying to scare me?"

"No. I'm trying to protect you. My visions always come true. You know that. They're not predictions; they're fact. And while I can't unlearn what I know about the future, I can try to keep you from going through the same thing."

Jason thought for a minute before giving me the answer I dreaded.

"I want to know," he said.

"Are you sure?"

"Yeah. I'm not afraid of the future, Crisa. I get what Liza was saying last semester about our Inherent Fates. Whatever happens in our lives is a reflection of who we are and our choices. Which means that whatever you've seen of my future is going to come to pass one way or the other as a result of me just being me. If that's the case, it'd be foolish for me to cower in fear of it. Don't you think?"

"I guess," I replied. I fidgeted for a moment, stalling. "So . . . you're absolutely sure then?"

*Please say no. Please say no. Please say no.*

"One hundred percent," he said.

Obliged to keep my word, I told him what I'd foreseen. I told him about the battle with the knights by the riverbank, about him, Blue, and SJ eventually being overpowered, and about how Blue was going to be nearly killed.

And there—in the cold, still infirmary—I finally told Jason the morbid secret I'd been preserving for so many weeks now. That the only reason Blue was fated to survive this attack was because he was going to sacrifice himself for her. She would be saved, but he would pay the price, dying by that riverbank while she lived on in his place.

When the story was done, he and I sat in silence. I wasn't sure for how long. All I knew was that it felt like time had frozen solid, or at the very least, to the density of frozen yogurt.

Jason stared out the window—lost in thought. I watched his face worriedly. Part of me wished I had kept my mouth shut. Part of me felt relieved to have finally told him. The majority of me just felt guilt seeping even deeper into my skin.

Like it wasn't bad enough that my conscious activities kept putting the people I cared about in danger. My unconscious ones were wreaking just as much havoc. I was like a plague. Everything and everyone I came in contact with was at risk. Which meant I really did have to get out of here. Now, more than ever, I was thankful for being sent home where I could be isolated from the greater world for a while.

"You okay?" I asked after some time had passed.

Jason didn't answer. I didn't blame him. It was a stupid question given the situation, but it was the only thing I could think to say.

"Did you tell Blue about this?" he asked.

"No."

"Good," he said. "I don't want her to know."

This surprised me. "Why?" I asked.

"Because it'll hurt her. When what happens, *happens*, she's going to blame herself and I can't change that. But I *can* prevent her from feeling like there was something she could've done to prevent it."

"Jason, she knows my visions can't be altered."

"You really think that'll keep her from trying? No way. I know her, Crisa. The second you tell her she'll become obsessed with trying to stop it. And then when she can't, she won't just feel blame, she'll get consumed by it."

He paused and took a breath. "Look, if I have to die to save her," he swallowed, "I want to be sure that she'll eventually be able to forgive herself for it. Which won't be possible if she knows what's coming. I need you to promise me you're not going to say anything to her, okay?"

"All right. I won't tell her. I promise. But, Jason, don't you want to talk about the main issue here? I told you that you're going to die. You must want to—"

"No," he said. "You already have enough on your plate to worry about, Crisa. I don't want you to worry about me too. I'm fine. I'll deal with this in my own time."

I nodded, understanding in more ways than one.

Jason glanced at his watch and stood to leave. "I have to go," he said. "I've got a midterm in Cavalier Rescues at two o'clock and I need to get back to campus."

"All right," I replied. "I guess I'll see you later?"

"Yeah," he said. "See you."

He moved swiftly for the door. As he grasped the handle on his way out, I called after him. "Jason."

He stopped.

"I'm sorry."

"Don't be," he responded solemnly, but sincerely. "What's coming isn't your fault, Crisa."

He left the room and I stared at the door for a minute after he'd gone—knowing that while he may have been right, it definitely didn't feel that way.

Eight exams, three days, and fifty classmates plaguing me with questions I refused to answer later, my day of departure had finally arrived.

It was early morning. The sun hadn't risen yet; the sky and everything else was gray and crisp. SJ, Blue, and I walked across the grounds to the field by the front entrance where we were meeting Lucky, who had been appointed as my ride home.

Yesterday Lady Agnue told me that the school guards had found three of the four magic hunters who'd attacked me. They had not managed to escape the stable before it collapsed during the fire. I assumed that the only hunter who'd gotten away was Parker. As their leader, he'd proven to be smarter and a lot harder to get rid of. My gut told me he was out there somewhere, having likely fled into the forest between Lady Agnue's and Lord Channing's. Over the last few days the school guards had apprehended six other hunters hiding in the forest, but not him.

Since the search of the forest was ongoing, the In and Out Spell continued to be periodically lowered and the perimeter of the campus very thoroughly guarded, making us feel secure meeting out in the open.

I spotted the boys and Lucky. My pet dragon's silvery skin blended in with the color of morning.

"Tell me again why we had to do this so early?" Blue yawned.

"I want to get out of here before any of the other students wake up," I explained. "You don't know how many of them have asked me about my magic in the last few days. It's been exhausting; I didn't have to work this hard to outrun Arian. Plus, I want to leave before Lady Agnue can get in a last word. Today's going to be unpleasant enough without more of that dragon lady's vile echoing in my ear."

Blue looked to Lucky then back to me. "You do realize that since you're the one with the dragon, *technically* that would make *you* the—"

"Blue."

"Right, sorry. Not helping."

I huffed in amusement at my ever-candid friend and put my arm around her shoulder. "You know what? Believe it or not, you are."

"Daniel and I checked the Lord Channing's storm tracker in the school's observatory this morning, Crisa," Jason said as we convened. "The weather looks good for the day. Should be smooth sailing."

"Thanks," I said.

The two of us exchanged a hug. This was one of the last farewells I had to make. I'd already said my goodbyes to SJ and Blue in our room, as I was not one for public displays of affection or big displays of emotion. Throughout the week I'd bid my adieus to Girtha, Marie Sinclaire, Madame Alexanders, and a few other friends as well. That only left Daniel.

I was worried an exchange of goodbyes might be awkward between us, but thankfully it wasn't. It was simple and curt.

"Good luck" was all Daniel said to me as I walked past him.

"You too" was all I said in return.

The cold air washed against my cheeks and I inadvertently shivered as I went by him.

With a mini black leather backpack slung over my fully recovered shoulder, I proceeded to climb on board Lucky's neck. When he raised it up a second later, I stared down at my friends.

"See you in a month," I said.

I was about to take off when SJ suddenly spoke. "Crisa," she said. "Please be careful."

An undertone of affection seeped through her words. It warmed me and gave me hope.

I nodded and gave her a slight smile. "I will."

With that, I turned my attention back to Lucky. It was time. "All right, boy. Let's go."

Prompted by a swift kick of my heel, Lucky took off into the sky. My hands clutched onto one of the large blunt spines along the back of his neck. The wind slapped my face. I clung on tightly as I adjusted to the ascent but soon relaxed as we leveled out.

I glanced over my shoulder. Even from up here everything was still bathed in a sleepy shade of wintery gray. Everything but the practice fields, that is. They were unmistakably black and their devastation was impossible to miss.

My heart all but stopped at the sight. The aftermath of the fire was burned into the grounds like a scar. The once green fields were charred and desolate. The obstacle courses and track were melted, destroyed. The barn and stables lay in shambles. Blackened, fire-stripped trees bent over like broken spirits protruding from layers of ash.

I forced myself to look away and my gaze fell upon the main building of the school instead. My friends had been reduced to specks. The academy itself was still as a toadstool. Not a single light shone from the windows as my classmates slept on, undisturbed.

In that moment I was reminded of the last time I'd left school on a mission. It seemed like an adventure that began an eternity ago even though it had only been a few months. Everything about my current state of departure was different from what it'd been last fall.

Back then I was in the dark. I didn't know about my magic, my visions, or my fate. Now I had answers that I'd long been after, and more that I hadn't even known to ask for. Moreover, I was in possession of something vital that I didn't have the last time—a strong sense of self. This advantage alone filled me with courage, fight, and confidence.

As I looked ahead at the streaks of gold breaking through the horizon, I knew that while I was afraid of the threats out there waiting for me—antagonists, magic hunters, the future—I was not afraid to face them.

If they wanted to come after me, let them. I wasn't the same lost, confused little girl they'd encountered last semester. I'd changed. And I was ready. Which meant that I was open to their challenge. The only question in my head that remained was who would be the first taker?

# CHAPTER 19

# House of Glass

fter almost a full day of flying I was glad to see the fantastic sight of my home kingdom of Midveil in the distance.

On the outskirts, colorful villages dotted the lush green hills like specks of confetti. Conversely, Midveil's urban citadel was dazzling and modern—made of sleek silver, polished chrome, and huge panes of glass. My family's castle resided at the heart of it. Giant shards of glass jutted out decoratively, making the whole compound shine and reflect light at every angle.

The castle staff had been notified of the mode of transport I'd be arriving on, so the guards were not surprised to see a massive dragon land in the courtyard in front of the main entrance.

The guards saluted in greeting. I tightened the shoulder straps on my backpack, checked to make sure my wandpin was still tucked to my bra strap, then slid down Lucky's left wing.

I patted my trusty dragon on the nose in gratitude as the guards began to lead him through a tunnel to the back of the castle.

I made my way to the stairs at the main entrance. The walk up to the front door was arduous. Even after having made the climb several thousand times in my life, the 372 stairs still made my thighs hurt. By the time I got up to the front door, I seriously needed a glass of water.

Of course, the staircase was only partially to blame for the dryness in my throat and my pounding heart. To be honest, the idea of coming home and seeing my family (particularly my parents) always made me a bit nervous.

I loved my mom and dad, but since they only saw me during the summer and during other brief breaks since I'd started attending Lady Agnue's six years ago, I felt slightly disconnected from them.

My mom—the famous Cinderella—always tried to be there for me when she could. She was loving in that way. Whenever I was home, she spent as much time with me as possible between her queenly duties and did all that she could to be motherly in those brief, precious moments.

I was close with my two brothers too. Pietro (the eldest) was significantly older than me; he'd just turned twenty-seven. I enjoyed hanging out with him, though admittedly not as much as my other brother Alex. Pietro could be fun, but his default mode was to protect and defend. He behaved big brotherly in accordance with the more traditional sense of the role. This used to annoy me more when I was younger, but as I grew and made it *very* clear he needed to chill out, he reined in the act a little. Now we had fun, just the parent-approved kind of fun. I could tell he still wanted to protect me, however he restrained the impulse as much as possible for the sake of our relationship.

I appreciated that he tried, but I only spent time with him one-on-one every so often so as not to push my luck. I also didn't share any of my problems or more mischief-based pursuits with him. It was always in the back of my mind that he was a bit too responsible to understand, let alone let me get away with anything.

My other brother Alexander Knight was on the opposite side of the big brother spectrum. Growing up, Alex hadn't just helped me get into trouble; he'd encouraged it. And for this, I adored him more than he knew.

I was bashful as a child. I may have felt the same way then that I did now about Book's pomp and circumstance, and my traditional princess role, but in my early years I was far too timid to express any sentiments of defiance.

Alex had been the one to help me work past that. He constantly pushed me, messed with me, and smack-talked me until I learned to fight back. Through his amiable provocation, my smart mouth found a voice, my inner strength found its confidence, and my spirit came to relish the sassy rebelliousness that characterized me today.

In the past couple of years, when my attitude became a subject of conversation at our dinner table, Alex always joked that he had created a monster. However, what he didn't say was that he was proud of who I'd become. And what I didn't say in return was how much I appreciated him for helping me get there.

This was our weird, wonderful dynamic. I was always glad to see him and knew it wouldn't be hard for us to reconnect, despite the long absences. Unlike with Pietro or my mother and father, the distance between Alex and I was easily bridged because there was no pretense or sense of duty between us. There was just a big brother messing with his little sister, and a little sister never ceasing to challenge the big brother and trying to knock him down a few pegs.

Two guards opened the grand doors at the top of the stairs and I stepped inside my glass palace. Within the majestic foyer was a staircase as enormous as the one outside. This set of steps wound its way downward though, which had never made any sense to me.

*Seriously, instead of having a castle layout that had you climb up a bunch of stairs only to descend an equal number of stairs upon arrival, why not build the place on ground level? Our castle's architect must've either been an idiot or a masochist.*

As my hand eased down the silver railing, I began to feel anxious. I knew what awaited me at the end of this massive descent—the throne room. Moreover, I knew who waited for me there—my mom and dad.

Ugh. How could I even begin to describe my father?

He was the beloved king of Midveil, a realm-renowned former prince charming, and a great man on all counts. The thing about such great men, though, was that they were a bit hard to relate to. Especially when you were the rambunctious daughter of one.

When I was younger, my dad and I had gotten along really well. I think he liked me better when I was less strong-willed.

And I understood why. King or not, it was easier to get along with someone when they did exactly what you told them and never went against anything you said. But voicing the opinions of your own mind and heart when they were not in accord with that person's wishes . . . Well, it made for some tense dinner conversation to say the least.

Under the advice of my mother and brothers, I tried to hold my tongue and behave when I was home. But restraining myself that way made me feel like I was not being true to myself. I hated holding back. I hated feeling like the only way my father and I would ever have peace in our relationship was if I pretended to be meek.

My combat boots hit marble, which echoed through the high-ceilinged entryway. I stopped at the doors of the throne room, wringing the cuffs of the jacket I wore over my dress.

The doors that stood between me and my official homecoming were no less than twelve feet tall. Each door was etched with the image of a sleeping lion. Decorative silver crystals shone like stars above the lions' heads. My family's crest was imprinted directly beneath the slumbering creatures with the words *Aut viam inveniam aut faciam.*

I touched the words to give me strength, as if trying to absorb the wisdom of the phrase. The door felt cold. After a minute I found the courage to go inside. Plastering a smile on my face, I pushed the doors open.

"Guess who's back?" I called across the room.

My mom and dad—seated on their thrones and in deep conversation with their advisors—looked up.

"Crisanta," my mom said happily. She nodded to the men she'd been talking to and stood to meet me. Her long, bouncy, blonde hair was curled to perfection. The bustled fuchsia gown she wore matched the color of the stones in her crown and stud earrings.

My mother wrapped her arms around me in a tight hug. Only when she pulled away did she notice my new 'do.

"Pumpkin, what did you do to your hair?" she asked, running

her fingers through my shoulder-length cut. Then she glanced at my outfit. "And what are you wearing?"

The way she said it made me feel kind of insulted. I mean, I knew my mom was not a fan of my style. She didn't like my love of boots and made it a point to have my closet restocked with gowns and flowy day dresses whenever I returned to school. But still, I thought my outfit today was cute.

Over my black leggings I wore my favorite lace-up, black leather combat boots, which came up a few inches below the knee. My dress was a blood red, long-sleeved number with a whimsical skirt streaked with navy and black. On top of that I donned one of my favorite jackets. It was black with leather trimming on the sleeves, shoulders, and elbows.

"Sorry, Mom. I had to pick something wind resistant for flying," I said. "And my hair . . . Well, I was ready for a change."

My mom's blue eyes studied me for a moment, then she resumed hugging me.

"You look lovely, dear." She glanced back at my father who was still in serious discussion with his advisors. She lowered her tone to a whisper. "But how about we put away the leather for the duration of your stay. You know how your father feels about the way you present yourself within the castle and the kingdom."

I nodded. "I know, Mom. Fancy dresses and best behavior. I'll try my best."

My mother smiled and patted me on the head. "That is all I ask. Now go say hello to your father."

I peeked over her shoulder at my dad, who finally seemed to be wrapping up his conversation. I gulped inadvertently. "He looks busy. Maybe I'll come back later."

"Crisanta."

*Too late.*

My father rose and I approached him. His advisors bowed respectfully and moved through a curtained-off door on the left that led to my parents' royal work chambers. I stood before my father and gave a small curtsy before closing the distance between us.

"Hi, Dad."

The two of us exchanged a rigid hug before he sat back down on his throne and looked me over. It wasn't in the curious way my mom had, but in the way a bidder studied an item submitted to his auction house—appraising me, as it were. This made me feel uncomfortable, but I met his eyes confidently as he sized me up.

I looked a lot more like my father than my mother. His hair was brown, his nose was rounded and on the larger side, and he had a sharp, proud chin that contradicted the smooth, heart-shaped curve of his face. I could see myself in him and I didn't like it.

I did not want to be molded in his image. He was a good man and everything—smart, strong, resourceful, and a natural, respected leader who took charge and made tough choices when they needed to be made. Nevertheless, my father was so conventional, shrewdly unforgiving, and relentlessly stern that he made Lena Lenore seem compassionate.

Despite my aversion to following in his footsteps, I knew perfectly well that I was stubborn, proud, and headstrong, just like him. What could I say—in a lot of ways I was my father's daughter, an understanding that never ceased to irk me.

My father rubbed the knuckle of his pointer finger under his chin as he exhaled pensively. I knew the tick well. He usually did this right before passing judgment on my behavior.

I writhed in the silence.

"Your mother and I were very upset to receive that letter from your headmistress, Crisanta. Your dismissal from school is very disappointing."

"*Disappointing?*" I snapped.

My mother gently put a hand on my shoulder. I took a breath.

"Dad," I continued more evenly. "Didn't you get my follow-up letter explaining what really happened—why Lady Agnue *had* to send me home?"

"We did."

"Okay, then you know that I wasn't kicked out of school. I came home because of my magic."

I waited for some sort of reaction from him or my mother. Making the decision to tell my family about my powers had been a big deal. I knew there was no point in keeping it a secret anymore. While knowledge of my *Pure* Magic was (and needed to be) kept confidential, the word about my general magic was out. All the teachers and students at Lady Agnue's—and Lord Channing's by extension—already knew. The Fairy Godmothers were aware. The antagonists had known for months. It seemed like half the realm was already in on the secret, so there was no use in pretending around my parents. Still, I had been nervous about divulging the truth. Candidly sharing that piece of myself felt odd. Everyone else who knew about my magic had found out on their own or by accident. This was the first time I had made the call to directly tell someone. Getting no reaction at all from my mom and dad was sort of disappointing. I wasn't the type to crave attention, but I'd definitely expected some here. People didn't just have magic. Fairy Godmothers were typically the only non-villains who did. Those with Mer blood (i.e., mermaids and the few descendants of the famous Little Mermaid) tended to have a magical ability. But then, people with Mer blood weren't entirely human. I was something new. So why weren't my parents saying anything?

I studied their faces. It was hard to gauge what they were thinking. Eventually I broke the silence. "You know, I was almost killed last week because of those magic hunters Lady Agnue told you about," I said. "I was sent home because she thinks it is safer for me and the other kids if I stay here until they catch all the hunters and improve campus security."

"I am aware of that, Crisanta," my father responded at last. "But it is not as though these details about what happened can be divulged to the public. Your family and your school know about your magic, but the greater public does not. Consequently, by all appearances it *does* seem as though you were kicked out of the academy. And *that* matters."

"By *that*, you mean our family's image. That's what matters?" I clarified.

"Of course. What else did you think I meant?"

"I don't know. How about me? Don't I matter?"

"Crisanta . . ." my mom warned under her breath.

"What?" I shrugged. "It's a perfectly reasonable question considering that after learning that I have magic and a bunch of hunters kidnapped and almost killed me for it, my father's only issue with the situation is how my leaving school looks to Midveil's constituents."

My father gave me one of his silent, powerful stares, which I had not become immune to, even after all these years. I looked away and took a slight step back.

My father cleared his throat and was about to respond when the throne room doors opened and a few of my dad's head advisors entered. The two men wore silvery-gray suits and sky blue ties. The tall, gingery blonde woman in the center wore a similar-colored pantsuit.

I did a double take upon seeing the woman.

Ever since my friends and I had discovered the corrupt practices of the kingdoms' ambassadors at the last Century City Summit, I'd dreaded eventually seeing our family's ambassador again.

Susannah Marberg (Sooz, as everyone except my dad called her) had been our Midveil ambassador since I was a preteen. I'd always considered her loyal, kind, and totally awesome. She balanced working for my parents with various outside commitments including mentoring underprivileged children and competing in equestrian tournaments.

Since she'd been a part of our lives for so long and lived in the castle because of her ambassador role, I'd always looked up to her like an unofficial big sister. At least I used to. Now I felt anger whenever I thought of her.

She'd been in the room at the Capitol Building along with the ambassadors of the other twenty-five kingdoms when my friends and I had eavesdropped on the Summit—the bi-annual meeting held by the ambassadors to discuss important matters of state. That meant Sooz knew about the very protagonist conspiracy we were bent on stopping. It also meant she'd been doing it for her entire career, most likely without my parents' knowledge.

I dreaded coming face to face with her now, having to confront the feelings of betrayal I felt toward her and what she stood for.

Thankfully, the woman who entered was not Susannah—simply a woman of comparable hair color and height. I exhaled in relief as the advisors approached my father.

"We'll discuss this later, Crisanta," he said, waving me to step aside and let them pass. "Go settle in and send your brother my way when you find him. Alex and I are to attend an agriculture committee hearing this evening before dinner."

My mother took me by the arm before I could say anything else.

"Sorry," I said under my breath once we'd left the throne room. "I guess that 'behaving myself' thing was an empty promise."

My mother didn't reply as we moved down the hall and approached the glass lift that would take us to the upper floors of the castle's southern wing. Its transparent doors slid open and I stepped inside, but my mother did not join me. I looked at her, feeling guilty.

My shoulders slumped. "I really am sorry, Mom. I know I let my temper get the better of me where Dad is concerned and I shouldn't, but he just . . ." I sighed again. "I didn't mean to tick him off. I've had a rough week. Hopefully I won't be a burden on you for very long and I'll be out of your hair before—"

"Crisanta," my mother interrupted.

I blinked.

"You are not a burden—not on me, not on your father, not on any of us. What you are is our daughter, and we will do whatever we have to in order to protect you now that things have . . . changed."

My mother took one of my hands in hers. "How long have you had it?" she asked carefully. "The magic, I mean."

"I'm not entirely sure," I admitted. "A long time. Emma put it there before she disappeared, so it could've been any time before my seventh birthday."

"But how long have you known of its existence?" she clarified.

I shrugged. "A few months. It all happened really fast. I'm still figuring it out."

My mom suddenly hugged me again. "I am sorry about what happened to you back at school, my sweet girl. It must have been awful."

I closed my eyes as fire, hay, and hunters flashed across my memory.

"It was," I answered. "But I'm okay. At least I will be. I just need time to process."

"I understand that, Crisanta," my mother replied slowly. "Just know that if you ever require anything else, or *anyone* else to help you, do not be shy to reach out. I know how you are about such things. You internalize; it is your way. But it is not always the best way. Sharing a load with someone can make carrying it so much easier. Whether it is me, your brothers, or perhaps one of your friends from school, I encourage you to find someone with whom you feel comfortable enough to share your problems before they overwhelm you."

My heart ached.

I'd already had someone like that. And it did make carrying the load a lot easier. But Daniel didn't want the job anymore. After he pushed me away, it would take a lot for me to feel comfortable sharing my faith with someone again.

"Mom, I'm fine," I lied. "Honestly, I'm not overwhelmed."

"And I am glad to hear that, Pumpkin. I only worry that it may not always be the case."

"All right, Mom. I promise that if it ever becomes too much, I'll take your advice and find someone I trust to talk to. Okay?"

"Okay," my mother replied. She stepped back then bit her lip and glanced away. The doors to the lift began to shut, but I put my arm up to block them.

"What's that look for?" I asked.

"Nothing," she responded sadly. "I only hope that this is not another one of your empty promises. I can protect you from a lot, pumpkin, as can your father, your brothers, and these walls. But I cannot protect you from yourself. That is something you alone are charged with."

I tilted my head, absorbing her words.

"Go," she said, her tone changing from solemn to spritely.

"Dinner is in two hours and I am sure you want to relax after such a long flight."

I nodded and the doors to the lift began to close again.

"Remember," my mom called. "Attire is formal."

As the translucent box began to rise to the eighth floor, my mother disappeared from sight and I was left facing nothing but my own glassy reflection and fading thoughts of Daniel.

# CHAPTER 20

# My Brother, The Future King

nd so I was all, 'Guess what, Dad? I have magical powers that people are trying to murder me for.' And he was like, 'That's nice, Crisanta. Remind your brother we have a meeting, will you.' I mean seriously, what the heck, right?"

I flopped backward on the royal blue sofa in Alex's bedroom and glared up at the ceiling. I'd spent way too much time staring up at it over the years as I complained about how crazy our dad made me. So much so, that I pretty much had everything about it committed to memory, even the tile count—793, in case you were wondering.

My brother was polishing one of the many swords in his room. He kept his armor in here, along with plenty of weapons, but the blade currently in his hand was his favorite. It was a sword called Oathcrusher which he'd received five years ago as a present for his sixteenth birthday.

He kept polishing the blade as he walked over to the couch. The shadow of his slim but muscular five-foot-ten frame passed over me.

"Crisa, you know how Dad is," Alex responded. "He's all business. He cares, he just doesn't know how to show it. And anyway, can you really blame him for his reaction? You didn't exactly present the information in the greatest of ways. How would you like it if your kid told you that she had magical powers and was getting sent home from school because she was kidnapped and almost killed?"

I blew a strand of hair out of my face and sat up. Alex was a good listener most of the time, but his advice always made me feel a little foolish—like I was a whiny child. He was right, of course, but that didn't mean I had to like it.

"Yeah, I guess," I admitted. "I just hate how whenever we have a conversation he has to say something that ticks me off. Our relationship is fine when we're not speaking."

"I'm not sure that counts," Alex commented as he finished shining his sword.

"Oh, what would you know, Mr. Perfect?" I asked mockingly.

Alex threw the polishing rag in my face. I swatted it away. He came over and gave me an affectionate pat on the head followed by a not-so-welcome noogie that riled up my hair.

"Shake it off, Crisa," he said. "Come on. I know what'll make you feel better. They just re-did the floors in the sword-fighting arena out back. It's been ages since we've had a match and I know you're dying to see if you can finally beat me."

I raised my eyebrows. "Hey, I've beaten you before."

"You mean I've let you win before."

"Ha ha," I scoffed. "Mr. Perfect thinks he's so invincible with a sword, does he? Well, I've got news for you, bro. I've been practicing a lot lately and I know all of your moves. Prepare to be totally owned."

"You only *think* you know all my moves," Alex countered, mischief in his aqua-blue eyes. "I've got a few new tricks up my sleeve that oughta put you in your place."

I smiled.

"So do I," I replied coyly. "For one, I won't be using a sword in the arena today."

With a forceful spin, I sent Alex's sword flying.

"And that, I believe, is three to two!" I boasted gleefully, as Alex went to collect *Oathcrusher* from the sidelines.

"How long did you say you've been practicing with that spear?" he asked when he came back over.

"A few months," I grinned. "I'm pretty awesome, aren't I?"

"You're decent," he said. "I guess I'll have to stop going easy on you."

"Right." I rolled my eyes. "Tell yourself what you need to, bro. I'm still gonna hand your pride back to you on a silver platter."

Alex and I began another round of combat. Instantly my lighthearted, post-match feelings of triumph gave way to the focused intensity I needed for such a challenge.

My brother was an amazing swordfighter. He was a natural and had won our kingdom's annual tournament for the last four years running. Strong, fast, ruthless—I admired him for his aptitude as much as I feared him for it when we were sparring.

Alex, Daniel, and Arian were the three most skilled sword-fighters I'd ever encountered. Which was why (my talents and new confidence aside) I still had to watch myself where my brother was concerned, especially since he'd been the one to teach me how to fight in the first place. In that way Alex had an advantage over Arian and Daniel. He knew my style, strengths, and weaknesses in combat better than anyone.

My boots skidded against the ground as I blocked Alex's latest strike. He redirected quickly and came back toward my sternum. I stepped out of the way and spun around. He pivoted as I came in with a strike of my own. He blocked my blow with the shield in his other hand as I countered. I swung; he ducked.

Alex and I went in for a shot simultaneously and ended up pushing each other back. We both staggered a bit as we regained our balance. Alex was faster to recover though, and he rushed at me again.

"I thought I heard someone in here," said a familiar voice from behind.

The voice distracted me and I didn't react in time to block Alex's maneuver. I tried to redirect his strike, but he swung his shield around and rammed me in the ribs. The jolt caused me to lose my grip and my spear tumbled to the ground.

"Pietro!" I yanked off my helmet and spun around to glower at my other brother, who'd slipped into the arena. "You distracted me."

"Sorry," he said, rubbing the back of his neck. "Didn't mean to. I was looking for Alex." He turned to the prince in question. "Dude, Dad sent me to find you. He says you're fifteen minutes late for the agriculture meeting."

"Wouldn't be the first time," Alex said as he stowed his sword.

He took off his helmet and ran a gloved hand through his blond hair. I smiled to myself as I marveled at how—despite his thick eyebrows and rugged features—he looked so much like my mother.

"Dad'll get over it," Alex said, a touch of endearing arrogance twinkling in his eyes.

I sighed. "How are you his favorite again?" I asked as he took off his armor.

"Beats me," he shrugged. "But I'm not complaining. I'll see you guys at dinner. I'm gonna head over."

"Wait, what about our match?" I asked. "We're tied three to three."

"Rain check," he said. "We'll finish later. It's not like the outcome was going to be a surprise."

"Is that so?" I put my hands on my hips.

Alex riled up my hair again as he walked by. "Why don't you ask the scoreboard?"

He gestured to the dry-erase board on the right side of the room where he and I had kept track of our victories against one another since we were little (a remnant of our childhood that we insisted on preserving no matter how many times our parents renovated the arena). The ratio of his wins to mine was highly in his favor. A scowl crossed my face as he left the room.

"And there goes our future king," Pietro said as he came over to me.

"Yes, in all his humble glory," I scoffed, picking up my spear and leaning against the chrome-plated wall.

Pietro and I stood side by side for a moment in quietude. I noted that he was a bit tanner than the last time I'd seen him. Apart from that, he was exactly the same—his thick black hair, his dark brown eyes, his naturally bronzed skin. He was the tallest of the three of us but unlike Alex and me, he looked nothing like either of our parents.

"Glad to see you too by the way," Pietro eventually said. "Thanks for coming to say hi."

My eyebrows shot up. "Oh, sorry, my bad! I was going to come by your room after I saw Alex, but he challenged me to a fight, and you know I couldn't say no to that. He'd think I was chicken. Plus, I was dying to show him what I could do with my spear and I—"

"Crisa, relax," Pietro said, smiling. "It's fine. I'm just glad you're home. I was really worried when Mom told us what happened at Lady Agnue's. You okay?"

"Yeah, I'm fine. How much did she tell you?"

"Everything. Although, knowing you, I gather that the 'everything' you offered up in that letter is not actually everything in its entirety. Am I right?"

"You gather correctly," I replied.

"So I guess there's no point in asking what else is new with you then?" He bumped my shoulder affectionately.

"Again, bro, spot on." I bumped his shoulder back. "But enough about me. What's new with you and the rest of the family?"

"With me? Nothing that exciting. I started seeing this girl from the citadel. She's pretty great—strong opinions, ambitious, interested in politics, wears *a lot* of leather. The new recruits to the King's Guard have their final exam next week, so I've been whipping them into shape. And I think I finally figured out a more effective system for organizing our weapon's vault. As for the rest of the family . . . Well, Dad passed a decree to build a few new water towers in the city, what with the lack of rain lately. Mom is planning a couple of diplomacy visits next month. Oh, and *Alex* has a girlfriend."

My eyes nearly popped out of my head. "What? You're joking!" I exclaimed.

"I'm not. I mean, I haven't met her or anything, but he's definitely got one."

"If you haven't met her then how do you know?"

"You can just tell. I've seen him sneaking off. He's been swinging between broody moods and giddy highs. And he's been spending a lot more time in the palace gym working out."

"That's all circumstantial," I responded defensively.

"But not coincidental," Pietro argued. "Trust me, Crisa. He has a girlfriend. It's a guy thing. More than that, it's a brother thing. He's acting like I did when I first started going out with Rita, and Andy, and Mara, and, well, you get the idea."

"No way," I insisted, shaking my head adamantly. "We just hung out together for, like, an hour. And we write every now and again while I'm at school. He would have told me."

"Hey, opting to keep things to yourself isn't a trait exclusive to you in this family. That kid doesn't like to open up to anyone if he can help it either."

"I guess . . ." I said.

*Why didn't Alex tell me that he has a girlfriend?*

I bit my lip. The notion bothered me. As averse as I was to sharing or letting others in, I'd always been less guarded toward Alex. I didn't tell anyone everything (with the exception of that stint with Daniel). However, I did tell Alex some things and that was a big deal to me, the queen of lone wolves. I'd even considered telling him about my magic before I'd been forced to reveal the truth because of the hunters. The fact that he felt the need to keep something as silly as a relationship from me was kind of insulting.

I mean, come on. My secrets were fair to keep. They involved homicidal antagonists, Fairy Godmother conspiracies, government corruption, magic-based diseases, and visions that affected the fate of our realm. Not really casual big-brother-little-sister talk. But Alex having a girlfriend was not exactly world-altering news that he needed to keep to himself.

"Whatever." I shrugged. "I don't know if I believe it anyway."

Pietro let out a slight laugh at my reaction.

"What?" I asked.

"Nothing," he said. "It's just funny, isn't it? How annoying it is when people you care about get weird about sharing personal stuff. There's a word I'm thinking of here. It starts with a K. Oh, it's on the tip of my tongue. Can you help me out there, Crisa?"

"Karma?" I replied, shooting him a glare.

"That's it."

He grinned, showing off his perfectly white teeth. Then he straightened up and moved for the door. "Be on time for dinner, okay, sis?" he said. "You and I don't have the luxury of never falling out of Dad's good graces like that other kid does, and you've already had a rough week."

"Yeah, I will. Thanks." Then emotion spurred inside of me. "Pietro, hold on."

I put my spear down and jogged up to my brother, stood on my toes, and threw my arms around him. "I'm glad to see you too."

In the confines of my childhood bedroom, it was like time had stood still over the last decade.

The pink canopy over my bed draped in elegant swooshes. Dolls and stuffed bears sat on shelves gathering dust despite the best efforts of the castle's cleaning staff. The bluish-gray paint on the walls simulated the sky in springtime. An assortment of jeweled tiaras in various sizes and colors glistened atop my vanity. It all seemed like the landscape of a memory.

Truthfully, the only thing that seemed to have changed over the years was the size of the gowns hanging in my closet. As I'd expected, it had been fully re-stocked by my mother since my last visit. My closet was overflowing with enough frilled and sequined fabric to open up a boutique in the high-end shopping district of the citadel.

I began to get ready for dinner. Unlike my mother (and every other princess in existence) I did not have ladies-in-waiting to help me dress. I had ladies-in-waiting—their names were Minnie, Paprika, and Daphne—but I didn't have them aid me with basic things that I thought every girl should be able to do for herself. Respecting my preferences, the ladies stayed out of my room for the most part and kept busy during the day assisting other people in the castle unless I requested otherwise.

For this evening I selected a simple, mint-colored dress to wear to tonight's dinner. It had no jewels, no glitter, and no petticoat. It was rather plain with the exception of a sparkling, golden belt. To finish—and make my parents happy—I accessorized with an equally understated gold tiara.

I was glad to have found something that met my comfort and style requirements while also satisfying the formal dress code for dinner. However, the contentment I'd managed to secure with this outfit instantly vanished when I opened up my shoe closet. Pumps, stilettos, and wedges filled the space like an orthopedic surgeon's worst nightmare. My brows furrowed with irritation as I searched the closet, under the bed, and all of my secret nooks for the pairs of boots I'd left behind upon my return to school last fall.

Alas, I found none. My mom had located and removed them all. Which meant I had two choices. Wear the black combat boots I'd arrived in, which my parents would clearly be able to see beneath the hem of my dress, or rough it with a pair of these forsaken heels.

Ordinarily I would have gladly chosen the former, but I decided against it tonight. I had promised my mom that I would try not to provoke my dad; I could power through an evening of foot discomfort for him. She'd certainly sacrificed the same thing that historic night they'd met at the ball. If she could do it in *glass* stilettos, I figured I could manage with a pair of satin ones.

Ready for dinner, I slipped out of my room.

The halls of my castle were somewhat creepy at night. As I wandered back toward the lift, I proceeded with more caution than should have been natural for a person in their own home.

My heels clicked against the floors, the sound ricocheting off the ceiling. A cold draft blew from some open window. My reflection followed me like a ghost as it was captured by the glass walls of the triangular-shaped corridor. It felt like walking through the innards of a kaleidoscope-themed funhouse.

Even though the downstairs dining room was made from the same materials—glass and shimmering metal—the room glowed with warmth from the candelabras and chandeliers. I was the last to arrive at dinner. My parents and both my brothers looked up as I entered.

"Hi," I said as normally as possible.

I strolled over to my seat—to the left of my dad (who sat at the head of the table) and across from my mother who sat on his right. The chair was as hard as I remembered. The entire thing shined silver and lacked armrests or cushions of any sort. Its back was uncompromisingly erect and stretched at least a foot above my head when I was seated.

"Now we can eat," my father said, signaling to one of the servers at the back of the room. A moment later a long parade of staff began wheeling in tonight's dishes.

Once we'd been served I felt some of my tensions ease away. For one, the food was great. And two, I didn't have to worry about talking, let alone arguing, when my mouth was full. Sadly, it was between courses that our family table fell open to disaccord.

"So, Crisanta," my mother began benignly. "How is school? Aside from the events of last week, that is."

"Fine," I answered. "I think I did well on my midterms. I've been working as a TA for my potions professor this semester. And I made the Twenty-Three Skidd team."

"Lady Agnue's has a Twenty-Three Skidd team now? That's awesome," Alex commented as he motioned for me to pass the salt.

"Not exactly," I responded. "Lord Channing's opened up tryouts for the boys' teams to everyone. Blue, Daniel, and I all tried out and got in."

"Who's Daniel?" Pietro asked.

I stopped cutting my steak. "What?"

"Who is Daniel?" my mother repeated.

"He's . . . he's a friend of mine," I said quickly. "He started school back in the fall. His protagonist book appeared really late and he ended up becoming Jason's roommate."

"I thought Mark was Jason's roommate."

"He was, but he's not at school this year. Lord Channing said he was taking a leave of absence."

"What happened? He get kicked out for having magic too?" Alex joked.

"Honestly, I don't know," I admitted. "And for the zillionth time, I wasn't kicked out. I was—"

"I know, I know. Settle down." Alex smirked. "I was messing with you. Seriously though, congrats on making the team. That's a big deal."

A small wave of gratification passed over me. At least Alex was acknowledging the accomplishment, even if the rest of my family didn't seem interested.

"Thanks," I said. "It is."

"Yeah, it's really cool," Pietro agreed. "But changing the subject, there's something I have to ask, Crisa. Something that you didn't explain in your letter. What can your magic do?"

"Pietro . . ." My mother gave him a disapproving gaze.

"What? I'm interested to know. If magic hunters are after her for it, it's bound to be something good."

I was filled with an odd combination of satisfaction and reluctance. I was proud of what I could do. I loved how powerful and boss I felt whenever I used my magic. It was also certainly nice to have someone take an interest in it. My father had barely blinked when I'd brought it up this afternoon. Liza treated it like it was a dangerous problem I needed to control. Lenore was trying to use it to get me tossed into Alderon. Lady Agnue and SJ made me feel ashamed of it. And the rest of my friends talked about it matter-of-factly like it was no big deal. As a result, the idea of showing off my power to my brother and the rest of my family was kind of appealing. Maybe someone here would actually recognize it for the super cool gift that it was if they had a proper demonstration.

Then again, I was timid about sharing. For while I was related to everyone at this table, I had to remember that they were not anywhere near as accepting as my friends. Those guys—for the most part—wanted me to be myself. My family—at the very least my parents—wanted me to be a girl who lived up to their expectations. I was afraid that I could not be both. But I was not too afraid to try.

"It's life," I conceded. "My magic can bring anything to life. Once it has, the objects I animate follow my commands."

"What? No way. Prove it," Alex said. He put his steak knife in front of my place setting. "Here, bring this to life."

I flicked my eyes to my mom. Despite her objection of Pietro raising the topic, she seemed curious and nodded for me to go ahead. I looked to my dad for the same kind of encouragement. He gave no such reassurance. He just eyed me carefully.

"All right then," I responded.

I exhaled deeply (more for the sake of calming my nerves than for channeling my magic). I placed two fingers over the handle of the knife and concentrated, making sure to focus on bringing it to life temporarily like Liza had taught me.

*Come to life and follow my lead until I release you*, I instructed.

My hand glowed and the golden energy infused into the knife. A second later, the cutlery rose off the table and floated in front of me—ready to obey my commands until I let it go.

Using my fingers like a symphony conductor, I proceeded to make the knife move. I made it hover across the table and cut a few slices of meat from the prime rib on the center platter. I had it spread butter on the sourdough that sat on each of our five bread plates. Then I had it dance overhead—twirling about in a sweeping figure-eight motion like a death-defying trapeze artist.

I was enjoying my family's jaw-dropping response as I whirled the knife faster and faster, when suddenly a voice across the room cut my glory short.

"Am I interrupting something?"

Startled, I lost concentration. Susannah Marberg, our kingdom's ambassador, had entered the dining room. When I saw her, my control was abruptly cut off from the knife. I didn't get the chance to end the temporary life I'd given it in a thought-out, conscious way. The bitter, betrayed emotions I felt toward Susannah replaced my focus and my magic—reading my feelings—sent the blade hurling across the room. It plunged into the wall not six inches from Sooz's head.

"Crisanta!" my mother exclaimed.

"Dude, what the heck?" Pietro seconded.

"I'm sorry! I'm sorry!" I said, grimacing. "It was an accident, I just—"

"Lost control," my father finished. He folded his hands and leaned forward, looking at me sternly. "You clearly do not have as much of a handle on these powers as you'd like to think. You nearly took off Miss Marberg's head."

"It's fine. I'm fine!" Sooz exclaimed as she walked over to our table.

She usually didn't join us for dinner so I hadn't expected to see her. The hairs on my arms stood erect as she came closer. She stopped behind my chair and put her hand on my shoulder. I cringed at her touch, but she did not notice.

"Crisanta obviously did not mean it, and aside from the fright, the demonstration was quite exhilarating," Sooz said.

"Yeah," Alex scoffed. "That's one word for it."

"Susannah, please," my father said, waving her off. "Crisanta, based on what I just saw, I don't want you using your powers within the palace anymore. Are we clear?"

"Dad, I said I was sorry," I protested. "And it's pretty important that I practice. Otherwise how am I ever going to get better?"

I wasn't going to tell my father, but there was another reason I had to use my powers regularly. It was called Magic Build-Up. If I went too long without using them, my powers would build and explode out of me like a painful tidal wave.

"Maybe getting better should not be your main concern," my father replied. "As is, your powers have already attracted magic hunters to your school. If you make your abilities stronger, the danger you court will only increase. So no magic in the palace. I mean it, Crisanta."

"Mom?" I turned to her for support, but she shook her head sadly.

"I am sorry, Pumpkin. But I think your father is right."

"I can't believe this," I pushed my chair out, shrugging off Sooz's hand in the process. "I'm going to my room."

"Would you like a guard to escort you?" my mother called as I stomped toward the exit.

I paused in the doorway and ripped out the steak knife speared there. "What do you think?"

I stormed out, cursing the ground beneath my feet. When I reached the lift, I decided not to board. On second thought I was not going to sulk in my room like a pouting child. I treaded down a long corridor through the indoor arboretum, the hall of the human-sized chessboard, and the third largest conference room until I reached the Hall of Transparency. Constructed entirely of glass, this space was intended to be a place for self-reflection (and literal reflection, I guess). There was nothing in the wide room except for a white sofa housed within an alcove. I'd come in here to lie on that sofa many times growing up, but tonight I walked past it. It was not the place of solace I sought. That resided in the room right beyond.

I stepped into our castle's grand library. It was square and had many staircases—some functional leading to other levels and some decorative leading absolutely nowhere. I strode across the white carpet until I made it to the shelves that held the topography books.

I removed my heels and placed them on one of the end tables. Then I reached up to a high shelf and pulled out the third book in the series with a forceful yank while my other hand turned a lion-shaped bookend on the shelf immediately below. The moment I did this, sounds of latches and bolts echoed across the room. I turned and watched as the fireplace pushed itself inward and off to the side—revealing an old brick-and-mortar tunnel.

Our castle, like all good ones, had its share of secret passageways. Their locations and access points had been kept in our family for generations—passed down from each ruler to his or her offspring.

My dad was a stickler for the rules, so he had never shared the information with us. Luckily, my grandfather had always had a flare for mischief. Before he'd passed on, he'd taken great pride in teaching Alex, Pietro, and I these wonderful clandestine routes within the castle.

He'd shown us six secret passageways, but when I was nine

Alex and I inadvertently discovered a seventh. It was unlike the others in that while those six connected to different rooms within the building, or outside to the castle grounds, the seventh tunnel ran so far and deep it could take you all the way to the streets of the citadel or the mountains surrounding our kingdom.

Alex and I knew that if our parents ever found out about the tunnel they'd have it sealed off, so we'd formed a pact to never tell anyone about the route—not our friends, not our mom, not even Pietro. We'd also made a vow to never use the passageway without the other person present. It was an old tunnel, after all, and it was safer not to venture into it alone. Plus, it made sharing the secret more fun.

This was not the passageway I intended to enter now. The tunnel in the library led outside.

I put the book I'd dislodged back in place, grabbed one of the removable candelabras from its holster on the wall, and stepped into the tunnel. Inside, I pulled a lever that triggered the closure of the bookcase. Once it was sealed, I began my trek through the darkness.

The dirt crunched beneath my bare feet and I kept the candelabra high to see any cobwebs in the way. At the end of the tunnel I put my hand on a brick and pushed. The wall moved to the side. Moonlight streamed into the tunnel. I stowed the candelabra for my return trip, blowing out the flames and securing it in a holster beside a carved-out cubby that held a box of matches. From there, I shimmied out of the opening and then pushed the wall shut behind me.

I'd been deposited into our castle's hedge maze. It was a huge place, but I had the path committed to memory like every other part of the grounds. Making my way through, I passed lion-shaped topiaries, modern sculptures, and two gazebos before I found the exit that would lead me to the part of the campus I'd been after.

A few acres of level, pristine grass lay in front of me. In the past, this section of the grounds—the main lawn—had been used for everything from equestrian tournaments to garden parties for visiting diplomats. My parents even had their wedding reception here. At the moment, it was being used exclusively as Lucky's new home.

My beloved dragon was lying in the middle of the field, the moonlight reflecting off his scales. As I came nearer, he opened his golden eyes curiously and lifted his head. He looked like he was about to jump up, but I motioned for him to stay.

"Hey, boy. How's your night been?" I asked as I patted him on the snout.

He huffed happily and I smiled.

I sat down on the grass next to him, leaning against his side. I was comfortable for the most part, as his body was strangely soft despite the roughness of his scales. The night was not that cold, but a whisper of wind picked up once in a while, causing me to shiver. Lucky seemed to sense my discomfort and he moved one of his wings to shelter me from the breeze.

"Good boy," I said as I pet him.

Glad for his company and his concern, I lay there and stared up at the sky until I drifted off to sleep.

# CHAPTER 21

# Backstories & Stories Yet to Come

atalie looked older in this dream.

Her hair was longer, swept into a messy bun that showed off her cheekbones. Her face appeared more mature. And she wore touches of eye makeup that accentuated her naturally elegant features.

She was in a loft apartment filled with artwork. There was one mural so grand it took up the entire left wall. Apart from the colorful pieces, the apartment also contained a cot, a maroon couch, a small kitchen in the corner, and a desk piled high with papers, spiral journals, and textbooks. On the shelves were knickknacks, a silver alarm clock, and a decorative cardinal flag with "University of Southern California" written on it in gold lettering.

The wooden floor was covered by a protective tarp that surrounded an oddly shaped bench in the middle of the room. Natalie was sitting on this bench, bent over a large canvas.

There was a knock at the door.

Natalie glanced up as Ryan came in holding an envelope. She smiled and pushed a strand of loose hair out of her eyes—inadvertently brushing some yellow paint across her cheek.

"The mail came," Ryan announced as he walked over to check out the canvas she'd been concentrating on.

"Thank you, Postmaster General," she said as she picked up a thin paintbrush and carefully swept a shade of citrine over her canvas. "Just put it on the counter. I'll look at it later."

"Nat," Ryan said seriously. "It's from them."

Natalie's eyes widened. She froze for a second, yellow paint dripping onto her already-stained jeans. Then she set down the brush and studied the envelope in Ryan's hand. There was both dread and excitement in her expression.

"It's small," she commented. "If it was an acceptance, it would be bigger—like with your acceptance to Columbia."

"That's not a set rule, though," Ryan argued. "That was medical school. They had to shove a lot of pamphlets and junk in there. This is an apprenticeship at the Met. Maybe they believe in minimalism."

Natalie took the envelope from Ryan and brushed her left thumb over the words above the return address: *The Metropolitan Museum of Art*.

"I can't look," Natalie said. "What if it's a no? If I don't open it, I can go on pretending like there's still a possibility that everything will work out—that all our plans are possible. If I open it and it's a no, that's it. And if that's the case, then what?"

Ryan sat down on the bench beside her. "Then we'll make new plans," he said. "Either way, I'm here with you."

Natalie stood and tore open the envelope. She turned away from Ryan as her eyes darted across the sheet of paper inside. Then she stopped reading. Her eyes went blank as she stared straight ahead.

"What?" Ryan asked, standing up. "What does it say?"

Natalie didn't turn around. "I got it," she said softly, as if she could barely believe it herself.

"What?"

She spun around—her face lit with joy. "I got it! I got the apprenticeship! I got the job!" Natalie jumped into Ryan's arms and he whirled her around ecstatically. They spun and spun as the room melted into bright white light.

In a torrid flurry, images began to flash through my dreamscape. I saw a lagoon with mermaids, water sparkling in the early morning light rimmed by a tall and smooth, lavender-colored cliffside. A ship I'd committed to memory from my textbooks at school, the *Jolly Roger*, bobbed along the ocean. There were temple ruins with strange markings surrounded by jungle. Kids of various ages flew across open sky. And lastly, a platter of nachos.

My vision flashes weren't always connected, but based on my geographical and general knowledge of Neverland from mapmaking, I had an inkling these images were all linked to the same realm. Except the nachos. I didn't know how those fit in.

The flashes continued from there, but they began to change into something darker that made my subconscious cringe. The barn burning in the practice fields. Arrows splicing into lanterns. The purple color in my veins.

I realized these new images were not visions of the future. They were memories. Bad ones. Horrific scenes that I had repressed streamed through my mind without mercy. After a flood of the cruel images, my mind stalled upon Parker's horrible eyes boring into me as I desperately tried to push away his dagger at my throat. Then I woke up.

I couldn't seem to get enough air and my heart was racing. As I sat alert, I discovered that my own hand was grabbing my throat. I speedily released it, trying to shake away the troubled memories, but my head throbbed. I closed my eyes, blocking out the powder blue sky. The bright morning sun beat against my face as I tried to center myself.

*Keep it together. What happened with the hunters doesn't matter anymore. You're here. They're gone. You're fine.*

I opened my eyes again and blinked hard as I adjusted to the daylight. Lucky was still snoozing, but I could see workers and guards across the grounds in the distance. Based on the position of the sun, I guessed it was midmorning.

I knew no one would be looking for me. The rest of my family usually had their days booked solid from the instant they got up. I did not have a schedule as I was not supposed to be here.

I crawled out from under Lucky's wing and stretched. Then I heard a familiar voice.

"We'll need at least five tables for the buffet line. Use the big ones. You know how the attendees of the War Games Convention can eat. And I'd like a stage for the dual demonstrations. Can someone get me a copy of the waiver the participants signed last year?"

I tiptoed around Lucky's snout and saw Sooz marching through one of the castle's outer corridors with a slew of staff following her like an entourage. They were headed toward the fields. I glanced around and decided to make a run for it.

With as much stealth as conceivable for a girl on a lawn in a floor-length dress, I hastened back toward the entrance of the hedge maze and darted inside. My bare feet moved quickly across the stone path.

After a couple of minutes I stopped to rest at the edge of a fountain, grateful for having made it here unseen. I was in no mood for another interaction with that traitor, Sooz. Until I had a better idea of how to handle the situation, I wanted to keep my distance from her.

I continued to sit in the maze for a while. The sun hit my cheeks as I took in the sounds of birds, the trickling of the fountain, and the gagecho croaking to my right.

All kingdoms in Book had native animals unique to their part of the land. In Midveil, that was the gagecho. Gagechos were identical to geckos with the exception of two qualities. First, they were a pale blue color with splashes of silver on their scales. Second, they had the special ability of copying sounds, like a mockingbird. Gagechos were able to absorb whatever sound they'd most recently heard and project it back, their vocal chords able to match it perfectly in every way. Hence the "echo" in *gagecho*.

I found the ability charming and hilarious. If a gagecho caught you off guard it could give you quite a fright, but other than that the creatures were cute and harmless.

I looked at the one sunbathing beside me on the fountain. He was small, even for his kind. He must've been a baby. The tiny creature turned his face in my direction—his itty-bitty black eyes blinking up at me curiously.

"Hey, what's your story?" I asked him.

The baby gagecho tilted his head. His throat inflated and deflated a few times with rapid succession and then—

"Hey, what's your story?"

I grinned at the reptile's spot-on imitation of my voice, right down to the sarcastic inflection.

The gagecho zipped back into the bushes of the maze. As he did so, I garnered he had the right idea. A walk outside felt like a nice way to kill some time, much more so than heading back to the palace. But first, something had to be done about my long dress. I took out my wandpin.

*Lapellius.*

*Knife.*

I used the blade to cut the skirt of my gown above the knees—transforming it into a much shorter dress that would be easier to move about in. Storing my wandpin back in its clandestine place, I continued ahead.

The maze was beautiful in the daytime, like a world all its own. Other than the sounds of fountains and singing birds, everything remained quiet and serene. The rose bushes were in full bloom and the bougainvillea canopies draped gracefully over the walkways. I wandered through their seclusion for a while until I came to the great mausoleum near the rear of the maze. It was constructed of thick white stone and marble. Steps led up to a set of glistening crystal doors situated beneath an immense gold clock. I walked up the steps and pushed the doors open.

Few people ever came in here. While the structure was breathtaking, it was also very somber. In this magnificent compound lay the dead of my family.

The place wasn't stocked wall to wall with coffins or anything. Actually, there was just one. It was made of porcelain and resided in the center of the round room, directly beneath a massive rotunda skylight. Even this one wasn't in use, though. The thing was more symbolic than anything else. Across its smooth, crème-colored lid and sides were the names of all my ancestors, written in gold and silver leaf. That was the tradition in Midveil, you see. Whenever members of one's family passed away, their names were carved into some sort of ancestral gravestone. This was our family coffin.

The mausoleum's rounded walls were lined with golden drawers that looked like paneled tiles. Each drawer had a name carved into it. Sealed within the drawers were the cremated remains of all the lost members of the Knight family—from its first recorded, ancient founding members, to my dad's parents.

The tile was cold beneath my feet as I wandered across the room to the family coffin. I gingerly grazed the names carved on the porcelain lid with my fingertips, paying my respects.

I exited the mausoleum through the crystal doors on the other side and stepped back into the sunshine. To the left was a slope thick with bushes and forest. If you climbed that, eventually you'd end up somewhere on the main grounds, perhaps behind the kitchens, or even as far away as the stables if you maneuvered through it long enough.

That was not the traditional route out of here, though. Upon exiting the mausoleum you had two marked trails to choose from. An old brick path stretched from the back doors and split in opposite directions. One route headed into the remaining part of the hedge maze. The second led to the edge of the grounds, specifically to an old shed where my father and brothers stored their winter hunting equipment. This was the path I chose.

Weeping willows grew all around the modest, normally ignored wooden shed. The only time this place was used was when Alex, Pietro, and my dad came to raid it for their annual hunting trip to the mountains in late December. I had never been invited on any of these trips. I'd invited myself once or twice, but that was hardly the same thing.

Since their last trip had been months ago, this place hadn't been disturbed for some time. From one great willow bough next to the shed hung a rickety tree swing. The wood of the swing was painted light blue. Vines had grown around the chains, extending from the tree overhead. I took a seat and pushed against the aged brick floor to teeter on my toes.

My eyes wandered to the wishing well to the right of the shed. I loved that well. Not just for its antiquated design, but because it was special to Alex and me. He and I had a tradition of each throwing a coin into it whenever we used our *secret* secret passageway, which could be found inside that very shed.

Aside from collecting and storing hunting supplies in

December, no one ever came out here. As such, as I balanced on my toes and looked around the secluded spot, an idea occurred to me.

*Hm. I guess this is where I'll be spending most my time for the next few weeks.*

After all, my dad did say no magic in the *palace* . . .

# CHAPTER 22

# The Dangers of Showing Off

re you ready to have your mind blown?" I asked Alex as he sat on the tree swing.

"Selling it pretty hard there, aren't you?" he asked in return. "I saw you almost decapitate Sooz with a flying knife. How do you expect to top that?"

"Just watch," I said.

I walked about thirty feet away from him, then paused—mentally preparing for the scope of what I intended to do. I stepped back another three feet to give myself a touch more space, then knelt and placed my hand on the brick path that led to the hunting shed.

Since my return home I'd been keeping busy. Sometimes this involved work; other times it involved leisure, like giving Pietro lessons on how to fly Lucky. But the activity that captured the greatest amount of my attention was coming out here every day to practice my magic and take lessons with Liza via Mark Two. Without the distraction of school or magic hunters or even friends, I'd been able to fully dedicate no less than six hours a day to the endeavor. As a result, I was amazed at how drastically my strength and control over my powers had increased in just seven days. It was enough now that I actually felt comfortable having an audience, which was a pretty big deal for me.

In all the time I'd been training with Liza, I had never practiced in front of others. Not even my friends. I'd been too self-conscious, worried that I might not have sufficient control over my magic and end up looking foolish . . . like I had at dinner the other night.

Today, though, I was so confident in myself, and the work I'd put into my progress, that I felt like showing someone I trusted. That someone was Alex. I'd clued him in on my secret activities and had invited him to come and see what I could do firsthand.

I pressed my fingers firmly onto the brick path. With a steady exhale, I cleared my mind of emotion and concentrated my magic the way I'd been practicing. The glow crept out of me and seeped into the first brick before spreading to the other bricks in the path ahead. There were about a hundred of them, and they all vibrated for a second (as if experiencing a private earthquake) before yanking themselves from the ground and flying around me like a flock of geese circling the eye of a storm.

"Not bad," Alex commented. "But can you make them do anything else?"

"Can I make them do anything else?" I scoffed. "Keep your eyes peeled, bro. Here comes the good part."

*Okay. Steady.*

*You've been practicing this split-focus, telepathic deal with your powers with Liza all week. If she says you're finally ready to start letting yourself off the leash in that regard, then you totally are.*

*You can do this.*

I began to command the bricks to work together to form new shapes. First I had them reconfigure themselves into a large wall. Then I began firing a few at a target board I'd nailed to a tree a couple of days ago. As the bricks hit the mark spot-on, I redirected another aspect of my focus to the remaining mass.

*Stairs*, I thought. *Build me continuous stairs.*

At once, the bricks worked together to construct a levitating staircase, which I began to climb. Higher and higher I rose as it kept growing—the steps I'd already used moving to the front of the line to build new ones for me to escalate even farther.

I'd managed to rise a solid twenty feet above the ground while still maintaining control over the firing bricks. It was impressive, and I was ecstatic at the scope of the feat. But I started to feel tired. I was experiencing the warning signs of Magic Exhaustion. My control over the bricks was beginning to falter and my mental reflexes became less sharp. It was growing harder to breathe and stay upright.

I should've taken this as my cue to immediately lower myself to the ground. However, I was so close to thirty feet (the record I'd been trying to break for the last three days, which I measured with specific markers I'd carved into a tree) that I refused to yield. If I just held my concentration a bit longer . . .

A bead of sweat ran down my forehead and my hand quivered as the glow it emanated flickered on and off.

*Twenty-six feet . . . Twenty-seven feet . . . Twenty-eight feet . . .*
*Come on. Almost there.*

Alas, it seemed that was as far as I could push myself today. My glow disappeared all at once. The firing bricks I'd temporarily given life to fell, including the ones beneath my feet. I yelped with panic as I plummeted to the ground.

*Eep!*

"Platform! Platform!" I commanded desperately as I flailed. I was able to will a final wisp of magic out of me and a half-dozen bricks levitated under my feet like a piece of floating floor just in time.

I landed on the makeshift platform with a light thud. It descended the last twenty feet with me crouched upon it. When I reached ground level the bricks returned to normal like the others. My magic was exhausted. It would take about a day for my powers to recharge.

I stood wearily, grasping my head. It felt like lead, as did my bones. My skin felt thin and floppy like plastic wrap.

*Ugh. I hate Magic Exhaustion.*

"You okay?" Alex asked. He'd come to my side and grabbed my arm to keep me from tipping over.

"Um, yeah . . ." I grunted. "Just tired."

"You used too much magic at once. I guess you know your limits now, huh?"

"My limits for *today*," I corrected as I he and I went to sit down on the swing. "I've been pushing myself every day this week. You'd be surprised at how far I've already come. With more practice, I could—"

"Get yourself killed," Alex interjected. "You almost fell thirty feet. If you hadn't gotten control at the last second, you would've cracked your skull."

"I guess it's a good thing I always come through in a clutch then, huh?" I joked.

"Crisa."

"Alex, come on," I sighed. "Look, there's a reason you're the only person I told that I was practicing out here. I thought you'd be supportive. Or at a minimum, not be an over-concerned nark and try to stop me from pursuing this."

"All right, all right. Do what you want. Just watch it, okay? I don't want to come out here one day and find my sister splattered on the floor like roadkill."

"Lovely image," I huffed. "Thanks."

"You're welcome," he replied. "Have it at the forefront of your mind next time you're practicing. Then maybe you won't get cocky and push yourself before you're ready."

"Yeah, yeah. If you're done lecturing, didn't you say you had a surprise for me too?" I asked.

"You sure you're feeling up to it? You look pretty pale and wobbly."

"I'm fine. Fast healer, you know. Now seriously, what's the big surprise that required me to wear our kingdom's colors today?" I gestured down at my light gray leggings and the powder blue, long-sleeved dress and silver belt that I wore.

"All right, are you ready to have *your* mind blown?" Alex reached into his back pocket and pulled out two rectangular-shaped pieces of brightly colored parchment. He handed me one and I held it up to the sunlight.

*"Twenty-Three Skidd Finals / Game Five: Midveil Patriots*
*vs. Tunderly Giants*
*Saturday, March 21st @ 3:00 p.m."*

"Shut up!" I punched him in the arm. "You got us tickets to a Twenty-Three Skidd finals match?"

"I did, *and* I got us outfield seats. But if we're going to make the game, we have to move. Come on."

"Wait." I bit my lip. "There's no way Mom and Dad are gonna let me go. The reason Lady Agnue sent me here was for protection. They're not going to let me leave the grounds, let alone go to a massive public event with thousands of people and huge security challenges."

"Oh, young one," Alex said mockingly, "what makes you think we're doing this above board?" He gestured toward the shed.

I grinned. "What was I thinking?"

There was a bucket of old coins near the wishing well and I picked out two for us to throw in. It was a silly tradition, but we'd been doing it since we were little and I cherished anything Alex and I shared.

"Let's do this," I said as I jogged back to him. I held out his coin, but much to my surprise he didn't take it. I tilted my head. "What's wrong?"

"Nothing. Just . . . aren't we getting too old for the wishing well thing?"

"Um, no. I don't think so."

"Well, I do," he said coldly. "Throw one in if you want, but I'm not going to. We only started doing it because we were wishing for a way out of the castle right before we found this tunnel. To keep throwing coins and making wishes for the sake of that one moment is stupid."

Without further explanation, Alex entered the shed, leaving me standing there holding two coins and feeling idiotic.

All I could do was sigh and throw both coins into the well. One wish for my brother—that he'd get over whatever weirdness had possessed him so we could enjoy our day together. And one wish for me—that in my absence my friends were finally safe, and that when we were reunited in three weeks I would have enough control over my magic to keep them that way no matter what obstacles we faced in the future.

I glanced at my hands. The palms pulsed like I'd recently touched something hot and nearly gotten burned. I clenched them into fists with resolve. I had to keep pushing myself. I would become better, stronger, and more powerful. I had to.

I followed Alex into the shed. It was musty inside and smelled of aged venison. Various saddles, stirrups, and holsters were racked on the wall on the left while specially made crossbows, archer bows, and precision bows were racked on the right. Interspersed among them were mounted stuffed heads from previous kills, which I tried my best not to look at as I pursued Alex to the meat storage lockers along the back wall.

Lockers one and two were much bigger. As such, they were the ones used to temporarily store meat in the weeks after my brothers and father's trips. They had been cleaned and modernized with the latest in icebox and electrical cooling apparatuses over the years, unlike the third locker, which had been broken for a long time.

This third fridge had rusted handles and seriously yellowed edges. Like the other two much sleeker fridges, it appeared bolted to the floor and back wall. But Alex and I knew better. My brother opened the door. A gust of rancid wind hit us like a tidal wave. We simultaneously scrunched our noses.

The racks inside were empty (except for the mold clinging to the rims and a couple of boxes of baking soda on the bottom rack). Alex reached out for the box closest to the right and moved it aside. Behind the box was an old thermometer.

Alex rotated it a quarter turn to the left then to the right 360 degrees then to the left again all the way around. A large sound like a deadbolt moving emanated from the fridge. We stepped away and watched as the fridge jittered then laboriously moved to the side, revealing the trapdoor beneath.

Alex and I climbed twelve feet down a ladder before our boots hit solid ground. Using the light that shone through the trapdoor for guidance, Alex removed a matchbook from his pocket and lit a couple of portable candelabras mounted on the wall. He handed me one and pulled a lever that triggered the fridge up top to slide back into place.

Now the only light came from the candelabras that he and I were holding. Alex in front, me loyally behind, the two of us began our descent beneath the earth.

It would have been eerie had we not made the trip so many times. The walls were curved and bluish gray. We ducked beneath straggling roots and thick cobwebs. A metal track ran along the bottom in a straight route.

Once upon a time this tunnel must've been a part of an elaborate mining operation. I didn't know how long ago it had been put out of commission. But given that all other tunnels connecting to this route were buried, and no one else in the city seemed to know of its existence, I assumed that it had been centuries ago. All that remained was this one passage.

The tunnel ahead, like the tunnel behind, plunged into inky blackness. Neither Alex nor I hesitated though. The place brought back too many memories of our shared adventures for me to feel anything less than content as we forged on.

The journey to the exit would take about fifteen minutes on foot. Halfway there, I decided that this was the perfect opportunity to ask Alex about something that had been swirling in the corners of my mind since last week.

"Alex," I began timidly. "You don't have a girlfriend, do you?"

Even in the dim light I could see his muscles tense. I walked a bit faster to keep pace with him and try to read his expression. He didn't look directly at me. He opened his mouth as if he was about to say something, but rapidly closed it again.

"How'd you find out?" he eventually said.

My heart sank. He had been keeping the truth from me. I just couldn't understand why. So what if he was dating some trick? It wasn't exactly a universe-altering development. Why hadn't he told me?

I didn't ask him this, of course. The fact that he hadn't said anything to me on his own made me realize that our dynamic had changed. I thought about what had happened with the wishing well a few minutes ago. I didn't want to do anything that might distance us further, so instead of drilling him with accusatory questions, I tried for some more basic, benign ones.

"Who is she?" I asked.

"She's just someone," he replied as we turned a corner and began an even steeper descent.

"How descriptive," I said mockingly. "Sure sounds like something special."

He gave me a quick smile that looked devious in this light. "Actually, she is. I've never felt like this about someone before, Crisa. She's smart, confident, unafraid of anything, and she pushes me to look at things from a bigger perspective."

"So why are you keeping her a secret?"

"Because she's different than the rest of us."

"Different how? You mean she's not a protagonist?"

"Not exactly," he responded. "She just sees a lot of flaws in the way the realm is being run and wants to change things. And you know how older generations like our parents can be with regards to change. They're afraid of it. They like tradition and keeping things the way they are. They'd think her stance was extremist or something when it's really just logical. So that's why I don't want Mom or Dad or anyone to know about her until the time is right. They wouldn't approve."

"But Pietro's brought home girls that our parents didn't approve of. Remember that chick with the Griffin-tracking obsession? Or Laura, the girl who only wore slipper-sandals?"

"Yeah, but Pietro's not next in line to be king. I am. And I want this to be the girl I someday rule with."

I think I threw up in my mouth a little.

"Whoa, slow your roll there, Jack. How long have you two been dating exactly?"

"A couple of months." He shrugged.

My eyes nearly bugged out of my head. "A couple of months! Are you insane? You can't know you love somebody after a couple of months, let alone know you want to spend the rest of your life with them. Alex, that's ridiculous."

"No. It's not, Crisa. I know it might seem fast, but I'm sure of my feelings."

"That's what you said when you first tried banana pancakes and swore they were the greatest breakfast food in the history of time. Then what happened? Three weeks later you tried pumpkin pancakes and changed your allegiance."

"That's totally different. You can't compare breakfast foods to girlfriends."

"You can if they are both examples of your exaggerated, in-the-moment proclamations of true love," I argued. "You didn't know at the time of the banana pancakes that something greater would come along, so you thought they were as good as it gets. The same thing applies here. You've never had deep feelings for a girl before, so you're assuming that what you're feeling now is as good as it gets."

"Oh, what do you know?" Alex scoffed. "You're the last person I should be talking to about this. You've never even been into someone that way before."

"Maybe not," I countered. "But maybe that's why I'm the perfect person to talk about it with. My brain is totally objective, *unlike yours*."

Alex seemed angry with me. He clearly had not taken kindly to my outspoken counsel. We walked in silence for a while, but eventually I decided to extend an olive branch. I did not like being at odds with him. I had so few true allies in the world—especially in this castle—that I couldn't afford to lose his support. I also felt the obligation to be there for him just as he had always been there for me over the years. I tried to break the tension with a calmer approach.

"Look, I'm happy you found someone, all right," I said carefully. "But if she really means that much to you, I think you should introduce her to us. It's got to be better than all this sneaking around."

Alex shook his head. "Trust me, Crisa. Mom and Dad would never let me be with this girl no matter how I feel about her. They're too stuck in their own ways. They would never understand what we envision for Midveil's future or accept that things around here need to change."

"Well, if that's the case then what's your end game here?" I asked. "You can't go on keeping your secret girlfriend a secret forever. At some point you're going to have to choose."

Alex paused when we reached a split in the tunnel. "I already did," he said bluntly.

We had arrived at a two-way intersection. He handed me his candelabra and stepped toward the wall in front of us instead of taking one of the routes that extended on either side.

I was not surprised. The tunnel to our right went into the residential part of Midveil's citadel. The path to the left let out on the outskirts of the city near the base of the mountains. On foot that trek took about twenty minutes. But with the aid of the track and several mining carts that were still operational further down, you could get there in less than five.

Alex pushed a sequence of bricks on the wall in front of us like a code. The wall shifted and I extinguished our candelabras and hung them up before sliding through the newly created gap.

It took a minute to adjust to the brightness of the outside world. We were in an alley full of dumpsters. Alex and I closed the tunnel before heading toward the main street. As we merged with the crowd of the citadel, I was grateful for about the hundredth time this week for the loyalty of my ladies-in-waiting, particularly Minnie.

After the horrid "heels only" discovery in my closet, I had asked Minnie to go into town and pick me up a few pairs of boots. The gray, lace-up pair I wore now came to my knees and allowed for the agility and quick-to-jump-out-of-the-way finesse necessary for a trip across Midveil's bustling city center.

Today was the first time in a while that I felt like myself again—leggings, boots, comfy dress, and no tiara. Since I'd come home I had been donning far more regal attire than I usually did at school. I didn't have much of a choice in the matter since my mom had restocked my closet with traditional, princess-appropriate dresses while I was away. I didn't mind. Dressing a little more formally was a small price to pay to keep my mom happy on my short visits home. But Minnie helped me get any non-conventional princess clothing I needed, like the simple dress and pair of leggings I wore today.

After receiving it, I'd put in a follow-up request that she and my ladies-in-waiting create another dress for me—something sturdy, lightweight, and short-sleeved. I would need an outfit for the day my friends and I departed Midveil on our mission to find Paige Tomkins. I couldn't exactly go on an epic quest in a fancy gown. And after all the shenanigans we got into on our last adventure, I thought it would be best to wear something custom-made to be durable.

With another quick hop-and-evade maneuver, I avoided a carriage as Alex and I jaywalked across the traffic-laden street. The glass buildings glittered as we passed. I grinned widely. I loved the hullabaloo of the citadel. I relished the noise and the crowds and the feeling of life that pulsed from every nook and cranny like my own powers pulsed through my system when I got them raring.

To reach the stadium that hosted our kingdom's Twenty-Three Skidd matches we went by one of the citadel's more upscale districts. There were designer boutiques, salons, and trendy cafes where local hipsters sipped beverages from crystal goblets, listened to local bands, and ate gluten-free beignets. The citadel's most prestigious theater boasted advertisements for a sold-out performance of Midveil's favorite musicians, the Viomin String Quartet. An imported carriage dealership promoted 20 percent off its first-year leases.

A slew of buildings made up the restaurant borough that came next and beyond that was the business district, which was the busiest part of the citadel.

The buildings here were taller, sharper, and inherently grandiose. I stared up at the largest of them—Midveil Plaza. Every level of the building was solid glass, allowing people on the streets to see straight into every office and conference room from the ground floor to the top. Marble columns lined the entryway like giants; a powder blue Midveil flag draped between the lead pair.

The sight of the flag made my memory flash back to that dream I kept having about the burning building, the one where I dug through wreckage to find my kingdom's flag. I thought about the debris that rained down, the fire. Then I remembered the last fire I'd been trapped in. Like a leak in a dam, a spill of anxiety suddenly rushed in. For a moment the noise and crowds of the citadel felt overwhelming, suffocating. Then I pushed away the panic that the memory of Parker and the magic hunters caused.

*The hunters were in the past*, I reminded myself. That was there and I was here. As for the nightmare, tons of buildings in Midveil displayed flags and the majority of our structures—from these grand towers to the poorest shops at the edge of the citadel— were made of glass and metal. I had no way of knowing where this vision would come to fruition. Which in turn meant that it was useless to obsess over it until my dreams provided me with more clues.

I forced myself back to the present as Alex and I approached Midveil's Twenty-Three Skidd stadium. The structure was twice as big as the one at Lord Channing's. Banners and posters for the Midveil Patriots adorned the outer walls of the arena alongside Midveil flags. Tailgating tents in powder blue and silver for our team and forest green and yellow for the Tunderly Giants were set up all over the massive outdoor plaza leading up to the main entrance.

The smell of burgers, pickles, and grilled onions wafted under my nose while the sounds of laughter and merchandise sellers filled my ears. Children carrying tiny flags rode on the shoulders of adults. Men with strong abdominals and flabby bellies alike had gone shirtless in order to paint their favorite team players' colors and numbers on their skin. A line snaked up to an area where fans could get autographs from Gruffaw the Lion, Midveil's team mascot.

It was total madness and I utterly adored it, just like I adored Alex for knowing how much it meant to me to be here.

# CHAPTER 23

# A New Match

ome on! What was that?" I shouted angrily as a Patriot player fell from his Pegasus to the net below.

The hundreds of other fans in our section were equally riled. The score was now 15–14 to the Giants' advantage. Midveil and Tunderly had been bitter rivals for many years, and as the second half of the game commenced, it became increasingly violent.

Just like at school, the projection orbs flying through the sky captured up-close images of everything that happened. These visuals were shown across different sizes of holographic screens that floated several hundred feet above the center of the arena. The magic tech made the whole event seem larger than life.

"Go! Go! Go!" Patriots' fans chanted as Sam Ginchansky, the star player of our team, plunged toward the goal. I jumped up and down so much that most of the popcorn in my tub fell to the floor.

"Shoot it!" I screeched.

Ginchansky bobbed and weaved expertly past a couple of opponents before swinging his lacrosse sword and hurling the ball into the goal.

Everyone around me freaked out. Alex high-fived the dude on his right while I launched myself into a full chest bump with the guy on my left.

Ginchansky's face filled all eight of the arena's holographic screens. He lifted his visor and gave a wink and a smile to the crowd. The stadium went wild.

As the teams readied for the next play, the fans began to settle back into their seats. I threw one arm around Alex and hugged him.

"What's that for?" he asked.

"Nothing. Just thanks. You must've had to go through a lot of trouble to score these tickets, and you have no idea how much I appreciate it."

He shrugged off my arm like big brothers typically did. "Sure thing," he replied. "I thought it'd be nice for us to squeeze in some mismanaged adventure while we still had the chance. And, anyway, this match seemed like it'd be a good one."

"A good one?" I repeated. "Have we been watching the same game? This is the greatest thing ever!"

"I'm glad you're having fun," he said, smiling. Then he glanced at the fallen popcorn on the ground. "Maybe a little too much fun?"

"What? Oh." I grinned. "My bad. I'll get more."

As I stood up, Alex leaned in. "Remember," he whispered. "Keep a low profile."

"Relax," I whispered back. "I'm not exactly wearing a tiara."

For security purposes it was vital that my brother and I go unnoticed, us being who we were. But I didn't think there was anything to worry about. I was gone at school most of the year, so I was hardly recognizable. And Alex hadn't made a lot of public appearances in Midveil lately, as he'd been travelling with my dad across the realm to better his skills in foreign affairs and diplomacy.

The two of us blended in well; we were dressed in regular clothes and Patriot team colors like every other Midveil citizen present. Alex also wore sunglasses and a hat that shadowed his face. He'd bought an extra hat for me at the entrance of the stadium, which he'd slapped on my head without asking if I wanted it.

Another thing that helped our cover was the fact that we'd gotten seats in the outfield with the rowdiest fans. No one would think to find us here. Of course, blending in wasn't the only reason Alex had procured tickets in this section. Even if we hadn't been trying to stay under the radar, we still would have preferred it this way. The dignitaries in the box seats could keep their finger sandwiches, bubbly water, and polite clapping. Alex and I liked it out here where the beverages were of the slushy variety, the smell of processed nacho cheese permeated the air, and the fans caused a lively ruckus.

Nonetheless, I heeded Alex's advice as I pushed my way out of our row. Chips and pretzel crumbs crunched beneath my boots as I jogged up the stairs.

The wide cement corridors that wound around the arena were fairly deserted, except for the occasional person looking for an open snack stand. Many vendors had abandoned their posts in order to go and watch the game.

As I walked along, I thought about how happy I was in that moment. My magic training was going great. I'd only fought with my father a couple of times since coming back. Pietro and I had been bonding as I taught him how to fly Lucky. And here I was with Alex, having an amazing time watching my favorite sport. I loved the experience so much that my heart only throbbed slightly at the reminder of the Twenty-Three Skidd team I'd left behind.

Had it not been for the spark that came next, I would have spent the rest of the afternoon in the delusion that things in Midveil might always remain this good.

Way down by Section C something caught my eye. It came from the left where there was a curtained-off tunnel that led to the higher floors of the arena. Following my instinct, I slowly brushed aside the heavy curtain. At first everything seemed in order. However, a second later I saw it again in the center of the tunnel—a floating flurry of red sparks.

"What in the . . ."

Suddenly the flurry expanded like a baby cyclone. The glittering swarm took on the familiar shape of a woman.

I jumped back.

"I thought I might find you here," Lenore said as she restored her wand to ring form and slid it onto her finger. "Instructed to stay within the castle walls or not, I know what a fan you are of this sport, *and* disobeying direct orders."

The intimidating Godmother Supreme was wearing a white pantsuit today—high-waisted trousers paired with a fitted, deep

V-neck blazer. A silk silver top poked out from beneath it. Her silver shoes were high as ever.

She wore the look well. Lenore wore every look well.

"I'd be impressed by the detective work if I didn't already know you like spying on me to make sure I stay in line," I said to the Godmother dryly. "What do you want, Lenore?"

"To talk to you," she replied simply. "And to make sure that you have been keeping up with your end of our bargain."

"You expect a lot considering what you almost did to me and my school."

Lenore raised her eyebrows as if she genuinely didn't know what I was talking about. "How do you mean?"

"What do you mean how do I mean?" I spat. "You said as long as I didn't say anything about your skeevy protagonist selection practices that you'd leave me and my friends alone. Yet you, a Fairy Godmother of all things, helped magic hunters break into Lady Agnue's to try and have me kidnapped and almost got SJ, Blue, and the rest of the students killed in the process."

"Crisanta, that is absurd," Lenore responded. "While I am not denying that I have, on more than one occasion, workshopped how to get rid of you without being detected or violating the limitations of my power, I had nothing to do with the attack on your school."

"Oh yeah," I scoffed. "Then what were you doing so close to the grounds that night? How did you know our school was in trouble and that the In and Out Spell needed to be lowered?"

"Some of my Godmothers and I were patrolling the area near the schools for the same reason we are currently investigating Midveil and several other kingdoms across the realm," Lenore answered. "There is disorder afoot. A faction of commons is growing tired with the structure of the realm—protagonist selection, the exclusivity of the academies, even the treatment of Alderon. Your little friend Daniel is from Century City. I'm sure he must've told you about what's been going on there—the flag burnings, the missing persons, the murders."

I gulped but kept my expression neutral. "He mentioned

something."

"The danger is growing," Lenore continued. "These commons want to tear down the system we've built to keep Book running smoothly. They believe our realm's division of power is unfair and wish to be on the same level as protagonists, treated as if they are just as important when it just isn't so. As we have in the past, my Godmothers and I are working with the kingdoms' ambassadors to find the source of the discontent and silence the threat before it grows too extreme."

I always got slightly nervous whenever Lenore was this forthcoming with me. The last time she'd been completely open had been right before she'd tried to take my magic away. This frank conversation made me wonder what she wanted from me now. Nevertheless, I was not in the habit of cowering to her. And I was too angry over what happened at Lady Agnue's to show restraint either.

"If that's the case, allow me to narrow the search for you," I replied. "I'm looking at one of those sources of discontent right now."

"Amusing," Lenore scoffed. "But so far from the point it's laughable. I am not the enemy here, Crisanta. Contrary to what you might believe, I am the one trying to protect this world from destruction, from—"

"Change," I interrupted. "Yeah, I get it. Good luck with that, Lenore."

I turned my back and started to march out of the tunnel. In a flash the Godmother Supreme appeared in front of me, blocking my path.

"Make no mistake, Crisanta. I came to you today for more than just a routine check-in," the Godmother said.

*What'd I tell you? I had a feeling this was going somewhere unfavorable.*

Yet, once again, my spite and spirit outweighed my common sense.

"What, decide to skip the middle man and just end me yourself?" I crossed my arms. "Go ahead and try, Lenore. I dare you."

She glowered at me. Her hazel eyes burned deeply into

my skin, but I held my stance. Although it was ill-advised to threaten one of our realm's most powerful people, let alone a Fairy Godmother, I knew she couldn't hurt me. She'd told me so herself.

"Oh, that's right. You can't, can you?" I said sassily. "All that power and you can't use it to bring any serious, direct harm to me. Ironic, isn't it? You're such a fan of rules, but they're preventing you from doing the very thing that I know you're itching to do."

Lenore abruptly pulled the ring from her finger. She morphed it into her wand. I gulped, but chose not to reach for my own. Lenore still wanted something from me; I could tell from the way she was looking at me. As long as this was the case, I decided not to react. I didn't want her to think I was easily intimidated.

"I would watch that anger of yours, Crisanta," she said condescendingly. "Emotion clouds your judgment. If you continue to believe ridiculous notions like I was responsible for the magic hunter attack on your school, you'll fall down a rabbit hole from which you cannot escape."

My arms remained crossed with defiance. I was not buying what she was selling. Lenore could deny it all she wanted, but I was far from being naïve enough to believe her. I was certain that she was responsible for the magic hunters' attack on Lady Agnue's. Which meant she was to blame for the horror that had ensued that night—a horror that kept haunting me.

"That matter aside," Lenore went on, "there is a reason I came to you today."

Lenore waved her wand and with a scatter of red sparks a piece of parchment materialized out of thin air. She handed it to me. I was surprised and suspicious, but took it from her and began to read.

"*Daphne Reigns, Serge Wells, Aggie Black, Connor Erickson . . .* What is this?" I asked, holding up the list of two dozen names.

"Suspects under investigation," Lenore replied. "These are people with access to the Midveil palace who Susannah Marberg and I believe may be involved with the brewing commons rebellion. The list mainly consists of cleaning or kitchen staff members, but there is also a lady-in-waiting, a couple of men in the King's Guard, a groundskeeper, and . . ." Lenore nodded for me to keep reading.

I scanned the list of names until I reached the last one. "Pietro Knight? You can't be serious."

"Unfortunately, I am."

"How dare you, Lenore. That happens to be my brother you're talking about."

"*Adopted* brother if memory serves," Lenore corrected.

This infuriated me even more. I attempted to shove the list back at the Godmother, but she refused to take it.

"Keep it," she said. "Susannah or I will check back in with you in a couple of weeks to see if you have noticed anything peculiar about the people on this list."

"In case it's escaped your notice, Lenore, I care as little for Susannah as I do for you. Frankly, I hope someone eventually gains the power to overturn the lot of you. So why in Book would I ever do any of your dirty work?"

"Simple," Lenore responded with a shrug. "While you may not agree with the ways in which my colleagues and I run the realm, I hardly think you want any harm to befall your kingdom, let alone your own family. That is how these things start, you know. You may think me a ruthless traditionalist, and that change is a good thing. However, shifts in the world hardly ever occur without some casualties.

"Unless you want your kingdom and your family to be among the casualties of this commons rebellion, you will help us. The unrest is real and it is growing. We believe that the next phase in the commons' plan is to overthrow several kingdoms and eliminate their current rulers. I fear that if swift action is not taken soon, we will not be able to stop this conflict at its conception like we have with so many others over the years."

"What other conflicts?"

"Exactly," Lenore said.

She pushed past me to take her leave. "Just keep your eyes peeled, Crisanta, and keep your head down. What we've discussed today is merely one example of the many measures my associates and I will take to safeguard the old order. Mercy is never a priority when it comes to realm governance. The other higher-ups and I do not take kindly to those who mean to challenge us. Do you understand, my dear? There is nothing that will prevent me from protecting Book from chaos, from disruption, from—"

"From change?" I interrupted again.

Lenore smiled. "No dear, from *you*."

With that, the Godmother waved her wand. Sparks began to consume her and I stepped back. "Bear that in mind the next time you think yourself untouchable enough to test me," she said. Her face faded into a red glimmer, but her voice still remained. "After all, you wouldn't want anything as awful as those magic hunters to befall you again, would you?"

In a flash, the red sparks vanished and I was left scowling at empty space.

The cheers from the arena echoed louder as I merged back into the main corridor. They blurred around me like noise pollution. My glee had been sullied by Lenore's threats and propositions.

The commons rebellion had worried me when Daniel first mentioned it, but I hadn't dwelled on the matter. It seemed so far away at the time—at school, surrounded by other problems in the immediate vicinity, it was easy not to think about ones far away and out of my control. Now, though, it was different. I was out in the world, exposed to its greater problems and threats. The situation Lenore had described was scary, and she'd made it personal by implying that my family and kingdom were at risk.

I made it back to our row in the stands, but discovered Alex was gone. The score was 19–18 with Midveil in the lead. Despite this advantage, the energy of the game did not feel as infectious as before.

I stared down at the list Lenore had given me, specifically at Pietro's name. Part of me wanted to help Lenore. Much as I hated her and Sooz, I was smart enough to know that if they were coming to *me* for help, the threat was serious. But seeing my brother's name on that list irritated me to such a degree that it gave me misgivings. They were obviously wrong to consider him a suspect, and if they were wrong about that, what else were they wrong about? I had seen no hint of unrest in Midveil.

After a moment, I made the impulsive decision to crumple the note and throw it on the ground. It fell between the cracks of the row of seats in front of me—out of sight and out of mind.

"What happened to the popcorn?" Alex asked, reappearing by my side with a tray of nachos. "I figured I'd run into you on the way back from the snack stand, but didn't see you anywhere."

"I got sidetracked," I replied, speaking the truth. "Care to share?"

"Ugh, fine." He extended the tray. "But next time you're on your own."

"Yeah, yeah," I replied as I shoved a chip into my mouth. "Just pass the guacamole."

# CHAPTER 24

## *Surreptitious Knights*

idveil won the match, I ate three candy apples and half a plate of nachos, and on the way back to the castle I found a rock shaped like a bear that I thought intriguing enough to stuff into my pocket and take with me.

Despite Lenore's efforts, it turned out to be a lovely day. And it remained such until we returned home and I entered my bedroom. As I was putting the interestingly shaped rock on my fireplace mantle, I saw something on my bedspread.

It was a note. When I unfolded it, I discovered it was the same list Lenore had given me, which I'd discarded back at the arena. I scowled at the thing, scrunched it up again, and tossed it in the trash. Alas, the document did not take the hint. Over the next several days the list reappeared when I was least expecting it. I found it in my left boot in the morning, within the pages of a library book on another day, and even stuffed in my sandwich at lunch one afternoon. Evidently Lenore had written the list on magic paper, which meant it could not be destroyed or lost until it served its purpose.

As the days ticked on, serve its purpose it did. The more I looked at the list, the more I was forced to realize that my decision to disregard it had been rash. I had reacted with emotion, not logic on the day of the Twenty-Three Skidd match. Lenore filled me with such spite, and that spite made me want to do the exact opposite of whatever she wanted. Now that I had the chance to think about things without being blinded by rage, my mind had changed. My concern over the commons rebellion outweighed my dislike for the Godmother Supreme. And my concern for the implications such a rebellion might have on my family and kingdom outmatched my own personal vendettas.

I started to pay closer attention to the people on Lenore's list. When I passed them in the corridors or on the grounds, I watched them more carefully. In doing so, I was disappointed and troubled when I did, in fact, witness peculiar behavior. Sometimes this could be as simple as one of them passing a note in the hallways or loitering in some random room in the castle. On other occasions, the behavior manifested in more disconcerting manners. The first example of this occurred on a Wednesday while I was reading in the arboretum.

It was in the death of the afternoon. I was sitting on a high branch of a ficus tree with a book in my hand. I used to dread climbing. However, our adventure to find the Author had been jam-packed with all sorts of challenges, climbing included, so I was trying to work past my weakness to be better prepared for next time.

As I sat there, two palace staff members, Daphne Reigns (one of my ladies-in-waiting) and Aggie Black, slipped into the arboretum. Both girls were on Lenore's watch list. They didn't see me and, thinking that they were alone, conversed openly.

"Did you receive word from her?" Aggie whispered.

I looked down. The two girls were nervous—glancing around to make sure no one was coming. Even from up here I thought Aggie seemed sweaty. There was dirt and twigs on her apron, so I assumed she'd been running around outside. This seemed a bit suspicious, as she was normally assigned to work in the kitchen.

"Yes," Daphne replied as she tucked a strand of strawberry-blonde hair behind one ear and checked over her shoulder. "I received a message this morning. She says our master is still securing members of the King's Guard. He needs a bit longer so we can fully count on them to cooperate the day that phase two commences."

Aggie nodded. "And what about the princess? Her presence here was never intended. Have they taken that into account?"

"Yes. He insists that she is to remain unharmed, but our lady says not to concern ourselves with that technicality. In fact, between you and me, she has instructed us with ensuring that—"

I heard footsteps. The girls stopped talking and scurried out of the arboretum. I stayed in my position for a couple of minutes until I was sure they were gone. When all was silent again, I snapped my book shut, scampered down the tree, and took off toward my room, Daphne and Aggie's words ringing in my ears.

*It couldn't be,* I insisted to myself as I rode the lift. *It just couldn't be.*

While I had elected to keep my eyes peeled for the people on Lenore's list, the one person I'd refused to spy on was my brother. Pietro was no traitor. He was a prince and a protagonist, the trusted leader of the King's Guard, and my brother. There was absolutely no reason to doubt him or his loyalty . . . until I had overheard Aggie and Daphne's conversation.

Desperate to talk to someone objective, I bolted the door to my bedroom, pulled out my Mark Two, and called Liza. When she answered, I described what Lenore had told me at the Twenty-Three Skidd match and what had happened with Daphne and Aggie. I hoped that my magical mentor could give me some information about Pietro's protagonist book that would reassure me of his future actions and fate, and calm my doubts about him. Regrettably, what Liza offered ended up being the opposite of reassuring.

"What do you mean, he doesn't have a book?" I exclaimed.

"I'm sorry, Crisa. But it's the truth," Liza said. "Not all royals are born with books. You learned that last semester. And anyway, it is my understanding that Pietro is not even really royalty. He is adopted, is he not?"

"Yes," I begrudgingly admitted. "Technically he is not royal born; he is common born. The Scribes did not unveil a protagonist book when he was a baby like they do with all royal children. But later when he was five, the Scribes came to my parents with a protagonist book. They said the Author chose him as a common protagonist and he could attend Lord Channing's."

"The Scribes clearly had a book forged for him, Crisa," Liza replied. "I realize it must be upsetting, but you shouldn't be so surprised. After all, SJ doesn't have a book."

I groaned and began pacing the room. "First my best friend, then Pietro. Next you're going to tell me that Alex doesn't have a book either."

Liza didn't respond, which made me stop.

"Liza?"

A pained expression appeared on her face. Then she nodded.

"Are you kidding me?"

"I am afraid not," she sighed.

"Why didn't you say something before?"

"For this exact reason," she explained. "I knew how you'd react. Furthermore, you told me how knowledge of not having a book created friction with SJ. I didn't want to cause you any more distress, especially knowing what's coming, and knowing that soon enough you will—"

"Stop," I said, cutting her off angrily. "I was serious when I said I don't want to know what you've seen of my fate, Liza. It's bad enough having to see the future on my own—witness the horrors awaiting others. I don't want any more unnatural awareness influencing my path. You can think that decision cowardly or unwise if you like, but I don't care.

"If there really is so much riding on me and my choices, I can't afford to be weighed down by worrying about the future. I have to make decisions without being afraid. As for my brothers . . ." I paused and took a breath. "I'm sorry I yelled at you for not telling me sooner. You were right to keep this from me."

"Perhaps I was before," Liza replied steadily. "But the reason I told you about Pietro now was because, based on what you've told me, I fear you may need to reconsider how you regard him. My sister is a lot of things, Crisa, but foolish is not one of them. If she suspects your brother, then I think maybe it would be best if you kept your mind open to the idea that the people in your life may not be who you think they are. Pietro could very well be a part of the commons rebellion."

I felt a knot form in my throat. "And you and Lenore could

very well be totally wrong," I argued. "Maybe this whole threat isn't even as severe as Lenore thinks." I was trying to convince myself as much as her. "I mean, I know what's been happening in Century City is bad. But our realm is huge and the commons rebellion activities have only been occurring in that one part. When Lenore and I talked she made it sound like the whole realm could be in danger, just like she implied its been threatened by rebellions in the past. But she was clearly exaggerating on that front. I've never heard of a single rebellion in Book posing a danger to our entire realm. If such a thing existed, we would know."

"You mean just like you used to *know* that 'The Author' controlled your lives and that your fate was out of your control?"

My eyes narrowed. "What are you saying?"

"Crisa," Liza continued, "until recently you have lived in a bubble that the Fairy Godmothers and realm higher-ups created for you. Everything you knew, in essence, was a lie. What makes you think that there isn't more about the realm that they've kept from you to maintain order?"

I stared hard at her reflection.

"There is so much that people don't know, Crisa," Liza sighed, "and you've only scratched the surface. These mutterings of unrest and rebellion my sister discussed with you are one such example, the likes of which I can assure you are *very* real. I've been around for close to two centuries, so I know what Lena is talking about. Moreover, I am privy to the details of her work that she keeps from the greater populace.

"There have been many attempts at rebellion over the years by commons, Crisa—attempts to overthrow Godmothers, and royals, and protagonist selection. But each time these conflicts grow big enough to call attention to themselves, Lena and the other realm leaders put a stop to them. That is the only reason you don't know about their existence.

"But if Lena has come to you with this information—and is asking for your help—that can only mean that things are different this time. Which is why I must advise you to believe her, and to take the matter seriously even where Pietro is concerned. The commons rebellion may be limited to Century City right now, but it could spread in the blink of an eye. For all you know, it already has and is just waiting to catch fire."

"Alex, have you noticed anything weird going on with Pietro lately?" I asked as I leaned against the wall of the gymnasium.

My brother looked up from the bench press and furrowed his eyebrows. "What do you mean?"

"I'm not sure," I admitted all too truthfully. "I'm just asking."

"Well," Alex puffed as he continued his workout. "Nothing comes to mind. He started dating some girl who's a real handful. I met her about a month ago. She wears *a lot* of leather and she chewed my ear off about the latest bill passed by the Midveil Parliament. Beyond that, though, I can't think of anything out of the ordinary. He spends most of his time with the King's Guard."

"Yeah." I nodded. "I know."

"And . . . twenty!" Alex announced as he finished his last set.

As he re-racked the weights, I detected something out of place. Or rather, something missing from its place.

"Alex, where are your wristbands?" I asked.

For years, Alex had worn several bands around his left wrist. They were mementos that he never took off. One was a leather bracelet that he and his friends had commissioned when a mate of theirs had been killed in a carriage accident years ago. It bore the boy's name and the date of his passing. Alex and the others wore the bands as a forever reminder of their lost friend.

Another band was a simple knotted piece of red rope that had been taken from the garland placed upon Alex's head the first year he'd won Midveil's annual sword fighting tournament—the day everyone in the kingdom first began respecting him as their future king.

Finally, the third wristband Alex usually wore was a thin gold one inscribed with our family's motto. It had been mine, but I'd given it to him when he'd first gone to Lord Channing's, hoping that as he went off into the big, exciting world and learned to be a hero, he wouldn't forget me—his small, unremarkable sister.

He promised that he never would. And true to his word, every summer when he came home from school he made time to hang out with me, mentor me, and teach me sword skills. We'd spent so much time together over the years that I'd come to think of him as not just my brother, but my close friend.

It became our tradition to take turns wearing the sentimental gold wristband. At the end of summer before classes started again one of us would pass the keepsake on to the other to be worn until the next year.

I had given it to him last September before I'd returned to school, so he should have been wearing it now. The fact that he wasn't, and that the two other bands were nowhere to be seen, instantly threw me. Had he not been wearing them this whole time? I thought back. I couldn't remember if I'd seen them on his wrist since coming back. I'd just assumed they were there.

"I got rid of them," Alex replied.

"Got rid of them?" I exclaimed.

"Relax," he said. "I didn't throw them out. I put them away. They're in my room, so you can have your bracelet back if you want."

"I don't understand," I stammered. "Why don't you want to wear them anymore? You've always worn them. I thought they mattered to you."

"They do," he said. "But it's like you said, I've *always* worn them. And, well, I got tired of carrying around the weight."

"It's not like they're shackles, Alex," I protested. "They're memories. They're your past."

"Same thing." He shrugged as he reached for his water bottle. "Especially when you're trying to look to the future. Trust me."

When he finished chugging his water, he looked at me sadly. "You're disappointed, aren't you?"

"I guess I'm confused," I replied. "I want to know what happened with you. What changed?"

"What happened was that I grew up, Crisa," Alex said as he grabbed his stuff and headed for the door. "Maybe it's time you do the same."

I stood in the gym alone for a few minutes before I made

my way into the hall and decided to go outside to see Lucky. I stopped in my tracks when I heard Pietro's voice. Cautiously, I poked my head around the corner.

Pietro was standing at the end of the corridor talking with Aggie Black. The arched ceilings cast shadows over the pair as they conversed.

"Did you find out?" Pietro asked Aggie, glancing behind him to make sure no one was following.

I held my breath as Aggie responded.

"Yes," she replied. "And I'll make sure she gets the message. But, your highness, I still don't see why you cannot do this. You have much more access. Wouldn't it be simpler for you to simply explain the truth to her yourself?"

"I don't want her getting involved past what's required," Pietro responded. "I've said it before and I'll say it again, I want her protected. Furthermore, until I'm certain of who can and cannot be trusted around here, I don't want to send up any unnecessary red flags. I already feel like I'm being watched, that they suspect I know something. So until I have what we need, I cannot afford to take any chances with showing my hand."

Footsteps echoed in the distance, halting Pietro's conversation with the girl.

"Go," he said. "Make your move when you're certain the conditions are right."

I heard two pairs of shoes in motion. The daintier pair moving farther away had to be Aggie's. Which meant that the ones rapidly coming my way were Pietro's.

I stood up straight. He'd be next to me in seconds. There was no time to retreat so I cantered forward, "accidentally" running into him as he rounded the corner.

"Oh, uh, sorry," I said as I moved around him.

"Crisa. Hey!" he said. "What's up?"

"Um, nothing." I replied. "What's up with you?"

"Same old, same old. Where've you been? We hung out almost every day the week you came back when you were teaching me to fly your dragon. But since our last lesson I feel like the only time I see you is at dinner."

I thought quickly. I didn't want him to know I'd been avoiding him since Lenore planted those suspicions in my head, which I inadvertently had.

"I've been busy." I said. "Take home schoolwork, you know? Lady Agnue didn't exactly send me away for a vacation."

"Fair enough," my brother replied. "Still, it'd be cool to hang out with my little sis while she's home. You want to hit the combat room later and do some sparring? Maybe after dinner?"

"Um, you know, I actually pulled a muscle earlier so . . . maybe some other time?"

"Definitely," he responded.

A few members of the King's Guard came into view down the hall, nodding to Pietro. I noticed his expression darken ever so slightly.

"I gotta go," he said. "You sure you're okay? You look kind of pale."

"I'm fine. That, um, muscle I pulled really hurts," I replied. "Now go on. You have better things to do than worry about me. Those guys are waiting for you, aren't they?"

He smiled and patted me on the head. "Yeah, but give me a shout if you ever need me. In the meantime, whatever you're doing, be careful. One misstep and you could really get hurt."

"Yeah," I said. "You're preaching to the choir."

Pretty much every part of my body pulsed with exhaustion.

I'd been pushing myself with my magic training every day, but today I'd increased my efforts in order to better distract myself from the brewing doubts I had about Pietro and my anger toward Alex.

Honestly, I didn't know which of my brothers was rattling me more. My observations connecting Pietro to the commons rebellion weirded me out, but he was my brother. Adopted or not, he would not betray me or my parents or my kingdom. I knew him too well to believe that . . . at least without proof. Alex, meanwhile, was just annoying me. One minute he and I were best buds, the next he was cold and callous. The whole thing gave me emotional whiplash.

I thought on this as I made my way back to the castle through the stables. This was a mistake. I didn't think twice about it at first, but as the smell of wood and hay filled my nose, dark memories ignited.

I tried to push the magic hunters to the rear of my mind, but I couldn't keep them at bay. My body tensed as I remembered the feeling of being drugged by those Poppies, the heat of the fire, and the arrows flying so close to my skin.

Suddenly a horse in the stall to my right whinnied loudly and rose on his hind legs, his front hooves rising above me. Startled, I slipped and fell. My vision blurred for a second and my heart raced. I shut my eyes to drive the sensation away, but images of horses stampeding and wooden beams crashing down flashed through my mind. The smells of burnt wood, sweat, and ash seemed too real. They suffocated me as I remembered being flattened to the ground—lying helplessly with a hunter's boot pressed into my back.

*No.*

I forced my eyes open and willed myself to look around at my surroundings for a reality check.

*It's just a horse.*

*This is just a stable.*

*And those are just memories.*

I got up and dusted myself off. I hated being plagued by these fears. Maybe my mother was right. Maybe I did need to talk to someone. Opening up about my worries to Daniel had really helped in my previous trying times. Just because he had betrayed my trust didn't mean everyone I let in would. It was only a matter of picking the right person.

I hurriedly exited the stables. Not feeling like going back to the castle anymore, I found my way to Lucky on the main lawn. He was enjoying his afternoon nap.

I lay on the grass beside him. It was about as close to a peaceful place as I could find around here. Or so I thought. The curse of an overactive mind was that it didn't matter the exact setting; thoughts would follow you everywhere.

My brain simmered on the commons rebellion.

In all my years as a protagonist I had been unhappy with the way our realm was run. I didn't like the Author deciding who I would be, putting my life on a single track without my having a say. But at least my track had been a blessed one, full of tiaras and gowns and castles. Commons didn't have that.

I recalled a conversation Daniel and I had last semester. He asserted that antagonists were brave because they were commons who'd chosen to disregard the wishes of the Author and the realm's higher-ups to be something more than basic ensemble characters. I'd disagreed with his statement, but he'd countered with, *"Are you sure you don't just feel that way because you're a protagonist? You've never had to struggle and fight like a common. You don't know what a desperate person—someone poor or pushed around—might do to feel important, let alone feed their families."*

It was true that the lives of main characters were much more regulated and controlled than the commons'. We had to go to specific schools, act a certain way, and learn certain skills so we could grow up to be certain people. The commons didn't have to deal with that type of micromanagement. The drawback was that our realm's higher-ups didn't care about managing them at all. If commons had problems, they didn't get Fairy Godmothers to fix them. If they desired an education, they couldn't count on the government to provide one. If their lives were difficult, their needs would be at the bottom of the ambassadors' docket—always underneath those of protagonists.

Given that, I could understand why discontent might grow over the years. These rebelling commons wanted a world where they weren't treated like second-class citizens. They wanted to matter and have the right to be the main characters of their own stories. Now they were pushing back against people like Lena Lenore who stood in the way.

The words of the Fairy Godmother Supreme about the commons rebellion whispered at the corners of my mind. *"They believe our realm's division of power is unfair and wish to be on the same level as protagonists, treated as if they are just as important when it just isn't so."*

Lenore's statement expressed the views of those who controlled

Book. So it was no wonder this was happening. If I were in the commons' shoes, I would be ticked off. Being thought of that way would suck.

In retrospect this brewing commons rebellion had always only been a matter of time. After all—even with the good fortune of a privileged upbringing—I could only put up with the realm's rules and the Author's limitations for so long. After nearly seventeen years, I had been pushed too far and decided things needed to change. Hence my quest to find the Author. Now a faction of commons felt the same way and was fighting back. I could understand that. I could empathize with that. *However*, what I could not understand nor empathize with was people hurting others on their way to accomplishing this agenda.

There had been murders in Century City. People were missing. And Lenore said she and the higher-ups believed the next phase of the commons' plan was to overthrow several kingdoms and eliminate their current rulers. Although I didn't like Lenore and I didn't like the way the realm was run, I did not endorse anything that would put innocent people at risk, let alone my family, my friends, and my friends' families. I believed in change, but not like this.

"Crisa?"

I opened my eyes. A gingery-blonde head blocked the sunlight and spilled a shadow over me.

"Sooz." I sat up and tried to get to my feet, but the tiredness I'd been feeling from Magic Exhaustion caused me to falter.

"Are you all right?" she reached out to help but I curtly brushed her hand away.

"Fine," I snapped. "Just a bit dizzy."

I patted Lucky on the side to wish him goodbye. He opened one golden eye and exhaled. I started to march away. Sooz followed.

"Can I help you with something?" I asked.

"I wanted to see how you were doing."

"Again, I'm fine," I replied.

"Good. And, well, I also wanted to ask you a question."

"Ask away," I said without slowing down.

"Okay. Here it is then," Sooz said slowly. "Crisa, have you been avoiding me?"

That made me stop. We'd reached a corridor running alongside the castle. It was held up on either side by tall, slender columns. The floor was tiled in various shades of blue glass that shined in the light.

I turned to meet Sooz's gaze and studied her critically. Due to the fact that I *had* been avoiding her, I hadn't really gotten a chance to see how she'd changed in the months that I'd been gone. It felt like I was looking at her for the first time in a while.

Her hair was long like it had been when I was much younger and she'd let me play with it to practice my braiding. It seemed she'd put on some weight, probably from spending too much time at a desk working through her breaks. The bags under her eyes were darker; she'd had more stress and less sleep.

Despite the external factors, the greatest difference in Sooz's appearance came from the way she looked at me. We'd had an unofficial big sister/little sister relationship for years. When she used to look at me, her eyes had always been filled with kindness, understanding, and warmth. Now her eyes seemed harder. She gazed at me with hesitation, suspicion, and a touch of fear—the same way I looked at her.

"No," I lied. "I haven't been avoiding you. It's a big castle. Other than at dinner, I don't even see my own parents most of the time."

"Yes, but square-footage aside, we both know that you don't cross paths with your parents by your own design, not chance. Which again, is what makes me believe you are intentionally doing the same with me."

"You're making something out of nothing." I shrugged as I resumed walking. "Why would I be avoiding you?"

"Maybe because you know what the other ambassadors and I have been doing to influence protagonist selection?"

I stopped again.

"Lenore told me that you and your friends found out," she explained. "That you've known since the last Summit meeting but have been keeping it a secret."

I'd been trying so hard every day to keep my anger toward Sooz bottled up, resisting the urge to express to her the many things that I wanted to. But her provocation was just the nudge I needed.

"Did Lenore also mention that the only reason we're keeping it a secret is because she is blackmailing me?" I asked.

"Yes," Sooz sighed, sort of remorsefully. "That was mentioned."

I put my hands on my hips and the fury I'd been harboring lashed out like a cornered dog. "Then I guess the following should go without saying. Though—since I still can't believe what a rotten traitor you are—I'll say it anyway. You're despicable, Susannah. Our kingdom trusts you. My family trusts you. I trusted you. How can you go along with what the head Fairy Godmothers and the other ambassadors are doing? Forging protagonist books for royals, destroying protagonist books to meet some stupid quota, helping Lenore with her agenda—it's not right. You're a coward for standing by all these years and letting it happen."

"I know the amount of trust your family places in me," Sooz replied fervently. "And it was in honor of that trust—the oath of service to them and to you—that I've done my duty. Your brothers and your best friend were born without books, Crisa. Had the ambassadors and I not rigged the system, they would have been cast as commons and seen as lepers in the royal community. Pietro already has a difficult enough time getting respect in noble circles what with his adoption. Can you imagine how he'd have been treated growing up if he'd just been a common?

"And consider SJ and Alex. They are both first in line for their thrones, but how secure would those positions be if not for the intervention of the ambassadors? Think about it. What kingdom would want a common as a ruler? None. Because while protagonists are something special—leaders, heroes, champions—commons are just that: common.

"So I ask you, Crisa, was it really so despicable to destroy three commons' books in order to make room at the academies for SJ and your brothers? Was it really so cowardly to forge books for three of the people you care about most in the world when doing so saved them from a life of ridicule and persecution? And if given the choice, would you have done any different?"

I stared at Sooz. Since learning the truth about protagonist selection I'd never even considered that the ambassadors had been doing the right thing. They had no authority to mess with people's fates. But having lived through the awful insecurity that SJ's lack of a protagonist book caused, I wondered how convinced I was in regards to my answer to Sooz's question. This was the well-being of my brothers and my best friend we were talking about. So if given the choice, would I really *have* done any differently?

My mind swirled with conflict for a moment. And then the storm cleared, and I saw things clearly.

Since we found out she didn't have a book, I'd been telling SJ that she didn't need one to be special. With or without one, she was an exemplary princess, a skilled potionist, and a brilliant inventor. I didn't say this to make her feel better; they were truths that anyone could see.

Meanwhile, knowing I had a book—let alone discovering the serious nature of my prologue prophecy—hadn't made me special. It'd gotten me noticed, sure, but what made me special was my character—my strengths, my weaknesses, my choices, my spirit. I didn't need the validation of some higher power to tell me what those traits would allow me to amount to. I knew by my own accord. And SJ should've known the same.

Therefore, although I wanted the best for her, and Alex, and Pietro, I felt certain that if they hadn't been selected as protagonists they would have still become the same people that they were today. Maybe their roads would have been harder. And maybe they would've had to prove themselves more regularly. But if they were the people I knew them to be, it wouldn't have mattered. The world would have eventually seen them for what they were and what they were meant to be, heedless of the class they were born into. They would've been protagonists. Not because "the Author" or the realm's higher-ups deemed them to be, but because their characters warranted it.

"You know what, Sooz," I finally said. "I get where you're coming from. My experience with SJ has shown me what kind of effect not having a protagonist book can have on a person's self-esteem."

"So you understand that what the other ambassadors and I are doing is for the best?" Sooz asked earnestly, a touch of hope in her voice. "You can forgive me?"

"I didn't say that," I replied. "I understand your reasons, but that doesn't mean I think you're right."

Sooz crossed her arms and looked down on me with the intimidating glare she used when trying to close a deal with government officials. I was unfazed. I'd faced too many monsters to cower to one in a teal sweater and matching pumps.

I mirrored her stance. "I understand why you forged the books for Alex, Pietro, and SJ," I said bluntly. "When those you care about are on the line even the most ethical people have trouble seeing straight. But that doesn't change the fact that it is wrong and you've had over five years of service as an ambassador to realize that. Five years to realize that what you're all doing is wrong." I paused for a moment and sighed. "It took me five seconds, Sooz."

A couple of my mother's ladies-in-waiting came down the corridor then. They paused their conversation and bowed as they passed. When their footsteps had dissipated, I nodded to Sooz. "I should go," I said. "You and I have nothing left to discuss."

As I made to move past her, Susannah suddenly reached out and grabbed me by the wrist. I tried to shake her off; but she did not let go. She held onto me with a surprisingly tight grip.

"We do have one more thing left to discuss, Crisa. The matter of the list Lenore gave you."

All the gentleness with which she'd been handling our conversation was gone. She was all business now, done wasting her time trying to get me on her side.

"You mean the list of people the two of you are accusing of treachery? Isn't it a bit hypocritical for you to have input on such a thing?" I asked as I glowered at her.

"Hilarious," Sooz scoffed. "Just tell me. Have you noticed anything peculiar about the people on the list or not?"

My rage had built up enough again to provoke me into wanting to say nothing just to spite her, but thankfully logic won out this round. Whether I liked it or not, the Godmother Supreme had been onto something that day in the shadows of the Twenty-Three Skidd stadium. There was something suspicious going on within the walls of Midveil Castle. If Lenore was right about the next phase of the commons rebellion involving overthrowing kingdoms and eliminating rulers, I had to do what I could to minimize the risk to my family. Even if that meant cooperating with the likes of her and Sooz.

"Daphne Reigns, Aggie Black, Donald Smith, Blaine Weldhouse, and John Coolson," I said bitterly. "Those are the people on your list that I've noticed acting weird. If you and your wand-wielding boss are looking into people around the palace, I'd start with them."

"And what about Pietro?" Sooz asked, squeezing my wrist tighter. "Our sources say he might be one of the main players in this, the one giving the orders."

Ire surged through me and I vehemently shook off Sooz's grip. "Well, your sources are wrong. He has nothing to do with this. And so help me, Sooz, if you or Lenore go anywhere near him, or tell anyone else your suspicions about his loyalties, you won't have to worry about the commons starting a rebellion. I don't care what either of you do to me, I'll tell everyone the truth about protagonist selection and start a rebellion myself. Got it?"

I turned and stormed away.

"You're letting your feelings for him cloud your judgment, Crisa," she called. "If you were really as morally noble as you are pretending to be, you'd see the signs."

I didn't look at her. But as I continued down the corridor, I couldn't help but wonder if she was right.

# CHAPTER 25

## The Message

t had been one of those days.

Much to my own surprise, I hadn't felt like practicing magic today. I'd been pushing myself hard for the past three weeks and I'd woken up feeling totally drained.

This wasn't only because of the physical exertion involved with channeling magic; another side effect of my increased practice was more nightmares. The amount of power I used directly correlated with the clarity and number of visions that filled my head. As a result, my sleep had been pretty eventful since coming home.

And yet . . . even this wasn't the true cause of my exhaustion and stress.

By now I was more or less used to seeing the future in my dreams. And I'd been expecting the consequence of increased dreams with more magic. What I had not anticipated was being plagued with flashes of the past. It was those suffocating memories that caused me the most distress. Images of the magic hunters and their brutal attack continued seeping into my slumber. When they came back they short-circuited my visions of the future, eventually waking me up in fear and panic.

Like this morning. Everything was going fine in dreamland. I was having a stream of vision flashes that, like several previous nights, seemed connected by the theme of Neverland. I saw tiny fairies with multi-colored, flashing wings. Pirates milling around a dock. And—extremely on the nose—an alleyway that led to a storefront window with the sign "Neverland's Best Souvenir Shop." Then something peculiar happened. I was in a void and a man appeared.

The only person who'd ever spoken to me in a dream directly, not as a part of a vision, had been Liza. This was something new and therefore interesting. The man was about sixty and had a long, wispy, white beard. He wore a silver-and-dark-blue robe with a utility belt that held an assortment of leather pouches. In his hand was a crazy staff that ended in a ridged, twisted point like a mining drill.

"Finally," he said. "I've been trying to reach you for an eternity, but this darn cave blocks my projection."

"Sorry?" I said. "Who are you?"

"Not important, Crisanta. I'm here to talk to you about where you go next. You and your friends need to go to Never—"

I was flattened to the ground. All of a sudden my dream was overpowered by memories of the magic hunters. My body was on the floor of the barn with the hunters holding me down; I could feel the ache of the arrow wound I'd sustained. I struggled and looked up. Parker approached. The flames and shadows behind him were even more malicious than I remembered. I tried to escape the memory, but continued reliving flashes of it until leering images of Parker eventually woke me with a jolt of terror.

As I lay in bed, I realized the time had come to heed my mother's advice and let someone in. It was a difficult decision to make, and I was reluctant to make it at all given the afterburn of Daniel pushing me away. But I desperately needed to talk to someone. If I didn't, I knew soon enough my fears might cause me to crack.

By the afternoon I'd decided I would talk to Alex. His recent mood swings had been throwing me, but he had always been my friend, a good brother, and a kind of mentor. I trusted that when it mattered most he was someone I could put my trust in. Now I simply needed the right opportunity to do it.

"Crisanta?"

I lifted my head on hearing my mother's voice on the other side of my bedroom door.

In lieu of doing some of the take home schoolwork Lady Agnue had assigned me, I'd been reading my Shadow Guardians book for the majority of the afternoon, swaddled up on my bed in a large wool sweater. I'd brought the book with me from Lady Agnue's but had been concentrating so hard on my magic over the last few weeks that I had yet to touch it. Until today it'd been hidden in one of my desk drawers beneath a pile of miscellaneous letters, postcards, and receipts I'd collected over the years. Today there was a storm brewing outside, so it seemed like the right time to put a pin in my magic practice in favor of some reading.

I hadn't found anything interesting in the Shadow Guardians book since that big discovery back at school. However, I did come across a picture of an actual Shadow. It was my first exposure to what the creatures looked like and—in a word—it was horrifying. The Shadow was black, jagged, and flat like an evil ink stain. It had a crooked, blood-red mouth and shining slit eyes. Just seeing it in the book made me shudder and I quickly turned the page.

When I heard my mom's voice at the door my eyes immediately darted to the untouched pot of tea on the platter on my nightstand. Every day my ladies-in-waiting brought me afternoon tea at my mother's request. She loved the stuff, and whenever I was home she tried to force me to drink it because she thought it was more ladylike than the coffee or hot chocolate I preferred. Despite her efforts, I avoided the beverage whenever possible. Both Pietro and I hated tea.

Not wanting to hurt my mother's feelings, I launched myself from the bed and grabbed the pot—long grown cold—by the handle.

"Hold on a second, Mom!" I called.

I thrust open the balcony doors and dumped the contents over the side of the railing. Then I scurried back inside, latched the doors, and put the pot back on the platter.

"Come in," I said.

The door handle turned and I had a mini panic attack when I saw the Shadow Guardians book still lying on my comforter. I thrust the text under the bed then hopped back on the mattress before the door opened.

My mother strode in smiling. "Studying hard, Pumpkin?"

"Yup, sure am," I said, trying to look as casual as possible surrounded by the paperwork I'd been using to translate the Shadow Guardians book. Hopefully my mother thought it was part of my homework.

"Well, perhaps you can take a short break," my mom continued. "You have mail." She held out an envelope in her hand.

This got me excited. I had been corresponding with Blue and Jason during my stay at home. They'd kept me updated on the various happenings around school. More importantly, they'd given me updates about their Wonderland mapmaking progress. Naturally these messages were encoded. Jason had taken a code decryption course last year and had shown me and Blue some of the basics. I was easily able to translate the jumbled text in their letters for the news I sought.

"Who from?" I asked.

"Chance Darling," she responded.

The eagerness in my expression sank. "Oh." I took the envelope from my mother and noticed that the golden seal on the outside was broken. "You opened it."

"I know how much trouble you have opening envelopes," my mother replied.

I chose not to rebut this comment. She wasn't wrong, but it sucked that this literally gave her a free pass to look at my mail. I took out the folded letter and read:

> *Dear Crisanta,*
>
> *I wanted to come and visit you after I heard what happened the night of the fire at Lady Agnue's. However, knowing how fond you are of my presence, I decided that you did not need to feel any worse.*
>
> *Within this brief message, I cannot properly tell you how I felt when I learned what almost occurred. So I shall not attempt to. A fact for which I am sure you just released a huge sigh of relief.*
>
> *Instead, I shall say this. Please be well, and know that you*

*are missed. I will be thinking of you and hope that, even if it is for just a moment, this letter allows you to think of me too. In a non-irritated manner, that is.*

*Sincerely Yours,*

*Chance Darling*

*P.S. I have not forgotten my promise to prove my affections for you are genuine. By the time you return to school, I believe I will have finally found a way.*

I felt my lips curve into a small smile as I folded the note. This was due in part to his relentlessness, and also in part to the gladness over being reminded of school and life outside this castle. The smile vanished when I looked up at my grinning mother.

"So . . ." she said, overly cheerfully.

"So . . ." I echoed back.

"You did not tell me that Chance Darling was courting you. He is a lovely boy, and the Darlings are a wonderful family. I always told his parents when we used to visit them up north that the two of you would make a lovely couple."

"Mom!" I groaned. "What's happening with Chance and me is my business. And anyway, we're not a couple."

"You mean he is not attempting to court you?" my mother asked, confused.

"No. He definitely is," I responded.

"Then what is the problem?"

"The problem is that I don't want him to. We're too different. I could never actually," I grimaced, "*date* someone like him. I don't even know if I like him as a person, let alone as a boy."

My mother nodded. "That is fair enough. Love at first sight is not a happenstance for every person like it was for your father and me. Some people attain true love through friendship that deepens over time. Perhaps that is the route you are meant to take."

"Yeah, sure," I said, scooting my mother out of the room before the conversation could get any more awkward. "That's got to be it. Look, we'll talk later, Mom. I have schoolwork to do."

"All right, Pumpkin. I shall see you at dinner."

"Yup, sounds good. Bye now."

I closed the door behind her and locked it.

*And I thought my conversation with Alex about dating had been uncomfortable.*

Though I supposed the next conversation I needed to have with him would be even harder.

"When did you become such a good swimmer?"

I wiped away the water in my eyes with one hand as I held on to the edge of our indoor swimming pool with the other. Alex was looking down at me. He was dripping too, but with sweat. He must've been working out in the gym next door.

My brother's face warbled in the reflection of the pool's waters. The fluorescent pink lights at the bottom made his hair look blonder and his eyes seem paler.

"Last semester I had some aquatic-related adventures in Adelaide," I explained. "I promised myself that I would try to get a pool installed at Lady Agnue's after that. She said no, of course, and I never got a chance to try the one at Lord Channing's. But that doesn't mean I can't make use of the one here. Figured I might as well add another skill to my repertoire, you know."

Alex nodded and took a piece of paper out of his pocket—the note I'd slid under his door this morning.

"Care to explain?"

"I wanted to talk to you," I said reluctantly. "Do you have a minute?"

He pulled over a bench and sat. I leaned both arms against the edge of the pool and let my chin rest against them with a sigh. This was it. This was to be my first attempt at letting someone in on my vulnerabilities since Daniel. I bit back the uncertainty. It had to be done. I not only needed someone to trust; I needed to know that I *could* trust someone again.

"I've been having a lot of stressful dreams," I admitted to Alex, finally voicing the truth. "Ever since the magic hunter attack, I can't seem to make them stop. I think I'm suppressing a lot about that night and I really need someone to talk to. I need someone to listen and not judge me for it, or try to be overprotective, or make me feel weak and small. I need someone to just be there for me." I glanced up at my brother. "Can I trust you to do that, Alex? If I let you in, can I count on you not to let me down?"

"Crisa, of course you can," my brother said evenly. "You can trust me with anything. I would never betray your trust and I would never let you down. You know that."

I gulped and steadied myself.

"All right then. Here's the truth," I said. "I know I act like nothing bothers me, but it's not true." I stared into the water as the memories came back and emotion welled up in my throat. "That night with the hunters was terrifying," I said in a whisper. "It wasn't only the fire and the arrows—the hunters also dosed me with a Poppy Potion. To be drugged like that was the scariest experience of my life because all of my strength, my weapons, my fighting skill, and my magic, didn't matter. They weren't enough to save me. If my friend Girtha hadn't shown up when she did, I would have been killed. It's not the first time I've had a brush with death—but before I didn't have so much riding on me. I can't go into it with you right now, but there are a lot of people relying on me these days. And that night makes me wonder . . . how can I possibly hope to protect others when I can't even protect myself?"

There was a drawn out pause before Alex responded.

"Maybe you need to stop thinking about others."

I perked up with a touch of indignation. "What?"

"Crisa, you're young and you've only begun defining your story. If you keep worrying so much about how your destiny affects others, then you're never going to be able to take care of yourself properly and give *yourself* what you need to survive."

I genuinely didn't know how to reply. Alex's point wasn't totally invalid, but it was definitely a lot colder than what I'd been expecting.

I knew I spent more time worrying about others than I did about myself. But I cared about others more than I cared about myself. My friends, Natalie Poole, my family, my realm—they mattered more than I did. How could I compare my one life to the importance of securing the well-being of an entire world? And how could I exist in a world where the people I loved had been destroyed by the plots entangling me?

The answer: I couldn't.

"For what it's worth," Alex continued, "you don't have to be scared here."

"I know, I know," I said as I heaved myself out of the pool. I covered my silvery bathing suit with a fluffy white robe and tried to get warm. "The magic hunters can't get to me here. We have walls and guards and weapons coming out of our ears. That's why Lady Agnue sent me home."

"True," Alex replied as he stood up. "But you also have me."

Despite my sogginess, he gave me a solid hug. The last of the stress I'd been holding onto melted away and was replaced with warmth. Alex may have been acting odd lately, but it was good to know I could still count on him. While his advice hadn't been the best, I appreciated him listening. And I appreciated him loving me too.

I think it was fair to say that I was beginning to develop an unnatural trepidation toward envelopes.

The one Lady Agnue handed me back at school had been the ultimate bearer of bad news, telling me I would have to return home. I hadn't minded the letter Chance had sent me at first. However, the interest it caused my mother to take in my non-existent love life made me super uncomfortable. And then there was the matter of the message I'd found on my bedroom floor this morning. Someone had slid it under my door during the night.

The envelope it came in was unmarked. A small note on the inside contained the following instructions:

> *Exit the courtyard through the stables. Grab a shovel.*
> *Take the Jacaranda path until you reach the twelfth tree*
> *on your right. Turn off the path and head down the hill.*
> *Find the wild jasper berry bushes growing near the back of*
> *the mausoleum. Careful; they're poisonous.*

*Then dig.*
*You'll know where.*

Needless to say, I was both intrigued by and suspicious of the message.

I also couldn't understand why the note-writer had insisted that I take such a convoluted path to the mausoleum. I had half a mind to ignore the instructions and use my own method of getting there through the hedge maze. I also had half a mind not to go at all. I mean, secret messages slipped in the dead of night beneath one's bedroom door hardly screamed trustworthy.

Still, my curiosity tended to surpass precaution in situations like this, so I decided to skip breakfast, grab my wandpin, and head in pursuit of whatever I was meant to find on the outskirts of the grounds.

The palace was busy today. Very busy. There was a big event going on in our ballroom that was keeping most of the staff occupied. People hustled and bustled around me with their own missions. And yet, someone still managed to take notice that I was up to something.

"Oh there you are, Pumpkin. I was looking for you," my mother said.

I'd been about to slip through a side door that led out back when she came around the corner. "Have you had breakfast?" she asked me.

"Um, no. I wasn't hungry."

"Not hungry?" my mother's brow furrowed with concern. "That is not like you. Are you sick? There is something going around the palace, you know."

She tried to put the back of her hand on my forehead, but I stepped out of reach. "I'm fine. Did you need something, Mom?"

"Yes. I wanted to ask you to help me with the final arrangements for the banquet we are having for the King and Queen of Tunderly."

"Mauvrey's parents?"

*My archenemy's parents?*

"Yes," my mother replied. "You would know that if you came to any of the advisor forums or party planning committee meetings I invited you to in the last few weeks. But I digress. The point is that the Weatheralls are coming as a prelude to our kingdoms' partnership for Vicennalia Aurora festivities next month. It is a grand celebration that happens every twenty-five years when—"

"Yeah, I know what it is," I interjected. "But what does it have to do with me exactly?"

"Well, I thought it might be good practice for you," my mother replied. "You have been back nearly a month and we have spent so little time together. We should see to your princess duties every now and then, do you not agree?"

"Fine, Mom," I huffed. "When will the Weatheralls be here?"

"In three days. So I will need you to start assisting me tomorrow morning at eight o'clock sharp, all right?"

"Okay, but fair warning—arrival of the Weatheralls withstanding—my friends will also be arriving here in three days. Remember? They're coming in for a visit."

I couldn't believe it'd almost been a month since I left Lady Agnue's. It felt like another world ago. I was both excited and nervous about seeing my friends again. I missed them, but I missed the old versions of our friendships, not the fragile ones we had now. I'd left on such odd terms with each of them—SJ and me fighting, Daniel and I in a weird place post him pushing me away, Jason having learned that I foresaw his death, and me not being able to tell Blue about it. I didn't know what it was going to be like reuniting with them.

"Lady Agnue and Lord Channing gave them permission to leave school?" my mother asked, surprised.

"Spring break starts next week."

"Oh, yes. With you being home I had forgotten. I have been so busy lately. How many of your friends are we expecting again?"

"Four," I responded. "SJ, Blue, and Jason—all of whom you've met—and the guy I mentioned a few weeks back, Daniel. They're coming here for a couple days and then we're going to go stay with Jason on his farm in Coventry for the rest of the break. I mentioned it over breakfast a couple weeks ago."

Staying with Jason was a lie, but not even a professional interrogator would've been able to see through my veil of deception.

I felt bad lying to my mom, but it was necessary. Students were free to leave campus over spring break, so our headmasters wouldn't know we were embarking on another quest—this time to find Paige Tomkins. However, my friends and I needed a cover for our parents.

Via encoded letter, we'd decided what we were going to tell them. Our parents knew that Blue lived in a cottage with her mother in Harzana and would not have room for four teenage houseguests. Involving my family or SJ's in the lie was tricky because they were both royalty and could potentially talk to each other. And none of our families had met Daniel, so we doubted they would be okay with us staying with a stranger. Thus, Jason's home was to be our alibi. Our families had met him and my friends and I had actually stayed at his farm once before. He came from a good family that lived on a large property, and his brother Jack was a protagonist.

We'd all told our respective families we were staying with him, and he'd told his family he was remaining at school during spring break to train for his Hero Finals, which plenty of male protagonists actually did.

"Very well," my mother said, buying my lie. "I shall remind your father and ensure the staff prepare rooms and attire." She began to stride down the corridor but then paused.

"Oh, and Crisanta," she said over her shoulder. "I am still capable of detecting that look of mischief in your eyes. Whatever you are up to this morning, do stay out of trouble."

I couldn't help but smile. "Yes, Mom."

She smiled slightly too. "I do hope that is not another hollow promise, Pumpkin. Your expression suggests otherwise."

I felt a tad resentful for how easily my mother could read me, but truly grateful for how understanding she was of my nature.

Once outside, I walked east through the stone courtyard until I reached the stables. Following the note's instructions, I entered.

I was about halfway to the other side when I glanced around at the rafters, the horses, the hay—and realized something. I was not scared anymore.

Being in here before had filled me with PTSD-level panic. Now I felt nothing. In fact, now that I thought about it, last night had been the first night in a while that I hadn't dreamed of the magic hunter attack. Relief flowed through me.

The anxiety was gone. Talking with Alex really had helped. While I was still concerned about the hunters and the threat they posed, I was no longer crippled by the fear. I'd let the memory go. By letting someone in, I'd let that night go.

At the end of the stables, I grabbed a shovel from an unlocked supply shed and pushed through the exit. The Jacaranda trees were blooming and I took in their pale purple grandeur in the light of the spring day. When I reached the twelfth tree in the row, I strode off the path to the right and looked down. Leaning my free hand against the bark of the tree, I gazed at the slope.

A good portion of our castle's perimeter was natural forest that had never been developed. I had always been grateful for this. Living in a compound so unnaturally rigid and architecturally flawless, I'd always enjoyed having unruly wild life encircling us.

As I stared into the forest's depths, I began to question this endeavor. I didn't know who had sent that note. I didn't know what I was going to find down this path. Yet, I was driven onward by my interest to see the mission through and discover what lay at its conclusion.

I moved down the hill, my knowledge of the grounds guiding me in the direction of the mausoleum. It must have been ten minutes before I eventually saw it peeking through the trees.

I headed round back. A number of jasper berry bushes grew here, the likes of which I had long been warned to be careful around.

As my mother had keenly pointed out, I did like to eat. So when I was younger it had been necessary to repeatedly tell me not to go eating whatever wild berries I came across on the palace grounds. Many plants (like the nearly translucent white berries on these bushes) were incredibly poisonous.

With this logic in mind, the mud around these bushes should've been undisturbed. The only person who had the impulse to wander around the outskirts of the palace was me, and I had been trained since my toddler princess days to avoid playing near toxic plants. However, as I studied the ground, I was surprised to discover footprints in the dirt. The leaves were flatter in these spots, the earth scattered in a way that seemed unnatural. I knelt and looked closer.

*Yup, someone's definitely been through here. More than once by the looks of it.*

I followed the prints as best I could through the domain of jasper berry bushes, the occasional gagecho darting over my path.

The note said that I would know when to dig. After a minute, I realized it was right. Beneath the threshold of an overbearing bush to my left, I found a patch of disturbed ground.

I bent down to inspect further. The pungent scent of jasper berries filled my nose and for a moment I allowed myself to breathe it in. Despite the toxic nature of the berries, their sweet yet sharp, wintery fragrance had always seemed quite lovely to me.

I analyzed the area beneath the bushes. The dirt was loose, and seemed to have been patted into a mound. Someone had buried something here.

Shovel in hand, I began to dig. It did not take me long to hit something. I leaned over to see what'd I'd uncovered. Lying in the earth was a wooden box. It was no bigger than a jewelry chest and latched shut with a small lock.

I put down the shovel and reached for it. As I did, the lid began to rumble. I jumped back slightly and stared into the hole. The box was jiggling as if something were trapped inside, something tiny and angry that very much wanted to get out.

*Lapellius.*

Placing my wand on the ground at the ready—I pulled the box out of the hole. The thing only jerked around more upon my touch. I set it on a pile of leaves as I picked up my wand.

*Knife.*

I held up my unbreakable blade, ready to slice the lock and

possibly stab at whatever came out of the box if necessary. With a swift motion I chopped off the lock. The lid flew upward instantly as a shiny something shot out of the box. Actually, a whole lot of shiny somethings.

A cluster of tiny glass shards flew into the air. They swarmed around like a small, but loyal team of mosquitoes, whirring furiously, but with purpose. I watched as the pieces grouped together and began to take a more specific shape—slowly going from a flying squad of glass particles to an actual figure.

I squinted as I tried to make out the shape.

*A dog?*

*A dragon?*

*A horse?*

*No. It couldn't be.*

The pieces of glass locked together and I saw what it truly was.

*A glass Pegasus.*

I couldn't believe that SJ's glass Pegasus figurine that I'd sent after Mauvrey was flying around me. It'd been gone so long that I'd started to think it had gotten lost or destroyed. But it turned out I'd only been partially right. It *had* been destroyed, but it hadn't lost its way. It'd been trapped here, buried beneath the ground of my home in Midveil no less.

Realization struck. The understanding felt like acid coursing through my veins. If this glass creature was here, then that meant that Mauvrey had been here. And if this trail of footprints ran true, that meant she'd been in the castle.

# CHAPTER 26

# Matters of Trust

lex?"

I knocked hesitantly on my brother's bedroom door. He did not answer, but it creaked open regardless. He must've forgotten to lock it on his way out.

After my discovery of the glass Pegasus, I'd raced all the way back to the castle. I had come to an abrupt halt, however, when I realized I did not know where I was running to.

No one apart from my friends and Lady Agnue knew the truth about Mauvrey. And I didn't exactly have the most concrete proof that she'd been here. The glass Pegasus figurine would've been my only evidence, but I didn't even have that anymore. A minute after putting itself back together, the thing had flown off—still committed to its original mission of finding Mauvrey's final destination so it could show me the way to her.

Even without proof though, I knew I had to tell someone what I'd learned—especially since Mauvrey's parents were going to be here in a few days. I felt certain that this couldn't be a coincidence. It just couldn't be.

Given how helpful it had been to let Alex in on my magic hunter issues, I figured he was the best person to trust with this too. He did say I could count on him for anything.

Alas, it seemed I'd missed him this morning. He'd told us over dinner that he would be attending the annual War Games Convention being held in our palace ballroom today and would be gone for the whole of the afternoon.

The War Games Convention was an annual gathering of

players in the military industry. There were fighting demon-strations, weapons vendors, seminars, duel demonstrations, and Q&A panels with military leaders and famed tacticians. If it had to do with war and battle strategy, it was featured at the convention.

Alex and Pietro loved that sort of thing and had gone every year since they'd graduated from Lord Channing's. I'd never been. When I was little I was not allowed; you had to be at least fourteen years old to attend. After I'd passed the age requirement I'd always been at school when it was held. I would finally have a chance to check it out this year. Hopefully I would run into Alex while I was there.

I should've closed Alex's door and gone on my way, but I found myself compelled to step inside my brother's room. For a couple of minutes, I wandered around perusing his sword collection, his various medals of honor and accolades, and the suit of polished armor in the corner by the royal blue velvet drapes.

I paused by his fireplace. Lying abandoned in a rusty, curved dish atop the mantle were my brother's formerly precious wristbands. Seeing the golden bracelet we'd shared for so many years gathering dust made me both sad and angry. I plucked it from the dish and wiped off the dust on my skirt.

I held the bracelet in my hand. The engraved words had faded over time, and the gold was slightly tarnished.

Feeling bitter, I clasped the thing around my left wrist—resolving to hang onto it until my brother came to his senses. Alex may have been acting bizarre recently, but I had to believe he would get over it. Our talk by the swimming pool yesterday had confirmed that the brother I loved was still in there.

I left the room and headed downstairs to the War Games Convention. Our palace ballroom—the center of the event—was packed with visitors. There were booths set up everywhere like a mini marketplace. Specialists in everything from troop training maneuvers to shield forging were presenting their wares and striking deals. A stage had been erected at the front where a convincing swordfighting demonstration was underway. People mingled everywhere, many of them in some type of uniform. I marveled at the sight and wandered into the hullaballoo.

I was admiring a booth specializing in knives and daggers that Blue would have loved when two palace staff members caught my attention. Aggie Black and Blaine Weldhouse (a parliament scribe who was also on Lenore's list) were standing at a booth at the end of the row.

I began to make my way over to them, pushing through the crowds. I saw Aggie slip some money to Blaine. Blaine shook the hand of a bearded vendor and subtly passed him the currency. He leaned in to whisper something in the vendor's ear.

*What were they up to?*

"Excuse me." I bobbed and weaved around a group of bespectacled men who were blocking my path. "Excuse me."

I finally maneuvered my way over to the booth where I'd seen Aggie and Blaine, but they'd vanished into the crowd by then. The banner hanging above the tent read "Crossbows Etc." The booth's bearded proprietor was standing underneath it behind a table.

"Hey, those two people you were just talking to," I said directly, "what did they want?"

"I'm sorry, young lady," the bearded man responded. "I don't know what you mean."

"Like heck you don't," I countered. "I saw that guy hand you money. What was it for?"

"Dear girl, here at Crossbows Etc., we offer a variety of services including custom-made weaponry, private or group classes, and tours of our facility and museum featuring the history of crossbowmanship. We *also* offer our sincerest client-vendor confidentiality. It's in our mission statement." He pointed to a lacquered, fancy sign mounted in the corner of the tent.

"We at Crossbows Etc. promise you the best in weapons, weapons training, and weapons history alongside our oath to protect your confidentiality at every turn and shot," I read aloud.

I rolled my eyes. *Ugh. Seriously?*

I guess I had to go with Plan B. I hated playing the princess card, but I had to know what Aggie and Blaine were up to.

"Look, buddy," I said. "I respect your oath; I do. I've got a thing for privacy myself. But are you aware of who you're talking to? I'm Crisanta Knight—princess around these parts. So why don't you do yourself a favor and tell me what I wanna know before I go get my dad. I don't think the king of Midveil would be particularly pleased to find out some random guy at a convention is impeding a royal investigation."

The bearded man pointed down at the very table I had my hands firmly planted on. I looked at the stacks of pamphlets and business cards there. On the front page of the pamphlets—below the mission statement and above the copyright symbol—was a small blurb accompanied by my family's royal seal.

"Personally endorsed by the King & Queen of Midveil as the leaders in the industry for more than ten years," I read.

My eyes narrowed into a glare.

"Listen, Beardy," I said, "Endorsement or not, this is important. Tell me what I want to know, or so help me I—"

"Crisa?"

I turned around to find Pietro and a few of his friends from the King's Guard in casual dress. All of them but Pietro were holding to-go cups in their hands.

"What's going on?" my brother asked, raising an eyebrow as he looked from me to the bearded vendor.

"Nothing," I replied. "I was just telling this jerk-wad that he needs to get the stick out of his—"

"Crisa." Pietro held up his hand and stepped past me. "I'm sorry, General Savoy," he said as he shook hands with the bearded man. "My sister can get a bit . . . overzealous. But she means well."

"Not a problem," Savoy responded with a chuckle. "I find her expressiveness adorable. Princesses with strong opinions are endearing and amusing, like cats wearing sweaters."

"I'm sorry, what?" I started to lunge toward the table, but Pietro grabbed my shoulder and held me back.

"Come on, Crisa," he said, steering me away. "Let it go."

Savoy winked at me as we left, causing me to ball up my fists even tighter.

"Give me two minutes, guys," Pietro told his friends as he pulled me aside.

"Dude, what the heck?" I asked. "I was in the middle of something. How could you just jump in and side with *that guy*?"

"Crisa, General Savoy was one of dad's most trusted advisors and generals for over two decades. They are still good friends and more importantly he is a chief supplier for the King's Guard and the Midveil military. Offending him is not an option, even if it means swallowing your pride."

"This wasn't about my pride, Pietro. He has information I need."

"About what?"

"About . . ."

I cut myself off. Since the other day, I'd caught a few more glimpses of Pietro talking with Aggie. Their interactions never lasted for more than thirty seconds, and they were always too far off for me to eavesdrop. Even so, it was becoming harder for me to stand by my assertion to Sooz that he was not involved with the commons rebellion.

"It's nothing," I answered. "I was just looking into something."

Pietro nodded. "All right. I have to talk business with a few guys at the Invasive Troop Strategy booth, so I have to go. Just do me a favor and don't go picking any more fights with the guests. I know it's a War Games Convention, Crisa, but that doesn't mean you have to take the theme so literally."

He patted me on the head and marched off with his friends. I glanced back toward the Crossbows Etc. booth, tempted to re-engage my target despite Pietro's wishes. But my bearded foe was no longer present and the curtains had been drawn shut across the booth. A sign hung over them that read:

"*Booth Closed for Lunch Break. Trespassers Will Be Shot.*"

Undeterred, I shimmied up to the side of the booth. I pulled a corner of the curtain back and stole a quick peek within.

*Empty.*

When I was sure no one was looking, I slipped inside. Hurriedly I began to poke around. There were unopened stacks of business cards, finely polished weapons on display pedestals, and flipbooks of glowing customer testimony. To my left, I found a travelling trunk of personal items, which had to be General Savoy's luggage.

I managed to pick the lock in under a minute and swiftly began going through the contents.

An extra suit with bronze, military-grade cufflinks lay on the top. Below that were some peppermint sticks and a few books (*A Bridge Not Far Enough* by General Thomas A. Malloy, *Appear; Attack; Destroy!* by Commander Joe Gregorious Foghorn, and *An Affair to Never Forget* by Lady Nora Ephnaron).

The third book in the stack made me raise an eyebrow. Unlike the other novels, this one was old and weathered. More peculiar still was the difference in the covers. While the Malloy and Foghorn books featured great explosions, Miss Ephnaron's displayed a romantic image of a man and woman holding hands in front of a lopsided, yellow-and-black cottage. The cottage, which had a twisted gray chimney and matching shutters, was near the woods and had flowers floating around it. The illustration seemed familiar somehow. I couldn't place it, but I felt certain I'd seen it before. Maybe in a book or on a postcard? Intrigued, I picked it up for closer inspection. There was an inscription on the inside flap:

> *"Past summer's end and winter's fire,*
> *In the rains of spring and autumn tire,*
> *Keep my heart and always recall,*
> *Where Gravity froze, and we did fall."*
> – With Love, L.

*Curious*, I thought to myself as I placed the book back in the trunk.

I kept digging and discovered two things of interest on the bottom layer. There was an oak cigar box with the message "With Love, L." engraved on the top, and a case of medals of honor that my father had likely bestowed upon Savoy throughout his career.

I was about to close the trunk when I noticed the lining of the lid had an unnatural bulge. I ran my hand along the edge until I felt the seam curve over a concealed zipper.

*A hidden compartment.*

I opened it and found a collection of folders. Flipping through them, I saw weapon designs, group lesson schedules, and inventory logs—none of which were of particular interest. But there was still something left in the compartment. I pulled out a booklet, which contained a list of orders. *Bingo.*

Unlike the other documents, the entries in this logbook were written in code. Random letters filled each row like gibberish except for the two columns on the right—one that listed dates and times of purchases and another that detailed amounts paid.

I flipped to the last recorded purchase. It had today's date and the time noted was ten minutes ago. This must be the transaction that Aggie and Blaine had made.

The monetary figure caused my eyes to widen. That was *a lot* of money. Sadly, I couldn't read the coded writing on the page, which would've told me what the transaction was for.

A rustling noise outside the booth caught my attention. There was no time to waste. Still, I had to know what Aggie and Blaine paid for.

Thinking quickly, I grabbed a quill and copied the gibberish from their transaction onto the palm of my hand. Then I skipped back to a page in the order log from the previous year. This page was encoded like all the others and had no telling information relevant to today's events, but it was all I needed nonetheless. I gently tore it out—careful not leave a crease or shred of the page behind.

Every cipher had a solution; I only needed to solve it. And to do that, I simply required time and a sample of the code. I'd certainly had my fair share of deciphering and translating text recently with my Shadow Guardians book, and Jason had taught me about decoding last year. How hard could this be?

The general would certainly notice if today's purchase log disappeared. But I didn't think he'd miss a page from last year. I folded the page, shoved it in my pocket, and slipped out of the booth. Merging into the traffic of the convention again, I calmly made my way out of the ballroom. Our library had plenty of books on cryptography. One of them had to illustrate a way to break the kind of cipher Savoy was employing.

As I made my way through the castle—further and further from the convention—the crowds began to thin. By the time I made it to the Hall of Transparency, I was completely alone. Or so I thought. When I was about to open the door to the library, I heard a familiar creaking coming from inside. I entered just in time to see the fireplace sliding back into place.

"Alex?"

He extinguished a candelabra and turned around hastily. "Crisa! What're you doing here?"

"In the library? Um, I was planning on reading. What about you? I thought you were at the convention for the day."

"I was. I just needed some air."

"So you snuck out through here? There's access to the main lawn through the ballroom, you know."

"Obviously," Alex said. "But I needed some space too. Don't you use this tunnel to get to your secret practice spot every day instead of one of the normal castle exits?"

"Well, yeah, but I'm trying not to get caught. With Mom, Dad, and even Pietro on my case, I have to take extra precaution when it comes to hiding my magic-related activities. You're *you*, though. Why do you need to hide?"

"I'm not hiding, Crisa. I have a lot of important things to deal with right now and I'm trying to handle them on my own."

I softened, knowing exactly how he felt. "I get it. I'm sorry. I didn't mean to pry."

He nodded and moved toward the door.

"Hey, Alex," I said, putting my hand on his arm right before he passed me. "I was actually hoping I could talk to you for a sec. I discovered something by the mausoleum and I—"

"Sorry, Crisa," he interrupted. "I don't have time to talk. I have my own things to worry about today."

I swallowed my disappointment. He'd really helped me the other day by listening to my worries. Maybe I could show him that this could be a two-way street.

My brother started out the door again.

"Alex . . ."

He stopped.

"Maybe I could help with whatever's bothering you. I know letting people in isn't really either of our styles. But I've come to realize that bottling stuff up may not always be the wisest course of action. Opening up to you the other day really made a difference to me. So if you ever wanted to talk—"

"Crisa," he interrupted again, this time more sharply. "You're right."

"I am?"

"Letting people in isn't either of our styles. So what's say we keep our business to ourselves. You needed to vent the other day and that's fine. But I don't have time to make that a regular thing. I have a world of pressure on me with training to be the future king and dealing with Pietro and handling stuff with the commons rebellion, which—I don't know if you've heard since you spend all day magic training—is actually growing pretty serious outside these walls. Asking me to take on your problems too is selfish. I expect more from you."

Alex left the library before I could muster a reply. It was just as well. At the moment I was speechless.

I thought I could trust my brother. I'd made the difficult choice to let him in, but in the end he didn't want my trust or the closeness that came with it. It was a burden to him just as it had been a burden to Daniel.

I felt the hurt and sadness inside of me harden—solidifying around my heart like toffee around a candied apple.

I'd spent last semester pushing people away but eventually learned that letting them in made me stronger. Now the universe was denying me that gift. Every person I put my faith in shoved it right back in my face.

Which meant that I was alone. Whatever was happening with Mauvrey, Pietro, General Savoy, and the commons on Lenore's list—I had to tackle these issues by myself and hope that it was enough.

# CHAPTER 27

# Friends for Dinner

hen you wake up face down in a textbook, it's usually a sign you've been reading too long.

I spent the afternoon in the library searching through dozens of books on cryptography, code deconstruction, and ciphers, along with a few books on General Savoy himself to hunt for clues about context. After an intermission that included changing into a gown and having a quiet, tense dinner with my family, I'd returned to the library and continued my quest for answers.

As noted by the pool of drool on the pages in front of me, and the late hour, it was fair to say the quest had yet to prove fruitful. Still, I refused give up. I just needed some rest. I would regroup and try again tomorrow.

I put the stolen page from Savoy's log and a scrap of paper with the code I'd copied from my hand in my pocket, closed my books, and headed upstairs to my bedroom.

My eyelids were heavy and my reflexes slow as I ran a brush through my hair. That's when I saw something in the reflection of the mirror. Another note had just been slipped beneath my door.

I put the brush down and hurried over. It was a simple scrap of parchment folded in half. I opened it and discovered a message:

*Tunnel #5*
*Night after next @ half past two.*
*Come alone.*

I threw my door open and dashed into the hall in search of

whoever'd left the message. I looked left; then right. At the far end of the corridor I saw the shadow of a figure hurrying away.

"Hey!" I shouted.

The shadow froze. Then it took off running.

"Hey, stop!" I called after the speeding silhouette.

I bolted down the moonlit hallway—my reflection in the glass hurrying to keep up with me. I managed to skid around the corner right after the lift descended. In one last attempt to cut off the suspect, I bee-lined for the stairwell and raced down the floors one staircase at a time.

*Eight . . . seven . . . six . . . five . . . four . . . three . . . two . . .*

Panting heavily, I burst out of the first-floor stairwell only to come face-to-face with an empty lift. There was no sign of the shadow I'd been pursuing. Whoever it had been had vanished without a trace.

"Roses or orchids?"

"Whichever," I yawned as I looked up from the place settings I was supposed to be inspecting. I was sitting with drooped shoulders at a table in one of the palace rec rooms. The walls were covered in a design of fancy silver florets. Powder blue carpet matched the open curtains. Light beaming in from tall windows made the selection of gorgeous china and goblets in front of me glimmer. But even their sheen was not enough to keep me completely alert. Yesterday's late night research in the library was taking its toll. To my mother, though, my tiredness probably came across as disinterest.

"Crisanta," she nagged. "I realize that this is not your favorite way to spend the day, but could you please try and take an interest. There will be many important diplomats, royalty, and protagonists attending this banquet. And some day when you are queen of your own castle, these kinds of things will be vital for you to know."

"All right, I'm sorry," I said. "What was the question again?"

"Do you think we should use roses or orchids in the centerpieces for our welcome banquet for the Weatheralls on Saturday?"

With a sigh, I cast my gaze across the long table blooming with dozens of different flower arrangements.

"Neither," I said decidedly. "Roses are too played out, and orchids aren't native to Midveil so they'll cost an arm and a leg. I say we go with lilacs." I picked up a stem of lilac and admired the clusters of dark purple flowers. "They're pretty, fragrant, and have a nice draping quality about them."

I glanced at the selection of other flowers on the table. "Pair them with deep purple and bright green hydrangeas. I passed by the craft room earlier in the week and saw castle staff working on décor for the banquet that looked like big, poofy hydrangea balls, so these flowers will match. You can also add white peonies for contrast and . . . What are these?" I picked up the placard in front of a vase of purple flowers that resembled pompom balls. "Alliums," I said. "Stick them all into one of those tall vases."

I made a makeshift bouquet of the flowers I had mentioned and dropped them into a tall vase. "There," I declared, showing my mother the centerpiece. "That's what I think. Feel free to criticize."

Much to my surprise, my mother simply smiled and took the vase from my hands. "Beautiful," she said. "Margaret." She gestured to one of her ladies-in-waiting. "Make them all exactly like this, please."

"Yes, your majesty." Margaret took the vase from my mother and headed out of the room in a hurry.

"That was very well done, Pumpkin," my mother said. "Your arrangement is lovely. And I appreciate how well it matches the Vicennalia Aurora, which has inspired this whole banquet."

"What do my flowers have to do with the Aurora?" I asked. "I thought it was some sort of magic-fluctuation event?"

"It is," my mother responded. "But that is not the only reason it is celebrated. On the night of the Vicennalia Aurora, when the clock strikes half past seven and the magic fluctuation reaches its peak, the sky will be filled with the most beautiful aurora of natural lights. They streak across the night in waves of purple and green and white and pink for a single hour before vanishing for another twenty-five years. It is a rare and breathtaking event for all of Book, as it can be seen from anywhere. That is why so many kingdoms usually partner together to share in the festivities. Your centerpiece design reflects the key colors of the Aurora."

"Lucky guess, I guess." I shrugged.

"Even so, I am impressed, Pumpkin," my mother replied. "I do not know why you fight me so much on these kinds of activities when you have such . . ."

Suddenly my mother put her hand to her head and faltered as if she were about to faint.

"Mom!" I rushed to her side and grabbed her arm.

She steadied herself. "I am terribly sorry. I do not know what came over me."

"Are you feeling okay?"

"I think I am catching whatever cold has been going around the castle," she replied as I helped her into a chair. "I have been feeling a bit ill these last few days."

"How ill exactly?"

"It comes and goes. It was mainly stomach cramps at first. However, since this morning I have been feeling fatigued and my vision blurred for a moment just now."

"You should lie down," I said. "I'll stay here and finish the banquet prep on my own."

"No, no," my mother insisted. "I am fine. As I said, it comes and it goes. I only need a moment to compose myself, and perhaps a hot cup of tea." She called to a staff member standing in the corner. "Celia, can you have my afternoon tea prepared now, please?"

"Yes, majesty." Celia headed for the kitchens as my mother sat up straight, trying to regain her composure. She fixed the crown on her head, which had tilted.

"I adore the tea the kitchen staff has been preparing this season," she said, tucking a loose strand of blonde hair behind her ear. "How do you like it, Pumpkin?"

"Um, yeah," I lied, having never actually tasted the stuff. "It's the tops."

"And so nice on the throat since I have been feeling ill," my mother continued. "One of my ladies mentioned to me the other day how drastically under the weather some of the staff has been feeling. And with the demanding nature of Saturday's events, she thought it might be a good, preventative measure to have them drink it as well. I have had some of this special brew sent to the King's Guard common room and the servants' quarters every afternoon this week. Tea is not just good for the soul, you know, Crisanta; it is excellent for your health."

I nodded, even though tea just made me nauseous.

"The tea pairs wonderfully with those almond biscuits your Aunt Jemma sends us from her annual trip to the Middlebrook countryside," my mother continued. "We just received a fresh box. Would you like to join me for tea in the courtyard?"

"Um, I would . . ." I started to say, "but I actually have a project going in the library right now. Do you mind if I head over there while you take your break and then come back to help you with the rest of this banquet stuff? I can meet you in, like, half an hour?"

"Fine, dear," my mother said wistfully. "But half an hour sharp. We have crystal and orchestra numbers to select next."

"Gotcha. Orchestra numbers. Looking forward to it."

I dashed out of the room—glad to have avoided choking down any tea, and sad that in ducking teatime I'd missed out on Aunt Jemma's almond biscuits.

I woke on Friday morning feeling like storm clouds were brewing over my head.

All my worries about Pietro, Alex pushing me away, and the commons rebellion were beginning to make me nervous. Thankfully, my mother gave me the afternoon off from princess duty so she could rest from the cold she seemed to be developing.

Instead of continuing to try and crack Savoy's code in the library, I took a break of my own and returned to my hideaway at the back of the grounds to practice magic. At least there I could celebrate one of the few things that had gone right since my return to Midveil.

My powers had grown incredibly strong in the last four weeks.

As the golden glow swirled around me and magic flowed through my veins, I felt amazing. It gave me a greater sense of confidence about the upcoming mission my friends and I would make to the Wonderlands to find Paige Tomkins. On our last quest I had felt consistently bad about not being able to protect them from the harm that followed me. Now I felt formidable. Now I felt like my enemies had more to worry about than I did.

Normally Liza would coach me during my practice sessions through the Mark Two, but today I'd chosen to make my final session a solitary one. Liza always tried to stop me from pushing myself to my limit. She didn't like me experiencing Magic Exhaustion and felt that doing so only put me more at risk for Magic Burn Out. Me? I liked pushing my limits. It was the only way I could go even further the following day.

With my friends meant to arrive tomorrow and our journey set to begin the day after that, I figured this would be my last chance to see what I was truly capable of. I didn't mind if that meant achieving a hefty episode of Magic Exhaustion. So what if I wouldn't have use of my powers for another twenty-four hours? Tomorrow my whole day was going to be dedicated to the banquet, so I didn't need magic. I would be back at full force by the time we departed on Sunday.

By early evening, I was very close to my limits. Twilight had started to fall and my golden glow was diminishing like the sun's rays. My strength, too, was depleting. My bones hurt and I was feeling increasingly faint. And yet, I didn't push myself far enough for the exhaustion to overtake me. Not because of fear or restraint, but because of timing. It was half past six. Dinner was soon and I needed to get back.

I rapidly returned to the castle to shower and change. The moment I stepped inside, Minnie scurried up to me.

"Princess, you have guests," Minnie said.

"Guests?" I repeated.

"Yes. They flew in about ten minutes ago on a large plank of wood. One is a boy with an axe, and the other a girl with a blue-colored cloak. They say they're your friends."

I threw my arms around Jason, then Blue. "I thought you guys weren't coming until tomorrow!"

My friends were waiting in the library where Minnie had instructed them to wait after my mother had cleared them for entrance at the front gate.

I thought there might be some weirdness between us when I first saw them, especially with Jason since our last conversation had involved my vision of his death. But in that moment all my bad thoughts were buried beneath my pure gladness to see them.

"That's when SJ and Daniel are arriving," Blue replied after I'd squeezed her thoroughly. "Those pansies wanted to take the magic train to get here, but Jason and I thought we might give flying a shot. It worked for you, didn't it?"

"Yes, but I had a dragon. You guys used *this* thing." I gestured to my enchanted wooden plank, which was flying around the library excitedly. "I can't believe you broke it out of the school dungeon to fly it here. How did that even work?"

"I've been sneaking down to the dungeon for weeks now," Blue explained. "I wanted to see if I could train old Woody here to behave. I know it follows your orders because you're the one that brought it to life. But Lucky trusts us enough to listen to all of us now, so I figured the same could work in this case."

"I guess your theory paid off."

"Sort of. The thing still goes berserk whenever it's left alone for too long, or it's stressed out. But if I talk to it nicely, it *usually* listens to me." Blue waved the wooden plank over to us. "Yo, Woody! Come here!"

The wooden plank darted over and levitated by Blue's head. Jason gestured to some of the modifications he'd made. "I installed pop-up backrests, seatbelts, and cushions for comfort. It was kind of double dipping for one of my carpentry classes." He shrugged.

"Smart." I grinned. "But we gotta lock that thing up before it hurts someone."

"Fair enough," Blue replied. "But before that there's something I'm dying to show you." Blue reached inside her tan backpack and pulled out a rolled-up piece of parchment.

"What's that?"

"Our completed map of Camelot," Jason said. "I finished it a few days ago. SJ is handling the others, but I thought you might like to see one of the final products." He unrolled the map on one of the library tables. I smiled widely as I took in its completion— tiny roads connecting major cities, forests and mountains labeled everywhere, even markers for potential hazards like monsters— the details were amazing.

"This is great," I replied. "Did you—"

"Hit the deck!" Jason tackled me to the ground. The wooden plank almost decapitated me as it flew across the room.

I checked to make sure the coast was clear before I got up from the carpet. "Thanks," I said. Then I turned my attention to Blue. "I thought you had that thing under control?"

The wooden plank was swirling around the library ceiling doing figure eights.

"You know the things you bring to life are temperamental," Blue said. "Unless Jason and I are giving it direct orders, it kind of does whatever it wants."

"Well, that's not safe. We're in a castle made of glass. What if it—Awgh!"

The wooden plank collided with a high shelf and several books came clattering down. I jumped out of the way to avoid getting hit with a geology textbook.

"Okay, I get what you're saying," Blue responded. "But I don't want to shove it in another dungeon. We can't keep treating it like a prisoner. That thing may be made of wood, Crisa, but it is alive."

I sighed. Then my brow furrowed with an idea. "You're right. But what if it wasn't?"

I stepped to the middle of the room and held up my hand. I still had a little magic left in me. Maybe there was something I could do. Something I'd been wanting to try.

"Hey, over here!" I called to the wooden plank. The thing immediately swerved and started to descend.

"Back at school, Liza taught me how to give life to things

temporarily," I explained to Jason and Blue, who were watching me closely. "By visualizing a clear end point, the objects I enchant finish their tasks then return to normal. Given that, I think I might be able to draw the life back from Woody by visualizing its end point in the same way, even if it is after the fact."

When the wooden plank was at my level, I reached my hand out to touch it. For a moment, I had second thoughts. I felt bad about symbolically killing the thing—taking its life force—and Liza had warned me not to attempt the trick. Then again, in retrospect Liza hadn't asked me *not* to do it. She told me I *couldn't* do it. And that was a while ago. Now my magic was much stronger, so maybe I could.

I eased closer like a tamer approaching a wild horse. I stretched out my hand until my palm touched the flat surface of the plank. With a deep breath, I projected my magic.

The idea was simple enough. If I could give life, why couldn't I take it back? I pictured the wooden plank being disenchanted, pictured the life leaving it. I thought about the mission I'd once given it, and how that mission was over. I willed the power to reverse back into me.

Power surged through my body. A golden glow throbbed around the wooden plank. A feeling of near exhaustion came rushing in soon after. My legs began to quiver and my head buzzed and ached. For a second I thought the pain might be too much to handle, but I managed to hold true. With clenched teeth and eyes shut tight, I used the last of my power. Magic Exhaustion hit and I collapsed to my knees. A moment after I did, I heard a loud thud in front of me. My eyes flew open to find the wooden plank lying on the carpet. It didn't move.

"Are you okay?" Jason asked, helping me to my feet.

I was light-headed, my chest throbbed, and it felt like every vein inside me had been injected with low-grade acid. And yet, when I stood and nudged the wooden plank with my boot and it didn't stir, I felt more powerful than ever. I'd done it. My magic really could take life away as easily as it could give it.

"That was weird," Blue commented.

"Well, it's the first time I've tried to reverse my powers of life,"

I replied, rubbing my head. "It was hardly a performance-ready trick."

"No, your magic aura," Blue explained. "It changed at the end there. The color fluctuated a bit; the gold flashed darker for a sec."

I didn't have an explanation for that. My eyes had been closed at the end, so I hadn't seen what she was talking about.

"It was probably just the lighting," Jason commented, gesturing around at the library. "The sun is going down and it's getting darker in here."

"Right," I said, remembering the time. "We have to get ready for dinner." I walked over to the table to roll up the map. Before I did, I took one last look at its impressiveness.

"So cool," I said, handing it back to Jason. "Are they all this detailed?"

"Unfortunately no," Blue admitted. "In the end we weren't able to find anything useful about Limbo or Cloud Nine. Those realms remain a mystery so, Book not counting, we only have seven fully composed maps of the Wonderlands."

"We'll work with what we have," I said. "It's still a great advantage, and it took a lot of hard work. You guys must've really been busy over the last month."

"That's an understatement," Blue scoffed. "So much has happened since you left. The Twenty-Three Skidd practices, Lady Agnue's new regulations, that thing with the librarian and the accidental trap door, Chance Darling's project—"

Jason elbowed Blue abruptly.

"Chance's project?" I repeated.

"Never mind," Blue responded. "It's not important."

"You're a horrible liar," I said.

"And you're a good one," she countered. "Every week when I wrote to you, I asked if you were okay, and you said yes every time. But we've only been talking for two minutes and I can already see the truth written all over your face. Something's wrong."

I sighed. "A lot has happened. And none of it is anything I wanted to discuss via letter. Especially since I didn't know who might intercept it along the way."

"You're worried about someone in your castle?" Jason asked.

"I'm worried about *a lot* of someones in my castle. For starters, Mauvrey. She's been here."

"What!" Both my friends' faces elongated with shock and worry.

"Yeah, that was my reaction too," I said. "I found SJ's glass Pegasus figurine buried outside the other day. I'm not sure what that translates to in terms of timing, but it was tracking Mauvrey, so that means she was definitely here at some point."

"Is that what's been bugging you?" Jason asked.

"I'm afraid that's only the tip of the iceberg. Have you heard that there's a commons rebellion brewing?"

"Unfortunately," Jason responded. "Lady Agnue's and Lord Channing's didn't tell us, but Daniel corresponds regularly with his girlfriend in Century City. She's been keeping him up-to-date about the situation."

Blue's eyebrows rose. "Daniel has a girlfriend?"

"Who do you think was sending him those letters?" Jason said.

"I don't know, I didn't ask. I assumed it was his family."

"Back on topic . . ." I said, eager to change the subject away from Daniel and his girlfriend. "Lenore and the higher-ups think the commons' next move is to eliminate royal rulers in an effort to overthrow kingdoms. She believes some of my palace staff members are part of the plot. And . . . my brother Pietro might be involved with the rebellion too."

"Wow," Blue commented. "That is a lot. Anything else we should know?"

I released a sigh. "Well, I've been receiving anonymous notes from someone in the castle. My other brother Alex is acting like a jerk for no reason. Mauvrey's parents are coming for a royal visit tomorrow. And to top it off, I'm trying to decrypt a code that may be related to the rebellion."

"Dang," Jason commented. "Sounds like you've been busy too."

"You don't know the half of it," I said. "And if you're up for a challenge, I could really use some help. But first, we've got to change for dinner. My parents don't like tardiness."

"You're going to shower too, right?" Blue asked as we left the library.

"Um, yeah. Why?"

"You smell like magic sweat."

I raised my eyebrows. "Is that a thing?"

"Yeah. You've only smelled this way a few times before, so I'm guessing you were practicing magic pretty hard earlier."

I was a little offended, but curious nonetheless. "What do I smell like?"

"Glitter and cheese."

I looked to Jason and he shrugged. "She's not wrong."

Jason and Blue were dressed in the full formal attire that my mom had arranged for them. My own black dress glided along the spotless floor on our way to the dining room. The skirt was light, but the nerves I carried were heavy.

"Some advice before we go in," I said. "I know it goes against all our instincts, but try not to speak unless spoken to. Answer questions with as few syllables as possible. And don't bring up anything that has to do with politics, modern music, energy drink potions, or your opinion on the effectiveness of bronze versus iron cannons. Got it?"

"Aw, there go all the talking points I prepped on the ride over." Blue rolled her eyes. "Relax, Crisa. It's dinner with your parents. I'm sure we can handle it."

"See, that's the thing," I insisted. "It's not dinner with my parents. It's dinner with the king and queen of Midveil."

"Isn't that the same thing?" Jason asked.

"Yes and no," I replied. "They're . . ." I shook my head. "You know what, just trust me. Think of it as a reconnaissance mission. You get in, try not to draw attention to yourself, then get out."

As I expected, Blue and Jason were soon taken aback by the grand stiffness of both our dining room and my family. They were used to the formal, fancy balls our schools held, and the structured traditionalism taught by the staff. But since neither of my friends were royalty, they hadn't been ready for how different my home was from theirs.

Blue and I had visited Jason over the summer a few years back and had relished being with his family. I loved the way they talked and laughed and lived so openly with one another. Blue and her mom in Harzana lived with similar light-hearted warmth. It was awesome, and I had nothing comparable on my home turf. All I had was a lot of glass, tiaras, and guards. Although I did notice that there were fewer of the latter around today.

Pietro informed us that the reason for their diminished presence was that many were out sick. Evidently the flu bug going around the palace had been growing nastier, resulting in fewer men and women reporting for work each day. I assumed this was the same illness that my mother was currently suffering from, but trying to hide.

Once we'd completed the formal introductions, my friends and I settled into our chairs and began to eat. Blue and Jason seemed to be heeding my advice about not speaking unless spoken to. Alex was doing his part by not speaking at all. Pietro and my dad had a lengthy conversation about how to best accommodate for the shortage of King's Guard members at the royal banquet tomorrow.

For the first half of dinner my mother—looking exceptionally pale, but too proud to acknowledge it—barely made a peep apart from an occasional raspy cough into her silk, powder blue napkin. But eventually her need to play hostess overpowered her body's desire to conserve energy.

"So, Blue," she said softly. "Crisanta tells us that you made one of the Lord Channing's Twenty-Three Skidd teams as well?"

"That's right," Blue responded as she reached for the bread. "I'm on Jason's team, the Crusaders. We're in first place right now."

I froze, holding a forkful of mashed potatoes in midair. "Blue, you didn't tell me that."

She glanced away. "Sorry. Must've forgot to mention it."

"That's pretty impressive," Pietro said, overlooking the brief, awkward pause. "Training with the other common protagonists at Lady Agnue's must really keep you in good fighting shape."

Blue smirked. "Yeah, well, with this one away for the past month I've had to work extra hard not to lose my edge," she said, gesturing to me as she continued eating.

"What do you mean by that?" my mother asked.

"Crisa's the best training partner at school," Blue went on, oblivious to the severe expression that had appeared on my mother's face. "Strong, fast, merciless—I mean, it's a wonder those hunters that attacked her last month didn't lose a— Ow!"

I had elbowed Blue in the ribs and now gave her a stern scowl.

"Sorry," she said. "I'll shut up now."

"No, please," my father said in a suspiciously calm manner. "I would love to hear just how capable Crisa is at the common protagonist extracurriculars offered at your school. After all, it is not as though we send her there to be educated for her future royal duties."

"Dad, I'm sure she's still learning what she's supposed to," Pietro spoke up in my defense.

"Pietro, this does not concern you. I was talking to your sister," my dad replied. "Surely if she can defend herself so admirably against magic hunters, she can defend the shirking of her royal responsibilities."

"Relax, Dad," I responded, keeping my voice even. "I work out with Blue during my free periods. I'm still taking all of my princess classes. They *are* mandatory."

"Mandatory?" my father mused. "That word has no meaning when it comes to you. You discard rules like kitchen scraps. I specifically told you that you were not to practice magic on the grounds. Yet, I learned from one of the gardeners this afternoon that you were seen doing just that this very day."

I bit my lip.

*Caught red-handed. Well, golden, glowing handed.*

*No wonder my father was being short with me.*

"Technically, you said not to practice magic in the *palace*, not on the grounds," I replied with a guilty, nervous grin.

The atmosphere turned tense. My mother, Pietro, and my

friends eyed my father for his reaction, while Alex alone watched me for mine.

My father simply shook his head. "Disappointing," he said.

"My utilizing my magic?" I asked slowly. "Or just me?"

He looked at me sternly and rubbed the knuckle of his pointer finger under his chin like he always did when he judged me. "Does it make a difference?" he asked. "Both are unpredictable, unruly, and dangerously irresponsible."

It felt like I'd gotten punched in the heart. Shame, embarrassment, and anger flushed my cheeks red. I abruptly pushed my chair out and stood. I'd had enough.

"Excuse me," I said, throwing my napkin down on my place setting. I walked out of the room. I heard the scrape of two other chairs as Blue and Jason followed.

"Crisa, you okay?" Jason asked as he and Blue caught up with me in the hall.

"Fine," I responded, continuing to walk briskly.

"But aren't you—"

"Crisa!" Alex called.

I turned around as he jogged up to us. "What do you want?" I asked.

"Are you okay? Dad was pretty hard on you in there."

"Oh, you noticed? Yeah, well, thanks for trying to mitigate. Oh, wait, that's right. You were silent as a board in there. But what else is new?"

Alex looked to Blue and Jason. "Give us a minute," he said.

They glanced at me and I gave them a dismissive wave. "It's fine. I'll meet you in the library in two minutes. Take the path I showed you before dinner."

As my friends continued down the corridor, I crossed my arms and glared at Alex. "What?"

"Look, I know I've been acting kind of weird lately—"

"Weird?" I repeated. "Try awful. What happened, Alex? We were fine and then all of a sudden we weren't. Did I do something?"

"No. It's like I was telling you the other day, I've had a lot of stuff to—"

"Deal with? You keep saying that," I huffed.

"Yeah, well, what I didn't mention was that it has to do with Pietro," Alex said cautiously.

This got my attention. And it made the hairs on the back of my neck stand up. "What about Pietro?" I asked.

Alex glanced behind him to make sure we were alone and then lowered his voice. "I can't get into it right now, but I think he and I are about to become a lot less civil. And until I can be sure where his allegiances lie, I don't want to put you in a position that could compromise you."

"Compromise me how?" I asked, matching his volume.

"A lot is about to happen, Crisa," Alex said, choosing his words carefully. "And I know you love Pietro, and that he's always looked out for you. But when things change very soon, I don't want you to get in the middle of it. Confrontation with him will be unavoidable, and I'm ready for it. But I want to make sure that whatever happens you're not caught in the crossfire. With what's coming, I owe it to you to at least protect you from that."

"Alex, you're not making any sense," I said. "What's coming? Is this about the commons rebellion?"

Alex nodded. I opened my mouth to reply, but one of Alex's squires scurried down the hall toward us.

"Sire," he said, "the king requests that you return to the dining room right away."

"I'm busy," Alex said. "Tell him I'll get there when I get there."

The squire took off running as I shook my head. "Honestly, how is it that you can say stuff like that to Dad and he still thinks of you as the apple of his eye while he looks at me like I'm a bruised cantaloupe at the back of the pantry?"

"Dad's blind," Alex said bluntly. "He doesn't see what's right in front of him and that's his downfall."

"Whatever," I said. "That's not important right now. We need to finish talking about this thing with the commons."

"*Everything* that's happening right now is important, Crisa," Alex responded. "And it's not smart for us to talk about this so openly. I don't know who I can trust around here."

"You can trust *me*," I said, adamantly.

Alex took a step back. "Not with this, Crisa."

I uncrossed my arms and my expression softened. "Why not?" I asked. "Why don't you want to let me in?"

"Because you're not ready for it," he said sternly. "You've changed since last summer, Crisa. I'm not only talking about your magic powers. I've noticed the difference in your personality— your confidence bordering on cockiness, your growing sense of defiance, your willingness to fight back even if it puts you in harm's way. While that change isn't necessarily a bad thing, it does make your future actions less predictable and your future character a lot less . . . reliable."

"What are you saying? You think that just because I'm not the exact same person I was before, you can't count on me?"

"I'm saying that I don't know if I can count on who you're turning into," Alex responded. "Maybe I can. Maybe this new you will be as loyal to me as the old you always has been. But until I can be sure, with everything that's coming I can't afford to take a gamble."

"So in addition to the whole 'protecting me' nonsense, you've been pushing me away because you think I'm *a risk* to you?" I asked in disbelief. "That because I've changed you might not be able to rely on me? Alex, that's ridiculous. You know there's nowhere you could go that I wouldn't follow. You're my brother. More than that, you're . . . you."

Alex sighed. "I want to trust you, Crisa. And soon enough you'll know the truth. But for now, please stop digging. I know you hate being kept in the dark, and hate following orders even more, but it's for the best. Big changes are coming. The less you know, the less likely you are to make rash judgments or choices preemptively, and the more likely it'll be that, when the time comes, I will be able to rely on you and keep you safe."

My brother put his hands on my shoulders and looked down on me. "Please, Crisa. I was telling you the truth that day at the swimming pool. You can trust me. I'll never betray you and I'll never let you down. I promise. Have faith in that and just this once, stand down."

I stared at him. "You do realize that in asking me to twiddle my thumbs while you handle whatever it is you're dealing with, you're asking me to go against everything you've spent years trying to teach me, right? You're asking me to keep my mouth shut and my head down amid all this crazy when you're the one who taught me to do the opposite."

"I taught you to be smart too, Crisa," he said. "If you were, you'd listen to me now."

"You taught me to fight back, Alex," I countered, shrugging off his grip. "So that's exactly what I'm going to keep doing. Hold onto your secrets and push me away if you want. But I'm just as invested in what's happening inside and outside this castle's walls as you are. And with or without your help, I'm going to get to the bottom of it."

I started to walk down the corridor.

"Crisa," Alex called.

I paused.

"If you keep on this path, I can't promise I'll be able to protect you."

"Good," I said without looking back. "Because I never asked you to."

# CHAPTER 28

# Gravity

ou know, somehow I thought that being in a giant glass castle would be a tad more exciting."

Blue rolled her eyes and flung away another cryptography book. The text fell pretty loudly onto the table beside Jason, but he did not look up from what he was reading. He was really good at keeping his concentration where studying was concerned. Plus, I reckoned he was used to Blue's disruptive behavior.

"Hey, you guys said you wanted to help," I commented as I tossed aside my own text and stretched out like a cat.

"Help, yes," Blue replied. "Go blind from reading tiny decrypting codes? Not so much. We've tried dozens of these cipher keys, Crisa. And every time we apply one to that page you tore from Savoy's logbook, it only translates to gobbledygook. Finding the one that'll work is like searching for a needle in a hundred haystacks. Only it's worse. Can we please take a break and talk about something else for a minute?"

"Like what?"

"I don't know," she groaned. "Something less frustrating."

"Well, I'm open to suggestions," I said.

Blue flopped backward onto the white couch—her head dangling upside down over one of the armrests. She bit her lip as she mulled it over. Then all at once she flipped back up—her eyes gleaming with curiosity.

"Here's a question," she began. "Crisa, why isn't Pietro next in line to be king? Succession dictates that the firstborn is first in line for a throne, right? Take SJ's family. She's the eldest of her siblings. So she's in line to be queen of her kingdom. If Pietro is the eldest of your parents' kids, why isn't he Midveil's next ruler instead of Alex?"

This caused Jason to glance up from his book—evidently he was interested in the answer as well.

I sighed. The knowledge was pretty common in Midveil, and among diplomatic circles, but a lot of outsiders didn't know the truth behind our family's line of succession. We preferred it that way for Pietro's sake. I had never even talked about it with my friends at school.

"It's because Pietro isn't technically my parents' kid," I explained. "Nor is he technically my brother. He's adopted."

I begrudgingly told Blue and Jason the story of Pietro's origins. As Lenore and Susannah had pointed out recently, Pietro was not a natural born Knight. In truth, he was a natural born Langston.

My mother had grown up with two stepsisters. But only one of those sisters was wicked. While the oldest of the pair was a real nasty piece of work, the younger sister, Merriweather Langston, had always been indifferent, but not unkind to my mother during her pre-Prince Charming days. After the night of the fateful ball, Merriweather actually delivered a tip to the castle that the prince should investigate their family's suburb for the owner of the glass slipper.

As such, after my parents married my mother forgave her younger stepsister and invited her to be a lady-in-waiting at the castle. In the years that followed, Merri not only served as a loyal, trusted lady-in-waiting to my mother, but as a dear friend. After Merri married and became pregnant with her first child, my mother pledged to be the baby's godmother.

Tragically, Merri's husband became ill in the months before her delivery and passed away in his sleep. Whether what happened next was a result of heartbreak, medical complications, or the same illness that took her husband, Merri, too, died upon giving birth to her son—Pietro.

With my mother's love and promise to Merri, as well as her compassion and commitment to the child, my parents did the only thing they could. They adopted the baby, giving life to Pietro

Knight—a prince in name, but not in blood. A royal who would always be a part of the noble court, but would never be king. And a man who would be the most loyal of sons and leaders, but who the public (despite our best efforts) would never treat exactly the same as the prince who was born to my parents six years later—my brother Alex.

It was fairly obvious to both Blue and Jason that I was uncomfortable telling this story. I didn't look them in the eye once and fidgeted with a couch cushion the whole time like a nervous tick. When I'd finished, they did not probe the subject further. The three of us settled back into our research without another word.

The quietude of this renewed reading lasted another half an hour before Jason looked up from his research. "Guys," he said. "I think I might've found that needle in a hundred haystacks."

I almost fell off my sofa. "What? Let me see!"

Blue and I rushed over to the table Jason was hunched over. In front of him were two books—a cryptography text and a book on military history. He pointed to the open cryptography text, specifically at a large graph on the left page, which was twenty-seven columns wide and twenty-seven rows tall.

"It's called a Vigenère Cipher," Jason explained. "It's a combination of several Caesar Ciphers where each letter shift depends on a keyword."

"Okay, but what makes you think this is the cipher Savoy used?" I asked.

"For one, the fact that it is way more complicated than the other ciphers we found," Jason responded. "Since a person can only crack it with a specific keyword, it makes the cipher impossible for anyone to break at random. With his long military history and a reputation for ruthless tactics, a guy like Savoy has got to have enemies. It would make sense that he would use something like this to protect his secrets. Then of course, there's also this clue."

Jason pushed the military history book closer to me. "Savoy went through the Midveil Military Training Academy about thirty years ago. According to these records, the leader of the academy during that time was General Lucas Vigenère—cousin to the inventor of the Vigenère Cipher."

I stared at a black-and-white image of a graduating class of students. The caption identified the stern-faced man on the far right as Savoy. The man slapping him proudly on the back was General Vigenère.

"It makes sense, right?" Jason said. "This has got to be it."

"Maybe so," Blue replied. "But even if it is, we're still going to need that keyword in order to solve it."

"I know," Jason admitted. "But maybe we can figure it out. We've already been reading Savoy's biographies to find some kind of code key."

"You really think it'll be that easy?" Blue asked.

"I didn't say anything about easy," Jason replied. "I'm saying it's possible."

"Where do we begin?"

"I would start with the names of important family members in his life," Jason said. "Even for a man like Savoy, passwords are always rooted in something personal."

Jason picked up one of the smaller-sized books from a pile at the edge of his table. "This book on military generals mentions that Savoy's immediate family consisted of three brothers, two sisters, his parents, and his grandparents on his mother's side. We could go through the census records and try their names first."

"We could . . ." I said slowly. "But first I want to try something else. Blue, I saw you reading a biography about Savoy. Did it mention anything about his wife?"

"Yeah," she responded. "They were married for over twenty-five years before she passed away from Crawley's Disease. Her name was Loretta."

This confirmed my suspicions.

"Try 'Loretta' first," I told Jason. "When I was snooping through Savoy's stuff I found a book and a cigar box with the inscription 'With Love, L.' If he lost her to an illness, he is carrying those things around as mementos. If the keyword is rooted in something personal, I would put money down that it's related to her."

"It's worth a shot," Jason said. "Pass me the page you took from his log and I'll give it a go."

I handed him the document and he began to work on translating the first two coded phrases on the page. Blue and I waited anxiously as he plugged the keyword "LORETTA" into the Vigenère Cipher. After a minute of tense waiting, he looked up with defeat on his face.

"I'm sorry, Crisa. That's not it," Jason said.

"Are you sure?"

"Yeah, look." Jason twisted around and handed me the paper he'd used to write the attempted translation.

"See. Gibberish," he said as I took in the disappointing results. "But don't worry. We'll keep trying. I'm still confident this is the right cipher. We just need to try different passwords. Between the three of us, I know we can crack it."

I glanced at a silver clock hanging on the mantle over the fireplace.

"Make that the two of you," I said remorsefully. "I have to go. It's almost time for me to have my secret meeting with whomever sent me that note I received the other night."

"Crisa, are you sure you should even go?" Blue asked. "With all the shady stuff happening with this commons rebellion, and Mauvrey, and your brothers, it could be a trap."

"Oh, I'm assuming it's a trap," I replied. "That way if it is, then I'm already on guard. If it's not, then I'll just be pleasantly surprised."

"Crisa."

"Blue, stop worrying. She'll be fine," Jason interceded. "She has her wand and her magic."

"You're half right," I said. "I exhausted my magic when I disenchanted the wooden plank." I gestured at the inanimate slab, which we'd propped against a wall in the corner. "I was already pretty drained from so much practice earlier, but that last trick finally did it. Now my magic has to reboot. Using my powers again isn't an option until tomorrow evening."

"Are you nuts?" Blue said. "If you don't have your powers then you're definitely not going alone."

"Blue," I said adamantly. "First off, I still have my wand. Second, this isn't a group decision; it's mine. I have to go alone otherwise it might spook whoever this person is from coming forward. And I have too many questions right now to take that risk." I flicked my eyes to the clock again. Quarter past two. "If I'm not back in half an hour, you're more than welcome to come storming the tunnel after me," I said, gesturing to a diagram on an end table, which I'd drawn earlier to show them how to access and operate the different castle passages. "But for now you're going to have to let me go, okay?"

Blue looked like she wanted to argue, but held in the impulse. "Fine," she grunted. "But thirty minutes exactly, you got it?"

"Yes, yes." I nodded.

"Here." Jason took his watch off and handed it to me. "Take this."

I strapped the watch to my wrist and gave my friends a confident look. "All right. You guys keep focusing on finding that keyword and I'll be back to help soon."

My friends reluctantly went back to their code-cracking as I left the library. The stranger's note had indicated we were to meet in the fifth of the castle's secret tunnels. I started to make my way to the room that would allow me access to it from inside the castle—the hall of the human-sized chessboard.

As expected, my route there was deserted. Most of the palace was asleep. The only people who wouldn't be were the King's Guard members assigned to the graveyard shift. But since many had called in sick, the men healthy enough to be on duty were appointed to patrol more important parts of the castle.

I entered the hall I sought. It was haunting at this hour. Not to say it wasn't creepy during the day; giant chess rooms tended to have that effect. Under the glass ceiling's nighttime luminescence though, the eerie aura magnified.

Clouds covered much of the moon tonight in thick, cumulus gray. The only warmth in the room came from the candelabras that lined the walls. These walls were four enormous mirrored panels that were thirty feet in height and double that in length. They reflected the vibrant orange hues of the candelabra flames, the chess pieces themselves, and my own person in an infinite pattern on all sides.

I stepped toward the center of the room—my footsteps echoing off the tile as I moved. The floor was checkered in massive onyx and chrome tiles. The onyx corresponded with the black chess pieces and the chrome with the white ones. The pieces were about five feet tall and hollow—constructed of a colored acrylic and titanium combo with a felt-lined bottom—making them easy to push along the smooth, life-size board.

I began to glide the chrome knights on the board to specific empty spaces on the right side and the onyx knights to spaces on the left. My final step was moving the far-right chrome pawn and the far-left onyx pawn two places forward and three places to the side.

The moment that last pawn slid into place, the floor began to vibrate. I stepped several paces back and braced myself. Every tile on the board (my own included) began to shift. The whole of the board was now in motion—rearranging itself like a large, living puzzle.

Several of the tiles in the center began to sink, transforming into the first steps in the spiral staircase concealed beneath the room.

*Here we go.*

Once the floor had settled, I grabbed a candelabra off the wall and entered the passage. When I was seven stairs down, the tile overhead jolted and moved again. I glanced up as the room was sealed off.

Of all the secret tunnels tucked within the castle, Tunnel number five was the least used. The most obvious reason for this was that unlocking this hidden stairwell required the specific, elaborate positioning of some very large pieces, making it a lot harder to access without drawing attention to yourself.

The other reason this route was not frequently utilized was that upon hitting the seventh stair down, a trigger was activated. This caused a chain reaction that reset the chessboard up top. The stairs that had been tile rose up, the opening reverted and closed itself off, and the pieces went back to their proper places.

The only way out of this tunnel now was at the other end. Which meant one way or another I would be seeing this clandestine meeting through.

Everything down here was black—my candelabra only able to illuminate one or two steps in front of me. I followed the twisting staircase with caution. My eyes strained on every outline and my ears listened for sounds aside from my own footsteps. At the bottom of the stairs I continued carefully through the tunnel until I sensed I was at about the midway point.

I glanced at Jason's watch in the candlelight. It was half past two exactly—my meet-up should begin any second.

I drew my wandpin in my free hand and clutched it tightly as I waited. While I couldn't use my powers to bring life to anything right now, I was beyond grateful that I could still use my wand. Until recently I didn't believe that Magic Exhaustion would allow it. After all, the reason my wand only worked for me was because it sensed my Fairy Godmother-based magic. And every time I operated it I used a small amount of that magic. Thus, Magic Exhaustion should have robbed me of the capability.

However, a couple of weeks ago after a training session left me with Magic Exhaustion, I used my wand without thinking and it worked. I asked Liza about this and she reminded me that since my wand had been separately enchanted to morph into whatever weapon I chose, it didn't need my magic to perform that function. The wand only needed the tiniest bit of my magic to detect me as its Fairy Godmother owner.

This still hadn't seemed like a complete explanation. Magic Exhaustion meant I was exhausted of magic, right? So I shouldn't have had any. But after I probed the matter sufficiently, Liza admitted something to me. Magic Exhaustion was not as absolute as she'd once led me to believe. In truth, it was like any other type of exhaustion. It didn't mean your strength vanished completely; it only meant you'd extremely fatigued it. Like runners after a marathon, their muscles might be weak and their bodies depleted, but that didn't mean they'd lost the ability to run. Magic Exhaustion didn't take away my power; it only reduced it to such a miniscule level that I couldn't perform any significant feat (i.e. bring anything to life intentionally). But there was still magic left in me—a small amount, sure, but enough to satisfy my wand's requirements.

I glanced at my watch.

Hmm.

While I had been punctual for this sketchy rendezvous, it seemed the meeting's instigator did not value timeliness with the same regard. I continued to wait there for him or her as the minutes ticked on.

At 2:40 a.m. I realized that whoever was meant to meet me was probably not going to show. And with my half hour almost up, I decided to call it a night, lest I risk Blue and Jason marauding through the castle passages looking for me.

I began my way down the tunnel anew, journeying toward the exit. My pace was ginger and slow at first. Then I heard a scream.

The horrifying, high-pitched cry echoed off the curved walls of the tunnel. I jumped in surprise, nearly dropping my candelabra. The sound had come from the tunnel exit where I was headed.

The scream came a second time and I started running toward it. As I ran, I heard it again and again and again. It sounded so close now that I felt I was about to collide with whoever was making it. But then I turned a corner and saw the exit to the tunnel twenty feet away. It was wide open. There was no sign of anyone in distress.

The bluish glow of night spilled into the tunnel. I was transfixed for a moment then the same scream projected around me and I almost leapt out of my skin. It was so loud and near. It sounded like it was coming from my feet.

I glanced down, confused. Something silver next to my shoe caught my eye. I crouched low and lit up the ground with my candelabra. It was a small gagecho, his pupils orange from the reflection of the flames. His throat pumped. And then the frightened female scream I'd been chasing erupted from his tiny mouth.

This gagecho had been producing the awful sound.

At first I was relieved. After all, the tone of that scream had made it sound like someone was getting murdered. But then I understood something and my relief rushed away.

Gagechos mimicked whatever noise they'd most recently heard. So if this one had copied a scream, then at some point someone down here *had* screamed. And I had a feeling I knew who it was.

There was no explanation for why the opening on this side of the tunnel was ajar. No one ever used this passage. If the gagecho had heard a scream close by, it probably belonged to the person who'd intended to meet me.

Feeling worried, I exited the tunnel and closed it behind me.

What had happened to this girl who'd sent me the message and wanted to speak with me in such a secretive manner?

And what had she wanted to tell me?

These questions looped around my brain as I scurried past the stables and skirted around the grounds until I made it to the main lawn. I saw Lucky asleep in the distance but did not stop to say hello. I darted into the hedge maze then eventually made it back to the library via the secret passage. My friends were halfway to the door when I emerged from the fireplace. The thirty-minute deadline had expired a couple of minutes ago and they were about to come after me.

I explained what had happened in the tunnels, my skin crawling.

"You saw no trace of this girl at all?" Blue clarified.

"No." I shook my head as I sat there, dazed. "Just that awful scream."

"Well, you shouldn't let it get to you," Jason tried to console me. "It's not like you know what happened to her."

"How many things would cause a person to scream like that?" I countered. I plopped my head back against one of the plush couch pillows. "Please tell me that you guys cracked Savoy's cipher while I was gone?"

"Sorry, chief," Blue said. "No luck. We've tried every family member's name but all the translations ended up being gobbledy-gook."

"Did you try things other than family names?"

"We tried the city he was born in, his nickname in the military, titles of his favorite books, direct quotes from his biographies, his sheep and hunting dogs' names, his—"

"Wait, hold on," I said, sitting up straighter. "His favorite books."

I thought back to that romantic novel I'd found in Savoy's trunk—the outlier of his possessions. It had been a gift from his wife. But unlike the cigar box, which was practical, I couldn't understand why he'd felt compelled to keep it with him. He clearly wasn't going to read it. And while the inscription inside was lovely, if he wanted it close by for sentimental purposes he could've just as easily torn out the page and kept it with him. There had to be a reason why he kept the book in its entirety.

I thought back to the book's cover—that lopsided yellow-and-black cottage with the flowers floating near it. It had seemed so familiar. But why?

My eyes wandered about the room as my brain searched for a trigger that would bring back whatever piece of information I was having trouble zeroing in on. That's when I saw it. Our midnight snacks were on the center table—a bowl of chocolate truffles, some pretzels, and Aunt Jemma's almond biscuits.

That was all it took.

Every year, my Aunt Jemma sent those cookies while she was on her annual trip to the Middlebrook countryside. However, every now and then she'd send other things too, like souvenir key chains, commemorative lace doilies, or postcards.

"Holy bananas! I know where I've seen it!"

"Seen what?" Jason asked.

"Hold on, I'll be right back," I said as I leapt off the couch.

I dashed out of the library and sped to the lift. I couldn't get to my room fast enough. When I arrived, I opened the bottom left hand drawer of my desk. I moved my Shadow Guardians book out of the way then dug around through the papers there—old letters, random notes, school report cards, receipts, and various postcards.

I pulled out a postcard I'd received from Aunt Jemma two

years ago during one of her trips to Middlebrook. I must have subconsciously remembered it this whole time, maybe even glanced at it when I had stored my Shadow Guardians book in here.

I flipped the text part of the postcard over in my hand to reveal the front image. It featured the exact same cottage as the cover of Savoy's book, right down to the chimney and the flowers floating around the exterior. The only difference was that at the top of this picture in bright yellow, cursive print was the words: "Greetings from the Famous Gravity Spot! — *Gravity, Middlebrook.*"

I remembered now. The Gravity Spot was this weird location Aunt Jemma had visited during one of her trips. According to legend, it had once been the sight of a great Fairy Godmother battle. And because of all the magic used there at the time, it had been left with this odd enchanted energy that made everything within a certain weight range float upon entering its gravity field.

The wheels in my head continued to turn as I connected the dots.

*Gravity . . .* I thought to myself. I closed my eyes and recalled the inscription in Savoy's book.

> *"Past summer's end and winter's fire,*
> *In the rains of spring and autumn tire,*
> *Keep my heart and always recall,*
> *Where Gravity froze, and we did fall."*
> – With Love, L.

I'd wondered why Savoy's wife had chosen to capitalize the word "gravity" in the final line of her poem. I'd assumed that it was because it was important. The truth though, was that in addition to being important, she'd capitalized it because it was *a name*.

I quickly made my way back to Blue and Jason in the library.

"Guys," I said, panting to catch my breath. "In all those history texts you've been reading that referenced Savoy, did any of them mention a place called Gravity, Middlebrook?"

"Um, that sounds kind of familiar," Jason said as he went over to grab a book from the table. "Give me a second." I waited with bated breath as he flipped and scanned pages.

"Here it is," he said, holding up the book. "I knew I'd read that name somewhere. Gravity, Middlebrook, is where Savoy met his wife. She was born there and one year when he and his troops were passing through—accompanying the king on a royal visit—he wandered into this place called the Gravity Spot where she worked. The rest is history."

"That it's then," I gasped, as I took the book from him and read the passage for myself. "That's what the password for the cipher is. *Gravity.* Savoy didn't just keep that book I told you about because of the inscription; he kept it because it was a memento of the place where the two of them first met. Based on how old it was, he might've even gotten it on the day in question."

Blue immediately went for a piece of parchment and began to plug the two coded columns of the logbook page into the Vigenère Cipher. Jason and I waited nervously as she worked in silence. After a minute, she looked up.

"It worked," she said. "The keyword actually worked!"

The three of us huddled over Blue's results to see for ourselves. Sure enough, the keyword of "GRAVITY" had yielded an actual translation.

### "PRODUCTS PURCHASED | PURCHASER"

"You're brilliant!" Blue said excitedly.

"Technically, I'm just a girl who broke into a suitcase and held onto a postcard way too long. But I'll take it," I replied, grinning. "Now come on, plug that keyword into the entry that corresponds with Aggie and Blaine's transaction. If the information for these other columns is 'Products Purchased' and 'Purchaser,' then it should tell us what they spent all that money on and who they bought it for."

Jason brought over the coded entry in question and laid it on the table in front of Blue who immediately started copying it down on a clean sheet. She scribbled furiously as she decrypted the code. After about thirty seconds she abruptly stopped writing.

"Blue, what's wrong?" Jason asked. "Did it work? Does the translation make sense?"

"Um, yeah, it worked," she said. "As to whether it makes sense or not, that's not something I can answer."

"Blue, you're scaring me," I said. "Show me what the translation says."

She didn't meet my eyes, but held up the paper.

"PRODUCTS PURCHASED | PURCHASER"
"SNIPER SERVICES | P. KNIGHT"

My heart stopped beating.

No.

No, no, no, no. It couldn't be, but it was. It was right in front of me written in black and white. There was only one member of the Knight family whose name started with a P.

"Pietro . . ." I swallowed hard as the truth settled in my throat like a lump of coal.

"I guess evil skipped a generation," Blue commented sadly.

"What?" I stuttered.

"Pietro is adopted, Crisa. You may think of him as your brother, but he's not. His aunt and grandmother were Cinderella's wicked stepsister and stepmother. There's evil in his blood. Maybe that explains this."

The lump in my throat burned. I felt angry, vengeful, and hopelessly sad. Without saying another word to my friends, I traipsed over to the couch and lay down, staring up at the ceiling.

"Crisa?" Jason said.

"I need a minute," I managed.

I needed more than a minute, actually. But with the big banquet tomorrow and a treacherous brother sleeping in the castle, I didn't think the universe would afford me any more than that. Why would it? It was not in the habit of showing mercy. Tonight was no exception.

# CHAPTER 29

# End of the Line

y gown for the banquet was a romantic work of art. The powder blue, floor-length ensemble was made of two pieces with the upper part in the style of a conservative crop top. It had an A-line silhouette and a mock turtleneck with a matching, lightweight cape that flowed off the shoulders and draped behind me to the floor. My favorite part of the dress was the shimmering white dove with spread wings that was embroidered into the crop top.

I stepped away from the mirror to collect my wandpin. Once I'd secured it in place, I opened the top drawer of my desk and pulled out the gold wristband Alex and I used to share. Despite my unease about our relationship, I proceeded to fasten the band around my left wrist for luck. After what Blue, Jason, and I had discovered last night, I needed Alex and I to be on the same team.

Aggie and Blaine had purchased "Sniper Services" for "P. Knight," confirming my doubts once and for all that Pietro was involved with the commons rebellion.

The revelation cut me deep. It felt like my heart had a large crack in it. His betrayal was the hardest thing I'd ever had to stomach. And yet, the understanding did not cause me great shock or devastation. In retrospect—despite my attempts to ignore Lenore and Susannah's accusations—because of Pietro's recent shady behavior, I think I had been suspicious of him for a long time. Ever since my talk with Liza when she advised me to be careful with how I regarded him, it felt as though I'd been subconsciously preparing myself for something like this.

Part of me wanted Pietro to be severely punished. But my love for him was still there, even if my faith in him wasn't. This had to be handled another way.

For starters, I was not turning the condemning information about Pietro over to Lenore. I would not let the Godmother Supreme silence my brother the way she had silenced all other attempted uprisings and their advocates in the past. Traitor or not, he was my brother. My friends and I would proceed delicately.

In spite of the emotions storming around inside my head, I promised myself that I would remain calm. It was like with my magic; I was in command of my power when I remained steady and focused. And that's what I had to be right now—steady and focused. I needed my mind to be clear and my heart under control if I was to handle whatever was coming today.

Everything felt so random, yet so connected. Mauvrey had come to my castle at some point. Her parents were arriving from Tunderly. Pietro had purchased the services of a sniper. My mother was getting increasingly sick by the day. A debilitating illness was spreading through the King's Guard and palace staff. My mysterious note sender had failed to show up at our meeting. A gagecho echoed screams in the tunnel.

And then there was today. Many high-ranking protagonists and royals were attending the banquet being held in honor of the Weatheralls and our kingdoms' Vicennalia Aurora partnership. With so many VIPs in one place at one time, I had a strong feeling that whatever had been building these last few weeks was set to culminate in the hours to come. All we had to do was figure out what was in store and what we were going to do about it. Not showing our hand regarding Pietro was key to that.

"Hey, you ready?"

I turned to find Jason in my doorway. I was not surprised to see my friend dressed so formally, as my mother had fully ensured my friends would be properly attired for their stay. I *was* surprised by how well the style fit him. Jason always looked good at our school balls, but the regal, Mideveilian touches on his suit made my friend appear more princely than I'd ever seen him.

A fancy sheath with a sword hung at his side. This was a customary look for royal/protagonist functions, but I'm sure he would've preferred to have his trusty axe with him. Given my anxiety over today's events, I would've preferred that too.

"Yeah, I'm ready," I said as I met him in the doorway. "Where's Blue?"

"I knocked on her door, but she said she needed more time and that she'd meet us in the ballroom. Something about her dress's skirt being big enough to house a travelling circus. Does that mean anything to you?"

I gestured at my dress. "Do you see what I have on?"

My cape swooshed behind me as Jason and I began our way down the corridor. Daylight streamed through the glass in angelic streaks.

"Other than the stuff with the maps, how's everything been going?" I asked awkwardly. "Most of our letters dealt with quest business, and I feel like we've been dealing with my junk nonstop since you got here so I haven't gotten a chance to ask."

"School's fine." Jason shrugged. "Like Blue said, our Twenty-Three Skidd team's in first right now. If we keep up the good work I think we could win the year. Your team is in third. Oh, and you should know that instead of selecting another person from tryouts, Javier and Gordon are holding your spot. When you get back, it's yours if you want it."

I felt a moment of unexpected, unbridled happiness. I'd figured that they'd given away my spot on the Seven Suns to a runner-up. Knowing it would be waiting for me when I returned to school made me giddy with joy.

I swallowed my smile quickly though. It was misplaced right now given the circumstances, and given that this hadn't been where I was going with the conversation.

"That's really great," I replied. "But what I meant was how's everything been going with you? I mean, handling what I told you—"

"About me dying?"

He said it so bluntly I was surprised.

"I guess I'm handling it as well as anyone could," Jason continued. "Since you have no idea when it's going to happen, I'm just trying not to think about it."

"How's that working out for you?"

He raised his eyebrows. "How do you think?"

I wrung my hands from the guilt. "In case I haven't said it enough, I'm sorry, Jason. You shouldn't have to deal with this. It's not fair."

"You *have* said it enough, Crisa. And your apology is as unnecessary now as it was a month ago. Life—even the fairytale kind—isn't always fair. I should no more have to deal with knowing I'm going to die than you should have to deal with foreseeing it. But that's the lot we were given. All we can do is try our best to move forward, do some good, and make a difference in the ways we can while we have the chance. If we just feel sorry for ourselves then we might as well lay down and die right now because we've already given up."

I was filled with tremendous respect for Jason. How could he be so brave in the face of this? How could he hold it together and keep his head so level? He was amazing. And he inspired me to be the same.

"You're still sure you don't want to tell Blue, though?" I asked as we entered the lift at the end of the hall. I hoped that he'd had a change of heart in regards to this. Not telling Blue was killing me. I'd assured her at the close of last semester that I wouldn't keep secrets from her anymore. I didn't like not living up to that promise.

"Definitely," he said. "No more than I want you to keep asking me if I'm okay. I'm not, but I accept it. As should you."

"Are you sure?" I pressed. "Because while I get where you're coming from, I think that she would—"

"No, Crisa," he said gently.

The lift came to a halt on the ground floor. Its glass doors slid open but we didn't step out immediately.

"Whatever happens—and however this ends up playing out—you can't tell her. You promised."

"I know, Jason, but I just . . ." I sighed. "You know what?

Never mind. I won't say anything. Just like I won't keep asking you if you're all right."

"Thanks," he said with sincerity. "I appreciate it."

We stepped out of the lift and were immediately swept into the traffic of the corridor. The hall leading to the ballroom was bustling with kitchen staff carrying fully loaded platters, decorators draping columns with colored garlands, florists filling vases, and bakers wielding trays of cakes.

I leapt to the side as Sooz and her posse of event planners came marching through. She nodded to me but didn't slow her stride.

I looked up and saw a castle attendant hanging an oversized, decorative hydrangea ball from the ceiling—one of many dangling throughout the corridor. I smiled when he saw me, but he didn't return the greeting. Instead he gave me a sort of stern, narrow-eyed glare. It sent a weird feeling up my spine.

As Jason and I entered the ballroom, I was astounded by how beautiful it looked. Despite having grown up here, I was always amazed by the way the place could transform from event to event, and the lavish splendor of royal affairs never failed to impress me. Dozens of tables outfitted in silks and glittering runners were set up. The floral centerpieces I'd designed sat upon them proudly. The chairs had off-white cushions made of shimmery fabric. Four exquisitely sharp and ornate glass chandeliers surrounded a fifth, much larger, one in the center. Decorative silks that matched the tablecloths and runners interconnected the beautiful light fixtures and also dangled from the mezzanine alcoves above my head.

High up along the room's back wall there were ten mini alcoves that connected to two levels of hidden mezzanines. Lighting technicians worked from there to create atmospheric magic during important functions. We also typically positioned guards in a few of the alcoves to keep an eye on proceedings. The only access to these mezzanines was through a single door concealed behind a decorative tapestry by the windows.

I glanced up at a guard in one of the alcoves. He was staring across the room with a tense expression on his face. I followed his line of sight. Alex and my father were standing on the stage on the far side of the room where my family, the Weatheralls, and I would be sitting for the banquet. The two of them were talking with some of their advisors. Both were in formal dress with military regalia decorating their coats and sashes, swords stowed in elegant sheaths at their sides, and polished shoes reflecting the daylight pouring in from outside. I felt this light against my face as Jason and I glided across the room.

The left side of the ballroom was checkered with windows of various sizes and shapes placed at different elevations—it reminded me of the geometric intricacy of honeycombs. Two chrome doors at the center led to the main lawn. Guards stood in front of them now, so Jason and I kept to the back wall. The lowest windows were at about my chest height. Through one I could see the beautiful spring day, and Lucky, who was sleeping in the sun.

I had assured my parents that he would not be a problem today. Lately Lucky spent most of his time sleeping. I guess he thought we were on vacation. Still, my parents had mentioned "their daughter's pet dragon" in the invitations they'd sent out. They couldn't risk any of our guests being surprised and having a panic attack or—more likely, given how many Lord Channing's alumni and protagonists were coming—*launching* an attack.

When I returned my gaze to the entrance of the ballroom I spotted Pietro. His formal attire emphasized his rank as a captain in the King's Guard. His coat was black with silver buttons and a silver sash. His uniform had several medals of honor pinned to it, and there was a cobalt stripe on his sash and epaulettes to signify his higher rank. A long sword swung from a sheath attached to his belt.

Pietro made a beeline for me the moment he saw us. My body tensed. Jason touched my arm as if to remind me to stay strong. I appreciated it, and remained committed to keeping my cool.

"Crisa," Pietro said. "Mom wants to see you in her room. She says it's important."

"All right." I nodded. "What's wrong? I thought she'd be here already."

"She isn't feeling well and needs your help."

I turned to Jason. "Man the fort for me, will you?"

I headed out the door, anxious to check on my mother, but realized that Pietro was following me.

"Was there something else?" I asked.

"No, just. . ." He looked around the bustling hall. "I'm worried, Crisa. Too many of my men are out sick today. I'm going to have my work cut out for me."

"Well, if there are no unforeseen circumstances, I can't imagine your worry is necessary, Pietro," I said with an edge.

"Yeah. I suppose not." He flicked his eyes back to the ballroom. "Look, the guests are going to start arriving in the next twenty minutes and the Weatheralls will be here about an hour after that. When they get here, do me a favor and be on the lookout for anything out of the ordinary. Keep your eyes open, okay?"

"Believe me," I said. "They're open."

"Pietro!" One of my brother's right-hand guards came jogging over. "Rafael just started hacking up. He's too sick to work. You're going to have to reassign someone to the east entrance."

"I cannot catch a break today," my brother groaned. He shook his head, frustrated. Then he looked to me. "I'll see you later. I have to deal with this. Remember what I said."

I continued down the hall only to be accosted by one of my ladies-in-waiting. An all-but-confirmed traitor from Lenore's list, Daphne Reigns was one of the last people I wanted to see right now. She cantered across the corridor as I dodged another florist. "Princess!" she called.

She came jogging up to me carrying a to-go cup. "I noticed that you did not drink the tea we brought you this morning. With such a big day ahead, I thought I'd bring you some to enjoy while you're on the move."

I rolled my eyes. The fact that she was harassing me with something so trivial inflamed my mood. "Thanks, but I'll pass," I said.

"But, princess—"

"Daphne, I'm serious. Get out of my way."

For an instant Daphne appeared more resentful than hurt.

She promptly let me pass, though I barely took ten steps before another lady-in-waiting called my name.

"Princess!"

"I'm a little busy right now, Minnie," I responded without slowing down.

"So, I guess we'll just turn around and go home then?" a familiar voice said.

I froze. Then I whirled around. The instant I saw Daniel and SJ standing there, I forgot the millions of things I had to worry about. My face broke into a wide grin.

"You made it!"

I felt the instinct to rush in and embrace my friends, but I caught myself. Although I was glad they were here, I quickly remembered that my relationship with both of them had soured before I left school. SJ was probably still unhappy with me and Daniel had put up a wall between us. The memory hit me like an unwelcome slap.

They were still my good friends, though. And I *had* missed them. So I tried my best to pretend that there wasn't any awkwardness between us. I gave SJ a small hug, which she returned, and bumped Daniel on the shoulder playfully.

"Thank you, Minnie," I said. "Will you go find Jason in the ballroom and tell him the others have arrived and will meet up with him shortly?"

"Yes, princess," Minnie said with a curtsy.

When she'd gone, Daniel looked me up and down, taking in my ensemble. "So this is the real you? *Princess* is it?"

"Please," I scoffed. "This is all pretense. Now this . . ."

I lifted the hem of my skirt to reveal my boots and leggings. "*This* is the real me. And it's 'Knight' to you, Daniel. Call me princess again and I'll have you thrown in the stockade."

"Do you actually have a stockade?" he asked, a hint of concern in his voice.

"You know, I'm not going to answer that." I smirked. "Anyway, you guys need to hurry and change. This thing's going to start soon and I—"

"Blue!" SJ called.

I turned around as my friend sashayed up to us in a strapless, pure white gown with a skirt of feathers.

"You look beautiful," SJ said.

"I look like a goose," Blue countered.

"Let's agree to disagree," I said. "Blue, can you show Daniel and SJ to their rooms—they're next to yours—and fill them in on the way? I've really gotta go check on my mom. I'll meet you guys in the ballroom in ten, all right?"

"You got it, chief," Blue said. She leaned in and lowered her voice to a whisper. "And not to alarm you, but on my way here I saw this bearded dude that one of the guards addressed as General Savoy."

"You're joking."

"'Fraid not. Our new friend is here, which means your hunch was probably right. Whatever those 'Sniper Services' Pietro bought are, they're probably being delivered today."

"If you see him again, stay on him," I said.

I took the east lift to my parents' suite on the fifth floor. As I approached, the guards announced my entrance. Once they'd let me in, they immediately shut the doors behind me.

"Mom?" I called.

I heard coughing, but no response. I followed the noise into my mother's massive walk-in closet.

My mother was sitting on a stool in a gorgeous sapphire blue gown. Her hair was twisted up regally with a crown of actual sapphires, matching her earrings. She was leaning over her vanity, clutching a wad of tissues.

"Mom?" I repeated.

She turned around. Her eyes were slightly red. Her face was droopy and paler than normal, and her lips were dry like she was dangerously close to dehydration.

"Pumpkin, oh good, I am glad you are here," she said as she straightened up and threw her tissues in the trash. "I need to ask a favor. I am afraid my cold is a bit worse today, so I am going to need you to introduce the Weatheralls on my behalf at the start of the banquet. All you have to do is say a few words of welcome to the room—tying in the importance of the Vicennalia

Aurora and how it brings us all together. Can you do that for me?"

"Um, yeah, sure," I said. "But, Mom, are you even well enough to go to the banquet? You don't look so good."

"I am fine, sweetie, just a bit under the weather." My mom clutched her stomach with one hand and grasped onto the edge of her vanity with the other. She seemed to be trying to keep herself from fainting.

I was about to protest again but one of my mother's ladies-in-waiting (a chubby redhead named Abigail) came rushing into the room. "Your majesty," she said, curtsying to us both. "Something's happened. The king requests the presence of you and the princess in the royal work chambers immediately."

"What's wrong?" I asked as we followed her out of the room.

"I'm not sure, princess," Abigail replied, "but the king insists that the two of you be escorted there by guards."

The men posted outside my mother's room marched us to the throne room downstairs. My apprehension grew. I had no idea what was so urgent that my father had felt it necessary to call on us like this.

The royal work chambers were private quarters that my mother and father used when conducting extremely confidential business. I'd only ever been in there a handful of times over the years, and on most of those occasions I'd been snooping.

The grand stairs to the castle's main entrance were on my right as we walked through the foyer. The railings were wrapped with garland, sparkling silver ribbon, and bunches of small violet flowers my mother had told me were called Sweet Williams.

Staff members were busily putting the finishing touches on the castle's festive appearance. They continued to hang ornamental green and purple hydrangea balls from the ceiling. I noticed Blaine Weldhouse within their ranks and for a second I was tempted to kick the ladder out from under his feet, even if it meant bringing a dozen or so painstakingly hung decorations down with him.

My mother and I were ushered into the throne room before I could act on the impulse. We walked across the room then through the curtained door beside the thrones on the back wall, entering the royal work chambers. The guards stopped at the forest green curtains and closed the door behind us from the outside.

Inside the room were my father, Alex, Sooz, Pietro, Rod Davis and Anthony Graystone (two other captains from the King's Guard), and a woman I didn't recognize. She had majestic, thick black hair, tan skin, and was crying into Pietro's shoulder. He had one arm around her.

"What happened?" I asked as I stepped toward my father at his mahogany desk. "Who's that?" I pointed to the unfamiliar woman.

"Crisa, this is Evette Black," Sooz said with great solemnity. "Pietro's girlfriend."

My expression cringed with confusion from the unexpectedness. The woman in question broke away from Pietro's shoulders and turned to me. Her dark brown eyes were bloodshot and her nose was red from sniffling. Other than those factors, she was very pretty, muscular, and exotic-looking. Also, both Pietro and Alex had been right in their earlier descriptions of her. She did wear a lot of leather.

"Evette," my mother said with a cordial nod.

As my mom crossed the forest green carpet to take a seat, my father explained why we were all gathered here.

"Miss Black's younger sister Agatha is a server at the palace," he said with great graveness in his tone.

"Aggie," Evette whispered. "Her name was Aggie."

"Was?" I repeated. "What do you mean *was*?"

"Aggie was found dead this morning," my father responded. "Captain Davis discovered her body in the stables when he was making his rounds. It looked like she had been dragged there, but we're not sure from where. Nor are we sure who killed her and why. The castle physician believes it happened last night between two and four in the morning."

My mother and I were speechless. We all were. The only sound in the room was Evette's muffled sobbing on Pietro's fancy jacket.

I had my own instance of near fainting then, and I steadied myself against a mahogany bookcase. That awful, blood-curdling scream I'd heard last night from the gagecho belonged to a girl. And that tunnel was so close to the stables. I was convinced that Aggie Black was the person who'd wanted to meet me last night, which meant she'd left me the note that lead me to discover Mauvrey had been in the castle. But the poor girl was killed when she was coming to find me and then her body was dragged out to the stables so she wouldn't be found immediately. That gagecho must've heard her dying scream when she was killed.

I had to resist the urge to throw up.

"The guests will be arriving any minute," Sooz said curtly, breaking the silence. "It is too late to cancel. All we can do is keep this quiet until after the banquet. Once the king and queen of Tunderly depart, we can resume the investigation, but for now we must keep up appearances."

"Dad . . ." Pietro started to say.

My father held up his hand. "I'm sorry, Pietro, but Miss Marberg is right. There are too many protagonists and diplomats arriving. We cannot let it leak that there has been a murder in the castle. The panic would be disastrous."

He turned his attention to Evette. "Miss Black, we will find whoever did this to your sister, I promise you. But I am afraid that for the next twenty-four hours, the matter must be kept silent. Information about Aggie cannot leave this room."

Evette gave a small nod as Pietro held her tighter and addressed my father.

"I get it, Dad. But the fact remains that a murder did happen on the grounds. And since the gates have been closed since last night, the murderer is likely still *on* the grounds."

"Sir, if I may." Anthony Graystone stepped forward. Graystone was tall and solidly built like Pietro. His shoulders alone were hero-worthy. But his face was not handsome. It was too sharp, his Adam's apple too large, and his hair too slick.

"Davis and I can tighten security around the castle entrance," Graystone said. "If we reassign men near the gates, we could catch anyone trying to sneak off the grounds."

"Fine," Pietro said. "But don't take any men away from the back exits. And I want a guard in every one of the main watchtowers and double the security in the ballroom."

"Sir," Davis (shorter and humbler looking than Graystone) interrupted. "I don't think we have the manpower to—"

"Just get it done," Pietro said.

They saluted my brother and dashed out of the room. My mother coughed violently.

"Cin," Sooz said, addressing my mother. "Are you all right?"

"Fine," she insisted as she stood. My mom crossed to the other side of the room and took Evette's hands in hers. "I am so sorry about your sister. As the king said, we will find who did this. In the meantime, you may use the guest quarters adjacent to Pietro's room to rest. My ladies will keep you company and get you anything you need, and I will have a guard posted outside your room."

"Thank you, majesty," Evette said softly.

"I'll take her there now," Pietro said. Then he paused and pivoted toward Alex. "I just had a thought. Get word to Graystone and Davis; tell them they can divert eight men from the western corridor and twelve from the southern corridor to use in the ballroom. I want one stationed in every one of the overhead alcoves in the mezzanines and the remainder at the ready on the back stairs, just in case."

"I'll go tell them now," Alex said as he exited the room.

I thought he gave me a weird stare as he passed, but I could've been imagining it. Pietro and Evette left the room a moment later and my mother followed. She was still wobbling like she might faint.

"Mom," I touched her arm. "Please go lie down. The world won't end if you miss this banquet. Isn't there enough going on for you to realize that it probably isn't safe to be walking around right now, especially if you're feeling like you might pass out?"

"Crisanta, for the last time, I am *fine*. There are more important things for us to worry about than my slight illness. Just go get me a cup of tea from the kitchen and then join me in the ballroom. Guests have started arriving and they need to be greeted."

"Mom, enough with the tea. You need to—"

"Mind your mother, Crisanta," my father interjected. "She's right. There are too many things to worry about to waste time arguing. Now go."

I rolled my eyes in frustration then glanced at Sooz and gave her a look indicating she should follow me out.

The castle's main doors had been opened while we were in our meeting. In just five minutes the place had become a splendid madhouse. Guests were arriving in throngs. A spectacle of fine ladies and gentleman filled the foyer. They came pouring down the staircase—smiling, laughing, and greeting one another as they flowed gracefully toward the ballroom. I tried my best to remain unnoticed as I slipped into an adjacent hallway and waited.

Sooz found me soon after and I ushered her into the nearest empty room, which happened to be the music room.

I didn't trust Sooz anymore, but I knew that in this case we were on the same side. I may have had a very different idea about keeping order than she and Lenore did, but none of us wanted a commons rebellion. So I let our feud slide for a moment and leveled with her—taking "the enemy of my enemy is my friend" approach.

"Crisa, this better be good," Sooz said, crossing her arms. "Do you have any idea what's happening right now?"

"More than most," I said. "Sooz, Aggie may have been on Lenore's list of suspects, and I did see her multiple times saying and doing suspicious things, but she tipped me off earlier in the week in regards to something really major. Then she sent me a note telling me to meet her last night but never showed. So now I'm wondering if maybe she wasn't so much participating in the commons rebellion as she was spying on it. And the reason she wanted to meet me in such a secretive way was because she was trying to warn me about something. Only someone found out and killed her before she got the chance.

"It's plausible," Sooz said slowly. "And if you're right, and she was trying to warn you last night, chances are it probably had something to do with today's events."

"Agreed. We should go talk to Evette. Maybe she knows what her sister was up to and can shed some light."

"I'll go. You help your mother. And if you see anything suspicious, let me know. The Weatheralls will be arriving in little less than an hour and I have a bad feeling."

"Welcome to my world."

Sooz headed for the east lift to find Evette and I continued my way down the corridor. I'd help my mother, but first I needed to regroup with my friends. Skirts and capes and feathers of every color impeded my way as I shimmied through the mass. Eventually I made it to the ballroom where my friends were waiting.

SJ and Daniel had changed. Daniel was dressed in regal attire and looked as dapper as Jason. His personal sword was in a sheath at his side, fitting in with the proper regalia.

SJ wore a silver silk gown with a high collar that made her neck look swan-like. A small crossbody bag was slung across her chest, bulging with whatever she had stuffed inside.

"Where have you been?" Blue asked. "We were getting worried."

"A palace staffer named Aggie Black was found dead this morning. She was the one leaving me the notes. Her older sister—who's been dating Pietro—is here. Our kingdom's ambassador, Susannah, just went to go talk to her. I think my mom is on death's door. And the Weatheralls are arriving in half an hour. I'm probably leaving something out, but I think that's more than enough to keep us busy for a few minutes."

"What can we do?" SJ asked earnestly.

I was somewhat surprised by SJ's genuine tone and desire to help. But I guess it was like with the magic hunter attack at school—when things got serious we could put aside our differences and remember what mattered, one another included.

"Divide and conquer," I said. "Blue, find Savoy and follow him. I don't want that guy out of your sight. Jason, track down Blaine Weldhouse—the dude I pointed out to you yesterday—and find out what those Sniper Services he purchased are for. I'm done playing games. We need answers. Don't cause a scene, but beyond that, I don't care how you make him talk. SJ, can you keep your eyes on my mom until I get back? And, Daniel . . ."

He may have been the person I felt the farthest from right now, but I knew when it came to combat and conflict, he could be relied upon. It was no different than when our relationship first started. We'd fought our way out of plenty of dangers together without being close. If our friendship had returned to that original state, I knew he would fight just as hard.

"See that tapestry back there?" I said, gesturing to the large floral wall hanging at the back of the ballroom. "Behind it is a staircase that leads to the mezzanines connected to these alcoves." I nodded up. "Pietro is having Alex divert more men to guard them, but I need you to stand watch until those reinforcements arrive. Okay?"

My friends all accepted their duties without hesitation. Despite what was going on with us personally, we were like a well-oiled machine when united for a common cause.

I felt a small pang of gladness. I was happy to be reminded of how well we worked as a team. It'd been a while since we had, and I missed it.

We went our separate ways. I hastened into the corridor and headed toward the main kitchen. It was swarming with waiters, caterers, and cooks zipping about getting food ready. Thankfully, they were so consumed with their work they paid me no mind. As I made my way past them I was tempted to help myself to a platter of shrimp dumplings and a few mini crème brûlées, but I mentally scolded myself for the gluttony. I had to focus. Trivial a task as it was, I had to prepare some tea for my mother then get back to the ballroom to defend against any threats that dared emerge.

I rushed through the meat locker and pantry to a back kitchen with industrial sized fridges. Inside the center fridge I found a large jug marked "Seasonal Tea Brew," which I lugged onto the counter. I grabbed a teakettle from the cookware closet and used some matches in one of the drawers to light the stove. Hastily, I poured the cold, translucent liquid into the kettle. As I waited for it to boil, I looked out the side door. The wildlife of the castle's forest could be seen through the window.

"Crisa?"

I whirled around, startled to find Pietro there.

"Pietro, what are you doing here?"

"I have to tell you something. I didn't want to involve you, but I think we're past me being able to protect you."

"Are you talking about the commons rebellion?"

Pietro's eyes widened. "How did you—"

"Ugh, give me some credit, will you? I swear, everyone around here thinks I'm either dense or helpless. I know what's going on, Pietro." I was too frustrated to hold in my suspicions and anger any longer. "Aggie was trying to warn me about something to do with the rebellion last night, but was killed before she could. What I don't know is what your involvement in all of this is."

"My involvement?" Pietro repeated.

"I've seen you whispering to Aggie in the shadows when you thought no one was looking. I've heard rumors and spotted the signs. Sooz warned me. Lenore and Alex warned me. I never fully believed them, but now I know better. What are you planning for today, Pietro? What are those 'Sniper Services' you purchased? How did you get mixed up with this rebellion? And give me one good reason why I shouldn't turn you over to Mom and Dad."

Pietro looked stunned. "Crisa, I don't understand half of what you're talking about, but I'm *not* a part of the commons rebellion. I'm trying to stop it."

"What?"

"After I'd been dating Evette for a while, her sister confided in me. She'd heard rumblings of a commons rebellion faction within the palace that was plotting to overthrow Mom and Dad. We devised a plan where Aggie would slowly worm her way into the group, get them to trust her as one of their own, and then spy on them for me. That's why she and I would meet in secret sometimes—so she could fill me in on the information she'd acquired. If you saw her dealing with anyone else that looked suspicious, it was because she was playing the part, continuing her undercover work on my behalf."

My heart had gone numb and cold since I thought Pietro was the enemy. Learning that he wasn't a traitor filled me with untold relief and resuscitated the part of me that had stopped beating. It was like someone had given me an electric shock.

I believed what he was saying. It was a brother-sister thing, but it was also an intuition thing. I'd already faced many antagonists and characters with wicked intent. I saw none of their maleficence in Pietro. He was good. It hit me all at once. All I had to do was look into his eyes to truly know that. I felt ashamed. I'd let the Godmother Supreme's suspicions, as well as those of Susannah, Liza, and Alex influence me when I should have trusted my own instincts from the beginning.

"So you knew about the meeting last night? The notes left under my door?"

"I needed Aggie to warn you because I couldn't," Pietro explained. "Some of the members of the commons rebellion suspected I was on to them, and Aggie told me a while back that they were watching you too. I couldn't talk to you directly without tipping my hand, so she had to do it."

"That first note Aggie left me had me go to the mausoleum and dig up a glass Pegasus figurine. I sent that figurine after Mauvrey Weatherall a while back and ordered it to follow her until it could lead me to wherever she'd gone. What does she have to do with this?"

"We found out a few weeks ago that Mauvrey Weatherall is one of the main characters pulling the strings behind all this. Aggie only saw her on the grounds once; it was by the mausoleum. She witnessed Mauvrey destroy that Pegasus and bury it. Later, Aggie overheard Daphne Reigns mention that it had something to do with you. We figured that leaving you a note was a good way to tip you off about her presence without drawing too much attention to ourselves."

*Mauvrey was helping to orchestrate the commons rebellion?*

But Mauvrey worked for the antagonists. That meant the

antagonists were invested in the commons rebellion and were the ones gunning for our kingdoms to be overthrown. It went with their MO—eliminating rulers and protagonists, causing chaos, and tearing Book apart. And that had to be why this rebellion was more serious than the previous threats the Godmothers had been able to extinguish in the past. This time the commons had the shrewd and devious brilliance of the antagonists to guide their cause.

The only thing that didn't make sense was why the antagonists were helping the commons. That was a piece of the puzzle that didn't fit. Antagonists were far from the compassionate type. Why invest their time and resources in this rebellion when they already had their own pawns and plans for destroying the realm? It felt like I was missing something.

"What about last night?" I asked Pietro.

"Aggie was supposed to warn you about today so you'd be fully prepared. I didn't know she never made it."

"All right then, Pietro. Just tell me, for the love of Book what *is* going on today?"

Pietro gave a worried look. "I'm not a hundred percent sure. Aggie said that she and Blaine were instructed to hire Sniper Services from Savoy. Only I don't know who they're planning to take out. The commons rebellion may be targeting rulers, but different types of government officials and protagonists in Century City have been murdered over the last couple months. With so many important people here today, anyone could be Mauvrey's next target. That's why this sickness spreading through the King's Guard couldn't have come at a worse time. The odds are against us. I need your help—and your friends' help too, if you think they can handle it."

"You'll never meet a more formidable set of protagonists," I said proudly. "I've already filled them in on the threats and they've got our back. I'll update them on what you just told me, and we will be ready to act if we see anything."

"I don't want you guys to get in any danger. You're just kids," Pietro said. "If you see something suspicious, tell me and I'll—"

"Pietro." I waved my hand to cut him off. "We're kids, but we're also main characters. We don't need your protection. Trust me. You have no idea what we're capable of."

Pietro sized me up. "All right, Crisa. I'm counting on you. Between you, your friends, and Alex, I think we have enough extra manpower to spot and stop any trouble before it happens. With the twenty other guards I told Alex to assign to the ballroom, we should be covered." He released a huff and swallowed audibly. "I've really got to get back now." My brother put his hand on my shoulder for a second then made for the door.

My head was working on overdrive trying to process all this new information. I had almost all of the answers I needed. All but one.

"Pietro," I said.

My brother paused with his hand against the door.

"I snooped around the stall of Crossbows Etc. at the War Games Convention. In Savoy's log—where he recorded the Sniper Services that Blaine and Aggie paid for—it said that the purchaser was P. Knight. That's why I thought it was you behind this. If it wasn't, why did Savoy record it that way?"

"I can't explain that, Crisa," my brother responded, shaking his head. "Maybe Blaine told Savoy to put my name down to try and frame me in case their deal went sour."

I looked into my brother's dark brown eyes. He was being sincere. He wasn't hiding anything. For the first time in a long time, I felt that someone was being completely honest with me. It was a nice change of pace.

I approached my brother and put my hand on his arm. "I believe you," I said. "And I'm sorry if for a while there I didn't. You deserve more than that."

The teakettle whistled—alarming us not to waste any more time.

"I'm going to go check on the security by the rear exits one more time before the banquet starts," he said. "You good?"

"Yeah," I said. "I'll see you in there."

I raced to the teakettle. With all that was going on, I couldn't believe that I still had to make a stupid cup of tea for my mother.

I really hoped she would be okay, and that this detour was worth it. I poured the boiling liquid into a to-go cup.

The smell hit me hard. The intensity of it felt like a hammer falling upon my memory. The tea had a very specific scent about it—sweet yet sharp, but something else too. I inhaled deeper. I knew I'd smelled this somewhere before, somewhere recent. The fragrance was so familiar, so impressionable, so wintery?

*Wait.*

*Sweet, sharp, wintery.*

My eyes darted down at the translucent liquid. Suddenly I recognized what the smell was.

*Jasper berries!*

I dropped the cup. My hands were shaking.

This tea—the tea that my mom had been drinking, that had been given to the King's Guard and the castle staff, that my own attendants had been attempting to serve me every day—it was *jasper berry* tea. A half dozen light bulbs went off in my head.

It wasn't some random flu bug or virus sweeping the palace. Almost everyone in the castle was being poisoned! All the liquid in that jug from the fridge was poison tea made from the toxic jasper berries that grew by the mausoleum.

This must have been a part of the commons' plan the entire time. Mauvrey and her followers must've decided that in order to get close to their target, they would need to weaken the palace security. This poisoned tea had reduced the number of guards and attendants by 60 percent, even taking my ever-vigilant mother out of action.

No one had suspected a thing. Why would they? Tea was tea. The only reason I recognized that scent was because I'd been surrounded by the jasper berry bushes the other day as I dug around behind the mausoleum.

It was a good thing that Pietro and I hated tea. If we didn't, the stuff would have surely made us sick as well, and increased the odds that Mauvrey and her common followers would succeed.

Suddenly I heard a thud on the side door. Then something crashed through the window. I jumped back, shielding my face as glass shattered inward and an object just as transparent plowed through. It was SJ's Pegasus figurine! The tiny thing flew in from outside and darted around excitedly. It seemed to be motioning for me to follow.

*Mauvrey.*

The Pegasus was supposed to return to me once it'd found my princess nemesis and could lead me back to her. If it was here now, I had a bad feeling she was close.

The Pegasus zoomed out through the hole in the window. I picked up the hem of my skirt and started after it. When the figurine reached the edge of the lawn, it plummeted downhill into the wild, forested area of the palace grounds. Dead leaves crackled under my boots as my cape and dress snagged on crooked tree limbs—tearing jagged slits into the fabric. I wasn't sure how far I'd run until I found the jasper berry bushes. Their distinct smell confirmed my theory about the tea's origins.

The Pegasus made a wide, left turn and I followed it to the mausoleum's front entrance. The doors were open and the Pegasus darted inside. I clambered up the stairs under the shadow of the shining clock that indicated it was 11:15 a.m. My boots echoed off the tile as I entered. There was no one in the mausoleum, but the Pegasus was flying around our family coffin obsessively.

I walked toward it with trepidation. That bad feeling I'd been having all day amplified with every step. The coffin was bolted shut, as usual. Steeling my nerves, I unfastened the lock and threw back the lid.

Mauvrey lay inside—still as ice. Seeing her again made my heart stop with a conflicting combination of wariness and fiery hatred.

Her eyes were shut. She was so still I wasn't sure if she was asleep or dead. Her blonde hair spilled around her pale face and shimmery dark purple zip-up jacket. Her hands were folded over her chest.

I was dumbstruck, perplexed, and then surprised beyond all reason when Mauvrey's eyes suddenly shot open. Her spooky black Shadow Guardian irises looked up at me. Before I could move, her closed fist opened and she blew a handful of sparkly powder in my face.

I stumbled back, coughing at the cloud of powder. I didn't know what it was, but it had gotten in my nose, eyes, and mouth, which were now burning and freezing at the same time.

Mauvrey sat up in the coffin like she'd risen from a nap. Her eyes returned to their normal blue shade and she smiled at me.

"You are too easy, you know that?" she said as she climbed out.

"Says the girl who couldn't even kill me last semester," I spluttered, continuing to choke.

I clutched my throat and felt myself stagger. My knees were weak and I was losing balance.

"I would not fight it, Crisa," Mauvrey said confidently. She tossed her hair and straightened her jacket. "That powder is a specially ground Poppy Potion designed to make its victims fall asleep for a full day."

On cue, my knees gave out and I fell to the floor. The veins in my arms were flooded with that awful, familiar purple glow. Thankfully, the rear doors of the mausoleum burst open. Three guards in Midveil uniform came marching over, one of whom was Anthony Graystone.

For a moment I thought I was saved. But when Mauvrey grinned, I knew I was in more trouble than I thought.

"About time," Mauvrey said. "Help me get her into the coffin."

I was too dizzy, drained, and disoriented to conjure a comeback or any of my usual sass. The guards swiftly hoisted me up and placed me in the tomb. I gritted my teeth, trying to will my body to resist, but it was useless. I was barely able to twitch my thumb as Graystone bound my wrists.

Mauvrey met my furious gaze and sighed. "Oh, do not give me that look, Crisa," she said. "All this unpleasantness would not be necessary if you would have done what you were supposed to for once in your life and drunk that stupid tea. Now instead of being slowly poisoned with dignity like your mother, you will simply be incapacitated in this lovely coffin for the day.

"It is a shame really," she continued. "Part of me would have genuinely liked for you to see what comes next. I have spent so much time preparing for today. And since I cannot be in the room myself when phase two commences, I would have liked to have had you there, watching as your world shatters, both literally and figuratively."

Despite the heaviness consuming me, I garnered every bit of strength I had left to utter one hard word.

"How?" I spat bitterly.

Mauvrey seemed to relish my fighting back. Her eyes sparkled with malicious glee as she leaned into the coffin. Her face was right next to mine; her breath skimmed my cheek.

"Oh, my dear nemesis," she whispered. "It was never a matter of *how*. It was always a matter of *who*."

Mauvrey righted herself and smiled.

"Sweet dreams, Crisa," she said.

She blew me a sarcastic kiss and gave me a small wave just before shutting the lid of the coffin—sealing me within its darkness as the Poppy Potion kicked in.

CHAPTER 30

# Phase Two

y eyes burst open and I gasped for breath.

I didn't know how long I'd been asleep, but I felt certain that only a short time had passed. Definitely not the full twenty-four hours Mauvrey said the potion would last. However, no amount of time spent in a coffin was good when your home and family were in danger. I had to get out of there.

The inside of the coffin was not completely black. The last of the purple in my veins was fading away under the golden glow pulsing through my arms. My body was fighting back, like it had the night of the magic hunters.

I pounded my bound hands against the lid of the coffin like a caged animal. Then I took a deep breath and reined in my fear. I needed to be calm to find a way out.

This Poppy Potion was different from the one the magic hunters used. I could feel it. While that potion had left me feeling woozy when I'd woken, I didn't feel that way now.

I lifted my bound hands and reached inside my dress for my wandpin.

*Lapellius.*

The wand morphed in my hands, its off-white glow lighting the tightly condensed space.

*Knife.*

The end of the wand I was holding turned into a leather grip and a blade sprouted on the other side. I put the grip in between my teeth and sliced through the bindings on my wrists.

My hands free, I pushed up on the lid of the coffin with my full force. It would not budge. Mauvrey and our guards (or her guards, apparently) must have bolted it shut once they'd put me inside.

I placed my palms against the lid and concentrated.

*Come alive and open up,* I commanded as I willed my magic to return.

Nothing happened.

*Come on. Wake up and let me out,* I ordered again—focusing as hard as I could.

My fingertips glowed meekly for a second, but their golden light extinguished immediately like a candle in the wind. I huffed in frustration. My Magic Exhaustion was still in play. If it took the normal twenty-four hours to reboot, I would not have control over my powers until tonight. I could operate my wand, but that was it.

I scowled and slammed my hand against the lid in another burst of frustration. I'd spent the last month training my magic to be strong so I could protect the people I cared about. Now *everyone* I cared about was in danger and I couldn't use my magic to help them, let alone myself.

After another grunt I forced myself to regain focus and think about my actual options. I could transform my wand into an axe or a hammer, but I had barely six inches of space between my body and the coffin's lid. I would surely do more damage to myself than the coffin.

Then I had another thought. My wand was as unbreakable as it was bound to transform into whatever weapon I willed it into. So theoretically, the lack of space could help me escape.

*Wand.*

I positioned my trusty weapon with its tip sandwiched just below the lid next to the latch. My hand gripped the wand firmly to keep it in place. Hopefully this would work.

*Spear.*

The wand expanded from both ends like it normally did, undeterred by the limitations of the coffin. With a loud snap, the spear extended to it full five feet in length and brutally broke the latch on the outside, setting me free.

*Yes!*

*Wand.*

I hopped out of the deathtrap. The mausoleum was empty. Mauvrey and her men were long gone. The glass Pegasus had also vanished. Now that it'd completed its mission, it'd probably flown off somewhere.

I burst through the crystal front doors of the mausoleum. When I'd run down the stairs I spun around to catch a glimpse of the clock. I'd barely been asleep forty minutes! It was five to noon, which meant the Weatheralls had probably already arrived, the banquet was about to begin, and I didn't have long to stop Mauvrey and the commons from getting to their phase two.

*Lapellium.*

Clutching my glittering wandpin tightly, I sprinted back to the castle. I plowed through the forest area, across the stretch of lawn, then through the open side door to the rear kitchen. I raced through the pantry, meat locker, and main kitchen. It was still busy, but the foods and faces whizzed by in a blur. I ducked beneath a final tray before pushing past the set of doors that led to the hallway. It was relatively empty now. The guests must've already taken their seats. Only a few staff members patrolled the halls like they customarily did, acting as runners in case anybody needed anything.

"Crisa!"

Blue and Jason appeared out of nowhere.

"Mauvrey's here," I panted. "She's gonna make her move and some of my family's guards are working for her. We need to figure out who she's targeting."

"We know who she's targeting," Jason said. "It's her parents. I found that Blaine guy and got the information like you asked."

"How did you manage that?"

"A broken arm or two. Does it matter? Snipers are about to take out the Weatheralls."

"The Weatheralls? Mauvrey's eliminating her own parents?" I was shocked for a moment, but there was little time to ponder the depths of Mauvrey's evilness.

I brought my mind back to the task at hand, running through options of where the snipers could possibly—

I snapped my fingers. "I know exactly where the shooters will be positioned," I said. "Hurry. We need to get to the ballroom."

"Crisa, wait. There's something else," Blue said quickly. "Savoy saw that I was following him. He attacked me, so I had to fight back."

"Are you okay?"

"What? Yeah, fine, but that's not the point. He was amused when Jason and I told him we knew about the sniper attack on the Weatheralls, laughing about how we didn't know the half of it. So we tried . . . alternative means to get him to talk. The one thing we managed to get out of him was about that name in his logbook, P. Knight."

"Blue, Pietro already told me the truth. He has nothing to do with any of this. He's on our side and Savoy must've put his name in that log to set him up."

"No, that's just it," Jason insisted. "It's not a set-up. It's the right name, but we pegged the wrong guy."

"What are you saying?"

Blue looked pained as her eyes met mine. "When Savoy wrote P. Knight as the buyer, he didn't mean Pietro Knight. He meant *Prince* Knight."

"That's the same thing," I argued.

"Crisa," Jason said evenly. "There is more than one Prince Knight."

And that's when a piece of me died.

A hundred small signs that I'd written off added up to the conclusion that I'd been too obstinate to see. Alex's secretiveness, his coldness, his sneaking around. All his talk about not knowing who he could trust, about how he and Pietro were soon going to be at odds, about how he was keeping me in the dark because he wasn't sure how I would react to the "big changes" coming soon.

Then there was his mysterious girlfriend he seemed so reluctant to talk about. The girlfriend that he'd met a couple months ago and he hadn't introduced to any of us because he knew Mom and Dad would never approve of her "ideas" for the realm.

*Mauvrey.*

The girl he was seeing and taking his cues from this whole time had been Mauvrey. I knew it with a certainty as clear as the day outside. She had just told me that the secret to her coup within the castle hadn't been a matter of how, but *who*. As in, *who* would have the connections, resources, and power to pull all of this off without getting caught?

*Alex.*

A clock struck noon. The chimes echoed in a low register that sent chills through my body. Time was up.

"Come on," I said to my friends. "We have a traitor to stop."

My friends and I dashed down the corridor. My heart pounded with the same deep resonance as the clock telling us to hurry. Voices swirled around my head.

*"You're letting your feelings for him cloud your judgment, Crisa. If you were really as morally noble as you are pretending to be, you'd see the signs."*

*"I think maybe it would be best if you kept your mind open to the idea that the people in your life may not be who you think they are."*

Both Sooz and Liza had been right. They'd just had the wrong brother.

Fury and regret rose inside me with each step. My mind flooded with the memory of the day I'd confronted Alex about his girlfriend; that last day before everything between us had begun to fall apart.

*"Trust me, Crisa."* Alex had said. *"Mom and Dad would never let me be with this girl no matter how I feel about her. They're too stuck in their own ways. They would never understand what we envision for Midveil's future or accept that things around here need to change."*

*"Well, if that's the case then what's your end game here?"* I'd asked. *"You can't go on keeping your secret girlfriend a secret forever. At some point you're going to have to choose."*

*"I already did."*

How could I have been so blind?

My friends and I arrived at the ballroom as the clock ceased chiming. A pair of guards opened the doors for us to a sea of applause.

Ladies, gentleman, diplomats, heroes, damsels, protagonists, and high caliber commons filled the palace ballroom. All of them were on their feet, facing the front. Their attention was focused on the stage where the king and queen of Tunderly were ascending to their seats. Daniel and SJ spotted us and jogged over. We moved past the guards positioned along the back wall, heading toward the tapestry where the door to the mezzanines was hidden.

I gripped my wandpin so tightly that it made a dent in my hand.

"Those reinforcements your brother Alex was supposed to send never showed," Daniel said through the applause.

"Not surprising considering that he's in on it," I replied. "He's working with Mauvrey and the commons. One or more of those guards up in the mezzanines are snipers they hired to take out Mauvrey's parents. We need to find them and stop them before it's too late."

"There's got to be at least six guards on each level. We'll need to move quickly."

"Then let's go," I said. "Blue, stay by the front entrance in case an attacker plans to burst in through there. Everybody else, come on. We're almost out of—"

"And now to officially welcome you to today's grand event," Sooz announced from the stage, "please welcome the lovely and bold, Princess Crisanta Katherine Knight!" She gestured to the rear of the room where my friends and I were standing and every pair of eyes turned toward me.

It threw me for a moment, but as applause sounded in my name, I knew what I had to do. "Go," I muttered to my friends beneath the large smile I plastered on my face. "I'll stall."

I began to stride to the front of the room, faking confidence and charm as the cheers continued and the eyes of every person followed my practiced princess gait. When I took to the stage, I saw Blue move for the door as the rest of my friends disappeared behind the tapestry to search the mezzanines for the threat. The spotlight shone down on me and I took a deep breath.

For a girl who did not like being the center of attention, standing on a stage in front of two hundred of Book's elite was a lot to handle. The old me would not have been able to manage it. Much as I liked to talk, I had never been a big fan of public speaking. I think it was because I'd never been confident enough in myself. That had changed recently. As I stepped into the light, I steadfastly held my ground. My character was strong as steel now. Add to that, I had a fire burning inside me that was committed to fighting against the invaders in my home and protecting those they meant to hurt.

The applause began to die once I took center stage. My mother nodded to me. Despite my complete lack of preparation, I let my voice fill the space. I was nothing if not good at speaking my mind and improvising in tight situations.

"Good afternoon and welcome," I said to the room in my most vivacious tone. "On behalf of my entire family, I want to thank you all for being here today."

Applause broke out again. I quickly scanned the room. I had an empty chair waiting for me on the opposite side of the table next to my mother. My brothers were seated on the left with Alex at the end and Pietro beside him. The Weatheralls were between my mother and father in the center.

It'd been years since I'd seen the Weatheralls in person, but they looked more or less how I remembered.

Mauvrey's mother (the queen of Tunderly and Book's famous Sleeping Beauty) was every bit as beautiful as her fairytale's namesake suggested. Her long, strawberry-blonde hair fell in perfect loose curls. She wore a massive, spiky golden crown and an amber, long-sleeved gown trimmed in black lace.

The queen's face was very much like Mauvrey's—from her spritely nose to her flawless complexion. The only notable difference was her eyes. Mauvrey's mother had light hazel eyes, whereas her daughter (when she wasn't allowing her evil black Shadow Guardian irises to shine through) had intense blue ones.

The king of Tunderly had similarly blue eyes. His blond hair was more akin to my nemesis's as well. There was also this way he furrowed his brow that reminded me of how Mauvrey used to look in class when she was absorbed in one of our lessons.

"It is such a treat to have the king and queen of Tunderly visit us," I went on, gesturing to the smiling pair. "Especially as we prepare for the long-awaited Vicennalia Aurora."

At the mere mention of the celebration the crowd applauded yet again, like they simply could not bottle up their enthusiasm any longer. It was a bit annoying, but more applause meant more stalling time.

I squinted through the stage lights as best I could to have a good look around the ballroom. I could see guards and several lighting technicians filling up the alcoves throughout the mezzanines. I also saw the shadows of three bodies darting behind them, searching.

My friends were trying to snuff out the crossbow snipers who were supposed to take out Mauvrey's parents. But with all the guards armed, it would be a difficult task to pick out a rogue shooter hiding in plain sight. They needed more time but I didn't know how much I could give them.

The cheers faded and I continued dragging the situation out, grateful I'd paid attention during Madame Lisbon's Damsels in Distress lesson on crowd pleasing.

"The Vicennalia Aurora is a time of great unity in our realm," I continued. "Occurring every twenty-five years, people from all walks of life share in this celebration of something bigger— something that defies kingdom borders, country treaties, and archetype distinction."

Alex sat unassumingly at the end of the table. He was watching me. There was a touch of confusion in his expression, like he was surprised to see me. Given that he was probably aware of his girlfriend's plans to lock me in a coffin, my appearance at the banquet must've been a shock.

I walked closer to the Weatheralls out of protective instinct and pivoted toward the audience. The words I spoke next inadvertently came straight from the heart. I didn't know what triggered them. Maybe it was the intense emotions bubbling inside me. Or maybe they just needed to be said.

"The Vicennalia Aurora is a great example of how no matter how different we are, our stories are all connected. Every decision we make and every action we take has the power to affect change and consequence. And as we move forward, in order to ensure that the next twenty-five years are prosperous ones, we must heed the understanding that comes with this. We have just as much responsibility to lead lives that are good as we do to intervene when others make choices that aren't. We have a responsibility to stand up, step outside of our own little worlds, and stop those who would wish others harm."

I'd been addressing the audience as a whole, but as I spoke my final words my eyes fell upon Alex, and I spoke just for him.

"The Vicennalia Aurora reminds us that our stories are not about us alone," I said. "So it would be a mistake to assume that when malevolence creeps from the shadows, it will go unchallenged. For true protagonists—heroes, princesses, and so on—will *never* turn a blind eye, even if they put themselves at risk. Because at the end of the day, it is as much their shared duty as it is their shared nature to stop threats when they see them."

Alex glared at me as I spoke my last words. He knew that I knew. I could see it in his eyes. Then everything happened quickly.

Alex raised an index finger from the table and nodded to the back of the room. It was a signal. I knew it as surely as I knew that if I didn't react fast, someone's life would pay the price. My gaze darted to where Alex was looking. The stage lights were at just the right angle for me to catch a glance at a guard in a side alcove on the second level of the mezzanine who'd removed the crossbow from his back.

*Lapellius.*

*Shield.*

My wand spiraled out and I lunged in front of Tunderly's king and queen. An arrow that'd been fired from the mezzanine squarely hit my shield a half second later. I exchanged a glance with Tunderly's king, who'd I just saved from being executed. Several gasps and short screams were emitted by guests, but over them I heard the decisive sound of a powerful punch from across the room. I looked over my shield and peered through the lights to catch a glimpse of Daniel knocking out the guard who'd taken the shot.

Everything in the room was silent for a beat. I swiftly stood up and shouted to the guards positioned along the back wall.

"Guards!" I gestured at the alcove and gave an order that was arguably clichéd, but still satisfying to say. "Seize him!"

All twelve men did not move. A cold feeling tingled up my arms as I registered a very distinct, sarcastic sound. I glanced back at Alex. He was slow clapping. As if I couldn't hate him any more right now. He gave a small shrug as he stood and walked over to the center of the stage, squaring me off.

"Nice sentiments, little sister. But you're forgetting something," he said. "If a protagonist wants to challenge malevolence, they better remember not to underestimate it. It has a way of sneaking up on you."

Alex turned his head toward the guards at the back of the room and said the three words that proved he was right.

"Fire at will!"

Like a fleet of foxes released in a hen house, so came the attack that followed. The guards began firing arrows, not just at the head table, but into the crowd. The sadistic extent of Mauvrey and Alex's plan was far greater than any of us had anticipated.

I wanted to do nothing more than run the fifteen feet that separated me from my brother and tackle him. I wanted to grab him by his finely pressed shirt collar and slam his head against the table with all my might. But I couldn't. An arrow had just skimmed my father's shoulder. Protect first; revenge second.

I gripped the edges of the table and flipped it on its side to provide cover for my parents and the Weatheralls. They ducked behind it as screams erupted around the ballroom.

My mother and Tunderly's queen remained behind the table while the two kings drew their weapons and sprang into action. Both men had plenty of fighting experience and could protect themselves. My father was moving a bit slower, though. I didn't blame him. He'd just found out his son was a traitor. The pain of that must've been immeasurable.

I looked on at the chaos. People were running in every direction, terrified. Arrows were fired from all over. The first wave of the panicked mass reached the main doors at the far end of the ballroom. Horror sunk in my chest when they started banging against them desperately. The doors would not open. They must have been locked from the outside. Looks like the same went for the chrome doors on the left that led to the main lawn. A couple of guards were defending them, but I saw one guest—probably a hero of some sort—fight past their defense only to discover those doors wouldn't budge either. The people in here were fish in a barrel.

We had to take out the attackers. And we had to get everyone out of the ballroom.

At that moment I was grateful to have friends who were so in sync with me. The instant the pandemonium had exploded they'd begun a counterattack.

Blue was zipping around the ballroom—using the tables for cover as she collected finely sharpened steak knives from each place setting and hurled them at the shooters. It was clearly difficult for her to take clean shots with so many innocents darting around, but she was hardly a novice. By the time my feet hit the floor in front of the stage she'd already taken out four guards on the ground level.

I ducked an arrow then skidded across the edge of a table to protect a Ravelli diplomat who was about to be sliced open by a guard wielding a sword. I slammed my shield against the guard's blade then kicked him in the shin before mercilessly smashing my shield into his face.

To my left, two guards closed in on a pair of ladies begging for mercy. I grabbed plates from the nearest table and flung them discus-style at the attackers' heads. The china crashed into their skulls. I unlatched the cape from my dress and threw it at the nearest guard's face, temporarily blinding him.

*Sword.*

I slashed my sword at the guard and spun around to strike the man behind him.

*Shield.*

I kept both attackers' blades at bay and kicked the closest guard's knee before leaping back and spinning low.

*Spear.*

My weapon elongated and I swept one guard off his feet. I returned the spear to a shield and rose to protect myself from the second. He kicked me in the chest and I was thrust against the edge of a table. The wind was temporarily knocked out of me, but my aggression only amplified.

I was about to re-engage when a purple marble suddenly impacted the ground between the two guards. The moment it hit the floor, it released a powerful bolt of lightning that barbequed the guards where they stood.

I glanced up to where the projectile had come from. SJ was standing in one of the mezzanine's alcoves on the second level firing her homemade portable potions at the remaining guards.

I'd never seen her utilize a lightning potion before. It must've been new. I looked around and recognized the remnants of other portable potions she'd used before. Several guards across the ballroom were frozen in large chunks of ice thanks to her ice potions. A couple more guards were trapped in large blobs of green goo courtesy of her slime potions.

SJ was not alone in the eagle-eye defensive. Daniel and Jason were darting in and out of the other alcoves to combat and disarm remaining rogue snipers.

While the crowds that surrounded me may not have realized it, thanks to my valiant friends, the terror would soon be over. The downpour of arrows was growing lighter by the second and we were about to bust out of here.

SJ drew back her slingshot (which she must've been carrying in her purse along with the portable potions) and took aim at the doors.

The orb she released was another kind I was familiar with—an explosion portable potion. When the potion made impact with the top part of the doors, a burst of fire and red smoke blasted out. Both doors were shot off their hinges and our panicked guests started pouring out of the ballroom.

"Crisa, duck!"

I didn't question the voice and instinctively hit the deck. A millisecond later an arrow pierced the window behind me. I sheltered my face with my shield as glass shattered around me.

My eyes darted back to where the warning had come from. Alex.

He was engaged in a ruthless swordfight with Pietro and clearly couldn't afford to be distracted. Even so, he'd let his normally unshakeable focus slip for a second to protect me from getting shot.

Of everything that had come to pass in the past hour, nothing filled me with quite as much hatred as that gesture.

*How dare Alex pretend that he still cares about me!*

*Look at what he's done! Look at what he's brought to our home!*

I herded the sea of people toward the exit—protecting them with Blue and SJ as they made their way out.

As I moved, I saw that my father and the king of Tunderly were still fighting their own battles. Six guards, including Anthony Graystone, had taken to the stage and were coming at them with violent intent. My father and Mauvrey's father were not easy targets. Despite being outnumbered, they were far from outmatched. Both moved swiftly and vehemently as they protected their queens.

I caught a glimpse of my father slashing his sword so strongly into one of the guards that it pierced straight through him like a shish kabob. I cringed, but did not look away. And in the next instant I was glad for it. My father's sword had become so deeply lodged in the guard that he was unable to pull it free in time.

I stepped in. I think my instinct had guessed at the series of events faster than my brain had absorbed them. I bent down and grabbed a fallen arrow from the floor.

*Bow.*

I sent the arrow across the room right as Anthony Graystone lunged at my father. It shot straight into Graystone's shoulder—sending him tumbling.

My father stole a glimpse at me for a second, but neither of us said a word. He ripped his sword free and went back to fighting while I picked up a few more arrows and sent them flying toward any other malicious guards I could spot.

Half the guests were in the corridor now—bolting for the main entrance of the palace. The arrows had stopped raining from above and with one final knife to the arm (courtesy of Blue) the last of the guards on our level was defeated.

The screaming simmered down. I was relieved to see that my mother, father, and the Weatheralls were opponent-free as well. However, my heart stopped when I saw Pietro lying motionless on the floor.

"Pietro!" I ran to him.

The people rushing around us blurred into a haze as I dropped to my knees next to him. My brother was still, like Mauvrey in that casket. He didn't appear to be obviously bleeding. I really hoped he had just been knocked out. I felt his neck for a pulse and found one.

Instinct set in fast. I was never one for handling matters with a delicate touch. I grabbed my unconscious brother by the shirt collar and slapped him across the face.

"Pietro!"

That did it. The shock jolted him awake. He sat up with a groan.

"Ugh. I'm okay. Where's Alex?" he grunted, reaching for his sword.

"I'm not sure," I said. "But he's not going to get away."

Pietro looked at me for a second like he really believed me. And honestly, I really believed me too. Our parents were safe. The king and queen of Tunderly were safe. The guards who'd attacked us had all been taken care of while the palace guests were escaping.

But then came the noise—a very distinct *series* of noises that shook my confidence as surely as they shook the building itself.

Explosions began to blast through the castle corridors. People started screaming again and I found myself bearing bitter witness to the truth behind Alex's words.

One should never underestimate the power of malevolence.

# CHAPTER 31

# Shattered

xplosives had been hidden in the decorative hydrangea flower balls, which were hanging pretty much everywhere.

They erupted into balls of fire and engulfed the rooms and hallways with acrid smoke. They didn't combust all at once, thank goodness. But there was no telling when the next one would go off, so the mass of people caught in the crosshairs had no idea which way to run.

Three explosions unfolded in the corridors followed by two in the ballroom. I was tossed to the floor then dove out of the way to dodge a chunk of ceiling that came crashing down. Other guests in the vicinity hid under tables to avoid the debris and glass that fell.

Daniel, SJ, and Jason came barreling out of the hidden door behind the tapestry. Jason helped Pietro to his feet and Daniel helped me to mine. Six more explosions were set off in violent succession from various points throughout the hall.

People who had been in the doorway were pushed back into the ballroom from the sheer force of the combustion. Dark gray smoke flooded in. Whole panes of windows shattered spraying shards everywhere.

I heard shouts and cries and moans coming from beyond the ballroom. Despite every instinct telling me otherwise, I ran toward them. I leapt over fallen chairs and pushed my way into the desecrated hall. My friends were right behind me.

I felt sick to my stomach at what I saw.

People near me were freaking out. But at the other end of the hall guests lay scattered around a giant pile of rubble blocking the stairs that led to the main door. Some of them were moving. The more naïve, childlike part of my heart convinced my head that those who weren't had just been knocked unconscious. Anything else didn't seem possible. I hadn't known enough darkness yet to accept the alternative.

The ceiling shook again.

*Shield.*

I protected my skull and SJ's from a shard of glass that would have otherwise impaled us. The aftershock threw me off balance. Jason caught me and righted me without hesitation.

"What do we do?" he asked.

I wondered the same thing. There was no way out. The explosions had buried the front door and it was impossible to pass down the hall to any of the building's other exits; they were unbearably far away and there were too many people.

We needed a way out. We needed to *make* a way out.

"SJ!" I shouted. "Can you contain this?" I gestured to the spreading fires and the crumbling columns that threatened to collapse.

She nodded and dug into her bag of portable potions. She began releasing ice potions to contain the fires and slime potions to help prevent structural collapse of the building.

"Here!" I tossed Blue my shield. "Cover her. I need thirty seconds."

Blue shielded SJ as Daniel and Jason aided the guards (the ones not on Mauvrey and Alex's payroll) in protecting the other guests as best they could.

I raced back into the ballroom at full speed. My boots crushed the corpses of floral centerpieces and formerly fine china. I bobbed and weaved around the disintegrating room—dodging the collapse of another chandelier and several chunks of roof—until I reached the left wall. The chrome doors were still locked, so I grabbed a chair and chucked it at the lowest window, smashing a hole through it.

I rushed forward. The window was at my chest level. I leaned out and brought my fingers to my lips and whistled. It was high-pitched and desperate. I flicked my eyes over to the stage where my parents and the Weatheralls were. My mother had been knocked to the ground by the latest explosion, which made my heart lurch. The king of Tunderly was shielding his queen from the rubble that continued to rain over the room. I took another glance out the window and saw what was coming.

"Get down!" I shouted.

I raced away from the wall and braced myself for imminent impact. A moment later Lucky's scaly, silver body rammed through the side of the ballroom—responding to my summons. He demolished the windows, the doors, and the rest of the wall, creating a gaping hole to the outside.

My loyal pet shook glass and metal from his scaly head then blinked his golden eyes at me expectantly.

"Good boy!" I yelled. "Now back outside! Go!"

Lucky looked confused but excited to help. He stretched his wings and bounded outside.

"Through here!" I called to the people in the ballroom, gesturing to the newly created opening, which led to the safety of the main lawn. It did not take long for the guests to seize the opportunity. My friends could see what I'd done and they began herding people in the corridor this way. In their dusty suits and ball gowns, people came stampeding toward the exit.

The explosions continued without mercy as guests emptied onto the main lawn. After ensuring that my parents had made it out, I re-entered the hallway to find SJ firing her last portable potion at a side wall that would've otherwise collapsed on top of the duke and duchess of Whoozalee.

Daniel and Jason helped the noble couple to their feet as Blue returned my shield. We continued assisting people out of the death trap corridor. As I guided my second cousin Violet to the ballroom doors, that's when I saw them.

My friends and I had been concentrating so hard on the people between the ballroom and the main doors that we hadn't thought to look back. It had escaped my notice that there were some servants in the deeper parts of the castle that needed assistance. Not all of our palace staff was on team Mauvrey and Alex. Many of them had been in the kitchen, and I imagined most had escaped through there when the explosions started. However, a few had been in the halls when the attack was unleashed.

I went to aid a handful of staff members farther down the hall. Some were trapped beneath collapsed columns or other debris; others were on their hands and knees from the impact of the explosions. Obstacles and rubble stood in my way, but I was not waylaid for long.

I found myself actually feeling grateful for the number of near-death experiences I'd had in recent months. It seemed I'd built up a certain level of tolerance to the chaos. I moved faster, responded quicker, and I was far less shaken by the ordeal than I would have been had my life not grown so accustomed to cruel peril.

After assisting six servants out of the wreckage, in the corner of my eye I saw a maid struggling against a fallen piece of ceiling; it had pinned her leg to the ground. Pietro was attempting to boost it off her. I rushed over and gritted my teeth as I helped him lift it. The maid slid out and Pietro scooped her up.

"Minnie," the maid moaned as she reached out. I pivoted to where she was gesturing. A few yards away my lady-in-waiting Minnie lay on the ground, rubble around her. I sprinted over. I put my finger to Minnie's neck to check for a pulse, but I felt nothing.

*Oh no.*

*No, no, no.*

"Crisa, come on!" Pietro shouted.

I put my wand down and held Minnie's hand in mine as I checked her wrist for a pulse. Still nothing.

*Come on, Minnie,* I thought earnestly, closing my eyes in prayer. *Be alive. Please, please be alive.* My heart raced as I willed with all my faith that she would breathe. Somehow—by a miracle—she did. I heard a rush of air return to her body and my eyes burst open to see hers glance up at me.

"Princess?"

"Hi, Minnie."

"I thought I was going to die."

"Well, you're not. That's an order. Now up you go."

Minnie hobbled to her feet, but seemed fine to walk on her own after that. I grabbed my wand and made to follow her and Pietro at first, but then I hesitated. At that very moment I saw Alex. He was by the lift in the distance, much farther down the hall.

We both stood there for a beat—a hundred yards between us that felt like a hundred miles. Staring. Wondering. Deciding.

"Alex!" I yelled.

He ran. I ran after him.

"Crisa!" I heard Blue call. I spun around. She and Daniel were at the threshold of the ballroom, waiting for me. Both of them had someone draped over their shoulders, fireman-rescue style.

I thought about coming to my senses and rejoining them, but fate intervened and a set of hydrangea balls hanging between us erupted. That entire section of ceiling came tumbling down. I was tossed back against the wall. I felt my head hit glass, but steadied myself with hardly a hesitation.

My access to the ballroom had been completely cut off by debris. I was not going to be able to get through. But it wouldn't have mattered if I could. My brother and I had unfinished business.

"Just get out!" I yelled to Blue and Daniel through the avalanche. "I'll be fine."

Alex was getting further away with every passing second and I had to catch up with him.

The wreckage of the explosions cut across every part of the corridor. There were fewer of the deadly hydrangea balls deeper within the castle, but they were still present in every room—some already having erupted and unleashed their damage, others threatening to do the same at any time.

*Dang, why did our castle decorators have to be so frickin' thorough?*

I jumped over fallen trees in the arboretum. A series of explosions went off right as I entered the chess hall, which sent several human-sized pieces flying. A wall-sized mirror shattered; a shard skinned my upper arm as I raced by.

My pace only quickened as I sped through the adjacent

conference room then into the Hall of Transparency. Finally, I made it to the library. It was engulfed in flames. They'd caught on the white carpet and draping Vicennalia Aurora-colored silks that hung whimsically from the ceiling. There wasn't much time before the remaining hydrangea balls in here would take the rest of the place down.

Alex was standing across the room. I'd been certain he was headed this way. I had pieced the remaining segments of the puzzle together. He was going to use the fireplace tunnel to escape to the hedge maze, then follow the path past the mausoleum and use our secret passageway in the hunting shed to flee the grounds with Mauvrey and his men.

It made perfect sense. That was how Mauvrey had made it onto the property unseen. Alex had shown her the tunnel. And since no one else knew about the route, they would get away unseen. By everyone but me, that is.

"Alex, stop!"

My brother was about to go through the passage in the fireplace. There were three of our guards with him. The men lunged at me, but Alex raised his hand to keep them from attacking.

"Stand down!"

"But, sir! Mauvrey gave us orders—"

"And now *I'm* giving you orders. Go through the tunnel to the exit and get to the mountains. Tell Mauvrey I'll be there soon."

My brother's men left us alone.

I wanted to wring Alex's neck, or slap him in the face, or kick him in the shin. I wanted to make him suffer. I wanted to make him feel even a quarter of the horror I was feeling. But in that terrible moment, I couldn't bring myself to do any of it. All I could muster was a single plea.

"Alex, please. Don't do this."

"That's not an option," he replied. "I've made my choice. I love Mauvrey, Crisa. And I believe in what she's doing."

"What she's doing is insane!" I shouted. "She just tried to take out her own parents. Her men were killing innocent people. She tried to kill *me* last semester! And she's in cahoots with the antagonists! She's a monster! How can you take her side?"

"What she's done is a means to an end, Crisa. I don't like that this was necessary, but it *was* necessary. Our class system can't go on like this anymore, separating people into protagonists, commons, and antagonists. The time has come for change. But the people pulling the strings behind the realm's curtains—the ambassadors, the Godmothers, the royals—they don't see that. And they crush anyone who tries to take a stand against them. Do you have any idea how many people have been killed over the years for even thinking of rebelling?"

"Do you have any idea how many people were killed today because of you and your Shadow Guardian girlfriend?"

The library shook from a nearby explosion. Alex paused.

"Crisa—"

"Shut up!" I said, squeezing my wand tighter. "I don't want to hear your excuses anymore. You're a liar! You told me I could trust you; that you'd never let me down or betray me! *And I believed you!*"

"I'm sorry, Crisa. But this is the way it is," he said firmly. "I didn't want to tell you the truth before because I was afraid you would react like this. That you would choose them instead of me."

"If by 'them' you mean the good guys, then yeah, Alex. I choose them."

"Well, you've picked your side and I've picked mine. Fight me all you want, but I know mine is the right one."

"How can you be so stupid?" My voice cracked. "You're a traitor!"

"I'm also your brother. As angry as you are, you know you can't erase that."

A dark calm came over me as I clenched my wand even harder. "You stopped being my brother when your selfishness nearly killed Mom, Dad, and Pietro."

He shrugged as if we were quibbling over something insignificant like assembly instructions for a desk chair. "If that's how you feel, then fine. But I'm not changing my mind."

There was no time for a reply. Two of the remaining hydrangea balls in the room combusted simultaneously. My shoulders slammed against a bookshelf behind me, rattling my skull.

Scattered texts stoked the fire on the ground. Smoke filled the room and I saw cracks spreading across the ceiling with deadly intent. Alex was suddenly much closer.

"Come on!" he said, gesturing to the fireplace. "We gotta go!"

He moved toward me, but I pulled out of his reach. "Fat chance!" I coughed. "I'm not going anywhere with you!"

"Crisa!" he protested.

I drew back farther.

*Spear.*

"Stay away from me!" I said, pointing the blade directly at him.

"Crisa, the room is coming down. The rest of this floor is a death zone. You'll never make it to another exit in time; you'll be buried alive. We have to escape through this tunnel. Now."

"So Mauvrey can stab me through the heart like you stabbed me in the back? I don't think so."

"Seriously, Crisa? Come on, I would never let her kill you! I told Mauvrey that from the beginning. She was okay with taking out her parents, but you, Mom, Dad, and Pietro were only supposed to be captured. You can't really think I'm capable of that kind of evil."

I took another step back, spear still raised and eyes locked with his. "Alex, you just helped one of the most malicious people I've ever met destroy our family and burn down our home. For goodness' sake, you let her use a Poppy Potion to drug me when I confided in you that it was one of the things in the world I was most scared of. I have no idea what kind of evil you're capable of."

Plaster and glass fell from the ceiling and the fire burned stronger, but I refused to lower my guard.

Alex's eyes narrowed. "I am not going to let you get yourself killed in here. You're coming with me."

"Make me."

"Fine." Alex drew his sword. His eyes were trained on my spear—intent on disarming me and forcing me to go with him. I didn't want to fight him, but I would have rather gotten killed than follow him anywhere ever again.

He came at me. I used the distance between us to my advantage and jabbed him in the chest with the dull end of my spear, keeping him at bay. He rushed at me again. I tried to repeat the move but he was ready for it this time. He seized the staff with his free hand and pulled me forward.

I grabbed the hand that held his sword. I tried to kick his knee outward, but he anticipated that; he knew my go-to moves whenever I was backed in a corner. Alex side-stepped and twisted my arm to pin it behind my back, but I slammed my elbow into his jaw and got away.

I found myself against the wall with no more space to withdraw. My brother saw his opportunity and moved in. I saw my opportunity too. It was brief, but it was there. Had Alex been any of the many antagonists, magic hunters, or monsters I'd faced in the past, I would have taken it and won the fight. However, Alex wasn't any of those things. Alex was Alex. Despite the rage and betrayal I felt, I couldn't change that. And that instinct kept me from taking the shot.

My hesitation made me vulnerable. I lost the room to get in a solid block with my spear and had to change my wand into a sword. It was a mistake. With the spear, my brother and I were much more evenly matched. With swords, I paled in comparison.

Alex countered my block and struck at me anew. I parried. He struck again. I bounded out of the way. The two of us fought until my sword was knocked from my hand.

He thought he had me then, but my adrenaline was pumping. The moment the sword left my fingers, I grabbed his wrist and kicked him in the thigh. He thrust me off, stepped in, and punched me in the ribs. Hard.

I buckled—the wind knocked out of me. Alex took that chance to grab me by the back of the neck and herd me toward the tunnel.

"Go!" he ordered.

I glanced at the open passage then up at the ceiling about to give way. My eyes darted to the door on the other side of the room. Alex read my mind as I made a break for it. He seized my wrist, his hand around the gold bracelet we used to share. His sword was at my throat and his aqua-blue eyes were inches from mine for a second. Then he abruptly let go.

Alex's face winced with pain at the sound of searing flesh. I backed up to the door, confused, but not taking my sights off him. His hand was burning from where he'd touched me. It was literally exuding steam like a teakettle. His body contorted with jagged movements like an exorcism until his shoulders and face were yanked back.

Alex's eyes turned piercing black and an equally dark, ghostly essence emerged from his body. It was ghastly. The top part of the creature had a crooked, blood red mouth and slit eyes. The bottom part still clung to my brother's body like a parachute attached to someone in free fall. I recognized it with horror the way a witness might identify a murderer from a line-up.

The thing made a disturbing screeching sound then sunk back into my brother. Indiscernible whispers emanated from his body like an eerie aftereffect.

"You're a Shadow Guardian," I gasped.

Alex's eyes had returned to their regular shade of blue. Right then the final hydrangea balls in the room exploded. My brother leapt to the side. I dove for my sword and rolled to the door as a huge beam collapsed, glass shattered, and bookshelves fell over. When the shaking stopped long enough for me to get to my feet, I found that a smoking barrier of rubble had fallen between us. I could still see him, but he could not get to me.

Before he could even try, I fled the room.

*Shield.*

Glass and ceiling continued to fall. The castle was a total wreck. The corridor back to the kitchens was blocked, as was my access to the ballroom. I heard a loud crash and the doorway I'd just come through got buried. My only option now was the passage that led to the western part of the castle. It was a long route, and probably decorated with hydrangea balls, but it was my only shot. I picked myself up and went for it.

Sweat dripped from my forehead as I struggled to breathe. There was carbon dioxide in my lungs and searing heat on my skin. I flew through a hall lined with burning columns and Midveil flags, all the while shielding my head from the wreckage that fell.

My heart slammed against my chest from exhaustion and

pain. These halls that I'd walked through a thousand times were being incinerated, my big brother was to blame, and I was a minute away from being buried alive. I was running through a nightmare.

And that's when I realized that this *had been* one of my nightmares. I'd had this very dream several times.

I launched myself out of the way as a beam came tumbling down. My hands hit the ash-covered, marble floor. I coughed and started to pick myself up, but hesitated when I saw something powder blue. I grasped at it and pulled it free.

It was Midveil's flag—meant to be here as surely as I was.

"Aut viam inveniam aut faciam."

The charred words around the insignia filled me with more fire than the room.

The memory of my dreams surged through me. And—knowing what came next—when the distinct sound of cracks echoed behind me, I rolled out of the way, managing to dodge the falling column I'd foreseen. It smashed into heavy pieces on the ground. I lunged to get up, but one of the chunks had landed on my dress and was pinning me down.

I struggled and tried not to give in to the panic, shock, and hurt that caused a disobedient tear to stream down my cheek. The roof was threatening to give way. My eyes darted to a ten-foot-high mirror nearby then at the hydrangea balls just beyond it. With shrewd understanding I knew what was about to happen.

*Oh, crud.*

I transformed my shield into a knife and cut my dress above the knee, freeing myself. I broke into a sprint seconds before another hydrangea ball exploded. The shockwave caused much of the ceiling to come loose and the mirror to erupt.

*Shield.*

When I was safe from the scattering shards, I made a break for my mother's private study. That would be my escape. I sped through the havoc until I reached it.

The room was filled with smoke, but no hydrangea balls. More importantly, there was a door at the back that led to a patio. I rushed over, but discovered it was locked.

"Come on!" I yelled angrily, rattling the silver frame, which protected the glass like an exoskeleton and kept me from smashing through.

Using my wand to hack through the door would take too long. If I stayed in here more than another thirty seconds, I would suffocate. Fear and desperation pulsed through me. Without thinking, I raised my right hand.

"Let. Me. Out," I commanded.

Abruptly my palm lit up like a lantern. The door glowed and then it shot outward in one solid blow. Relief rushed through me and I burst outside.

I stopped to take a deep, replenishing breath, inhaling the fresh air. I returned my wand to its pin form and thanked the universe that my magic had worked. I didn't understand how. It should've been rebooting for another six hours. But that didn't matter right now. I was free but this was far from over. I bolted around the crumbling castle until I reached the evacuation area outside the ballroom.

Several Fairy Godmothers had arrived and were using their magic to put out the fires and stabilize the building to keep the upper floors from coming down. Innumerable guests were dotted across the main lawn. I spotted my father, Pietro, and my mother in her sapphire gown being escorted by several Godmothers to an area farther away. I also saw my friends, and just past them, my pet dragon.

"Crisa, where are you going?" SJ shouted as I raced by.

"Alex, Mauvrey, and their men have been using a secret passageway to get in and out of the castle," I explained as my friends kept pace with me. "I know where it leads and I think I can cut them off."

I brought my fingers to my lips and whistled. Lucky came bounding over. Without wasting another second, I threw my leg over his neck. "Go!" I said. With a kick of my heel, I spurred him into the sky.

I knew that Alex, Mauvrey, and the others were using the seventh passage, and Alex had mentioned in the library that they were meeting by the mountains. That meant they were taking the extension of the route that led outside the citadel. With any luck, I could beat them there.

I navigated Lucky due north. He flew quickly, his wings flapping violently, but I didn't hear them. All I heard was the sound of the blood pumping in my ears and the white noise of adrenaline that buzzed inside me like electricity.

When the forest was in sight, I scanned the area for the cave where the seventh passage let out. Sure enough, I spotted scattered dots of men at the base of the mountains just ahead.

I urged Lucky to land. His claws and body plowed into the dirt. Their jolt shook the ground and the nerves of the two dozen people gathered there. I was already sliding off his neck before Lucky came to a complete stop.

That's when I saw it—a glowing silver splotch at the threshold of the mountains. It was floating there in free space, barely big enough for a grown person to step through. Though I hadn't seen one for some time, there was no mistaking it for what it was.

*A wormhole. A tear in the realm's outer In and Out Spell.*

A handful of disloyal men from the King's Guard, a few kitchen staff, and Daphne Reigns continued to dash through the portal—vanishing from view. Who knew how many more had already escaped before I'd gotten there.

The only ones who stalled at the sight of me were Alex and Mauvrey. I glowered at them, and in that moment the sheen of the portal caused me to notice something on Mauvrey's wrist. It was a rose gold watch with a leather band that looked suspiciously like a Hole Tracker.

*It can't be.*

The pair of them stood there for a second, watching me. They looked amused, impressed, and vaguely surprised that I'd managed to follow them. However, as the last of their men disappeared through the wormhole, it seemed they didn't want to stick around to find out what I was planning to do next. Alex tore his gaze away from me and stepped through the hole. Mauvrey gave me a condescending wave and followed.

I sprinted toward the tear in our realm as it started to get smaller and smaller. Despite my best efforts, the silvery opening sealed itself off and vanished mere seconds before I reached it.

It was gone. Mauvrey was gone. And Alex . . .

Alex was gone.

The part of me that had died the moment I'd accepted Alex was a liar and a traitor felt like a black hole inside my chest. Now that I was alone and without enemies to fight, the pain was too crushing to bear.

I fell to my knees as my heart finished breaking. Then I cried out. The sound was anguished and blood-curdling, echoing off the mountains. When it was out of me—purged—I knelt there in silence, hanging my head from the weight of the hatred and betrayal I had to carry going forward.

# CHAPTER 32

# The Ever Aftermath

he fires were out by the time I returned to the castle. SJ and Blue rushed to meet me as I slid off Lucky's neck. I braced myself for their questions.

I hadn't come back to the castle right away. Instead, I'd taken a bit of time to pull myself together. I felt deafeningly fractured. What had just happened—the internal shattering I'd just endured—was unlike anything I'd ever experienced. And I could not allow my friends, my family, or anyone else to see me that way.

There were two reasons behind this. First, there was no one left I felt comfortable enough with to share that fragile side of myself. I had friends and family, but letting someone see you at your most shattered was hard. The closest I'd ever come to being destroyed before this was last semester when all my doubts nearly consumed me. Daniel had witnessed my vulnerability at that time, and he helped me get through it, but I could not count on him to help me through this, not anymore.

The other, more important reason I'd elected to suck in my pain was for the good of everyone around me. My friends and I were about to embark on a dangerous journey to find Paige Tomkins, pinning us against the antagonists once more. They needed a clearheaded leader. My family was dealing with the aftermath of our home's destruction and the betrayal of one of our own. They needed a steady pillar of support. And the rest of the realm, as well as people beyond it like Natalie Poole, were still in jeopardy. They needed a hero brave enough to fight. What none of them needed was what I felt like at the moment—a girl with a broken heart.

I steadied my shaking nerves and channeled the coldest, most logical part of me to take over. I willed myself to be what I needed to be. I would not let anyone see me cry, I would not let my strength or focus falter because of what my brother had done, and I would not allow myself to appear broken.

"What happened?" Blue asked when she and SJ reached me. Her once pristine white dress was torn all over and covered in ash.

I shook my head bitterly. "He got away," I said. "Where are Jason and Daniel?"

"Checking the other floors of the castle," Blue explained. "The upper levels weren't destroyed by the explosions. The Godmothers reinforced the structure before it could come to that. Now they're escorting out the people who were trapped up there during the attack so we can do a final head count of the survivors."

*Survivors.*

The word sent a shiver up my spine, but I buried it like I'd buried the feelings I'd experienced on the mountainside.

"What about my parents?" I asked. "Are they okay?"

"Not completely," SJ admitted. "They are safe, as are the king and queen of Tunderly. But your mother passed out. I imagine it was from the shock."

"It's not," I said.

She and Blue led me to where my parents, Sooz, and a few Godmothers and guards were gathered. My mother was lying on a blanket—her eyes closed and her breathing steady. My father knelt beside her worriedly.

Sooz glanced up when she saw me approaching. "Crisa, are you—"

"Fine. But my mom's not. She and a lot of the King's Guard and palace staff members have been poisoned with jasper berries."

My father's eyes bugged in panic as I explained what I'd uncovered about the tea and the berries. He took my mother's hand and brushed the blonde hair out of her pale face.

"Can the Godmothers whip up some sort of antidote?" I asked.

"Antidotes cannot simply be poofed into existence, my dear," a dark-haired Godmother replied. "Our powers are not designed to work like a pharmacy. If what you're saying is true, then an antidote will need to be brewed, and quickly."

"Does anyone know if the palace physician is still alive?" Sooz asked the guards.

A tall, redheaded guard shook his head. "I'm sorry, ma'am. One of the guards found his body when they were doing a sweep of the main corridor a few minutes ago."

"Well, find someone else," my father barked. "There are at least two-hundred protagonists gathered on this lawn. Someone here has to be capable of brewing an antidote."

"I know someone," Blue interrupted. She gestured to SJ.

SJ gulped, but nodded. "I may be able to help."

"Get the princess to the physician's lab immediately," Sooz ordered one of the Godmothers. "It is safe to return inside?"

"Yes, ma'am."

"Then hurry. Assist her with whatever she needs."

SJ took off with a couple of Godmothers in tow. I turned back to my parents. I was a bit surprised that my father was just sitting here. He was the king. Our castle just suffered a disaster. Our kingdom had come under attack. A bunch of people required a leader. He should've been at his most proactive right now. After all, he was in charge. Yet he remained beside my mother.

"Dad," I began slowly, "don't people need you?"

My father didn't meet my gaze. "Your brother is running point on this."

"My brother . . ."

The words almost caught in my throat. My father seemed to have the same second thoughts about his phrasing.

"Pietro," he clarified. "The King's Guard and the Fairy Godmothers are reporting to him. I have placed him in charge for now."

"Why?"

"Because he is better suited for it at the moment than I am." My dad's eyes flicked from my mother to me. I saw the fear and worry consuming him and realized he was right. At this moment he was not in the proper state of mind to command. For the first time that I could remember, he looked like a man, not a king.

I understood. His son—more than that, the apple of his eye, his protégé, and, frankly, his favorite child—had just betrayed him in the lowest possible way. And the woman he loved more than anything in the world—more than his kingdom and more than his own life—had been poisoned.

"She'll be all right, Dad," I told him as I bent down and put my hand on his shoulder. "All of them will be. SJ's the best potionist at school. She will come through."

He looked at me with a solemn, vulnerable expression. "You have faith in her?" he asked.

"I do."

"Then so do I."

I felt someone come up behind me. "Crisa, I think we better talk," Sooz said softly.

I patted my mother on the hand and motioned for Blue to follow me. We moved away from the crowd so we could speak in private.

I tried to block out the sound of sobs coming from the groups of people around us. I also tried not to look at the palace, but smoke still drifted from it and the giant hole in the side of the ballroom offered a clear view of the wreckage inside.

"I would feel better if you and I spoke alone," Sooz said, glaring at Blue.

"Well, I would prefer if my home wasn't in pieces and my brother wasn't a traitor," I snapped. I was surprised by the hostility in my tone and reined it in, clearing my throat. "Blue knows everything, Sooz. She can hear this."

"Fine then," Sooz replied. "Pietro is handling things right now and I have to report to him shortly, but I want you to fill me in on what happened on your end."

I still did not trust Sooz as a person, or as an ambassador. But I decided to be honest with her. We were on the same team for the moment; we had to work as a united front. Too much had happened today with my enemies out in the open. I didn't have time for enemies in the shadows as well. I would confront my issues with her and the ambassadors another day.

I filled Sooz in about Alex and Mauvrey, how the antagonists got into the castle through the secret tunnel, and that they escaped through a wormhole that appeared in the realm's outer In and Out Spell. In exchange, Sooz told me what she'd learned.

"It seems that Alex and Mauvrey have been planning this for a while," Sooz said. "They had many commons working for them and wanted to inflict as much damage in the most public way possible. This destruction was a part of a multifaceted attack."

"Multifaceted?" Blue repeated.

"Midveil was not the only kingdom hit by the commons rebellion today," Sooz explained. "That is why it took so long for me to summon the Godmothers here to contain the situation. Similar attacks occurred all over the realm at the exact same time. The Godmothers were spread too thinly and couldn't respond fast enough.

"Middlebrook, Salinas, Tunderly, Gallant, Coventry—they were all assaulted today in some way. Tunderly and Salinas suffered attacks on their palaces like we did. The other three kingdoms had bombings in the commercial and business districts of their citadels."

Susannah shook her head. "We have been monitoring these threats of rebellion for some time, but we never anticipated anything like this. There have been attempted attacks and coups in the past, but they've never been on such a massive scale. Commons have never had the means, nor leadership, to be this coordinated. I just don't understand how this happened."

"I do," I replied. "The commons weren't acting alone. Mauvrey has been working with the antagonists for months now. And if she was the one pulling the strings behind the attack on our kingdom, we can assume that the antagonists were probably behind the other attacks too."

"You think the antagonists are sponsoring the commons rebellion?" Sooz said. "How? Why? What could they possibly have to gain by helping them?"

"I don't think it's about helping them," I said. "I think it's about weakening the protagonists as much as possible before the antagonists make their real play."

"What do you mean?"

Blue and I exchanged a look. We couldn't keep this to ourselves anymore. My deals with Lady Agnue and Lenore be darned. The five of us needed help, and we needed our realm's higher-ups to know what we were really dealing with.

Blue and I proceeded to tell Sooz everything we'd learned when we were captured by the antagonists last December and held in their capital of Valor. We explained to her about meeting the antagonist queen Nadia, the antagonists' plot to overthrow the realm and eliminate all protagonists, Arian and his ongoing hunt for protagonists who might affect this plan, the fact that a number of these antagonists were Shadow Guardians (which allowed them to get through certain In and Out Spells), and their hunt for the missing Fairy Godmother Paige Tomkins.

"Lady Agnue threatened me into silence," I told Sooz as I finished the story. "She didn't want anyone to know."

"What could your headmistress possibly have on you that you'd keep silent about this?" Sooz replied.

I hesitated. I may have wanted us to be on the same side, but I was not about to trust this woman with my deepest secret. I didn't want one more person using my Pure Magic against me.

Sensing my discomfort, Sooz withdrew the question. "You know what, it doesn't matter. I appreciate you telling me. I know you're angry with me about the whole protagonist selection thing, but I'm glad you understand we have bigger fish to fry at the moment." Sooz glanced back at the disheveled castle. "You realize that I have to tell all the ambassadors about this, and the Godmothers too."

"I know," I said. "And I'm glad. It's time they knew what we are up against. I'll face Lady Agnue in my own time, but frankly, after what just happened, I think even she would understand why I had to speak up."

"Our headmistress isn't going to lay a finger on you," Blue

asserted, putting her hand on my shoulder. She glanced at Sooz and narrowed her eyes. "*Right?*"

"Right," Sooz said. "I don't care what your secret is, Crisa. I care about protecting this realm, even if you and I have different takes on how that should be accomplished." Sooz bit her lip and thought hard for a moment. "But these Shadow Guardians that can cross In and Out Spells," she said. "How many are there?"

"I can think of at least three," I muttered. "But I have no idea how many are actually out there. Only someone working with them might know."

"Then it is a good thing we caught such a person," Susannah said, motioning toward the stables. "Our men pulled Anthony Graystone out of the wreckage. He's injured, but he's alive."

*Graystone.*

I clenched my fists. "They're interrogating him?"

"Yes. Some members of the King's Guard are handling it while Pietro is seeing to other matters, but they haven't gotten anything out of him yet."

"Then they're not doing it properly. Take me to him. Now."

"Crisa," Sooz interjected. "Princesses are not suited for interrogations. Your father would object. And your brother is the one in charge. I should get him first or at least tell him that—"

"Susannah," I said firmly. "This guy helped coordinate an attack on my home, almost killed my dad, and shut me in a coffin. I don't need your approval or permission. He's mine. So take me to him or get out of my way."

Sooz, Blue, and I stepped into the palace stables. Several guards were congregated in one of the larger stalls around Anthony Graystone. He was chained to the wall, his arms and legs tightly restrained.

"Leave us," I ordered the guards.

A mustached guard named Darrel approached me cautiously. "Your highness, I don't think it would be wise to—"

"That wasn't a request," I interrupted. "I said *leave us.*"

They looked to Sooz and she nodded warily.

The men bowed. "We'll be right outside if you need us, princess," Darrel said.

I regarded Sooz and Blue. "You better leave too."

"Crisa," Blue interrupted. "You really think it's such a good idea for you to be alone with this guy? You said it yourself, he helped Mauvrey put you in a coffin and almost killed your dad."

"You're worried he might try something?"

"No." Blue leaned in. "I'm worried you will. I've never seen you look so . . ." She flicked her eyes away, unable to finish the sentence. There was a window across from us. In it, I could see my reflection and I understood what she was saying. My expression was all venom. My face had never seemed so steely and my eyes had never held such darkness.

I took a deep breath then faced my friend. "I'm fine, Blue. Go. I've got this."

She patted my arm supportively, and she and Sooz reluctantly stepped outside. When the stable doors closed, my eyes focused on the man chained before me.

His once perfectly pressed shirt was bloodied where my arrow had hit his shoulder. There was some soot on his face, some filth in his hair, and a lack of regret in his expression. In fact, he seemed almost amused as I came closer to him.

"Well, well, a private visit from the princess," he mused. "I guess I must have a noose in my near future if the guards are granting me my last request."

I cocked my head.

"You must be a masochist if I'm your last request, Graystone," I said. "I'm hardly here to show mercy. Frankly, I'm not even here as a princess. If I was, then I couldn't do this."

I punched him in the shoulder. Hard. Right where the wound was.

He grimaced. I was a mere foot from him, but the chains around his wrists kept him from lunging at me like I knew he wanted to.

"Now then," I continued, straightening my dress and locking

eyes with him. "Let's get on with this before I show you just how un-princess-like I can be. Tell me what you know about the antagonists. For starters, how many have become Shadow Guardians and are working with the commons rebellion?"

Graystone spat to the side. A little blood hung from his lip. "More than you can count," he said spitefully.

"I can count pretty high. Why don't you ballpark it for me?"

His eyes darted between the hay-covered wooden floor and me. I sighed and took out my wand as I started to pace.

*Lapellius.*

*Knife.*

"Come on, Anthony," I said as I tapped the blade against the palm of my hand. "And here I thought you might make this easy for both of us."

I suddenly lunged at his face with my knife. His eyelids flew shut and he shouted in fright until he heard a thud beside his ear. When Graystone opened his eyes, he saw that I'd actually stabbed the wall two inches from his cheek. A scare tactic. I pulled out my blade, noting his fear and surprise and the nervous beads of sweat that had begun to slide down his forehead.

"Now do you want to tell me something useful or should I practice my knife-throwing skills?" I asked menacingly as I retraced my steps. "I'm hardly as good as my friend Blue, but my aim can be pretty spot on when I'm properly motivated."

Graystone hesitated.

"No? Perhaps a different kind of motivation." I twirled the knife in my hand and transformed it into a spear. I stood three feet from him. Then I drew back my arm.

"All right, all right," Graystone said, panicked.

I lowered my arm.

"Look," he sighed, "I honestly don't know how many Shadow Guardian antagonists got out of Alderon. I know each attack that happened today was coordinated by at least one, so maybe a half dozen or so. Only one in every hundred people can carry a Shadow. That's one of the reasons the antagonists are partnering with commons. They need allies that aren't restricted by Alderon's

In and Out Spell, and they know a lot of commons are more than willing to see protagonists burn." His gaze drifted away and I could tell he was holding something back.

"*And?*" I asked presumptively.

"Antagonists aren't the only ones carrying Shadows," Anthony admitted. "Other people high up in commons rebellion leadership have taken on the creatures so they can get in and out of Alderon and coordinate with the people there. Your brother is one example. He took a Shadow a month ago."

I turned my face so that Graystone wouldn't see my expression falter.

"Do you know what they're planning next?" I asked, still facing away from him. "What the rebellion's next target is?"

"No," he replied. "I know there is something big coming, something to do with the Vicennalia Aurora. But that's it. I was only involved in the plans for the attack on Midveil. The architects of the master plan were never here in the palace. Mauvrey and Alex ran the show, but they were taking instructions from someone else."

I stepped toward him. "Who?"

"All I have is a name. Arian."

*Arian.*

Of course he was involved in this. Why did I have to get such a multitasker for an archenemy? Only Arian could conduct a manhunt for a missing Fairy Godmother while helping Nadia plan to overtake the realm and still manage to orchestrate multifaceted commons rebellion attacks throughout the realm.

"I saw Alex and the others escape through a wormhole by the mountains," I continued, changing the subject. "Where did it take them?"

"I don't know."

I raised my arm, the point of my spear aimed directly at him. "Anthony, I swear—"

"No, really," he insisted. Suddenly his face didn't look so slick; just pathetic.

"They only told us that the portal created by the wormhole

would take us to another realm once the attack was underway and it was time to flee the city," he said.

"But how did they know it was going to be there?"

"It was Mauvrey. She has some kind of special watch," he responded—confirming my suspicions about the Hole Tracker I'd seen her wearing before she'd leapt through the wormhole. "She, this Arian guy, and other antagonists are using them to realm-hop. Something about finding some woman named Paige."

"Anything else?" I asked.

He shook his head.

"Good," I said. "Then I guess we're done here."

I returned my spear to its wand form and began to head for the door.

"Oh, actually there is one more thing, princess," Graystone said, stopping me in my tracks. "See, Mauvrey had a bad feeling you'd escape somehow. And in the event that any of us were caught, she requested that we pass along a message to you."

"And what is that?" I asked slowly.

Graystone smirked. "See you soon."

# CHAPTER 33

## Honesty

hen I finished with Graystone, I came outside to find that Sooz had left to take care of some other matters. Only Blue was waiting for me.

Once I'd told her what Graystone had shared, we went to work assisting Pietro with whatever he needed. I hoped that at some point I might run into Debbie, that she was one of the Fairy Godmothers flitting about here. But when I asked another Godmother I was told she had been assigned to a different attacked kingdom. I was sad to hear this. I could have used her friendly face right now.

Our school's first aid training came in handy as we helped with the wounded. We assisted people with getting back to their carriages and onto their horses. And we coordinated with the Godmothers to take stock of how many staff and King's Guard members we had left.

The only task I was reluctant to undertake was going inside the castle to search for survivors. I did it, of course. But it was difficult. As I stepped through the gargantuan hole in the ballroom, I felt a deep pain in my chest. The pain was like ice, and that ice only grew colder as I walked through the ballroom and entered the disarray of the corridor.

Smoke still floated from the wreckage. Debris lay everywhere with glass scattered over everything like sharp snowfall. I treaded gingerly around the disarray, reminding myself to hold it together.

*No emotion. No breaking down. Do not let anyone see you cry.*

When I came across my first survivor, I was relieved. I pulled one of Alex's squires out of the mess, lifting a column off his leg. The boy was coughing a lot, and he had a broken leg, but otherwise he was fine. I helped him hobble outside to the medical tent Pietro had set up.

I journeyed back inside to continue my search. Soon after I came across my first non-survivor.

I'd never seen a dead person before. This woman was lying on the ground—dust on her face and debris on her dress. Her eyes were open, her face forever frozen in an expression of shock. I approached her slowly and felt for a pulse. There was nothing. Her skin was the temperature of snow. The black hole feeling returned to my chest, but I didn't fold.

Part of me thought I should have shown some grand display of sobbing or emotion. But surprisingly I didn't. I supposed I'd already seen so much horror today, my heart was wrung dry of all the sadness it could expel. Maybe that's what that black hole feeling was. Emptiness.

I closed the woman's eyes and closed my own for a moment as I touched her hand and said a silent prayer. Then I kept going. Because that's all I could do.

Jason's words from that morning came back to me in a rush:

*"All we can do is try our best to move forward, do some good, and make a difference in the ways we can while we have the chance."*

A couple hours later, SJ finished brewing her antidote to the jasper berry tea. My friends and I helped administer it to the sick. Once we were done, the five of us regrouped outside.

"How are you doing?" SJ asked me, genuine concern in her voice.

"Dumb question," Blue said. "How do you *think* she's doing?"

I waved off her defensiveness. "It's fine. I'm fine."

"*You're fine?*" Jason repeated, doubtfully.

"I'm handling it," I corrected. I straightened up and cleared my throat. "We need to leave. Mauvrey and Alex took a wormhole. Graystone said they were going after Paige. I think it's best if we didn't wait any longer to do the same. We have our maps. We're ready."

"You don't want to be here to help your family?" Jason asked. "We understand if you need to take a couple days to rest and—"

"No," I cut him off. "I don't need to rest. I need to do something. And the best way for me to help my family is to stop Alex from wreaking any more havoc. We leave in an hour. But first, we need to tell my parents the truth. Sooz already knows everything about the antagonists. Blue and I told her so we'd be on the same page as all the ambassadors and the Godmothers. My parents deserve my honesty too. The secret is out, so there is no sense in holding back anymore."

"Except about your Pure Magic," Blue said. "It's too dangerous for anyone else to know about that yet. We don't know what they'd do to you."

"Agreed," I said. "And we shouldn't say anything about Liza being the Author, or the protagonist selection conspiracy. Lenore would make us suffer if we told anyone about either. Besides, we need Sooz and the other ambassadors on our side to deal with the antagonists and the commons rebellion."

"All right," Jason said. "While you talk to your parents, I'll see about securing us a ride out of here. Lucky might not be a good option if we're going through a wormhole. We'll be headed into the Wonderlands and won't be able to take him with us, which means we'd have to abandon him in whatever city we access our wormhole from. With all the chaos the realm has seen today, I don't think leaving an unsupervised dragon somewhere is a good idea."

"Fair point," said Blue. "I'll go see if there's anything else Pietro needs before we leave."

"I shall check on the patients who drank the antidote I brewed," SJ added.

"And I'll go with you," Daniel said to me. I gave him a confused look and his expression softened. "To tell your parents," he clarified. "You shouldn't have to do it alone."

The gesture surprised me, considering his stance on our relationship. But I did not question it. His instinct was good. I didn't want to tell my parents alone.

"Um, all right," I said. "Everyone meet back here in an hour. Make sure you are ready to go."

My friends parted ways, all except Daniel and me. He followed me across the main lawn to a private medical tent that the Fairy Godmothers had poofed up for my parents. My mother was recuperating inside as SJ's antidote kicked in. The Weatheralls had their own tent next door. Tunderly's king had broken his arm in the fight, and SJ had also helped the castle nurses whip up a bone-mending potion that was healing him and the other people with damaged limbs.

I didn't say anything to Daniel on the way to the tent. I also kept in front of him as we walked. I was committed to staying strong and not letting anyone see how I truly felt. Daniel had always possessed a talent for seeing through me, but now that he and I weren't the friends we used to be I couldn't let him.

"Mom, how are you feeling?" I asked my mother as I entered the tent. She was awake and a little color had returned to her face. My father was sitting in a chair next to her. A couple of our castle's nurses moved about the room, and a cluster of Godmothers were talking in the corner.

"Crisanta, I am doing much better," she replied. "I cannot believe how quickly this potion is working. Your friend SJ is truly a remarkable young lady."

"I know," I said. *I just wish she did.*

"Um, this is Daniel." I gestured to the hero on my left. "I know you guys haven't formally met. He's my friend from school."

"Your majesty," Daniel said, bowing to my mother then my father. "Sir."

My mother gave a small smile and my father stood for a moment to shake Daniel's hand.

"Mom, Dad," I continued. "My friends and I have to go. What I said to you the other day about us staying with Jason was a lie. We actually have another mission."

"To stop the antagonists," my mother interrupted. "We know. Sooz was in here a short while ago and she told us what you told her—the truth about everything."

I cringed. "Are you mad?" I asked.

I expected them to blow up at me for throwing myself into danger so readily, and for lying. I also anticipated a slew of worry. My parents hadn't reacted well to magic hunters trying to kill me at school. I figured they'd freak out if they knew just how many people wanted me dead because of my prologue prophecy (something else Blue and I had detailed to Sooz).

"We are not mad, Crisanta," my mother replied, much to my disbelief. "Shocked perhaps. Concerned for you, certainly. But not mad. How could we be? You have an entire kingdom of wickedness after you in addition to magic hunters, and you have had the strength and resolve to fight back. Speaking as a protagonist, I could not be more inspired by your courage. And speaking as your mother, I could not be more proud."

Her words filled me with warmth, humility, and surprise. While I didn't actively seek the approval of others, getting my mother's blessing was something truly special.

*Deep down, no matter how self-accepting or accomplished we are, we always crave the approval of our parents to some degree.*

"Did Sooz tell you about Paige Tomkins?" I asked, trying not to let my mother's sentiments overwhelm me.

"The Fairy Godmother that the antagonists are looking for?" my father clarified. "Does Alex have something to do with that as well?"

Hearing my father say my brother's name with such a hateful inflection made me pause.

"Yes," Daniel replied on my behalf. "He and Mauvrey Weatherall have left Book to search for her in the other magical realms known as the Wonderlands. But we believe we have a means to beat them to it."

I nodded. "My friends and I have this thing called a Hole Tracker, which allows us to find wormholes that lead to other Wonderlands. We've been mapping out the Wonderlands for several months so that when we went after Paige we wouldn't be flinging ourselves into the unknown and our search would be more efficient. While I was at home, Daniel, SJ, Jason, and Blue finished the task. Now that the maps are ready we want to leave right away to stop Alex and the other antagonists before it's too late."

Sooz entered the tent. Her eyes widened when she saw me. "I was just speaking with your friend Jason about securing you proper transport," she began steadily, then faltered. "Uh, Crisa, I hope you're not upset that I told your parents what you told me."

"I'm not," I said. "It's time everybody knew. In fact, I was in the middle of explaining to them that my friends and I are going after Paige and Alex."

"Crisanta," my mother interjected. "I understand why you think you have to do this, and like I said, I am immeasurably proud of you. But the five of you are mere children. I cannot wholeheartedly approve of you going on such a perilous quest."

"Mom," I said evenly. My expression was soft, but my tone immovable. "I didn't tell you all of this because I wanted your permission. With all due respect, I don't need it. My friends and I are doing this one way or the other. We may be kids, but we have the responsibility to take action and the power to do it. So I'm not asking you to let me go. I'm telling you that—unfortunately—you don't have a choice."

My father took my mother's hand and spoke to her gently. "She will be okay," he told her. "Crisanta can take care of herself. And her friends will take care of her too." He looked at Daniel. *"Right?"*

"Yes, sir," Daniel said with a stern nod. He seemed a bit intimidated by my dad's intense stare. I'd never seen Daniel look intimidated before. It was kind of nice.

"You have our blessing, Crisanta," my father continued, regarding me directly. "Whether you need it or not, you have it. Go find this Paige woman and keep her from the antagonists. Stop Alex, no matter what it takes."

The humanizing grief I'd seen in my father earlier was gone. His tone and stature had become king-like again. His face reflected the same hardness I saw in myself. I could tell that he'd had a chance to process what happened and was resolving to bury his own heart and be what he needed to be, just as I was. As I'd always believed, I really was my father's daughter.

He stood up straight. "I have already spoken with Pietro and the Weatheralls. Since Tunderly's palace was also attacked, neither our home nor the Weatheralls' is safe for the moment. The Godmothers were able to eliminate the leaders of the commons rebellion that instigated the Tunderly attack. And the ones responsible for the chaos here are either dead, in custody, or have escaped with Alex. But for now, we must temporarily relocate until the castles are safe and all remaining staff and King's Guard have been cleared of suspicion."

"We've made arrangements for the Weatheralls to stay with the Yazkavore royal family and for your parents to stay with the Darlings in Clevaunt," Sooz said to me. "They're the closest kingdoms, and since both are located in the North Mountains, they are heavily fortified. We'll have Fairy Godmothers assigned there, as well as to all the other castles in the realm until this commons rebellion is stopped."

"Good," I said. "Because something big is coming. Anthony Graystone confirmed that the antagonists are the ones guiding the commons rebellion, and that they have something planned for the Vicennalia Aurora. We need to be ready."

"We will be," Sooz said.

My mother pulled herself up slightly so she was sitting upright. "When will you depart?"

"Right away," I said. "I came to say goodbye. For now."

"Not just yet," my mother said. "Daniel, Susannah, all of you." She glanced around at the Godmothers and nurses in the tent. "Will you excuse us for a minute?"

Daniel touched my arm, which caused me to flinch. "I'll be outside."

"No," I said. "Go change out of your suit. I'll meet you and the others when I'm done."

He nodded and left the tent. Then it was just me and my parents.

I was wary at first about why they wanted to be alone, but then my mother opened her arms and motioned for me to come to her. A small piece of my vulnerability fell through and I allowed myself to lean into it. My mother enveloped me in a hug that we both really needed. When we reluctantly pulled away, she tucked a loose strand of hair behind my ear. "Be careful, Crisanta," she said. Her eyes were glassy, but still so much like steel. "This road is a dangerous one. And we have already lost one child today."

My father came to stand in front of me then. I tensed a bit. Despite the fact that he'd convinced my mother that I could handle this mission, interactions with him rarely ended well. I expected some comment that might lessen my resolve and make me feel small. I expected him to do that thing where he rubbed the knuckle of his pointer finger under his chin as he silently judged me. I expected him to berate me. But he didn't.

"You know that I love you, Crisanta."

He said it sternly, but the inflection in his tone made it seem like a question.

I nodded.

"I do," I said. Then I felt the truth slip out of me. "You just don't like me very much."

My father exchanged a glance with my mother before returning his focus to me. "You couldn't be further from the truth," he responded. "I am harder on you. It's true. And maybe I have always taken it easier on Alex, but it is because you are so different."

"I know," I said with a sigh. "He was the perfect son and prince who did what you expected. And I'm the weird rebel princess who always answers back."

"No, that's not what I mean," my father corrected. "Contrary to what you might think, Crisanta, I've always been tougher on you because you possess something that neither of your brothers has. Your mother and I have seen it in you since you were young. There is a rare fire in your heart that can drive you to achieve more than what is expected of you. They can teach protagonists a lot of things at Lady Agnue's and Lord Channing's, but they cannot teach that. Alex never had it. He was strong and intelligent, but that drive—that yearning and potential to be something more— was always missing. So I kept him close and tried to encourage him as best I could. If he was going to be the next king of Midveil, I had to make sure he was ready. You didn't need me the way that he did."

My heart ached. "But I did need you," I said softly. "You and I have so much in common. Do you know how much it's always hurt that you treat me as a second to Alex?" My voice cracked. "If what you're saying is true and you thought I had the potential to become something more, then why were you so hard on me all the time?"

"Because I wanted you to be ready," my father said. "Having potential is a dangerous thing on its own, Crisanta. It is as much a blessing as it is a curse because it means you stand out, and there will always be people who view you as a threat because of it. But for you specifically, it is an even greater challenge. Princesses are supposed to grow up to fulfill certain expectations, live certain lives. I've always suspected you had the ability to surpass those archetypes, but I knew that as you got older the number of people and obstacles working against you would only increase. While showing encouragement and support to Alex was how I thought I could help him achieve his best self, I felt that giving you opposition early on—but in a safe place—would condition you to fight back.

"I wanted to make sure you could handle whatever the world threw at you. I wasn't being hard on you because I wanted to break you. I wanted you to be ready, to be strong enough to face the challenges and people who *will* try to break you. Perhaps it was not the kindest lesson to lay upon your childhood, and I am sorry if it caused you to feel like I didn't love or care for you as much as Alex—that was not my intention. It was the only way I could think to prepare you for the life you are headed toward. The life, it seems, that has already found you."

I was too shocked to speak. Too shocked to move. There was so much buzzing about inside me that I could barely stand.

I knew I wanted to cry, but I didn't shed a tear. I knew I wanted to say something, but I didn't have the words. This long-awaited explanation about the rocky relationship with my father filled me with an indescribable warmth.

He didn't dislike me. In his own weird, tough-love kind of way, he'd just wanted to help me become the person I'd always been aspiring toward.

And the thing was . . . his efforts had paid off. Over the years the way he treated me *had* taught me to fight back. It made me grow thick skin and a steel spine so that when I went out into the real world I was ready for much heartier foes. The defiance and strong will I'd developed at home gave me the nerve and experience I needed to stand against true opposition to my character development, like Lady Agnue, Mauvrey, Lena Lenore, and countless others. My dad had been conditioning me to face these enemies all along. He'd been trying to help me become *this girl* all along.

I studied my father. We shared so many qualities—the pride that made us stand tall, the fire that made us strong, and the genuine love and desire to help those we cared about. For once, I did not feel remorse about being so much like him.

I took a step forward and gave my father a hug—not the rigid, timid kind we occasionally exchanged, but a real, loving hug. As his arms wrapped around me too, and my face pressed into his chest, I told him something I hadn't said in a long time.

"I love you, Dad."

# CHAPTER 34

# Journeys Ahead

y parents and the Weatheralls needed a safe way to get to their temporary castles in Clevaunt and Yazkavore. Since Fairy Godmothers could only teleport so far—unlike Liza, who had an all-powerful mastery of teleportation—and no one could guarantee their safety if they travelled by carriage or the magic train, I'd offered them Lucky as a means of transport.

My mother was not a fan of the idea of dragon travel. She had quite a few things to say on the matter. Alas, it was the only way. Her protests did not change that.

Pietro was going to fly my parents and the Weatheralls to their respective safe havens straight away. It was a good thing that I'd taught him how to fly Lucky earlier in the month. After I bid farewell to my mother and father, he was the last person I had to say goodbye to.

"So you're coming back here after you drop off Mom and Dad in Clevaunt and the Weatheralls in Yazkavore?" I clarified.

"Yeah," Pietro said. "I'm going to supervise the reconstruction of the castle and security clearance of all our remaining guards and staff."

"You'll be here alone?"

"Evette is going to stay with me. I asked Mom and Dad for permission. I think it'll be good for us to have each other to talk to, what with everything that's happened."

Pietro's eyes had a glaze of sadness over them, and I could tell he was tired. But there was nothing short of strength and determination in his expression. Our father had laid a huge responsibility upon his shoulders, and while Pietro may not have ever trained to be king like Alex, he knew what it meant to be a leader, take charge, and defend others. He was ready for this. I had no doubt he would perform under pressure. Having Evette there to give him support was an added bonus.

"Good," I said. "I'm glad you have someone."

"And what about you?"

"What about me?"

"You have someone, right? To talk to I mean, and help you deal with all of this?"

"I'll deal with it just fine on my own, Pietro. Don't worry about me."

He gave me a tight hug and then patted my head, mustering a smile. "I'll always worry about you, baby sister. Since you refuse to do it, someone else has to."

My brother started back toward Lucky where my parents and the king of Tunderly were preparing to go. I headed for the tower that housed my bedroom to get myself ready. Suddenly Mauvrey's mother came around the corner. She paused when she saw me.

"Crisanta," she said.

"Your majesty," I responded, bowing a bit. "I . . . I wish you safe travels."

"Thank you," she said. "I cannot say I have ever flown on a dragon before."

"Don't worry. Lucky is a friendly dragon. You'll be fine." I gave her a warm smile and a small curtsy, intending to keep going, but she moved in front of me.

"Forgive me," the queen said, "but all afternoon I have found myself in dire need to speak with you, but with just as much fatigue over not knowing the proper thing to say."

"People we love broke our hearts today, your majesty," I replied softly. "I'm not sure there is a proper thing to say."

The queen made a small motion between a nod and a head shake. Her expression was empty. The only thing I was able to ascertain for certain was that she'd been crying.

"I should probably get going," I said, trying to escape the awkward lapse. "I have a couple of things to prepare before we depart."

"Crisanta," the queen repeated, preventing me from taking another step. "If you catch up with your brother, what do you plan on doing with him?"

The question caught me off guard. I had to think for a moment before answering. "I don't know," I replied honestly. "I hate him, but part of me wants to believe that the person I've always known is still in there, that—Shadow Guardian or not—somehow he can be saved."

"And what about Mauvrey?" the queen asked. "I know my daughter has done terrible things, not just to us today, but to you personally. Do you believe she can be saved?"

This inquiry threw me even more. Mauvrey was evil. She was an antagonist-supporting witch who—in a few short months— had poisoned me, tried to kill me, and locked me in a coffin. Even before any of that stuff went down she'd been a toxic presence in my life for years. But she hadn't always been that way. Just like Alex, she had changed. So theoretically, did that mean she could change back?

"I don't know, your majesty," I responded. "I suppose that's up to her."

"Do me one favor then?" the queen said. "If there is ever a time that your path crosses hers and you see a chance to help her break free of whatever darkness has hold of her, please promise me that you will take it."

I thought about the request. The odds seemed impossible. Mauvrey hadn't simply been possessed by darkness, after all; she'd chosen and embraced it. Still, this was her mother, and she needed a glimmer of hope that her only child might not be lost forever. Who was I to deny her of that?

"I promise," I said.

And I meant it.

I watched Lucky zoom into the sky from the balcony of my bedroom. His scales flickered in the afternoon sunlight and he was out of sight in less than a minute.

Since my room was on a higher floor of the castle, it had not been damaged by the ground level explosions. I'd asked one of the Godmothers to teleport me up here so I could change. My friends had gotten back to their guest rooms in the same way.

My dragon gone, I headed for the closet. There was a garment bag in there—sandwiched among the dresses—that Minnie had delivered to my room earlier in the week. It was the sturdy dress that I'd requested be made for my journey to the Wonderlands.

I don't know exactly what I'd been expecting, but the outfit was significantly more beautiful and colorful than anything I thought I'd get when I requested something durable and lightweight. I guess comfort, function, and fashion really could coexist.

I slipped the dress on over my black leggings. It was a lavender-and-orange masterpiece. The neckline and waist were highlighted in royal purple with elegant, curled embroidery running up the bodice. The bottom seam of the dress was finished with jagged black fabric that matched the off-the-shoulder sleeves, and the royal purple collar was popped high.

It felt a bit strange to be wearing something so bright and colorful when my mood was dark and the situation was bleak, but I didn't fight it.

"That'll do," I mused as I caught a glimpse of myself in the mirror.

I threw on the black military jacket I'd arrived in a month ago, secured my wandpin to my bra strap, grabbed my backpack from under the bed, and went over to my desk.

I took my Mark Two out of the top drawer and shoved it inside the bag with my dream journal, which I'd brought with me from Lady Agnue's. There was a secret compartment at the back of the drawer where I kept a small sack of gold that I'd earned from allowances and odd jobs over the years. I packed it as an emergency fund for our trip. Next, I pulled out a couple of items that were already inside the bag.

The first was my SRB. SRB stood for Soap on a Rope-Like

Bracelet. SJ had invented it last semester and given one to each member of our group. The bracelets were laced with a special potion that kept the wearer clean and fresh. If we got dirty or wet in any way while wearing them, the SRBs instantly cleaned and dried us off with a flurry of silver sparks. Needless to say they were the ideal accessory for a long quest.

The other item I removed from my backpack was my Hole Tracker. This fantastical watch-like device showed its wearer when and where the nearest wormholes were going to open up, creating portals to other realms. It had been generously gifted to me by a White Rabbit named Harry (the son of the famous White Rabbit from the *Alice in Wonderland* stories). White Rabbits were charged with guarding wormhole portals from unauthorized access, using their Hole Trackers to find and get to the openings whenever they could.

I thought that Harry's gift would give us an advantage over the antagonists. Now I knew better. My enemies had Hole Trackers too.

I secured the Tracker around my left wrist beside the SRB and the gold wristband that I used to share with Alex. For a moment, I studied the wristband and considered removing it. Then I decided to leave it alone. Keeping it was like keeping hope alive that Alex wasn't entirely lost.

Plus, the wristband had an adverse effect on him that might come in handy. I opened the bottom left drawer and picked up my Shadow Guardians book, flipping to a page I'd read long ago when circumstances were so much different. I scanned the passage then my original translation right beside it.

"As Shadows draw their power from darkness . . . they can be weakened by light in the same sense . . . Shadow Guardians stay away from items that embody human symbols of light, such as selflessness, kindness, hope, and faith. Some examples include family mementos and items of deep sentimental value to the human host."

I sighed and closed the book.

It all made sense now. The reason Alex hadn't wanted to throw coins into the wishing well. The reason he had stopped wearing all his sentimental wristbands. The reason his hand had burned so drastically when his skin made contact with our shared gold bracelet. It was because the objects were toxic to him, or at least to the Shadow inside of him.

I shut the book, much like I was shutting the portion of my story that involved this place. Once I'd stored the text back in my drawer, I marched to the balcony. For one last time I glanced back at the space. My room looked like a foreign world now, even more than it had upon my arrival a month ago. It was like a museum dedicated to a girl who used to live there and the innocent world she once existed in.

I leaned out over the balcony and gave a signal to the Fairy Godmother who was waiting for me on the grass below. On seeing my wave, she used her magic wand to teleport me back to ground level. A cloud of red smoke consumed my form; when it dissipated, I was standing beside her.

I thanked the Godmother, whose name was Elsie, and went to meet my friends. Sooz had made arrangements for five Pegasi from Midveil's Twenty-Three Skidd arena to be brought over to the castle. They were on loan to us for getting to our next destination. It was time to find the nearest wormhole and begin our hunt for Paige Tomkins.

I approached my friends and the steeds. Blue was petting the mane of a pretty hazel Pegasus. "So where's the nearest wormhole supposed to open?" she asked when she saw me coming, gesturing to the Hole Tracker on my wrist.

"Century City," I responded, having already checked. I pushed a button on the device and a holographic map projected in front of me. A small, glowing silver circle appeared in the Century City portion of the map with holographic coordinates and a time stamp next to it.

"Aren't the holes usually marked in black?" Daniel commented

"Yeah," I said. "But all those times we used the Hole Tracker before, the holes connected to Earth. Maybe the color changes depending on the realm the hole leads to?"

"So where does that one lead?" SJ asked.

"I don't know," I responded. "This thing shows the coordinates and times of the next holes, but not details about their destinations."

"Well, that is not terribly useful," SJ replied.

"What can I say, I don't really know how to work this Hole Tracker properly. Harry didn't give me instructions. From messing around with it, I discovered that it flashes brighter when we get closer to a hole. There is a more specific proximity sensor I can turn on as well that tells me how far we are in terms of feet and miles. I can also flip through time settings to see when future holes are opening up. But I can't see where the holes are going, and it only displays vague maps of the realm we are currently in, not any others. Just look." I tilted my chin at the holographic projection. "I probably wouldn't even know this was Century City, let alone somewhere in Book, if it wasn't for the coordinates and the big labels at the top. That's why it was so important for us to make those Wonderland maps in the first place. The maps on the Hole Tracker are barely better than wandering around blind."

"All right then." SJ sighed. "What time is this Century City wormhole opening up?"

"Six o'clock tonight," I said.

"Which means we better get going," Blue said, giving her hazel steed a final pat. "It's a long flight from here to Century City. Come on, people, we're burning daylight."

Jason rubbed his hands together. "Century City: Round Two. Any chance this will go smoother than our last visit?"

I huffed in amusement. "With our track record, I wouldn't count on it."

# CHAPTER 35

# Not So Happy Returns

louds blew past us. The sky dipped from brilliant blue to gray. The temperature dropped. But while the world changed around me, everything within stayed static. I had a thousand things to think about, but my mind was blank.

My friends didn't talk to me much on the way. Maybe they knew that's what I wanted. Maybe they knew that's what I needed.

After hours of flying, I looked down to see our realm's capital, Century City. When my friends and I had arrived here last semester, I was awestruck by its architectural grandeur. Now it no longer impressed me. The intricately shaped skyscrapers seemed duller. The aromas wafting up from the bakeries and coffee shops didn't smell as sweet. Even the people, who once bustled about with such animation and intrigue, no longer appeared interesting. They all looked like ants.

My friends and I steered our Pegasi toward the Capitol Building—a majestic-looking structure with a white cupola at the center of the city where government affairs were handled.

An immense gold statue of a dragon stood in the middle of a roundabout outside the Capitol. The statue was without equal in scale and scariness. Its hind legs were like sequoia trees on steroids. Its menacing eyes and massive face were frozen in an eternal state of rage. Its three-hundred-foot wingspan stretched over the surrounding streets.

We landed our steeds in front of the steps that led up to the Capitol Building. Several guards were waiting at the top to take them from us.

When we'd settled on our plans in Midveil, the Fairy Godmothers there had communicated via Mark Twos with several Godmothers stationed in Century City. Those Godmothers had informed the Capitol Building guards to receive our Pegasi on arrival. They would see to it that the steeds were returned safely to Midveil.

Once we'd handed over our rides, my friends and I walked away from the Capitol Building under the shadow of the enormous gold dragon.

I pushed the button on my Hole Tracker to check where we had to go. I kept my eyes on the watch and not the dragon as we crossed the street and passed beneath it. The statue had a weird effect on me every time I saw it. It was just so gigantic and sinister-looking that it made me feel off-balance.

On the other side of the street people were closing up their stalls in the outdoor marketplace. According to my Hole Tracker, we were very close to our destination. If I had to guess, the wormhole we sought would open near one of those shops. The silver circle that glowed fervently on my Tracker all but affirmed it.

There were twenty tiny, continuously moving circles on the face of my watch with multiple hands pointing to them. These circles flashed gold, silver, orange, or red, once in a while one turned black. I'd selected the silver circle that corresponded with our destination, and as a result it now took up the face of the watch and pulsed vividly.

"We're close, but we've still got forty minutes until six o'clock," I informed my friends.

"Since we have a little time before the wormhole opens, do you guys mind if I make a short stop somewhere?" Daniel asked suddenly.

"Where?" Jason asked.

"It's a couple of blocks over. You don't need to come with. I can go on my own."

"*Where?*" I repeated.

"To visit a friend," Daniel said, rubbing the back of his neck.

"We'll go with you," Blue offered.

"Again, that's not necessary," Daniel insisted.

"Maybe not for you, but for us that's a different story," Blue countered. "Come on, man. We all dig your whole mysterious, brooding, lone wolf deal. But friends oughta share a little something about their personal lives every now and again. Stop being so weird. Crisa just introduced us to her entire family. And after seeing them in action, trust me, you've got nothing to worry about."

I wasn't sure if I should feel insulted by the remark. Daniel seemed annoyed and reluctant. He gave me a quick glance that I couldn't quite read. Eventually he nodded, conceding to Blue's demand. Refusal wasn't typically an option with her.

"Fine," he said. "Come on."

Daniel led us through the city, taking a lot of shortcuts. He knew his way around like a local because he was. Before being chosen as a protagonist and being sent to Lord Channing's, Century City had been his home. He'd lived here as a common all his life until he'd been accepted to Lord Channing's only seven months ago.

Steam rose from a manhole, misting over a line of freshly laundered linen above me. I gazed up and saw more of these lines crisscrossing over the alley like a trapeze artist's playground.

We turned and came upon a street of smaller houses sandwiched between much taller buildings. Daniel headed toward a pale yellow dwelling. When the five of us reached its rickety front porch, he stopped and faced us.

He gave me that same enigmatic expression as before, then addressed our whole group. "Just don't make a big deal out of this, okay?"

We nodded at his cryptic tone. I had never seen Daniel so flustered, so nervous. He was normally unfazed by anything. What could possibly have him this on edge?

Daniel knocked on the door. A female voice called out, "Coming!"

A moment later the door swung open. A girl stood in front of us. She had beautiful wavy black hair. Her rich brown eyes were like chocolate truffles against her light olive skin. I recognized her instantly.

"Daniel!" she gasped.

He smiled bashfully as her eyes met his. "Hey, Kai."

Kai was perched on the arm of the chair Daniel was sitting in. Her hand was absentmindedly running through his hair. It was weird to see someone be close to him and have him like it.

She'd ushered us into her home once Daniel had introduced each of us, but after our brief presentation and an abbreviated explanation as to the reason for our visit, she hadn't taken her eyes off my friend. Nor had she allowed her body to migrate more than two feet from his.

I felt uncomfortable. The girl who Daniel had known his entire life, the girl he loved, the girl his prologue prophecy predicted I could undo—I was looking right at her. An odd combination of guilt and nausea washed over me as I watched her. Daniel may not have blamed me for what his prophecy said, but once a guy tells you that his girlfriend could come to a permanent end because of you, it's hard to feel relaxed in her living room.

"So . . ." Blue broke the silence. "I'd like to say Daniel's told us all about you, Kai. But who are we kidding. Until yesterday, I didn't even know you existed."

"I knew," Jason commented. "Daniel told me about you a couple months ago."

I didn't chime in that I knew. Best to stay away from the topic.

Kai tore her eyes away from her boyfriend to smile at Jason. "Yes, well, Daniel's never been one for sharing."

"That's an understatement," Blue replied. "So tell us, girlfriend of Daniel, what's your story?"

"*Blue*," Daniel protested.

"It's fine, Daniel," Kai interceded. "Let's see, my story . . ." She shrugged modestly while continuing to toy with Daniel's hair. "It's not that exciting, not like you protagonists, I'm sure. I've lived here my whole life. I'm an only child. My dad works the night shift for Capitol Building security. I like to bake. And I tutor the neighborhood kids in reading and arithmetic whenever I'm not working."

"Where do you work?" Jason asked as he studied the collectible metal figurines on the fireplace mantle.

"I'm an assistant at one of the city's forges," she said as she settled in closer to Daniel. "I've been working there since I was twelve, but for the last few years the head bladesmith has taken me on as his official apprentice."

"That's awesome," Jason responded. "Can you fight too?"

Kai nodded. "Mr. Torres says you can't make a proper sword unless you understand the sword. He's been giving me lessons since I started working with him. I've gotten pretty good."

"Good? She's amazing," Daniel cut in, looking at her proudly. "She would give half the guys at Lord Channing's a run for their money."

My eyes narrowed. I was inexplicably annoyed by the exchange.

I wandered into the kitchen to refill the water glass Kai had given me upon arrival. As the tap water ran into the cup, I stared out the slightly dirty window. Over the tin roof of the adjacent dwelling I could make out the cupola of the Capitol Building. Its windows were dark. Its white stone grew more shadowy as twilight approached.

When my glass was full, I went out the back door. Kai was nice enough, but I needed some air. I sat in one of the beat-up lawn chairs outside, watching a Chartreux cat inspecting the contents of an overturned trashcan. My mind wandered for what felt like seconds, but it must've been longer. I was startled when the door behind me opened.

"Hey, it's a quarter to six," Jason said, his head peeking out. "We're getting ready to go."

"Um, okay. Coming."

I got up to go back inside, but Jason blocked my way. "Crisa . . ." he said. "I get that what happened today was awful, and I understand why you would want to put it behind you. But I'm worried about you. Are you sure you're okay to just charge on like this?"

A bit of emotion sent a tremor up my throat, but my resolve reined it in.

"I appreciate your concern, Jason. I really do," I said. "But do you remember what you said to me this morning before the attack when I asked you how you were? You said you didn't want me to keep asking if you were okay. That you weren't, but you accepted that, and you wanted me to as well. The same goes for me. With what just happened with my home and my brother . . ."

My throat began to tighten.

I gulped down the surge and remained steady. "Look. It's hard enough for me to have lived through it once. I don't want to rehash it, especially when doing so could distract me from what's important—finding Paige and stopping the antagonists. You should understand that better than anyone. I've been taking my cues from you and how you've handled yourself since I told you about my vision."

Silence hung between us. A tin can rolled along the ground, chased by the cat.

Jason sighed. "Fair enough," he said. "I'll accept that and leave you be if that's what you want."

"It is," I said semi-certainly. "And should any of the others bring up the subject, I'd appreciate it if you spread the word."

Jason put his hand on my shoulder for a moment, then let me pass. I returned inside the house and set my glass down on the counter before we made our way back into the living room. Kai was giving Daniel a kiss goodbye. It wasn't a peck either. It was a legitimate, vulnerable, deeply personal kiss.

I froze. My eyes darted to the ground. I'd never been a fan of public displays of affection. But this one in particular made my stomach lurch in a way that even today's events hadn't yet managed.

I followed SJ, Blue, and Jason out the door, where we waited until Daniel joined us a minute later, Kai at his side. We all thanked Kai for her hospitality and then turned to walk back the way we'd come. Daniel was behind me. At least, I thought he was. When I disembarked the steps I turned around and saw that he was still standing in the doorway, facing Kai with his back to me. His arms were around her waist. Her arms were around his neck as she whispered something in his ear. She pulled him close to her by his jacket collar, then gave him another kiss.

I grimaced.

Once she let go, she saw my staring and blushed awkwardly. "Best be on your way," she said to Daniel, smiling. She glanced past his shoulder. "It was nice meeting you, Crisa. Do me a favor and keep an eye on him for me. He can take care of himself just fine, but that doesn't mean he wouldn't benefit from someone else looking out for him too."

"Sure. You bet," I said, throwing in an awkward salute for some unknown reason.

Kai closed her front door. Blue and Jason began to lead us back to the city center, having memorized the path on our way here. Daniel and I were at the rear of the group.

"So . . ." Daniel said as we jaywalked across a busy street. "That happened."

"Yup, sure did," I muttered.

"Any comments?"

"Nope."

"Good."

It was barely five minutes to six when we returned to where we'd started. In the shadowy twilight the silhouette of the dragon statue was chilling. Again, I tried not to look at it more than I needed to.

All the vendors had left the marketplace with their wares, but the stalls themselves remained. Navy curtains swayed slightly in the early evening breeze. Hollowed out of goods and filled with shadows, they were pretty eerie.

The silver circle on the face of my Hole Tracker glowed brighter as we continued our search for the wormhole. The more it glowed, the closer I knew we were getting.

I turned on the proximity sensor, which activated a small holographic compass over the watch. As we wove through the marketplace, the compass displayed updates. One hundred feet away N/E. Fifty feet away N/E. Thirty feet away N.

We hurriedly followed the Hole Tracker's guidance. When

the clock struck six, the Tracker indicated we were ten feet away. We were standing on the sidewalk between an empty booth and an antiques shop—one of many in this part of the capital. The silver circle that represented the hole we were tracking burned so brightly I thought the entire watch might catch fire. I glanced around. Between the stalls I could still see the giant dragon statue in the roundabout, but nothing else caught my eye. Where was the wormhole?

"Maybe the hole is inside," Jason said, gesturing to the antiques shop.

I approached the glass storefront and my Hole Tracker shone with enthusiasm. "I think you're right," I said.

"I got it," Blue announced. Without being asked, she drew one of her throwing knives and bent down in front of the shop entrance to pick the lock.

"Blue, we are only a few a hundred yards away from the Capitol Building," SJ griped in a hushed tone. "There are guards all over this city. You are going to get us shot or arrested before we have even begun our quest."

"Relax, SJ," Blue said, concentrating on the lock. "Century City is the safest place to live in the realm. No guard is going to waste time patrolling an empty marketplace."

Blue wasn't wrong. Ordinarily, the crime rate in Century City was so close to zero it might as well be a negative number. But with the recent commons rebellion attacks, I wondered if the silence in the streets wasn't so much because the guards weren't worried about crime, but because the civilians were worried about wandering out at night.

Blue cracked the lock and pushed the door open. We hurried inside, closing the door behind us. The antiques shop was packed with wooden spinning wheels, bronze clocks, and aged furniture. The aisles were so tight and cluttered I felt like if I made a wrong move and bumped into a lamp, one of the piles of junk would come crashing down in an avalanche and bury me. I shuddered. Antiques shops were super creepy. I never understood why Century City had so many of them. How much competition could there be in the old, smelly stuff industry?

My friends and I diligently searched the shop for the wormhole. My Hole Tracker began glowing crazily near the back. I stopped. I was standing in front of a floor-length antique mirror. I walked toward it.

Out of inexplicable instinct, I held out my hand to touch the cold surface of the mirror. My fingers passed right through it—disappearing from view and causing the mirror to ripple like unsettled water. I extended my hand farther to test the phenomenon; it sank through all the way up to my shoulder.

"Guys, I think I've got something."

The others came over and were stunned to see what I'd discovered.

"I think this is it," I said hesitantly.

"Why doesn't it *look* like a portal, though?" Jason asked.

"I don't know," I admitted. "Maybe not all portals to the Wonderlands look the same. The one I first met Harry by was a giant silver hole in the ground beneath a tree."

"That makes sense," Blue said. "Think about the *Alice in Wonderland* stories. She went through a hole under a tree the first time, then a looking glass the second time. Maybe wormholes adapt to wherever they appear."

"So . . . we're just supposed to jump through?" Daniel asked.

I observed the reflection of our group in the mirror. My friends were uncertain and seemed to be looking to me for the final say-so.

"Let's go," I said.

And with no more delay, I took a literal and figurative leap of faith through the looking glass.

# CHAPTER 36

## Once Upon a Tavern

t felt like I'd been ejected into open space.

The portal this wormhole created dropped us into a large, black abyss that smelled like garden soil. My friends and I tumbled through darkness. My body flailed and my boots scraped against what felt like dirt walls and roots. After about twenty seconds, the dark chasm abruptly opened into a massive room.

I fell onto a comically large bed and rolled out of the way to avoid being landed on by Blue and Jason, who came tumbling down in the next instant. The impact of their landing launched me off the mattress and onto the ground.

Blue and Jason sprang out of the way as SJ and Daniel dropped in after them. Their landing ricocheted Jason onto the floor beside me while Blue fell off the bed's other end.

I groaned. I think we all did. Once I was on my feet again, I stared up at the hole in the ceiling we'd fallen through. It was twenty feet above ground. The area surrounding it, like the curved walls that led there, was made of earth. Straggling vines dangled near the dark ejection point and a veil of spectral fog wafted over it, matching the layer of mist at our level.

Throughout the strange, circular room this light mist hovered over the floor, coming up to the middle part of my lower leg. I gazed around. Fourteen doors lined the rounded walls. Each door was unique in design—and closed. One was constructed of ice and framed with holly and garland. Another was dark and wooden with vines sprouting orange tiger lilies. Two were small—

no bigger than a foot in height—while a couple others were over ten feet tall with titanium and steel reinforcements.

The bed was the only thing in the room, and it merely consisted of a thick white mattress on a metal bedframe.

"Is everyone okay?" Jason asked.

We all nodded, except for Blue who was still lying on the floor. She pulled something out from under the bed. "Hey, look what I found."

She was holding a latched wooden box. Inside, the lid was lined with a half dozen secured vials labeled "Drink Me" and the bottom was made up of the same number of sealed Tupperware containers labeled "Eat Me."

"It's like in *Alice in Wonderland*," she said. "We must need to take these if we want to get through a few of those doors," she said. "The big and the little ones, anyway."

"Okay, but what is this place?" Daniel asked.

I walked up to a door with curiosity—the one with the holly and garland. It was normal-sized. The door itself was made of ice, but the handle was smooth and silver. I reached out for it and pulled. The moment I did, a frosty wind slammed the door the rest of the way open. A blizzard began to immediately blow into the room—forcing me back and onto the floor.

"Whoa!"

The others rushed to help me close it. A landscape covered in snow was on the other side of the doorway. In the distance I could see the glow of a village. The smell of sugar cookies blended in with the wind that blew against us until we managed to shut the door again.

"What was that?" Jason asked as he leaned against the icy doorframe.

"I think it might have been another realm," I responded.

I moved for the next door in the sequence (a forest green one with a gold floral design etched into it). It may have been a bad idea, but I threw it open before the others could stop me. I was glad I did. It gave me confirmation.

Through the open door we could see the inside of the antiques shop we'd just been in. Every tchotchke was there—cloaked in the dark seclusion of the store.

"I think these are all portals," I said in awe, closing the door back to Book.

"How does that make any sense?" SJ asked, still dusting flakes of snow from her black suede jacket and camel-colored pants.

"It doesn't," I admitted. "But when has that ever stopped our story before?"

"So if these doors are all portals to other Wonderlands," Jason clarified, "then we just have to pick one to begin our search."

"Exactly," I said. "Only I think we should look for a door to Neverland. We should start our quest in that realm."

"Why there?" Blue asked. My other friends looked at me curiously.

"While I was in Midveil I had a lot of vision flashes relating to Neverland," I explained. "Once I even had this old man appear to me in a dream the way Liza used to. I don't know who he is, but I think he wanted us to go to Neverland."

"Isn't it kind of a gamble to base our search on a vision of some guy you don't even know?" Blue asked.

"It was dreams of Liza last semester that helped me discover my magic, which was what saved us from being killed in Alderon," I countered. "My gut tells me we should listen here too."

My friends exchanged silent glances before Jason eventually responded. "All right. Neverland it is. Let's spread out. One of these doors has to lead there."

My friends and I began opening and closing doors. I had to get down on my hands and knees to check the tiny doors while Jason gave Blue a boost to turn the knob of a giant one.

Soon enough it was SJ who found our exit portal. "Here," she said, calling us over to the last door she'd opened—the dark wooden one with the vines and orange tiger lilies growing around it. "This door leads to Neverland."

"How can you tell?" Jason asked as we approached.

"See for yourself."

We all crowded the doorframe and looked through. The door

opened into an alleyway, but a storefront window at the end of the lane had a sign that read "Neverland's Best Souvenir Shop." That's when I became certain that our course was true. I'd seen that sign in a vision.

"Huh. Well, that's fairly self-explanatory," Blue said. Then without any hesitation she stepped through the doorway.

"Blue!" SJ said, reaching out.

She landed on the street in front of us. "What?" she said. "Come on, it's just a doorway. No need to freak out."

SJ apprehensively tightened the straps on the small black backpack she was wearing. "It is a doorway to another realm," she argued, gradually stepping over the threshold into the alleyway. "It is not exactly the same thing as stepping from a living room into a kitchen."

The rest of us followed. Daniel was the last one out, and he closed the door behind him. When he did, it was replaced with a silver, swirling wormhole that levitated in the alley.

"I guess on this side the portals resemble normal wormholes." He shrugged.

Suddenly the wormhole sealed itself up and every trace of it disappeared.

"No turning back now, I suppose," I said.

The five of us journeyed out of the alley and found ourselves in a bustling portside town. We stood under a red awning and observed the Wonderland we'd arrived in.

Despite the sun going down, small businesses were charged with activity. Storefronts were decorated with multi-colored paper lanterns while twinkling lights lit up the windows and doorframes. Fireflies flickered around like curious spectators.

From my Wonderland mapping I knew that Neverland had several busy portside towns, but there were elements about this place that I hadn't expected. For starters, there were only adults, which baffled me since I knew for a fact that Neverland was home to plenty of kids who came here to avoid getting older. Then there were the shops surrounding us. They sold goods that we'd never seen before. Banners hung from store windows advertising things we didn't understand.

"Sale on Microwaves!"

"Half off Dehumidifiers!"

"Buy one, get one free Falafels!"

For a second I wondered if we were really in Neverland. Then I looked out at the sea beyond the boardwalk and spotted a familiar ship. The sides of the vessel were painted red and black. My friends spotted it too.

To get a better look, we wandered along the boardwalk where mechanical telescopes were mounted. I pressed my eye to peer through one then rotated the mechanism until I had a clear visual of the ship. The enormous sails were silky white, the mast was bronze, and a single flag adorned with skull and crossbones flew from the crow's nest

Each of my friends took a turn at the telescope and they all concurred. We'd all spent time staring at an illustration of that boat in our textbooks when we'd been cramming for midterms.

"We're definitely in the right place," Jason said as he looked up from the telescope. "That's the *Jolly Roger*, Captain Hook's Ship."

"Okay, so we're in Neverland," Daniel said. "Where should we start our search for Paige?"

Blue lifted her chin, closed her eyes, and took a deep whiff of the air. Then she pointed back up the boardwalk at a tavern on the edge of town. "There," she said.

"Why?" SJ asked.

"Because that's where the smell of burgers is coming from," Blue replied.

"Blue, we have hardly begun our quest. Do you really think this is an appropriate time for a meal break?"

"Considering that the last thing I ate was a chicken dumpling off the floor of Crisa's ballroom after the attack this afternoon, yes," Blue said. "Besides, the sun is going down and we need to come up with a solid plan for how to proceed. Dinner is the perfect chance to regroup." She glanced at me for half a second. "A lot has happened today."

My stomach rumbled loudly the moment Blue mentioned food. It had been forever since my last meal and I was starving.

"Blue's right," I said. "We should regroup and get some dinner. It's not like taking a half hour to eat is going to kill us."

On the corner of two streets—one marked "Buena Vista" and another "Alameda"—we entered a pub called "Once Upon a Tavern."

It was a quaint place with low wooden ceilings, dark green vinyl booths, and antique light fixtures. The windows were stained glass. Every bar stool had legs with intricate vine designs.

I noticed a few framed signatures hanging on the walls of the establishment. Beneath each frame was an empty table. I was surprised that no one was sitting at them. The tavern was bustling with activity and there was barely any standing room.

Evidently my friends and I shared the same thought. Led by Blue and Jason, we wormed our way through the crowds to one of the aforementioned tables. Just as we were about to sit, a burly man with a round nose and white whiskers appeared before us. His nametag read "Manager."

"What do you five think you're doing?"

"Sitting," Blue replied.

"Not here you're not," the man said. "Ain't you got any respect?" He pointed to the framed signature behind the table.

It was indiscernible, but then I noticed a plaque directly beneath it that held the same name in professional engraving.

"*Walt Disney,*" I read aloud. The last name struck a chord of familiarity. I was pretty sure I'd heard it while I was on Earth last semester.

The manager took off the bowler hat he was wearing and brought it to his chest. "Wonderful man. Bless his soul. This was his regular table, see. And like all the other valued storytellers, we save 'im a spot here permanently. So, off you go." He shooed us away from the table. "There are a few stools at the bar. Come with me, but keep your heads down."

We trailed the manager through the crowded tavern until we reached the far end of the bar. We passed several other permanently reserved, empty tables along the way. I was able to make out the names on some of the plaques, including "J. M. Barrie," "Steven Spielberg," and "J. Howard."

I knew J. M. Barrie was the writer responsible for Earth's first adaptation of *Peter Pan*. The other names were unfamiliar.

We sat down at the bar as the manager came behind the counter. He began to clean some glasses as he lowered his voice to speak to us. "You're more than welcome to stay; business is business after all. But if anyone asks, you're all twenty-one," he whispered.

"Don't worry," I said. "We weren't planning on drinking."

"No, it's not that," he said. "Ale flows like rainwater around these parts, so I couldn't stop you if I tried. I just don't want anyone to know that you're kids."

"Why?"

"Because kids aren't allowed. The only kids in Neverland are the Lost Boys and Girls that live in the Neverwood, some Indian children, and of course Pan. If any of the pirates got wind you were here, they'd feed you to the crocodiles. They're not too fond of your kind."

"Like adults are *so* much better," Blue scoffed.

The manager glared at her. "Just eat quick and get out. And don't to talk to anyone."

"We're teenagers, not toddlers," Blue replied. "You don't have to warn us not to talk to strangers."

"I do when the repercussions could affect every other realm," the manager responded.

"How's that?" Jason asked.

The manager sighed. He leaned against the bar and nodded to a man wearing jeans and a t-shirt with a big, gold-colored WB logo printed on it.

"See that fella over there? He's one of the storytellers in Neverland on temporary visa. Word is, he's doing early research for a big adaptation back in his home realm. So we gotta be nice or he won't give us the goods he's brought with him. That means no tampering with his research."

"What do you mean, research?" I asked.

"The White Rabbits have an agreement with the higher-ups in most of the Wonderlands," the manager replied. "Every now and then, they'll select a few storytellers from other realms like Earth and allow them to visit us for a short period of time. These storytellers hear our tales, do research on our realm and its main players, and then take that information back to their world to make stories they can turn a buck on. In exchange, they give us technological advancements from their worlds.

"How do you think we ended up with stuff like electricity, churros, indoor plumbing, jeans, and tacos? Those things weren't invented in our realms—they're innovations brought to us by them storytellers. It's a good gig, and we don't want to screw it up. So don't tamper with the system. The storytellers in Neverland are only to have access to characters and plot lines *about* Neverland. That's all their visas are good for unless the White Rabbits give 'em access to somewhere else. I don't know where you kids are from, but you've got that protagonist look about you, which means you don't belong in someone else's story, got it?"

We nodded.

"Good," he said as he handed us menus. "Now what can I get you? Might I recommend the Tiger Lily tiger prawns with honey dipping sauce? They're so good, it's sinful."

I was quite satisfied with our visit to the tavern, particularly in regards to the house special, Neverland Nachos.

The manager had directed us to a machine in the corner of the bar called an ATM to change our Book money into Neverland currency to pay for the meal. We ended up exchanging a good portion of our funds that way. We didn't need Book money on this quest, and the ATM had an option labeled "ONC" that converted money into currency valid in Oz, Neverland, and Camelot.

As the sun continued to recede outside the windows, the place got busier. I was glad for the delicious distraction of the fattening foods we were enjoying. I'd been through so much today; I really needed a break from the—

"He's coming!"

My head snapped in the direction of the tavern's front window where one of the waiters had pressed his face against the stained glass. "Assume positions!" he shouted.

People began moving and items were swiftly hidden. The bar counter was wiped down. Several parties evacuated the tables and chairs they'd been using. A waiter grabbed the framed Disney signature and stuffed it beneath a booth cushion. Even the manager jumpily began mixing drinks into glasses.

"What's going on?" I asked as he poured some whiskey.

"The captain's coming. Remember what I told you about keeping your head down. And whatever you do, don't—"

The door burst open. Every person in the tavern silently turned to acknowledge the new arrivals, but all were careful not to make direct eye contact.

A tall, lean man sporting well-trimmed facial hair and a short black ponytail swaggered in with twelve others behind him. It was obvious they were pirates. And by the looks of their leader's hand (or lack thereof), it was obvious that he was Hook. Captain Hook.

"Chawkovsky!" Hook bellowed.

The manager who'd been helping us zipped around the bar and came out to greet the Captain.

"Are my men's drinks prepared?" Hook asked.

Chawkovsky nodded. "Yes, sir. They're waiting for you at the bar. I'll have servers bring them over momentarily."

"Good," Hook replied. "On the house, as always?"

Chawkovsky nodded even faster. "Yes, sir. Of course, sir."

"Very good, man. Very good. At ease." Hook smiled and gestured around to the patrons. "All of you at ease. We're here to drink and be merry, are we not? Go about your business, please, and we too shall drink and be merry. As long as there aren't any swine from Disney in here."

A patron standing by the bar subtly zipped up his jacket, concealing his t-shirt of a cartoon mouse wearing red shorts and white gloves.

"Of course not, Captain," Chawkovsky said nervously. "We all know how you feel about that lot."

"Right then." Hook nodded. "Let's have a look for ourselves

just to be sure, shall we?" Hook marched over to the storyteller wearing the WB shirt. "You're not from around here. Which studio do you represent?"

"Um, Warner Brothers," the man replied, shaking a little.

Hook smiled and patted the storyteller on the shoulder. "Good lad, no need to be nervous. You just be sure that my character is represented valiantly in your next adaptation and all will be well. Make me look foolish, however . . ." Hook scraped his hook against the marble countertop. The awful sound made the patrons cringe.

"You'd be surprised how many of your kind haven't made it home because I disapproved of their pitches," Hook said. "So, tell me. Am I going to be disappointed with yours?"

"Um, no sir," WB guy quaked. "In fact, you're not even the villain my writers want to focus on. We're thinking of focusing more on Blackbeard. You'd be a secondary character."

Hook's eyebrows shot up and he snatched WB guy by the back of the neck and slammed his face into the counter.

"Do I look like a secondary character to you?" he barked. He shoved his hook under WB guy's chin. "Next time, do more research."

The pirate viciously lifted his hook to strike.

"Hey! Leave him alone!" I shouted.

Hook, his twelve men, my friends, and every other person in the tavern turned and stared.

"Crisa," Blue whispered between gritted teeth.

Hook released WB guy's neck and the storyteller coughed gratefully. The captain took a few steps closer to get a better look at me. The crowds parted on cue.

It was hard to say whether Hook was more outraged by the remark, surprised by its source, or intrigued by the fact that I had chosen to hold my ground rather than leap behind the bar and go into hiding.

"Well, now," Hook said as he eyed me. "Who do we have here?"

"They're no ones," Chawkovsky tried to intervene. "They're just travelers."

"And how old are these travelers exactly?"

"Um, twenty-one," Chawkovsky stammered.

Hook narrowed his eyes and seized the manager by his shirt collar. "Do I look like an imbecile to you? I didn't become a captain in Neverland without being able to recognize a protagonist when I see one. And I didn't get a twelve-year-old for an archenemy without being able to note the difference between a kid and an adult. They. Smell. Like. Children."

"I thought he was a pirate, not a bloodhound," Daniel muttered under his breath.

Hook pushed Chawkovsky out of the way.

"Crisa, now would be a good time for a magical distraction," Jason whispered urgently.

"I know, I'm working on it," I said.

I tried to focus and make the power flow out of me. Alas, hard as I concentrated, my magic would not manifest. I was still in the reboot stage of Magic Exhaustion. The twenty-fours I needed had not been fulfilled. Not quite yet.

I frowned in surprise. I knew I usually needed the complete twenty-four hours, but for some reason I'd been able to call upon my powers to burst out of my mother's study this afternoon. During other times when I had reached Magic Exhaustion, I could only access the tiniest amount of power to operate my wand. And even that was by accident, or instinct. I shouldn't have been able to harness that much magic on purpose earlier, but I had. I didn't know why that was, but I wished whatever mojo I'd channeled then could come back now. Regrettably, it didn't.

"I can't do it," I muttered. "My powers are still tapped out."

"Take them to the ship!" the captain ordered.

Hook's twelve men drew their weapons and began to shove their way toward us.

"Then I guess we do this the old-fashioned way," Blue said. She took one last swig of her root beer then thrust the glass to the ground, causing it to shatter. Several heads turned in her direction and she responded by swiftly rotating to the nearest bar patron and punching him in the face.

"Bar fight!" she yelled. And like that, it was on.

Immediately the patrons were up in arms as if they'd been waiting for this all night. Maybe they also craved a distraction from Hook's pirates. Or maybe they wanted to satisfy a long time urge to take a shot at them in the confusion.

Swords were drawn, bar stools went flying, punches swung left and right, pirates slammed into tables. Chaos erupted so quickly that I began to wonder if maybe adults shouldn't be allowed in here either.

"Get down!"

Daniel and I ducked beneath a table to avoid the body of a drunken hermit who had been thrown over the counter.

As we made our way to the door, my friends and I had the opportunity to land a few punches ourselves. A smile slipped across my lips. After a long, strenuous day, letting off steam with a good bar fight was strangely liberating. While my heart still ached from the tragedies I'd experienced in Midveil, the fun of slamming an antagonistic pirate in the back with a bar stool made me feel oddly alive again.

After Jason head-butted a guy with a gold tooth and Blue kicked another pirate so powerfully he flew through the window, we managed to make it out of the tavern unscathed. We stumbled out into the street and kept running until we were a safe distance from the establishment.

When we stopped at the dock to catch our breaths, Blue shot me an exasperated look. "Did you have to do that?" she panted.

"Hook would've killed that guy," I protested. "What was I supposed to do?"

"Not get *us* almost killed would've been a good start," she replied. "We've got bigger problems and responsibilities riding on us, Crisa, and a lot of people who need our help. What you did in there was reckless. Enjoyable or not, that wasn't our fight."

"Blue, you're right. We've got a lot of big things riding on us. But that doesn't mean we should ignore the smaller problems that cross our path. Just because we didn't owe WB guy anything doesn't mean this wasn't our fight. The fact that we were there and could do something about it makes it our fight."

Blue shook her head and sighed. "Ugh, I hate how—"

"*Noble* I am sometimes? Yeah, I got it. But nobility has nothing to do with this; it's just a matter of right and wrong. SJ agrees with me, don't you, SJ?"

I glanced around. Only then did we notice that our group was short one princess.

"Where's SJ?" I gasped.

Daniel nudged me in the shoulder and nodded in the direction we'd come from. "There."

Coming down the boardwalk was Hook and his band of men. And constrained by several pirates within their ranks was SJ.

# CHAPTER 37

# Hooked on a Feeling

hat's the plan?" Daniel whispered to me as we were escorted onto the *Jolly Roger*.

"Rescue SJ, get off the ship, and feed Hook's other hand to a crocodile if there's time."

"I meant a plan for how to do that."

The ship swayed lightly beneath my feet. "I'm still working on that part."

We'd had to surrender to Hook in order to keep him from slitting SJ's throat. Now our hands were bound and we were being taken aboard his ship as prisoners, which he seemed to be enjoying. Us, less so.

"Toss these protagonists in the brig," Hook ordered. "When we get far enough from shore, we'll feed them to the beast."

We were led single file through a trap door and a narrow set of stairs. The atmosphere below deck was shadowy and damp. There were four dark cells—two on each side with a small walkway between them. The five of us were shoved into the first cell on the right and bolted inside.

The pirates had confiscated all our stuff, including our backpacks and my friends' weapons. Luckily, my disguised wandpin had been safe from the reaping. Once the pirates had left, I jimmied my bound hands up to grasp it, then I morphed the wandpin into a knife, which we all used to cut the ropes restraining us.

"Well, this is just great. You *had* to go and get captured, didn't you, SJ?" Blue groaned as she sat on the wooden bench inside the cell. She kicked aside a dead rat carcass like it was nothing then started carving her initials into the side of the boat with the one throwing knife she'd managed to slip into her boot before her utility belt was confiscated.

SJ looked peeved. Then the boat lurched forward. We'd set sail.

"Look, what's done is done," I said. "Let's focus on getting out of here."

"The only way out of here is through the digestive tract of a crocodile."

We hadn't noticed the man sitting in the far corner of the adjacent cell. He had matted blond hair, a dusty black blazer, and navy pants. He leaned against the wall next to the bars.

"That's if you're a storyteller, anyway," he continued. "If you're a kid, then he's probably going to throw you overboard point blank. So, which of the two are you?"

"The latter," Jason replied. "But I'm pretty sure we got tossed in here for being protagonists."

This got the scruffy man's attention. "Protagonists!" He moved closer and clutched the bars of his cell. "Finally, some inspiration! You know, the only character I've talked to in the last couple of days was a lame antagonist from some realm called Book. And he wasn't even interesting. All I ever got out of him before Hook killed him was that he'd found some lead in his search for a woman named Paige."

My eyebrows shot up. "I don't suppose you mean Paige *Tomkins*?"

"Yeah, yeah, that was it. Anyway, I'm glad to have some interesting characters to talk to. So how 'bout it guys? Where are you from? Who are you? What's your story?"

"Who we are doesn't matter," Jason said earnestly. "Who was this antagonist? What did he say about Paige's location?"

"You answer my questions first," the man replied. "I've been down here since Hook found out my studio wanted to do a musical adaptation of *Peter Pan* that involved the Hook character performing a tap number. The guy had a fit, stole my storyteller visa and Hole Tracker, and locked me in here. The only reason I haven't been fed to the croc like the two producers I was travelling with is that I agreed to work on a manuscript painting him as a swashbuckling hero.

"But that manuscript will never sell in Hollywood, and if I get out of here someday, I'd like to at least have something of production value to take back to Paramount. So tell me your story and I'll tell you mine. If you wanna find out where this Paige is, give me the scoop." He pointed at SJ through the bars. "Starting with you."

SJ furrowed her brow. "The manager at the tavern told us not to speak to storytellers. He said that doing so could have repercussions on other realms."

"SJ, he has a lead about where Paige is. We need whatever information he's got," Jason insisted. "It's not like we could get tossed in jail for it. We're already in one."

"All right, all right," SJ sighed. She uncrossed her arms. "My name is SJ Kaplan. I am the daughter of Snow White and Prince Edward, future queen of the land of Dobb, and apparently a helpless damsel in distress that got captured by the bad guys in the last scene." She shot a glare at Blue.

"Daughter of Snow White?" the writer repeated. "Pass. Snow White stories are going to saturate the market in a few years. A friend of mine has a dark-vibe screenplay he wants to sell to Universal Pictures where he envisions a big star like Charlize Theron playing the wicked queen. And these two guys I know at ABC are planning a TV show where the main character is the daughter of Snow White. She's going to be a badass with a red leather jacket. Sorry, kid, you're just not original enough." He rubbed his chin and turned to me. "Now you've got a distinct look about you—bright eyes, brave face. Tell me your story."

SJ clenched her fists. For a second I thought she might shoot laser beams out of her eyes. What I was less certain of, though, was whether she would aim them at the writer or at me.

"Um, pass," I said. "You don't want to hear about me. My story's too complicated."

"So I'll trim the word count on the manuscript. Come on. Give me something and I'll tell you what you wanna know."

I looked at SJ. From the expression on her face, she was

probably wishing that she had a portable potion to fire right now. Nevertheless, she exhaled irritably and gestured from me to the writer. "Go ahead."

"All right . . . fine," I agreed reluctantly as I turned toward the writer. "But you don't know what you're getting into."

"Which makes it all the more intriguing."

"I'm only giving you the short version and I'm only saying it once, so pay attention," I told him flatly. "My name is Crisanta Knight. My mother is Cinderella. My brother is a back-stabbing traitor. A whole lot of people out there want to kill me. And I've got magical powers. There. Satisfied?"

"Hold on, hold on," the writer said as he scribbled in a notebook that he'd pulled from his pocket. "What was that last part? Did you say you have magical powers?"

"Yup."

"Can you show me?"

"Nope."

"Why not?"

I shrugged. "They're all dried up right now. I kind of used them too much yesterday and they need time to reboot."

The writer grinned ear-to-ear at his scribbles. "See," he said addressing SJ, but pointing at me with his pen. "That's what I call an innovative protagonist."

*Really, man? I'm already in the doghouse with SJ. Could you make things any worse?*

I ignored SJ's furious face and wheeled back to the writer. "It's your turn now. I gave you what you wanted. What do you know about Paige?"

"Fair enough." The writer shrugged. "I think I can work with what you've told me. So anyway, this antagonist told me that he'd found proof that this woman he was looking for—Paige Tomkins—wasn't in Neverland. She was in another realm."

"Which one?" Daniel asked.

"Oz."

My friends and I exchanged a look. I hurriedly turned on my Hole Tracker, which thankfully the pirates hadn't thought to confiscate. The holographic map now displayed a blobby image of an island labeled "Neverland" at the top. A little dot highlighted our offshore location, but there was no sign of a hole opening anywhere on the island. I passed my index finger in a circular motion around the face of the Hole Tracker to scroll the time settings forward until I found the next wormhole.

"There," I said, pointing at the silvery circle. "The next portal opens tomorrow at five past ten in the morning."

"I guess your hunch about coming here first was spot on," Jason said to me. "Finding this writer guy is the ultimate clue."

I furrowed my brow. He was right. The writer had just given us a very distinct plan for how to proceed. But I couldn't help but feel like there was more to it than that. Had the old man in my dream really only wanted us to come here to find this writer, or was there another reason?

Blue pivoted to the writer. "Did this antagonist say if he'd told anybody else about—"

Blue cut herself off at the sound of the trap door swinging open. I turned off my Hole Tracker and morphed my wand back to its clandestine wandpin state—much to the awe of our writer cellmate—then clutched it tightly in the palm of my hand. Three dirty-looking pirates arrived at our cell and went to work unlatching its many bolts.

"The captain wants the girl with the combat boots, the girl with the blue cape, and the blond boy up on deck," snarled the lead pirate.

Crud. I hadn't had time to hatch an escape plan. Without our weapons, the odds were rough. The only thing I knew for certain was that my wand could be used in one of its unbreakable forms to slice through the locks outside our cell. But our time was up before I'd thought of what we should do after that. Now I had to make a decision.

I could keep my weapon for my own personal protection and hope to the heavens that I would find a way back down here to free Daniel and SJ. Or I could leave the wand with them and trust that they would find a way to save us once they'd escaped.

The latter was definitely a smarter way to go, but I didn't know if I wanted to trust Daniel or SJ with my wand. They had both hurt me deeply and pushed me away, and my wand wasn't just my prized possession; it was an extension of myself.

Nevertheless, I realized that the issues between us were personal problems, the kind we'd all agreed to put aside so we could work together on our mission. And we could definitely do that. The attack on my home this afternoon was the perfect example. We'd barely been reunited an hour and SJ and Daniel hadn't hesitated to jump into battle with me. Our natural pull toward teamwork and fighting the bigger enemy made us strong. Obviously some instincts—protecting your friends most of all— surpassed personal feuds.

As our cell door was unlatched, I backed up a few steps so that I was standing directly in front of Daniel. Exhaling deeply, I moved my wandpin behind my back.

*Lapellius.*

*Knife.*

Once I felt the leather grip of the knife solidify in my hand, I subtly passed it to Daniel. His warm hand brushed mine as the weapon went from my possession to his. I craned my neck to see him tuck it inside his jacket as our cell door clanged open.

"Come on, let's go," the lead pirate beckoned.

"Why just the three of us?" Jason asked as we were herded out.

"Simple," the second pirate responded. "Combat boots defied him, blue cape started the fight back at the tavern, and you head-butted his first mate. The captain is thinking of keeping your other two friends as unpaid deck hands."

"Over our dead bodies," Daniel scoffed as he and SJ were locked back inside the cell.

"Don't worry, kid," the lead pirate called back. "That's always Plan B."

As we were led away, I glanced at Daniel. I knew he couldn't hear my thoughts, but he still knew how to read the emotion in my eyes. *Please don't let me down*, I implored.

# CHAPTER 38

# Polly Want a Beat Down?

 stepped onto the deck of the *Jolly Roger*. The sun had nearly set after an impossibly long day. Clouds had moved in; they looked like the rainstorm variety. Their darkness made the sky completely gray, save for a thin sliver of red clinging to the horizon.

My magic should have been coming back soon, but I still couldn't muster a spark. With my luck, it wouldn't finish rebooting until this fight was over.

Pirates crowded around the trap door as we emerged. Behind them was a collection of gunpowder barrels. Gas lanterns lit the deck of the *Jolly Roger*, casting malevolent shadows on the crew. These men had looked comically formidable back at the tavern. It was hard to take anyone with gold teeth and leather trousers too seriously. But in this light, their sinister stock had gone up significantly. I was glad they hadn't noticed our hands weren't bound anymore. I felt vulnerable enough as it was.

The pirate ship was surging through the evening tide. The water was choppy, another sign of the oncoming storm. The deck felt unstable beneath my feet as we were paraded through the gathering of seafaring men, several of whom were sporting my friends' weapons. They must've been proud of the score. However, the pirates had no idea what those weapons were really capable of.

A few months ago Jason, Blue, and SJ had saved a Fairy Godmother's life. In return, she'd given them magical rewards. Blue had been gifted with enchanted throwing knives. She used to carry several strapped to a utility belt alongside her hunting knife, but they ran out quickly. Now the utility belt was charmed to replenish the knives as she threw them.

Jason had his trusty axe enchanted. He had grown extremely skilled with it over the years, but his only regret was that it was more of an offensive tool than a defensive one. Accordingly, the Godmother made it so that if he said or thought the word "protect," the axe would create a small protective force field to temporarily shield whatever was within a three-foot radius.

SJ's gift was a little more complicated. It had to do with the sack she kept her portable potions in. But I'll explain more about that later.

As my friends and I passed a chubby crewmate who had taken Blue's hunting knife and utility belt for himself, she almost blew a gasket at the sight of him picking his teeth with the point of her favorite blade. She lunged at him instinctively, but was held back by several men. The pirates cackled as she was pushed along. The ship pitched upon hitting a particularly large wave.

Our group stopped at the port side of the ship. Hook and his first mate were standing atop the three-step staircase that led to the plank. Hook pointed at me. I was shoved forward as I remembered this exact moment from a long-ago nightmare.

I stole a glance behind me. Through the feet of the crowd I saw the trap door leading to the brig. A tiny glint caught my eye. The blade of my knife was carefully cutting through the latches. Daniel and SJ were coming, but they needed a distraction.

I glowered at the first mate (and the conceited parrot sitting on his shoulder) before addressing Hook. "Really?" I said, raising my eyebrows. "No wonder Warner Brothers wants to make you a secondary character. You haven't updated your act in ages."

"Excuse me?" Hook said, flabbergasted.

"You heard me," I continued, elongating my words with dramatic flair as I bought my friends some time. "Your routine's tired, Hook. Any pirate worth his salt these days has more than just a plank, a parrot, and a few men with peg legs to do his bidding. Why do you think I didn't hesitate to call you out back at the tavern?"

I took a few daring steps closer to Hook, my stance and tone remaining confident. "You're not scary. You're a relic of a fairytale gone by. You either need to change to keep up with the times, or move over and let a new villain step in and fill your water-resistant shoes. Take it from a protagonist from the *present* generation— clinging to the past is a cowardly move when the world is ripe for new stories."

I took another look-see and saw that Daniel, SJ, and our writer friend were peeking their heads out of the brig. The pirates had all gathered around the plank drama and weren't paying the slightest attention to the trap door behind them.

When I turned back, the captain was standing directly in front of me. Hook's narrow, burning blue eyes locked with mine for an instant as the rest of the deck remained fear-sickeningly silent. All of a sudden, Hook grabbed me by the collar, lifted me off the ground, and threw me forward onto the plank ahead.

*Ow.*

The board shook beneath me. I placed my hands on its splintery surface and eased to my hands and knees. When I looked down, I saw a pair of menacing yellow eyes in the ever-blackening water and gasped.

A colossal, scaly body rose to the surface. Unlike my dream of this scene, I could make out the crocodile perfectly. The beast was swimming in circles twenty feet beneath the plank. He opened his mouth to show me his innumerable sharp teeth and snorted impatiently into the water.

To the tune of the ticking clock I heard emanating from his gut, I carefully got to my feet. The storm was nearing and the waves were growing fitful.

I turned around to face the crew and their captain as a crack of lighting snapped in the distance, lighting up the clouds. In the shadows behind the masses, three bodies moved swiftly. Two of them ducked past the sail of the foremast while the other headed to the front of the ship. I tried to call my magic again, but the golden glow would not come.

"Do you want to know why those incorrigible storytellers keep re-adapting characters like me, my dear?" Hook asked cockily.

"It's because we're classics. Oh sure, new protagonists can seem flashy and exciting, but you will never be remembered like we are. You're but a passing ship in the night that cannot possibly hope to hold water in the long run. And speaking of holding water, I do hope you're a fast swimmer, because my old friend gets antsy when I tease him with fresh meat."

I analyzed the surroundings. Midterms at school had sharpened my knowledge of this pirate ship. In the falling twilight, I saw Daniel. He had scaled the bowsprit—the long spar that extended from the front of a ship like the horn of a unicorn. It looked like he was cutting the forestays that were tied there, the ropes that connected up to the foremast at a forty-five-degree angle.

*Awgh!*

A hefty pirate had stomped on the other side of the plank, causing it to bounce and me to almost topple off. I stretched out my arms and barely kept my balance.

Hook smiled. "You're only prolonging the inevitable," he said.

*If I had a ruby slipper for every time a villain told me that.*

Suddenly I noticed that the edges of the lowest foremast sail were on fire.

"I don't have to prolong the inevitable," I said. "I just have to prolong the distraction. And ship passing through the night or not, that's one of my specialties."

Hook rolled his eyes. "Mr. Gropper," he gestured to his first mate, "force her off, will you? I grow tired of her attitude. Honestly, children are the worst."

"You've clearly never met a teenager."

Mr. Gropper began to force me back with a harpoon. I tried to conjure my magic once more. My fingertips tingled like seductive matches teasing a spark. I was close to being rebooted—I could feel it—but hard as I tried, the glow and power refused to return. My only hopes now were the ones I'd placed in SJ and Daniel. The ticking of the crocodile beneath me was growing louder, no doubt from excitement over my imminent fall.

*Come on, SJ. The gunpowder barrels are right there,* I thought desperately.

*Please tell me you thought to—*
*KABOOM!*

The lower portion of the foremast buckled under the fury of an explosion. The pirates immediately lost interest in me. They dashed about as burning beams tumbled to the deck like falling torches.

My relief escalated a second later when Daniel came to my rescue. Holding the rope that had once served as a forestay, he swung down from the bowsprit and whisked me off the plank, old-school hero style. Holding me by the waist, he swooped us over the railing closer to the stern and released the rope before the reciprocal force swung us back over the water. We fell in a heap onto an elevated platform overlooking the chaos-stricken deck.

"Thanks," I coughed. "But couldn't you have stuck the landing?"

"Maybe if you hadn't eaten so many Neverland Nachos," he countered.

We rushed to the main deck. It looked like both Jason and Blue had taken leave of their escorts and managed to repossess their weapons. The two of them fought back-to-back in spectacular synchronization. He struck; she ducked. He spun; she swung. They moved with conjoined grace despite being on a burning boat that was sloshing against sizeable waves.

Our only way off the *Jolly Roger* was the lifeboats on the other side of the ship. We had to make our way to them. Several men came charging toward Daniel and me. He took my knife out of his pocket and tossed it to me.

*Spear.*

My blade morphed; the silver shine of its body caught the light of the fire around us. I twirled the staff as the attackers drew near—knocking one in the teeth while deflecting the strikes of two others. Daniel engaged a fourth pirate with a powerful jab-uppercut-hook combo that would've humbled even Girtha.

As that pirate went down, I thrust a kick to my left, turned, and slammed my staff onto the back of another assailant. My grip reversed and I rammed my spear's dull end into the gut of a different pirate. Finally, I flipped my grip to bring the staff down upon the first man a second time. He collapsed to the deck with a thud.

Daniel and I sidestepped around each other—trading partners. He swung the back of his fist into the second attacker while I whirled around and smacked my staff into the temple of the third. Daniel dropped his pirate with a swift elbow between the shoulders while I took mine down with the other end of my spear.

Without saying a word, he and I swiftly bumped fists then parted ways. For a moment I was surprised. We used to do that when we worked together on Twenty-Three Skidd maneuvers and I guess it had come back like a reflex, a remnant of how comfortable we used to be as a duo. It was weird. It was unexpected.

As Daniel reclaimed his sword from one of the fallen pirates and headed to help SJ, I moved portside to aid our writer friend who was literally on the ropes.

The writer was desperately clinging to the rigging of the mainmast—climbing it like a rope ladder in order to escape two crewmates.

*Wand.*

The waves were getting more intense. Holding my weapon between my teeth, I scaled after them—clinging to the moist, prickly ropes to keep from being thrown off.

Writer boy made it to the first beam of the mainmast. Immediately after hoisting himself up, he began to climb the strip of rigging that led to the next beam. The two pirates kept on his tail. I had caught up to one at that point. I reached out, grabbed him by the belt, and yanked—pulling him off the rigging. He fell as I continued to climb.

I mounted the beam at the same time as the second pirate. We were on opposite sides of the mainmast. The writer was farther up, continuing to scurry higher like a panicked baby bear.

I didn't have the space or the balance for my spear here, so I transformed my wand into a sword. I wrapped my left hand around a section of rigging and used it to swing to the other side of the beam.

Weapon drawn, the pirate came to meet me. Our blades clashed—high, low, low, high, thrust, side, parry—until the ship was jolted upward by a huge wave.

I'd been keeping my hand entangled within the rigging as we fought. While I lost my footing when the wave hit, I ricocheted back into the ropes a second later. The suddenness caused the sword to fly out of my hand. It clattered to the deck below.

*Crud.*

The pirate did not have the same luck. He fell overboard—sword and all—crashing into the increasingly violent waters.

Glancing at the progressing battle beneath me, I noticed Daniel was in trouble. He was at the rear of the ship fighting several attackers at once. Wholly preoccupied with their threat, and not getting toasted by the spreading fires, he didn't notice the assailants on the stern about to attack him from behind.

Fear coursing through me, I didn't think. I shot out my hand that wasn't clinging to the rigging. Golden light lit it up like a small comet and I aimed it at a large beam projecting from the stern. Following my will to protect Daniel, the beam broke against its bindings and swung around like a massive club. In one fell swoop, it slammed into all six men who had been encroaching him and thrust them overboard.

Daniel looked up at me for an instant, but something caught his attention back on deck. "Look out!" he hollered.

I moved my head just in time to evade a dagger that had been hurled at me. The dagger stabbed the mast. Straining my neck, I spotted the man who'd thrown it. Hook. He had another blade at the ready. I tried to get out of the way, but with the tossing of the ship, my left foot—like my hand and arm—had gotten entangled within the ropes. I was stuck, caught like a fly in a spider's web. I struggled to get free. Hook took aim.

"Hey!"

Hook and I turned to the voice as Blue's balled up fist came smashing into his face. The captain was launched backward from the strength of the blow—tripping and tumbling over a pile of ropes in the process.

I finished detangling my wrist and ankle, but the moment I

did the *Jolly Roger* hit a powerful swell. The entire ship thrust up like a bucking bronco and I was sent flying off the mainmast and over the water.

I screamed, and rightfully so. I thought I was totally done for—doomed to drown in the torrent sea or wake up in a crocodile's stomach next to an alarm clock.

Remarkably though, I did not find myself crushed by waves or being swallowed; I found myself flying. Ten feet before hitting the sea, someone grabbed my arm and hauled me into the sky. I looked up and saw a boy silhouetted in the light of the lightning laced sky. He lowered me into the safety of the crow's nest high up.

The boy had blond hair, an impish smile, and was wearing a forest green, leather vest over his long sleeve. I opened my mouth to say something, but he held up a hand. "Hang on," he said.

He zipped away with the speed of a hummingbird. Not five seconds later, he returned and floated in front of me, holding up my wand in its sword form. "You dropped this," he said. "I'm Peter."

I smiled gratefully and took the sword. "Nice to meet you, Peter."

*"Pan!"*

We both glanced down to see a disgruntled Hook barking at the flying hero.

Peter shrugged. "Give me a sec, will ya? The old guy gets fussy if I don't pay attention to him."

His bright blue eyes sparked with mischief and he dove down so fast the updraft caused my hair and skirt to flutter. I leaned over the railing to watch the scene below.

"Hook! I missed you!" Peter called as he swooped low. He drew a sword from the sheath strapped to his back as he came to meet his foe. "I love what you've done with the place. I've been telling you for years this hull needs a good redecorating."

"Come here, boy! If my ship goes down, I'm taking you with me!"

"Them be fighting words, Paps," Peter said as he flew around the captain—paying no mind to the fire or the freaked-out pirates abandoning ship and jumping into lifeboats. "Why don't you put your money where your mustache is? I'll tell you what, I win and you treat my crew to a platter of Neverland Nachos. You win, and I'll let you feed me to the crocs."

"Have at thee then!" Hook bellowed.

The two of them proceeded to engage in one of the coolest, weirdest sword fights I'd ever seen. Hook was much bigger and stronger than Peter. And he was an incredibly talented swordsman—his agility, precision, and ability to improvise around the chaotic deck were ridiculous. But Peter was also extremely skilled. A lot of his movement suggested natural talent, but there was a finesse to his strikes that hinted at some sort of formal training.

Peter made up for Hook's age and experience with his jumpy, erratic movements, utilizing his flight to gain better positions throughout the duel. I couldn't help but gawk at the sight. I mean, come on. This was a classic. Peter Pan fighting Captain Hook? What kid hadn't daydreamed about this at some point?

While Peter and the captain sparred across the deck, Hook's first mate, Mr. Gropper, was clambering over burning debris to reach them. I realized he intended to strike Peter from behind while the kid was distracted.

I rapidly climbed out of the crow's nest and maneuvered across the beam directly underneath it until I reached a stay that ran close to the deck.

*Bow.*

My sword morphed into an archer's bow and I used it to zipline down the sturdy rope. I landed between Peter and the first mate who'd been about to make his move. I slammed the side of my bow into Mr. Gropper's neck. Before he could recover, I spun around and back-kicked him then drove a powerful punch into his nose. He went sprawling across the deck.

It had started to drizzle by that point. All of a sudden a powerful explosion rocked the ship. The flames must've finally reached the remaining barrels of gunpowder. A violent domino effect of explosions was set in motion, and the pirates bolted for the remaining lifeboats. Through the smoke and bedlam I could see SJ, Daniel, Blue, Jason, and our rescued writer on the other side of the *Jolly Roger* trying to maneuver toward the lifeboats as well. I headed straight for them, but a great chunk of the mainmast came crashing down between us.

I threw myself back to avoid getting crushed. When I stood up, I couldn't see the others anymore. The rain had picked up and was beginning to extinguish the flames. Out of nowhere Peter came flying around the side of the ship to meet me. "Come on, we gotta go!"

"We can't!" I shouted. "My friends!"

"Don't worry, that's why I brought *my* friends!" Peter gestured toward the sky.

At first I didn't know what he was talking about. But then I saw them. A dozen other children flew up to the ship. They swooped down and disappeared behind the debris blocking the stern from view. Seconds later, they shot back into the sky in pairs—each carrying one of my friends by the arms.

Peter smiled that boyish smile of his and extended his hand. "Shall we?"

# CHAPTER 39

I was pleasantly surprised to discover how forward-thinking Neverland had become.

My friends, the writer (whose name was Mitchell Kapner), and I had been rescued by Peter Pan's band of Lost Boys *and Girls*. The notion put a satisified smile on my face.

Our destination was hidden deep within the Neverland forest, known as the Neverwood. We flew about halfway there then completed the remainder of the journey on foot. The rain turned to a drizzle then eventually stopped. Afterward, much to the amazement of our new friends, our SRBs returned our clothes to their pristine states with a flutter of silver sparks.

I chatted with various Lost Boys and Girls along the way. The trek was long and I wished I could hover above the ground like they and Peter did. My backpack—which my friends had managed to retreive from the pirates, along with the rest of our things—started to feel heavy after a while. Or maybe it was just the weight I was carrying from my problems. It had been a ridiculously long and arduous day. If my life really was a book, the last ten hours could've easily filled a half dozen chapters.

We arrived at a dense row of trees. Peter pushed aside a branch to reveal our endpoint. "Welcome to the Hideaway," he said. "Or Camp Awesome. There's been some back and forth about the name."

Our group stepped into a large campground. There was a flat area with a fire pit to the left surrounded by dozens of plump cushions. Lost Boys and Girls were laying out place settings at an immensely long table on the far right. In the middle of the camp were various obstacle courses. Overhead there were treehouses, rope bridges that connected the trees in a chaotic zigzag pattern, and strings of lanterns that glowed dimly. The luminescent energy inside the lanterns sparkled and pulsed like a heartbeat. In the next moment I discovered why.

A multitude of fairies came zipping through the trees. They stopped at each lantern and shook their wings. Sprinkles of lime green magic fluttered from the fairies, and the lanterns began to glow stronger until they were restored to their full brightness.

When the camp was brightly lit with lime green light, the fairies swarmed around Peter affectionately. They didn't speak, but their wings changed colors and flashed in a code that Peter must've been able to decipher, because he kept offering responses.

"Yup, the whole thing."

"He had it coming."

"Defintiely not."

"Sweat and roast beef with a hint of saltwater."

Blue cleared her throat and all the fairies whipped their heads toward us. It was kind of intimidating. For tiny, cute creatures, they could sport some pretty sour faces.

"Oh, right," Peter said. "Guys, these are my new friends— Blue, Daniel, SJ, Jason, and the great Crisanta Knight. She saved my life, you know. Kept me from getting sliced and diced by Hooky's wormy first mate, Gropper."

I couldn't help but blush; getting complimented by *the* Peter Pan was humbling. Even the fairies were impressed. Their wings glowed pink and began to flutter with extra speed. They flew around me happily and then buzzed around my friends with equal glee.

"They're glad to meet you," Peter translated. "And they want to thank you, Crisa, for your service to the team."

"It was nothing," I said bashfully. "You saved me first and I—"

The sound of a whistle abruptly rang through the camp. All the fairies stopped mingling and darted to where one specific fairy was waiting at the head of the long dining table. She was slender and red-haired with a cute nose—reminding me a bit of my own Fairy Godmother back home, Debbie.

The fairy saluted her troops and they returned the gesture. She buzzed instructions to them with the colors of her flashing wings.

The rest of the fairies took off, heeding her orders. When they'd gone she flew over and extended her tiny hand to me. It looked like she wanted to shake or something, so I extended my pointer finger. She shook it and winked before taking off into the trees.

"She was sweet," SJ commented.

"To Crisa," Blue corrected. "She was pretty direct with those other fairies."

"That's Tinkerbell," Peter explained. "She's the fairy leader and doesn't cut the others any slack when there's work to be done. You gotta respect a leader who rules with an iron fist. She's the nicest when she's off the clock, though."

"Seriosuly?" Blue cocked an eyebrow. "All the stories I've read say she can be pretty jealous of other girls and vindictive like a wet cat."

"Blue," SJ groaned.

Peter shrugged. "She used to be. Then she started going to therapy. Now, come on," he continued. "I want to show you guys the rest of the camp." He addressed the Lost Boys and Girls with us. "Who wants do the honors?"

"I will," called Madison, one of the Lost Girls in our group.

She grinned and flew across the clearing. She stopped next to a particularly large tree, gesturing for us to follow. Madison shoved an arm into the branches and pulled on something hidden, which made a sound like a cord being yanked to open a curtain. In response, a chorus of mechanical snaps echoed through the area and a section of the tree trunk suctioned open like a sliding door—revealing a hollow center. We stepped closer and discovered a slide inside.

I was peering down the entryway when a Lost Boy pushed me from behind with a gleeful hoot. I fell forward—tumbling through the dark passageway. After a few seconds, I plummeted into the light. I landed on a massive trampoline and was jettisoned into a plastic ball pit with assorted pillows and thousands of feathers.

When I surfaced, I found myself looking up at the curious faces of a dozen younger children. I was about to open my mouth when I was interrupted by the sound of another squish on the trampoline. A body landed in the pit next to me.

Blue popped out of the balls and feathers, spitting one of the latter out of her mouth.

"That was awesome!" she said as we climbed out of the pit.

I felt something solid and prickly poking into my side. I turned around to find a seven-year-old nudging me in the ribcage with a mace. "State your business here, intruder," the child said assertively through his missing three front teeth.

Blue and I looked around to find that all the kids had encircled us and were pointing their respective weapons in our direction. Before I could say anything, SJ, Jason, and Daniel landed in the pit. Peter and the Lost Boys and Girls came flying through the passage right behind them.

"Pan!" all the kids shouted excitedly

"We caught intruders," the toothless one announced as he poked me with his mace again.

"Hey, watch it," I said.

"You watch it," he challenged as his gums whistled. "I am Thaddeus Thunderbolt—Conqueror of PogPie Valley."

I stooped to his level. Both figuratively and literally.

"Yeah, well, I'm Crisanta Knight," I said, crossing my arms. "Conqueror of Anybody Who Gets on My Nerves."

"Troops!" Peter said. "At ease. These are not intruders; they're our new friends. They helped me beat Hook today."

The mood in the room changed instantly. All the menacing tiny faces were replaced with smiles of interest and delight. Even little Thaddeus seemed glad to have us, although he didn't put away his mace.

The kids bombarded us with questions as they gave us a tour of their bunker. It was like a palace constructed from the blueprints of a child's sugar-high daydream. The floor was a blend of wooden boards mixed with ball pits, stretches of trampoline, and hopscotch squares. The high ceiling was decorated with strings of confetti, mobiles, arts-and-crafts cut-outs, and hoops hanging every which way. Multi-level bunkbeds were embedded in the hideout's walls. Each bed was decorated with its own unique flair and none were properly made.

In the activity areas, there were pillow-and-blanket forts for playing cards and holding secret meetings. Slides and rope ladders crossed this way and that. Hardcore crafting areas, mountain ranges of toys, a plethora of board games, and small, mismatched shoes, were littered everywhere. There was even a whole nook dedicated to glitter.

"So what do you think?" Peter asked as we bounced from trampoline to trampoline across the room. "This is one of three underground bunkers in the Hideaway."

"It's epic," Jason commented, making a front flip on the trampoline beside me.

"What about you, Mitchell? What do you think?" I called back.

No response.

"Mitchell?" I turned in mid jump to discover he wasn't behind us.

"He can't come down here," Peter said, floating next to me. "We let him into the camp because he's a friend of yours and an enemy of Hook's. But down here is just for kids. Big people—even big people we like—have to stay up top. That's the rule. Even our adult friend AP lives by it. Anyway, ol' Mitch isn't alone. My first lieutenant showed him to the Wendy House where our Honorary Mother lives. She'll keep him company til we get back."

"Honorary Mother?" SJ repeated. "You mean Wendy Darling is still here?"

Peter shook his head. "Nah, she left a long time ago. We've had lots of Honorary Mothers since then. It's a title that gets passed on to the oldest girl in the camp at any given time. We've called the bunker those girls live in the Wendy House since the Darlings visited us, though."

"Hold up," Blue leapt from her trampoline over to mine so

she was closer to the conversation. "I think I missed something. Who's AP?"

"Nice to meet you," AP said, extending a firm handshake to each of us.

AP was a handsome man who looked about thirty-five. I recognized his face. I'd seen it in a dream once. The man was lean and muscular with honey blond hair, bright blue eyes, and an endearing, impish smile. He almost looked like a grown-up version of our host, Peter.

"SJ Kaplan, princess of Dobb," SJ said, shaking AP's hand.

Last in line, I extended my hand. "Crisanta Knight, princess of Midveil," I said.

AP's congenial expression faltered.

"You're a Knight," he said, stating the obvious. "A Knight of royal blood."

"Um, yeah. I guess so."

He shook my hand, but continued to stare at me.

"So if you're an adult," Blue asked AP, "why do you live with the Lost Boys and Girls?"

AP cleared his throat and turned to Blue. "When I first came to Neverland I tried living with the adults in one of the portside towns," he explained. "But the pirates kept hassling me to join their crews. And then kept trying to kill me for not wanting to. They're scum who prey on the weak and ravage this land of its magic properties. I wasn't about to team up with the likes of them."

"So we offered AP the opportunity to team up with us," Peter said, flying overhead to help a tiny fairy carry a large loaf of bread to the enormous dining table. "I know it's unorthodox, but he proved himself worthy. A long while back there was one adventure I thought I might not make it back from."

Peter gestured for us to sit. It looked like dinner was ready and all thirty Lost Boys and Girls were settling along the benches and beginning to dig in. We took our seats at the head of the table.

"Hook and his men had me and a handful of my troops

cornered," Peter went on as we started passing food. "He'd laid a trap for me. We all would have been killed, but AP here saved us. He is the most awesome sword fighter I've ever seen. When the battle was done and we'd escaped, he offered to train me and the other kids in sword fighting so we could be better matched against the pirates. That's how we've all gotten so skilled over the years. In exchange, he lives at the edge of our camp and is an honorary member of the Lost Boys and Girls." Peter gave a sly grin. "Despite his disadvantage."

"Disadvantage?" Jason asked as he helped himself to a big serving of mashed potatoes. Despite our partial dinner earlier, he was clearly hungry. I didn't blame him. So was I. Whooping pirate butt can really work up an appetite.

"He means that I'm an adult," AP replied with a huff of amusement.

"Question," I said. "You said you *came* to Neverland. Obviously I'm glad you ended up staying if it helped to improve everyone's combat skills. But before you met Peter and teamed up with the Lost Boys and Girls, if the pirates were hassling you that much, why didn't you just go back to where you came from? I'm assuming you're from another Wonderland, right?"

A shadow passed over AP's eyes, like a sad thought. Peter quickly swallowed and interceded on behalf of his adult friend.

"I got it, man," Peter said. He pivoted toward me. "Lost Boys and Girls come to Neverland for different reasons. For most of them, it's because they have no place to call home in their own realms—no parents, no family. So they find their way here and we give them a home. Others like me are here to escape what adulthood has in store for us."

"What did adulthood have in store for you?" Daniel asked.

Peter paused for a second, but swiftly shook his blond head. "It doesn't matter. The point is that I left. The third reason people come to Neverland—kids *and* adults—is because it's the only place where they can keep on living. That's the case for both AP and our current Honorary Mother."

"How familiar are you with the different realm time zones?" AP asked, picking up the conversation.

"We know that Earth moves twenty times faster than Book," Blue replied.

"And Book moves about four and a half times faster than the ONC—the time zone that Oz, Neverland, and Camelot run on," AP responded. "But Neverland is special. While this realm is on the same time *zone* as Oz and Camelot—a year here is equal to a year there—the physics of time are different. Every sunset and sunrise in Neverland may correlate to those of Oz and Camelot, but the people here don't feel their effects. That is why the citizens of Neverland don't age. In Neverland, while the days move forward, biological time is frozen. And because of that, people from other realms with mortal injuries or sicknesses can come here to preserve their lives. You can still die from instant killings like, say, if Hook were to stab you. But you can't die from any kind of mortal harm that needs time to do its work—a disease, an injury that doesn't claim your life right away, even poison."

"This realm keeps your biological clock from ticking forward," Peter summarized. "So the mortally injured or ill can live forever."

"People like me," AP said. "Years ago, I was stabbed with a poisoned blade during a great battle in my home realm. I thought I was dead, but when I woke up I was here. I didn't know that Neverland could save me, and I'm not entirely sure how I came through a portal to end up in this land. But so long as I stay, my wound cannot kill me because it is frozen in time. If I leave Neverland, I will die instantly."

Our little group went silent, despite the gleeful conversation of the children further down the table.

"I'm so sorry," I said after a beat.

"It was my own fault," AP admitted solemnly. "The man who stabbed me in the back was my half-brother. I should have seen it coming."

It felt like someone kicked me in the stomach. My friends' eyes lingered on me. I focused on my breathing and ignored the burning pain in my chest where my heart used to be.

"Trust me," I said with a sigh. "It's not your fault. People tend to have blind spots when it comes to family."

CHAPTER 40

# Lost Boy and Girl

ith the next wormhole not due to open until the morning and no immediate threats at our door, we temporarily let our guard down. Despite the serious nature of the topic that began our dinner discussion, our group began to enjoy the evening.

Everyone in the Hideaway was so nice and full of life and innocence that my friends and I couldn't help but forget our troubles. The food was great. The laughter was frequent. And the conversation flowed as freely as the chocolate milk.

The whole camp wanted to hear all about us. They wanted to know where we'd come from, how'd we gotten here, where we were going next. We told them about our search for Paige Tomkins in the Wonderlands, and the antagonists trying to stop us. Then we entertained them with tales of our previous perilous adventures.

I felt kind of bad that Mitchell wasn't around to take notes for his manuscript. But apparently he'd really hit it off with the camp's Honorary Mother and she'd agreed to give him a lengthy interview. They were taking their dinner in her private bunker and probably wouldn't be coming out any time soon.

Jason and Blue told the Lost Boys and Girls about the Therewolves we'd encountered in the Forbidden Forest last fall. SJ detailed our trip to the Earth island of Bermuda where we found the Little Mermaid's daughter. Then Daniel and I wowed them with a description of our time fighting the Pied Piper, the villainous Goldilocks, and the giant lobster-esque creature known as the Magistrake.

During our tag-team account of the adventures the two of us had shared in Alderon, I suddenly realized what was happening. Just like on Hook's ship when we'd inadvertantly bumped fists, he and I were falling into old habits. We finished each other's sentences, poked fun, and were genuinely smiling at one another.

When I became aware of this, I felt a tingle of electricity in my spine like a warning. I drew back after that, reining in how much I allowed myself to connect with him. I wasn't sure if Daniel had noticed how chummy we were being with each other, but he definitely noticed when I pulled away.

We got to know various Lost Boys and Girls over dinner, and even some of the fairies. Although we couldn't speak their light-blinking language, they were fairly good mimers and took to answering yes or no with one or two wing flashes.

The person who proved hardest to get to know was Peter himself. He was happy to talk about anything to do with Neverland and readily shared stories about the escapades he'd had on the island over the years. But unlike the other kids, who easily talked about where they came from and what had brought them here, whenever we asked Peter a question that pertained to anything before his arrival in Neverland, he dodged the subject with a joke, a sassy comment, or simply by flying away.

"Don't take it too hard," young Thaddeous said as he reached in front of me to grab a bowl of macaroni salad. "He's always like that. None of us know who he was before he came here or why he left his home. The only thing we do know is that he's from Camelot."

"Camelot?" SJ asked, leaning in. Peter was on the other side of the table and out of earshot, but she seemed wary talking about him behind his back. "How do you know that?"

"We learned it the old-fashioned way: eavesdropping," Thaddeus replied. "A while back, we heard him and AP talking about it. AP's from Camelot too."

"Why didn't Peter just say so?" I asked.

"We're not supposed to tell outsiders any details about Peter or AP," Thaddeus responded. "It's nothing personal. We just need to protect them so they can keep protecting us. Once you've proven trustworthy and get your Team Pan membership card, maybe they'll be more open with you."

"A membership card?" Daniel said with a half laugh. "You've got to be kidding."

Thaddeus frowned. He put down his spoon and opened his worn leather vest. Sewn on the inside pocket was a small patch with a fancy bronze *P* insignia and the words *Members Only*. "Does this look like I'm kidding?"

He closed his jacket and tilted his chin at me, his expression super serious. "I'm only telling you this proprietary information because I like you. You're cute and aggressive. That's my kind of gal."

"Watch out, Chance Darling," Blue teased.

My friends burst out laughing as my cheeks turned red. Before I could reply to Thaddeus, Peter stood up and started banging a knife on his cup at the other end of the table.

"Attention, attention!" he called, raising his cup. "A toast to our new friends. They fought bravely, burnt down the *Jolly Roger*, and gave Hook a thorough beat-down."

Everyone cheered, hooted, and stomped their feet.

"I'd also like to particularly thank Crisa for saving my life," he continued. "Crisanta Knight, without you I would've been a goner. And so—as is custom for true heroes around these parts—the troop will now give you a nickname so that your legend may live on in the Neverwood forever. Any suggestions, gang?"

"Destroyer of Worlds!" shouted one girl.

"Pirate Pulverizer!" shouted another.

"Conqueror of the Crocodile!" yelled a boy with bright red hair.

"Hey, my nickname's the Conqueror," protested Thaddeus.

"Yeah, but you're the Conqueror of PogPie Valley," argued the ginger.

"Still, I'm the only Conqueror 'round here," Thaddeus argued.

"Says who?"

"Says me!"

"Guys," Peter interrupted. "Let's settle this later in the mud-pit. For now, we need teamwork. Come on, everybody. Give me something original."

"The Page Turner," Blue said suddenly.

Everyone turned toward her. She shrugged. "Girl's always moving the story forward."

"Blue," I murmured between gritted teeth.

I was so embarrased that I wanted the earth to swallow me whole.

"I like it!" Peter announced. He raised his cup anew. "Here's to Crisanta Knight, the Page Turner!"

The others followed his lead. "Crisanta Knight, the Page Turner!"

They clinked their cups, stomped their feet, and chugged down their beverages while I bit my lip and met SJ's jealous glare across the table.

After the feast, everyone gathered around a large bonfire. Peter and the Lost Boys and Girls reenacted the fight on Hook's ship for the rest of the camp. There were improvised flying swordfights and a few boys even put on a crocodile costume and chased the kid playing Hook around the makeshift theater circle.

The rest of us laughed at the spectacle while snacking on treats and candies being passed around the campfire. These kids really knew how to let loose.

As the warmth fused into my skin, I allowed myself to feel happy. After everything that had happened with Midveil and my brother, I was surprised and glad that I still could.

"You know," Jason mused beside me as he took a large cookie from the plate being passed around. "I get that we've been almost killed a half dozen times today, and that we have a lot of enemies waiting for us once we leave here, but I gotta say, I'm having a good time."

"That's under-selling it," Blue exclaimed as she took a cookie of her own. "This is an excellent quest. I just checked two things off my bucket list—burning down a boat and punching Captain Hook in the face."

"You have some really specific things on your bucket list," I commented as Peter and a few girls flew overhead, still playing pirate.

Blue shrugged with a smile. "Hey, a girl's gotta dream big, right?"

"Dude, I saved Peter Pan," I responded in a more hushed tone as I looked around to make sure SJ wasn't anywhere nearby. "That wasn't on my bucket list, and I didn't like all the attention Peter surprised me with at dinner, but it's still ferociously cool."

"Don't I know it," Blue said. "I'm totally jealous."

"Me too," Jason agreed. "This was my favorite book when I was younger. I still can't believe we're actually—"

"Jason, man, get over here!" Peter called as he flew by. "Show 'em how you man-handled that dude with the eye patch."

"Jason! Jason! Jason!" the other kids chanted as they clapped their hands together.

"All right, all right." He grabbed his axe from its sheath and clambered to his feet.

The whole camp cheered as he stepped inside the circle.

"Have at thee, dastardly pirate!" he called to a Lost Boy with a sword and a fake eye patch. The boy grinned and charged. Much to the delight of the other children, the two of them danced around one another in exaggerated battle.

"They love him," I said to Blue as we watched their game of pretend.

"Who wouldn't? He's a great guy."

"And *you* totally love him," I teased.

Blue's eyes nearly popped out of her skull and she smacked me hard on the arm. Still, I cracked a grin.

"I don't *love* him," she said in an irritated whisper. "I just have above-average female feelings for him. So *shut up*."

I tried to mask my smile. "I know," I said with a shrug. "I was just getting you back for earlier."

"Earlier?"

"That comment you made when Thaddeus was hitting on me. Oh, and the Page Turner thing. I was not a fan of that either."

"Fair enough," Blue said. "But that Chance Darling remark

was hilarious, and you know it. And as for the Page Turner thing, you need to stop being so shy of the limelight. You're great, Crisa. And you've done a lot of really impressive stuff. You should be proud of it *and* proud of yourself."

"Maybe . . ." I mused with a light smile.

I gazed back at the bonfire contentedly. Then my good mood vanished when some kids added a large bunch of kindling and the flames suddenly leapt taller. They flashed in my pupils, igniting a memory that tore away my peace.

In the light of the bonfire flames I saw a thousand bad things at once and I felt every emotion that went with them. The terrible events of the day flashed before me. Mauvrey's malicious grin right before she slammed the lid of the coffin, that Shadow screeching and clinging to Alex, the bodies lying in the corridor of my castle . . .

I started to hyperventilate.

"Hey, are you okay?" Blue's expression was concerned as she reached for me.

I drew back. "I'm fine," I said.

But I wasn't. The fire was too hot. The noises were too loud. I stood brusquely. "I'm going to get some air."

I darted out of range before Blue could offer to come with me. I hastened my way across the camp to the perimeter of trees and then through them. I zigzagged farther and farther from the camp until the light and laughter of the Hideaway were a distant haze. Then I sank to the ground. Tears welled up inside of me, but I held them back, trying to hold myself together. I took deep, deep breaths and clutched my knees to my chest.

My heart rate calmed after a minute and I felt like I could breathe again. My head leaned against a cold tree trunk. I rested there with my eyes closed and hoped the chilly air would freeze the fire churning inside me.

"Crisa?"

I opened my eyes. Daniel was standing in front of me. Fireflies floated near his silhouette, making him look strangely surreal. What was more surreal, though, was hearing my name from his lips. He'd only ever called me Crisa once, and that was when I was about to fall into a giant lava pit. The fact that he'd used it now put me on edge.

Without being invited, Daniel sat on a thick tree root across from me. He focused on the dirt for a while. After an awkwardly long lull, he looked at me carefully. "How are doing? You've been acting like you're fine. But after everything, I don't see how you could be."

*Dude, did he just ask me a personal question? Isn't that against our rules?*

"I'm dealing with it," I said.

"You mean you're burying it?" he countered.

"Same difference," I replied. "Not that it's anything you need to concern yourself with."

I could tell by his expression that my coldness may have been a bit much, but I didn't apologize. He had it coming.

Eventually I got tired of the silence. This was the first time we'd been alone together in a while and it made me uncomfortable. I wasn't ready to go back to the Hideaway yet, and if he wasn't going to leave, I had to at least try and diffuse the weirdness with some casual chatter.

"I was surprised that Kai's house was the only stop you wanted to make in Century City," I noted, changing the subject.

"Why's that?" he asked.

"I don't know," I mused. "I guess I figured you might've wanted to visit your home, your family."

"Not much of a home to go back to," he replied. "I've been on my own since I was nine."

I tilted my head. "What do you mean you've been on your own?"

"My parents . . ." he said slowly, like even remembering the words caused him pain. "They died in a fire when I was a kid. My sister too. She was only five."

I sat completely still and stared at Daniel. Shadows crossed his strong features. The vague, distant light of the Hideaway did nothing to lessen the darkness in his eyes, or the piece of truth he'd just shared.

"Why are you telling me this?" I asked slowly. "I thought we agreed we weren't going to talk about personal stuff with each other anymore."

"I know," Daniel said, looking away. "I'm sorry."

I stared at him.

"Not sorry that I told you about my family," he clarified. "Sorry that I pushed you away in the first place." He shook his head and I didn't move. My breath caught in my throat.

"Crisa . . ." he said. "I hated letting you in last semester. Since I lost my family, I've gotten used to keeping people at a distance. Other than Kai, there is no one I'm really close to. But when we were forced to trust each other on our Author quest, something happened. I realized I didn't mind having someone to talk to, having *you* to talk to. And that freaked me out. I've done things on my own for most of my life—I didn't want to get soft relying on someone else. So I pushed you away. I made the choice to sever our connection before I got too used to it. But now . . . I know that was a mistake."

At last Daniel lifted his head. He held my gaze with his dark brown eyes and I tried my best not to let them knock me off balance.

"Jason's a good friend, and I've told him a bit about Kai and my life before school. But talking to him isn't the same as talking with you. You and I haven't known each other much longer, but we opened up to each other during all that time we spent together. And when you went back to Midveil, I finally came to terms with the truth."

"Which is?" I asked hesitantly.

"I miss being friends with you. *Really* being friends with you. Not this shallow relationship we've had since I suggested we treat each other differently. I'm sorry I did that. I know the timing is terrible and I know you're probably mad, but I think we should go back to how it was before. That's what I want. But I don't know if it's what you want."

My heart softened, for there was a part of me that desperately wanted exactly that. I felt so alone right now. I wanted to be able to talk to Daniel and have his words fill my heart with resolve and reassurance like they once had.

But when I considered letting him back in, a tremor of anger and fear reverberated through me. I couldn't do it. Not again.

I'd trusted Daniel that way before and he'd thrown it back in my face and stomped on my faith like it was nothing. His apology didn't change that, nor did it erase how much I resented him for leaving me on my own.

And then there was Alex.

After Daniel had turned me away, I'd opened up to my brother and shared my deepest feelings with him. Then he'd betrayed me in the same way. Like Daniel, he'd made me think that I had someone I could count on. And he'd ended up stabbing me in the back and creating a chasm between us that could never be bridged. He'd burned me and broken me and now I had an emptiness inside that was impossible to fill.

Every person I'd ever allowed myself to be truly vulnerable with had hurt me and pushed me away. I just couldn't bear the thought of going through that one more time. My heart had fractured into a hundred pieces from the betrayal of my brother and the destruction of my home. I would not risk another crack.

In retrospect, it was stupid to wear your heart on your sleeve where it could break. I was tucking it back in where no one would ever see it again.

"It's not what I want, Daniel," I said, standing resolutely and staring at him with a hard expression. "I think we're better like this. I'm sorry if you don't feel that way, but I've made up my mind. *You* put that distance between us when you chose to push me away, and I'm too tired to cross it again."

# CHAPTER 41

## Malice

 was in an infirmary. The windows were open, allowing the sunset to spill through and cast different shades on the room.

There were many cots. The first few dozen were in plain view while the ones farther down had long navy curtains separating them for patient privacy. All the beds were occupied by unconscious people, mostly men in tunics worn under armor, but also some women in brown robes. Additional sleeping bodies were strewn across the floor, the occasional nurse lying amongst them. The veins on all their arms glowed sickly purple like they'd been exposed to Poppies or some form of Poppy Potion.

Arian was on the far end of the room. He stepped into a curtained-off area. I followed him. When I was on the other side of the curtain, I discovered he was talking to dream me. They were standing on opposite sides of a cot, an unconscious girl lying between them. She had wavy black hair and wore a mint green jacket; however the angle of my perspective blocked her face. My vision focused on the exchange happening between dream me and Arian.

Dream me wore a brilliant red dress with ripped hems over her leggings and boots. She also donned a torn navy, military-styled jacket that had seen better days. A sword sheath was strapped across her shoulder and her hand glowed fervently gold with the aura of magic. Her face was filled with spite.

Arian, meanwhile, had a calm demeanor and placid expression

on his face, cool and confident as ever. His cruel handsomeness and malevolent presence remained intimidating—even in a dream. Seeing him made my bones rattle with spite. My hatred for him ran deep, no matter if I was awake or asleep.

His black Shadow Guardian eyes drifted down to the body lying in the cot.

"An awful lot of trouble to go through to kill me, Arian," dream me said. "Why not just do it right here?" She gestured at the infirmary, provoking him. "Afraid you can't beat me on your own?"

"I'm not trying to kill you today," Arian said, walking around the cot back into the aisle. He began heading toward the large doors at the front of the infirmary. Dream me trailed him.

"I actually need you to do something for me," he said.

"What's that?"

Dream me stood frozen in the center of the walkway ten feet behind him. He gestured with a tilt of his head for her to follow. "Come on. I'll explain on the way."

My vision shifted to Natalie Poole.

The hazel-haired teenager was in a graveyard. The sky was gray and leaves were blowing everywhere. Three ravens were perched on a tree in the corner. The grass was deep green like it'd recently rained.

Natalie wore a black dress and a bright yellow coat. Ryan Jackson stood beside her with an arm tight around her shoulder. Her head rested against his chest. They stood in front of a gravestone with the name James Poole carved into the stone.

Again my dream changed. I saw a blonde woman face-planted in the dirt. She wore a light blue shirt and khaki skirt. While the woman's face remained hidden, I saw that her arms had a green tint. They also didn't resemble regular arms. It was almost as if they were partially made of straw. A hazy background surrounded the girl that looked like thick walls of cornstalks. And the vague cawing of crows resonated throughout the scene.

The vision started to blur even more, but before I transitioned away, I saw a crow land on the woman's head. The crow had a gray collar outfitted with a little mechanism that held a blinking red light. In the crow's beak was a weirdly glistening object like a sponge. Just after the crow landed on the woman's head, a purple energy exuded from her skull. It was absorbed into the crow's sponge, as if attracted to it.

The crow took off at that point—sponge now glowing. I saw movement in the background by the cornstalks, but my subconscious was moving into the next scene.

Now I was in a cave with dream me, Daniel, and a man of about sixty. I recognized him. He was the same old man who had spoken to me in my dreams and compelled me to go to Neverland. His white, wispy beard hung down to his hips. He wore the same silver-and-dark-blue robe and utility belt I'd seen before. And in his hand, he still grasped that long, weird staff.

Unlike the dream where he'd talked to me directly, this was a normal vision. He had no idea that I was there.

The three of us were in a massive cave with a high ceiling and a bluish hue. There was a small pond in the middle filled with silvery water. A fountain protruded from its center, spewing a steady stream. The floor was composed of reddish stone, but bright indigo rocks dotted the whole space. Meanwhile, huge clumps of pale blue phosphorescent moss grew all over and provided light.

Dream me was studying the walls of the cavern. They were covered in drawings, words, and diagrams that had been crafted with some form of indigo charcoal, no doubt sourced from the peculiar rocks. I floated into her body and looked through her eyes. I recognized certain words on the wall, like *Century City*, *Pure Magic*, and *Chance Darling*. I also saw some words and phrases I didn't understand, like *Big Bear*, *Dreamland*, and *Simia Crown*.

My eyes stopped on an image that sent a myriad of emotions rippling through me. It was a sketch of me facing off with Mauvrey. I was grabbing her by throat, pinning her against a wall and strangling her. The expression on my face was nothing short of ruthless.

Flashes replaced the scene. A bronze statue of a swan. A brick bookstore with concrete steps and simple, white pillars framing the entrance. Daniel and Kai in a dark forest, arguing. The shadow of Natalie Poole running up a narrow stairwell, distant applause behind her. And then back to Arian.

He opened a trap door and descended the stairs to a room of black stone. He wore a cruel sneer on his face. The scene blurred as he came nearer. I felt my heart beat louder and louder—its palpations were deafening. Arian was only two feet away. The scene went dark. Everything was silent for a second. Then a scream—my scream—pierced the void and I was jolted awake.

I sat up in bed. The children in the Lost Boys and Girls' bunker were still asleep. The room was not completely dark. Magical, fairy dust-powered nightlights lit the ceiling.

I was in the bottom bed of a spare bunk; Blue was on the top. Twisting slightly, I saw Jason sleeping peacefully in the bottom bunk across from me. Lying on his sheets was a flashlight that he hadn't turned off before falling asleep. Over his body lay the unrolled Oz map he'd been studying.

Based on Mitchell's tip, we would need to go to Oz next. As such—and given that we didn't know where our next wormhole would deposit us in that enchanted realm—Jason had stayed up late trying to commit our Oz map to memory. Not just the names of cities and roads, but also our notes. Neatly written on the back of each elaborate map were important references about the realm, including customs, cultural preferences, and types of magical creatures. I was grateful all that research had borne such great fruit, and that we didn't have to worry about carrying these maps around with us thanks to SJ's magic bag.

As I mentioned earlier, SJ, Jason, and Blue had all been given a reward for saving that Fairy Godmother last semester. SJ's gift was the sack she carried her portable potions in. My friend always kept her portable potions in the same dainty velvet bag, which she hung from her belt beside the slingshot she used to fire them with. Unfortunately, only so many portable potions could fit inside, so she had asked the Fairy Godmother to enchant her sack to remedy the problem.

Though it was no bigger than a sandwich bag, the sack now had a sort of reality-bending wormhole inside it. SJ simply had to think about a specific object in a specific location, stick her hand in the sack, and she would be able to pull out what she desired.

There were a few catches to the enchantment. For starters, SJ had to know the exact location of the object. If she wanted a hairbrush from our room but didn't remember which drawer she'd stuck it in, it was no good. Also, the object had to exist. She couldn't stick her hand inside and draw out a miscellaneous sandwich that hadn't been made. But she *could* concentrate on the granola bars we kept in my nightstand and pull out one of those. Lastly, whatever she pulled out had to be small enough to fit through the mouth of the bag. SJ could also send things back through the bag by the same principles.

The enchantment came in handy for a lot of reasons, like providing us with supplies, emergency food, and, of course, our maps. As part of our initial plan, when our Wonderland maps were complete, SJ and Blue were meant to hide them in a secret compartment behind a false wall we'd built into her closet over winter break. With the exception of the Camelot map Jason had brought to Midveil to show me as a sneak preview, it was my understanding that all our rolled-up maps were stashed there now. At some point before we'd left Midveil, SJ had restored the Camelot map to this hiding place via the charmed sack, and tonight she'd pulled out the Oz map for Jason to peruse by the same means.

This enchantment was particularly helpful because it allowed SJ a much greater stock of portable potions. While my friends had been working on their maps of the Wonderlands over the last month, SJ had also been aggressively brewing different kinds of potions in preparation for our journey. They were hidden in bulk in the same secret compartment as the maps. By concentrating on their location and the exact potion she wanted, SJ could now pull out tons of ammo without needing to worry about rebrewing on the go like she had on our previous mission.

A few minutes had passed since my dream had woken me up, but I was by no means calmed down. I sighed and stared up at the bunk above me. My heart was pounding too fast for me to go back to sleep. I was awake, and in the silence my thoughts threatened to wander to bad places. Fearing that unkind topics would cause me to suffer a panic attack like I had during the bonfire, I decided not to just lay here and simmer.

I reached into my backpack at the foot of the bed and drew out my Mark Two. Then I slipped stealthily from the bed into my boots and maneuvered across the room, avoiding toys and trampolines. Throughout the bunker there were human-sized clear tubes. They looked like they didn't belong with the rest of the décor, but they served an important purpose. While the slide was the only way to enter this sanctum, these tubes were the way out. Before dinner Peter had shown my friends and me how to work them.

Carefully I stepped onto the silver platform of the closest tube and pressed a red button. I took in the tranquil room, the peacefully slumbering Lost Boys and Girls, and Blue and Jason before the platform silently lifted me out of sight.

There hadn't been enough spare beds in this bunker to house all five members of my group. Daniel and SJ ended up sleeping in one of the other bunkers. I was slightly relieved when things had worked out this way. Between the added jealousy my attention from Mitchell and Peter seemed to be causing SJ, and my confrontation with Daniel in the woods, I didn't want to deal with either of them right now. When the five of us were together, concentrating on a common mission or fight, we could operate fine and gloss over the flaws in our dynamics. But in close quarters those flaws were far more obvious. The frost in our situations rivaled the windy torrents from that snowy realm I'd accidentally opened a Wonderland door to earlier.

The tube-like elevator I was in ran up the innards of a large tree that'd been hollowed out. When my platform reached the top of the tube, the area in front of me slid aside. I stepped through and emerged in the campground. Like Peter had shown us, I pulled on a specific branch of the tree and the door slid shut again. I marveled at how it blended in with the bark of the trunk. It was like it was never there.

Checking my Hole Tracker, I discovered it was one in the morning. The bonfire had died long ago and every child and fairy was tucked away in bed.

The canopy of trees blocked the sky, so I decided to find a spot where I might see the stars and not feel so claustrophobic. I knew my friends wouldn't have liked the idea of me wandering off alone, but I was not afraid. Frankly, I dared anyone or anything out there to even *try* crossing me. With the mood I was in, and the day I'd just had, they wouldn't stand a chance.

A few lanterns projected a faint fairy glow over the Hideaway, but beyond that the woods were dark, save for a few fireflies. I drew my wandpin.

*Lapellius.*

My wand grew in my hand and illuminated the area in front of me as I wandered through the woods. I stopped at a mighty tree with strong enough branches to serve as footholds.

I transformed my wand into a bow so I could climb by its light and swung it around my shoulder. Summoning my strength, I ascended higher and higher up the branches. Eventually I broke through the canopy into the open air of night.

The view was beautiful. The storm we'd seen earlier had vanished. Above me was the most wondrous sight I'd ever seen— millions of stars twinkling against the humbling blackness of sky.

I gave myself another boost and settled onto a thick branch so I could take a good look around. The forest's canopy created a sea of dark green in every direction. The ocean sparkled in the distance. The large white moon was rising over the horizon. I breathed in the breathtaking scene, trying to quiet the emotions in my heart and the visions in my head.

With the moon providing sufficient luminescence, I restored my bow to a wandpin and pulled my Mark Two from my jacket pocket. I didn't know what time, or even what day, it was in Book. AP had explained that Book ran about four and a half times faster than the ONC time zone, but I was too tired to attempt the math.

Liza always answered my calls. I hoped this would be no exception. I really needed someone to talk to. Someone who was not directly connected to the horror I'd seen today and who could distract me with another topic.

I flipped open my magic compact. "Liza."

The compact buzzed for about a minute before Liza answered the call. Her hair was frazzled, and she had serious bags under her eyes. I didn't comment on either; I was just happy she'd answered and that the call had gone through despite us being in different realms.

*That's some good reception.*

"Crisa?" Liza yawned. Then her eyes took on a more panicked gleam. "Are you okay?"

"Fine," I said. "I only wanted to talk. Just because I call you after-hours doesn't mean the world is on fire."

Liza exhaled with relief. "Well, what do you expect me to think when you call me so late? The last time you buzzed me at this hour your school was on fire and you'd nearly been kidnapped by magic hunters. After what happened in Midveil . . ."

"You heard about that, huh?"

"Crisa, the whole realm heard about that. Lena filled me in on the specifics though. I'm only glad you weren't hurt."

"Yeah, aren't we all," I muttered.

"You told your ambassador Susannah about the antagonists, what they're planning for the realm and why they want to kill you," Liza stated matter-of-factly.

"I did."

"Now everyone knows about your magic."

"They do."

"How are you feeling about that?" Liza asked. "I mean, the ambassadors and the Godmothers haven't spread the news about the antagonist threat to the greater realm; they're keeping that to themselves for the time being, so your prophecy is also remaining proprietary. But *everyone* knows about your powers now. Since your school already knew, the higher-ups saw no reason to try and cover it up anymore. According to Lena, your magic has become top gossip in every kingdom. You're one of the first non-Fairy Godmother, non-villain characters to wield magic. And not counting your realm's famed Little Mermaid and her half breed children who possess a touch of Mer magic, you're absolutely the first princess to have it. Aren't you concerned about how being outed will affect your life?"

"Not really," I admitted. "Obviously I can't let anyone know I have *Pure* Magic. I'm taking that secret to the grave because if I don't, I'll get sent to Alderon and reach the grave way sooner than I'd prefer. But gossip can't hurt me. My enemies already know about my powers. While I don't like the extra attention, I like hiding even less. And honestly, with everything that's going on, I think it might be a good idea to put on a confident face and show those enemies that I'm not scared to show my power. Now if they want to challenge me, it won't be in the shadows."

"I respect your decision," Liza said. "And I understand why you might want to take a more proactive stance . . ." Her voice dropped away and I arched an eyebrow.

"What?"

"Crisa, other than the general chat, is there another reason you called me? Did you want to talk about what happened today?"

For a moment I considered confiding in her. Liza and I weren't friends exactly. She was my mentor; she was hard on me a lot of the time, but I knew she cared. Well, she cared about me not turning evil. I wasn't sure if she cared about me as a person yet. We hadn't known each other that long. I felt like I trusted her with a lot, but as I opened my mouth to voice some of my troubles, I was reminded of the promise I'd made to myself earlier.

*Remember Daniel. Remember Alex.*

*Do not live with your heart on your sleeve. Protect it. Protect yourself.*

"No. I'm fine," I assured her again. "I just . . ."

My mind shuffled through various topics of conversation that would not trudge up any unpleasant feelings, but might warrant a call at such an inconvenient hour.

"Oh, I wanted to be honest with you about something," I said. "I sort of disobeyed your advice."

Liza's expression turned suspicious and concerned. *"What did you do?"*

"Nothing bad," I said defensively. "You know that wooden plank I enchanted in December? Blue and Jason brought it to Midveil, and it was a hazard. Since I've gotten so much more powerful recently, I decided to try that reverse trick of my magic. I took the life from the wood instead of giving it. I know you said I couldn't do it. But it turns out it wasn't that hard. Removing life from the plank was as simple as giving it life in the first place. So no harm, no foul, right?"

Liza didn't reply immediately. A hard, worried frown had settled on her face.

"Crisa, I told you specifically not to do that," she said.

"Technically, you told me I *couldn't* do that. And I totally could, so what's the big deal?"

"The big deal is that we have been working for months to try and give you control over your powers in the hopes that you won't get corrupted like pretty much everyone else who's ever been in your situation."

"What does that have to do with this?"

Liza sighed. "Do you know what a Malice Line is, Crisa?"

I frowned as I remembered that Lenore had used the term at the start of the semester when she'd come to visit me in Lady Agnue's office.

"Your sister said something about it once," I responded. "After I showed her what my powers could do, she warned me to be careful of it. But she didn't tell me why, much less what it is."

"The power of Pure Magic appeals to the darkness in our hearts," Liza began. "By giving into that, carriers of Pure Magic are consumed. But the stronger a person's heart is, the longer they can avoid this fate. What marks the first sign of turning dark is crossing the Malice Line, which occurs when you use your powers to inflict mortal harm on another living being. For example, if I were to use my powers of teleportation to teleport someone's heart from inside their chest into my hand, killing them, I would cross the Malice Line."

"You could do that?" I gulped.

"Of course. I am much more powerful than you know, Crisa. But I hold back because using my power for dark purposes would be crossing a line. *That* line specifically."

"So me taking life from that wooden plank . . ."

"You crossed the Malice Line, Crisa," Liza confirmed. "Crossing it once isn't going to make you wicked. But crossing it the first time is a trigger. It makes your magic stronger, hungrier, more easily corruptible. And with your specific power . . ." Liza shook her head. "Giving life is a rare, beautiful ability, Crisa. But the reverse of that—taking life—is a dark power. Arguably the *darkest* power. That's why even Fairy Godmothers, and genies before they vanished, cannot brandish it, because no one should wield such godly influence. An ability like that is too strong. The more times you cross the Malice Line by taking life, the closer you will come to succumbing to its pull, and your Pure Magic Disease."

*And I thought I couldn't be in any more trouble than I already was. That'll show me.*

I felt the urge to chuck my Mark Two out into the sea of trees. Having my home destroyed, my family betrayed, and my friendships tested in one day wasn't enough. Apparently, fate deemed that today was also a good day for me to cross a major threshold toward darkness.

The fact that I'd made the choice myself was the real kicker. I'd taken this destructive step on my own. Now there was no going back and my magic was only going to be harder to control. I groaned internally. Maybe it would just be easier to be evil.

"I think I'm going to call it a night, Liza. I'm kind of beat."

Liza looked at me sympathetically, as if remembering for a moment that I wasn't just a student for her to instruct, but a person—a kid—who sometimes needed a hand to hold and not just a kick in the butt. "Okay, Crisa," she said. "But remember, crossing the Malice Line once won't break you. Every time you cross it, it will just destabilize you a little more. But you're not going to do that anymore, right?"

"Right," I muttered, staring at the trees.

"Keep me updated?"

"I will. Good night, Liza."

"Crisa . . ."

I met her gaze.

"I'm sorry about your brother."

I nodded at her, accepting her condolences, but didn't say anything else.

I snapped the compact shut and sat there with my back pressed against the tree trunk for a few minutes with my eyes closed. As I was drifting off, my Mark Two began to buzz. Liza must've forgotten to tell me something, or she realized she'd let me off too easy and wanted to get in another round of nagging. I dug the compact out of my pocket and flipped it open.

"Yes, Liza?"

"Liza? Make a new friend, Crisa?"

I was startled to see Mauvrey's smug face in the mirror.

"Mauvrey! What the heck? How did you get a Mark Two?"

"Crisa, after everything you have seen me orchestrate, do you really think I would have trouble acquiring a simple piece of magic tech a few weeks before it hits the market?

"What do you want?" I spat.

"I wanted to check up on you, see how you were doing."

"I'm peachy," I replied.

"And how are your parents; did they make it out all right? I do hope they were not too shaken up."

"They're a whole lot better than yours, I'm sure," I countered. "Alex may have betrayed my parents today, but at least he didn't try to have them taken out by sniper."

"Crisa, I needed my parents out of the way so that I could inherit my crown and exert influence over Tunderly in time to aid Nadia and Arian with their plan for the realm. It hurt to give the order, but that was my cost for power. It was a calculated, acceptable loss."

"You're a monster, you know that?"

"It is just politics, Crisa."

"It's patricide, Mauvrey. And it's another reason why I'm more than happy to hunt you down and make you pay for it."

"As fun as that sounds," Mauvrey continued, "you and I both have more important tasks to see to at the moment."

"I don't know what you mean."

"Oh please, Crisa. There is no need to beat around the bush. I know you are going after Paige Tomkins as surely as you know Arian and his antagonists are doing the same."

"Aren't you chasing her as well?" I asked.

"I have another important mission on my hands, one that I cannot complete without your brother's help. He is very special, you know. A Knight of royal blood destined for something great. With any luck, soon he and I will be on the verge of claiming a fantastic destiny."

"With any luck, you won't run into me along the way. I don't know why Arian and your antagonist friends want Paige, Mauvrey, but my friends and I are going to find her first and do whatever it takes to protect her. If you get in our way, I *will* take you down."

Mauvrey smiled that smug, venomous smile of hers. I had to resist the urge to crush the compact from the hatred that pulsed through me.

"I am sure we are going to have some fun conflicts in the future then," she said. "Sleep well, Crisa. Try not to get killed on your quest. I was really hoping to murder you myself when this is all over." She glanced over her shoulder for a second, then back at me. "Oh, hold on. Looks like your big brother wants to say hi."

"Mauvrey, I don't want to—"

It was too late. Her image had vanished and Alex's face appeared in my Mark Two.

"Hey," he said.

The single syllable was enough to send a jolt of pain through my body. I steadied my tone, trying to keep him from seeing how much his presence affected me.

"What?" I replied.

Alex paused for a second.

"I'm glad you got out of the castle," he responded. "I was worried you'd be trapped in there."

"Aw, how sweet," I hissed. "Aren't you just the most thoughtful."

Alex huffed as he took in my glower. "Resentment doesn't suit you."

"Yeah, well, empathy doesn't really suit you either. So why don't you just shove that feigned concern down your throat and tell me why you really wanted to talk to me? I know it wasn't to check on my well-being."

"I want to warn you about something," Alex said.

"It's a little too late for that, bro."

"Crisa, would you listen to me for a second?"

"Why should I? I don't even know who you are. You're involved with Mauvrey and you're helping the antagonists launch a commons rebellion. For goodness' sake, you've got a Shadow living inside of you like a parasite! Is there any part of the old you that's even there anymore?"

"Of course there is. Crisa, I'm still here. Hard as it may be for you to believe with the recent choices I've made, it's true. The person who helped you learn to fight, who looked out for you as a kid, who cares for you and will always try to protect you even when you don't want me to—that person's not gone. I promise you that's still me."

"Your promises don't mean anything to me. Not after everything you've done."

"Yes they do," Alex said, holding my gaze. "I can see it in your eyes and hear it in your voice. You want to believe me. I can tell."

I didn't say anything. I didn't know if I had the strength to deny it.

"Crisa," Alex continued. "Arian has sent teams to different Wonderlands to find Paige Tomkins—splitting them up to cover more ground. They started searching a few weeks ago, but haven't found anything. So far they've eliminated Toyland, Cloud Nine, Xanadu, and Book in its entirety. Mauvrey and I aren't helping them with the search. We're with Arian and some of his men tonight, but tomorrow morning we go our separate ways again. Mauvrey and I have business in Camelot and that's where we're headed. Arian's plan is to do a sweep of Oz next, then Neverland. So if you're in either of those two realms right now, watch your back."

*Hm.* If Arian was still divide-and-conquering his forces, that meant the antagonist Mitchell mentioned hadn't warned anyone else about Paige's whereabouts before Hook fed him to the crocodile. That was important. Then another thought occurred to me and I bit my lip.

"Why are you telling me this? Aren't you on their side? Why give me the heads up?"

"Because despite the fact that I've chosen my side, that doesn't mean I want to see anything happen to you. Arian's main goal right now is to find Paige Tomkins, but he wants you too. All his men are under orders to bring you in alive if they find you on their hunt."

"Well, that's a step up from kill on sight," I huffed in cynical amusement. "Are you telling me your boss doesn't want me dead anymore?"

"No, he definitely does. But not right away. Mauvrey was instructed to capture you because he needs you as a . . ." Alex cut himself off. "Look, whether you prove useful or not, if they catch you, they will kill you eventually and I won't be able to stand in their way. But I *can* protect you by doing my best to make sure your paths don't cross in the first place."

"How do I know this isn't a trick?" I asked suspiciously. "Arian and Mauvrey know I'm after Paige and you're with them. How can I trust anything you say?"

"I can't answer that," Alex said. "You just have to."

Alex looked over his shoulder. "I've gotta go. Mauvrey's coming back. But, Crisa, before I go, remember that no matter what I've done, I would never hurt you."

Alex's image vanished as he hung up the call.

I didn't know what to believe. I let go of my rage, punching a branch with my balled-up fist. The pain jolted back the tears that had welled up in my eyes.

I'd grown up fine-tuning my ability to see through Alex's poker face, to read his tells, to know when he was being truly vulnerable and when he was simply pretending to be.

The fact that he'd become this monster under my watch made me wonder if I could trust my instincts about him at all. Maybe I was too close to the situation. Maybe I wanted so badly to believe him, to believe *in* him, that I could no longer count on my own judgment where he was concerned.

Shoving my compact back inside my pocket, I decided to climb back down. I'd been gone long enough and it was time to return to camp.

As I descended by the light of my bow once more, I wondered why the antagonists wanted to capture me and not simply kill me like before. It definitely explained the incident in the mausoleum with Mauvrey. I'd thought it was strange how she'd chosen to incapacitate me with that Poppy Potion instead of taking me out then and there. Now I understood why. She'd put me in that coffin because she was saving me. For Arian.

The understanding made me gulp.

Somehow I liked it better when Arian was trying to kill me. At least then I knew what he wanted. Now it was anybody's guess.

# CHAPTER 42

## The Portalscape

y a remarkable stroke of luck, the next wormhole out of Neverland was going to appear a short walk from the Hideaway.

My friends and I got up with plenty of time and had breakfast with the Lost Boys and Girls. AP talked with Daniel about some sword fighting moves that he favored. Jason continued to pour over the Oz map with Blue at his side. SJ gave some of the campers a demonstration of what her portable potions could do. As the kids cheered the eruption of an ice potion she'd just fired, I spotted her smiling at their reaction. It was good to see. The kids were impressed because she was impressive.

SJ based so much of her self-esteem on her former "perfect princess" persona, which she believed a lack of a protagonist book robbed her of. But she was missing the big picture. Although being exceptional at the traditional aspects of our archetype had earned her top marks and respect at school for many years, her ability to sing, curtsy, and communicate with animals had never been what I'd admired her for. My friend was brilliant. She was smart and creative in a way that was beyond reproach. I knew for certain that the antagonists would have beaten us long ago if it weren't for her. I would have died long ago if it weren't for her.

I only hoped that one day she would move past her disappointment about not being chosen as a protagonist and accept how wonderful she was. I also hoped she would come to realize that blaming me for what she'd lost wasn't the answer.

I didn't want to keep being the object of her bitterness. I hated it. I felt bad that she was going through a rough situation, but every time I replayed that first fight in our room or saw a resentful look in her eyes whenever I got any attention, it made me mad. Like I didn't have enough problems. I didn't need her trying to fill me with guilt or saddle me with blame for her problems too. Plus . . . I needed her. Not just because she made our team stronger but also because she was my friend. And I missed her as much as I resented her for pushing me away.

"You ready to go?" Blue asked, trotting up next to me. "It's almost wormhole time."

"Yeah. We just need to get SJ."

"No problem." Blue pivoted. "SJ!" she hollered.

Startled, SJ misfired and launched a jade potion toward an unsuspecting Mitchell as he was heading through the forest. It exploded against a tree behind him and the slime it emitted caught his back leg. He tripped and stumbled forward. The children laughed. Blue and I rushed over; SJ reached him first. She stowed her slingshot and bent down to take a look at his trapped leg.

Mitchell struggled against the slime. "Nice shot, mini Snow White," he said. "Can you get me out of this?"

SJ put her hands on her hips and stood up. "Sorry, Mitchell. Why not ask a more *innovative* protagonist to help you?" she said with a feigned smile. "Oh look, here comes one now. Crisa, care to give him a hand?"

SJ trotted off without another glance back.

"What's with your friend?" Mitchell asked.

"She's going through something," I explained, trying to yank his leg out of the slime.

"And she has to take it out on me?"

"What did you expect?" Blue said as she drew her hunting knife and started cutting away the gunk. "You seriously insulted her last night on Hook's ship. You basically called her boring."

I used my wand in the form of a knife to help Blue slice away at Mitchell's ensnarement. When the writer was free, he leapt up and tried to wipe the slime off his blazer.

"Good luck on your quest," he told us, ignoring Blue's comment. "I'll probably be heading home soon myself, but I have a few follow up questions for these guys' Honorary Mother." He stuck out his hand. "It was nice meeting you both. Maybe someday I'll write a story that'll put your names on the big screen."

"Big screen of what?" Blue asked, shaking his hand.

Mitchell smiled. "Never mind. Just good luck." He shook my hand too and continued on his journey into the woods.

"I don't like that guy," Blue said decidedly.

I shrugged. "I'm undecided. Writers can be tricky."

My friends and I bid our farewells to the Lost Boys and Girls and the fairies before meeting up with Peter, AP, and Tinkerbell, who led us through the forest to the spot where my Hole Tracker indicated the next wormhole would appear. Jason mentioned that we were lucky the coordinates fell where they did; according to our map, a bit further south and we might come upon any number of dangers. Wild animals, booby-trapped ancient tribal ruins, and certain-death sinkholes could be found on the island. The Neverwood wasn't all fairies and feasts.

When we arrived at the right spot, it was several minutes past ten o'clock. My Hole Tracker beamed excitedly. I pulled up the holographic map to double check our position. The silvery wormhole glistened upon it.

Out of curiosity, I scrolled through the time settings and learned that two other holes would be opening in the next few hours on different parts of the island. Unlike the silver wormhole that was going to open up any second in front of us, my Hole Tracker displayed one of these future holes as orange and the other as red.

It made me wonder again about the difference. Did the color somehow correspond to where the wormhole's portal would take you? I supposed this would be as good a test as any. If our oncoming silver wormhole took us back to that weird crossroads of doors leading to other realms, then it would certainly appear that way.

"Knock 'em dead," Peter said. Tinkerbell seconded the sentiment with bright wing flashes. "Come back and visit us sometime. It's been fun fighting alongside you."

"Be careful in Oz," AP warned. "That place is more dangerous than Neverland. The landscape is diverse with obstacles and monstrous creatures at every turn. I know you weren't able to meet the Hideaway's Honorary Mother, but she's spent a great deal of time in Oz and has told us of her many harrowing adventures there."

"Any specific advice?" Blue asked.

"Be wary of the witch in the North Mountains. She is trapped there, but has vicious winged minions doing her bidding across the land."

My friends and I exchanged a look.

*Which witch was he talking about? I thought the Wicked Witch of Oz had been defeated long ago. And she was from the* west.

"Oh, and mind the Poppies," AP added. "They grow in abundance there."

Like a knife being shoved through the dimension, a jagged silver slit suddenly appeared in the air twenty feet above us. The tear widened to form a sparkling circular wormhole five feet in diameter.

"Time to go," Peter said. "I'll give you guys a lift."

One by one, Peter flew us up to the hole. I watched each of my friends vanish into its depths. Peter came for me last. He took me by the hand and we zipped into the air, pausing for a moment to float over the wormhole.

"Crisanta Knight," AP called.

I twisted around to see him better.

"Watch out for your blind spots."

I nodded solemnly then glanced at Peter. "See you next time, kid."

"See you next time, bigger kid." He winked.

Peter Pan let go of my hand and I fell into the abyss once more.

Like the portal we'd entered via the looking glass in Century City, this one dropped into a dark, dingy plummet. As I tumbled, I touched roots and dirt until the abyss abruptly opened up and spit me out in the same way as before.

I landed on the springy, thick mattress. After I sat up and blew the hair out of my face, I looked around the massive room with the fourteen doors. My friends and I weren't alone. There was a White Rabbit in the room. The others were talking to him. My focus narrowed in on the rabbit's black vest and alert ears. His back was turned to me, but I recognized him instantly.

"Harry!"

Upon hearing his name, Harry the White Rabbit pivoted around. His ears perked up and he immediately hopped over.

"Crisa!"

The amicable Harry grinned broadly. I hadn't seen him since that night we met in the Forbidden Forest all those months ago. His jeans were dark blue and he wore a mock tuxedo t-shirt under his vest. He also wore a Hole Tracker like the one he'd given me, though his looked shiny and new.

"Making good use of the gift I gave you, I see," he said, nodding to my watch. "Your friend Jacob over here was just explaining that you're trying to get to Oz."

"That's right. But his name is Jason," I corrected, hopping off the bed and going over to properly introduce my friends. "And this is Blue, Daniel, and SJ." I gestured to each of them. "Guys, this is Harry. I told you about him last semester."

"Hey," Harry said. Then he turned his attention back to me. "You're lucky you didn't run into any other White Rabbits while you were passing through this intersection. If any of my co-workers had caught you here crossing worlds without a storyteller visa, they would have gone ballistic."

"Where is *here*, exactly?" Daniel asked. "When we went through wormholes last semester, we went straight into another realm. The ones we've taken over the last couple of days keep leading us here."

"Oh, sorry," Harry said. "I probably should've warned you before I gave you the Hole Tracker, Crisa. There are two types of holes. One kind creates a temporary tear in a realm's outer In and Out Spell, thus opening a portal that leads directly from one land to the next. Those only stay open for a few minutes and are usually in super random, hard-to-reach places."

"Like the black hole we took in the middle of the ocean to Earth last semester," Blue commented. "We never would have found that wormhole without the help of a mermaid and the magic taffy we used to breathe underwater."

Harry didn't know what she was talking about, but he agreed with the gist of her point. "Yeah. So anyway, since the short opening time and unsavory locations of these Pop-Up Portals deter people from using them, we White Rabbits don't usually monitor them. The holes we try to keep track of are the ones that lead directly to the Portalscape. That's this place." He gestured around the room. "A Wonderland in its own right.

"Basically, when a Portalscape Portal appears, it stays open for ten to fifteen minutes. People who go through end up here with access to doors that lead to all the Wonderlands. That's why White Rabbits try to guard Portalscape Portals, because having unfettered access to all fourteen core magic realms is dangerous and could have consequences on any number of worlds."

"How bad could it be?" Jason said.

"Have you ever seen the movie *The Nightmare Before Christmas*?"

"Is Bruce Willis in it?" Blue asked.

"The actor?" Harry replied. "Definitely not."

"Then no."

"Well, rent it at a video store if you're ever on Earth looking to kill some time. Dude who came up with the story, Tim Burton, traveled through here a while back on a storyteller visa, and let's just say the protagonist in his movie demonstrates the bad juju that can go down if characters wander out of their worlds and into someone else's without being checked."

"But this is the second time we've accessed a Portalscape Portal and we didn't run into a White Rabbit either time," Daniel interceded. "Are you guys sleeping on the job?"

Harry's hair bristled. "No," he said indignantly. "First off, that wormhole you just came through was mine; I was running late to it is all. And second, these last few days have been hard on my kind. Not all White Rabbits have the ability to guard holes. There are only up to a dozen of us on duty at a time. And with the approach of the Vicennalia Aurora, more holes than usual have been opening up. The magic instability of the Vicennalia Aurora makes the walls between worlds a lot weaker, so more wormholes form. Unfortunately, we're not able to cover them all. Though like I said, that's a lucky break for you because trying to get past a White Rabbit without the proper visa is dangerous. You *do not* want to mess with us. On that note . . ."

Harry opened his vest and pulled out a zip-up wallet from an inner pocket. I spotted two things inside the wallet—a beautiful golden stamp and a little black stick that looked like a miniature wand. "It was my bad for not thinking to do this when I gave you the Hole Tracker in the first place, Crisa," he said as he drew the stamp. "I was uh . . . distracted, I guess. I'm just glad that one of my co-workers didn't catch you portal-hopping and tear you to shreds." He motioned for me to extend my hand.

When I did, he placed the face of the stamp against the back of it. "All access," he said. "No expiration."

The stamp glowed and then flashed a myriad of different colors. When I pulled my hand away, I saw a sparkling crest marked on my skin. It faded a moment later.

"Now if you ever run into a White Rabbit while portal-hopping, you can show him your hand and he'll use his scanner wand to see that you have an all-access storyteller visa stamp." Harry waved for the rest of my friends to come forward. "Let me get the rest of you guys squared away too."

My friends formed a line and Harry repeated the stamping process as he went on talking. "This is actually kind of exciting for me. I've never given an all-access storyteller visa to anyone before. It's very rare that we do. The whole point of this system is that White Rabbits only allow reputable storytellers from other lands through. They bring technology and innovations from other worlds and we provide them with literary material, which they use to turn a profit back home. The last guy we gave all-access to was this awesome dude named Walt Disney. He was about as reputable as they come, so we let him have at it."

"On a related topic," SJ said as she received her stamp. "Harry, why do portals show up in different colors on the Hole Tracker?"

"Simple," Harry said. "The colors indicate what type of portal you're dealing with and where it will take you. Portalscape Portals are silver and will always bring you right here to the Portalscape. Pop-Up Portals, which we don't typically guard because, like I said, they tend to turn up in really obscure and dangerous places, are either red or orange—red for counterclockwise jumps and orange for clockwise jumps."

"What do you mean clockwise and counterclockwise?" Jason asked Harry.

The White Rabbit had finished stamping my friends' hands and began to put his supplies back in his vest pocket. "The Pop-Up Portals aren't random," he explained. "When you're using them within the boundaries of the Wonderlands, they take you in a circular pattern that matches the layout of the Portalscape. Take this door, for example," Harry said as he hopped over to a bright yellow door. "It takes you to Oz. The next Wonderland in the sequence is Limbo." Harry pointed at a glittery, red wooden door to his right. Then he stood in front of the following door in the sequence—a rounded, silver one. "After Limbo is the Portalscape."

Harry continued to hop around the room like a tour guide, pointing to the different doors. "Following that we have Xanadu, then the Super Dome, Atlantis, the North Pole, *your* Book, *my* Wonderland, Toyland, The Giants' Keep, Neverland, Camelot, Cloud Nine, and then it's back to Oz again. See? Full circle."

"So all Wonderland holes move in this cycle?" SJ clarified. "The wormholes that form Pop-Up Portals in Book will always lead to Wonderland, holes in Oz will always lead to Limbo, and so on?"

"No, see that's what I was trying to explain with the orange and red portals," Harry said. "The holes can move clockwise and counterclockwise. So a hole in Camelot, for instance, could take you forward to Cloud Nine or backward to Neverland."

"Orange for clockwise jumps in the cycle, red for counterclockwise ones," I said, finally getting it. "Noted. Anything else we should know before we get going?"

"Well, there are a bunch of really specific functions on your Hole Tracker, but since you're probably not planning on becoming a hole guardian like us White Rabbits, there's no need to overwhelm you. I should just warn you that Portalscape Portals will always appear silver on the Tracker, but sometimes they blend in with the environment around them, like mirrors, tree stumps, deep puddles, and the occasional wardrobe. Also, a word to the wise on those black holes your friend mentioned—"

Suddenly we heard a terrible roar from up above. It came from the chasm we'd dropped out of.

"What was that?" Blue asked.

"Someone without a storyteller visa is trying to get past a White Rabbit guarding a Portalscape Portal." Harry shrugged. "I told you not to mess with us."

The roars continued and I also heard the distant sounds of yelling and fighting. They set my friends and I on edge, but Harry seemed undisturbed by it.

"Like I was saying," he continued. "The black holes lead to non-Wonderland realms. Since those realms don't exist in a sequence like these do," he gestured around the massive room, "they're a more erratic form of travel."

Harry took my wrist and twisted two knobs on my Hole Tracker. A series of holographic user settings popped up and he made a few rapid selections that were too fast for me to keep track of. When he was done, he twisted the two knobs again.

"There," he said. "Now when a black hole shows up on your Tracker, you can find out what non-Wonderland realm it leads to by clicking on it."

The whole room shook with another roar. This one was louder and angrier. Dirt and sediment began to fall from the ceiling.

"Will do, Harry," I said. "Thanks for the help."

"For you, any time," Harry said.

He nervously thumped the ground with his foot and looked away. It might have just been my eyes playing tricks on me, but for a second I thought I saw the area beneath his whiskers grow slightly pink.

*Was he blushing?*

Harry cleared his throat. "Best of luck. And don't lose that Hole Tracker. When you're not using it for tracking down missing persons, use it to come visit me in Wonderland, okay? You still owe me that rain check."

"Definitely," I said.

*ROAR!!!!!*

This time, Harry looked up. We all did. When no other sound followed, we assumed that the fight was over. Then the bed in the middle of the Portalscape flashed with a bright white light.

"Oh no . . ." Harry said.

The bed flashed fourteen more times in quick succession.

"Harry, what's wrong?" I asked.

"Someone must've killed a White Rabbit," he said in shock, his eyes full of panic. "That's never happened before! By the count of those flashes, fifteen unauthorized users are on their way down here."

Now it was my turn to say "Oh, no."

I spun to face my friends. "Alex made contact with me through my Mark Two last night," I said quickly. "He told me that he and Mauvrey are headed to Camelot and Arian is going to Oz. I think this could be them."

"Crisa! Why didn't you tell us that before?" Blue angrily punched me in the arm. "We've been chatting in here like we had all the time in the world!"

"I'm sorry!" I said. "But we gotta go now." I bolted for the yellow door that led to Oz, my friends behind me. "Harry," I said, glancing back. "Watch out for the people headed down here. They're—"

That's when I saw her. Falling through the chasm in the roof was Mauvrey—her blonde hair rippling around her. Our eyes met.

I yanked open the door to Oz. In front of me was a lot of rubble and what looked like the ruins of an old building.

"Go!" I ushered my friends through, holding the door open for them.

Mauvrey landed on the mattress with a rough thud. Another two bodies were ejected from the chasm in the roof after her—Alex and Arian. Mauvrey opened her mouth to say something, but rolled off the far side of the mattress so she wouldn't get squashed. I started to step through the door.

"Crisa!" Harry called after me. "To find your way in Oz, make sure to follow the Y—"

"The Yellow Brick Road, I got it!" I said.

"No, Crisa. The *YUR!*"

His confusing statement caused me to hesitate. But I immediately came to my senses when Arian landed. Unlike everyone else I'd seen arrive, he was not fazed by the abrupt plummet. When his feet touched the mattress, he bounced off it like a trampoline and landed in a crouched position on the floor of the Portalscape.

He rose and locked eyes with me. He drew his sword.

*Aw, crud.*

# CHAPTER 43

# Ruins

hen I stepped through the yellow door to Oz, I found myself in a city of ruins. Massive chunks of debris, slabs of concrete, and piles of iron were everywhere. This place had once been a fine metropolis, but now it was a deserted wasteland. It didn't look like the Oz from storybooks.

I waved for my friends to take cover. "They're coming!" I shouted.

The warning came too late. Arian, Alex, and Mauvrey emerged from the Portalscape Portal with twelve men behind him. My friends and I ran around the side of a collapsed apartment building. We jumped through one of the broken windows and bobbed and weaved through its decaying innards. It was dark and extremely creepy, but the antagonists continued their chase. After climbing through several sections of the building, we ducked behind a dusty, glass-covered countertop, which appeared to be the remnants of a kitchen island.

"Kill them all except Crisanta Knight!" I heard Arian call.

The five of us listened avidly to the sound of our enemies' footsteps. Daniel shot me a look. "Since when do they not want to kill you?" he whispered.

"Mauvrey said they needed me for something," I whispered back. "That's why she didn't kill me in Midveil."

The footsteps started to recede. My friends and I took that as our cue to carefully keep going. We eased our way through a window in the adjacent room and stepped out into the open. We had about six seconds to take in our surroundings.

"Blue!" Daniel tackled Blue to the ground. An arrow narrowly missed them both and plunged into the wall behind us. I flicked my eyes in the direction from which it'd come. I could see two archers taking aim in a building across the way. I also spotted red and gold shapes sitting on windowsills on the building ledges.

*Were those birds?*

Two more arrows were fired. Jason ducked one; SJ sidestepped the other. We took off—desperately avoiding additional shots.

"They must have split up," Jason said as we slid for cover beneath a fallen slab of concrete the size of a dragon's torso. "Probably figured it would be easier to cross us off their list from different vantage points."

I searched around for ideas but was not inspired. All I saw was a plump red bird the size of a goose sitting atop a tilted street lamp. It was fully scarlet except for a golden neck pouch that protruded from its chest like an inflated balloon.

"We're sitting ducks and as a group we're an easy target," I said drawing my wandpin and morphing it into a shield. "There's five of us and fifteen of them. We need to split up to split their focus."

"Okay, but what's our endgame?" Jason asked, pulling his axe from its sheath.

"That is," Daniel said, pointing to a building a half-mile away. Cliffs ringed that side of the ruined city and a tall building leaned against them. The building looked like it had been affected by an explosion at some point, but not enough to cause it to topple. It rested against the cliff at a seventy-degree angle.

"It's the only building that reaches the top of the cliffs," Daniel said. "We split up, scale it, and once we've made it, SJ blows it down with an explosion portable potion and the antagonists have no way of following us."

A weird and unexpected sound like a mini sonic boom suddenly pierced the air. It caused everything in the vicinity to quiver.

"What was that?" Blue asked.

"Not sure," SJ said. "But there is no way we can reach the top of that building with enough lead time. It is too tall. They will shoot us down long before then."

"No they won't," I said. "Because I'm going to distract the biggest threats. Arian wants me for something, and it's obviously important enough for Mauvrey and Alex to divert their plans. They were supposed to go to Camelot, but they came after me instead. I can distract them and buy you guys time."

"Crisa, you can't do that on your own," Jason protested.

"I can and I will. Because I have a score to settle *and* I'm fully recharged." I held up my hand and golden energy sparked around it.

"Behind the concrete!" another voice yelled, distinctly closer.

"We need to move now," I said.

My friends drew their weapons and braced themselves for the conflict ahead.

"See you at the top," Blue said to me. She turned her attention to the task at hand and her eyes blazed with fire. "Break."

We ran free of our cover. Daniel and Blue headed left while SJ bolted straight ahead and Jason went around back. Arrows whizzed through the air in their wake, but my friends moved swiftly. They would need to approach the building from different angles to keep from being shot and not give away our play.

I straightened up and began to walk into the open. I did not run. I did not hide. I strutted out in plain sight. I held my shield tightly in my hand, but I had faith I would not need to use it. They wanted me alive.

"Arian!" I shouted.

My voice echoed off the ruins. I could spot four different archers—two in the building we'd seen before, another in a structure further west, and a third on the fire escape of an apartment complex across from me.

Then I saw Arian. He emerged from beneath the remains of a crumbling, concrete bridge between two buildings. I stepped forward to meet him. He did the same. A moment later, Alex showed himself. He'd heard my call and had climbed out the window of a disheveled storefront. Finally, I saw Mauvrey. She was on the second floor of a wrecked structure. She started moving toward me as well.

It was working. The three leaders of this attack were focused on me, and the same could be said for the four archers in the vicinity. That meant there were only eight antagonists out there with the potential to waylay my friends.

Another mini sonic boom echoed through the city. The dirt trembled beneath my boots as the surrounding area vibrated from the disturbance.

Arian, Alex, and Mauvrey were only forty feet from me now, approaching from different directions. A flock of red birds with golden neck pouches flew across the sky, casting temporary shadows over our confrontation.

Arian and my brother had their swords drawn. Mauvrey had no weapon, but I noticed something different about her. My royal archenemy wore the same outfit as yesterday—shimmery purple jacket, black skinny jeans, high-heeled boots. But now she also donned a pair of bronze-colored fingerless gloves. They caught the light, making me think they were partly made of metal. She wore a belt containing a knife sheath and a small, handheld crossbow like I'd seen Goldilocks use a while back.

I addressed each of them in turn. "Arian. Alex. Princess of Darkness."

"Long time no see, Knight," Arian said.

"Did you miss me?"

Alex took another step closer.

"Uh-uh." I raised my hand and waggled a finger. "Not another move, bro."

My hand erupted in golden light.

Alex and I locked eyes as I tried to keep my expression even. While I could put on a good poker face, inside I was bursting with anger and sadness at the sight of him. I knew these strong emotions had the potential to make me use my magic to lash out. And despite my current show of power and confidence, I definitely didn't want that. My glowing hand was a bluff. I hadn't mentioned this to my friends before we split up, but I wanted to avoid using my magic against Alex and Mauvrey.

Liza consistently warned about the dangers of letting emotion fuel Pure Magic. That's why I was always supposed to have a clear mind and be fully concentrating when I used it. If I didn't, I risked losing control.

Having recently crossed the Malice Line, I didn't want to tempt my power again if I could help it. Which meant I needed to avoid using my powers here. The emotion swelling inside me now was ten times more vindictive than it had been in Alderon, the last time I'd lost control. I could feel the magic itching to assert its dominance and cloud my focus. I had to be strong and hold back. Harnessing my Pure Magic in this state could be as damaging to me as it would be to my enemies.

"What do you want with me?" I asked. I pivoted toward Mauvrey. "You could have killed me yesterday and you didn't. What could you possibly need me for that would have stopped you?"

"We needed a spare," Mauvrey replied with a shrug.

"A spare what?"

Arian began to walk toward me again. Alex followed his lead.

"Hey, I said stay put." My hand flared with more energy—some of it was my doing, but I knew it was more of an instinctive emotional reaction. The feelings I had about seeing my brother again after all he'd done were deep and intense.

"You forget that Alderon is full of witches and warlocks, Knight," Arian said, unfazed by my threat. "They all have Pure Magic Disease. Which means I know that you're going to try and avoid using magic when your emotions are too strong. Don't want to make your heart disintegrate into darkness any faster, do you?"

I wasn't sure how Arian knew my magic was pure. I didn't think I'd ever mentioned that. But I realized maybe he didn't know for certain and only suspected like Lenore did. He was testing for my reaction, and he was near enough now that he saw the change in my expression.

"Yeah, that's what I thought," he said with a smirk. "Alex, take her down. Mauvrey, give her a shock then tie her up once she's knocked out. You can keep her in Camelot until we're sure we don't need her."

Arian started to walk away.

"Not gonna fight me yourself, Arian?" I called as Alex and Mauvrey closed in.

"Not today, Knight," he responded. "I have a Fairy Godmother to find. But I think I'll kill one or two of your friends first. Not because I have to, but because I deeply want to."

The anger I'd been holding in snapped. Golden energy shot out of my palm into a pile of rubble across from Arian. The mass of concrete, dirt, and cement shook. The pieces floated off the ground and joined together to form a lumpy, eight-foot-tall creature made of debris.

I didn't specifically ask for this creature to rise, nor did I give it the direct order to attack, but it seemed I didn't need to. Like with the incident of the knife I'd almost killed Sooz with, my magic could read the will of my emotion as easily as it could my express commands. If the latter failed to react quick enough or exert enough control, the former took over. The heart outweighed the head.

The rubble monster leapt in Arian's direction. Arian jumped out of the way to evade the creature's pummeling fists. The earth shook from its violent impact.

Alex was within striking distance then. He came at me with his sword. I ducked and swooped around his other side, throwing a kick. Alex deflected the kick with his hand, forcing my foot to the left with a powerful thrust. I did not let the move throw me off balance. I spun with it, threw my other boot up, and launched into a spinning back-kick that went straight into his ribs and knocked him to the dirt.

I trotted speedily backward. "Catch me if you can, traitors!" I taunted. Then I pivoted and bolted away.

Arian was occupied with my rubble monster, but Alex and Mauvrey came after me with full force. Transforming my shield into a wand, I made a beeline across the street—maneuvering through the city's ruins with my pursuers hot on my tail. I sprinted around collapsed structures, through compressed buildings, and in and out of crumbling alleyways.

Eventually I ducked into an alleyway piled with debris. Mini mountains of brick and metal were in my way. A red and gold bird was perched on a windowsill two stories up. As I skidded down the slope of a dismembered piece of wall, the bird ruffled its feathers and unleashed a new level of chaos.

Now I knew where the mini sonic booms were coming from.

The bird stood, elongated its neck, and jerked it in-and-out again in a quick motion. This movement caused the bird's golden neck sack to deflate and release a sonic boom into the air. The boom crashed into the upper half of the building to my left, smashing the wall to smithereens. The sound also produced an earthquake that made me lose my footing. Sections of wall rained down and I thrust my body away and covered my head, protecting myself.

I couldn't see Alex and Mauvrey now. They'd probably had to leap back to avoid the boom's destruction.

I picked up my wand, which had fallen from my grip, and picked up my pace. When I emerged from the alley, I discovered I'd closed about half the distance to the desired cliffside building. A burst of fire drew my attention to a tower a hundred feet away. Several explosions had gone off.

*SJ.*

She must've been firing portable potions at the antagonist archers, but the structure they were in was clearly not structurally sound enough to take the hits. The building began to lean in my direction and was poised to collapse.

I pushed my legs to their maximum speed to outrun it. The building's shadow consumed me—growing bigger and bigger as it drew closer to impact until—

*KER-SMASH!*

I was able to clear the crash zone in time, but the collision caused a shockwave that rippled through the rubble. I was launched forward, colliding with a wall of concrete.

*Ow* . . .

I partially blacked out. I could still hear the sounds of the scene, but my vision was spotty and it felt like everything was moving at the speed of syrup. By the time I regained full consciousness, I saw that the shockwave had not only taken me down, it'd made several smaller structures fall and disturbed a flock of red birds that'd been flying overhead. All seven of them released sonic booms as they darted through taller ruins. Everything shook viciously.

I looked up to see Mauvrey only fifteen feet away. Adrenaline coursed through my body in the nick of time. My nemesis shot out her hand and her metallic glove released a pair of thin, shimmering wires that would have wrapped around my arm had I not moved in that instant. Instead, they bounced off the wall behind me. She closed her fingers around her palm with two rapid pulses and the wires immediately reeled in.

*What the what?*

"You like?" she said. "They are called trapper gloves. Arian has been training me with them for a long time. They have a lot of applications, for example . . ." Mauvrey shot out her hand as a red bird swooped ten feet overhead. The wires from her trapper gloves sprung out and latched onto the bird. Mauvrey crossed her pointer and middle fingers. The moment she did, a charge of electricity bolted up the wires. The bird smoked like an overcooked hamburger. Then Mauvrey jerked her arm down and slammed the creature into the ground. She released the charred, unconscious bird and whipped the wires back to her glove like a fishing line.

*So that's what Arian meant by "shock her."*

Suddenly Mauvrey was a much greater threat than I'd ever considered.

*Shield.*

My wand transformed and I blocked the wires that ejected from Mauvrey's other glove. She moved in closer and mocked me as we fought. "So how is the remodeling going?" she asked. "I hear my castle in Tunderly will reopen soon, but yours may take weeks. I suppose that is the downside of utilizing so much glass in castle construction."

*Spear.*

I gritted my teeth and lashed out. She ducked beneath my weapon and weaved to the side. I tried to stab her again, but she evaded me with ease. It only made me angrier. I usually moved faster than my opponents; it was one of my advantages.

But Mauvrey was quicker than me. She was light on her feet and moved with a fluidity that I did not know how to counter.

We parried closer to the collapsed building lying in the street. I literally had my back to the crumbling wall, and there was a large, partly shattered window directly behind me. I felt like a sitting duck. These trapper gloves were difficult to evade.

"You know, Crisa," Mauvrey sneered. "I really must tell you how glad I am things worked out with your brother. I was worried at first when Arian asked me to manipulate him over to our side. I thought it would be hard to change the heart of a hero. But it looks like that coldness and cruelty was inside him all along. He was never the person you thought he was. I simply brought out who he was truly meant to be."

I wanted to grab Mauvrey by the neck and throttle her like that cave drawing in one of my visions had depicted. I also wanted to give her a good slap.

My magic itched to be released, but I contained the urge to use it. It was bad enough that I'd let some slip while clouded with fury at Arian. Any amount of power I unleashed toward Mauvrey (who I hated in a much more personal way) would be fueled entirely by loathing and vengeance, and I couldn't risk that. I couldn't risk feeding the dark hunger of my Pure Magic. I would have to beat Mauvrey the old-fashioned way.

Standing ten feet away from me, Mauvrey shot her left glove wires at my legs. I leapt up to avoid them, but, anticipating that, she released her right glove wires at a higher angle. They latched around my left arm like metallic tentacles. She thought she had me, but I wrapped my hand around the wires and yanked with all my might before she could activate the electricity. The force pulled Mauvrey right off her feet and sent her toward me. I redirected her incoming body with my other hand to throw her through the window behind me.

She flew into the building with a brutal thud. The wires grew limp when she hit the ground and I shook them off. I bounded through the window after her, my shadow falling over her body as she groaned. She moved, but barely.

"You brought out who I was really meant to be too, Mauvrey,"

I said plainly. "After all, a hero can't properly rise without the right villain bringing out the best in them."

I temporarily put my wand back in pin form and grabbed Mauvrey by her golden hair. Then I punched her in the face. Hard.

My nemesis sprawled on the floor, knocked out. I felt a wave of satisfaction flood over me, but also more venom. A punch in the face was too good for Mauvrey, and me giving it to her was not as fulfilling as I thought it would be. She had wronged me more than a simple beating could compensate for.

A scream suddenly pierced the city. It was loud, it was pained, and it was Blue's. I jumped back through the window and ran toward the cliffs. More sonic booms resonated behind me. I was able to scale a great deal of distance until Alex suddenly emerged. He appeared at an intersection of rusty vehicles and storefronts with smashed windows. Red birds sat on street lamps and upturned carriages throughout the wasteland.

"Crisa." He eyed my wand.

"Alex." I eyed his sword. "So is this the part where we fight?"

"I don't want to."

"You just want to capture me and take me to Arian."

"It's necessary."

"So is this." I morphed my wand, twirling it in my hand as it changed so that when my spear elongated I came out swinging. Alex met me head on.

Our weapons collided fiercely. "You can't beat me—you know that," Alex said as he struck and I evaded. He and I parried through the debris-laden ground as red birds watched.

I leapt onto a chunk of concrete to get a higher position.

*Shield.*

*Spear.*

*Shield.*

*Sword.*

*Spear.*

"You're weaker than I am," Alex said. He swung his sword low and I jumped over it, coming onto ground level once more.

"I'm not weak," I said angrily, clashing my weapon with his.

I hooked my left fist. "You are!" The punch landed square on his cheek. For once I had the upper hand and I advanced on my brother with no mercy.

"You were too weak to resist Mauvrey's manipulation. You were too weak to protect your family. You were too weak to pick the right side!" I thrust all my weight into my staff and rammed him in the chest with the dull end. He tripped, falling back on some rocks. I stood over him. With a swift follow-up kick, I knocked the sword clear out of his hand. It clacked against the ground, out of reach.

A tense moment hung between us.

"So now what?" Alex asked, keeping one eye on me and one on the weapon pointed at his chest. "Are you going to kill me?"

The hardness in my tone and face softened. As furious as I was with Alex, as much as I detested him and everything he'd done, I did not want to hurt him. I couldn't. I loved him. I hated that I still did, but it was true. And if I sought vengeance on him now, it would cement the rift between us.

Naïve as it may have been, part of me hoped that Mauvrey was wrong. That this wasn't who my brother was meant to be. He'd been deceived. He'd been tricked. He could come back. After all, he had warned me about Arian last night. Which meant some part of him still cared for me.

"No," I responded with a sigh. "I'm going to reason with you."
*Wand.*

I crouched down and squared him off at a safe distance. "Mauvrey's mother asked me if I thought she could be saved and I told her I didn't know. But I want to believe that you still can be, Alex. And this is your chance. Please. Don't keep working for Arian. Don't go with Mauvrey to Camelot. You can still change. Be the person I used to admire. Be the person I called my brother and my friend."

There was a long beat where neither of us moved or said anything. Then two wires curtly whipped around my right arm. I barely realized they were there before an electric shock bolted through them.

"Argh!" My jacket cushioned some of the effect, but the shock definitely hurt. My wand slipped from my hand as I was jolted several feet back into the dirt and wreckage. My entire sleeve was smoking and I felt dazed. Alex rose and collected his sword. A red bird—who clearly did not grasp the gravity of the situation— fluttered over and landed on a piece of cement beside me. It blinked its emerald eyes with disinterest.

Mauvrey's wires released my arm and reeled back to her trapper gloves. She stood on a big chunk of rubble and looked down while Alex came closer and paused in front of me. For a moment, hope sparked in my heart. He seemed unsure. Then hope was extinguished.

"Hit her again," he said to Mauvrey. "She needs to be knocked out. Otherwise she'll keep fighting."

Mauvrey smiled at me smugly. "You got it, babe." She raised her hand.

"Get away from her!" SJ's voice shouted furiously. A lightning portable potion landed at Mauvrey's feet. Instantly an intense capsule of electricity encased her and she screamed before collapsing to the ground, knocked out by the surge. I didn't know where SJ was, but I saw my opportunity and took it. I lunged for the red bird and grabbed it by the neck. I hugged it against my chest then squeezed the bird's throat.

The result was precisely what I'd hoped for. The bird discharged a sonic boom directly at Alex. It was so loud it nearly popped my eardrums, but it propelled Alex off his feet. He flew through the air and collided with a pillar.

I let go of the bird and it shook its feathers irately before flying off.

SJ came into view, as did Jason, both running to my aid. Jason picked up my wand while SJ helped me to my feet. "Thanks," I said. "You saved me."

She didn't respond, nor did she meet my gaze.

"Let's go. We're close now," Jason said.

I removed my smoldering jacket and threw it to the ground. Jason tossed me my wand and we took off running. "Does anyone know what happened to Blue?" I asked. "I heard her scream earlier."

"No," Jason said. "But I'm worried. Crisa, can you enchant one of these slabs of concrete and fly us to the top of the cliffs?"

The idea had occurred to me earlier as a means to outrun Arian and Mauvrey, but I didn't take it for fear of the whole "magic overtaking me via emotion" thing. My heart was even worse off now—freshly devastated by my latest exchange with Alex.

"No good," SJ objected before I could respond. "Before I ran into the both of you, I took out one of Arian's men. He was communicating by Mark Two at the time. Arian guessed our play, Crisa. He told all his men to divert their attention to that building. If we fly up there, we will be open targets and completely exposed. Our only chance is to go inside the building and work our way up through the stairs."

We ducked beneath another fallen bridge. "And if the antagonists are already inside the building?" Jason asked.

We skidded around a sharp turn. The huge cliffs were right in front of us. The enormous building was a staggering, crumbling monster. I saw something in my peripheral vision.

"They're not," I said. "They're right there." I gestured to four attackers running toward us.

"And there." SJ pointed at two men drawing their bows from an adjacent building eight stories up. "Crisa!"

"Got it!" I turned my wand to a shield and blocked a set of arrows launched at us. "All right, let's climb this—"

"And there!" Jason grabbed my arm and pulled me against him. His axe projected its shimmering force field and protected us from arrows fired by men standing on a bridge. Shots evaded, we rushed into the building.

The archers from the adjacent structure were too far off to pursue us on foot, but between the three on the bridge and the four on the ground, we had a seven-man tail. My friends and I had a head start, but this was going to be one heck of a chase.

We dove through the first slanted room of the building— leaping over moldy furniture and broken light fixtures. Eventually we entered a hall. At the end of it we found a staircase. The building was leaning at a seventy-degree angle, so climbing it was awkward, but easier than climbing thirty stories straight up a normal structure I suppose.

Our pursuers entered the stairwell when we were on the seventh floor. Our feet pounded on the steps with a noise like a stampede. It made my adrenaline pump harder—all those hammering footsteps filling my skull and causing the hairs on my arm to stand erect.

Rubble and wreckage littered the stairwell and made it treacherous. But it wasn't until the twenty-second floor that we reached an impassible problem. There was a gaping hole where the stairs should've been. There was no way up. If we were going to continue, we would have to find another way.

"Here!" Jason pushed open the door that connected the stairwell to the hallway. We followed his lead through the mangled corridor. He kicked open another door at the far end and we dashed for a shattered window that led straight to the fire escape.

Jason leapt out, trailed by SJ, then me. We were so high up it was ridiculous. The wind blew my hair back as I stared down at the drop. The fire escape was made of rickety, rusted iron. The edge of the cliff was only eight floors up. We clambered toward it as fast as we could. We managed to ascend three more flights before our enemies appeared on the fire escape. They started to follow us, but then the red birds returned. A whole flock was flying in a V shape like a boomerang. They broke off in different directions and a few veered toward us.

"Incoming!" I shouted.

Three birds released sonic booms. One boom hit the cliffs, spraying rock at us. A second collided with the lower half of the building, causing the structure to buckle. The third blasted into the fire escape between us and our pursuers. Several parts of the fire escape were shaken loose from the building and jutted out to the side. I heard shouts from men plummeting to their doom. The antagonists had been thrown from the building.

SJ lost her balance a few steps above me and fell. I released one hand from the railing and grabbed her, forcefully shoving her back to her feet. "Keep going!" I yelled.

We continued to scale the floors of the building.

*Twenty-seven . . .*
*Twenty-eight . . .*
*Twenty-nine . . .*

The edge of the cliff was within our reach. But the structural damage from the latest burst of sonic booms was not through with us yet. The top half of the building lurched, scraping against the cliffside and preparing to collapse completely.

Jason reached the thirtieth floor and took the leap from the fire escape to the cliff. He made it. SJ went next. Jason grabbed her hand and pulled her in. I scrambled up the steps. The building kept sinking. I prepared to launch myself for the cliff, but the building couldn't hold out any longer. Its weight pitched the entire structure to the side in one abrupt movement and I fell off. I dropped two stories in half a second, but managed to grab hold of one of the fire escape's protruding railings.

My heart was in my throat. As I dangled in the open air, I could see the faces of SJ and Jason high above. I saw Daniel too. He'd made it there before us.

They were too far off to help. I had to find a way to help myself. There was only one option. I closed my eyes and shut out all the chaos. Difficult as it was, I forced myself to push away all my feelings of fury and loathing and sadness for Alex and Arian and Mauvrey. I let the calm and the focus in, and channeled my strength and clarity. Concentration overpowered the emotion inside me. With a steady exhale, I opened my eyes and allowed my magic to flow—not hungrily or vindictively, which would put me at risk, but with complete control.

Golden light streamed from my slipping fingers into the metal railing then spread to the fire escape. A moment later the metal gingerly began to move upward. Like a stem growing into a flower, the railing I clung to lifted me up with care until I rose over the cliff. It curved down like a bashful leaf and set me beside my friends before bending back the way it'd come. My friends were stunned.

"That was amazing," SJ said in awe.

"I've been practicing," I replied. "Where's Blue?"

"Over there." Daniel pointed to where Blue was resting

beneath a tree. "She got hit pretty hard, but she'll be okay. SJ," he said, "bring it down."

"Gladly." SJ drew her slingshot and fired six consecutive red portable potions at lower parts of the structure. Explosions boomed. The sound was deafening and the resulting fire cast up an orange and red glow.

The entire building went crashing down, taking its final resting place with the ruins below.

# CHAPTER 44

# A Man Called Julian

thought you said she was okay!" I said to Daniel as I rushed to Blue's side. My friend was lying propped up against a tree trunk. There was a broken arrow within her grip, which I guess she'd ripped out herself. She had been shot just above the collarbone and blood was soaking into her shirt.

"I said she *will* be okay," Daniel replied. "SJ, show her what you've got."

SJ knelt next to Blue and opened her potions sack. "After you were shot by the magic hunters at Lady Agnue's, Crisa, I thought it might be a good idea to make some healing potions. I took the antidote that Madame Alexanders applied to your shoulder and found a way to enhance it." She pulled out a little bottle filled with pinkish liquid that looked like grapefruit juice. "Instead of healing Blue's wound in a few days, this will do the job in four or five hours."

"SJ, that's incredible," I responded.

"Blue, this is going to sting," SJ said, uncorking the bottle. "A lot."

SJ pulled back Blue's shirt to reveal the jagged wound and poured the liquid over the injury. Blue clenched her teeth and shut her eyes, resisting the urge to scream. She grabbed my hand and squeezed it so hard I thought my fingers might come off.

The liquid bubbled when it made contact with her skin and I heard the sound of sizzling—like searing steak in a pan. After a minute the blood began to evaporate. When it was gone, the area where the wound had been was covered in a splotch of glowing pink goo.

Blue let go of my hand and adjusted her shirt. Her SRB caused silver sparks to clean up the material like it had been freshly laundered.

"How do you feel?" I asked.

Blue glanced up at Jason. There was deep concern in his face. She blushed a bit.

"A bit embarrassed that one of Arian's goons managed to shoot me, but I'll live. It feels like a horse kicked me in the shoulder, but it beats the way I felt five minutes ago."

"The wound will continue to mend and the skin will sew itself back together over the next few hours," SJ said as the two of us helped our friend to her feet. "But you will be fine."

"How many of those antidotes you got in there?" Jason asked, pointing at SJ's potions sack.

"Unfortunately, only one more," SJ replied. "It took me many tries to make it. The other bottle is in our closet's secret compartment. I can draw it out the next time one of us gets injured."

"You say that like it's inevitable," Jason said.

"Isn't it?" Daniel responded.

"SJ . . ." Jason said, a spark of hope in his eyes. "Can it heal any kind of injury?"

"No," she said. "It cannot cure a fatal wound—only flesh wounds and minor injuries."

"Oh."

Jason looked bummed and I knew why. He'd had the same thought I did. For a moment, we'd both hoped that maybe it could save him. Maybe this potion was a way to cheat the death I'd foreseen. Alas, it wasn't. With a sigh, Jason gestured to SJ. "Can I have the map please?"

SJ opened her magic potions sack, shoved her hand inside, then pulled out a rolled-up piece of parchment that was at least three times the height of the sack itself.

"So where are we?" Daniel asked.

"Well, that was the Ruined City," Jason explained, unrolling the map. "Right here." He pointed at a spot on the southwestern side of the document. "Those birds we saw were Strumpet Birds. They settled in the area a couple of decades ago and all the people had to evacuate. The birds destroyed the city in a matter of years. So this forest up here should be the Forest of Merriment." He tilted his chin at the trees in front of us. "Once we pass through it, we'll reach the Yellow Brick Road and we can follow that to the Emerald City. I figure we should start by asking the Wizard for help. He might have some idea where we can find a missing Fairy Godmother."

"Solid plan," Blue said, stretching her arm. "I guess it's off to see the Wizard then."

Jason rolled up the map, but held onto it.

"Hey, Jason," I said, checking to make sure my wandpin was still in place, then adjusting my backpack. "Is there anything on that map about a YUR?"

"Um, no. What's that?"

"I don't know. Something that Harry said. I guess we'll find out later."

We made our way through the Forest of Merriment and found the Yellow Brick Road. The forest was not as merry as I would've hoped. Actually, it was kind of dark and spooky. The Yellow Brick Road, however, was as rich and sunnily colored as the stories promised.

Referring to the map when we came to forks in the road, the five of us followed the bright yellow path for a long time. It led us through many parts of Oz, including the Elder's Pass, Spider Pixie Canyon, and Lilac Meadows.

As we proceeded down the Yellow Brick Road into the Forest of Saltar, I was surprised that we didn't run into anyone. In fact, we hadn't seen a single other soul on the road all day. I thought it was a bit weird given that this was supposed to be the main road through Oz that led to the realm's capital.

There were a couple of other peculiarities as well. We came across several large crimson insignias imprinted in the Yellow

Brick Road. And on more than one occasion, I could've sworn the road was trembling, as if something was passing through the earth beneath us.

I took the distraction of the long trek as a blessing. It helped me cast aside the thoughts of Alex that gnawed at my mind and heart. I didn't know what was worse: that he'd turned on me again in the Ruined City, or that I was stupid enough to believe that he might not. Had I been so delusional to think that he still cared for me? Was Mauvrey right about his true nature? Should I give up and treat him strictly like an enemy from here on out?

By midday, we had emerged from the Forest of Saltar and into the open again. I could see the Emerald City from here, like a beacon on a hill. Glassy buildings that reminded me of Midveil projected into the sky. They all had a greenish tint and were pointed at the tops like stalagmites. The tower at the center was significantly grander than the others and resembled a streak of frozen, vertical lightning.

As we entered the final stretch to the city, I was dismayed that the path was lined on either side by plains of familiar flowers.

*Poppies.*

The bright red-and-black-spotted flowers encircled the city like a moat. A notable mist floated above them. I remembered seeing traces of that same mist in the jars in Madame Alexanders's lab cases at school. I supposed the greater the number of flowers, the more mist they produced.

"Watch your step," I said as the path began to cut through their domain.

The Poppy moat was at least a half mile in radius. Tall towers with spinning blades were placed throughout it. Each one was made of bronze and copper and extended at least three hundred feet in the air. They looked like solar-powered wind turbines for gathering energy, the likes of which I'd seen when my family and I had visited other kingdoms in Book.

At the center of each turbine was a glowing scarlet sphere. The more I looked at them, the more I thought the towers resembled flowers; the spheres were like stamen and the spinning blades that surrounded them were like sharp petals.

Every few minutes the spheres projected shimmering beams of light into the sky. Different tower spheres lit up at different times in a pattern that I could not follow. When we were halfway through the Poppy moat, SJ suddenly paused and put her hand to her chest as if she was about to faint.

"What's wrong?" I asked.

"I think it is the flowers," she said, taking a heavy breath. "I read in our potions textbook that in the wild, Poppies can exude drowsy gas. I have been feeling it more and more with each step."

"So that's what that mist is," I commented.

"I feel it too," Jason said, rubbing his tired, unfocused eyes. "What about you guys?"

Daniel and Blue confessed that they'd been feeling symptomatic as well. Their expressions appeared as exhausted as SJ's and Jason's. I observed them with worry and guilt since I seemed to be immune to the effects.

"We'll be inside soon," I said, gesturing to the wall surrounding the city. "Come on. We're almost there."

The wall around the Emerald City hadn't looked that intimidating from afar. As we'd gotten closer though, I realized it was terribly formidable. The thing was no less than six hundred feet tall and wrapped around the entire city. Unlike the glass towers within, the wall was made of solid concrete.

I wondered what could warrant such serious security measures. As we approached the large iron door in the wall at the end of the path, I saw a black whir flying in the distance and got my answer. At first it looked like a massive bird. But then I remembered that giant birds didn't have arms, legs, and bat wings.

SJ pointed to the sky. "Is that . . . ?"

Blue nodded. "Flying monkey."

The others and I watched as the creature flew toward the city. For a moment I was afraid for the civilians within. But when the creature tried to enter the city's domain from the sky, it was electrocuted. A sizzling, formerly invisible, emerald barrier above the walls revealed itself and shocked the flying monkey, causing it to screech and ricochet back into the sky. It must've been some kind of In and Out Spell.

Hastily I marched up to the grand iron door and knocked forcefully. "Hello?"

A tiny window above the door slid open. "State your business," said a small man wearing a large fedora.

"We're here to see the Wizard," Jason responded.

The man nodded. "Hold up your hands."

We lifted our palms for him to see. The small man disappeared behind the window and a blinking machine replaced him. It was metallic and the size of a kickball, and it was attached to a metal tentacle that allowed it to stretch out the window. It released a wave of bright red light that scanned us from head to toe.

"Scanning for dark magic," the machine said in a baritone register. When it finished, it recoiled back through the window, leaving us on the road, puzzled.

We waited. That's when I glanced up and noticed the flying monkey had not gone back into the clouds after being shocked. Rather, it had circled around the city and was coming toward us. Fast.

Blue banged on the door. "Excuse me!"

The window opened again. The small man peeked out and looked down at us. "Your background checks are still running. It'll be another minute."

"We don't have another minute!" Blue shouted.

"Sorry, those are the rules," the small man said. He shut the window again with little regard for the peril we were in.

The flying monkey screeched. It was fifty feet away from us and closing. SJ drew a silver portable potion from her bag and took aim.

Forty feet.

She fired her slingshot. The portable potion shot into the sky, but the flying monkey swerved and evaded it.

Twenty feet.

As the ice potion exploded in a distant part of the Poppy field, Blue pulled one of her throwing knives and hurled it at the creature with her uninjured arm. The flying monkey dodged the knife then dove for our group.

There was nowhere to go. The Poppies had us corralled on both sides and the wall barricaded us from behind. Jason was the farthest out on the road, and he was looking frantically at the door of Oz, waiting for the little man to let us in. I knew what was about to happen and raced forward and shoved him aside just as the flying monkey swooped in and would have snatched him up. The creature's claws clasped around my upper arms instead. We darted into the sky, but I didn't wait for us to get very high. I grabbed my wandpin, transformed it into a dagger, then stabbed one of the creature's paws. It shrieked and I was released. I landed in the field of Poppies with a semi-cushioned thud.

*Lapellium.*

I sat up and rubbed my right arm. It had some of the flying monkey's blood on it, which my SRB quickly cleaned off. The scratches from the monkey's claws remained though. I looked around. The injured flying monkey had retreated into the clouds. My friends were only a few dozen yards away.

"You okay?" Jason called.

My arm veins had begun to pulsate purple from touching the flowers, but as I'd come to expect, their toxins had no power over me.

"Fine!" I called back.

I waded through the flowers back to the road—dusting loose petals off me as I made my way. As I walked, the Poppies' purple glow in my arms was chased away by my own golden one. By the time I reached the road again, both glows had faded entirely.

The gargantuan iron door embedded in the wall finally opened. After we'd entered, it sealed itself shut again. The moment it closed, the light returned to my friends' eyes and the exhaustion disappeared from their faces. With the mist of the Poppies behind them, their symptoms were gone.

We were in a long tunnel with a small kiosk in front of us.

"Sorry about the delay."

We turned and spotted the fedora-clad man who'd spoken to us through the window. He was sliding down a ladder against the door that led to a high perch. "The scan is usually pretty fast," he continued on his way to the kiosk. "But *your* results," he nodded at me, "were inconclusive the first time, so we had to run it again. The machine sometimes has trouble telling the difference between Pure Magic and dark magic. I'll need you to fill out a few forms before entering the city." He opened up the door to his kiosk, slipped inside, and then regarded us through his new post.

"Really?" I asked.

"It's policy. Now come, come."

He waved me forward and handed me a holographic clipboard that looked like it was made of pure energy and a quill the size of a lightning rod. For the next couple of minutes, I answered a bunch of census questions and a few personal ones, not taking them seriously at all.

Height: *Depends on size of boots.*

Weight: *None of your business.*

Mental State: *TBD.*

I handed the clipboard and quill back to the guard with a fake smile. "Can we go now?"

He nodded and presented us with a city map, a brochure of the city's best attractions, and a yellow ticket stub with the number thirty-five written on it.

Jason gave our Oz map back to SJ for storage and accepted the materials. I took a deep breath and readied myself for the venture ahead.

It was time to see the Wizard *and* see if he really was as wonderful as the stories said. I hoped so. At this point he was our only lead to finding Paige.

The Emerald City was nothing short of amazing.

It seemed modesty and frugality were two words this metropolis had never heard of. Every building was decorated in expensive-looking crystals. Every carriage and horse's saddle was encrusted with gems. And every person was a vision of colorful silk, lace, and velvet.

The ladies' day dresses cascaded behind them as they sashayed along the streets. Their necks were adorned with fine jewels that looked like second skins. The men's coattails flounced about in an equally grand way—their colorful, whimsically patterned bow ties matching perfectly with their pocket handkerchiefs. Fancy hats seemed to be a common theme for both men and women, as was the use of fine gloves. Needless to say, we felt totally under-dressed.

We followed the map the man at the wall had given us to get to the Emerald Tower, where the Wizard lived. As we crossed the streets I was struck by the number of posters of the Wizard throughout the city; his face could be seen on everything from park benches to decorative window hangings. The ads lauded the greatness of the Wizard and were captioned with boastful phrases like "The Wizard Believes in You," "The Wizard: Savior of Oz," and "We are Defended; We are Cared for; We are Under the Watchful Watch of the Wizard." While these advertisements varied, at the bottom of each was always the same tagline:

*"The Wizard is good; the Wizard protects us; all hail the Wizard."*

The propaganda had the opposite effect on me and made me wary of the man before even meeting him.

"Hey, I appreciate what you did back there," Blue whispered to me as we passed a flower vendor insisting on the freshness of his daisies.

"Hmm?"

Blue glanced ahead to make sure the others were out of earshot. "For Jason," she said. "I screwed up with that flying monkey. I had him in my sights and I missed. You know I have much better aim with my right arm, but my injury is still healing. If you hadn't done what you did, Jason would've gotten hurt because I failed to protect him."

"Blue, you didn't fail. You missed. So did SJ. It happens."

Blue shook her head and sighed. "I'm just glad you're forever looking out for us. I can't tell you what it means to know you always have our backs."

Blue smiled and slapped me on the shoulder. I returned the smile, but timidly. Guilt chomped my insides like a piranha. Blue constantly made me out to be so noble, but I didn't think she'd feel that way if she knew that I'd told Jason he was going to die and that I was keeping it from her, thus keeping her from trying to prevent it.

She definitely would not see me in the same light if she knew the truth.

The five of us arrived at another wall. This one encircled the Emerald Tower—the great, jagged building I'd seen from far off. The barrier was concrete like the one around the city with doors constructed of dark green metal. A gatekeeper (also wearing a fedora) waved us through. I was a bit surprised at the ease of entry.

We followed a metallic path that led up to the front doors of the Tower. I spotted no less than thirty guards on patrol, each in golden armor. Inside the Tower, more guards guided us until we reached a line with several dozen people in it.

"What's with the line?" I asked the closest guard.

"These are the Wizard's appointments for the day," the guard explained. "Do you have a ticket?"

Jason handed the guard the bright stub we'd been given upon entering the city.

"Number thirty-five," the guard read aloud. "Should be about twenty minutes. Back of the line please."

When it was finally our turn, we were ushered into a grand room that reminded me of my parents' throne room in Midveil, only gaudier. The floor was gold tile. Fountains at the end of the room spouted water that flashed different colors thanks to spotlights in the ceiling. Thick marble columns holding blazing torches led up to the throne.

Upon that throne sat a man. He was in his late twenties with curly black hair, perfectly groomed eyebrows, and a confident smile. There was a sort of cockiness in the way he positioned himself in his seat. Mischief glinted in his eyes.

"You may now state your business before his majesty the Wizard of Oz," a guard bellowed. He saluted the man on the throne and repeated the phrase we'd seen plastered across the city: "The Wizard is good; the Wizard protects us; all hail the Wizard."

"Welcome!" The Wizard said, beckoning us to move closer.

"Somehow, I thought he'd be older," Blue whispered in my ear as we approached.

"I heard that," the Wizard said as he rose from his throne.

Much to my surprise, he walked across the room and came to meet us. He shook each of our hands in turn. "Most visitors from other realms tend to expect that," he continued. "I suppose you also think the only things I'm capable of handing out are hearts, brains, and courage?"

"Well . . ." was all Blue could say.

"Don't worry," the Wizard said with a kindly smile. "I'm just joking. The majority of people who come from other realms expect someone older because they are familiar with the Wizard before me. However, my father passed away years ago, so I'm hoping my legacy will catch on soon."

"Wizard is a family name?" Daniel asked, raising an eyebrow.

"More like a family business," the Wizard responded. "My name is my own. And it is Julian. Although, I am quite partial to 'His Great and Powerful-ness.'"

"How did you know we were from another realm?" SJ asked.

Julian grinned, happy that she'd caught on. "You entered the Emerald City through the main doors. The only people who do that are not from around here. Plus, when you were scanned you did not come up in any of our records. Tell me, are you storytellers here on visa, did you fall through a portal by accident, or none of the above?"

"Uh, none of the above," I answered. "We're actually here on a mission."

Julian headed back toward his throne. "Color me intrigued. I do love a good mission. Though I must say, you are a bit younger than most protagonists that typically pass through here. What is your objective?"

"We're searching for a Fairy Godmother named Paige Tomkins who went missing from our realm ten years ago," Jason explained. "We got a tip that she's in Oz and thought you might be able to shed some light."

Julian didn't say anything for a long moment and kept his back to us.

"So . . ." Daniel said. "Can you help us or not?"

"I can do better than that, my dear boy," Julian replied, finally finding his voice. He spun around, causing his coattails to whip. "I can tell you where she is."

My eyes nearly bugged out of my head. "You're not serious."

"Oh, I am very serious," Julian said. "Well, at least most of the time. But definitely this time. Now, while I cannot say for certain that your Paige Tomkins is in Oz, I do know where she would be if she was. There is an area at the base of the North Mountains called the Plain of the Forgotten. And within it, there is one place in particular called the Maze of the Mindless. People there are able to hide in plain sight; their memory is forgotten. So if your Godmother friend was looking for a good place to conceal herself, the best place in Oz would be there."

"All right," I said steadily. "Thanks. We'll head for the Plain of the Forgotten then."

"Excellent," Julian replied, clapping his hands together. "See my assistant for directions. She can also validate your parking if you need it. Otherwise, I wish you protagonists well and hope you find what you're looking for."

Julian pulled a lever by his throne. It opened a set of doors to the left. Guards emerged and herded us toward the exit. I glanced back at Julian. He gave me a confident, closed-mouth smile and a slight politician's wave.

We were escorted into a hallway. A woman with big boobs and a pointed face like a possum was sitting at a cherry wood desk. She wore an emerald pencil skirt and a slinky, silver silk top. "You need directions?" she asked.

SJ withdrew our map of Oz from her potions sack. Upon unrolling it, I saw that the Plain of the Forgotten was already labeled on the document; it was at the base of the North Mountains like Julian said. But the woman at the desk showed us a shortcut that would get us there faster. When she was done, we moved for the exit of the Emerald Tower. As we passed through the front doors, Daniel spoke under his breath so the guards wouldn't hear.

"Does anyone feel like that was too easy?"

# CHAPTER 45

# StalkWalkers

he Plain of the Forgotten was a long carpet of yellowed desert grass that stretched through a thin forest of crooked trees. The trees were black like they'd been charred. Mangled roots gripped their trunks into the ground. Entangled vines hung off branches like serpents.

On the other side of the plain was a massive cornfield. It rested beneath the watchful shadow of the North Mountains. The plain continued on either side of the cornfield—the tree density getting thicker farther out—but the corn grew so close together that there seemed to only be one way to enter the cornfield. This entrance was housed under a tall metallic arch with "Maze of the Mindless" woven in dark wire over the top.

According to Julian, if Paige was in Oz she was here. He'd seemed certain of it. So my friends and I forged ahead into the maze.

Even with the blue sky overhead, it was eerie. The corn stalks stretched nine feet in height. The North Mountains loomed over us like an overlord of nature—purple and gray and ominous. Adding to the weirdness, every couple of turns we ran into creepy-looking scarecrows. Some were attached to traditional wooden stakes. Others were propped against copper stakes with an assortment of silver and copper wires securing them tightly.

There were two kinds of scarecrows. The first was a homogeneous type—wearing a traditional outfit of a plaid shirt, overalls, and a straw hat. These scarecrows were the ones attached to plain wooden stakes. The second kind of scarecrow—the ones bound to metal stakes—wore torn remains of fine dresses, suits, leather jackets, and other clothing. While the homogenous scarecrows had frightening grins sewn into their burlap faces, the heterogeneous ones donned scared, lifelike expressions.

I walked up to one of the heterogeneous scarecrows. She was wearing a light blue shirt and khaki skirt. Blonde straw hung around her worn face. Her expression was wistful. In studying her more closely, I noticed that her specific kind of scarecrow wasn't simply made of straw. The heterogeneous scarecrows' limbs were a weird mutation of straw and skin and burlap. It was like someone had crossbred a scarecrow with a human. A mossy, green rash grew on the top layer of straw-skin, which spread over the scarecrow's entire body.

A chill went through my blood. There were way too many similarities with this place and my recent dream of that crow absorbing purple energy from the woman face-planted in a cornfield. Was this the same setting?

I leaned in to analyze the scarecrow further. Suddenly she looked up. Her eyes blinked and met mine. "Hello."

Startled, I jumped back and rammed into Jason and Daniel.

We all stared at the scarecrow. She stared back. "Who are you?" she asked.

Daniel took a step forward. "What in the . . ."

"Noodles!" the scarecrow blurted.

My friends and I glanced at each other.

"I'm sorry, did you say noodles?" Jason asked.

The scarecrow nodded. "Yes, I was supposed to have some for lunch today you see and I . . ." her eyes rolled to the side like lost marbles. "Some time you see. See you some time. Time you saw me. Me oh my oh me?"

Blue snapped her fingers in the lady scarecrow's face. "Hey, you. Eyes in front."

Lady scarecrow raised her head and furrowed her straw brow. "I'm sorry. I drifted off, didn't I?"

"Um, something like that," I responded. "What . . . what *are* you?"

"What am I? This morning I was a *who*, now I am a *what*. Isn't that sad?"

"She's gone loopy again," Blue huffed.

"Not just yet," lady scarecrow insisted. "Probably any minute I will, but for the moment I have my marbles. Most of them anyway . . ." She nodded at her arms, which were bound to the copper stake. "I used to be called Bridget; now I am called scarecrow seventy-eight."

"I don't understand," Blue said.

"I don't understand much of anything anymore," Bridget replied sadly. "But I'll help you. See those mountains up there?" She tilted her chin at the North Mountains.

"Yes," SJ said.

"That's where the Wicked Witch lives. And we are hers."

"Hold up," Blue interjected. "The Wicked Witch of the West is *dead*. That's not an opinion; it's a fact. It's been catalogued in at least a hundred different storybooks."

"The Wicked Witch of the West is not dead. She is gone. But that's neither here nor there. Her sister Glinda the Good has come to power. Now Glinda is known as the Wicked Witch of the North."

"Anyone following this?" Blue asked.

"Barely," Jason responded.

"Pay attention," Bridget said, her tone growing more urgent. "When Glinda's minions catch you here, they will turn you into one of us. Like they did to me this very morn."

"Which brings us back to the question—what exactly *are* you?" Daniel asked.

"I am a brainless scarecrow," Bridget said. "Glinda cannot leave the North Mountains, but she has minions that spy on the realm for her. She sometimes sends these minions to capture Ozians. The nobodies are kept as prisoners. Others are brought here and turned into brainless scarecrows. Glinda likes to collect people's minds, you see. So when we become brainless scarecrows, her minions gather our minds and bring them back to her for her collection."

A second chill quaked my bones. The energy that crow had

absorbed from the woman in my dream, that woman had been Bridget and that energy must've been her mind. While I was sleeping safely in Neverland last night, I'd foreseen this poor woman's early morning doom in this very cornfield.

I recalled a dream I'd had long ago of a sponge being wrung out in a river in the mountains. A pair of feminine hands had held the sponge, and it exuded the same purple energy. My gaze darted to the North Mountains looming over us.

*Glinda.*

"That's . . ." I didn't even know the word for it. It was terrible, terrifying, and rather disturbing, but none of the words seemed to do the situation justice.

"Their memory is forgotten," Daniel thought out loud. "That's what the Wizard said about the people in the Maze of the Mindless. We assumed he meant that others forgot about them. But if their minds have been taken, the people here are the ones doing the forgetting. Julian tricked us."

"It looks like," Blue said. "But that doesn't mean Paige isn't here. The woman's been gone for ten years. Maybe she was turned into a brainless scarecrow?"

Hm. If Paige had been turned into a brainless scarecrow, I honestly didn't know what that meant for us. Blue got closer to Bridget and poked her in the arm.

"What's the life span of these things?" Blue asked.

"How long have you been trapped here, Bridget?" I rephrased.

"I am not sure. There is no way to tell time in the stalks."

"Is there a way to reverse it? To help you?" Jason asked.

Bridget tilted her head. Her eyes got that distant look again and she began mumbling. "Help you? Yes, yes, help you."

"Bridget?" SJ repeated.

Our scarecrow friend struggled to focus, but her eyes began to quiver in their burlap sockets. Whatever clarity she'd possessed in the last minute was quickly leaving her.

"The stalks," she mumbled. "The stalks are bad, get out of the stalks or they'll be mad. And you'll be sad. Get out while you can or the crows will know and . . . *Noodles!*"

Bridget's grin distorted as her head dropped to her chest and she continued to quietly mumble to herself about noodles and shampoo.

"Bridget?" Blue poked her in the straw-skin arm again, but our scarecrow friend did not respond anymore.

"I think we lost her," Jason said.

Blue put her fingers to Bridget's neck. "She has a pulse. So she's still alive."

"What do you think she meant by 'get out while you can or the crows will know'?" Jason asked as the five of us continued through the maze, reluctantly leaving poor Bridget behind.

"I don't know," Daniel responded. "She probably was trying to warn us to watch out for the Wicked Witch of the North."

"But she said *they'll* be mad, not *she'll* be mad." I commented. "Bridget must've meant something else."

"I am beginning to wonder whether or not it is wise to continue our exploration of this place," SJ interjected. "The pronoun of the threat is irrelevant. If Glinda's 'minions' find us, we will either become prisoners or get transformed into one of these brainless scarecrows. Maybe we should head back?"

"Calm yourself, Negative Nancy," Blue replied. "We've done a lot more with a lot less."

"Yes, and how many times have those situations ended well?"

Blue shrugged. "All right, not that often. But we didn't come all the way to Oz so we could give up in a cornfield. This is the only solid lead we've got. We have to follow it and see if we can find Paige."

"And just how do you suggest we do that? This place is enormous."

"Why don't we just ask someone," I suggested, as we came across another scarecrow.

I turned to the hay dummy in question. Like Bridget, he was a disturbing amalgam of skin, straw, and burlap. His body was mounted to a metal stake and his skin had the same mossy, green rash coating. He wore the ragged remains of a suit—matching pocket-square and all—and had brown straw for hair and leather shoes.

"Might as well." Blue shrugged, approaching him. "Hey, scarecrow guy. Do you know where we might find a Paige?"

The scarecrow tilted his head and a goofy, creepy grin spread across his face. "Paige . . ." he mused.

"That's right." Blue nodded. "Paige Tomkins. She's supposed to be around here somewhere. Any idea where we could find her?"

"Paige, page, page of a book. The pager buzzed the business schnook. By the book; business crook. Pretty Paige and the pages she took."

"I'm guessing that's a no," Daniel said.

"So let's try another," Blue replied. She stomped over to a dummy in the corner. This was one of the homogenous scarecrows—red plaid shirt, old overalls, and a torn straw hat complimented by an unsettling smile sewn into his face.

"Yo, scarecrow," Blue continued. "Do *you* know where we might find a rogue Fairy Godmother hiding out here?"

The creature did not answer. He didn't move or mumble.

"This one's different," Blue commented, studying him. "He doesn't have that green rash and just looks like a normal scarecrow, no skin." Blue moved to poke him in his hay chest, but before she could, a high-pitched voice shouted for her to stop.

"Don't touch him!"

A tiny white mouse wearing a light blue suit jacket scurried out of one of the thick stalk walls. He stood on his hind legs next to Blue's boot and waved his petite paws in warning.

"Please, keep away," he said. "If you touch it, it'll wake up. Then the crows will come and signal the others to wake up as well."

SJ knelt to address the mouse. "What do you mean? These scarecrows are victims of the witch, are they not?"

"Some of these dummies are brainless scarecrows that used to be people," the mouse explained, climbing onto the hand SJ offered. She lifted him to eye level as he continued. "But the others—the ones that look like normal scarecrows—are StalkWalkers. They're the keepers of this maze and are minions of the witch, just like the crows that live here. If trespassers are detected, the crows will wake the StalkWalkers to hunt down intruders. The first time I saw it happen I was only a mousling. It was awful. Those poor villagers."

The little mouse's expression went dead for a second. "Please go. You're not safe here."

"Trust me," I said. "It's not safe for us out there either. But maybe you can help us so we can get out of here without being detected. How well do you know this place?"

"Pretty well." The mouse shrugged. "My family has lived in the area for a few generations and a team of my subjects and I have been mapping the maze for years. I'm Donahue Van Winklevolt III—prince of my people and future Mouse King. But you can just call me Kevin. I always really liked the name Kevin."

"Um, okay, Kevin," I said. "We're looking for someone. She's a Fairy Godmother named Paige Tomkins. The Wizard told us we might find her here, but we don't know where to look. We think she might've been turned into a brainless scarecrow."

"I've had a few conversations with a nice scarecrow named Paige over the years. She's more coherent than the other brainless scarecrows. The smarter and more powerful the person was before getting transformed, the more likely they are able to be a bit lucid sometimes."

"Can you take us to her?"

"I really shouldn't," Kevin responded. "I can stay undetected pretty well here because of my size. But it's a miracle you guys haven't been found by the crows yet. You should leave now before it is too late."

"See," SJ said.

"Oh, hush, SJ," Blue said. "Kevin, we're not leaving until you take us to Paige. So lead the way."

"All right, but don't say I didn't warn you." Kevin motioned for SJ to set him back on the ground. "Just keep your heads down and move fast. The crows could appear at any time."

Kevin began to scuttle through the maze and we hurried after him. We swiftly made our way through the cornfield for a few minutes before the mouse stopped in a small clearing. On one side was another StalkWalker. Across from it was a petite brainless scarecrow bound to a copper stake. Her straw hair was short and black, her burlap sack face was vaguely heart shaped, and she wore a silver dress that may have once been beautiful, but now looked like cobwebs.

I'd seen a picture of Paige before, in a file Arian had on her. *Was this the same woman?*

I walked slowly toward the brainless scarecrow. "Paige?"

She did not stir.

"Paige Tomkins?" I tried again.

The scarecrow lifted her head and met my green eyes with her navy ones. They were dull, but the color matched the glittering navy scarf around her neck. "Paige . . ." she repeated back to me. "Paige is a good name. Paige is my name. It was my mother's name, but now it's mine. I am Paige. You are who?"

It was her. This former Fairy Godmother had been reduced to a slightly smelly amalgamation of hay, straw, and mossy green human tissue.

"Paige," I started slowly. "My name is Crisanta Knight. I'm Emma's goddaughter."

Paige's eyes seem to lift with clarity at the mention of Emma's name.

"Emma? Crisanta? You're bigger than I thought. I promised to help Emma protect a little girl; you're big."

"It's been a long time," I replied. "You've been gone a long time."

Paige hung her head for a moment and sighed. "I have, haven't I?" She looked at the five of us. "I remember Crisanta, but I also recognize you." Paige nodded to Jason. "When I was at the Fairy Godmother Agency, I worked on the case file of your brother Jack. You are all protagonists, aren't you?"

Jason seemed stunned. "Um, yeah. We're protagonists."

"Antagonists have come looking for me. Some have found me. But none get what they want. That's why I put myself here, you see. No one can hide forever, so I hid myself and what they want from me in separate places."

"What do you mean you put yourself here?" Jason asked.

"What are you hiding in a separate place?" Blue added.

"And why are the antagonists looking for you?" I threw in, hoping she could answer all three pressing questions.

"Your questions share an answer," Paige replied, her voice gaining clarity with each sentence. "At the Fairy Godmother Agency, my job was to hold many secrets in my head, like the knowledge of the genies. Long ago, genies were common. But when their magic threatened the balance of the realm, the Godmothers decided to remove them. We set a trap and the genies were caught.

"To protect everyone, an enchantment wiped the memories of all involved. All but me. I was chosen to guard the knowledge. Only I would know where the genies were imprisoned, where they are all *still* imprisoned. But people started coming after me because of it, people who wanted to find the genies and use their power. I got scared about what would happen if they found me, so I ran. I ran for a very long time—always hiding and looking over my shoulder—until one day I came to Oz and learned about the brainless scarecrows. I knew they were my best option. If the witch took my brain, the knowledge I carried within it would be safe."

*Holy cow. That's what the antagonists were after. They wanted to find Paige because they wanted to find Book's genies. And if that happened—*

"Can you imagine what kind of havoc that would wreak on the realm?" SJ said, reading my mind. "Every genie grants three wishes. Even one under the control of the antagonists would be devastating, but all of them?"

"All that stuff with Crisa and the prophecies and the Eternity Gate might not even matter," Blue said. "Genies might not have the power to take life—just like Fairy Godmothers—but the antagonists could lay waste to everyone and everything in a bunch of other colorful ways. We'd be doomed."

"Which means we need to find Paige's memories before they do," Jason responded.

"Hold on," Daniel said, turning his attention to Paige. "If the witch has your knowledge, your memories, how are you able to tell us any of this?"

Paige attempted a shrug. "A person's mind can't be removed

entirely. As long as it's still out there, I'm still connected to it. But I can only get surface memories. And the clarity never lasts. I probably only have another minute before my mind goes wonky again."

"Well, we're getting you out of here before that," Blue declared.

"I can't leave," Paige said as Blue walked closer to her. "These metal stakes we're tied to are electric. If we try to get free, they'll instantly ignite and we'll be swallowed in fire. The whole maze will probably go up in flames as a result."

"There has to be a way to shut them down. Just give us a minute. We'll figure something out," I said as I began to examine the stake with Blue.

"I gave you answers because you are protagonists—whom Fairy Godmothers are pledged to serve—and because of my promise to Emma many years ago," Paige said. "But you must go. This is a trap. The Wizard sends people who are looking for me to the Maze of the Mindless so they'll get captured by StalkWalkers and turned into brainless scarecrows. Only the Wizard actually knows how to regain my memories. But no one ever returns from the maze to press him for more answers. You have to leave before you meet the same fate as the others he's sent here. Kevin, tell them."

"I did," Kevin squeaked. "They're not afraid of the Stalk-Walkers."

"Then they've never seen one," Paige replied. She looked over my shoulder. "But I have a feeling they're about to."

Blue and I turned around slowly. A crow was perched on one of the cornstalks behind SJ, Jason, and Daniel. It sat there looking at us curiously, its beady eyes shining. A gray collar around its neck held a little mechanism with a blinking red light. We all stood still.

"Blue?" I muttered.

"I'm on it," she whispered back.

Blue slowly inched her hand toward her utility belt and removed a throwing knife from its holster. The crow suddenly opened its mouth to caw, but Blue's knife sailed through the air before the bird could make a peep. The blade made a direct hit, and the crow was knocked back into the cornfield, dead.

"That took care of that," Blue said.

My face went dark. "Somehow I don't think so."

On the edge of the clearing, seven crows were now perched upon the cornstalks. They eyed us threateningly. There was no time to think of a plan. There wasn't even time for Blue to fire off more throwing knives to thin out the bunch. The crows opened their beaks and cawed.

At first it was just the one screech, which they all exerted in deafening unison. But moments later, we began to hear their calls from all over the cornfield. Dozens upon dozens of unseen crows called out in response to the signal these had set off. The noise escalated until the cornfield echoed in their low-pitched screams.

"Go! Now!" Paige shouted. "The StalkWalkers are waking up!"

Across from us, the StalkWalker planted in the ground began to slowly lift its head. Its eyes glowed bright green and its smile distorted into a menacing glower. The ropes binding the creature to its wooden stake began to come undone on their own. *Wait, no.* Those weren't even ropes. They were tendril-like extensions of the StalkWalker. *Creepy.*

"Come on!" Kevin squeaked. "I can get you out of here, but we need to move!"

"What about Paige?" Blue said above the murderous screeching of the crows.

"No one can help me," she answered. "I can't be saved!"

"Guys!" Jason shouted. The StalkWalker was almost loose.

"Go!" Paige urged again.

"Fine, but we're coming back for you," I said as I began to back up with the others. "I promise you that; you hear me, Paige? We *will* save you."

The StalkWalker ripped itself free and landed in a crouched position, the last of its rope-like extensions wriggling around its straw hands.

"Run!" Kevin squeaked.

Our guide took off through the maze with us charging after him. The crows filled the sky, swarming overhead like a cyclone. The cornstalk walls seemed to be shaking. We turned a corner and skidded to a stop. Six StalkWalkers stood directly in front of us. They charged—arms outstretched, eyes viciously viridescent, and mouths full of . . .

*Holy crud! What is that?*

Crackling inside the StalkWalkers' crooked mouths was some kind of green magic that conducted itself like sparks of electricity.

Kevin u-turned and continued to lead us, but he was clearly growing frantic. The brainless scarecrows laughed goofily as we raced past them. SJ's portable potions would have come in handy, but the StalkWalkers were too fast, too close, and too erratic for her to get a clean shot. Running was all we had time for. Alas, even that was starting to fail us. Our lead was diminishing. The crows cawed louder. My heart pounded faster. The stalks rustled harder. And then, from out of the cornstalk wall, a straw hand shot out. Rope-like tendrils whipped around my wrist and yanked me into the depths of the cornstalks.

*Eeep!*

I struggled, but couldn't regain my footing; the cornstalks smacked me in the face and distorted my vision. I was pulled with the speed of a trout hooked on a fishing line. When the dragging stopped, three StalkWalkers stood over me. Two of them held me down. The third released its rope tendrils from my wrist and hovered in front of my face. I looked into its flaming green eyes as it opened its mouth wider—showing me the snapping green magic inside.

I thrashed about and shouted for help, but it was too late. The StalkWalker sank its sharp teeth into my left shoulder. I screamed. Suddenly, a sword and axe slashed through the stalks around me. Daniel and Jason appeared behind their gleaming weapons and sliced the heads off the StalkWalkers.

Daniel stretched out his hand. "Come on!"

I took it and he, Jason, and I pushed back through the stalks until we reached the others. SJ managed to fire off one of her ice potions, freezing four oncoming StalkWalkers where they stood. We resumed our flight, zigzagging through twists and turns, veering out of the way of monsters when they cut us off, and dodging to avoid more of their arms, which kept popping out of the stalk walls.

The enraged crows were now taking shots at us too—their claws outstretched to tear our hair and skin. As we rounded a turn, I felt myself falter a bit. I glanced at my arm. The area where the StalkWalker had bitten me was turning green. And the black, slit-like bite marks were emanating small sparks of green magic. The wound stung violently.

"Awgh!" I lashed out and swatted another crow.

I transformed my wand into a shield to protect my head as best I could, but doing so impaired my vision and made running for my life a lot more difficult. A large cluster of StalkWalkers was only thirty feet behind us.

"There! Up ahead!" Blue pointed to the arched entrance of the maze. It was only twenty feet away, but blocked by a dozen StalkWalkers.

"Everyone stand back!" SJ shouted.

She grabbed another ice potion from her sack and launched it at the barricade. With a giant implosion, all the StalkWalkers were encased in frost. The five of us leapt over their icy collection and dashed out of the Maze of the Mindless with Kevin scurrying right behind.

"Will they keep following us?" SJ asked Kevin when we'd put about forty feet between the entrance and us.

The mouse shook his head. "No. Just listen."

Much to our relief, the caw of the crows had died down. The birds had flown off and disappeared into the cornfield. No StalkWalkers emerged from the archway.

"Glinda has enchanted her crows to patrol certain areas. Same with the flying monkeys," Kevin said. "She might be evil, but she's very organized. When there are no more threats within their domain, the minions retreat."

"That's lucky," Blue said as we gazed back at the death trap we'd escaped.

"Yeah," I gulped, looking down at the greenish rash on my shoulder and the green energy that kept snapping off it. "Lucky."

"Knight, you okay?" Daniel asked as he came to my side.

"Um, I . . . I can't feel my arm," I said, only then realizing this for myself. I started to feel dizzy, and sick, and heavy. "I . . ."

The world was spinning. Colors blended together like an exotic smoothie. My friends were jumbled blobs of ink. Daniel's concerned, garbled face was the last thing I saw.

# CHAPTER 46

# YUR

atalie, it's eight o'clock on a Saturday morning. Did we really have to come to a museum today?" Ryan asked, exasperated as he pursued Natalie up a massive, winding staircase.

"One, the Getty is not *a* museum; it's *the* museum," Natalie responded. "And two, yes, we did. You're just lucky I know the staff so well that they let us in before it officially opens."

Natalie bounded up the last few steps, her loose maple hair bouncing off her shoulders. When she reached the top, she turned back and put her hands on her hips victoriously.

"We've been putting this assignment off for weeks and it's due next Monday," she said. "If we're going to finish our art history report on the Baroque period, we have to pick a painting for our final subject study today."

"Couldn't we have just looked up these pictures online, though? Why did we have to drive all the way out here?"

"Simple," Natalie replied as Ryan joined her atop the stairs. "You love track, right? Well, which do you prefer—running on the beach or running on a treadmill at a crowded 24 Hour Fitness?"

"The beach, obviously," Ryan answered. "The atmosphere changes the whole experience."

"It's the same thing with paintings," Natalie said, gesturing around her. "Seeing a tiny three-by-five screenshot of a beautiful painting on a computer screen is nothing like seeing it in real life hanging in a gallery—the curves of the paint, the brush strokes, the colors and subtle hue changes—" Natalie stopped talking when she noticed Ryan smirking at her.

"What?"

"Nothing," he said. "You really love this stuff, don't you?"

"If by 'this stuff' you mean art, then yes. I do. I always have. I probably feel about paintings the same way you feel about running—like I can never get enough, like they make me feel alive, like they're not just a hobby, they're—"

"A passion," Ryan finished.

"Exactly." Natalie nodded.

The pair continued down the empty hallway.

"So you come here a lot?" Ryan asked after a minute.

"Whenever I get the chance," she replied wistfully. "But between school and scholarship applications and taking care of my mom and my two after-school jobs, I don't get to come as often as I used to."

"I'm sorry," Ryan said.

"It's not your fault," Natalie responded. "And anyway, maybe I don't get to make a lot of new memories here, but I've got some great old ones. My first memory ever is of here, actually. When I was five, my parents brought me to the Getty for the first time and I remember playing in the gardens out back. After that, my dad brought me here every weekend he could get off work. He's the one that got me into art history."

"You must know every painting on these walls by heart then," Ryan commented as they rounded a corner.

"Maybe the permanent collections," Natalie said. "But the Getty gets a lot of visiting collections from across the world. My favorite painting, for example, hasn't been here since my seventh birthday."

"Which one's that?"

Natalie opened her mouth to speak, but her lips tightened. "Forget it; you don't care."

"I wouldn't ask if I didn't," Ryan countered. "Come on, tell me what it is."

"Never mind. We should change the subject before my nerdiness knocks you down a social peg."

Ryan frowned but dropped the subject.

Eventually the pair saw a sign that read "Wonders of the Baroque Period." They entered a part of the museum that housed a long stretch of oil paintings. They walked in silence for a few minutes before Ryan stopped and pointed.

"Check out the mustache on that guy," he said.

Natalie took a look at the painting of a middle-aged, heavily-mustached man. "Yeah, not very flattering. It's a good thing they never identified the subject of this Rembrandt. His descendants would've been seriously embarrassed."

"Makes for a good laugh, though. Wanna do our report on him?"

"Rembrandt's *A Polish Nobleman*? Pass. There are way better paintings from the 1600s to choose from. Rembrandt is too predictable a choice. And the colors he uses depress me. I want us to pick something with a little more heart."

"All right, what would you suggest?" Ryan asked.

Natalie pursed her lips and looked around. After a moment, her eyes widened and she smiled. "This one."

She trotted across the room and paused at a painting. It was of a young girl. She wore a bronze dress and her hair was wrapped in a pale blue and yellow headscarf. Her face was radiant—flawless, glowing skin, pink lips that caught the light, and the most elegant nose. The girl was looking over her shoulder and seemed to be torn between saying something and keeping silent—her mouth barely open as she held syllables on her tongue. Her eyes bore a hint of mystery, contemplation, sadness, and also the hidden joy of a secret. A single plump pearl earring hung from her left ear and shined like her eyes.

"Johannes Vermeer's *Girl with a Pearl Earring*," Natalie said as she and Ryan came to stand before it. "This is my favorite Baroque piece. See how Vermeer uses red and brown ochres to define shadows on the subject's face and create definition and depth? And check out the warmth of the colors in her clothes. Then there's that look in her eyes. It's my favorite quality about the painting."

"What kind of special colors did he use to do that?"

Natalie shook her head. "It's not about the colors," she said. "That's why I like this painting so much. It not only exemplifies artistic skill, it exemplifies soul, which can't be broken down to technique or a specific kind of paint. While we can analyze the rest of the factors of the work, soul can't be scrutinized that way. You can't explain it; you just feel it."

Natalie scowled when she glanced over and saw Ryan smirking at her again. "Stop looking at me like that."

"Sorry—it's cool to see someone get so excited about something. I think the last time I saw Tara get that passionate about anything was . . ." He paused for a second. "You know, I can't think of an example."

"Well, that's what you get for dating a blonde robot with the personality of frozen yogurt."

"Hey, we talked about this. I know you guys don't like each other, but no bad-mouthing my girlfriend to my face, okay?"

"Sorry." Natalie sighed. "It slipped out. But if you wanted to be in a Tara-Bashing-Free-Zone, you shouldn't have partnered with me on this project."

"True, but you owe me. I helped you study for that chemistry test last month, and now I need you to return the favor by sharing some of your art history wisdom with me. You're the smartest kid in the class and I'm barely passing."

This time Natalie smirked. "Say it again."

"You're the smartest kid in class."

"No, not that. The other thing."

"What? That I'm barely passing? Why?"

"No reason." She shrugged. "It's just nice to be reminded that even Mr. Perfect isn't perfect at *everything*."

Ryan rolled his eyes. "I hate it when you call me that. I'm *not* perfect."

"Clearly," Natalie scoffed, bemused. "I only want to make sure *you* know that. A healthy dose of humility is good for guys like you every now and again."

"Well, Miss Humility, are we done here? I've got other places to be that don't involve schoolwork."

"Almost done," Natalie said. "I just want you to do one thing before we go."

"What's that?"

"I want you to really look at this painting," Natalie said seriously. "This is important. Look at this girl and forget everything I've told you, and everything you've learned at school, and tell me what you see."

Ryan crossed his arms and focused on the painting. He stared at its pale, enigmatic subject for a few beats before Natalie leaned over to him.

"So?"

He turned and met Natalie's eyes. "You know what I see, Natalie? I see a girl who's smart, passionate, and truly original, but is trying her best to keep those parts of herself a secret because she's afraid of what the world would do to her if she ever owned up to them."

I opened my eyes to find a mouse staring at me.

I yelped with surprise and launched myself upright. The mouse squeaked and dove off my chest. It landed in the grass beside me, blinked, then scampered off without a word.

Fully awake, I glanced around at my surroundings. I was lying in a field of wildflowers. About twenty feet to my left was a tiny city. And by "tiny city" I didn't mean in population; I meant in proportion.

The buildings could not have been more than five feet tall. Even the ones that were intended to be skyscrapers were barely taller than me. In short (pun intended), it was adorable. A plethora of mice in colorful jackets and hats scurried about the itty-bitty metropolis—looking like moving marshmallows.

My contentment at the cute sight was cut short by the searing pain in my left shoulder. The exact spot where the StalkWalker had bitten me was bandaged up, but the area around the wound was much greener now; the entire upper half of my arm was inked with a sketchy, green rash. What's worse? Beneath the greenish tint was not skin.

I poked my bicep and almost had a heart attack. The area that should have felt like my arm felt far squishier and pricklier. My eyes narrowed. It was straw! The upper half of my left arm was turning to straw!

Immediately I leapt to my feet, but nearly fell over again from the dizziness. The lower half of my arm was still human, but the green discoloration was spreading and I found it difficult to flex my fingers.

I was on top of a hill. In the distance, I could still see the North Mountains and the Plain of the Forgotten. We hadn't gone very far, maybe a couple of miles.

I peeled back my bandage slightly. The black bite marks had grown deeper and projected sparks of the magic green energy the monster had injected into me. I covered up the wound just as the mouse I'd scared off returned with my friends, Kevin, and several other mice.

"Glad you're up," Jason said. "Now we can get going. You've been asleep for half an hour and we have to move quickly if we're gonna get you to the Wizard before that spreads." He pointed at my gross arm. "Kevin says traditional antidotes like the one SJ made won't work on that. The StalkWalker's bite is one part poison, one part nasty magic."

I clutched my head and blinked hard, trying to process Jason's words. My vision was vibrating slightly—the colors of the sky, fields, and petite city kept merging together, making it hard to focus.

"Wait. Sorry. What's happening to my arm?" I asked.

"You were bitten by a StalkWalker," Kevin replied. "But your friends got you out before too much of their spark was injected into you, so you still have a chance to make it to the Wizard before . . ."

"Before what?"

Blue grimaced. "Before you turn into a brainless scarecrow."

"*What?*" I freaked out.

"Calm down," Kevin said. "The Wizard has a cure and you should have no trouble getting to him before it spreads beyond repair. In the meantime, we have applied some ointment to the injury to slow down the transformation and keep most of your vitals in check."

"Do you think you are well enough to travel?" SJ asked.

"Considering the alternative if I don't, yeah," I responded. "Let's move."

Unfortunately, that was easier said than done. I took one step forward and almost fell over again. Luckily Daniel caught me by my good arm and held me upright. I appreciated the save, but felt weird being this close to him. It was only last night that I'd rejected his apology and told him I didn't want to return our friendship to the way it was. He had to be mad at me, or semi-hurt at the very least.

I pulled away from Daniel, but realized that while I could stand, walking was a lot more difficult. "Guys, I don't know if I can make it all the way back to the Emerald City on foot," I said.

"Don't worry," Kevin interceded. "You won't be. Follow us. We'll show you a better way." Our mousey friend and his rodent companions scampered down the hill. Blue, Jason, and SJ followed them.

Daniel looked at me. "Do you want me to carry you?"

"Do you want me to smack you?"

He smirked. "All right, just put your arm around my neck and hold on to me at least. The last thing you want to do is to go rolling down this hill and add embarrassment to injury, right?"

"Right," I admitted begrudgingly.

"Well, come on," Daniel said as he leaned over enough for me to wrap my good arm around his shoulders.

My emotions tensed. He was far too close for comfort, but I went along with it. Together, we made our way to the base of the hill. I spotted a crimson insignia etched into the Yellow Brick Road. Kevin and his mouse friends sat in pairs on the bricks that surrounded the insignia, forming the shape of a hexagon.

"When Glinda took power," Kevin explained, "many Ozians began to vanish. Even though she can't leave the North Mountains, her flying monkeys can, and they can swoop in at any time and make off with you. Soon it no longer became safe for us to use the Yellow Brick Road. So the Wizard established the Yellow Underground Railroad. The YUR for short. Each stop is marked by one of these emblems and requires a touch code to gain access."

Kevin addressed his mousy cohorts. "Ready team? Let's show 'em."

On three, all the assembled mice jumped in the air and came down on their bricks at the same time. The six bricks lit up with a bright, temporary flash.

Kevin and his gang proceeded to hop around the bricks in a synchronized pattern. Every brick they landed on lit up. I watched the sequence closely. When the fifteenth brick in the series had been activated, the crimson insignia flashed. When it did, the mice hurried off the road.

The bricks around the blazing insignia began to retract. They pulled away like a living trap door, revealing a yellow staircase that descended below the earth.

We followed Kevin down the steps in awe. Directly beneath the Yellow Brick Road was an underground railway system. The walkway was gray tile, the benches and tracks were sleek silver, and the walls were made of some kind of reflective, green-tinted metal.

A yellow subway suddenly zoomed out of the tunnel behind us with a rush of wind that blew my hair and dress into a tizzy, just like it blew Blue's cape and SJ's braided ponytail.

"Perfect timing," Kevin said.

The transport came to a stop in front of us. When its doors slid open, a handful of people stepped out in addition to six mice, a porcupine with a top hat accompanied by his lady porcupine, and three dwarves. They nodded cordially to our group before walking past us and up the stairs.

*Huh. So this was the YUR that Harry mentioned.*

"The Emerald City is the fifth stop on this route," Kevin said. "When you get off, follow the other passengers to the surface and you'll be good to go."

"Thank you, Kevin," SJ said. "You have been most kind and helpful."

"And thanks for the patch-up job too," I added, gesturing to my bandage. "That and the major save back in the Maze of the Mindless."

"Any time," Kevin responded. "There are two types of mice out there—those that care, and those that don't. And if I'm going to be Mouse King one day, my court and I have a responsibility to always be the former."

"That is very honorable," SJ commented.

"Yeah, well, my great-grandfather cast a shadow on my family's rule a long time ago when he led a mass genocide across Toyland, so I wouldn't say our actions are honorable so much as they are recompense. Since his passing we've tried to repair our relationship with the realm by being as kind to others as possible, but most aren't so open to our help. Obviously, they still don't trust us. I just hope one day our efforts to change speak for themselves and people believe we're not what we once were, you know?"

I bent down and crouched in front of Kevin so as to better look him the eye. "Don't worry," I said simply. "They will."

The five of us boarded the crowded subway. The seats were neither choice, nor together. Jason and Blue headed for a couple in back. SJ rode solo up front. The last two empty seats were by a window in the middle. Daniel sat first. I hesitated, but with no other place to go, I sat next to him. After about a minute, the glass doors slid shut and the subway started to move again.

Seated across the aisle was a noblewoman who I imagined was also headed for the Emerald City. She wore a floor-length, indigo velvet dress with a bustle on the rear that made it difficult for her to sit. The bustle did balance out the hat she wore, though. Which was unfathomably large.

Behind SJ was a family of White Rabbits—two babies, two parents, and one teenager wearing a beanie with cutouts for his ears. He reminded me of Harry, only more withdrawn. He seemed very distracted by some sort of handheld game he was playing.

In the seats behind Daniel and me, there were a dozen dwarves in work attire. I was particularly interested in one that had orange eyebrows the size of caterpillars, but I turned away in a hurry when he noticed my staring.

"How you holding up, Knight?" Daniel asked.

"Um, fine," I said. "Just keeping a low profile."

"Is that even possible for you?"

"I think my chances only get smaller the more I morph into a mutated scarecrow," I replied as I waggled my super gross arm to illustrate the point.

Regrettably, I made the gesture right as a small blond boy walked by. He saw my arm and his eyes widened. He wailed for his mother before running back to the other side of the car.

Feeling self-conscious, I pivoted away from the stares of the other commuters.

"Here," Daniel said with a sigh. He removed his dark brown leather jacket and offered it to me. "You can borrow it until you're decent again."

I was a bit shocked by the gesture. The last thing I expected was his kindness after being pretty stern with him last night. We hadn't really talked since then. I was surprised he was acting so normal and so nice.

"Uh, thanks," I responded slowly, putting the jacket on. "And while we're on the subject, thanks for before as well."

"Before?"

"Yeah. I owe you and Jason a thank you for your help back in the cornfield. I thought I was done for."

"Knight, you've beaten plenty of enemies and monsters. I doubt you would have been taken down by a scarecrow in the end."

"Nonetheless," I continued, "I appreciate you coming back for me. Especially after the way I . . . After I said that . . ." I exhaled with frustration at my inability to speak. "Well anyway, thanks."

"Knight, it's no big deal." He shrugged. "Forget it."

"How can I?" I asked, exasperated by his calmness. "And more importantly, how can *you*? I made it clear I don't want to be friends like we used to be. Not to mention I was kind of a jerk to you last night after you told me about your family. So why are you still being so nice to me?"

"For starters, you've had a pretty rough day. While you were asleep, Jason and SJ told Blue and me about how you were almost captured by Alex and Mauvrey in the Ruined City. I imagine confronting them after everything they've done must've hurt."

*It did. More than I can say.*

"So I figure you don't need me giving you grief about last night on top of it," Daniel said. "And while I wish you felt differently, I get why you think we can't go back to the way things were. We had something good and I screwed it up. I didn't just break your trust; I shoved it back in your face. That's a hard thing to forgive and I shouldn't have expected you to, least of all on the day your entire home life fell apart. That's why I'm not mad about your decision. Let's just forget I said anything and move forward, okay?"

"Okay," I responded. I fixed my gaze on the floor of the subway.

"One more thing, Knight . . ."

I glanced up.

"For the record, whatever kind of friends we are, we are still friends. Which means I'll always come back for you. Whether you want me to or not."

I studied him for a second as I tried to understand his words. They were kind and altruistic; genuine and welcome; spoken plainly and without caveat.

I felt dizzy again as the pain in my arm pulsed. The ache caused me to wince and blink as my vision faltered and drowsiness filled my head.

"I think I'm going to close my eyes for a minute," I said to Daniel. "Wake me when we get there?" He nodded and I leaned my head back against the seat as my eyelids sank like heavy curtains.

# CHAPTER 47

## The Cure

ver the next half hour, dreams flashed through my head. They were jumbled and faster than usual, possibly because of the StalkWalker poison coursing through my veins.

An enormous goose stared down at me. A bunch of pumpkins flew through a mist-covered forest. Chance Darling and Daniel swordfought in a combat arena, which must've been at their school. Lastly, a huge dragon with black scales and red eyes snarled, emanating pure, untempered hatred.

I woke with the ferocity of the creature's expression burned into my brain. Right as I stirred, the subway's intercom came on.

"Attention passengers: we are now arriving in the Emerald City. Please make sure you take all belongings and small children with you and remember: the Wizard is good; the Wizard protects us; all hail the Wizard."

"A bit overzealous with his message, isn't he?" I yawned as I stretched to life.

"At least he's consistent," Daniel said, nodding to the fleet of propaganda posters lining the walls of the station.

The sliding doors opened and our group merged with the other commuters migrating to the south end of the platform. The first two passengers who arrived at the back wall worked together to twist a series of green levers. On the final pull, the wall shook and moved to the side, revealing another bright yellow staircase. Light and sound from the city above flooded in.

I was dismayed to see a robotic sphere scanning passengers

at the top of the stairs, much like the one on the outer wall of the city. Just before the robot turned in our direction, I whirled around Daniel and stood perfectly still behind him. The robot's red light scanned over him, but I was able to elude its eye. I walked carefully in step with Daniel so the machine wouldn't see me, then spun around his other side as it went on to scan SJ.

Temporary adrenaline made up for my wooziness and I hustled up the rest of the stairs as fast as I could. I was in no mood to fill out more paperwork, and I didn't know if the StalkWalker poison inside of me would be considered dark magic and set off an alert.

On the streets we hailed a cab-carriage and before long we arrived back at the Emerald Tower. Unfortunately, the great doors were now closed.

"Yo, you with the hat!" Blue called to the fedora-donning gatekeeper peeking out from his watchtower. "Open up. We need a follow-up appointment with the Wizard!"

The gatekeeper darted inside the watchtower. There was silence for a few seconds, then some miscellaneous clanging sounds before he stuck his head out again and looked down at us.

"I'm sorry, miss," he responded. "General visiting hours are over for the day."

"But this is an emergency," Jason called. "Can you tell the Wizard the protagonists he talked to earlier about Paige Tomkins need to see him?"

"His Great and Powerful-ness already knows you are here," the gatekeeper responded. "He does not wish to see you. So please, have a nice day and be on your way. The Wizard is good; the Wizard protects us; all hail the—"

"The Wizard is either going to open these doors, or call security when we break them down. Either way, we're seeing him!" I shouted.

"Miss, please. He doesn't have time—"

"*Time?* I'm turning into a scarecrow, you jackwagon. He's going to make time."

The gatekeeper scurried inside his post, shut the window, and lowered the blinds.

"Stand back," I said as the hand of my good arm began to glow prematurely.

"Crisa, you sure that's a good idea?" Jason asked. "Can you even control your magic when you're like this?"

"I guess we'll find out." I pressed my good hand over the gap between the two front doors so I was touching them both. I took a deep breath, ignoring the pain of the StalkWalker poison, driving my weakness away.

*Focus. Just focus.*

I exerted all the strength I had at my disposal.

*Open. Take us to the Wizard. And protect us from any guards who might try and stop us along the way.*

Golden energy flowed through me as I gave the doors temporary life—meekly at first, but then in a burst that spread over their entire framework. The doors quivered, then flung open.

My friends and I stepped through the entrance. There were guards in golden armor at the ready on the other side, but their threat was meaningless. Both doors dramatically ripped off their hinges. One dropped to the floor at our feet; the other shot forward and created a barrier from the guards. The five of us leapt aboard the flattened door, which levitated off the ground and continued moving once we'd stepped on. As we proceeded toward the Emerald Tower, the second door shielded us from the guards trying to stop us.

It was rather incredible. Although my outright commands had been short and sweet, now that my magic had been so heavily trained, it was like the objects I gave life to could read paragraphs' worth of intention and vision without me needing to specify everything. They responded to my will on a much more cognitive level.

When we arrived at the throne room we found the entrance locked shut. The levitating door allowed us to dismount before converting itself into a battering ram. It wasn't long before we busted in. That door having completed its task, it went inanimate again. Instead of giving it more life, I placed my hand on the one attached to the throne room doorway and infused fresh energy into it.

"Seal the entrance until I say otherwise," I commanded.

The door shut curtly behind us with a loud slam.

I turned around. Julian was sitting on his throne, looking alarmed. He reached for the lever near his seat, but Blue hurled one of her throwing knives at him—pinning the sleeve of his jacket to the wall.

"I don't think that'll be necessary," she said as we approached.

Julian glanced at the knife piercing his fine silk jacket—gulping as he appreciated Blue's precision. Her own shoulder wound had clearly healed.

"Children!" Julian said, darting his eyes back to us. "I wasn't expecting you."

"Clearly," I said. "You sent us to that cornfield like cows to slaughter. Paige told us herself when we found her; you send anyone looking for her to the Maze of the Mindless so they'll be turned into brainless scarecrows."

Our host shrugged. "It was nothing personal. Paige and I have an arrangement. When she came to Oz she requested my help and paid me well for it. She told me her plan about getting turned into a scarecrow. All she asked of me was that whenever people came searching for her I would send them straight to the maze. She knew anyone who went after her would never make it past the StalkWalkers. I was simply holding up my end of the bargain."

"By pretending to help us when you were really sending us to a death sentence," Daniel clarified.

"Exactly," Julian agreed. "Not the most honorable of actions—I admit—but when I strike a deal I live up to the terms, regardless of their moral ambiguity." An intrigued smile crept across his lips. "How *did* you make it out, by the way? No one ever has. The fact that you did is quite impressive."

"We had help," Jason responded. "Paige trusted us and warned us to get out. Then the heir to the mouse throne led the way. We also had SJ's portable potions, which pack a punch."

"Portable potions?" Julian said, freeing his sleeve before coming over to us. "Sounds interesting. Would you show me?"

The room shook a bit as Julian's guards banged on the door.

"Only if you give us something first," SJ replied. "Two somethings actually. First and foremost, we were told you have an antidote for the bite of a StalkWalker. Crisa needs it. Now."

Julian's gaze shifted toward me. I removed Daniel's jacket—revealing my arm. Julian's eyebrows shot up, as did mine when I realized the poison had spread to my hand. It was now half straw, half skin.

"My, you do need a little of my special potion, don't you? Follow me. My workshop is in the other room."

Julian led us to a door on the far right of the throne room. Before going through, he pressed an intercom button on the wall. "Sasha, tell the guards they can stop trying to break in here," he said. "I'm fine. And they're probably scuffing the floor."

"Yes, Your Great and Powerfulness. Right away," the intercom responded.

"Come along," Julian said, leading us into the room beyond.

We entered the most elaborate potions lab I'd ever seen. Glass tubes ran everywhere, twisting along the walls and ceiling, interconnected by various orbs. Glistening tables were covered with fine platinum equipment. A large fireplace roared in the corner with green flames. Vials and bottles containing colorful liquids and goop lined the wall between massive cabinets. It looked like the blood samples of a rainbow. I was awestruck. I could only imagine how SJ felt.

None of this, though, could compare to the large cauldron at the center of the room. It bubbled with a magma-like substance, glowed like a mutant tadpole, and smelled vaguely of lemon zest.

Julian went over to one of the cabinets. He opened it, withdrew a jar, and gestured for me to sit on a stainless steel stool. I handed Daniel back his jacket and took a seat as Julian placed the jar on the table and put on a pair of blue rubber gloves. "Rubber doesn't conduct electricity," he explained as he removed the bandage from my arm.

The wound sparked with defiance, making me want to gag, but Julian was not fazed. He scooped up a handful of the jar's navy paste and spread it over my upper arm. The antidote did its work quicker than I could have imagined.

Instantly, the magic sparks around the bite marks disappeared. The green rash receded up my arm until it was gone completely. My skin and bone solidified, the feeling came back to my hand, and I soon felt strong again.

Satisfied, Julian ran a cloth under the sink and wiped the blue paste from my arm. To my delight, practically every trace of the wound was gone. All that was left were the bite marks themselves, and they'd shrunk to the size of thin pencil lines.

I hopped off the stool and flexed my fingers. "Wow, that worked fast," I said. "Thanks."

"You're welcome, my dear," Julian replied. "I'm glad you got here when you did. Another couple of hours and there would have been nothing I could do for you. This antidote only works in the early phase of brainless scarecrow transformation. Now, SJ is it?" he turned to my friend. "If I could just have a look at those portable potions of yours . . ."

SJ crossed her arms. "I believe I said there were *two* things you needed to give us."

Julian couldn't help but grin. "Yes, of course. And what was the second?"

"Answers," she replied flatly. "Paige told us that you are the only person who knows how to regain her memories."

"Yes, that's true."

"So how do we do it?"

Julian rubbed his neck and grimaced. "Honestly it's a fool's errand. I'd be doing you more harm than good by telling you."

"With all due respect . . ." I began. "Actually, forget respect. We came here for information and you're going to give it to us. We're trying to *protect* Paige. She wouldn't have told us the truth if she didn't trust us. We're the good guys here. If the bad guys find out how to recover Paige's memories and learn where our realm's genies are, we're all toast. You *have* to help us."

"You talk a mean game, protagonist," Julian responded.

"Crisa," I corrected.

"Ever think about going into politics?"

"I'll check out the booth at my school's next career fair. Now, how do we get Paige's memories back?"

Julian pressed a button on the back wall—another intercom. "Eva, I'm in the lab. I've got some protagonists who survived a visit to Paige Tomkins and are now asking about Glinda and the Passage Perelous. Can you come in here?"

We waited in silence for a half minute before a metallic door slid open. An elegant woman strode in. She wore an ink-colored, floor-length gown with long sleeves decorated in tiny dark-blue crystals. Her décolletage plunged in a deep, if not scandalous, neckline. The woman's black hair was pulled back into a half-ponytail of loose curls. Her fair complexion contrasted with her dark blue eyes.

"So," she said, "you want to know about my sister."

Had I been drinking a beverage, I would have spit it out.

"Your *sister*?" I said. "But that would mean you're—"

"The former Wicked Witch of the West," the woman replied coolly. "But you can just call me Eva."

Jason tilted his head. "But aren't you supposed to be—"

"Dead?" Blue interrupted.

"Blue!" SJ piped.

"What?" Blue countered. "You know it's true. It's in every version of *The Wizard of Oz* anyone's ever read. The Wicked Witch of the West always melts when Dorothy hits her with a pail of water."

"Yes, well, that is the trouble with such popular stories isn't it," Eva mused, her slender fingers tracing the countertop. "People just keep retelling them over and over again. There is a new twist here and there to freshen up the adaption, but no one ever asks the most obvious question."

"And that would be?" Daniel asked.

"What happened next?"

Eva stood beside Julian and slid her arm through his. "If they did, my husband would not be the only one with the knowledge you are currently after."

Blue and I exchanged a look. "He's your husband?" we echoed.

"It's a simple story, really," Eva went on. "Dorothy's bucket of water did not destroy me. I mean, honestly, how people can even believe that in the first place is beyond me. I was a powerful witch. If water was all it took, no one would've ever had to destroy me. All they would've had to do was wait until the rainy season. But I digress. The point is, the water melted me, yes, but that reaction was only a temporary state while the water did what it was intended to do—cure me of my Pure Magic."

I couldn't formulate a single syllable. A rush of hope filled my heart.

"I thought Pure Magic Disease couldn't be cured," Blue said slowly, watching me out of the corner of her eye.

"For the most part that's true," Eva replied. "But every rule has an exception. All three of my sisters and I were carriers of Pure Magic Disease. It made our magic strong, but—guessing by the expressions on your faces—you know that such power comes with a price."

Eva sighed. "The disease affected my two older sisters first, the former Wicked Witches of the East and South—Dara and Louise. Dara was killed when Dorothy dropped a house on her. Louise was killed by her subjects during the Great Tin Man Revolt.

"My Pure Magic began to turn me on my twenty-third birthday," Eva went on. "There was an incident—a boyfriend dumped me and in my rage I lost control over my powers. Dark emotion overtook my mental clarity, and I used my abilities for revenge, inflicting mortal harm on my ex. I convinced myself at the time that this incident was an outlier, but I was never the same after it happened. I'd crossed what is called a Malice Line. The wickedness came more easily after that; over time my abilities became increasingly governed by fury, not focus. And then, well, that's all she wrote. Or I suppose I should say that's all *he* wrote. I should have never let that L. Frank Baum leave here without signing a non-disclosure agreement."

"Dear, you know the innovations that he and the other storytellers on visa have traded with us over the years have been invaluable to our economy's growth," Julian said.

Eva rolled her eyes and turned toward him. "Yes, I know. But do all of them really have to profit from adaptations that make me so horrid and ugly?"

"They're just stories, Eva."

Daniel cleared his throat, interceding before their conversation could drift more off topic. "I'm sorry. But what does all this have to do with why the water didn't melt you?"

"Everything, my dear boy," Julian said. "If it were not for that bucket of water, Eva would still be the terrible witch she was before. Dorothy did not simply splash her with any random liquid. Before coming to face her, our friend from Kansas went on a quest to obtain special water with magical properties."

"Not that Mr. Baum put that in his first book because apparently it interfered with the flow of his third act." Eva scoffed. "Writers. They can crank out a dozen sequels to one idea, but have a fit over the word count."

"Back to the point though . . ." Julian continued. "My father, the former Wizard of Oz, told Dorothy that there was only one sure-fire way to defeat the Wicked Witch of the West, and that was by curing her of her Pure Magic. The sole opportunity for which was rapidly approaching—the Vicennalia Aurora. Have you heard of it?"

"We have, actually," I said. "My family was preparing for it before . . ."

My mind went blank for a second. A swift succession of violent images flashed through my head. Fire, collapsing structures, antagonists, Mauvrey, Alex. I swallowed down the agony of my memories and gathered the strength to continue the conversation.

"It's happening in a month, right?" I asked.

"It might be a few weeks away in your realm," Eva responded. "However, ours is right around the corner. Time in Oz, Neverland, and Camelot moves much slower than in other realms, like Book and the Superdome for instance. While the Vicennalia Aurora will occur in every Wonderland simultaneously at half past seven, it will be at different points in each realm's individual timeline."

"What some people don't know is that the Vicennalia Aurora is more than a mere celebration," Julian chimed in. "It is a day when magic in all the Wonderlands is in flux."

"I'm aware," I responded.

"Care to recap for those of us who aren't?" Blue asked.

"Certainly." Julian nodded. "The Vicennalia Aurora is a name we came up with to define the massive energy fluctuation that periodically courses through the Wonderlands. For the ONC— the time zone that affects Oz, Neverland, and Camelot—the fluctuation occurs about every five and a half years. For other realms this varies. For example, with Book I believe the event only transpires every twenty-five years.

"Because of the fluctuation, on the night of the Vicennalia Aurora the magic in every Wonderland is unstable. Enchantments and curses can be easier or harder to break, certain types of magic can become stronger while others become weaker, and people with Pure Magic are more vulnerable as their powers grow more erratic. This is why the Vicennalia Aurora is the only time that people with Pure Magic can be cleansed by the sole cure for their disease—The Four Waters of Paradise."

Blue bit her lip. "Hold on, I've heard that term before. It's from *Le Morte d'Arthur*, Sir Mallory's tales of Camelot and the Knights of the Round Table. We were reading it in class this semester. The Four Waters of Paradise were used to cure Sir Gawain when he'd been mortally wounded in battle."

"Very good," Eva replied with a nod. "Those waters come from a special spring on the Isle of Avalon, which lies in a dangerous part of Camelot. The waters are the purest, most potent form of magical cleanser that has ever existed and accordingly, are the only way to cleanse a person of Pure Magic.

"Dorothy was able to brave the journey through Camelot, collect a vial of the water from the spring, and bring it back to Oz," Eva explained. "All she had to do was mix it with a bucket of regular water and dose me with it. Which she succeeded in doing.

"The cure melted me down at first, but that was merely a side effect. The properties of the waters were able to work their way through me and every blood cell was thoroughly washed before I magically solidified again. When I did, I was cured. I still possessed the ability that came with my Pure Magic, but it was no longer as powerful and I was no longer tied to the disease. I was free from the darkness."

Oh, wow . . . I'd never heard such wonderful news. Liza was

wrong. Lenore was wrong. Everyone in my realm who knew about Pure Magic was wrong. Maybe the magic itself couldn't be removed, but there was a remedy to my disease that would keep my heart from turning dark. I could be saved. The hope burned inside me so strongly it felt like my arteries had caught fire.

I was going to find the cure.

"Though while I was saved," Eva went on, "the same could not be said for my younger sister. Glinda possessed Pure Magic as well, but for a long time we all thought she'd beaten the disease. She was so good, you see—so noble, kind-hearted, determined to stay above wickedness. However, about a year ago she began to turn. Her heart struggled against it, but eventually she was claimed by the darkness inside her. The rest you already know. Her minions have terrorized Oz since she went full evil seven months ago. And they will continue to wreak havoc if no one challenges her. Thank goodness for Paige, though. She is the reason that Glinda is trapped in the North Mountains and can't unleash wickedness on the realm firsthand. Her mountainous lair is protected by a powerful enchantment. Are you familiar with the concept of In and Out Spells?"

Jason nodded. "More than most."

"Right, well, In and Out Spells are complicated magic," Eva said. "While many Fairy Godmothers can muster small, temporary versions on their own, the large and permanent ones usually require a team. However, Julian is the greatest potionist in all of Oz. So when Paige came to us, he created a powerful potion to combine with Paige's magic, and the magic of the pixies in our realm, to form a hybrid. The resulting In and Out Spell over the North Mountains is not as strong—people can go in, but not out, and it doesn't prevent other living creatures like crows and flying monkeys from passing through. But it holds Glinda back, and that is enough for now."

"This is where we come in, isn't it?" Blue said bluntly.

"Yes," Eva replied. "You survived the Maze of the Mindless. But if you truly want to retrieve the knowledge that Paige has lost, you will need to journey past the In and Out Spell around the North Mountains into Glinda's lair where she keeps her memory stone—it contains the memories off all the brainless scarecrows. The problem, of course, is that even if you manage to defeat her and free the memories, you would have no way of getting out. The In and Out Spell would prevent you from leaving."

"Actually, it wouldn't," Daniel said. "We're immune to In and Out Spells."

"Not true," SJ said.

We all pivoted toward her.

"I thought you told us we'd be immune to all In and Out Spells after we broke the one around the Indexlands last semester," I commented.

"Yes, but that refers to all *traditional* In and Out Spells that have already been created. The one around the North Mountains is not an ordinary In and Out Spell. It has been mixed with potions and pixie magic to create some sort of new hybrid. Our immunity will not cover that. If we enter the North Mountains, we will be trapped as surely as Glinda."

"Which means that if you want the memory stone, and want to escape Glinda's lair, you will need to make the journey during the Vicennalia Aurora," Julian said. "The magic flux can make enchantments easier to break, so the Vicennalia Aurora will be your only window to pass back through the In and Out Spell unharmed."

"But the magic flux is unpredictable," I argued. "It can make certain types of magic stronger or weaker. How can we know for sure that this In and Out Spell will be affected in the latter way? What if the Aurora actually makes it more powerful and we're trapped forever?"

"The magic flux is unpredictable *to an extent*," Julian clarified. "While the flux's effects are at their peak during the Aurora, in the days leading up to the event you can begin to see signs of how the flux will manifest. Paige, the pixies, and I also created another, less powerful In and Out Spell over the crest of the city. It begins at the top of the outer wall. We reformulated this spell with the sole intention of doing what the first spell did not—keep out animals like flying monkeys and crows. We thought we were successful, but recently birds have been getting through, including the crows that work as Glinda's minions. Like that one." He pointed at an open window high up on the laboratory wall.

There was a shady crow perched there staring at us. It had a gray collar on its neck with a tiny black box and blinking red light at the center. Julian threw a paperweight at it. The bird dodged the projectile and flew off before our host could chuck another.

"Glinda has many crows outfitted with video cameras," Eva enlightened. "They spy on us and report back to her. The second In and Out Spell is supposed to keep them from getting into the Emerald City, but several have made it through in the past two days. This In and Out Spell is weakening because of the Aurora. That's a clear sign that when the event actually occurs, all similar spells will be penetrable."

My thoughts darted to Alderon. Did that mean the In and Out Spell around the antagonists' kingdom would be penetrable during the Vicennalia Aurora? Lady Agnue said that Lena Lenore always stationed Fairy Godmothers there to reinforce the spell during the event, but I wondered if it would be enough.

"Past the North Mountains In and Out Spell, there is one much bigger catch to getting what you want," Julian said, picking up the conversation anew.

"Why am I not surprised?" Blue huffed.

"The memory stone where Glinda keeps her stolen minds is not an ordinary rock," Julian explained. "Glinda created it from a combination of Jacobee stone, Avalonian glass, and magic to absorb the memories of the brainless scarecrows and keep them trapped inside like bees in a hive . . ."

Hm, if my dreams connected the way I thought, I imagined that had to be the mystical stone filled with green and purple lights that I'd dreamed about earlier in the semester.

"The stone is all but impenetrable," Julian continued. "Before the North Mountains In and Out Spell went up, we sent several armies there to try and rescue the minds of the citizens who'd been turned into scarecrows, but the few survivors who made it back recounted that even our strongest weapons and magic attacks could not pierce it. I suspect that there is only one thing in the Wonderlands that can."

"Which is?" I asked.

"Excalibur," Eva answered solemnly. "It is the most powerful and feared blade in the Wonderlands. Nothing in all the realms is stronger. It can cut through anything, enhances the strength of whoever wields it, and since it was forged from the magic of Avalon, it is immune to magic attacks and possession."

"I thought Excalibur was lost after King Arthur died," SJ said.

"You say lost; I say hidden," Julian replied. "When Arthur died, the sword was returned to the spirit who gifted it to him—the Lady of the Lake. She, the sword, and the Four Waters of Paradise can all be found on the Isle of Avalon. But the Isle of Avalon is almost impossible to get to. It is hidden in the Passage Perelous—an extremely dangerous part of Camelot that has more perils than any place in any of the realms."

"Why am *I* not surprised," SJ huffed, echoing Blue.

"Time is also working against you," Eva commented. "Where you're from the Vicennalia Aurora may be weeks away, but for the ONC it will occur after the sun sets five days from today."

"Five days!" Daniel repeated.

*Five days?* Was that all we had? Our mission to find the Author had taken weeks. How in the name of Book were we going to do this?

"Aside from that," Julian continued, "even if you could get to Excalibur, it might not matter. The Lady of the Lake has made it so that only certain people can claim it. In the seven years since King Arthur has died, no one has managed to do so. What does that tell you?"

"That we'll have to try really, really hard," I joked.

"No." Julian sighed, a look of sadness in his eyes. "It tells you that going after Excalibur is a foolish quest. Dorothy and her allies were able to find and collect the waters from the Isle of Avalon once, but things are different now. In hindsight, I suppose I didn't take luck into account when I looked at their past success."

Julian's voice had grown raspy on the last few syllables, and he glanced at the floor for a moment. Eva put a pale, delicate hand on his shoulder.

"Hey, you okay?" Daniel asked.

Julian stood up straight and cleared his throat.

"Yes, sorry about that," he said. "Look, the point is that I don't advise you go to Camelot. The Passage Perelous is suicide."

"Maybe," I responded. "But it's also necessary."

Julian appeared truly remorseful, but he did not argue any further. Instead, he went to a different cabinet and took out a weathered book and a rolled-up piece of parchment, laying them on a table for us to take a gander. "This is my most up-to-date book on Camelot," Julian explained. "And this is the last map we were able to procure of the land. Maybe they'll help."

"We actually have a map," SJ said. She reached into her magic potions sack and took out the document in question. We looked at our map and Julian's map side by side. They were surprisingly similar.

"Not bad," Julian said. "This looks even more detailed than mine. No one has a complete map of Camelot anymore; they went out of print after Arthur passed. Mine is an antique. Yours?"

"We put it together from a bunch of research and cataloging we did of Camelot, King Arthur, and the Knights of the Round Table," Jason responded.

"Resourceful. I like it. You may just want to note the following though." Julian grabbed a quill from an inkwell and circled four areas in the top section of our map. He then drew a line around another part of the map and made squiggly lines just above it.

A flicker of light and shadow caught my attention—causing me to glance up at the high window. Another crow had parked itself outside the lab and was peering down at us. I glared at it and Eva promptly hurled a sponge at the window, shooing the bird away.

Julian held up our map and pointed at the changes. "These areas I've circled are hot zones for the Questor Beast—a nasty creature you don't want to mess with that lives in the Passage Perelous."

I saw Blue cringe, but I didn't know why.

"The line I've drawn there is my understanding of where you can enter the Passage Perelous," Julian said. "And the squiggles just beyond mark the Shifting Forest. I wish there was a way to go around that, but you have to go through if you want to reach the Isle of Avalon. That's where Dorothy and my . . ." Julian cleared his throat. "That's where the Four Waters of Paradise were discovered." He picked up the book he'd brought out. "This book on Camelot has some sections on other monsters in the Passage Perelous and ways King Arthur and the Knights of the Round Table beat them in the past. It won't help you claim the sword, but it might help you get to the Isle. I recommend starting with the chapter on Arthur."

Julian turned to the right page and handed over the open-faced book. My face dropped. We all gasped when we saw the picture on the first page of the chapter.

Blue snatched the book. "Holy crud, is that—"

"AP," I said.

The portrait of King Arthur on the page was an exact match for the man we'd met at the Lost Boys and Girls camp in Neverland. From his blond hair to the powerful glint in his eyes, every detail was a perfect match.

"King Arthur Pendragon," SJ said in awe, "is AP."

"He's not dead," Blue marveled.

Julian and Eva exchanged a shocked look. "What do you mean he's not dead?" she asked. "Of course he is."

"No, we met him," I said, taking the book from Blue. "He's alive and he's in Neverland." I thought back to the conversations we'd had with him. "AP said he couldn't leave Neverland because he'd been mortally injured in his home realm and the only reason he wasn't dead was because of Neverland's weird time properties."

"And he said that he was killed by his half-brother," Jason chimed in. "King Arthur was killed by his half-brother, Mord-red."

"We met King Arthur!" Blue stated, still struck by the realization.

"And we're going to meet him again," I said. "If Arthur is the only person known to have claimed Excalibur, then he is the only person who can tell us how to do it now." I shut the book and tossed it to Jason. Then I checked my Hole Tracker. I brought up its map and scrolled through the time settings. "There aren't any

Portalscape Portals opening until tomorrow morning, but there is a clockwise Pop-Up Portal opening in two hours. If we want to conserve time—which we need to, given that we only have five days—we should take that. The Wonderland realm sequence goes Oz, Limbo, Portalscape. Once we get to Limbo, our odds are better because we can take another clockwise Pop-Up Portal or a Portalscape Portal and end up in the same place. Then we just take the door straight to Neverland."

"Sounds like a plan," Jason said.

Julian stepped closer to me and studied my Hole Tracker's holographic map, specifically where the shining orange hole of the Pop-Up Portal was being displayed. "I know that area. This hole may be close to some very dangerous territory, but there is a YUR line that runs nearby. If you travel that way it should take you no more than twenty minutes to get there."

"Would the five of you like something to eat before you go?" Eva offered. "If you are embarking on such a harrowing undertaking, the least we can do is make sure you have snacks."

"I'll take that," Blue said. "I definitely burned up my fair share of calories fighting bad guys today."

Julian looked sad again, like he truly regretted saying anything at all. "If the five of you are sure you have to do this, I'm not going to stop you. But remember, you must make it back in five days or you'll miss the Vicennalia Aurora and your chance at rescuing Paige's memories."

"We'll make it back in time," I assured him. "We'll find Arthur, reach Avalon, claim the sword, and get Paige's memory back before the Aurora is over."

*And maybe find the Four Waters of Paradise and cure my Pure Magic in the process*, I hoped.

"I've said it before and I'll say it again, kid," Julian replied, his smile returning. "With all that confidence, you should seriously consider a career in politics, if you survive this."

"Right," I said hesitantly. "Something to look forward to."

# CHAPTER 48

## Ozma

t was two hours until the wormhole opened and only a twenty-minute journey to get there, so we had a moment for a break. After a swift meal, SJ gave Julian some pointers in the ways of the portable potion. Jason and Blue went to read the Camelot book Julian had given us. And Daniel, well, I wasn't sure where he went, but I didn't go looking.

It was making me uncomfortable how nice he was being. His kindness made it a lot harder to keep him at a cold distance. This afternoon I'd realized how easy it would be for me to forgive him and fall into the way things once were. But no matter how tempting, I knew that was a bad idea. A second chance with Daniel would mean a second chance at getting hurt. After all, I had offered Alex a do-over, given him the opportunity to make amends and overcome his betrayal in the Ruined City, but he'd broken my heart again. Who was to say Daniel wouldn't do the same?

After telling the throne room door it could stop barricading people out, I wandered through the majestic Emerald Tower to kill our remaining time. The halls were silent, as if the Tower was being forced to keep its mouth shut. The walls were made of green crystal, the ceilings were high, and a silvery carpet ran through most of the corridors.

As I explored alone, I had to work extra hard to keep my angry, morose thoughts about Alex at bay. Part of me couldn't believe that the destruction of my home had only happened yesterday. We'd experienced so much in the last twenty-four hours that it felt like an eternity ago. But if I allowed myself to think about Alex's betrayal—like I did now—the wounds felt raw and fresh.

I wondered if I would feel this way forever, if this was the kind of pain that could never truly heal. More than anything, I wondered if Alex was completely lost. I'd tried to extend him a hand this morning, and he'd rejected it. But did that mean I should give up on him entirely? Despite his recent malevolence, my heart urged me not to. It compelled me to believe that perhaps twenty-four hours of acting like an antagonist did not erase twenty-one years of him being a protagonist, and being my brother.

I came upon a huge silver door decorated with intricate ironwork. The hallway was an otherwise dead-end, so I turned the brass knob. At first, nothing happened. But then the brass began to warm beneath my fingers. A few seconds later, my hand abruptly started to glow, which confused me since I hadn't summoned my magic.

A small burst of golden light was sucked from my hand and into the door. I watched as the energy flooded through the ironwork like rainwater in the cracks of a sidewalk. A beautiful star design appeared. It flashed brightly for a moment then disappeared. I heard the slide of a bolt and the door opened. Weird.

I stepped inside the room. It was lit by a small skylight and some ever-glowing candlesticks that floated around. Every corner was filled with clutter. There were golden armoires collecting dust, tiaras stored in glass cases, dolls that hadn't been played with in an eternity, and an old fountain shaped like a Star Bird. My attention was drawn to two pieces in the odd collection: a steel shoebox and a throne.

The box was encrusted with many jewels, but a number of chains were wrapped around it to keep it tightly closed. The chains met at the top of the box and were secured through a lock. When I touched the lock, the same phenomenon that occurred with the door repeated. My hand temporarily glowed, then the energy was absorbed into the lock. The box lit up and spoke. "Magic detected. Welcome back, Your Great and Powerful-ness."

Before I had time to process the statement, the chains on the box fell away and the lid popped open. Inside, I discovered a single object—a right shoe.

The shoe was silver with a big red bow at the front. In the center of the bow was a magnificent ruby. I picked up the slipper and turned it over in my hand. There were a few words engraved into the leather at the bottom: Property of Dorothy Gale.

*Hmm. Blue would be disappointed. The different texts regarding* The Wizard of Oz *never agreed on what color Dorothy's magic, home-seeking shoes were. But Blue, like many others, always believed they were ruby red.*

As I wondered where the famous shoe's mate was, I suddenly realized that the ruby in the center of the bow had begun to blink. Then, just as unexpectedly, the slipper flew out of my hands. It began zipping around the room like an angry bird until it crashed through the skylight and flew off. I jumped out of the way to avoid being struck by the glass shards, and fell backward into the lap of the small throne behind me.

*What the heck was that?*

As I sat up, I noticed a name sewn into the throne in small crystals—*Ozma*. I stood and took a closer look at the seat. It was smaller than the throne that belonged to Julian, but more decorative. The cushions were a rich shade of emerald and the gold framework was twisted into intricate spirals and accentuated by glistening gemstones.

I put my pointer finger on the lettering of the O in Ozma and traced the name, wondering about its origins.

"Being reminded of her hurts him too much."

I nearly leapt out of my skin. I whirled around to find Eva standing in the doorway. "That's why Julian keeps all her stuff in here," she continued as she approached.

"I don't understand," I said. "Who is she?" I nodded to the throne. "Who is Ozma?"

"Julian's sister."

"The Wizard of Oz has a sister?"

"Yes," Eva replied. "She was his younger sister. She was also Oz's ruler while Julian was her advisor and second in command. That's the way our royal linage laws work in Oz. The youngest child in the family is the one who inherits the crown. Any other siblings serve as advisors who study magic and master potions for the betterment of the land. That's why Julian has that grand lab and is so fascinated with your friend's portable potions. Before he inherited the throne from Ozma, potions were his main responsibility. He's truly one of the most skilled potionists in all the realms."

I glanced back at the name on the throne then took in the dusty objects in the room with fresh eyes. "So if Julian rules Oz now," I asked, "what happened to Ozma?"

"We don't know exactly," Eva responded. "Before Paige helped us create the In and Out Spell around the North Mountains, Glinda's terror and magic were destroying Oz. She proved too strong to be defeated by traditional means. So Ozma, Dorothy, Julian, and I concluded that the only way to stop her was the same way they stopped me: the Four Waters of Paradise. Six months ago, we agreed that he and I would remain here to safeguard Oz while Dorothy and Ozma embarked on a journey to Camelot to bring back the cure before this next Vicennalia Aurora. But something terrible must have happened, because we haven't heard from them since.

"At first we tried to stay optimistic. Ozma and Dorothy had gone missing before. They were both fearless, despite being so young. Whenever war or threats reared their ugly heads throughout Oz, the two of them went straight into the line of fire to save whoever needed saving or quell the conflict before it escalated. In the process, they've been kidnapped and imprisoned on multiple occasions—sometimes for weeks at a time. But they always eventually escaped or were rescued. So Julian and I held out hope. But that grew harder to sustain as the weeks went on. After a month, we sent scouts to Camelot to try and find Ozma and Dorothy, but the searches were fruitless. After four months passed, we began to accept the horrid truth that they might not return ever again."

"That's why Julian was so against us going to Camelot," I thought aloud.

Eva nodded. "Camelot has always been a dangerous place, but since Arthur's passing it has become even more perilous. He and

Gwenivere left no heirs, so the crown has changed hands from one ruthless ruler to the next. Camelot is in chaos—civil wars have broken out, magic hunters have run amok, and monsters are on the rise with fewer noble knights to slay them. Any number of threats could've killed Ozma and Dorothy, and Julian blames himself."

I continued looking around the room, appreciating the dolls and books and tiaras for what they were—remnants of a lost girl. "Has he gone to Camelot to search for her himself?" I asked.

"He cannot," Eva replied. "With Ozma gone, he is the only heir to the throne of Oz. If something were to happen to him, the realm would fall into chaos just as Camelot did. While it hurts him to not go after Ozma himself, Julian is doing what's right by staying in the Emerald City."

"So since he can't save her, he shoved all the memories of her in here?" I asked. "To try and forget about her?"

"In a way, yes. He could never completely forget Ozma. They were terribly close. However, he simply couldn't go on living with the constant reminder that he'd left her out there to fend for herself. We had her things moved into this room to put her out of his mind."

"Seems pretty cold to me," I said defensively. "Shutting out memories of the past so he could go off and be someone else."

"You don't know how hard it was for him, how much he still loves her," Eva said gently in his defense. "Don't let his smiles and charisma fool you; he carries his responsibility to her every day. Pushing his affection for her out of sight is the only way he can keep functioning as the person he needs to be."

"What about the person she needed him to be?" I muttered under my breath.

"What?"

"Nothing," I said, shaking my head.

Maybe I was being too harsh on Eva and Julian. Brother-sister relationships were a sensitive topic for me these days. I shouldn't let my own sadness and regret color my opinions of these people's lives.

"I'm gonna head to the throne room. My friends and I should go soon, and this place is depressing," I said.

Eva nodded and followed me out. After she closed the door, she pressed her hand onto the brass knob. The glow repeated like it had with me—filling the ironwork with light. Then I heard the sound of a bolt slide back into place.

*Did the door have some sort of magic trigger?*

"You never mentioned what your power is," I commented, as Eva and I walked down the corridor together. "You said after you were cured of your Pure Magic Disease you still retained the ability that came with it."

"That's correct. My sisters and I mastered the combining of potions and magic a long time ago, so we are able to cast a myriad of magic spells. However, my inherent power is fire."

"Fire?"

Eva stopped and held out her hand in a balled-up fist. When she uncurled her fingers, a bright ball of fire suddenly flashed into existence—levitating inches above her palm. I took a step back. The orange hues of the flame sphere flickered vibrantly in Eva's hand. The memory of a dream I had a long time ago clicked in the back of my brain.

I remembered a woman with dark hair holding a ball of fire. I now knew that this vision had been of Eva. I also recalled seeing Eva's face flash across my dreamscape the night I'd been taken by the magic hunters. It'd only been for a moment, but the memory was clear.

"The power comes in handy," Eva continued. She balled up her fist again—causing the fire to vanish like it was nothing more than a magic trick. "And with Julian's water magic, we balance each other out. He really is my perfect other half."

"Wait. His *water magic*?"

"That's right. Julian is more than our land's most talented potionist and spiritual leader, Crisa. And Ozma was more than a benevolent princess and Oz's ruler. Both my husband and his sister are descended from the Fairies of Neverland. Prior to her passing, their mother was the Fairy Queen Lurline. Ozma and Julian were both born with a touch of Fairy Magic that manifested to give them powers. Lurline was a water fairy, so they each possess a little water magic. Julian has never been very skilled with magic though, so he prefers to keep it a secret. He is far more gifted with potions."

I felt like my head was bursting with everything I'd learned in the last couple of hours. Risking an information overload, I found the will to ask one more question.

"What about Glinda?" I said. "What is her power?"

"My sister's Pure Magic manifested into a power much more impressive and versatile than mine," Eva replied. "She can generate force fields of energy."

My senses tingled again.

*That dream I had of the mountain fortress, and the work camp, and the flying monkey, and the high-heeled shoes—*

"And you?" Eva asked, interrupting my train of thought. "What is your power?"

"Excuse me?"

"You were able to get inside Ozma's room. Those doors are sealed with a magic lock—they can only be opened by someone with magic."

"I guess you missed the whole kermuckus with the gate and throne room doors," I said. "I can bring things to life. I'm actually really proud of the power, and I like using it, but I'm worried about what might happen if I . . ."

Eva observed the fear in my face. "You have Pure Magic Disease, don't you?"

"Yeah," I responded solemnly. Then I perked up. "But if the Four Waters of Paradise cured you, they could cure me too right?"

The idea that I could be cured had been swirling around my brain like a beautiful tornado since Eva told us her story. If I could cure the disease and still retain my magic, it meant I would never have to worry about turning dark. I'd be free to lead the charge against Arian and Nadia without fearing how my fate was tied to theirs. I only had to find the waters before the Vicennalia Aurora.

"Yes," Eva replied. "You can be cured by the waters, Crisa. Whether you will succeed in finding them by the Aurora, however, is a horse of a very different color."

I sighed. That was not the encouragement I needed.

"Crisa . . ." Eva said then. "If you do find the waters, I'd like you to bring some back for Glinda as well."

I raised an eyebrow. "But she's—"

"Wicked? I realize that. But while she is evil now, and has done some terrible things, she wasn't always that way. I believe she can change back. She is my family and I am not giving up on her, no matter what she's done."

A lump formed in my throat, but I forced it down. While I wanted to believe Eva's sister could change—like I wanted to believe my brother could change—I still didn't know if that was a wise wish or a fool's faith.

CHAPTER 49

# *Flower Power*

n our way back to the Emerald City's YUR station, I told my friends about Ozma, and also Eva and Julian's magic. As I was wrapping up the tale, we passed through a bustling agora. Among the stalls we discovered a booth selling Mark Two magic compact mirrors.

I was surprised, as those weren't set to debut in our realm for a little while longer. But the shopkeeper told us that the Wizard had sources in other realms scouting for fresh innovations that would allow Ozians to get the best technology first.

This was too good an opportunity to pass up. My four friends each purchased a Mark Two, and I bought a couple of extras for emergencies, which I stuffed in my backpack alongside my own. I was grateful that we'd converted the majority of our money to ONC currency at the ATM in Neverland.

We made it to the entrance of the station and fell in line behind other Ozians going down to the YUR. I glanced up and spotted another crow with a camera collar. He flew overhead and landed on top of a lamppost across the street.

*Was he watching us?*

Descending below street level, we found that the platform was a lot busier now and my friends and I struggled against the wave of civilians. The subway doors slid open just as we arrived. Passengers simultaneously exited and entered the car without concern for who had the right of way. I felt totally disoriented, and yet I thought I registered something in my peripheral vision. I was almost certain I caught a glimpse of . . .

I turned my head, but the person I thought I'd seen was nowhere in sight.

*Must be imagining things.*

My friends and I were the last ones to board. Once inside, I turned to face the platform. That's when I laid eyes on him.

Arian.

It was uncanny how seeing him sent a surge of hatred and fear up my spine. The hairs on the back of my neck stood on end and my breath caught in my throat.

Arian had a half dozen men with him, but I didn't see Mauvrey and Alex. When Arian spotted me, his eyes widened and he started to push his way toward the subway car. I automatically tried to take a step back, but it was too crowded.

Suddenly I felt the subway car jolt. The doors suctioned together, sealing shut in front of my face only a few feet before Arian reached them.

He and I locked gazes through the glass for a moment, but there wasn't time for anything else. The subway sped away and plunged into the tunnel before either of us could make a move.

"Was that Arian?" Blue asked, apparently having seen him as well.

I nodded. "If he's here to find Paige, he probably had the same thought as we did about seeing the Wizard."

"That's good," Jason said. "The Wizard will send him to the Maze of the Mindless. With any luck, maybe he and his antagonist buddies will get turned into brainless scarecrows."

"It's a nice thought, but Arian's too good," I said. "We should assume that he'll make it through the maze, and when he does, he'll come back for Julian and force him to reveal the truth. At which point we'll all be after the same thing."

"Avalon," SJ said.

"Excalibur," Blue added.

"The location of all of Book's genies," Daniel finished.

This whole day had been moving so fast—*scarecrows and subways and witches, oh my*—I hadn't had time to properly reflect on the knowledge Paige had imparted.

It was crazy to think that our realm's entire genie population was trapped somewhere. They had vanished from Book so long ago. The history books had several theories about what happened to them: they'd gone extinct after thousands of years of life, their powerful magic had burned them out, they'd migrated to another realm. No one was sure; that's why there were so many conflicting books on the subject. I'd even written a paper last semester about the differing theories. I got a B+.

I don't think anyone ever suspected that the Fairy Godmothers were responsible for the disappearance. Now that I knew what the Godmothers were willing to do to maintain control over the realm however, I had no trouble believing it.

"I can't even begin to think how much destruction the antagonists would cause if they got to the genies," Jason said. "Even if there were only ten genies left, at three wishes a piece, that's thirty powerful, magical ways Arian and Nadia can attack the realm. They won't need to wait for Natalie to open the Eternity Gate."

"Maybe that was their plan all along," Daniel said. "The deal with Natalie and the Eternity Gate isn't meant to happen for another nine months. What if that's their back-up plan and Paige and the genies have been their primary objective this whole time?"

"No, I do not believe so," SJ cut in. "Genies have restrictions on their magic just like Fairy Godmothers do. They cannot bring things to life or take life. They cannot affect free will. They cannot penetrate In and Out Spells. So perhaps the two efforts are linked—complementary to one another. When the Eternity Gate opens, all normal magic that is active will be suspended. That includes In and Out Spells, Fairy Godmother Magic, and the power of other magical creatures, *like* genies. Therefore, I think that even if Arian and the antagonists found out where the genies are being kept now, they would not set them free until after Natalie opens the Eternity Gate. If their magic is not active when the Gate opens, they will not be affected. So after the fact—when the Gate is open and the Fairy Godmothers' magic is temporarily suspended—the antagonists can release the genies and use their powers without anyone to stop them."

"If the antagonists do that when the In and out Spell around Alderon is lowered, they will have an army of magical power to take on the rest of the realm," Blue finished. "They will have the genies, plus all the witches and warlocks in Alderon with Pure Magic Disease. Meanwhile, the only magic we'll have left on our side is—"

"Me," I concluded.

The others grimaced and I didn't blame them.

"We have to get to the genies first," I said.

The fact that we were the only ones getting off at this stop should've been our first clue that something was wrong.

We arrived at the station closest to where my Hole Tracker and our Oz map indicated the next wormhole would open. The specific coordinates were less than a mile from this spot, and the wormhole itself was scheduled to appear in about twenty minutes—making it an optimal place for us to disembark.

When the intercom announced our arrival at "S.H. Station: Home of the Poppy Plains," my friends and I thought it was peculiar how the other passengers shifted in their seats nervously as we rose to exit. They avoided eye contact with us, all except for one young girl who met my gaze and mouthed the words "good luck" as the sliding doors closed.

The subway sped away into the tunnel, leaving us in the deserted station. There was not a single other living soul on the platform, and it looked like there may not have been for some time.

We worked the levers by the staircase in the way we'd seen back in the Emerald City station. The road above opened and we ascended the staircase. On the surface, an enormous sea of Poppies surrounded the Yellow Brick Road. It made the flower moat surrounding the Emerald City look pathetic. There were tens of thousands of flowers here in an assortment of colors. Red, purple, pink, orange, yellow—the colors stretched out in massive stripes like a rainbow.

A dense fog rose up from the great number of Poppies. The drowsy gas was thick and mysterious-looking.

My Hole Tracker's proximity sensor beckoned us forward and we proceeded down the skinny sliver of Yellow Brick Road toward a forest in the distance. The entry to the YUR automatically sealed itself off in our wake.

More crows passed overhead, giving me a bad feeling. They only circled a few times before flying off. The others were too distracted by the drowsy gas to notice.

I found myself feeling both elated and guilty at how easy this was for me. For anyone else, walking along a thinly laid strip of Yellow Brick Road fenced by Poppies would have felt like traversing a wire over shark-infested waters. To me, such fears were inconsequential. Past a few purple veins, Poppies caused no harm on me.

Unfortunately, my friends did not share this immunity. The fog of drowsy gas around the Emerald City had affected them slightly. The strength of the fog here had a much stronger impact. As we continued, my friends slumped. The drowsy gas influenced them more and more the further we passed through the plain.

"This drowsy gas sucks," Blue commented when we were halfway across. "I literally feel myself getting dizzier with each step; it's like my muscles are weakening."

"Not only that," SJ added, her breathing ragged and shallow. "My mental acuity is losing its strength. It is like the foggier the landscape grows, the foggier my mindscape becomes in turn. Do the rest of you feel it?"

The boys and Blue were in consensus; the drowsy gas wasn't just making them physically tired, it was affecting their mental sharpness as well.

"Why can't you feel it, Crisa?" Blue asked.

"I don't know," I admitted. "It must have something to do with my magic."

"Of course it does," SJ huffed, still mentally alert enough to channel her spite and jealousy.

I shrugged off the comment. It was all I could do. Even after everything with Alex and Mauvrey and Arian, the pettiness of SJ's bitterness toward me still filled me with resentment. Short of pushing her into the Poppy fields for an extended nap, my only option was to keep distance between us.

We arrived at the forest fifteen minutes before the wormhole opened. Each tree was at least a hundred feet tall and a muddy shade of gray. The twisted trunks were thick with dark red leaves crowding the branches. They formed a canopy overhead that made the sky look blood red as we passed beneath them.

The fog of the Poppies persisted through the forest, wrapping itself around the trees like ghostly police tape.

Scattered throughout the forest were various swamps. Aside from the occasional dirty bubble that emerged from their murky waters, they remained still and eerie. No wildlife in sight. My lethargic friends had to watch their step as we moved along. We kept to the Yellow Brick Road and did not wander from its path even though we'd left the Poppies behind.

Further into the forest we encountered remnants of abandoned old houses. The paint on the outsides had faded. Windows were dirty or cracked. Wooden shutters and roofs were dark and withered from rot. Doors hung open on their hinges, creaking as a light breeze moved them back and forth.

My skin felt cold and my nerves stood on end. Everything about this place felt off. I didn't like it. What I liked even less was the moldy pumpkin I suddenly rammed my foot into.

I couldn't help but squeak in surprise. This hauntingly silent atmosphere had me in such an anxious state that the gourd had completely caught me off guard.

The pumpkin rolled over a few feet and came to a stop when it collided with a slab of gray stone. A gravestone.

I cautiously approached the slab and knelt before it. The thing was covered in moss, dust, and cobwebs, but I was still able to see writing underneath. I brushed away the dirt until the engraving was legible.

"Ichabod Crane," I read aloud.

*Why does that name sound familiar?*

"Blue." I tilted my head up at her. "This name, I know I've heard it before. Where's it from?"

In all the years I'd known Blue, one of her favorite passions had been fairytale history. And accordingly, one of her favorite pastimes had been sharing her research with us. She was definitely our group's expert on the subject. She talked so much about her findings that I had to tune her out sometimes out of necessity. However, some things did stick and I was glad. The info had come in handy in the past, and had even saved my life.

Blue furrowed her eyebrows and squinted at the gravestone. "I . . ." She bit her lip before shaking her head. "I'm sorry; it's those dang Poppies. My brain's cloudier than this forest. I know that name too. But I just . . . can't remember . . ."

I glanced back at the stone, then the pumpkin that had led me to it—bright orange beneath its mildew, a chunk missing from where a rat must've bitten into it, two brownish spots of discoloration near the top.

"It's fine," I said, putting my hand on my friend's shoulder. "It doesn't matter. We need to keep going."

And keep going we did. We journeyed deeper into the grasp of the forest—the fog escalating all the while, especially closer to the swamps. We came across more and more pumpkins and gravestones. The gourds blocking our paths were at various stages of decomposition, but were always lying close to grave markers.

What was stranger still was that we began to hear rustling sounds behind us. Every time we turned around though, there was nothing there except pumpkins. I felt like we were being followed, or at the very least being watched.

*Ten minutes to the wormhole.*

"Hey, what's that?" Jason pointed to a building ahead. It was hard to make out at first. The Poppy fog was incredibly thick.

Moving closer, I saw the building for all its spookiness. The foreboding structure was about twelve feet high with a swamp pool positioned behind it. It was sandwiched tightly between two trees that leaned inward, as if reaching for each other. These trees were different from the others in the forest. Their bark was black and they sprouted bright yellow flowers.

The dwelling itself was cracked in half, but in an upside down V shape so that the opening was big at the bottom and small at the top. Its insides were completely shrouded in darkness. I didn't want to go anywhere near it. Alas, I realized we would have to. According to my Hole Tracker, that was our destination. Our wormhole would appear shortly within that ominous-looking structure, creating a portal to the next realm in the Wonderland sequence, Limbo.

In no hurry to enter the building until we absolutely needed to, my friends and I drifted around the clearing. In the distance, despite the thick fog and foliage, we could see glimmers of pink, red, and purple Poppies. We were near the other end of the forest.

"Look over there," SJ said suddenly.

Something shimmered about fifty feet from the Yellow Brick Road. One of the trees was not natural. It was made of bronze. We strayed from the path and walked toward it.

From base to branches, the bronze tree was covered in engravings. Each inscription had the name of a person, followed by the name of a specific place and a realm in parentheses. My fingers traced the words with curiosity.

*Nicole Weathersbee (Tarrytown, New York; Earth)*
*Sir Aronheart (the Forest Savauge; Camelot)*
*Reese Klein (Tarrytown, New York; Earth)*
*Bo'sun Smee (the Neverwood; Neverland)*
*Ichabod Crane (Tarrytown, New York; Earth)*

"Hey, it's that name again," I exclaimed.

Daniel studied the tree. "This is a memorial," he said decidedly. "All these names probably correspond with the tombstones we've been seeing. I spotted the name 'Sir Aronheart' on a grave a ways back."

"Why are there so many from this Tarrytown place?" Jason asked.

"I don't know," I responded. "But the engraving for 'Bo'sun

Smee' says he's from Neverland. You don't suppose that Smee is the same Smee who—"

"It is. Or rather, it must be," SJ interjected. "Bo'sun is another word for first mate. How many first mates from Neverland named *Smee* do you know?"

"That would explain why Captain Hook's first mate was a different dude than in the stories," Blue commented. "I'd been wondering about that. Smee must have died here. That guy Mr. Gropper replaced him."

"All these people from other realms, they must've gone through some kind of wormhole that led them to Oz," I said as I took a couple of steps back. "But why are their graves here? And what killed—Awgh!"

I tripped and landed on my butt at the tree's bronze roots. I twisted around to see what had caused me to stumble.

*Ugh, another stupid pumpkin.*

Something shone in the dirt and leaves behind me.

*What's this?*

I rolled the pumpkin out of the way and got on my hands and knees. Right at the foot of the tree was a black marble plaque with weathered golden writing.

> *"Tarrytown . . . This sequestered glen has long been known by the name of 'Sleepy Hollow' . . . A drowsy, dreamy influence seems to hang over the land, and to pervade the very atmosphere."*
>
> — *Washington Irving,*
> The Legend of Sleepy Hollow

"Sleepy Hollow . . ." Blue repeated in a daze. Then her eyebrows shot up. "Oh, crud. Guys, we arrived at S.H. station. We're in Sleepy Hollow. The *original* Sleepy Hollow."

"What do you mean the original?" Jason asked.

"The adaptations I've read for the tale of Sleepy Hollow are set in different locations," Blue explained. She pushed her hands out from her head, eyes clenched, as if she were straining to mentally and physically pierce the Poppy fog to try and explain what she knew. "The most well-known version was written by this guy named Washington Irving and takes place in Tarrytown, New York. It's an Earth town that's been haunted for hundreds of years and is nicknamed Sleepy Hollow. But if *this* Sleepy Hollow has all the gravestones, and . . . ."

Her eyes darted back to the creepy building between the trees. "The portal . . . of course! It makes perfect sense!"

"Blue, you are babbling," SJ said. "What makes perfect sense?"

"Everything," Blue said. "Don't you see?" Blue turned to me. "Crisa, if your watch says a hole is going to open up here, then maybe holes have opened up in this area before. That would explain all the Sleepy Hollow adaptations out there and Tarrytown's namesake."

"Its namesake?"

"A place called Tarrytown, New York, doesn't get a nickname like Sleepy Hollow without a reason. I think it's because of the Poppy plains around this forest. They've been making us sleepy and our thoughts hazy since we got here. It's plausible that this sleepy effect has been seeping through into other realms whenever a portal opens up.

"I mean, just take a gander at Irving's description of Tarrytown: 'a drowsy, dreamy influence seems to hang over the land, and to pervade the very atmosphere.' Can you think of anywhere else that fits that description? I'll give you a hint." Blue opened her arms wide and gestured around us. "It's surrounded on all sides by an ocean of sleep-inducing flowers."

"So if *this* Sleepy Hollow created the Sleepy Hollow legends in other realms," I clarified, "then all these people with gravestones here are—Awgh!"

Again, I'd tripped over a pumpkin. The same pumpkin.

*How did it manage to move back into my path?*

I picked up the rotten thing to inspect it. The gourd was identical to the first one I'd stumbled over by Ichabod Crane's tombstone. It had the exact same missing chunk with corresponding rodent bite marks, mildew formations, and pair of brown spots.

"Blue, remind me. How does the rest of that Sleepy Hollow story go?" I asked steadily.

Blue squinted as she tried to focus through the Poppy fog. "The Hollow is known for having a lot of ghosts, but the main one it's famous for is the Headless Horseman. He rides around carrying his severed head in his arms. The unfortunate souls he encounters lose their heads and get added to his collection."

"Charming," SJ scoffed.

"There's something else too," Jason interceded. "I remember reading a picture book version of this story when I was younger. In the illustrations, the Headless Horseman was depicted as this big shadowy figure with his head concealed in a sack he carried around. But sitting on top of his shoulders where his head should've been . . . was a pumpkin."

Our gazes all drifted to the orange object I held in my hands. Then we heard the same rustling sound from before and our eyes darted to the forest behind us. An army of pumpkins had gathered about sixty feet away. They remained still while we looked at them, but they hadn't been there a few minutes ago. Which meant they'd definitely moved.

"How long until the wormhole opens, Crisa?" Jason asked, a note of worry in his voice.

I checked my Hole Tracker. "Just under two minutes."

"Then I suggest you start running."

The deep, taunting voice came from the rotting gourd in my hands. I dropped the pumpkin, which made an "oomph" sound as it landed in the leaves.

"Did that pumpkin just speak?" SJ gasped.

I poked it with the tip of my boot, rolling it over. Two eyes and a mouth had formed on its bruised surface.

"It did before it was so *crudely* dumped," the pumpkin responded. "Honestly, you lose your body and it's like no one respects you anymore. But I digress. The hunt is about to commence."

"The hunt?" Daniel repeated.

"Yes. Once our master returns, he'll be so glad to have so many fresh bodies."

"What are you talking about?" I demanded.

"The rules are simple," the pumpkin replied. "All you have

to do is get past our master. If you make it to the portal and go through before it closes, you're safe. You get hit and you become like the rest of us."

I started to open my mouth to ask another question, but the pumpkin interceded—grinning with his crooked mouth. "Us pumpkin heads are the weapon of choice for the Headless Horseman. Get hit by one of us when we're lit up by his fire and brimstone, and *BAM!* Your body disintegrates and all that's left of you is your head, which swiftly turns into a pumpkin."

"That is horrific!" SJ exclaimed. "How can you be smiling about such a thing?"

The pumpkin probably would have shrugged if he'd had shoulders. Since he didn't, his eyes rotated in their rotting sockets.

"It's nothing personal. How can it be? We're not people. We used to be. My name was Ichabod. I was a teacher back in New York just trying to win the heart of the girl of my dreams when I got caught in the Horseman's path. Alas, that is the past and this is the present. And you would be surprised how quickly you lose your humanity when you're no longer human. We are starved for entertainment around here, and chasing the innocents that the Pop-Up Portals regurgitate is the only thing we have to look forward to. And on that note . . . I suggest you start running. He has really good aim."

The face of my Hole Tracker flashed brightly. A wormhole was forming. We all turned on our heels and looked at the creepy dwelling between the black trees. An orange hole appeared. It spiraled clockwise and grew bigger and bigger until it was the size of a garden shed.

"Have fun," Ichabod said with an evil laugh, rolling away to join the rest of the gourds. The pumpkins were now assembled like a tight-knit battalion a mere forty feet away.

Once the Pop-Up Portal steadied, it levitated for only a moment before its vivid interior began to waver like unsettled water. A figure emerged from within. The new arrival to the Hollow was cast in shadow due to the brightness of the portal behind him. But who, or rather *what*, he was was unmistakable.

He was mounted atop a black horse with a glistening silver mane, and he wore a black cloak and set of leather gloves. A crimson scarf was tied around his neck—above which was nothing but air. No doubt his head was concealed in the velvety sack tied to the horse's platinum saddle.

Menacingly still for a moment, the rider looked at us. Or at least I assumed he did. It was really hard to tell with him being *headless* and all.

His horse snorted, releasing a cloud of olive green smoke.

The rider held out his hand. Just above his leather-cased palm, a ball of fire appeared. Unlike the one I'd seen Eva produce, this flame was brilliant green. It levitated above his hand for a second as every pumpkin in range revealed a malicious face and was consumed from within by the same green fire. Igniting like a hundred enormous, viridescent fireflies, they floated off the ground. And then they starting coming at us.

They shot off in swift succession like cannonballs. My friends and I dove behind the bronze tree for cover. Peering around the trunk, I saw the Headless Horseman clench his fist and extinguish the ball of fire in his hand before galloping after us. His horse's eyes had taken on the same kelly green shade as the flaming gourds.

Despite our initial shared cover, my friends and I were driven further away from each other and the wormhole as we evaded the attack of the pumpkins. They were coming at us from all directions, and we were forced to scatter through the forest.

The fog simultaneously worked in our favor and worked against us. In the last few minutes—maybe a result of nearing nightfall—it'd grown incredibly dense. It was so thick now that I couldn't see more than ten feet in front of our noses. This made the pumpkins' assaults blind. I appreciated the advantage, but the consequence was that the sleep-inducing effects of the Poppies increased as well. With the fog so dense, the drowsiness was significantly slowing my friends down.

Daniel and I were both behind a particularly large tree at the moment. While I felt totally wired from head to toe—alert and vigilant as ever—I could see weakness in his body and a dazed expression on his face.

"Oz sucks," Daniel panted.

"You're telling me? I almost turned into a scarecrow this afternoon."

A pair of pumpkins collided with a tree to our left. Daniel shook his head like a tired student trying not to fall asleep at his desk. He was doing his best to fight the fog's effects, but the pressure to succumb was strong. His eyes started to close and I shook his arm in panic.

"Hey," I whispered sharply. "Wake up!"

His consciousness returned with a jolt. "Sorry," he said.

We spotted SJ, Blue, and Jason nearby. Pumpkins were pelting the tree they were hiding behind. The moment there was a ceasefire, they dashed over, coming to a crouch beside us.

"I . . ." SJ blinked hard and teetered on her feet. Her slingshot was clutched in her hand and she had an ice potion in the other. "I cannot get a clear shot," she said. "Even if I had one, there is a good chance I would miss. With all this Poppy fog, I am barely hanging on."

The piercing whinny of the Horseman's steed shook the forest.

"We have to get out of here," Jason said.

Blue nodded in the direction we'd come from. "The wormhole? Ichabod said if we make it through the portal, we're home free."

"Too risky," I replied. "It's a long way back to that house where the wormhole opened, and without being able to see where we're going, we'd be running blind. We need to make a break for the exit of the Hollow." I pointed at the colorful Poppies poking through openings in the fog bank. We were at the edge of the forest now. The Yellow Brick Road continued a few yards to our left. "We'll find another hole to use later. Not getting decapitated or turned into a pumpkin takes precedence."

"Can't you just use your magic?" Blue asked.

I shook my head. "It wouldn't help here. I can't exactly command a tree to protect us when it wouldn't be able to see any better than we can."

Another whinny sounded. A half dozen pumpkins pummeled a tree five feet away. Icy air filled my lungs as adrenaline soaked my muscles.

"So we run," Jason said.

"We run," I agreed.

"When?"

I took out my wand and transformed it from its hairpin state. "Now."

The five of us leapt from our cover and bolted. We couldn't see any of the trees or buildings before coming within a few feet of them. On more than one occasion we had to throw ourselves to the ground to avoid an incoming gourd.

My friends struggled. As if avoiding the erratic attack of the pumpkins wasn't hard enough, their dulled alertness inhibited our progress. I periodically stopped in my tracks to make sure I hadn't lost any of them.

"SJ!" I morphed my wand to a shield and jumped in front of her.

The shield spiraled out just in time to protect us from a pumpkin that came hurtling out of the fog. The pumpkin ricocheted off my shield and tumbled to the ground—its flaming face contorted and momentarily dazed.

"Blue!" Jason shouted.

I turned to see him save Blue in a similar manner. Leaping in front of her with his weapon at the ready, Jason used his axe's force field to protect them mere milliseconds before a pumpkin would have struck Blue's head. Not bad for a guy with Poppy-diminished reflexes. I guess his instinct to protect Blue was too strong for the Poppies to suppress completely.

Through the thick fog, I began to see the outline of a large figure rapidly approaching and I heard the clopping of metal horseshoes echoing around its advance.

"Go!" I shouted.

In a frenzied race, we headed for the edge of the forest—feet splashing in murky swamp water and crunching violently through piles of leaves. I swept aside a spider web the size of a tablecloth and burst into the open.

The Yellow Brick Road gleamed and a fresh sea of Poppies surrounded us on both sides. Because of the open air, the fog was much thinner here—allowing us to see what lay ahead—but the drowsy effects were still present.

We continued to sprint away from Sleepy Hollow; it was only a matter of time before the pumpkins and the Horseman pursued us out here. When we'd put about eighty feet between us and the forest line, SJ abruptly stopped. "Hold on," she said, pointing to the sky. "What is that?"

We skidded to a halt and looked up to where she was signaling. I squinted at the little black specks decorating the skyline—inbound for us at five hundred feet away.

"Crows?" Jason asked, holding his hand up to get a better look.

"Not only that." Blue strained her eyes. "Crows *and* flying monkeys."

She was right. Some of the black specks had fatter, sharper wings and long torsos that extended into tails.

"What the heck are crows and flying monkeys doing out here?" Daniel asked.

I connected the dots. "Glinda's crow spies have been watching us since the Emerald Tower. Remember? It started with the one in the window of Julian's potions lab. They must've reported back to the witch and she sent her flying monkeys to stop us before we could leave Oz."

"So how are we—"

"Hit the deck!"

A pumpkin shot out of the billowing fog and I dove into the field of Poppies, taking Blue with me. We plunged into the pink flowers. But while I stood up a second later, she remained motionless from the moment the petals touched her skin.

"Oh, no!" I hurried to her side, but it was too late. Her eyelids were closed and the veins in her arms were pulsing purple. She'd been exposed.

The others moved to come to her aid, but I held up my hand to stop them. "Stay on the path!"

I stashed away my wandpin then swung Blue's arm over my neck and lifted her up, dragging her out of the Poppies and back onto the road.

"She only touched them for a minute," Jason said, worried. "How long will she be out?"

"I don't know," I said. I glanced up at the incoming crows and flying monkeys then turned my head to see the shadowy figure of the Horseman emerging from the forest. We were trapped—enemy monsters in both directions and Poppies that would instantly incapacitate my friends everywhere else.

"Now would be a good time for a plan, Knight," Daniel said.

"Well, I'm open to suggestions," I snapped.

"Crisa," SJ suddenly gasped. "Look."

I turned to see what she was gesturing at. The pumpkin that had assailed Blue and me had passed out. It lay asleep in the spot where it'd crashed into the Poppies. The flames around it had extinguished. Its gnarled eyes and mouth were closed. What's more? It was faintly glowing purple and seemed to be snoring.

"The Poppies work on enchanted creatures too," I thought aloud. "I have an idea! It's crazy . . ."

"But?" Daniel pressed.

"But nothing," I replied. "It's just crazy. Everybody get behind me."

Jason lifted Blue into his arms and my friends stepped behind me. I dropped to my knees—my hands pressed flat against the Yellow Brick Road.

I'd practiced a version of this trick so many times at home in Midveil that part of me felt sure it would work. At the same time, I'd never tried it on this scale. What if I didn't have the strength? My control over my powers had improved drastically in the last few weeks, but the job at hand was massive. I hoped that all my training with Liza had made me ready. If it hadn't, there wasn't going to be another chance.

The shadowy shape coming out of the fog was accompanied by a dozen green, floating blobs—pumpkins getting ready to target us.

*Deep breath, Crisa. You can do this.*

I cleared my head of all emotion and concentrated—allowing my creative will and commands to flood into the bricks, infusing them with temporary life and purpose.

*Please let this work.*

Golden energy purged from my fingertips into the road like

an electric charge. Every yellow brick in the path ahead began to shake and light up.

The long road broke apart. Each brick came to life individually and rose into the air. They levitated in front of me en masse as the Headless Horseman and a squadron of gourds came into view. Six pumpkins rushed forward, beelining toward my group. I directed six bricks to meet them before they got anywhere near us.

*Fire.*

Each brick assaulted a pumpkin like a miniature cannonball. They either shot through their assigned targets—splattering pumpkin pieces everywhere—or hit them with enough force to cause them to veer off course and topple into the Poppies for a nap.

The Horseman directed more and more pumpkins to attack the way a conductor commanded his orchestra. As the gourds came flying out of the forest, I made my glowing bricks meet them dead-on in the same way. It was difficult at first. I'd never sustained so much power and split my focus in so many different directions. But my magic was only getting started.

Soon enough, my power and concentration came like a reflex. Golden light pulsed through me as my magic burned at its fullest potential. In that enhanced state, I created an opportunity for us to advance. I had not forgotten about the imminent threat of the flying monkeys. Knowing that we could not deflect their aerial attack with all the other obstacles in play, I realized our only way out was onward and upward.

While I continued to keep the Horseman's pumpkin assaults at bay, I directed a hundred bricks to come to our aid in an alternative way. The bricks read my mind and merged to construct a staircase in midair.

"We're going for the portal!" I shouted to my friends. "Climb!"

The spilt-focus of my magic was unstoppable then. As I continued to command portions of my protective golden brick storm to deter the Horseman's flaming pumpkins, I willed the rest to unceasingly construct a staircase. Without pause, each time we scaled a portion of stairs, the bricks immediately broke apart and flew to the front of our charge to build even more steps—flawlessly continuing our advance.

We passed over the Horseman's figurative head. I redirected my offensive bricks downward like a straight-up rainstorm. When we'd made it past him and were high over the trees, I commanded the staircase to take us down.

The flock of flying monkeys was fifty feet away.

*Lower. Faster,* I ordered the bricks.

We descended into the depths of the forest once again. It was tricky at first, the tops of the trees being so thick and all, but we shimmied through the branches and after the highest layers the descent was easy.

We touched down. Fog surrounded us on all sides as the screeching of the flying monkeys closed in. I looked up. The creatures were having trouble breaking through the trees due to their large, crooked wings. The crows, however, were darting through. I shot off several bricks at the first ones that plunged in.

"The portal!" SJ said.

I glanced over my shoulder and spotted it. Just a short distance away was the circular, orange body of the wormhole.

"Go!" I ordered the others. "I'll cover you."

My friends bolted for the hole. I clenched my fists—golden light flaming around them. But then I stumbled. Tiredness hit me fast and hard. I was suddenly out of breath. My glow was rescinding and my skin had begun to pale. I was about to reach Magic Exhaustion.

A pumpkin exploded against a nearby tree, causing me to jump back. I tried to build a protective wall from the closest bricks, but pain charged through me and I decided to stop. I could feel I only had a little magic left, so I had to conserve what I had.

I made after my friends as fast as I could, pausing to send the occasional brick to collide with a crow. Regrettably, my defense cost me time. Soon SJ, Daniel, Blue, and Jason were but shadows in the fog. A second later their silhouettes were gone completely. The only beacon that remained was the orange hole.

Green explosions lit up around me. Although the fog was

inhibiting the view of the Horseman, it didn't mean he was going to stop taking shots.

The trees above shook wildly. At last three flying monkeys successfully maneuvered through the branches. They descended quickly, claws outstretched.

*I guess this is it.*

I called all of my remaining concentration and power.

*Protect.*

Every brick within my control circled protectively around my body and shot up into the trees like a giant fist, hitting the flying monkeys and knocking them away like a powerful hook punch.

The move took me down too, but in a different way. My knees buckled and I collapsed to the forest floor. I tried to summon more magic, but it was gone. Every part of me begged for rest. This was the worst case of Magic Exhaustion I'd ever experienced. My body wanted me to sleep, to give in to the tiredness, but I couldn't do that. Not now. I clenched my teeth, pulled myself to my feet, and somehow found the strength to run.

Crows in my wake, searching for me through the fog, I sped over root, vine, and stump—desperately spurring my legs on. The wormhole appeared to be closing. It was shrinking in size and brightness before my eyes.

A pumpkin crashed into a tree three feet to my right. Stealing a glimpse, I discovered the Horseman and his shadowy steed had broken through the fog and were galloping at full speed toward me. He had one gloved hand driving his beast forward and the other raised to control the flaming pumpkins at his heels. He was about to take one final blow.

I arrived at the creepy house not a moment too soon and dove for the hole. My vision was consumed by a vivid, tangerine flash. Then I crashed onto whatever ground waited for me on the other side.

The world was going dim. It looked like I was in an all-white room, but I didn't have the clarity to note more than that. The sparkling wormhole was sealing itself off behind me, but I could still hear the sounds of metal horseshoes and the screeching of flying monkeys. They echoed in the back of my mind as Magic Exhaustion took over and I passed out.

## CHAPTER 50

# Limbo Stuck

irtha was following Chance Darling through a dark desert terrain. A forest green sky almost entirely clogged by clouds hung overhead. Lightning flashed bright yellow and rumbling thunder provided a continuous soundtrack.

Random junk levitated in the air—wilting flowers, old running shoes, fluttering documents. There were also pale gray ghostly images floating around. They were stretched out and mangled, but looked human—if the human form was put through a pasta maker and then hung out in the breeze. Many of the ghosts occasionally opened their mouths to let out a wail, but no sound escaped their phantom lips.

"Does it weird you out that she was never who you thought she was?" Girtha asked the prince as they continued their trek.

Chance considered the question for a moment before responding. "A bit," he replied. "It makes me wonder how different she is going to be once she wakes up."

"You don't still care for her do you?" Girtha asked. My large, sturdy friend was keeping an eye on the troubling surroundings, but the other was trained on the prince.

He was still handsome—I had a feeling he would always be—but his face had changed. The smugness in his expression and the cockiness in his eyes that used to characterize him had vanished. I saw the same earnestness in him that I saw in Daniel when he'd tried to convince me to forgive him last night, or when he talked about Kai.

"No," Chance responded. "You know where my heart belongs now. I just don't know if it will ever matter."

Chance hadn't stopped walking this whole time; his back had been to Girtha. I saw his face elongate in some form of sadness.

"I know she cares for me," he said. "She may try to underplay it, but I have spent enough time studying the curves of her face and the crinkles of her eyes to see that she does have feelings for me. But . . ."

The prince finally ceased walking. He sighed and turned to Girtha. "I worry that I was too late from the start. What if the reason she has not given me her heart is because she already gave it to someone else?"

The peculiar dream faded. My subconscious rose into the mysterious sky then I opened my eyes. There was an aching sensation pulsing through my bones and a great dizziness in my head. This wasn't an ordinary case of Magic Exhaustion. The pain felt different, more severe. Like I may have come pretty close to Magic Burn Out.

I stood up slowly. The realm I'd landed in appeared to be an enormous white room. My friends were nowhere in sight. I checked my Hole Tracker to see how long I'd been out, but the hands on the watch had stopped. I tried to bring up the holographic map to check for wormhole activity, but that didn't work either. In fact, none of the Hole Tracker's functions were operational.

I pulled my Mark Two out of my backpack and attempted to call the others, but all I got was static. My body continued to tremble from fatigue as I looked around the white space. I realized then that I wasn't actually in a room. At first glance it might've seemed that way, but there were no walls or doors or windows. This wasn't a room; this was a void. I'd had enough nightmares to recognize one when I saw it.

*Hmm. I wonder if this is a dream.*

I held up my hand to my face. It felt solid. And the pain in my body was too real to have been a manifestation.

*It doesn't feel like a dream.*

*But if I'm not in one of my visions, then where am I? This is supposed to be Limbo, but this is a void, not a Wonderland. Am I in the right place?*

"This void is Limbo. And you are definitely in the right place."

I spun around to find a beaver behind me. He was carmine red with a black nose and dark eyes. He held a piece of bark in his paws, which he nibbled on, and was floating in midair.

*Wow. I've seen some strange things today, but this is the most ridiculous—*

"Hey, watch what you think," the beaver said.

I blinked. "Did you just hear my thoughts?"

"Well, you can hear them. Why can't I?"

"Um, because they're *mine*," I responded.

The beaver shrugged. "Fair enough."

He continued to float around me—bobbing like a beach ball on an ocean wave. I stared at him curiously—expecting him to say more—but he remained silent, chewing contentedly on his piece of bark.

I cleared my throat. "So, I'm looking for my friends. They came through a little while ago. Any thoughts on how I might find them and leave this place?"

"I have plenty of thoughts," the beaver replied with a touch of sass. "But since you did not share yours with me, why should I share mine with you?"

"Ugh, fine," I groaned. "Help yourself, but first help me. You can poke around my brain all you want, but tell me how I can get out of here."

"The answer to the question is in the location," the beaver said, floating upside down.

"What?"

"You're in Limbo."

"So you mentioned."

The beaver righted himself and looked me in the eye. "You don't get it. The only way to find your way *through* Limbo is by facing your own Limbo first."

"It's been a long day, Bucky, and I don't have time for riddles. You're gonna have to be more specific."

My host finished chewing his bark and snapped the claws on his tiny paws. In a bright flash, a striped limbo stick about the size of a spear appeared. It floated horizontally in front of my face and had sparkly streamers protruding from both ends.

"In life, people are constantly finding themselves lost in some form of Limbo," the beaver explained thoughtfully. "It might be related to relationships, work, personal growth, or emotions. This realm—this Wonderland—is where all those anxieties dwell. If you want to find your way out, you must first face what is blocking you."

The beaver motioned at the Limbo stick with his tail and nodded. "But first thing's first—grasp onto the stick with your hand."

I reached out my hand but paused before I touched the stick.

"Oh, come now," the beaver huffed. "No need to fear. The stick just needs to get a reading on you before you can play. It doesn't hurt. Honest."

I sighed and grabbed the Limbo stick. The moment I did, a bolt of energy zapped me like a fully charged lightning rod.

"Ow!" I leapt back, rubbing my hand. "You said that it wouldn't hurt!"

"That was a lie."

"Yeah, clearly." I scowled.

A Limbo stick stand suddenly shimmered into existence in front of me, holding up either end of the stick on the highest of its five notches. An image began to materialize right beyond the set-up. It was a hologram of a human figure. One I recognized.

"Blue?" I said as the image solidified. The image did not respond. She just stood there staring at me with her arms crossed.

"What is this?" I asked the beaver.

"According to the Limbo Stick of Destiny, you are currently lost in five different states of Limbo," the beaver responded. "Each notch on the Limbo stick stand represents one of those states. You play the game by facing them one at a time—admitting what it is about those states of Limbo that bothers you, and then coming to an understanding of what you need to do to work through them. Pass all the levels and your way out of here will be revealed."

"How does that make any sense," I retorted. "I mean, what's the point? Thinking about my problems isn't going to magically fix them."

"No," the beaver admitted. "But a state of Limbo isn't the kind of problem that can simply go away like magic. In order to overcome it, it must first be explored."

I glared at him.

He levitated over the Limbo stick and patted it with his tail confidently. "Trust me. Sometimes all a person needs to find their way through Limbo is to start by admitting that they're in it. The rest will come naturally."

"What's with the different levels of difficulty then?" I asked, gesturing to the notches in the Limbo stick stand. "I played Limbo at a barbeque once. The further you went in the competition, the lower the notches got, making each round harder than the last. How does that correlate here?"

The beaver shrugged again. "Some states of Limbo are more difficult than others. The more difficult the state of Limbo, the more challenging the bar."

I put my hands on my hips as I examined the lower notches on the Limbo stick stand. "I don't know if I can bend that far."

"You'd be surprised how much a person can bend when they want to," the beaver replied. "And anyway, you shouldn't complain. All your states of Limbo are relationship-based, and those are the easiest to fix. Most people have to deal with personal growth-related Limbos, and those are the roughest. But you seem perfectly fine in that department. You must have a high degree of self-acceptance."

"I should hope so," I huffed in amusement. "I spent a whole bunch of chapters and multiple story arcs in my last adventure getting to that point."

"Good for you," the beaver commented. "Too bad I can't say the same for that little black-haired girl who was just in here. The personal growth Limbo she had to face had a pretty low notch."

"Little black-haired girl . . ." I paused. "Skin white as snow? Slingshot at her hip?"

"That's the one," the beaver replied.

"Is she okay?" I asked earnestly. "Did she make it through?"

"Can't tell you that," the beaver answered as he began to float around me again. "You make it through and you'll find out for yourself."

I scowled again, but decided to accept the beaver's terms. One thing I'd learned on my adventures was that things went a lot smoother when you didn't fight the crazy; you just leaned into it.

"Fine," I said, turning back to the image of Blue. She stared at me. There was hurt, but also anger in her eyes. It made me cringe and I looked away. The beaver bobbed over to me.

"Just look at her," he urged more delicately. "You know what's bothering you. Let your feelings flow."

With a deep breath, I pivoted and faced Blue again. I let the truth shatter the dam that held back my anxieties. I knew I was in a state of Limbo with Blue because of my vision that Jason was going to die. It was killing me to keep this terrible secret from her, especially since she had serious feelings for him, but I had promised Jason that I wouldn't say a word.

I met the eyes of my bold, fierce-hearted friend. She didn't look like a hologram anymore; she looked like flesh and blood. I sighed and held her stern, sad gaze. "I don't want to disappoint you, Blue," I started slowly, talking to her as if she were really there. "I don't want to be the girl I was last semester—the girl who kept secrets from her friends and hurt them. But this isn't like last semester. I'm not guarding the truth to protect myself like I used to. I'm legitimately doing it to protect you because Jason is right. If you knew the truth, it would kill you when he dies. You'd be racked with guilt for the rest of your life because you were unable to stop it from happening. And neither Jason nor I want that for you. So I'm sorry, but I'm not sorry that I am keeping this secret. I'm doing it for your own good. Telling you the truth would be selfish because it would do nothing but appease my own guilt."

Understanding—and an acceptance of that understanding—secured itself inside me.

I exhaled steadily. "Jason's decision was the right call. And I am making the right call by supporting it. Because you would do the same for me."

I unexpectedly found myself flinging my head back and walking beneath the Limbo stick, going straight through Blue's flickering image. As I passed through her, it felt like I was taking a breath of fresh air.

When I pulled myself upright a moment later, I discovered both her and the stick were no longer behind me. The Limbo stick and stand had teleported ahead of me anew, but the stick was at a lower level this time. An image of Jason appeared immediately beyond it.

*Jason.*

I studied him—*really* looked at him for the first time in a long time. In retrospect, since I'd told him about my vision I'd avoided taking him in so completely. Doing so brought too much pain. The sorrow in his eyes—usually full of kindness and sympathy—was a reminder of the burden I'd saddled him with.

The guilt and sadness I'd been suppressing rose in my throat and I no longer shied away from the state of Limbo between us.

"I feel like somehow what's coming for you is my fault," I admitted, talking to the image of Jason as though it were real, just like I had with Blue's. "I mean, I know that it's not. And you've told me more than once that I shouldn't blame myself for seeing what I did, but that doesn't mean I don't feel like I'm responsible. I feel like I'm letting you down, like I'm not fighting for you like I should be."

I started to pace a bit. "I've been mad, Jason. Mad at the future. Mad at you for making me share it with you when I could've held onto the burden for both of us. But mainly . . . I think I've been mad at myself for believing there was nothing I could do about it."

I paused and thought on my own words.

*Was there something I could do about it?*

Yes, my visions always came true. Yes, there had never been a time when I'd been able to disprove that. And, yes, I definitely saw Jason die. But "always" and "never" and "definitely" were not the finite terms I once considered them to be.

I had *always* thought that my father disliked me, my brother was a good-hearted hero, and Girtha and I would be enemies forever. I had *never* thought that SJ would be jealous of me, Chance could possess genuine feelings for me, or that there might be a way to cure my Pure Magic Disease. And overall, I *definitely* didn't think that after seventeen years of living my life that I would be where I was at this very moment.

Nevertheless, all remained true. Didn't that mean something?

Up til recently I'd believed certain things were a certain way. I believed that the Author controlled our lives. I believed the Godmothers were embodiments of goodness who looked out for our best interests. I believed I was just a princess and could never be a hero. I believed Alex was a great big brother, a loyal son, and a worthy future king. But I had been wrong. I'd learned and done so many impossible things recently that the idea that anything was set in stone was ridiculous. So maybe that meant that Jason's fate *could* be unwritten.

And if that were true, then what was I doing wasting time wallowing? Perhaps believing I could change his future was irrational and illogical and crazy. But then again, most of my most brilliant moments were.

A vow settled in my stomach, and then I spoke it into existence.

"No matter how small a chance, Jason, I know there is a chance that the future I've seen can be altered. I can feel it in my heart as surely as I can feel the magic pulsing through my veins. And I'd rather spend our remaining time together being driven by that shred of hope than conceding that fate is out of our control."

I ducked beneath the Limbo stick with ease. Like before, I felt a weight lift from my shoulders, this one heavier.

The stick and stand proceeded to flash in front of me again. An image of SJ stood behind them now. She glared at me and I glared at her in return. Our Limbo was not my fault, after all. She'd been the one to create this distance between us. She'd been the one to act irrationally. And she'd been the one who'd been so consumed by her own insecurities lately that she was pushing me away, like . . . like . . .

Realization suddenly struck me. It fell hard as a hammer and was utterly humbling and brutally swift. SJ was behaving like *I* used to. I'd been so frustrated with the situation I hadn't seen it. Now it was clear as day. In this empty space with no one and nothing to focus on but us, I could sense the familiarity. I was on the opposite end of a battle I'd once instigated. All this time I'd been upset with SJ for letting her unreasonable doubts cloud her judgment and wreak havoc upon our friendship. But I'd done the exact same thing last semester.

The only difference was that when I was going through my personal trauma, SJ hadn't pushed me away. Despite the fact that my words and actions hurt her, she'd tried to help me through it. She'd let me know that she was there for me. She'd been patient, and stood by me, and put up with my foolishness because she knew I couldn't force my heart and mind to change; they had to get there on their own.

And while she was going through her own internal turmoil, what had I done? I'd resented her for it. I'd let her stew on her own because that's what she told me she wanted. And I'd done absolutely nothing to try and help her through her problems. Which meant that while the insecurities SJ was feeling may not have been my fault, the distance between us certainly was. And I had the responsibility to fix it.

I ducked beneath the Limbo stick. I didn't remember making the motion; it just happened. When I emerged on the other side, I began to feel nostalgic for Sleepy Hollow. At least the demons there could be dealt with through brute force, unlike this emotional muck that stung like the aftermath of spicy curry.

The Limbo stick was much lower now. The image that appeared in front of me was my brother's. Unlike my friends' hologram, Alex's expression wasn't stern, sad, or hurt; he was smirking. He was looking at me like he always did—with a mixture of pride, mischief, and charm glinting in his eyes.

Seeing him normal like that made me angry. Nothing was normal anymore. And it was all because of him. He'd ruined everything. Our family, our kingdom, our relationship—he'd set it ablaze. He'd betrayed us.

I didn't know how to make sense of that. I was confused about how to proceed. As horrible and treacherous as Alex had been, a desperate, naïve part of my soul still had faith in him. I wanted to believe that he could be saved, that he could be the brother I once knew and loved, that he could come back. But as I stared at his expression, and compared it to the cold, ruthless one I'd faced in Midveil and in the Ruined City, I finally accepted the truth.

I could never trust my brother again. Whether I liked it or not, the Alex I knew was gone. There was no changing that. There was no bringing him home. My brother had died that day along with the innocent victims of his attack.

It was the hardest truth I'd realized so far, but I accepted it with as much certainty as the others. I swooped beneath the daunting Limbo stick as I swallowed the sadness in my throat.

I surfaced on the other side to face the final level of Limbo waiting for me—Daniel. I was surprised and turned around to look at the beaver.

"I thought you said the levels of this Limbo stick correspond to the difficulty level of my states of Limbo."

"That's right," the beaver said, floating closer.

"So why is Daniel my last level? My brother Alex hurt me more than anyone ever has. Daniel and I have a rocky relationship, but it's nothing compared to the internal havoc that my brother has caused me."

"The difficulty level doesn't always correlate to the level of pain," the beaver explained. "It correlates with how easy it is for you to find clarity. Whoever this Daniel is to you, the issues you have with him are a lot more uncertain than your feelings about your brother."

I glanced back at Daniel, and in a moment of humility I knew the beaver was right. While seeing each of the others had triggered very distinct, immediate emotions, Daniel's face had no such bearing on me. I felt so many conflicting things about him at once that it was like sensory overload. The Limbo stick seemed impossibly low. There was no way I could bend myself to cross beneath it.

"I can't do this," I said to the beaver, whose face had taken a turn for the judgmental. "The bar is too low."

"Only because you've set it there," he responded. "You want to get out of here? Face him." The beaver wagged his tail at Daniel. "If you don't, you'll be stuck in more ways than one."

I grunted. Daniel had been a constant roadblock for me since we'd met. It was only fitting that he'd eventually become a physical one—smugly standing between me and my way out of this Wonderland.

I bit my lip. I didn't even know where to start. But then, wasn't that always the case with us? I never knew where to begin, just like I never knew where to draw the line. Daniel knew, though. And he'd truly hurt me when he'd drawn it earlier in the semester.

I'd always been prone to bottling things up and keeping people at a distance. He'd been the first person to help me get out of my own way. Trusting him had made me feel stronger, safer, and happier. When he pushed me away so abruptly, I didn't just lose a friend I cared for, I lost a vital part of my support system.

It was terrifying to be vulnerable with another person. It was going out on a limb—sharing a piece of your soul in good faith that the person you entrusted it to would build you up, not break you down. But that's exactly what Daniel had done; he'd broken me down. I'd come to rely on him and he had shattered my faith that I could lean on someone. When I finally got past his betrayal and let myself trust someone else that way again, I ended up getting crushed by Alex. It made me wonder if trusting people so completely was a bad idea.

I had to remain strong for so many things—my realm, my friends, Natalie Poole, Paige Tomkins, and countless others. I didn't want to risk the chance that someone might hurt me like that a third time. I didn't know if I could take it. What if the next time I was betrayed, my heart shattered irreparably?

If I let Daniel in again then I was inviting in the opportunity for more pain. But if I took that chance, if I gave *him* another chance . . . I was inviting in something else too, wasn't I?

My heart skipped a beat as I gazed at the boy before me. *Friendship.*

That's what I would be inviting into my life if I trusted him. Real friendship. Not the shallow kind where you talked about homework and the weather, but the real kind where you opened your spirit to someone and shared what really mattered about yourself.

I knew in my heart that I missed what he'd been to me—someone who forced me to share, who got me to trust, and who taught me to let people in. Someone who—in the worst, but also the best possible way—made me feel more connected to life than my powers ever had.

*Wasn't that worth the risk?*

In life, the things that mattered most rarely came easily. But if you were brave enough to accept their challenge, and courageous enough to keep fighting for them even when it got difficult, the reward could be wonderful.

That's what I wanted for Daniel and me.

During our Author quest we'd become friends, but not in the natural way. We'd trusted each other because we had to, not because we wanted to. If we were to move forward now, it had to be a choice made of free will. That was the only way for this to work. We could no longer be forced friends; we had to be *real* friends.

The road to that would be even harder, and there would be way more obstacles ahead. But at that moment—staring into his strong, defiant eyes—I knew that it would be worth it.

He was worth it.

My chin swiftly passed beneath the bar. I gracefully swept under the Limbo stick as my last bit of internal Limbo was overcome. Then I rammed into Daniel. Not an image of him, but the real thing.

"Daniel!" I exclaimed. I grabbed his arms to make sure he was real.

He looked just as startled to see me. "Knight, where'd you come from?"

I gestured back at the Limbo stick and the floating beaver, but both had vanished. When I turned to face Daniel again, SJ, Blue, and Jason were standing behind him.

Jason stepped forward. "I take it you met the beaver?"

I nodded.

"Us too," Blue said. "He was weird."

I was glad to see that she was conscious again after her Poppy-touching episode.

"But we all passed his test, right?" I said. "Otherwise we wouldn't have found each other again."

"That's true," Jason replied. "But shouldn't we have also found a way out of here? We're still trapped."

I looked around and saw something new in the middle of the room. It was a white ladder.

I glanced at the Hole Tracker on my wrist. It was working again. An orange circle pulsed brightly on its face. A Pop-Up Portal was inbound for our location. When we reached the base of the ladder, a glimmering orange wormhole appeared at the top—spiraling in a clockwise direction as it opened.

This was our way out.

My friends climbed up the ladder and passed through the portal. I took a final observation of the white void we were leaving behind. As I did, the beaver reappeared. He was upside down and chewing on a different piece of bark. He waved at me with one paw and his tail.

I waved back. Then I jumped through the portal, secretly grateful for having been graced with his presence. Thanks to Limbo, I had put some of my worries behind me and now felt renewed. I had a clean outlook on my relationships and problems, and intended to make some major changes in the very near future.

# CHAPTER 51

# The Missing Girl

e entered the next realm in the Wonderland sequence, the Portalscape. After that we immediately headed for the door to Neverland—the dark wooden one with the vines and orange tiger lilies. We had to find Arthur as soon as possible and learn more about Excalibur so that we might retrieve it and use it to free Paige's mind from Glinda's memory stone.

The five of us passed through the door into a dense area of forest. We compared our coordinates on my Hole Tracker map with our Wonderland map of Neverland. It allowed us to understand what part of the Neverwood we were in, but sadly that wasn't enough.

"No one actually knows where the Lost Boys and Girls camp is hidden," Jason explained, reiterating something I'd already gleaned from my own research of the realm earlier in the semester.

"Not surprising," Blue commented. "If anyone could find out where it was, then the pirates would storm the camp."

"True," Jason said, "but it makes things more difficult for us. They didn't have any maps at the Hideaway—I asked—and no one would point it out on our map either. That little kid with the mace told me that all location information is proprietary."

"I checked the Hole Tracker when we were there," I said. "The blob that signifies where we are showed up about here." I pointed to an area a bit northeast from where we were on the holographic map. "But with the size of this forest, that generality isn't the most helpful."

"There has to be a way to figure it out," Blue said. "We need to find AP; I mean Arthur."

"I have an idea," Jason replied. He pointed at a part of our map close to where we were. "That's Fairy Hollow. The entrance to the secret fairy kingdom is supposed to be there. Its invisible, and fairies are able to turn themselves invisible when they approach it. But if we go there, maybe one of the fairies from the Lost Boys and Girls camp will recognize us and can show us the way back to camp."

"It's worth a shot," Daniel said.

We forged ahead in the cold dusk. I regretted losing my jacket in the Ruined City and was tempted to ask Daniel if I could borrow his again. Then I mentally slapped myself for the thought.

When we arrived at Fairy Hollow, nothing looked out of the ordinary. It was a wooded glen with a bunch of boulders lying about.

"The fairy kingdom is probably underground," SJ asserted. "We need to get their attention."

"How do we do that?" Jason asked.

"I vote for the direct approach," Blue said. She stepped forward into the center of the clearing and started shouting. "Fairies! Come out! We need your help! We're friends of Peter and Tinkerbell! Help us! Please!"

Startled birds squawked and fled the trees.

"Blue!" SJ protested.

But Blue's direct approach worked. Several small, whirring balls of light emerged from the boulders. They floated above us and then morphed into fairy form. There were three of them, and one of them was Tinkerbell. She recognized us and zipped over to me excitedly. Her wings flashed as she tried to communicate. I didn't understand her language, but I got the gist of her expression and body language.

"It's nice to see you too. We didn't expect to be back so soon either," I said. "Listen, Tink, we need to get back to the camp. Can you take us there?"

She nodded with a smile and flew into the forest with the other two fairies. We followed quickly. After a solid twenty-minute trek, we pushed through some branches and found a familiar setting. The Hideaway.

Some Lost Boys and Girls were in the early stages of dinner preparation. Others were busy playing in the tree houses up top. Peter flew into camp from the other side and spotted us. A giant grin spread across his face and he flew over.

"Hey! You're back! Did you find that Paige woman you were looking for?"

"Yeah, we did," I replied. "And she pointed us in the direction of our next mission. That's why we're here. We need to talk to AP."

"You're in luck," Peter said. "He and I just got back from an expedition to Mermaids' Lagoon. There he is now." Peter pointed across the camp to where AP was walking. I called out to him.

"Yo, Arthur!"

He froze in his tracks and stared at me. I crossed my arms and tilted my chin toward the table. "Can we talk?"

Arthur did not want to have our conversation out in the open. He took us to his own bunker, which was on the edge of camp. We entered through a tree trunk like the kids' bunkers, but instead of a slide, this one had a staircase inside that twisted beneath the earth.

Arthur's bunker was completely different from the other dwellings in the Hideaway. The furniture was straight, lacquered, and constructed of dark mahogany. The decorations were simple and well-made. A whole wall in the back was dedicated to hunting equipment. A collection of swords was mounted on the right. And by a bed in the corner resided a suit of knightly armor that was worn and scratched like it'd seen a hundred battles.

Peter had escorted us here alongside Arthur. On the way we'd given them the briefest of recaps, an introduction to a much deeper conversation we needed to have. It seemed important to delicately ease our way into the topic of Excalibur.

Arthur gestured for us to sit. My friends and I took chairs surrounding his round table. And yes, I appreciated the irony of that.

"I'll leave you guys alone," Peter said, once we'd settled in Arthur's quarters. "I have business up top. I already know Arthur's story, and you can catch me up on the specifics of yours at dinner." He zipped back up the stairwell to the entrance and disappeared.

"I keep my true identity a secret because it's as dangerous to the children here as it is to me," Arthur began. "If it got back to Camelot that I was still alive, the people ruling now would likely send forces to bring me back. Obviously this would kill me, as the only thing keeping me alive is Neverland's unique time properties. And anyone who tried to stand in the way would be at risk."

"Were you telling the truth about not knowing how you got here?" I asked.

"Not quite. My trusted advisor, wizard, and friend Merlin had me swear many years ago that if I knew I was not long for this world, I would have one of my Knights of the Round Table return me to the Isle of Avalon and push me out onto the lake in a boat. Merlin said it was because I needed to return Excalibur to the Lady of the Lake, who bestowed it to me—a ritual that all past kings who wheeled Excalibur underwent. She would keep the blade safe until someone else worthy came to claim it. But now I think Merlin may have known more than he let on. He had the power to see the future. He may have foreseen that a wormhole would open on the lake and take me here, saving me."

"So the sword . . ." Daniel said.

"It remains under the care of the Lady of the Lake until someone else claims it."

"How can you be sure someone hasn't already?" I asked.

"Because I am connected to the sword. Excalibur was originally forged for the Pendragon bloodline, so Camelot's kings would always have a strong weapon at their side. It is hard to explain, but I can still feel it out there like a part of me in some other place. The sword is meant to imbue us with great power. However, any man or woman can wield Excalibur and the weapon will grant them enhanced strength just as well. That is why there are so many traps and tests on the way to retrieving the blade. Its owner must be worthy. Should it fall into the wrong hands, the results could be devastating. Each king before me has had to traverse these obstacles to prove himself worthy and claim the sword. I advise you to be wary of these perilous tests on your way to the Isle. I assume that is why you came back to see me, is it not? You want to claim Excalibur?"

"The woman we were looking for—Paige—has lost her memories to the Wicked Witch of the North, Glinda," Jason responded. "The only way to set them free is to use Excalibur to shatter Glinda's unbreakable memory stone during the Vicennalia Aurora. When we saw a picture of you in a book about Camelot and figured out who you are, we thought you might be able to help us."

"That I can," he said solemnly. "And that I will. I have met many valiant men and women during my rule in Camelot, but none of them fit the bill to claim Excalibur. Then you five came along. When I met you," he met the eyes of everyone in our group, but lingered on mine for a second longer, "I had an instinct that you might be the ones the Lady of the Lake has been waiting for. You are all honorable and brave, and a valiant team of equally strong, but diversely skilled heroes. Moreover, your timing is right. A long time ago, Merlin told me a prophecy, one that would inevitably become famous in our land. It is known as the Great Lights Prophecy."

"You have prophecies in your realm too?" Daniel asked.

"We used to," Arthur said. "Merlin was the only one in our land with the ability to see the future, but he vanished years ago. His Great Lights Prophecy refers to the Vicennalia Aurora. It predicts that Excalibur will be found and the rightful king of Camelot restored when the Great Lights—what we call the Vicennalia Aurora—occurs. You showing up here a few days before that event cannot be mere coincidence. I think the time has come for the prophecy to be fulfilled and you are the ones to see it through."

"But be warned," Arthur continued. "The journey to Avalon is incredibly dangerous. You'll have to cross the infamous Passage Perelous. And should you survive, the Isle itself is full of enchanted traps and obstacles, and it is guarded by the Lady of the Lake, who is a challenge herself. If you make it to Avalon, she will ask much of you. You must show her respect and do exactly as she says. If you deviate from her instructions, you will die. If the other spirits of the lake deem you unworthy, you will die. If you do not watch your step even for one second, you will also probably die."

*Ugh. Don't magical quests ever let you off with a warning?*

"If you persevere and actually manage to claim Excalibur," Arthur concluded, "you will have to sacrifice something precious in exchange—a decision."

"A decision?" Blue repeated. "I don't understand."

"If you claim Excalibur there will come a time when one decision will define your future and you will not choose wisely. You won't know when it will come to pass, but it *will* come to pass. For me, it was when I decided to ignore Merlin's advice to kill my half-brother Mordred many years ago. Merlin had a vision that Mordred would turn dark, but I didn't listen. Mordred was my family and I cared for him. I chose to let him live. In the end, that cost me my life. When Mordred stabbed his blade into my body, the Lady of the Lake appeared before me. And I knew that this was my sacrificed decision. I had finally paid the price."

A buzzer went off near the entrance of Arthur's bunker. Footsteps echoed down the stairwell and a moment later a girl emerged. She was the oldest person aside from Arthur that I'd seen at the Lost Boys and Girls camp—somewhere in her early twenties. Her hair was dark brown, her eyes were light brown, and she was tall.

I recognized her thin, strong face. I'd seen it before in a dream.

"Hello there," she said to us in an accent I had never heard before. She pivoted toward the King of Camelot. "Arthur, Peter advised me about what is going on. He said these children just came from Oz and that they are planning on going to Camelot as part of a plan to challenge Glinda. I thought I would aid the effort by sharing my wisdom on both subjects."

"What do you know about Glinda and Camelot?" Blue asked.

"Quite a lot actually. My name is Dorothy. Dorothy Gale."

"*What?*" Blue exclaimed.

I was equally stunned. How many misplaced protagonists were there in Neverland?

I wasn't sure what surprised me more—Dorothy's presence or the way she'd been presented. Encountering Arthur and Peter and other important characters on this journey had been big, *ta-dah* moments. Dorothy had waltzed in here and introduced herself like she was joining us for a card game

She sat down beside Jason. With me, my four fairytale friends, King Arthur, and the new addition of Dorothy Gale, it felt like a literary power table. Mitchell—our writer friend—would have died from happiness. Too bad he wasn't here. On our way to Arthur's bunker, Peter mentioned that Mitchell had already taken a wormhole home.

"Peter and the other campers call me their Honorary Mother because I'm the oldest at camp, and with all the adventures I've been on, I am pretty good at telling stories," Dorothy explained. "I've been in Neverland for many months for the same reason as Arthur. I sustained a fatal wound and accidentally ended up here. Now I cannot return to Oz because if I left Neverland, my injury would kill me."

"Did you get hurt while you were looking for the Four Waters of Paradise?" Jason asked.

Dorothy raised an eyebrow. "How did you know?"

"We've been to see the Wizard of Oz—Julian," I said.

"Wait! You've been to see Julian?" Dorothy exclaimed. "Tell me, is Ozma all right? Did she make it back to Oz?"

"We were under the impression you were together," I replied. "What happened? Ozma's not in Oz."

Dorothy's face grew ghostly white. "I cannot believe Ozma hasn't returned. I thought for certain my slipper would do the job."

"Your slipper?" Blue said.

"My magic jeweled slippers," Dorothy clarified. "Since my first visit to Oz I've worn them on every adventure. While their main function is to transport their wearer back home with three clicks of the heel, they also have a handy secondary function. You can record a message into the ruby jewel on each slipper. With two clicks of the heel, the shoe with the message will fly wherever you want it to go. Once its message has been played, it will come back to reunite with its mate. The jewels are drawn together like a homing beacon."

Dorothy leaned forward in her seat and laced her fingers together, her expression serious. "Many months ago, I went to Camelot with Ozma in search of the Four Waters of Paradise. We were successful getting to Avalon and finding the waters, but on our return through the Passage Perelous we were attacked by the Questor Beast. It is Camelot's most notorious monster—a horrible, multi-headed creature that spits acid and has poison coursing through every vein in its body. If you so much as get scratched by it, you're a goner."

"I've seen renderings of it in a few old texts about Camelot and in a book that Julian recently showed us," Blue said, strangely solemn. "I kind of hoped the illustrators were exaggerating."

"I can tell you that anything you may have seen or read is nothing but a vast *under*exaggeration," Dorothy responded.

"She's right," Arthur said. "There is no other monster like it in all the realms. Many of Camelot's bravest knights have been killed by it. The Questor Beast has ravaged the land around Avalon for centuries. I myself tried to hunt it several times and failed."

I raised an eyebrow with curiosity as I watched Blue's reaction. Her face was pale and her expression was still. She seemed worried, but also angry—like when you resented something you knew you could not escape.

"The creature's attack caught us off guard," Dorothy continued. "We dropped the bottle containing the Four Waters of Paradise and some spilled onto one of my slippers. As a result, the shoes could not transport us home."

"Why's that?" Daniel asked.

"The Four Waters of Paradise are the strongest form of magic purifier in existence," Dorothy explained. "That is why they are able to cure Pure Magic Disease. Luckily, both shoes didn't get wet, as that would have caused all their magic to be wiped clean. But since, like I said, one shoe was damaged, the pair couldn't be used to send us home. Ozma and I had to make a break for it on foot. Sadly, we weren't able to get away. The monster was too fast and the fog was too thick. We didn't know up from down or left from right. The Hole Tracker we'd been using had also gotten wet, so we were running completely blind.

"We found a cave in the forest where we could temporarily hide from the Questor Beast. I took off my slippers and clicked the heels together twice. While the damaged slipper prevented us from returning home, the shoes' secondary function still worked. I recorded a message for Julian and Eva then directed the good slipper back to Oz. I knew that once the message was delivered they would send help to collect us, but it wouldn't matter if we were both dead. So after I sent the slipper off, I decided to buy Ozma a chance to escape."

Dorothy released a long, sad sigh.

"Before Ozma could stop me, I gave her the other slipper, told her to stay hidden until she had an opportunity to flee, drew my sword, and ran off to lure the monster away."

"You left her," I said.

"I had no choice. I had to make sure Ozma was safe. She isn't just Oz's ruler, she is like a little sister to me. She's been my dearest friend since I rescued her and returned her to the throne a couple years ago. So I did what was necessary. Alas, I did not foresee what happened next. The Questor Beast pursued me through the fog. When it finally revealed itself, I managed to cut off one of its heads. But there were still four more to contend with. The monster snapped and bit while I sliced and dodged. Eventually it pounced and I was struck.

"The heads of the Questor Beast have the ability to fire their fangs like knives. These fangs contain a venom that kills within a minute. One of the fangs cut my arm and the poison instantly began to spread through me. I figured that was it. But then I tripped and stumbled down a hill. Just before I passed out, I saw a bright red light. Next thing I knew, I woke up in Neverland."

"You fell through a portal," Daniel said.

"A counterclockwise portal," Blue added.

"Unintentionally, but yes," Dororthy replied. "The Questor Beast fang was still lodged in my shoulder when I woke, but the effects of its venom had stopped. A few Lost Boys and Girls found me and I have been here ever since."

"So that's the reason you didn't return to Oz," I said.

"Yes," Dorothy said sadly. "I'm trapped here because if I were to ever leave this realm, my body clock would tick forward once more and the Questor Beast's poison would finish me off. However, while I can never go back, I've held out hope that in the aftermath of my failure, Julian and his forces were able to retrieve Ozma from Camelot after receiving my slipper message. If she's still missing, then my slipper never made it."

"It did," I said abruptly.

Every head at the table turned in my direction.

"How do you know?" Daniel asked.

"When I was exploring the Emerald Tower, I found a storage room where Julian has put all of Ozma's stuff. The slipper was locked in a box." I turned to Dorothy. "Did he know about the slipper's homing and message storing capabilities?"

"Yes, of course," Dorothy replied. "When the slipper reached him he would've immediately known to listen to my message, and then he could have followed that slipper back to the one I left with Ozma. Why in Oz would he lock it up instead? That makes no sense."

My eyes narrowed at the unpleasant tingle of déjà vu. "Maybe he didn't want to find Ozma."

"What do you mean?"

"You said you returned Ozma to Oz's throne a couple of years ago, right?"

"That's right. She was stolen by a witch when she was a baby. The witch raised her as a servant with no memory of who she was until I rescued her."

"So am I correct in assuming that Julian was the sole sovereign of Oz until his younger sister came along and was declared the rightful ruler? And since then he's just been her second in command?"

"That's true, but I don't see where you are going with this," Dorothy said.

"Where I'm going with this is that maybe Julian didn't use the slipper to find Ozma because he didn't *want* her to return to Oz. "

Dorothy gasped. "That's a horrible thing to say. Julian would never betray Ozma. He's her older brother. She adored him and he adored her."

"So?" I said bluntly. "That doesn't mean anything. If he decided the throne of Oz was what he wanted and didn't care about the price, then it's perfectly conceivable that he could double cross Ozma to get it. Don't believe me if you want, but the facts are there. The slipper was in his storage room. The box it was locked in would only open to the touch of magic, which Julian has. And when I opened it, it said, 'Welcome back, Your Great and Powerfulness.' Do you know anybody else who goes by that humble nickname?"

"Well, no. But I just don't think Julian is capable of that kind of evil."

I leaned my hands against the table and looked Dorothy in the eye. "*Everyone* is capable of evil," I replied. "They just need the right push."

I felt someone's hand on my arm.

"Knight . . ." Daniel said softly.

"What?" I asked, frowning at him.

"Nothing," he said, withdrawing quickly. "Nevermind."

I cleared my throat and continued, steadying my tone a bit. "Dorothy, I know it is difficult, but you need to make room for the possibility that Julian intentionally left Ozma in Camelot and chose to keep the throne for himself."

Dorothy's face was wrought with conflict as her glassy eyes met my hard ones. "That's a very cold, dark theory."

"Yes," I admitted. "But that doesn't mean it isn't right."

# CHAPTER 52

# Intermission

fter our talk with King Arthur and Dorothy, I checked my Hole Tracker. There wasn't another wormhole of any kind opening until 8:30 a.m. the day after tomorrow, which meant we were stuck in Neverland.

I was dismayed by the news. The sun had gone down, so we only had five more sunsets before the Vicennalia Aurora. We had less than a week to find Excalibur, return to Oz, and free Paige's mind from the memory stone. Time was of the essence and it was highly inconvenient that we had to waste a full day waiting in Neverland.

Then again, if I was honest with myself, I was also secretly relieved. I was glad we had a day to rest. I felt guilty thinking that, but it was true. With the myriad of obstacles in Camelot that Arthur and Dorothy had described, I knew more trials would soon be upon us. I was grateful we were being forced to take a breather before diving in again.

Neverland was the perfect place for a day off. Between the big feasts, the amicable company, and the fun and games, it was the ideal environment for an exhausted, recently heartbroken protagonist to recover.

I sat with Blue around the bonfire—my belly full of pancakes, chocolate milk, and cured meats. Daniel and Jason were on the opposite side of the bonfire circle. I could see their faces through the flames and they were laughing about something. I wasn't sure why, but seeing Daniel smile made me smile.

SJ was off talking with Dorothy somewhere. The two had really hit it off. Dorothy had a lot of potions experience from her time spent in Oz working with Julian, plus she had a rather colorful backstory. For starters, apparently she wasn't from Kansas; that was just a creative choice one of the earliest storytellers who'd written about Oz made to make her more relatable to his audience. She was from some place on Earth called England. I was sure Blue would probably ask her a million questions about it tomorrow, but for now my cloaked friend seemed more interested in relaxing than research. A first for her. I guess she must've been exhausted too.

I felt a bit bad about upsetting Dorothy with my talk regarding Julian. On SJ's suggestion, we'd decided to drop the matter for now. There wasn't anything we could do to *prove* Julian was guilty, and we still didn't know for sure what had happened to Ozma. I was pretty firm in my beliefs about his treachery, but the uncertainty was clearly making Dorothy uneasy, especially given that she could not leave Neverland.

"What are you thinkin' about?" Blue asked. Her cheek was bulging from the enormous lollipop she'd taken from the candy dish being passed around.

"The journey ahead," I replied. "And how glad I am for this intermission."

"Intermission?"

"Yeah, you know, the break we're experiencing from our quest."

"We finished our quest, Crisa," Blue said. "We found Paige, which was what we wanted to do at the start."

"Technically that's true, but I feel like this story with Paige is incomplete. Finding her only opened our eyes to the bigger quest of freeing her mind, which we've barely even begun."

Blue took the lollipop out of her mouth. "Not all stories are tied with a perfect bow at the end, Crisa. Especially not those with so many characters and story arcs in play. I'm calling a wrap on our current venture. The day after tomorrow we'll take the next wormhole and navigate our way through this new story that's unfolding. We'll best Camelot and every obstacle it has to offer and find a better ending, and you're going to lead us there like you always have."

"That's an awful lot of confidence to place in me, Blue," I commented.

"Well, you deserve it."

"Because *I'm so noble*?" I teased.

"No," she said simply. "Because you're my friend. And I know you'll always do right by me and protect us to the best of your ability."

I smiled. My Limbo with Blue was gone. I no longer felt guilt about keeping Jason's secret and I fully agreed with what Blue had just said. I would always do right by her. And I would protect her, SJ, Jason, and Daniel with all that I had.

I put one of my arms around my best friend and gave her a playful side hug as we watched the improv play being performed around the fire. Blue popped the lollipop back in her mouth and tilted her head in Jason and Daniel's direction.

"Do you think he knows that I like him?" she asked.

I was surprised she'd brought up the topic. Jason was a sensitive subject for Blue and she usually got defensive when I mentioned anything about her crush.

"I doubt it," I replied. "You guys have always been good friends, so your closeness and protectiveness of one another is nothing new. I'm not even sure SJ and I would know if you hadn't told us."

"That's good," Blue said. "I don't want him to know yet. I need to play it cool. Though I wish I hadn't made an idiot of myself earlier in front of him."

"What are you talking about?"

"In Sleepy Hollow." She pulled the lollipop from her mouth again. "I totally humiliated myself. Falling asleep in the middle of a fight, being *carried* to safety by Jason—I'm so embarrased."

"Oh, come now," I said. "I hate the idea of being seen as a damsel in distress as much as you do. But if I can make peace with getting saved every now and then when I truly need it, you can deal with this. I guarantee you that Jason doesn't think any less of you for needing help today. He just wants to protect you."

"Getting saved isn't the issue here, though," Blue said. "The problem is that I embarrassed myself in front of a boy I like."

"How's that any different from embarrassing yourself in front of a boy you don't like?"

"I don't know. It just is." She huffed then looked at me. My grin caused her to break into a smile too.

"We have evil to fight and people to save and we're talking about boys." She shook her head and laughed. "We're hopeless, Crisa."

"No, we're human," I said, still smiling. "And I think that means we're anything but."

I excused myself from the bonfire to make a couple of calls on my Mark Two.

The first was to Liza. I wanted to update my magical mentor on where we were, what was happening, and where we were going next. I also told her about how I had used my magic recently. She was proud of me for being wise enough to restrain the majority of my magic when I was feeling such strong emotions in the Ruined City. But she was upset that I'd pushed myself to such an extreme state of Magic Exhaustion in Oz.

When the conversation and nagging were done, I promised that we would talk soon. Liza said goodbye with her all-too-familiar final words.

"Try and stay out of trouble, Crisa."

I smirked wryly. "I'll do my best."

When the call concluded, I stared out at the darkness. I'd climbed up a tree again, but tonight the sky was not clear. A ceiling of cold-bearing clouds blocked the moon and stars. I took a breath and gathered the strength and calm to make my final call.

"Alex," I said.

I knew Mauvrey had a Mark Two so I'd hoped Alex had one of his own. My compact started ringing and a moment later, he answered.

"Crisa." He sounded surprised.

"Hey," I responded.

My emotion didn't rise and my heart didn't beat faster on seeing him this time. I think finally facing the truth about how I felt in Limbo had allowed me to move past that. I wasn't completely healed, but I wasn't heartbroken anymore either. I'd accepted what had happened and I'd accepted who he'd become. By letting go of the hope that my brother was still the person he used to be and that he could come back, I'd found peace. It was a sad, cold kind of peace, but I preferred it to the rage that had clouded my focus these last couple of days.

"I wanted to ask you something," I said, getting straight to the point. "Why were you and Mauvrey headed to Camelot? You said you weren't helping with the search for Paige Tomkins. I want to know what other reason you could have for going there."

This had been bothering me since my friends and I had learned about Excalibur and changed course. We didn't know that we needed to go to Camelot until we discovered that Excalibur could free Paige's memories. And we didn't know about needing to free Paige's memories until we found her in the Maze of the Mindless and she explained the whole situation with the brainless scarecrows, Glinda, and the memory stone.

So why were Alex and Mauvrey already on their way to Camelot this morning? Arian hadn't found Paige yet. By now he'd probably located her, escaped the maze, and forced Julian to share the same information about Excalibur and Glinda's memory stone, but he hadn't known earlier. Which meant the antagonists had another, separate mission in Camelot.

"He wanted us to retrieve something," Alex said with a shrug.

"Wow. Real cryptic," I said, rolling my eyes. "And here I thought you'd moved past beating around the bush after you let your girlfriend electrocute me." I released an exasperated sigh. "Different question then. What do I have to do with your new mission? In the Ruined City, Mauvrey said you needed me as 'a spare.'"

Alex didn't answer that question either. He paused as a shadow of guilt passed over his face. "Crisa," he said. "About what happened in the Ruined City—"

"Save it," I cut him off. "I accept who you've become, Alex.

You don't need to explain it, because I don't really care. There are allies and there are enemies, and today I finally accepted which you are. Let's stop pretending that we're anything more to each other, all right? I think it would save time."

He hesitated for a moment but finally nodded. "Fine," he said. "If we're enemies, then I don't owe you any answers. But I'll tell you something, Crisa. Whatever happens next, I stand by what I've said. We may be on different sides, but I will try to protect you whenever possible. I won't always be able to, like today when Arian's orders complicated things, but I'll try."

"Knock yourself out," I responded. "It doesn't matter to me anymore."

I truly meant it. I finally saw Alex Knight clearly for the first time in a long time.

"Arian found Paige today," Alex said after a moment.

I shrugged easily. "I figured as much."

"He said he ran into you in the Emerald City, so I take it you probably found her as well."

"You figure correctly. Which means now your little task force has more than one reason for being in Camelot." I paused. "You know, soon enough I'll figure out what your other reason for being there is."

"I know," he said.

"Then I guess there's only one thing left to say. See you soon, bro."

I hung up my Mark Two without further regard for my brother. He was going to continue to be a main player in my story; it was unavoidable. But from now on I would not mistake his character in it. He was an antagonist. I was a protagonist. Not because we were chosen by anyone, but because we'd chosen the roles for ourselves. The thought sat strongly with me as I breathed in the evening air.

Soon I'd climb back down the tree and rejoin the chaotic world, but up here, there was stillness that seemed to go on forever. I let it absorb into my spirit like lotion on the skin.

My thoughts drifted to other realms.

I hoped that my parents were okay. The quest I was on and

the enemies I had to fight kept me from thinking too much about all we'd lost in Midveil. I didn't know if my parents were sufficiently distracted staying at Chance Darling's family castle. Once I returned from this mission I needed to connect with them. Now that they were short one child, I owed it to them to step up for the family.

I was glad that Pietro was there for my parents. He was a true brother and prince. We were all lucky to have him. While I still felt kind of bad for suspecting him of treachery, that story arc—and realizing his true goodness—had made me feel closer to him than ever before.

Funny how people kept surprising me.

Although several characters I cared for had turned on me over the course of the last few months, I could not overlook the fact that there were others who had changed for the better, and who I was glad to give more room in my life to, like Girtha back at school and maybe . . . maybe even Chance.

I smiled slightly at the thought of him, the prince I'd left behind. I didn't know if I hoped he would succeed or fail in his endeavor to prove himself to me. Nor did I know how he would even go about it. But after everything that had happened, I knew not to rule anything out.

# CHAPTER 53

# A Knight of Royal Blood

"Open the cave, Nyneve."

An old woman stood in the middle of a forest facing a massive cave. A large stone blocked the cave's opening. The woman had gray, wavy hair like unraveled yarn and a complexion like raw chicken.

Behind her were seven men. I instantly recognized them as magic hunters. This elder facing the cave was clearly their prisoner.

One of the hunters raised a bow and aimed it at her. "Now," he barked.

The woman's blue eyes were wide with dread and her cracked lips quivered. "I am warning you one last time," she said, pivoting. "Moving this stone will bring you nothing but destruction. He is too powerful. You are no match."

The magic hunters were unmoved. "Open it," a hunter with a red scarf said curtly. "We'll see who is outmatched."

Shaking with nervousness, the old woman turned to face the stone blocking the cave once more. Slowly, she brought her hands up and placed them on its unnaturally smooth surface. After a few moments the stone began to emanate a pale green glow. As the viridescence increased, the cave trembled. The old woman seemed petrified, as if a monster was about to be set free.

If this was the case, I did not get to witness it. My dreams shifted to a different setting. Century City.

I was running. Screaming and crashing sounds emanated from behind me, but I did not look back. I continued racing through the streets until I reached a familiar outdoor market—

the one my friends and I had passed through the night we found our first Portalscape Portal.

People were in panic everywhere trying to escape from something, but I didn't know what. Tents and stalls tipped over. Antiques crashed against the pavement. Barrels, sacks, and crates fell in my path like roadblocks. I kept going—leaping, bobbing, and weaving through everything with my eyes trained on one thing. A mirror. It was in the window of an antiques store, but not the same one as before. I knew I needed to get to it.

Scene change.

A net abruptly launched on top of me. Everything was dark; my world had been consumed by an obsidian void that concealed the rest of the scene, but I felt the ropes tighten against my skin. The net began to be yanked back, pulling me along with it.

Suddenly I was underwater. The net was gone and Daniel was below me, being dragged into the darkness by something that had him by the ankle.

*Daniel!*

I swam after him. Faster and faster I kicked. Deeper and deeper I dove. The waters were blackening with every passing second and I was losing him. Desperately I reached out until . . .

"Did you really think I'd forgotten about you?" Arian's voice said.

I woke with a start.

I was in one of the Lost Boys and Girls' bunkers, but I was alone. I guess the kids were early risers. Out of the corner of my eye I saw something twinkle behind a bed.

"Um, hello?" I said.

A trio of bashful fairies showed themselves. They floated over to me, smiling happily.

With a yawn and a rub of my eyes, I stood and stretched. Something tugged on the hem of my skirt, and I looked down to see a fourth fairy trying to get my attention.

"What is it?" I asked.

The fairy flew up to join the other three. The four of them whirred around excitedly, their wings changing from pink to green to yellow as they gestured upward.

"All right," I said as I ran my fingers through my hair and cracked my knuckles. "I can take a hint. It's time to get up."

I rose to ground level with my fairy posse. It was a beautiful day. Sunlight streamed through the trees, permeating the leafy cover of the camp in golden streaks. The campers were already up and about. Lost Boys and Girls ate, dueled, flew, and played.

Peter came flying over to me with a big grin on his face. "Good. They got you up."

One of the fairy's wings flashed lavender three times.

"She says you're a heavy sleeper," Peter translated. The fairy flashed her wings white twice, then red and blue once. Peter laughed. "And that you talk in your sleep."

"I'm aware," I said. "Thanks for the wake-up call. I was so tired I might've slept the whole day. I guess I should go find my friends. Have you seen them?"

Peter nodded. "That's why I sent the fairies to get you," he explained. "Your friends are getting a flying lesson and they didn't want you to miss out."

When I arrived at the cliffs where my friends were standing, I wasn't sure if I was more fascinated by the gorgeous view of the forest below or the fact that Blue was presently flying across the sky at full speed. She was soaring with two Lost Girls. Her smile was so wide she could've given the Cheshire Cat a run for his money.

"This is amazing!" she said as she did a backflip in the air. "You guys gotta try it!"

"Gladly," I said, alerting my friends to my presence.

Blue spotted me and flew back to the cliffs with the Lost Girls at her side.

"Look who decided to join us," Daniel said. "Have a nice sleep, did you?"

"Yeah, lovely as always," I said as I approached the cliff's edge. "I see you guys wasted no time in taking advantage of the perks Neverland has to offer."

"Figured we might as well since we're stuck her here til tomorrow morning," Jason responded.

"Hey, this is Neverland—not the alleyway behind a fried fish restaurant," Peter commented. "Being stuck here isn't exactly something you should be bummed about."

"Don't take it personally, Pete," I said. "We're just on a deadline. We've only got five more sunsets until the Vicennalia Aurora."

"Well, try to have fun today anyway," Peter said. "I get the whole 'save the world' mumbo jumbo. But since you can't do anything about it now, you should enjoy your time here. You guys are kids too, you know, even if you have big responsibilities. Try acting like it. At least every now and then."

Peter winked and jumped off the cliff. He fell from sight for a moment then zoomed into the sky and disappeared in the clouds.

"Back to business," said the Lost Girl named Madison, who we'd met previously. "Like you saw with your friend Blue, once the fairy dust has been applied, you just need to concentrate really hard on wonderful thoughts—those things that fill your heart completely and utterly with happiness and joy—then scrunch your nose and we have liftoff. Are the rest of you ready to try?"

We nodded.

"Okay, fairies. Hit 'em with a few good shakes."

The fairies buzzed over our heads and fluttered their wings extra fast.

Glittering bits of magic that looked like gleaming snowflakes rained down. The instant each sparkle touched our skin, it evaporated, leaving a feeling of warmth and lightness. I scrunched up my nose and focused on thoughts of joy.

After a few beats, SJ started to float off the ground, followed by Daniel. They grinned at one another and joined Blue in the air. Jason and I, however, seemed unable to rise. No matter how hard we tried, we stayed grounded.

The magic should have worked the same for everyone, so I assumed the problem lay with us. Honestly it made sense. This magic required completely joyful thoughts to work, and it was tough to keep those in my head for very long. I had plenty of happy memories, but each came with the price of being reminded of a responsibility or heartache.

If I thought of childhood fun—games of tag and chase, exploring the tunnels beneath my castle, learning to use a sword for the first time—it reminded me of Alex. Thinking of the first time I rode a Pegasus reminded me of the pain of getting my prologue prophecy. Making the Twenty-Three Skidd team at Lord Channing's caused me to think about how I never got to play a match because of the magic hunter attack. It was all very depressing.

My feet were firmly planted on the dirt while my friends flew about in front of me. I glanced over at Jason. He was equally stuck. It wasn't hard to figure out why. Despite his generally optimistic outlook, it must've been difficult to let joy overflow his system when he knew the details of his not-too-distant death. As with me, his happiness was found in moments, not in the long term.

"What's wrong with you guys?" Blue asked, flying over.

"I can't do it," I admitted.

"Me neither," Jason sighed.

Madison flew in close and studied us for a second. "Hmph," she mumbled. "I haven't seen this in a while. Your good thoughts are being stifled. You have so many dark ones that they're weighing you down like an anchor. That's why you can't fly. The unhappy thoughts aren't letting the wonderful ones take over. You can't completely let go."

The other Lost Girl—Tiffany, I think—nodded in agreement. "Madison's right. Joyful thoughts create feelings of light-hearted, high-spiritedness inside you, which cause your body to become light and rise higher. If your soul is too heavy, then it can't achieve this state. Looks like you're grounded. For now, anyway."

Jason and I exchanged a disappointed look.

"Hey, no big deal, Crisa," Blue said after an awkward beat. "You've got magical powers, so you don't need fairy dust. Just enchant a rock or something and you and Jason can join us up here on your own private hoverboard."

"My powers are still exhausted from Sleepy Hollow," I replied. "They probably won't be recharged until later tonight."

"Right. Well, maybe a little rest for you is a good thing," Blue said steadily. "We'll probably face a lot of wacko monsters and antagonists in Camelot, which means we'll need you working at full magical capacity."

I nodded, appreciating her diplomatic, silver-lined response. "Yeah, I think I'll just go hang out with the kids back at camp."

"Me too," Jason said. "You guys have fun."

"You sure you're okay?" Blue asked him. "Is something bothering you? Crisa can be angsty sometimes, but you're usually so upbeat. I'm surprised you can't fly either."

"Don't worry about it." He shrugged. "I'm having an off day. Now go on and take a good soar for us," he said, putting his arm around my shoulder. "We landlubbers have other things to do."

Jason and I were left standing on the cliff's edge as our friends bolted into the clouds. We started walking back to camp. A squirrel appeared on our path. It had a piece of wood in its mouth. Seeing it reminded me of that floating beaver in Limbo, chewing on his bark.

I glanced sideways at Jason. It had felt really good embracing my Limbo realizations with Blue and Alex last night. I was ready to continue the trend.

"I've decided I'm not going to let you die," I said bluntly.

Jason stopped and gave me a confused look. "What are you talking about?" he said. "I'm going to die by that river. You saw it."

"Yes," I replied. "I just mean I'm not going to let it happen."

"Crisa," he said dejectedly. "Your visions come true. They *always* come true. It's not like with Liza's prologue prophecies where there can be multiple interpretations. Your dreams show the future exactly for what it is. Another way is impossible."

"Impossible is irrelevant," I said firmly. "Just look at where we are, Jason. Look at what we've done and seen. Fairies and headless horsemen and flying kids and zombie scarecrows. We live in a world of impossible things and impossible people, but we accept them as fact every day. Our very origins make us impossible. I mean, beanstalks that grow through the sky and slippers made of glass comfortable enough to dance in? If we can believe in all those impossible things, what makes you so certain that we can't change the future I've seen?"

Jason stared at me for a long while. There was a forlorn look in his eyes that was hard to read. After a moment, he fixed his gaze on the ground. "Crisa, I get what you're saying, but I don't . . . I don't want to get my hopes up. Hope is—"

"A dangerous thing," I finished. "I know. But it's also a powerful thing. I haven't given up hope that we can save you, Jason, and neither should you. We can do the impossible, because we already are the impossible."

Jason and I locked eyes. After a long moment, he squeezed my shoulder and gave me a small smile. "I'm going to find Thaddeus," he said. "I promised I'd show him some moves with my axe." He started to walk away but glanced back before stepping through the trees. "I don't know if I'm willing to bet on the impossible here, Crisa. But I would bet on you. So if you think there is a way, then I'm not going to give up hope either."

With that, he was gone. And I smiled.

*I will save you, Jason. I promise.*

I headed into the woods, intending to wander around aimlessly for a while. However, as I was passing through a particularly dense area of the forest, I suddenly fell through a giant hole in the ground that had been concealed beneath a false carpet of branches and leaves—some sort of animal trap.

I plummeted five feet, but grabbed hold of one of the vines on the side of the ditch before I fell the remaining ten. I began pulling myself up, but the vine started to break. My fingers reached for the edge of the pit.

*Just a touch closer . . .*

The vine tore. I grasped for the dirt in desperate reflex, but someone grabbed my hand before I could fall. I looked up to see Arthur.

"Hold on," he said, blue eyes shining. "I've got you. Give me your other hand."

As he reached down, his sleeve was pushed up and I spotted a birthmark on the skin of his left forearm—a cross with a star-shaped freckle in the top right quadrant.

Arthur pulled me up and out of the pit. Dude must've had a lot of upper body strength. He lifted me as if I weighed nothing at all, which definitely wasn't true after last night's feast.

"Thanks," I said. "Lucky for me you were out here."

"Not quite luck, just good timing," Arthur replied. "This is my trap. There is a large bear that's been posing a danger to some of the children. I was coming to see if I'd captured it."

"Sorry to disappoint," I said. "All you caught was me."

Arthur shrugged. "According to Peter, you're a formidable opponent. So I suppose I will still count that as a win."

I grinned. "I'm glad to see that even after a royal becomes a king, he never fully outgrows that prince charming quality."

"And I am glad to know that a girl called Knight lives up to the name in more ways than one. Your friends' stories about you at the feast the other night gave me the impression that you are exceptionally brave. And when I went into town yesterday, I heard talk of a young lady matching your description who saved a storyteller at Once Upon a Tavern. The story goes that she stood up to Hook without hesitation in order to protect a man she didn't even know."

"Stories are sometimes embellished," I said. "Honestly, that was nothing. Anybody would've done the same."

"No, Crisanta. They wouldn't have. But the fact that you believe that says more about your character than I think you realize. You are honorable—a trait that is increasingly rare. And that, in truth, is one of the reasons why I have been so forthcoming with you and your friends about Excalibur and how to claim it."

Arthur gestured to a nearby log. It was overgrown with moss and had a few mushrooms sprouting from it. He sat on one end and indicated for me to take the spot across from him. I acquiesced. It was weird that he was treating me like an equal since he was a king and a legend, but I felt comfortable talking with him. He was kind and direct, his presence authoritative and strong, yet warm and compelling.

"There are many challenges and dangers involved with trying to reach Excalibur; hence why no one has claimed the sword in the seven years since I was killed," Arthur said. "But there is also another reason no one has succeeded. None of them were meant to. I mentioned last night that one of Merlin's most well-known prophecies is the Great Lights Prophecy. However, there is more to it than what I have said."

Arthur held my gaze as he recited the prophecy from memory:

> *"A game of four kings*
> *Three of them lost*
> *A struggle for the realm*
> *Where one king pays the cost.*
>
> *This fate will be forged*
> *By one Knight alone*
> *Born of royal blood*
> *Heir to the lion's throne.*
>
> *The Oath pledged to Camelot's king*
> *Endowed with the quest*
> *And blessed by the Boar's Mouth*
> *With strength to pass the test.*
>
> *The Lake shall be crossed*
> *And the Sword will be found*
> *To the rightful king returned*
> *When Great Lights strike the ground."*

"So now do you see?" Arthur asked me.

I shook my head.

"I learned about all the Wonderlands during my studies as a young man," Arthur said. "I acquired knowledge on their customs, structures, and rulers. It may have been a long time ago, but in my studies of Book, I now distantly remember learning that the rulers of the kingdom called Midveil were the Knight family. And if I recall correctly, their symbol was a lion."

I blinked.

"I used to think that the Knight of the prophecy was one of my Knights of the Round Table," Arthur continued. "But after meeting you, I now believe that the 'Knight' mentioned in the prophecy is not a title but a name. *Your* name. You are literally a Knight of royal blood. More than that, you are exceptionally honorable and have that most precious thing—the heart of a hero. With the Great Lights meant to strike in a few days, I suspect that you, Crisanta Knight, might be the one destined to retrieve Excalibur and return it to me once you have finished utilizing it for your quest."

I didn't know how Arthur expected me to react to this, but all I could manage was, "You've got to be joking."

"I am not," Arthur replied.

"I don't get it. Why didn't you say any of this last night?"

"I thought I would do you the kindness of having this conversation with you in private. I can sense that you are not a fan of attention. Am I correct?"

Embarrassed, I nodded. Then I let out a weighty sigh. "Most people used to write me off because they didn't expect anything great from me. That hurt at times, but I liked being left alone. Now though—between my magic, my visions, and my prophecy— sometimes I feel like people talk about me all the time. It makes me feel uncomfortable, especially around . . . certain people. So yeah, I do appreciate you not announcing to the entire room that apparently I might be destined to retrieve Excalibur too."

"I figured as much," Arthur replied. "Although I would advise you not to be so reluctant in the future. Humility and insecurity are easily confused in the heart, but reap two very different results in the soul."

"You don't understand," I said, shaking my head. "The crazier things get, the more people seem to look to me to lead. I don't have a problem with that. I'm good at thinking on my feet and making plans, and I actually like being a leader. But since it happens so often, I feel kind of awkward about the attention it gets me and how it affects my friends. I don't want to overshadow their abilities and valor. One of them is already super ticked off at me for hogging the spotlight. I'd like to not push them away any further if I can help it."

Arthur gave me a stern but sympathetic look. "Hiding who you are for the service of others is no more beneficial to them than it is to you, Crisanta," he said. "You cannot be afraid to step into the light, even if it means you stand in it alone. Oftentimes that is the price of being a leader. And that, I assure you, is something I understand more than most."

My eyes widened as mortification caught in my throat.

*Right. Duh.*

*Here I am complaining about the price of being a leader to the king of Camelot. This guy used to lead one of the most powerful realms of all time!*

"You know, you remind me a bit of myself," Arthur said kindly.

I didn't think I could have blushed any more fiercely, or been any more surprised.

"You're a young hero on the verge of a changing world. There's so much responsibility on your shoulders, so many unprecedented possibilities, and so many people and choices depending on you."

Arthur took a breath and continued.

"Leadership is a burden, Crisanta. And no matter how well-equipped we are, when it is thrust upon us at such a young age, the responsibility can be hard to bear. I know, for I have been there. I was only sixteen when I became king of Camelot. I had to deal with a lot of resistance to my rule right from the start—greedy kings, treacherous courtiers, wars of great scale, and bloodshed that all but wiped my heart clean of faith. So trust me when I say that I know what you are going through. More than that, trust what I am about to tell you.

"The greatest trait that you and I share is the same quality that made you step in and save that storyteller in the tavern. You have honor, Crisanta Knight—a rare combination of strength of heart, soundness of mind, and integrity of soul that makes you stand up for what you know is right—no matter the personal cost. This characteristic cannot be taught any more than it can be learned; it is simply innate. And in your case, as it was with mine, I believe it will make you rise to the challenge of what is coming, and be triumphant."

Arthur got up and stood in front me. "On that note, other than being a Knight of royal blood, there are two other prerequisites to being the subject of the Great Lights Prophecy. One is to be blessed by the Boar's Mouth, which is in my castle in the Camelot citadel. I will tell you more about this later. The other requirement is that you have to pledge The Oath to the King of Camelot."

I cleared my throat. "What kind of an oath?" I asked.

"It's not just *an* oath," Arthur said. "It's *The* Oath, otherwise known as the Pentecostal Oath. It is the all-binding pledge of allegiance that men and women take to serve Camelot and become Knights of the Round Table."

*Is this going where I think it's going?*

"The Knights of my Round Table have always been selected based on three qualities: supreme combatant skill, bravery, and unwavering honor."

*Oh snap. This is totally going where I think it's going.*

"As you have proven to possess all of the above, I find it to be both my duty and my privilege to help you complete this prerequisite and move you one step closer to being the subject of the prophecy meant to claim Excalibur. I would like to extend to you an invitation to take The Oath and join the most sacred bond of loyal service in Camelot—the Knights of the Round Table."

He gestured to a spot in front of him. "Please kneel."

*You better believe I'm going to kneel!*

Arthur removed the sword from the sheath at his belt and brought the side of its blade to rest upon my right shoulder.

"Candidate for knighthood, I now put before you the sacred bond of our congregation, The Pentecostal Oath. As a Knight of the Round Table, you, Crisanta Knight, hereby swear to defend the realm of Camelot—her lands, people, and sovereign—from all those who pose a threat. You promise to give mercy to those who ask for it, resist cruelty, malice, and self-interest, and agree to offer succor to any and all innocent souls who require it. These are the duties you are charged with. And to the best of your ability, you shall be sworn to their standard forevermore, upon pain of forfeiture.

"In accepting the responsibility and title 'Knight of the Round

Table,' you eternally bind yourself to uphold the name and legacy it carries. You pledge yourself to the service of others, no matter the personal cost. You commit yourself to protect Camelot and her interests with all of your mortal ability. And you swear to be honor-bound from now until the end of days. Knowing this, Crisanta Knight, do you accept The Oath?"

I looked up at Arthur. His eyes were serious and powerful. I solemnly pondered the severity of his words and the legacy and responsibility they carried with them. I also for a moment wished Blue and Jason were here, as I was secretly geeking out over how cool this was.

Filled with an odd rush of pride and humility, I answered King Arthur with more certainty than I'd felt in a long time.

"I do," I said

Arthur nodded and moved his sword to my other shoulder then back again.

"Then Crisanta Knight," he said, "Page Turner, Princess of Midveil—I officially dub thee a Knight of the Round Table."

# CHAPTER 54

# The Promise

t had been a mixed day. The morning hadn't started out so hot, what with the intense nightmares and the disappointing revelation that I couldn't fly. But the afternoon was full of cool, weird surprises, including getting knighted by Arthur and receiving a one-on-one training session from the king to further fine-tune my fighting abilities.

At first it was intimidating to duel with Arthur. One, he was a king. Two, he had *way* more experience. But despite these factors, he proved to be a great teacher and gave me some really solid tips about my footwork and stance. Turns out he'd been personally training Peter in sword combat for years. The flying kid was undeniable proof of Arthur's ability to help others improve.

After our lengthy session, Arthur wanted to check a few more of his traps in the forest. Before we parted ways he asked that my friends and I meet him at his bunker before dinner to discuss my knighthood, the prophecy, and Excalibur in anticipation of our departure tomorrow.

Once he'd gone, I spent the majority of the remaining afternoon playing with the Lost Boys and Girls alongside Jason—getting into mischief and becoming involved in some really elaborate games of capture the flag in the tree houses above camp. I did take a break at one point to go scribble my latest visions in my dream journal. I'd had it in my backpack since Midveil but hadn't gotten a chance to pen down any of my new dreams.

SJ, Daniel, and Blue were off flying all day. They returned

when the sun started to go down, and we headed for Arthur's bunker. They needed to know what had transpired between the king and I, and I needed to get over myself. Arthur was right; it was time I stopped shying away from the obligations of being a leader.

The king of Camelot was already back from his hunting trip when we knocked on his tree. Once we were all settled inside his bunker, I filled my friends in on everything.

I was grateful that Arthur was there to help with the explanation. SJ refused to make eye contact with me after we got into the whole "destined to claim Excalibur" thing, but I let it go. I was planning on talking to her later as part of my ongoing mission to do justice to the realizations I'd had in Limbo.

When all Arthur info had been shared, I bridged into the next topic—one that I'd mulled over throughout the afternoon.

"I think Alex and Mauvrey are also going after Excalibur," I said, sharing my latest theory with my friends. "My brother fits the description of the Knight in the prophecy the same way I do. Maybe that's the reason they were headed to Camelot yesterday. When I confronted Mauvrey in the Ruined City, she said Arian had asked her to manipulate Alex over to their side. This could be the reason. The antagonists want Excalibur."

"But what about The Oath?" Daniel asked, turning toward Arthur. "To be a Knight of the Round Table, you have to pledge that oath to the king of Camelot."

"Camelot must have a new king," Arthur replied. "Perhaps your antagonists believe pledging The Oath to him will satisfy the Boar's Mouth."

"What's the Boar's Mouth?" Blue asked.

"It's a sacred statue in Camelot's citadel castle," Arthur explained. "Before going on a great quest, men and women present themselves to the statue and get blessed by it. If they don't, it is a bad omen and they have no hope of succeeding. But the statue only responds to those who are confirmed Knights of the Round Table. And as you say, Daniel, you only become such a knight by pledging The Pentecostal Oath to the king of Camelot."

"But if you're not dead, then technically *you're* still the king of

Camelot," Blue said. "Regardless of who's sitting on the throne, if the old ruler of a kingdom is still alive there can't be a true new ruler."

"I'm not sure if the statue will see it that way," Arthur responded. "It could very well accept the new king. However, if it doesn't, it won't respond to Alex's request for a blessing. Then your antagonists—as well as the new ruler of Camelot—will know I am alive."

"If The Oath to the new king does work though, the Boar's Mouth will bless Alex?" Jason clarified.

"I can't say for certain," Arthur responded. "The Boar's Mouth blesses a knight's quest based on what it sees in the knight's soul. If the Boar's Mouth does not believe your brother is worthy or capable of the quest, then he will not be blessed. This would disqualify him from being the Knight of the prophecy."

"So that's why she did it . . ." I thought aloud.

My friends turned to me.

"I couldn't understand why Arian and the antagonists wanted to capture me instead of kill me. Mauvrey said it was because they needed a spare. I think she meant a spare Knight."

I closed my eyes and recalled my conversation with Mauvrey over the Mark Two the other night.

"She said, 'I have another important mission on my hands, one that I cannot complete without your brother's help. He is very special, you know. A Knight of royal blood destined for something great. With any luck, soon he and I will be on the verge of claiming a fantastic destiny'."

I opened my eyes. "If Mauvrey and Alex's mission this whole time was Excalibur, then that's why they didn't kill me when they had the chance. Arian doesn't want to get rid of me until they're sure Alex fits all the requirements of the prophecy. I'm their back-up plan."

"But why do they need Excalibur?" Jason asked. "They need it now to free Paige's memories, but what was their original motivation for going after it?"

"I don't know," I admitted. "But I'm sure we'll find out soon enough."

A loud banging sound echoed from the stairwell; someone was knocking on the tree trunk door. "Feast's on!" a boy called down.

Arthur regarded us. "You heroes have a great quest ahead, but there will be time for heroics and sacrifice later. Tonight, you deserve peace and some good fun. Come."

We followed the king up the steps. Blue leaned back and whispered in my ear. "I bet you feel pretty stupid."

My eyebrows scrunched together in confusion. "Why?"

"I recall *someone* claiming King Arthur was a total jerk at the start of Damsels in Distress class this semester."

I let out a half chuckle, remembering when Madame Lisbon tried to make me read that chapter from *Le Morte d'Arthur*. "Well, it's hardly the first time I've been wrong."

Our serious thoughts about the future were temporarily put on hold. It was dinnertime, which meant another three hours of feasting and campfire games.

During the meal I kept stealing glances at SJ and Daniel. We were leaving Neverland tomorrow morning, and I didn't want to embark on the next leg of this quest without having a proper talk with each of them. I decided to start with SJ. As the Lost Boys and Girls finished eating and headed to the bonfire, I spotted her chatting with Dorothy.

Anxiety filled my stomach. It'd been a long time since I attempted a deep conversation with SJ. We'd been distant since that first fight at Lady Agnue's all those weeks ago. I couldn't believe we'd gotten to a point where I actually felt nervous about talking to a girl who was once—and still hopefully was—my best friend.

Alex's thin gold wristband caught the sheen of the fairy light and bonfire. Despite my closure with him, I'd decided to keep wearing it. No longer as a reminder of the brother I'd lost, but as a reminder of where I came from. I ran a finger over my family motto etched into the metal.

*Aut viam inveniam aut faciam.*

I'd grown up seeing those words on the crest of every Midveil flag. To me, the words offered sound advice on how to live life. Their wisdom was practically engrained in my DNA.

*Aut viam inveniam aut faciam.*

"I will either find a way, or I will make one," I read aloud, translating the words glistening on my wrist.

The phrase meant that while the path we forge might not be an easy one, we should pave it with the strength to fight and the belief that we could be better. With these words and their message burning inside me, I made my way over to SJ and Dorothy.

"Hey," I said.

"Hi, Crisa," Dorothy replied.

"Dorothy," I said casually, "do you mind if I borrow SJ for a minute?"

"Not at all," she replied. "I have to talk to Peter anyway."

Dorothy gave me a wink and a small wave as she sashayed away. SJ turned to face me.

"What is it?" she asked. "Is something wrong?"

"Does something have to be wrong for you and I to talk these days?"

"I suppose not." She shrugged. "It is just you and I have not had that much to say to each other as of late."

"Which is exactly why I want to talk to you," I replied. "SJ, I'm tired of this. I'm tired of us being a thousand miles away from each other when we're both standing right here. I want this coldness between us to be done."

SJ crossed her arms defensively. "Crisa, if you expect me to push aside my feelings and simply apologize—"

"No, that's not it at all," I said. "SJ, I don't want to ask you for an apology. I want to offer you one." I paused and spoke with utter sincerity. "I'm sorry for how I've been treating you."

SJ raised her delicate eyebrows. Her jaw was tight and her eyes were hard. "Crisa, I have said some pretty terrible things to you. I hurt you and frankly . . . I was trying to."

Her expression softened and a veil of shame grazed her features ever so slightly. "But as my trials in Limbo so *keenly* pointed out, I have been blaming you for my problems unjustly. I needed to put a face to my strife and I chose yours. I was suffering and I resented that you were thriving, so I tried to lighten my anguish by passing some on to you. It was an awful thing to do. So why in the realm would you be seeking my forgiveness?"

"Because I wasn't there for you when I should have been," I replied. "Look, whether I understand what you're going through with the protagonist selection thing or not is irrelevant. What matters is that you are my best friend and you're frustrated and angry and confused, just like I was last semester. Only back then, instead of pushing me away out of pride or spite, you showed me empathy and understanding so that I could work through what was bothering me. You had faith that I would find myself again. And at the very least, I owe you the same thing. This whole time, I've been resenting you for how you feel when I should've been there for you like you were for me. So that is why I owe you an apology. You've never been anything but a true friend to me, even when I was putting distance between us. And I want you to forgive me for not returning that loyalty when you needed it the most."

SJ's face was a combination of sadness, disbelief, and guilt. Eventually she uncrossed her arms and glanced at the dirt. "I hate feeling this way," she whispered somberly. "All this anger, this insecurity—it brings me no more pleasure to bear than it does you to witness, you know."

"I know."

SJ's shoulders fell. Her walls started to come down. "What is the matter with me?" she said with a remorseful groan, bringing her fingers to her temple. "I have been so terrible to you—so terrible in general. All my life I have been a person of sound logic and reason, but I have allowed both to falter under these feelings of jealousy and doubt and defeat. Worse still, even now as I admit to such irrationalities, I still cannot talk myself out of feeling them. I must be losing my mind, or losing myself or . . ."

She wrapped her arms around herself protectively. "I feel like the girl I was before may not be capable of coming back."

A beat passed. Then I shrugged.

"So what?" I said.

SJ looked up. "Excuse me?"

"I mean, okay, so maybe we can't go back to who we were

before," I continued. "But that doesn't mean we can't rebuild. In rising out of the rubble and forging ahead, we can become something new, something better even."

I put my hand on my friend's shoulder. "SJ, I am certain of two things. One, whomever you choose to be going forward—protagonist book or not—I know it will be someone fantastic. Because that's what you are, SJ. You're fantastic. And you're brilliant, and kind, and brave. And it's not because the Author, or Lady Agnue's, or your royal pedigree made you that way. It's because you made yourself that way."

SJ's gaze timidly met mine. "And the second thing?" she asked.

"Whomever you choose to be, and however long it takes you to decide, I will be there for you. No matter the realm, no matter the time zone, no matter what else is going on in the world—from now on you can always count on me to stand with you, just like you've always stood with me."

SJ's eyes were glassy. It seemed at odds with the steeliness in her expression, yet strangely fitting. After a moment, she cleared her throat and gave me a small, grateful look.

"Thank you, Crisa," she said.

I took her hand in mine and gave it a light squeeze. "Hey, it's what best friends are for, right?"

A raucous burst of laughter suddenly came from the bonfire. Whatever joke had been told had just sent a roar of good cheer through the camp.

"I think I shall go join the others," SJ said with a hint of a smile. "If we are going to be fighting monsters for the next few days, I suppose it would be foolish not to enjoy what downtime we have left . . . Care to join me?"

"I'd love to, but in a minute. I actually have some stuff to talk to Daniel about." I glanced around the campground, noticing he'd vanished from view. "Did you see where he went?"

SJ nodded toward the woods. "He slipped away a minute ago through there."

"Then I guess that's where I'm headed," I said. "Wish me luck?"

"Crisa, you do not need luck with Daniel. You never have. You just need a little push."

I turned and sighed. "Will you at least get me started then?"

SJ released a short huff of amusement, then gave me a slight push from behind. "Off you go," she said. "And might I say, it is about darn time."

I smiled over my shoulder, heading in the direction of the woods.

This was it. There was never going to be a right time or setting to make peace with Daniel. Now was as good a moment as any.

I kept walking until the lights of the camp's lanterns faded. In the throng of the forest I was wonderstruck to discover something even more beautiful in their place. Hundreds of fireflies—*way* more than the last time I was here—flickered about the tall trees like tiny, shiny stars. It was by their glow that I found Daniel. I saw him through the trees sitting on a log, looking stoic and pensive.

"Hey," I said as I moseyed over to him.

Daniel turned in my direction, a bit surprised. "Hey," he responded. "What are you doing out here?"

I leaned against a tree trunk and sighed nonchalantly. "I needed a breather. I'm a fan of pageantry and shenanigans as much as the next girl, but it's been a long few days, and frankly I'd kill for a little headspace."

"So why exactly are you talking to me then?" he asked.

I shrugged. "Self-destructive tendencies," I suggested.

He smirked. "So that's what we are to each other now—self-destructive tendencies?"

"For the moment," I said slowly. "But to be honest, that's sort of why I came to find you. I've been doing some thinking."

"Knight, you're always doing some thinking," he said bluntly. "Don't get me wrong, it saves our skins half the time, but it also leads to fights in the woods where we say things we can't take back. So why don't I just stop you right there before history repeats itself."

I felt the sting of his words like sunburn on my cheeks. Nevertheless, I hung on to my resolve. "But see, that's just it. I came out here to tell you that I don't want history to repeat itself. I want to take some things back. One thing in particular in fact: I changed my mind. I want us to try again."

"Knight—"

"Daniel, please let me finish. If I don't say this now, I'll lose the nerve."

Daniel shut his mouth and gestured for me to continue. I slowly closed the gap between us and returned my heart to my sleeve where it belonged.

"For the last few months my life has been a series of burning bridges," I said steadily. "Some disintegrated without my provocation, others burned despite my best efforts, and I'm ashamed to say I set fire to some myself. Like the one between you and me. I've spent so much energy burning it down again and again out of fear. And . . . I don't want to live that way anymore. I want us to be friends, Daniel. Real friends. I accept your apology for instigating the distance between us, and I hope you'll accept mine for being a jerk to you the other night when you tried to mend it. If you still want us to let each other in, then it's what I want too."

The fireflies buzzed. They made it feel like the world was moving around us.

"I don't know if we can," he eventually said.

My heart sank.

"Why not?" I asked.

"It's the way we are, Knight. We don't change. At least not in regards to each other. I don't care what that beaver in Limbo showed me—the way you reacted when I tried to apologize proved that. We've done our best, but we can't seem to be open with one another without it being forced or provoked."

"What about what you told me two nights ago?" I asked softly. "About your family? I didn't force that out of you."

"No, you didn't," he said. "But you threw it back in my face when you told me you wanted us to keep our distance. How do you think I felt after that? I trusted you with one of the most private things about me, and you acted like it was nothing. I'm not sure there's anything you can say to undo that."

I stood there in a swell of conflict as regret swirled within.

"You're right," I admitted. "I was awful that night. You let yourself be fully vulnerable with me and I didn't appreciate it. So

. . . let me offer you something in recompense—not provoked, not forced, and definitely not expecting anything in return." I took a breath. "Alex."

"What about him?"

"I want to tell you the truth about what he did to me. A truth that I haven't shared with anyone because the wound is too deep."

I steadied my nerves and found the courage to speak openly.

"I know I put on a good face, but the truth is that I've been devastated since the attack. No one has ever hurt me like he did. A part of me *died* that day, Daniel. I have never—" The hurt was so intense that I felt my body start to shake involuntarily. I wrapped my arms around myself tightly and took a deep breath.

"I have never been so destroyed. He didn't just break my heart; he broke my world."

My voice grew raspy as a knot formed in my chest and my throat burned. That was the problem with feelings. When you kept them caged, they didn't seem that threatening, but when you let them out you ran the risk of their power running rampant.

"I have been too afraid to say anything and let the pain show," I continued, the words pouring out of me now. "Everyone expects so much of me. Everywhere we go, the list of things I'm supposed to do, and people I'm supposed to save, and prophecies I can't outrun, only grows. So I keep all my emotion bottled up. I hide my pain, my regret, my . . . sorrow."

I felt a tear escape.

I had underestimated how hard it would be to voice these thoughts into existence. While I may have found closure with how I regarded Alex and who he'd become, it still stung deeply to think about the day my castle burned and how it had felt to crumple on that mountainside and scream at the sky. All the feelings I'd buried in order to focus on our mission and my responsibilities quivered inside me like a thousand snowy peaks on the verge of an avalanche.

"I have to hide these feelings from everyone," I said, my throat closing up. "If I think about it too much, I want to break down and cry. And . . ." My voice cracked and I cracked. The flood of tears I'd been holding back since Midveil came rushing out at last. "What kind of leader does that?" I gasped through a sob.

Daniel—who hadn't moved this whole time—didn't wait another second. When the last word escaped my lips and my tears broke, he closed the distance between us and put his arms around me, embracing me in a tight, warm hug. It was the most surprising thing he'd ever done. And yet I didn't hesitate at his advance in the slightest. I hugged him back and buried my face deep into his chest as more tears fell.

Neverland stood still for a few long moments. I could hear Daniel's heart beating—slow, steady, safe. It called me away from the brink.

After another minute, the two of us finally stepped back. The connection passed and we didn't linger on it. We didn't need to. Moments like that didn't require explanation or analysis. They were too pure and too precious.

Daniel started walking and he gestured for me to follow. I wiped my eyes with the back of my hand and went to his side. We strolled through the forest in silence for a while until he eventually spoke. "You shouldn't be so hard on yourself, Knight," he said. "I know there's a lot at stake with the realm and the antagonists and Paige and a million other things, but you're human. No one would blame you if you took a minute to act like it every once in a while."

"That's easy for you to say," I said wistfully.

"Actually, it's not. I may not have magical powers or visions of the future, but I get what it feels like to have another person's fate relying on you."

"You mean Kai?" I asked carefully.

Daniel nodded. "I constantly worry about her and how my decisions will affect her fate. But I'm not going to let that overshadow what's happening with me now, because what's going on now is just as important as what's coming. They both matter, and they need to be treated that way—emotional stuff and all."

"You're talking about balancing my long game with my short game," I said, clearing my throat and willing the shrewder, more rational side of me to come forward.

"Exactly," Daniel said. "It's like fighting a war—you keep your eye on the end goal, but keep your head in the battle at hand. Because no matter how smart or strong you are, if you focus solely on one element and ignore the others, you'll lose."

I stepped over a particularly large tree root. "Easier said than done," I commented.

"It's not that complicated, Knight. Just do it."

"Daniel, I'm not a machine you can turn on and off. I'm gonna need a little more than that." A thought crossed my mind. "How do you do it? How do you keep your head balanced between everything that's eating you alive in the present with what you're worried about in the future?"

Daniel shrugged. "I don't know. Just take a deep breath once in a while and stop thinking that you need to be this impenetrable rock all the time. You're a lot of impressive things, Knight. That's the whole reason you have so many people after you. But just because you have power and potential doesn't mean you need to expect the world of yourself every second of every day. You need to remind yourself that everything's going to be okay. That *you're* going to be okay."

"The deep breath thing I can do, Daniel," I said hesitantly. "The rest of it though . . . Again, that's easier said than done."

"Then I'll help you."

Daniel stepped in front of me and looked me straight in the eyes. We didn't stand face-to-face like this very often, so I sometimes forgot he was so tall, and that his eyes were such a deep shade of brown. He put both his hands on my shoulders and I tensed, not quite sure where this was going. Then without warning, he started shaking my shoulders roughly.

"Everything's going to be okay! You're going to be okay!"

"All right, all right!" I said, my face breaking into a grin. "I get it!"

Daniel stopped the shoulder quake and smiled back at me.

I punched him in the arm playfully. "Point taken. I'll try it your way and won't be so hard on myself from now on. Just don't do that again."

"We'll see," he said. "If I see you getting stuck in your head, I may have to."

"Yeah, well I suppose there are worse things."

"Than shoulder quakes?"

"No, than having someone who cares enough to give you one. Someone who hopefully accepts my apology about the other night and believes that we *can* change?"

Daniel stared at me for a second then at last agreed. "Friends like we were before?" he asked, holding out his hand.

I paused.

"No," I said decidedly. "Not like we were before. Let's be better. No more of this back and forth thing. No more doubts. No going backward ever again. Real friends who don't run away when things get hard. Let's really go forward."

Daniel gave me a warm look that could've melted a frost giant. "Deal," he said.

I extended my hand and pressed it against his. We shook on it and I felt like something finally clicked into place. Daniel and I were finally ready to be the kind of friends we'd always had the potential to be if we'd ever given it a proper chance.

"If we're going to be real friends," Daniel said as we continued our walk, "I want to promise you something."

"Oh? What's that?"

"I want to promise to be what you don't always admit you need—someone to remind you that when the world gets too heavy, you don't have to hold it up on your own."

My heart felt lighter at the thought. It was one of the nicest offers I'd ever gotten.

"If you're going to promise me that then I want to promise you something in return, Daniel," I said. "I want to promise you that so long as you and I are friends, I will do everything in my power to help you protect Kai."

I hadn't seen Daniel look so taken aback in a while. His expression was part surprise, part appreciation, and part something I didn't recognize.

"You don't have to, Knight," he said. "I told you, I don't—"

"Blame me for your prophecy. I know. But just because I may not be directly responsible for what it says doesn't mean that I can't do my part to influence the outcome. It's like you said, sometimes I need someone to remind me that I don't have to hold up the world on my own. Well, my friend, the same goes for you. This deal about relying on one another is a two-way street. And though you hate to admit it as much as I do, you're not alone in this either. So let me help you like you're offering to help me."

I grabbed his arm. "Come on, what do you say?"

"Fine, Knight," he said begrudgingly. "You can help."

"Well, don't sound too excited about it."

Daniel shook his head. "I'm sorry. I appreciate the offer. She just means a lot to me."

"Why do you think I'm offering?" I replied steadily. "If she means a lot to you, then I want to do everything I can to make sure nothing happens to her."

He hesitated another moment, but then his face relaxed and the trust between us solidified once and for all. "All right, Knight. Fine. Thank you. I really do appreciate it."

"You're welcome," I said. "And don't worry, Daniel. I keep my promises. Kai will be safe. I give you my word."

# CHAPTER 55

# Line Eight

he Getty Museum was packed.

Couples, whole families, students on field trips, and groups of tourists wandered across the premises. They made their way through the museum with an explorer's vigor as they took in the artwork of old and new masters. A blond man in his thirties and a young girl of about seven stood out in the throng. Her curly maple hair sprung off her shoulders as she scaled the stairs like a track star.

*Young Natalie Poole.*

Her father struggled to keep up with her. As he followed her sequined sneakers, he smiled just as brightly as she did.

The two of them proceeded through a packed alcove of the museum marked by a sign that read "The Works of Vincent Van Gogh."

There was hardly any standing room. Natalie's father hoisted her up onto his shoulders so she could tower over the masses and see the paintings better. The look on her face was priceless as she took in each work. Her grin was wide. Her eyes shone. This glad expression mirrored her father's. The two clearly shared a love for the artistic treasures they were beholding.

The man eventually led small Natalie to a less crowded part of the room. He was holding her by the hand now. "See this one, Nat. This is my favorite. Van Gogh painted it in 1890 just before he died."

She gazed up at where her father was pointing. Her tie-dyed shirt had a plastic button with the words "Birthday Girl" printed on it. She tilted her head and bit her lip as she studied the work.

"He looks so sad," she said.

She stepped closer to where the painting was mounted—her face steady, her eyebrows raised with curiosity and wonder. "What's it called?"

Natalie's father knelt down to his daughter's level and patted her hair. "It's called *The*—"

"*Knight!* Wake up!"

My eyelids jolted open as I was ripped away from the dream. Daniel was kneeling over me—his hands on my shoulders from having shaken me out of my sleep. There was an urgency in his expression. Noise and commotion filled my ears as the Lost Boys and Girls in the bunker swarmed around us.

"What's wrong?" I asked, clambering up.

"They found us," Daniel said.

Sheets and pillows went flying. An alarm wailed. Fairies zoomed all over. Orders were hollered as kids gathered weapons and bolted for the exits that led up to camp.

Realization struck me like lightning and my eyes widened.

"Who? Arian? Mauvrey? Alex?"

Daniel grabbed my hand and began pulling me through the chaos.

"All of them," he said.

# End of Book Four

# ABOUT THE AUTHOR

Geanna Culbertson is the award-winning author of *The Crisanta Knight Series*. Culbertson is also a regular speaker at schools for an array of age groups (from elementary schools to major universities).

Culbertson is a proud alumna of the University of Southern California where she earned her B.A. in Public Relations and triple minor degrees in Marketing, Cinematic Arts, and Critical Approaches to Leadership. She is a part of only 1.3% of her graduating class to earn the double distinction of Renaissance Scholar and Discovery Scholar. Her Discovery Scholar thesis "Beauty & the Badass: Origins of the Hero-Princess Archetype" earned her acclaim in the School of Cinematic Arts, and helped fuel her female protagonist focused writing passions.

In addition to authoring *The Crisanta Knight Series* (set to be eight books with the final release in spring 2021), Culbertson is a full-time manager at a leading industry digital marketing firm, representing over 30 clients across the nation. When Culbertson is not working or writing, she can likely be found performing volunteer work at her local karate studio where she teaches martial arts (she is a black belt), going on adventures with her mother and best friend, and indulging her love of delicious food across the land.

# TABLE OF CONTENTS

[xxi]

> This darksome burn, horseback brown,
> His rollrock highroad roaring down,
> In coop and in comb the fleece of his foam
> Flutes and low to the lake falls home.

Others enjoy the interplay of Germanic and Italic colorations, as in Shakespeare's Sonnet CXVI:

> Let me not to the marriage of true minds
> Admit impediments . . . .

The physical condition of the language that was in place by about 1250 invited exploitation by poets of many sorts. Indo-European languages share certain basic features and change according to certain common patterns; by 1250 the general changes in English had a permanent effect on what poets could do. One tremendous change, which began many centuries ago and is still going on, has to do with the typical word-making and word-changing mechanism of a language.

Consider the Latin word *video:* it is made up from a stem (*vid-*, "see") plus a suffix (*-eo*) meaning something like "first-person singular present indicative": the English translation, "I see," must state the pronoun (1) as a separate word that (2) comes before the verb. Likewise, the *vidi* in Julius Caesar's famous claim *Veni, vidi, vici* requires two or three separate English words for an adequate translation: "I saw" or "I have seen." The drift—from single words with inflections on the right side, to collections of single words arranged on the left—has affected what we do with nouns, verbs, adjectives, and adverbs. The process had led to a language with many more monosyllables than Latin had and with many more polysyllabic words that can be stressed on the final syllables. Latin had no such words.

This is not the place to go into the details of such evolutionary developments. Indeed, there are still controversies about the whole affair. It seems, even so, that, about a thousand years ago, Indo-European languages were reaching a state in which three devices were newly available to verse-markers: (1) there were syllables that could be distinguished and measured by *quality* or accent, rather than by *quantity* or duration (as had been the uniform custom in the verse measures of Sanskrit, Greek, and Latin); (2) there were such contours of single words and of word groups—like article-plus-noun and auxiliary-plus-verb—that the accentual rhythm could be called "rising": these are chiefly the so-called *iambs* that are found in most English poems (as in the finale of Tennyson's "Ulysses": "To strive, to seek, to find, and not to yield."); (3) rhyme. Rhyme works better when the rhyming stressed syllable is not followed by unstressed material. To seize a local example, my daughter's name, "Caroline," is easier to find rhymes for than is the name of the state we live in, "North Carolina."

Now, the mood of rising that we hear in the customary rhythms of poetry coexists with the mood of falling that we find among the customary sentiments of poetry—even poetry designed for children—so that terrific torque or tension is set up in the process. There is a similar tension inherent in the double vocabulary of English, where, for example, "velocity" is a relatively abstract technical term with four little uniform syllables and "speed" is very different.

There is yet another tension available in rhyme itself, which invites us to consider words that have a common sound, yet tease us with antithetical meanings, as in the "making" and "breaking" in Dylan Thomas's "A Refusal to Mourn the Death, by Fire, of a Child in London." Rhyme, let us not forget, is much better at accenting difference and tension than is alliteration, which gives mostly the effect of sliding along the slippery slope of selfsame sounds.

Poets have been helped by the richness of the English language, but to convey their own individual visions in works of art, they have had to fashion their own individual techniques. The greatest successes are on vivid display in the pages that follow.

One can read the poets as they are arranged here, in chronological order; one can read their poems according to rank (an Appendix lists them in order of number of times they have been anthologized); or one can sample them at random. Some statistics may be interesting. Poets represented by ten or more poems are Shakespeare (29), Anonymous (21), Donne (19), Blake (18), Dickinson (14), Yeats (14), Wordsworth (13), Hopkins (12), Tennyson (11), Hardy (11), Frost (11), Keats (10). There are 160 poets here, 139 of whom are named; the 21 anonymous writers were all British. That three-quarters of the poems are British makes sense, because British poetry has been with us three times as long as American poetry in English. The breakdown by century is certainly interesting:

| Century | Number of poems |
|---------|-----------------|
| XIII-XV | 23 |
| XVI | 70 |
| XVII | 69 |
| XVIII | 47 |
| XIX | 169 |
| XX | 122 |

It is interesting to note that most seventeenth-century poems included here are from the first half of the century, while most of the eighteenth-century poems come from the last quarter of the century. Short lyrics were not much in fashion between 1660 and 1760. The nineteenth century seems to have been a golden age for poetry from first to last; I do not believe that the twentieth will ever look so good. I am not the first to remark that the very greatest writers of the twentieth century work in prose.

There is little poetry on today's radio or television, even with the advent of cable, and the newspapers report that about thirty percent of our adult population is functionally illiterate. That cannot augur anything good for poetry, but I remain hopeful, nevertheless, and I believe that this collection proves that our own generation's taste in poetry is fine indeed. I would like to thank all the poets, critics, and editors whose judgment has propelled these works into the position of the "Top 500 Poems" in English. I also have some personal thanks of my own and offer a tribute to a number of friends who put up with me even when I would say (as I heard myself say one day), "That poem that wasn't entitled 'A Farewell to Arms' maybe wasn't written by George Peele after all." Let me list their names as a way of expressing my gratitude for their forbearance and generosity: Reid Barbour, Elizabeth Core, Sally Greene, Anne Hall, Anne Harmon, Hilary Holladay, Edith Hazen, Paul Jones, Robert Kirkpatrick, Jerry Mills, John Frederick Nims, and James Raimes.

Dear Caroline: This is *it!* The Cuccu and the Tiger are waiting, and so much else. Read!

# Cuckoo Song

Sumer is icumen in,
  Lhudé sing cuccu;
Groweth sed and bloweth med
  And springth the wudé nu.
    Sing cuccu!
Awé bleteth after lomb,
  Lhouth after calvé cu;
Bulluc sterteth, bucké verteth;
  Murie sing cuccu.
    Cuccu, cuccu,
  Wel singés thu, cuccu,
  Ne swik thu naver nu.
Sing cuccu nu! Sing cuccu!
Sing cuccu! Sing cuccu nu!

---

*The creature that Spenser called "The merry Cuckow, messenger of Spring" sings out his bell-like mating call at spring's threshold. The bird perches also at the threshold of anthologies: Nashe's "Spring, the Sweet Spring" (p. 120) with its vivid bird-chorus leads off Palgrave's* Golden Treasury *(1861) and this admirable poem—originally scored as an extraordinary six-voice round—comes first in Quiller-Couch's* Oxford Book of English Verse *(1900). (Note that: "nu" is "now"; "lhude" is "loud"; "med" is "meadow"; "awé" is "ewe"; "verteth" is "breaks wind"; "swik" is "be silent.")*

Chaucer, who is customarily ranked as the third greatest English poet (after Shakespeare and Milton) was a
vintner's son who gave distinguished military and civil
service to his country. He was the earliest notable poet
to be buried in the Poets' Corner of Westminster Abbey.

## *General Prologue*
## *to* The Canterbury Tales

When April with its sweet showers
Has pierced the drought of March to the root
And bathed every plant-vein in such liquid
As has the power to engender the flower;
When Zephyr also with its sweet breath
Has in every grove and field inspired
The tender crops, and the young sun
Has run half its course in Aries the Ram,
And small fowls make melody
That sleep all the night with open eye
(Nature pierces them so in their hearts) —
Then people long to go on pilgrimages
And palmers to seek foreign shores
To distant shrines, known in sundry lands;
And specially from every shire's end
Of England they travel to Canterbury
To seek the holy blissful martyr
That has helped them when they were sick.
  It happened that one day in that season
 As I lay at the Tabard Inn in Southwark
Ready to travel on my pilgrimage
To Canterbury with a most devout heart,
There came at night into that lodging-place
Twenty-nine in a group

Of sundry people, by chance fallen
Into fellowship, and they were all pilgrims
Wanting to ride toward Canterbury.
The chambers and stables were roomy,
And we were very well accommodated.
Soon, when the sun had set,
I had spoken to every one of them
So that I was immediately in their fellowship.
And we agreed to get up early
To make our way to the place I have described to you.
Nonetheless, while I have some time and room
Before passing further into this tale,
It seems reasonable to me
To tell you the condition
Of each of them, as it seemed to me,
And what they were, and of what rank,
And also in what array they were.
   I will first begin, then, with a knight. . . .

from The Canterbury Tales

---

*Chaucer's six-hundred-year-old English is still understandable to readers without a specialized education, but my rough-and-ready translation may be helpful. The general opening to the Tales leads up to a pilgrim-by-pilgrim introduction.*

# Sir Patrick Spens

### I. THE SAILING

The king sits in Dunfermline town
  Drinking the blude-red wine;
"O whare will I get a skeely skipper
  To sail this new ship o' mine?"

O up and spak an eldern knight,
  Sat at the king's right knee;
"Sir Patrick Spens is the best sailor
  That ever sail'd the sea."

Our king has written a braid letter,
  And seal'd it with his hand,
And sent it to Sir Patrick Spens,
  Was walking on the strand.

"To Noroway, to Noroway,
  To Noroway o'er the faem;
The king's daughter o' Noroway,
  'Tis thou must bring her hame."

The first word that Sir Patrick read
  So loud, loud laugh'd he;
The neist word that Sir Patrick read
  The tear blinded his e'e.

"O wha is this has done this deed
  And tauld the king o' me,
To send us out, at this time o' year,
  To sail upon the sea?

"Be it wind, be it weet, be it hail, be it sleet,
  Our ship must sail the faem;
The king's daughter o' Noroway,
  'Tis we must fetch her hame."

They hoysed their sails on Monenday morn
  Wi' a' the speed they may;
They hae landed in Noroway
  Upon a Wodensday.

### II. THE RETURN

"Mak ready, mak ready, my merry men a'!
  Our gude ship sails the morn."
"Now ever alack, my master dear,
  I fear a deadly storm.

"I saw the new moon late yestreen
  Wi' the auld moon in her arm;
And if we gang to sea, master,
  I fear we'll come to harm."

They hadna sail'd a league, a league,
  A league but barely three,
When the lift grew dark, and the wind blew loud,
  And gurly grew the sea.

The ankers brak, and the topmast lap,
  It was sic a deadly storm:
And the waves cam owre the broken ship
  Till a' her sides were torn.

"Go fetch a web o' the silken claith,
  Another o' the twine,
And wap them into our ship's side,
  And let nae the sea come in."

They fetch'd a web o' the silken claith,
    Another o' the twine,
And they wapp'd them round that guide ship's side,
    But still the sea came in.

O laith, laith were our gude Scots lords
    To wet their cork-heel'd shoon;
But lang or a' the play was play'd
    They wat their hats aboon.

And mony was the feather bed
    That flatter'd on the faem;
And mony was the gude lord's son
    That never mair cam hame.

O lang, lang may the ladies sit,
    Wi' their fans into their hand,
Before they see Sir Patrick Spens
    Come sailing to the strand!

And lang, lang may the maidens sit
    Wi' their gowd kames in their hair,
A-waiting for their ain dear loves!
    For them they'll see nae mair.

Half-owre, half-owre to Aberdour,
    'Tis fifty fathoms deep;
And there lies gude Sir Patrick Spens,
    Wi' the Scots lords at his feet!

*The poem presents its dramatically elliptical narration in the simplest ballad measure with superlative economy of design: just a few quick bold strokes and a thoroughgoing reliance on concrete detail. We are not told that the king was worried in some vague way; he is drinking and asking for help. Four brief speeches (king, knight, Sir Patrick, a nameless sailor) and then a focus on the marvelous detail of "cork heel'd shoon" (the last word in medieval chic) and floating hats. (Note that: "skeely" is "skillful"; "lift" is "sky"; "lap" is "sprang"; "laith" is "unwilling"; "aboon" is "above"; "flatter'd" is "floated," "tossing"; "kames" is "combs.")*

# *Western Wind*

Western wind, when wilt thou blow?
The small rain down can rain.
Christ, that my love were in my arms,
And I in my bed again.

---

*In homage to this poem, which is among the very oldest in this anthology, the fine poet and editor John Frederick Nims has given the title* Western Wind *to a most useful and entertaining anthology of poetry.*

# Edward, Edward

"Why does your brand so drop with blood,
    Edward, Edward?
Why does your brand so drop with blood,
  And why so sad go ye, O?"
"O I have killed my hawk so good,
    Mother, mother;
O I have killed my hawk so good,
  And I have no more but he, O."

"Your hawk's blood was never so red,
    Edward, Edward;
Your hawk's blood was never so red,
  My dear son, I tell thee, O."
"O I have killed my red-roan steed,
    Mother, mother;
O I have killed my red-roan steed,
  That went so fair and free, O."

"Your steed was old, and ye have more,
    Edward, Edward;
Your steed was old, and ye have more,
  Some other dole ye dree, O."
"O I have killed my father dear,
    Mother, mother;
O I have killed my father dear,
  Alas, and woe is me, O!"

"And what penance will ye dree for that,
  Edward, Edward?
What penance will ye dree for that,
  My dear son, now tell me, O."
"I'll set my foot in yonder boat,
  Mother, mother,
I'll set my foot in yonder boat,
  And I'll fare o'er the sea, O."

"And what will ye do with your towers and your hall,
  Edward, Edward?
And what will ye do with your towers and your hall,
  That were so fair to see, O?"
"I'll let them stand till down they fall,
  Mother, mother;
I'll let them stand till down they fall,
  For here never more must I be, O."

"And what will ye leave to your bairns and your wife,
  Edward, Edward?
And what will ye leave to your bairns and your wife,
  When ye go o'er the sea, O?"
"The world's room: let them beg through life,
  Mother, mother;
The world's room: let them beg through life,
  For them never more will I see, O."

"And what will you leave to your own mother dear,
  Edward, Edward?
And what will ye leave to your own mother dear,
  My dear son, now tell me, O?"
"The curse of hell from me shall ye bear,
  Mother, mother;
The curse of hell from me shall ye bear,
  Such counsels ye gave to me, O!"

*Compared with "Sir Patrick Spens," (p. 10) this ballad shows a quantum advance in sophistication and polish: the stanza is more complex, and the design is stripped to a set of quick* ex post facto *exchanges between a mother and a son. (Note that: "brand" is "sword"; "dree" is "suffer.")*

# *Thomas the Rhymer*

True Thomas lay oer yond grassy bank
   And he beheld a ladie gay,
A ladie that was brisk and bold,
   Come riding oer the fernie brae.

Her skirt was of the grass-green silk,
   Her mantel of the velvet fine,
At ilka tett of her horse's mane
   Hung fifty silver bells and nine.

True Thomas he took off his hat,
   And bowed him low down till his knee:
"All hail, thou mighty Queen of Heaven!
   For your peer on earth I never did see."

"O no, O no, True Thomas," she says,
   "That name does not belong to me;
I am but the queen of fair Elfland,
   And I'm come nere for to visit thee.

"But ye maun go wi me now, Thomas,
   True Thomas, ye maun go wi me,
For ye maun serve me seven years,
   Thro weel or wae as may chance to be."

She turned about her milk-white steed,
   And took True Thomas up behind,
And aye wheneer her bridle rang,
   The steed flew swifter than the wind.

For forty days and forty nights
   He wade thro red blude to the knee,
And he saw neither sun nor moon,
   But heard the roaring of the sea.

O they rade on, and further on,
   Until they came to a garden green:
"Light down, light down, ye ladie free,
   Some of that fruit let me pull to thee."

"O no, O no, True Thomas," she says,
   "That fruit maun not be touched by thee,
For a' the plagues that are in hell
   Light on the fruit of this countrie.

"But I have a loaf here in my lap,
   Likewise a bottle of claret wine,
And now ere we go farther on,
   We'll rest a while, and ye may dine."

When he had eaten and drunk his fill,
   "Lay down your head upon my knee,"
The lady sayd, "ere we climb yon hill,
   And I will show you fairlies three.

"O see not ye yon narrow road,
   So thick beset wi thorns and briers?
That is the path of righteousness,
   Tho after it but few enquires.

"And see not ye that braid braid road,
   That lies across yon lillie leven?
That is the path of wickedness,
   Tho some call it the road to heaven.

"And see not ye that bonny road,
   Which winds about the fernie brae?
That is the road to fair Elfland,
   Where you and I this night maun gae.

"But Thomas, ye maun hold your tongue,
    Whatever you may hear or see,
For gin ae word you should chance to speak,
    You will neer get back to your ain countrie,"

He has gotten a coat of the even cloth,
    And a pair of shoes of velvet green,
And till seven years were past and gone
    True Thomas on earth was never seen.

---

*A certain Thomas of Erceldoun, who lived in the thirteenth century, was reputed to possess prophetic powers as well as talent as a poet. (Note that: "lock" is "tuft"; "fairlies" is "marvels"; "maun" is "must.")*

Anonymous

# The Wife of Usher's Well

There lived a wife at Usher's Well,
　And a wealthy wife was she;
She had three stout and stalwart sons,
　And sent them o'er the sea.

They hadna been a week from her,
　A week but barely ane,
But word came to the carlin wife
　That her three sons were gane.

They hadna been a week from her,
　A week but barely three,
Whan word came to the carlin wife
　That her sons she'd never see.

'I wish the wind may never cease,
　Nor fashes in the flood,
Till my three sons come hame to me,
　In earthly flesh and blood.'

It fell about the Martinmass,
　When nights are lang and mirk,
The carlin wife's three sons came hame,
　And their hats were o the birk.

It neither grew in syke nor ditch,
　Nor yet in ony sheugh;
But at the gates o Paradise
　That birk grew fair eneugh.

'Blow up the fire, my maidens,
　Bring water from the well;
For a' my house shall feast this night,
　Since my three sons are well.'

And she has made to them a bed,
　She's made it large and wide,
And she's taen her mantle her about,
　Sat down at the bed-side.

Up then crew the red, red cock,
　And up and crew the gray;
The eldest to the youngest said,
　' 'Tis time we were away.'

The cock he hadna crawd but once,
　And clappd his wings at a',
When the youngest to the eldest said,
　'Brother, we must awa.'

'The cock doth craw, the day doth daw,
　The channerin worm doth chide;
Gin we be mist out o our place,
　A sair pain we maun bide.'

'Fare ye weel, my mother dear!
　Farewell to barn and byre!
And fare ye weel, the bonny lass
　That kindles my mother's fire!'

---

*Martinmas, November 11, falls not long after All Soul's Night. The hats of birch ("birk"), as scholars have noted, would be out of season in November. (Note that: "carlin" is "old peasant"; "fashes" is "disturbances"; "sike" is "field"; "sheugh" is "furrow"; "channerin" is "fretting"; "gin" is "if"; "byre" is "stable.")*

# As You Came
## from the Holy Land of Walsingham

As you came from the holy land
  Of Walsingham,
Met you with my true love
  By the way as you came?

How shall I know your true love
  That have met many one,
As I went to the holy land
  That have come, that have gone?

She is neither white nor brown
  But as the heavens fair,
There is none hath a form so divine
  in the earth or the air.

Such an one did I meet, good sir,
  Such an angel-like face,
Who like a queen, like a nymph, did appear
  By her gate, by her grace.

She hath left me here all alone,
  All alone as unknown,
Who sometimes did me lead with herself,
  And me loved as her own.

What's the cause that she leaves you alone
  And a new way doth take,
Who loved you once as her own
  And her joy did you make?

I have loved her all my youth,
  But now old, as you see;
Love likes not the falling fruit
  From the withered tree.

Know that love is a careless child
  And forgets promise past;
He is blind, he is deaf when he list
  And in faith never fast.

His desire is a dureless content
  And a trustless joy;
He is won with a world of despair
  And is lost with a toy.

Of womankind such indeed is the love,
  Or the word love abused,
Under which many childish desires
  And conceits are excused.

But true love is a durable fire
  In the mind ever burning;
Never sick, never old, never dead,
  From itself never turning.

---

*If, as some scholars still believe, Sir Walter Ralegh wrote this poem, he must have done so by adapting an existing popular song; the tone and design suggest a time before the sixteenth century. Walsingham in Norfolk has long been sacred to pilgrims. Robert Lowell's "Quaker Graveyard in Nantucket" has a section called "Our Lady of Walsingham," about the shrine in Walsingham Priory.*

# Corpus Christi Carol

*Lully, lulley; lully, lulley;*
*The fawcon hath born my make away.*

He bare hym up, he bare hym down;
He bare hym into an orchard brown.

In that orchard ther was an hall,
That was hangid with purpill and pall.

And in that hall ther was a bede;
Hit was hangid with gold so rede.

And yn that bed ther lythe a knyght,
His wowndes bledyng day and nyght.

By that bedes side ther kneleth a may,
And she wepeth both nyght and day.

And by that beddes side ther stondith a ston,
'Corpus Christi' wretyn theron.

---

*Here, in a poem at least five hundred years old, pagan and Christian elements are combined so economically that only the sketchiest lineaments remain. The ever-bleeding wounds recall the Fisher King of Grail lore (see T. S. Eliot's "Waste Land," p. 968) as well as the Body of Christ (which is what "Corpus Christi" means). The poem, which may be a remnant or a fragment or a blend of more than one earlier poem, has been justifiably classified as both carol and ballad. (Note that: "make" is "mate"; "may" is "maid.")*

# The Three Ravens

There were three ravens sat on a tree,
  *Downe a downe, hay down, hay downe*
There were three ravens sat on a tree,
  *With a downe*
There were three ravens sat on a tree,
They were as black as they might be,
  *With a downe derrie, derrie, derrie, downe, downe.*

The one of them said to his mate,
"Where shall we our breakfast take?"

"Down in yonder greene field,
There lies a knight slain under his shield.

"His hounds they lie down at his feete,
So well they can their master keepe.

"His haukes they flie so eagerly,
There's no fowle dare him come nie."

Downe there comes a fallow doe,
As great with yong as she might goe.

She lift up his bloudy hed,
And kist his wounds that were so red.

She got him up upon her backe,
And carried him to earthen lake.

She buried him before the prime,
She was dead herselfe ere even-song time.

God send every gentleman
Such haukes, such hounds, and such a leman.

---

*Ravens and crows are everywhere in ancient and medieval literature, dark emblems of survival and disposal. In one of his late poems, W. B. Yeats said, "Another Troy must rise and set, / Another lineage feed the crow" in the same decade (the 1930s) as Eisenstein's epic film* Alexander Nevsky *with its unforgettable pictures of carrion-feeders scavenging after a battle. In 1971, Ted Hughes, later to be Poet Laureate of England, published several crow poems in* Crow: From the Life and Songs of the Crow. *(Note that: "leman" is "lover.")*

# Tom o' Bedlam's Song

·❖·❖·❖·❖·

From the hag and hungry goblin
That into rags would rend ye,
The spirit that stands by the naked man
In the Book of Moons defend ye,
That of your five sound senses
You never be forsaken,
Nor wander from yourselves with Tom
Abroad to beg your bacon,
 *While I do sing, Any food, any feeding,*
 *Feeding, drink, or clothing;*
 *Come dame or maid, be not afraid,*
 *Poor Tom will injure nothing.*

Of thirty bare years have I
Twice twenty been enraged,
And of forty been three times fifteen
In durance soundly caged
On the lordly lofts of Bedlam
With stubble soft and dainty,
Brave bracelets strong, sweet whips ding dong
With wholesome hunger plenty,
 *And now I sing, etc.*

With a thought I took for Maudlin
And a cruse of cockle pottage,
With a thing thus tall, sky bless you all,
I befell into this dotage.
I slept not since the Conquest,
Till then I never waked,
Till the roguish boy of love where I lay
Me found and strip't me naked.
 *And now I sing, etc.*

When I short have shorn my sow's face
And swigg'd my horny barrel,
In an oaken inn I pound my skin
As a suit of gilt apparel;
The moon's my constant mistress
And the lovely owl my marrow;
The flaming drake and the night crow make
Me music to my sorrow.
    *While I do sing, etc.*

The palsy plagues my pulses
When I prig your pigs or pullen,
Your culvers take, or matchless make
Your Chanticleer or Sullen.
When I want provant with Humphrey
I sup, and when benighted,
I repose in Paul's with waking souls
Yet never am affrighted.
    *But I do sing, etc.*

I know more than Apollo,
For oft when he lies sleeping
I see the stars at bloody wars
In the wounded welkin weeping;
The moon embrace her shepherd,
And the Queen of Love her warrior,
While the first doth horn the star of morn,
And the next the heavenly Farrier.
    *While I do sing, etc.*

The gypsies, Snap and Pedro,
Are none of Tom's comradoes,
The punk I scorn and the cutpurse sworn,
And the roaring boy's bravadoes.
The meek, the white, the gentle
Me handle, touch, and spare not;
But those that cross Tom Rynosseross
  Do what the panther dare not.
    *Although I sing, etc.*

With an host of furious fancies
Whereof I am commander,
With a burning spear and a horse of air,
To the wilderness I wander.
By a knight of ghosts and shadows
I summon'd am to a tourney
Ten leagues beyond the wide world's end:
Methinks it is no journey.
    *Yet will I sing, etc.*

---

*The "mad song" gives a writer the chance to play with interesting irrational combinations. Thomas D'Urfey wrote one in 1688 ("I'le Sail upon the Dog-Star") that also uses "roaring boy." Tom o' Bedlam, a stock madman through the sixteenth century, is the guise that Edgar adopts in* King Lear. *(Note that: "cruse" is "bowl"; "prig" is "steal"; "punk" is "whore.")*

# Adam Lay I-bounden

Adam lay i-bounden,
  Bounden in a bond;
Four thousand winter
  Thought he not to long;
And al was for an appel,
  An appel that he took,
As clerkes finden writen
  In here book.

Ne hadde the appel take been,
  The appel take been,
Ne hadde never our Lady
  A been hevene-queen.
Blessed be the time
  That appel take was!
Therefore we moun singen
  *"Deo Gracias!"*

---

*From data in the Old Testament, one can calculate that the Creation occurred in 4004 B.C. This little song expresses the sentiment known as the Fortunate Fall. (Note that: "Deo Gracias" is "Thanks be to God.")*

# Lord Randal

>>>>>>>

"O where hae ye been, Lord Randal, my son?
O where hae ye been, my handsome young man?"
"I hae been to the wild wood; mother, make my bed soon,
For I'm weary wi' hunting, and fain wald lie down."

"Where gat ye your dinner, Lord Randal, my son?
Where gat ye your dinner, my handsome young man?"
"I din'd wi' my true-love; mother, make my bed soon,
For I'm weary wi' hunting, and fain wald lie down."

"What gat ye to your dinner, Lord Randal, my son?
What gat ye to your dinner, my handsome young man?"
"I gat eels boil'd in broo; mother, make my bed soon,
For I'm weary wi' hunting, and fain wald lie down."

"What became of your bloodhounds, Lord Randal, my son?
What became of your bloodhounds, my handsome young man?"
"O they swell'd and they died; mother, make my bed soon,
For I'm weary wi' hunting, and fain wald lie down"

"O I fear ye are poison'd, Lord Randal, my son!
I fear ye are poison'd, my handsome young man!"
"O yes! I am poison'd; mother, make my bed soon,
For I'm sick at the heart, and I fain wald lie down."

---

*As with "Edward, Edward" (p. 15), the story here is developed through a dialogue between a mother and son.*

# The Cherry-Tree Carol

Joseph was an old man,
  and an old man was he,
When he wedded Mary,
  in the land of Galilee.

Joseph and Mary walked
  through an orchard good,
Where was cherries and berries,
  so red as any blood.

Joseph and Mary walked
  through an orchard green,
Where was berries and cherries,
  as thick as might be seen.

O then bespoke Mary,
  so meek and so mild:
"Pluck me one cherry, Joseph,
  for I am with child."

O then bespoke Joseph,
  with words most unkind:
"Let him pluck thee a cherry
  that brought thee with child."

O then bespoke the babe,
  within his mother's womb:
"Bow down then the tallest tree,
  for my mother to have some."

Then bowed down the highest tree
  unto his mother's hand;
Then she cried, "See, Joseph,
  I have cherries at command."

O then bespake Joseph:
  "I have done Mary wrong;
But cheer up, my dearest,
  and be not cast down."

Then Mary plucked a cherry,
  as red as the blood,
Then Mary went home
  with her heavy load.

Then Mary took her babe,
  and sat him on her knee,
Saying, "My dear son, tell me
  what this world will be."

"O I shall be as dead, mother,
  as the stones in the wall;
O the stones in the streets, mother,
  shall mourn for me all.

"Upon Easter-day, mother,
  my uprising shall be;
O the sun and the moon, mother,
  shall both rise with me."

---

*In spite of its rather rough mixture of elements from various scriptural and popular sources, this carol remains touching.*

# The Lord Is My Shepherd

❖❖❖❖❖

The Lord is my shepherd; I shall not want.
  He maketh me to lie down in green pastures: he leadeth me
    beside the still waters.
  He restoreth my soul: he leadeth me in the paths of
    righteousness for his name's sake.
  Yea, though I walk through the valley of the shadow of
    death, I will fear no evil: for thou art with me; thy rod
    and thy staff they comfort me.
  Thou preparest a table before me in the presence of mine
    enemies: thou anointest my head with oil; my cup runneth
    over.
  Surely goodness and mercy shall follow me all the days of my
    life: and I will dwell in the house of the Lord for ever.

                                              Psalm XXIII

---

*About half of the 150 Psalms in the Bible are attributed to David, famed as "the sweet psalmist of Israel" (Second Samuel XXIII:1). The Twenty-third is probably the best-known poem in the Old Testament and perhaps even the whole Bible. It is classified as a "song of trust," like one of the songs that David sang to pacify and heal King Saul.*

# I Sing of a Maiden

I sing of a maiden
  That is makèles:
King of all kings
  To her son she ches.

He came all so still
  There his mother was,
As dew in Aprìl
  That falleth on the grass.

He came all so still
  To his mother's bower,
As dew in Aprìl
  That falleth on the flower.

He came all so still
  There his mother lay,
As dew in Aprìl
  That falleth on the spray.

Mother and maiden
  Was never none but she;
Well may such a lady
  Goddès mother be.

---

*Much pre-Reformation popular art, including songs, hymns, and prose texts, is devoted to the Blessed Virgin Mary. (Note that: "makeles" is "matchless," "mateless"; "chees" is "close"; "swich" is "such.")*

# A Lyke-Wake Dirge

><><><><

This ae nighte, this ae nighte,
  —*Every nighte and alle,*
Fire and fleet and candle-lighte,
  *And Christe receive thy saule.*

When thou from hence away art past,
  —*Every nighte and alle,*
To Whinny-muir thou com'st at last;
  *And Christe receive thy saule.*

If ever thou gavest hosen and shoon,
  —*Every nighte and alle,*
Sit thee down and put them on;
  *And Christe receive thy saule.*

If hosen and shoon thou ne'er gav'st nane
  —*Every nighte and alle,*
The whinnes sall prick thee to the bare bane;
  *And Christe receive thy saule.*

From Whinny-muir when thou may'st pass,
  —*Every nighte and alle,*
To Brig o' Dread thou com'st at last;
  *And Christe receive thy saule.*

From Brig o' Dread when thou may'st pass.
  —*Every nighte and alle,*
To Purgatory fire thou com'st at last;
  *And Christe receive thy saule.*

If ever thou gavest meat or drink,
   *—Every nighte and alle,*
The fire sall never make thee shrink;
   *And Christe receive thy saule.*

If meat or drink thou ne'er gav'st nane,
   *—Every nighte and alle,*
The fire will burn thee to the bare bane;
   *And Christe receive thy saule.*

This ae nighte, this ae nighte,
   *—Every nighte and alle,*
Fire and fleet and candle-lighte,
   *And Christe receive thy saule.*

---

*A "lyke" is a corpse, a "wake" a night watch kept over it. A "whinny-muir" is a moor with thorny shrubs. The economy of charity and punishment is not strictly Biblical, but the idea appealingly makes sense. If you never feed the hungry or clothe the naked, you are in for some answerable treatment come post-mortem time. (Note that: "bane" is "bone"; "brig" is "bridge.")*

Anonymous

# My Love in Her Attire

My love in her attire doth show her wit,
It doth so well become her:
For every season she hath dressings fit,
For winter, spring, and summer.
No beauty she doth miss,
When all her robes are on;
But Beauty's self she is,
When all her robes are gone.

---

*This is an amorous but discreet poem of praise fit to stand alongside Herrick's
"Upon Julia's Clothes" (p. 173).*

# The Demon Lover

"O where have you been, my long, long love,
  This long seven years and more?"
"O I'm come to seek my former vows
  Ye granted me before."

"O hold your tongue of your former vows,
  For they will breed sad strife;
O hold your tongue of your former vows
  For I am become a wife."

He turn'd him right and round about,
  And the tear blinded his ee;
"I wad never hae trodden on Irish ground,
  If it had not been for thee.

"I might have had a king's daughter,
  Far, far beyond the sea;
I might have had a king's daughter,
  Had it not been for love o' thee."

"If ye might have had a king's daughter,
  Yersell ye had to blame;
Ye might have taken the king's daughter,
  For ye kend that I was nane.

"If I was to leave my husband dear,
  And my two babes also,
O what have you to take me to,
  If with you I should go?"

"I hae seven ships upon the sea,
  The eighth brought me to land;
With four-and-twenty bold mariners,
  And music on every hand."

She has taken up her two little babes,
  Kiss'd them baith cheek and chin;
"O fair ye weel, my ain two babes,
  For I'll never see you again."

She set her foot upon the ship,
  No mariners could she behold;
But the sails were o' the taffetie,
  And the masts o' the beaten gold.

She had not sail'd a league, a league,
  A league but barely three,
When dismal grew his countenance,
  And drumlie grew his ee.

They had not sailed a league, a league,
  A league but barely three,
Until she espied his cloven foot,
  And she wept right bitterlie.

"O hold your tongue of your weeping," says he,
  "Of your weeping now let me be;
I will show you how the lilies grow
  On the banks of Italy."

"O what hills are yon, yon pleasant hills,
  That the sun shines sweetly on?"
"O yon are the hills of heaven," he said,
  "Where you will never win."

"O whaten a mountain is yon?" she said,
  "All so dreary wi' frost and snow?"
"O yon is the mountain of hell," he cried,
  "Where you and I will go."

He struck the tapmast wi' his hand,
  The foremast wi' his knee;
And he brak that gallant ship in twain,
  And sank her in the sea.

---

*The motif of the return of the dead lover has appeared as recently as the movie* Ghost *in 1990, although the film lover was human and benevolent and not at all demonic. See also the "demon lover" in Coleridge's "Kubla Khan" (p. 430). (Note that: "kend" is "knew"; "drumlic" is "gloomy.")*

Anonymous

# *Weep You No More, Sad Fountains*

❖❖❖❖

Weep you no more, sad fountains;
  What need you flow so fast?
Look how the snowy mountains
  Heaven's sun doth gently waste.
    But my sun's heavenly eyes
      View not your weeping,
      That now lies sleeping
    Softly, now softly lies
      Sleeping.

Sleep is a reconciling,
  A rest that peace begets.
Doth not the sun rise smiling
  When fair at ev'n he sets?
    Rest you then, rest, sad eyes,
      Melt not in weeping,
      While she lies sleeping
    Softly, now softly lies
      Sleeping.

---

*This verse form is a striking demonstration of the art of diminution. Thanks to the flexibility of English syntax, "A rest that peace begets" means both "rest begets peace" and "peace begets rest."*

# *The Unquiet Grave*

❦❦❦

"The wind doth blow today, my love,
  And a few small drops of rain;
I never had but one true love,
  In cold grave she was lain.

"I'll do as much for my true love
  As any young man may;
I'll sit and mourn all at her grave
  For a twelvemonth, and a day."

The twelvemonth and a day being up,
  The dead began to speak,
"Oh who sits weeping on my grave,
  And will not let me sleep?"

" 'Tis I, my love, sits on your grave
  And will not let you sleep,
For I crave one kiss of your clay-cold lips
  And that is all I seek."

"You crave one kiss of clay-cold lips,
  But my breath smells earthy strong;
If you have one kiss of my clay-cold lips
  You time will not be long:

" 'Tis down in yonder garden green,
  Love, where we used to walk,
The finest flower that ere was seen
  Is withered to a stalk.

"The stalk is withered dry, my love,
    So will our hearts decay;
So make yourself content, my love,
    Till God calls you away."

---

*As in many situations — including that in* Romeo and Juliet — *the woman has more sense than the man; it does not matter that the man is alive and the woman is not.*

# Waly, Waly

>>>>>>>

O waly, waly, up the bank,
  And waly, waly, down the brae,
And waly, waly, yon burn side,
  Where I and my love were wont to gae.

I leant my back upon an oak,
  I thought it was a trusty tree;
But first it bent, and then it broke,
  Just as my love proved false to me.

O waly, waly, love is bonny,
  A little while when it is new;
But when it's old, it waxes cold,
  And fades away like morning dew.

O wherefore should I busk my head?
  O wherefore should I comb my hair?
For my true love has me forsook,
  And says he'll never love me more.

Now Arthur's Seat shall be my bed,
  The sheets shall ne'er be filled by me:
Saint Anthony's well shall be my drink,
  Since my true love has forsaken me.

Martinmas wind, when wilt thou blow,
  And shake the green leaves off the tree?
O gentle death, when wilt thou come?
  For of my life I am weary.

'Tis not the frost, that freezes fell,
  Nor blowing snow's inclemency;
'Tis not such cold that makes me cry,
  But my love's heart grown cold to me.

When we came in by Glasgow town,
  We were a comely sight to see,
My love was clad in black velvet,
  And I myself in cramasie.

But had I wist, before I kissed,
  That love had been so ill to win,
I'd locked my heart in a case of gold,
  And pinned it with a silver pin.

And oh! if my young babe were born,
  And set upon the nurse's knee,
And I my self were dead and gone:
  For a maid again I'll never be.

---

*The vague exclamation "Waly" (related to "wellaway" and "welladay") turns up in many versions of this ballad; some of them lack almost all specific detail (except a reference to Glasgow near the end), others are linked up with the story known as "Jamie Douglas," which concerns a domestic tragedy of the late seventeenth century. (Note that: "cramasie" is "crimson.")*

# JOHN SKELTON 1460?–1529

Skelton tutored Prince Henry (later Henry VIII) and held the academic title "poet laureate" (though not the official position, which was not instituted until later). His poetry has considerable range, but he is remembered mostly as the author of jolly doggerel and vitriolic satire.

## To Mistress Margaret Hussey

Merry Margaret,
  As midsummer flower,
Gentle as falcon
Or hawk of the tower:
With solace and gladness,
Much mirth and no madness,
All good and no badness;
    So joyously,
    So maidenly,
    So womanly
      Her demeaning
      In every thing,
      Far, far passing
      That I can indite,
      Or suffice to write
Of Merry Margaret
  As midsummer flower,
Gentle as falcon
Or hawk of the tower.
  As patient and still
And as full of good will
As fair Isaphill,
Coriander,
Sweet pomander,
Good Cassander,

Steadfast of thought,
Well made, well wrought,
Far may be sought
Ere that ye can find
So courteous, so kind
As Merry Margaret,
    This midsummer flower,
Gentle as falcon
Or hawk of the tower.

from The Garlande of Laurell

---

*Skelton had other styles, including a most dignified manner for some religious poems, but the distinctive pattern here—short lines, percussive rhythm, a piling-on of rhymes, ostensibly slipshod execution—is what has become known as Skeltonic. After five centuries, the charm, vigor, and audacity endure. (Note that: "Isaphill" is "Hypsipyle of Lemnos.")*

Wyatt was born into a noble family in Kent, educated at Cambridge, and employed as a courtier and diplomat by Henry VIII. He was thought to have been associated with Anne Boleyn before her marriage to the king, and he was imprisoned briefly after her downfall. He soon found his way back, however, into the king's favor. Wyatt may rank as the foremost English poet in terms of technical inventiveness, since he was the first to use terza rima and ottava rima and was among the first to write sonnets (all the forms mentioned here came from Italy). In friendship and in literary relations, Wyatt is commonly linked with the Earl of Surrey.

# They Flee from Me
# That Sometime Did Me Seek

They flee from me that sometime did me seek
With naked foot stalking in my chamber.
I have seen them gentle, tame and meek
That now are wild and do not remember
That sometime they put themselves in danger
To take bread at my hand; and now they range
Busily seeking with a continual change.

Thanked be fortune, it hath been otherwise
Twenty times better, but once in special,
In thin array after a pleasant guise,
When her loose gown from her shoulders did fall
And she caught me in her arms long and small,
Therewithal sweetly did me kiss
And softly said, "Dear heart, how like you this?"

It was no dream: I lay broad waking.
But all is turned thorough my gentleness
Into a strange fashion of forsaking.
And I have leave to go of her goodness
And she also to use newfangleness.
But since that I so kindly am served
I fain would know what she hath deserved.

---

*These paradoxes and complexities may foreshadow the Metaphysical poetry that was to flourish almost a hundred years later. Tottel's* Miscellany *entitles this poem "The Lover Showeth How He Is Forsaken of Such as He Sometime Enjoyed" and "corrects" the seventeenth line to read "Into a bitter fashion of forsaking."*

# *The Lover Complaineth the Unkindness of His Love*

My lute awake! perform the last
Labour that thou and I shall waste,
And end that I have now begun;
For when this song is sung and past,
My lute be still, for I have done.

As to be heard where ear is none,
As lead to grave in marble stone,
My song may pierce her heart as soon;
Should we then sigh, or sing, or moan?
No, no, my lute, for I have done.

The rocks do not so cruelly
Repulse the waves continually,
As she my suit and affection,
So that I am past remedy:
Whereby my lute and I have done.

Proud of the spoil that thou hast got
Of simple hearts thorough love's shot,
By whom, unkind, thou hast them won,
Think not he hath his bow forgot,
Although my lute and I have done.

Vengeance shall fall on thy disdain,
That makest but game on earnest pain;
Think not alone under the sun
Unquit to cause thy lovers plain,
Although my lute and I have done.

Perchance thee lie withered and old,
The winter nights that are so cold,
Plaining in vain unto the moon;
Thy wishes then dare not be told;
Care then who list, for I have done.

And then may chance thee to repent
The time that thou hast lost and spent
To cause thy lovers sigh and swoon;
Then shalt thou know beauty but lent,
And wish and want as I have done.

Now cease, my lute! this is the last
Labour that thou and I shall waste,
And ended is that we begun;
Now is this song both sung and past:
My lute, be still, for I have done.

---

*The long title was added to this poem in Richard Tottel's* Miscellany *fifteen years after Wyatt's death. The meaningful rhyme of "old," "cold," and "told," by the way, recurs in the first, fifteenth, and last stanzas of Keats's "Eve of St. Agnes" (p. 551). (Note that: "unquit" is "unrevenged"; "plain" is "complain"; "list" is "like.")*

# Whoso List to Hunt

Whoso list to hunt, I know where is an hind,
But as for me, helas, I may no more.
The vain travail hath wearied me so sore,
I am of them that farthest cometh behind.
Yet may I by no means my wearied mind
Draw from the deer, but as she fleeth afore
Fainting I follow. I leave off therefore
Since in a net I seek to hold the wind.
Who list her hunt, I put him out of doubt,
As well as I may spend his time in vain.
And graven with diamonds in letters plain
There is written her fair neck round about:
"Noli me tangere for Caesar's I am,
And wild for to hold though I seem tame."

---

*Reading this brilliant but enigmatic poem, one will probably find it hard to resist the temptation to identify the "deer" who belongs to Caesar with Anne Boleyn, who belonged for a time to Henry VIII. This, incidentally, is the earliest sonnet in this anthology and among the first in English. (Note that: "list" is "like"; "noli me tangere" is "I do not want you to touch me," "touch me not.")*

Ralegh was chiefly known as a military, political, and
diplomatic genius and also as a charismatic adventurer.
He wrote history and poetry of a most distinguished
order. For all his brilliance and patriotic service, however, James I still ordered Ralegh's execution, and he
was beheaded.

# The Nymph's Reply to the Shepherd

If all the world and love were young,
And truth in every shepherd's tongue,
These pretty pleasures might me move
To live with thee and be thy Love.

But Time drives flocks from field to fold;
When rivers rage and rocks grow cold;
And Philomel becometh dumb;
The rest complains of cares to come.

The flowers do fade, and wanton fields
To wayward Winter reckoning yields:
A honey tongue, a heart of gall,
Is fancy's spring, but sorrow's fall.

Thy gowns, thy shoes, thy beds of roses,
Thy cap, thy kirtle, and thy posies,
Soon break, soon wither—soon forgotten,
In folly ripe, in reason rotten.

Thy belt of straw and ivy-buds,
Thy coral clasps and amber studs,—
All these in me no means can move
To come to thee and be thy Love.

But could youth last, and love still breed,
Had joys no date, nor age no need,
Then these delights my mind might move
To live with thee and be thy Love.

---

*It is probable but not certain that Ralegh wrote this reply to Marlowe's "Passionate Shepherd to His Love" (p. 82), where there is further commentary on the responses.*

# The Lie

Go, Soul, the body's guest,
Upon a thankless arrant:
Fear not to touch the best;
The truth shall be thy warrant:
Go, since I needs must die,
And give the world the lie.

Say to the court, it glows
And shines like rotten wood;
Say to the church it shows
What's good, and doth no good:
If church and court reply,
Then give them both the lie.

Tell potentates, they live
Acting by others' action;
Not loved unless they give,
Not strong but by affection:
If potentates reply,
Give potentates the lie.

Tell men of high condition
That manage the estate,
Their purpose is ambition,
Their practice only hate:
And if they once reply,
Then give them all the lie.

Tell them that brave it most
They beg for more by spending,
Who, in their greatest cost,
Seek nothing but commending:
And if they make reply,
Then give them all the lie.

Tell zeal it wants devotion,
Tell love it is but lust;
Tell time it metes but motion,
Tell flesh it is but dust:
And wish them not reply,
For thou must give the lie.

Tell age it daily wasteth;
Tell honour how it alters;
Tell beauty how she blasteth;
Tell favour how it falters:
And as they shall reply,
Give every one the lie.

Tell wit how much it wrangles
In tickle points of niceness;
Tell wisdom she entangles
Herself in over-wiseness:
And when they do reply,
Straight give them both the lie.

Tell physic of her boldness;
Tell skill it is pretension;
Tell charity of coldness;
Tell law it is contention:
And as they do reply,
So give them still the lie.

Tell fortune of her blindness;
Tell nature of decay;
Tell friendship of unkindness;
Tell justice of delay:
And if they will reply,
Then give them all the lie.

Tell arts they have no soundness,
But vary by esteeming;
Tell schools they want profoundness,
And stand too much on seeming:
If arts and schools reply,
Give arts and schools the lie.

Tell faith it's fled the city;
Tell how the country erreth;
Tell manhood shakes off pity
And virtue least preferreth:
And if they do reply,
Spare not to give the lie.

So when thou hast, as I
Commanded thee, done blabbing
—Although to give the lie
Deserves no less than stabbing—
Stab at thee he that will,
No stab thy soul can kill.

---

*Like Waller's "Go, Lovely Rose" (p. 200), "The Lie" begins as an "envoy" or "sending poem" with orders to a representative. Unlike Waller's poem, however, Ralegh's turns into a telling inventory of all that is wrong with the world—true in 1608 and still true, four centuries later.*

# Even Such Is Time

Even such is time that takes in trust
Our youth, our joys, our all we have,
And pays us but with age and dust,
Who in the dark and silent grave,
When we have wandered all our ways,
Shuts up the story of our days.
But from this earth, this grave, this dust,
My God shall raise me up, I trust.

---

*Just as musical themes return to their tonic or keynote, Ralegh's rhymes run
from "trust" through "dust" (twice) and back to "trust."*

# The Passionate Man's Pilgrimage

Give me my scallop-shell of quiet,
My staff of faith to walk upon,
My scrip of joy, immortal diet,
My bottle of salvation,
My gown of glory, hope's true gage,
And thus I'll take my pilgrimage.

Blood must be my body's balmer,
No other balm will there be given,
Whilst my soul like a white palmer
Travels to the land of heaven,
Over the silver mountains,
Where spring the nectar fountains;
And there I'll kiss
The bowl of bliss,
And drink my eternal fill
On every milken hill.
My soul will be a-dry before,
But after it will ne'er thirst more.

And by the happy blissful way
More peaceful pilgrims I shall see,
That have shook off their gowns of clay
And go apparelled fresh like me.
I'll bring them first
To slake their thirst,
And then to taste those nectar suckets,
At the clear wells
Where sweetness dwells,
Drawn up by saints in crystal buckets.

And when our bottles and all we
Are filled with immortality,
Then the holy paths we'll travel,
Strewed with rubies thick as gravel,
Ceilings of diamonds, sapphire floors,
High walls of coral and pearl bowers.

From thence to heaven's bribeless hall
Where no corrupted voices brawl,
No conscience molten into gold,
Nor forged accusers bought and sold,
No cause deferred, nor vain-spent journey,
For there Christ is the King's Attorney,
Who pleads for all without degrees,
And he hath angels, but no fees.

When the grand twelve million jury
Of our sins with sinful fury
'Gainst our souls black verdicts give,
Christ pleads his death, and then we live.
Be thou my speaker, taintless pleader,
Unblotted lawyer, true proceeder;
Thou movest salvation even for alms,
Not with a bribed lawyer's palms.

And this is my eternal plea
To him that made heaven, earth and sea:
Seeing my flesh must die so soon,
And want a head to dine next noon,
Just at the stroke when my veins start and spread,
Set on my soul an everlasting head.
Then am I ready, like a palmer fit,
To tread those blest paths which before I writ.

*Pilgrimages have fascinated English writers since the Middle Ages: Chaucer, of course, Spenser, Bunyan, T. S. Eliot (whose* Four Quartets *consists of ghostly visits that have been called "totemic pilgrimages"), down to Philip Larkin, whose "Church Going" (p. 1068) represents a secular—but nonetheless passionate—pilgrimage. Ralegh's poem, which, in 1604, seemed to presage his beheading in 1618, combines a nearly Spenserian allegory of equipment and symbols with a sharp courtier's satire of earthly politics. Ralegh's authorship of this poem has recently been seriously questioned.* The New Oxford Book of Sixteenth-Century Verse *lists the poem as anonymous, maybe "written by a recusant . . . ." (Note that: "scrip" is "bag"; "gage" is "pledge"; "suckets" is "confections"; "angels" is "gold coins.")*

# EDMUND SPENSER c.1552–1599

Spenser, educated at Pembroke Hall, Cambridge, earned his living in various appointive political positions. His magnum opus, *The Faerie Queene*, was begun in 1579 and never finished. In addition to its six books (and part of another), Spenser wrote a number of shorter works, including the twelve eclogues of *The Shepheardes Calender* and the 89 sonnets of *Amoretti*.

## One Day I Wrote Her Name upon the Strand

>>>>>>>

One day I wrote her name upon the strand;
But came the waves, and washed it away:
Again, I wrote it with a second hand;
But came the tide, and made my pains his prey.
Vain man, said she, that dost in vain assay
A mortal thing so to immortalize;
For I myself shall like to this decay,
And eke my name be wiped out likewise.
Not so, quoth I; let baser things devise
To die in dust, but you shall live by fame:
My verse your virtues rare shall eternize,
And in the heavens write your glorious name.
   Where, whenas death shall all the world subdue,
   Our love shall live, and later life renew.

Sonnet LXXV
from Amoretti

---

*The sonnets of Spenser's* Amoretti *(1595) show the pleasures of convention—repeating sentiments and figures also used in this volume in sonnets by Sidney, Shakespeare, and others, and not so very different in the mid-twentieth-century popular song "Love Letters in the Sand"—with the complementary pleasures of* invention—*notable here in the engaging original rhyme scheme of the uniquely "Spenserian" sonnet (ababbcbccdcdee), a graceful compromise between the Italian and English forms.*

# Prothalamion

Calm was the day, and through the trembling air
Sweet-breathing Zephyrus did softly play,
A gentle spirit, that lightly did delay
Hot Titan's beams, which then did glister fair;
When I (whom sullen care,
Through discontent of my long fruitless stay
In princes' court, and expectation vain
Of idle hopes, which still do fly away
Like empty shadows, did afflict my brain)
Walked forth to ease my pain
Along the shore of silver-streaming Thames;
Whose rutty bank, the which his river hems,
Was painted all with variable flowers,
And all the meads adorned with dainty gems
Fit to deck maidens' bowers,
And crown their paramours
Against the bridal day, which is not long:
   Sweet Thames run softly, till I end my song.

There in a meadow by the river's side
A flock of nymphs I chancèd to espy,
All lovely daughters of the flood thereby,
With goodly greenish locks all loose untied
As each had been a bride;
And each one had a little wicker basket
Made of fine twigs entrailèd curiously,
In which they gathered flowers to fill their flasket,
And, with fine fingers, cropped full feateously
The tender stalks on high.
Of every sort which in that meadow grew
They gathered some; the violet, pallid blue,
The little daisy that at evening closes,
The virgin lily and the primrose true,
With store of vermeil roses,

To deck their bridegrooms' posies
Against the bridal day, which was not long:
   Sweet Thames run softly, till I end my song.

With that I saw two swans of goodly hue
Come softly swimming down along the Lee;
Two fairer birds I yet did never see;
The snow which doth the top of Pindus strew
Did never whiter shew,
Nor Jove himself, when he a swan would be
For love of Leda, whiter did appear;
Yet Leda was, they say, as white as he,
Yet not so white as these, nor nothing near;
So purely white they were
That even the gentle stream, the which them bare,
Seemed foul to them, and bade his billows spare
To wet their silken feathers, lest they might
Soil their fair plumes with water not so fair,
And mar their beauties bright,
That shone as heaven's light,
Against their bridal day, which was not long:
   Sweet Thames run softly, till I end my song.

Eftsoons the nymphs, which now had flowers their fill,
Ran all in haste to see that silver brood
As they came floating on the crystal flood;
Whom when they saw, they stood amazèd still
Their wondering eyes to fill;
Them seemed they never saw a sight so fair,
Of fowls so lovely that they sure did deem
Them heavenly born, or to be that same pair
Which through the sky draw Venus' silver team;
For sure they did not seem
To be begot of any earthly seed,
But rather angels, or of angels' breed;
Yet were they bred of summer's-heat, they say,
In sweetest season, when each flower and weed
The earth did fresh array;

So fresh they seemed as day,
Even as their bridal day, which was not long:
   Sweet Thames run softly, till I end my song.

Then forth they all out of their baskets drew
Great store of flowers, the honour of the field,
That to the sense did fragrant odours yield,
All which upon those goodly birds they threw,
And all the waves did strew,
That like old Peneus' waters they did seem
When down along by pleasant Tempe's shore,
Scattered with flowers, through Thessaly they stream,
That they appear, through lilies' plenteous store,
Like a bride's chamber-floor.
Two of those nymphs meanwhile two garlands bound
Of freshest flowers which in that mead they found,
The which presenting all in trim array,
Their snowy foreheads therewithal they crowned,
Whilst one did sing this lay
Prepared against that day,
Against their bridal day, which was not long:
   Sweet Thames run softly, till I end my song.

"Ye gentle birds! the world's fair ornament,
And heaven's glory, whom this happy hour
Doth lead unto your lovers' blissful bower,
Joy may you have, and gentle heart's content
Of your love's couplement;
And let fair Venus, that is queen of love,
With her heart-quelling son upon you smile,
Whose smile, they say, hath virtue to remove
All love's dislike, and friendship's faulty guile
For ever to assoil.
Let endless peace your steadfast hearts accord,
And blessed plenty wait upon your board,
And let your bed with pleasures chaste abound,
That fruitful issue may to you afford,
Which may your foes confound,

And make your joys redound
Upon your bridal day, which is not long:
   Sweet Thames run softly, till I end my song."

So ended she; and all the rest around
To her redoubled that her undersong,
Which said their bridal day should not be long:
And gentle Echo from the neighbour ground
Their accents did resound.
So forth those joyous birds did pass along,
Adown the Lee that to them murmured low,
As he would speak but that he lacked a tongue,
Yet did by signs his glad affection show,
Making his stream run slow.
And all the fowl which in his flood did dwell
Gan flock about these twain, that did excel
The rest, so far as Cynthia doth shend
The lesser stars. So they, enrangèd well,
Did on those two attend,
And their best service lend
Against their wedding day, which was not long:
   Sweet Thames run softly, till I end my song.

At length they all to merry London came,
To merry London, my most kindly nurse,
That to me gave this life's first native source,
Though from another place I take my name,
An house of ancient fame:
There when they came whereas those bricky towers
The which on Thames' broad aged back do ride,
Where now the studious lawyers have their bowers,
There whilom wont the Templar knights to bide,
Till they decayed through pride:
Next whereunto there stands a stately place,
Where oft I gainèd gifts and goodly grace
Of that great lord, which therein wont to dwell,
Whose want too well now feels my friendless case;
But ah! here fits not well

Old woes, but joys to tell
Against the bridal day, which is not long:
  Sweet Thames run softly, till I end my song.

Yet therein now doth lodge a noble peer,
Great England's glory and the world's wide wonder,
Whose dreadful name late through all Spain did thunder,
And Hercules' two pillars standing near
Did make to quake and fear:
Fair branch of honour, flower of chivalry!
That fillest England with thy triumphs' fame,
Joy have thou of thy noble victory,
And endless happiness of thine own name
That promiseth the same;
That through thy prowess and victorious arms
Thy country may be freed from foreign harms,
And great Eliza's glorious name may ring
Through all the world, filled with thy wide alarms,
Which some brave Muse may sing
To ages following,
Upon the bridal day, which is not long:
  Sweet Thames run softly, till I end my song.

From those high towers this noble lord issuing,
Like radiant Hesper when his golden hair
In the ocean billows he hath bathèd fair,
Descended to the river's open viewing,
With a great train ensuing.
Above the rest were goodly to be seen
Two gentle knights of lovely face and feature,
Beseeming well the bower of any queen,
With gifts of wit and ornaments of nature
Fit for so goodly stature,
That like the twins of Jove they seemed in sight
Which deck the baldric of the heavens bright;
They two, forth pacing to the river's side,
Received those two fair brides, their love's delight,
Which, at the appointed tide,

Each one did make his bride
Against their bridal day, which is not long:
  Sweet Thames run softly, till I end my song.

---

*Spenser published his "Epithalamion" in 1595 in honor of his own wedding. The next year, he coined "Prothalamion" as a name for a "Spousall Verse" or a betrothal poem celebrating a ceremony technically somewhat in advance of the nuptials proper. It was a double wedding involving the two eldest daughters of the Earl of Worcester and their fiancés. The river-refrain returns in T. S. Eliot's "Waste Land" (p. 968). (Note that: "entrayléd" is "interlaced"; "flasket" is "basket"; "breede" is "race"; "whylome" is "formerly"; "tyde" is "time.")*

Sidney's charismatic presence pervades the literature of England at the end of the sixteenth century and the beginning of the seventeenth; and even this book honors not only Sidney's poetry but also his birthplace (in Jonson's "To Penshurst") and his sister (in Browne's "On the Countess Dowager of Pembroke"). Although his life was short and busy, Sidney wrote a prose romance, an important critical treatise, and many poems, all in his spare time, as it were. He died in battle in the Netherlands and was buried in St. Paul's Cathedral.

## *With How Sad Steps, O Moon, Thou Climb'st the Skies!*

With how sad steps, O moon, thou climb'st the skies,
   How silently, and with how wan a face.
   What, may it be that even in heavenly place
   That busy archer his sharp arrows tries?
Sure, if that long-with-love-acquainted eyes
   Can judge of love, thou feel'st a lover's case;
   I read it in thy looks; thy languished grace
   To me, that feel the like, thy state descries.
Then, even of fellowship, O moon, tell me,
   Is constant love deemed there but want of wit?
   Are beauties there as proud as here they be?
Do they above love to be loved, and yet
   Those lovers scorn whom that love doth possess?
   Do they call virtue there ungratefulness?

Sonnet XXXI
from Astrophil and Stella

---

*One can be so troubled by love that the woes are projected onto everything around, even celestial objects. The moon's pallor and mutability make it an apt correlative for any number of emotional states. Loony tunes are nothing new and will never go out of style. About four centuries after Sidney, Philip Larkin wrote a moon poem called "Sad Steps."*

# Leave Me, O Love,
# Which Reachest But to Dust

Leave me, O Love, which reachest but to dust,
  And thou, my mind, aspire to higher things!
Grow rich in that which never taketh rust:
  Whatever fades but fading pleasure brings.
Draw in thy beams, and humble all thy might
  To that sweet yoke where lasting freedoms be,
Which breaks the clouds and opens forth the light,
  That doth both shine and give us sight to see.
O take fast hold; let that light be thy guide
  In this small course which birth draws out to death;
And think how evil becometh him to slide,
  Who seeketh heaven, and comes of heavenly breath.
    Then farewell, world; thy uttermost I see;
    Eternal Love, maintain thy life in me.

---

*Some earlier editors placed this poem as Sonnet CX in the sonnet sequence* Astrophil and Stella, *but now there is general agreement that it belongs at the end of the volume called* Certain Sonnets.

# My True Love Hath My Heart

My true love hath my heart, and I have his,
　　By just exchange, one for the other given.
I hold his dear, and mine he cannot miss,
　　There never was a better bargain driven.
His heart in me keeps me and him in one,
　　My heart in him his thoughts and senses guides;
He loves my heart, for once it was his own,
　　I cherish his, because in me it bides.
His heart his wound receivèd from my sight,
　　My heart was wounded with his wounded heart;
For as from me on him his hurt did light,
　　So still methought in me his hurt did smart.
　　　Both equal hurt, in this change sought our bliss:
　　　My true love hath my heart and I have his.

from Arcadia

---

*The tricky story-within-a-story in Book III of* Arcadia *is too complicated to be summarized; suffice it to say that a young woman sings this lovely song to a young man.*

# Loving in Truth,
## and Fain in Verse My Love to Show

()◀▬▶()

Loving in truth, and fain in verse my love to show,
That she, dear she, might take some pleasure of my pain,
Pleasure might cause her read, reading might make her know,
Knowledge might pity win, and pity grace obtain,
I sought fit words to paint the blackest face of woe:
Studying inventions fine, her wits to entertain,
Oft turning others' leaves, to see if thence would flow
Some fresh and fruitful showers upon my sunburn'd brain.
But words came halting forth, wanting Invention's stay;
Invention, Nature's child, fled stepdame Study's blows;
And others' feet still seemed but strangers in my way.
Thus, great with child to speak, and helpless in my throes,
Biting my truant pen, beating myself for spite:
"Fool," said my Muse to me, "look in thy heart and write!"

Sonnet I
from Astrophil and Stella

---

*This first sonnet in the* Astrophil and Stella *cycle may seem to advise one to
indulge in unfettered creative writing, but the poem itself is a marvel of artifice
and craft. It is a very rare sort of sonnet, rhyming* ababababcdcdee *and using
hexameters—lines with six iambic feet—rather than the usual pentameters.
(Note that: "trewand" is "truant.")*

# Come Sleep! O Sleep, the Certain Knot of Peace

Come, Sleep, O Sleep, the certain knot of peace,
  The baiting-place of wit, the balm of woe,
The poor man's wealth, the prisoner's release,
  The indifferent judge between the high and low;
With shield of proof shield me from out the press
  Of those fierce darts Despair at me doth throw:
O make in me those civil wars to cease;
  I will good tribute pay, if thou do so.
Take thou of me smooth pillows, sweetest bed,
  A chamber deaf to noise and blind to light,
A rosy garland and a weary head;
  And if these things, as being thine by right,
    Move not thy heavy grace, thou shalt in me,
    Livelier than elsewhere, Stella's image see.

Sonnet XXXIX
from Astrophil and Stella

An exercise in finding clever ways to praise and court sleep, this poem is also an expression of the power of love. (Note that: "baiting" is "resting.")

# GEORGE PEELE c.1558–c.1597

Peele seems to have been one of those engaging hell-raisers that distinguish certain expansive ages of literature. He was himself a performer as well as a playwright and lyric poet. He also specialized in that type of poem known as "gratulatory."

## *His Golden Locks Time Hath to Silver Turned*

His golden locks time hath to silver turned;
  O time too swift, O swiftness never ceasing!
His youth 'gainst time and age hath ever spurned,
  But spurned in vain; youth waneth by increasing.
Beauty, strength, youth are flowers but fading seen;
Duty, faith, love are roots, and ever green.

His helmet now shall make a hive for bees,
  And, lovers' sonnets turned to holy psalms,
A man-at-arms must now serve on his knees,
  And feed on prayers, which are age his alms:
But though from court to cottage he depart,
His saint is sure of his unspotted heart.

And when he saddest sits in homely cell,
  He'll teach his swains this carol for a song—
"Blest be the hearts that wish my sovereign well,
  Curst be the souls that think her any wrong."
Goddess, allow this agèd man his right,
To be your beadsman now that was your knight.

from Polyhymnia

*This poem, which was first printed as part of Peele's "Polyhymnia," was long thought to be Peele's work, written for the ceremony in 1590 when the Queen's Champion, Sir Henry Lee, aged sixty, gave up his position. It has recently been persuasively argued, however, that the poem is not by Peele but by Lee himself. The poem has also been titled "A Farewell to Arms," by which name it was presumably known to Ernest Hemingway in the 1920s.*

# Whenas the Rye Reach to the Chin

When as the rye reach to the chin,
And chopcherry, chopcherry ripe within,
Strawberries swimming in the cream,
And school-boys playing in the stream;
  Then O, then O, then O my true love said,
    Till that time come again,
  She could not live a maid.

from The Old Wives' Tale

---

*This song seems to be an amiable riddle, along the lines of "blue moon" and "month of Sundays."*

Canonized in 1970, Southwell is the only saint among
the poets in this book. He was educated by Jesuits on
the continent and took holy orders. Back in England,
he was arrested on his way to celebrate Mass. He was
imprisoned and brutally tortured before being executed.
Most of his poems were written during his three-year
imprisonment.

# The Burning Babe

≫≫≫≫≫≫

As I in hoary winter's night stood shivering in the snow,
Surprised I was with sudden heat which made my heart to glow;
And lifting up a fearful eye to view what fire was near,
A pretty Babe all burning bright did in the air appear;
Who, scorched with excessive heat, such floods of tears did shed,
As though his floods should quench his flames which with his
  tears were fed.
"Alas!" quoth he, "but newly born in fiery heats I fry,
Yet none approach to warm their hearts or feel my fire but I.
My faultless breast the furnace is, the fuel wounding thorns;
Love is the fire, and sighs the smoke, the ashes shame and
  scorns;
The fuel justice layeth on, and mercy blows the coals;
The metal in this furnace wrought are men's defiled souls;
For which, as now on fire I am to work them to their good,
So will I melt into a bath to wash them in my blood."
With this he vanished out of sight and swiftly shrunk away,
And straight I called unto mind that it was Christmas Day.

---

*In the limited scope of sixteen lines, Southwell combines many traditions and
conventions: the seven-stress line of folk ballads, the alliteration of Old English,
the sustained allegory of Medieval theology, the piercing vision of mysticism, and
the heritage of solstitial observances, including Christmas.*

# SAMUEL DANIEL 1562–1619

Daniel wrote tragedies and masques as well as the sonnet sequence *Delia*, which is the source of his poem in this anthology. He also engaged in literary controversy, answering Thomas Campion's *Observations in the Art of English Poesie* with his robust *A Defence of Ryme.*

## Care-Charmer Sleep, Son of the Sable Night

Care-charmer Sleep, son of the sable Night,
    Brother to Death, in silent darkness born,
Relieve my languish, and restore the light;
    With dark forgetting of my cares return.
And let the day be time enough to mourn
    The shipwreck of my ill-adventured youth;
Let waking eyes suffice to wail their scorn
    Without the torment of the night's untruth.
Cease, dreams, th' images of day-desires,
    To model forth the passions of the morrow;
Never let rising sun approve you liars,
    To add more grief to aggravate my sorrow.
        Still let me sleep, embracing clouds in vain,
        And never wake to feel the day's disdain.

from Delia

---

*Without claiming for Daniel the last word in Freudian sophistication, we may still admire the way he could recognize that dreams deal with "our day-desires," often in ways that disturb our needed repose.*

# MICHAEL DRAYTON 1563–1631

Drayton, who, like Shakespeare, came from Warwick-
shire, was a Jack of all poetic genres, excelling in the
sonnet and also in historical and topographical poems;
moreover, he collaborated on various dramatic works.
He was among the earliest of the professional men of
letters and is buried, fittingly, in Westminster Abbey.

## Since There's No Help, Come Let Us Kiss and Part

Since there's no help, come let us kiss and part;
Nay, I have done, you get no more of me,
And I am glad, yea, glad with all my heart
That thus so cleanly I myself can free;
Shake hands for ever, cancel all our vows,
And when we meet at any time again,
Be it not seen in either of our brows
That we one jot of former love retain.
Now at the last gasp of Love's latest breath,
When, his pulse failing, Passion speechless lies,
When Faith is kneeling by his bed of death,
And Innocence is closing up his eyes,
    Now if thou wouldst, when all have given him over,
    From death to life thou mightst him yet recover.

Sonnet LXI
from Idea

---

*It is thought that Anne Goodere, daughter of Drayton's patron, was the inspi-
ration for his* Idea *or* Ideas Mirrour *(1594). Drayton's language is plainer
than Shakespeare's, and the introductory sonnet of* Idea *sounds quite modern:
"My verse is the true image of my mind." The first three lines of this sonnet
consist exclusively of ordinary monosyllables.*

# CHRISTOPHER MARLOWE 1564-1593

Marlowe was born at Canterbury, educated at Cambridge, and murdered at Deptford, presumably in a quarrel over the bill at a tavern. In the swift blaze of his career, Marlowe produced a half-dozen tragedies as well as translations from Ovid. In an age of matchless greatness in literature, only Shakespeare was greater than Marlowe.

## *The Passionate Shepherd to His Love*

Come live with me and be my love,
And we will all the pleasures prove
That valleys, groves, hills, and fields,
Woods, or steepy mountain yields.

And we will sit upon the rocks,
Seeing the shepherds feed their flocks
By shallow rivers, to whose falls
Melodious birds sing madrigals.

And I will make thee beds of roses
And a thousand fragrant posies;
A cap of flowers and a kirtle
Embroidered all with leaves of myrtle;

A gown made of the finest wool
Which from our pretty lambs we pull;
Fair linèd slippers for the cold,
With buckles of the purest gold;

A belt of straw and ivy buds,
With coral clasps and amber studs.
And if these pleasures may thee move,
Come live with me and be my Love.

The shepherds' swains shall dance and sing
For thy delight each May morning.
If these delights thy mind may move,
Then live with me and be my Love.

---

*This gentle pseudo-pastoral was first published in 1599, some years after Marlowe's death, in a collection called* The Passionate Pilgrim. *The next year,* England's Helicon *included this poem along with a reply that may be by Sir Walter Ralegh (see "The Nymph's Reply to the Shepherd," p. 55). In 1633 John Donne's "Bait" began, "Come live with me and be my love, / And we will some new pleasures prove . . . ."*

In spite of his eminence as the greatest English poet and one of the greatest poets ever in the world, we know little about Shakespeare's life. His father was a prominent citizen of Stratford-upon-Avon. When Shakespeare was eighteen he married a somewhat older woman, Anne Hathaway, who gave birth to a daughter six months after the wedding. During the 1590s Shakespeare worked in the London theater as actor and playwright. Early in his career, he wrote some long poems, and it is probable that the sonnets that make up more than half of his poems in this book were written during the 1590s. His three dozen plays, for which he is most famous, are grouped as histories or chronicle plays, comedies, romances, and tragedies.

# That Time of Year
# Thou Mayst in Me Behold

That time of year thou mayst in me behold
When yellow leaves, or none, or few, do hang
Upon those boughs which shake against the cold,
Bare ruin'd choirs where late the sweet birds sang.
In me thou see'st the twilight of such day
As after sunset fadeth in the west,
Which by and by black night doth take away,
Death's second self, that seals up all in rest.
In me thou see'st the glowing of such fire,
That on the ashes of his youth doth lie,
As the death-bed whereon it must expire,
Consum'd with that which it was nourish'd by.
   This thou perceiv'st, which makes thy love more strong,
   To love that well which thou must leave ere long.

Sonnet LXXIII

*It is as though the measured pace of poetry implicitly says, "The clock is ticking, the meter is running." Music and poetry are themselves reminders of time, and time's passing leads finally to a state of inexorable mortality, ever clearer as one ages. But, as Wallace Stevens was to say in "Sunday Morning" (p. 920) dozens of decades later, "Death is the mother of beauty": the meter-matrix of mortality gives birth to much great poetry.*

# Shall I Compare Thee to a Summer's Day?

()◀━▶()

Shall I compare thee to a summer's day?
Thou art more lovely and more temperate:
Rough winds do shake the darling buds of May,
And summer's lease hath all too short a date;
Sometime too hot the eye of heaven shines,
And often is his gold complexion dimm'd;
And every fair from fair sometime declines,
By chance or nature's changing course untrimm'd:
But thy eternal summer shall not fade
Nor lose possession of that fair thou ow'st;
Nor shall Death brag thou wand'rest in his shade,
When in eternal lines to time thou grow'st;
   So long as men can breathe or eyes can see,
   So long lives this, and this gives life to thee.

Sonnet XVIII

---

*Elizabethan sonneteers inherited a packet of conventions from Italian precursors, most notably Francesco Petrarch. "Petrarchan" designates the rhetoric of love poems involving fanciful comparisons and fantastic exaggeration. But this sonnet, like Sonnet CXXX, "My mistress' eyes are nothing like the sun," on p. 97, could be called anti-Petrarchan, since it begins by denying comparisons. The final claim—that the very verse we are reading is what confers eternal life—is a convention derived from Horace's Odes. (Note that: "ow'st" is "ownest.")*

# Let Me Not
## to the Marriage of True Minds

Let me not to the marriage of true minds
Admit impediments. Love is not love
Which alters when it alteration finds,
Or bends with the remover to remove.
O, no! it is an ever-fixèd mark
That looks on tempests and is never shaken;
It is the star to every wand'ring bark,
Whose worth's unknown, although his height be taken.
Love's not Time's fool, though rosy lips and cheeks
Within his bending sickle's compass come;
Love alters not with his brief hours and weeks,
But bears it out even to the edge of doom.
    If this be error and upon me proved,
    I never writ, nor no man ever loved.

Sonnet CXVI

---

*Shakespeare's Julius Caesar claims to be as "constant as the northern star"—
that is, the Pole Star that seems not to move while all other stars revolve around
it and which can still be used in informal navigation. Ink has been spilt over the
reading of line 8, which probably refers to the star (whose elevation or celestial
altitude can be known by instruments) but may refer to the bark (ship).*

# Fear No More the Heat o' the Sun

Fear no more the heat o' the sun
   Nor the furious winter's rages;
Thou thy worldly task hast done,
   Home art gone, and ta'en thy wages:
Golden lads and girls all must,
As chimney-sweepers, come to dust.

Fear no more the frown o' the great,
   Thou art past the tyrant's stroke;
Care no more to clothe and eat;
   To thee the reed is as the oak:
The scepter, learning, physic, must
All follow this, and come to dust.

Fear no more the lightning flash,
   Nor the all-dreaded thunder stone;
Fear not slander, censure rash;
   Thou hast finished joy and moan:
All lovers young, all lovers must
Consign to thee, and come to dust.

No exorciser harm thee!
Nor no witchcraft charm thee!
Ghost unlaid forbear thee!
Nothing ill come near thee!
Quiet consummation have;
And renownèd be thy grave!

from Cymbeline

---

*In the fourth act of* Cymbeline, *the princes Guiderius and Arviragus "say" this funeral song over the supposedly dead body of the supposed boy Fidele—really the living body of the woman Imogen. (Shakespeare's theater, which had no actresses, specialized in plots involving change or confusion of sex; there were, in addition, many make-believe deaths.)*

# *When Icicles Hang by the Wall*

When icicles hang by the wall,
   And Dick the shepherd blows his nail
And Tom bears logs into the hall,
   And milk comes frozen home in pail,
When blood is nipp'd and ways be foul,
Then nightly sings the staring owl,
To-whit!
To-who!—a merry note,
While greasy Joan doth keel the pot.

When all aloud the wind doth blow,
   And coughing drowns the parson's saw,
And birds sit brooding in the snow,
   And Marian's nose looks red and raw,
When roasted crabs hiss in the bowl,
Then nightly sings the staring owl,
To-whit!
To-who!—a merry note,
While greasy Joan doth keel the pot.

from Love's Labour's Lost

---

*Two songs are sung at the end of* Love's Labour's Lost, *one associated with "Ver, the Spring" and the cuckoo ("When daisies pied and violets blue") and this complementary companion piece, associated with "Hiems, Winter" and the owl. Marian, or at least her nose "red and raw," is immortal, and forever will "greasy Joan" be at her pot. (Note that: "keel" is "stir"; "crabs" is "crab apples.")*

# Full Fathom Five Thy Father Lies

>>>>>>>

Full fathom five thy father lies;
   Of his bones are coral made;
Those are pearls that were his eyes:
   Nothing of him that doth fade
But doth suffer a sea-change
Into something rich and strange.
Sea-nymphs hourly ring his knell:
Ding-dong.
Hark! now I hear them,—ding-dong, bell.

from The Tempest

---

*In* The Tempest, *the spirit Ariel sings this little song to Ferdinand, who believes that his father has been drowned in a shipwreck. Ferdinand is mistaken, as Ariel knows, so that the potential cruelty in the message is softened somewhat.*

# When to the Sessions
# of Sweet Silent Thought

When to the sessions of sweet silent thought
I summon up remembrance of things past,
I sigh the lack of many a thing I sought,
And with old woes new wail my dear time's waste.
Then can I drown an eye, unus'd to flow,
For precious friends hid in death's dateless night,
And weep afresh love's long since cancell'd woe,
And moan th' expense of many a vanish'd sight.
Then can I grieve at grievances foregone,
And heavily from woe to woe tell o'er
The sad account of fore-bemoaned moan,
Which I new pay as if not paid before.
    But if the while I think on thee, dear friend,
    All losses are restor'd and sorrows end.

Sonnet XXX

---

*Here we see an exoskeleton as distinct as a grasshopper's: "When . . . Then . . . Then . . . But . . . ." The vocabulary owes much to the no-nonsense realms of law and commerce. This sonnet is a complaint, a favorite type of writing with English poets from Chaucer to the present. Here, as in celebrated soliloquies in* Macbeth *and* Hamlet, *Shakespeare seems to relish the chance to inventory the woes of the world. This poem, by the way, is the source of the title of the English translation of Marcel Proust's* À la recherche du temps perdu. *(Note that: "tell" is "count.")*

# Oh Mistress Mine

Oh mistress mine! where are you roaming?
Oh! stay and hear; your true love's coming,
  That can sing both high and low.
Trip no further, pretty sweeting;
Journeys end in lovers meeting,
  Every wise man's son doth know.

What is love? 'tis not hereafter;
Present mirth hath present laughter;
  What's to come is still unsure:
In delay there lies no plenty;
Then come kiss me, sweet and twenty,
  Youth's a stuff will not endure.

from Twelfth Night

---

*This song from* Twelfth Night, *sung by the clown Feste, is like sea-foam. It oscillates cheerfully between nonsense and platitude, finally sounding the familiar refrain of* carpe diem — *"seize the day."*

# The Expense of Spirit in a Waste of Shame

The expense of spirit in a waste of shame
Is lust in action; and, till action, lust
Is perjured, murderous, bloody, full of blame,
Savage, extreme, rude, cruel, not to trust;
Enjoyed no sooner but despisèd straight;
Past reason hunted, and no sooner had,
Past reason hated as a swallowed bait
On purpose laid to make the taker mad;
Mad in pursuit, and in possession so;
Had, having, and in quest to have, extreme;
A bliss in proof, and proved, a very woe,
Before, a joy proposed; behind, a dream.
    All this the world well knows, yet none knows well
    To shun the heaven that leads men to this hell.

*Sonnet CXXIX*

---

*The antiquity of these stoic sentiments is also attested by Ben Jonson's hard-hitting translation of a fragment by Petronius, a member of Nero's entourage: "Doing a filthy pleasure is, and short; / And done we straight repent us of the sport . . . ."*

# When, in Disgrace with Fortune and Men's Eyes

✕✕✕✕✕

When, in disgrace with fortune and men's eyes,
I all alone beweep my outcast state,
And trouble deaf heaven with my bootless cries,
And look upon myself, and curse my fate,
Wishing me like to one more rich in hope,
Featured like him, like him with friends possessed,
Desiring this man's art, and that man's scope,
With what I most enjoy contented least;
Yet in these thoughts myself almost despising,
Haply I think on thee, and then my state,
Like to the lark at break of day arising
From sullen earth, sings hymns at heaven's gate;
   For thy sweet love remembered such wealth brings
   That then I scorn to change my state with kings.

*Sonnet XXIX*

---

*T. S. Eliot appropriated a phrase from this sonnet for "Ash-Wednesday," in which Shakespeare's line becomes "Desiring this man's gift and that man's scope." The "Yet" at the head of line 9 marks the "turn" (volta) that distinguishes the architecture of the classic sonnet.*

# *When Daisies Pied*

When daisies pied and violets blue,
   And lady-smocks all silver-white,
And cuckoo-buds of yellow hue
   Do paint the meadows with delight,
The cuckoo then, on every tree,
Mocks married men, for thus sings he,
     "Cuckoo;
    Cuckoo, cuckoo": Oh word of fear,
    Unpleasing to a married ear!

When shepherds pipe on oaten straws,
   And merry larks are plouwmen's clocks,
When turtles tread, and rooks, and daws,
   And maidens bleach their summer smocks,
The cuckoo then, on every tree,
Mocks married men, for thus sings he,
     "Cuckoo;
    Cuckoo, cuckoo": Oh word of fear,
    Unpleasing to a married ear!

from Love's Labour's Lost

---

*These lines, along with their companion piece "When Icicles Hang by the Wall"
(p. 89), come at the end of* Love's Labour's Lost. *The pun on "cuckoo" and
"cuckold" is a reminder that the words are related, supposedly because of the
behavior of the female bird.*

# It Was a Lover and His Lass

It was a lover and his lass,
  With a hey, and a ho, and a hey nonino,
That o'er the green corn field did pass
  In springtime, the only pretty ring time,
When birds do sing, hey ding a ding, ding:
Sweet lovers love the spring.

Between the acres of the rye,
  With a hey, and a ho, and a hey nonino,
These pretty country folks would lie,
  In springtime, etc.

This carol they began that hour,
  With a hey, and a ho, and a hey nonino,
How that a life was but a flower
  In springtime, etc.

And therefore take the present time,
  With a hey, and a ho, and a hey nonino;
For love is crownèd with the prime
  In springtime, etc.

from As You Like It

*Two pages sing this song to Touchstone and Audrey in the last act of* As You Like It. *Touchstone comments afterwards, "Truly, young gentlemen, though there was no great matter in the ditty, yet the note was very untuneable" (with "ditty," related to "diction," meaning the words).*

# My Mistress' Eyes
## Are Nothing like the Sun

❖❖❖❖

My mistress' eyes are nothing like the sun;
Coral is far more red than her lips' red;
If snow be white, why then her breasts are dun;
If hairs be wires, black wires grow on her head.
I have seen roses damasked, red and white,
But no such roses see I in her cheeks,
And in some perfumes there is more delight
Than in the breath that from my mistress reeks.
I love to hear her speak, yet well I know
That music hath a far more pleasing sound;
I grant I never saw a goddess go:
My mistress when she walks treads on the ground.
   And yet by heaven I think my love as rare
   As any she belied with false compare.

Sonnet CXXX

---

*In somewhat the same key as Sonnet XVIII ("Shall I compare thee to a summer's day?" on p. 86), this poem amounts to a denial of a set of conventional metaphors. The exaggerated figures of praise for a beloved woman come from many sources, to be sure, but the sonnets of Petrarch are the chief source for Renaissance poets.*

# Poor Soul,
## the Center of My Sinful Earth

Poor soul, the center of my sinful earth,
My sinful earth, these rebel powers that thee array,
Why dost thou pine within and suffer dearth,
Painting thy outward walls so costly gay?
Why so large cost, having so short a lease,
Dost thou upon thy fading mansion spend?
Shall worms, inheritors of this excess,
Eat up thy charge? Is this thy body's end?
Then, soul, live thou upon thy servant's loss,
And let that pine to aggravate thy store.
Buy terms divine in selling hours of dross,
Within be fed, without be rich no more.
   So shalt thou feed on Death, that feeds on men,
   And Death once dead, there's no more dying then.

Sonnet CXLVI

---

*The theme of the "death of death" returns in John Donne's Holy Sonnet X ("Death, be not proud," p. 125) and, in varied form, in Dylan Thomas's "Refusal to Mourn the Death, by Fire, of a Child in London" (p. 1054).*

# Hark! Hark! the Lark

>>>>>>>

Hark! hark! the lark at heaven's gate sings,
  And Phoebus 'gins arise,
His steeds to water at those springs
  On chaliced flowers that lies;
And winking Mary-buds begin
  To ope their golden eyes:
With every thing that pretty is,
  My lady sweet, arise!
  Arise, arise!

from Cymbeline

---

*In need of a wooing song, the lewd Cloten commands his musicians: "First, a very excellent good-conceited thing; after, a wonderful sweet air with admirable rich words to it . . . ."*

# Take, O Take Those Lips Away

Take, O take, those lips away,
That so sweetly were forsworn;
And those eyes, the break of day,
Lights that do mislead the morn:
But my kisses bring again
Bring again:
Seals of love but sealed in vain,
—Sealed in vain!

from Measure for Measure

---

*This song is sung by Mariana and a boy in "the moated grange" (see Tennyson's "Mariana," p. 654).*

# Farewell!
## Thou Art Too Dear for My Possessing

Farewell! thou art too dear for my possessing,
  And like enough thou know'st thy estimate:
The charter of thy worth gives thee releasing;
  My bonds in thee are all determinate.
For how do I hold thee but by thy granting?
  And for that riches where is my deserving?
The cause of this fair gift in me is wanting,
  And so my patent back again is swerving.
Thyself thou gav'st, thy own worth then not knowing,
  Or me, to whom thou gav'st it, else mistaking;
So thy great gift, upon misprision growing,
  Comes home again, on better judgement making.
    Thus have I had thee, as a dream doth flatter,
    In sleep a king, but, waking, no such matter.

Sonnet LXXXVII

---

*From the beginning, this sonnet vacillates between two realms, the erotic and the commercial, a traffic facilitated in part by the multiple meanings of "dear" and "possessing."*

# *Where the Bee Sucks, There Suck I*

Where the bee sucks, there suck I;
In a cowslip's bell I lie;
There I couch when owls do cry.
On the bat's back I do fly
After summer merrily.
Merrily, merrily shall I live now
Under the blossom that hangs on the bough.

from The Tempest

---

*The "airy spirit" Ariel sings this happy song, looking forward to being freed from service to Prospero.*

# When That I Was
## and a Little Tiny Boy

xxxxxx

When that I was and a little tiny boy,
  With hey, ho, the wind and the rain,
A foolish thing was but a toy,
  For the rain it raineth every day.

But when I came to man's estate
  With hey, ho, the wind and the rain,
'Gainst knaves and thieves men shut their gate,
  For the rain it raineth every day.

But when I came, alas! to wive,
  With hey, ho, the wind and the rain,
By swaggering could I never thrive,
  For the rain it raineth every day.

But when I came unto my beds,
  With hey, ho, the wind and the rain,
With toss-pots still had drunken heads,
  For the rain it raineth every day.

A great while ago the world begun,
  With hey, ho, the wind and the rain,
But that's all one, our play is done,
  And we'll strive to please you every day.

from Twelfth Night

---

*The clown Feste sings these verses at the end of* Twelfth Night. *The serious possibilities lurking in the design and the refrain are explored by Thomas Hardy in "During Wind and Rain" (p. 784) and by Robert Frost in "The Wind and the Rain." Twelfth Night falls in early January.*

# Full Many a Glorious Morning Have I Seen

Full many a glorious morning have I seen
Flatter the mountain-tops with sovereign eye,
Kissing with golden face the meadows green,
Gilding pale streams with heavenly alchemy;
Anon permit the basest clouds to ride
With ugly rack on his celestial face,
And from the forlorn world his visage hide,
Stealing unseen to west with this disgrace:
Even so my son one early morn did shine
With all-triumphant splendour on my brow;
But, out, alack! he was but one hour mine,
The region cloud hath mask'd him from me now.
    Yet him for this my love no whit disdaineth;
    Suns of the world may stain when heaven's sun staineth.

Sonnet XXXIII

---

*Renaissance poets were in love with concentric patterns whereby a human life is likened to the progress of a day or a year. In this sonnet, the comparison is buttressed by a pun on "eye" and "I" and, perhaps, on "sun" and "son."*

# No Longer Mourn For Me When I Am Dead

No longer mourn for me when I am dead
Than you shall hear the surly sullen bell
Give warning to the world that I am fled
From this vile world, with vilest worms to dwell:
Nay, if you read this line, remember not
The hand that writ it; for I love you so,
That I in your sweet thoughts would be forgot,
If thinking on me then should make you woe.
O, if, I say, you look upon this verse
When I perhaps compounded am with clay,
Do not so much as my poor name rehearse,
But let your love even with my life decay;
    Lest the wise world should look into your moan,
    And mock you with me after I am gone.

Sonnet LXXI

---

*It is fitting that a poem about life and death should follow an elementary design of simple sounds: "No . . . Nay . . . Oh . . . Lest . . . ."*

# Tired with All These,
# for Restful Death I Cry

◆◆◆◆

Tired with all these, for restful death I cry,
As, to behold desert a beggar born,
And needy nothing trimm'd in jollity,
And purest faith unhappily forsworn,
And gilded honour shamefully misplac'd,
And maiden virtue rudely strumpeted,
And right perfection wrongfully disgrac'd,
And strength by limping sway disabled,
And art made tongue-tied by authority,
And folly, doctor-like, controlling skill,
And simple truth miscall'd simplicity,
And captive good attending captain ill:
   Tir'd with all these, from these would I be gone,
   Save that, to die, I leave my love alone.

Sonnet LXVI

---

*The meaning and technique are both remarkable here: the poem is a bill of complaints (a familiar device in Shakespeare's tragedies as well), and ten of the fourteen lines begin with the same word.*

# Like as the Waves
# Make towards the Pebbled Shore

Like as the waves make towards the pebbled shore,
So do our minutes hasten to their end;
Each changing place with that which goes before,
In sequent toil all forwards do contend.
Nativity, once in the main of light,
Crawls to maturity, where with being crowned,
Crooked eclipses 'gainst his glory fight,
And Time that gave doth now his gift confound.
Time doth transfix the flourish set on youth
And delves the parallels in beauty's brow,
Feeds on the rarities of nature's truth,
And nothing stands but for his scythe to mow:
   And yet to times in hope my verse shall stand,
   Praising thy worth, despite his cruel hand.

Sonnet LX

---

*Like Sonnet LXV ("Since Brass, nor Stone, nor Earth, nor Boundless Sea," on p. 110), this poem makes a conventional claim for the ability of poems of praise to endure and to preserve love.*

# When Daffodils Begin to Peer

>>>>>>>

When daffodils begin to peer,
  With heigh! the doxy, over the dale,
Why, then comes in the sweet o' the year;
  For the red blood reigns in the winter's pale.

The white sheet bleaching on the hedge,
  With heigh! the sweet birds, O, how they sing!
Doth set my pugging tooth on edge,
  For a quart of ale is a dish for a king.

The lark, that tirra-lirra chants,
  With heigh! with heigh! the thrush and the jay,
Are summer songs for me and my aunts,
  While we lie tumbling in the hay.

from The Winter's Tale

---

*Autolycus the rogue sings this lusty number: both "doxy" and "aunts" refer to prostitution.*

# How like a Winter
## Hath My Absence Been

How like a winter hath my absence been
From thee, the pleasure of the fleeting year!
What freezings have I felt, what dark days seen!
What old December's bareness everywhere!
And yet this time removed was summer's time.
The teeming autumn, big with rich increase,
Bearing the wanton burthen of the prime,
Like widowed wombs after their lords' decease;
Yet this abundant issue seemed to me
But hope of orphans and unfathered fruit;
For summer and his pleasures wait on thee,
And, thou away, the very birds are mute;
    Or, if they sing, 'tis with so dull a cheer
    That leaves look pale, dreading the winter's near.

Sonnet XCVII

---

*The "wanton burden" evidently means the fruit or harvest of wantonness. (Note that: "prime" is "the spring"; "cheer" is "disposition.")*

# Since Brass, nor Stone, nor Earth, nor Boundless Sea

Since brass, nor stone, nor earth, nor boundless sea,
But sad mortality o'ersways their power,
How with this rage shall beauty hold a plea,
Whose action is no stronger than a flower?
O how shall summer's honey breath hold out
Against the wrackful siege of batt'ring days,
When rocks impregnable are not so stout,
Nor gates of steel so strong but time decays?
O fearful meditation, where alack,
Shall Time's best jewel from Time's chest lie hid?
Or what strong hand can hold his swift foot back,
Or who his spoil of beauty can forbid?
    O none, unless this miracle have might,
    That in black ink my love may still shine bright.

Sonnet LXV

---

*Brass, made of copper and zinc, has long been a symbol of durability; it has also come to mean money, shamelessness, and audacity. Here and elsewhere (as in Sonnet LV: "Not marble, nor the gilded monuments / Of princes, shall outlive this powerful rhyme"), Shakespeare enters the formulaic boastful claim about the ability of his art to preserve his love.*

# Come Away, Come Away, Death

Come away, come away, death,
  And in sad cypress let me be laid.
Fly away, fly away, breath;
  I am slain by a fair cruel maid.
My shroud of white, stuck all with yew,
    O! prepare it.
My part of death, no one so true
    Did share it.

Not a flower, not a flower sweet,
  On my black coffin let there be strown;
Not a friend, not a friend greet
  My poor corpse, where my bones shall be thrown.
A thousand thousand sighs to save,
    Lay me, O! where
Sad true lover never find my grave,
    To weep there.

from Twelfth Night

---

*Twelfth Night begins with the Duke's "If music be the food of love, play on . . . ." He asks the clown to sing again "the song we had last night" and calls it "old and plain." He also says it is "silly sooth," meaning "simple truth."*

# Come unto These Yellow Sands

Come unto these yellow sands,
　And then take hands:
Court'sied when you have, and kissed,
　The wild waves whist, —
Foot it featly here and there;
And, sweet sprites, the burden bear.
　　Hark, hark!
　　　Bow, wow,
　　The watch-dogs bark:
　　　Bow, wow.
　　Hark, hark! I hear
The strain of strutting chanticleer
Cry, Cock-a-diddle-dow!

from The Tempest

---

*After hearing this song sung by an invisible Ariel, Ferdinand muses in words later echoed in T. S. Eliot's "Waste Land" (p. 968):*

*Sitting on a bank,*
*Weeping again the King my father's wrack,*
*This music crept by me upon the waters . . . .*

# Tell Me Where Is Fancy Bred

()◀━━▶()

Tell me, where is fancy bred,
Or in the heart, or in the head?
How begot, how nourished?
  Reply, reply.
It is engend'red in the eyes,
With gazing fed; and fancy dies
In the cradle where it lies.
  Let us all ring fancy's knell.
  I'll begin it—Ding, dong, bell.

All: Ding, dong, bell.

from The Merchant of Venice

---

*The stage direction in* The Merchant of Venice *reads, "A song the whilst Bassanio comments on the caskets to himself." As elsewhere in Shakespeare, "fancy" here means "love" or perhaps "fond infatuation."*

# THOMAS CAMPION 1567–1620

Campion was a trained physician, a musician competent enough to compose music for his own poems, a bold and expressive poet in English and Latin, and a vigorous controversialist in some of the ongoing literary wars of his time. Among the poets in this anthology, he stands virtually alone in his ability to write a memorable lyric not based on recurring syllabic accent.

## My Sweetest Lesbia

My sweetest Lesbia, let us live and love,
And though the sager sort our deeds reprove,
Let us not weigh them. Heaven's great lamps do dive
Into their west, and straight again revive,
But soon as once set is our little light,
Then must we sleep one ever-during night.

If all would lead their lives in love like me,
Then bloody swords and armor should not be;
No drum nor trumpet peaceful sleeps should move,
Unless alarm came from the camp of love.
But fools do live, and waste their little light,
And seek with pain their ever-during night.

When timely death my life and fortune ends,
Let not my hearse be vexed with mourning friends,
But let all lovers, rich in triumph, come
And with sweet pastimes grace my happy tomb;
And, Lesbia, close up thou my little light,
And crown with love my ever-during night.

---

*Here Campion is imitating, and in part translating, an early poem of Catullus to his "Lesbia" (whose real name was Clodia). The poem has been translated into English by many others, including Richard Crashaw in the seventeenth century and John Frederick Nims in the twentieth.*

# Rose-cheeked Laura

⬥⬥⬥⬥

Rose-cheeked Laura, come,
Sing thou smoothly with thy beauty's
Silent music, either other
    Sweetly gracing.

Lovely forms do flow
From concent divinely framèd;
Heav'n is music, and thy beauty's
    Birth is heavenly.

These dull notes we sing
Discords need for helps to grace them;
Only beauty purely loving
    Knows no discord,

But still moves delight,
Like clear springs renewed by flowing,
Ever perfect, ever in them-
    selves eternal.

---

*This lyric is one of the most successful of the many Elizabethan experiments in basing versification on principles drawn from classical antiquity. It contains no rhyme, the rhythm is based on quantity (length of syllable) as well as quality (accent), lines are made up of different kinds of foot, and a word may be broken at the end of a line—a very rare occurrence in serious poetry. (Note that: "concent" is "harmonious music-making.")*

# *There Is a Garden in Her Face*

There is a garden in her face,
  Where roses and white lilies grow;
A heavenly paradise is that place,
  Wherein all pleasant fruits do flow.
There cherries grow which none may buy,
  Till "Cherry-ripe" themselves do cry.

Those cherries fairly do enclose
  Of orient pearl a double row,
Which when her lovely laughter shows,
  They look like rosebuds filled with snow.
Yet them nor peer nor prince can buy,
  Till "Cherry-ripe" themselves do cry.

Her eyes like angels watch them still;
  Her brows like bended bows do stand,
Threatening with piercing frowns to kill
  All that attempt with eye or hand
Those sacred cherries to come nigh,
  Till "Cherry-ripe" themselves do cry.

---

*Campion plays with many conventions, including the music and lore of street-vendors' cries (which can still be heard) and the farfetched comparisons of erotic verse from Italy and France (which also can still be heard). In chapter 24 of* Tess of the d'Urbervilles, *Thomas Hardy describes Angel Clare's reaction to Tess's beautiful face by saying, "He had never before seen a woman's lips and teeth which forced upon his mind with such persistent iteration the old Elizabethan simile of roses filled with snow"; and the line "Late roses filled with early snow" returns in T. S. Eliot's "East Coker"* (Four Quartets).

# Thrice Toss These Oaken Ashes in the Air

>>>>>>>

Thrice toss these oaken ashes in the air;
Thrice sit thou mute in this enchanted chair;
Then thrice three times tie up this true love's knot,
And murmur soft: "She will, or she will not."

Go burn these poisonous weeds in yon blue fire,
These screech-owl's feathers and this prickling briar,
This cypress gathered at a dead man's grave,
That all thy fears and cares an end may have.

Then come, you fairies, dance with me a round;
Melt her hard heart with your melodious sound.
In vain are all the charms I can devise;
She hath an art to break them with her eyes.

---

*Poets are fond of lists, catalogues, and superstitions, especially those involving numbers. This may be all in fun, but it makes a convincing love poem as well as a valuable collection of data for folklorists.*

# THOMAS NASHE 1567–1601

The life of the anti-Puritan satirist Thomas Nashe looks like a perfect example of Thomas Hobbes's formulation of human life in a state of nature: solitary, nasty, brutish, poor, and short. Nashe has, nevertheless, an appealing charm and impressive inventiveness, and he managed, in a short and vexed life, to distinguish himself in comic drama, satire, and prose fiction, writing one of the very earliest adventure novels, *The Unfortunate Traveler; or, The Life of Jack Wilton.*

## *Adieu, Farewell, Earth's Bliss*

Adieu, farewell earth's bliss;
This world uncertain is;
Fond are life's lustful joys;
Death proves them all but toys;
None from his darts can fly;
I am sick, I must die.
  Lord, have mercy on us!

Rich men, trust not in wealth,
Gold cannot buy you health;
Physic himself must fade.
All things to end are made,
The plague full swift goes by;
I am sick, I must die.
  Lord, have mercy on us!

Beauty is but a flower
Which wrinkles will devour;
Brightness falls from the air;
Queens have died young and fair;
Dust hath closed Helen's eye.
I am sick, I must die.
  Lord, have mercy on us!

Strength stoops unto the grave,
Worms feed on Hector brave;
Swords may not fight with fate,
Earth still holds ope her gate.
"Come, come" the bells do cry.
I am sick, I must die.
   Lord, have mercy on us.

Wit with his wantonness
Tasteth death's bitterness;
Hell's executioner
Hath no ears for to hear
What vain art can reply.
I am sick, I must die.
   Lord, have mercy on us.

Haste, therefore, each degree,
To welcome destiny;
Heaven is our heritage,
Earth but a player's stage;
Mount we unto the sky.
I am sick, I must die.
   Lord, have mercy on us.

     from Summer's Last Will and Testament

---

*Nashe's comedy* Summer's Last Will and Testament *contains two songs that have outlasted their original setting: "Spring, the Sweet Spring" (p. 120) and this litany. A formal church litany involves clergy and congregation alternating supplications and responses. We can hear Nashe, notoriously witty, wanton, bitter, and artful, in the castigation of "vain art" and in the plangent couplet about "Wit with his wantonness." (Note that: "fond" is "foolish"; "toys" is "trifles.")*

# Spring, the Sweet Spring

Spring, the sweet spring, is the year's pleasant king;
Then blooms each thing, then maids dance in a ring,
Cold doth not sting, the pretty birds do sing,
 "Cuckoo, jug-jug, pu-we, to-witta-woo!"

The palm and may make country houses gay,
Lambs frisk and play, the shepherds pipe all day,
And we hear aye birds tune this merry lay,
 "Cuckoo, jug-jug, pu-we, to-witta-woo."

The fields breathe sweet, the daisies kiss our feet,
Young lovers meet, old wives a-sunning sit,
In every street these tunes our ears do greet,
 "Cuckoo, jug-jug, pu-we, to-witta-woo!"
 Spring, the sweet spring!

from Summer's Last Will and Testament

---

*Although leading off Palgrave's* Golden Treasury *(1861) certainly added to this song's fame, it is meritorious in its own right. Most of Great Britain is hundreds of miles farther north than most of the United States, so that—the Gulf Stream notwithstanding—winter is usually cold, dark, and damp, and spring is always welcome. (Note that, "cuckoo . . .," is "the conventional cry of cuckoo, nightingale, lapwing, and owl.")*

Tichborne came from a prominent Catholic family and took part in the Babington conspiracy to assassinate Queen Elizabeth. With others in the group, he was arrested, tried, and gruesomely executed. His age at the time of his death is not certainly known, but it is probable that he was no more than eighteen.

## *Tichborne's Elegy*

Elegy Written with His Own Hand in the Tower before His Execution

My prime of youth is but a frost of cares,
　My feast of joy is but a dish of pain,
My crop of corn is but a field of tares,
　And all my good is but vain hope of gain:
The day is past, and yet I saw no sun,
And now I live, and now my life is done.

My tale was heard, and yet it was not told,
　My fruit is fall'n, and yet my leaves are green,
My youth is spent, and yet I am not old,
　I saw the world, and yet I was not seen:
My thread is cut, and yet it is not spun,
And now I live, and now my life is done.

I sought my death, and found it in my womb,
　I looked for life, and saw it was a shade,
I trod the earth, and knew it was my tomb,
　And now I die, and now I was but made:
My glass is full, and now my glass is run,
And now I live, and now my life is done.

Tichborne was hanged and quartered on September 20, 1586. He was in the spring of life, and he died just before the autumnal equinox—as is reflected in the "prime" and "frost" of the opening of his elegy, supposedly written on the eve of execution. Hilary Holladay has noticed that the poem contains eighteen lines, one for each year of the poet's life. Of the 180 words in the poem, 179 are outright monosyllables, and even the lone exception ("fallen") is sounded and counted as a monosyllable ("fall'n").

# SIR HENRY WOTTON 1568–1639

Wotton served as secretary to the Earl of Essex and
later, between 1604 and 1624, was involved in various
diplomatic and intelligence-gathering positions. His literary writings were not published until twelve years
after his death.

## On His Mistress, the Queen of Bohemia

You meaner beauties of the night
   That poorly satisfy our eyes
More by your number than your light,
   You common people of the skies,
   What are you when the moon doth rise?

You wandering chanters of the wood
   That warble forth Dame Nature's lays,
Thinking your passions understood
   By weaker accents, what's your praise
   When Philomel her voice doth raise?

You violets that first appear,
   By your pure purple mantles known,
Like the proud virgins of the year,
   As if the spring were all your own,
   What are you when the rose is blown?

So, when my mistress shall be seen
   In form and beauty of her mind,
By virtue first, then choice, a queen,
   Oh tell if she were not designed
   The eclipse and glory of her kind?

*Elizabeth of Bohemia, daughter of James I of England, was Wotton's employer—and that is what "Mistress" here means. In 1620 Wotton was a diplomat temporarily in her service. The success of his poem owes something to a balancing act: the diplomat indulges in exaggerated praise but tempers that extremism by using rhetorical questions that have a subtler effect than outright declarations. (A slightly later poem addressed to Elizabeth of Bohemia and attributed to "G. H." may be by George Herbert.)*

# JOHN DONNE 1572–1631

Donne was a Roman Catholic but later, while studying
law, joined the Church of England. He was a traveler,
diplomat, and courtier. Rather late in life, he became a
preacher and was soon famous for his sermons; he was
made Dean of St. Paul's in 1621. As the poems in this
anthology demonstrate, Donne could write, with equal
facility and depth, passionate poems of secular love and
passionate poems of sacred love, both sorts informed by
large-minded wit.

## Death, Be Not Proud

()◄██►()

Death, be not proud, though some have callèd thee
Mighty and dreadful, for thou art not so;
For those whom thou think'st thou dost overthrow
Die not, poor Death, nor yet canst thou kill me.
From rest and sleep, which but thy pictures be,
Much pleasure; then from thee much more must flow,
And soonest our best men with thee do go,
Rest of their bones, and soul's delivery.
Thou'rt slave to fate, chance, kings, and desperate men,
And dost with poison, war, and sickness dwell;
And poppy or charms can make us sleep as well
And better than thy stroke; why swell'st thou then?
One short sleep past, we wake eternally,
And death shall be no more: Death, thou shalt die.

Holy Sonnet X

---

*Three of Donne's Holy Sonnets are included in this anthology: this one, the
seventh (p. 128), and the fourteenth (pp. 126). They are much alike, especially
in their common reliance on imperatives, dramatic paradoxes, and subtle-seeming
ratiocination.*

# Batter My Heart, Three-Personed God

Batter my heart, three-personed God; for, you
As yet but knock, breathe, shine, and seek to mend;
That I may rise, and stand, o'erthrow me, and bend
Your force, to break, blow, burn, and make me new.
I, like an usurped town, to another due,
Labour to admit you, but oh, to no end,
Reason your viceroy in me, me should defend,
But is captived, and proves weak or untrue,
Yet dearly I love you, and would be loved fain,
But am bethrothed unto your enemy,
Divorce me, untie, or break that knot again,
Take me to you, imprison me, for I
Except you enthrall me, never shall be free,
Nor ever chaste, except you ravish me.

Holy Sonnet XIV

---

*Before Donne, the sonnet was a relatively unholy secular love lyric that could become intensely erotic and also lightheartedly satirical. And it could exploit love's capacity for exaggeration and paradox. Donne's Holy Sonnets lift the level of love from secular to sacred but keep the dramatic emphasis on paradox.*

# The Good Morrow

·◇·◇·◇·◇·

I wonder by my troth, what thou, and I
    Did, till we loved? were we not weaned till then,
But sucked on country pleasures, childishly?
    Or snorted we in the seven sleepers' den?
'Twas so; but this, all pleasures fancies be.
If every any beauty I did see,
Which I desired, and got, 'twas but a dream of thee.

And now good-morrow to our waking souls,
    Which watch not one another out of fear;
For love, all love of other sights controls,
    And makes one little room, an every where.
Let sea-discoverers to new worlds have gone,
Let maps to other, worlds on worlds have shown,
Let us possess one world, each hath one, and is one.

My face in thine eye, thine in mine appears,
    And true plain hearts do in the faces rest,
Where can we find two better hemispheres
    Without sharp North, without declining West?
Whatever dies, was not mixed equally;
If our two loves be one, or, thou and I
Love so alike, that none do slacken, none can die.

---

*John Dryden and Samuel Johnson doubted the wisdom of using intellectual arguments in love poetry. In our time, on the other hand, T. S. Eliot has praised Donne for preserving a unity of sensibility missing in Dryden, who so sharply separated mind from heart. For Donne, mind and heart were one, and love could employ the idiom of physics, and vice versa.*

# At the Round Earth's Imagined Corners

At the round earth's imagined corners, blow
Your trumpets, angels, and arise, arise
From death, you numberless infinities
Of souls, and to your scattered bodies go,
All whom the flood did, and fire shall o'erthrow,
All whom war, dearth, age, agues, tyrannies,
Despair, law, chance, hath slain, and you whose eyes,
Shall behold God, and never taste death's woe.
But let them sleep, Lord, and me mourn a space,
For, if above all these, my sins abound,
'Tis late to ask abundance of thy grace,
When we are there; here on this lowly ground,
Teach me how to repent; for that's as good
As if thou hadst sealed my pardon, with thy blood.

Holy Sonnet VII

*We can glimpse here something of Donne's fondness for paradox and education: this poet knows that the earth is round, with "corners" that are merely imaginary; he also knows that angels are not bound by literal laws of physics. Angels, like the vernacular today, still observe "the four corners of the world."*

# Go and Catch a Falling Star

＞＞＞＞＞＞＞

Go and catch a falling star,
  Get with child a mandrake root,
Tell me where all past years are,
  Or who cleft the Devil's foot,
Teach me to hear mermaids singing,
  Or to keep off envy's stinging,
    And find
    What wind
Serves to advance an honest mind.

I thou be'st borne to strange sights,
  Things invisible to see,
Ride ten thousand days and nights,
  Till age snow white hairs on thee.
Thou, when thou return'st, wilt tell me
  All strange wonders that befell thee,
    And swear
    Nowhere
Lives a woman true, and fair.

If thou find'st one, let me know,
  Such a pilgrimage were sweet;
Yet do not, I would not go,
  Though at next door we might meet;
Though she were true, when you met her,
  And last, till you write your letter,
    Yet she
    Will be
False, ere I come, to two, or three.

Like many of the Holy Sonnets, this poem begins with a robust series of imperatives. The impossible things are more or less conventional, but the terms are joined by certain dark underlying similarities (the devil is a sort of falling star, the mandrake root is supposedly anthropomorphic); conceivably, the prevalence of dishonesty and inconstancy is a result of the Fall.

# The Sun Rising

Busy old fool, unruly sun,
   Why dost thou thus,
Through windows, and through curtains call on us?
Must to thy motions lovers' seasons run?
      Saucy pedantic wretch, go chide
      Late school-boys, and sour prentices,
   Go tell court-huntsmen that the King will ride,
   Call country ants to harvest offices;
Love, all alike, no season knows, nor clime,
Nor hours, days, months, which are the rags of time.

      Thy beams, so reverend, and strong
      Why shouldst thou think?
I could eclipse and cloud them with a wink,
But that I would not lose her sight so long:
      If her eyes have not blinded thine,
      Look, and tomorrow late, tell me,
   Whether both th' Indias of spice and mine
   Be where thou left'st them, or lie here with me.
Ask for those kings whom thou saw'st yesterday,
And thou shalt hear, All here in one bed lay.

      She's all states, and all princes, I,
      Nothing else is.
Princes do but play us; compared to this,
All honor's mimic; all wealth alchemy.
      Thou sun art half as happy as we,
      In that the world's contracted thus;
   Thine age asks ease, and since thy duties be
   To warm the world, that's done in warming us.
Shine here to us, and thou art everywhere;
This bed thy center is, these walls, thy sphere.

The playful overstatement here about the sun's mistaken self-image "so reverend and strong" resembles the much more serious statement in Holy Sonnet X (p. 125) about death's mistaken self-image as "Mighty and dreadful." Donne delights in deflation of the overrated, so that the genuinely worthy—in this case, sexual love—can be suitably praised.

# A Valediction: Forbidding Mourning

As virtuous men pass mildly away,
   And whisper to their souls to go,
Whilst some of their sad friends do say,
   The breath goes now, and some say, no:

So let us melt, and make no noise,
   No tear-floods, nor sigh-tempests move,
'Twere profanation of our joys
   To tell the laity our love.

Moving of the earth brings harms and fears,
   Men reckon what it did and meant,
But trepidation of the spheres,
   Though greater far, is innocent.

Dull sublunary lovers' love,
   Whose soul is sense, cannot admit
Absence, because it doth remove
   Those things which elemented it.

But we by a love so much refined
   That our selves know not what it is,
Interassurèd of the mind,
   Care less eyes, lips, and hands to miss.

Our two souls therefore, which are one,
   Though I must go, endure not yet
A breach, but an expansion,
   Like gold to airy thinness beat.

If they be two, they are two so
   As stiff twin compasses are two,
Thy soul, the fixed foot, makes no show
   To move, but doth if th' other do.

And though it in the center sit,
   Yet when the other far doth roam,
It leans, and hearkens after it,
   And grows erect as that comes home.

Such wilt thou be to me, who must
   Like th' other foot, obliquely run;
The firmness makes my circle just,
   And makes me end where I begun.

---

*Here, in one of Donne's many poems of parting and farewell ("valediction"), we see what is probably the most celebrated of the so-called Metaphysical conceits: conceptualizations that range far afield for metaphoric likenesses. With remarkable wit and virtuosity, Donne succeeds in likening lovers to a metal drafting instrument.*

# A Hymn to God the Father

Wilt Thou forgive that sin where I begun,
  Which was my sin, though it were done before?
Wilt Thou forgive that sin through which I run,
  And do run still, though still I do deplore?
    When Thou hast done, Thou hast not done,
      For I have more.

Wilt Thou forgive that sin which I have won
  Others to sin and made my sin their door?
Wilt Thou forgive that sin which I did shun
  A year, or two, but wallowed in a score?
    When Thou hast done, Thou hast not done,
      For I have more.

I have a sin of fear, that when I have spun
  My last thread, I shall perish on the shore;
Swear by thyself that at my death Thy Son
  Shall shine as He shines now, and heretofore;
    And having done that, Thou hast done,
      I fear no more.

---

*Seeing God as the Father prompts Donne to join "Son" and "Sun." The poet's own name enters into the punning, since "thou hast done" sound like "thou hast Donne."*

# *The Ecstasy*

Where, like a pillow on a bed,
 A pregnant bank swelled up, to rest
The violet's reclining head,
 Sat we two, one another's best.
Our hands were firmly cèmented
 With a fast balm, which thence did spring,
Our eye-beams twisted, and did thread
 Our eyes, upon one double string;
So t'intergraft our hands, as yet
 Was all the means to make us one,
And pictures in our eyes to get
 Was all our propagation.
As 'twixt two equal armies, fate
 Suspends uncertain victory,
Ours souls (which to advance their state
 Were gone out) hung 'twixt her, and me.
And whilst our souls negotiate there,
 We like sepulchral statues lay;
All day, the same our postures were,
 And we said nothing, all the day.
If any, so by love refined,
 That he soul's language understood,
And by good love were grown all mind,
 Within convenient distance stood,
He (though he knew not which soul spake,
 Because both meant, both spake the same)
Might thence a new concoction take,
 And part far purer than he came.
"This ecstasy doth unperplex"
 (We said) "and tell us what we love;
We see by this, it was not sex;
 We see, we saw not what did move:
But as all several souls contain
 Mixture of things, they know not what,

Love, these mixed souls doth mix again,
   And makes both one, each this and that.
A single violet transplant,
   The strength, the color, and the size,
(All which before was poor, and scant)
   Redoubles still, and multiplies.
When love, with one another so
   Interinanimates two souls,
That abler soul, which thence doth flow,
   Defects of loneliness controls.
We then, who are this new soul, know
   Of what we are composed, and made,
For, the atomies of which we grow,
   Are souls, whom no change can invade.
But oh alas, so long, so far
   Our bodies why do we forbear?
They are ours, though they are not we; we are
   The intelligences, they the sphere.
We owe them thanks, because they thus,
   Did us, to us, at first convey,
Yielded their forces, sense, to us,
   Nor are dross to us, but allay.
On man heaven's influence works not so,
   But that it first imprints the air,
So soul into the soul may flow,
   Though it to body first repair.
As our blood labors to beget
   Spirits, as like souls as it can,
Because such fingers need to knit
   That subtle knot, which makes us man:
So must pure lovers' souls descend
   To affections, and to faculties,
Which sense may reach and apprehend,
   Else a great prince in prison lies.
To our bodies turn we then, that so
   Weak men on love revealed may look;
Love's mysteries in souls do grow,
   But yet the body is his book.

And if some lover, such as we,
   Have heard this dialogue of one,
Let him still mark us, he shall see
   Small change, when we're to bodies gone."

---

*As Donne would have known, "ecstasy" comes from Greek* ekstasis, *the opposite of* stasis. *The various meanings of* ekstasis *include "distraction" and "trance," along with the idea of being moved in space (as the lovers' souls "were gone out" in the fourth stanza of Donne's poem). See also the ecstatic moments in Hopkins's "Windhover" (p. 790) and Hardy's "Darkling Thrush" (p. 770). Martin Heidegger said, "Time is ecstasy." (Note that: "atomies" is "indivisible units.")*

# The Canonization

For God's sake hold your tongue, and let me love,
  Or chide my palsy, or my gout,
  My five grey hairs, or ruined fortune flout;
With wealth your state, your mind with arts improve,
    Take you a course, get you a place,
    Observe his Honor, or his Grace;
Or the king's real, or his stamped face
  Contemplate; what you will, approve,
  So you will let me love.

Alas, alas, who's injured by my love?
  What merchant's ships have my sighs drowned?
  Who says my tears have overflowed his ground?
When did my colds a forward spring remove?
    When did the heats which my veins fill
    Add one more to the plaguy bill?
Soldiers find wars, and lawyers find out still
  Litigious men, which quarrels move,
  Though she and I do love.

Call us what you will, we are made such by love;
  Call her one, me another fly,
  We're tapers too, and at our own cost die,
And we in us find the eagle and the dove
    The phœnix riddle hath more wit
    By us; we two being one are it.
So to one neutral thing both sexes fit,
  We die and rise the same, and prove
  Mysterious by this love.

We can die by it, if not live by love,
   And if unfit for tomb or hearse
   Our legend be, it will be fit for verse;
And if no piece of chronicle we prove,
    We'll build in sonnets pretty rooms;
    As well a well-wrought urn becomes
The greatest ashes, as half-acre tombs,
   And by these hymns all shall approve
   Us canonized for love:

And thus invoke us, "You, whom reverend love
   Made one another's hermitage;
   You, to whom love was peace, that now is rage;
Who did the whole world's soul contract, and drove
    Into the glasses of your eyes
    (So made such mirrors, and such spies,
That they did all to you epitomize);
   Countries, towns, courts beg from above
   A pattern of your love."

*With many erotic puns (especially the equation of death and orgasm) and much sexual lore, Donne here presents a tissue of exaggerations that confirm the strength of his love. We remember that "stanza" in Italian means "room" and that Cleanth Brooks's distinguished study of paradox in poetry is called* The Well-Wrought Urn.

# The Flea

Mark but this flea, and mark in this,
How little that which thou deniest me is;
Me it sucked first, and now sucks thee,
And in this flea our two bloods mingled be;
Thou know'st that this cannot be said
A sin, or shame, or loss of maidenhead,
　Yet this enjoys before it woo,
　And pampered swells with one blood made of two,
　And this, alas, is more than we would do.

Oh stay, three lives in one flea spare,
Where we almost, nay more than married are.
This flea is you and I, and this
Our marriage bed and marriage temple is;
Though parents grudge, and you, we are met,
And cloistered in these living walls of jet.
　Though use make you apt to kill me
　Let not to that, self-murder added be,
　And sacrilege, three sins in killing three.

Cruel and sudden, hast thou since
Purpled thy nail in blood of innocence?
Wherein could this flea guilty be,
Except in that drop which it sucked from thee?
Yet thou triumph'st, and say'st that thou
Find'st not thy self nor me the weaker now;
　'Tis true; then learn how false fears be:
　Just so much honor, when thou yield'st to me,
　Will waste, as this flea's death took life from thee.

There just has to be an element of aimless showing off in "The Flea," as though Donne had been challenged to make something out of nearly nothing. Since it is inconceivable that any coy mistress could be swayed by an argument so silly, one may conclude that the poet is merely demonstrating the strength of his passion, devotion, and ingenuity. (Note that: "use" is "habit.")

# Hymn to God My God, in My Sickness

Since I am coming to that holy room
  Where, with thy choir of saints for evermore,
I shall be made thy music; as I come
  I tune the instrument here at the door,
  And what I must do then, think now before.

Whilst my physicians by their love are grown
  Cosmographers, and I their map, who lie
Flat on this bed, that by them may be shown
  That this is my southwest discovery
  *Per fretum febris*, by these straits to die,

I joy, that in these traits, I see my West,
  For, though their currents yield return to none,
What shall my West hurt me? As West and East
  In all flat maps (and I am one) are one,
  So death doth touch the resurrection.

Is the Pacific Sea my home? Or are
  The Eastern riches? Is Jerusalem?
Anyan, and Magellan, and Gibraltar,
  All straits, and none but straits, are ways to them,
  Whether where Japhet dwelt, or Cham, or Shem.

We think that Paradise and Calvary,
  Christ's cross and Adam's tree, stood in one place;
Look, Lord and find both Adams met in me;
  As the first Adam's sweat surrounds my face,
  May the last Adam's blood my soul embrace.

So, in his purple wrapped, receive me, Lord;
  By these his thorns give me his other crown;
And, as to others' souls I preached thy word,
  Be this my text, my sermon to mine own:
  Therefore that he may raise the Lord throws down.

---

*The great circumnavigators of the sixteenth century, whose adventures continued into Donne's day, established the virtual unity of West and East, a seeming paradox with religious implications for the believer who sees Christ's death on Good Friday "touching" the Resurrection on Easter Sunday (see also Donne's "Good Friday, 1613. Riding Westward," p. 153). According to medieval lore, the "tree" of Adam's fall and the "tree" of the Crucifixion stood in the same place; and Creation, Fall, and Crucifixion all took place in April. (Note that: "per fretum febris" is "through the strait of fever.")*

# Sweetest Love, I Do Not Go

Sweetest love, I do not go
  For weariness of thee,
Nor in hope the world can show
  A fitter love for me;
    But since that I
Must die at last, 'tis best
To use myself in jest
    Thus by feigned deaths to die.

Yesternight the sun went hence,
  And yet is here today;
He hath no desire nor sense,
  Nor half so short a way.
    Then fear not me,
But believe that I shall make
Speedier journeys, since I take
    More wings and spurs than he.

O how feeble is man's power,
  That, if good fortune fall,
Cannot add another hour
  Nor a lost hour recall!
    But come bad chance,
And we join to it our strength,
And we teach it art and length,
    Itself o'er us to advance.

When thou sigh'st thou sigh'st not wind,
  But sigh'st my soul away;
When thou weep'st, unkindly kind,
  My life's blood doth decay.
    It cannot be
That thou lov'st me as thou say'st,
If in thine my life thou waste:
  That art the best of me.

Let not thy divining heart
  Forethink me any ill;
Destiny may take thy part,
  And may thy fears fulfil.
    But think that we
Are but turned aside to sleep:
They who one another keep
  Alive, ne'er parted be.

*This song is one of Donne's many valedictions: formal farewells or poems of parting. At the end of the poem, Donne indulges in a delicate trick of verbal magic to argue that the lovers are never parted.*

# A Nocturnal upon St. Lucy's Day, Being the Shortest Day

>>>>>>>

'Tis the year's midnight, and it is the day's,
Lucy's, who scarce seven hours herself unmasks;
   The sun is spent, and now his flasks
   Send forth light squibs, no constant rays;
     The world's whole sap is sunk;
The general balm the hydroptic earth hath drunk,
Whither, as to the bed's-feet, life is shrunk,
Dead and interred; yet all these seem to laugh,
Compared with me, who am their epitaph.

Study me then, you who shall lovers be
At the next world, that is, at the next spring:
   For I am every dead thing,
   In whom love wrought new alchemy.
     For his art did express
A quintessence even from nothingness,
From dull privations, and lean emptiness:
He ruined me, and I am re-begot
Of absence, darkness, death: things which are not.

All others, from all things, draw all that's good,
Life, soul, form, spirit, whence they being have;
   I, by Love's limbeck, am the grave
   Of all, that's nothing. Oft a flood
     Have we two wept, and so
Drowned the whole world, us two; oft did we grow
To be two Chaoses, when we did show
Care to aught else; and often absences
Withdrew our souls, and made us carcasses.

But I am by her death (which word wrongs her)
Of the first nothing the elixir grown;
  Were I a man, that I were one
  I needs must know; I should prefer,
    If I were any beast,
Some ends, some means; yea plants, yea stones detest,
And love; all, all some properties invest;
If I an ordinary nothing were,
As shadow, a light and body must be here.

But I am none; nor will my sun renew.
You lovers, for whose sake the lesser sun
  At this time to the Goat is run
  To fetch new lust, and give it you,
    Enjoy your summer all;
Since she enjoys her long night's festival,
Let me prepare towards her, and let me call
This hour her Vigil, and her Eve, since this
Both the year's, and the day's deep midnight is.

---

*St. Lucy's Day is December 13, and in Donne's time the winter solstice was observed on December 12. Although the solstice is the shortest day (that is, having the least daylight), it is the moment of the sun's rebirth, and the daylight hours will increase for six months until the summer solstice. It was once noted that "solar heroes," or divinities, are born in December, under the sign of Capricorn. (Note that: "hydroptic" is "dropsical," "insatiably thirsty"; "limbeck" is "alembic"; "goat" is "Capricorn.")*

# The Funeral

Whoever comes to shroud me, do not harm
      Nor question much
That subtle wreath of hair which crowns my arm;
The mystery, the sign you must not touch,
      For 'tis my outward Soul,
Viceroy to that, which then to heaven being gone,
      Will leave this to control,
And keep these limbs, her Provinces, from dissolution.

For if the sinewy thread my brain lets fall
      Through every part
Can tie those parts, and make me one of all;
These hairs which upward grew, and strength and art
      Have from a better brain,
Can better do it; except she meant that I
      By this should know my pain,
As prisoners then are manacled, when they're condemned to die.

Whate'er she meant by it, bury it with me,
      For since I am
Love's martyr, it might breed idolatry,
If into others' hands these Relics came;
      As 'twas humility
To afford to it all that a Soul can do,
      So, 'tis some bravery,
That since you would save none of me, I bury some of you.

---

*Both "The Funeral" and "The Relic" (p. 151) concern a wreath or bracelet of the lover's hair to be worn by the speaker in the grave.*

# The Apparition

When by thy scorn, O murderess, I am dead,
And that thou think'st thee free
From all solicitation from me,
Then shall my ghost come to thy bed,
And thee, feigned vestal, in worse arms shall see;
Then thy sick taper will begin to wink,
And he, whose thou art then, being tired before,
Will, if thou stir, or pinch to wake him, think
   Thou call'st for more,
And in false sleep will from thee shrink,
And then, poor aspen wretch, neglected thou
Bathed in a cold quicksilver sweat wilt lie
   A verier ghost than I;
What I will say, I will not tell thee now,
Lest that preserve thee; and since my love is spent,
I had rather thou shouldst painfully repent,
Than by my threatenings rest still innocent.

---

*Donne would have been aware that the Latin* apparitio *means not only "appearance" but also "attendance" and "service"; the meaning of "ghost" is newer. Quicksilver (mercury), an apt figure to describe postcoital sweat, also calls up uses in alchemy (to refine precious metal from ore) and medicine (to treat syphilis).*

# *The Relic*

When my grave is broke up again
Some second guest to entertain,
(For graves have learned that woman-head
To be to more than one a bed)
    And he that digs it, spies
A bracelet of bright hair about the bone,
    Will he not let us alone,
And think that there a loving couple lies,
Who thought that this device might be some way
To make their souls, at the last busy day,
Meet at this grave, and make a little stay?

    If this fall in a time, or land,
    Where mis-devotion doth command,
    Then, he that digs us up will bring
    Us to the Bishop and the King,
    To make us relics; then
Thou shalt be a Mary Magdalen, and I
    A something else thereby;
All women shall adore us, and some men;
And since at such time, miracles are sought,
I would have that age by this paper taught
What miracles we harmless lovers wrought.

First, we loved well and faithfully,
Yet knew not what we loved, nor why,
Difference of sex no more we knew,
Than our guardian angels do;
　　Coming and going, we
Perchance might kiss, but not between those meals;
　　Our hands ne'er touched the seals,
Which nature, injured by late law, sets free;
These miracles we did; but now alas,
All measure, and all language, I should pass,
Should I tell what a miracle she was.

---

*Shakespeare presumably put a curse on those who would disturb his bones (as Yorick's are disturbed in* Hamlet). *Donne seems to accept the situation, since the reuse of graves was a common practice. The line "A bracelet of bright hair about the bone" still has plenary power to shock and move.*

# Good Friday, 1613. Riding Westward

Let man's soul be a sphere, and then in this
The intelligence that moves, devotion is;
And as the other spheres, by being grown
Subject to foreign motions, lose their own,
And being by others hurried every day
Scarce in a year their natural form obey,
Pleasure or business, so, our souls admit
For their first mover, and are whirled by it.
Hence is't that I am carried towards the west
This day, when my soul's form bends toward the east.
There I should see a sun, by rising set,
And by that setting, endless day beget;
But that Christ on this cross did rise and fall,
Sin had eternally benighted all.
Yet dare I almost be glad I do not see
That spectacle of too much weight for me.
Who sees God's face, that is self life, must die;
What a death were it then to see God die!
It made his own lieutenant, Nature, shrink;
It made his footstool crack, and the sun wink.
Could I behold those hands which span the poles
And tune all spheres at once; pierced with those holes?
Could I behold that endless height, which is
Zenith to us and to our antipodes,
Humbled below us? or that blood which is
The seat of all our souls, if not of his,
Make dirt of dust, or that flesh which was worn
By God for his apparel, ragged and torn?
If on these things I durst not look, durst I
Upon his miserable mother cast mine eye,
Who was God's partner here, and furnished thus
Half of that sacrifice which ransomed us?
Though these things, as I ride, be from mine eye,

They are present yet unto my memory,
For that looks towards them; and thou look'st towards me,
O Savior, as thou hang'st upon the tree;
I turn my back to thee but to receive
Corrections, till thy mercies bid thee leave.
Oh, think me worth thine anger, punish me,
Burn off my rusts, and my deformity;
Restore thine image, so much, by thy grace,
That thou mayst know me, and I'll turn my face.

---

*One major axis of this turning poem is that from East to West, with a reminder, on a Good Friday, that the words "east" and "Easter" (and eos, Greek for "dawn") are related. Although "sun" and "son" are not etymologically related, they are joined by a common pun, especially when the Son of God rises at sunrise on Easter Sunday.*

# *The Anniversary*

All kings, and all their favorites,
   All glory of honors, beauties, wits.
The sun itself, which makes times, as they pass,
Is elder by a year, now, than it was
When thou and I first one another saw:
All other things, to their destruction draw,
   Only our love hath no decay;
This, no tomorrow hath, nor yesterday;
Running, it never runs from us away,
But truly keeps his first, last, everlasting day.

   Two graves must hide thine and my corse,
   If one might, death were no divorce;
Alas, as well as other princes, we
(Who prince enough in one another be)
Must leave at last in death, these eyes, and ears,
Oft fed with true oaths, and with sweet salt tears;
   But souls where nothing dwells but love
(All other thoughts being inmates) then shall prove
This, or a love increasèd there above,
When bodies to their graves, souls from their graves remove.

   And then we shall be thoroughly blest,
   But we no more, than all the rest;
Here upon earth, we are kings, and none but we
Can be such kings, nor of such subjects be;
Who is so safe as we? where none can do
Treason to us, except one of us two.
   True and false fears let us refrain,
Let us love nobly, and live, and add again
Years and years unto years, till we attain
To write threescore: this is the second of our reign.

It is typical of some lovers to act as their own fanatic accountants who know the day—or in some cases the hour or even the very minute—when they met or fell in love or became engaged. Donne's cleverness plays with the notion of time standing still and love persisting even as time runs on.

# BEN JONSON 1572–1637

Ben Jonson is the earliest English writer who is routinely called by a nickname, a familiarity that seems justified by Jonson's vigor, charm, and good humor. He was a successful playwright, producing tragedies as well as comedies; a translator, conversationalist, and critic of great learning and distinction; and, above all, a lyric poet whose grace and energy are the equal of his best classical precursors.

# *Drink to Me Only with Thine Eyes*

Drink to me only with thine eyes,
  And I will pledge with mine;
Or leave a kiss but in the cup,
  And I'll not look for wine.
The thirst that from the soul doth rise
  Doth ask a drink divine;
But might I of Jove's nectar sup,
  I would not change for thine.

I sent thee late a rosy wreath,
  Not so much honoring thee
As giving it a hope that there
  It could not withered be.
But thou thereon didst only breathe,
  And sent'st it back to me;
Since when it grows, and smells, I swear,
  Not of itself, but thee.

---

*It is unlikely that many among the general reading public will know poems in this collection as true lyrics, songs meant to be sung. But this gem of Jonson's, his Song: To Celia, is still, after almost four hundred years, one of the loveliest and most popular of songs in English.*

# On My First Son

•❖•❖•❖•❖•

Farewell, thou child of my right hand, and joy;
My sin was too much hope of thee, loved boy.
Seven years thou wert lent to me, and I thee pay,
Exacted by thy fate, on the just day.
Oh, could I lose all father now! For why
Will man lament the state he should envy?
To have so soon 'scaped world's and flesh's rage,
And, if no other misery, yet age?
Rest in soft peace, and, asked, say here doth lie
Ben Jonson his best piece of poetry;
For whose sake, henceforth, all his vows be such,
As what he loves may never like too much.

---

*Jonson's son, who died on his seventh birthday, was a junior. As Jonson knew, "Benjamin" means "son of the right hand" or "favorite." He also knew that "poem" means "thing made" or "product," so that one may speak of one's poetry as children and of one's children as poetry.*

# Hymn to Diana

Queen and huntress, chaste and fair,
Now the sun is laid to sleep,
Seated in thy silver chair,
State in wonted manner keep:
  Hesperus entreats thy light,
  Goddess excellently bright.

Earth, let not thy envious shade
Dare itself to interpose;
Cynthia's shining orb was made
Heaven to clear when day did close:
  Bless us then with wishèd sight,
  Goddess excellently bright.

Lay thy bow of pearl apart,
And thy crystal-shining quiver;
Give unto the flying hart
Space to breathe, how short soever:
  Thou that mak'st a day of night,
  Goddess excellently bright.

from Cynthia's Revels

---

*Like "Slow, Slow, Fresh Fount" (p. 164), this is a song from* Cynthia's Revels. *Hesperus sings the hymn to Cynthia (or Diana), virgin goddess of the moon
and the hunt.*

# Still to Be Neat

>>>>>>

Still to be neat, still to be dressed,
As you were going to a feast;
Still to be powdered, still perfumed:
Lady, it is to be presumed,
Though art's hid causes are not found,
All is not sweet, all is not sound.

Give me a look, give me a face,
That makes simplicity a grace;
Robes loosely flowing, hair as free:
Such sweet neglect more taketh me
Than all the adulteries of art;
They strike mine eyes, but not my heart.

from The Silent Woman

---

*Robert Herrick, who called Jonson "Saint Ben," helped himself to parts of this marvelous song from one of Jonson's plays. The "sweet" and "neglect" are used also in Herrick's "Delight in Disorder" (p. 174), and "taketh" (was ever a mot more juste?) also graces Herrick's "Upon Julia's Clothes" (p. 173).*

# The Triumph of Charis

See the Chariot at hand here of Love,
  Wherein my Lady rideth!
Each that draws is a swan or a dove,
  And well the car Love guideth
As she goes, all hearts do duty
    Unto her beauty;
And enamour'd do wish, so they might
    But enjoy such a sight,
That they still were to run by her side,
Thorough swords, thorough seas, whither she would ride.

Do but look on her eyes, they do light
  All that Love's world compriseth!
Do but look on her hair, it is bright
  As Love's star when it riseth!
Do but mark, her forehead's smoother
    Than words that soothe her;
And from her arch'd brows such a grace
    Sheds itself through the face,
As alone there triumphs to the life
All the gain, all the good, of the elements' strife.

Have you seen but a bright lily grow
  Before rude hands have touch'd it?
Have you mark'd but the fall of the snow
  Before the soil hath smutch'd it?
Have you felt the wool of the beaver,
    Or swan's down ever?
Or have smelt of the bud of the brier,
    Or the nard in the fire?
Or have tasted the bag of the bee?
O so white, O so soft, O so sweet is she!

from A Celebration of Charis in Ten Lyric Pieces

*The phrase "or swan's down ever" occurs also at the end of Ezra Pound's* Pisan Cantos. *This "triumph" is the fourth part of Jonson's "Celebration of Charis in Ten Lyric Pieces." No person has been identified as the original of "Charis," whose name means "grace." (Note that: "whether" is "whithersoever"; "nard" is "spikenard," an aromatic plant.)*

# Epitaph on S. P.

Weep with me, all you that read
  This little story;
And know, for whom a tear you shed
  Death's self is sorry.
'Twas a child that so did thrive
  In grace and feature,
As Heaven and Nature seemed to strive
  Which owned the creature.
Years he numbered scarce thirteen
  When Fates turned cruel,
Yet three filled Zodiacs had he been
  The Stages' jewel;
And did act (what now we moan)
  Old men so duly,
As sooth the Parcae thought him one,
  He played so truly.
So, by error, to his fate
  They all consented;
But, viewing him since, alas, too late!
  They have repented;
And have sought, to give new birth,
  In baths to steep him;
But, being so much too good for earth,
  Heaven vows to keep him.

*The boy-actor Salomon Pavy acted in some of the plays that Jonson wrote for the Children of Queen Elizabeth's Chapel. (Note that: "Parcae" is "the Fates.")*

# Slow, Slow, Fresh Fount, Keep Time with My Salt Tears

Slow, slow, fresh fount, keep time with my salt tears;
　　Yet slower yet, oh faintly gentle springs:
List to the heavy part the music bears,
　　"Woe weeps out her division when she sings."
　　Droop herbs and flowers;
　　Fall grief in showers;
　　"Our beauties are not ours":
　　　　Oh, I could still,
Like melting snow upon some craggy hill,
　　Drop, drop, drop, drop,
Since nature's pride is, now, a withered daffodil.

from Cynthia's Revels

---

*In* Cynthia's Revels, *the nymph Echo sings this pretty echoic song for Narcissus, metamorphosed into a flower related to the daffodil. (Note that: "division" is "subdividing one long note into several shorter ones.")*

# Come, My Celia, Let Us Prove

Come, my Celia, let us prove
While we may the sports of love;
Time will not be ours forever,
He at length our good will sever.
Spend not then his gifts in vain.
Suns that set may rise again,
But if once we lost this light,
'Tis with us perpetual night.
Why should we defer our joys?
Fame and rumor are but toys.
Cannot we delude the eyes
Of a few poor household spies?
Or his easier ears beguile,
So removèd by our wile?
'Tis no sin love's fruit to steal,
But the sweet theft to reveal:
To be taken, to be seen,
These have crimes accounted been.

from Volpone

---

*Volpone includes this song in his assault on the virtuous wife Celia, to whose husband, Corvino, the "easier ears" in line 13 belong. The model for the beginning of the poem seems to be much the same lines from Catullus as inspired Campion's "My Sweetest Lesbia" (p. 114).*

# To Penshurst

Thou art not, Penshurst, built to envious show,
Of touch or marble; nor canst boast a row
Of polished pillars, or a roof of gold;
Thou hast no lantern whereof tales are told,
Or stair, or courts; but stand'st an ancient pile,
And, these grudged at, art reverenced the while.
Thou joy'st in better marks, of soil, of air,
Of wood, of water; therein thou art fair.
Thou hast thy walks for health, as well as sport;
Thy mount, to which the dryads do resort,
Where Pan and Bacchus their high feasts have made,
Beneath the broad beech and the chestnut shade,
That taller tree, which of a nut was set
At his great birth where all the Muses met.
There in the writhèd bark are cut the names
Of many a sylvan, taken with his flames;
And thence the ruddy satyrs oft provoke
The lighter fauns to reach thy Lady's Oak.
Thy copse too, named of Gamage, thou hast there,
That never fails to serve thee seasoned deer
When thou wouldst feast, or exercise, thy friends.
The lower land, that to the river bends,
Thy sheep, thy bullocks, kine, and calves do feed;
The middle grounds thy mares and horses breed.
Each bank doth yield thee conies; and the tops,
Fertile of wood, Ashore and Sidney's copse,
To crown thy open table, doth provide
The purpled pheasant with the speckled side;
The painted partridge lies in every field,
And for thy mess is willing to be killed.
And if the high-swollen Medway fail thy dish,
Thou hast thy ponds that pay thee tribute fish,
Fat agèd carps that run into thy net,
And pikes, now weary their own kind to eat,

As loath the second draught or cast to stay,
Officiously at first themselves betray;
Bright eels that emulate them, and leap on land
Before the fisher, or into his hand.
Then hath thy orchard fruit, thy garden flowers,
Fresh as the air, and new as are the hours.
The early cherry, with the later plum,
Fig, grape, and quince, each in his time doth come:
The blushing apricot and woolly peach
Hang on thy walls, that every child may reach.
And though thy walls be on the country stone,
They're reared with no man's ruin, no man's groan;
There's none that dwell about them wish them down,
But all come in, the farmer and the clown,
And no one empty-handed, to salute
Thy lord and lady, though they have no suit.
Some bring a capon, some a rural cake,
Some nuts, some apples; some that think they make
The better cheeses bring 'em, or else send
By their ripe daughters, whom they would commend
This way to husbands, and whose baskets bear
An emblem of themselves in plum or pear.
But what can this (more than express their love)
Add to thy free provisions, far above
The need of such? whose liberal board doth flow
With all that hospitality doth know;
Where comes no guest but is allowed to eat,
Without his fear, and of thy lord's own meat;
Where the same beer and bread, and selfsame wine,
That is his lordship's shall be also mine.
And I not fain to sit (as some this day
At great men's tables), and yet dine away.
Here no man tells my cups; nor, standing by,
A waiter doth my gluttony envy,
But gives me what I call, and lets me eat;
He knows below he shall find plenty of meat.
Thy tables hoard not up for the next day;
Nor, when I take my lodging, need I pray

For fire, or lights, or livery; all is there,
As if thou then wert mine, or I reigned here:
There's nothing I can wish, for which I stay.
That found King James when, hunting late this way
With his brave son, the prince, they saw thy fires
Shine bright on every hearth, as the desires
Of thy Penates had been set on flame
To entertain them; or the country came
With all their zeal to warm their welcome here.
What (great I will not say, but) sudden cheer
Didst thou then make 'em! and what praise was heaped
On thy good lady then! who therein reaped
The just reward of her high housewifery;
To have her linen, plate, and all things nigh,
When she was far; and not a room but dressed
As if it had expected such a guest!
These, Penshurst, are thy praise, and yet not all.
Thy lady's noble, fruitful, chaste withal.
His children thy great lord may call his own,
A fortune in this age but rarely known.
They are, and have been, taught religion; thence
Their gentler spirits have sucked innocence.
Each morn and even they are taught to pray,
With the whole household, and may, every day,
Read in their virtuous parents' noble parts
The mysteries of manners, arms, and arts.
Now, Penshurst, they that will proportion thee
With other edifices, when they see
Those proud, ambitious heaps, and nothing else,
May say, their lords have built, but thy lord dwells.

*So-called topographical poetry, of which "To Penshurst" is one of the greatest examples in English, has persisted since the seventeenth century, exercising a poet's skills in architecture, history, rhetoric, and the arts of verse-writing. Penshurst, in Kent, enjoyed the superlative distinction of being the seat of the Sidneys, one of the most illustrious families of Elizabethan and Jacobean England. (Note that: "touch" is "touchstone," a fine marble; "lantherne" is a glassed-in room like a greenhouse on top of a house; "clowne" is "rural peasant," "rustic"; "penates" is "household gods"; "proportion" is "compare.")*

# JOHN WEBSTER c.1578–c.1632

In the manner of the Elizabethan theater, John Webster freely collaborated—with William Rowley, Thomas
Dekker, Thomas Heywood, John Marston, and Cyril
Tourneur—but his most famous tragedies were his
alone: *The White Devil* and *The Duchess of Malfi.* Of the
poets in this book, Webster was the only one who was
also a coachmaker.

# Call for the Robin Redbreast
# and the Wren

Call for the Robin Redbreast and the Wren,
Since o'er shady groves they hover,
And with leaves and flowers do cover
The friendless bodies of unburied men.
Call unto his funeral Dole
The Ante, the field-mouse, and the mole
To rear him hillocks, that shall keep him warm,
And (when gay tombs are robb'd) sustain no harm,
But keep the wolf far thence, that's foe to men,
For with his nails he'll dig them up agen.

from The White Devil

---

*"Webster was much possessed by death," according to T. S. Eliot's "Whispers of
Immortality". This end of Cornelia's song or dirge from Webster's* White Devil
*also appears, varied slightly, in Eliot's "Waste Land" (p. 968).*

Browne's narrative and lyric poems have been important models for many writers, including Milton and
Keats.

## On the Countess Dowager of Pembroke

❖❖❖❖

Underneath this sable hearse
Lies the subject of all verse:
Sidney's sister, Pembroke's mother:
Death, ere thou has slain another,
Fair and learned and good as she,
Time shall throw a dart at thee.

Marble piles let no man raise
To her name: for after days
Some kind woman born as she,
Reading this, like Niobe,
Shall turn marble, and become
Both her mourner and her tomb.

---

*Mary Herbert, Countess of Pembroke (1561–1621), was the younger sister of Sir Philip Sidney. She was also one of the most accomplished people in an age of prodigious accomplishment. A poet and translator herself, she befriended and helped many writers, including Samuel Daniel and Ben Jonson.*

# ROBERT HERRICK 1591–1674

Superficially, Herrick was a good deal like his contemporary George Herbert: a poet and clergyman educated at Cambridge. But, markedly unlike the pious and saintly Herbert, Herrick was a much better secular poet than a sacred one. In his marvelously constructed lyrics there is an appreciation of nature and the physical—including the body, with and without clothes.

## To the Virgins, to Make Much of Time

Gather ye rose-buds while ye may,
   Old Time is still a-flying;
And this same flower that smiles today,
   Tomorrow will be dying.

The glorious lamp of heaven, the sun,
   The higher he's a-getting,
The sooner will his race be run,
   And nearer he's to setting.

That age is best which is the first,
   When youth and blood are warmer;
But being spent, the worse, and worst
   Times, still succeed the former.

Then be not coy, but use your time,
   And while ye may, go marry;
For having lost but once your prime,
   You may for ever tarry.

---

*This gem of a poem is a good deal like Andrew Marvell's* carpe diem *poem "To His Coy Mistress" (p. 229). Unlike Marvell's clever pseudo-syllogism, however, Herrick's little song simply asserts some pretty hackneyed propositions, including a variant of "time flies," followed by the imperatives "be not coy," "use your time," and "go marry."*

Robert Herrick

# Upon Julia's Clothes

>>>>>>>

Whenas in silks my Julia goes,
Then, then, methinks, how sweetly flows
That liquefaction of her clothes.

Next, when I cast mine eyes and see
That brave vibration each way free,
O how that glittering taketh me!

---

*The highlights of the poem are the surprisingly technical "liquefaction" and the brilliant stroke (abetted by alliteration) of "brave vibration" ("brave" as in "brave new world," meaning "splendid").*

# Delight in Disorder

A sweet disorder in the dress
Kindles in clothes a wantonness.
A lawn about the shoulders thrown
Into a fine distractión;
An erring lace, which here and there
Enthralls the crimson stomacher;
A cuff neglectful, and thereby
Ribbons to flow confusèdly;
A winning wave, deserving note,
In the tempestuous petticoat;
A careless shoestring, in whose tie
I see a wild civility;
Do more bewitch me than when art
Is too precise in every part.

---

*Herrick cleverly says that poetry, a model of order, could be used to praise erotic disorder. In saluting disorder (praise echoed in our time by Roland Barthes), Herrick practices what he preaches by exhibiting modest disorder in rhetoric, logic, grammar, and versification.*

# *To Daffodils*

Fair daffodils, we weep to see
  You haste away so soon:
As yet the early-rising sun
  Has not attained his noon.
     Stay, stay,
    Until the hasting day
      Has run
    But to the evensong;
And, having prayed together, we
    Will go with you along.

We have short time to stay, as you,
  We have as short a spring;
As quick a growth to meet decay,
  As you, or anything.
     We die,
    As your hours do, and dry
      Away,
    Like to the summer's rain;
Or as the pearls of morning's dew
    Ne'er to be found again.

---

*It makes sense that a poem about the brevity of life, whether floral or human, should be in short lines made up mostly of notably short words—molecular syllables like "see," "so," "day," "do," "die."*

# The Argument of His Book

I sing of brooks, of blossoms, birds and bowers,
Of April, May, of June and Jùly-flowers;
I sing of May-poles, hock-carts, wassails, wakes,
Of bridegrooms, brides and of their bridal cakes;
I write of youth, of love, and have access
By these to sing of cleanly wantonness;
I sing of dews, of rains, and piece by piece
Of balm, of oil, of spice and ambergris;
I sing of times trans-shifting, and I write
How roses first came red and lilies white;
I write of groves, of twilights, and I sing
The Court of Mab, and of the Fairy King;
I write of hell; I sing (and ever shall)
Of heaven, and hope to have it after all.

---

*"Argument" here means the subject matter. Herrick speaks truly: he wrote several hundred poems on a great variety of subjects and kept his head and heart through it all.*

# Corinna's Going a-Maying

Get up, get up for shame! The blooming morn
Upon her wings presents the god unshorn.
  See how Aurora throws her fair,
  Fresh-quilted colors through the air.
  Get up, sweet slug-a-bed, and see
  The dew bespangling herb and tree!
Each flower has wept and bowed toward the east
Above an hour since, yet you not dressed;
  Nay! not so much as out of bed?
  When all the birds have matins said
  And sung their thankful hymns, 'tis sin,
  Nay, profanation, to keep in,
Whenas a thousand virgins on this day
Spring, sooner than the lark, to fetch in May.

Rise and put on your foliage, and be seen
To come forth, like the springtime, fresh and green,
  And sweet as Flora. Take no care
  For jewels for your gown or hair.
  Fear not; the leaves will strew
  Gems in abundance upon you.
Besides, the childhood of the day has kept,
Against you come, some orient pearls unwept.
  Come, and receive them while the light
  Hangs on the dew-locks of the night;
  And Titan on the eastern hill
  Retires himself, or else stands still
Till you come forth. Wash, dress, be brief in praying;
Few beads are best when once we go a-Maying.

Come, my Corinna, come; and, coming, mark
How each field turns a street, each street a park,
  Made green and trimmed with trees; see how
  Devotion gives each house a bough
  Or branch: each porch, each door, ere this,
  An ark, a tabernacle is,
Made up of white-thorn neatly interwove,
As if here were those cooler shades of love.
  Can such delights be in the street
  And open fields, and we not see't?
  Come, we'll abroad; and let's obey
  The proclamation made for May,
And sin no more, as we have done, by staying;
But, my Corinna, come, let's go a-Maying.

There's not a budding boy or girl this day
But is got up and gone to bring in May.
  A deal of youth, ere this, is come
  Back, and with white-thorn laden home.
  Some have dispatched their cakes and cream,
  Before that we have left to dream;
And some have wept, and wooed, and plighted troth,
And chose their priest, ere we can cast off sloth.
  Many a green-gown has been given,
  Many a kiss, both odd and even,
  Many a glance, too, has been sent
  From out the eye, love's firmament;
Many a jest told of the keys betraying
This night, and locks picked; yet we're not a-Maying!

Come, let us go, while we are in our prime,
And take the harmless folly of the time!
  We shall grow old apace, and die
  Before we know our liberty.
  Our life is short, and our days run
  As fast away as does the sun.
And, as a vapor or a drop of rain,
Once lost, can ne'er be found again,
  So when or you or I are made
  A fable, song, or fleeting shade,
  All love, all liking, all delight
  Lies drowned with us in endless night.
Then, while time serves and we are but decaying,
Come, my Corinna, come, let's go a-Maying.

---

*Here is a* carpe diem *poem urging the almost literal seizure of the day (see Herrick's "To the Virgins, to Make Much of Time," p. 172). Since "Corinna" could be a diminutive of "Cora," another name for Persephone, the poem gains a dimension from classical myth that adds complexity and profundity, although the mischievous Herrick is not above mildly lewd jests about keys and locks. Some of the arguments, and even some of the language, come out of the mouths of "the ungodly" in the Old Testament.*

# The Night-Piece to Julia

Her eyes the glow-worm lend thee,
The shooting stars attend thee;
  And the elves also,
  Whose little eyes glow
Like the sparks of fire, befriend thee.

No will-o'-th'-wisp mislight thee,
Nor snake or slow-worm bite thee;
  But on, on thy way,
  Not making a stay,
Since ghost there's none to affright thee.

Let not the dark thee cumber;
What though the moon does slumber?
  The stars of the night
  Will lend thee their light
Like tapers clear without number.

Then, Julia, let me woo thee,
Thus, thus to come unto me;
  And when I shall meet
  Thy silv'ry feet
My soul I'll pour into thee.

---

*Even in parts of the world with advanced civilization, enchanting rural lore persists, four hundred years after Herrick's birth. Glow-worms and shooting stars have a special place in literature, from Shakespeare's* Midsummer-Night's Dream *and Marvell's* "Mower to the Glow-Worms" *(p. 244) to Robert Frost's* "Fireflies in the Garden." *(Note that: "slow-worm" is "small lizard" or (the earlier and more probable meaning) "an adder.")*

# Grace for a Child

Here a little child I stand,
Heaving up my either hand;
Cold as Paddocks though they be,
Here I lift them up to Thee,
For a Benizon to fall
On our meat, and on us all. *Amen.*

---

*The seven other poems by Herrick in this anthology come from a book called* Hesperides; *this child's prayer is from Herrick's more pious collection,* Noble Numbers. *(Note that: "Paddocks" are "toads" or "frogs"; a "Benizon" is a "blessing.")*

# HENRY KING, BISHOP OF CHICHESTER 1592–1669

King, who was friendly with John Donne and Isaak
Walton, in time became Bishop of Chichester.

## Exequy on His Wife

Accept, thou shrine of my dead Saint!
Instead of dirges this complaint;
And for sweet flowers to crown thy hearse,
Receive a strew of weeping verse
From thy griev'd friend, whom thou might'st see
Quite melted into tears for thee.
   Dear loss! since thy untimely fate
My task hath been to meditate
On thee, on thee: thou art the book,
The library whereon I look
Though almost blind. For thee (lov'd clay!)
I languish out, not live the day,
Using no other exercise
But what I practise with mine eyes.
By which wet glasses I find out
How lazily time creeps about
To one that mourns: this, only this
My exercise and bus'ness is:
So I compute the weary hours
With sighs dissolved into showers.
   Nor wonder if my time go thus
Backward and most preposterous;
Thou hast benighted me. Thy set
This eve of blackness did beget,
Who wast my day, (though overcast
Before thou had'st thy noon-tide passed)
And I remember must in tears,

Thou scarce had'st seen so many years
As day tells hours. By thy clear sun
My love and fortune first did run;
But thou wilt never more appear
Folded within my hemisphere:
Since both thy light and motion
Like a fled star is fall'n and gone;
And twixt me and my soul's dear wish
The earth now interposed is,
With such a strange eclipse doth make
As ne'er was read in almanake.

I could allow thee for a time
To darken me annd my sad clime,
Were it a month, a year, or ten,
I would thy exile live till then;
And all that space my mirth adjourn
So thou wouldst promise to return;
And putting off thy ashy shroud
At length disperse this sorrow's cloud.

But woe is me! the longest date
Too narrow is to calculate
These empty hopes. Never shall I
Be so much blest, as to descry
A glimpse of thee, till that day come
Which shall the earth to cinders doom,
And a fierce fever must calcine
The body of this world, like thine
(My Little World!). That fit of fire
Once off, our bodies shall aspire
To our souls' bliss: then we shall rise,
And view ourselves with clearer eyes
In that calm region, where no night
Can hide us from each other's sight.

Meantime, thou hast her earth: much good
May my harm do thee. Since it stood
With Heaven's will I might not call
Her longer mine, I give thee all
My short-liv'd right and interest

In her, whom living I lov'd best:
With a most free and bounteous grief,
I give thee what I could not keep.
Be kind to her, and prithee look
Thou write into thy Doomsday book
Each parcel of this rarity
Which in thy casket shrin'd doth lie:
See that thou make thy reck'ning straight,
And yield her back again by weight;
For thou must audit on thy trust
Each grain and atom of this dust:
As thou wilt answer Him, that lent,
Not gave thee, my dear monument.

    So close the ground, and 'bout her shade
Black curtains draw, my bride is laid.
    Sleep on (my love!) in thy cold bed
Never to be disquieted,
My last good night! Thou wilt not wake
Till I thy fate shall overtake:
Till age, or grief, or sickness must
Marry my body to that dust
It so much loves; and fill the room
My heart keeps empty in thy tomb.
Star for me there; I will not fail
To meet thee in that hollow vale.
And think not much of my delay;
I am already on the way,
And follow thee with all the speed
Desire can make, or sorrows breed.
Each minute is a short degree
And ev'ry hour a step towards thee.
At night when I betake to rest,
Next morn I rise nearer my west
Of life, almost by eight hours' sail,
Than when sleep breath'd his drowsy gale.
    Thus from the sun my bottom steers,
And my days' compass downward bears.
Nor labour I to stem the tide,

Through which to thee I swiftly glide.
  'Tis true; with shame and grief I yield,
Thou, like the van, first took'st the field,
And gotten hast the victory
In thus adventuring to die
Before me; whose more years might crave
A just precedence in the grave.
But hark! My pulse, like a soft drum
Beats my approach, tells thee I come;
And slow howe'er my marches be,
I shall at last sit down by thee.
  The thought of this bids me go on,
And wait my dissolution
With hope and comfort. Dear! (forgive
The crime) I am content to live
Divided, with but half a heart,
Till we shall meet and never part.

---

*In lines admired by Edgar Allan Poe and T. S. Eliot, Henry King memorialized his dead wife. As was typical at the time, King uses some of the witty devices of the Metaphysicals (such as employing technical terms from geometry: sixty minutes of arc equal one degree). But King's most durable achievement is the registration of passionate love and profound theology. (Note that: "straw" is "scattering"; "calcine" is "burn to dust"; "bottom" is "sea-going craft.")*

# GEORGE HERBERT 1593–1633

After a time as an apprentice courtier, Herbert took
orders in his early thirties and spent the remaining few
years of his life as a most devout clergyman and a religious poet of great intellect and passion. Herbert's poetry, mostly contained in *The Temple; or, Sacred Poems
and Private Ejaculations,* was not published until after his
death.

# *Love Bade Me Welcome*

Love bade me welcome; yet my soul drew back,
　　Guilty of dust and sin.
But quick-eyed Love, observing me grow slack
　　From my first entrance in,
Drew nearer to me, sweetly questioning
　　If I lacked any thing.

"A guest," I answered, "worthy to be here";
　　Love said, "You shall be he."
"I the unkind, ungrateful? Ah my dear,
　　I cannot look on Thee."
Love took my hand, and smiling did reply,
　　"Who made the eyes but I?"

"Truth Lord, but I have marred them: let my shame
　　Go where it doth deserve."
"And know you not," says Love, "who bore the blame?"
　　"My dear, then I will serve."
"You must sit down," says Love, "and taste My meat."
　　So I did sit and eat.

Like "The Collar" (p. 188), this "Love" (one of three poems Herbert wrote with that title) is a brightly colored, highly dramatized account of a conflict between a person and a principle—a man and a god. The Love here seems to be a pagan Eros, but this Lord merges with the Christian God: the God who is Love. Something of medieval "light" philosophy may persist in the notion that Love made eyes in the first place. (Louis L. Martz points out a question from Psalm XCIV: "He that formed the eye, shall he not see?")

# The Collar

>>>>>>>

I struck the board, and cried, No more.
I will abroad.
What? shall I ever sigh and pine?
My lines and life are free; free as the road,
Loose as the wind, as large as store.
Shall I be still in suit?
Have I no harvest but a thorn
To let me blood, and not restore
What I have lost with cordial fruit?
Sure there was wine
Before my sighs did dry it: there was corn
Before my tears did drown it.
Is the year only lost to me?
Have I no bays to crown it?
No flowers, no garlands gay? all blasted?
All wasted?
Not so, my heart: but there is fruit,
And thou hast hands.
Recover all thy sigh-blown age
On double pleasures: leave thy cold dispute
Of what is fit, and not. Forsake thy cage,
Thy rope of sands,
Which petty thoughts have made, and made to thee
Good cable, to enforce and draw,
And be thy law,
While thou didst wink and wouldst not see.
Away, Take Heed,
I will abroad,
Call in thy death's head there: tie up thy fears.
He that forbears
To suit and serve his need,
Deserves his load.

But as I raved and grew more fierce and wild
　　At every word,
Me thought I heard one calling, *Child!*
　　And I replied, *My Lord.*

---

*Herbert puns on "collar/choler." The "board" struck in the first line is a table—a usage surviving today only in such locutions as "bed and board"; in this poem it refers not only to the table for meals but also to that used for Holy Communion.*

# Virtue

Sweet day, so cool, so calm, so bright,
The bridal of the earth and sky:
The dew shall weep thy fall tonight;
    For thou must die.

Sweet, rose, whose hue angry and brave
Bids the rash gazer wipe his eye:
Thy root is ever in its grave,
    And thou must die.

Sweet spring, full of sweet days and roses,
A box where sweets compacted lie;
My music shows ye have your closes,
    And all must die.

Only a sweet and virtuous soul,
Like seasoned timber, never gives;
But though the whole world turn to coal,
    Then chiefly lives.

---

*As Louis L. Martz observes, "Virtue" is constructed according to a process of deepening the meaning of "sweet," from the simple sensual pleasure (in Herbert's day as much a matter of smell as of taste) to a moral asset of the soul.*

# The Pulley

When God at first made man,
Having a glass of blessings standing by,
"Let us," said He, "pour on him all we can:
Let the world's riches, which dispersed lie,
    Contract into a span."

So Strength first made a way;
Then Beauty flowed, then Wisdom, Honor, Pleasure:
When almost all was out, God made a stay,
Perceiving that alone of all His treasure
    Rest in the bottom lay.

"For if I should," said He,
"Bestow this jewel also on My creature,
He would adore My gifts instead of Me,
And rest in Nature, not the God of Nature:
    So both should losers be.

"Yet let him keep the rest,
But keep them with repining restlessness:
Let him be rich and weary, that at least,
If goodness lead him not, yet weariness
    May toss him to My breast."

---

*Although related to any number of fanciful Creation myths, including the Hebrew and the Greek, Herbert's "Pulley" is a charmingly original explanation of why we are so restless. Restively, the poet puns on various senses of "rest" as verb and noun.*

# *Redemption*

Having been tenant long to a rich lord,
   Not thrivìng, I resolvèd to be bold,
   And make a suit unto him, to afford
A new small-rented lease, and cancel the old.
In heaven at his manor I him sought:
   They told me there, that he was lately gone
   About some land, which he had dearly bought
Long since on earth, to take possession.
I straight returned, and knowing his great birth,
   Sought him accordingly in great resorts,
   In cities, theaters, gardens, parks, and courts.
At length I heard a ragged noise and mirth
   Of thieves and murderers: there I him espied,
   Who straight, "Your suit is granted," said, and died.

---

*Of the eight Herbert poems here, only two are sonnets—this and "Prayer the Church's Banquet" (p. 195). This poem uses the sonnet form for a parable that combines homely domestic details, theological concepts, and the melodramatic structure that Herbert and many other preachers like.*

# Easter Wings

Lord, who createdst man in wealth and store,
Though foolishly he lost the same,
Decaying more and more
Till he became
Most poor:
With Thee
O let me rise
As larks, harmoniously,
And sing this day Thy victories:
Then shall the fall further the flight in me.

My tender age in sorrow did begin:
And still with sicknesses and shame
Thou did'st so punish sin,
That I became
Most thin.
With thee
Let me combine
And feel thy victory:
For, if I imp my wing on thine,
Affliction shall advance the flight in me.

---

*Herbert composed a few poems that belong to the tradition of the* carmen fig-
uratum *or figure poem — that is, one whose shape on the page suggests its subject
or theme. There are some ancient Greek examples, and Richard Willes published
several (in Latin) in 1573. Among the moderns, the most notable practitioners
of shaped poetry in English have been E. E. Cummings, Dylan Thomas, and
John Hollander. Herbert makes a stanza that suggests the shape of wings and
also the form of his argument; the stanza grows poorest and thinnest with the
words "Most poor" and "Most thin." (Note that: "imp" is "graft.")*

# Jordan

Who says that fictions only and false hair
Become a verse? Is there in truth no beauty?
Is all good structure in a winding stair?
May no lines pass, except they do their duty
  Not to a true, but painted chair?

Is it no verse, except enchanted groves
And sudden arbours shadow coarse-spun lines?
Must purling streams refresh a lover's loves?
Must all be veiled, while he that reads, divines,
  Catching the sense at two removes?

Shepherds are honest people; let them sing:
Riddle who list, for me, and pull for prime:
I envy no man's nightingale or spring;
Nor let them punish me with loss of rhyme,
  Who plainly say, *My God, My King.*

---

*Herbert wrote two poems entitled "Jordan" having to do with poetry itself, as though to let the baptismal River Jordan replace the Pierian Spring of the secular Muses of classical antiquity. Such artful rejection of artfulness—the crafty denial of craft—is among the oldest of rhetorical gimmicks. (Note that: "pull for prime" is to try to draw a lucky card in the game called primero.)*

# Prayer the Church's Banquet

Prayer, the Church's banquet; Angels' age,
God's breath in man returning to his birth,
The soul in paraphrase, heart in pilgrimage,
The Christian plummet, sounding heaven and earth;
Engine against th' Almighty, sinner's tower,
Reversed thunder, Christ-side-piercing spear,
The six-days' world-transposing in an hour,
A kind of tune, which all things hear and fear;
Softness, and peace, and joy, and love, and bliss,
Exalted Manna, gladness of the best;
Heaven in ordinary, man well dressed,
The milky way, the bird of Paradise,
    Church-bells beyond the stars heard, the souls blood,
    The land of spices; something understood.

---

*In one of his richest and boldest poems, Herbert uses the sonnet form (fairly rare for him) to provide a catalogue of subjects with no verb or predicate of any kind. More than any other poem in this anthology, this one is a pure list, like a paradigmatic outline for a sermon or lecture.*

# Thomas Carew 1595–1639

Carew, a lawyer's son, was educated in the law at Oxford and the Middle Temple. He is included among the
Courtly poets who specialized in lighthearted lyrics in
praise of love.

## Ask Me No More Where Jove Bestows

Ask me no more where Jove bestows,
When June is past, the fading rose;
For in your beauty's orient deep
These flowers, as in their causes, sleep.

Ask me no more whither do stray
The golden atoms of the day;
For in pure love heaven did prepare
Those powders to enrich your hair.

Ask me no more whither doth haste
The nightingale when May is past,
For in your sweet dividing throat
She winters, and keeps warm her note.

Ask me no more where those stars light
That downwards fall in dead of night,
For in your eyes they sit, and there
Fixed become, as in their sphere.

Ask me no more if east or west
The phoenix builds her spicy nest,
For unto you at last she flies
And in your fragrant bosom dies.

The "causes" here come from Aristotle, for whom anything results from the operation of four causes (final, formal, material, efficient). Things inhere in their causes; so roses may be said to "sleep" in theirs. "Dividing" is a technical term in music; in Carew's day an atom ("uncuttable") was an indivisible particle.

# To My Inconstant Mistress

When thou, poor Excommunicate
   From all the joys of Love, shalt see
The full reward and glorious fate
   Which my strong faith shall purchase me,
   Then curse thine own inconstancy!

A fairer hand than thine shall cure
   That heart which thy false oaths did wound;
And to my soul a soul more pure
   Than thine shall by Love's hand be bound,
   And both with equal glory crown'd.

Then shalt thou weep, entreat, complain
   To Love, as I did once to thee;
When all thy tears shall be as vain
   As mine were then: for thou shalt be
   Damn'd for thy false apostasy.

---

*Carew adds technical terms from Christian theology to themes dating back to Catullus and Propertius.*

# SIR WILLIAM DAVENANT 1606–1668

Davenant (also called D'Avenant) was said to be Shakespeare's godson, and rumors persisted that he was Shakespeare's natural son as well. He was a busy and varied man of letters, producing comedies, tragedies, and the heroic poem *Gondibert*, which is still readable. He was made poet laureate and knighted by Charles I. A loyal Cavalier, he was imprisoned in the Tower in the early 1650s, saved supposedly by Milton. Davenant returned the favor during the Restoration, when Milton was jailed.

## *The Lark Now Leaves His Watery Nest*

>>>>>>

The lark now leaves his watery nest,
    And climbing, shakes his dewy wings;
He takes this window for the east,
    And to implore your light, he sings,
Awake, awake, the morn will never rise,
Till she can dress her beauty at your eyes.

The merchant bows unto the seaman's star,
    The ploughman from the sun his season takes;
But still the lover wonders what they are,
    Who look for day before his mistress wakes.
Awake, awake, break through your veils of lawn,
Then draw your curtains, and begin the dawn.

---

*This* aubade *(morning song) is reminiscent of Shakespeare's "Hark! Hark! the Lark" (p. 99). The phrase "watery nest" is also found in Shakespeare's "Rape of Lucrece".*

A complex man surviving in most complex times, Waller was a politician in the good and bad senses. He was a lawyer and, at sixteen, a member of Parliament, seeming to support the Parliamentarians but really a Royalist who, when exposed in 1643, displayed treachery, cowardice, and faithlessness. No matter: his lovely poetry shines with a clear light and true voice, and all the double-crossing and crookedness evaporate.

## Go, Lovely Rose

Go, lovely rose,
Tell her that wastes her time and me
That now she knows,
When I resemble her to thee,
How sweet and fair she seems to be.

Tell her that's young
And shuns to have her graces spied,
That, hadst thou sprung
In deserts where no men abide,
Thou must have uncommended died.

Small is the worth
Of beauty from the light retired:
Bid her come forth,
Suffer herself to be desired,
And not blush so to be admired.

Then die, that she
The common fate of all things rare
    May read in thee,
How small a part of time they share
    That are so wondrous sweet and fair.

---

*This is an "envoy," a sending poem acting as a go-between for a poet who for some reason cannot address his or her love directly. Waller's contemporary Henry Lawes set "Go, Lovely Rose" to music.*

# On a Girdle

That which her slender waist confined,
Shall now my joyful temples bind;
No monarch but would give his crown,
His arms might do what this has done.

It was my heaven's extremest sphere,
The pale which held that lovely deer;
My joy, my grief, my hope, my love,
Did all within this circle move!

A narrow compass! and yet there
Dwelt all that's good, and all that's fair!
Give me but what this riband bound,
Take all the rest the sun goes round!

---

*Here "girdle" means a belt or sash and not the modern elasticized foundation garment.*

# JOHN MILTON 1608–1674

Milton, who is customarily ranked as the second-greatest poet in English (after Shakespeare), was born in London and educated at Cambridge. Thereafter he spent several years in retirement, preparing himself for great things. For about the middle twenty years of his life, he took on some unpoetic chores as Latin Secretary to Cromwell's Council of State. His sight was failing during his State service, and by 1652 he was totally blind. His greatest work, *Paradise Lost,* was published in 1667, *Paradise Regained* and *Samson Agonistes* four years later.

## *Lycidas*

Yet once more, O ye laurels, and once more,
Ye myrtles brown, with ivy never-sere,
I come to pluck your berries harsh and crude,
And with forc'd fingers rude
Shatter your leaves before the mellowing year.
Bitter constraint and sad occasion dear
Compels me to disturb your season due:
For Lycidas is dead, dead ere his prime
Young Lycidas, and hath not left his peer.
Who would not sing for Lycidas? he well knew
Himself to sing, and build the lofty rhyme.
He must not float upon his watery bier
Unwept, and welter to the parching wind
Without the meed of some melodious tear.
  Begin then, Sisters of the sacred well
That from beneath the seat of Jove doth spring;
Begin, and somewhat loudly sweep the string:
Hence with denial vain, and coy excuse.
So may some gentle Muse
With lucky words favor my destin'd urn,
And as he passes, turn

And bid fair peace be to my sable shroud.
For we were nurs'd upon the self-same hill,
Fed the same flock, by fountain, shade and rill.
    Together both, ere the high lawns appear'd
Under the glimmering eyelids of the morn,
We drove afield, and both together heard
What time the gray-fly winds her sultry horn,
Battening our flocks with the fresh dews of night,
Oft till the ev'n-star bright
Toward heav'n's descent had slop'd his burnish'd wheel.
Meanwhile the rural ditties were not mute
Temper'd to the'oaten flute:
Rough Satyrs danc'd, and Fauns with cloven heel
From the glad sound would not be absent long,
And old Dametas lov'd to hear our song.
    But O the heavy change, now thou art gone,
Now thou art gone, and never must return!
Thee shepherd, thee the woods and desert caves
With wild thyme and the gadding vine o'ergrown
And all their echoes mourn.
The willows and the hazel copses green
Shall now no more be seen
Fanning their joyous leaves to thy soft lays.
As killing as the canker to the rose,
Or taint-worm to the weanling herds that graze,
Or frost to flowers that their gay wardrobe wear
When first the whitethorn blows,
Such, Lycidas, thy loss to shepherd's ear.
    Where were ye Nymphs when the remorseless deep
Clos'd o'er the head of your lov'd Lycidas?
For neither were ye playing on the steep,
Where your old bards the famous Druids lie,
Nor on the shaggy top of Mona high,
Nor yet where Deva spreads her wizard stream.
Ay me, I fondly dream!
Had ye been there . . . for what could that have done?
What could the Muse herself that Orpheus bore,
The Muse herself, for her enchanting son?

Whom universal nature did lament,
When by the rout that made the hideous roar
His gory visage down the stream was sent,
Down the swift Hebrus to the Lesbian shore.
  Alas! What boots it with uncessant care
To tend the homely slighted shepherd's trade,
And strictly meditate the thankless Muse?
Were it not better done as others use,
To sport with Amaryllis in the shade,
Hid in the tangles of Neaera's hair?
Fame is the spur that the clear spirit doth raise
(That last infirmity of noble mind)
To scorn delights and live laborious days;
But the fair guerdon where we hope to find,
And think to burst out into sudden blaze,
Comes the blind Fury with th'abhorred shears
And slits the thin-spun life. "But not the praise,"
Phoebus repli'd, and touch'd my trembling ears.
"Fame is no plant that grows on mortal soil,
Nor in the glistering foil
Set off to th'world, nor in broad rumor lies;
But lives, and spreads aloft by those pure eyes
And perfect witness of all-judging Jove:
As he pronounces lastly on each deed,
Of so much fame in Heav'n expect thy meed."
  O fountain Arethuse, and thou honor'd flood,
Smooth-sliding Mincius, crown'd with vocal reeds,
That strain I heard was of a higher mood.
But now my oat proceeds,
And listens to the herald of the sea
That came in Neptune's plea.
He ask'd the waves, and ask'd the felon winds,
"What hard mishap hath doom'd this gentle swain?"
And question'd every gust of rugged wings
That blows from off each beaked promontory.
They knew not of his story,
And sage Hippotades their answer brings
That not a blast was from his dungeon stray'd;

The air was calm, and on the level brine
Sleek Panope with all her sisters play'd.
It was that fatal and perfidious bark,
Built in th'eclipse, and rigg'd with curses dark,
That sunk so low that sacred head of thine.
    Next Camus (reverend sire) went footing slow,
His mantle hairy and his bonnet sedge
Inwrought with figures dim, and on the edge
Like to that sanguine flower inscrib'd with woe.
"Ah! Who hath reft" (quoth he) "my dearest pledge?"
Last came, and last did go,
The pilot of the Galilean lake.
Two massy keys he bore of metals twain
(The golden opes, the iron shuts amain).
He shook his mitr'd locks, and stern bespake:
"How well could I have spar'd for thee, young swain,
Enough of such as for their bellies' sake
Creep and intrude and climb into the fold?
Of other care they little reckoning make
Than how to scramble at the shearers' feast
And shove away the worthy bidden guest.
Blind mouths! that scarce themselves know how to hold
A sheephook, or have learn'd ought else the least
That to the faithful herdman's art belongs!
What recks it them? What need they? They are sped.
And when they list their lean and flashy songs
Grate on their scrannel pipes of wretched straw,
The hungry sheep look up, and are not fed,
But swoll'n with wind and the rank mist they draw,
Rot inwardly, and foul contagion spread:
Besides what the grim wolf with privy paw
Daily devours apace, and little said.
But that two-handed engine at the door
Stands ready to smite once, and smites no more."
    Return, Alpheus, the dread voice is pass'd
That shrunk thy streams; return, Sicilian Muse,
And call the vales and bid them hither cast
Their bells and flowerets of a thousand hues.

Ye valleys low, where the mild whispers use
Of shades and wanton winds and gushing brooks,
On whose fresh lap the swart star sparely looks,
Throw hither all your quaint enamel'd eyes
That on the green turf suck the honey'd showers,
And purple all the ground with vernal flowers.
Bring the rathe primrose that forsaken dies,
The tufted crow-toe and pale jessamine,
The white pink, and the pansy freak'd with jet,
The glowing violet,
The musk-rose and the well-attir'd woodbine,
With cowslips wan that hang the pensive head,
And every flower that sad embroidery wears;
Bid amaranthus all his beauty shed,
And daffodillies fill their cups with tears
To strew the laureate hearse where Lycid lies.
For so, to interpose a little ease,
Let our frail thoughts dally with false surmise;
Ay me! whilst thee the shores and sounding seas
Wash far away, where e'er thy bones are hurl'd,
Whether beyond the stormy Hebrides,
Where thou perhaps under the humming tide
Visit'st the bottom of the monstrous world,
Or whether thou, to our moist vows deni'd,
Sleep'st by the fable of Bellerus old,
Where the great vision of the guarded Mount
Looks toward Namancos and Bayona's hold.
Look homeward Angel now, and melt with ruth,
And O ye dolphins, waft the hapless youth.
　　Weep no more, woeful shepherds, weep no more;
For Lycidas your sorrow is not dead,
Sunk though he be beneath the watery floor:
So sinks the daystar in the ocean bed,
And yet anon repairs his drooping head
And tricks his beams and with new-spangl'd ore
Flames in the forehead of the morning sky;
So Lycidas sunk low, but mounted high
Through the dear might of him that walk'd the waves,

Where other groves and other streams along
With nectar pure his oozy locks he laves
And hears the unexpressive nuptial song
In the bless'd kingdoms meek of joy and love.
There entertain him all the saints above
In solemn troops and sweet societies,
That sing, and singing in their glory move,
And wipe the tears for ever from his eyes.
Now, Lycidas, the shepherds weep no more.
Henceforth thou art the genius of the shore
In thy large recompense, and shalt be good
To all that wander in that perilous flood.
   Thus sang the uncouth swain to th'oaks and rills,
While the still morn went out with sandals gray;
He touch'd the tender stops of various quills,
With eager thought warbling his Doric lay.
And now the sun had stretch'd out all the hills,
And now was dropp'd into the western bay;
At last he rose, and twitch'd his mantle blue,
Tomorrow to fresh woods and pastures new.

---

*"Pastor" originally meant "shepherd," and the fiction of such pastoral elegies as "Lycidas" is that the dead subject—usually a poet—is a shepherd lamented by others. Samuel Johnson, doubting Milton's sincerity, said, "Where there is leisure for fiction there is little grief." But the poem is still read and loved. (Note that: "scrannel" is "flimsy"; "unexpressive" is "ineffable.")*

# On His Deceased Wife

Methought I saw my late espoused saint
  Brought to me like Alcestis from the grave,
  Whom Jove's great son to her glad husband gave,
  Rescued from Death by force, though pale and faint.
Mine, as whom washed from spot of childbed taint
  Purification in the Old Law did save,
  And such as yet once more I trust to have
  Full sight of her in heaven without restraint,
Came vested all in white, pure as her mind.
  Her face was veiled; yet to my fancied sight
  Love, sweetness, goodness, in her person shined
So clear as in no face with more delight.
  But, O! as to embrace me she inclined,
  I waked, she fled, and day brought back my night.

---

*Milton wrote nothing more personal or more touching. This account of a blind widower's dream may be about Milton's first wife, Mary, who died just after giving birth in 1652, or his second wife, Katherine, who died a few months after giving birth in 1658. Most scholars favor the choice of Katherine, since Milton never set eyes on her.*

# On His Blindness

()◀━━▶()

When I consider how my light is spent,
Ere half my days, in this dark world and wide,
And that one talent which is death to hide
Lodged with me useless, though my soul more bent
To serve therewith my Maker, and present
My true account, lest he returning chide,
"Doth God exact day labor, light denied?"
I fondly ask; by Patience, to prevent
That murmur, soon replies: "God doth not need
Either man's work or his own gifts; who best
Bear his mild yoke, they serve him best. His state
Is kingly: thousands at his bidding speed
And post o'er land and ocean without rest.
They also serve who only stand and wait."

---

*By 1652 Milton was completely blind. He was aware of connections with other blind men, preeminently Homer and Samson. (The last word of* Samson Agonistes *is "spent.") (Note that: "fondly" is "foolishly.")*

# On the Late Massacre in Piedmont

Avenge, O Lord, thy slaughtered saints, whose bones
Lie scattered on the Alpine mountains cold;
Even them who kept thy truth so pure of old
When all our fathers worshipped stocks and stones,
Forget not: in thy book record their groans
Who were thy sheep and in their ancient fold
Slain by the bloody Piemontese, that rolled
Mother with infant down the rocks. Their moans
The vales redoubled to the hills, and they
To heaven. Their martyred blood and ashes sow
O'er all the Italian fields where still doth sway
The triple tyrant; that from these may grow
A hundredfold, who, having learnt thy way,
Early may fly the Babylonian woe.

---

*The Waldenses or Waldensians, a dissenting sect founded by Peter Waldo in the twelfth century, continue to live in the French and Italian Alps. In the sixteenth century they accepted the Protestant doctrine of the Reformation. The massacre took place on April 24, 1655. (Note that: "stocks" is "idols"; "triple tyrant" is the Pope.)*

# L'Allegro

Hence loathèd Melancholy
  Of Cerberus and blackest Midnight born,
In Stygian cave forlorn
  'Mongst horrid shapes, and shrieks, and sights unholy,
Find out some uncouth cell,
  Where brooding Darkness spreads his jealous wings,
And the night-raven sings;
  There under ebon shades and low-browed rocks,
As ragged as thy locks,
  In dark Cimmerian desert ever dwell.
But come thou Goddess fair and free,
In Heaven ycleaped Euphrosyne,
And by men, heart-easing Mirth,
Whom lovely Venus at a birth
With two sister Graces more
To ivy-crownèd Bacchus bore;
Or whether (as some sager sing)
The frolic wind that breathes the spring,
Zephyr with Aurora playing,
As he met her once a-Maying,
There on beds of violets blue,
And fresh-blown roses washed in dew,
Filled her with thee, a daughter fair,
So buxom, blithe, and debonair.
Haste thee Nymph, and bring with thee
Jest and youthful jollity,
Quips and cranks, and wanton wiles,
Nods, and becks, and wreathèd smiles,
Such as hang on Hebe's cheek,
And love to live in dimple sleek;
Sport that wrinkled Care derides,
And Laughter holding both his sides.
Come, and trip it as ye go
On the light fantastic toe,

And in thy right hand lead with thee,
The mountain nymph, sweet Liberty;
And if I give thee honor due,
Mirth, admit me of thy crew
To live with her, and live with thee,
In unreprovèd pleasures free:
To hear the lark begin his flight,
And singing startle the dull night,
From his watchtower in the skies,
Till the dappled dawn doth rise;
Then to come in spite of sorrow,
And at my window bid good morrow,
Through the sweetbrier, or the vine,
Or the twisted eglantine;
While the cock with lively din,
Scatters the rear of darkness thin,
And to the stack or the barn door,
Stoutly struts his dames before;
Oft listening how the hounds and horn
Cheerly rouse the slumbering morn,
From the side of some hoar hill,
Through the high wood echoing shrill.
Some time walking not unseen
By hedgerow elms, on hillocks green,
Right against the eastern gate,
Where the great sun begins his state,
Robed in flames and amber light,
The clouds in thousand liveries dight;
While the ploughman near at hand
Whistles o'er the furrowed land,
And the milkmaid singeth blithe,
And the mower whets his scythe,
And every shepherd tells his tale
Under the hawthorn in the dale.
Straight mine eye hath caught new pleasures
Whilst the lantskip round it measures:
Russet lawns and fallows gray,
Where the nibbling flocks do stray,

Mountains on whose barren breast
The laboring clouds do often rest,
Meadows trim with daisies pied,
Shallow brooks and rivers wide.
Towers and battlements it sees
Bosomed high in tufted trees,
Where perhaps some beauty lies,
The cynosure of neighboring eyes.
Hard by, a cottage chimney smokes,
From betwixt two agèd oaks,
Where Corydon and Thyrsis met,
Are at their savory dinner set
Of herbs and other country messes,
Which the neat-handed Phyllis dresses;
And then in haste her bower she leaves,
With Thestylis to bind the sheaves;
Or if the earlier season lead,
To the tanned haycock in the mead.
Sometimes with secure delight
The upland hamlets will invite,
When the merry bells ring round,
And the jocund rebecks sound
To many a youth and many a maid,
Dancing in the chequered shade;
And young and old come forth to play
On a sunshine holiday,
Till the livelong daylight fail;
Then to the spicy nut-brown ale,
With stories told of many a feat,
How fairy Mab the junkets eat;
She was pinched and pulled, she said,
And he, by friar's lanthorn led,
Tells how the drudging goblin sweat,
To earn his cream-bowl duly set,
When in one night, ere glimpse of morn,
His shadowy flail hath threshed the corn
That ten day-laborers could not end;
Then lies him down the lubber fend,

And stretched out all the chimney's length,
Basks at the fire his hairy strength;
And crop-full out of doors he flings,
Ere the first cock his matin rings.
Thus done the tales, to bed they creep,
By whispering winds soon lulled asleep.
Towered cities please us then,
And the busy hum of men,
Where throngs of knights and barons bold
In weeds of peace high triumphs hold,
With store of ladies, whose bright eyes
Rain influence, and judge the prize
Of wit or arms, while both contend
To win her grace whom all commend.
There let Hymen oft appear
In saffron robe, with taper clear,
And pomp, and feast, and revelry,
With masque and antique pageantry:
Such sights as youthful poets dream
On summer eves by haunted stream.
Then to the well-trod stage anon,
If Jonson's learnèd sock be on,
Or sweetest Shakespeare, Fancy's child,
Warble his native wood-notes wild;
And ever against eating cares,
Lap me in soft Lydian airs,
Married to immortal verse,
Such as the meeting soul may pierce
In notes with many a winding bout
Of linkèd sweetness long drawn out,
With wanton heed and giddy cunning,
The melting voice through mazes running,
Untwisting all the chains that tie
The hidden soul of harmony;
That Orpheus' self may heave his head
From golden slumber on a bed
Of heaped Elysian flowers, and hear
Such strains as would have won the ear

Of Pluto, to have quite set free
His half-regained Eurydice.
These delights if thou canst give,
Mirth, with thee I mean to live.

---

*Milton, like Browning, delighted in complementary companion poems, a classification that suits* Paradise Lost *and* Paradise Regained *as well as the pair of set pieces "L'Allegro" ("The Mirthful Man") and "Il Penseroso" ("The Thoughtful Man"). (Note that: "buxom" is "jolly"; "dight" is "decked," "dressed"; "secure" is "carefree"; "friar's lantern" is "will-o'-the-wisp"; "lubber" is "crude"; "weeds" is "clothing.")*

# Il Penseroso

Hence vain deluding Joys,
  The brood of Folly without father bred,
How little you bestead,
  Or fill the fixèd mind with all your toys;
Dwell in some idle brain,
  And fancies fond with gaudy shapes possess,
As thick and numberless
  As the gay motes that people the sunbeams,
Or likest hovering dreams,
  The fickle pensioners of Morpheus' train.
But hail thou Goddess, sage and holy,
Hail divinest Melancholy,
Whose saintly visage is too bright
To hit the sense of human sight,
And therefore to our weaker view
O'erlaid with black, staid Wisdom's hue;
Black, but such as in esteem
Prince Memnon's sister might beseem,
Or that starred Ethiop queen that strove
To set her beauty's praise above
The sea nymphs, and their powers offended;
Yet thou art higher far descended:
Thee bright-haired Vesta long of yore
To solitary Saturn bore;
His daughter she (in Saturn's reign
Such mixture was not held a stain).
Oft in glimmering bowers and glades
He met her, and in secret shades
Of woody Ida's inmost grove,
Whilst yet there was no fear of Jove.
Come pensive Nun, devout and pure,
Sober, steadfast, and demure,
All in a robe of darkest grain,
Flowing with majestic train,

And sable stole of cypress lawn,
Over thy decent shoulders drawn.
Come, but keep thy wonted state,
With even step and musing gait,
And looks commercing with the skies,
Thy rapt soul sitting in thine eyes;
There held in holy passion still,
Forget thyself to marble, till
With a sad leaden downward cast,
Thou fix them on the earth as fast.
And join with thee calm Peace and Quiet,
Spare Fast, that oft with gods doth diet,
And hears the Muses in a ring
Aye round above Jove's altar sing.
and add to these retired Leisure,
That in trim gardens takes his pleasure;
But first and chiefest, with thee bring
Him that yon soars on golden wing,
Guiding the fiery-wheelèd throne,
The Cherub Contemplation;
And the mute Silence hist along,
'Less Philomel will deign a song,
In her sweetest, saddest plight,
Smoothing the rugged brow of Night,
While Cynthia checks her dragon yoke,
Gently o'er th' accustomed oak;
Sweet bird that shunn'st the noise of folly,
Most musical, most melancholy!
Thee, chauntress, oft the woods among,
I woo to hear thy evensong;
And missing thee, I walk unseen
On the dry smooth-shaven green,
To behold the wandering moon,
Riding near her highest noon,
Like one that had been led astray
Through the heavens' wide pathless way;
And oft, as if her head she bowed,
Stooping through a fleecy cloud.

Oft on a plat of rising ground
I hear the far-off curfew sound,
Over some wide-watered shore,
Swinging slow with sullen roar;
Or if the air will not permit,
Some still, removèd place will fit,
Where glowing embers through the room
Teach light to counterfeit a gloom,
Far from all resort of mirth,
Save the cricket on the hearth,
Or the bellman's drowsy charm,
To bless the doors from nightly harm.
Or let my lamp at midnight hour
Be seen in some high lonely tower,
Where I may oft outwatch the Bear,
With thrice-great Hermes, or unsphere
The spirit of Plato to unfold
What worlds or what vast regions hold
Th' immortal mind that hath forsook
Her mansion in this fleshly nook;
And of those daemons that are found
In fire, air, flood, or under ground,
Whose power hath a true consent
With planet or with element.
Sometime let gorgeous Tragedy
In sceptered pall come sweeping by,
Presenting Thebes, or Pelops' line,
Or the tale of Troy divine,
Or what (though rare) of later age
Ennobled hath the buskined stage.
But, O sad Virgin, that thy power
Might raise Musaeus from his bower,
Or bid the soul of Orpheus sing
Such notes as, warbled to the string,
Drew iron tears down Pluto's cheek,
And made Hell grant what love did seek;
Or call up him that left half told
The story of Cambuscan bold,

Of Camball, and of Algarsife,
And who had Canace to wife,
That owned the virtuous ring and glass,
And of the wondrous horse of brass,
On which the Tartar king did ride;
And if aught else great bards beside
In sage and solemn tunes have sung,
Of tourneys and of trophies hung,
Of forests and enchantments drear,
Where more is meant than meets the ear.
Thus Night oft see me in thy pale career,
Till civil-suited Morn appear,
Not tricked and frounced as she was wont
With the Attic boy to hunt,
But kerchiefed in a comely cloud,
While rocking winds are piping loud,
Or ushered with a shower still,
When the gust hath blown his fill,
Ending on the rustling leaves,
With minute-drops from off the eaves.
And when the sun begins to fling
His flaring beams, me Goddess bring
To archèd walks of twilight groves,
And shadows brown that Sylvan loves,
Of pine or monumental oak,
Where the rude axe with heavèd stroke
Was never heard the nymphs to daunt,
Or fright them from their hallowed haunt.
There in close covert by some brook,
Where no profaner eye may look,
Hide me from Day's garish eye,
While the bee with honied thigh,
That at her flowery work doth sing,
And the waters murmuring,
With such consort as they keep,
Entice the dewy-feathered Sleep;
And let some strange mysterious dream
Wave at his wings in airy stream

Of lively portraiture displayed,
Softly on my eyelids laid.
And as I wake, sweet music breathe
Above, about, or underneath,
Sent by some spirit to mortals good,
Or th' unseen Genius of the wood.
But let my due feet never fail
To walk the studious cloister's pale,
And love the high embowèd roof,
With antic pillars massy proof,
And storied windows richly dight,
Casting a dim, religious light.
There let the pealing organ blow
To the full-voiced choir below,
In service high and anthems clear,
As may with sweetness, through mine ear,
Dissolve me into ecstasies,
And bring all Heaven before mine eyes.
And may at last my weary age
Find out the peaceful hermitage,
The hairy gown and mossy cell,
Where I may sit and rightly spell
Of every star that heaven doth show,
And every herb that sips the dew;
Till old experience do attain
To something like prophetic strain.
These pleasures Melancholy give,
And I with thee will choose to live.

---

*It seems significant that "Il Penseroso," though beginning and ending with the same words as "L'Allegro," should be longer by two dozen lines. Readers of long poems seem to prefer the dark to the light, putting* Paradise Lost *and* Dante's Inferno *ahead of* Paradise Regained *and the* Paradiso; *but, among short poems, "L'Allegro" is somewhat more popular than "Il Penseroso." (Note that: "bestead" is "profit"; "hit" is "affect"; "hist" is "summon"; "plat" is "plot"; "virtuous" is "powerful"; "frounced" is "curled"; "dight" is "decked," "dressed"; "spell" is "speculate.")*

# SIR JOHN SUCKLING 1609–1642

The son of a knight who had served as Secretary of State and Comptroller of the Household under James I, Suckling was born in Middlesex and educated at Cambridge. He was a loyal supporter of Charles I; he fled to the Continent early in the Civil War and died in Paris, purportedly a suicide. John Aubrey credits Suckling with the invention of cribbage.

# *Why So Pale and Wan, Fond Lover?*

>>>>>>>

Why so pale and wan, fond lover?
  Prithee, why so pale?
Will, when looking well can't move her,
  Looking ill prevail?
  Prithee, why so pale?

Why so dull and mute, young sinner?
  Prithee, why so mute?
Will, when speaking well can't win her,
  Saying nothing do't?
  Prithee, why so mute?

Quit, quit, for shame; this will not move,
  This cannot take her.
If of herself she will not love,
  Nothing can make her:
  The devil take her!

from Aglaura

---

*This easy song has a good deal of prosodic sophistication as well as rhetorical drama: in one dimension, the speaker works against the lover (who may be himself); in another, the speaker and lover work together against the woman. And the percussively reiterated questions work against the final imperative, "Quit, quit."*

# ANNE BRADSTREET c.1612–1672

Anne Bradstreet was the daughter of one governor of the Massachusetts Bay Colony (Thomas Dudley) and the wife of another (Simon Bradstreet). She came to America at age eighteen, raised eight children, and lived to see her work published in 1650 as *The Tenth Muse Lately Sprung Up in America*.

## To My Dear and Loving Husband

If ever two were one, then surely we.
If ever man were loved by wife, then thee;
If ever wife was happy in a man,
Compare with me, ye women, if you can.
I prize thy love more then whole mines of gold,
Or all the riches that the East doth hold.
My love is such that rivers cannot quench,
Nor aught but love from thee, give recompense.
Thy love is such I can no way repay,
The heavens reward thee manifold, I pray.
Then while we live, in love let's so persever
That when we live no more, we may live ever.

---

*Anne Bradstreet considered her poems her "offspring" (see Jonson's "On My First Son," p. 158). Three centuries after the first publication of her poems, John Berryman produced* Homage to Mistress Bradstreet.

Lovelace was gifted, handsome, amiable, and wealthy, but he lost everything in supporting the Royalist cause. His most durable poems reflect the circumstances of his turbulent life: he really was in prison (in 1642, for supporting the King), and he really did go to the wars, fighting and being wounded.

## To Lucasta, Going to the Wars

Tell me not, Sweet, I am unkind
  That from the nunnery
Of thy chaste breast and quiet mind,
  To war and arms I fly.

True, a new mistress now I chase,
  The first foe in the field;
And with a stronger faith embrace
  A sword, a horse, a shield.

Yet this inconstancy is such
  As you too shall adore;
I could not love thee, Dear, so much,
Loved I not Honour more.

---

*The real name of Lovelace's fiancée was Lucy Sacheverell. He did, in fact, love honor more than Lucy-Lucasta, and he did, in fact, go to war. When, by an error, his death was reported to her, she married somebody else. The quaint argument may seem silly today when ideals of chivalry and honor have just about perished.*

# To Althea, from Prison

When Love with unconfinèd wings
  Hovers within my gates,
And my divine Althea brings
  To whisper at the grates;
When I lie tangled in her hair
  And fetter'd to her eye,
The birds that wanton in the air
  Know no such liberty.

When flowing cups run swiftly round
  With no allaying Thames,
Our careless heads with roses bound,
  Our hearts with loyal flames;
When thirsty grief in wine we steep,
  When healths and draughts go free—
Fishes that tipple in the deep
  Know no such liberty.

When, like committed linnets, I
  With shriller throat shall sing
The sweetness, mercy, majesty,
  And glories of my King;
When I shall voice aloud how good
  He is, how great should be,
Enlargèd winds, that curl the flood,
  Know no such liberty.

Stone walls do not a prison make,
  Nor iron bars a cage;
Minds innocent and quiet take
  That for an hermitage;
If I have freedom in my love
  And in my soul am free,
Angels alone, that soar above,
  Enjoy such liberty.

---

*Lovelace wrote this song while incarcerated for his Royalist views in 1642. Lovelace can coin memorable paradoxical phrases—e.g., "Stone walls do not a prison make"—but there is nothing farfetched about the sentiment. His eloquence is matched only by his sincerity.*

# The Grasshopper

O thou that swing'st upon the waving hair
  Of some well-filled oaten beard,
Drunk every night with a delicious tear
  Dropp'd thee from heav'n where now th' art rear'd;

The joys of earth and air are thine entire,
  That with thy feet and wings dost hop and fly;
And when thy poppy works, thou dost retire
  To thy carv'd acorn-bed to lie.

Up with the day, the sun thou welcomest then,
  Sport'st in the gilt plats of his beams,
And all these merry days mak'st merry men,
  Thyself, and melancholy streams.

But ah the sickle! golden ears are cropp'd,
  Ceres and Bacchus bid good night;
Sharp frosty fingers all your flow'rs have topp'd,
  And what scythes spar'd, winds shave off quite.

Poor verdant fool, and now green ice! thy joys,
  Large and as lasting as thy perch of grass,
Bid us lay in 'gainst winter rain, and poise
  Their floods with an o'erflowing glass.

Thou best of men and friends! we will create
  A genuine summer in each other's breast;
And spite of this cold time and frozen fate,
  Thaw us a warm seat to our rest.

Our sacred hearths shall burn eternally
  As vestal flames; the North-wind, he
Shall strike his frost-stretch'd wings, dissolve, and fly
  This Ætna in epitome.

Dropping December shall come weeping in,
  Bewail th' usurping of his reign;
But when in showers of old Greek we begin,
  Shall cry he hath his crown again.

Night as clear Hesper shall our tapers whip
  From the light casements where we play,
And the dark hag from her black mantle strip,
  And stick there everlasting day.

Thus richer than untempted kings are we,
  That asking nothing, nothing need:
Though lord of all what seas embrace, yet he
  That wants himself is poor indeed.

---

*The cautionary fable invoked here reaches from Aesop in the 6th century, B.C., to the episode of the Ondt and the Gracehoper in James Joyce's* Finnegans Wake *(1939). Since Lovelace was loyal to the Crown, the grasshopper may stand for the Cavaliers in "this cold time" after the establishment of the Commonwealth in 1649. (Note that: "gilt-plats" is "gold-colored meadows"; "poise" is "counterbalance"; "strike" is "fold.")*

# ANDREW MARVELL 1621–1678

Marvell was born in Yorkshire and educated at Cambridge. Like Edmund Waller, he was a Member of Parliament, and in a busy career he served both the court of Charles II and the Cromwellians. Marvell assisted Milton for a time in the Latin Secretaryship to the Council of State. Marvell was a celebrated controversialist and satirist as well as a splendid lyric poet.

## To His Coy Mistress

Had we but world enough and time,
This coyness, Lady, were no crime.
We would sit down and think which way
To walk, and pass our long love's day.
Thou by the Indian Ganges' side
Shouldst rubies find; I by the tide
Of Humber would complain. I would
Love you ten years before the Flood,
And you should, if you please, refuse
Till the Conversion of the Jews.
My vegetable love should grow
Vaster than empires, and more slow.
An hundred years should go to praise
Thine eyes, and on thy forehead gaze,
Two hundred to adore each breast,
But thirty thousand to the rest.
An age at least to every part,
And the last age should show your heart.
For, Lady, you deserve this state,
Nor would I love at lower rate.

But at my back I always hear
Time's winged chariot hurrying near,
And yonder all before us lie
Deserts of vast eternity.

Thy beauty shall no more be found,
Nor in thy marble vault shall sound
My echoing song; then worms shall try
That long preserved virginity,
And your quaint honor turn to dust,
And into ashes all my lust.
The grave's a fine and private place,
But none, I think, do there embrace.
　　Now therefore, while the youthful hue
Sits on thy skin like morning glew,
And while thy willing soul transpires
At every pore with instant fires,
Now let us sport us while we may;
And now, like amorous birds of prey,
Rather at once our time devour
Than languish in his slow-chapped power.
Let us roll all our strength and all
Our sweetness up into one ball
And tear our pleasures with rough strife
Thorough the iron gates of life.
Thus, though we cannot make our sun
Stand still, yet we will make him run.

---

*T. S. Eliot noticed that this great poem of seduction has a lucidly logical struc-
ture: (1) If we had time, you could hold out; (2) We don't have time; (3) "Now
therefore . . . ." Like Herrick's "To the Virgins, to Make Much of Time" (p.
172), this poem belongs to the category of* carpe diem: *seize the day. The poem
also partakes of that special kind of erotic encomium called a* blason, *usually
a top-to-toe inventory of physical attractions (but see also Hopkins's "Habit of
Perfection," p. 800).*

# The Garden

How vainly men themselves amaze
To win the palm, the oak, or bays,
And their incessant labors see
Crown'd from some single herb or tree,
Whose short and narrow-vergèd shade
Does prudently their toils upbraid;
While all flowers and all trees do close
To weave the garlands of repose!

Fair Quiet, have I found thee here,
And Innocence, thy sister dear?
Mistaken long, I sought you then
In busy companies of men:
Your sacred plants, if here below,
Only among the plants will grow:
Society is all but rude
To this delicious solitude.

No white nor red was ever seen
So amorous as this lovely green.
Fond lovers, cruel as their flame,
Cut in these trees their mistress' name:
Little, alas! they know or heed
How far these beauties hers exceed!
Fair trees, wheresoe'er your barks I wound,
No name shall but your own be found.

When we have run our passion's heat,
Love hither makes his best retreat:
The gods, that mortal beauty chase,
Still in a tree did end their race;
Apollo hunted Daphne so
Only that she might laurel grow;
And Pan did after Syrinx speed
Not as a nymph, but for a reed.

What wondrous life in this I lead!
Ripe apples drop about my head;
The luscious clusters of the vine
Upon my mouth do crush their wine;
The nectarine and curious peach
Into my hands themselves do reach;
Stumbling on melons, as I pass,
Ensnared with flowers, I fall on grass.

Meanwhile the mind from pleasure less
Withdraws into its happiness;
The mind, that ocean where each kind
Does straight its own resemblance find;
Yet it creates, transcending these,
Far other worlds, and other seas;
Annihilating all that's made
To a green thought in a green shade,

Here at the fountain's sliding foot,
Or at some fruit-tree's mossy root,
Casting the body's vest aside,
My soul into the boughs does glide;
There, like a bird, it sits and sings,
Then whets and combs its silver wings,
And, till prepared for longer flight,
Waves in its plumes the various light.

Such was that happy Garden-state
While man there walked without a mate:
After a place so pure and sweet,
What other help could yet be meet!
But 'twas beyond a mortal's share
To wander solitary there:
Two paradises 'twere in one,
To live in Paradise alone.

How well the skillful gard'ner drew
Of flowers and herbs, this dial new!
Where, from above, the milder sun
Does through a fragrant zodiac run:
And, as it works, th' industrious bee
Computes its time as well as we.
How could such sweet and wholesome hours
Be reckon'd but with herbs and flowers!

---

*In ridiculing the use of certain trees for emblematic purposes (palms for athletes, bays for poetry) and highlighting the cruelty of carving in the bark of trees, Marvell offers a revisionist reading of ancient myths, suggesting that metamorphoses, such as those of Daphne and Syrinx, were by design, and that Adam's loss of paradise dated from the introduction of Eve.*

# The Definition of Love

◆◆◆◆

My love is of a birth as rare
As 'tis for object strange and high;
It was begotten by despair
Upon impossibility.

Magnanimous despair alone
Could show me so divine a thing,
Where feeble hope could ne'er have flown,
But vainly flapped its tinsel wing.

And yet I quickly might arrive
Where my extended soul is fixed,
But fate does iron wedges drive,
And always crowds itself betwixt.

For fate with jealous eye does see
Two perfect loves, nor lets them close;
Their union would her ruin be,
And her tyrannic power depose.

And therefore her decrees of steel
Us as the distant poles have placed,
Though love's whole world on us doth wheel,
Not by themselves to be embraced;

Unless the giddy heaven fall,
And earth some new convulsion tear,
And, us to join, the world should all
Be cramped into a planisphere.

As lines, so loves, oblique may well
Themselves in every angle greet;
But ours so truly parallel,
Though infinite, can never meet.

Therefore the love which us doth bind,
But fate so enviously debars,
Is the conjunction of the mind,
And opposition of the stars.

---

*As scholars have noted, the defining at work here is not only the familiar affair of telling what something is, but it is also the setting of a limit or boundary. This love, offspring of Despair and Impossibility, is utterly thwarted. (Note that: "close" is "unite"; "planisphere" is a flat two-dimensional representation of three-dimensional reality.)*

# Bermudas

Where the remote Bermudas ride,
In the Ocean's bosom unespied,
From a small boat, that rowed along,
The listening winds received this song:

"What should we do but sing His praise,
That led us through the watery maze,
Unto an isle so long unknown,
And yet far kinder than our own?
Where He the huge sea-monsters wracks
That lift the deep upon their backs,
He lands us on a grassy stage,
Safe from the storms' and prelates' rage:
He gave us this eternal Spring
Which here enamels everything,
And sends the fowls to us in care
On daily visits through the air:
He hangs in shades the orange bright,
Like golden lamps in a green night,
And does in the pomegranates close
Jewels more rich than Ormus shows;
He makes the figs our mouths to meet,
And throws the melons at our feet;
But apples plants of such a price
No tree could ever bear them twice.
With cedars, chosen by His hand
From Lebanon, He stores the land,
And makes the hollow seas, that roar,
Proclaim the ambergris on shore.
He cast (of which we rather boast)
The Gospel's pearl upon our coast;
And in these rocks for us did frame
A temple where to sound His name.

Oh! let our voice His praise exalt,
Till it arrive at Heaven's vault,
Which, thence (perhaps) rebounding, may
Echo beyond the Mexique bay."

Thus sung they, in the English boat,
A holy and a cheerful note;
And all the way, to guide their chime,
With falling oars they kept the time.

---

*Juan de Bermúdez discovered the island group that bears his name early in the sixteenth century. Reports of the fine vegetation and weather formed part of the inspiration of Shakespeare's* Tempest. *Some Puritans known to Marvell sought refuge there. Marvell travelled all over Europe, including Denmark and Russia, but never visited the islands. (Note that: "apples" is "pineapples.")*

# An Horatian Ode
## upon Cromwell's Return from Ireland

>>>>>>>

The forward Youth that would appear
Must now forsake his Muses dear,
    Nor in the Shadows sing
    His Numbers languishing.
'Tis time to leave the Books in dust,
And oyl th' unused Armours rust:
    Removing from the Wall
    The Corslet of the Hall.
So restless Cromwel could not cease
In the inglorious Arts of Peace,
    But through adventrous War
    Urged his active Star:
And, like the three-fork'd Lightning, first
Breaking the Clouds where it was nurst,
    Did thorough his own Side
    His fiery way divide.
For 'tis all one to Courage high
The Emulous or Enemy;
    And with such to inclose
    Is more then to oppose.
Then burning through the Air he went,
And Pallaces and Temples rent:
    And Caesars head at last
    Did through his Laurels blast.
'Tis Madness to resist or blame
The force of angry Heavens flame;
    And, if we would speak true,
    Much to the Man is due:
Who, from his private Gardens, where
He liv'd reserved and austere,
    As if his highest plot
    To plant the Bergamot,

Could by industrious Valour climbe
To ruine the great Work of Time,
   And cast the Kingdoms old
   Into another Mold.
Though Justice against Fate complain,
And plead the antient Rights in vain:
   But those do hold or break
   As Men are strong or weak.
Nature that hateth emptiness,
Allows of penetration less:
   And therefore must make room
   Where greater Spirits come.
What Field of all the Civil Wars
Where his were not the deepest Scars?
   And Hampton shows what part
   He had of wiser Art:
Where, twining subtile fears with hope,
He wove a Net of such a scope,
   That Charles himself might chase
   To Caresbrooks narrow case:
That thence the *Royal Actor* born
The Tragick Scaffold might adorn,
   While round the armed Bands
   Did clap their bloody hands.
*He* nothing common did, or mean,
Upon the memorable Scene:
   But with his keener Eye
   The Axes edge did try:
Nor call'd the Gods with vulgar spight
To vindicate his helpless Right,
   But bow'd his comely Head
   Down, as upon a Bed.
This was that memorable Hour
Which first assur'd the forced Pow'r.
   So when they did design
   The Capitols first Line,
A bleeding Head where they begun,
Did fright the Architects to run;

And yet in that the State
Foresaw its happy Fate.
And now the Irish are asham'd
To see themselves in one Year tam'd:
   So much one Man can do,
   That does both act and know.
They can affirm his Praises best,
And have, though overcome, confest
   How good he is, how just,
   And fit for highest Trust:
Nor yet grown stiffer with Command,
But still in the Republick's hand:
   How fit he is to sway
   That can so well obey.
He to the Commons Feet presents
A Kingdome, for his first years rents:
   And, what he may, forbears
   His Fame to make it theirs:
And has his Sword and Spoyls ungirt,
To lay them at the Publick's skirt.
   So when the Falcon high
   Falls heavy from the Sky,
She, having kill'd, no more does search,
But on the next green Bow to pearch;
   Where, when he first does lure,
   The Falckner has her sure.
What may not then our Isle presume
While Victory his Crest does plume;
   What may not others fear,
   If thus he crown each Year!
A Caesar he ere long to Gaul,
To Italy an Hannibal,
   And to all States not free
   Shall Clymacterick be.
The Pict no shelter now shall find
Within his party-colour'd Mind;
   But from this Valour sad
   Shrink underneath the Plad:

Happy if in the tufted brake
The English Hunter him mistake,
　　Nor lay his Hounds in near
　　The Caledonian Deer.
But thou the Wars and Fortunes Son
March indefatigably on,
　　And for the last effect
　　Still keep thy Sword erect:
Besides the force it has to fright
The Spirits of the shady Night;
　　The same Arts that did gain
　　A Pow'r must it maintain.

---

*Frank Kermode and Keith Walker have said of Marvell's state of mind in the spring of 1650, when Oliver Cromwell came back from his expedition to Ireland, "The reason why there is so much uncertainty about his position is that . . . he expressed himself not in prose but in poetry, with a higher degree of obliquity and a concern for more than topical significance. 'An Horatian Ode on Cromwell's Return from Ireland' is a manifestly great poem, yet it is also baffling to anybody who wants simply to know where the poet stood with Cromwell in 1650." (Note that: "bergamot" is a pear-shaped citrus fruit; "climacteric" is "crucial time.")*

# The Picture of Little T. C.
# in a Prospect of Flowers

See with what simplicity
This nymph begins her golden days!
  In the green grass she loves to lie,
And there with her fair aspect tames
The wilder flowers, and gives them names;
  But only with the roses plays,
    And them does tell
What colour best becomes them, and what smell.

  Who can foretell for what high cause
This darling of the gods was born?
  Yet this is she whose chaster laws
The wanton Love shall one day fear,
And, under her command severe,
  See his bow broke and ensigns torn.
    Happy who can
Appease this virtuous enemy of man!

  O then let me in time compound
And parley with those conquering eyes,
  Ere they have tried their force to wound;
Ere with their glancing wheels they drive
In triumph over hearts that strive,
  And them that yield but more despise:
    Let me be laid,
Where I may see thy glories from some shade.

Meantime, whilst every verdant thing
Itself does at thy beauty charm,
Reform the errors of the Spring;
Make that the tulips may have share
Of sweetness, seeing they are fair,
And roses of their thorns disarm;
But most procure
That violets may a longer age endure.

But O, young beauty of the woods,
Whom Nature courts with fruits and flowers,
Gather the flowers, but spare the buds;
Lest Flora, angry at thy crime
To kill her infants in their prime,
Do quickly make the example yours;
And ere we see,
Nip in the blossom all our hopes and thee.

---

*The title initials are thought to belong to a child named Theophila Cornewall. Her first name, which means "Beloved of God," may be referred to in line 10 ("darling of the gods"). Marvell's curious title has caught the fancy of modern poets: consider Charles Tomlinson's "Picture of J. T. in a Prospect of Stone" and John Ashbery's "Picture of Little J. A. in a Prospect of Flowers."*

# The Mower to the Glow-Worms

Ye living lamps, by whose dear light
The nightingale does sit so late
And studying all the summer night,
Her matchless songs does meditate;

Ye country comets, that portend
No war, nor prince's funeral,
Shining unto no higher end
Than to presage the grasses' fall;

Ye glow-worms, whose officious flame
To wandering mowers shows the way,
That in the night have lost their aim,
And after foolish fires do stray;

Your courteous lights in vain you waste,
Since Juliana here is come,
For she my mind hath so displaced
That I shall never find my home.

---

*At various stages of their lives, members of the well-named Lampyridae family
are called glow-worms, fireflies, lightning bugs, and lightning beetles. Poets from
all over the world have loved them for centuries. They are magnets for all sorts
of lore and literature. Marvell gets a good deal of charm and information into
a short, modest poem. (Note that: "foolish fires"—ignes fatui in Latin—is the
spooky light from burning marsh-gas, also called "will-o'-the-wisp" and "jack-
o'-lantern"; "officious" is "obliging.")*

# A Dialogue between the Soul and Body

SOUL:

      O who shall from this dungeon raise
A soul enslaved so many ways?
With bolts of bones, that fettered stands
In feet; and manacled in hands:
Here blinded with an eye; and there
Deaf with the drumming of an ear;
A soul hung up, as 'twere, in chains
Of nerves, and arteries, and veins;
Tortured, besides each other part,
In a vain head and double heart.

BODY:

      O who shall me deliver whole
From bonds of this tyrannic soul?
Which, stretched upright, impales me so
That mine own precipice I go;
And warms and moves this needless frame
(A fever could but do the same);
And, wanting where its spite to try,
Has made me live to let me die;
A body that could never rest,
Since this ill spirit it possessed.

SOUL:

What magic could me thus confine
Within another's grief to pine?
Where whatsoever it complain,
I feel, that cannot feel, the pain.
And all my care itself employs
That to preserve, which me destroys;
Constrained not only to endure
Diseases, but, what's worse, the cure;
And ready oft the port to gain,
Am shipwrecked into health again.

BODY:

But physic yet could never reach
The maladies thou me dost teach:
Whom first the cramp of hope does tear;
And then the palsy shakes of fear;
The pestilence of love does heat;
Or hatred's hidden ulcer eat;
Joy's cheerful madness does perplex,
Or sorrow's other madness vex;
Which knowledge forces me to know,
And memory will not forgo.
What but a soul could have the wit
To build me up for sin so fit?
So architects do square and hew
Green trees that in the forest grew.

---

*There is bibliographical evidence that much of Marvell's poem has been lost. The loss is all the more regrettable in view of Marvell's genius in giving both contestants such interesting and original arguments. (Note that: "needless" is "not in need"; "physic" is "medicine.")*

# HENRY VAUGHAN 1622–1695

Since Henry Vaughan and his twin brother Thomas
were born in a part of Wales once inhabited by a tribe
called the Silures, Vaughan styled himself a "Silurist."
He studied both law and medicine, and his poems are
saturated with religious feeling. Vaughan was extraordinarily devoted to the memory of George Herbert and
modelled his own writings on those in Herbert's *The
Temple*. Vaughan's passionate feelings affected Wordsworth very strongly, a century after Vaughan's death.

## *The Retreat*

Happy those early days! when I
Shined in my angel-infancy.
Before I understood this place
Appointed for my second race,
Or taught my soul to fancy ought
But a white, celestial thought,
When yet I had not walked above
A mile or two, from my first love,
And looking back (at that short space)
Could see a glimpse of his bright face;
When on some *gilded cloud* or *flower*
My gazing soul would dwell an hour,
And in those weaker glories spy
Some shadows of eternity;
Before I taught my tongue to wound
My conscience with a sinful sound,
Or had the black art to dispense
A sev'ral sin to ev'ry sense,
But felt through all this fleshly dress
Bright *shoots* of everlastingness.
    O, how I long to travel back
And tread again that ancient track!

That I might once more reach that plain,
Where first I left my glorious train;
From whence th' inlightened spirit sees
That shady city of palm trees;
But (ah!) my soul with too much stay
Is drunk, and staggers in the way.
Some men a forward motion love,
But I by backward steps would move,
And when this dust falls to the urn
In that state I came, return.

---

*"Retreat" means both a movement backward and a place of shelter. Vaughan plays also on the "re-" prefix that means both "back" and "again" in the title and the last word. This poem is a precursor of Wordsworth's "Intimations" ode (p. 400).*

# The World

()◀▬▶()

I saw Eternity the other night,
Like a great ring of pure and endless light,
  All calm, as it was bright;
And round beneath it, time in hours, days, years,
  Driven by the spheres
Like a vast shadow moved; in which the world
  And all her train were hurled:
The doting lover in his quaintest strain
  Did there complain;
Near him, his lute, his fancy, and his flights,
  Wit's sour delights,
With gloves and knots, the silly snares of pleasure,
  Yet his dear treasure,
All scattered lay, while he his eyes did pour
  Upon a flower.

The darksome statesman, hung with weights and woe,
Like a thick midnight-fog, moved there so slow,
  He did not stay, nor go;
Condemning thoughts, like sad eclipses, scowl
  Upon his soul,
And clouds of crying witnesses without
  Pursued him with one shout;
Yet digged the mole, and lest his ways be found
  Worked underground,
Where he did clutch his prey, but One did see
  That policy;
Churches and altars fed him; perjuries
  Were gnats and flies;
It rained about him blood and tears, but he
  Drank them as free.

The fearful miser on a heap of rust
Sat pining all his life there, did scarce trust
  His own hands with the dust,
Yet would not place one piece above, but lives
  In fear of thieves.
Thousands there were as frantic as himself,
  And hugged each one his pelf:
The downright epicure placed heav'n in sense,
  And scorned pretense;
While others, slipped into a wide excess,
  Said little less;
The weaker sort slight trivial wares enslave,
  Who think them brave;
And poor, despised Truth sat counting by
  Their victory.

Yet some, who all this while did weep and sing,
And sing and weep, soared up into the ring;
  But most would use no wing.
O fools, said I, thus to prefer dark night
  Before true light!
To live in grots and caves, and hate the day
  Because it shows the way;
The way which from this dead and dark abode
  Leads up to God;
A way where you might tread the sun, and be
  More bright than he!
But as I did their madness so discuss,
  One whispered thus:
This ring the Bridegroom did for none provide
  But for His bride.

---

*Even after 350 years, Vaughan's genius retains its peculiar power to astonish. The grandeur of "I saw Eternity" is balanced by the colloquial humility of "the other night." Throughout, the poem—a detailed gloss on First John II:16–17— keeps both the grand vision and the common touch; each element validates the other. (Note that: "brave" is "flashy.")*

# They Are All Gone into the World of Light

They are all gone into the world of light!
  And I alone sit ling'ring here;
There very memory is fair and bright,
  And my sad thoughts doth clear.

It glows and glitters in my cloudy breast,
  Like stars upon some gloomy grove,
Or those faint beams in which this hill is dressed,
  After the sun's remove.

I see them walking in an air of glory,
  Whose light doth trample on my days:
My days, which are at best but dull and hoary,
  Mere glimmering and decays.

O holy Hope! and high Humility,
  High as the heavens above!
These are your walks, and you have showed them me,
  To kindle my cold love.

Dear, beauteous Death! the jewel of the just,
  Shining nowhere, but in the dark;
What mysteries do lie beyond thy dust,
  Could man outlook that mark!

He that hath found some fledged bird's nest, may know
  At first sight if the bird be flown;
But what fair well or grove he sings in now,
  That is to him unknown.

And yet, as angels in some brighter dreams
   Call to the soul when man doth sleep,
So some strange thoughts transcend our wonted themes,
   And into glory peep.

If a star were confin'd into a tomb,
   Her captive flames must needs burn there;
But when the hand that locked her up, gives room,
   She'll shine through all the sphere.

O Father of eternal life, and all
   Created glories under Thee!
Resume Thy spirit from this world of thrall
   Into true liberty.

Either disperse these mists, which blot and fill
   My perspective, still, as they pass:
Or else remove me hence unto that hill
   Where I shall need no glass.

---

*Most of Vaughan's material here is biblical, but the imagery of the last stanza relies on the technology of the mid-seventeenth century. "Perspective" means "telescope"; the "glass" at the end is primarily a telescope but also secondarily alludes to the metal mirror in First Corinthians XIII in the Bible (about seeing "through a glass darkly").*

# *Peace*

❖❖❖❖

My soul, there is a country
   Far beyond the stars,
Where stands a winged sentry
   All skillful in the wars.
There, above noise and danger,
   Sweet Peace sits crowned with smiles,
And One born in a manger
   Commands the beauteous files.
He is thy gracious friend,
   And (Oh, my Soul awake!)
Did in pure love descend
   To die here for thy sake.
If thou canst get but thither,
   There grows the flower of peace,
The rose that cannot wither,
   Thy fortress and thy ease;
Leave then thy foolish ranges;
   For none can thee secure
But One who never changes,
   Thy God, thy life, thy cure.

---

*As is typical of Vaughan's best poems, "Peace" combines a cosmic vision with ordinary diction, as in the most memorable passage "If thou canst get but thither . . . ." (we still say "get" in this sense).*

# The Night

Through that pure Virgin-shrine,
That sacred veil drawn o'er thy glorious noon
That men might look and live as glow-worms shine,
        And face the moon,
    Wise Nicodemus saw such light
    As made him know his God by night.

    Most blest believer he!
Who in that land of darkness and blind eyes
Thy long-expected healing wings could see,
        When thou didst rise,
    And what can never more be done
    Did at midnight speak with the Sun!

    O who will tell me where
He found thee at that dead and silent hour!
What hallowed solitary ground did bear
        So rare a flower,
    Within whose sacred leaves did lie
    The fullness of the Deity.

    No mercy-seat of gold,
No dead and dusty *Cherub*, nor carv'd stone,
But his own living works did my Lord hold
        And lodge alone;
    Where *trees* and *herbs* did watch and peep
    And wonder, while the *Jews* did sleep.

    Dear night! this worlds defeat;
The stop to busie fools; cares check and curb;
The day of Spirits; my souls calm retreat
        Which none disturb!
    *Christs* progress, and his prayer time;
    The hours to which high Heaven doth chime.

Gods silent, searching flight:
When my Lords head is fill'd with dew, and all
His locks are wet with the clear drops of night;
    His still, soft call;
  His knocking time; The souls dumb watch,
  When Spirits their fair kinred catch.

Were all my loud, evil days
Calm and unhaunted as is thy dark Tent,
Whose peace but by some *Angels* wing or voice
    Is seldom rent;
  Then I in Heaven all the long year
  Would keep, and never wander here.

But living where the Sun
Doth all things wake, and where all mix and tyre
Themselves and others, I consent and run
    To ev'ry myre,
  And by this worlds ill-guiding light,
  Erre more then I can do by night.

There is in God (some say)
A deep, but dazling darkness; As men here
Say it is late and dusky, because they
    See not all clear;
  O for that night! where I in him
  Might live invisible and dim.

---

*The reference to John III:2 in the Bible concerns Nicodemus, who "came to Jesus by night, and said unto him, Rabbi, we know that thou art a teacher come from God: for no man can do these miracles that thou doest, except God be with him." T. S. Eliot's "Mr. Eliot's Sunday Morning Service" quotes the final words of Vaughan's poem. (Note that: "kinred" is "kindred.")*

# JOHN DRYDEN 1631–1700

During the quarter-century between Milton's death in 1674 and his own death in 1700, Dryden was the most considerable and accomplished poet in England. A product of Westminster and Cambridge, he was brilliant as a dramatist, a critic, a translator, and a satirist. Now and then he looked back to the work of Chaucer, Shakespeare, and Jonson, occasionally attempting modernized adaptations of earlier work, but he also looked ahead—so much so that he is often regarded as an eighteenth-century poet, even though he died in the seventeenth century.

# To the Memory of Mr. Oldham

≫≫≫≫≫

Farewell, too little and too lately known,
Whom I began to think and call my own;
For sure our souls were near allied, and thine
Cast in the same poetic mold with mine.
One common note on either lyre did strike,
And knaves and fools we both abhorred alike.
To the same goal did both our studies drive:
The last set out the soonest did arrive.
Thus Nissus fell upon the slippery place,
While his young friend performed and won the race.
O early ripe! to thy abundant store
What could advancing age have added more?
It might (what Nature never gives the young)
Have taught the numbers of thy native tongue.
But satire needs not those, and wit will shine
Through the harsh cadence of a rugged line.
A noble error, and but seldom made,
When poets are by too much force betrayed.
Thy gen'rous fruits, though gathered ere their prime,
Still showed a quickness; and maturing time
But mellows what we write to the dull sweets of rhyme.

Once more, hail, and farewell! farewell, thou young
But ah! too short, Marcellus of our tongue!
Thy brows with ivy and with laurels bound;
But fate and gloomy night encompass thee around.

---

*John Oldham (1653–1683) died young after publishing* Satire against Virtue *(1679) and* Satires upon the Jesuits *(1681). (Note that: "Nisus" is a youth who fell into a pool of blood; "Marcellus" is the illustrious nephew of Augustus who died at age twenty. Both Nisus and Marcellus are in Virgil's* Aeneid.*)*

# Mac Flecknoe

All human things are subject to decay,
And, when Fate summons, monarchs must obey:
This Flecknoe found, who, like Augustus, young
Was called to empire and had governed long;
In prose and verse was owned, without dispute
Through all the realms of Nonsense, absolute.
This agèd prince, now flourishing in peace
And blessed with issue of a large increase,
Worn out with business, did at length debate
To settle the succession of the state;
And pondering which of all his sons was fit
To reign, and wage immortal war with wit,
Cried: " 'Tis resolved; for nature pleads that he
Should only rule who most resembles me:
Sh——— alone my perfect image bears,
Mature in dullness from his tender years.
Sh——— alone, of all my sons, is he
Who stands confirmed in full stupidity.
The rest to some faint meaning make pretense,
But Sh——— never deviates into sense.
Some beams of wit on other souls may fall,
Strike through and make a lucid inverval,
But Sh———'s genuine night admits no ray,
His rising fogs prevail upon the day;
Besides his goodly fabric fills the eye,
And seems designed for thoughtless majesty:
Thoughtless as monarch oaks that shade the plain
And, spread in solemn state, supinely reign.
Heywood and Shirley were but types of thee,
Thou last great prophet of tautology.
Even I, a dunce of more renown than they,
Was sent before but to prepare thy way;
And coarsely clad in Norwich drugget came
To teach the nations in thy greater name.

My warbling lute, the lute I whilom strung
When to King John of Portugal I sung,
Was but the prelude to that glorious day,
When thou on silver Thames didst cut thy way
With well-timed oars before the royal barge,
Swelled with the pride of thy celestial charge;
And big with hymn, commander of an host,
The like was ne'er in *Epsom* blankets tossed.
Methinks I see the new Arion sail,
The lute still trembling underneath thy nail;
At thy well-sharpened thumb from shore to shore
The treble squeaks for fear, the basses roar;
Echoes from Pissing-Alley Sh — — — call,
And Sh — — — they resound from A — — — Hall.
About thy boat the little fishes throng
As at the morning toast that floats along.
Sometimes as prince of thy harmonious band
Thou wield'st thy papers in thy threshing hand.
St. André's feet ne'er kept more equal time,
Not even the feet of thy own *Psyche's* rhyme,
Though they in number as in sense excel;
So just, so like tautology they fell,
That, pale with envy, Singleton forswore     ⎫
The lute and sword which he in triumph bore   ⎬
And vowed he ne'er would act Villerius more."  ⎭
Here stopped the good old sire, and wept for joy
In silent raptures of the hopeful boy.
All arguments, but most his plays, persuade
That for anointed dullness he was made.
    Close to the walls which fair Augusta bind
(The fair Augusta much to fears inclined),
An ancient fabric, raised t' inform the sight,
There stood of yore and Barbican it hight.
A watchtower once; but now, so Fate ordains,
Of all the pile an empty name remains.
From its old ruins brothel-houses rise,
Scenes of lewd loves and of polluted joys.
Where their vast courts the mother-strumpets keep,

And, undisturbed by watch, in silence sleep.
Near these a Nursery erects its head,
Where queens are formed and future heroes bred;
Where unfledged actors learn to laugh and cry,  ⎫
Where infant punks their tender voices try,       ⎬
And little Maximins the gods defy.                    ⎭
Great Fletcher never treads in buskins here,
Nor greater Jonson dares in socks appear;
But gentle Simkin just reception finds
Amidst this monument of vanished minds;
Pure clinches the suburbian muse affords,
And Panton waging harmless war with words.
Here Flecknoe, as a place to fame well known,
Ambitiously designed his Sh — — —'s throne.
For ancient Dekker prophesied long since  ⎫
That in this pile should reign a mighty prince,  ⎬
Born for a scourge of wit and flail of sense;  ⎭
To whom true dullness should some *Psyches* owe,
But worlds of *Misers* from his pen should flow;
*Humorists* and *Hypocrites* it should produce,
Whole Raymond families and tribes of Bruce.
　　Now Empress Fame had published the renown
Of Sh — — —'s coronation through the town.
Roused by report of Fame, the nations meet
From near Bunhill and distant Watling Street.
No Persian carpets spread th' imperial way,
But scattered limbs of mangled poets lay;
From dusty shops neglected authors come,
Martyrs of pies and relics of the bum.
Much Heywood, Shirley, Ogleby there lay,
But loads of Sh — — — almost choked the way.
Bilked stationers for yeomen stood prepared,
And H — — — was Captain of the Guard.
The hoary Prince in majesty appeared,
High on a throne of his own labors reared.
At his right hand our young Ascanius sate,
Rome's other hope and pillar of the state.
His brows thick fogs, instead of glories, grace,

And lambent dullness played around his face.
As Hannibal did to the altars come,
Sworn by his sire a mortal foe to Rome;
So Sh———— swore, nor should his vow be vain,
That he till death true dullness would maintain,
And in his father's right and realm's defense
Ne'er to have peace with wit nor truce with sense.
The King himself the sacred unction made,
As king by office, and as priest by trade:
In his sinister hand instead of ball
He placed a mighty mug of potent ale;
*Love's Kingdom* to his right he did convey,
At once his scepter and his rule of sway,
Whose righteous lore the Prince had practiced young,
And from whose loins recorded *Psyche* sprung.
His temples last with poppies were o'erspread,
That nodding seemed to consecrate his head.
Just at that point of time, if fame not lie,
On his left hand twelve reverend owls did fly:
So Romulus, 'tis sung, by Tiber's brook
Presage of sway from twice six vultures took.
Th' admiring throng loud acclamations make,
And omens of his future empire take.
The sire then shook the honors of his head,
And from his brows damps of oblivion shed
Full on the filial dullness:long he stood    ⎫
Repelling from his breast the raging god;    ⎬
At length burst out in this prophetic mood:  ⎭
"Heavens bless my son, from Ireland let him reign
To far Barbadoes on the western main;
Of his dominion may no end be known,
And greater than his father's be his throne.
Beyond *Love's Kingdom* let him stretch his pen."
He paused, and all the people cried, "Amen."
"Then thus," continued he, "my son, advance
Still in new impudence, new ignorance.
Success let others teach, learn thou from me
Pangs without birth and fruitless industry.

Let *Virtuosos* in five years be writ,
Yet not one thought accuse thy toil of wit.
Let gentle George in triumph tread the stage,
Make Dorimant betray, and Loveit rage;
Let Cully, Cockwood, Fopling, charm the pit,
And in their folly show the writer's wit.
Yet still thy fools shall stand in thy defense,
And justify their author's want of sense.
Let 'em be all by thy own model made
Of dullness, and desire no foreign aid,
That they to future ages may be known
Not copies drawn but issue of thy own.
Nay, let thy men of wit, too, be the same,
All full of thee and differing but in name;
But let no alien S—dl—y interpose
To lard with wit thy hungry *Epsom* prose.
And when false flowers of rhetoric thou wouldst cull,
Trust nature, do not labor to be dull;
But write thy best, and top; and in each line
Sir Formal's oratory will be thine.
Sir Formal, though unsought, attends thy quill
And does thy northern dedications fill.
Nor let false friends seduce thy mind to fame
By arrogating Jonson's hostile name.
Let Father Flecknoe fire thy mind with praise,
And Uncle Ogleby thy envy raise.
Thou art my blood, where Jonson has no part;
What share have we in nature or in art?
Where did his wit on learning fix a brand
And rail at arts he did not understand?
Where made he love in Prince Nicander's vein,
Or swept the dust in *Psyche's* humble strain?
Where sold he bargains, whip-stitch, kiss my arse,
Promised a play and dwindled to a farce?
When did his muse from Fletcher scenes purloin,
As thou whole Etherege dost transfuse to thine?
But so transfused as oil on waters flow,
His always floats above, thine sinks below.

This is thy province, this thy wondrous way,
New humors to invent for each new play;
This is that boasted bias of thy mind
By which one way, to dullness, 'tis inclined,
Which makes thy writings lean on one side still,
And in all changes that way bends thy will.
Nor let thy mountain belly make pretense
Of likeness; thine's a tympany of sense.
A tun of man in thy large bulk is writ,
But sure thou 'rt but a kilderkin of wit.
Like mine thy gentle numbers feebly creep,
Thy tragic muse gives smiles, thy comic sleep.
With whate'er gall thou sett'st thyself to write,
Thy inoffensive satires never bite.
In thy felonious heart though venom lies,
It does but touch thy Irish pen, and dies.
Thy genius calls thee not to purchase fame
In keen iambics but mild anagram;
Leave writing plays, and choose for thy command
Some peaceful province in acrostic land.
There thou may'st wings display and altars raise,
And torture one poor word ten thousand ways.
Or, if thou wouldst thy different talents suit,
Set thy own songs and sing them to thy lute."
He said, but his last words were scarcely heard, ⎫
For Bruce and Longville had a trap prepared, ⎬
And down they sent the yet declaiming bard. ⎭
Sinking, he left his drugget robe behind,
Borne upwards by a subterranean wind.
The mantle fell to the young prophet's part,
With double portion of his father's art.

*Dryden insults Thomas Shadwell (1642?–1692) by making him out to be the son ("Mac") of Richard Flecknoe (who died about 1678), a Roman Catholic priest and minor poet whose only positive fame comes from his having written one of the first English operas. (He is nastily caricatured in Andrew Marvell's "Flecknoe, an English Priest at Rome.") For reasons unknown, Dryden constructs an elaborate mock-epic to ridicule not only Shadwell's work but his person as well (he was fat and addicted to opium). The contagious style of "Mac Flecknoe" occupied the center of English satiric verse from Dryden's heyday in the 1670s right through Byron's 150 years further on. (Note that: "fabric" is "building"; "clinches" is "puns"; "stationers" is "printers and publishers"; "sinister" is "left"—the literal meaning; "kilderkin" is "small cask.")*

# A Song for St. Cecilia's Day, 1687

❖❖❖❖❖

### I

From harmony, from heavenly harmony
  This universal frame began:
  When Nature underneath a heap
    Of jarring atoms lay,
  And could not heave her head,
The tuneful voice was heard from high:
  "Arise, ye more than dead."
Then cold, and hot, and moist, and dry,
In order to their stations leap,
  And Music's power obey.
From harmony, from heavenly harmony
  This universal frame began:
  From harmony to harmony
Through all the compass of the notes it ran,
The diapason closing full in man.

### II

What passion cannot Music raise and quell!
  When Jubal struck the corded shell,
  His listening brethren stood around,
  And, wondering, on their faces fell
  To worship that celestial sound.
Less than a god they thought there could not dwell
  Within the hollow of that shell
  That spoke so sweetly and so well.
What passion cannot Music raise and quell!

### III

The trumpet's loud clangor
   Excites us to arms,
With shrill notes of anger,
   And mortal alarms.
The double double double beat
   Of the thundering drum
Cries: "Hark! the foes come;
Charge, charge, 'tis too late to retreat."

### IV

The soft complaining flute
In dying notes discovers
The woes of hopeless lovers,
Whose dirge is whispered by the warbling lute.

### V

Sharp violins proclaim
Their jealous pangs, and desperation,
Fury, frantic indignation,
Depth of pains, and height of passion,
   For the fair, disdainful dame.

### VI

But O! what art can teach,
   What human voice can reach,
The sacred organ's praise?
   Notes inspiring holy love,
Notes that wing their heavenly ways
   To mend the choirs above.

## VII

Orpheus could lead the savage race;
And trees unrooted left their place,
  Sequacious of the lyre;
But bright Cecilia raised the wonder higher:
When to her organ vocal breath was given,
An angel heard, and straight appeared,
  Mistaking earth for heaven.

### GRAND CHORUS

*As from the power of sacred lays*
  *The spheres began to move,*
*And sung the great Creator's praise*
  *To all the blest above;*
*So, when the last and dreadful hour*
*This crumbling pageant shall devour,*
*The trumpet shall be heard on high,*  ⎫
*The dead shall live, the living die,*  ⎬
*And Music shall untune the sky.*  ⎭

---

*For several years at the end of the seventeenth century, a London music society sponsored a celebration on November 22, the day of St. Cecilia, patron saint of music and, according to legend, inventor of the organ. Dryden's song was the official ode for the observance in 1687; "Alexander's Feast" (p. 268) performed the same honor in 1697.*

# Alexander's Feast;
# or, The Power of Music

## I

'Twas at the royal feast, for Persia won
    By Philip's warlike son:
    Aloft in awful state
    The god-like hero sate
        On his imperial throne:
    His valiant peers were placed around;
Their brows with roses and with myrtles bound.
    (So should desert in arms be crowned:)
The lovely Thaïs by his side,
Sat like a blooming Eastern bride
In flower of youth and beauty's pride.
        Happy, happy, happy pair!
    None but the Brave
    None but the Brave
    None but the Brave deserves the Fair.

### CHORUS

*Happy, happy, happy pair!*
*None but the Brave*
*None but the Brave*
*None but the Brave deserves the Fair.*

II

Timotheus placed on high
    Amid the tuneful choir,
    With flying fingers touched the lyre:
The trembling notes ascend the sky,
And heavenly joys inspire.
The song began from Jove;
Who left his blissful seats above,
(Such is the power of mighty Love.)
A dragon's fiery form belied the god:
Sublime on radiant spires he rode,
    When he to fair Olympia pressed,
    And while he sought her snowy breast:
Then, round her slender waist he curled,
And stamped an image of himself, a sovereign of the world.
The listening crowd admire the lofty sound,
"A present Deity," they shout around:
"A present Deity," the vaulted roofs rebound.
    With ravished ears
    The Monarch hears,
    Assumes the god,
    Affects to nod,
    And seems to shake the spheres.

CHORUS

*With ravished ears*
*The Monarch hears,*
*Assumes the god,*
*Affects to nod,*
*And seems to shake the spheres.*

III

The praise of Bacchus then the sweet musician sung,
Of Bacchus ever fair and ever young;
The jolly god in triumph comes;
Sound the trumpets, beat the drums:
Flushed with a purple grace
He shows his honest face;
Now give the hautboys breath: he comes, he comes!
"Bacchus, ever fair and young,
Drinking joys did first ordain;
Bacchus' blessings are a treasure;
Drinking is the soldier's pleasure;
Rich the treasure,
Sweet the pleasure;
Sweet is pleasure after pain."

CHORUS

*Bacchus' blessings are a treasure;*
*Drinking is the soldier's pleasure;*
*Rich the treasure,*
*Sweet the pleasure;*
*Sweet is pleasure after pain.*

IV

Soothed with the sound the King grew vain,
    Fought all his battles o'er again;
And thrice he routed all his foes, and thrice he slew the slain.
    The master saw the madness rise,
    His glowing cheeks, his ardent eyes;
    And while he heaven and earth defied,
    Changed his hand, and checked his pride.
        He chose a mournful Muse
        Soft pity to infuse:
    He sung Darius great and good,
       By too severe a fate,
   Fallen, fallen, fallen, fallen,
      Fallen from his high estate
And weltering in his blood;
    Deserted at his utmost need
    By those his former bounty fed;
    On the bare earth exposed he lies,
    With not a friend to close his eyes.

With downcast looks the joyless victor sate,
    Revolving in his altered soul
      The various turns of chance below;
    And, now and then, a sigh he stole,
    And tears began to flow.

CHORUS

*Revolving in his altered soul*
    *The various turns of chance below;*
*And, now and then, a sigh he stole,*
    *And tears began to flow.*

V

The mighty master smiled to see
That love was in the next degree:
'Twas but a kindred sound to move,
For pity melts the mind to love.
    Softly sweet, in Lydian measures
    Soon he soothed his soul to pleasures.
    "War," he sung, "is toil and trouble;
    Honour but an empty bubble.
      Never ending, still beginning,
    Fighting still, and still destroying;
      If the world be worth thy winning,
    Think, O think it worth enjoying.
      Lovely Thaïs sits beside thee,
      Take the good the Gods provide thee."

The many rend the skies with loud applause;
So Love was crowned, but Music won the cause.
    The Prince, unable to conceal his pain,
      Gazed on the Fair
      Who caused his care,
    And sighed and looked, sighed and looked,
    Sighed and looked, and sighed again:
At length, with love and wine at once oppressed,
The vanquished victor sunk upon her breast.

CHORUS

*The Prince, unable to conceal his pain,*
    *Gazed on the Fair*
    *Who caused his care,*
    *And sighed and looked, sighed and looked,*
    *Sighed and looked, and sighed again:*
*At length, with love and wine at once oppressed,*
*The vanquished victor sunk upon her breast.*

VI

Now strike the golden lyre again,
A louder yet, and yet a louder strain.
Break his bands of sleep asunder,
And rouse him, like a rattling peal of thunder.
   Hark, hark, the horrid sound
    Has raised up his head,
    As awaked from the dead,
   And amazed he stares around.
"Revenge, revenge!" Timotheus cries,
  "See the Furies arise!
  See the snakes that they rear,
  How they hiss in their hair,
 And the sparkles that flash from their eyes!
  Behold a ghastly band,
  Each a torch in his hand!
Those are Grecian ghosts that in battle were slain,
And unburied remain
Inglorious on the plain.
    Give the vengeance due
    To the valiant crew.
Behold how they toss their torches on high,
  How they point to the Persian abodes,
And glittering temples of their hostile gods!"
The Princes applaud with a furious joy,
And the King seized a flambeau, with zeal to destroy;
   Thaïs led the way
   To light him to his prey,
And, like another Helen, fired another Troy.


CHORUS

*And the King seized a flambeau, with zeal to destroy;*
   *Thaïs led the way*
   *To light him to his prey,*
*And, like another Helen, fired another Troy.*

### VII

Thus, long ago,
Ere heaving bellows learned to blow,
While organs yet were mute;
Timotheus, to his breathing flute
And sounding lyre,
Could swell the soul to rage, or kindle soft desire.
At last divine Cecilia came,
Inventress of the vocal frame;
The sweet Enthusiast, from her sacred store,
Enlarged the former narrow bounds,
And added length to solemn sounds,
With Nature's mother wit, and arts unknown before.
Let old Timotheus yield the prize,
Or both divide the crown;
He raised a mortal to the skies,
She drew an angel down.

### GRAND CHORUS

*At last divine Cecilia came,*
*Inventress of the vocal frame;*
*The sweet Enthusiast, from her sacred store,*
*Enlarged the former narrow bounds,*
*And added length to solemn sounds,*
*With Nature's mother wit, and arts unknown before.*
*Let old Timotheus yield the prize,*
*Or both divide the crown;*
*He raised a mortal to the skies,*
*She drew an angel down.*

---

*The title feast was held in Persepolis to celebrate Alexander's victory over the Persians. Some power—Dryden nominates the musician Timotheus—moved Alexander to burn Persepolis in retaliation for the Persians' burning of Athens. The notion of "another Troy," by the way, recurs in much of William Butler Yeats's poetry and verbatim in his "Two Songs from a Play." See the commentary on Dryden's "Song for St. Cecilia's Day," p. 265. (Note that: "admire" is "wonder at"; "hautboys" is "oboes"; "flambeau" is "torch.")*

# E D W A R D   T A Y L O R  c.1645–1729

Taylor, born in England, came to Massachusetts in
1668, studied at Harvard, and served as pastor and
physician in the town of Westfield for more than fifty
years. None of his poetry was published until 1939,
more than two centuries after his death.

## *Huswifery*

Make me, O Lord, Thy spining wheel complete.
  Thy Holy Word my distaff make for me.
Make mine affections Thy swift flyers neat
  And make my soul Thy holy spool to be.
  My conversation make to be Thy reel
  And reel the yarn thereon spun of Thy wheel.

Make me Thy loom then, knit therein this twine:
  And make Thy Holy Spirit, Lord, wind quills:
Then weave the web Thyself. The yarn is fine.
  Thine ordinances make my fulling mills.
  Then dye the same in heavenly colors choice,
  All pinked with varnished flowers of paradise.

Then clothe therewith mine understanding, will,
  Affections, judgment, conscience, memory,
My words, and actions, that their shine may fill
  My ways with glory and Thee glorify.
  Then mine apparel shall display before Ye
  That I am clothed in holy robes for glory.

---

*Taylor's devotional poems, among the earliest to be written in America, owe some
of their imagery and feeling to such English exemplars as Donne and Herbert.
The itemized domestic allegory of "Huswifery"—related to textile jobs like spinning, weaving, dyeing, and sewing—was a staple feature of sermons and didactic
verse.*

# JONATHAN SWIFT 1667–1745

*Gulliver's Travels* has conferred absolute immortality on Swift; on account of it and it alone he belongs with the greatest of writers. Historically, however, he is important for contributions to political thought, particularly on the treatment of Ireland. He was born and educated in Dublin and from 1713 served as Dean of St. Patrick's there. He is not known to have married, but he maintained close relationships with Esther Johnson ("Stella") and Esther Vanhomrigh ("Vanessa").

# A Description of the Morning

Now hardly here and there an hackney coach
Appearing, showed the ruddy morn's approach.
Now Betty from her master's bed had flown,
And softly stole to discompose her own;
The slipshod 'prentice from his master's door
Had pared the dirt, and sprinkled round the floor.
Now Moll had whirled her mop with dextrous airs,
Prepared to scrub the entry and the stairs.
The youth with broomy stumps began to trace
The kennel's edge, where wheels had worn the place.
The small-coal man was heard with cadence deep,
Till drowned in shriller notes of chimney sweep:
Duns at his lordship's gate began to meet;
And brickdust Moll had screamed through half the street.
The turnkey now his flock returning sees,
Duly let out a-nights to steal for fees:
The watchful bailiffs take their silent stands,
And schoolboys lag with satchels in their hands.

---

*This vision of a modern urban morning—first published in* The Tatler *in 1709—should be compared with Blake's "London" (p. 361), written almost a century later. (Note that: "kennel" is "gutter," "sewer"; "duns" is "bill collectors.")*

# ALEXANDER POPE 1688–1744

Pope was the greatest English poet for a third of the
eighteenth century: from about 1711, when he wrote
his "Essay on Criticism," until his death thirty-three
years later. He was most successful as a translator of
Homer, but his reputation rests largely on his genius as
a satirist, especially in the mock-epic mode displayed in
"The Rape of the Lock" and *The Dunciad*. As the "Epistle to Dr. Arbuthnot" demonstrates, Pope was among
the finest epistolary poets in English.

## *Know Then Thyself*

Know then thyself, presume not God to scan,
The proper study of mankind is Man.
Placed on this isthmus of a middle state,
A being darkly wise and rudely great:
With too much knowledge for the Sceptic side,
With too much weakness for the Stoic's pride,
He hangs between; in doubt to act or rest,
In doubt to deem himself a God or Beast,
In doubt his mind or body to prefer;
Born but to die, and reasoning but to err;
Alike in ignorance, his reason such
Whether he thinks too little or too much:
Chaos of thought and passion, all confused;
Still by himself abused, or disabused;
Created half to rise and half to fall;
Great lord of all things,yet a prey to all;
Sole judge of truth, in endless error hurled;
The glory, jest, and riddle of the world!
   Go, wondrous creature! mount where science guides:
Go, measure earth, weigh air, and state the tides:
Instruct the planets in what orbs to run,
Correct old time and regulate the Sun;
Go, soar with Plato to th' empyreal sphere,

To the first good, first perfect, and first fair;
Or tread the mazy round his follow'rs trod
And quitting sense call imitating God—
As Eastern priests in giddy circles run,
And turn their heads to imitate the Sun.
Go, teach Eternal Wisdom how to rule:
Then drop into thyself, and be a fool!
   Superior beings, when of late they saw
A mortal man unfold all nature's law,
Admired such wisdom in an earthly shape,
And showed a NEWTON as we show an ape.
   Could he, whose rules the rapid comet bind,
Describe or fix one movement of his mind?
Who saw its fires here rise and there descend,
Explain his own beginning or his end?
Alas, what wonder: man's superior part
Unchecked may rise, and climb from art to art,
But when his own great work is but begun,
What reason weaves by passion is undone.

from An Essay on Man

---

*These eighteen lines open the second epistle (of four) in "An Essay on Man,"
described in Pope's Argument as being "Of the Nature and State of Man, with
respect to Himself, as an Individual."*

# Epistle to Dr. Arbuthnot

•❖•❖•❖•❖•

P. Shut, shut the door, good John! (fatigued, I said),
Tie up the knocker, say I'm sick, I'm dead.
The Dog Star rages! nay 'tis past a doubt
All Bedlam, or Parnassus, is let out:
Fire in each eye, and papers in each hand,
They rave, recite, and madden round the land.

    What walls can guard me, or what shades can hide?
They pierce my thickets, through my grot they glide,
By land, by water, they renew the charge,
They stop the chariot, and they board the barge.
No place is sacred, not the church is free;
Even Sunday shines no Sabbath day to me:
Then from the Mint walks forth the man of rhyme,
Happy to catch me just at dinner time.

    Is there a parson, much bemused in beer,
A maudlin poetess, a rhyming peer,
A clerk foredoomed his father's soul to cross,
Who pens a stanza when he should engross?
Is there who, locked from ink and paper, scrawls
With desperate charcoal round his darkened walls?
All fly to Twit'nam, and in humble strain
Apply to me to keep them mad or vain.
Arthur, whose giddy son neglects the laws,
Imputes to me and my damned works the cause:
Poor Cornus sees his frantic wife elope,
And curses wit, and poetry, and Pope.

    Friend to my life (which did not you prolong,
The world had wanted many an idle song)
What drop or nostrum can this plague remove?
Or which must end me, a fool's wrath or love?
A dire dilemma! either way I'm sped,
If foes, they write, if friends, they read me dead.
Seized and tied down to judge, how wretched I!
Who can't be silent, and who will not lie.

To laugh were want of goodness and of grace,
And to be grave exceeds all power of face.
I sit with sad civility, I read
With honest anguish and an aching head,
And drop at last, but in unwilling ears,
This saving counsel, "Keep your piece nine years."
  "Nine years!" cries he, who high in Drury Lane,
Lulled by soft zephyrs through the broken pane,
Rhymes ere he wakes, and prints before term ends
Obliged by hunger and request of friends:
"The piece, you think, is incorrect? why, take it,
I'm all submission, what you'd have it, make it."
  Three things another's modest wishes bound,
My friendship, and a prologue, and ten pound.
  Pitholeon sends to me: "You know his Grace,
I want a patron; ask him for a place."
Pitholeon libeled me—"but here's a letter
Informs you, sir, 'twas when he knew no better.
Dare you refuse him? Curll invites to dine,
He'll write a *Journal*, or he'll turn Divine."
Bless me! a packet—" 'Tis a stranger sues,
A virgin tragedy, an orphan Muse."
If I dislike it, "Furies, death, and rage!"
If I approve, "Commend it to the stage."
There (thank my stars) my whole commission ends,
The players and I are, luckily, no friends.
Fired that the house reject him," " 'Sdeath, I'll print it,
And shame the fools—Your interest, sir, with Lintot!"
Lintot, dull rogue, will think your price too much.
"Not, sir, if you revise it, and retouch."
All my demurs but double his attacks;
At last he whispers, "Do; and we go snacks."
Glad of a quarrel, straight I clap the door,
"Sir, let me see your works and you no more."
  'Tis sung, when Midas' ears began to spring
(Midas, a sacred person and a king),
His very minister who spied them first,
(Some say his queen) was forced to speak, or burst.

And is not mine, my friend a sorer case,
When every coxcomb perks them in my face?
  A. Good friend, forbear! you deal in dangerous things.
I'd never name queens, ministers, or kings;
Keep close to ears, and those let asses prick;
'Tis nothing — — —P. Nothing? if they bite and kick?
Out with it, *Dunciad!* Let the secret pass,
That secret to each fool, that he's an ass:
The truth once told (and wherefore should we lie?)
The queen of Midas slept, and so may I.
  You think this cruel? take it for a rule,
No creature smarts so little as a fool.
Let peals of laughter, Codrus! round thee break,
Thou unconcerned canst hear the mighty crack.
Pit, box, and gallery in convulsions hurled,
Thou stand'st unshook amidst a bursting world.
Who shames a scribbler? break one cobweb through,
He spins the slight, self-pleasing thread anew:
Destroy his fib or sophistry, in vain;
The creature's at his dirty work again,
Throned in the center of his thin designs,
Proud of a vast extent of flimsy lines.
Whom have I hurt? has poet yet or peer
Lost the arched eyebrow or Parnassian sneer?
And has not Colley still his lord and whore?
His butchers Henley? his freemasons Moore?
Does not one table Bavius still admit?
Still to one bishop Philips seem a wit?
Still Sappho — — —A. Hold! for God's sake—you'll offend.
No names—be calm—learn prudence of a friend.
I too could write, and I am twice as tall;
But foes like these! — — —P. One flatterer's worse than all.
Of all mad creatures, if the learn'd are right,
It is the slaver kills, and not the bite.
A fool quite angry is quite innocent:
Alas! 'Tis ten times worse when they repent.
  One dedicates in high heroic prose,
And ridicules beyond a hundred foes;

One from all Grub Street will my fame defend,
And, more abusive, calls himself my friend.
This prints my letters, that expects a bribe,
And others roar aloud, "Subscribe, subscribe!"
    There are, who to my person pay their court:
I cough like Horace, and, though lean, am short;
Ammon's great son one shoulder had too high,
Such Ovid's nose, and "Sir! you have an eye—"
Go on, obliging creatures, make me see
All that disgraced my betters met in me.
Say for my comfort, languishing in bed,
"Just so immortal Maro held his head":
And when I die, be sure you let me know
Great Homer died three thousand years ago.
    Why did I write? what sin to me unknown
Dipped me in ink, my parents', or my own?
As yet a child, not yet a fool to fame,
I lisped in numbers, for the numbers came.
I left no calling for this idle trade,
No duty broke, no father disobeyed.
The Muse but served to ease some friend, not wife,
To help me through this long disease, my life,
To second, Arbuthnot! thy art and care,
And teach the being you preserved, to bear.
    A. But why then publish? P. Granville the polite,
And knowing Walsh, would tell me I could write;
Well-natured Garth inflamed with early praise,
And Congreve loved, and Swift endured my lays;
The courtly Talbot, Somers, Sheffield, read;
Even mitered Rochester would nod the head,
And St. John's self (great Dryden's friends before)
With open arms received one poet more.
Happy my studies, when by these approved!
Happier their author, when by these beloved!
From these the world will judge of men and books,
Not from the Burnets. Oldmixons, and Cookes.
    Soft were my numbers; who could take offense
While pure description held the place of sense?

Like gentle Fanny's was my flowery theme,
A painted mistress, or a purling stream.
Yet then did Gildon draw his venal quill;
I wished the man a dinner, a sat still.
Yet then did Dennis rave in furious fret;
I never answered, I was not in debt.
If I want provoked, or madness made them print,
I waged no war with Bedlam or the Mint.
   Did some more sober critic come abroad?
If wrong, I smiled; if right, I kissed the rod.
Pains, reading, study are their just pretense,
And all they want is spirit, taste, and sense.
Commas and points they set exactly right,
And 'twere a sin to rob them of their mite.
Yet ne'er one sprig of laurel graced these ribalds,
From slashing Bentley down to piddling Tibbalds.
Each wight who reads not, and but scans and spells,
Each word-catcher that lives on syllables,
Even such small critics some regard may claim,
Preserved in Milton's or in Shakespeare's name.
Pretty! in amber to observe the forms
Of hairs, or straws, or dirt, or grubs, or worms!
The things, we know, are neither rich nor rare,
But wonder how the devil they got there.
   Were others angry? I excused them too;
Well might they rage; I gave them but their due.
A man's true merit 'tis not hard to find;
But each man's secret standard in his mind,
That casting weight pride adds to emptiness,
This, who can gratify? for who can guess?
The bard whom pilfered pastorals renown,
Who turns a Persian tale for half a crown,
Just writes to make his barrenness appear,
And strains from hard-bound brains eight lines a year:
He, who still wanting, though he lives on theft,
Steals much, spends little, yet has nothing left;
And he who now to sense, now nonsense leaning,
Means not, but blunders round about a meaning:

And he whose fustian's so sublimely bad,
It is not poetry, but prose run mad:
All these, my modest satire bade translate,
And owned that nine such poets made a Tate.
How did they fume, and stamp, and roar, and chafe!
And swear, not Addison himself was safe.

   Peace to all such! but were there one whose fires
True Genius kindles, and fair Fame inspires;
Blessed with each talent and each art to please,
And born to write, converse, and live with ease:
Should such a man, too fond to rule alone,
Bear, like the Turk, no brother near the throne;
View him with scornful, yet with jealous eyes,
And hate for arts that caused himself to rise;
Damn with faint praise, assent with civil leer,
And without sneering, teach the rest to sneer;
Willing to wound, and yet afraid to strike,
Just hint a fault, and hesitate dislike;
Alike reserved to blame or to commend,
A timorous foe, and a suspicious friend;
Dreading even fools; by flatterers besieged,
And so obliging that he ne'er obliged;
Like Cato, give his little senate laws,
And sit attentive to his own applause;
While wits and Templars every sentence raise,
And wonder with a foolish face of praise—
Who but must laugh, if such a man there be?
Who would not weep, if Atticus were he?

   What though my name stood rubric on the walls
Or plastered posts, with claps, in capitals?
Or smoking forth, a hundred hawkers' load,
On wings of winds came flying all abroad?
I sought no homage from the race that write;
I kept, like Asian monarchs, from their sight:
Poems I heeded (now berhymed so long)
No more than thou, great George! a birthday song.
I ne'er with wits or witlings passed my days
To spread about the itch of verse and praise;

Nor like a puppy daggled through the town
To fetch and carry sing-song up and down;
Nor at rehearsals sweat, and mouthed, and cried,
With handkerchief and orange at my side;
But sick of fops, and poetry, and prate,
To Bufo left the whole Castalian state.
　　Proud as Apollo on his forkéd hill,
Sat full-blown Bufo, puffed by every quill;
Fed with soft dedication all day long,
Horace and he went hand in hand in song.
His library (where busts of poets dead
And a true Pindar stood without a head)
Received of wits an undistinguished race,
Who first his judgment asked, and then a place:
Much they extolled his pictures, much his seat,
And flattered every day, and some days eat:
Till grown more frugal in his riper days,
He paid some bards with port, and some with praise;
To some a dry rehearsal was assigned,
And others (harder still) he paid in kind.
Dryden alone (what wonder?) came not nigh;
Dryden alone escaped this judging eye:
But still the great have kindness in reserve;
He helped to bury whom he helped to starve.
　　May some choice patron bless each gray goose quill!
May every Bavius have his Bufo still!
So when a statesman wants a day's defense,
Or Envy holds a whole week's war with Sense,
Or simple Pride for flattery makes demands,
May dunce by dunce he whistled off my hands!
Blessed be the great! for those they take away,
And those they left me—for they left me Gay;
Left me to see neglected genius bloom,
Neglected die, and tell it on his tomb;
Of all thy blameless life the sole return
My verse, and Queensberry weeping o'er thy urn!
Oh, let me live my own, and die so too!
("To live and die is all I have to do")

Maintain a poet's dignity and ease,
And see what friends, and read what books I please;
Above a patron, though I condescend
Sometimes to call a minister my friend.
I was not born for courts or great affairs;
I pay my debts, believe, and say my prayers,
Can sleep without a poem in my head,
Nor know if Dennis be alive or dead.
   Why am I asked what next shall see the light?
Heavens! was I born for nothing but to write?
Has life no joys for me? or (to be grave)
Have I no friend to serve, no soul to save?
"I found him close with Swift"—"Indeed? no doubt"
Cries prating Balbus, "something will come out."
'Tis all in vain, deny it as I will.
"No, such a genius never can lie still,"
And then for mine obligingly mistakes
The first lampoon Sir Will or Bubo makes.
Poor guiltless I! and can I choose but smile,
When every coxcomb knows me by my style?
   Cursed be the verse, how well soe'er it flow,
That tends to make one worthy man my foe,
Give Virtue scandal, Innocence a fear,
Or from the soft-eyed virgin steal a tear!
But he who hurts a harmless neighbor's peace.
Insults fallen worth, or Beauty in distress,
Who loves a lie, lame Slander helps about,
Who writes a libel, or who copies out:
That fop whose pride affects a patron's name,
Yet absent, wounds an author's honest fame;
Who can your merit selfishly approve,
And show the sense of it without the love;
Who has the vanity to call your friend,
Yet wants the honour, injured, to defend;
Who tells whate'er you think, whate'er you say,
And, if he lie not, must at least betray:
Who to the *Dean,* and *silver bell* can swear,
And sees at *Cannons* what was never there;

Who reads, but with a lust to misapply,
Make satire a lampoon, and fiction, lie.
A lash like mine no honest man shall dread,
But all such babbling blockheads in his stead.
    Let *Sporus* tremble—"What? that thing of silk,
Sporus, that mere white curd of ass's milk?
Satire or sense, alas! can Sporus feel?
Who breaks a butterfly upon a wheel?"
Yet let me flap this bug with gilded wings,
This painted child of dirt that stinks and stings;
Whose buzz the witty and the fair annoys,
Yet wit ne'er tastes, and beauty ne'er enjoys:
So well-bred spaniels civilly delight
In mumbling of the game they dare not bite.
Eternal smiles his emptiness betray,
As shallow streams run dimpling all the way.
Whether in florid impotence he speaks,
And, as the prompter breathes, the puppet squeaks;
Or at the ear of Eve, familiar toad,
Half froth, half venom, spits himself abroad,
In puns, or politics, or tales, or lies,
Or spite, or smut, or rhymes, or blasphemies.
His wit all seesaw, between *that* and *this*,
Now high, now low, now master up, now miss,
And he himself one vile antithesis.
Amphibious thing! that acting either part,
The trifling head, or the corrupted heart,
Fop at the toilet, flatterer at the board,
Now trips a Lady, and now struts a Lord.
Eve's tempter thus the Rabbins have exprest,
A cherub's face, a reptile all the rest;
Beauty that shocks you, parts that none will trust,
Wit that can creep, and pride that licks the dust.
    Not Fortune's worshipper, nor fashion's fool,
Not lucre's madman, nor ambition's tool,
Not proud, nor servile; be one poet's praise,
That, if he pleased, he pleased by manly ways:
That flattery, even to kings, he held a shame,

And thought a lie in verse or prose the same.
That not in fancy's maze he wandered long,
But stooped to truth and moralized his song:
That not for fame, but virtue's better end,
He stood the furious foe, the timid friend,
The damning critic, half-approving wit,
The coxcomb hit, or fearing to be hit;
Laughed at the loss of friends he never had,
The dull, the proud, the wicked, and the mad;
The distant threats of vengeance on his head,
The blow unfelt, the tear he never shed;
The tale revived, the lie so oft o'erthrown,
The imputed trash, and dulness not his own;
The morals blackened when the writings 'scape,
The libeled person, and the pictured shape;
Abuse, on all he loved, or loved him, spread,
A friend in exile, or a father, dead;
The whisper, that to greatness still too near,
Perhaps, yet vibrates on his SOVEREIGN's ear—
Welcome for thee, fair Virtue! all the past:
For thee, fair Virtue! welcome even the *last!*
    "But why insult the poor, affront the great?"
A knave's a knave, to me, in every state:
Alike my scorn, if he succeed or fail,
Sporus at court, or Japhet in a jail,
A hireling scribbler, or a hireling peer,
Knight of the post corrupt, or of the shire;
If on a pillory, or near a throne,
He gain his Prince's ear, or lose his own.
Yet soft by nature, more a dupe than wit,
Sappho can tell you how this man was bit:
This dreaded satirist Dennis will confess
Foe to his pride, but friend to his distress,
So humble, he has knocked at Tibbald's door,
Has drunk with Cibber, nay, has rhymed for Moore.
Full ten years slandered, did he once reply?
Three thousand suns went down on Welsted's lie.
To please a mistress one aspersed his life;

He lashed him not, but let her be his wife:
Let Budgell charge low Grubstreet on his quill,
And write whate'er he pleased, except his will;
Let the two Curlls of town and court, abuse
His father, mother, body, soul, and Muse.
Yet why? that father held it for a rule,
It was a sin to call our neighbor fool;
That harmless mother thought no wife a whore:
Hear this, and spare his family, James Moore!
Unspotted names, and memorable long,
If there be force in virtue, or in song.
    Of gentle blood (part shed in honor's cause,
While yet in Britain honor had applause)
Each parent sprung — — —A. What fortune,
    pray? — — —P. Their own,
And better got than Bestia's from the throne.
Born to no pride, inheriting no strife,
Nor marrying discord in a noble wife,
Stranger to civil and religious rage,
The good man walked innoxious through his age.
No courts he saw, no suits would ever try,
Nor dared an oath, nor hazarded a lie.
Unlearn'd, he knew no schoolman's subtle art,
No language but the language of the heart.
By nature honest, by experience wise,
Healthy by temperature, and by exercise;
His life, though long, to sickness passed unknown,
His death was instant, and without a groan.
Oh, grant me thus to live, and thus to die!
Who sprung from kings shall know less joy than I.
    O friend! may each domestic bliss be thine!
Be no unpleasing melancholy mine:
Me, let the tender office long engage,
To rock the cradle of reposing Age,
With lenient arts extend a mother's breath,
Make Languor smile, and smooth the bed of Death,
Explore the thought explain the asking eye,
And keep a while one parent from the sky!

On cares like these if length of days attend,
May heaven, to bless those days, preserve my friend,
Preserve him social, cheerful, and serene,
And just as rich as when he served a Queen!
    A. Whether that blessing be denied or given,
Thus far was right—the rest belongs to Heaven.

---

*In a mode and style much indebted to Horace, Pope's epistle to his distinguished friend and physician is a dialogue inside a letter. The imagined responses of Arbuthnot identify him as the addressee and the interlocutor who boosts the movement of the satire, so that some editors label speeches in the poem "P." and "A." The dialogue of the epistle, is as much of a confessional autobiography as Pope cared to commit to paper. (Note that: "sped" is "ruined"; "snacks" is "shares"; "Templars" is "law students"; "rubric" is "in red"; "claps" is "posters"; "bit" is "deceived.")*

# An Essay on Criticism

#### PART 1

'Tis hard to say, if greater want of skill
Appear in writing or in judging ill;
But of the two less dangerous is the offense
To tire our patience than mislead our sense.
Some few in that, but numbers err in this,
Ten censure wrong for one who writes amiss;
A fool might once himself alone expose,
Now one in verse makes many more in prose.
 'Tis with our judgments as our watches, none
Go just alike, yet each believes his own.
In poets as true genius is but rare,
True taste as seldom is the critic's share;
Both must alike from Heaven derive their light,
These born to judge, as well as those to write.
Let such teach others who themselves excel,
And censure freely who have written well.
Authors are partial to their wit, 'tis true,
But are not critics to their judgment too?
 Yet if we look more closely, we shall find
Most have the seeds of judgment in their mind:
Nature affords at least a glimmering light;
The lines, though touched but faintly, are drawn right.
But as the slightest sketch, if justly traced, ⎫
Is by ill coloring but the more disgraced, ⎬
So by false learning is good sense defaced: ⎭
Some are bewildered in the maze of schools,
And some made coxcombs Nature meant but fools.
In search of wit these lose their common sense,
And then turn critics in their own defense:
Each burns alike, who can, or cannot write,
Or with a rival's or an eunuch's spite.
All fools have still an itching to deride,

And fain would be upon the laughing side.
If Maevius scribble in Apollo's spite,
There are who judge still worse than he can write.
  Some have at first for wits, then poets passed,
Turned critics next, and proved plain fools at last.
Some neither can for wits nor critics pass,
As heavy mules are neither horse nor ass.
Those half-learn'd witlings, numerous in our isle,
As half-formed insects on the banks of Nile;
Unfinished things, one knows not what to call,
Their generation's so equivocal:
To tell them would a hundred tongues require,
Or one vain wit's, that might a hundred tire.
  But you who seek to give and merit fame,
And justly bear a critic's noble name,
Be sure yourself and your own reach to know,
How far your genius, taste, and learning go;
Launch not beyond your depth, but be discreet,
And mark that point where sense and dullness meet.
  Nature to all things fixed the limits fit,
And wisely curbed proud man's pretending wit.
As on the land while here the ocean gains,
In other parts it leaves wide sandy plains;
Thus in the soul while memory prevails,
The solid power of understanding fails;
Where beams of warm imagination play,
The memory's soft figures melt away.
One science only will one genius fit,
So vast is art, so narrow human wit.
Not only bounded to peculiar arts,
But oft in those confined to single parts.
Like kings we lose the conquests gained before,
By vain ambition still to make them more;
Each might his several province well command,
Would all but stoop to what they understand.
  First follow Nature, and your judgment frame
By her just standard, which is still the same;
Unerring Nature, still divinely bright,

One clear, unchanged, and universal light,
Life, force, and beauty must to all impart,
At once the source, and end, and test of art.
Art from that fund each just supply provides,
Works without show, and without pomp presides.
In some fair body thus the informing soul
With spirits feeds, with vigor fills the whole,
Each motion guides, and every nerve sustains;
Itself unseen, but in the effects remains.
Some, to whom Heaven in wit has been profuse,
Want as much more to turn it to its use;
For wit and judgment often are at strife,
Though meant each other's aid, like man and wife.
'Tis more to guide than spur the Muse's steed,
Restrain his fury than provoke his speed;
The wingèd courser, like a generous horse,
Shows most true mettle when you check his course.

Those rules of old discovered, not devised,
Are Nature still, but Nature methodized;
Nature, like liberty, is but restrained
By the same laws which first herself ordained.

Hear how learn'd Greece her useful rules indites,
When to repress and when indulge our flights:
High on Parnassus' top her sons she showed,
And pointed out those arduous paths they trod;
Held from afar, aloft, the immortal prize,
And urged the rest by equal steps to rise.
Just precepts thus from great examples given,
She drew from them what they derived from Heaven.
The generous critic fanned the poet's fire,
And taught the world with reason to admire.
Then criticism the Muse's handmaid proved,
To dress her charms, and make her more beloved:
But following wits from that intention strayed,
Who could not win the mistress, wooed the maid;
Against the poets their own arms they turned,
Sure to hate most the men from whom they learned.
So modern 'pothecaries, taught the art

By doctor's bills to play the doctor's part,
Bold in the practice of mistaken rules,
Prescribe, apply, and call their masters fools.
Some on the leaves of ancient authors prey,
Nor time nor moths e'er spoiled so much as they.
Some dryly plain, without invention's aid,
Write dull receipts how poems may be made.
These leave the sense their learning to display,
And those explain the meaning quite away.
   You then whose judgment the right course would steer,
Know well each ancient's proper character;
His fable, subject, scope in every page;
Religion, country, genius of his age:
Without all these at once before your eyes,
Cavil you may, but never criticize.
Be Homer's works your study and delight,
Read them by day, and meditate by night;
Thence form your judgment, thence your maxims bring,
And trace the Muses upward to their spring.
Still with itself compared, his text peruse;
And let your comment be the Mantuan Muse.
   When first young Maro in his boundless mind
A work to outlast immortal Rome designed,
Perhaps he seemed above the critic's law,
And but from Nature's fountains scorned to draw;
But when to examine every part he came,
Nature and Homer were, he found, the same.
Convinced, amazed, he checks the bold design, ⎫
And rules as strict his labored work confine ⎬
As if the Stagirite o'erlooked each line. ⎭
Learn hence for ancient rules a just esteem;
To copy Nature is to copy them.
   Some beauties yet no precepts can declare,
For there's a happiness as well as care.
Music resembles poetry, in each ⎫
Are nameless graces which no methods teach, ⎬
And which a master hand alone can reach. ⎭
If, where the rules not far enough extend

(Since rules were made but to promote their end)
Some lucky license answers to the full
The intent proposed, that license is a rule.
Thus Pegasus, a nearer way to take,
May boldly deviate from the common track.
From vulgar bounds with brave disorder part,
And snatch a grace beyond the reach of art,
Which without passing through the judgment, gains
The heart, and all its end at once attains.
In prospects thus, some objects please our eyes, ⎫
Which out of Nature's common order rise, ⎬
The shapeless rock, or hanging precipice. ⎭
Great wits sometimes may gloriously offend,
And rise to faults true critics dare not mend;
But though the ancients thus their rules invade
(As kings dispense with laws themselves have made)
Moderns, beware! or if you must offend
Against the precept, ne'er transgress its end;
Let it be seldom, and compelled by need;
And have at least their precedent to plead.
The critic else proceeds without remorse,
Seizes your fame, and puts his laws in force.

    I know there are, to whose presumptuous thoughts
Those freer beauties, even in them, seem faults.
Some figures monstrous and misshaped appear,
Considered singly, or beheld too near,
Which, but proportioned to their light or place,
Due distance reconciles to form and grace.
A prudent chief not always must display
His powers in equal ranks and fair array,
But with the occasion and the place comply,
Conceal his force, nay seem sometimes to fly.
Those oft are stratagems which errors seem,
Nor is it Homer nods, but we that dream.

    Still green with bays each ancient altar stands
Above the reach of sacrilegious hands,
Secure from flames, from envy's fiercer rage,
Destructive war, and all-involving age.

See, from each clime the learn'd their incense bring!
Here in all tongues consenting paeans ring!
In praise so just let every voice be joined,
And fill the general chorus of mankind.
Hail, bards triumphant! born in happier days,
Immortal heirs of universal praise!
Whose honors with increase of ages grow,
As streams roll down, enlarging as they flow;
Nations unborn your mighty names shall sound,
And worlds applaud that must not yet be found!
Oh, may some spark of your celestial fire,
The last, the meanest of your sons inspire
(That on weak wings, from far, pursues your flights,
Glows while he reads, but trembles as he writes)
To teach vain wits a science little known,
To admire superior sense, and doubt their own!

PART 2

Of all the causes which conspire to blind
Man's erring judgment, and misguide the mind,
What the weak head with strongest bias rules,
Is pride, the never-failing vice of fools.
Whatever Nature has in worth denied,
She gives in large recruits of needful pride;
For as in bodies, thus in souls, we find
What wants in blood and spirits swelled with wind:
Pride, where wit fails, steps in to our defense,
And fills up all the mighty void of sense.
If once right reason drives that cloud away,
Truth breaks upon us with resistless day.
Trust not yourself: but your defects to know,
Make use of every friend—and every foe.
   A little learning is a dangerous thing;
Drink deep, or taste not the Pierian spring.
There shallow draughts intoxicate the brain,
And drinking largely sobers us again.
Fired at first sight with what the Muse imparts,
In fearless youth we tempt the heights of arts,

While from the bounded level of our mind
Short views we take, nor see the lengths behind;
But more advanced, behold with strange surprise
New distant scenes of endless science rise!
So pleased at first the towering Alps we try,
Mount o'er the vales, and seem to tread the sky,
The eternal snows appear already past,
And the first clouds and mountains seem the last;
But, those attained, we tremble to survey
The growing labors of the lengthened way,
The increasing prospect tires our wandering eyes,
Hills peep o'er hills, and Alps on Alps arise!
   A perfect judge will read each work of wit
With the same spirit that its author writ:
Survey the whole, nor seek slight faults to find
Where Nature moves, and rapture warms the mind;
Nor lose, for that malignant dull delight,
The generous pleasure to be charmed with wit.
But in such lays as neither ebb nor flow,
Correctly cold, and regularly low,
That, shunning faults, one quiet tenor keep,
We cannot blame indeed—but we may sleep.
In wit, as nature, what affects our hearts
Is not the exactness of peculiar parts;
'Tis not a lip, or eye, we beauty call,
But the joint force and full result of all.
Thus when we view some well-proportioned dome
(The world's just wonder, and even thine, O Rome!),
No single parts unequally surprise,
All comes united to the admiring eyes:
No monstrous height, or breadth, or length appear;
The whole at once is bold and regular.
   Whoever thinks a faultless piece to see,
Thinks what ne'er was, nor is, nor e'er shall be.
In every work regard the writer's end,
Since none can compass more than they intend;
And if the means be just, the conduct true,
Applause, in spite of trivial faults, is due.

As men of breeding, sometimes men of wit,
To avoid great errors must the less commit,
Neglect the rules each verbal critic lays,
For not to know some trifles is a praise.
Most critics, fond of some subservient art,
Still make the whole depend upon a part:
They talk of principles, but notions prize,
And all to one loved folly sacrifice.
    Once on a time La Mancha's knight, they say,
A certain bard encountering on the way,
Discoursed in terms as just, with looks as sage,
As e'er could Dennis, of the Grecian stage;
Concluding all were desperate sots and fools
Who durst depart from Aristotle's rules.
Our author, happy in a judge so nice,
Produced his play, and begged the knight's advice;
Made him observe the subject and the plot,
The manners, passions, unities; what not?
All which exact to rule were brought about,
Were but a combat in the lists left out.
"What! leave the combat out?" exclaims the knight.
"Yes, or we must renounce the Stagirite."
"Not so, by Heaven!" he answers in a rage,
"Knights, squires, and steeds must enter on the stage."
"So vast a throng the stage can ne'er contain."
"Then build a new, or act it in a plain."
    Thus critics of less judgment than caprice,
Curious, not knowing, not exact, but nice,
Form short ideas, and offend in arts
(As most in manners), by a love to parts.
    Some to conceit alone their taste confine,
And glittering thoughts struck out at every line;
Pleased with a work where nothing's just or fit,
One glaring chaos and wild heap of wit.
Poets, like painters, thus unskilled to trace
The naked nature and the living grace,
With gold and jewels cover every part,
And hide with ornaments their want of art.

True wit is Nature to advantage dressed,
What oft was thought, but ne'er so well expressed;
Something whose truth convinced at sight we find,
That gives us back the image of our mind.
As shades more sweetly recommend the light,
So modest plainness sets off sprightly wit;
For works may have more wit than does them good,
As bodies perish through excess of blood.
  Others for language all their care express,
And value books, as women men, for dress.
Their praise is still—the style is excellent;
The sense they humbly take upon contènt.
Words are like leaves; and where they most abound,
Much fruit of sense beneath is rarely found.
False eloquence, like the prismatic glass,
Its gaudy colors spreads on every place;
The face of Nature we no more survey,
All glares alike, without distinction gay.
But true expression, like the unchanging sun, ⎫
Clears and improves whate'er it shines upon; ⎬
It gilds all objects, but it alters none. ⎭
Expression is the dress of thought, and still
Appears more decent as more suitable.
A vile conceit in pompous words expressed
Is like a clown in regal purple dressed:
For different styles with different subjects sort,
As several garbs with country, town, and court.
Some by old words to fame have made pretense,
Ancients in phrase, mere moderns in their sense.
Such labored nothings, in so strange a style,
Amaze the unlearn'd, and make the learned smile;
Unlucky as Fungoso in the play, ⎫
These sparks with awkward vanity display ⎬
What the fine gentleman wore yesterday; ⎭
And but so mimic ancient wits at best,
As apes our grandsires in their doublets dressed.
In words as fashions the same rule will hold,
Alike fantastic if too new or old:

Be not the first by whom the new are tried,
Nor yet the last to lay the old aside.
   But most by numbers judge a poet's song,
And smooth or rough with them is right or wrong.
In the bright Muse though thousand charms conspire,
Her voice is all these tuneful fools admire,
Who haunt Parnassus but to please their ear,   ⎫
Not mend their minds; as some to church repair,  ⎬
Not for the doctrine, but the music there.      ⎭
These equal syllables alone require,
Though oft the ear the open vowels tire,
While expletives their feeble aid do join,
And ten low words oft creep in one dull line:
While they ring round the same unvaried chimes,
With sure returns of still expected rhymes;
Where'er you find "the cooling western breeze,"
In the next line, it "whispers through the trees";
If crystal streams "with pleasing murmurs creep,"
The reader's threatened (not in vain) with "sleep";
Then, at the last and only couplet fraught
With some unmeaning thing they call a thought,
A needless Alexandrine ends the song
That, like a wounded snake, drags its slow length along.
Leave such to tune their own dull rhymes, and know
What's roundly smooth or languishingly slow;
And praise the easy vigor of a line
Where Denham's strength and Waller's sweetness join.
True ease in writing comes from art, not chance,
As those move easiest who have learned to dance.
'Tis not enough no harshness gives offense,
The sound must seem an echo to the sense.
Soft is the strain when Zephyr gently blows,
And the smooth stream in smoother numbers flows;
But when loud surges lash the sounding shore,
The hoarse, rough verse should like the torrent roar.
When Ajax strives some rock's vast weight to throw,
The line too labors, and the words move slow;
Not so when swift Camilla scours the plain,

Flies o'er the unbending corn, and skims along the main.
Hear how Timotheus' varied lays surprise,
And bid alternate passions fall and rise!
While at each change the son of Libyan Jove
Now burns with glory, and then melts with love;
Now his fierce eyes with sparkling fury glow,
Now sighs steal out, and tears begin to flow:
Persians and Greeks like turns of nature found
And the world's victor stood subdued by sound!
The power of music all our hearts allow,
And what Timotheus was is Dryden now.

    Avoid extremes; and shun the fault of such
Who still are pleased too little or too much.
At every trifle scorn to take offense:
That always shows great pride, or little sense.
Those heads, as stomachs, are not sure the best,
Which nauseate all, and nothing can digest.
Yet let not each gay turn thy rapture move;
For fools admire, but men of sense approve:
As things seem large which we through mists descry,
Dullness is ever apt to magnify.

    Some foreign writers, some our own despise;
The ancients only, or the moderns prize.
Thus wit, like faith, by each man is applied
To one small sect, and all are damned beside.
Meanly they seek the blessing to confine,
And force that sun but on a part to shine,
Which not alone the southern wit sublimes,
But ripens spirits in cold northern climes;
Which from the first has shone on ages past,
Enlights the present, and shall warm the last;
Though each may feel increases and decays,
And see now clearer and now darker days.
Regard not then if wit be old or new,
But blame the false and value still the true.

    Some ne'er advance a judgment of their own,
But catch the spreading notion of the town;
They reason and conclude by precedent,

And own stale nonsense which they ne'er invent.
Some judge of authors' names, not works, and then
Nor praise nor blame the writings, but the men.
Of all this servile herd the worst is he
That in proud dullness joins with quality,
A constant critic at the great man's board,
To fetch and carry nonsense for my lord.
What woeful stuff this madrigal would be
In some starved hackney sonneteer or me!
But let a lord once own the happy lines,
How the wit brightens! how the style refines!
Before his sacred name flies every fault,
And each exalted stanza teems with thought!
    The vulgar thus through imitation err;
As oft the learn'd by being singular;
So much they scorn the crowd, that if the throng
By chance go right, they purposely go wrong.
So schismatics the plain believers quit,
And are but damned for having too much wit.
Some praise at morning what they blame at night,
But always think the last opinion right.
A Muse by these is like a mistress used,
This hour she's idolized, the next abused;
While their weak heads like towns unfortified,
'Twixt sense and nonsense daily change their side.
Ask them the cause; they're wiser still, they say;
And still tomorrow's wiser than today.
We think our fathers fools, so wise we grow;
Our wiser sons, no doubt, will think us so.
Once school divines this zealous isle o'erspread;
Who knew most sentences was deepest read.
Faith, Gospel, all seemed made to be disputed,
And none had sense enough to be confuted.
Scotists and Thomists now in peace remain
Amidst their kindred cobwebs in Duck Lane.
If faith itself has different dresses worn,
What wonder modes in wit should take their turn?
Oft, leaving what is natural and fit,

The current folly proves the ready wit;
And authors think their reputation safe,
Which lives as long as fools are pleased to laugh.
  Some valuing those of their own side or mind,
Still make themselves the measure of mankind:
Fondly we think we honor merit then,
When we but praise ourselves in other men.
Parties in wit attend on those of state,
And public faction doubles private hate.
Pride, Malice, Folly against Dryden rose,
In various shapes of parsons, critics, beaux;
But sense survived, when merry jests were past;
For rising merit will buoy up at last.
Might he return and bless once more our eyes,
New Blackmores and new Milbourns must arise.
Nay, should great Homer lift his awful head,
Zoilus again would start up from the dead.
Envy will merit, as its shade, pursue,
But like a shadow, proves the substance true;
For envied wit, like Sol eclipsed, makes known
The opposing body's grossness, not its own.
When first that sun too powerful beams displays,
It draws up vapors which obscure its rays;
But even those clouds at last adorn its way,
Reflect new glories, and augment the day.
  Be thou the first true merit to befriend;
His praise is lost who stays till all commend.
Short is the date, alas! of modern rhymes,
And 'tis but just to let them live betimes.
No longer now that golden age appears,
When patriarch wits survived a thousand years:
Now length of fame (our second life) is lost,
And bare threescore is all even that can boast;
Our sons their fathers' failing language see,
And such as Chaucer is shall Dryden be.
So when the faithful pencil has designed
Some bright idea of the master's mind,
Where a new world leaps out at his command,

And ready Nature waits upon his hand;
When the ripe colors soften and unite,
And sweetly melt into just shade and light;
When mellowing years their full perfection give,
And each bold figure just begins to live,
The treacherous colors the fair art betray,
And all the bright creation fades away!
   Unhappy wit, like most mistaken things,
Atones not for that envy which it brings.
In youth alone its empty praise we boast,
But soon the short-lived vanity is lost;
Like some fair flower the early spring supplies,
That gaily blooms, but even in blooming dies,
What is this wit, which must our cares employ?
The owner's wife, that other men enjoy;
Then most our trouble still when most admired,
And still the more we give, the more required;
Whose fame with pains we guard, but lose with ease,
Sure some to vex, but never all to please;
'Tis what the vicious fear, the virtuous shun,
By fools 'tis hated, and by knaves undone!
   If wit so much from ignorance undergo,
Ah, let not learning too commence its foe!
Of old those met rewards who could excel,
And such were praised who but endeavored well;
Though triumphs were to generals only due,
Crowns were reserved to grace the soldiers too.
Now they who reach Parnassus' lofty crown
Employ their pains to spurn some others down;
And while self-love each jealous writer rules,
Contending wits become the sport of fools;
But still the worst with most regret commend,
For each ill author is as bad a friend.
To what base ends, and by what abject ways,
Are mortals urged through sacred lust of praise!
Ah, ne'er so dire a thirst of glory boast,
Nor in the critic let the man be lost!

Good nature and good sense must ever join;
To err is human, to forgive divine.
　But if in noble minds some dregs remain
Nor yet purged off, of spleen and sour disdain,
Discharge that rage on more provoking crimes,
Nor fear a dearth in these flagitious times.
No pardon vile obscenity should find,
Though wit and art conspire to move your mind;
But dullness with obscenity must prove
As shameful sure as impotence in love.
In the fat age of pleasure, wealth, and ease
Sprung the rank weed, and thrived with large increase:
When love was all an easy monarch's care,
Seldom at council, never in a war;
Jilts ruled the state, and statesmen farces writ;
Nay, wits had pensions, and young lords had wit;
The fair sat panting at a courtier's play,
And not a mask went unimproved away;
The modest fan was lifted up no more,
And virgins smiled at what they blushed before.
The following license of a foreign reign
Did all the dregs of bold Socinus drain;
Then unbelieving priests reformed the nation,
And taught more pleasant methods of salvation;
Where Heaven's free subjects might their rights dispute,
Lest God himself should seem too absolute;
Pulpits their sacred satire learned to spare,
And Vice admired to find a flatterer there!
Encouraged thus, wit's Titans braved the skies,
And the press groaned with licensed blasphemies.
These monsters, critics! with your darts engage,
Here point your thunder, and exhaust your rage!
Yet shun their fault, who, scandalously nice,
Will needs mistake an author into vice;
All seems infected that the infected spy,
As all looks yellow to the jaundiced eye.

PART 3

Learn then what morals critics ought to show,
For 'tis but half a judge's task, to know.
'Tis not enough, taste, judgment, learning, join;
In all you speak, let truth and candor shine:
That not alone what to your sense is due
All may allow; but seek your friendship too.

Be silent always when you doubt your sense;
And speak, though sure, with seeming diffidence:
Some positive, persisting fops we know,
Who, if once wrong, will needs be always so;
But you, with pleasure own your errors past,
And make each day a critic on the last.

'Tis not enough, your counsel still be true;
Blunt truths more mischief than nice falsehoods do;
Men must be taught as if you taught them not,
And things unknown proposed as things forgot.
Without good breeding, truth is disapproved;
That only makes superior sense beloved.

Be niggards of advice on no pretense;
For the worst avarice is that of sense.
With mean complacence ne'er betray your trust,
Nor be so civil as to prove unjust.
Fear not the anger of the wise to raise;
Those best can bear reproof, who merit praise.

'Twere well might critics still this freedom take;
But Appius reddens at each word you speak,
And stares, tremendous! with a threatening eye,
Like some fierce tyrant in old tapestry.
Fear most to tax an honorable fool,
Whose right it is, uncensured to be dull;
Such, without wit, are poets when they please,
As without learning they can take degrees.
Leave dangerous truths to unsuccessful satyrs,
And flattery to fulsome dedicators,
Whom, when they praise, the world believes no more,
Than when they promise to give scribbling o'er.

'Tis best sometimes your censure to restrain,
And charitably let the dull be vain:
Your silence there is better than your spite,
For who can rail so long as they can write?
Still humming on, their drowsy course they keep,
And lashed so long, like tops, are lashed asleep.
False steps but help them to renew the race,
As, after stumbling, jades will mend their pace.
What crowds of these, impenitently bold,
In sounds and jingling syllables grown old,
Still run on poets, in a raging vein,
Even to the dregs and squeezings of the brain,
Strain out the last dull droppings of their sense,
And rhyme with all the rage of impotence.
    Such shameless bards we have, and yet 'tis true,
There are as mad, abandoned critics too.
The bookful blockhead, ignorantly read,
With loads of learned lumber in his head.
With his own tongue still edifies his ears,
And always listening to himself appears.
All books he reads, and all he reads assails,
From Dryden's *Fables* down to Durfey's *Tales*.
With him, most authors steal their works, or buy;
Garth did not write his own *Dispensary*.
Name a new play, and he's the poet's friend,
Nay showed his faults—but when would poets mend?
No place so sacred from such fops is barred,
Nor is Paul's church more safe than Paul's churchyard:
Nay, fly to altars; *there* they'll talk you dead:
For fools rush in where angels fear to tread.
Distrustful sense with modest caution speaks, ⎫
It still looks home, and short excursions makes; ⎬
But rattling nonsense in full volleys breaks, ⎭
And never shocked, and never turned aside,
Bursts out, resistless, with a thundering tide.
    But where's the man, who counsel can bestow,
Still pleased to teach, and yet not proud to know?
Unbiased, or by favor, or by spite:

Not dully prepossessed, nor blindly right;
Though learned, well-bred; and though well-bred, sincere;
Modestly bold, and humanly severe:
Who to a friend his faults can freely show,
And gladly praise the merit of a foe?
Blessed with a taste exact, yet unconfined;
A knowledge both of books and humankind;
Gen'rous converse; a soul exempt from pride;
And love to praise, with reason on his side?
   Such once were critics; such the happy few,
Athens and Rome in better ages knew.
The mighty Stagirite first left the shore,
Spread all his sails, and durst the deeps explore;
He steered securely, and discovered far,
Led by the light of the Mæonian star.
Poets, a race long unconfined, and free,
Still fond and proud of savage liberty,
Received his laws; and stood convinced 'twas fit,
Who conquered nature, should preside o'er wit.
   Horace still charms with graceful negligence,
And without method talks us into sense;
Will, like a friend, familiarly convey
The truest notions in the easiest way.
He, who supreme in judgment, as in wit,
Might boldly censure, as he boldly writ,
Yet judged with coolness, though he sung with fire;
His precepts teach but what his works inspire.
Our critics take a contrary extreme,
They judge with fury, but they write with fle'me.
Nor suffers Horace more in wrong translations
By wits, than critics in as wrong quotations.
   See Dionysius Homer's thoughts refine,
And call new beauties forth from every line!
   Fancy and art in gay Petronius please,
The scholar's learning, with the courtier's ease.
   In grave Quintilian's copious work, we find
The justest rules, and clearest method joined:
Thus useful arms in magazines we place,

All ranged in order, and disposed with grace,
But less to please the eye, than arm the hand,
Still fit for use, and ready at command.
    Thee, bold Longinus! all the nine inspire,
And bless their critic with a poet's fire.
An ardent judge, who, zealous in his trust,
With warmth gives sentence, yet is always just;
Whose own example strengthens all his laws,
And is himself that great sublime he draws.
    Thus long succeeding critics justly reigned,
License repressed, and useful laws ordained.
Learning and Rome alike in empire grew;
And arts still followed where her eagles flew;
From the same foes, at last, both felt their doom,
And the same age saw learning fall, and Rome.
With tyranny, then superstition joined,
As that the body, this enslaved the mind;
Much was believed, but little understood,
And to be dull was construed to be good;
A second deluge learning thus o'errun,
And the monks finished what the Goths begun.
    At length Erasmus, that great, injured name
(The glory of the priesthood, and the shame!),
Stemmed the wild torrent of a barb'rous age,
And drove those holy Vandals off the stage.
    But see! each Muse, in Leo's golden days,
Starts from her trance, and trims her withered bays!
Rome's ancient Genius, o'er its ruins spread,
Shakes off the dust, and rears his reverend head.
Then sculpture and her sister-arts revive;
Stones leaped to form, and rocks began to live;
With sweeter notes each rising temple rung;
A Raphael painted, and a Vida sung.
Immortal Vida: on whose honored brow
The poet's bays and critic's ivy grow:
Cremona now shall ever boast thy name,
As next in place to Mantua, next in fame!

But soon by impious arms from Latium chased,
Their ancient bounds the banished Muses passed;
Thence arts o'er all the northern world advance,
But critic-learning flourished most in France:
The rules a nation, born to serve, obeys;
And Boileau still in right of Horace sways.
But we, brave Britons, foreign laws despised,
And kept unconquered—and uncivilized;
Fierce for the liberties of wit, and bold,
We still defied the Romans, as of old.
Yet some there were, among the sounder few
Of those who less presumed, and better knew,
Who durst assert the juster ancient cause,
And here restored wit's fundamental laws.
Such was the Muse, whose rules and practice tell,
"Nature's chief masterpiece is writing well."
Such was Roscommon, not more learned than good,
With manners gen'rous as his noble blood;
To him the wit of Greece and Rome was known,
And every author's merit, but his own.
Such late was Walsh—the Muse's judge and friend,
Who justly knew to blame or to commend;
To failings mild, but zealous for desert;
The clearest head, and the sincerest heart.
This humble praise, lamented shade! receive,
This praise at least a grateful Muse may give:
The Muse, whose early voice you taught to sing,
Prescribed her heights, and pruned her tender wing,
(Her guide now lost) no more attempts to rise,
But in low numbers short excursions tries:
Content, if hence the unlearned their wants may view,
The learned reflect on what before they knew:
Careless of censure, nor too fond of fame;
Still pleased to praise, yet not afraid to blame;
Averse alike to flatter, or offend;
Not free from faults, nor yet too vain to mend.

*Pope produced his effervescent essay at about the age of twenty. The period around 1710 was probably the last time anybody writing literary criticism in Europe could in effect limit his inquiry to poetry. Pope's main exemplars are Horace and Boileau, to whom he acknowledges his debt. A verse essay on verse labors under the double burden of needing to succeed as precept and as example. (Note that: "to tell them" is "to tally them"; "science" is "branch of knowledge"; "doctors' bills" is "prescriptions"; "receipts" is "recipes"; "tempt" is "attempt"; "clown" is "hick"; "flagitious" is "scandalously evil"; "lumber" is "trash"; "fle'me" is "phlegm"; "low numbers" is "humble poems.")*

We think so much of Samuel Johnson, the imposing "Doctor Johnson," that we call his day the Age of Johnson, reflecting chiefly his stature both as a great lexicographer and prose-writer and as the subject of what is indisputably the most wonderful literary biography in the language. We are likely to forget the Samuel Johnson who was also among the finest poets of his age. Although he died more than 200 years ago, his example remains brightly in view when we think about the history of periodical writing, biography, dictionaries, the profession of the writer, and the place of the "man of letters."

# A Short Song of Congratulation

≫≫≫≫≫

Long-expected one and twenty
　　Ling'ring year at last is flown,
Pomp and pleasure, pride and plenty,
　　Great Sir John, are all your own.

Loosened from the minor's tether;
　　Free to mortgage or to sell,
Wild as wind, and light as feather
　　Bid the slaves of thrift farewell.

Call the Bettys, Kates, and Jennys
　　Every name that laughs at care,
Lavish of your grandsire's guineas,
　　Show the spirit of an heir.

All that prey on vice and folly
　　Joy to see their quarry fly:
Here the gamester light and jolly,
　　There the lender grave and sly.

Wealth, Sir John, was made to wander,
  Let it wander as it will;
See the jockey, see the pander,
  Bid them come, and take their fill.

When the bonny blade carouses,
  Pockets full, and spirits high,
What are acres? What are houses?
  Only dirt, or wet or dry.

If the guardian or the mother
  Tell the woes of willful waste,
Scorn their counsel and their pother,
  You can hang or drown at last.

---

*Johnson included this marvel of irony in a letter to Hester Thrale, saying, "You have heard in the papers how Sir J. Lade is come to age, I have enclosed a short song of congratulation, which you must not show to any body . . . ." Sir John was a notorious hell-raiser. He happened to be Mrs. Thrale's nephew, and he came to no good.*

# On the Death of Mr. Robert Levet, a Practiser in Physic

Condemned to Hope's delusive mine,
    As on we toil from day to day,
By sudden blasts or slow decline
    Our social comforts drop away.

Well tried through many a varying year,
    See Levet to the grave descend;
Officious, innocent, sincere,
    Of every friendless name the friend.

Yet still he fills affection's eye,
    Obscurely wise and coarsely kind;
Nor, lettered Arrogance, deny
    Thy praise to merit unrefined.

When fainting nature called for aid,
    And hovering death prepared the blow,
His vigorous remedy displayed
    The power of art without the show.

In Misery's darkest cavern known,
    His useful care was ever nigh,
Where hopeless Anguish poured his groan,
    And lonely Want retired to die.

No summons mocked by chill delay,
    No petty gain disdained by pride;
The modest wants of every day
    The toil of every day supplied.

His virtues walked their narrow round,
   Nor made a pause, nor left a void;
And sure the Eternal Master found
   The single talent well employed.

The busy day, the peaceful night,
   Unfelt, uncounted, glided by;
His frame was firm—his powers were bright,
   Though now his eightieth year was nigh.

Then with no fiery throbbing pain,
   No cold gradations of decay,
Death broke at once the vital chain,
   And freed his soul the nearest way.

---

*By as much as Sir John Lade (in "A Short Song of Congratulation," p. 312) falls short of decency, Robert Levet—sometimes styled "Doctor" although he was not licensed—exceeded normal expectations. Although ungainly and grotesque, Levet had a good heart and knew enough about medicine to be of help to those in need. He lived for many years in Johnson's house. (Note that: "officious" is "kind," "performing good works.")*

# The Vanity of Human Wishes:
# The Tenth Satire of Juvenal Imitated

❖❖❖❖❖

Let Observation with extensive View,
Survey Mankind, from *China to Peru*;
Remark each anxious Toil, each eager Strife,
And watch the busy Scenes of crouded Life;
Then say how Hope and Fear, Desire and Hate,
O'erspread with Snares the clouded Maze of Fate,
Where wav'ring Man, betray'd by vent'rous Pride,
To tread the dreary Paths without a Guide;
As treach'rous Phantoms in the Mist delude,
Shuns fancied Ills, or chases airy Good.
How rarely Reason guides the stubborn Choice,
Rules the bold Hand, or prompts the suppliant Voice,
How Nations sink, by darling Schemes oppress'd,
When Vengeance listens to the Fool's Request.
Fate wings with ev'ry Wish th' afflictive Dart,
Each Gift of Nature, and each Grace of Art,
With fatal Heat impetuous Courage glows,
With fatal Sweetness Elocution flows,
Impeachment stops the Speaker's pow'rful Breath,
And restless Fire precipitates on Death.

But scarce observ'd the Knowing and the Bold,
Fall in the gen'ral Massacre of Gold;
Wide-wasting Pest! that rages unconfin'd,
And crouds with Crimes the Records of Mankind,
For Gold his Sword the Hireling Ruffian draws,
For Gold the hireling Judge distorts the Laws;
Wealth heap'd on Wealth, nor Truth nor Safety buys,
The Dangers gather as the Treasures rise.

Let Hist'ry tell where rival Kings command,
And dubious Title shakes the madded Land,
When Statutes glean the Refuse of the Sword,
How much more safe the Vassal than the Lord,

Low sculks the Hind beneath the Rage of Pow'r,
And leaves the wealthy Traytor in the *Tow'r*,
Untouch'd his Cottage, and his Slumbers sound,
Tho' Confiscation's Vulturs hover round.
    The needy Traveller, serene and gay,
Walks the wild Heath, and sings his Toil away.
Dos Envy seize thee? crush th' upbraiding Joy,
Increase his Riches and his Peace destroy,
Now Fears in dire Vicissitude invade,
The rustling Brake alarms, and quiv'ring Shade,
Nor Light nor Darkness bring his Pain Relief,
One shews the Plunder, and one hides the Thief.
    Yet still one gen'ral Cry the Skies assails,
And Gain and Grandeur load the tainted Gales;
Few know the toiling Statesman's Fear or Care,
Th' insidious Rival and the gaping Heir.
    Once more, *Democritus*, arise on Earth,
With chearful Wisdom and instructive Mirth,
See motly Life in modern Trappings dress'd,
And feed with varied Fools th' eternal Jest:
Thou who couldst laugh where Want enchain'd Caprice
Toil crush'd Conceit, and Man was of a Piece;
Where Wealth unlov'd without a Mourner dy'd;
And scarce a Sycophant was fed by Pride;
Where ne'er was known the Form of mock Debate,
Or seen a new-made Mayor's unwieldly State;
Where Change of Fav'rites made no Change of Laws,
And Senates heard before they judg'd a Cause;
How wouldst thou shake at *Britain's* modish Tribe,
Dart the quick Taunt, and edge the piercing Gibe?
Attentive Truth and Nature to descry,
And pierce each Scene with Philosophic Eye.
To thee were solemn Toys or empty Shew,
The Robes of Pleasure and the Veils of Woe:
All aid the Farce, and all thy Mirth maintain,
Whose Joys are causeless, or whose Griefs are vain.
    Such was the Scorn that fill'd the Sage's Mind,
Renew'd at ev'ry Glance on Humankind;

How just that Scorn ere yet thy Voice declare,
Search every State, and canvass ev'ry Pray'r.
　　Unnumber'd Suppliants croud Preferment's Gate,
Athirst for Wealth, and burning to be great;
Delusive Fortune hears th' incessant Call,
They mount, they shine, evaporate, and fall.
On ev'ry Stage the Foes of Peace attend,
Hate dogs their Flight, and Insult mocks their End.
Love ends with Hope, the sinking Statesman's Door
Pours in the Morning Worshiper no more;
For growing Names the weekly Scribbler lies,
To growing Wealth the Dedicator flies,
From every Room descends the painted Face,
That hung the bright *Palladium* of the Place,
And smoak'd in Kitchens, or in Auctions sold,
To better Features yields the Frame of Gold;
For now no more we trace in ev'ry Line
Heroic Worth, Benevolence Divine:
The Form distorted justifies the Fall,
And Detestation rids th' indignant Wall.
　　But will not *Britain* hear the last Appeal,
Sign her Foes Doom, or guard her Fav'rites Zeal;
Through Freedom's Sons no more Remonstrance rings,
Degrading Nobles and controuling Kings;
Our supple Tribes repress their Patriot Throats,
And ask no Questions but the Price of Votes;
With Weekly Libels and Septennial Ale,
Their Wish is full to riot and to rail.
　　In full-blown Dignity, see *Wolsey* stand,
Law in his Voice, and Fortune in his Hand:
To him the Church, the Realm, their Pow'rs consign,
Thro' him the Rays of regal Bounty shine,
Turn'd by his Nod the Stream of Honour flows,
His Smile alone Security bestows:
Still to new Heights his restless Wishes tow'r,
Claim leads to Claim, and Pow'r advances Pow'r;
Till Conquest unresisted ceas'd to please,
And Rights submitted, left him none to seize.

At length his Sov'reign frowns—the Train of State
Mark the keen Glance, and watch the Sign to hate;
Where-e'er he turns he meets a Stranger's Eye,
His Suppliants scorn him, and his Followers fly;
Now drops at once the Pride of aweful State,
The golden Canopy, the glitt'ring Plate,
The regal Palace, the luxurious Board,
The liv'ried Army, and the menial Lord.
With Age, with Cares, with Maladies oppress'd,
He seeks the Refuge of Monastic Rest.
Grief aids Disease, remember'd Folly stings,
And his last Sighs reproach the Faith of Kings.

    Speak thou, whose Thoughts at humble Peace repine,
Shall *Wolsey's* Wealth, with *Wolsey's* End be thine?
Or liv'st thou now, with safer Pride content,
The wisest Justice on the Banks of *Trent?*
For why did *Wolsey* near the Steeps of Fate,
On weak Foundations raise th' enormous Weight?
Why but to sink beneath Misfortune's Blow,
With louder Ruin to the Gulphs below?

    What gave great *Villiers* to th' Assassin's Knife,
And fix'd Disease on *Harley's* closing Life?
What murder'd *Wentworth*, and what exil'd *Hyde*,
By Kings protected, and to Kings ally'd?
What but their Wish indulg'd in Courts to shine,
And Pow'r too great to keep or to resign?

    When first the College Rolls receive his Name,
The young Enthusiast quits his Ease for Fame;
Through all his Veins the Fever of Renown
Burns from the strong Contagion of the Gown;
O'er *Bodley's* Dome his future Labours spread,
And *Bacon's* Mansion trembles o'er his Head.
Are these thy Views? proceed, illustrious Youth,
And Virtue guard thee to the Throne of Truth!
Yet should thy Soul indulge the gen'rous Heat,
Till captive Science yields her last Retreat;
Should Reason guide thee with her brightest Ray,
And pour on misty Doubt resistless Day;

Should no false Kindness lure to loose Delight,
Nor Praise relax, nor Difficulty fright;
Should tempting Novelty thy Cell refrain,
And Sloth effuse her opiate Fumes in vain;
Should Beauty blunt on Fops her fatal Dart,
Nor claim the Triumph of a letter'd Heart;
Should no Disease thy torpid Veins invade,
Nor Melancholy's Phantoms haunt thy Shade;
Yet hope not Life from Grief or Danger free,
Nor think the Doom of Man revers'd for thee:
Deign on the passing World to turn thine Eyes,
And pause awhile from Letters, to be wise;
These mark what Ills the Scholar's Life assail,
Toil, Envy, Want, the Patron, and the Jail.
See Nations slowly wise, and meanly just,
To buried Merit raise the tardy Bust.
If Dreams yet flatter, once again attend,
Hear *Lydiat's* life, and *Galileo's* end.

   Nor deem, when Learning her last Prize bestows
The glitt'ring Eminence exempt from Foes;
See when the Vulgar 'scape, despis'd or aw'd,
Rebellion's vengeful Talons seize on *Laud.*
From meaner Minds, tho' smaller Fines content
The plunder'd Palace or sequester'd Rent;
Mark'd out by dangerous Parts he meets the Shock,
And fatal Learning leads him to the Block:
Around his Tomb let Art and Genius weep,
But hear his Death, ye Blockheads, hear and sleep.
   The festal Blazes, the triumphal Show,
The ravish'd Standard, and the captive Foe,
The Senate's Thanks, the Gazette's pompous Tale,
With Force resistless o'er the Brave prevail.
Such Bribes the rapid *Greek* o'er *Asia* whirl'd,
For such the steady *Romans* shook the World;
For such in distant Lands the *Britons* shine,
And stain with Blood the *Danube* or the *Rhine;*
This Pow'r has Praise, that Virtue scarce can warm,
Till Fame supplies the universal Charm.

Yet Reason frowns on War's unequal Game,
Where wasted Nations raise a single Name,
And mortgag'd States their Grandsires Wreaths regret,
From Age to Age in everlasting Debt;
Wreaths which at last the dear-bought Right convey
To rust on Medals, or on Stones decay.
   On what Foundation stands the Warrior's Pride,
How just his Hopes let *Swedish Charles* decide;
A Frame of Adamant, a Soul of Fire,
No Dangers fright him, and no Labours tire;
O'er Love, o'er Fear extends his wide Domain,
Unconquer'd Lord of Pleasure and of Pain;
No Joys to him pacific Scepters yield,
War sounds the Trump, he rushes to the Field;
Behold surrounding Kings their Pow'rs combine,
And One capitulate, and One resign;
Peace courts his Hand, but spreads her Charms in vain;
"Think Nothing gain'd," he cries, "till nought remain,
On *Moscow's* Walls till *Gothic* Standards fly,
And All be mine beneath the Polar Sky."
The March begins in Military State,
And Nations on his Eye suspended wait;
Stern Famine guards the solitary Coast,
And Winter barricades the Realms of Frost;
He comes, nor Want nor Cold his Course delay; —
Hide, blushing Glory, hide *Pultowa's* Day:
The vanquish'd Hero leaves his broken Bands,
And shews his Miseries in distant Lands;
Condemn'd a needy Supplicant to wait,
While Ladies interpose, and Slaves debate.
But did not Chance at length her Error mend?
Did no subverted Empire mark his End?
Did rival Monarchs give the fatal Wound?
Or hostile Millions press him to the Ground?
His Fall was destin'd to a barren Strand,
A petty Fortress, and a dubious Hand;
He left the Name, at which the World grew pale,
To point a Moral, or adorn a Tale.

All Times their Scenes of pompous Woes afford,
From *Persia's* Tyrant to *Bavaria's* Lord.
In gay Hostility, and barb'rous Pride,
With half Mankind embattled at his Side,
Great *Xerxes* comes to seize the certain Prey,
And starves exhausted Regions in his Way;
Attendant Flatt'ry counts his Myriads o'er,
Till counted Myriads sooth his Pride no more;
Fresh Praise is try'd till Madness fires his Mind,
The Waves he lashes, and enchains the Wind;
New Pow'rs are claim'd, new Pow'rs are still bestow'd,
Till rude Resistance lops the spreading God;
The daring *Greeks* deride the Martial Shew,
And heap their Vallies with the gaudy Foe;
Th' insulted Sea with humbler Thoughts he gains,
A single Skiff to speed his Flight remains;
Th' incumber'd Oar scarce leaves the dreaded Coast
Through purple Billows and a floating Host.
    The bold *Bavarian*, in a luckless Hour,
Tries the dread Summits of *Cesarean* Pow'r,
With unexpected Legions bursts away,
And sees defenceless Realms receive his Sway;
Short Sway! fair *Austria* spreads her mournful Charms,
The Queen, the Beauty, sets the World in Arms;
From Hill to Hill the Beacons rousing Blaze
Spreads wide the Hope of Plunder and of Praise;
The fierce *Croatian*, and the wild *Hussar*,
With all the Sons of Ravage croud the War;
The baffled Prince in Honour's flatt'ring Bloom
Of hasty Greatness finds the fatal Doom,
His foes Derision, and his Subjects Blame,
And steals to Death from Anguish and from Shame.
    Enlarge my Life with Multitude of Days,
In Health, in Sickness, thus the Suppliant prays;
Hides from himself his State, and shuns to know,
That Life protracted is protracted Woe.
Time hovers o'er, impatient to destroy,
And shuts up all the Passages of Joy:

In vain their Gifts the bounteous Seasons pour,
The Fruit Autumnal, and the Vernal Flow'r,
With listless Eyes the Dotard views the Store,
He views, and wonders that they please no more;
Now pall the tastless Meats, and joyless Wines,
And Luxury with Sighs her Slave resigns.
Approach, ye Minstrels, try the soothing Strain,
Diffuse the tuneful Lenitives of Pain:
No Sounds alas would touch th' impervious Ear,
Though dancing Mountains witness'd *Orpheus* near;
Nor Lute nor Lyre his feeble Pow'rs attend,
Nor sweeter Musick of a virtuous Friend,
But everlasting Dictates croud his Tongue,
Perversely grave, or positively wrong.
The still returning Tale, and ling'ring Jest,
Perplex the fawning Niece and pamper'd Guest,
While growing Hopes scarce awe the gath'ring Sneer,
And scarce a Legacy can bribe to hear;
The watchful Guests still hint the last Offence,
The Daughter's Petulance, the Son's Expence,
Improve his heady Rage with treach'rous Skill,
And mould his Passions till they make his Will.

Unnumber'd Maladies his Joints invade,
Lay Siege to Life and press the dire Blockade;
But unextinguish'd Av'rice still remains,
And dreaded Losses aggravate his Pains;
He turns, with anxious Heart and cripled Hands,
His Bonds of Debt, and Mortgages of Lands;
Or views his Coffers with suspicious Eyes,
Unlocks his Gold, and counts it till he dies.

But grant, the Virtues of a temp'rate Prime
Bless with an Age exempt from Scorn or Crime;
An Age that melts with unperceiv'd Decay,
And glides in modest Innocence away;
Whose peaceful Day Benevolence endears,
Whose Night congratulating Conscience cheers;
The gen'ral Fav'rite as the gen'ral Friend:
Such Age there is, and who shall wish its End?

Yet ev'n on this her Load Misfortune flings,
To press the weary Minutes flagging Wings:
New Sorrow rises as the Day returns,
A Sister sickens, or a Daughter mourns.
Now Kindred Merit fills the sable Bier,
Now lacerated Friendship claims a Tear.
Year chases Year, Decay pursues Decay,
Still drops some Joy from with'ring Life away;
New Forms arise, and diff'rent Views engage,
Superfluous lags the Vet'ran on the Stage,
Till pitying Nature signs the last Release,
And bids afflicted Worth retire to Peace.
But few there are whom Hours like these await,
Who set unclouded in the Gulphs of Fate.
From *Lydia's* Monarch should the Search descend,
By *Solon* caution'd to regard his End,
In Life's last Scene what Prodigies surprise,
Fears of the Brave, and Follies of the Wise?
From *Marlb'rough's* Eyes the Streams of Dotage flow,
And *Swift* expires a Driv'ler and a Show.
The teeming Mother, anxious for her Race,
Begs for each Birth the Fortune of a Face:
Yet *Vane* could tell what Ills from Beauty spring;
And *Sedley* curs'd the Form that pleas'd a King.
Ye Nymphs of rosy Lips and radiant Eyes,
Whom Pleasure keeps too busy to be wise,
Whom Joys with soft Varieties invite,
By Day the Frolick, and the Dance by Night,
Who frown with Vanity, who smile with Art,
And ask the latest Fashion of the Heart,
What Care, what Rules your heedless Charms shall save,
Each Nymph your Rival, and each Youth your Slave?
Against your Fame with Fondness Hate combines,
The Rival batters, and the Lover mines.
With distant Voice neglected Virtue calls,
Less heard and less, the faint Remonstrance falls;
Tir'd with Contempt, she quits the slipp'ry Reign,
And Pride and Prudence take her Seat in vain.

In croud at once, where none the Pass defend,
The harmless Freedom, and the private Friend.
The Guardians yield, by Force superior ply'd;
To Int'rest, Prudence; and to Flatt'ry, Pride.
Here Beauty falls betray'd, despis'd, distress'd,
And hissing Infamy proclaims the rest.
   Where then shall Hope and Fear their Objects find?
Must dull Suspence corrupt the stagnant Mind?
Must helpless Man, in Ignorance sedate,
Roll darkling down the Torrent of his Fate?
Must no Dislike alarm, no Wishes rise,
Nor Cries invoke the Mercies of the Skies?
Enquirer, cease, Petitions yet remain,
Which Heav'n may hear, nor deem Religion vain.
Still raise for Good the supplicating Voice,
But leave to Heav'n the Measure and the Choice.
Safe in his Pow'r, whose Eyes discern afar
The secret Ambush of a specious Pray'r.
Implore his Aid, in his Decisions rest,
Secure whate'er he gives, he gives the best.
Yet when the Sense of sacred Presence fires,
And Strong Devotion to the Skies aspires,
Pour forth thy Fervours for a healthful Mind,
Obedient Passions, and a Will resign'd;
For Love, which scarce collective Man can fill;
For Patience sov'reign o'er transmuted Ill;
For Faith, that panting for a happier Seat,
Counts Death kind Nature's Signal of Retreat:
These Goods for Man the Laws of Heav'n ordain,
These Goods he grants, who grants the Pow'r to gain;
With these celestial Wisdom calms the Mind,
And makes the Happiness she does not find.

So powerfully does Johnson adapt Juvenal's dignified satirical manner that the poem can reach back to such familiar examples from classical antiquity as Xerxes and Alexander, can graciously include a touching sketch of the senile Swift (who had died in 1745, just four years before Johnson's poem was written), and can reach forward to our own time. Johnson's "remembered folly stings" is very probably one ancestor of Eliot's "fools' approval stings" in "Little Gidding" (p. 987). (Note that: "lenitives" are substances that lighten pain.)

# THOMAS GRAY 1716–1771

Gray was born in London and educated at Eton and Cambridge. Although he held a law degree, he devoted his life to the study of language and literature. Toward the end of his life he was made Professor of Modern History at Cambridge. Gray could be regarded as a bridge, or at least a bridge-builder, between the neo-classical values of the Augustan Age and the romantic values of the later eighteenth century, and also between the interest of scholarly learning and the fascination of great popularity.

# Elegy Written in a Country Churchyard

The curfew tolls the knell of parting day,
The lowing herd wind slowly o'er the lea,
The plowman homeward plods his weary way,
And leaves the world to darkness and to me.

Now fades the glimmering landscape on the sight,
And all the air a solemn stillness holds,
Save where the beetle wheels his droning flight,
And drowsy tinklings lull the distant folds;

Save that from yonder ivy-mantled tower
The moping owl does to the moon complain
Of such as, wand'ring near her secret bower,
Molest her ancient solitary reign.

Beneath those rugged elms, that yew tree's shade,
Where heaves the turf in many a mold'ring heap,
Each in his narrow cell for ever laid,
The rude forefathers of the hamlet sleep.

The breezy call of incense-breathing morn,
The swallow twitt'ring from the straw-built shed,
The cock's shrill clarion, or the echoing horn,
No more shall rouse them from their lowly bed.

For them no more the blazing hearth shall burn,
Or busy houswife ply her evening care;
No children run to lisp their sire's return,
Or climb his knees the envied kiss to share.

Oft did the harvest to their sickle yield,
Their furrow oft the stubborn glebe has broke;
How jocund did they drive their team afield!
How bowed the woods beneath their sturdy stroke!

Let not Ambition mock their useful toil,
Their homely joys, and destiny obscure;
Nor Grandeur hear with a disdainful smile
The short and simple annals of the poor.

The boast of heraldry, the pomp of pow'r,
And all that beauty, all that wealth e'er gave,
Awaits alike th' inevitable hour.
The paths of glory lead but to the grave.

Nor you, ye Proud, impute to these the fault,
If Mem'ry o'er their tomb no trophies raise,
Where through the long-drawn aisle and fretted vault
The pealing anthem swells the note of praise.

Can storied urn or animated bust
Back to its mansion call the fleeting breath?
Can Honor's voice provoke the silent dust,
Or Flatt'ry soothe the dull cold ear of Death?

Perhaps in this neglected spot is laid
Some heart once pregnant with celestial fire;
Hands that the rod of empire might have swayed,
Or waked to ecstasy the living lyre.

But Knowledge to their eyes her ample page
Rich with the spoils of time did ne'er unroll;
Chill Penury repressed their noble rage,
And froze the genial current of the soul.

Full many a gem of purest ray serene,
The dark unfathomed caves of ocean bear:
Full many a flower is born to blush unseen,
And waste its sweetness on the desert air.

Some village Hampden, that with dauntless breast
The little tyrant of his fields withstood;
Some mute inglorious Milton here may rest,
Some Cromwell, guiltless of his country's blood.

Th' applause of list'ning senates to command,
The threats of pain and ruin to despise,
To scatter plenty o'er a smiling land,
And read their hist'ry in a nation's eyes.

Their lot forbade; nor circumscribed alone
Their glowing virtues, but their crimes confined;
Forbade to wade through slaughter to a throne,
And shut the gates of mercy on mankind.

The struggling pangs of conscious truth to hide,
To quench the blushes of ingenuous shame,
Or heap the shrine of Luxury and Pride
With incense kindled at the Muse's flame.

Far from the madding crowd's ignoble strife,
Their sober wishes never learned to stray;
Along the cool sequestered vale of life
They kept the noiseless tenor of their way.

Yet ev'n these bones from insult to protect
Some frail memorial still erected nigh,
With uncouth rhymes and shapeless sculpture decked,
Implores the passing tribute of a sigh.

Their name, their years, spelt by th' unlettered Muse,
The place of fame and elegy supply:
And many a holy text around she strews,
That teach the rustic moralist to die.

For who to dumb Forgetfulness a prey,
This pleasing anxious being e'er resigned,
Left the warm precincts of the cheerful day,
Nor cast one longing ling'ring look behind?

On some fond breast the parting soul relies,
Some pious drops the closing eye requires;
Ev'n from the tomb the voice of Nature cries,
Ev'n in our ashes live their wonted fires.

For thee, who mindful of th' unhonor'd dead
Dost in these lines their artless tale relate;
If chance, by lonely contemplation led,
Some kindred spirit shall inquire thy fate,

Haply some hoary-headed swain may say,
"Oft have we seen him at the peep of dawn
Brushing with hasty steps the dews away
To meet the sun upon the upland lawn.

"There at the foot of yonder nodding beech
That wreathes its old fantastic roots so high,
His listless length at noontide would he stretch,
And pore upon the brook that babbles by.

"Hard by yon wood, now smiling as in scorn,
Mutt'ring his wayward fancies he would rove,
Now drooping, woeful wan, like one forlorn,
Or crazed with care, or crossed in hopeless love.

"One morn I missed him, on the customed hill,
Along the heath and near his fav'rite tree;
Another came; nor yet beside the rill,
Nor up the lawn, nor at the wood was he;

"The next with dirges due in sad array
Slow through the churchway path we saw him borne.
Approach and read (for thou can'st read) the lay,
Graved on the stone beneath yon aged thorn."

The Epitaph

*Here rests his head upon the lap of Earth*
*A youth to Fortune and to Fame unknown.*
*Fair Science frowned not on his humble birth,*
*And Melancholy marked him for her own.*

*Large was his bounty, and his soul sincere,*
*Heav'n did a recompence as largely send:*
*He gave to Mis'ry all he had, a tear,*
*He gained from Heav'n ('twas all he wished) a friend.*

*No farther seek his merits to disclose,*
*Or draw his frailties from their dread abode,*
*(There they alike in trembling hope repose),*
*The bosom of his Father and his God.*

---

*Gray's lines reach us through phrases that are virtually proverbial ("purest ray serene"), through such titles as Hardy's* Far from the Madding Crowd *and Humphrey Cobb's* Paths of Glory, *and through overt echoes and allusions in poems by T. S. Eliot, John Crowe Ransom, Hart Crane, Philip Larkin, and George Starbuck. The meditation set in a sacred place continues through Wordsworth's "Tintern Abbey" (p. 407), Hardy's "Darkling Thrush" (p. 770), Eliot's "Little Gidding" (p. 987), and Larkin's "Church Going" (p. 1068). (Note that: "rude" is "uneducated"; "glebe" is "ground"; "provoke" is "call forth" (literally); "madding" is "milling.")*

# Ode on the Death of a Favorite Cat, Drowned in a Tub of Gold Fishes

Twas on a lofty vase's side,
Where China's gayest art had dyed
　　The azure flowers that blow;
Demurest of the tabby kind,
The pensive Selima reclined,
　　Gazed on the lake below.

Her conscious tail her joy declared;
The fair round face, the snowy beard,
　　The velvet of her paws,
Her coat, that with the tortoise vies,
Her ears of jet, and emerald eyes,
　　She saw; and purr'd applause.

Still had she gazed; but 'midst the tide
Two angel forms were seen to glide,
　　The Genii of the stream:
Their scaly armor's Tyrian hue
Thro' richest purple to the view
　　Betray'd a golden gleam.

The hapless Nymph with wonder saw:
A whisker first and then a claw,
　　With many an ardent wish,
She stretch'd in vain to reach the prize.
What female heart can gold despise?
What Cat's averse to fish?

Presumptuous Maid! with looks intent
Again she stretch'd, again she bent,
  Nor knew the gulf between.
(Malignant Fate sat by, and smil'd)
The slipp'ry verge her feet beguil'd,
  She tumbled headlong in.

Eight times emerging from the flood
She mew'd to ev'ry watry God,
  Some speedy aid to send.
No Dolphin came, no Nereid stirr'd:
Nor cruel *Tom*, nor *Susan* heard.
  A Fav'rite has no friend!

From hence, ye Beauties, undeceiv'd,
Know, one false step is ne'er retriev'd,
  And be with caution bold.
Not all that tempts your wand'ring eyes
And heedless hearts, is lawful prize;
  Nor all, that glisters, gold.

---

*Gray's "Elegy" (p. 327) is somber and earnest; this "Ode" is flippant and airy.
It belongs among the animal fables whose pedigree goes back to Aesop and comes
forward to the bestiary maintained in today's cartoons. The favorite cat belonged
to the estimable Horace Walpole. (Note that: "blow" is "bloom.")*

# WILLIAM COLLINS 1721-1759

Collins was a gifted and learned poet, but he had to work during unfavorable times and amid uncongenial surroundings. He was subject to melancholia and died insane.

## *Ode to Evening*

If aught of Oaten Stop, or Pastoral Song
May hope, chaste Eve, to soothe thy modest ear,
   Like thy own solemn springs,
   Thy springs and dying gales,
O nymph reserved, while now the bright-haired sun
Sits in yon western tent, whose cloudy skirts,
   With brede ethereal wove,
   O'erhang his wavy bed;
Now air is hushed, save where the weak-ey'd bat
With short shrill shriek flits by on leathern wing,
   Or where the beetle winds
   His small but sullen horn,
As oft he rises midst the twilight path,
Against the pilgrim borne in heedless hum:
   Now teach me, Maid composed,
   To breathe some softened strain,
Whose numbers stealing through thy darkening vale
May not unseemly with its stillness suit;
   As musing slow, I hail
   Thy genial loved return!
For when thy folding star arising shows
His paly circlet, at his warning lamp
   The fragrant Hours, and elves
   Who slept in flowers the day,

And many a nymph who wreathes her brows with sedge,
And sheds the freshening dew, and, lovelier still,
 The Pensive Pleasures sweet,
 Prepare thy shadowy car.
Then lead, calm votaress, where some sheety lake
Cheers the lone heath, or some time-hallowed pile,
 Or upland fallows grey,
 Reflect its last cool gleam.
But when chill blustering winds or driving rain
Forbid my willing feet, be mine the hut
 That from the mountain's side
 Views wilds and swelling floods,
And hamlets brown, and dim-discovered spires,
And hears their simple bell, and marks o'er all
 Thy dewy fingers draw
 The gradual dusky veil.
While Spring shall pour his showers, as oft he wont,
And bathe thy breathing tresses, meekest Eve!
 While Summer loves to sport
 Beneath thy lingering light;
While sallow Autumn fills thy lap with leaves,
Or Winter, yelling through the troublous air,
 Affrights thy shrinking train,
 And rudely rends they robes;
So long, sure-found beneath the sylvan shed,
Shall Fancy, Friendship, Science, rose-lipped Health,
 Thy gentlest influence own,
 And hymn thy favourite name!

---

*Collins modelled his ode on some of Horace's. Marvell's "Horatian Ode upon Cromwell's Return from Ireland" (p. 238) also uses an English adaptation of Horace's so-called Alcaic stanza, two longer lines followed by two shorter ones. Unlike Marvell, however, Collins courageously imitated his Roman exemplar in writing an unrhymed lyric (the earliest in this anthology) and producing thereby a bewitchingly peculiar music. (Note that: "brede" is "embroidery"; "folding-star" is "evening star.")*

# How Sleep the Brave

How sleep the brave who sink to rest
By all their country's wishes blest!
When Spring, with dewy fingers cold,
Returns to deck their hallowed mold,
She there shall dress a sweeter sod
Than Fancy's feet have ever trod.

By fairy hands their knell is rung,
By forms unseen their dirge is sung;
There Honor comes, a pilgrim gray,
To bless the turf that wraps their clay,
And Freedom shall awhile repair,
To dwell a weeping hermit there!

---

*In 1745 and early 1746 the British army suffered defeat in one battle in Belgium and two in Scotland. This is Collins's "Ode Written in the Beginning of the Year 1746."*

Goldsmith was educated at Trinity College, Dublin, but failed to be ordained, even though his father was a clergyman. He received some medical training and worked for a time as a physician. He became a successful professional writer, distinguishing himself as a journalist, historian, biographer, and all-round literary author, producing not only the poems in this anthology but popular plays (such as *She Stoops to Conquer*) and *The Vicar of Wakefield*, one of the most beloved novels in English.

## When Lovely Woman Stoops to Folly

❖❖❖

When lovely woman stoops to folly,
  And finds too late that men betray,
What charm can soothe her melancholy,
  What art can wash her guilt away?

The only art her guilt to cover,
  To hide her shame from every eye,
To give repentance to her lover,
  And wring his bosom—is to die.

from The Vicar of Wakefield

*This song from Goldsmith's novel* The Vicar of Wakefield *also contributes a few lines to T. S. Eliot's* "Waste Land" *(p. 968).*

# An Elegy on the Death of a Mad Dog

Good people all, of every sort,
  Give ear unto my song;
And if you find it wond'rous short,
  It cannot hold you long.

In Islington there was a man,
  Of whom the world might say,
That still a godly race he ran,
  Whene'er he went to pray.

A kind and gentle heart he had,
  To comfort friends and foes;
The naked every day he clad,
  When he put on his clothes.

And in that town a dog was found,
  As many dogs there be,
Both mongrel, puppy, whelp, and hound,
  And curs of low degree.

This dog and man at first were friends;
  But when a pique began,
The dog, to gain some private ends,
  Went mad and bit the man.

Around from all the neighboring streets
  The wond'ring neighbors ran,
And swore the dog had lost its wits,
  To bite so good a man.

The wound it seem'd both sore and sad
   To every Christian eye;
And while they swore the dog was mad,
   They swore the man would die.

But soon a wonder came to light,
   That showed the rogues they lied:
The man recover'd of the bite,
   The dog it was that died.

                    from The Vicar of Wakefield

---

*Like "When Lovely Woman Stoops to Folly" (p. 338), this variant on the folk-irony of The Biter Bit is a number from* The Vicar of Wakefield, *performed as incidental (and parodic) entertainment by a member of the vicar's family. Sir Walter Scott, a generation younger than Goldsmith, could produce comparably durable verses in respectable prose works. Charles Kingsley, in a smaller way, could do something of the sort a hundred years later. Peacock, Waugh, and DeVries, among the comedians, could handle parodies from time to time. By now, the art has all but died; among contemporary novelists, just about the only practitioner writing passable song-lyrics is Thomas Pynchon.*

# The Deserted Village

≫≫≫≫≫

SWEET AUBURN! loveliest village of the plain,
Where health and plenty cheered the laboring swain,
Where smiling spring its earliest visit paid,
And parting summer's lingering blooms delayed.
Dear lovely bowers of innocence and ease,
Seats of my youth, when every sport could please,
How often have I loitered o'er thy green,
Where humble happiness endeared each scene!
How often have I paused on every charm,
The sheltered cot, the cultivated farm,
The never-failing brook, the busy mill.
The decent church that topped the neighboring hill,
The hawthorn-bush, with seats beneath the shade,
For talking age and whispering lovers made!

How often have I blessed the coming day,
When toil remitting lent its turn to play,
And all the village train, from labor free,
Led up their sports beneath the spreading tree,
While many a pastime circled in the shade,
The young contending as the old surveyed;
And many a gambol frolicked o'er the ground,
And sleights of art and feats of strength went round;
And still, as each repeated pleasure tired,
Succeeding sports the mirthful band inspired;
The dancing pair that simply sought renown,
By holding out, to tire each other down;
The swain mistrustless of his smutted face,
While secret laughter tittered round the place;

The bashful virgin's sidelong looks of love,
The matron's glance that would those looks reprove, —
These were thy charms, sweet village! sports like these,
With sweet succession, taught e'en toil to please;
These round thy bowers their cheerful influence shed,
These were thy charms, — but all these charms are fled!

Sweet smiling village, loveliest of the lawn,
Thy sports are fled, and all thy charms withdrawn;
Amidst thy bowers the tyrant's hand is seen,
And desolation saddens all thy green;
One only master grasps the whole domain,
And half a tillage stints thy smiling plain;
No more thy glassy brook reflects the day,
But, choked with sedges, works its weedy way;
Along thy glades, a solitary guest,
The hollow-sounding bittern guards its nest;
Amidst thy desert walks the lapwing flies,
And tires their echoes with unvaried cries.
Sunk are thy bowers in shapeless ruin all,
And the long grass o'ertops the mouldering wall,
And, trembling, shrinking from the spoiler's hand,
Far, far away thy children leave the land.

Ill fares the land, to hastening ills a prey,
Where wealth accumulates and men decay:
Princes and lords may flourish, or may fade;
A breath can make them, as a breath has made;
But a bold peasantry, their country's pride,
When once destroyed, can never be supplied.

A time there was, ere England's griefs began,
When every rood of ground maintained its man;
For him light Labor spread her wholesome store,
Just gave what life required, but gave no more;
His best companions, innocence and health;
And his best riches, ignorance of wealth.

But times are altered; trade's unfeeling train
Usurp the land and dispossess the swain;
Along the lawn, where scattered hamlets rose,
Unwieldy wealth and cumbrous pomp repose,
And every want to luxury allied,
And every pang that folly pays to pride.
Those gentle hours that plenty bade to bloom,
Those calm desires that asked but little room,
Those healthful sports that graced the peaceful scene,
Lived in each look, and brightened all the green,—
These, far departing, seek a kinder shore,
And rural mirth and manners are no more.

Sweet Auburn! parent of the blissful hour,
Thy glades forlorn confess the tyrant's power.
Here, as I take my solitary rounds,
Amidst thy tangling walks and ruined grounds,
And, many a year elapsed, return to view
Where once the cottage stood, the hawthorn grew,
Remembrance wakes, with all her busy train,
Swells at my breast, and turns the past to pain.

In all my wanderings round this world of care,
In all my griefs—and God has given my share—
I still had hopes my latest hours to crown,
Amidst these humble bowers to lay me down;
To husband out life's taper at the close,
And keep the flame from wasting by repose;
I still had hopes—for pride attends us still—
Amidst the swains to show my book-learned skill,
Around my fire an evening group to draw,
And tell of all I felt and all I saw;
And, as a hare, whom hounds and horns pursue,
Pants to the place from whence at first she flew,
I still had hopes, my long vexations past,
Here to return,—and die at home at last.

O blest retirement! friend to life's decline,
Retreats from care, that never must be mine,
How blest is he who crowns in shades like these
A youth of labor with an age of ease;
Who quits a world where strong temptations try,
And, since 't is hard to combat, learns to fly!
For him no wretches, born to work and weep,
Explore the mine, or tempt the dangerous deep;
No surly porter stands in guilty state,
To spurn imploring famine from the gate:
But on he moves to meet his latter end,
Angels around befriending virtue's friend;
Sinks to the grave with unperceived decay,
While resignation gently slopes the way;
And, all his prospects brightening to the last,
His heaven commences ere the world be past.

Sweet was the sound, when oft, at evening's close,
Up yonder hill the village murmur rose;
There, as I passed with careless steps and slow,
The mingling notes came softened from below;
The swain responsive as the milkmaid sung,
The sober herd that lowed to meet their young;
The noisy geese that gabbled o'er the pool,
The playful children just let loose from school;
The watch-dog's voice that bayed the whispering wind,
And the loud laugh that spoke the vacant mind, —
These all in sweet confusion sought the shade,
And filled each pause the nightingale had made.
But now the sounds of population fail,
No cheerful murmurs fluctuate in the gale,
No busy steps the grass-grown foot-way tread,
But all the bloomy flush of life is fled.
All but yon widowed, solitary thing,
That feebly bends beside the plashy spring;
She, wretched matron, forced in age, for bread,
To strip the brook with mantling cresses spread,

To pick her wintry fagot from the thorn,
To seek her nightly shed, and weep till morn;
She only left of all the harmless train,
The sad historian of the pensive plain.

Near yonder copse, where once the garden smiled,
And still where many a garden-flower grows wild;
There, where a few torn shrubs the place disclose,
The village preacher's modest mansion rose.
A man he was to all the country dear,
And passing rich with forty pounds a year;
Remote from towns he ran his godly race,
Nor e'er had changed, nor wished to change, his place;
Unskilful he to fawn, or seek for power,
By doctrines fashioned to the varying hour;
Far other aims his heart had learned to prize,
More bent to raise the wretched than to rise.
His house was known to all the vagrant train.
He chid their wanderings, but relieved their pain;
The long-remembered beggar was his guest,
Whose beard descending swept his aged breast.
The ruined spendthrift, now no longer proud,
Claimed kindred there, and had his claims allowed;
The broken soldier, kindly bade to stay,
Sate by his fire, and talked the night away;
Wept o'er his wounds, or tales of sorrow done,
Shouldered his crutch, and showed how fields were won.
Pleased with his guests, the good man learned to glow,
And quite forgot their vices in their woe;
Careless their merits or their faults to scan,
His pity gave ere charity began.

Thus to relieve the wretched was his pride,
And e'en his failings leaned to Virtue's side;
But in his duty prompt at every call,
He watched and wept, he prayed and felt for all;

And, as a bird each fond endearment tries,
To tempt its new-fledged offspring to the skies,
He tried each art, reproved each dull delay,
Allured to brighter worlds, and led the way.

  Beside the bed where parting life was laid,
And sorrow, guilt, and pain by turns dismayed,
The reverend champion stood. At his control,
Despair and anguish fled the struggling soul;
Comfort came down the trembling wretch to raise,
And his last faltering accents whispered praise.

  At church, with meek and unaffected grace,
His looks adorned the venerable place;
Truth from his lips prevailed with double sway,
And fools, who came to scoff, remained to pray.
The service past, around the pious man,
With steady zeal, each honest rustic ran;
E'en children followed with endearing wile,
And plucked his gown, to share the good man's smile.
His ready smile a parent's warmth expressed,
Their welfare pleased him, and their cares distressed;
To them his heart, his love, his griefs were given,
But all his serious thoughts had rest in heaven.
As some tall cliff, that lifts its awful form,
Swells from the vale, and midway leaves the storm,
Though round its breast the rolling clouds are spread,
Eternal sunshine settles on its head.

  Beside yon straggling fence that skirts the way,
With blossomed furze unprofitably gay,
There, in his noisy mansion, skilled to rule,
The village master taught his little school;
A man severe he was, and stern to view,
I knew him well, and every truant knew;
Well had the boding tremblers learned to trace
The day's disasters in his morning face;

Full well they laughed with counterfeited glee
At all his jokes, for many a joke had he;
Full well the busy whisper circling round
Conveyed the dismal tidings when he frowned;
Yet he was kind, or, if severe in aught,
The love he bore to learning was in fault.
The village all declared how much he knew,
'T was certain he could write, and cipher too;
Lands he could measure, times and tides presage,
And e'en the story ran that he could gauge;
In arguing too, the parson owned his skill,
For, e'en though vanquished, he could argue still,
While words of learnèd length and thundering sound
Amazed the gazing rustics ranged around;
And still they gazed, and still the wonder grew
That one small head could carry all he knew.


But past is all his fame. The very spot
Where many a time he triumphed is forgot.—
Near yonder thorn, that lifts its head on high,
Where once the sign-post caught the passing eye,
Low lies that house where nut-brown draughts inspired,
Where graybeard mirth and smiling toil retired,
Where village statesmen talked with looks profound,
And news much older than their ale went round.
Imagination fondly stoops to trace
The parlor splendors of that festive place,—
The whitewashed wall; the nicely sanded floor;
The varnished clock that ticked behind the door;
The chest, contrived a double debt to pay,
A bed by night, a chest of drawers by day;
The pictures placed for ornament and use;
The twelve good rules; the royal game of goose;
The hearth, except when winter chilled the day,
With aspen boughs and flowers and fennel gay;
While broken teacups, wisely kept for show,
Ranged o'er the chimney, glistened in a row.

Vain, transitory splendor! could not all
Reprieve the tottering mansion from its fall?
Obscure it sinks, nor shall it more impart
An hour's importance to the poor man's heart;
Thither no more the peasant shall repair
To sweet oblivion of his daily care;
No more the farmer's news, the barber's tale,
No more the woodman's ballad shall prevail;
No more the smith his dusky brow shall clear,
Relax his ponderous strength, and lean to hear;

The host himself no longer shall be found
Careful to see the mantling bliss go round;
Nor the coy maid, half willing to be prest,
Shall kiss the cup to pass it to the rest.

Yes! let the rich deride, the proud disdain,
These simple blessings of the lowly train;
To me more dear, congenial to my heart,
One native charm, than all the gloss of art.
Spontaneous joys, where nature has its play,
The soul adopts, and owns their first-born sway;
Lightly they frolic o'er the vacant mind,
Unenvied, unmolested, unconfined:
But the long pomp, the midnight masquerade,
With all the freaks of wanton wealth arrayed, —
In these, ere triflers half their wish obtain,
The toiling pleasure sickens into pain;
And, e'en while fashion's brightest arts decoy,
The heart, distrusting, asks if this be joy.

Ye friends to truth, ye statesmen, who survey
The rich man's joys increase, the poor's decay,
'T is yours to judge, how wide the limits stand
Between a splendid and a happy land.

Proud swells the tide with loads of freighted ore,
And shouting Folly hails them from her shore;
Hoards e'en beyond the miser's wish abound,
And rich men flock from all the world around.
Yet count our gains. This wealth is but a name
That leaves our useful products still the same.
Not so the loss. The man of wealth and pride
Takes up a space that many poor supplied;
Space for his lake, his park's extended bounds,
Space for his horses, equipage, and hounds:
The robe that wraps his limbs in silken sloth
Has robbed the neighboring fields of half their growth;
His seat, where solitary sports are seen,
Indignant spurns the cottage from the green;
Around the world each needful product flies,
For all the luxuries the world supplies:
While thus the land, adorned for pleasure all,
In barren splendor feebly waits the fall.

As some fair female unadorned and plain,
Secure to please while youth confirms her reign,
Slights every borrowed charm that dress supplies,
Nor shares with art the triumph of her eyes,
But when those charms are past, — for charms are frail, —
When time advances, and when lovers fail,

She then shines forth, solicitous to bless,
In all the glaring impotence of dress;
Thus fares the land by luxury betrayed,
In nature's simplest charms at first arrayed,
But verging to decline, its splendors rise,
Its vistas strike, its palaces surprise;
While, scourged by famine from the smiling land,
The mournful peasant leads his humble band;
And while he sinks, without one arm to save,
The country blooms, — a garden and a grave.

Where then, ah! where shall poverty reside,
To 'scape the pressure of contiguous pride?
If to some common's fenceless limits strayed
He drives his flock to pick the scanty blade,
Those fenceless fields the sons of wealth divide,
And e'en the bare-worn common is denied.
If to the city sped;—what waits him there?
To see profusion that he must not share;
To see ten thousand baneful arts combined
To pamper luxury and thin mankind;
To see each joy the sons of pleasure know
Extorted from his fellow-creature's woe.
Here while the courtier glitters in brocade,
There the pale artist plies the sickly trade;
Here while the proud their long-drawn pomps display,
There the black gibbet glooms beside the way.
The dome where Pleasure holds here midnight reign,
Here, richly decked, admits the gorgeous train:
Tumultuous grandeur crowds the blazing square,
The rattling chariots clash, the torches glare.
Sure scenes like these no troubles e'er annoy!
Sure these denote one universal joy!
Are these thy serious thoughts?—Ah, turn thine eyes
Where the poor houseless shivering female lies.
She once, perhaps, in village plenty blest,
Has wept at tales of innocence distrest;
Her modest looks the cottage might adorn,
Sweet as the primrose peeps beneath the thorn;
Now lost to all: her friends, her virtue fled,
Near her betrayer's door she lays her head,
And, pinched with cold, and shrinking from the shower,
With heavy heart deplores that luckless hour,
When idly first, ambitious of the town,
She left her wheel and robes of country brown.

Do thine, sweet Auburn, thine, the loveliest train,
Do thy fair tribes participate her pain?
E'en now, perhaps, by cold and hunger led,
At proud men's doors they ask a little bread!

Ah, no! To distant climes, a dreary scene,
Where half the convex world intrudes between,
Through torrid tracks with fainting steps they go,
Where wild Altama murmurs to their woe.
Far different there from all that charmed before,
The various terrors of that horrid shore, —
Those blazing suns that dart a downward ray,
And fiercely shed intolerable day;
Those matted woods where birds forget to sing,
But silent bats in drowsy clusters cling;
Those poisonous fields with rank luxuriance crowned,
Where the dark scorpion gathers death around;
Where at each step the stranger fears to wake
The rattling terrors of the vengeful snake;
Where crouching tigers wait their hapless prey,
And savage men more murderous still than they;
While oft in whirls the mad tornado flies,
Mingling the ravaged landscape with the skies.
Far different these from every former scene,
The cooling brook, the grassy vested green,
The breezy covert of the warbling grove,
That only sheltered thefts of harmless love.

Good Heaven! what sorrows gloomed that parting day
That called them from their native walks away;
When the poor exiles, every pleasure past,
Hung round the bowers, and fondly looked their last,
And took a long farewell, and wished in vain
For seats like these beyond the western main;
And shuddering still to face the distant deep,
Returned and wept, and still returned to weep.
The good old sire the first prepared to go
To new-found worlds, and wept for others' woe;
But for himself in conscious virtue brave,
He only wished for worlds beyond the grave.
His lovely daughter, lovelier in her tears,
The fond companion of his helpless years,

Silent went next, neglectful of her charms,
And left a lover's for her father's arms.
With louder plaints the mother spoke her woes,
And blessed the cot where every pleasure rose;
And kissed her thoughtless babes with many a tear,
And clasped them close, in sorrow doubly dear;
Whilst her fond husband strove to lend relief
In all the silent manliness of grief.

O luxury! thou curst by Heaven's decree,
How ill exchanged are things like these for thee!
How do thy potions, with insidious joy,
Diffuse their pleasures only to destroy!
Kingdoms by thee, to sickly greatness grown,
Boast of a florid vigor not their own.
At every draught more large and large they grow,
A bloated mass of rank, unwieldy woe;
Till, sapped their strength, and every part unsound,
Down, down they sink, and spread a ruin round.

Even now the devastation is begun,
And half the business of destruction done;
Even now, methinks, as pondering here I stand,
I see the rural virtues leave the land.
Down where yon anchoring vessel spreads the sail
That idly waiting flaps with every gale,
Downward they move, a melancholy band,
Pass from the shore, and darken all the strand.
Contended toil, and hospitable care,
And kind connubial tenderness, are there;
And piety with wishes placed above,
And steady loyalty, and faithful love.
And thou, sweet Poetry, thou loveliest maid,
Still first to fly where sensual joys invade;
Unfit, in these degenerate times of shame,
To catch the heart, or strike for honest fame;
Dear charming nymph, neglected and decried,
My shame in crowds, my solitary pride;

Thou source of all my bliss and all my woe,
That found'st me poor at first, and keep'st me so;
Thou guide, by which the nobler arts excel,
Thou nurse of every virtue, fare thee well!
Farewell; and O, where'er thy voice be tried,
On Torno's cliffs, or Pambamarca's side,
Whether where equinoctial fervors glow,
Or winter wraps the polar world in snow,
Still let thy voice, prevailing over time,
Redress the rigors of the inclement clime;
Aid slighted truth with thy persuasive strain;
Teach erring man to spurn the rage of gain;
Teach him, that states of native strength possest,
Though very poor, may still be very blest;
That trade's proud empire hastes to swift decay,
As ocean sweeps the labored mole away;
While self-dependent power can time defy,
As rocks resist the billows and the sky.

---

*One line from "The Deserted Village"—"And still they gazed, and still the wonder grew"—seems to be one model of a line in T. S. Eliot's "Waste Land": "And still she cried, and still the world pursues" (see p. 968). The general melancholy of wasted lands and deserted villages touches both British and American poetry from the eighteenth century onward (see Robert Frost's "Directive," p. 908). (Note that: "vacant" is "idle," "vacationing"; "guage" is "estimate the capacity"; "labored mole" is "breakwater constructed with much labor.")*

# WILLIAM COWPER 1731–1800

Cowper could produce effective satires and engaging historical pieces and he was a fine letter-writer, but for the purposes of this anthology he was most successful as an author of hymns. Cowper (sounded "Cooper," by the way) seems to have been a sweet-tempered man but was tormented by depression and mania most of his adult life.

# *Light Shining out of Darkness*

God moves in a mysterious way,
   His wonders to perform;
He plants his footsteps in the sea,
   And rides upon the storm.

Deep in unfathomable mines
   Of never-failing skill,
He treasures up his bright designs,
   And works his sovereign will.

Ye fearful saints fresh courage take,
   The clouds ye so much dread
Are big with mercy, and shall break
   In blessings on your head.

Judge not the Lord by feeble sense,
   But trust him for his grace;
Behind a frowning providence,
   He hides a smiling face.

His purposes will ripen fast,
   Unfolding ev'ry hour;
The bud may have a bitter taste,
   But sweet will be the flow'r.

Blind unbelief is sure to err,
  And scan his work in vain;
God is his own interpreter,
  And he will make it plain.

---

*With Isaac Watts, Charles Wesley, A. M. Toplady, and many others, the
eighteenth century was one of the greatest ages of Protestant hymn-writing.
Cowper wrote the famous* Olney Hymns *with John Newton, curate of Olney.
Newton is best remembered today for "Amazing Grace."*

# The Poplar Field

The poplars are felled, farewell to the shade
And the whispering sound of the cool colonnade,
The winds play no longer, and sing in the leaves,
Nor Ouse on his bosom their image receives.

Twelve years have elapsed since I last took a view
Of my favourite field and the bank where they grew,
And now in the grass behold they are laid,
And the tree is my seat that once lent me a shade.

The blackbird has fled to another retreat
Where the hazels afford him a screen from the heat,
And the scene where his melody charmed me before,
Resounds with his sweet-flowing ditty no more.

My fugitive years are all hasting away,
And I must ere long lie as lowly as they,
With a turf on my breast, and a stone at my head,
Ere another such grove shall arise in its stead.

'Tis a sight to engage me, if any thing can,
To muse on the perishing pleasures of man;
Though his life be a dream, his enjoyments, I see,
Have a being less durable even than he.

---

*A century after Cowper's poem, Gerard Manley Hopkins wrote one much like it on the same subject: "Binsey Poplars."*

# PHILIP FRENEAU 1752–1832

Freneau came along just in time to take part in literary
activities related to the American Revolution, and he
lived long enough to keep up the production of patriotic
and satirical verses through the War of 1812. Early in
the life of the Republic he was an adherent of Thomas
Jefferson and such an enemy of Alexander Hamilton
that George Washington complained about "that rascal
Freneau."

# The Indian Burying Ground

In spite of all the learned have said,
   I still my old opinion keep;
The posture, that we give the dead,
   Points out the soul's eternal sleep.

Not so the ancients of these lands —
   The Indian, when from life released,
Again is seated with his friends,
   And shares again the joyous feast.

His imaged birds, and painted bowl,
   And venison, for a journey dressed,
Bespeak the nature of the soul,
   Activity, that knows no rest.

His bow, for action ready bent,
   And arrows, with a head of stone,
Can only mean that life is spent,
   And not the old ideas gone.

Thou, stranger, that shalt come this way,
   No fraud upon the dead commit —
Observe the swelling turf, and say
   They do not lie, but here they sit.

Here still a lofty rock remains,
  On which the curious eye may trace
(Now wasted, half, by wearing rains)
  The fancies of a ruder race.

Here still an aged elm aspires,
  Beneath whose far-projecting shade
(And which the shepherd still admires)
  The children of the forest played!

There oft a restless Indian queen
  (Pale Shebah, with her braided hair)
And many a barbarous form is seen
  To chide the man that lingers there.

By midnight moons, o'er moistening dews;
  In habit for the chase arrayed,
The hunter still the deer pursues,
  The hunter and the deer, a shade!

And long shall timorous fancy see
  The painted chief, and pointed spear,
And Reason's self shall bow the knee
  To shadows and delusions here.

---

*Freneau seems to be deliberately echoing the form and content of Gray's "Elegy Written in a Country Churchyard" (p. 327) with these alternately rhyming quatrains (although Freneau's meter is a foot shorter than Gray's heroic pentameter). But these "rude forefathers" are not laid out as though asleep; these members of a "ruder race" are buried in a sitting position.*

Blake was a splendid graphic artist as well as a literary genius. After an early period of relatively unsophisticated lyrics, he produced visionary poems of remarkable scope and originality. His influence has increased steadily since his death, and among his literary descendants can be counted D. G. Rossetti, W. B. Yeats, and Allen Ginsberg.

# The Tiger

Tiger, Tiger, burning bright
In the forests of the night;
What immortal hand or eye,
Could frame thy fearful symmetry?

In what distant deeps or skies
Burnt the fire of thine eyes!
On what wings dare he aspire?
What the hand, dare seize the fire?

And what shoulder, & what art,
Could twist the sinews of thy heart?
And when thy heart began to beat,
What dread hand? & what dread feet?

What the hammer? what the chain?
In what furnace was thy brain?
What the anvil? what dread grasp
Dare its deadly terrors clasp?

When the stars threw down their spears
And water'd heaven with their tears:
Did he smile his work to see?
Did he who made the Lamb make thee?

Tiger, Tiger, burning bright,
In the forests of the night:
What immortal hand or eye,
Dare frame thy fearful symmetry?

from Songs of Experience

---

*"The Tiger," from the celebrated* Songs of Experience *(1794), is, indeed, a song of experience, vividly and memorably. Its powerful rhythm seems pounded out on an instrument of percussion, something that beats like a heart or a hammer, both of which are named in the poem. The mighty beast is the whole world of experience outside ourselves, a world of igneous creation and destruction. Faced with such terrifying beauty, the poet can only ask; the poem is nothing but one wondering question after another.*

# London

()◀▶()

I wander thro' each charter'd street,
Near where the charter'd Thames does flow.
And mark in every face I meet
Marks of weakness, marks of woe.

In every cry of every Man,
In every Infants cry of fear,
In every voice: in every ban,
The mind-forg'd manacles I hear,

How the Chimney-sweepers cry
Every blackning Church appalls,
And the hapless Soldiers sigh
Runs in blood down Palace walls,

But most thro' midnight streets I hear
How the youthful Harlots curse
Blasts the new-born Infants tear
And blights with plagues the Marriage hearse.

from Songs of Experience

---

*"The Tiger" (p. 359) contains no "I" and no statements; "London" centers on
an "I" and is nothing but statements in a strikingly original idiom that fore-
shadows surrealist combinations of sensory images.*

# And Did Those Feet in Ancient Time

And did those feet in ancient time
Walk upon England's mountains green?
And was the holy Lamb of God
On England's pleasant pastures seen?

And did the Countenance Divine
Shine forth upon our clouded hills?
And was Jerusalem builded here,
Among these dark Satanic Mills?

Bring me my Bow of burning gold:
Bring me my Arrows of desire:
Bring me my Spear: O clouds unfold!
Bring me my Chariot of fire!

I will not cease from Mental Fight,
Nor shall my Sword sleep in my hand,
Till we have built Jerusalem
In England's green & pleasant Land.

from Milton

*Blake's words (some of which furnished the movie title* Chariots of Fire) *are very likely the most inspiriting ever written by an Englishman for Englishmen. A tradition of rugged struggle extends from Milton and Bunyan in the seventeenth century, through Blake and Wordsworth in the eighteenth and nineteenth, down to our own time in writers as diverse as W. B. Yeats and Joyce Cary.*

# Piping down the Valleys Wild

❖❖❖❖

Piping down the valleys wild
Piping songs of pleasant glee
On a cloud I saw a child,
And he laughing said to me,

"Pipe a song about a Lamb";
So I piped with merry chear.
"Piper pipe that song again"—
So I piped, he wept to hear.

"Drop thy pipe thy happy pipe
Sing thy songs of happy chear";
So I sung the same again
While he wept with joy to hear.

"Piper sit thee down and write
In a book that all may read"—
So he vanish'd from my sight.
And I pluck'd a hollow reed,

And I made a rural pen,
And I stain'd the water clear,
And I wrote my happy songs
Every child may joy to hear.

from Songs of Experience

*Blake introduces his* Songs of Innocence *with a song of innocence of sorts— innocence without idiocy, innocence with sophistication. There is weeping with laughter (as fits babies and adults alike), and there must be misgiving in recognizing that the passage from piping and singing to writing is a downward motion that involves a stain on clarity.*

# The Sick Rose

O Rose, thou art sick.
The invisible worm
That flies in the night
In the howling storm

Has found out thy bed
Of crimson joy,
And his dark secret love
Does thy life destroy.

from Songs of Experience

---

*The conjunction of "joy" and "destroy" echoes Book IX of* Paradise Lost, *in which another flying enemy invades a paradise. Milton's epic is mostly unrhymed, but "destroy" and "joy" end consecutive lines in one of Satan's soliloquies.*

# The Lamb

Little Lamb, who made thee?
  Dost thou know who made thee?
Gave thee life, and bid thee feed
By the stream and o'er the mead;
Gave thee clothing of delight,
Softest clothing, woolly, bright;
Gave thee such a tender voice,
Making all the vales rejoice?
  Little Lamb, who made thee?
  Dost thou know who made thee?

  Little Lamb, I'll tell thee,
  Little Lamb, I'll tell thee:
He is called by thy name,
For he calls himself a Lamb,
He is meek, and he is mild;
He became a little child.
I a child, and thou a lamb,
We are called by his name.
  Little Lamb, God bless thee!
  Little Lamb, God bless thee!

from Songs of Experience

---

*Blake so designed* Songs of Experience *that many of the poems therein work as companion pieces to some in* Songs of Innocence, *in some cases even sharing the same title. "The Lamb" is the emblem of innocence, corresponding to "The Tiger" (p. 359) as the emblem of experience.*

# Ah! Sun-Flower

Ah Sun-flower! weary of time,
Who countest the steps of the Sun,
Seeking after that sweet golden clime
Where the traveller's journey is done;

Where the Youth pined away with desire,
And the pale Virgin shrouded in snow,
Arise from their graves and aspire,
Where my Sun-flower wishes to go.

from Songs of Experience

---

It is characteristic of the Songs of Experience to saturate a natural creature with human emotions and to translate all such creatures into symbols of human desire.

# Hear the Voice of the Bard

Hear the voice of the Bard!
Who Present, Past and Future, sees
Whose ears have heard
The Holy Word,
That walk'd among the ancient trees.

Calling the lapsed Soul
And weeping in the evening dew;
That might controll
The starry pole;
And fallen, fallen light renew!

O Earth, O Earth, return!
Arise from out the dewy grass;
Night is worn,
And the morn
Rises from the slumberous mass.

Turn away no more:
Why wilt thou turn away
The starry floor
The wat'ry shore
Is giv'n thee till the break of day.

from Songs of Experience

*Blake, recalling the ancient attribution of vatic powers and public duties to the bard—a specialized term retaining a Celtic dignity well into the nineteenth century, thanks to Thomas Gray's "The Bard" (1757)—placed this invocation at the beginning of* Songs of Experience.

# Auguries of Innocence

To see a World in a Grain of Sand
And a Heaven in a Wild Flower,
Hold Infinity in the palm of your hand
And Eternity in an hour.

A Robin Redbreast in a Cage
Puts all Heaven in a Rage.
A dove house fill'd with doves and Pigeons
Shudders Hell thro' all its regions.
A dog starv'd at his Master's Gate
Predicts the ruin of the State.
A Horse misus'd upon the Road
Calls to Heaven for Human blood.
Each outcry of the hunted Hare
A fibre from the Brain does tear.
A Skylark wounded in the wing,
A Cherubim does cease to sing.
The Game Cock clip'd and arm'd for fight
Does the Rising Sun affright.
Every Wolf's and Lion's howl
Raises from Hell a Human Soul.
The wild deer, wand'ring here and there,
Keeps the Human Soul from Care.
The Lamb Misus'd breeds Public strife
And yet forgives the Butcher's Knife.
The Bat that flits at close of Eve
Has left the Brain that won't Believe.
The Owl that calls upon the Night
Speaks the Unbeliever's fright.
He who shall hurt the little Wren
Shall never be belov'd by Men.
He who the Ox to wrath has mov'd
Shall never be by Woman lov'd.

The wanton Boy that kills the Fly
Shall feel the Spider's enmity.
He who torments the Chafer's sprite
Weaves a Bower in endless Night.
The Catterpiller on the Leaf
Repeats to thee thy Mother's grief.
Kill not the Moth nor Butterfly,
For the Last Judgement draweth nigh.
He who shall train the Horse to War
Shall never pass the Polar Bar.
The Beggar's Dog and Widow's Cat,
Feed them and thou wilt grow fat.
The Gnat that sings his Summer's song
Poison gets from Slander's tongue.
The poison of the Snake and Newt
Is the sweat of Envy's Foot.
The Poison of the Honey Bee
Is the Artist's Jealousy.
The Prince's Robes and Beggar's Rags
Are Toadstools on the Miser's Bags.
A truth that's told with bad intent
Beats all the Lies you can invent.
It is right it should be so;
Man was made for Joy and Woe;
And when this we rightly know
Thro' the World we safely go.
Joy and Woe are woven fine,
A Clothing for the Soul divine;
Under every grief and pine
Runs a joy with silken twine.
The Babe is more than swaddling Bands;
Throughout all these Human Lands
Tools were made, and Born were hands,
Every Farmer Understands.
Every Tear from Every Eye
Becomes a Babe in Eternity;
This is caught by Females bright
And return'd to its own delight.

The Bleat, the Bark, Bellow and Roar
Are Waves that Beat on Heaven's Shore.
The Babe that weeps the Rod beneath
Writes Revenge in realms of death.
The Beggar's Rags, fluttering in Air,
Does to Rags the Heavens tear.
The Soldier, arm'd with Sword and Gun,
Palsied strikes the Summer's Sun.
The poor Man's Farthing is worth more
Than all the Gold on Afric's Shore.
One Mite wrung from the Labrer's hands
Shall buy and sell the Miser's Lands:
Or, if protected from on high,
Does that whole Nation sell and buy.
He who mocks the Infant's Faith
Shall be mock'd in Age and Death.
He who shall teach the Child to Doubt
The rotting Grave shall ne'er get out.
He who respects the Infant's faith
Triumphs over Hell and Death.
The Child's Toys and the Old Man's Reasons
Are the Fruits of the Two seasons.
The Questioner, who sits so sly,
Shall never know how to Reply.
He who replies to words of Doubt
Doth put the Light of Knowledge out.
The Strongest Poison ever known
Came from Caesar's Laurel Crown.
Nought can deform the Human Race
Like to the Armour's iron brace.
When Gold and Gems adorn the Plow
To peaceful Arts shall Envy Bow.
A Riddle or the Cricket's Cry
Is to Doubt a fit Reply.
The Emmet's Inch and Eagle's Mile
Make Lame Philosophy to smile.
He who Doubts from what he sees
Will ne'er Believe, do what you Please.

If the Sun and Moon should doubt,
They'd immediately Go out.
To be in a Passion you Good may do,
But no Good if a Passion is in you.
The Whore and Gambler, by the State
Licenc'd, build that Nation's Fate.
The Harlot's cry from Street to Street
Shall weave Old England's winding Sheet.
The Winner's Shout, the Loser's Curse,
Dance before dead England's Hearse.
Every Night and every Morn
Some to Misery are Born.
Every Morn and every Night
Some are Born to sweet delight.
Some are Born to sweet delight,
Some are Born to Endless Night.
We are led to Believe a Lie
When we see not Thro' the Eye
Which was Born in a Night to perish in a Night
When the Soul Slept in Beams of Light.
God Appears and God is Light
To those poor Souls who dwell in Night,
But does a Human Form Display
To those who Dwell in Realms of day.

---

*These miscellaneous sayings, from a notebook kept in 1803, were not published
until 1863, many years after Blake's death. More than any of his Romantic
contemporaries or successors, Blake kept up the Augustan habit of registering
moral truths in epigrams, rather like Alexander Pope and Benjamin Franklin.*

# How Sweet I Roam'd from Field to Field

〰〰〰

How sweet I roam'd from field to field
And tasted all the summer's pride,
Till I the Prince of Love beheld
Who in the sunny beams did glide!

He show'd me lilies for my hair,
And blushing roses for my brow;
He led me through his gardens fair,
Where all his golden pleasures grow.

With sweet May dews my wings were wet,
And Phoebus fir'd my vocal rage;
He caught me in his silken net,
And shut me in his golden cage.

He loves to sit and hear me sing,
Then, laughing, sports and plays with me;
Then stretches out my golden wing,
And mocks my loss of liberty.

---

*Blake's* Poetical Sketches *(1783) consists of poems written from Blake's adolescence, in some cases as early as 1769. Of Blake's poems in this anthology, this song is the earliest.*

# The Little Black Boy

()◀━▶()

My mother bore me in the southern wild,
And I am black, but O! my soul is white;
White as an angel is the English child,
But I am black as if bereav'd of light.

My mother taught me underneath a tree,
And sitting down before the heat of day,
She took me on her lap and kissèd me,
And pointing to the east, began to say:

"Look on the rising sun: there God does live,
And gives his light, and gives his heat away;
And flowers and trees and beasts and men receive
Comfort in morning, joy in the noon day.

"And we are put on earth a little space,
That we may learn to bear the beams of love,
And these black bodies and this sun-burnt face
Is but a cloud, and like a shady grove.

"For when our souls have learn'd the heat to bear,
The cloud will vanish; we shall hear his voice,
Saying, 'Come out from the grove, my love & care,
And round my golden tent like lambs rejoice.' "

Thus did my mother say, and kissèd me;
And thus I say to little English boy:
When I from black and he from white cloud free,
And round the tent of God like lambs we joy,

I'll shade him from the heat till he can bear
To lean in joy upon our father's knee;
And then I'll stand and stroke his silver hair,
And be like him, and he will then love me.

from Songs of Experience

---

*"The Little Black Boy" is in the same heroic quatrain as Gray's "Elegy" (p. 327). Although not a stanza much used by Blake, it serves here to ennoble its subject.*

# A Poison Tree

I was angry with my friend:
I told my wrath, my wrath did end.
I was angry with my foe:
I told it not, my wrath did grow.

And I water'd it in fears,
Night and morning with my tears;
And I sunnèd it with smiles,
And with soft deceitful wiles.

And it grew both day and night,
Till it bore an apple bright;
And my foe beheld it shine,
And he knew that it was mine,

And into my garden stole
When the night had veil'd the pole;
In the morning glad I see
My foe outstretch'd beneath the tree.

from Songs of Experience

---

*Blake retells the legend of the deadly apple in terms that will reappear in Eliot's "Gerontion" (p. 984): "These tears are shaken from the wrath-bearing tree."*

# The Chimney Sweeper

•◇•◇•◇•◇•

When my mother died I was very young,
And my father sold me while yet my tongue
Could scarcely cry *'weep' 'weep' 'weep' 'weep'*!
So your chimneys I sweep, & in soot I sleep.

There's little Tom Dacre, who cried when his head,
That curled like a lamb's back, was shaved; so I said,
"Hush Tom never mind it, for when your head's bare,
You know that the soot cannot spoil your white hair."

And so he was quiet, & that very night,
As Tom was asleeping he had such a sight—
That thousands of sweepers Dick, Joe, Ned & Jack,
Were all of them locked up in coffins of black;

And by came an Angel who had a bright key,
And he opened the coffins & set them all free;
Then down a green plain leaping, laughing they run,
And wash in a river and shine in the sun.

Then naked & white, all their bags left behind,
They rise upon clouds, and sport in the wind.
And the angel told Tom, if he'd be a good boy,
He'd have God for his father & never want joy.

And so Tom awoke, and we rose in the dark,
And got with our bags & our brushes to work.
Though the morning was cold, Tom was happy & warm;
So if all do their duty, they need not fear harm.

from Songs of Innocence

Blake wrote two poems called "The Chimney Sweeper": this one in Songs of Innocence and another in Songs of Experience. This poem is longer than its companion piece and perhaps more naive. Chimney sweepers' work was dirty and dangerous; since the spaces were small and confined, younger children were in demand.

# To the Evening Star

Thou Fair-haired Angel of the Evening,
Now, whilst the sun rests on the mountains, light
Thy bright torch of love; thy radiant crown
Put on, and smile upon our evening bed!
Smile on our loves; and while thou drawest the
Blue curtains of the sky, scatter thy silver dew
On every flower that shuts its sweet eyes

In timely sleep. Let thy West Wind sleep on
The lake; speak silence with thy glimmering eyes,
And wash the dusk with silver. Soon, full soon,
Dost thou withdraw; then the wolf rages wide,
And the lion glares through the dun forest:
The fleeces of the flocks are covered with
Thy sacred dew: protect them with thine influence.

---

*The evening star is the planet Venus, named for the Roman goddess of love. Although this is an early poem of Blake's, it is technically very mature and advanced: a sonnet by virtue of its fourteen lines but with no rhyme or regular rhythm. Lines ending "the" and "with" are common nowadays but were nearly unprecedented in 1783. Blake's decision to avoid rhyme in an evening poem may owe something to Collins's unrhymed "Ode to Evening" (p. 335).*

# The Garden of Love

>>>>>>>

I went to the Garden of Love,
And saw what I never had seen:
A Chapel was built in the midst,
Where I used to play on the green.

And the gates of this Chapel were shut,
And "Thou shalt not" writ over the door;
So I turn'd to the Garden of Love
That so many sweet flowers bore;

And I saw it was filled with graves,
And tomb-stones where flowers should be;
And Priests in black gowns were walking their rounds,
And binding with briars my joys and desires.

from Songs of Experience

*This song of experience recounts the familiar dilemma: our biological nature is thwarted by much of our civil law and established religion. The strain between the antithetical parts of human life gives torque to Blake's work in all media.*

# The Clod and the Pebble

"Love seeketh not Itself to please,
Nor for itself hath any care,
But for another gives its ease,
And builds a Heaven in Hell's despair."

So sang a little Clod of Clay
Trodden with the cattle's feet,
But a Pebble of the brook
Warbled out these metres meet:

"Love seeketh only Self to please,
To bind another to Its delight,
Joys in another's loss of ease,
And builds a Hell in Heaven's despite."

from Songs of Experience

*Blake could invent an original fable as engaging as any in folklore but without
an overload of obvious allegory. Wisdom literature commonly proffers contra-
dictory advice (as in Proverbs XXVI: "Answer not a fool according to his folly"
and "Answer a fool according to his folly").*

# Holy Thursday

'Twas on a Holy Thursday, their innocent faces clean,
The children walking two & two, in red & blue & green,
Grey-headed beadles walked before with wands as white as
    snow,
Till into the high dome of Paul's they like Thames' waters flow.

O what a multitude they seemed, these flowers of London town!
Seated in companies they sit with radiance all their own.
The hum of multitudes was there, but multitudes of lambs,
Thousands of little boys & girls raising their innocent hands.

Now like a mighty wind they raise to Heaven the voice of song,
Or like harmonious thunderings the seats of Heaven among.
Beneath them sit the aged men, wise guardians of the poor;
Then cherish pity, lest you drive an angel from your door.

from Songs of Innocence

---

*Blake wrote two poems entitled "Holy Thursday," in* Songs of Innocence *and
in* Songs of Experience. *The more popular is this one from* Songs of Innocence. *Holy Thursday (Ascension Day) was celebrated in London by having
poor children from charity schools march to St. Paul's Cathedral for a special
service.*

# Mock On, Mock On, Voltaire, Rousseau

Mock on, mock on, Voltaire, Rousseau;
Mock on, mock on, 'Tis all in vain.
You throw the sand against the wind,
And the wind blows it back again.

And every sand becomes a Gem
Reflected in the beams divine;
Blown back, they blind the mocking Eye,
But still in Israel's paths they shine.

The Atoms of Democritus
And Newton's Particles of light
Are sands upon the Red sea shore,
Where Israel's tents do shine so bright.

---

*Democritus and Newton probably do not deserve to be grouped with mockers like Voltaire and Rousseau, but it is not Blake's business to be fair or exact. Scientists and philosophical skeptics are drawn into an irresistible vortex where they receive the same scorn as that heaped on Israel's enemies in the Old Testament.*

# ROBERT BURNS 1759–1796

Burns is honored as the national poet of Scotland. He was genuinely convivial and modest in company but also intelligent enough to master his craft—chiefly as a writer or re-writer of songs—and to understand the eighteenth-century fashion for the primitive and the rustic. His engaging face can still be seen on cigar boxes and shortbread tins.

## A Red, Red Rose

O my Luve's like a red, red rose,
  That's newly sprung in June:
O my Luve's like the melodie
  That's sweetly played in tune!

As fair art thou, my bonnie lass,
  So deep in luve am I;
And I will luve thee still, my dear,
  Till a' the seas gang dry.

Till a' the seas gang dry, my dear,
  And the rocks melt wi' the sun;
I will luve thee still, my dear,
  While the sands o' life shall run.

And fare thee weel, my only Luve,
  And fare thee weel a while!
And I will come again, my Luve,
  Though it were ten thousand mile.

*This, Burns's most famous poem, is among the purest expressions of love in any literature.*

# To a Mouse on Turning Her Up in Her Nest with the Plough, November, 1785

Wee, sleekit, cow'rin', tim'rous beastie,
O, what a panic's in thy breastie!
Thou need na start awa sae hasty,
  Wi' bickering brattle!
I wad be laith to rin an' chase thee,
  Wi' murd'ring pattle!

I'm truly sorry Man's dominion
Has broken Nature's social union,
An' justifies that ill opinion
  Which makes thee startle,
At me, thy poor, earth-born companion,
  An' fellow-mortal!

I doubt na, whiles, but thou may thieve;
What then? poor beastie, thou maun live!
A daimen icker in a thrave
  'S a sma' request:
I'll get a blessin wi' the lave,
  An' never miss 't!

Thy wee-bit housie, too, in ruin!
It's silly wa's the win's are strewin!
An' naething, now, to big a new ane,
  O' foggage green!
An' bleak December's winds ensuin,
  Baith snell an' keen!

Thou saw the fields laid bare an' waste,
An' weary Winter comin fast,
An' cozie here, beneath the blast,
   Thou thought to dwell,
Till crash! the cruel coulter past
   Out thro' thy cell.

That wee-bit heap o' leaves an' stibble,
Has cost thee monie a weary nibble!
Now thou's turn'd out, for a' thy trouble,
   But house or hald,
To thole the winter's sleety dribble,
   An' cranreuch cauld!

But Mousie, thou are no thy lane,
In proving foresight may be vain:
The best laid schemes o' mice an' men,
   Gang aft a-gley,
An' lea'e us nought but grief an' pain,
   For promis'd joy!

Still, thou art blest, compar'd wi' me!
The present only toucheth thee:
But Och! I backward cast my e'e,
   On prospects drear!
An' forward, tho' I canna see,
   I guess an' fear!

---

*It was like Burns to find the deepest meaning in the humblest creatures, such as lice or mice. His description of the mouse is like Uncle Toby's treatment of the fly in Sterne's* Tristram Shandy.

# John Anderson, My Jo

John Anderson my jo, John,
　When we were first acquent;
Your locks were like the raven,
　Your bony brow was brent;
But now your brow is beld, John,
　Your locks are like the snaw;
But blessings on your frosty pow,
　John Anderson my Jo.

John Anderson my jo, John,
　We clamb the hill the gither;
And mony a canty day, John,
　We've had wi' ane anither:
Now we maun totter down, John,
　And hand in hand we'll go;
And sleep the gither at the foot,
　John Anderson my Jo.

*This is one of the many poems that Burns produced by rewriting an anonymous work from folklore.*

# The Banks o' Doon

◆◇◆◇◆

Ye flowery banks o' bonnie Doon,
  How can ye blume sae fair!
How can ye chant, ye little birds,
  And I sae fu' o' care!

Thou'll break my heart, thou bonnie bird
  That sings upon the bough;
Thou minds me o' the happy days
  When my fause Luve was true.

Thou'll break my heart, thou bonnie bird
  That sings beside thy mate;
For sae I sat, and sae I sang,
  And wist na o' my fate.

Aft hae I roved by bonnie Doon
  To see the woodbine twine,
And ilka bird sang o' its love;
  And sae did I o' mine.

Wi' lightsome heart I pu'd a rose,
  Frae aff its thorny tree;
And my fause luver staw the rose,
  But left the thorn wi' me.

---

*The Doon is a river in Burns's native Ayrshire in the western Lowlands. When Gerard Manley Hopkins decided to write about a stream in Scotland, in "Inversnaid" (p. 799), he modelled some of his diction on Burns's (including the word* burn, *which means "brook.")*

# For A' That and A' That

Is there for honest poverty
That hings his head, and a' that?
The coward slave, we pass him by;
We dare be poor for a' that!
For a' that, and a' that,
Our toils obscure, and a' that;
The rank is but the guinea stamp—
The man's the gowd for a' that!

What tho' on hamely fare we dine,
Wear hodden gray, and a' that?
Gie fools their silks, and knaves their wine—
A man's a man for a' that!
For a' that, and a' that,
Their tinsel show, and a' that;
The honest man, though e'er sae poor,
Is king o' men, for a' that!

Ye see yon birkie, ca'd a lord,
Wha struts, an' stares, an' a' that—
Tho' hundreds worship at his word,
He's but a coof for a' that;
For a' that, and a' that,
His riband, star, and a' that;
The man of independent mind,
He looks an' laughs at a' that.

A prince can mak a belted knight,
A marquis, duke, and a' that;
But an honest man's aboon his might —
Gude faith, he mauna fa' that!
For a' that, and a' that,
Their dignities, an' a' that;
The pith o' sense, and pride o' worth,
Are higher rank than a' that.

Then let us pray that come it may, —
As come it will for a' that, —
That sense and worth, o'er a' the earth,
May bear the gree, an' a' that.
For a' that, and a' that,
It's comin' yet, for a' that —
That man to man, the warld o'er,
Shall brithers be for a' that.

---

*Intellectual poets of the seventeenth century delighted in paradox; some of their eighteenth-century successors delighted in less complicated affirmations of equality and identity. We now glibly repeat such verdicts as Burns's "A man's a man for a' that," but the sentiment was far from cant or cliché two centuries ago.*

# Holy Willie's Prayer

>>>>>>>

O Thou that in the heavens does dwell!
Wha, as it pleases best Thysel,
Sends ane to heaven and ten to hell,
  A' for Thy glory!
And no for ony gude or ill
  They've done before Thee!

I bless and praise Thy matchless might,
When thousands Thou has left in night,
That I am here before Thy sight,
  For gifts and grace,
A burning and a shining light
  To a' this place.

What was I, or my generation,
That I should get such exaltation?
I, wha deserved most just damnation
  For broken laws,
Sax thousand years ere my creation,
  Thro' Adam's cause!

When from my mother's womb I fell,
Thou might hae plunged me deep in hell,
To gnash my gooms, and weep, and wail,
  In burning lakes,
Where damned devils roar and yell,
  Chained to their stakes.

Yet I am here, a chosen sample,
To shew Thy grace is great and ample;
I'm here, a pillar o' Thy temple,
    Strong as a rock,
A guide, a buckler, and example,
    To a' Thy flock.

O Lord, Thou kens what zeal I bear,
When drinkers drink, and swearers swear,
And singin' here, and dancin' there,
    Wi' great an' sma';
For I am keepet by Thy fear,
    Free frae them a'.

But yet, O Lord, confess I must,
At times I'm fashed wi' fleshly lust;
And sometimes too, in warldly trust,
    Vile Self gets in;
But Thou remembers we are dust,
    Defiled wi' sin.

O Lord! yestreen, Thou kens—wi' Meg—
Thy pardon I sincerely beg!
O may't ne'er be a living plague,
    To my dishonor!
And I'll ne'er lift a lawless leg
    Again upon her.

Besides, I farther maun allow,
Wi' Leezie's lass, three times—I trow—
But Lord, that Friday I was fou
    When I cam near her;
Or else, Thou kens, Thy servant true
    Wad never steer her.

Maybe Thou lets this fleshy thorn
Buffet Thy servant e'en and morn,
Lest he o'er proud and high should turn,
   That he's sae gifted;
If sae, Thy hand maun e'en be borne
   Until Thou lift it.

Lord, bless Thy Chosen in this place,
For here Thou has a chosen race:
But God, confound their stubborn face,
   And blast their name,
Wha bring Thy rulers to disgrace
   And public shame.

Lord mind Gaun Hamilton's deserts!
He drinks, and swears, and plays at cartes,
Yet has sae mony taking arts
   Wi' Great and Sma',
Frae God's ain priest the people's hearts
   He steals awa.

And when we chastened him therefore,
Thou kens how he bred sic a splore,
And set the warld in a roar
   O' laughing at us—
Curse Thou his basket and his store,
   Kail and potatoes.

Lord, hear my earnest cry and prayer
Against that Presbytry of Ayr!
Thy strong right hand, Lord, make it bare
   Upon their heads!
Lord visit them, and dinna spare,
   For their misdeeds!

O Lord, my God, that glib-tongued Aiken!
My very heart and flesh are quaking
To think how I sat, sweating, shaking,
   And pissed wi' dread,
While he wi' hingin lip and sneaking
   Held up his head!

Lord, in Thy day o' vengeance try him!
Lord, visit them that did employ him!
And pass not in Thy mercy by them,
   Nor hear their prayer;
But for Thy people's sake destroy them,
   And dinna spare!

But Lord, remember me and mine
Wi' mercies temporal and divine!
That I for grace and gear may shine,
   Excelled by nane!
And a' the glory shall be Thine!
   AMEN! AMEN!

---

*"Holy Willie" was William Fisher, a Kirk (Scottish church) Elder who, according to Burns, "was much and justly famed for that polemical chattering which ends in tippling orthodoxy, and for that spiritualized bawdry which refines to liquorish devotion." The hypocrite's prayer is offered up after he has been bested in a church court by Gavin Hamilton and Robert Aiken.*

In his long and eventful life, Wordsworth had more to do with the nature of English poetry than any other poet of the past two centuries. Educated at Cambridge, he spent time in France at the height of the Revolution. Legacies and sinecures enabled Wordsworth and his sister Dorothy to live simply, without needing to earn a living. They occupied dwellings in Dorset, then in Somerset, near Coleridge, then at Grasmere in the Lake Country, and finally—in 1813, after he had married Mary Hutchinson—at Rydal Mount. An on-again-off-again friendship with Coleridge was clearly the most important association of Wordsworth's literary life. The two collaborated on the volume called *Lyrical Ballads, with a Few Other Poems*, containing Coleridge's "The Rime of the Ancient Mariner" and a number of Wordsworth's poems, including the meditative masterpiece "Tintern Abbey." Wordsworth was much honored in his later years and from 1843 until his death was Poet Laureate.

## The World Is Too Much with Us

The world is too much with us; late and soon,
Getting and spending, we lay waste our powers:
Little we see in Nature that is ours;
We have given our hearts away, a sordid boon!
This Sea that bares her bosom to the moon;
The winds that will be howling at all hours,
And are up-gathered now like sleeping flowers;
For this, for everything, we are out of tune;

It moves us not.—Great God! I'd rather be
A Pagan suckled in a creed outworn;
So might I, standing on this pleasant lea,
Have glimpses that would make me less forlorn;
Have sight of Proteus rising from the sea;
Or hear old Triton blow his wreathèd horn.

---

*The form of this sonnet refers back to sixteenth- and seventeenth-century pre-cursors. Some of the details refer back as well: the description of Proteus (the Old Man of the Sea) recalls Milton's description of the same figure; that of the sea-god Triton recalls Spenser's.*

# I Wandered Lonely as a Cloud

I wandered lonely as a cloud
That floats on high o'er vales and hills,
When all at once I saw a crowd,
A host, of golden daffodils;
Beside the lake, beneath the trees,
Fluttering and dancing in the breeze.

Continuous as the stars that shine
And twinkle on the milky way,
They stretched in never-ending line
Along the margin of a bay:
Ten thousand saw I at a glance,
Tossing their heads in sprightly dance.

The waves beside them danced; but they
Out-did the sparkling waves in glee:
A poet could not but be gay,
In such a jocund company:
I gazed—and gazed—but little thought
What wealth the show to me had brought:

For oft, when on my couch I lie
In vacant or in pensive mood,
They flash upon that inward eye
Which is the bliss of solitude;
And then my heart with pleasure fills,
And dances with the daffodils.

---

*A doctrine of simple-hearted harmony with rural nature was a foundation-stone of Romanticism, and Wordsworth was the most eloquent exponent of that belief. One could conceivably force complications into such poetry, because it is profound, but the essential feeling is as simple as it is familiar.*

# Composed upon Westminster Bridge, September 3, 1802

Earth has not anything to show more fair;
Dull would he be of soul who could pass by
A sight so touching in its majesty:
This City now doth, like a garment, wear
The beauty of the morning; silent, bare,
Ships, towers, domes, theaters, and temples lie
Open unto the fields, and to the sky;
All bright and glittering in the smokeless air.
Never did sun more beautifully steep
In his first splendor, valley, rock, or hill;
Ne'er saw I, never felt, a calm so deep!
The river glideth at his own sweet will:
Dear God! the very houses seem asleep;
And all that mighty heart is lying still!

---

*According to Wordsworth's sister, the actual experience occurred on July 31, 1802. The "City" of London is the financial district, a square mile that includes London Bridge and is distinguished by fine commercial and religious buildings. It is much the same neighborhood as that in T. S. Eliot's "Waste Land" (p. 968).*

# The Solitary Reaper

Behold her, single in the field,
Yon solitary Highland Lass!
Reaping and singing by herself;
Stop here, or gently pass!
Alone she cuts and binds the grain,
And sings a melancholy strain;
O listen! for the Vale profound
Is overflowing with the sound.

No Nightingale did ever chaunt
More welcome notes to weary bands
Of travelers in some shady haunt,
Among Arabian sands:
A voice so thrilling ne'er was heard
In spring-time from the Cuckoo-bird,
Breaking the silence of the seas
Among the farthest Hebrides.

Will no one tell me what she sings? —
Perhaps the plaintive numbers flow
For old, unhappy, far-off things,
And battles long ago:
Or is it some more humble lay,
Familiar matter of today?
Some natural sorrow, loss, or pain,
That has been, and may be again?

Whate'er the theme, the Maiden sang
As if her song could have no ending;
I saw her singing at her work,
And o'er the sickle bending: —
I listened, motionless and still;
And, as I mounted up the hill,
The music in my heart I bore,
Long after it was heard no more.

---

*Although deriving most of his material from his own experience, Wordsworth acknowledged that this vision of a lone working-woman singing in Gaelic came from Thomas Wilkinson's* Tour of Scotland. *The poet asks, "Will no one tell me what she sings?" because he cannot understand her language.*

# Ode: Intimations of Immortality from Recollections of Early Childhood

### I

There was a time when meadow, grove and stream,
The earth and every common sight,
   To me did seem
  Apparelled in celestial light,
The glory and the freshness of a dream.
It is not now as it hath been of yore; —
  Turn wheresoe'er I may,
   By night or day,
The things which I have seen I now can see no more.

### II

  The Rainbow comes and goes,
  And lovely is the Rose,
  The Moon doth with delight
Look round her when the heavens are bare,
  Waters on a starry night
  Are beautiful and fair;
The sunshine is a glorious birth;
But yet I know, where'er I go,
That there hath past away a glory from the earth.

### III

Now, while the birds thus sing a joyous song,
  And while the young lambs bound
   As to the tabor's sound,
To me alone there came a thought of grief:
A timely utterance gave that thought relief,
   And I again am strong:

The cataracts blow their trumpets from the steep;
No more shall grief of mine the season wrong;
I hear the Echoes through the mountains throng,
The Winds come to me from the fields of sleep,
   And all the earth is gay
     Land and sea
   Give themselves up to jollity,
     And with the heart of May
   Doth every Beast keep holiday; —
     Thou child of Joy,
Shout round me, let me hear thy shouts, thou happy
Shepherd-boy!

### IV

Ye blessèd Creatures, I have heard the call
   Ye to each other make; I see
The heavens laugh with you in your jubilee;
   My heart is at your festival,
   My head hath its coronal,
The fulness of your bliss, I feel—I feel it all.
   Oh evil day! if I were sullen
   While Earth herself is adorning,
     This sweet May-morning,
   And the Children are culling
     On every side,
   In a thousand valleys far and wide,
   Fresh flowers; while the sun shines warm,
And the Babe leaps up on his Mother's arm: —
   I hear, I hear, with joy I hear!
   —But there's a Tree, of many, one,
A single Field which I have looked upon,
Both of them speak of something that is gone:
   The Pansy at my feet
   Doth the same tale repeat:
Whither is fled the visionary gleam?
Where is it now, the glory and the dream?

### V

Our birth is but a sleep and a forgetting:
The Soul that rises with us, our life's Star,
   Hath had elsewhere its setting,
     And cometh from afar:
   Not in entire forgetfulness,
   And not in utter nakedness,
But trailing clouds of glory do we come
   From God, who is our home:
Heaven lies about us in our infancy!
Shades of the prison-house begin to close
   Upon the growing Boy,
But He beholds the light, and whence it flows,
   He sees it in his joy;
The Youth, who daily farther from the east
   Must travel, still is Nature's Priest,
   And by the vision splendid
   Is on his way attended;
At length the Man perceives it die away,
And fade into the light of common day.

### VI

Earth fills her lap with pleasures of her own;
Yearnings she hath in her own natural kind,
And even with something of a Mother's mind,
   And no unworthy aim
   The homely Nurse doth all she can
To make her Foster-child, her Inmate Man,
   Forget the glories he hath known,
And that imperial palace whence he came.

### VII

Behold the Child among his new-born blisses,
A six years' Darling of a pigmy size!
See where 'mid work of his own hand he lies,
Fretted by sallies of his mother's kisses,
With light upon him from his father's eyes!
See, at his feet, some little plan or chart,

Some fragment from his dream of human life,
Shaped by himself with newly-learned art;
 A wedding or a festival,
 A mourning or a funeral;
  And this hath now his heart,
 And unto this he frames his song:
  Then will he fit his tongue
To dialogues of business, love, or strife;
 But it will not be long
 Ere this be thrown aside,
 And with new joy and pride
The little Actor cons another part;
Filling from time to time his "humorous stage"
With all the Persons, down to palsied Age,
That Life brings with her in her equipage;
 As if his whole vocation
 Were endless imitation.

### VIII

Thou whose exterior semblance doth belie
 Thy Soul's immensity;
Thou best Philosopher, who yet dost keep
Thy heritage, thou Eye among the blind,
That, deaf and silent, read'st the eternal deep,
Haunted for ever by the eternal mind, —
 Mighty Prophet! Seer blest!
 On whom those truths do rest,
Which we are toiling all our lives to find,
In darkness lost, the darkness of the grave;
Thou, over whom thy Immortality
Broods like the Day, a Master o'er a Slave,
A Presence which is not to be put by;
Thou little Child, yet glorious in the might
Of heaven-born freedom on thy being's height,
Why with such earnest pains dost thou provoke
The years to bring the inevitable yoke,
Thus blindly with thy blessedness at strife?
Full soon thy Soul shall have her earthly freight,

And custom lie upon thee with a weight,
Heavy as frost, and deep almost as life!

## IX

  O joy! that in our embers
  Is something that doth live,
  That nature yet remembers
  What was so fugitive!
The thought of our past years in me doth breed
Perpetual benediction; not indeed
For that which is most worthy to be blest;
Delight and liberty, the simple creed
Of Childhood, whether busy or at rest,
With new-fledged hope still fluttering in his breast:—
  Not for these I raise
  The song of thanks and praise;
 But for those obstinate questionings
  Of sense and outward things,
  Fallings from us, vanishings;
 Blank misgivings of a Creature
Moving about in worlds not realized,
High instincts before which our mortal Nature
Did tremble like a guilty Thing surprised:
  But for those first affections,
  Those shadowy recollections,
 Which, be they what they may,
Are yet the fountain-light of all our day,
Are yet a master-light of all our seeing;
 Uphold us, cherish, and have power to make
Our noisy years seem moments in the being
Of the eternal Silence: truths that wake,
 To perish never:
Which neither listlessness, nor mad endeavour,
  Nor Man nor Boy,
Nor all that is at enmity with joy,
Can utterly abolish or destroy!
 Hence in a season of calm weather
  Though inland far we be,

Our Souls have sight of that immortal sea
 Which brought us hither,
 Can in a moment travel thither,
And see the Children sport upon the shore,
And hear the mighty waters rolling evermore.

X

Then sing, ye Birds, sing, sing a joyous song!
 And let the young Lambs bound
 As to the tabor's sound!
We in thought will join your throng,
 Ye that pipe and ye that play,
 Ye that through your hearts today
 Feel the gladness of the May!
What though the radiance which was once so bright
Be now for ever taken from my sight,
 Though nothing can bring back the hour
Of splendour in the grass, of glory in the flower;
 We will grieve not, rather find
 Strength in what remains behind;
 In the primal sympathy
 Which having been must ever be;
 In the soothing thoughts that spring
 Out of human suffering;
 In the faith that looks through death,
In years that bring the philosophic mind.

XI

And O, ye Fountains, Meadows, Hills, and Groves,
Forbode not any severing of our loves!
Yet in my heart of hearts I feel your might
I only have relinquished one delight
To live beneath your more habitual sway.
I love the Brooks which down their channels fret,
Even more than when I tripped lightly as they;
The innocent brightness of a new-born Day
 Is lovely yet;
The Clouds that gather round the setting sun

Do take a sober colouring from an eye
That hath kept watch o'er man's mortality;
Another race hath been, and other palms are won.
Thanks to the human heart by which we live,
Thanks to its tenderness, its joys, and fears,
To me the meanest flower that blows can give
Thoughts that do often lie too deep for tears.

---

*According to Wordsworth's own testimony, he wrote the last seven stanzas of this poem two years after the first four. The poem looks back to Vaughan's "Retreat" (p. 247) and has more intimate connections with Coleridge's "Dejection: An Ode" (p. 458). The concentration on childhood and the suggestion of "a prior state of existence" also relate the poem to Yeats's "Among School Children" (p. 860).*

# Lines Composed a Few Miles above Tintern Abbey

Five years have passed; five summers, with the length
Of five long winters! and again I hear
These waters, rolling from their mountain-springs
With a sweet inland murmur.—Once again
Do I behold these steep and lofty cliffs,
Which on a wild secluded scene impress
Thoughts of more deep seclusion; and connect
The landscape with the quiet of the sky.
The day is come when I again repose
Here, under this dark sycamore, and view
These plots of cottage-ground, these orchard-tufts,
Which, at this season, with their unripe fruits,
Are clad in one green hue, and lose themselves
Mid groves and copses. Once again I see
These hedge-rows, hardly hedge-rows, little lines
Of sportive wood run wild; these pastoral farms
Green to the very door; and wreathes of smoke
Sent up, in silence, from among the trees,
With some uncertain notice, as might seem,
Of vagrant dwellers in the houseless woods,
Or of some hermit's cave, where by his fire
The hermit sits alone.

              Those beauteous forms,
Through a long absence, have not been to me
As is a landscape to a blind man's eye:
But oft, in lonely rooms, and mid the din
Of towns and cities, I have owed to them,
In hours of weariness, sensations sweet,
Felt in the blood, and felt along the heart,
And passing even into my purer mind

With tranquil restoration: — feelings too
Of unremembered pleasure; such, perhaps,
As have no slight or trivial influence
On that best portion of a good man's life;
His little, nameless, unremembered acts
Of kindness and of love. Nor less, I trust,
To them I may have owed another gift,
Of aspect more sublime; that blessed mood,
In which the burthen of the mystery,
In which the heavy and the weary weight
Of all this unintelligible world
Is lightened: — that serene and blessed mood,
In which the affections gently lead us on,
Until, the breath of this corporeal frame,
And even the motion of our human blood
Almost suspended, we are laid asleep
In body, and become a living soul:
While with an eye made quiet by the power
Of harmony, and the deep power of joy,
We see into the life of things.
                      If this
Be but a vain belief, yet, oh! how oft,
In darkness, and amid the many shapes
Of joyless day-light; when the fretful stir
Unprofitable, and the fever of the world,
Have hung upon the beatings of my heart,
How oft, in spirit, have I turned to thee
O sylvan Wye! Thou wanderer through the woods,
How often has my spirit turned to thee!

And now, with gleams of half-extinguished thought,
With many recognitions dim and faint,
And somewhat of a sad perplexity,
The picture of the mind revives again:
While here I stand, not only with the sense
Of present pleasure, but with pleasing thoughts
That in this moment there is life and food
For future years. And so I dare to hope

Though changed, no doubt, from what I was, when first
I came among these hills; when like a roe
I bounded o'er the mountains, by the sides
Of the deep rivers, and the lonely streams,
Wherever nature led; more like a man
Flying from something that he dreads, than one
Who sought the thing he loved. For nature then
(The coarser pleasures of my boyish days,
And their glad animal movements all gone by,)
To me was all in all.—I cannot paint
What then I was. The sounding cataract
Haunted me like a passion: the tall rock,
The mountain, and the deep and gloomy wood,
Their colours and their forms, were then to me
An appetite: a feeling and a love,
That had no need of a remoter charm,
By thought supplied, or any interest
Unborrowed from the eye.— That time is past,
And all its aching joys are now no more,
And all its dizzy raptures. Not for this
Faint I, nor mourn nor murmur: other gifts
Have followed, for such loss, I would believe,
Abundant recompence. For I have learned
To look on nature, not as in the hour
Of thoughtless youth, but hearing oftentimes
The still, sad music of humanity,
Not harsh nor grating, though of ample power
To chasten and subdue. And I have felt
A presence that disturbs me with the joy
Of elevated thoughts; a sense sublime
Of something far more deeply interfused,
Whose dwelling is the light of setting suns,
And the round ocean, and the living air,
And the blue sky, and in the mind of man,
A motion and a spirit, that impels
All thinking things, all objects of all thought,
And rolls through all things. Therefore am I still
A lover of the meadows and the woods,

And mountains; and of all that we behold
From this green earth; of all the mighty world
Of eye and ear, both what they half-create,
And what perceive; well pleased to recognize
In nature and the language of the sense,
The anchor of my purest thoughts, the nurse,
The guide, the guardian of my heart, and soul
Of all my moral being.
                           Nor, perchance,
If I were not thus taught, should I the more
Suffer my genial spirits to decay:
For thou art with me, here, upon the banks
Of this fair river; thou, my dearest friend,
My dear, dear friend, and in thy voice I catch
The language of my former heart, and read
My former pleasures in the shooting lights
Of thy wild eyes. Oh! yet a little while
May I behold in thee what I was once,
My dear, dear sister! And this prayer I make,
Knowing that Nature never did betray
The heart that loved her, 'tis her privilege,
Through all the years of this our life, to lead
From joy to joy: for she can so inform
The mind that is within us, so impress
With quietness and beauty, and so feed
With lofty thoughts, that neither evil tongues,
Rash judgments, nor the sneers of selfish men,
Nor greetings where no kindness is, nor all
The dreary intercourse of daily life,
Shall e'er prevail against us, or disturb
Our cheerful faith that all which we behold
Is full of blessings. Therefore let the moon
Shine on thee in thy solitary walk;
And let the misty mountain winds be free
To blow against thee: and in after years,
When these wild ecstasies shall be matured
Into a sober pleasure, when thy mind

Shall be a mansion for all lovely forms,
Thy memory be as a dwelling-place
For all sweet sounds and harmonies; Oh! then,
If solitude, or fear, or pain, or grief,
Should be thy portion, with what healing thoughts
Of tender joy wilt thou remember me,
And these my exhortations! Nor, perchance,
If I should be, where I no more can hear
Thy voice, nor catch from thy wild eyes these gleams
Of past existence, wilt thou then forget
That on the banks of this delightful stream
We stood together; and that I, so long
A worshipper of Nature, hither came,
Unwearied in that service: rather say
With warmer love, oh! with far deeper zeal
Of holier love. Nor wilt thou then forget,
That after many wanderings, many years
Of absence, these steep woods and lofty cliffs,
And this green pastoral landscape, were to me
More dear, both for themselves, and for thy sake.

---

*In a poem that is essentially an ode in all but name, Wordsworth expresses the profound meanings of a pilgrimage or return to a special sacred place—a theme that animates much poetry in English, from Chaucer's* Canterbury Tales *(p. 8) through Gray's "Elegy Written in a Country Churchyard" (p. 328) to such distinguished modern work as Eliot's "Little Gidding" (p. 987) and Larkin's "Church Going" (p. 1068).*

# Lucy

Comprising:
*She Dwelt among the Untrodden Ways,*
*I Traveled among Unknown Men,*
*Strange Fits of Passion Have I Known,*
*Three Years She Grew in Sun and Shower*
*A Slumber Did My Spirit Seal*

(I)

She dwelt among the untrodden ways
    Beside the springs of Dove,
A Maid whom there were none to praise
    And very few to love:

A violet by a mossy stone
    Half hidden from the eye!
Fair as a star, when only one
    Is shining in the sky.

She lived unknown, and few could know
    When Lucy ceased to be;
But she is in her grave, and oh,
    The difference to me!

(II)

I traveled among unknown men,
    In lands beyond the sea;
Nor, England! did I know till then
    What love I bore to thee.

'Tis past, that melancholy dream!
    Nor will I quit thy shore
A second time; for still I seem
    To love thee more and more.

Among thy mountains did I feel
  The joy of my desire;
And she I cherished turned her wheel
  Beside an English fire.

Thy mornings showed, thy nights concealed,
  The bowers where Lucy played;
And time too is the last green field
  That Lucy's eyes surveyed.

(III)

Strange fits of passion have I known:
And I will dare to tell,
But in the Lover's ear alone,
What once to me befell.

When she I loved looked every day
Fresh as a rose in June,
I to her cottage bent my way,
Beneath an evening-moon.

Upon the moon I fixed my eye,
All over the wide lea;
With quickening pace my horse drew nigh
Those paths so dear to me.

And now we reached the orchard-plot;
And, as we climbed the hill,
The sinking moon to Lucy's cot
Came near, and nearer still.

In one of those sweet dreams I slept,
Kind Nature's gentlest boon!
And all the while my eyes I kept
On the descending moon.

My horse moved on; hoof after hoof
He raised, and never stopped:
When down behind the cottage roof,
At once, the bright moon dropped.

What fond and wayward thoughts will slide
Into a Lover's head!
"O mercy!" to myself I cried,
"If Lucy should be dead!"

(IV)

Three years she grew in sun and shower;
Then Nature said, "A lovelier flower
   On earth was never sown;
This child I to myself will take;
She shall be mine, and I will make
   A lady of my own.

"Myself will to my darling be
Both law and impulse: and with me
   The girl, in rock and plain,
In earth and heaven, in glade and bower,
Shall feel an overseeing power
   To kindle or restrain.

"She shall be sportive as the fawn
That wild with glee across the lawn
   Or up the mountain springs;
And hers shall be the breathing balm,
And hers the silence and the calm
   Of mute insensate things.

"The floating clouds their state shall lend
To her; for her the willow bend;
   Nor shall she fail to see
Even in the motions of the storm
Grace that shall mould the maiden's form
   By silent sympathy.

"The stars of midnight shall be dear
To her; and she shall lean her ear
   In many a secret place
Where rivulets dance their wayward round,
And beauty born of murmuring sound
   Shall pass into her face.

"And vital feelings of delight
Shall rear her form to stately height,
   Her virgin bosom swell;
Such thoughts to Lucy I will give
While she and I together live
   Here in this happy dell."

Thus Nature spake—The work was done—
How soon my Lucy's race was run!
   She died, and left to me
This heath, this calm and quiet scene;
The memory of what has been,
   And never more will be.

(V)
A slumber did my spirit seal;
   I had no human fears:
She seemed a thing that could not feel
   The touch of earthly years.

No motion has she now, no force;
   She neither hears nor sees;
Rolled round in earth's diurnal course,
   With rocks, and stones, and trees.

---

*These five lyrics, along with a sixth called "Lucy Gray," are customarily grouped as "the Lucy poems." Although "I Traveled among Unknown Men" was slightly later than the others, Wordsworth said that it belonged after "She Dwelt among the Untrodden Ways." No actual persons or occasions mentioned in the poem have been identified with any certainty.*

# It Is a Beauteous Evening

It is a beauteous evening, calm and free,
The holy time is quiet as a Nun
Breathless with adoration; the broad sun
Is sinking down in its tranquillity;
The gentleness of heaven broods o'er the Sea:
Listen! the mighty Being is awake,
And doth with his eternal motion make
A sound like thunder—everlastingly.
Dear Child! dear Girl! that walkest with me here,
If thou appear untouched by solemn thought,
Thy nature is not therefore less divine:
Thou liest in Abraham's bosom all the year;
And worshipp'st at the Temple's inner shrine,
God being with thee when we know it not.

*The "dear Girl" in this sonnet is thought to be Wordsworth's natural daughter Caroline, who was about ten years old when the poem was written in the late summer of 1802.*

# London, 1802

>>>>>>>

Milton! thou should'st be living at this hour:
England hath need of thee; she is a fen
Of stagnant waters; altar, sword, and pen,
Fireside, the heroic wealth of hall and bower
Have forfeited their ancient English dower
Of inward happiness. We are selfish men;
Oh raise us up, return to us again
And give us manners, virtue, freedom, power.
Thy soul was like a star, and dwelt apart;
Thou hadst a voice whose sound was like the sea:
Pure as the naked heavens, majestic, free,
So didst thou travel on life's common way,
In cheerful godliness; and yet thy heart
The lowliest duties on herself did lay.

---

*After Milton, the sonnet form went into a 130-year hibernation, stirring now and then in Gray or Bowles but not fully reawakening until Wordsworth. Inspired by reading Milton's polemical prose, he addressed this ringing appeal to his mighty precursor as sonnet-writer and as moral exemplar.*

# My Heart Leaps Up

My heart leaps up when I behold
    A rainbow in the sky:
So was it when my life began;
So is it now I am a man;
So be it when I shall grow old,
    Or let me die!
The Child is father of the Man;
And I could wish my days to be
Bound each to each by natural piety.

---

*The last three lines of this prismatic poem reappear as the epigraph of Words-worth's "Ode: Intimations of Immortality from Recollections of Early Childhood" (p. 400).*

# Surprised by Joy

Surprised by joy—impatient as the wind
  I turned to share the transport—Oh! with whom
  But thee, deep buried in the silent tomb,
That spot which no vicissitude can find?
Love, faithful love, recalled thee to my mind—
  But how could I forget thee? Through what power,
  Even for the least division of an hour,
Have I been so beguiled as to be blind
To my most grievous loss!—That thought's return
  Was the worst pang that sorrow ever bore,
Save one, one only, when I stood forlorn,
  Knowing my heart's best treasure was no more;
That neither present time, nor years unborn
  Could to my sight that heavenly face restore.

*Wordsworth said that this tender poem was suggested by memories of his daughter Catherine, who died in 1812 at the age of four.*

# She Was a Phantom of Delight

She was a phantom of delight
When first she gleamed upon my sight;
A lovely apparition, sent
To be a moment's ornament;
Her eyes as stars of twilight fair;
Like twilight's, too, her dusky hair;
But all things else about her drawn
From May-time and the cheerful dawn;
A dancing shape, an image gay,
To haunt, to startle and waylay.

I saw her upon nearer view,
A Spirit, yet a Woman too!
Her household motions light and free,
And steps of virgin liberty;
A countenance in which did meet
Sweet records, promises as sweet;
A creature not too bright or good
For human nature's daily food;
For transient sorrows, simple wiles,
Praise, blame, love, kisses, tears, and smiles.

And now I see with eye serene
The very pulse of the machine;
A being breathing thoughtful breath,
A traveller between life and death;
The reason firm, the temperate will,
Endurance, foresight, strength, and skill;
A perfect Woman, nobly planned,
To warn, to comfort, and command;
And yet a Spirit still, and bright
With something of angelic light.

*Wordsworth wrote this poem about his wife.*

# Resolution and Independence

There was a roaring in the wind all night;
The rain came heavily and fell in floods;
But now the sun is rising calm and bright;
The birds are singing in the distant woods;
Over his own sweet voice the stock-dove broods;
The jay makes answer as the magpie chatters;
And all the air is filled with pleasant noise of waters.

All things that love the sun are out of doors;
The sky rejoices in the morning's birth;
The grass is bright with rain-drops;—on the moors
The hare is running races in her mirth;
And with her feet she from the plashy earth
Raises a mist; that, glittering in the sun,
Runs with her all the way, wherever she doth run.

I was a Traveler then upon the moor;
I saw the hare that raced about with joy;
I heard the woods and distant waters roar;
Or heard them not, as happy as a boy:
The pleasant season did my heart employ:
My old remembrances went from me wholly;
And all the ways of men, so vain and melancholy.

But, as it sometimes chanceth, from the might
Of joy in minds that can no further go,
As high as we have mounted in delight
In our dejection do we sink as low;
To me that morning did it happen so;
And fears and fancies thick upon me came;
Dim sadness—and blind thoughts, I knew not, nor could name.

I heard the sky-lark warbling in the sky;
And I bethought me of the playful hare:
Even such a happy Child of earth am I;
Even as these blissful creatures do I fare;
Far from the world I walk, and from all care;
But there may come another day to me—
Solitude, pain of heart, distress, and poverty.

My whole life I have lived in pleasant thought,
As if life's business were a summer mood;
As if all needful things would come unsought
To genial faith, still rich in genial good;
But how can he expect that others should
Build for him, sow for him, and at his call
Love him, who for himself will take no heed at all?

I thought of Chatterton, the marvellous Boy,
The sleepless Soul that perished in his pride;
Of Him who walked in glory and in joy
Following his plough, along the mountain-side:
By our own spirits are we deified:
We Poets in our youth begin in gladness;
But thereof come in the end despondency and madness.

Now, whether it were by peculiar grace,
A leading from above, a something given,
Yet it befell that, in this lonely place,
When I with these untoward thoughts had striven,
Beside a pool bare to the eye of heaven
I saw a Man before me unawares:
The oldest man he seemed that ever wore grey hairs.

As a huge stone is sometimes seen to lie
Couched on the bald top of an eminence;
Wonder to all who do the same espy,
By what means it could thither come, and whence;
So that it seems a thing endued with sense:
Like a sea-beast crawled forth, that on a shelf
Of rock or sand reposeth, there to sun itself;

Such seemed this Man, not all alive nor dead,
Nor all asleep—in his extreme old age:
His body was bent double, feet and head
Coming together in life's pilgrimage;
As if some dire constraint of pain, or rage
Of sickness felt by him in times long past,
A more than human weight upon his frame had cast.

Himself he propped, limbs, body, and pale face,
Upon a long grey staff of shaven wood:
And, still as I drew near with gentle pace,
Upon the margin of that moorish flood
Motionless as a cloud the old Man stood,
That heareth not the loud winds when they call;
And moveth all together, if it move at all.

At length, himself unsettling, he the pond
Stirred with his staff, and fixedly did look
Upon the muddy water, which he conned,
As if he had been reading in a book:
And now a stranger's privilege I took;
And, drawing to his side, to him did say,
"This morning gives us promise of a glorious day."

A gentle answer did the old Man make,
In courteous speech which forth he slowly drew:
And him with further words I thus bespake,
"What occupation do you there pursue?
This is a lonesome place for one like you."
Ere he replied, a flash of mild surprise
Broke from the sable orbs of his yet-vivid eyes.

His words came feebly, from a feeble chest,
But each in solemn order followed each,
With something of a lofty utterance drest—
Choice word and measured phrase, above the reach
Of ordinary men; a stately speech;
Such as grave Livers do in Scotland use,
Religious men, who give to God and man their dues.

He told, that to these waters he had come
To gather leeches, being old and poor:
Employment hazardous and wearisome!
And he had many hardships to endure:
From pond to pond he roamed, from moor to moor;
Housing, with God's good help, by choice or chance;
And in this way he gained an honest maintenance.

The old Man still stood talking by my side;
But now his voice to me was like a stream
Scarce heard; nor word from word could I divide;
And the whole body of the Man did seem
Like one whom I had met with in a dream;
Or like a man from some far region sent,
To give me human strength, by apt admonishment.

My former thoughts returned: the fear that kills;
And hope that is unwilling to be fed;
Cold, pain, and labour, and all fleshly ills;
And mighty Poets in their misery dead.
—Perplexed, and longing to be comforted,
My question eagerly did I renew,
"How is it that you live, and what is it you do?"

He with a smile did then his words repeat;
And said that, gathering leeches, far and wide
He travelled; stirring thus about his feet
The waters of the pools where they abide.
"Once I could meet with them on every side;
But they have dwindled long by slow decay;
Yet still I persevere, and find them where I may."

While he was talking thus, the lonely place,
The old Man's shape, and speech—all troubled me:
In my mind's eye I seemed to see him pace
About the weary moors continually,
Wandering about alone and silently.
While I these thoughts within myself pursued,
He, having made a pause, the same discourse renewed.

And soon with this he other matter blended,
Cheerfully uttered, with demeanour kind,
But stately in the main; and when he ended,
I could have laughed myself to scorn to find
In that decrepit Man so firm a mind.
"God," said I, "be my help and stay secure;
I'll think of the Leech-gatherer on the lonely moor!"

---

*For a poem about the humblest of humankind—an infirm old man with one of the worst jobs anybody has ever had—Wordsworth deliberately chose a stanza called Rhyme Royal, which had been associated with kings. Wordsworth's poem is travestied in "I'll Tell Thee Everything I Can" by "Lewis Carroll" (p. 755).*

# SIR WALTER SCOTT 1771–1832

Beginning in 1797 and continuing for thirty-five years, Scott published at least one book a year, and sometimes two: poetry, historical fiction, collections of folklore, and editions and biographies of earlier writers. Although the direct influence of his verse has diminished somewhat since the nineteenth century, his importance is still strongly felt in opera, historical fiction, and antiquarian studies. It is also worth noting that the modern sense of "glamour" comes from Scott.

## Proud Maisie

Proud Maisie is in the wood,
  Walking so early;
Sweet Robin sits on the bush,
  Singing so rarely.

"Tell me, thou bonny bird,
  When shall I marry me?"
"When six braw gentlemen
  Kirkward shall carry ye."

"Who makes the bridal bed,
  Birdie, say truly?"
"The grey-headed sexton
  That delves the grave duly.

"The glowworm o'er grave and stone
  Shall light thee steady.
The owl from the steeplesing,
  'Welcome, proud lady.' "

from The Heart of Midlothian

---

*Scott seems to have been the last writer who produced still-readable novels containing poems that qualify for an anthology based on popularity. "Proud Maisie," from chapter 40 of* The Heart of Midlothian, *is the last song sung by Madge Wildfire.*

# Breathes There the Man
# with Soul So Dead

❧❧❧❧

Breathes there the man with soul so dead,
  Who never to himself hath said,
  This is my own, my native land!
Whose heart hath ne'er within him burn'd,
As home his footsteps he hath turn'd
  From wandering on a foreign strand!
If such there breathe, go, mark him well;
For him no Minstrel raptures swell;
High though his titles, proud his name,
Boundless his wealth as wish can claim;
Despite those titles, power, and pelf,
The wretch, concentred all in self,
Living, shall forfeit fair renown,
And, doubly dying, shall go down
To the vile dust, from whence he sprung,
Unwept, unhonour'd, and unsung.

from The Lay of the Last Minstrel

---

*These lines open canto 6 of "The Lay of the Last Minstrel." Today, two centuries later, Scotland ("Caledonia") still inspires patriotic fervor. Any number of immensely popular romances amply demonstrate that the land continues to impress us as wild, rugged, and exciting. The turning point of Edward Everett Hale's "Man without a Country," by the way, comes when the hero, Philip Nolan, reads these lines by Scott.*

# Lochinvar

Oh, young Lochinvar is come out of the West, —
Through all the wide Border his steed was the best,
And, save his good broadsword, he weapon had none, —
He rode all unarmed, and he rode all alone.
So faithful in love, and so dauntless in war,
There never was knight like the young Lochinvar.

He stayed not for brake, and he stopped not for stone,
He swam the Eske river where ford there was none,
But, ere he alighted at Netherby gate,
The bride had consented, the gallant came late;
For a laggard in love, and a dastard in war,
Was to wed the fair Ellen of brave Lochinvar.

So boldly he entered the Netherby hall,
Among bridesmen, and kinsmen, and brothers, and all.
Then spoke the bride's father, his hand on his sword,
(For the poor craven bridegroom said never a word),
"Oh, come ye in peace here, or come ye in war,
Or to dance at our bridal, young Lord Lochinvar?"

"I long wooed your daughter, my suit you denied; —
Love swells like the Solway, but ebbs like its tide; —
And now am I come, with this lost love of mine,
To lead but one measure, drink one cup of wine.
There are maidens in Scotland more lovely by far,
That would gladly be bride to the young Lochinvar."

The bride kissed the goblet, the knight took it up,
He quaffed off the wine, and he threw down the cup.
She looked down to blush, and she looked up to sigh,
With a smile on her lips,and a tear in her eye.
He took her soft hand ere her mother could bar:
"Now tread we a measure," said young Lochinvar.

So stately his form, and so lovely her face,
That never a hall such a galliard did grace;
While her mother did fret, and her father did fume,
And the bridegroom stood dangling his bonnet and plume,
And the bridemaidens whispered, " 'Twere better by far
To have matched our fair cousin with young Lochinvar."

One touch to her hand, and one word in her ear,
When they reached the hall-door, and the charger stood near;
So light to the croupe the fair lady he swung,
So light to the saddle before her he sprung!
"She is won! we are gone! over bank, bush, and scaur;
They'll have fleet steeds that follow," quoth young Lochinvar.

There was mounting 'mong Græmes of the Netherby clan;
Forsters, Fenwicks, and Musgraves, they rode and they ran;
There was racing and chasing on Cannobie Lee,
But the lost bride of Netherby ne'er did they see.
So daring in love, and so dauntless in war,
Have ye e'er heard of gallant like young Lochinvar?

from Marmion

*In the chivalric tale "Marmion," Lady Heron sings "Lochinvar," which Scott based on a folk ballad.*

Paradoxically, the most philosophical of philosophical
critics, fit for the company of Plato and Bacon, is also
the least philosophical of poets, fit for the company of
the anonymous authors of "Sir Patrick Spens" and
other ballads. The son of a vicar, Coleridge received a
spotty but stimulating education and led a particularly
vexed life, which included a dependency on opium. He
was, however, most fortunate in his associations; he
was close to Charles Lamb, William Wordsworth, and
Robert Southey, and he was supported for several years
by the philanthropy of Josiah and Thomas Wedgwood,
still famous for their china.

# Kubla Khan

In Xanadu did Kubla Khan
A stately pleasure-dome decree:
Where Alph, the sacred river, ran
Through caverns measureless to man
   Down to a sunless sea.
So twice five miles of fertile ground
With walls and towers were girdled round;
And here were gardens bright with sinuous rills,
Where blossomed many an incense-bearing tree;
And here were forests ancient as the hills,
Enfolding sunny spots of greenery.

But oh! that deep romantic chasm which slanted
Down the green hill athwart a cedarn cover!
A savage place! as holy and enchanted
As e'er beneath a waning moon was haunted
By woman wailing for her demon-lover!
And from this chasm, with ceaseless turmoil seething,
As if this earth in fast thick pants were breathing,
A mighty fountain momently was forced:
Amid whose swift half-intermitted burst
Huge fragments vaulted like rebounding hail,
Or chaffy grain beneath the thresher's flail:
And 'mid these dancing rocks at once and ever
It flung up momently the sacred river.
Five miles meandering with a mazy motion
Through wood and dale the sacred river ran,
Then reached the caverns measureless to man,
And sank in tumult to a lifeless ocean:
And 'mid this tumult Kubla heard from far
Ancestral voices prophesying war!

    The shadow of the dome of pleasure
    Floated midway on the waves;
    Where was heard the mingled measure
    From the fountain and the caves.
It was a miracle of rare device,
A sunny pleasure-dome with caves of ice!

A damsel with a dulcimer
In a vision once I saw:
It was an Abyssinian maid,
And on her dulcimer she played,
Singing of Mount Abora.
Could I revive within me
Her symphony and song,
To such a deep delight 'twould win me,
That with music loud and long,
I would build that dome in air,
That sunny dome! those caves of ice!
And all who heard should see them there,
And all should cry, Beware! Beware!
His flashing eyes, his floating hair!
Weave a circle round him thrice,
And close your eyes with holy dread,
For he on honey-dew hath fed,
And drunk the milk of Paradise.

*We meet in Coleridge a genius-level mentality (here, in 1797, about twenty-five years of age), with his deep desires given special form and color by fabulously comprehensive reading and profound thinking. The desires take the form of a Paradise, which literally means "a walled enclosure." Then, reading about another walled enclosure devoted to pleasure and lulled by both opium and the charms of repeated sounds in exotic words, the genius falls asleep and dreams this poem.*

# The Rime of the Ancient Mariner

>>>>>>>

IN SEVEN PARTS

*Facile credo, plures esse Naturas invisibles quam visibiles in rerum universitate. Sed horum* [sic] *omnium familiam quis nobis enarrabit? et gradus et cognationes et discrimina et singulorum munera? Quid agunt? quae loca habitant? Harum rerum notitiam semper ambivit ingenium humanum, nunquam attigit. Juvat, inverea, non diffiteor, quandoque, in animo, in tabulâ, majoris et melioris mundi imaginem contemplari: ne mens assuefacta hodiernae vitae minutiis se contrahat nimis, et tota subsidat in pusillas cogitationes. Sed veritati interea invigilandum est, modusque servandus, ut certa ab incertis, diem a nocte, distinguamus.* —T. BURNET

## PART I

*An ancient Mariner meeteth three Gallants bidden to a Wedding feast, and detaineth one.*

It is an ancient Mariner
And he stoppeth one of three.
—"By thy long gray beard and glittering
    eye,
Now wherefore stopp'st thou me?

The Bridegroom's doors are opened wide,
And I am next of kin;
The guests are met, the feast is set:
May'st hear the merry din."

He holds him with his skinny hand,
"There was a ship," quoth he.
"Hold off! unhand me, graybeard loon!"
Eftsoons his hand dropped he.

*The Wedding Guest is spellbound by the eye of the old seafaring man, and constrained to hear his tale.*

He holds him with his glittering eye—
The Wedding Guest stood still,
And listens like a three years' child:
The Mariner hath his will.

[433]

The Wedding Guest sat on a stone:
He cannot choose but hear;
And thus spake on that ancient man,
The bright-eyed Mariner.

"The ship was cheered, the harbor cleared,
Merrily did we drop
Below the kirk, below the hill,
Below the lighthouse top.

*The Mariner tells how the ship sailed southward with a good wind and fair weather, till it reached the line.*

The Sun came up upon the left,
Out of the sea came he!
And he shone bright, and on the right
Went down into the sea.

Higher and higher every day,
Till over the mast at noon —"
The Wedding Guest here beat his breast,
For he heard the loud bassoon.

*The Wedding Guest heareth the bridal music; but the Mariner continueth his tale.*

The bride hath placed into the hall,
Red as a rose is she;
Nodding their heads before her goes
The merry minstrelsy.

The Wedding Guest he beat his breast,
Yet he cannot choose but hear;
And thus spake on that ancient man,
The bright-eyed Mariner.

*The ship driven by a storm toward the South Pole.*

"And now the STORM-BLAST came and he
Was tyrannous and strong;
He struck with his o'ertaking wings,
And chased us south along.

With sloping masts and dipping prow,
As who pursued with yell and blow
Still treads the shadow of his foe,
And forward bends his head,
The ship drove fast, loud roared the blast,
And southward aye we fled.

And now there came both mist and snow,
And it grew wondrous cold:
And ice, mast-high, came floating by,
As green as emerald.

*The land of ice, and of fearful
sounds where no living thing
was to be seen.*

And through the drifts the snowy clifts
Did send a dismal sheen:
Nor shapes of men nor beasts we ken—
The ice was all between.

The ice was here, the ice was there,
The ice was all around:
It cracked and growled, and roared and
howled,
Like noises in a swound!

*Till a great sea bird, called the
Albatross, came through the
snowfog, and was received
with great joy and hospitality.*

At length did cross an Albatross,
Thorough the fog it came;
As if it had been a Christian soul,
We hailed it in God's name.

It ate the food it ne'er had eat,
And round and round it flew.
The ice did split with a thunder-fit;
The helmsman steered us through!

And lo! the Albatross proveth a bird of good omen, and followeth the ship as it returned northward through fog and floating ice.

And a good south wind sprung up behind;
The Albatross did follow,
And every day, for food or play,
Came to the mariners' hollo!

In mist or cloud, on mast or shroud,
It perched for vespers nine;
Whiles all the night, through fog-smoke
    white,
Glimmered the white Moon-shine."

The ancient Mariner inhospitably killeth the pious bird of good omen.

"God save thee, ancient Mariner!
From the fiends, that plague thee thus! —
Why look'st thou so?" — With my crossbow
I shot the ALBATROSS.

PART II

The Sun now rose upon the right:
Out of the sea came he,
Still hid in mist, and on the left
Went down into the sea.

And the good south wind still blew behind,
But no sweet bird did follow,
Nor any day for food or play
Came to the mariners' hollo!

His shipmates cry out against the ancient Mariner, for killing the bird of good luck.

And I had done a hellish thing,
And it would work 'em woe:
For all averred, I had killed the bird
That made the breeze to blow.
Ah wretch! said they, the bird to slay,
That made the breeze to blow!

*But when the fog cleared off, they justify the same, and thus make themselves accomplices in the crime.*

Nor dim nor red, like God's own head,
The glorious Sun uprist:
Then all averred, I had killed the bird
That brought the fog and mist.
'Twas right, said they, such birds to slay,
That bring the fog and mist.

*The fair breeze continues; the ship enters the Pacific Ocean, and sails northward, even till it reaches the Line.*

The fair breeze blew, the white foam flew,
The furrow followed free;
We were the first that ever burst
Into that silent sea.

*The ship hath been suddenly becalmed.*

Down dropped the breeze, the sails
    dropped down,
'Twas sad as sad could be;
And we did speak only to break
The silence of the sea!

All in a hot and copper sky,
The bloody Sun, at noon,
Right up above the mist did stand,
No bigger than the Moon.

Day after day, day after day,
We stuck, nor breath nor motion;
As idle as a painted ship
Upon a painted ocean.

*And the Albatross begins to be avenged.*

Water, water, everywhere,
And all the boards did shrink;
Water, water, everywhere,
Nor any drop to drink.

The very deep did rot: O Christ!
That ever this should be!
Yea, slimy things did crawl with legs
Upon the slimy sea.

About, about, in reel and rout
The death-fires danced at night;
The water, like a witch's oils,
Burnt green, and blue and white.

And some in dreams assuréd were
Of the Spirit that plagued us so;
Nine fathom deep he had followed us
From the land of mist and snow.

*A Spirit had followed them; one of the invisible inhabitants of this planet, neither departed souls nor angels; concerning whom the learned Jew, Josephus, and the Platonic Constantinopolitan, Michael Psellus, may be consulted. They are very numerous, and there is no climate or element without one or more.*

And every tongue, through utter drought,
Was withered at the root;
We could not speak, no more than if
We had been choked with soot.

*The shipmates, in their sore distress, would fain throw the whole guilt on the ancient Mariner: in sign whereof they hang the dead sea bird round his neck.*

Ah! well-a-day! what evil looks
Had I from old and young!
Instead of the cross, the Albatross
About my neck was hung.

PART III

There passed a weary time. Each throat
Was parched, and glazed each eye.
A weary time! a weary time!
How glazed each weary eye,
When looking westward, I beheld
A something in the sky.

At first it seemed a little speck,
And then it seemed a mist;
It moved and moved, and took at last
A certain shape, I wist.

A speck, a mist, a shape, I wist!
And still it neared and neared:
As if it dodged a water sprite,
It plunged and tacked and veered.

With throats unslaked, with black lips
    baked,
We could nor laugh nor wail;
Through utter drought all dumb we stood!
I bit my arm, I sucked the blood,
And cried, a sail! a sail!

With throats unslaked, with black lips
    baked,
Agape they heard me call:
Gramercy! they for joy did grin,
And all at once their breath drew in,
As they were drinking all.

*And horror follows. For can it be a ship that comes onward without wind or tide?*

See! see! (I cried) she tacks no more!
Hither to work us weal;
Without a breeze, without a tide,
She steadies with upright keel!

The western wave was all aflame.
The day was well nigh done!
Almost upon the western wave
Rested the broad bright Sun;
When that strange shape drove suddenly
Betwixt us and the Sun.

*It seemeth him but the skeleton of a ship.*

And straight the Sun was flecked with bars,
(Heaven's Mother send us grace!)
As if through a dungeon grate he peered
With broad and burning face.

*And its ribs are seen as bars on the face of the setting Sun.*

Alas! (thought I, and my heart beat loud)
How fast she nears and nears!
Are those *her* sails that glance in the Sun,
Like restless gossameres?

*The Specter-Woman and her Deathmate, and no other on board the skeleton ship.*

Are those *her* ribs through which the Sun
Did peer, as through a grate?
And is that Woman all her crew?
Is that a DEATH? and are there two?
Is DEATH that woman's mate?

*Like vessel, like crew!*

*Her* lips were red, *her* looks were free,
Her locks were yellow as gold:
Her skin was as white as leprosy,
The Nightmare LIFE-IN-DEATH was she,
Who thicks man's blood with cold.

*Death and Life-in-Death have diced for the ship's crew, and she (the latter) winneth the ancient Mariner.*

The naked hulk alongside came,
And the twain were casting dice;
"The game is done! I've won! I've won!"
Quoth she, and whistles thrice.

*No twilight within the courts of the Sun.*

The Sun's rim dips; the stars rush out:
At one stride comes the dark;
With far-heard whisper, o'er the sea,
Off shot the specter-bark.

*At the rising of the Moon,*

We listened and looked sideways up!
Fear at my heart, as at a cup,
My lifeblood seemed to sip!
The stars were dim, and thick the night,
The steersman's face by his lamp gleamed
    white;
From the sails the dew did drip —
Till clomb above the eastern bar
The hornéd Moon, with one bright star
Within the nether tip.

*One after another,*

One after one, by the star-dogged Moon,
Too quick for groan or sigh,
Each turned his face with ghastly pang,
And cursed me with his eye.

*His shipmates drop down dead.*

Four times fifty living men,
(And I heard nor sigh nor groan)
With heavy thump, a lifeless lump,
They dropped down one by one.

The souls did from their bodies fly—
They fled to bliss or woe!
And every soul, it passed me by,
Like the whizz of my cross-bow!

PART IV

"I fear thee, ancient Mariner!
I fear thy skinny hand!
And thou art long, and lank, and brown,
As is the ribbed sea-sand.

I fear thee and thy glittering eye,
And thy skinny hand, so brown."—
Fear not, fear not, thou Wedding Guest!
This body dropped not down.

Alone, alone, all, all alone,
Alone on a wide wide sea!
And never a saint took pity on
My soul in agony.

The many men, so beautiful!
And they all dead did lie:
And a thousand thousand slimy things
Lived on; and so did I.

I looked upon the rotting sea,
And drew my eyes away;
I looked upon the rotting deck,
And there the dead men lay.

I looked to heaven, and tried to pray;
But or ever a prayer had gushed,
A wicked whisper came, and made
My heart as dry as dust.

I closed my lids, and kept them close,
And the balls like pulses beat,
For the sky and the sea, and the sea and
    the sky
Lay like a load on my weary eye,
And the dead were at my feet.

*But the curse liveth for him in the eye of the dead men.*

The cold sweat melted from their limbs,
Nor rot nor reek did they:
The look with which they looked on me
Had never passed away.

An orphan's curse would drag to hell
A spirit from on high;
But oh! more horrible than that
Is the curse in a dead man's eye!
Seven days, seven nights, I saw that curse,
And yet I could not die.

The moving Moon went up the sky,
And nowhere did abide;
Softly she was going up,
And a star or two beside—

*In his loneliness and fixedness he yearneth towards the journeying Moon, and the stars that still sojourn, yet still move onward; and everywhere the blue sky belongs to them, and is their appointed rest, and their native country and their own natural homes, which they enter unannounced, as lords that are certainly expected and yet there is a silent joy at their arrival.*

Her beams bemocked the sultry main,
Like April hoar-frost spread;
But where the ship's huge shadow lay,
The charméd water burnt alway
A still and awful red.

*By the light of the Moon he beholdeth God's creatures of the great calm.*

Beyond the shadow of the ship,
I watched the water snakes:
They moved in tracks of shining white,
And when they reared, the elfish light
Fell off in hoary flakes.

Within the shadow of the ship
I watched their rich attire:
Blue, glossy green, and velvet black,
They coiled and swam; and every track
Was a flash of golden fire.

*Their beauty and their happiness.*

*He blesseth them in his heart.*

O happy living things! no tongue
Their beauty might declare:
A spring of love gushed from my heart,
And I blessed them unaware:
Sure my kind saint took pity on me,
And I blessed them unaware.

*The spell begins to break.*

The self-same moment I could pray;
And from my neck so free
The Albatross fell off, and sank
Like lead into the sea.

PART V

Oh sleep! it is a gentle thing,
Beloved from pole to pole!
To Mary Queen the praise be given!
She sent the gentle sleep from Heaven,
That slid into my soul.

*Be grace of the holy Mother, the ancient Mariner is refreshed with rain.*

The silly buckets on the deck,
That had so long remained,
I dreamt that they were filled with dew;
And when I awoke, it rained.

My lips were wet, my throat was cold,
My garments all were dank;
Sure I had drunken in my dreams,
And still my body drank.

I moved, and could not feel my limbs;
I was so light—almost
I thought that I had died in sleep,
And was a blessèd ghost.

*He heareth sounds and seeth strange sights and commotions in the sky and the element.*

And soon I heard a roaring wind:
It did not come anear;
But with its sound it shook the sails,
That were so thin and sere.

The upper air burst into life!
And a hundred fire-flags sheen,
To and fro they were hurried about!
And to and fro, and in and out,
The wan stars danced between.

And the coming wind did roar more loud,
And the sails did sigh like sedge;
And the rain poured down from one black
    cloud;
The Moon was at its edge.

The thick black cloud was cleft, and still
The Moon was at its side:
Like waters shot from some high crag,
The lightning fell with never a jag,
A river steep and wide.

*The bodies of the ship's crew
are inspirited, and the ship
moves on;*

The loud wind never reached the ship,
Yet now the ship moved on!
Beneath the lightning and the Moon
The dead men gave a groan.

They groaned, they stirred, they all uprose,
Nor spake, nor moved their eyes;
It had been strange, even in a dream,
To have seen those dead men rise.

The helmsman steered, the ship moved on;
Yet never a breeze up-blew;
The mariners all 'gan work the ropes,
Where they were wont to do;
They raised their limbs like lifeless tools—
We were a ghastly crew.

The body of my brother's son
Stood by me, knee to knee:
The body and I pulled at one rope,
But he said nought to me.

*But not by the souls of the
men, nor by demons of earth
or middle air, but by a blessèd
troop of angelic spirits, sent
down by the invocation of the
guardian saint.*

"I fear thee, ancient Mariner!"
Be calm, thou Wedding Guest!
'Twas not those souls that fled in pain,
Which to their corses came again,
But a troop of spirits blest:

For when it dawned—they dropped their
arms,
And clustered round the mast;
Sweet sounds rose slowly through their
mouths,
And from their bodies passed.

Around, around, flew each sweet sound,
Then darted to the Sun;
Slowly the sounds came back again,
Now mixed, now one by one.

Sometimes a-dropping from the sky
I heard the sky-lark sing;
Sometimes all little birds that are,
How they seemed to fill the sea and air
With their sweet jargoning!

And now 'twas like all instruments,
Now like a lonely flute;
And now it is an angel's song,
That makes the heavens be mute.

It ceased; yet still the sails made on
A pleasant noise till noon,
A noise like of a hidden brook
In the leafy month of June,
That to the sleeping woods all night
Singeth a quiet tune.

Till noon we quietly sailed on,
Yet never a breeze did breathe:
Slowly and smoothly went the ship,
Moved onward from beneath.

*The lonesome Spirit from the South Pole carries on the ship as far as the Line, in obedience to the angelic troop, but still requireth vengeance.*

Under the keel nine fathom deep,
From the land of mist and snow,
The spirit slid: and it was he
That made the ship to go.
The sails at noon left off their tune,
And the ship stood still also.

The Sun, right up above the mast,
Had fixed her to the ocean:
But in a minute she 'gan stir,
With a short uneasy motion—
Backwards and forwards half her length
With a short uneasy motion.

Then like a pawing horse let go,
She made a sudden bound:
It flung the blood into my head,
And I fell down in a swound.

*The Polar Spirit's fellow demons, the invisible inhabitants of the element, take part in his wrong; and two of them relate, one to the other, that penance long and heavy for the ancient Mariner hath been accorded to the Polar Spirit, who returneth southward.*

How long in that same fit I lay,
I have not to declare;
But ere my living life returned,
I heard and in my soul discerned
Two voices in the air.

"Is it he?" quoth one, "Is this the man?
By him who died on cross,
With his cruel bow he laid full low
The harmless Albatross.

The spirit who bideth by himself
In the land of mist and snow,
He loved the bird that loved the man
Who shot him with his bow."

The other was a softer voice,
As soft as honey-dew:
Quoth he, "The man hath penance done,
And penance more will do."

PART VI

FIRST VOICE:

"But tell me, tell me! speak again,
Thy soft response renewing—
What makes that ship drive on so fast?
What is the ocean doing?"

SECOND VOICE:

"Still as a slave before his lord,
The ocean hath no blast;
His great bright eye most silently
Up to the Moon is cast—

If he may know which way to go;
For she guides him smooth or grim.
See, brother, see! how graciously
She looketh down on him."

*The Mariner hath been cast into a trance; for the angelic power causeth the vessel to drive northward faster than human life could endure.*

FIRST VOICE:

"But why drives on that ship so fast,
Without or wave or wind?"

SECOND VOICE:

"The air is cut away before,
And closes from behind.

Fly, brother, fly! more high, more high!
Or we shall be belated:
For slow and slow that ship will go,
When the Mariner's trance is abated."

*The supernatural motion is retarded; the Mariner awakes, and his penance begins anew.*

I woke, and we were sailing on
As in a gentle weather:
'Twas night, calm night, the moon was high;
The dead men stood together.

All stood together on the deck,
For a charnel-dungeon fitter:
All fixed on me their stony eyes,
That in the Moon did glitter.

The pang, the curse, with which they died,
Had never passed away:
I could not draw my eyes from theirs,
Nor turn them up to pray.

*The curse is finally expiated.* And now this spell was snapped: once more
I viewed the ocean green,
And looked far forth, yet little saw
Of what had else been seen —

Like one, that on a lonesome road
Doth walk in fear and dread,
And having once turned round walks on,
And turns no more his head;
Because he knows, a frightful fiend
Doth close behind him tread.

But soon there breathed a wind on me,
Nor sound nor motion made:
Its path was not upon the sea,
In ripple or in shade.

It raised my hair, it fanned my cheek
Like a meadow-gale of spring —
It mingled strangely with my fears,
Yet it felt like a welcoming.

Swiftly, swiftly flew the ship,
Yet she sailed softly too:
Sweetly, sweetly blew the breeze —
On me alone it blew.

Oh! dream of joy! is this indeed
The lighthouse top I see?
Is this the hill? is this the kirk?
Is this mine own countree?

We drifted o'er the harbor-bar,
And I with sobs did pray—
O let me be awake, my God!
Or let me sleep alway.

The harbor-bay was clear as glass,
So smoothly it was strewn!
And on the bay the moonlight lay,
And the shadow of the Moon.

The rock shone bright, the kirk no less,
That stands above the rock:
The moonlight steeped in silentness
The steady weathercock.

And the bay was white with silent light,
Till rising from the same,
Full many shapes, that shadows were,
In crimson colors came.

A little distance from the prow
Those crimson shadows were:
I turned my eyes upon the deck—
Oh, Christ! what saw I there!

Each corse lay flat, lifeless and flat,
And, by the holy rood!
A man all light, a seraph-man,
On every corse there stood.

This seraph-band, each waved his hand:
It was a heavenly sight!
They stood as signals to the land,
Each one a lovely light;

This seraph-band, each waved his hand,
No voice did they impart—
No voice; but oh! the silence sank
Like music on my heart.

But soon I heard the dash of oars,
I heard the Pilot's cheer;
My head was turned perforce away
And I saw a boat appear.

The Pilot and the Pilot's boy,
I heard them coming fast:
Dear Lord in Heaven! it was a joy
The dead men could not blast.

I saw a third—I heard his voice:
It is the Hermit good!
He singeth loud his godly hymns
That he makes in the wood.
He'll shrieve my soul, he'll wash away
The Albatross's blood.

PART VII

*The Hermit of the Wood*

This Hermit good lives in that wood
Which slopes down to the sea.
How loudly his sweet voice he rears!
He loves to talk with mariners
That come from a far countree.

He kneels at morn, and noon, and eve—
He hath a cushion plump:
It is the moss that wholly hides
The rotted old oak stump.

The skiff-boat neared: I heard them talk,
"Why, this is strange, I trow!
Where are those lights so many and fair,
That signal made but now?"

*Approacheth the ship with wonder.*

"Strange, by my faith!" the Hermit said—
"And they answered not our cheer!
The planks looked warped! and see those
    sails,
How thin they are and sere!
I never saw aught like to them,
Unless perchance it were

Brown skeletons of leaves that lag
My forest-brook along;
When the ivy tod is heavy with snow,
And the owlet whoops to the wolf below,
That eats the she-wolf's young."

"Dear Lord! it hath a fiendish look,"
The Pilot made reply,
"I am a-feared"—"Push on, push on!"
Said the Hermit cheerily.

The boat came closer to the ship,
But I nor spake nor stirred;
The boat came close beneath the ship,
And straight a sound was heard.

*The ship suddenly sinketh.*

Under the water it rumbled on,
Still louder and more dread:
It reached the ship, it split the bay;
The ship went down like lead.

*The ancient Mariner is saved*
*in the Pilot's boat.*

Stunned by that loud and dreadful sound,
Which sky and ocean smote,
Like one that hath been seven days drowned
My body lay afloat;
But swift as dreams, myself I found
Within the Pilot's boat.

Upon the whirl, where sank the ship,
The boat spun round and round;
And all was still, save that the hill
Was telling of the sound.

I moved my lips—the Pilot shrieked
And fell down in a fit;
The holy Hermit raised his eyes,
And prayed where he did sit.

I took the oars: the Pilot's boy,
Who now doth crazy go,
Laughed loud and long, and all the while
His eyes went to and fro.
"Ha! ha!" quoth he, "full plain I see,
The Devil knows how to row."

And now, all in my own countree,
I stood on the firm land!
The Hermit stepped forth from the boat,
And scarcely he could stand.

The ancient Mariner earnestly entreateth the Hermit to shrieve him; and the penance of life falls on him.

"O shrieve me, shrieve me, holy man!"
The Hermit crossed his brow.
"Say quick," quoth he, "I bid thee say—
What manner of man art thou?"

Forthwith this frame of mine was
    wrenched
With a woeful agony,
Which forced me to begin my tale;
And then it left me free.

And ever and anon throughout his future life an agony constraineth him to travel from land to land;

Since then, at an uncertain hour,
That agony returns:
And till my ghastly tale is told,
This heart within me burns.

I pass, like night, from land to land;
I have strange power of speech;
That moment that his face I see,
I know the man that must hear me:
To him my tale I teach.

What loud uproar bursts from the door!
The wedding guests are there:
But in the garden-bower the bride
And bridemaids singing are:
And hark the little vesper bell,
Which biddeth me to prayer!

O Wedding Guest! this soul hath been
Alone on a wide sea:
So lonely 'twas, that God himself
Scarce seeméd there to be.

O sweeter than the marriage feast,
'Tis sweeter far to me,
To walk together to the kirk
With a goodly company!

To walk together to the kirk,
And all together pray,
While each to his great Father bends,
Old men, and babes, and loving friends
And youths and maidens gay!

*And to teach, by his own example, love and reverence to all things that God made and loveth.*

Farewell, farewell! but this I tell
To thee, thou Wedding Guest!
He prayeth well, who loveth well
Both man and bird and beast.

He prayeth best, who loveth best
All things both great and small;
For the dear God who loveth us,
He made and loveth all.

The Mariner, whose eye is bright,
Whose beard with age is hoar,
Is gone: and now the Wedding Guest
Turned from the bridegroom's door.

He went like one that hath been stunned,
And is of sense forlorn:
A sadder and a wiser man,
He rose the morrow morn.

*"The Rime of the Ancient Mariner" is at once a fascinating adventure story and a parabolical analysis of ethics; a long poem and an economical narrative; a sober tragedy but also, being told by the mariner to a wedding guest, a jubilant epithalamium; a recalling and recounting of immemorial hauntings and myth-makings and a present-tense realization of absolute immediacy, beginning "It is . . . ." (Note that, in Part VII: "too" is "clump.")*

# Dejection: An Ode

Late, late yestreen I saw the new Moon
With the old Moon in her arms;
And I fear, I fear, my master, dear!
We shall have a deadly storm.
                              Ballad of Sir Patrick Spens

Well! If the Bard was weather-wise, who made
   The grand old ballad of Sir Patrick Spence,
      This night, so tranquil now, will not go hence
Unrosed by winds, that ply a busier trade
Than those which mould yon cloud in lazy flakes,
Or the dull sobbing draft, that moans and rakes
Upon the strings of this Æolian lute,
      Which better far were mute.
   For lo! the New-moon winter-bright!
   And overspread with phantom light,
   (With swimming phantom light o'erspread
   But rimmed and circled by a silver thread)
I see the old Moon in her lap, foretelling
   The coming-on of rain and squally blast.
And oh! that even now the gust were swelling,
   And the slant night-shower driving loud and fast!
Those sounds which oft have raised me, whilst they awed,
      And sent my soul abroad,
Might now perhaps their wonted impulse give,
Might startle this dull pain, and makie it move and live!

A grief without a pant, void, dark, and drear,
   A stifled, drowsy, unimpassioned grief,
   Which finds no natural outlet, no relief,
      In word, or sigh, or tear—
O Lady! in this wan and heartless mood,
To other thoughts by yonder throstle wooed,

All this long eve, so balmy and serene,
Have I been gazing on the western sky,
   And its peculiar tint of yellow green:
And still I gaze—and with how blank an eye!
And those thin clouds above, in flakes and bars,
That give away their motion to the stars;
Those stars, that glide behind them or between,
Now sparkling, now bedimmed, but always seen:
Yon crescent Moon, as fixed as if it grew
In its own cloudless, starless lake of blue;
I see them all so excellently fair,
I see, not feel, how beautiful they are!

   My genial spirits fail;
   And what can these avail
To life the smothering weight from off my breast?
   It were a vain endeavour,
   Though I should gaze for ever
On that green light that lingers in the west:
I may not hope from outward forms to win
The passion and the life, whose fountains are within.

O Lady! we receive but what we give,
And in our life alone does Nature live:
Ours is her wedding garment, ours her shroud!
   And would we aught behold, of higher worth,
Than that inanimate cold world allowed
To the poor loveless ever-anxious crowd,
   Ah! from the soul itself must issue forth
A light, a glory, fair luminous cloud
   Enveloping the Earth—
And from the soul itself must there be sent
   A sweet and potent voice, of its own birth,
Of all sweet sounds the life and element!

O pure of heart! thou need'st not ask of me
What this strong music in the soul may be!
What, and wherein it doth exist,
This light, this glory, this fair luminous mist,
This beautiful and beauty-making power.
    Joy, virtuous Lady! Joy that ne'er was given,
Save to the pure, and in their purest hour,
Life, and Life's effluence, cloud at once and shower,
Joy, Lady! is the spirit and the power,
Which wedding Nature to us gives in dower
    A new Earth and new Heaven,
Undreamt of by the sensual and the proud—
Joy is the sweet voice, Joy the luminous cloud—
    We in ourselves rejoice!
And thence flows all that charms or ear or sight,
    All melodies the echoes of that voice,
All colours a suffusion from that light.

There was a time when, though my path was rough,
    This joy within me dallied with distress,
And all misfortunes were but as the stuff
    Whence Fancy made me dreams of happiness:
For hope grew round me, like the twining vine,
And fruits, and foliage, not my own, seemed mine.
But now afflictions bow me down to earth:
Nor care I that they rob me of my mirth;
    But oh! each visitation
Suspends what nature gave me any my birth,
    My shaping spirit of Imagination.
For not to think of what I needs must feel,
    But to be still and patient, all I can;
And haply by abstruse research to steal
    From my own nature all the natural man—
    This was my sole resource, my only plan:
Till that which suits a part infects the whole,
And now is almost grown the habit of my soul.

Hence, viper thoughts, that coil around my mind,
　　Reality's dark dream!
I turn from you, and listen to the wind,
　　Which long has raved unnoticed. What a scream
Of agony by torture lengthened out
That lute sent forth! Thou Wind, that rav'st without,
　　Bare crag, or mountain-tairn, or blasted tree,
Or pine-grove whither woodman never clomb,
Or lonely house, long held the witches' home,
　　Methinks were fitter instruments for thee,
Mad Lutanist! who in this month of showers,
Of dark-brown gardens, and of peeping flowers,
Mak'st Devils' yule, with worse than wintry song,
The blossoms, buds, and timorous leaves among.
　　Thou Actor, perfect in all tragic sounds!
Thou mighty Poet, e'en to frenzy bold!
　　　What tell'st thou now about?
　　　'Tis of the rushing of an host in rout,
With groans, of trampled men, with smarting wounds—
At once they groan with pain, and shudder with the cold!
But hush! there is a pause of deepest silence!
　　And all that noise, as of a rushing crowd,
With groans, and tremulous shudderings—all is over—
It tells another tale, with sounds less deep and loud!
　　　A tale of less affright,
　　　And tempered with delight,
As Otway's self had framed the tender lay,—
　　　'Tis of a little child
　　　Upon a lonesome wild,
Not far from home, but she hath lost her way:
And now moans low in bitter grief and fear,
And now screams loud, and hopes to make her mother hear.

'Tis midnight, but small thoughts have I of sleep:
Full seldom may my friend such vigils keep!
Visit her, gentle Sleep! with wings of healing,
    And may this storm be but a mountain-birth,
May all the stars hang bright above her dwelling,
    Silent as though they watched the sleeping Earth!
        With light heart may she rise,
        Gay fancy, cheerful eyes,
    Joy lift her spirit, joy attune her voice;
To her may all things live, from the pole to pole,
Their life the eddying of her living soul!
    O simple spirit, guided from above,
Dear Lady! friend devoutest of my choice,
Thus may'st thou ever, evermore rejoice.

---

*On an April night in 1802, after hearing his friend Wordsworth recite the early part of his "Ode: Intimations of Immortality from Recollections of Early Childhood" (p. 400), Coleridge wrote a long verse-letter to Sara Hutchinson, sister of Wordsworth's fiancée. Coleridge was married, but in love with Sara. This ode is the result of a severe revision of that letter.*

# Frost at Midnight

The Frost performs its secret ministry,
Unhelped by any wind. The owlet's cry
Came loud—and hark, again! loud as before.
The inmates of my cottage, all at rest,
Have left me to that solitude, which suits
Abstruser musings: save that at my side
My cradled infant slumbers peacefully.
'Tis calm indeed! so calm, that it disturbs
And vexes meditation, with its strange
And extreme silentness. Sea, hill, and wood,
This populous village! Sea, and hill, and wood,
With all the numberless goings-on of life,
Inaudible as dreams! the thin blue flame
Lies on my low-burnt fire, and quivers not;
Only that film, which fluttered on the grate,
Still flutters there, the sole unquiet thing.
Methinks its motion in this hush of nature
Gives it dim sympathies with me who live,
Making it a companionable form,
Whose puny flaps and freaks the idling Spirit
By its own moods interprets, everywhere
Echo or mirror seeking of itself,
And makes a toy of Thought.

> But O! how oft,
How oft, at school, with most believing mind,
Presageful, have I gazed upon the bars,
To watch that fluttering *stranger*! and as oft
With unclosed lids, already had I dreamt
Of my sweet birthplace, and the old church tower,
Whose bells, the poor man's only music, rang
From morn to evening, all the hot fair-day,
So sweetly, that they stirred and haunted me
With a wild pleasure, falling on mine ear

Most like articulate sounds of things to come!
So gazed I, till the soothing things, I dreamt,
Lulled me to sleep, and sleep prolonged by dreams!
And so I brooded all the following morn,
Awed by the stern preceptor's face, mine eye
Fixed with mock study on my swimming book:
Save if the door half-opened, and I snatched
A hasty glance, and still my heart leaped up,
For still I hoped to see the *stranger's* face,
Townsman, or aunt, or sister more beloved,
My playmate when we both were clothed alike!

    Dear Babe, that sleepest cradled by my side,
Whose gentle breathings, heard in this deep calm,
Fill up the interspersèd vacancies
And momentary pauses of the thought!
My babe so beautiful! it thrills my heart
With tender gladness, thus to look at thee,
And think that thou shalt learn far other lore,
And in far other scenes! For I was reared
In the great city, pent 'mid cloisters dim,
And saw nought lovely but the sky and stars.
But *thou*, my babe! shalt wander like a breeze
By lakes and sandy shores, beneath the crags
Of ancient mountain, and beneath the clouds,
Which image in their bulk both lakes and shores
And mountain crags: so shalt thou see and hear
The lovely shapes and sounds intelligible
Of that eternal language, which thy God
Utters, who from eternity doth teach
Himself in all, and all things in himself.
Great universal Teacher! he shall mold
Thy spirit, and by giving make it ask.

Therefore all seasons shall be sweet to thee,
Whether the summer clothe the general earth
With greenness, or the redbreast sit and sing
Betwixt the tufts of snow on the bare branch
Of mossy apple tree, while the nigh thatch
Smokes in the sun-thaw; whether the eave-drops fall
Heard only in the trances of the blast,
Or if the secret ministry of frost
Shall hang them up in silent icicles,
Quietly shining to the quiet Moon.

---

*The Coleridges were living in a cottage at Nether Stowey in Somersetshire, not very far from Coleridge's "sweet birthplace" in Devonshire. The "cradled infant" in this poem is Hartley Coleridge, who was born in 1796. (He is also mentioned in Coleridge's "Nightingale.")*

Southey was extraordinarily productive and versatile, turning out many volumes of poetry, history, and biography. He and Samuel Taylor Coleridge were married to sisters and were friends for decades. From 1813 until his death thirty years later, Southey served as Poet Laureate. Byron made Southey one of his favorite targets for satire and outright abuse, much of which now seems exaggerated and undeserved.

## *The Battle of Blenheim*

It was a summer evening,
  Old Kaspar's work was done;
And he before his cottage door
  Was sitting in the sun,
And by him sported on the green
His little grandchild Wilhelmine.

She saw her brother Peterkin
  Roll something large and round,
That he beside the rivulet,
  In playing there, had found;
He came to ask what he had found,
That was so large, and smooth, and round.

Old Kaspar took it from the boy,
  Who stood expectant by;
And then the old man shook his head,
  And with a natural sigh,
'Tis some poor fellow's skull, said he,
Who fell in the great victory.

I find them in the garden, for
    There's many here about,
And often when I go to plough
    The ploughshare turns them out;
For many thousand men, said he,
Were slain in the great victory.

Now tell us what 'twas all about,
    Young Peterkin he cries,
And little Wilhelmine looks up
    With wonder-waiting eyes;
Now tell us all about the war,
And what they kill'd each other for.

It was the English, Kaspar cried,
    That put the French to rout;
But what they kill'd each other for,
    I could not well make out.
But everybody said, quoth he,
That 'twas a famous victory.

My father lived at Blenheim then,
    Yon little stream hard by;
They burnt his dwelling to the ground,
    And he was forced to fly:
So with his wife and child he fled,
Nor had he where to rest his head.

With fire and sword the country round
    Was wasted far and wide,
And many a childing mother then,
    And new-born infant, died.
But things like that, you know, must be
At every famous victory.

They say it was a shocking sight,
   After the field was won,
For many thousand bodies here
   Lay rotting in the sun;
But things like that, you know, must be
After a famous victory.

Great praise the Duke of Marlbro' won,
   And our good Prince Eugene. —
Why, 'twas a very wicked thing!
   Said little Wilhelmine. —
Nay—nay—my little girl, quoth he,
It was a famous victory.

And everybody praised the Duke
   Who such a fight did win. —
But what good came of it at last?
   Quoth little Peterkin. —
Why that I cannot tell, said he,
But 'twas a famous victory.

---

*The Duke of Marlborough and Prince Eugene of Austria commanded a combined force that defeated the French at Blenheim (Bavaria) in 1704. Southey's poem suggests the unwitting wisdom of innocent children compared with the thoughtlessness of an adult—a contrast sharpened by the increasingly ironic ring of the repeated "victory."*

In a long and varied career, Landor wrote much epic and dramatic poetry as well as several ingenious "imaginary conversations" of literary and political personages. The general reader, however, and the majority of anthologies that serve the general reader, will remember Landor exclusively as the author of lapidary lyrics that possess a quality of irreducible perfection.

## Rose Aylmer

Ah what avails the sceptered race,
  Ah what the form divine!
What every virtue, every grace!
  Rose Aylmer, all were thine.
Rose Aylmer, whom these wakeful eyes
  May weep, but never see,
A night of memories and of sighs
  I consecrate to thee.

---

*There really was a Rose Aylmer. The daughter of Baron Aylmer, she died in 1800.*

# Dirce

## Stand close around, ye Stygian set,
With Dirce in one boat convey'd,
Or Charon, seeing, may forget
That he is old, and she a shade.

from Pericles and Aspasia

---

*The last three words vividly show the strength of alliteration combined with ellipsis ("is" being omitted).*

# I Strove with None

I strove with none, for none was worth my strife:
Nature I loved, and next to Nature, Art:
I warmed both hands before the fire of Life;
It sinks; and I am ready to depart.

from The Last Fruit off an Old Tree

---

*These lines are a heroic quatrain in more than one sense. Such pure stoicism is rare in English. One of Robert Frost's later poems, "Lucretius Versus the Lake Poets," continues the discussion.*

# Past Ruined Ilion Helen Lives

❖❖❖❖

Past ruined Ilion Helen lives,
    Alcestis rises from the shades;
Verse calls them forth; 'tis verse that gives
    Immortal youth to mortal maids.

Soon shall Oblivion's deepening veil
    Hide all the peopled hills you see,
The gay, the proud, while lovers hail
    These many summers you and me.

---

*Innumerable verses from three millennia call Helen forth, and even Alcestis endures in Milton's "On His Deceased Wife" (p. 209) and, wholly transformed, in T. S. Eliot's* Cocktail Party.

# THOMAS CAMPBELL 1777–1844

Although Campbell, the son of a Scottish merchant,
was a prominent reformer and one of the founders of
London University, his reputation today is based solely
on a number of war-songs.

## *Hohenlinden*

On Linden, when the sun was low,
All bloodless lay the untrodden snow,
And dark as winter was the flow
  Of Iser, rolling rapidly.

But Linden saw another sight
When the drum beat at dead of night,
Commanding fires of death to light
  The darkness of her scenery.

By torch and trumpet fast arrayed,
Each horseman drew his battle blade,
And furious every charger neighed
  To join the dreadful revelry.

Then shook the hills with thunder riven,
Then rushed the steed to battle driven,
And louder than the bolts of heaven
  Far flashed the red artillery.

But redder yet that light shall glow
On Linden's hills of stainèd snow,
And bloodier yet the torrent flow
  Of Iser, rolling rapidly.

'Tis morn, but scarce yon level sun
Can pierce the war-clouds, rolling dun,
Where furious Frank and fiery Hun
    Shout in their sulphurous canopy.

The combat deepens. On, ye brave,
Who rush to glory, or the grave!
Wave, Munich! all thy banners wave,
    And charge with all thy chivalry!

Few, few shall part where many meet!
The snow shall be their winding-sheet,
And every turf beneath their feet
    Shall be a soldier's sepulchre.

---

*The "furious Frank" beat the "fiery Hun"; that is, the French defeated the
Austrians at Hohenlinden, Bavaria, in December of 1800. Winter battles were
rare.*

Moore, a professor of religion, published his one celebrated poem in the *Troy Sentinel* (in Troy, New York)
in time for Christmas 1823.

# A Visit from St. Nicholas

>>>>>>>

'Twas the night before Christmas, when all through the house
Not a creature was stirring, not even a mouse.
The stockings were hung by the chimney with care,
In hopes that St. Nicholas soon would be there;
The children were nestled all snug in their beds,
While visions of sugarplums danced in their heads;
And mamma in her 'kerchief, and I in my cap,
Had just settled our brains for a long winter's nap,
When out on the lawn there arose such a clatter,
I sprang from the bed to see what was the matter.
Away to the window I flew like a flash,
Tore open the shutters and threw up the sash.
The moon on the breast of the new-fallen snow
Gave the luster of mid-day to objects below,
When, what to my wondering eyes should appear,
But a miniature sleigh, and eight tiny reindeer,
With a little old driver, so lively and quick,
I knew in a moment it must be St. Nick.
More rapid than eagles his coursers they came,
And he whistled, and shouted, and called them by name:
"Now, *Dasher!* now, *Dancer!* now, *Prancer* and *Vixen!*
On, *Comet!* on, *Cupid!* on, *Donder* and *Blitzen!*
To the top of the porch! to the top of the wall!
Now dash away! dash away! dash away all!"
As dry leaves that before the wild hurricane fly,
When they meet with an obstacle, mount to the sky,
So up to the house-top the coursers they flew,
With the sleigh full of toys, and St. Nicholas too.

And then, in a twinkling, I heard on the roof
The prancing and pawing of each little hoof.
As I drew in my head, and was turning around,
Down the chimney St. Nicholas came with a bound.
He was dressed all in fur, from his head to his foot,
And his clothes were all tarnished with ashes and soot;
A bundle of toys he had flung on his back,
And he looked like a peddler just opening his pack.
His eyes—how they twinkled! his dimples how merry!
His cheeks were like roses, his nose like a cherry!
His droll little mouth was drawn up like a bow,
And the beard of his chin was as white as the snow;
The stump of a pipe he held tight in his teeth,
And the smoke it encircled his head like a wreath;
He had a broad face and a little round belly,
That shook, when he laughed, like a bowlful of jelly.
He was chubby and plump, a right jolly old elf,
And I laughed when I saw him, in spite of myself;
A wink of his eye and a twist of his head,
Soon gave me to know I had nothing to dread.
He spoke not a word, but went straight to his work,
And filled all the stockings; then turned with a jerk,
And laying his finger aside of his nose
And giving a nod, up the chimney he rose.
He sprang to his sleigh, to his team gave a whistle,
And away they all flew like the down of a thistle,
But I heard him exclaim, ere he drove out of sight,
" *Happy Christmas to all, and to all a good-night.*"

---

*This Santa, small and dressed in fur, may not quite match the icon of today, but Moore contributed as much to his development as any other creator. Christmas seems everlasting, but most of our modern practices come from the nineteenth century, especially from such writers as Moore and Dickens.*

# LEIGH HUNT 1784–1859

Hunt was eventually to publish an *Autobiography* and *Table Talk*. He was always an able versifier, but he will be most fondly remembered as a supporter of writers (including Keats and Byron) and as an editor of several periodicals, including the *Examiner*, the *Reflector*, and the *Indicator*.

## Jenny Kissed Me

Jenny kissed me when we met,
  Jumping from the chair she sat in.
Time, you thief, who love to get
  Sweets into your list, put that in.
Say I'm weary, say I'm sad;
  Say that health and wealth have missed me;
Say I'm growing old, but add—
  Jenny kissed me!

---

*Hunt, the story goes, was kissed by Jane Welsh Carlyle when he delivered the news that a piece written by her husband Thomas had been accepted by the publisher. Technically, the poem is a rondeau only by the most relaxed definition—but Hunt seems to have been a relaxed and sympathetic person.*

# Abou Ben Adhem

Abou Ben Adhem (may his tribe increase!)
Awoke one night from a deep dream of peace,
And saw, within the moonlight in his room,
Making it rich, and like a lily in bloom,
An Angel writing in a book of gold:

Exceeding peace had made Ben Adhem bold,
And to the Presence in the room he said,
"What writest thou?" The Vision raised its head,
And with a look made of all sweet accord
Answered, "The names of those who love the Lord."

"And is mine one?" said Abou. "Nay, not so,"
Replied the Angel. Abou spoke more low,
But cheerly still; and said, "I pray thee, then,
Write me as one that loves his fellow-men."

The Angel wrote, and vanished. The next night
It came again with a great wakening light,
And showed the names whom love of God had blessed,
And, lo! Ben Adhem's name led all the rest!

---

*This rather Dickensian story has enjoyed immense popularity since its first
appearance in an anthology in 1838. Like Shelley, Byron, Poe, and many others,
Hunt took advantage of a general taste for matters vaguely Asian.*

# GEORGE GORDON NOEL BYRON, 6TH BARON BYRON 1788–1824

Byron is uniquely distinguished for his personality and
life as much as for his poetry. He is, indeed, widely
regarded as a very great poet and especially as a wit
and satirist. Byron was not only a genius but also a
millionaire, a hero, a nobleman, a sinner, and a beauty.
Born into a tormented and tempestuous family, he succeeded to the family title when he was ten; his schooling
was at Harrow and Cambridge. By 1812 he was one of
the most famous poets in England. He married most
unhappily in 1815 and in the next year—hounded by
accusations of insanity and incest—exiled himself permanently. Byronism is still with us, as is the Byronic
hero: dark, moody, aloof, misanthropic, courageous,
brilliant, audacious, tortured.

## *So We'll Go No More a-Roving*

So, we'll go no more a-roving
  So late into the night,
Though the heart be still as loving,
  And the moon be still as bright.

For the sword outwears its sheath,
  And the soul outwears the breast,
And the heart must pause to breathe,
  And love itself have rest.

Though the night was made for loving,
  And the day returns too soon,
Yet we'll go no more a-roving
  By the light of the moon.

*In his earlier poetry, Byron, who was partly Scottish, followed the lead of such other Scots as Robert Burns and Sir Walter Scott in reviving old ballads and composing new ones—or, as here, of grafting new material onto old. Regretful decrepitude may seem a fatuous pose in a writer not yet thirty, but Byron had scarcely seven more years to live when he wrote this.*

# She Walks in Beauty

>>>>>>>

### I

She walks in Beauty, like the night
Of cloudless climes and starry skies;
And all that's best of dark and bright
Meet in her aspect and her eyes:
Thus mellowed to that tender light
Which Heaven to gaudy day denies.

### II

One shade the more, one ray the less,
    Had half impaired the nameless grace
Which waves in every raven tress,
    Or softly lightens o'er her face;
Where thoughts serenely sweet express,
    How pure, how dear their dwelling-place.

### III

And on that cheek, and o'er that brow,
    So soft, so calm, yet eloquent,
The smiles that win, the tints that glow,
    But tell of days in goodness spent,
A mind at peace with all below,
    A heart whose love is innocent!

---

*This lyric, like "The Destruction of Sennacherib" (p. 482), was written for the volume called* Hebrew Melodies *(1815) with traditional music adapted by Isaac Nathan. Most things about Byron are fabulously romantic, including the story that he met a lovely cousin by marriage at a ball and wrote "She Walks in Beauty" the next morning.*

# The Destruction of Sennacherib

The Assyrian came down like the wolf on the fold,
And his cohorts were gleaming in purple and gold,
And the sheen of their spears was like stars on the sea,
When the blue wave rolls nightly on deep Galilee.

Like the leaves of the forest when summer is green,
That host with their banners at sunset were seen:
Like the leaves of the forest when autumn hath blown,
That host on the morrow lay wither'd and strown.

For the Angel of Death spread his wings on the blast,
And breathed in the face of the foe as he pass'd
And the eyes of the sleepers wax'd deadly and chill,
And their hearts but once heaved, and forever grew still!

And there lay the steed with his nostril all wide,
But through it there roll'd not the breath of his pride;
And the foam of his gasping lay white on the turf,
And cold as the spray of the rock-beating surf.

And there lay the rider distorted and pale,
With the dew on his brow, and the rust on his mail:
And the tents were all silent, the banners alone,
The lances unlifted, the trumpet unblown.

And the widows of Ashur are loud in their wail,
And the idols are broke in the temple of Baal;
And the might of the Gentile, unsmote by the sword,
Hath melted like snow in the glance of the Lord!

The durability of this poem is shown by the opening of the Prologue of Tom Clancy's Sum of All Fears (1991): " 'Like a wolf on the fold.' In recounting the Syrian attack on the Israeli-held Golan Heights at 1400 hours, local time, on Saturday, October 6, 1973, most commentators automatically recalled Lord Byron's famous line."

# When We Two Parted

When we two parted
  In silence and tears,
Half broken-hearted
  To sever for years,
Pale grew thy cheek and cold,
  Colder thy kiss;
Truly that hour foretold
  Sorrow to this.

The dew of the morning
  Sunk chill on my brow—
It felt like the warning
  Of what I feel now.
Thy vows are all broken,
  And light is thy fame;
I hear thy name spoken,
  And share in its shame.

They name thee before me,
  A knell to mine ear;
A shudder comes o'er me—
  Why wert thou so dear?
They know not I knew thee,
  Who knew thee too well:—
Long, long shall I rue thee,
  Too deeply to tell.

In secret we met—
  In silence I grieve,
That thy heart could forget,
  Thy spirit deceive.
If I should meet thee
  After long years,
How should I greet thee?
  With silence and tears.

---

*Byron was twenty when he wrote these haunting lines. The emotion is definite and powerful even though the* dramatis personae *are no more than pronouns.*

# The Ocean

There is a pleasure in the pathless woods,
There is a rapture on the lonely shore,
There is society where none intrudes
By the deep sea, and music in its roar:
I love not man the less, but nature more,
From these our interviews, in which I steal
From all I may be, or have been before,
To mingle with the universe, and feel
What I can ne'er express, yet cannot all conceal.

Roll on, thou deep and dark blue Ocean,—roll!
Ten thousand fleets sweep over thee in vain;
Man marks the earth with ruin,—his control
Stops with the shore;—upon the watery plain
The wrecks are all thy deed, nor doth remain
A shadow of man's ravage, save his own,
When, for a moment, like a drop of rain,
He sinks into thy depths with bubbling groan,
Without a grave, unknelled, uncoffined, and unknown.

His steps are not upon thy paths,—thy fields
Are not a spoil for him,—thou dost arise
And shake him from thee; the vile strength he wields
For earth's destruction thou dost all despise,
Spurning him from thy bosom to the skies,
And send'st him, shivering in thy playful spray
And howling, to his gods, where haply lies
His petty hope in some near port or bay,
And dashest him again to earth:—there let him lay.

The armaments which thunderstrike the walls
Of rock-built cities, bidding nations quake
And monarchs tremble in their capitals,
The oak leviathans, whose huge ribs make
Their clay creator the vain title take
Of lord of thee and arbiter of war, —
These are thy toys, and, as the snowy flake,
They melt into thy yeast of waves, which mar
Alike the Armada's pride or spoils of Trafalgar.

Thy shores are empires, changed in all save thee;
Assyria, Greece, Rome, Carthage, what are they?
Thy waters wasted them while they were free,
And many a tyrant since; their shores obey
The stranger, slave, or savage; their decay
Has dried up realms to deserts: not so thou;
Unchangeable save to thy wild waves' play,
Time writes no wrinkles on thine azure brow;
Such as creation's dawn beheld, thou rollest now.

Thou glorious mirror, where the Almighty's form
Glasses itself in tempests; in all time,
Calm or convulsed, — in breeze, or gale, or storm,
Icing the pole, or in the torrid clime
Dark-heaving; boundless, endless, and sublime,
The image of Eternity, — the throne
Of the Invisible! even from out thy slime
The monsters of the deep are made; each zone
Obeys thee; thou goest forth, dread, fathomless, alone.

And I have loved thee, Ocean! and my joy
Of youthful sports was on thy breast to be
Borne, like thy bubbles, onward; from a boy
I wantoned with thy breakers, —they to me
Were a delight; and if the freshening sea
Made them a terror, 't was a pleasing fear;
For I was as it were a child of thee,
And trusted to thy billows far and near,
And laid my land upon thy mane, —as I do here.

from Childe Harold's Pilgrimage

---

*Henry James drolly ridiculed the Romantics who "besought the deep blue sea to roll." It may be absurd to encourage natural forces to keep up what they cannot help doing ("Shine on, harvest moon"), but we do it, perhaps as a way of fixing our place and role in the world.*

# There Was a Sound of Revelry by Night

There was a sound of revelry by night,
And Belgium's capital had gathered then
Her beauty and her chivalry, and bright
The lamps shone o'er fair women and brave men;
A thousand hearts beat happily; and when
Music arose with its voluptuous swell,
Soft eyes looked love to eyes which spake again,
And all went merry as a marriage-bell;
But hush! hark! a deep sound strikes like a rising knell!

Did ye not hear it?—No; 'twas but the wind,
Or the car rattling o'er the stony street;
On with the dance! let joy be unconfined;
No sleep till morn, when Youth and Pleasure meet
To chase the glowing Hours with flying feet.
But hark! that heavy sound breaks in once more,
As if the clouds its echo would repeat;
And nearer, clearer, deadlier than before!
Arm! arm! it is—it is—the cannon's opening roar!

Within a windowed niche of that high hall
Sate Brunswick's fated chieftain; he did hear
That sound, the first amidst the festival,
And caught its tone with Death's prophetic ear;
And when they smiled because he deemed it near,
His heart more truly knew that peal too well
Which stretched his father on a bloody bier,
And roused the vengeance blood alone could quell:
He rushed into the field, and, foremost fighting, fell.

Ah! then and there was hurrying to and fro,
And gathering tears, and tremblings of distress,
And cheeks all pale, which but an hour ago
Blushed at the praise of their own loveliness;
And there were sudden partings, such as press
The life from out young hearts, and choking sighs
Which ne'er might be repeated: who would guess
If evermore should meet those mutual eyes,
Since upon night so sweet such awful morn could rise!

And there was mounting in hot haste: the steed,
The mustering squadron, and the clattering car,
Went pouring forward with impetuous speed,
And swiftly forming in the ranks of war;
And the deep thunder peal on peal afar;
And near, the beat of the alarming drum
Roused up the soldier ere the morning star;
While thronged the citizens with terror dumb,
Or whispering with white lips,—"The foe! they come! they come!"

And wild and high the "Cameron's gathering" rose,
The war-note of Lochiel, which Albyn's hills
Have heard,—and heard, too, have her Saxon foes;
How in the noon of night that pibroch thrills
Savage and shrill! But with the breath which fills
Their mountain pipe, so fill the mountaineers
With the fierce native daring which instils
The stirring memory of a thousand years,
And Evan's, Donald's fame rings in each clansman's ears!

And Ardennes waves above them her green leaves,
Dewy with nature's tear-drops, as they pass,
Grieving, if aught inanimate e'er grieves,
Over the unreturning brave,—alas!
Ere evening to be trodden like the grass
Which now beneath them, but above shall grow
In its next verdure, when this fiery mass
Of living valor, rolling on the foe,
And burning with high hope, shall moulder cold and low.

Last noon beheld them full of lusty life,
Last eve in Beauty's circle proudly gay,
The midnight brought the signal-sound of strife,
The morn the marshalling in arms—the day
Battle's magnificently stern array!
The thunder-clouds close o'er it, which when rent
The earth is covered thick with other clay,
Which her own clay shall cover, heaped and pent,
Rider and horse,—friend, foe,—in one red burial blent!

Their praise is hymned by loftier harps than mine;
Yet one I would select from that proud throng,
Partly because they blend me with his line,
And partly that I did his sire some wrong,
And partly that bright names will hallow song!
And his was of the bravest, and when showered
The death-bolts deadliest the thinned files along,
Even where the thickest of war's tempest lowered,
They reached no nobler breast than thine, young, gallant Howard!

There have been tears and breaking hearts for thee,
And mine were nothing, had I such to give;
But when I stood beneath the fresh green tree,
Which living waves where thou didst cease to live,
And saw around me the wide field revive
With fruits and fertile promise, and the Spring
Come forth her work of gladness to contrive,
With all her reckless birds upon the wing,
I turned from all she brought to those she could not bring.

I turned to thee, to thousands, of whom each
And one as all a ghastly gap did make
In his own kind and kindred; whom to teach
Forgetfulness were mercy for their sake;
The Archangel's trump, not glory's, must awake
Those whom they thirst for; though the sound of Fame
May for a moment soothe, it cannot slake
The fever of vain longing, and the name
So honored, but assumes a stronger, bitterer claim.

They mourn, but smile at length; and, smiling, mourn;
The tree will wither long before it fall;
The hull drives on, though mast and sail be torn;
The roof-tree sinks, but moulders on the hall
In massy hoariness; the ruined wall
Stands when its wind-worn battlements are gone;
The bars survive the captive they inthrall;
The day drags through though storms keep out the sun;
And thus the heart will break, yet brokenly live on:

Even as a broken mirror, which the glass
In every fragment multiplies; and makes
A thousand images of one that was,
The same, and still the more, the more it breaks;
And thus the heart will do which not forsakes,
Living in shattered guise, and still, and cold,
And bloodless, with its sleepless sorrow aches,
Yet withers on till all without is old,
Showing no visible sign, for such things are untold.

from Childe Harold's Pilgrimage

---

*Byron shares with Thackeray the honor of superlatively realizing all the brilliance and irony of the Duchess of Richmond's ball on the eve of the Battle of Waterloo in June 1815 — probably the single most important event in nineteenth-century Europe.*

Charles Wolfe, then a student at Trinity College, Dublin, read Southey's prose account (published in 1817) of the death and burial of Sir John Moore, which had taken place in early 1809. Wolfe's poem on the subject is his only work to achieve any fame, but it was immensely celebrated—and debated and even parodied—all through the nineteenth century.

# The Burial of Sir John Moore
# after Corunna

Not a drum was heard, not a funeral note,
As his corse to the rampart we hurried;
Not a soldier discharged his farewell shot
O'er the grave where our hero we buried.

We buried him darkly at dead of night,
The sods with our bayonets turning,
By the struggling moonbeam's misty light
And the lanthorn dimly burning.

No useless coffin enclosed his breast,
Not in sheet or in shroud we wound him;
But he lay like a warrior taking his rest
With his martial cloak around him.

Few and short were the prayers we said,
And we spoke not a word of sorrow;
But we steadfastly gazed on the face of the dead,
And we bitterly thought of the morrow.

We thought, as we hollow'd his narrow bed
And smooth'd down his lonely pillow,
That the foe and the stranger would tread o'er his head,
And we far away on the billow!

Lightly they'll talk of the spirit that's gone,
And o'er his cold ashes upbraid him—
But little he'll reck, if they let him sleep on
In the grave where a Briton has laid him.

But half of our heavy task was done
When the clock struck the hour for retiring;
And we heard the distant and random gun
That the foe was sullenly firing.

Slowly and sadly we laid him down,
From the field of his fame fresh and gory;
We carved not a line, and we raised not a stone,
But we left him alone with his glory.

---

*A small English force, retreating before a French army ten times as great, was leaving from the port of La Caruña in northwest Spain; Lieutenant General Sir John Moore was killed during the embarkation and had to be buried in haste in an unmarked grave. A temporary monument was erected by England's Spanish allies, with a permanent tomb overlooking the Atlantic erected later.*

Shelley was born into a substantial Sussex family and
educated at Eton and Oxford, being expelled from the
latter because of an atheistic pamphlet. His life was
complex and turbulent, with an early marriage to Harriet Westbrook, whom he subsequently abandoned for
Mary Godwin, the daughter of William Godwin and his
first wife, Mary Wollstonecraft. After Harriet's suicide
in 1816, Shelley and Mary were married. Shelley was a
distinguished translator as well as a great lyric and dramatic poet. He drowned when his yacht *Ariel* foundered
in a storm off the Italian coast. His body, washed
ashore after a week, was cremated in the presence of
Byron and Leigh Hunt.

# Ozymandias

I met a traveler from an antique land
Who said: Two vast and trunkless legs of stone
Stand in the desert. Near them, on the sand,
Half sunk, a shattered visage lies, whose frown,
And wrinkled lip, and sneer of cold command,
Tell that its sculptor well those passions read
Which yet survive, stamped on these lifeless things,
The hand that mocked them and the heart that fed;
And on the pedestal these words appear:
"My name is Ozymandias, king of kings:
Look on my works, ye Mighty, and despair!"
Nothing beside remains. Round the decay
Of that colossal wreck, boundless and bare
The lone and level sands stretch far away.

*The joke seems to be on Ozymandias, of whose boasting nothing remains but some fragments in a legend, with an easy moral: take care how you brag. But maybe the joke is on somebody besides the king. For one thing, he, Ramses II of Egypt, may still endure as a mummy. And, even if the monumental statue is broken and the inscription sounds fatuous, what remains of anybody else of that age?*

# Ode to the West Wind

### I

O wild West Wind, thou breath of Autumn's being,
Thou, from whose unseen presence the leaves dead
Are driven, like ghosts from an enchanter fleeing,

Yellow, and black, and pale, and hectic red,
Pestilence-stricken multitudes: O Thou,
Who chariotest to their dark wintry bed

The winged seeds, where they lie cold and low,
Each like a corpse within its grave, until
Thine azure sister of the Spring shall blow

Her clarion o'er the dreaming earth, and fill
(Driving sweet buds like flocks to feed in air)
With living hues and odors plain and hill:

Wild Spirit, which art moving everywhere;
Destroyer and Preserver; hear, O hear!

### II

Thou on whose stream, mid the steep sky's commotion,
Loose clouds like earth's decaying leaves are shed,
Shook from the tangled boughs of Heaven and Ocean,

Angels of rain and lightning: there are spread
On the blue surface of thine aëry surge,
Like the bright hair uplifted from the head

Of some fierce Mænad, even from the dim verge
Of the horizon to the zenith's height,
The locks of the approaching storm. Thou dirge

Of the dying year, to which this closing night
Will be the dome of a vast sepulcher,
Vaulted with all thy congregated might

Of vapors, from whose solid atmosphere
Black rain, and fire, and hail will burst: O hear!

### III

Thou who didst waken from his summer dreams
The blue Mediterranean, where he lay,
Lulled by the coil of his chrystalline streams,

Beside a pumice isle in Baiæ's bay,
And saw in sleep old palaces and towers
Quivering within the wave's intenser day,

All overgrown with azure moss and flowers
So sweet, the sense faints picturing them! Thou
For whose path the Atlantic's level powers

Cleave themselves into chasms, while far below
The sea-blooms and the oozy woods which wear
The sapless foliage of the ocean, know

Thy voice, and suddenly grow gray with fear,
And tremble and despoil themselves: O hear!

### IV

If I were a dead leaf thou mightest bear;
If I were a swift cloud to fly with thee;
A wave to pant beneath thy power, and share

The impulse of thy strength, only less free
Than thou, O Uncontrollable! If even
I were as in my boyhood, and could be

The comrade of thy wanderings over Heaven,
As then, when to outstrip thy skiey speed
Scarce seemed a vision; I would ne'er have striven

As thus with thee in prayer in my sore need.
Oh, lift me as a wave, a leaf, a cloud!
I fall upon the thorns of life! I bleed!

A heavy weight of hours has chained and bowed
One too like thee: tameless, and swift, and proud.

V

Make me thy lyre, even as the forest is:
What if my leaves are falling like its own!
The tumult of thy mighty harmonies

Will take from both a deep, autumnal tone,
Sweet though in sadness. Be thou, Spirit fierce,
My spirit! Be thou me, impetuous one!

Drive my dead thoughts over the universe
Like withered leaves to quicken a new birth!
And, by the incantation of this verse,

Scatter, as from an unextinguished hearth
Ashes and sparks, my words among mankind!
Be through my lips to unawakened earth

The trumpet of a prophecy! O Wind,
If Winter comes, can Spring be far behind?

---

*Shelley wrote this ode in Italy, one autumn two or three years before his death.
The poem soars on the loftiness of elementary ideas: elements, seasons, points of
the compass. Normally these are differential and separate us from nature and
from one another. But here, in a complex and passionate synthesis, Shelley
connects the death of leaves in autumn to the birth of seeds to come in the spring.*

# *To a Skylark*

Hail to thee, blithe spirit!
   Bird thou never wert,
That from heaven, or near it,
   Pourest thy full heart
In profuse strains of unpremeditated art.

Higher still and higher,
   From the earth thou springest
Like a cloud of fire;
   The blue deep thou wingest,
And singing still dost soar, and soaring ever singest.

In the golden lightning
   Of the sunken sun,
O'er which clouds are bright'ning,
   Thou dost float and run,
Like an unbodied joy whose race is just begun.

The pale purple even
   Melts around thy flight;
Like a star of heaven
   In the broad daylight
Thou art unseen, but yet I hear thy shrill delight.

Keen as are the arrows
   Of that silver sphere,
Whose intense lamp narrows
   In the white dawn clear,
Until we hardly see, we feel that it is there.

All the earth and air
　　With thy voice is loud,
　　As, when night is bare,
　　From one lonely cloud
The moon rains out her beams, and heaven is overflowed.

　　What thou art we know not;
　　What is most like thee?
　　From rainbow clouds there flow not
　　Drops so bright to see,
As from thy presence showers a rain of melody.

　　Like a poet hidden
　　In the light of thought,
　　Singing hymns unbidden,
　　Till the world is wrought
To sympathy with hopes and fears it heeded not:

　　Like a high-born maiden
　　In a palace tower,
　　Soothing her love-laden
　　Soul in secret hour
With music sweet as love, which overflows her bower:

　　Like a glow-worm golden
　　In a dell of dew,
　　Scattering unbeholden
　　Its aerial hue
Among the flowers and grass, which screen it from the view:

　　Like a rose embowered
　　In its own green leaves,
　　By warm winds deflowered,
　　Till the scent it gives
Makes faint with too much sweet those heavy-winged thieves:

Sound of vernal showers
　　On the twinkling grass,
Rain-awakened flowers,
　　All that ever was,
Joyous, and clear, and fresh, thy music doth surpass.

Teach us, sprite or bird,
　　What sweet thoughts are thine:
I have never heard
　　Praise of love or wine
That panted forth a flood of rapture so divine.

Chorus hymeneal,
　　Or triumphal chaunt,
Matched with thine would be all
　　But an empty vaunt—
A thing wherein we feel there is some hidden want.

What objects are the fountains
　　Of thy happy strain?
What fields, or waves, or mountains?
　　What shapes of sky or plain?
What love of thine own kind? what ignorance of pain?

With thy clear keen joyance,
　　Languor cannot be:
Shadow of annoyance
　　Never came near thee:
Thou lovest, but never knew love's sad satiety.

Waking as asleep,
　　Thou of death must deem
Things more true and deep
　　Than we mortals dream,
Or how could thy notes flow in such a crystal stream?

We look before and after,
　And pine for what is not:
Our sincerest laughter
　With some pain is fraught;
Our sweetest songs are those that tell of saddest thought.

Yet if we could scorn
　Hate, and pride, and fear;
If we were things born
　Not to shed a tear,
I know not how thy joy we ever should come near.

Better than all measures
　Of delightful sound,
Better than all treasures
　That in books are found,
Thy skill to poet were, thou scorner of the ground!

Teach me half the gladness
　That thy brain must know,
Such harmonious madness
　From my lips would flow,
The world should listen then, as I am listening now.

---

*Shelley wrote "To a Skylark" in 1820 while living at Leghorn, Italy. Sixty-seven years later, visiting the place, Thomas Hardy wrote "Shelley's Skylark":*

> *Somewhere afield here something lies*
> *In Earth's oblivious eyeless trust*
> *That moved a poet to prophecies . . .*

# Music, When Soft Voices Die

∞∞∞∞∞

Music, when soft voices die,
Vibrates in the memory;
Odours, when sweet violets sicken,
Live within the sense they quicken.

Rose leaves, when the rose is dead,
Are heaped for the beloved's bed;
And so thy thoughts, when thou art gone,
Love itself shall slumber on.

---

*This poem, found in a notebook, was published after Shelley's death by his widow. Since the poem is probably unfinished, some of the obscurities may never be understood. The "beloved" seems to be the dead rose; "thy thoughts" seems to mean "my thoughts of thee."*

# To Night

### I

Swiftly walk o'er the western wave,
  Spirit of Night!
Out of the misty eastern cave,
Where, all the long and lone daylight,
Thou wovest dreams of joy and fear,
Which make thee terrible and dear, —
  Swift by thy flight!

### II

Wrap thy form in a mantle gray,
  Star-inwrought!
Blind with thine hair the eyes of Day;
Kiss her until she be wearied out,
Then wander o'er city, and sea, and land,
Touching all with thine opiate wand—
  Come, long-sought!

### III

When I arose and saw the dawn,
  I sighed for thee;
When light rode high, and the dew was gone,
And noon lay heavy on flower and tree,
And the weary Day turned to his rest,
Lingering like an unloved guest,
  I sighed for thee.

IV

Thy brother Death came, and cried,
  Wouldst thou me?
Thy sweet child Sleep, the filmy-eyed,
Murmured like a noontide bee,
Shall I nestle near thy side?
Wouldst thou me? —And I replied,
  No, not thee!

V

Death will come when thou art dead,
  Soon, too soon —
Sleep will come when thou art fled;
Of neither would I ask the boon
I ask of thee, beloved Night —
Swift be thine approaching flight,
  Come soon, soon!

---

*"To Night" was written in the year before Shelley's death and first published in
Posthumous Poems in 1824. The metaphors are magically protean: Day is
female in the second stanza, male in the third.*

# England in 1819

An old, mad, blind, despised, and dying king,
Princes, the dregs of their dull race, who flow
Through public scorn, — mud from a muddy spring, —
Rulers who neither see, nor feel, nor know,
But leech-like to their fainting country cling,
Till they drop, blind in blood, without a blow, —
A people starved and stabbed in the untilled field, —
An army, which liberticide and prey
Makes as a two-edged sword to all who wield, —
Golden and sanguine laws which tempt and slay;
Religion Christless, Godless—a book sealed;
A Senate, — Time's worst statute unrepealed, —
Are graves, from which a glorious Phantom may
Burst, to illumine our tempestuous day.

---

*This grammatically remarkable sonnet—twelve lines of subject before a two-line predicate—should be compared with Wordsworth's "London, 1802" (p. 417).*

# To____

One word is too often profaned
　　For me to profane it,
One feeling too falsely disdained
　　For thee to disdain it;
One hope is too like despair
　　For prudence to smother,
And pity from thee more dear
　　Than that from another.

I can give not what men call love,
　　But wilt thou accept not
The worship the heart lifts above
　　And the Heavens reject not, —
The desire of the moth for the star,
　　Of the night for the morrow,
The devotion to something afar
　　From the sphere of our sorrow?

---

*These lines, though included in Palgrave's* Golden Treasury *(1861) and Quiller-Couch's* Oxford Book of English Verse *(1900), seem to have fallen somewhat out of favor, perhaps because of obscurity and awkwardness. But those very qualities can also create a beautiful and lifelike indefiniteness.*

# *Adonais*

I

I weep for Adonais—he is dead!
  Oh weep for Adonais, though our tears
Thaw not the frost which binds so dear a head!
  And thou, sad Hour selected from all years
  To mourn our loss, rouse thy obscure compeers,
And teach them thine own sorrow! Say: "With me
  Died Adonais! Till the future dares
Forget the past, his fate and fame shall be
An echo and a light unto eternity."

II

Where wert thou, mighty Mother, when he lay,
  When thy son lay, pierced by the shaft which flies
In darkness? Where was lorn Urania
  When Adonais died? With veilèd eyes,
  Mid listening Echoes, in her paradise
She sate, while one, with soft enamoured breath,
  Rekindled all the fading melodies
With which, like flowers that mock the corse beneath,
He had adorned and hid the coming bulk of Death.

III

Oh weep for Adonais—he is dead!—
  Wake, melancholy Mother, wake and weep!—
Yet wherefore? Quench within their burning bed
  Thy fiery tears, and let thy loud heart keep,
  Like his, a mute and uncomplaining sleep;
For he is gone where all things wise and fair
  Descend. Oh dream not that the amorous deep
Will yet restore him to the vital air;
Death feeds on his mute voice, and laughs at our despair.

IV

Most musical of mourners, weep again!
   Lament anew, Urania!—He died
Who was the sire of an immortal strain,
    Blind, old, and lonely, when his country's pride
    The priest, the slave, and the liberticide,
Trampled and mocked with many a loathèd rite
    Of lust and blood. He went unterrified
Into the gulf of death; but his clear sprite
Yet reigns o'er earth, the third among the Sons of Light.

V

Most musical of mourners, weep anew!
   Not all to that bright station dared to climb:
And happier they their happiness who knew,
    Whose tapers yet burn through that night of time
    In which suns perished. Others more sublime,
Struck by the envious wrath of man or god,
    Have sunk, extinct in their refulgent prime;
And some yet live, treading the thorny road
Which leads, through toil and hate, to Fame's serene abode.

VI

But now thy youngest, dearest one has perished,
   The nursling of thy widowhood, who grew,
Like a pale flower by some sad maiden cherished,
    And fed with true-love tears instead of dew.
    Most musical of mourners, weep anew!
Thy extreme hope, the loveliest and the last,
    The bloom whose petals, nipped before they blew,
Died on the promise of the fruit, is waste;
The broken lily lies—the storm is overpast.

### VII

To that high Capital where kingly Death
  Keeps his pale court in beauty and decay
He came; and bought, with price of purest breath,
  A grave among the eternal.—Come away!
  Haste, while the vault of blue Italian day
Is yet his fitting charnel-roof, while still
  He lies as if in dewy sleepy he lay.
Awake him not! surely he takes his fill
Of deep and liquid rest, forgetful of all ill.

### VIII

He will awake no more, oh never more!
  Within the twilight chamber spreads apace
The shadow of white Death, and at the door
  Invisible Corruption waits to trace
  His extreme way to her dim dwelling-place;
The eternal Hunger sits, but pity and awe
  Soothe her pale rage, nor dares she to deface
So fair a prey, till darkness and the law
Of change shall o'er his sleep the mortal curtain draw.

### IX

Oh weep for Adonais!—The quick Dreams,
  The passion-wingèd ministers of thought,
Who were his flocks, whom near the living streams
  Of his young spirit he fed, and whom he taught
  The love which was its music, wander not—
Wander no more from kindling brain to brain,
  But droop there whence they sprung; and mourn
     their lot
Round the cold heart where, after their sweet pain,
They ne'er will gather strength or find a home again.

X

And one with trembling hands clasps his cold head,
    And fans him with her moonlight wings, and cries,
"Our love, our hope, our sorrow, is not dead!
    See, on the silken fringe of his faint eyes,
    Like dew upon a sleeping flower, there lies
A tear some dream has loosened from his brain."
    Lost angel of a ruined paradise!
She knew not 'twas her own,—as with no stain
She faded, like a cloud which had outwept its rain.

XI

One from a lucid urn of starry dew
    Washed her light limbs, as if embalming them;
Another clipped her profuse locks, and threw
    The wreath upon him, like an anadem
    Which frozen tears instead of pearls begem;
Another in her wilful grief would break
    Her bow and wingèd reeds, as if to stem
A greater loss with one which was more weak,—
And dull the bardèd fire against his frozen cheek.

XII

Another Splendour on his mouth alit,
    That mouth whence it was wont to draw the breath
Which gave it strength to pierce the guarded wit,
    And pass into the panting heart beneath
    With lightning and with music: the damp death
Quenched its caress upon his icy lips,
    And, as a dying meteor stains a wreath
Of moonlight vapour which the cold night clips,
It flushed through his pale limbs, and passed to its eclipse.

XIII

And others came. Desires and Adorations;
  Wingèd Persuasions, and veiled Destinies;
Splendours, and Glooms, and glimmering Incarnations
  Of Hopes and Fears, and twilight Fantasies;
  And Sorrow, with her family of Sighs;
And Pleasure, blind with tears, led by the gleam
  Of her own dying smile instead of eyes, —
  Came in slow pomp; — the moving pomp might seem
Like pageantry of mist on an autumnal stream.

XIV

All he had loved, and moulded into thought
  From shape and hue and odour and sweet sound,
Lamented Adonais. Morning sought
  Her eastern watch-tower, and her hair unbound,
  Wet with the tears which should adorn the ground,
Dimmed the aërial eyes that kindle day;
  Afar the melancholy Thunder moaned,
  Pale Ocean in unquiet slumber lay,
And the wild Winds flew round, sobbing in their dismay.

XV

Lost Echo sits amid the voiceless mountains,
  And feeds her grief with his rememberd lay;
And will no more reply to winds or fountains,
  Or amorous birds perched on the young green spray,
  Or herdsman's horn, or bell at closing day;
Since she can mimic not his lips, more dear
  Than those for whose disdain she pined away
Into a shadow of all sounds: — a drear
Murmur, between their songs, is all the woodmen hear.

XVI

Grief made the young Spring wild, and she threw down
  Her kindling buds, as if she Autumn were,
Or they dead leaves; since her delight is flown,
  For whom should she have waked the sullen Year?
  To Phoebus was not Hyacinth so dear,
Not to himself Narcissus, as to both
  Thou, Adonais: wan they stand and sere
Amid the faint companions of their youth,
With dew all turned to tears,—odour, to sighing ruth.

XVII

Thy spirit's sister, the lorn nightingale,
  Mourns not her mate with such melodious pain;
Not so the eagle, who like thee could scale
  Heaven, and could nourish in the sun's domain
  Her mighty youth with morning, doth complain,
Soaring and screaming round her empty nest,
  As Albion wails for thee: the curse of Cain
Light on his head who pierced thy innocent breast,
And scared the angel soul that was its earthly guest!

XVIII

Ah woe is me! Winter is come and gone,
  But grief returns with the revolving year.
The airs and streams renew their joyous tone;
  The ants, the bees, the swallows, re-appear;
  Fresh leaves and flowers deck the dead Seasons' bier;
The amorous birds now pair in every brake,
  And build their mossy homes in field and brere;
And the green lizard and the golden snake,
Like unimprisoned flames, out of their trance awake.

XIX

Through wood and stream and field and hill and ocean,
  A quickening life from the Earth's heart has burst,
As it has ever done, with change and motion,
  From the great morning of the world when first
  God dawned on chaos. In its stream immersed,
The lamps of heaven flash with a softer light;
  All baser things pant with life's sacred thirst,
Diffuse themselves, and spend in love's delight
The beauty and the joy of their renewèd might.

XX

The leprous corpse, touched by this spirit tender,
  Exhales itself in flowers of gentle breath;
Like incarnations of the stars, when splendour
  Is changed to fragrance, they illumine death,
  And mock the merry worm that wakes beneath.
Nought we know dies: shall that alone which knows
  Be as a sword consumed before the sheath
By sightless lightning? The intense atom glows
A moment, then is quenched in a most cold repose.

XXI

Alas, that all we loved of him should be,
  But for our grief, as if it had not been,
And grief itself be mortal! Woe is me!
  Whence are we, and why are we? of what scene
  The actors and spectators? Great and mean
Meet massed in death, who lends what life must borrow.
  As long as skies are blue and fields are green,
Evening must usher night, night urge the morrow,
Month follow month with woe, and year wake year to sorrow.

XXII

He will awake no more, oh never more!
"Wake thou," cried Misery, "childless Mother! Rise
Out of thy sleep, and slake in thy heart's core
    A wound more fierce than his, with tears and sighs."
    And all the Dreams that watched Urania's eyes,
And all the Echoes whom their Sister's song
    Had held in holy silence, cried "Arise";
Swift as a thought by the snake Memory stung,
From her ambrosial rest the fading Splendour sprung.

XXIII

She rose like an autumnal Night that springs
    Out of the east, and follows wild and drear
The golden Day, which, on eternal wings,
    Even as a ghost abandoning a bier,
    Had left the Earth a corpse. Sorrow and fear
So struck, so roused, so rapt, Urania;
    So saddened round her like an atmosphere
Of stormy mist; so swept her on her way,
Even to the mournful place where Adonais lay.

XXIV

Out of her secret paradise she sped,
    Through camps and cities rough with stone and steel
And human hearts, which, to her aery tread
    Yielding not, wounded the invisible
    Palms of her tender feet where'er they fell.
And barbèd tongues, and thoughts more sharp than they,
    Rent the soft form they never could repel,
Whose sacred blood, like the young tears of May,
Paved with eternal flowers that undeserving way.

### XXV

In the death-chamber for a moment Death,
  Shamed by the presence of that living Might,
Blushed to annihilation, and the breath
  Revisited those lips, and life's pale light
  Flashed through those limbs so late her dear delight.
"Leave me not wild and drear and comfortless,
  As silent lightning leaves the starless night!
Leave me not!" cried Urania. Her distress
Roused Death: Death rose and smiled, and met her vain
  caress.

### XXVI

"Stay yet awhile! speak to me once again!
  Kiss me, so long but as a kiss may live!
And in my heartless breast and burning brain
  That word, that kiss, shall all thoughts else survive,
  With food of saddest memory kept alive,
Now thou art dead, as if it were a part
  Of thee, my Adonais! I would give
All that I am, to be as thou now art: —
But I am chained to Time, and cannot thence depart.

### XXVII

"O gentle child, beautiful as thou wert,
  Why didst thou leave the trodden paths of men
Too soon, and with weak hands though mighty heart
  Dare the unpastured dragon in his den?
  Defenceless as thou wert, oh where was then
Wisdom the mirrored shield, or Scorn the spear?
  Or, hadst thou waited the full cycle when
Thy spirit should have filled its crescent sphere,
The monsters of life's waste had fled from thee like deer.

XXVIII

"The herded wolves bold only to pursue,
   The obscene ravens clamorous o'er the dead,
The vultures to the conqueror's banner true,
   Who feed where Desolation first has fed,
   And whose wings rain contagion,—how they fled,
When, like Apollo from his golden bow,
   The Pythian of the age one arrow sped,
And smiled!—The spoilers tempt no second blow,
They fawn on the proud feet that spurn them lying low.

XXIX

"The sun comes forth, and many reptiles spawn;
   He sets, and each ephemeral insect then
Is gathered into death without a dawn,
   And the immortal stars awake again.
   So is it in the world of living men:
A godlike mind soars forth, in its delight
   Making earth bare and veiling heaven; and, when
It sinks, the swarms that dimmed or shared its light
Leave to its kindred lamps the spirit's awful night."

XXX

Thus ceased she: and the Mountain Shepherds came,
   Their garlands sere, their magic mantles rent.
The Pilgrim of Eternity, whose fame
   Over his living head like heaven is bent,
   An early but enduring monument,
Came, veiling all the lightnings of his song
   In sorrow. From her wilds Ierne sent
The sweetest lyrist of her saddest wrong,
And love taught grief to fall like music from his tongue.

### XXXI

Midst others of less note came one frail form,
　A phantom among men, companionless
As the last cloud of an expiring storm,
　Whose thunder is its knell. He, as I guess,
　Had gazed on Nature's naked loveliness
Actaeon-like; and now he fled astray
　With feeble steps o'er the world's wilderness,
And his own thoughts along that rugged way
Pursued like raging hounds their father and their prey.

### XXXII

A pard-like Spirit beautiful and swift—
　A love in desolation masked—a power
Girt round with weakness; it can scarce uplift
　The weight of the superincumbent hour.
　It is a dying lamp, a falling shower,
A breaking billow;—even whilst we speak
　Is it not broken? On the withering flower
The killing sun smiles brightly: on a cheek
The life can burn in blood even while the heart may break.

### XXXIII

His head was bound with pansies overblown,
　And faded violets, white and pied and blue;
And a light spear topped with a cypress-cone,
　Round whose rude shaft dark ivy-tresses grew
　Yet dripping with the forest's noonday dew,
Vibrated, as the ever-beating heart
　Shook the weak hand that grasped it. Of that crew
He came the last, neglected and apart;
A herd-abandoned deer struck by the hunter's dart.

XXXIV

All stood aloof, and at his partial moan
  Smiled through their tears. Well knew that gentle band
Who in another's fate now wept his own.
  As in the accents of an unknown land
  He sang new sorrow, sad Urania scanned
The Stranger's mien, and murmured "Who art thou?"
  He answered not, but with a sudden hand
Made bare his branded and ensanguined brow,
Which was like Cain's or Christ's—oh that it should be so!

XXXV

What softer voice is hushed over the dead?
  Athwart what brow is that dark mantle thrown?
What form leans sadly o'er the white death-bed,
  In mockery of monumental stone,
  The heavy heart heaving without a moan?
If it be he who, gentlest of the wise,
  Taught, soothed, loved, honoured, the departed one,
Let me not vex with inharmonious sighs
The silence of that heart's accepted sacrifice.

XXXVI

Our Adonais has drunk poison—oh
  What deaf and viperous murderer could crown
Life's early cup with such a draught of woe?
  The nameless worm would now itself disown;
  It felt, yet could escape, the magic tone
Whose prelude held all envy, hate, and wrong,
  But what was howling in one breast alone,
Silent with expectation of the song
Whose master's hand is cold, whose silver lyre unstrung.

### XXXVII

Live thou, whose infamy is not thy fame!
   Live! fear no heavier chastisement from me,
Thou noteless blot on a remembered name!
   But be thyself, and know thyself to be!
   And ever at thy season be thou free
To spill the venom which thy fangs o'erflow:
   Remorse and self-contempt shall cling to thee,
Hot shame shall burn upon thy secret brow,
And like a beaten hound tremble thou shalt—as now.

### XXXVIII

Nor let us weep that our delight is fled
   Far from these carrion-kites that scream below.
He wakes or sleeps with the enduring dead;
   Thou canst not soar where he is sitting now.
   Dust to the dust: but the pure spirit shall flow
Back to the burning fountain whence he came,
   A portion of the Eternal, which must glow
Through time and change, unquenchably the same,
Whilst thy cold embers choke the sordid hearth of shame.

### XXXIX

Peace, peace! he is not dead, he doth not sleep!
   He hath awakened from the dream of life.
'Tis we who, lost in stormy visions, keep
   With phantoms an unprofitable strife,
   And in mad trance strike with our spirit's knife
Invulnerable nothings. We decay
   Like corpses in a charnel; fear and grief
Convulse us and consume us day by day,
And cold hopes swarm like worms within our living clay.

### XL

He has outsoared the shadow of our night.
 Envy and calumny and hate and pain,
And that unrest which men miscall delight,
 Can touch him not and torture not again.
 From the contagion of the world's slow stain
He is secure; and now can never mourn
 A heart grown cold, a head grown grey in vain—
Nor, when the spirit's self has ceased to burn,
With sparkless ashes load an unlamented urn.

### XLI

He live, he wakes—'tis Death is dead, not he;
 Mourn not for Adonais.—Thou young Dawn,
Turn all thy dew to splendour, for from thee
 The spirit thou lamentest is not gone!
 Ye caverns and ye forests, cease to moan!
Cease, ye faint flowers and fountains! and, thou Air,
 Which like a mourning-veil thy scarf hadst thrown
O'er the abandoned Earth, now leave it bare
Even to the joyous stars which smile on its despair!

### XLII

He is made one with Nature. There is heard
 His voice in all her music, from the moan
Of thunder to the song of night's sweet bird.
 He is a presence to be felt and known
 In darkness and in light, from herb and stone,—
Spreading itself where'er that Power may move
 Which has withdrawn his being to its own,
Which wields the world with never-wearied love,
Sustains it from beneath, and kindles it above.

### XLIII

He is a portion of the loveliness
   Which once he made more lovely. He doth bear
His part, while the One Spirit's plastic stress
   Sweeps through the dull dense world; compelling there
   All new successions to the forms they wear;
Torturing the unwilling dross, that checks its flight,
   To its own likeness, as each mass may bear;
And bursting in its beauty and its might
From trees and beasts and men into the heaven's light.

### XLIV

The splendours of the firmament of time
   May be eclipsed, but are extinguished not;
Like stars to their appointed height they climb,
   And death is a low mist which cannot blot
   The brightness it may veil. When lofty thought
Lifts a young heart above its mortal lair
   And love and life contend in it for what
Shall be its earthly doom, the dead live there,
And move like winds of light on dark and stormy air.

### XLV

The inheritors of unfulfilled renown
   Rose from their thrones, built beyond mortal thought
Far in the unapparent. Chatterton
   Rose pale, his solemn agony had not
   Yet faded from him: Sidney, as he fought,
And as he fell, and as he lived and loved,
   Sublimely mild, a spirit without spot,
Arose; And Lucan, by his death approved; —
Oblivion as they rose shrank like a thing reproved.

### XLVI

And many more, whose names on earth are dark,
But whose transmitted effluence cannot die
So long as fire outlives the parent spark,
Rose, robed in dazzling immortality.
"Thou art become as one of us," they cry;
"It was for thee you kingless sphere has long
Swung blind in unascended majesty,
Silent alone amid an heaven of song.
Assume thy wingèd throne, thou Vesper of our throng!"

### XLVII

Who mourns for Adonais? Oh come forth,
Fond wretch, and know thyself and him aright.
Clasp with thy panting soul the pendulous earth;
As from a centre, dart thy spirit's light
Beyond all worlds, until its spacious might
Satiate the void circumference: then shrink
Even to a point within our day and night;
And keep thy heart light, lest it make thee sink,
When hope has kindled hope, and lured thee to the brink.

### XLVIII

Or go to Rome, which is the sepulchre,
Oh not of him, but of our joy. 'Tis nought
That ages, empires, and religions, there
Lie buried in the ravage they have wrought;
For such as he can lend—they borrow not
Glory from those who made the world their prey;
And he is gathered to the kings of thought
Who waged contention with their time's decay,
And of the past are all that cannot pass away.

### XLIX

Go thou to Rome,—at once the paradise,
  The grave, the city, and the wilderness;
And where its wrecks like shattered mountains rise,
  And flowering weeds and fragrant copses dress
  The bones of Desolation's nakedness,
Pass, till the Spirit of the spot shall lead
  Thy footsteps to a slope of green access,
Where, like an infant's smile, over the dead
A light of laughing flowers along the grass is spread.

### L

And grey walls moulder round, on which dull Time
  Feeds, like slow fire upon a hoary brand;
And one keen pyramid with wedge sublime,
  Pavilioning the dust of him who planned
  This refuge for his memory, doth stand
Like flame transformed to marble; and beneath
  A field is spread, on which a newer band
Have pitched in heaven's smile their camp of death,
Welcoming him we lose with scarce-extinguished breath.

### LI

Here pause. These graves are all too young as yet
  To have outgrown the sorrow which consigned
Its charge to each; and, if the seal is set
  Here on one fountain of a mourning mind,
  Break it not thou! too surely shalt thou find
Thine own well full, if thou returnest home,
  Of tears and gall. From the world's bitter wind
Seek shelter in the shadow of the tomb.
What Adonais is why fear we to become?

LII

The One remains, the many change and pass;
  Heaven's light for ever shines, earth's shadows fly;
Life, like a dome of many-coloured glass,
    Stains the white radiance of eternity,
    Until Death tramples it of fragments. — Die,
If thou wouldst be with that which thou dost seek!
  Follow where all is fled! — Rome's azure sky,
Flowers, ruins, statues, music, words, are weak
The glory they transfuse with fitting truth to speak.

LIII

Why linger, why turn back, why shrink, my heart?
  Thy hopes are gone before: from all things here
They have departed; thou shouldst now depart.
    A light is past from the revolving year,
    And man and woman; and what still is dear
Attracts to crush, repels to make thee wither.
  The soft sky smiles, the low mind whispers near:
'Tis Adonais calls! Oh hasten thither!
No more let life divide what death can join together.

LIV

That light whose smile kindles the universe,
  That beauty in which all things work and move,
That benediction which the eclipsing curse
    Of birth can quench not, that sustaining Love
    Which, through the web of being blindly wove
By man and beast and earth and air and sea,
  Burns bright or dim, as each are mirrors of
The fire for which all thirst, now beams on me,
Consuming the last clouds of cold mortality.

LV

The breath whose might I have invoked in song
   Descends on me; my spirit's bark is driven
Far from the shore, far from the trembling throng
   Whose sails were never to the tempest given.
   The massy earth and spherèd skies are riven!
I am borne darkly, fearfully afar!
   Whilst, burning through the inmost veil of heaven,
The soul of Adonais, like a star,
Beacons from the abode where the Eternal are.

---

*Just as Auden was to write a Yeatsian poem on Yeats's death (p. 1028), Shelley wrote a Keatsian poem on Keats's. The Spenserian stanza in "Adonais" is the measure used in Keats's "Eve of St. Agnes" (p. 551). Such a pastoral elegy, inherited from the Greeks, has long been used by one poet who laments the passing of another, as is the case with Milton's "Lycidas" (p. 203). "Adonais" stands alone, however, since both Shelley and Keats are poets of the very first rank.*

# JOHN CLARE 1793–1864

Despite a life marked by poverty, misery, insanity, and confinement to asylums, Clare managed to be one of the most productive poets in English; his complete works are still not available 130 years after his death. Praised at one time as a rustic primitive on the model of Burns, he was later honored as a sainted madman on the model of Smart, Collins, and Cowper. In time, he may receive recognition as a very good poet, sometimes even a great one.

# *I Am*

>>>>>>>

I am: yet what I am none cares or knows:
    My friends forsake me like a memory lost,
I am the self-consumer of my woes—
    They rise and vanish in oblivious host,
Like shadows in love's frenzied stifled throes—
And yet I am, and live—like vapors tossed

Into the nothingness of scorn and noise,
    Into the living sea of waking dreams,
Where there is neither sense of life or joys,
    But the vast shipwreck of my life's esteems;
Even the dearest, that I love the best,
And strange—nay, rather stranger than the rest.

I long for scenes where man has never trod,
    A place where woman never smiled or wept—
There to abide with my Creator, God,
    And sleep as I in childhood sweetly slept,
Untroubling and untroubled where I lie,
The grass below—above the vaulted sky.

*You would have to have a very hard heart indeed not to feel pity for Clare and to hear the utter truth, sincerity, and pathos of "I Am," written (along with hundreds of other poems) while he was confined in the General Lunatic Asylum in Northampton, where he spent about the last third of his life.*

Bryant established himself as a poet in his teens and was generally regarded as the leading American poet from about 1825 until his death more than fifty years later. He was trained as a lawyer and employed as a journalist. Originally a Democrat, he later became one of the founders of the Republican Party.

## To a Waterfowl

Whither, 'midst falling dew,
While glow the heavens with the last steps of day,
Far, through their rosy depths, dost thou pursue
    Thy solitary way?

Vainly the fowler's eye
Might mark thy distant flight to do thee wrong,
As, darkly painted on the crimson sky,
    Thy figure floats along.

Seek'st thou the plashy brink
Of weedy lake, or marge of river wide,
Or where the rocking billows rise and sink
    On the chafed ocean side?

There is a Power whose care
Teaches thy way along that pathless coast, —
The desert and illimitable air, —
    Lone wandering, but not lost.

All day thy wings have fanned,
At that far height, the cold, thin atmosphere,
Yet stoop not, weary, to the welcome land,
  Though the dark night is near.

And soon that toil shall end;
Soon shalt thou find a summer home, and rest,
And scream among thy fellows; reeds shall bend,
  Soon, o'er thy sheltered nest.

Thou'rt gone, the abyss of heaven
Hath swallowed up thy form; yet, on my heart
Deeply hath sunk the lesson thou hast given,
  And shall not soon depart.

He who, from zone to zone,
Guides through the boundless sky thy certain flight,
In the long way that I must tread alone,
  Will lead my steps aright.

---

*Some modern readers resent having a poem spell out its moral and theological
"lesson" so baldly, but a work with so much accuracy of observation and grace
of form has earned the right to a bit of sententiousness. Matthew Arnold called
this "the most perfect brief poem in the language."*

# Thanatopsis

To him who in the love of Nature holds
Communion with her visible forms, she speaks
A various language; for his gayer hours
She has a voice of gladness, and a smile
And eloquence of beauty, and she glides
Into his darker musings, with a mild
And gentle sympathy, that steals away
Their sharpness, ere he is aware. When thoughts
Of the last bitter hour come like a blight
Over thy spirit, and sad images
Of the stern agony, and shroud, and pall,
And breathless darkness, and the narrow house
Make thee to shudder, and grow sick at heart;—
Go forth under the open sky, and list
To Nature's teachings, while from all around—
Earth and her waters, and the depths of air,—
Comes a still voice—Yet a few days, and thee
The all-beholding sun shall see no more
In all his course; nor yet in the cold ground,
Where thy pale form was laid, with many tears,
Nor in the embrace of ocean shall exist
Thy image. Earth, that nourished thee, shall claim
Thy growth, to be resolv'd to earth again;
And, lost each human trace, surrend'ring up
Thine individual being, shalt thou go
To mix forever with the elements,
To be a brother to th' insensible rock
And to the sluggish clod, which the rude swain
Turns with his share, and treads upon. The oak
Shall send his roots abroad, and pierce thy mould.
Yet not to thy eternal resting place
Shalt thou retire alone—nor couldst thou wish
Couch more magnificent. Thou shalt lie down
With patriarchs of the infant world—with kings

The powerful of the earth—the wise, the good,
Fair forms, and hoary seers of ages past,
All in one mighty sepulchre.—The hills
Rock-ribb'd and ancient as the sun,—the vales
Stretching in pensive quietness between;
The venerable woods—rivers that move
In majesty, and the complaining brooks
That make the meadows green; and pour'd round all,
Old ocean's grey and melancholy waste,—
Are but the solemn decorations all
Of the great tomb of man. The golden sun,
The planets, all the infinite host of heaven,
Are shining on the sad abodes of death,
Through the still lapse of ages. All that tread
The globe are but a handful to the tribes
That slumber in its bosom.—Take the wings
Of morning—and the Barcan desert pierce,
Or lose thyself in the continuous woods
Where rolls the Oregan, and hears no sound,
Save his own dashings—yet—the dead are there,
And millions in those solitudes, since first
The flight of years began, have laid them down
In their last sleep—the dead reign there alone.—
So shalt thou rest—and what if thou shalt fall
Unnoticed by the living—and no friend
Take note of thy departure? All that breathe
Will share thy destiny. The gay will laugh
When thou art gone, the solemn brood of care
Plod on, and each one as before will chase
His favourite phantom; yet all these shall leave
Their mirth and their employments, and shall come,
And make their bed with thee. As the long train
Of ages glide away, the sons of men,
The youth in life's green spring, and he who goes
In the full strength of years, matron, and maid,
The bow'd with age, the infant in the smiles
And beauty of its innocent age cut off,—
Shall one by one be gathered to they side,

By those, who in their turn shall follow them.
So live, that when thy summons comes to join
The innumerable caravan, that moves
To the pale realms of shade, where each shall take
His chamber in the silent halls of death,
Thou go not, like the quarry-slave at night,
Scourged to his dungeon, but sustain'd and sooth'd
By an unfaltering trust, approach thy grave,
Like one who wraps the drapery of his couch
About him, and lies down to pleasant dreams.

---

*Bryant began his sophisticated "view of death" as a teenager. The first version was shorter than this final version by about thirty lines but still displayed a mature stoicism and discipline. "Thanatopsis" has long been a favorite moral poem for Americans.*

# JOHN KEATS 1795-1821

No poet in this anthology produced more great poetry at an earlier age than John Keats. Both his parents died while he was very young. Keats was apprenticed to a surgeon, moved to London in 1815, and was qualified as a "dresser" and subsequently as a surgeon, in accordance with the medical regulations of the day. Keats's earliest poems were written under the influence of Edmund Spenser, and all of Keats's work shows something of a Spenserian blend of sensuousness and intellectual depth. Keats was never a formal critic of the sort who writes essays, reviews, and dissertations, but, in his marvelous letters, he displays one of the finest critical intelligences in English literature.

## To Autumn

### I

Season of mists and mellow fruitfulness,
　Close bosom-friend of the maturing sun;
Conspiring with him how to load and bless
　With fruit the vines that round the thatch-eves run;
To bend with apples the mossed cottage-trees,
　And fill all fruit with ripeness to the core;
　　To swell the gourd, and plump the hazel shells
　With a sweet kernel; to set budding more,
And still more, later flowers for the bees,
Until they think warm days will never cease,
　　For summer has o'er-brimmed their clammy cells.

II

Who hath not seen thee oft amid thy store?
  Sometimes whoever seeks abroad may find
Thee sitting careless on a granary floor,
  Thy hair soft-lifted by the winnowing wind;
Or on a half-reaped furrow sound asleep,
  Drowsed with the fume of poppies, while thy hook
    Spares the next swath and all its twinèd flowers:
And sometimes like a gleaner thou dost keep
  Steady thy laden head across a brook;
  Or by a cider-press, with patient look,
    Thou watchest the last oozings hours by hours.

III

Where are the songs of Spring? Ay, where are they?
  Think not of them, thou hast thy music too,—
While barrèd clouds bloom the soft-dying day,
  And touch the stubble-plains with rosy hue;
Then in a wailful choir the small gnats mourn
  Among the river swallows, borne aloft
    Or sinking as the light wind lives or dies;
And full-grown lambs loud bleat from hilly bourn;
  Hedge-crickets sing; and now with treble soft
  The red-breast whistles from a garden-croft;
    And gathering swallows twitter in the skies.

---

*Most of Keats's six great odes were written in May 1819; true to its subject, however, this, the last, was written just a day or two before the autumnal equinox of 1819. Keats makes autumn "the human season," not much like the super-human creativity of spring or the otherworldly extremism of summer and winter. The poet here exploits to the full his matchless genius for sensual realization—how things look and sound and also how they smell, taste, and feel. (Note that: "bourn" is "region"; "croft" is "small enclosed field.")*

# La Belle Dame sans Merci

O what can ail thee, Knight at arms,
  Alone and palely loitering?
The sedge has withered from the Lake
  And no birds sing!

O what can ail thee, Knight at arms,
  So haggard and so woe begone?
The Squirrel's granary is full
  And the harvest's done.

I see a lily on thy brow
  With anguish moist and fever dew,
And on thy cheeks a fading rose
  Fast withereth too—

I met a Lady in the Meads,
  Full beautiful, a faery's child
Her hair was long, her foot was light
  And her eyes were wild—

I made a Garland for her head,
  And bracelets too, and fragrant Zone
She look'd at me as she did love
  And made sweet moan—

I set her on my pacing steed
  And nothing else saw all day long
For sidelong would she bend and sing
  A faery's song—

She found me roots of relish sweet
And honey wild and manna dew
And sure in language strange she said
I love thee true—

She took me to her elfin grot
And there she wept, and sigh'd full sore,
And there I shut her wild wild eyes
With kisses four.

And there she lulled me asleep
And there I dream'd—Ah woe betide!
The latest dream I ever dreamt
On the cold hill side.

I saw pale Kings, and Princes too
Pale warriors, death pale were they all;
They cried, La belle dame sans merci
Hath thee in thrall.

I saw their starv'd lips in the gloam
With horrid warning gaped wide,
And I awoke, and found me here
On the cold hill's side.

And this is why I sojourn here
Alone and palely loitering;
Though the sedge is withered from the Lake,
And no birds sing—

# La Belle Dame sans Merci
## (Revised Version)

Ah, what can ail thee, wretched wight,
  Alone and palely loitering;
The sedge has wither'd from the lake,
  And no birds sing.

Ah, what can ail thee, wretched wight,
  So haggard and so woe-begone?
The squirrel's granary is full,
  And the harvest's done.

I see a lilly on thy brow,
  With anguish moist and fever dew;
And on thy cheek a fading rose
  Fast withereth too.

I met a Lady in the meads
  Full beautiful, a fairy's child;
Her hair was long, her foot was light,
  And her eyes were wild.

I set her on my pacing steed,
  And nothing else saw all day long;
For sideways would she lean, and sing
  A faery's song.

I made a garland for her head,
  And bracelets too, and fragrant zone;
She look'd at me as she did love,
  And made sweet moan.

She found me roots of relish sweet,
    And honey wild, and manna dew,
And sure in language strange she said,
    I love thee true.

She took me to her elfin grot,
    And there she gaz'd and sighed deep,
And there I shut her wild sad eyes—
    So kiss'd to sleep.

And there we slumber'd on the moss,
    And there I dream'd, ah woe betide
The latest dream I ever dream'd
    On the cold hill side.

I saw pale kings, and princes too,
    Pale warriors, death-pale were they all;
Who cry'd—"La belle Dame sans mercy
    Hath thee in thrall!"

I saw their starv'd lips in the gloom
    With horrid warning gaped wide,
And I awoke, and found me here
    On the cold hill side.

And this is why I sojourn here
    Alone and palely loitering,
Though the sedge is wither'd from the lake,
    And no birds sing.

---

*Keats's "Eve of St. Agnes" (p. 551) includes "an ancient ditty . . . In Provence called 'La belle dame sans merci.'" There is a medieval song with that title (which means "The Lovely Lady without Pity") by Alain Chartier. Like many of his Romantic contemporaries, Keats adapted the ballad stanza and also followed the ballad convention of casting the entire poem in the form of questions and answers. Keats wrote two versions of this strangely powerful story. Since they are short, and since critics disagree about which is better, both are given here.*

# On First Looking into Chapman's Homer

Much have I traveled in the realms of gold,
   And many goodly states and kingdoms seen;
   Round many western islands have I been
Which bards in fealty to Apollo hold.
Oft of one wide expanse had I been told
   That deep-browed Homer ruled as his demesne,
   Yet did I never breathe its pure serene
Till I heard Chapman speak out loud and bold.
Then felt I like some watcher of the skies
   When a new planet swims into his ken;
Or like stout Cortez when with eagle eyes
   He stared at the Pacific— and all his men
Looked at each other with a wild surmise—
   Silent, upon a peak in Darien.

---

*Keats made two very apt choices of metaphors for his exciting and inspiring glimpse of Homer, whose Greek he could not read, through the translations of George Chapman. Keats erred in giving Cortez credit for what Balboa had done, but it was still brilliant of the poet to connect the Renaissance explorers with later discoverers.*

# Ode to a Nightingale

## I

My heart aches, and a drowsy numbness pains
  My sense, as though of hemlock I had drunk,
Or emptied some dull opiate to the drains
  One minute past, and Lethe-wards had sunk.
'Tis not through envy of thy happy lot,
  But being too happy in thine happiness, —
    That thou, light-wingèd Dryad of the trees,
      In some melodious plot
Of beechen green, and shadows numberless,
  Singest of summer in full-throated ease.

## II

O for a draught of vintage! that hath been
  Cool'd a long age in the deep-delvèd earth,
Tasting of Flora and the country green,
  Dance, and Provençal song, and sunburnt mirth!
O for a beaker full of the warm South,
  Full of the true, the blushful Hippocrene,
    With beaded bubbles winking at the brim,
      And purple-stainèd mouth;
That I might drink, and leave the world unseen,
  And with thee fade away into the forest dim:

### III

Fade far away, dissolve, and quite forget
  What thou among the leaves hast never known,
The weariness, the fever, and the fret
  Here, where men sit and hear each other groan;
Where palsy shakes a few, sad, last gray hairs,
  Where youth grows pale, and specter-thin, and dies;
    Where but to think is to be full of sorrow
      And leaden-eyed despairs,
  Where Beauty cannot keep her lustrous eyes,
    Or new Love pine at them beyond to-morrow.

### IV

Away! away! for I will fly to thee,
  Not charioted by Bacchus and his pards,
But on the viewless wings of Poesy,
  Though the dull brain perplexes and retards:
Already with thee! tender is the night,
  And haply the Queen-Moon is on her throne,
    Clustered around by all her starry Fays;
      But here there is no light,
  Save what from heaven is with the breezes blown
    Through verdurous glooms and winding mossy ways.

### V

I cannot see what flowers are at my feet,
  Nor what soft incense hangs upon the boughs,
But, in embalmèd darkness, guess each sweet
  Wherewith the seasonable month endows
The grass, the thicket, and the fruit-tree wild;
  White hawthorn, and the pastoral eglantine;
    Fast fading violets cover'd up in leaves;
      And mid-May's eldest child,
  The coming musk-rose, full of dewy wine,
    The murmurous haunt of flies on summer eves.

VI

Darkling I listen; and for many a time
  I have been half in love with easeful Death,
Call'd him soft names in many a musèd rhyme,
  To take into the air my quiet breath;
Now more than ever seems it rich to die,
  To cease upon the midnight with no pain,
    While thou art pouring forth thy soul abroad
      In such an ecstasy!
    Still wouldst thou sing, and I have ears in vain —
    To thy high requiem become a sod.

VII

Thou wast not born for death, immortal Bird!
  No hungry generations tread thee down;
The voice I hear this passing night was heard
  In ancient days by emperor and clown:
Perhaps the self-same song that found a path
  Through the sad heart of Ruth, when, sick for home,
    She stood in tears amid the alien corn;
      The same that oft-times hath
    Charm'd magic casements, opening on the foam
    Of perilous seas, in faery lands forlorn.

VIII

Forlorn! the very word is like a bell
  To toll me back from thee to my sole self!
Adieu! the fancy cannot cheat so well
  As she is fam'd to do, deceiving elf.
Adieu! adieu! thy plaintive anthem fades
  Past the near meadows, over the still stream,
    Up the hill-side; and now 'tis buried deep
      In the next valley-glades:
  Was it a vision, or a waking dream?
    Fled is that music: — Do I wake or sleep?

Keats's "Ode on a Grecian Urn" (p. 546) is virtually selfless, hinting only at a vague plural first-person pronoun toward the end. This beautiful ode, on the other hand, smacks more of the Romantic concentration on the singular self, with "My" at the beginning and "I" near the end.

John Keats

# Ode on a Grecian Urn

·◇·◇·◇·◇·

Thou still unravished bride of quietness,
　Thou foster-child of silence and slow time,
Sylvan historian, who canst thus express
　A flowery tale more sweetly than our rhyme:
What leaf-fringed legend haunts about thy shape
　Of deities or mortals, or of both,
　　In Tempe or the dales of Arcady?
　What men or gods are these? What maidens loth?
What mad pursuit? What struggle to escape?
　　What pipes and timbrels? What wild ecstasy?

Heard melodies are sweet, but those unheard
　Are sweeter; therefore, ye soft pipes, play on;
Not to the sensual ear, but, more endeared,
　Pipe to the spirit ditties of no tone:
Fair youth, beneath the trees, thou canst not leave
　Thy song, nor ever can those trees be bare;
　　Bold Lover, never, never canst thou kiss,
Though winning near the goal—yet, do not grieve;
　　She cannot fade, though thou hast not thy bliss,
　For ever wilt thou love, and she be fair!

Ah, happy, happy boughs! that cannot shed
　Your leaves, nor ever bid the Spring adieu;
And, happy melodist, unwearièd,
　For ever piping songs for ever new;
More happy love! more happy, happy love!
　For ever warm and still to be enjoyed,
　　For ever panting, and for ever young;
All breathing human passion far above,
　　That leaves a heart high-sorrowful and cloyed,
　A burning forehead, and a parching tongue.

[546]

Who are these coming to the sacrifice?
　To what green altar, O mysterious priest,
Lead'st thou that heifer lowing at the skies,
　And all her silken flanks with garlands drest?
What little town by river or sea shore,
　Or mountain-built with peaceful citadel,
　　Is emptied of this folk, this pious morn?
And, little town, thy streets for evermore
　Will silent be; and not a soul to tell
　　Why thou art desolate, can e'er return.

O Attic shape! Fair attitude! with brede
　Of marble men and maidens overwrought,
With forest branches and the trodden weed;
　Thou, silent form, dost tease us out of thought
As doth Eternity: Cold Pastoral!
　When old age shall this generation waste,
　　Thou shalt remain, in midst of other woe
　Than ours, a friend to man, to whom thou say'st,
Beauty is truth, truth beauty,—that is all
　　Ye know on earth, and all ye need to know.

*Compared with his Romantic "Ode to a Nightingale" (p. 542), this ode seems closer to the Classical spirit. Its subject is an artifact from classical antiquity, and the handling of the subject has an impersonal quality, reflected in the structural poise of the poem. Because of some confusing punctuation, it is unclear whether the urn says all of the last two lines or just "Beauty is truth, truth beauty."*

# When I Have Fears

When I have fears that I may cease to be
  Before my pen has gleaned my teeming brain,
Before high-piled books, in charactery,
  Hold like rich garners the full ripened grain;
When I behold, upon the night's starred face,
  Huge cloudy symbols of a high romance,
And think that I may never live to trace
  Their shadows, with the magic hand of chance;
And when I feel, fair creature of an hour,
  That I shall never look upon thee more,
Never have relish in the faery power
  Of unreflecting love; — then on the shore
Of the wide world I stand alone, and think
Till love and fame to nothingness do sink.

*Keats parallels the typical Shakespeare sonnet in rhyme scheme, in the tightly efficient "When . . . then . . ." architecture, and even in particulars of wording ("wide world" echoes Shakespeare's ". . . the prophetic soul of the wide world . . ." in Sonnet CVII). One of the last books by the modern American poet John Berryman is called* Love and Fame *(1970).*

# Ode on Melancholy

>>>>>>>

I

No, no, go not to Lethe, neither twist
  Wolf's-bane, tight-rooted, for its poisonous wine;
Nor suffer thy pale forehead to be kiss'd
  By nightshade, ruby grape of Proserpine;
Make not your rosary of yew-berries,
    Nor let the beetle, nor the death-moth be
      Your mournful Psyche, nor the downy owl
A partner in your sorrow's mysteries;
    For shade to shade will come too drowsily,
      And drown the wakeful anguish of the soul.

II

But when the melancholy fit shall fall
  Sudden from heaven like a weeping cloud,
That fosters the droop-headed flowers all,
  And hides the green hill in an April shroud;
Then glut thy sorrow on a morning rose,
    Or on the rainbow of the salt sand-wave,
      Or on the wealth of globed peonies;
Or if thy mistress some rich anger shows,
    Emprison her soft hand, and let her rave,
      And feed deep, deep upon her peerless eyes.

III

She dwells with Beauty—Beauty that must die;
  And Joy, whose hand is ever at his lips
Bidding adieu; and aching Pleasure nigh,
  Turning to poison while the bee-mouth sips:
Ay, in the very temple of Delight
  Veil'd Melancholy has her sovran shrine,
    Though seen of none save him whose strenuous tongue
  Can burst Joy's grape against his palate fine;
His soul shall taste the sadness of her might,
  And be among her cloudy trophies hung.

---

*Although we may have outgrown the primitive pathology that regards melancholia as the result of too much black bile, we still recognize the condition as a true affliction of the spirit. Keats sounds quite modern in his rejection of the usual dark emblems, emphasizing instead that the better images for melancholy are those of beauty, joy, and life itself, since we know they must perish. Keats, somewhat like Blake, devised an original mythology with melancholy's shrine right in the temple of delight.*

# The Eve of St. Agnes

### I

St. Agnes' Eve—Ah, bitter chill it was!
The owl, for all his feathers, was a-cold;
The hare limped trembling through the frozen grass,
And silent was the flock in woolly fold:
Numb were the Beadsman's fingers, while he told
His rosary, and while his frosted breath,
Like pious incense from a censer old,
Seemed taking flight for heaven, without a death,
Past the sweet Virgin's picture, while his prayer he saith.

### II

His prayer he saith, this patient, holy man;
Then takes his lamp, and riseth from his knees,
And back returneth, meager, barefoot, wan,
Along the chapel aisle by slow degrees:
The sculptured dead, on each side, seem to freeze,
Emprisoned in black, purgatorial rails:
Knights, ladies, praying in dumb orat'ries,
He passeth by; and his weak spirit fails
To think how they may ache in icy hoods and mails.

### III

Northward he turneth through a little door,
And scarce three steps, ere Music's golden tongue
Flattered to tears this aged man and poor;
But no—already had his deathbell rung:
The joys of all his life were said and sung:
His was harsh penance on St. Angnes' Eve:
Another way he went, and soon among
Rough ashes sat he for his soul's reprieve,
And all night kept awake, for sinners' sake to grieve.

IV

That ancient Beadsman heard the prelude soft;
And so it chanced, for many a door was wide,
From hurry to and fro. Soon, up aloft,
The silver, snarling trumpets' 'gan to chide:
The level chambers, ready with their pride,
Were glowing to receive a thousand guests:
The carvèd angels, ever eager-eyed,
Stared, where upon their heads the cornice rests,
With hair blown back, and wings put cross-wise on their
    breasts.


V

At length burst in the argent revelry,
With plume, tiara, and all rich array,
Numerous as shadows haunting faerily
The brain, new-stuffed, in youth, with triumphs gay
Of old romance. These let us wish away,
And turn, sole-thoughted, to one Lady there,
Whose heart had brooded, all that wintry day,
On love, and winged St. Agnes' saintly care,
As she had heard old dames full many times declare.


VI

They told her how, upon St. Agnes' Eve,
Young virgins might have visions of delight,
And soft adorings from their loves receive
Upon the honeyed middle of the night,
If ceremonies due they did aright;
As, supperless to bed they must retire,
And couch supine their beauties, lily-white,
Nor look behind, nor sideways, but require
Of Heaven with upward eyes for all that they desire.

VII

Full of this whim was thoughtful Madeline:
The music, yearning like a God in pain,
She scarcely heard: her maiden eyes divine,
Fixed on the floor, saw many a sweeping train
Pass by—she heeded not at all: in vain
Came many a tiptoe, amorous cavalier,
And back retired; not cooled by high disdain,
But she saw not: her heart was otherwhere:
She sighed for Agnes' dreams, the sweetest of the year.

VIII

She danced along with vague, regardless eyes,
Anxious her lips, her breathing quick and short:
The hallowed hour was near at hand: she sighs
Amid the timbrels, and the thronged resort
Of whisperers in anger, or in sport;
'Mid looks of love, defiance, hate, and scorn,
Hoodwinked with faery fancy; all amort,
Save to St. Agnes and her lambs unshorn,
And all the bliss to be before tomorrow morn.

IX

So, purposing each moment to retire,
She lingered still. Meantime, across the moors,
Had come young Porphyro, with heart on fire
For Madeline. Beside the portal doors,
Buttressed from moonlight, stands he, and implores
All saints to give him sight of Madeline,
But for one moment in the tedious hours,
That he might gaze and worship all unseen;
Perchance speak, kneel, touch, kiss—in sooth such things have
   been.

X

He ventures in: let no buzzed whisper tell:
All eyes be muffled, or a hundred swords
Will storm his heart, Love's feverous citadel:
For him, those chambers held barbarian hordes,
Hyena foemen, and hot-blooded lords,
Whose very dogs would execrations howl
Against his lineage: not one breast affords
Him any mercy, in that mansion foul,
Save one old beldame, weak in body and in soul.

XI

Ah, happy chance! the aged creature came,
Shuffling along with ivory-headed wand,
To where he stood, hid from the torch's flame,
Behind a broad hall-pillar, far beyond
The sound of merriment and chorus bland:
He startled her; but soon she knew his face,
And grasped his fingers in her palsied hand,
Saying, "Mercy, Porphyro! hie thee from this place;
They are all here tonight, the whole blood-thirsty race!

XII

"Get hence! get hence! there's dwarfish Hildebrand;
He had a fever late, and in the fit
He curséd thee and thine, both house and land:
Then there's that old Lord Maurice, not a whit
More tame for his gray hairs—Alas me! flit!
Flit like a ghost away."—"Ah, Gossip dear,
We're safe enough; here in this arm-chair sit,
And tell me how"—"Good Saints! not here, not here;
Follow me, child, or else these stones will be thy bier."

### XIII

He followed through a lowly archèd way,
Brushing the cobwebs with his lofty plume,
And as she muttered "Well-a—well-a-day!"
He found him in a little moonlight room,
Pale, latticed, chill, and silent as a tomb.
"Now tell me where is Madeline," said he,
"O tell me, Angela, by the holy loom
Which none but secret sisterhood may see,
When they St. Agnes' wool are waving piously."

### XIV

"St. Agnes! Ah! it is St. Agnes' Eve—
Yet men will murder upon holy days:
Thou must hold water in a witch's sieve,
And be liege-lord of all the Elves and Fays,
To venture so: it fills me with amaze
To see thee, Porphyro!—St. Agnes' Eve!
God's help! my lady fair the conjuror plays
This very night: good angels her deceive!
But let me laugh awhile, I've mickle time to grieve."

### XV

Feebly she laugheth in the languid moon,
While Porphyro upon her face doth look,
Like puzzled urchin on an aged crone
Who keepeth closed a wonderous riddle-book,
As spectacled she sits in chimney nook.
But soon his eyes grew brilliant, when she told
His lady's purpose; and he scarce could brook
Tears, at the thought of those enchantments cold,
And Madeline asleep in lap of legends old.

### XVI

Sudden a thought came like a full-blown rose,
Flushing his brow, and in his painèd heart
Made purple riot: then doth he propose
A stratagem, that makes the beldame start:
"A cruel man and impious thou art:
Sweet lady, let her pray, and sleep, and dream
Alone with her good angels, far apart
From wicked men like thee. Go, go!—I deem
Thou canst not surely be the same that thou didst seem."

### XVII

"I will not harm her, by all saints I swear,"
Quoth Porphyro: "O may I ne'er find grace
When my weak voice shall whisper its last prayer,
If one of her soft ringlets I displace,
Or look with ruffian passion in her face:
Good Angela, believe me by these tears;
Or I will, even in a moment's space,
Awake, with horrid shout, my foemen's ears,
And beard them, though they be more fanged than wolves and
   bears."

### XVIII

"Ah! why wilt thou affright a feeble soul?
A poor, weak, palsy-stricken, churchyard thing,
Whose passing-bell may ere the midnight toll;
Whose prayers for thee, each morn and evening,
Were never missed."—Thus plaining, doth she bring
A gentler speech from burning Porphyro;
So woeful, and of such deep sorrowing,
That Angela gives promise she will do
Whatever he shall wish, betide her weal or woe.

XIX

Which was, to lead him, in close secrecy,
Even to Madeline's chamber, and there hide
Him in a closet, of such privacy
That he might see her beauty unespied,
And win perhaps that night a peerless bride,
While legioned faeries paced the coverlet,
And pale enchantment held her sleepy-eyed.
Never on such a night have lovers met,
Since Merlin paid his Demon all the monstrous debt.

XX

"It shall be as thou wishest," said the Dame:
"All cates and dainties shall be storèd there
Quickly on this feast-night: by the tambour frame
Her own lute thou wilt see: no time to spare,
For I am slow and feeble, and scarce dare
On such a catering trust my dizzy head.
Wait here, my child, with patience; kneel in prayer
The while: Ah! thou must needs the lady wed,
Or may I never leave my grave among the dead."

XXI

So saying, she hobbled off with busy fear.
The lover's endless minutes slowly passed;
The dame returned, and whispered in his ear
To follow her; with agéd eyes aghast
From fright of dim espial. Safe at last,
Through many a dusky gallery, they gain
The maiden's chamber, silken, hushed, and chaste;
Where Porphyro took covert, pleased amain.
His poor guide hurried back with agues in her brain.

### XXII

Her faltering hand upon the balustrade,
Old Angela was feeling for the stair,
When Madeline, St. Agnes' charmèd maid,
Rose, like a missioned spirit, unaware:
With silver taper's light, and pious care,
She turned, and down the agéd gossip led
To a safe level matting. Now prepare,
Young Porphyro, for gazing on that bed;
She comes, she comes again, like ring dove frayed and fled.

### XXIII

Out went the taper as she hurried in;
Its little smoke, in pallid moonshine, died:
She closed the door, she panted, all akin
To spirits of the air, and visions wide:
No uttered syllable, or, woe betide!
But to her heart, her heart was voluble,
Paining with eloquence her balmy side;
As though a tongueless nightingale should swell
Her throat in vain, and die, heart-stifled, in her dell.

### XXIV

A casement high and triple-arched there was,
All garlanded with carven imag'ries
Of fruits, and flowers, and bunches of knot-grass,
And diamonded with panes of quaint device,
Innumerable of stains and splendid dyes,
As are the tiger-moth's deep-damasked wings;
And in the midst, 'mong thousand heraldries,
And twilight saints, and dim emblazonings,
A shielded scutcheon blushed with blood of queens and kings.

### XXV

Full on this casement shone the wintry moon,
And threw warm gules on Madeline's fair breast,
As down she knelt for heaven's grace and boon;
Rose-bloom fell on her hands, together pressed,
And on her silver cross soft amethyst,
And on her hair a glory, like a saint:
She seemed a splendid angel, newly dressed,
Save wings, for heaven—Porphyro grew faint:
She knelt, so pure a thing, so free from mortal taint.

### XXVI

Anon his heart revives: her vespers done,
Of all its wreathèd pearls her hair she frees;
Unclasps her warmèd jewels one by one;
Loosens her fragrant bodice; by degrees
Her rich attire creeps rustling to her knees:
Half-hidden, like a mermaid in sea-weed,
Pensive awhile she dreams awake, and sees,
In fancy, fair St. Agnes in her bed,
But dares not look behind, or all the charm is fled.

### XXVII

Soon, trembling in her soft and chilly nest,
In sort of wakeful swoon, perplexed she lay,
Until the poppied warmth of sleep oppressed
Her soothèd limbs, and soul fatigued away;
Flown, like a thought, until the morrow-day;
Blissfully havened both from joy and pain;
Clasped like a missal where swart Paynims pray;
Blinded alike from sunshine and from rain,
As though a rose should shut, and be a bud again.

XXVIII

Stol'n to this paradise, and so entranced,
Porphyro gazed upon her empty dress,
And listened to her breathing, if it chanced
To wake into a slumberous tenderness;
Which when he heard, that minute did he bless,
And breathed himself: then from the closet crept,
Noiseless as fear in a wide wilderness,
And over the hushed carpet, silent, stepped,
And 'tween the curtains peeped, where, lo!—how fast she slept.

XXIX

Then by the bedside, where the faded moon
Made a dim, silver twilight, soft he set
A table, and, half anguished, threw thereon
A cloth of woven crimson, gold, and jet—
O for some drowsy Morphean amulet!
The boisterous, midnight, festive clarion,
The kettledrum, and far-heard clarinet,
Affray his ears, though but in dying tone—
The hall door shuts again, and all the noise is gone.

XXX

And still she slept an azure-lidded sleep,
In blanchèd linen, smooth, and lavendered,
While he from forth the closet brought a heap
Of candied apple, quince, and plum, and gourd;
With jellies soother than the creamy curd,
And lucent syrups, tinct with cinnamon;
Manna and dates, in argosy transferred
From Fez; and spicèd dainties, every one,
From silken Samarcand to cedared Lebanon.

### XXXI

These delicates he heaped with glowing hand
On golden dishes and in baskets bright
Of wreathéd silver: sumptuous they stand
In the retired quiet of the night,
Filling the chilly room with perfume light.
"And now, my love, my seraph fair, awake!
Thou art my heaven, and I thine eremite:
Open thine eyes, for meek St. Agnes' sake,
Or I shall drowse beside thee, so my soul doth ache."

### XXXII

Thus whispering, his warm, unnervèd arm
Sank in her pillow. Shaded was her dream
By the dusk curtains:—'twas a midnight charm
Impossible to melt as iced stream:
The lustrous salvers in the moonlight gleam;
Broad golden fringe upon the carpet lies:
It seemed he never, never could redeem
From such a steadfast spell his lady's eyes;
So mused awhile, entoiled in woofèd fantasies.

### XXXIII

Awakening up, he took her hollow lute—
Tumultuous—and, in chords that tenderest be,
He played an ancient ditty, long since mute,
In Provence called, "La belle dame sans merci":
Close to her ear touching the melody—
Wherewith disturbed, she uttered a soft moan:
He ceased—she panted quick—and suddenly
Her blue affrayèd eyes wide open shone:
Upon his knees he sank, pale as smooth-sculptured stone.

### XXXIV

Her eyes were open, but she still beheld,
Now wide awake, the vision of her sleep:
There was a painful change, that nigh expelled
The blisses of her dream so pure and deep,

At which fair Madeline began to weep,
And moan forth witless words with many a sigh;
While still her gaze on Porphyro would keep;
Who knelt, with joinèd hands and piteous eye,
Fearing to move or speak, she looked so dreamingly.

### XXXV

"Ah, Porphyro!" said she, "but even now
Thy voice was at sweet tremble in mine ear,
Made tunable with every sweetest vow;
And those sad eyes were spiritual and clear:
How changed thou art! how pallid, chill, and drear!
Give me that voice again, my Porphyro,
Those looks immortal, those complainings dear!
Oh leave me not in this eternal woe,
For if thou diest, my Love, I know not where to go."

### XXXVI

Beyond a mortal man impassioned far
At these voluptuous accents, he arose,
Ethereal, flushed, and like a throbbing star
Seen 'mid the sapphire heaven's deep repose
Into her dream he melted, as the rose
Blendeth its odor with the violet —
Solution sweet: meantime the frost-wind blows
Like Love's alarum pattering the sharp sleet
Against the windowpanes; St. Agnes' moon hath set.

### XXXVII

'Tis dark: quick pattereth the flaw-blown sleet:
"This is no dream, my bride, my Madeline!"
'Tis dark: the icèd gusts still rave and beat:
"No dream, alas! alas! and woe is mine!
Porphyro will leave me here to fade and pine, —
Cruel! what traitor could thee hither bring?
I curse not, for my heart is lost in thine,
Though thou forsakest a deceivèd thing; —
A dove forlorn and lost with sick unpruned wing."

### XXXVIII

"My Madeline! sweet dreamer! lovely bride!
Say, may I be for aye thy vassal blest?
Thy beauty's shield, heart-shaped and vermeil dyed?
Ah, silver shrine, here will I take my rest
After so many hours of toil and quest,
A famished pilgrim—saved by miracle.
Though I have found, I will not rob thy nest
Saving of thy sweet self; if thou think'st well
To trust, fair Madeline, to no rude infidel.

### XXXIX

"Hark! 'tis an elfin-storm from faery land,
Of haggard seeming, but a boon indeed:
Arise—arise! the morning is at hand;—
The bloated wassaillers will never heed;—
Let us away, my love, with happy speed;
There are no ears to hear, or eyes to see,—
Drowned all in Rhenish and the sleepy mead:
Awake! arise! my love, and fearless be,
For o'er the southern moors I have a home for thee."

### XL

She hurried at his words, beset with fears,
For there were sleeping dragons all around,
At glaring watch, perhaps, with ready spears—
Down the wide stairs a darkling way they found.—
In all the house was heard no human sound.
A chain-drooped lamp was flickering by each door;
The arras, rich with horseman, hawk, and hound,
Fluttered in the besieging wind's uproar;
And the long carpets rose along the gusty floor.

## XLI

They glide, like phantoms, into the wide hall;
Like phantoms, to the iron porch, they glide;
Where lay the Porter, in uneasy sprawl,
With a huge empty flagon by his side:
The wakeful bloodhound rose, and shook his hide,
But his sagacious eye an inmate owns:
By one, and one, the bolts full easy slide: —
The chains lie silent on the footworn stones; —
The key turns, and the door upon its hinges groans.

## XLII

And they are gone: ay, ages long ago
These lovers fled away into the storm.
That night the Baron dreamt of many a woe,
And all his warrior-guests, with shade and form
Of witch, and demon, and large coffin-worm,
Were long be-nightmared. Angela the old
Died palsy-twitched, with meager face deform;
The Beadsman, after thousand ave's told,
For aye unsought for slept among his ashes cold.

---

*Keats's first poem was an "Imitation of Spenser" in the complex nine-line Spenserian stanza that, after 200 years of disuse, found favor with Byron (see "The Ocean," p. 486, and "There Was a Sound of Revelry by Night," p. 489) and Shelley (see "Adonais," p. 509). The romantic story is based on the legend that, on St. Agnes' Eve (January 20), a maiden can obtain a vision of her husband-to-be by performing certain rituals. The legend and the winter setting gave Keats a chance to experiment with many kinds of sensuous poetry, both in verbal devices and in sound effects. The thirtieth stanza is justly celebrated for its unusual gustatory and tactile appeals. There is also a measure of verbal humor, as in the line "Out went the taper as she hurried in."*

# Bright Star

Bright star, would I were steadfast as thou art—
Not in lone splendor hung aloft the night,
And watching, with eternal lids apart,
Like nature's patient sleepless Eremite,
The moving waters at their priestlike task
Of pure ablution round earth's human shores,
Or gazing on the new soft fallen mask
Of snow upon the mountains and the moors:
No—yet still steadfast, still unchangeable,
Pillowed upon my fair love's ripening breast
To feel for ever its soft fall and swell,
Awake for ever in a sweet unrest;
Still, still to hear her tender-taken breath,
And so live ever—or else swoon to death.

---

*Keats began this sonnet in 1819 and later, not long before his death, copied a version in a volume of Shakespeare's poems. The "fair love" is Fanny Brawne.*

# Ode to Psyche

O Goddess! hear these tuneless numbers, wrung
  By sweet enforcement and remembrance dear,
And pardon that thy secrets should be sung
  Even into thine own soft-conchèd ear:
Surely I dreamed today, or did I see
  The wingèd Psyche with awakened eyes?
I wandered in a forest thoughtlessly,
  And, on the sudden, fainting with surprise,
Saw two fair creatures, couchèd side by side
  In deepest grass, beneath the whispering roof
  Of leaves and trembled blossoms, where there ran
    A brooklet, scarce espied:
'Mid hushed, cool-rooted flowers fragrant-eyed,
  Blue, silver-white, and budded Tyrian.
They lay calm-breathing on the bedded grass;
  Their arms embracèd, and their pinions too;
  Their lips touched not, but had not bade adieu,
As if disjoinèd by soft-handed slumber,
And ready still past kisses to outnumber
  At tender eye-dawn of aurorean love:
    The wingèd boy I knew
  But who wast thou, O happy, happy dove?
    His Psyche true!

O latest-born and loveliest vision far
Of all Olympus' faded hierarchy!
Fairer than Phoebe's sapphire-regioned star,
  Or Vesper, amorous glow-worm of the sky;
Fairer than these, though temple thou hast none,
    Nor altar heaped with flowers;
Nor Virgin choir to make delicious moan
    Upon the midnight hours;
No voice, no lute, no pipe, no incense sweet
  From chain-swung censer teeming;
No shrine, no grove, no oracle, no heat
  Of pale-mouthed prophet dreaming.

O brightest! though too late for antique vows,
  Too, too late for the fond believing lyre,
When holy were the haunted forest boughs,
  Holy the air, the water, and the fire;
Yet even in these days so far retired
  From happy pieties, thy lucent fans,
  Fluttering among the faint Olympians,
I see, and sing, by my own eyes inspired.
So let me be thy choir, and make a moan
    Upon the midnight hours;
Thy voice, thy lute, thy pipe, thy incense sweet
  From swingèd censer teeming:
Thy shrine, thy grove, thy oracle, thy heat
  Of pale-mouthed prophet dreaming.

Yes, I will be thy priest, and build a fane
   In some untrodden region of my mind,
Where branchèd thoughts, new grown with pleasant pain
   Instead of pines shall murmur in the wind:
Far, far around shall those dark-clustered trees
    Fledge the wild-ridgèd mountains steep by steep;
And there by zephyrs, streams, and birds, and bees,
    The moss-lain Dryads shall be lulled to sleep;
And in the midst of this wide quietness
A rosy sanctuary will I dress
With the wreathed trellis of a working brain,
    With buds, and bells, and stars without a name,
With all the gardener Fancy e'er could feign,
    Who, breeding flowers, will never breed the same;
And there shall be for thee all soft delight
    That shadowy thought can win,
A bright torch, and a casement ope at night,
    To let the warm Love in!

---

*Keats wrote five great odes in April and May 1819. Of this one, the first to be finished, he wrote in a letter to his sister and brother: "The following Poem—the last I have written is the first and the only one with which I have taken even moderate pains . . . . You must recollect that Psyche was not embodied as a goddess before the time of Apuleius the Platonist who lived after the Augustan age, and consequently the Goddess was never worshipped or sacrificed to with any of the ancient fervour . . . ."*

Like Edgar Allan Poe and others of their generation, Hood was a magazine writer; he also served as editor of a succession of periodicals, including one called *Hood's Magazine*. He is known for humorous verse and satire. His son, who is called "Tom" Hood, carried on the tradition with undiminished vigor.

## *I Remember, I Remember*

() ◄───► ()

I remember, I remember,
The house where I was born,
The little window where the sun
Came peeping in at morn;
He never came a wink too soon,
Nor brought too long a day,
But now, I often wish the night
Had borne my breath away!

I remember, I remember,
The roses, red and white,
The violets, and the lily-cups,
Those flowers made of light!
The lilacs where the robin built,
And where my brother set
The laburnum on his birthday, —
The tree is living yet!

I remember, I remember,
Where I was used to swing,
And thought the air must rush as fresh
To swallows on the wing;
My spirit flew in feathers then,
That is so heavy now,
And summer pools could hardly cool
The fever on my brow!

I remember, I remember
The fir trees dark and high;
I used to think their slender tops
Were close against the sky;
It was a childish ignorance,
But now 'tis little joy
To know I'm farther off from Heaven
Than when I was a boy.

---

*After the unrelenting thunderstorms of the early-nineteenth-century Romantics, the more temperate weather of such minor Victorians as Hood can come as a pleasant relief.*

It was only after his suicide that Beddoes's best-
remembered work, the play called *Death's Jest-Book, or
The Fool's Tragedy,* appeared. It was Elizabethan in
style, including such incidental lyrics as "Old Adam, the
Carrion Crow."

# Old Adam, the Carrion Crow

Old Adam, the carrion crow,
  The old crow of Cairo;
He sat in the shower, and let it flow
Under his tail and over his crest;
    And through every feather
    Leaked the wet weather;
And the bough swung under his nest;
For his beak it was heavy with marrow.
  Is that the wind dying? O no;
  It's only two devils, that blow
Through a murderer's bones, to and fro,
    In the ghosts' moonshine.

Ho! Eve, my grey carrion wife,
  When we have supped on king's marrow,
Where shall we drink and make merry our life?
  Our nest it is queen Cleopatra's skull,
    'Tis cloven and cracked,
    And battered and hacked,
But with tears of blue eyes it is full:
Let us drink then, my raven of Cairo.
  Is that the wind dying? O no;
  It's only two devils, that blow
  Through a murderer's bones, to and fro,
    In the ghosts' moonshine.

from Death's Jest Book

*Ezra Pound called Beddoes "Prince of morticians." In this lyric, the theme (seen earlier in "The Three Ravens," p. 26) is varied with an idiom that one must call* macabre *(a term it is hard to avoid when one is talking about Beddoes). The repeated "Is that the wind dying?" is echoed in the second part of T. S. Eliot's "Waste Land" (p. 968).*

# RALPH WALDO EMERSON 1803–1882

Emerson spent most of his long life in Massachusetts, where he was born. He was a schoolmaster and Unitarian pastor but from about the age of thirty earned his living as an essayist and lecturer. Although his poetry is respected, his fame rests much more on his peculiarly American labors as a thinker. It is to his credit that he was among the first to recognize the genius of Whitman.

## Concord Hymn

Sung at the Completion of the Battle Monument, July 4, 1837

By the rude bridge that arched the flood,
　Their flag to April's breeze unfurled,
Here once the embattled farmers stood
　And fired the shot heard round the world.

The foe long since in silence slept;
　Alike the conqueror silent sleeps;
And Time the ruined bridge has swept
　Down the dark stream which seaward creeps.

On this green bank, by this soft stream,
　We set to-day a votive stone;
That memory may their deed redeem,
　When, like our sires, our sons are gone.

Spirit, that made those heroes dare
　To die, and leave their children free,
Bid Time and Nature gently spare
　The shaft we raise to them and thee.

*This hymn, not at all typical of Emerson's work in prose or verse, seems to survive in spite of itself, an occasional poem that has so outlived its occasion that many readers will not know which Concord is involved, or why. Even more will not be able to remember any of the stanzas beyond the first, on which rests all of the poem's fame.*

# The Snow-Storm

❖❖❖❖

Announced by all the trumpets of the sky,
Arrives the snow, and, driving o'er the fields,
Seems nowhere to alight: the whited air
Hides hills and woods, the river, and the heaven,
And veils the farm-house at the garden's end.
The sled and traveller stopped, the courier's feet
Delayed, all friends shut out, the housemates sit
Around the radiant fireplace, enclosed
In a tumultuous privacy of storm.

Come see the north wind's masonry.
Out of an unseen quarry evermore
Furnished with tile, the fierce artificer
Curves his white bastions with projected roof
Round every windward stake, or tree, or door.
Speeding, the myriad-handed, his wild work
So fanciful, so savage, nought cares he
For number or proportion. Mockingly,
On coop or kennel he hangs Parian wreaths;
A swan-like form invests the hidden thorn;
Fills up the farmer's lane from wall to wall,
Maugre the farmer's sighs; and at the gate
A tapering turret overtops the work.
And when his hours are numbered, and the world
Is all his own, retiring, as he were not,
Leaves, when the sun appears, astonished Art
To mimic in slow structures, stone by stone,
Built in an age, the mad wind's night-work,
The frolic architecture of the snow.

---

*Emerson was steeped in humanity and humaneness, but in this poem, once he removed our species from the scene, he can appreciate that, in a few winter hours, nature can project both superhuman grandeur and uncanny frivolity.*

# The Rhodora

## On Being Asked, Whence is The Flower?

In May, when sea-winds pierced our solitudes,
I found the fresh Rhodora in the woods,
Spreading its leafless blooms in a damp nook,
To please the desert and the sluggish brook.
The purple petals, fallen in the pool,
Made the black water with their beauty gay;
Here might the red-bird come his plumes to cool,
And court the flower that cheapens his array.
Rhodora! if the sages ask thee why
This charm is wasted on the earth and sky,
Tell them, dear, that if eyes were made for seeing,
Then Beauty is its own excuse for being:
Why thou wert there, O rival of the rose!
I never thought to ask, I never knew:
But, in my simple ignorance, suppose
The self-same Power that brought me there brought you.

---

*Gray's "Elegy Written in a Country Churchyard" (p. 327) seems to accept the fact that "Full many a flower is born to blush unseen, / And waste its sweetness on the desert air." The sentiment that "Beauty is its own excuse for being" was comforting enough to serve as a motto of the Art-for-Art's-Sake movement late in the nineteenth century—to say nothing of the emblematic* Ars Gratia Artis *of such an un-Emersonian institution as the leonine Metro-Goldwyn-Mayer Studios.*

# Brahma

If the red slayer think he slays,
  Or if the slain think he is slain,
They know not well the subtle ways
  I keep, and pass, and turn again.

Far or forgot to me is near;
  Shadow and sunlight are the same;
The vanish'd gods to me appear;
  And one to me are shame and fame.

They reckon ill who leave me out;
  When me they fly, I am the wings;
I am the doubter and the doubt,
  And I the hymn the Brahmin sings.

The strong gods pine for my abode,
  And pine in vain the sacred Seven;
But thou, meek lover of the good!
  Find me, and turn thy back on heaven.

---

*These mystical paradoxes represent Emerson's version of certain principles of Hinduism, in which Brahma is the supreme divinity. Emerson's immediate source was the* Vishnu Purana, *but much the same doctrine can be found in the* Bhagavad-Gita *(and also in "The Dry Salvages" in T. S. Eliot's* Four Quartets*).*

# Fable

The mountain and the squirrel
Had a quarrel,
And the former called the latter " Little Prig";
Bun replied,
"You are doubtless very big;
But all sorts of things and weather
Must be taken in together,
To make up a year
And a sphere.
And I think it no disgrace
To occupy my place.
If I'm not so large as you,
You are not so small as I,
And not half so spry.
I'll not deny you make
A very pretty squirrel track;
Talents differ; all is well and wisely put;
If I cannot carry forests on my back,
Neither can you crack a nut."

---

*It takes a very special kind of imagination to conceive of a mountain that calls a squirrel "Little Prig," but Emerson possessed just such imagination and magnanimity.*

# Days

Daughters of Time, the hypocritic Days,
Muffled and dumb like barefoot dervishes,
And marching single in an endless file,
Bring diadems and fagots in their hands.
To each they offer gifts after his will,
Bread, kingdoms, stars, and sky that holds them all.
I, in my pleached garden, watched the pomp,
Forgot my morning wishes, hastily
Took a few herbs and apples, and the Day
Turned and departed silent. I, too late,
Under her solemn fillet saw the scorn.

---

*Emerson proudly cultivated the American style of talking about dervishes, diadems, and apples in the same breath.*

# ELIZABETH BARRETT BROWNING 1806–1861

When she was about thirty-two years old, Elizabeth Barrett Browning was seriously ill and remained an invalid for some years. In spite of the overprotection of a forbidding father, she became secretly engaged to Robert Browning and married him in 1846, when she was forty. They are the only married couple among the many poets in this anthology.

## How Do I Love Thee? Let Me Count the Ways

How do I love thee? Let me count the ways.
I love thee to the depth and breadth and height
My soul can reach, when feeling out of sight
For the ends of Being and ideal Grace.
I love thee to the level of every day's
Most quiet need; by sun and candle-light.
I love thee freely, as men strive for Right;
I love thee purely, as they turn from Praise.
I love thee with the passion put to use
In my old griefs, and with my childhood's faith.
I love thee with a love I seemed to lose
With my lost saints, — I love thee with the breath.
Smiles, tears, of all my life! — and, if God choose,
I shall but love thee better after death.

Sonnet XLII
from Sonnets from the Portuguese

---

*At first, Elizabeth Barrett Browning called her love poems "Sonnets Translated from the Bosnian," changing the title later to* Sonnets from the Portuguese, *as though to camouflage intensely personal poems as translations. It is possible that Robert Browning, knowing her earlier poem "Catarina to Camoëns" about famous Portuguese literary lovers, called her "the Portuguese."*

# HENRY WADSWORTH LONGFELLOW 1807-1882

Longfellow was a great teacher in two senses: he was an innovator in the teaching of modern languages at Harvard, and he graciously submitted his art to what he perceived to be the duty of poetry—to deliver academic and moral lessons. He was probably the greatest and most effective didactic poet ever to write in the United States; people who know almost no other poems will know "Listen, my children, and you shall hear. . . ." Longfellow is also notable as an innovator in developing a long unrhymed measure that was *not* blank verse; he wrote two fine long poems in unrhymed dactylic hexameter (*Evangeline* and *The Courtship of Miles Standish*) and an unforgettable epic in unrhymed trochaic tetrameter (*The Song of Hiawatha*).

## My Lost Youth

Often I think of the beautiful town
  That is seated by the sea;
Often in thought go up and down
The pleasant streets of that dear old town,
  And my youth comes back to me.
    And a verse of a Lapland song
    Is haunting my memory still:
"A boy's will is the wind's will,
And the thoughts of youth are long, long thoughts."

I can see the shadowy lines of its trees,
  And catch, in sudden gleams,
The sheen of the far-surrounding seas,
And islands that were the Hesperides
  Of all my boyish dreams.
    And the burden of that old song,
    It murmurs and whispers still:
"A boy's will is the wind's will,
And the thoughts of youth are long, long thoughts."

I remember the black wharves and the slips,
  And the sea-tides tossing free;
And Spanish sailors with bearded lips,
And the beauty and mystery of the ships,
  And the magic of the sea.
    And the voice of that wayward song
    Is singing and saying still:
"A boy's will is the wind's will,
And the thoughts of youth are long, long thoughts."

I remember the bulwarks by the shore,
  And the fort upon the hill;
The sun-rise gun, with its hollow roar,
The drum-beat repeated o'er and o'er,
  And the bugle wild and shrill.
    And the music of that old song
    Throbs in my memory still:
"A boy's will is the wind's will,
And the thoughts of youth are long, long thoughts."

I remember the sea-fight far away,
How it thundered o'er the tide!
And the dead captains, as they lay
In their graves, o'erlooking the tranquil bay,
Where they in battle died.
And the sound of that mournful song
Goes through me with a thrill:
"A boy's will is the wind's will,
And the thoughts of youth are long, long thoughts."

I can see the breezy dome of groves,
The shadows of Deering's Woods;
And the friendships old and the early loves
Come back with a Sabbath sound, as of doves
In quiet neighborhoods.
And the verse of that sweet old song,
It flutters and murmurs still:
"A boy's will is the wind's will,
And the thoughts of youth are long, long thoughts."

I remember the gleams and glooms that dart
Across the schoolboy's brain;
The song and the silence in the heart,
That in part are prophecies, and in part
Are longings wild and vain.
And the voice of that fitful song
Sings on, and is never still:
"A boy's will is the wind's will,
And the thoughts of youth are long, long thoughts."

There are things of which I may not speak;
   There are dreams that cannot die;
There are thoughts that make the strong heart weak,
And bring a pallor into the cheek,
     And a mist before the eye.
       And the words of that fatal song
       Come over me like a chill:
"A boy's will is the wind's will,
And the thoughts of youth are long, long thoughts."

Strange to me now are the forms I meet
   When I visit the dear old town;
But the native air is pure and sweet,
And the trees that o'ershadow each well-known street,
     As they balance up and down,
       Are singing the beautiful song,
       Are sighing and whispering still:
"A boy's will is the wind's will,
And the thoughts of youth are long, long thoughts."

And Deering's Woods are fresh and fair,
   And with joy that is almost pain
My heart goes back to wander there,
And among the dreams of the days that were,
     I find my lost youth again.
       And the strange and beautiful song,
       The groves are repeating it still:
"A boy's will is the wind's will,
And the thoughts of youth are long, long thoughts."

---

*Longfellow's language still lives in the title of Robert Frost's first book,* A Boy's Will *(1913); and "The Pasture," which opens Frost's volume, follows the un-usual* abbc *rhyme scheme of Longfellow's refrain.*

# Paul Revere's Ride

Listen, my children, and you shall hear
Of the midnight ride of Paul Revere,
On the eighteenth of April, in Seventy-five;
Hardly a man is now alive
Who remembers that famous day and year.

He said to his friend, "If the British march
By land or sea from the town tonight,
Hang a lantern aloft in the belfry arch
Of the North Church tower as a signal light, —
One, if by land, and two, if by sea;
And I on the opposite shore will be,
Ready to ride and spread the alarm
Through every Middlesex village and farm,
For the country folk to be up and to arm."

Then he said, "Good night!" and with muffled oar
Silently rowed to the Charlestown shore,
Just as the moon rose over the bay,
Where swinging wide at her moorings lay
The *Somerset*, British man-of-war;
A phantom ship, with each mast and spar
Across the moon like a prison bar,
And a huge black hulk, that was magnified
By its own reflection in the tide.

Meanwhile, his friend through alley and street
Wanders and watches, with eager ears,
Till in the silence around him he hears
The muster of men at the barrack door,
The sound of arms, and the tramp of feet,
And the measured tread of the grenadiers,
Marching down to their boats on the shore.

Then he climbed the tower of the Old North Church,
By the wooden stairs, with stealthy tread,
To the belfry-chamber overhead,
And startled the pigeons from their perch
On the sombre rafters, that round him made
Masses and moving shapes of shade, —
By the trembling ladder, steep and tall,
To the highest window in the wall,
Where he paused to listen and look down
A moment on the roofs of the town
And the moonlight flowing over all.

Beneath, in the churchyard, lay the dead,
In their night-encampment on the hill,
Wrapped in silence so deep and still
That he could hear, like a sentinel's tread,
The watchful night-wind, as it went
Creeping along from tent to tent,
And seeming to whisper, "All is well!"
A moment only he feels the spell
Of the place and the hour, and the secret dread
Of the lonely belfry and the dead;
For suddenly all his thoughts are bent
On a shadowy something far away,
Where the river widens to meet the bay, —
A line of black that bends and floats
On the rising tide, like a bridge of boats.

Meanwhile, impatient to mount and ride,
Booted and spurred, with a heavy stride
On the opposite shore walked Paul Revere.
Now he patted his horse's side,
Now gazed at the landscape far and near,
Then, impetuous, stamped the earth,
And turned and tightened his saddle girth;
But mostly he watched with eager search
The belfry's tower of the Old North Church,
As it rose above the graves on the hill,

Lonely and spectral and sombre and still.
And lo! as he looks, on the belfry height
A glimmer, and then a gleam of light!
He springs to the saddle, the bridle he turns,
But lingers and gazes, till full on his sight
A second lamp in the belfry burns!

A hurry of hoofs in a village street,
A shape in the moonlight, a bulk in the dark,
And beneath, from the pebbles, in passing, a spark
Struck out by a steed flying fearless and fleet;
That was all! And yet, through the gloom and the light,
The fate of a nation was riding that night;
And the spark struck out by that steed, in his flight,
Kindled the land into flame with its heat.
He has left the village and mounted the steep,
And beneath him, tranquil and broad and deep,
Is the Mystic, meeting the ocean tides;
And under the alders that skirt its edge,
Now soft on the sand, now loud on the ledge,
Is heard the tramp of his steed as he rides.

It was twelve by the village clock,
When he crossed the bridge into Medford town.
He heard the crowing of the cock,
And the barking of the farmer's dog,
And he felt the damp of the river fog,
That rises after the sun goes down.

It was one by the village clock,
When he galloped into Lexington.
He saw the gilded weathercock
Swim in the moonlight as he passed,
And the meeting-house windows, blank and bare,
Gaze at him with a spectral glare,
As if they already stood aghast
At the bloody work they would look upon.

It was two by the village clock,
When he came to the bridge in Concord town.
He heard the bleating of the flock,
And the twitter of birds among the trees,
And felt the breath of the morning breeze
Blowing over the meadows brown.
And one was safe and asleep in his bed
Who at the bridge would be first to fall,
Who that day would be lying dead,
Pierced by a British musket-ball.

You know the rest. In books you have read,
How the British Regulars fired and fled, —
How the farmers gave them ball for ball,
From behind each fence and farmyard wall,
Chasing the redcoats down the lane,
Then crossing the fields to emerge again
Under the trees at the turn of the road,
And only pausing to fire and load.
So through the night rode Paul Revere;
And so through the night went his cry of alarm
To every Middlesex village and farm, —
A cry of defiance, and not of fear,
A voice in the darkness, a knock at the door,
And a word that shall echo for evermore!
For, borne on the night-wind of the Past,
Through all our history, to the last,
In the hour of darkness and peril and need,
The people will waken and listen to hear
The hurrying hoof-beats of that steed,
And the midnight message of Paul Revere.

from Tales of a Wayside Inn

*Even now, more than a century after Longfellow's death, much of what many Americans think they know about certain episodes and personages of their own country's history—Miles Standish, the Acadians in Canada and Louisiana, Paul Revere, Native American lore and language—comes from Longfellow's memorable verses. Revere's ride took place on the night before the battle commemorated in Emerson's "Concord Hymn" (p. 573).*

# Chaucer

⊹⊹⊹⊹

An old man in a lodge within a park;
 The chamber walls depicted all around
 With portraitures of huntsman, hawk, and hound,
 And the hurt deer. He listeneth to the lark,
Whose song comes with the sunshine through the dark
 Of painted glass in leaden lattice bound;
 He listeneth and he laugheth at the sound,
 Then writeth in a book like any clerk.
He is the poet of the dawn, who wrote
 The Canterbury Tales and his old age
 Made beautiful with song; and as I read
I hear the crowing cock, I hear the note
 Of lark and linnet, and from every page
 Rise odors of ploughed field or flowery mead.

---

*Longfellow wrote rather educational sonnets on a number of great English poets, but they are much better poems than "educational" may suggest. Longfellow was one of the greatest American sonnet-writers of the nineteenth century.*

# JOHN GREENLEAF WHITTIER 1807–1892

Whittier was an ardent Quaker and Abolitionist. His
first master and exemplar was Burns, whose manner he
imitated. Later he wrote vigorous political poetry of a
propagandistic sort. From the end of the Civil War until
his death, Whittier concentrated on the rural scene. He
wrote the words of the familiar hymn "Dear Lord and
Father of Mankind."

## Barbara Frietchie

Up from the meadows rich with corn,
Clear in the cool September morn,

The clustered spires of Frederick stand
Green-walled by the hills of Maryland.

Round about them orchards sweep,
Apple and peach tree fruited deep,

Fair as the garden of the Lord
To the eyes of the famished rebel horde,

On that pleasant morn of the early fall
When Lee marched over the mountain-wall;

Over the mountains winding down,
Horse and foot, into Frederick town.

Forty flags with their silver stars,
Forty flags with their crimson bars,

Flapped in the morning wind: the sun
Of noon looked down, and saw not one.

Up rose old Barbara Frietchie then,
Bowed with her fourscore years and ten;

Bravest of all in Frederick town,
She took up the flag the men hauled down;

In her attic window the staff she set,
To show that one heart was loyal yet.

Up the street came the rebel tread,
Stonewall Jackson riding ahead.

Under his slouched hat left and right
He glanced; the old flag met his sight.

"Halt!"—the dust-brown ranks stood fast.
"Fire!"—out blazed the rifle-blast.

It shivered the window, pane and sash;
It rent the banner with seam and gash.

Quick, as it fell, from the broken staff
Dame Barbara snatched the silken scarf.

She leaned far out on the window-sill,
And shook it forth with a royal will.

"Shoot, if you must, this old gray head,
But spare your country's flag," she said.

A shade of sadness, a blush of shame,
Over the face of the leader came;

The nobler nature within him stirred
To life at that woman's deed and word;

"Who touches a hair of yon gray head
Dies like a dog! March on!" he said

All day long through Frederick street
Sounded the tread of marching feet:

All day long that free flag tossed
Over the heads of the rebel host.

Ever its torn folds rose and fell
On the loyal winds that loved it well;

And through the hill-gaps sunset light
Shone over it with a warm good-night.

Barbara Frietchie's work is o'er,
And the Rebel rides on his raids no more.

Honor to her! and let a tear
Fall, for her sake, on Stonewall's bier.

Over Barbara Frietchie's grave,
Flag of Freedom and Union, wave!

Peace and order and beauty draw
Round thy symbol of light and law;

And ever the stars above look down
On thy stars below in Frederick town!

---

*By the time Whittier's poem was published in 1864, General Jackson was dead. He was shot by his own men by mistake on May 3, 1863, and died a week later. At thirty-nine, he was less than half Barbara Frietchie's age when she died, aged ninety.*

# Snow-Bound; A Winter Idyl

≫≫≫≫≫

The sun that brief December day
Rose cheerless over hills of gray,
And, darkly circled, gave at noon
A sadder light than waning moon.
Slow tracing down the thickening sky
Its mute and ominous prophecy,
A portent seeming less than threat,
It sank from sight before it set.
A chill no coat, however stout,
Of homespun stuff could quite shut out,
A hard, dull bitterness of cold,
That checked, mid-vein, the circling race
Of life-blood in the sharpened face,
The coming of the snow-storm told.
The wind blew east; we heard the roar
Of Ocean on his wintry shore,
And felt the strong pulse throbbing there
Beat with low rhythm our inland air.

Meanwhile we did our nightly chores, —
Brought in the wood from out of doors,
Littered the stalls, and from the mows
Raked down the herd's-grass for the cows:
Heard the horse whinnying for his corn;
And, sharply clashing horn on horn,
Impatient down the stanchion rows
The cattle shake their walnut bows;
While, peering from his early perch
Upon the scaffold's pole of birch,
The cock his crested helmet bent
And down his querulous challenge sent.

Unwarmed by any sunset light
The gray day darkened into night,
A night made hoary with the swarm
And whirl-dance of the blinding storm,
As zigzag, wavering to and fro,
Crossed and recrossed the wingèd snow:
And ere the early bedtime came
The white drift piled the window-frame,
And through the glass the clothes-line posts
Looked in like tall and sheeted ghosts.

So all night long the storm roared on:
The morning broke without a sun;
In tiny spherule traced with lines
Of Nature's geometric signs,
In starry flake, and pellicle,
All day the hoary meteor fell;
And, when the second morning shone,
We looked upon a world unknown,
On nothing we could call our own.
Around the glistening wonder bent
The blue walls of the firmament,
No cloud above, no earth below, —
A universe of sky and snow!
The old familiar sights of ours
Took marvellous shapes; strange domes and towers
Rose up where sty or corn-crib stood,
Or garden-wall, or belt of wood;
A smooth white mound the brush-pile showed,
A fenceless drift what once was road;
The bridle-post an old man sat
With loose-flung coat and high cocked hat;
The well-curb had a Chinese roof;
And even the long sweep, high aloof,
In its slant splendor, seemed to tell
Of Pisa's leaning miracle.

A prompt, decisive man, no breath
Our father wasted: "Boys, a path!"
Well pleased, (for when did farmer boy
Count such a summons less than joy?)
Our buskins on our feet we drew;
With mittened hands, and caps drawn low,
To guard our necks and ears from snow,
We cut the solid whiteness through.
And, where the drift was deepest, made
A tunnel walled and overlaid
With dazzling crystal: we had read
Of rare Aladdin's wondrous cave,
And to our own his name we gave,
With many a wish the luck were ours
To test his lamp's supernal powers.
We reached the barn with merry din,
And roused the prisoned brutes within:
The old horse thrust his long head out,
And grave with wonder gazed about;
The cock his lusty greeting said,
And forth his speckled harem led;
The oxen lashed their tails, and hooked,
And mild reproach of hunger looked;
The hornëd patriarch of the sheep,
Like Egypt's Amun roused from sleep,
Shook his sage head with gesture mute,
And emphasized with stamp of foot.

All day the gusty north-wind bore
The loosening drift its breath before;
Low circling round its southern zone,
The sun through dazzling snow-mist shone.
No church-bell lent its Christian tone
To the savage air, no social smoke
Curled over woods of snow-hung oak.
A solitude made more intense
By dreary-voicëd elements,
The shrieking of the mindless wind,

The moaning tree-boughs swaying blind,
And on the glass the unmeaning beat
Of ghostly finger-tips of sleet.
Beyond the circle of our hearth
No welcome sound of toil or mirth
Unbound the spell, and testified
Of human life and thought outside.
We minded that the sharpest ear
The buried brooklet could not hear,
The music of whose liquid lip
Had been to us companionship,
And, in our lonely life, had grown
To have an almost human tone.

As night drew on, and, from the crest
Of wooded knolls that ridged the west,
The sun, a snow-blown traveller, sank
From sight beneath the smothering bank,
We piled, with care, our nightly stack
Of wood against the chimney-back, —
The oaken log, green, huge, and thick,
And on its top the stout back-stick;
The knotty forestick laid apart,
And filled between with curious art
The ragged brush; then, hovering near,
We watched the first red blaze appear,
Heard the sharp crackle, caught the gleam
On whitewashed wall and sagging beam,
Until the old, rude-furnished room
Burst, flower-like, into rosy bloom;
While radiant with a mimic flame
Outside the sparkling drift became,
And through the bare-boughed lilac-tree
Our own warm hearth seemed blazing free.
The crane and pendent trammels showed,
The Turks' heads on the andirons glowed;
While childish fancy, prompt to tell
The meaning of the miracle,

Whispered the old rhyme: *"Under the tree,*
*When fire outdoors burns merrily,*
*There the witches are making tea."*

The moon above the eastern wood
Shone at its full; the hill-range stood
Transfigured in the silver flood,
Its blown snows flashing cold and keen,
Dead white, save where some sharp ravine
Took shadow, or the sombre green
Of hemlocks turned to pitchy black
Against the whiteness at their back.
For such a world and such a night
Most fitting that unwarming light,
Which only seemed where'er it fell
To make the coldness visible.

Shut in from all the world without,
We sat the clean-winged hearth about,
Content to let the north-wind roar
In baffled rage at pane and door,
While the red logs before us beat
The frost-line back with tropic heat;
And ever, when a louder blast
Shook beam and rafter as it passed,
The merrier up its roaring draught
The great throat of the chimney laughed;
The house-dog on his paws outspread
Laid to the fire his drowsy head,
The cat's dark silhouette on the wall
A couchant tiger's seemed to fall;
And, for the winter fireside meet,
Between the andirons' straddling feet,
The mug of cider simmered slow,
The apples sputtered in a row,
And, close at hand, the basket stood
With nuts from brown October's wood.

What matter how the night behaved?
What matter how the north-wind raved?
Blow high, blow low, not all its snow
Could quench our hearth-fire's ruddy glow.
O Time and Change! — with hair as gray
As was my sire's that winter day,
How strange it seems, with so much gone
Of life and love, to still live on!
Ah, brother! only I and thou
Are left of all that circle now, —
The dear home faces whereupon
That fitful firelight paled and shone.
Henceforward, listen as we will,
The voices of that hearth are still;
Look where we may, the wide earth o'er,
Those lighted faces smile no more.
We tread the paths their feet have worn,
  We sit beneath their orchard trees,
  We hear, like them, the hum of bees
And rustle of the bladed corn;
We turn the pages that they read,
  Their written words we linger o'er,
But in the sun they cast no shade,
No voice is heard, no sign is made,
  No step is on the conscious floor!
Yet Love will dream, and Faith will trust,
(Since He who knows our need is just,)
That somehow, somewhere, meet we must.
Alas for him who never sees
The stars shine through his cypress-trees!
Who, hopeless, lays his dead away,
Nor looks to see the breaking day
Across the mournful marbles play!
Who hath not learned, in hours of faith,
  The truth to flesh and sense unknown,
That Life is ever lord of Death,
  And Love can never lose its own!

We sped the time with stories old,
Wrought puzzles out, and riddles told,
Or stammered from our school-book lore
"The Chief of Gambia's golden shore."
How often since, when all the land
Was clay in Slavery's shaping hand,
As if a far-blown trumpet stirred
The languorous sin-sick air, I heard:
*"Does not the voice of reason cry,*
  *Claim the first right which Nature gave,*
*From the red scourge of bondage fly,*
  *Nor deign to live a burdened slave!"*
Our father rode again his ride
On Memphremagog's wooded side;
Sat down again to moose and samp
In trapper's hut and Indian camp;
Lived o'er the old idyllic ease
Beneath St. Francois' hemlock-trees;
Again for him the moonlight shone
On Norman cap and bodiced zone;
Again he heard the violin play
Which led the village dance away.
And mingled in its merry whirl
The grandam and the laughing girl.
Or, nearer home, our steps he led
Where Salisbury's level marshes spread
  Mile-wide as flies the laden bee;
Where merry mowers, hale and strong,
Swept, scythe on scythe, their swaths along
  The low green prairies of the sea.
We share the fishing off Boar's Head,
  And round the rocky Isles of Shoals
  The hake-broil on the drift-wood coals;
The chowder on the sand-beach made,
Dipped by the hungry, steaming hot,
With spoons of clam-shell from the pot.
We heard the tales of witchcraft old,
And dream and sign and marvel told

To sleepy listeners as they lay
Stretched idly on the salted hay,
Adrift along the winding shores,
When favoring breezes deigned to blow
The square sail of the gundelow
And idle lay the useless oars.

Our mother, while she turned her wheel
Or run the new-knit stocking-heel,
Told how the Indian hordes came down
At midnight on Cocheco town,
And how her own great-uncle bore
His cruel scalp-mark to fourscore.
Recalling, in her fitting phrase,
   So rich and picturesque and free,
   (The common unrhymed poetry
Of simple life and country ways,)
The story of her early days, —
She made us welcome to her home;
Old hearths grew wide to give us room;
We stole with her a frightened look
At the gray wizard's conjuring-book,
The fame whereof went far and wide
Through all the simple country side;
We heard the hawks at twilight play,
The boat-horn on Piscataqua,
The loon's weird laughter far away;
We fished her little trout-brook, knew
What flowers in wood and meadow grew,
What sunny hillsides autumn-brown
She climbed to shake the ripe nuts down,
Saw where in sheltered cove and bay
The ducks' black squadron anchored lay,
And heard the wild-geese calling loud
Beneath the gray November cloud.

Then, haply, with a look more grave,
And soberer tone, some tale she gave
From painful Sewel's ancient tome,
Beloved in every Quaker home,
Of faith fire-winged by martyrdom,
Or Chalkley's Journal, old and quaint, —
Gentlest of skippers, rare sea-saint! —
Who, when the dreary calms prevailed,
And water-butt and bread-cask failed,
And cruel, hungry eyes pursued
His portly presence mad for food,
With dark hints muttered under breath
Of casting lots for life or death,
Offered, if Heaven withheld supplies,
To be himself the sacrifice.
Then, suddenly, as if to save
The good man from his living grave,
A ripple on the water grew,
A school of porpoise flashed in view.
"Take, eat," he said, "and be content;
These fishes in my stead are sent
By Him who gave the tangled ram
To spare the child of Abraham."

Our uncle, innocent of books,
Was rich in lore of fields and brooks,
The ancient teachers never dumb
Of Nature's unhoused lyceum.
In moons and tides and weather wise,
He read the clouds as prophecies,
And foul or fair could well divine,
By many an occult hint and sign,
Holding the cunning-warded keys
To all the woodcraft mysteries;
Himself to Nature's heart so near
That all her voices in his ear
Of beast or bird had meanings clear,
Like Apollonius of old,

Who knew the tales the sparrows told,
Or Hermes who interpreted
What the sage cranes of Nilus said;
A simple, guileless, childlike man,
Content to live where life began;
Strong only on his native grounds,
The little world of sights and sounds
Whose girdle was the parish bounds,
Whereof his fondly partial pride
The common features magnified,
As Surrey hills to mountains grew
In White of Selborne's loving view, —
He told how teal and loon he shot,
And how the eagle's egg he got,
The feats on pond and river done,
The prodigies of rod and gun;
Till, warming with the tales he told,
Forgotten was the outside cold,
The bitter wind unheeded blew,
From ripening corn the pigeons flew,
The partridge drummed i' the wood, the mink
Went fishing down the river-brink.
In fields with bean or clover gay,
The woodchuck, like a hermit gray,
    Peered from the doorway of his cell:
The muskrat plied the mason's trade,
And tier by tier his mud-walls laid;
And from the shagbark overhead
    The grizzled squirrel dropped his shell.
Next, the dear aunt, whose smile of cheer
And voice in dreams I see and hear, —
The sweetest woman ever Fate
Perverse denied a household mate,

Who, lonely, homeless, not the less
Found peace in love's unselfishness,
And welcome wheresoe'er she went,
A calm and gracious element,
Whose presence seemed the sweet income
And womanly atmosphere of home,—
Called up her girlhood memories,
The huskings and the apple-bees,
The sleigh-rides and the summer sails.
Weaving through all the poor details
And homespun warp of circumstance
A golden woof-thread of romance.
For well she kept her genial mood
And simple faith of maidenhood;
Before her still a cloud-land lay,
The mirage loomed across her way;
The morning dew, that dries so soon
With others, glistened at her noon;
Through years of toil and soil and care,
From glossy tress to thin gray hair,
All unprofaned she held apart
The virgin fancies of the heart.
Be shame to him of woman born
Who hath for such but thought of scorn.

There, too, our elder sister plied
Her evening task the stand beside;
A full, rich nature, free to trust,
Truthful and almost sternly just,
Impulsive, earnest, prompt to act,
And make her generous thought a fact,
Keeping with many a light disguise
The secret of self-sacrifice.
O heart sore-tried! thou hast the best

That Heaven itself could give thee, — rest,
Rest from all bitter thoughts and things!
  How many a poor one's blessing went
  With thee beneath the low green tent
Whose curtain never outward swings!

As one who held herself a part
Of all she saw, and let her heart
  Against the household bosom lean,
Upon the motley-braided mat
Our youngest and our dearest sat,
Lifting her large, sweet, asking eyes,
  Now bathed in the unfading green
And holy peace of Paradise.
Oh, looking from some heavenly hill,
  Or from the shade of saintly palms,
  Or silver reach of river calms,
Do those large eyes behold me still?
With me one little year ago: —
The chill weight of the winter snow
  For months upon her grave has lain;
And now, when summer south-winds blow
  And brier and harebell bloom again,
I tread the pleasant paths we trod,
I see the violet-sprinkled sod
Whereon she leaned, too frail and weak
The hillside flowers she loved to seek,
Yet following me where'er I went
With dark eyes full of love's content.
The birds are glad; the brier-rose fills
The air with sweetness; all the hills
Stretch green to June's unclouded sky;
But still I wait with ear and eye
For something gone which should be nigh,
A loss in all familiar things,
In flower that blooms, and bird that sings.
And yet, dear heart! remembering thee,
  Am I not richer than of old?

Safe in thy immortality,
  What change can reach the wealth I hold?
  What chance can mar the pearl and gold
Thy love hath left in trust with me?
And while in life's late afternoon,
  Where cool and long the shadows grow,
I walk to meet the night that soon
  Shall shape and shadow overflow,
I cannot feel that thou art far,
Since near at need the angels are;
And when the sunset gates unbar,
  Shall I not see thee waiting stand,
And, white against the evening star,
  The welcome of thy beckoning hand?

Brisk wielder of the birch and rule,
The master of the district school
Held at the fire his favored place,
Its warm glow lit a laughing face
Fresh-hued and fair, where scarce appeared
The uncertain prophecy of beard.
He teased the mitten-blinded cat,
Played cross-pins on my uncle's hat,
Sang songs, and told us what befalls
In classic Dartmouth's college halls.
Born the wild Northern hills among,
From whence his yeoman father wrung
By patient toil subsistence scant,
Not competence and yet not want,
He early gained the power to pay
His cheerful, self-reliant way;
Could doff at ease his scholar's gown
To peddle wares from town to town;
Or through the long vacation's reach
In lonely lowland districts teach,
Where all the droll experience found
At stranger hearths in boarding round,
The moonlit skater's keen delight,

The sleigh-drive through the frosty night,
The rustic-party, with its rough
Accompaniment of blind-man's-buff,
And whirling-plate, and forfeits paid,
His winter task a pastime made.
Happy the snow-locked homes wherein
He tuned his merry violin,
Or played the athlete in the barn,
Or held the good dame's winding-yarn,
Or mirth-provoking versions told
Of classic legends rare and old,
Wherein the scenes of Greece and Rome
Had all the commonplace of home,
And little seemed at best the odds
'Twixt Yankee pedlers and old gods;
Where Pindus-born Arachthus took
The guise of any grist-mill brook,
And dread Olympus at his will
Became a huckleberry hill.

A careless boy that night he seemed;
    But at his desk he had the look
And air of one who wisely schemed,
    And hostage from the future took
    In trained thought and lore of book.
Large-brained, clear-eyed, of such as he
Shall Freedom's young apostles be,
Who, following in War's bloody trail,
Shall every lingering wrong assail;
All chains from limb and spirit strike,
Uplift the black and white alike;
Scatter before their swift advance
The darkness and the ignorance,
The pride, the lust, the squalid sloth,
Which nurtured Treason's monstrous growth,
Made murder pastime, and the hell
Of prison-torture possible;
The cruel lie of caste refute,

Old forms remould, and substitute
For Slavery's lash the freeman's will,
For blind routine, wise-handed skill;
A school-house plant on every hill,
Stretching in radiate nerve-lines thence
The quick wires of intelligence;
Till North and South together brought
Shall own the same electric thought,
In peace a common flag salute,
And, side by side in labor's free
And unresentful rivalry,
Harvest the fields wherein they fought.

Another guest that winter night
Flashed back from lustrous eyes the light.
Unmarked by time, and yet not young,
The honeyed music of her tongue
And words of meekness scarcely told
A nature passionate and bold,
Strong, self-concentred, spurning guide,
Its milder features dwarfed beside
Her unbent will's majestic pride.
She sat among us, at the best,
A not unfeared, half-welcome guest,
Rebuking with her cultured phrase
Our homeliness of words and ways.
A certain pard-like, treacherous grace
Swayed the lithe limbs and drooped the lash,
Lent the white teeth their dazzling flash;
And under low brows, black with night,
Rayed out at times a dangerous light;
The sharp heat-lightnings of her face
Presaging ill to him whom Fate
Condemned to share her love or hate.
A woman tropical, intense
In thought and act, in soul and sense,
She blended in a like degree
The vixen and the devotee,

Revealing with each freak or feint
  The temper of Petruchio's Kate,
The raptures of Siena's saint.
Her tapering hand and rounded wrist
Had facile power to form a fist;
The warm, dark languish of her eyes
Was never safe from wrath's surprise.
Brows saintly calm and lips devout
Knew every change of scowl and pout;
And the sweet voice had notes more high
And shrill for social battle-cry.

Since then what old cathedral town
Has missed her pilgrim staff and gown,
What convent-gate has held its lock
Against the challenge of her knock!
Through Smyrna's plague-hushed thoroughfares,
Up sea-set Malta's rocky stairs,
Gray olive slopes of hills that hem
  Thy tombs and shrines, Jerusalem,
Or startling on her desert throne
The crazy Queen of Lebanon
With claims fantastic as her own,
Her tireless feet have held their way;
And still, unrestful, bowed, and gray,
She watches under Eastern skies,
  With hope each day renewed and fresh,
  The Lord's quick coming in the flesh,
Whereof she dreams and prophesies!

Where'er her troubled path may be,
  The Lord's sweet pity with her go!
The outward wayward life we see,
  The hidden springs we may not know.
Nor is it given us to discern
  What threads the fatal sisters spun,
  Through what ancestral years has run
The sorrow with the woman born,

What forged her cruel chain of moods,
What set her feet in solitudes,
  And held the love within her mute,
What mingled madness in the blood,
  A life-long discord and annoy,
  Water of tears with oil of joy,
And hid within the folded bud
  Perversities of flower and fruit.
It is not ours to separate
  The tangled skein of will and fate,
To show what metes and bounds should stand
Upon the soul's debatable land,
And between choice and Providence
Divide the circle of events;
But He who knows our frame is just,
Merciful and compassionate,
And full of sweet assurances
And hope for all the language is,
That He remembereth we are dust!

At last the great logs, crumbling low,
Sent out a dull and duller glow,
The bull's-eye watch that hung in view,
Ticking its weary circuit through,
Pointed with mutely warning sign
Its black hand to the hour of nine.
That sign the pleasant circle broke:
My uncle ceased his pipe to smoke,
Knocked from its bowl the refuse gray,
And laid it tenderly away;
Then roused himself to safely cover
The dull red brands with ashes over.
And while, with care, our mother laid
The work aside, her steps she stayed
One moment, seeking to express
Her grateful sense of happiness
For food and shelter, warmth and health,
And love's contentment more than wealth,

With simple wishes (not the weak,
Vain prayers which no fulfilment seek,
But such as warm the generous heart,
O'er-prompt to do with Heaven its part)
That none might lack, that bitter night,
For bread and clothing, warmth and light.

Within our beds awhile we heard
The wind that round the gables roared,
With now and then a ruder shock,
Which made our very bedsteads rock.
We heard the loosened clapboards tost,
The board-nails snapping in the frost;
And on us, through the unplastered wall,
Felt the light sifted snow-flakes fall.
But sleep stole on, as sleep will do
When hearts are light and life is new;
Faint and more faint the murmurs grew,
Till in the summer-land of dreams
They softened to the sound of streams,
Low stir of leaves, and dip of oars,
And lapsing waves on quiet shores.

Next morn we wakened with the shout
Of merry voices high and clear;
And saw the teamsters drawing near
To break the drifted highways out.
Down the long hillside treading slow
We saw the half-buried oxen go,
Shaking the snow from heads uptost,
Their straining nostrils white with frost.
Before our door the straggling train
Drew up, an added team to gain.
The elders threshed their hands a-cold,
    Passed, with the cider-mug, their jokes
    From lip to lip; the younger folks
Down the loose snow-banks, wrestling, rolled,
Then toiled again the cavalcade

O'er windy hill, through clogged ravine,
And woodland paths that wound between
Low drooping pine-boughs winter-weighed.
From every barn a team afoot,
At every house a new recruit,
Where, drawn by Nature's subtlest law,
Haply the watchful young men saw
Sweet doorway pictures of the curls
And curious eyes of merry girls,
Lifting their hands in mock defence
Again the snow-ball's compliments,
And reading in each missive tost
The charm with Eden never lost.

We heard once more the sleigh-bells' sound;
And, following where the teamsters led,
The wise old Doctor went his round,
Just pausing at our door to say,
In the brief autocratic way
Of one who, prompt at Duty's call,
Was free to urge her claim on all,
That some poor neighbor sick abed
At night our mother's aid would need.
For, one in generous thought and deed,
What mattered in the sufferer's sight
The Quaker matron's inward light,
The Doctor's mail of Calvin's creed?
All hearts confess the saints elect
Who, twain in faith, in love agree,
And melt not in an acid sect
The Christian pearl of charity!

So days went on: a week had passed
Since the great world was heard from last.
The Almanac we studied o'er,
Read and reread our little store
Of books and pamphlets, scarce a score;
One harmless novel, mostly hid

From younger eyes, a book forbid,
And poetry, (or good or bad,
A single book was all we had,)
Where Ellwood's meek, drab-skirted Muse,
    A stranger to the heathen Nine,
    Sang, with a somewhat nasal whine,
The wars of David and the Jews.
At last the floundering carrier bore
The village paper to our door.
Lo! broadening outward as we read,
To warmer zones the horizon spread
In panoramic length unrolled
We saw the marvels that it told.
Before us passed the painted Creeks,
    And daft McGregor on his raids
    In Costa Rica's everglades.
And up Taygetos winding slow
Rode Ypsilanti's Mainote Greeks,
A Turk's head at each saddle-bow!
Welcome to us its week-old news,
Its corner for the rustic Muse,
    Its monthly gauge of snow and rain,
Its record, mingling in a breath
The wedding bell and dirge of death:
Jest, anecdote, and love-lorn tale,
The latest culprit sent to jail;
Its hue and cry of stolen and lost,
Its vendue sales and goods at cost,
    And traffic calling loud for gain.
We felt the stir of hall and street,
The pulse of life that round us beat;
The chill embargo of the snow
Was melted in the genial glow;
Wide swung again our ice-locked door,
And all the world was ours once more!

Clasp, Angel of the backward look
    And folded wings of ashen gray

And voice of echoes far away,
The brazen covers of thy book;
The weird palimpsest old and vast,
Wherein thou hid'st the spectral past;
Where, closely mingling, pale and glow
The characters of joy and woe;
The monographs of outlived years,
Or smile-illumed or dim with tears,
   Green hills of life that slope to death,
And haunts of home, whose vistaed trees
Shade off to mournful cypresses
   With the white amaranths underneath
Even while I look, I can but heed
   The restless sands' incessant fall,
Importunate hours that hours succeed,
Each clamorous with its own sharp need,
   And duty keeping pace with all.
Shut down and clasp the heavy lids;
I hear again the voice that bids
The dreamer leave his dream midway
For larger hopes and graver fears;
Life greatens in these later years,
The century's aloe flowers to-day!

Yet, haply, in some lull of life,
Some Truce of God, which breaks its strife,
The worldling's eyes shall gather dew,
   Dreaming in throngful city ways
Of winter joys his boyhood knew;
And dear and early friends— the few
Who yet remain—shall pause to view
   These Flemish pictures of old days;
Sit with me by the homestead hearth,
And stretch the hands of memory forth
   To warm them at the wood-fire's blaze!
And thanks untraced to lips unknown
Shall greet me like the odors blown
From unseen meadows newly mown,

Or lilies floating in some pond,
Wood-fringed, the wayside gaze beyond;
The traveller owns the grateful sense
Of sweetness near, he knows not whence,
And, pausing, takes with forehead bare
The benediction of the air.

---

*Writing toward the end of the American Civil War in 1864–1865, Whittier looked back forty-five years to an episode from his childhood. The group at the Whittier homestead included the poet's parents, his brother and two sisters, an uncle and an aunt (both unmarried), a schoolmaster lodging with them, and an eccentric woman named Harriet Livermore, who, as even the tolerant Quaker Whittier had to concede, was "fantastic and mentally strained."*

Holmes was a Harvard medical doctor who practiced privately for many years; he also taught anatomy and physiology at Harvard and spent six years as dean of the university's medical school. In a long and productive literary life he produced criticism, fiction, conversation, and much occasional verse. It was also Holmes who named *The Atlantic Monthly*.

# The Deacon's Masterpiece;
# or, The Wonderful "One-Hoss Shay"
## A Logical Story

Have you heard of the wonderful one-hoss shay,
That was built in such a logical way
It ran a hundred years to a day,
And then, of a sudden, it—ah, but stay,
I'll tell you what happened without delay,
Scaring the parson into fits,
Frightening people out of their wits,—
Have you heard of that, I say?

SEVENTEEN HUNDRED AND FIFTY-FIVE.
*Georgius Secundus* was then alive,—
Snuffy old drone from the German hive.
That was the year when Lisbon-town
Saw the earth open and gulp her down,
And Braddock's army was done so brown,
Left without a scalp to its crown.
It was on the terrible, Earthquake-day
That the Deacon finished the one-hoss shay.

Now in building of chaises, I tell you what,
There is always *somewhere* a weakest spot, —
In hub, tire, felloe, in spring or thill,
In panel, or crossbar, or floor, or sill,
In screw, bolt, thoroughbrace, — lurking still,
Find it somewhere you must and will, —
Above or below, or within or without, —
And that's the reason, beyond a doubt,
A chaise *breaks down,* but doesn't *wear out.*

But the Deacon swore (as Deacons do,
With an "I dew vum," or an "I tell *yeou*")
He would build one shay to beat the taown
'N the keounty 'n' all the kentry raoun':
It should be so built that it *couldn'* break daown:
"Fur," said the Deacon, " 't's mighty plain
Thut the weakes' places mus' stan' the strain;
'N' the way t' fix it, uz I maintain, is only jest
T' make that place uz strong uz the rest."

So the Deacon inquired of the village folk
Where he could find the strongest oak,
That couldn't be split nor bent nor broke, —
That was for spokes and floor and sills;
He sent for lancewood to make the thills;
The crossbars were ash, from the straightest trees;
The panels of whitewood, that cuts like cheese,
But lasts like iron for things like these;
The hubs of logs from the "Settler's ellum," —
Last of its timber, — they couldn't sell 'em,
Never an axe had seen their chips,
And the wedges flew from between their lips,
Their blunt ends frizzled like celery-tips;

Step and prop-iron, bolt and screw,
Spring, tire, axle, and linchpin too,
Steel of the finest, bright and blue;
Thoroughbrace bison-skin, thick and wide;
Boot, top, dasher, from tough old hide
Found in the pit when the tanner died.
That was the way he "put her through."
"There!" said the Deacon, "naow she'll dew!"

Do! I tell you, I rather guess
She was a wonder, and nothing less!
Colts grew horses, beards turned gray,
Deacon and deaconess dropped away,
Children and grandchildren—where were they?
But there stood the stout old one-hoss shay
As fresh as on Lisbon-earthquake-day!

EIGHTEEN HUNDRED;—it came and found
The Deacon's masterpiece strong and sound.
Eighteen hundred increased by ten;—
"Hahnsum kerridge" they called it then.
Eighteen hundred and twenty came;—
Running as usual; much, the same.
Thirty and forty at last arrive,
And then come fifty, and FIFTY-FIVE.
Little of all we value here
Wakes on the morn of its hundredth year
Without both feeling and looking queer.
In fact, there's nothing that keeps its youth,
So far as I know, but a tree and truth.
(This is a moral that runs at large;
Take it.—You're welcome.—No extra charge.)

FIRST OF NOVEMBER, — the Earthquake-day. —
There are traces of age in the one-hoss shay,
A general flavor of mild decay,
But nothing local as one may say.
There couldn't be, — for the Deacon's art
Had made it so like in every part
That there wasn't a chance for one to start,
For the wheels were just as strong as the thills,
And the floor was just as strong as the sills,
And the panels just as strong as the floor,
And the whipple-tree neither less nor more,
And the back-crossbar as strong as the fore,
And spring and axle and hub *encore*.
And yet, *as a whole*, it is past a doubt
In another hour it will be *worn out!*

FIRST OF NOVEMBER, 'Fifty-five!
This morning the parson takes a drive.
Now, small boys, get out of the way!
Here comes the wonderful one-hoss shay,
Drawn by a rat-tailed, ewe-necked bay.
"Huddup!" said the parson. Off went they.
The parson was working his Sunday's text, —
Had got to *fifthly*, and stopped perplexed
At what the — Moses — was coming next.
All at once the horse stood still,
Close by the meet'n'-house on the hill.
— First a shiver, and then a thrill,
Then something decidedly like a spill, —
And the parson was sitting upon a rock,
At half-past nine by the meet'n'-house clock, —
Just the hour of the Earthquake shock!

—What do you think the parson found,
When he got up and stared around?
The poor old chaise in a heap or mound,
As if it had been to the mill and ground!
You see, of course, if you're not a dunce,
How it went to pieces all at once, —
All at once, and nothing first, —
Just as bubbles do when they burst.

End of the wonderful one-hoss shay.
Logic is logic. That's all I say.

from The Autocrat of the Breakfast Table

---

*In more ways than one — in tone, rhythm, attention to detail — Holmes here sounds as though he is anticipating Dr. Seuss (Theodore Seuss Geisel), who was almost a hundred years younger. Few consumers nowadays even bother to scoff at "dynamic obsolescence" whereby products are deliberately designed to fall apart, sometimes before they are paid for.*

# The Chambered Nautilus

This is the ship of pearl, which, poets feign,
  Sails the unshadowed main, —
  The venturous bark that flings
On the sweet summer wind its purpled wings
In gulfs enchanted, where the Siren sings,
  And coral reefs lie bare,
Where the cold sea-maids rise to sun their streaming hair.

Its webs of living gauze no more unfurl!
  Wrecked is the ship of pearl!
  And every chambered cell,
Where its dim dreaming life was wont to dwell,
As the frail tenant shaped his growing shell,
  Before thee lies revealed, —
Its irised ceiling rent, its sunless crypt unsealed!

Year after year beheld the silent toil
  That spread his lustrous coil;
  Still, as the spiral grew,
He left the past year's dwelling for the new,
Stole with soft step its shining archway through,
  Built up its idle door,
Stretched in his last-found home, and knew the old no more.

Thanks for the heavenly message brought by thee,
  Child of the wandering sea,
  Cast from her lap, forlorn!
From thy dead lips a clearer note is born
Than ever Triton blew from wreathèd horn!
  While on mine ear it rings,
Through the deep caves of thought I hear a voice that sings: —

Build thee more stately mansions, O my soul,
As the swift seasons roll!
Leave thy low-vaulted past!
Let each new temple, nobler than the last,
Shut thee from heaven with a dome more vast,
Till thou at length art free,
Leaving thine outgrown shell by life's unresting sea!

from The Autocrat of The Breakfast Table

---

*In the first decade of the nineteenth century, an ambitious (although flawed) program of universal free public education was started all across the English-speaking world. By 1830, a new literate audience was demanding not only something to read but also guidance in the intellectual and ethical value of the reading matter. Holmes—along with Bryant, Whittier, Longfellow, and Lowell—came along just in time to answer both needs. They were fine poets, but—much to the disgust of their even finer contemporary, Edgar Allan Poe—they felt pressured to announce their moral lessons overtly. These "schoolroom poets" were finally rejected so robustly by generations of resentful readers that few advocates survive who can see the wonderful aesthetic qualities in many of their poems.*

# Old Ironsides

Ay, tear her tattered ensign down!
Long has it waved on high,
And many an eye has danced to see
That banner in the sky;
Beneath it rung the battle shout,
And burst the cannon's roar; —
The meteor of the ocean air
Shall sweep the clouds no more!

Her deck, once red with heroes' blood,
Where knelt the vanquished foe,
When winds were hurrying o'er the flood,
And waves were white below,
No more shall feel the victor's tread,
Or know the conquered knee; —
The harpies of the shore shall pluck
The eagle of the sea!

O, better that her shattered hulk
Should sink beneath the wave;
Her thunders shook the mighty deep,
And there should be her grave;
Nail to the mast her holy flag,
Set every threadbare sail,
And give her to the god of storms,
The lightning and the gale!

---

*At twenty-one, Holmes wrote this rhetorical exercise in response to an announcement that the frigate* Constitution, *famous for exploits in the War of 1812, was to be scrapped. The ploy worked, the ship was spared and can still be seen in Boston, 160 years after Holmes's verse.*

# EDGAR ALLAN POE 1809–1849

Although he was born in Boston, Poe, having been orphaned at an early age, was raised in Virginia. In a pitifully short career as a literary editor and journalist, he made himself famous as a fabulous inventor—a true American Daedalus—so that it can be persuasively argued that Poe, just about singlehandedly, invented the short story, science fiction, detective fiction, the symbolist poem, and the New Criticism. Poe remains the American writer with just about the greatest influence: he understood humankind's deepest fears and desires. His shadow stretches over many literary provinces, from Jules Verne to Oscar Wilde to Vladimir Nabokov to the novels of Thomas Pynchon and the films of Stanley Kubrick.

# To Helen

()◆()

Helen, thy beauty is to me
   Like those Nicéan barks of yore,
That gently, o'er a perfumed sea,
   The weary, way-worn wanderer bore
   To his own native shore.

On desperate seas long wont to roam,
   The hyacinth hair, thy classic face,
Thy Naiad airs have brought me home
   To the glory that was Greece,
And the grandeur that was Rome.

Lo! in yon brilliant window-niche
   How statue-like I see thee stand,
The agate lamp within thy hand!
Ah, Psyche, from the regions which
   Are Holy-Land!

*Seemingly a conglomeration of imperfections, Poe's "To Helen" somehow, un-accountably, creates a living and durable work of art that for 150 years has been the greatest American lyric poem. In meter and rhyme, the stanzas don't match; "long wont" is a ludicrous dangling modifier; some of the rhymes are of types that Poe castigated in others ("face" and "Greece" rhyme too little, "roam" and "Rome" too much). Poe suggested that the subject was a young woman named Jane Stith Stanard, who died when Poe was fifteen. The classical trappings are both allusive and elusive, as though the poet preferred suggestion to assertion. Nobody has explained "Nicéan"; "Naiad" and "Psyche" remain indeterminate. The poem is, nevertheless, a gem. First drafted when the poet was fourteen, "To Helen" probably had a younger author than any other poem in this book.*

# The Raven

Once upon a midnight dreary, while I pondered, weak and
   weary,
Over many a quaint and curious volume of forgotten lore,
While I nodded, nearly napping, suddenly there came a
   tapping,
As of some one gently rapping, rapping at my chamber door.
" 'Tis some visitor," I muttered, "tapping at my chamber
   door—
         Only this, and nothing more."

Ah, distinctly I remember it was in the bleak December,
And each separate dying ember wrought its ghost upon the
   floor.
Eagerly I wished the morrow;— vainly I had sought to
   borrow
From my books surcease of sorrow— sorrow for the lost
   Lenore—
For the rare and radiant maiden whom the angels name
   Lenore—
         Nameless here for evermore.

And the silken sad uncertain rustling of each purple curtain
Thrilled me—filled me with fantastic terrors never felt before;
So that now, to still the beating of my heart, I stood
   repeating
" 'Tis some visitor entreating entrance at my chamber
   door;—
         This it is, and nothing more."

Presently my soul grew stronger; hesitating then no longer,
"Sir," said I, "or Madam, truly your forgiveness I implore;
But the fact is I was napping, and so gently you came
    rapping,
And so faintly you come tapping, tapping at my chamber
    door,
That I scarce was sure I heard you"—here I opened wide the
    door; —
   Darkness there, and nothing more.

Deep into that darkness peering, long I stood there
    wondering, fearing,
Doubting, dreaming dreams no mortal ever dared to dream
    before;
But the silence was unbroken, and the darkness gave no
    token,
And the only word there spoken was the whispered word,
    "Lenore!"
This I whispered, and an echo murmured back the word,
    "Lenore!"—
   Merely this, and nothing more.

Back into the chamber turning, all my soul within me
    burning,
Soon I heard again a tapping somewhat louder than before.
"Surely," said I, "surely that is something at my window
    lattice;
Let me see, then, what thereat is, and this mystery explore—
Let my heart be still a moment and this mystery explore; —
   'Tis the wind and nothing more!"

Open here I flung the shutter, when, with many a flirt and
  flutter,
In there stepped a stately raven of the saintly days of yore;
Not the least obeisance made he; not an instant stopped or
  stayed he;
But, with mien of lord or lady, perched above my chamber
  door —
Perched upon a bust of Pallas just above my chamber door —
  Perched, and sat, and nothing more.

Then this ebony bird beguiling my sad fancy into smiling,
By the grave and stern decorum of the countenance it wore,
"Though thy crest be shorn and shaven, thou," I said, "art
  sure no craven,
Ghastly grim and ancient raven wandering from the Nightly
  shore —
Tell me what thy lordly name is on the Night's Plutonian
  shore!"
  Quoth the raven, "Nevermore."

Much I marvelled this ungainly fowl to hear discourse so
  plainly,
Though its answer little meaning — little relevancy bore,
For we cannot help agreeing that no living human being
Ever yet was blessed with seeing bird above his chamber
  door —
Bird or beast upon the sculptured bust above his chamber
  door,
  With such name as "Nevermore."

But the raven, sitting lonely on the placid bust, spoke only
That one word, as if his soul in that one word he did outpour.
Nothing farther then he uttered — not a feather then he
  fluttered —
Till I scarcely more than muttered "Other friends have flown
  before —
On the morrow *he* will leave me, as my hopes have flown
  before."

Then the bird said "Nevermore."

Startled at the stillness broken by reply so aptly spoken,
"Doubtless," said I, "what it utters is its only stock and store
Caught from some unhappy master whom unmerciful Disaster
Followed fast and followed faster till his songs one burden
    bore—
Till the dirges of his Hope that melancholy burden bore
            Of 'Never—nevermore.' "

But the raven still beguiling all my sad soul into smiling,
Straight I wheeled a cushioned seat in front of bird and bust
    and door;
Then, upon the velvet sinking, I betook myself to linking
Fancy unto fancy, thinking what his ominous bird of yore—
What this grim, ungainly, ghastly, gaunt, and ominous bird of
    yore
            Meant in croaking "Nevermore."

This I sat engaged in guessing, but no syllable expressing
To the fowl whose fiery eyes now burned into my bosom's
    core;
This and more I sat divining, with my head at ease reclining
On the cushion's velvet lining that the lamplight gloated o'er,
But whose velvet violet lining with the lamplight gloating o'er,
            *She* shall press, ah, nevermore!

Then, methought, the air grew denser, perfumed from an
    unseen censer
Swung by angels whose faint foot-falls tinkled on the tufted
    floor.
"Wretch," I cried, "thy God hath lent thee—by these angels
    he hath sent thee
Respite—respite and nepenthe from thy memories of Lenore!
Quaff, oh quaff this kind nepenthe and forget this lost
    Lenore!"
            Quoth the raven, "Nevermore."

"Prophet!" said I, "thing of evil!—prophet still, if bird or
    devil!—
Whether Tempter sent, or whether tempest tossed thee here
    ashore,
Desolate, yet all undaunted, on this desert land enchanted—
On this home by Horror haunted—tell me truly, I implore—
Is there—*is* there balm in Gilead?—tell me—tell me, I
    implore!"
        Quoth the raven, "Nevermore."

"Prophet!" said I, "thing of evil—prophet still, if bird or devil!
By that Heaven that bends above us—by that God we both
    adore—
Tell this soul with sorrow laden if, within the distant Aidenn,
It shall clasp a sainted maiden whom the angels name
    Lenore—
Clasp a rare and radiant maiden whom the angels name
    Lenore."
        Quoth the raven, "Nevermore."

"Be that word our sign of parting, bird or fiend!" I shrieked,
    upstarting—
"Get thee back into the tempest and the Night's Plutonian
    shore!
Leave no black plume as a token of that lie thy soul hath
    spoken!
Leave my loneliness unbroken!—quit the bust above my door!
Take thy beak from out my heart, and take thy form from off
    my door!"
        Quoth the raven, "Nevermore."

And the raven, never flitting, still is sitting, still is sitting
On the pallid bust of Pallas just above my chamber door;
And his eyes have all the seeming of a demon's that is
　　dreaming,
And the lamp-light o'er him streaming throws his shadow on
　　the floor;
And my soul from out that shadow that lies floating on the
　　floor
　　　　　Shall be lifted— nevermore!

---

*No poem in this book has stimulated more poetic responses, direct or indirect, than "The Raven." From Mallarmé's* Igitur *and D. G. Rossetti's "Blessed Damozel" in the nineteenth century—and possibly as early as canto 13 of Longfellow's "Song of Hiawatha" just after Poe's death—artists have repeated or countered the terms of Poe's powerful vision. (See Stevens's "Thirteen Ways of Looking at a Blackbird," p. 932, and William Carlos Williams's "Red Wheelbarrow," p. 935. Farther afield, see T. S. Eliot's "Burnt Norton" and Robert Frost's "Dust of Snow.")*

# Annabel Lee

It was many and many a year ago,
  In a kingdom by the sea,
That a maiden there lived whom you may know
  By the name of Annabel Lee;
And this maiden she lived with no other thought
  Than to love and be loved by me.

*She* was a child and *I* was a child,
  In this kingdom by the sea,
But we loved with a love that was more than love—
  I and my Annabel Lee—
With a love that the wingèd seraphs of Heaven
  Coveted her and me.

And this was the reason that, long ago,
  In this kingdom by the sea,
A wind blew out of a cloud by night
  Chilling my Annabel Lee;
So that her high-born kinsmen came
  And bore her away from me,
To shut her up in a sepulchre
  In this kingdom by the sea.

The angels, not half so happy in Heaven,
  Went envying her and me:—
Yes! that was the reason (as all men know,
  In this kingdom by the sea)
That the wind came out of the cloud chilling
  And killing my Annabel Lee.

But our love it was stronger by far than the love
   Of those who were older than we—
   Of many far wiser than we—
And neither the angels in Heaven above
   Nor the demons down under the sea
Can ever dissever my soul from the soul
   Of the beautiful Annabel Lee:—

For the moon never beams without bringing me dreams
   Of the beautiful Annabel Lee;
And the stars never rise but I feel the bright eyes
   Of the beautiful Annabel Lee:
And so all the night-tide, I lie down by the side
Of my darling, my darling, my life and my bride
   In her sepulchre there by the sea—
   In her tomb by the side of the sea.

---

*Although it uses a relatively primitive ballad technique, "Annabel Lee" was one of Poe's last poems, and its power has lasted right into the modern age, all the way from the mid-century pop tune "Too Young" (a hit record for Nat "King" Cole) to, a few years later, Vladimir Nabokov's* Lolita.

# The City in the Sea

Lo! Death has reared himself a throne
In a strange city lying alone
Far down within the dim West,
Where the good and the bad and the worst and the best
Have gone to their eternal rest.
There shrines and palaces and towers
(Time-eaten towers that tremble not!)
Resemble nothing that is ours.
Around, by lifting winds forgot,
Resignedly beneath the sky
The melancholy waters lie.

No rays from the holy heaven come down
On the long night-time of that town;
But light from out the lurid sea
Streams up the turrets silently—
Gleams up the pinnacles far and free
Up domes—up spires—up kingly halls—
Up fanes—up Babylon-like walls—
Up shadowy long-forgotten bowers
Of sculptured ivy and stone flowers—
Up many and many a marvellous shrine
Whose wreathéd friezes intertwine
The viol, the violet, and the vine.

Resignedly beneath the sky
The melancholy waters lie.
So blend the turrets and shadows there
That all seem pendulous in air,
While from a proud tower in the town
Death looks gigantically down.

There open fanes and gaping graves
Yawn level with the luminous waves;
But not the riches there that lie
In each idol's diamond eye—
Not the gaily-jewelled dead
Tempt the waters from their bed;
For no ripples curl, alas!
Along that wilderness of glass—
No swellings tell that winds may be
Upon some far-off happier sea—
No heavings hint that winds have been
On seas less hideously serene.

But lo, a stir is in the air!
The wave—there is a movement there!
As if the towers had thrust aside,
In slightly sinking, the dull tide—
As if their tops had feebly given
A void within the filmy Heaven.
The waves have now a redder glow—
The hours are breathing faint and low—
And when, amid no earthly moans,
Down, down that town shall settle hence,
Hell, rising from a thousand thrones,
Shall do it reverence.

---

*Poe's imaginings, however exotic and elaborate, are firmly based in a sober recognition of realistic fears and desires (many more fears than desires). Besides, Poe's stories unfold with telling execution and masterful technique. Later poets may reject Poe's vulgarity, but almost nobody denies his tremendous influence and importance. Matter from "The City in the Sea" returns in works by T. S. Eliot: "wilderness of glass" comes back as "wilderness of mirrors" in "Gerontion" (p. 984); the upside-down city reappears in the fifth part of "The Waste Land" (p. 968).*

# *The Bells*

>>>>>>>

I

Hear the sledges with the bells —
Silver bells!
What a world of merriment their melody foretells!
How they tinkle, tinkle, tinkle,
In the icy air of night!
While the stars that oversprinkle
All the heavens, seem to twinkle
With a crystalline delight;
Keeping time, time, time,
In a sort of Runic rhyme,
To the tintinnabulation that so musically wells
From the bells, bells, bells, bells,
Bells, bells, bells, —
From the jingling and the tinkling of the bells.

II

Hear the mellow wedding bells —
Golden bells!
What a world of happiness their harmony foretells!
Through the balmy air of night
How they ring out their delight! —
From the molten-golden notes,
And all in tune,
What a liquid ditty floats
To the turtle-dove that listens, while she gloats
On the moon!
Oh, from out the sounding cells,

What a gush of euphony voluminously wells!
How it swells!
How it dwells
On the Future!—how it tells
Of the rapture that impels
To the swinging and the ringing
Of the bells, bells, bells,—
Of the bells, bells, bells, bells,
Bells, bells, bells,
To the rhyming and the chiming of the bells!

III

Hear the loud alarum bells—
Brazen bells!
What a tale of terror, now, their turbulency tells!
In the startled ear of night
How they scream out their affright!
Too much horrified to speak,
They can only shriek, shriek,
Out of tune,
In a clamorous appealing to the mercy of the fire,
In a mad expostulation with the deaf and frantic fire,
Leaping higher, higher, higher,
With a desperate desire,
And a resolute endeavor
Now—now to sit, or never,
By the side of the pale-faced moon.
Oh, the bells, bells, bells!
What a tale their terror tells
Of Despair!
How they clang, and clash, and roar!
What a horror they outpour

On the bosom of the palpitating air!
　　Yet the ear, it fully knows,
　　　　By the twanging
　　　　And the clanging,
　　How the danger ebbs and flows;
　Yet the ear distinctly tells,
　　　　In the jangling
　　　　And the wrangling,
　How the danger sinks and swells,
By the sinking or the swelling in the anger of the bells—
　　　　Of the bells,—
　Of the bells, bells, bells, bells,
　　Bells, bells, bells—
In the clamor and the clangor of the bells!

IV

　Hear the tolling of the bells—
　　　Iron bells!
What a world of solemn thought their monody compels!
　In the silence of the night,
　How we shiver with affright
At the melancholy menace of their tone!
　　For every sound that floats
　From the rust within their throats
　　　Is a groan.
　　And the people—ah, the people—
　They that dwell up in the steeple,
　　　All alone,
And who tolling, tolling, tolling,
　In that muffled monotone,
Feel a glory in so rolling
　On the human heart a stone—

They are neither man nor woman —
They are neither brute nor human —
    They are Ghouls: —
And their king it is who tolls: —
And he rolls, rolls, rolls,
    Rolls
    A paean from the bells!
And his merry bosom swells
    With the paean of the bells!
And he dances, and he yells;
Keeping time, time, time,
In a sort of Runic rhyme,
    To the paean of the bells —
    Of the bells: —
Keeping time, time, time,
In a sort of Runic rhyme,
    To the throbbing of the bells —
    Of the bells, bells, bells —
    To the sobbing of the bells,
    Keeping time, time, time,
    As he knells, knells, knells,
In a happy Runic rhyme,
    To the rolling of the bells —
    Of the bells, bells, bells: —
    To the tolling of the bells,
Of the bells, bells, bells, bells,
    Bells, bells, bells —
To the moaning and the groaning of the bells.

---

*What a tour de force! Poe's most entertaining poem is a curriculum driven by the powers of sound, all organized according to foursomes: metals, ages and Ages, seasons, and appropriate emotional registers, with verbal and acoustic coefficients.*

# The Haunted Palace

In the greenest of our valleys,
  By good angels tenanted,
Once a fair and stately palace
  (Radiant palace) reared its head.
In the monarch Thought's dominion
  It stood there!
Never seraph spread a pinion
  Over fabric half so fair.

Banners yellow, glorious, golden,
  On its roof did float and flow
(This, all this, was in the olden
  Time long ago);
And every gentle air that dallied
  In that sweet day,
Along the ramparts plumed and pallid,
  A wingèd odor went away.

Wanderers in that happy valley
  Through two luminous windows, saw
Spirits moving musically
  To a lute's well-tuned law;
Round about a throne where, sitting
  (Porphyrogene!)
In state his glory well befitting,
  The ruler of the realm was seen.

And all with pearl and ruby glowing
   Was the fair palace door,
Through which came flowing, flowing, flowing,
   And sparkling evermore,
A troop of echoes, whose sweet duty
   Was but to sing,
In voices of surpassing beauty,
   The wit and wisdom of their king.

But evil things, in robes of sorrow,
   Assailed the monarch's high estate
(Ah! let us mourn, for never morrow
   Shall dawn upon him, desolate);
And round about his home the glory
   That blushed and bloomed
Is but a dim-remembered story
   Of the old time entombed.

And travellers, now, within that valley,
   Through the red-litten windows see
Vast forms that move fantastically
   To a discordant melody;
While, like a ghastly rapid river,
   Through the pale door
A hideous throng rush out forever,
   And laugh—but smile no more.

             from The Fall of the House of Usher

---

*Roderick Usher sings what the narrator of "The Fall of the House of Usher" variously calls a rhapsody, an improvisation, a fantasia, and a ballad. A poem about a palace in a story about a house, with both structures patently symbolic and human, is an obvious case of an inner text that repeats and validates an outer. Such texts-within-texts are common in horror stories, all the way from* Frankenstein *to* Wuthering Heights *and beyond.*

# ALFRED TENNYSON, 1ST BARON TENNYSON 1809–1892

Tennyson is one of the greatest poets to hold the Lau-
reateship; his tenure in that position continued for
forty-two years, from 1850 until his death. He was born
in Lincolnshire and educated at Cambridge. A friend
there was the brilliant Arthur Hallam, whose death in
1833 stimulated Tennyson to write the noble and eloquent elegy *In Memoriam* (published in 1850). Tennyson
excelled in the short musical lyric, the dramatic monologue, the long narrative, and certain boldly mixed
forms for which we still lack accurate names, such as in
"The Princess" and "Maud."

## The Splendor Falls

The splendor falls on castle walls
  And snowy summits old in story;
The long light shakes across the lakes,
  And the wild cataract leaps in glory.
Blow, bugle, blow, set the wild echoes flying,
Blow, bugle; answer, echoes, dying, dying, dying.

O, hark, O, hear! how thin and clear,
  And thinner, clearer, farther going!
O, sweet and far from cliff and scar
  The horns of Elfland faintly blowing!
Blow, let us hear the purple glens replying,
Blow, bugle; answer, echoes, dying, dying, dying.

O love, they die in yon rich sky,
    They faint on hill or field or river;
Our echoes roll from soul to soul,
    And grow for ever and for ever.
Blow, bugle, blow, set the wild echoes flying,
And answer, echoes, answer, dying, dying, dying.

                                        from The Princess

---

*The subtitle of Tennyson's "Princess" is "A Medley"—and that is accurate: there are varying narrative levels along with several memorable songs (added in the third edition) that have achieved independent celebrity. This poem, "Tears, Idle Tears" (p. 649), and "Now Sleeps the Crimson Petal" (p. 650), along with "Sweet and Low," are known to many who do not know "The Princess" and to some who may not even know Tennyson.*

# Break, Break, Break

Break, break, break,
  On thy cold gray stones, O Sea!
And I would that my tongue could utter
  The thoughts that arise in me.

O, well for the fisherman's boy,
  That he shouts with his sister at play!
O, well for the sailor lad,
  That he sings in his boat on the bay!

And the stately ships go on
  To their haven under the hill;
But O for the touch of a vanished hand,
  And the sound of a voice that is still!

Break, break, break,
  At the foot of thy crags, O Sea!
But the tender grace of a day that is dead
  Will never come back to me.

---

*Lord Byron, one of Tennyson's earliest exemplars, had addressed the ocean memorably in* Childe Harold's Pilgrimage *(p. 486), and we accept the appropriateness of the gesture, although it may seem fruitless to command an inanimate object to do what it can't help doing anyway. It is probable that Tennyson's poem refers to the death of his friend Arthur Henry Hallam, also the subject of the great elegy* In Memoriam.

# Crossing the Bar

Sunset and evening star,
  And one clear call for me!
And may there be no moaning of the bar,
  When I put out to sea,

But such a tide as moving seems asleep,
  Too full for sound and foam,
When that which drew from out the boundless deep
  Turns again home.

Twilight and evening bell,
  And after that the dark!
And may there be no sadness of farewell,
  When I embark;

For though from out our bourne of Time and Place
  The flood may bear me far,
I hope to see my Pilot face to face
  When I have crossed the bar.

---

*Tennyson wrote this when he was eighty and, although he wrote other poems afterwards, asked that this one be placed at the end of all collections of his poetry. He showed a fine sense of fitness in writing the poem in the first place, with its noble stoicism and good Britannic sea imagery, and also in dictating its appropriate placement.*

# *Ulysses*

It little profits that an idle king,
By this still hearth, among these barren crags,
Matched with an agèd wife, I mete and dole
Unequal laws unto a savage race
That hoard, and sleep, and feed, and know not me.
I cannot rest from travel; I will drink
Life to the lees. All times I have enjoyed
Greatly, have suffered greatly, both with those
That loved me, and alone; on shore, and when
Through scudding drifts the rainy Hyades
Vexed the dim sea. I am become a name;
For always roaming with a hungry heart
Much have I seen and known—cities of men
And manners, climates, councils, governments,
Myself not least, but honored of them all—
And drunk delight of battle with my peers,
Far on the ringing plains of windy Troy.
I am a part of all that I have met;
Yet all experience is an arch wherethrough
Gleams that untraveled world whose margin fades
Forever and forever when I move.
How dull it is to pause, to make and end,
To rust unburnished, not to shine in use!
As though to breathe were life! Life piled on life
Were all too little, and of one to me
Little remains; but every hour is saved
From that eternal silence, something more,
A bringer of new things; and vile it were
For some three suns to store and hoard myself,
And this gray spirit yearning in desire
To follow knowledge like a sinking star,
Beyond the utmost bound of human thought.
    This is my son, mine own Telemachus,
To whom I leave the scepter and the isle—

Well-loved of me, discerning to fulfill
This labor, by slow prudence to make mild
A rugged people, and through soft degrees
Subdue them to the useful and the good.
Most blameless is he, centered in the sphere
Of common duties, decent not to fail
In offices of tenderness, a pay
Meet adoration to my household gods,
When I am gone. He works his work, I mine.
   There lies the port; the vessel puffs her sail;
There gloom the dark, broad seas. My mariners,
Souls that have toiled, and wrought, and thought with me—
That ever with a frolic welcome took
The thunder and the sunshine, and opposed
Free hearts, free foreheads—you and I are old;
Old age hath yet his honor and his toil.
Death closes all; but something ere the end,
Some work of noble note, may yet be done,
Not unbecoming men that strove with Gods.
The lights begin to twinkle from the rocks;
The long day wanes, the low moon climbs; the deep
Moans round with many voices. Come, my friends,
'Tis not too late to seek a newer world.
Push off, and sitting well in order smite
The sounding furrows; for my purpose holds
To sail beyond the sunset, and the baths
Of all the western stars, until I die.
It may be that the gulfs will wash us down;
It may be we shall touch the Happy Isles,
And see the great Achilles, whom we knew.
Though much is taken, much abides; and though
We are not now that strength which in old days
Moved earth and heaven, that which we are, we are—
One equal temper of heroic hearts,
Made weak by time and fate, but strong in will
To strive, to seek, to find, and not to yield.

*This complex Ulysses owes as much to Dante as to Homer, with further debt to Milton, whose Satan in* Paradise Lost *makes speeches including "will" and "not to yield." Ambiguities notwithstanding, Tennyson's poem remains inspirational, and its last line is carved on the memorial to the heroic members of Robert Falcon Scott's expedition to the Antarctic.*

# The Eagle

He clasps the crag with crooked hands;
Close to the sun in lonely lands,
Ringed with the azure world, he stands.

The wrinkled sea beneath him crawls;
He watches from his mountain walls,
And like a thunderbolt he falls.

---

*A brief, flawless, heraldic realization of a creature in all the spikily tangible properties of his creatureliness.*

# Tears, Idle Tears

❖❖❖❖

Tears, idle tears, I know not what they mean,
Tears from the depth of some divine despair
Rise in the heart, and gather to the eyes,
In looking on the happy autumn-fields,
And thinking of the days that are no more.

Fresh as the first beam glittering on a sail,
That brings our friends up from the underworld,
Sad as the last which reddens over one
That sinks with all we love below the verge;
So sad, so fresh, the days that are no more.

Ah, sad and strange as in dark summer dawns
The earliest pipe of half-awakened birds
To dying ears, when unto dying eyes
The casement slowly grows a glimmering square;
So sad, so strange, the days that are no more.

Dear as remembered kisses after death,
And sweet as those by hopeless fancy feigned
On lips that are for others; deep as love,
Deep as first love, and wild with all regret;
O Death in Life, the days that are no more.

from The Princess

---

*Extraordinary: an unrhymed song, although the terminal phrase in every fifth line returns as a refrain. There are a few other unrhymed songs in "The Princess," including "Now Sleeps the Crimson Petal" (p. 650). Tennyson said that he had written "Tears, Idle Tears" at Tintern Abbey (see Wordsworth's poem, p. 407).*

# Now Sleeps the Crimson Petal

Now sleeps the crimson petal, now the white;
Nor waves the cypress in the palace walk;
Nor winks the gold fin in the porphyry font.
The firefly wakens; waken thou with me.

Now droops the milk-white peacock like a ghost,
And like a ghost she glimmers on to me.

Now lies the Earth all Danaë to the stars,
And all thy heart lies open unto me.

Now slides the silent meteor on, and leaves
A shining furrow, as thy thoughts in me.

Now folds the lily all her sweetness up,
And slips into the bosom of the lake.
So fold thyself, my dearest, thou, and slip
Into my bosom and be lost in me.

from The Princess

Like "Tears, Idle Tears" (p. 649), this is a remarkable "blank verse lyric" (Tennyson's phrase), with a repeated word functioning as a refrain.

# The Charge of the Light Brigade

≫≫≫≫≫≫

I

Half a league, half a league,
Half a league onward,
All in the valley of Death
    Rode the six hundred.
"Forward the Light Brigade!
Charge for the guns!" he said.
Into the valley of Death
    Rode the six hundred.

II

"Forward, the Light Brigade!"
Was there a man dismayed?
Not though the soldier knew
    Someone had blundered.
Theirs not to make reply,
Theirs not to reason why,
Theirs but to do and die.
Into the valley of Death
    Rode the six hundred.

III

Cannon to right of them,
Cannon to left of them,
Cannon in front of them
    Volleyed and thundered;
Stormed at with shot and shell,
Boldly they rode and well,
Into the jaws of Death,
Into the mouth of hell
    Rode the six hundred.

IV

Flashed all their sabres bare,
Flashed as they turned in air
Sabring the gunners there,
Charging an army, while
    All the world wondered.
Plunged in the battery-smoke
Right through the line they broke;
Cossack and Russian
Reeled from the sabre-stroke
    Shattered and sundered.
Then they rode back, but not,
    Not the six hundred.

V

Cannon to right of them,
Cannon to left of them,
Cannon behind them
    Volleyed and thundered;
Stormed at with shot and shell,
While horse and hero fell.
They that had fought so well
Came through the jaws of Death,
Back from the mouth of hell,
All that was left of them,
    Left of six hundred.

VI

When can their glory fade?
O the wild charge they made!
    All the world wondered.
Honor the charge they made!
Honor the Light Brigade,
    Noble six hundred!

*Of the 673 soldiers who, on October 25, 1854, charged into the North Valley above Balaclava in the Crimea, 113 were killed, 134 were wounded, and 231 were missing and presumed captured. The order, scribbled in pencil by General Richard Airey, was perhaps unclear: "Lord Raglan the Commander-in-Chief wishes the cavalry to advance rapidly to the front, and try to prevent the enemy carrying away the guns . . . ." This poem has enjoyed much celebrity—or notoriety; its title was given to at least two films: Michael Curtiz's in 1936, starring Errol Flynn and having little to do with history, and Tony Richardson's in 1968.*

# *Mariana*

With blackest moss the flower-pots
  Were thickly crusted, one and all:
The rusted nails fell from the knots
  That held the pear to the gable-wall.
The broken sheds looked sad and strange:
  Unlifted was the clinking latch;
  Weeded and worn the ancient thatch
Upon the lonely moated grange.
    She only said, "My life is dreary,
      He cometh not," she said;
    She said, "I am aweary, aweary,
      I would that I were dead!"

Her tears fell with the dews at even;
  Her tears fell ere the dews were dried;
She could not look on the sweet heaven,
  Either at morn or eventide.
After the flitting of the bats,
  When thickest dark did trance the sky,
  She drew her casement-curtain by,
And glanced athwart the glooming flats.
    She only said, "The night is dreary,
      He cometh not," she said;
    She said, "I am aweary, aweary,
      I would that I were dead!"

Upon the middle of the night,
  Waking she heard the night-fowl crow:
The cock sung out an hour ere light:
  From the dark fen the oxen's low
Came to her: without hope of change,
  In sleep she seemed to walk forlorn,
  Till cold winds woke the gray-eyed morn

About the lonely moated grange.
    She only said, "The day is dreary,
      He cometh not," she said;
    She said, "I am aweary, aweary,
      I would that I were dead!"

About a stone-cast from the wall
    A sluice with blackened waters slept,
And o'er it many, round and small,
    The clustered marish-mosses crept.
Hard by a poplar shook alway,
    All silver-green with gnarlèd bark:
For leagues no other tree did mark
The level waste, the rounding gray.
    She only said, "My life is dreary,
      He cometh not," she said;
    She said, "I am aweary, aweary,
      I would that I were dead!"

And ever when the moon was low,
    And the shrill winds were up and away,
In the white curtain, to and fro,
    She saw the gusty shadow sway.
But when the moon was very low,
    And wild winds bound within their cell,
    The shadow of the poplar fell
Upon her bed, across her brow.
    She only said, "The night is dreary,
      He cometh not," she said;
    She said, "I am aweary, aweary,
      I would that I were dead!"

All day within the dreamy house,
    The doors upon their hinges creaked;
The blue fly sung in the pane; the mouse
    Behind the mouldering wainscot shrieked,
Or from the crevice peered about.
    Old faces glimmered through the doors,

Old footsteps trod the upper floors,
Old voices called her from without.
 She only said, "My life is dreary,
  He cometh not," she said;
 She said, "I am aweary, aweary,
  I would that I were dead!"

The sparrow's chirrup on the roof,
 The slow clock ticking, and the sound
Which to the wooing wind aloof
 The poplar made, did all confound
Her sense; but most she loathed the hour
 When the thick-moted sunbeam lay
Athwart the chambers, and the day
Was sloping toward his western bower.
 Then, said she, "I am very dreary,
  He will not come," she said;
 She wept, "I am aweary, aweary,
  Oh God, that I were dead!"

---

*This early poem, published when Tennyson was twenty-one, is about a subject that Tennyson was to devote many more poems to: the abandoned and the bereft. (See also Shakespeare's* Measure for Measure, *Act III, scene 1.)*

# The Lady of Shalott

PART I

On either side the river lie
Long fields of barley and of rye,
That clothe the wold and meet the sky;
And through the field the road runs by
    To many-towered Camelot;
And up and down the people go,
Gazing where the lilies blow
Round an island there below,
    The island of Shalott.

Willows whiten, aspens quiver,
Little breezes dusk and shiver
Through the wave that runs for ever
By the island in the river
    Flowing down to Camelot.
Four gray walls, and four gray towers,
Overlook a space of flowers,
And the silent isle imbowers
    The Lady of Shalott.

By the margin, willow-veiled,
Slide the heavy barges trailed
By slow horses; and unhailed
The shallop flitteth silken-sailed
    Skimming down to Camelot:
But who hath seen her wave her hand?
Or at the casement seen her stand?
Or is she known in all the land,
    The Lady of Shalott?

Only reapers, reaping early
In among the bearded barley,
Hear a song that echoes cheerly
From the river winding clearly,
  Down to towered Camelot:
And by the moon the reaper weary,
Piling sheaves in uplands airy,
Listening, whispers " 'Tis the fairy
  Lady of Shalott."

PART II

There she weaves by night and day
A magic web with colours gay.
She has heard a whisper say,
A curse is on her if she stay
  To look down to Camelot.
She knows not what the curse may be,
And so she weaveth steadily,
And little other care hath she,
  The Lady of Shalott.

And moving through a mirror clear
That hangs before her all the year,
Shadows of the world appear.
There she sees the highway near
  Winding down to Camelot:
There the river eddy whirls,
And there the surly village-churls,
And the red cloaks of market girls,
  Pass onward from Shalott.

Sometimes a troop of damsels glad,
An abbot on an ambling pad,
Sometimes a curly shepherd-lad,
Or long-haired page in crimson clad,
   Goes by to towered Camelot;
And sometimes through the mirror blue
The knights come riding two and two:
She hath no loyal knight and true,
   The Lady of Shalott.

But in her web she still delights
To weave the mirror's magic sights,
For often through the silent nights
A funeral, with plumes and lights
   And music, went to Camelot:
Or when the moon was overhead,
Came two young lovers lately wed;
"I am half sick of shadows," said
   The Lady of Shalott.

### PART III

A bow-shot from her bower-eaves,
He rode between the barley-sheaves,
The sun came dazzling through the leaves,
And flamed upon the brazen greaves
   Of bold Sir Lancelot.
A red-cross knight for ever kneeled
To a lady in his shield,
That sparkled on the yellow field,
   Beside remote Shalott.

The gemmy bridle glittered free,
Like to some branch of stars we see
Hung in the golden Galaxy.
The bridle bells rang merrily
   As he rode down to Camelot:
And from his blazoned baldric slung
A mighty silver bugle hung,
And as he rode his armour rung,
   Beside remote Shalott.

All in the blue unclouded weather
Thick-jewelled shone the saddle-leather,
The helmet and the helmet-feather
Burned like one burning flame together,
   As he rode down to Camelot.
As often through the purple night,
Below the starry clusters bright,
Some bearded meteor, trailing light,
   Moves over still Shalott.

His broad clear brow in sunlight glowed;
On burnished hooves his war-horse trode;
From underneath his helmet flowed
His coal-black curls as on he rode,
   As he rode down to Camelot.
From the bank and from the river
He flashed into the crystal mirror,
"Tirra lirra," by the river
   Sang Sir Lancelot.

She left the web, she left the loom,
She made three paces through the room,
She saw the water-lily bloom,
She saw the helmet and the plume,
   She looked down to Camelot.
Out flew the web and floated wide;
The mirror cracked from side to side;
"The curse is come upon me," cried
   The Lady of Shalott.

PART IV

In the stormy east-wind straining,
The pale yellow woods were waning,
The broad stream in his banks complaining,
Heavily the low sky raining
   Over towered Camelot;
Down she came and found a boat
Beneath a willow left afloat,
And round about the prow she wrote
   *The Lady of Shalott.*

And down the river's dim expanse
Like some bold seër in a trance,
Seeing all his own mischance—
With a glassy countenance
   Did she look to Camelot.
And at the closing of the day
She loosed the chain, and down she lay;
The broad stream bore her far away,
   The Lady of Shalott.

Lying, robed in snowy white
That loosely flew to left and right—
The leaves upon her falling light—
Through the noises of the night
   She floated down to Camelot:
And as the boat-head wound along
The willowy hills and fields among,
They heard her singing her last song,
   The Lady of Shalott.

Heard a carol, mournful, holy,
Chanted loudly, chanted lowly,
Till her blood was frozen slowly,
And her eyes were darkened wholly,
   Turned to towered Camelot.
For ere she reached upon the tide
The first house by the water-side,
Singing in her song she died,
   The Lady of Shalott.

Under tower and balcony,
By garden-wall and gallery,
A gleaming shape she floated by,
Dead-pale between the houses high,
   Silent into Camelot.
Out upon the wharfs they came,
Knight and burgher, lord and dame,
And round the prow they read her name,
   *The Lady of Shalott.*

Who is this? and what is here?
And in the lighted palace near
Died the sound of royal cheer;
And they crossed themselves for fear,
  All the knights at Camelot:
But Lancelot mused a little space;
He said, "She has a lovely face;
God in his mercy lend her grace,
  The lady of Shalott."

---

*Tennyson later used the same material in "Lancelot and Elaine" in* The Idylls of the King.

# Flower in the Crannied Wall

Flower in the crannied wall,
I pluck you out of the crannies,
I hold you here, root and all, in my hand,
Little flower—but *if* I could understand
What you are, root and all, and all in all,
I should know what God and man is.

---

*This poem is sometimes labelled a "fragment." Many works, especially those from 1800 on, concentrate on a single small creature to ponder large meanings.*

Browning was a varied poet for all of his long career, but his modern reputation owes most to his perfection of the dramatic monologue (although that designation applies to only two of his poems in this anthology: "My Last Duchess" and "The Bishop Orders His Tomb at St. Praxed's Church"). After their sensational elopement in 1846, he and his wife lived in Florence, Italy, until her death in 1861. He then returned to England, where he spent most of his remaining days.

# My Last Duchess

## Ferrara

That's my last Duchess painted on the wall,
Looking as if she were alive. I call
That piece a wonder, now: Frà Pandolf's hands
Worked busily a day, and there she stands.
Will 't please you sit and look at her? I said
"Frà Pandolf" by design, for never read
Strangers like you that pictured countenance,
The depth and passion of its earnest glance,
But to myself they turned (since none puts by
The curtain I have drawn for you, but I)
And seemed as they would ask me, if they durst,
How such a glance came there; so, not the first
Are you to turn and ask thus. Sir, 't was not
Her husband's presence only, called that spot
Of joy into the Duchess' cheek: perhaps
Frà Pandolf chanced to say "Her mantle laps
Over my lady's wrist too much," or "Paint
Must never hope to reproduce the faint
Half-flush that dies along her throat": such stuff
Was courtesy, she thought, and cause enough
For calling up that spot of joy. She had

A heart—how shall I say?— too soon made glad,
Too easily impressed; she liked whate'er
She looked on, and her looks went everywhere.
Sir, 't was all one! My favour at her breast,
The dropping of the daylight in the West,
The bough of cherries some officious fool
Broke in the orchard for her, the white mule
She rode with round the terrace—all and each
Would draw from her alike the approving speech,
Or blush, at least. She thanked men,—good! but
    thanked
Somehow—I know not how—as if she ranked
My gift of a nine-hundred-years-old name
With anybody's gift. Who'd stoop to blame
This sort of trifling? Even had you skill
In speech—(which I have not)—to make your will
Quite clear to such an one, and say, "Just this
Or that in you disgusts me; here you miss,
Or there exceed the mark"—and if she let
Herself be lessoned so, nor plainly set
Her wits to yours, forsooth, and made excuse,
—E'en then would be some stooping; and I choose
Never to stoop. Oh sir, she smiled, no doubt,
Whene'er I passed her; but who passed without
Much the same smile? This grew; I gave
    commands;
Then all smiles stopped together. There she stands
As if alive. Will 't please you rise? We'll meet
The company below, then. I repeat,
The Count your master's known munificence
Is ample warrant that no just pretense
Of mine for dowry will be disallowed;
Though his fair daughter's self, as I avowed
At starting, is my object. Nay, we'll go
Together down, sir. Notice Neptune, though,
Taming a sea horse, thought a rarity,
Which Claus of Innsbruck cast in bronze for me!

*It has been observed that the Duke's admiration for a bronze of Neptune Taming a Sea Horse shows his dedication to bullying. Just as he tried to dominate the earlier Duchess, he is trying now to monopolize his negotiations with the envoy. And now you can answer half of the famous English literature exam question: Name two works in which an Italian duchess is offered fruit. (The other is John Webster's* Duchess of Malfi, *where the duchess is offered the fruit of the apricot tree.)*

Robert Browning

# Home Thoughts from Abroad

### I

Oh, to be in England
Now that April's there,
And whoever wakes in England
Sees, some morning, unaware,
That the lowest boughs and the brushwood sheaf
Round the elm-tree bole are in tiny leaf,
While the chaffinch sings on the orchard bough
In England—now!

### II

And after April, when May follows,
And the whitethroat builds, and all the swallows!
Hark, where my blossomed pear-tree in the hedge
Leans to the field and scatters on the clover
Blossoms and dewdrops—at the bent spray's edge—
That's the wise thrush; he sings each song twice over,
Lest you should think he never could recapture
The first fine careless rapture!
And though the fields look rough with hoary dew,
All will be gay when noontide wakes anew
The buttercups, the little children's dower
—Far brighter than this gaudy melon-flower!

---

*Browning published this poem and a companion piece, "Home-Thoughts, from the Sea," in 1845, both imagined from the viewpoint of an Englishman in or near the southwest corner of the Continent. Even the wording "Home-Thoughts" is peculiarly English (or Germanic), different from a corresponding expression in a Romance language.*

# Meeting at Night

◆◆◆◆

1

The gray sea and the long black land;
And the yellow half-moon large and low;
And the startled little waves that leap
In fiery ringlets from their sleep,
As I gain the cove with pushing prow,
And quench its speed i' the slushy sand.

2

Then a mile of warm sea-scented beach;
Three fields to cross till a farm appears;
A tap at the pane, the quick sharp scratch
And blue spurt of a lighted match,
And a voice less loud, through its joys and fears,
Then the two hearts beating each to each!

---

*In* Dramatic Romances *(1845), this poem and "Parting at Morning" (p. 675)
were printed together as one work entitled "Night and Morning." The parts were
separated and re-titled in 1849.*

# The Year's at the Spring

❈❈❈

The year's at the spring,
And day's at the morn;
Morning's at seven;
The hillside's dew-pearled;
The lark's on the wing;
The snail's on the thorn:
God's in His Heaven—
All's right with the world!

from Pippa Passes

---

*Although Pippa's song, which comes in the first scene ("Morning") of the drama* Pippa Passes, *may seem ridiculously optimistic, Pippa is no Pollyanna, and her song is far from simple. The* abcdabcd *rhyme-scheme itself bears the stamp of complexity.*

# The Bishop Orders His Tomb
# at St. Praxed's Church

>>>>>>>

Vanity, saith the preacher, vanity!
Draw round my bed: is Anselm keeping back?
Nephews—sons mine . . . ah, God, I know not! Well—
She, men would have to be your mother once,
Old Gandolf envied me, so fair she was!
What's done is done, and she is dead beside,
Dead long ago, and I am Bishop since,
And as she died so must we die ourselves,
And thence ye may perceive the world's a dream.
Life, how and what is it? As here I lie
In this state-chamber, dying by degrees,
Hours and long hours in the dead night, I ask
'Do I live, am I dead?' Peace, peace seems all.
Saint Praxed's ever was the church for peace;
And so, about this tomb of mine. I fought
With tooth and nail to save my niche, ye know:
—Old Gandolf cozened me, despite my care;
Shrewd was that snatch from out the corner South
He graced his carrion with, God curse the same!
Yet still my niche is not so cramped but thence
One sees the pulpit o' the epistle-side,
And somewhat of the choir, those silent seats,
And up into the aery dome where live
The angels, and a sunbeam's sure to lurk:
And I shall fill my slab of basalt there,
And 'neath my tabernacle take my rest,
With those nine columns round me, two and two,
The odd one at my feet where Anselm stands:
Peach-blossom marble all, the rare, the ripe
As fresh-poured red wine of a mighty pulse.
—Old Gandolf with his paltry onion-stone,
Put me where I may look at him! True peach,

Rosy and flawless: how I earned the prize!
Draw close: that conflagration of my church
—What then? So much was saved if aught were missed!
My sons, ye would not be my death? Go dig
The white-grape vineyard where the oil-press stood,
Drop water gently till the surface sink,
And if ye fine . . . Ah God, I know not, I! . . .
Bedded in store of rotten fig-leaves soft,
And corded up in a tight olive-frail,
Some lump, ah God, of *lapis lazuli*,
Big as a Jew's head cut off at the nape,
Blue as a vein o'er the Madonna's breast . . .
Sons, all have I bequeathed you, villas, all,
That brave Frascati villa with its bath,
So, let the blue lump poise between my knees,
Like God the Father's globe on both his hands
Ye worship in the Jesu Church so gay,
For Gandolf shall not choose but see and burst!
Swift as a weaver's shuttle fleet our years:
Man goeth to the grave, and where is he?
Did I say basalt for my slab, sons? Black—
'Twas ever antique-black I meant! How else
Shall ye contrast my frieze to come beneath?
The bas-relief in bronze ye promised me,
Those Pans and Nymphs ye wot of, and perchance
Some tripod, thyrsus, with a vase or so,
The Saviour at his sermon on the mount,
Saint Praxed in a glory, and one Pan
Ready to twitch the Nymph's last garment off,
And Moses with the tables . . . but I know
Ye mark me not! What do they whisper thee,
Child of my bowels, Anselm? Ah, ye hope
To revel down my villas while I gasp
Bricked o'er with beggar's mouldy travertine
Which Gandolf from his tomb-top chuckles at!
Nay, boys, ye love me—all of jasper, then!
'Tis jasper ye stand pledged to, lest I grieve
My bath must needs be left behind, alas!

One block, pure green as a pistachio-nut,
There's plenty jasper somewhere in the world—
And have I not Saint Praxed's ear to pray
Horses for ye, and brown Greek manuscripts,
And mistresses with great smooth marbly limbs?
—That's if ye carve my epitaph aright,
Choice Latin, picked phrase, Tully's every word,
No gaudy ware like Gandolf's second line—
Tully, my masters? Ulpian serves his need!
And then how I shall lie through centuries,
And hear the blessed mutter of the mass,
And see God made and eaten all day long,
And feel the steady candle-flame, and taste
Good strong thick stupefying incense-smoke!
For as I lie here, hours of the dead night,
Dying in state and by such slow degrees,
I fold my arms as if they clasped a crook,
And stretch my feet forth straight as stone can point,
And let the bedclothes, for a mortcloth, drop
Into great laps and folds of sculptor's-work:
And as yon tapers dwindle, and strange thoughts
Grow, with a certain humming in my ears,
About the life before I lived this life,
And this life too, popes, cardinals and priests,
Saint Praxed at his sermon on the mount,
Your tall pale mother with her talking eyes,
And new-found agate urns as fresh as day,
And marble's language, Latin pure, discreet,
—Aha, ELUCESCEBAT quoth our friend?
No Tully, said I, Ulpian at the best!
Evil and brief hath been my pilgrimage.
All *lapis*, all, sons! Else I give the Pope
My villas! Will ye ever eat my heart?
Ever your eyes were as a lizard's quick
They glitter like your mother's for my soul,
Or ye would heighten my impoverished frieze,
Piece out its starved design, and fill my vase
With grapes, and add a vizor and a Term,

And to the tripod ye would tie a lynx
That in his struggle throws the thyrsus down,
To comfort me on my entablature
Whereon I am to lie till I must ask
"Do I live, am I dead?" There, leave me, there!
For ye have stabbed me with ingratitude
To death—ye wish it—God, ye wish it! Stone—
Gritstone, a-crumble! Clammy squares which sweat
As if the corpse they keep were oozing through—
And no more *lapis* to delight the world!
Well go! I bless ye. Fewer tapers there,
But in a row: and, going, turn your backs
—Ay, like departing altar-ministrants,
And leave me in my church, the church for peace,
That I may watch at leisure if he leers—
Old Gandolf, at me, from his onion-stone,
As still he envied me, so fair she was!

---

*Browning's Bishop remains a vivacious and compelling preacher to the end. In a mixture that may impress the innocent as hypocritical, he is a theologian, an aesthete, a politician, and an ardent lover of the physical.*

# Parting at Morning

Round the cape of a sudden came the sea,
And the sun looked over the mountain's rim:
And straight was a path of gold for him,
And the need of a world of men for me.

---

*This poem and "Meeting at Night" (p. 669) were originally printed together as one work in* Dramatic Romances *(1845). "Him" in the third line refers to the sun.*

# Two in the Campagna

I wonder do you feel to-day
    As I have felt, since, hand in hand,
We sat down on the grass, to stray
    In spirit better through the land,
This morn of Rome and May?

For me, I touched a thought, I know,
    Has tantalised me many times,
(Like turns of thread the spiders throw
    Mocking across our path) for rhymes
To catch at and let go.

Help me to hold it! First it left
    The yellowing fennel, run to seed
There, branching from the brickwork's cleft,
    Some old tomb's ruin: yonder weed
Took up the floating weft,

Where one small orange cup amassed
    Five beetles,—blind and green they grope
Among the honey-meal; and last,
    Everywhere on the grassy slope
I traced it. Hold it fast!

The champaign with its endless fleece
    Of feathery grasses everywhere!
Silence and passion, joy and peace,
    An everlasting wash of air—
Rome's ghost since her decease.

Such life there, through such lengths of hours,
  Such miracles performed in play,
Such primal naked forms of flowers,
  Such letting nature have her way
While heaven looks from its towers.

How say you? Let us, O my dove,
  Let us be unashamed of soul,
As earth lies bare to heaven above!
  How is it under our control
To love or not to love?

I would that you were all to me,
  You that are just so much, no more—
Nor yours, nor mine, nor slave nor free!
  Where does the fault lie? what the core
Of the wound, since wound must be?

I would I could adopt your will,
  See with your eyes, and set my heart
Beating by yours, and drink my fill
  At your soul's springs,—your part my part
In life, for good and ill.

No. I yearn upward, touch you close,
  Then stand away. I kiss your cheek,
Catch your soul's warmth,—I pluck the rose
  And love it more than tongue can speak—
Then the good minute goes.

Already how am I so far
  Out of that minute? Must I go
Still like the thistle-ball, no bar,
  Onward, whenever light winds blow,
Fixed by no friendly star?

Just when I seemed about to learn!
  Where is the thread now? Off again!
  The old trick! Only I discern—
  Infinite passion, and the pain
Of finite hearts that yearn.

---

*The Brownings visited the Campagna di Roma—an 800-square-mile "champaign" or waste plain with thought-provoking ruins and relics. The speaker of the poem does not have to be Robert Browning himself or, indeed, any man.*

# Edward Lear 1812–1888

Lear was an observant traveler and a gifted draftsman who began writing to add some text to drawings for children. He belonged to about the same generation as "Lewis Carroll" and Sir William Schwenck Gilbert, writers of humorous verse that reaches genuine nonsense on one side but also touches the realms of travesty, parody, and satire, and even now and then some horror and pathos.

## The Owl and the Pussy-Cat

The Owl and the Pussy-cat went to sea
  In a beautiful pea-green boat,
They took some honey, and plenty of money,
  Wrapped up in a five-pound note.
The Owl looked up to the stars above,
  And sang to a small guitar,
"O lovely Pussy! O Pussy, my love,
  What a beautiful Pussy you are,
    You are,
    You are!
  What a beautiful Pussy you are!"

Pussy said to the Owl, "You elegant fowl!
  How charmingly sweet you sing!
O let us be married! too long we have tarried:
  But what shall we do for a ring?"
They sailed away, for a year and a day,
  To the land where the Bong-Tree grows,
And there in a wood a Piggy-wig stood,
  With a ring at the end of his nose,
    His nose,
    His nose,
  With a ring at the end of his nose.

"Dear Pig, are you willing to sell for one shilling
  Your ring?" Said the Piggy, "I will."
So they took it away, and were married next day
  By the Turkey who lives on the hill.
They dined on mince, and slices of quince,
  Which they ate with a runcible spoon;
And hand in hand, on the edge of the sand,
  They danced by the light of the moon,
    The moon,
    The moon,
  They danced by the light of the moon.

---

*Nonsense notwithstanding, Lear somehow puts a good deal of compassion and a great deal of charm into a little song. In this love story with a happy ending, one may hear echoes of moon-music from Byron's "So We'll Go No More a-Roving" (p. 479) and Poe's "Annabel Lee" (p. 631). Lear uses his favorite made-up word "runcible" here for the first time; it later modifies a cat and a hat. It meant nothing special then but has come to be the name of a kind of pickle-fork.*

# The Jumblies

I

They went to sea in a Sieve, they did,
In a Sieve they went to sea:
In spite of all their friends could say,
On a winter's morn, on a stormy day,
In a Sieve they went to sea!
And when the Sieve turned round and round,
And every one cried, "You'll all be drowned!"
They called aloud, "Our Sieve ain't big,
But we don't care a button! we don't care a fig!
In a Sieve we'll go to sea!"
Far and few, far and few,
Are the lands where the Jumblies live;
Their heads are green, and their hands are blue,
And they went to sea in a Sieve.

II

They sailed away in a Sieve, they did,
In a Sieve they sailed so fast,
With only a beautiful pea-green veil
Tied with a riband by way of a sail,
To a small tobacco-pipe mast;
And every one said, who saw them go,
"O won't they be soon upset, you know!
For the sky is dark, and the voyage is long,
And happen what may, it's extremely wrong
In a Sieve to sail so fast!"
Far and few, far and few,
Are the lands where the Jumblies live;
Their heads are green, and their hands are blue,
And they went to sea in a Sieve.

III

The water it soon came in, it did,
 The water it soon came in;
So to keep them dry, they wrapped their feet
In a pinky paper all folded neat,
 And they fastened it down with a pin.
And they passed the night in a crockery-jar,
And each of them said, "How wise we are!
Though the sky be dark, and the voyage be long,
Yet we never can think we were rash or wrong,
While round in our Sieve we spin!"
 Far and few, far and few,
 Are the lands where the Jumblies live;
 Their heads are green, and their hands are blue,
 And they went to sea in a Sieve.

IV

And all night long they sailed away;
 And when the sun went down,
They whistled and warbled a moony song
To the echoing sound of a coppery gong,
 In the shade of the mountains brown.
"O Timballo! How happy we are,
When we live in a sieve and a crockery-jar;
And all night long in the moonlight pale,
We sail away with a pea-green sail,
 In the shade of the mountains brown!"
 Far and few, far and few,
 Are the lands where the Jumblies live;
 Their heads are green, and their hands are blue,
 And they went to sea in a Sieve.

V

They sailed to the Western Sea, they did,
 To a land all covered with trees,
And they bought an Owl, and a useful Cart,
And a pound of Rice, and a Cranberry Tart,
 And a hive of silvery Bees.

And they bought a Pig, and some green Jack-daws,
And a lovely Monkey with lollipop paws,
And forty bottles of Ring-Bo-Ree,
  And no end of Stilton Cheese.
    Far and few, far and few,
      Are the lands where the Jumblies live;
    Their heads are green, and their hands are blue,
      And they went to sea in a Sieve.

VI

And in twenty years they all came back,
  In twenty years or more,
And every one said, 'How tall they've grown!
For they've been to the Lakes, and the Torrible Zone,
  And the hills of the Chankly Bore;
And they drank their health, and gave them a feast
Of dumplings made of beautiful yeast;
And every one said, "If we only live,
We too will go to sea in a Sieve,—
  To the hills of the Chankly Bore!"
    Far and few, far and few,
      Are the lands where the Jumblies live;
    Their heads are green, and their hands are blue,
      And they went to sea in a Sieve.

---

*Is there not something heroic about the Jumblies' pluck as they sail out in bad weather in an unfit vessel "In spite of all their friends could say"? (See also "Sir Patrick Spens," p. 10.) Like Odysseus, they come home after twenty years of adventures in exotic-sounding places. Lear's two poems in this anthology begin to show how much he liked certain combinations, such as "beautiful pea-green."*

# EMILY BRONTË 1818–1848

Emily Brontë will always be known more for *Wuthering Heights* than for her poetry, but that is only because the novel is one of the greatest books in the language. She was an accomplished and versatile poet, and it is a pity that she died so young. Her older sister Charlotte is famous for *Jane Eyre*, their younger sister Anne for *Agnes Grey* and *The Tenant of Wildfell Hall*.

# *Remembrance*

()◆►()

Cold in the earth—and the deep snow piled above thee,
Far, far removed, cold in the dreary grave!
Have I forgot, my only Love, to love thee,
Severed at last by Time's all-severing wave?

Now, when alone, do my thoughts no longer hover
Over the mountains, on that northern shore,
Resting their wings where heath and fern-leaves cover
That noble heart for ever, ever more?

Cold in the earth—and fifteen wild Decembers
From those brown hills, have melted into spring—
Faithful indeed is the spirit that remembers
After such years of change and suffering!

Sweet Love of youth, forgive if I forget thee,
While the world's tide is bearing me along:
Other desires and darker hopes beset me,
Hopes which obscure, but cannot do thee wrong!

No later light has lightened up my heaven;
No second morn has ever shone for me:
All my life's bliss from thy dear life was given—
All my life's bliss is in the grave with thee.

But, when the days of golden dreams had perished,
And even Despair was powerless to destroy,
Then did I learn how existence could be cherished,
Strengthened, and fed without the aid of joy;

Then did I check the tears of useless passion,
Weaned my young soul from yearning after thine;
Sternly denied its burning wish to hasten
Down to that tomb already more than mine!

And, even yet, I dare not let it languish,
Dare not indulge in memory's rapturous pain;
Once drinking deep of that divinest anguish,
How could I seek the empty world again?

---

*For more than half of her thirty years, Emily Brontë, along with her younger sister Anne, wrote prose and verse about an imaginary northern realm they called Gondal. "Remembrance" contains passion, memory, dream, Time, and winter: the same elements that animate* Wuthering Heights.

# ARTHUR HUGH CLOUGH 1819-1861

One of Clough's poems in this anthology is gravely earnest, the other flippantly light, but both are about conduct, morality, and belief. Clough was a friend of Matthew Arnold and had the same Rugby-Oxford
orientation; although he early gave up Oxford and went
his own way. Arnold addressed "To a Republican
Friend, 1848" to Clough and commemorated Clough in
the pastoral "Thyrsis."

# Say Not the Struggle Nought Availeth

Say not the struggle nought availeth,
  The labor and the wounds are vain,
The enemy faints not, nor faileth,
  And as things have been they remain.

If hopes were dupes, fears may be liars;
  It may be, in yon smoke concealed,
Your comrades chase e'en now the fliers,
  And, but for you, possess the field.

For while the tired waves, vainly breaking,
  Seem here no painful inch to gain,
Far back through creeks and inlets making,
  Coming silent, flooding in, the main.

And not by eastern windows only,
  When daylight comes, comes in the light,
In front the sun climbs slow, how slowly,
  But westward, look, the land is bright.

---

*Clough sounds here like one of Charles Kingsley's brigadiers of Muscular Chris-
tianity.*

# The Latest Decalogue

Thou shalt have one God only; who
Would be at the expense of two?
No graven images may be
Worshipped, except the currency:
Swear not at all; for, for thy curse
Thine enemy is none the worse:
At church on Sunday to attend
Will serve to keep the world thy friend:
Honour thy parents; that is, all
From whom advancement may befall:
Thou shalt not kill; but need'st not strive
Officiously to keep alive:
Do not adultery commit;
Advantage rarely comes of it:
Thou shalt not steal; an empty feat,
When it's so lucrative to cheat:
Bear not false witness; let the lie
Have time on its own wings to fly:
Thou shalt not covet, but tradition
Approves all forms of competition.

---

*Clough could write a poem as wholesomely inspiring as "Say Not the Struggle
Nought Availeth" (p. 686), but he was also capable of producing a telling satire
as sharp and witty as attacks by Swift and Byron.*

# JULIA WARD HOWE 1819–1910

With her husband, Samuel G. Howe, Julia Ward
Howe edited an antislavery newspaper and was active
as a writer and lecturer in support of women's rights
and the abolition of slavery.

## The Battle Hymn of the Republic

❧❧❧

Mine eyes have seen the glory of the coming of the Lord;
He is trampling out the vintage where the grapes of wrath are
    stored;
He hath loosed the fateful lightning of His terrible swift sword;
His truth is marching on.
    Glory! Glory! Hallelujah!
    Glory! Glory! Hallelujah!
    Glory! Glory! Hallelujah!
    His truth is marching on.

I have seen Him in the watch fires of a hundred circling camps
They have builded Him an altar in the evening dews and damps;
I can read His righteous sentence by the dim and flaring lamps;
His day is marching on.
    Glory! Glory! Hallelujah!
    Glory! Glory! Hallelujah!
    Glory! Glory! Hallelujah!
    His day is marching on.

He has sounded forth the trumpet that shall never call retreat;
He is sifting out the hearts of men before His judgment seat;
Oh, be swift, my soul, to answer Him; be jubilant, my feet;
Our God is marching on.
    Glory! Glory! Hallelujah!
    Glory! Glory! Hallelujah!
    Glory! Glory! Hallelujah!
    Our God is marching on.

In the beauty of the lilies Christ was born across the sea,
With a glory in His bosom that transfigures you and me;
As He died to make men holy, let us die to make men free;
While God is marching on.
    Glory! Glory! Hallelujah!
    Glory! Glory! Hallelujah!
    Glory! Glory! Hallelujah!
    While God is marching on.

---

*Early in the American Civil War, Julia Ward Howe wrote these stirring new words to the tune (and somewhat to the spirit) of "John Brown's Body," an antebellum song about the abolitionist leader who was hanged in 1859. This battle hymn, published in a magazine in 1862, has long been associated with the Union side in the Civil War, although it has lost a good deal of its partisan or regional significance.*

# WALT WHITMAN 1819–1892

Whitman wrote a lot about himself, and most readers
are familiar with the outlines of his history: born on
Long Island, worked as a printer and journalist, especially for Democrat organs, travelled to New Orleans,
served as a wound-dresser during the Civil War, stayed
on in Washington for some years after the war, moving
finally to Camden, New Jersey, where he spent the last
19 years of his life. Whitman was uncommonly suscep-
tible to influences of every sort. In creating his prodigiously capacious idiom for American poetry, he used
slang, opera, phrenology, all religions and philosophies,
the oratorical manners of preachers and lecturers, free
association, the cutting-pasting assemblage of newspapers—in short, anything. He was always a democrat
(although during the Civil War changed his party allegiance from Democrat to Republican). He was hailed
by Emerson on the first appearance of *Leaves of Grass* in
1855; praise also came from W. M. Rossetti and Al-
gernon Charles Swinburne.

## A Noiseless Patient Spider

>>>>>>>

A noiseless patient spider,
I mark'd where on a little promontory it stood isolated,
Mark'd how to explore the vacant vast surrounding,
It launch'd forth filament, filament, filament, out of itself,
Ever unreeling them, ever tirelessly speeding them.

And you O my soul where you stand,
Surrounded, detached, in measureless oceans of space,
Ceaselessly musing, venturing, throwing, seeking the spheres to
    connect them,
Till the bridge you will need be form'd, till the ductile anchor
    hold,
Till the gossamer thread you fling catch somewhere, O, my
    soul.

Both Oliver Wendell Holmes's "Chambered Nautilus" (p. 620) of 1858 and Whitman's "Noiseless Patient Spider" of 1868 carefully observe the structure or behavior of a creature simpler than ourselves and go on to apply the zoological message with a moral "O my soul."

# O Captain! My Captain!

O Captain! my Captain! our fearful trip is done,
The ship has weather'd every rack, the prize we sought is won,
The port is near, the bells I hear, the people all exulting,
While follow eyes the steady keel, the vessel grim and daring;
But O heart! heart! heart!
O the bleeding drops of red,
Where on the deck my Captain lies,
Fallen cold and dead.

O Captain! my Captain! rise up and hear the bells;
Rise up—for you the flag is flung—for you the bugle trills,
For you bouquets and ribbon'd wreaths—for you the shores
a-crowding,
For you they call, the swaying mass, their eager faces turning;
Here Captain! dear father!
This arm beneath your head!
It is some dream that on the deck,
You've fallen cold and dead.

My Captain does not answer, his lips are pale and still,
My father does not feel my arm, he has no pulse nor will,
The ship is anchor'd safe and sound, its voyage closed and done,
From fearful trip the victor ship comes in with object won;
Exult O shores, and ring O bells!
But I with mournful tread,
Walk the deck my Captain lies,
Fallen cold and dead.

from Memories of President Lincoln

*Whitman's sheaf called* Memories of President Lincoln *contains this poem and three others:* "When Lilacs Last in the Dooryard Bloomed" *(p. 694),* "Hush'd Be the Camps Today," *and* "This Dust Was Once the Man." *Although* "O Captain! My Captain!" *may seem to regress to a simple mode of allegory characteristic more of Holmes and Longfellow, and although some critics regard the poem as among Whitman's worst and least typical, it may be in these tormented lines that Whitman best achieves the status he desired of a genuinely popular writer.*

# When Lilacs Last in the Dooryard Bloomed

### 1

When lilacs lastin the dooryard bloomed
And the great star early drooped in the western sky in the night,
I mourned, and yet shall mourn with ever-returning spring.

Ever-returning spring, trinity sure to me you bring,
Lilac blooming perennial and drooping star in the west,
And thought of him I love.

### 2

O powerful western fallen star!
O shades of night—O moody, tearful night!
O great star disappeared—O the black murk that hides the star!
O cruel hands that hold me powerless—O helpless soul of me!
O harsh surrounding cloud that will not free my soul.

### 3

In the dooryard fronting an old farmhouse near the whitewashed
    palings
Stands the lilac-bush tall-growing with heart-shaped leaves of rich
    green,
With many a pointed blossom rising delicate, with the perfume
    strong I love,
With every leaf a miracle—and from this bush in the dooryard,
With delicate-colored blossoms and heart-shaped leaves of rich
    green,
A sprig with its flower I break.

4

In the swamp in secluded recesses,
A shy and hidden bird is warbling a song.

Solitary the thrush,
The hermit withdrawn to himself, avoiding the settlements,
Sings by himself a song.

Song of the bleeding throat,
Death's outlet song of life, (for well dear brother I know,
If thou wast not granted to sing thou would'st surely die.)

5

Over the breast of the spring, the land, amid cities,
Amid lanes and through old woods, where lately the violets
    peeped from the ground, spotting the grey debris,
Amid the grass in the fields each side of the lanes, passing the
    endless grass,
Passing the yellow-speared wheat, every grain from its shroud in
    the dark-brown fields uprisen,
Passing the apple-tree blows of white and pink in the orchards,
Carrying a corpse to where it shall rest in the grave,
Night and day journeys a coffin.

6

Coffin that passes through lanes and streets,
Through day and night with the great cloud darkening the land,
With the pomp of the inlooped flags, with the cities draped in
    black,
With the show of the States themselves as of crape-veiled women
    standing,
With processions long and winding and the flambeaus of the
    night,
With the countless torches lit, with the silent sea of faces and the
    unbared heads,
With the waiting depot, the arriving coffin, and the sombre faces,
With dirges through the night, with the thousand voices rising
    strong and solemn,

With the mournful voices of the dirges poured around the coffin,
The dim-lit churches and the shuddering organs—where amid
 these you journey,
With the tolling tolling bells' perpetual clang,
Here, coffin that slowly passes,
I give you my sprig of lilac.

7

(Nor for you, for one alone,
Blossoms and branches green to coffins all I bring,

For fresh as the morning, thus would I chant a song for you, O
 sane and sacred death.

All over bouquets of roses,
O death, I cover you over with roses and early lilies,
But mostly and now the lilac that blooms the first,
Copious I break, I break the sprigs from the bushes,
With loaded arms I come, pouring for you,
For you and the coffins all of you, O death.)

8

O western orb sailing the heaven,
Now I know what you must have meant as a month since I
 walked,
As I walked in silence the transparent shadowy night,
As I saw you had something to tell as you bent to me night after
 night,
As you drooped from the sky low down as if to my side, (while
 the other stars all looked on,)
As we wandered together the solemn night, (for something I
 know not what kept me from sleep,)
As the night advanced, and I saw on the rim of the west how
 full you were of woe,
As I stood on the rising ground in the breeze in the cool
 transparent night,
As I watched where you passed and was lost in the netherward
 black of the night,

As my soul in its trouble dissatisfied sank, as where you, sad
   orb,
Concluded, dropped in the night, and was gone.

9

Sing on there in the swamp,
O singer bashful and tender, I hear your notes, I hear your call,
I hear, I come presently, I understand you,
But a moment I linger, for the lustrous star has detained me,
The star my departing comrade holds and detains me.

10

O how shall I warble myself for the dead one there I loved?
And how shall I deck my song for the large sweet soul that has
   gone?
And what shall my perfume be for the grave of him I love?

Sea-winds blown from east and west,
Blown from the Eastern sea and blown from the Western sea, till
there on the prairies meeting,
These and with these and the breath of my chant,
I'll perfume the grave of him I love.

11

O what shall I hang on the chamber walls?
And what shall the pictures be that I hang on the walls,
To adorn the burial-house of him I love?

Pictures of growing spring and farms and homes,
With the Fourth-month eve at sundown, and the grey smoke
   lucid and bright,
With floods of yellow gold of the gorgeous, indolent, sinking sun,
   burning, expanding the air,
With the fresh sweet herbage underfoot, and the pale green
   leaves of the trees prolific,
In the distance the flowing glaze, the breast of the river, with a
   wind-dapple here and there,

With ranging hills on the banks, with many a line against the
    sky, and shadows,
And the city at hand with dwellings so dense, and stacks of
    chimneys,
And all the scenes of life and the workshops, and the workmen
    homeward returning.

### 12

Lo, body and soul—this land,
My own Manhattan with spires, and the sparkling and hurrying
    tides, and the ships,
The varied and ample land, the South and the North in the light,
Ohio's shores and flashing Missouri,
And ever the far-spreading prairies covered with grass and corn.

Lo, the most excellent sun so calm and haughty,
The violet and purple morn with just-felt breezes,
The gentle soft-born measureless light,
The miracle spreading bathing all, the fulfilled noon,
The coming eve delicious, the welcome night and the stars,
Over my cities shining all, enveloping man and land.

### 13

Sing on, sing on you grey-brown bird,
Sing from the swamps, the recesses, pour your chant from the
    bushes,
Limitless out of the dusk, out of the cedars and pines.

Sing on dearest brother, warble your reedy song,
Loud human song, with voice of uttermost woe.

O liquid and free and tender!
O wild and loose to my soul—O wondrous singer!
You only I hear—yet the star holds me, (but will soon depart,)
Yet the lilac with mastering odor holds me.

14

Now while I sat in the day and looked forth,
In the close of the day with its light and the fields of spring, and
  the farmers preparing their crops,
In the large unconscious scenery of my land with its lakes and
  forests,
In the heavenly aerial beauty, (after the perturbed winds and the
  storms,)
Under the arching heavens of the afternoon swift passing, and
  the voices of children and women,
The many-moving sea-tides, and I saw the ships how they sailed,
And the summer approaching with richness, and the fields all
  busy with labor,
And the infinite separate houses, how they all went on, each with
  its meals and minutia of daily usages,
And the streets how their throbbings throbbed, and the cities
  pent—lo, then and there,
Falling upon them all and among them all, enveloping me with
  the rest,
Appeared the cloud, appeared the long black trail;
And I knew death, its thought, and the sacred knowledge of
  death.

Then with the knowledge of death as walking one side of me,
And the thought of death close-walking the other side of me,
And I in the middle as with companions, and as holding the
  hands of companions,
I fled forth to the hiding receiving night that talks not,
Down to the shores of the water, the path by the swamp in the
  dimness,
To the solemn shadowy cedars and ghostly pines so still.

And the singer so shy to the rest received me,
The grey-brown bird I know received us comrades three,
And he sang the carol of death, and a verse for him I love.

From deep secluded recesses,
From the fragrant cedars and the ghostly pines so still,
Came the carol of the bird.

And the charm of the carol rapt me,
As I held as if by their hands my comrades in the night,
And the voice of my spirit tallied the song of the bird.

*Come lovely and soothing death,*
*Undulate round the world, serenely arriving, arriving,*
*In the day, in the night, to all, to each,*
*Sooner or later delicate death.*

*Praised be the fathomless universe,*
*For life and joy, and for objects and knowledge curious,*
*And for love, sweet love—but praise! praise! praise!*
*For the sure-enwinding arms of cool-enfolding death.*

*Dark mother always gliding near with soft feet,*
*Have none chanted for thee a chant of fullest welcome?*
*Then I chant it for thee, I glorify thee above all,*
*I bring thee a song that when thou must indeed come, come unfalteringly.*

*Approach strong deliveress,*
*When it is so, when thou hast taken them I joyously sing the dead,*
*Lost in the loving floating ocean of thee,*
*Laved in the flood by thy bliss O death.*

*From me to thee glad serenades,*
*Dances for thee I propose saluting thee, adornments and feastings for*
*    thee,*
*And the sights of the open landscape and the high-spread sky are fitting,*
*And life and the fields, and the huge and thoughtful night.*

*The night in silence under many a star,*
*The ocean shore and the husky whispering wave whose voice I know,*
*And the soul turning to thee, O vast and well-veiled death,*
*And the body gratefully nestling close to thee.*

*Over the tree-tops I float thee a song,*
*Over the rising and sinking waves, over the myriad fields and the prairies*
*wide,*
*Over the dense-packed cities all and the teeming wharves and ways,*
*I float this carol with joy, with joy to thee, O death,*

15

To the tally of my soul,
Loud and strong kept up the grey-brown bird,
With pure, deliberate notes spreading filling the night.

Loud in the pines and cedars dim,
Clear in the freshness moist and the swamp-perfume,
And I with my comrades there in the night.
While my sight that was bound in my eyes unclosed,
As to long panoramas of visions.

And I saw askant the armies,
I saw as in noiseless dreams hundreds of battle-flags,
Born through the smoke of the battles and pierced with missiles I
saw them,
And carried hither and yon through the smoke, and torn and
bloody,
And at last but a few shreds left on the staffs, (and all in
silence,)
And the staffs all splintered and broken.

I saw battle-corpses, myriads of them,
And the white skeletons of young men, I saw them,
I saw the debris and debris of all the slain soldiers of war,
But I saw they were not as was thought,
They themselves were fully at rest, they suffered not,
The living remained and suffered, the mother suffered,
And the wife and the child and the musing comrade suffered,
And the armies that remained suffered.

16

Passing the visions, passing the night,
Passing, unloosing the hold of my comrades' hands,
Passing the song of the hermit bird and the tallying song of my
    soul,
Victorious song, death's outlet song, yet varying ever-altering
    song,
As low and wailing, yet clear the notes, rising and falling,
    flooding the night,
Sadly sinking and fainting, as warning and warning, and yet
    again bursting with joy,
Covering the earth and filling the spread of the heaven,
As that powerful psalm in the night I heard from recesses,
Passing, I leave thee lilac with heart-shaped leaves,
I leave thee there in the dooryard, blooming, returning with
    spring.

I cease my song for thee,
From my gaze on thee in the west, fronting the west, communing
    with thee,
O comrade lustrous with silver face in the night.
Yet each to keep and all, retrievements out of the night,
The song, the wondrous chant of the grey-brown bird,
And the tallying chant, the echo aroused in my soul,
With the lustrous and drooping star with the countenance full of
    woe,
With the holders holding my hand nearing the call of the bird,
Comrades mine and I in the midst, and their memory ever to
    keep, for the dead I loved so well,
For the sweetest, wisest soul of all my days and lands—and this
    for his dear sake,
Lilac and star and bird twined with the chant of my soul,
There in the fragrant pines and the cedars dusk and dim.

from Memories of President Lincoln

*It is hard to believe that the same poet wrote "O Captain! My Captain!"—with its simple rhyming and allegorizing—and "When Lilacs Last in the Dooryard Bloomed," so much more powerful, eloquent, and artistic. The threefold symbols of star, bird, and plant contain a profound awareness of grief within an even profounder awareness of the ever-returning seasons. Other great "April elegies" in this anthology are Milton's "On the Late Massacre in Piedmont" (p. 211), Hardy's "Convergence of the Twain" (p. 777), Yeats's "Easter, 1916" (p. 864), and Eliot's "Waste Land" (p. 968).*

# I Hear America Singing

I hear America singing, the varied carols I hear,
Those of mechanics, each one singing his as it should be blithe
    and strong,
The carpenter singing his as he measures his plank or beam,
The mason singing his as he makes ready for work, or leaves off
    work,
The boatman singing what belongs to him in his boat, the deck-
    hand singing on the steamboat deck,
The shoemaker singing as he sits on his bench, the hatter singing
    as he stands,
The wood-cutter's song, the plowboy's on his way in the
    morning, or at noon intermission or at sundown,
The delicious singing of the mother, or of the young wife at
    work, or of the girl sewing or washing,
Each singing what belongs to him or her and to none else,
The day what belongs to the day—at night the party of young
    fellows, robust, friendly,
Singing with open mouths their strong melodious songs.

---

*In various editions of* Leave of Grass *between 1860 and 1881, Whitman moved
this poem around and even changed its first line and its title, which was originally "American mouth-songs!"*

# Cavalry Crossing a Ford

A line in long array, where they wind betwixt green islands;
They take a serpentine course — their arms flash in the sun —
    hark to the musical clank;
Behold the silvery river — in it the splashing horses, loitering, stop
    to drink;
Behold the brown-faced men — each group, each person, a
    picture — the negligent rest on the saddles;
Some emerge on the opposite bank — others are just entering the
    ford — while,
Scarlet, and blue, and snowy white,
The guidon flags flutter gaily in the wind.

---

*With the clarity of documentary photography, Whitman renders an unadorned wartime scene. All the implicit horror of war is held in abeyance, however, while the artist concentrates on the elaborate interplay of elements and colors. The poem begins and ends with simple description; between, in the second, third, and fourth lines, the reader is invited into the action: "hark . . . Behold . . . Behold . . . ."*

# MATTHEW ARNOLD 1822–1888

The son of Dr. Thomas Arnold (headmaster of Rugby),
Matthew Arnold was appointed an inspector of schools
in 1851 and later held the Chair of Poetry at Oxford for
ten years. His aesthetic and cultural criticism is almost
as influential as his poetry.

## *Dover Beach*

The sea is calm tonight.
The tide is full, the moon lies fair
Upon the straits; — on the French coast the light
Gleams and is gone; the cliffs of England stand,
Glimmering and vast, out in the tranquil bay.
Come to the window, sweet is the night-air!
Only, from the long line of spray
Where the sea meets the moon-blanched land,
Listen! you hear the grating roar
Of pebbles which the waves draw back, and fling,
At their return, up the high strand,
Begin, and cease, and then again begin,
With tremulous cadence slow, and bring
The eternal note of sadness in.

Sophocles long ago
Heard it on the Ægæan, and it brought
Into his mind the turbid ebb and flow
Of human misery; we
Find also in the sound a thought,
Hearing it by this distant northern sea.

Matthew Arnold

The Sea of Faith
Was once, too, at the full, and round earth's shore
Lay like the folds of a bright girdle furled.
But now I only hear
Its melancholy, long, withdrawing roar,
Retreating, to the breath
Of the night-wind, down the vast edges drear
And naked shingles of the world.

Ah, love, let us be true
To one another! for the world, which seems
To lie before us like a land of dreams,
So various, so beautiful, so new,
Hath really neither joy, nor love, nor light,
Nor certitude, nor peace, nor help for pain;
And we are here as on a darkling plain
Swept with confused alarms of struggle and flight,
Where ignorant armies clash by night.

---

*Written in the middle of the nineteenth century, "Dover Beach" has some claim to be the first distinctly modern poem, perhaps even qualifying as "modernist" in the way it places an isolated neurotic on the edge of a highly charged symbolic scene. The lines are broken and uneven; some of the transitions are abrupt, almost surrealist.*

# The Scholar-Gipsy

Go, for they call you, shepherd, from the hill;
　Go, shepherd, and untie the wattled cotes!
　　No longer leave thy wistful flock unfed,
　Nor let thy bawling fellows rack their throats,
　　Nor the cropped herbage shoot another head.
　　　But when the fields are still,
　And the tired men and dogs all gone to rest,
　　And only the white sheep are sometimes seen
　　Cross and recross the strips of moon-blanched green,
Come, shepherd, and again begin the quest!

Here, where the reaper was at work of late—
　In this high field's dark corner, where he leaves
　　His coat, his basket, and his earthen cruse,
　And in the sun all morning binds the sheaves,
　　Then here, at noon, comes back his stores to use—
　　　Here will I sit and wait,
　While to my ear from uplands far away
　　The bleating of the folded flocks is borne,
　　With distant cries of reapers in the corn—
All the live murmur of a summer's day.

Screened is this nook o'er the high, half-reaped field,
　And here till sundown, shepherd! will I be.
　　Through the thick corn the scarlet poppies peep,
　And round green roots and yellowing stalks I see
　　Pale pink convolvulus in tendrils creep;
　　　And air-swept lindens yield
　Their scent, and rustle down their perfumed showers
　　Of bloom on the bent grass where I am laid,
　　And bower me from the August sun with shade;
And the eye travels down to Oxford's towers.

And near me on the grass lies Glanvil's book —
  Come, let me read the oft-read tale again!
  The story of the Oxford scholar poor,
Of pregnant parts and quick inventive brain,
    Who, tired of knocking at preferment's door,
      One summer-morn forsook
His friends, and went to learn the gipsy-lore,
  And roamed the world with that wild brotherhood,
  And came, as most men deemed, to little good,
But came to Oxford and his friends no more.

But once, years after, in the country-lanes,
  Two scholars, whom at college erst he knew,
  Met him, and of his way of life enquired;
Whereat he answered, that the gipsy-crew,
    His mates, had arts to rule as they desired
      The workings of men's brains,
And they can bind them to what thoughts they will.
  "And I," he said, "the secret of their art,
  When fully learned, will to the world impart;
But it needs heaven-sent moments for this skill."

This said, he left them, and returned no more. —
  But rumors hung about the country-side,
  That the lost Scholar long was seen to stray,
Seen by rare glimpses, pensive and tongue-tied,
    In hat of antique shape, and cloak of gray.
      The same the gipsies wore.
Shepherds had met him on the Hurst in spring;
  At some lone alehouse in the Berkshire moors,
  On the warm ingle-bench, the smock-frocked boors
Had found him seated at their entering,

But, 'mid their drink and clatter, he would fly.
  And I myself seem half to know thy looks,
    And put the shepherds, wanderer! on thy trace;
  And boys who in lone wheatfields scare the rooks
    I ask if thou hast passed their quiet place;
      Or in my boat I lie
  Moored to the cool bank in the summer-heats,
    'Mid wide grass meadows which the sunshine fills,
    And watch the warm, green-muffled Cumner hills,
  And wonder if thou haunt'st their shy retreats.

For most, I know, thou lov'st retired ground!
  Thee at the ferry Oxford riders blithe,
    Returning home on summer-nights, have met
  Crossing the stripling Thames at Bab-lock-hithe,
    Trailing in the cool stream thy fingers wet,
      As the punt's rope chops round;
  And leaning backward in a pensive dream,
    And fostering in thy lap a heap of flowers
    Plucked in shy fields and distant Wychwood bowers,
  And thine eyes resting on the moonlit stream.

And then they land, and thou art seen no more!
  Maidens, who from the distant hamlets come
    To dance around the Fyfield elm in May,
  Oft through the darkening fields have seen thee roam,
    Or cross a stile into the public way.
      Oft thou hast given them store
  Of flowers—the frail-leafed, white anemone,
    Dark bluebells drenched with dews of summer eves,
    And purple orchises with spotted leaves—
  But none hath words she can report of thee.

And, above Godstow Bridge, when hay-time's here
  In June, and many a scythe in sunshine flames,
    Men who through those wide fields of breezy grass
  Where black-winged swallows haunt the glittering Thames,
    To bathe in the abandoned lasher pass,
      Have often passed thee near
  Sitting upon the river bank o'ergrown;
    Marked thine outlandish garb, thy figure spare,
    Thy dark vague eyes, and soft abstracted air —
  But, when they came from bathing, thou wast gone!

At some lone homestead in the Cumner hills,
  Where at her open door the housewife darns,
    Thou hast been seen, or hanging on a gate
  To watch the threshers in the mossy barns.
    Children, who early range these slopes and late
      For cresses from the rills,
  Have known thee eying, all an April-day,
    The springing pastures and the feeding kine;
    And marked thee, when the stars come out and shine,
  Through the long dewy grass move slow away.

In autumn, on the skirts of Bagley Wood —
  Where most the gipsies by the turf-edged way
    Pitch their smoked tents, and every bush you see
  With scarlet patches tagged and shreds of gray,
    Above the forest-ground called Thessaly —
      The blackbird, picking food,
  Sees thee, nor stops his meal, nor fears at all;
    So often has he known thee past him stray,
    Rapt, twirling in thy hand a withered spray,
  And waiting for the spark from heaven to fall.

And once, in winter, on the causeway chill
  Where home through flooded fields foot-travelers go,
    Have I not passed thee on the wooden bridge,
  Wrapped in thy cloak and battling with the snow,
    Thy face tow'rd Hinksey and its wintry ridge?
      And thou hast climbed the hill,
  And gained the white brow of the Cumner range;
    Turned once to watch, while thick the snowflakes fall,
    The line of festal light in Christ-Church hall—
  Then sought thy straw in some sequestered grange.

But what—I dream! Two hundred years are flown
  Since first thy story ran through Oxford halls,
    And the grave Glanvil did the tale inscribe
  That thou wert wandered from the studious walls
    To learn strange arts, and join a gipsy-tribe;
      And thou from earth art gone
  Long since, and in some quiet churchyard laid—
    Some country-nook, where o'er thy unknown grave
    Tall grasses and white flowering nettles wave,
  Under a dark, red-fruited yew-tree's shade.

—No, no, thou hast not felt the lapse of hours!
  For what wears out the life of mortal men?
    'Tis that from change to change their being rolls;
    'Tis that repeated shocks, again, again,
      Exhaust the energy of strongest souls
      And numb the elastic powers.
  Till having used our nerves with bliss and teen,
    And tired upon a thousand schemes our wit,
    To the just-pausing Genius we remit
  Our worn-out life, and are—what we have been.

Thou hast not lived, why should'st thou perish, so?
   Thou hadst *one* aim, *one* business, *one* desire;
     Else wert thou long since numbered with the dead!
   Else hadst thou spent, like other men, thy fire!
     The generations of thy peers are fled.
       And we ourselves shall go;
   But thou possessest an immortal lot,
     And we imagine thee exempt from age
     And living as thou liv'st on Glanvil's page,
Because thou hadst—what we, alas! have not.

For early didst thou leave the world, with powers
   Fresh, undiverted to the world without,
     Firm to their mark, not spent on other things;
   Free from the sick fatigue, the languid doubt,
     Which much to have tried, in much been baffled, brings.
       O life unlike to ours!
   Who fluctuate idly without term or scope,
     Of whom each strives, nor knows for what he strives,
     And each half lives a hundred different lives;
   Who wait like thee, but not, like thee, in hope.

Thou waitest for the spark from heaven! and we,
   Light half-believers of our casual creeds,
     Who never deeply felt, nor clearly willed,
   Whose insight never has borne fruit in deeds,
     Whose vague resolves never have been fulfilled;
       For whom each year we see
   Breeds new beginnings, disappointments new;
     Who hesitate and falter life away,
     And lose tomorrow the ground won today—
Ah! do not we, wanderer! await it too?

Yes, we await it! but it still delays,
  And then we suffer! and amongst us one,
    Who most has suffered, takes dejectedly
  His seat upon the intellectual throne;
    And all his store of sad experience he
      Lays bare of wretched days;
  Tells us his misery's birth and growth and signs,
    And how the dying spark of hope was fed,
    And how the breast was soothed, and how the head,
  And all his hourly varied anodynes.

This for our wisest! and we others pine,
  And wish the long unhappy dream would end,
    And waive all claim to bliss, and try to bear;
  With close-lipped patience for our only friend,
    Sad patience, too near neighbor to despair—
      But none has hope like thine!
  Thou through the fields and through the woods dost stray,
    Roaming the countryside, a truant boy,
    Nursing thy project in unclouded joy,
  And every doubt long blown by time away.

O born in days when wits were fresh and clear,
  And life ran gaily as the sparkling Thames;
    Before this strange disease of modern life,
  With its sick hurry, its divided aims,
    Its head o'ertaxed, its palsied hearts, was rife—
      Fly hence, our contact fear!
  Still fly, plunge deeper in the bowering wood!
    Averse, as Dido did with gesture stern
    From her false friend's approach in Hades turn,
  Wave us away, and keep thy solitude!

Still nursing the unconquerable hope,
  Still clutching the inviolable shade,
    With a free, onward impulse brushing through,
  By night, the silvered branches of the glade—
    Far on the forest-skirts, where none pursue,
      On some mild pastoral slope
  Emerge, and resting on the moonlit pales
  Freshen thy flowers as in former years
  With dew, or listen with enchanted ears,
From the dark dingles, to the nightingales!

But fly our paths, our feverish contact fly!
  For strong the infection of our mental strife,
    Which, though it gives no bliss, yet spoils for rest;
  And we should win thee from thy own fair life,
    Like us distracted, and like us unblest.
      Soon, soon thy cheer would die,
  Thy hopes grow timorous, and unfixed thy powers,
    And thy clear aims be cross and shifting made;
    And then thy glad perennial youth would fade,
Fade, and grow old at last, and die like ours.

Then fly our greetings, fly our speech and smiles!
  —As some grave Tyrian trader, from the sea,
    Described at sunrise and emerging prow
  Lifting the cool-haired creepers stealthily,
    The fringes of a southward-facing brow
      Among the Aegean isles;
  And saw the merry Grecian coaster come,
    Freighted with amber grapes, and Chian wine,
    Green, bursting figs, and tunnies steeped in brine—
And knew the intruders on his ancient home,

The young light-hearted masters of the waves—
And snatched his rudder, he shook out more sail;
And day and night held on indignantly
O'er the blue Midland waters with the gale,
Betwixt the Syrtes and soft Sicily,
To where the Atlantic raves
Outside the western straits; and unbent sails
There, where down cloudy cliffs, through sheets of foam,
Shy traffickers, the dark Iberians come;
And on the beach undid his corded bales.

---

*Arnold's notes make clear that this poem was inspired by a passage from Joseph Glanvil's* Vanity of Dogmatizing *(1661). Arnold used the same stanza (meter and rhyme) later in "Thyrsis," his pastoral elegy on the death of his friend and fellow-poet Arthur Hugh Clough. Arnold seems to have modelled the stanza on that in some of Keats's odes.*

# WILLIAM ALLINGHAM 1824–1889

Allingham was known mostly as a poet and anthologist.
He was also a notable diarist, in which role he provides
information about many of his literary friends, including D. G. Rossetti and Tennyson.

## *The Fairies*

Up the airy mountain,
  Down the rushy glen,
We daren't go a-hunting
  For fear of little men;
Wee folk, good folk,
  Trooping all together;
Green jacket, red cap,
  And white owl's feather!

Down along the rocky shore
  Some make their home,
They live on crispy pancakes
  Of yellow tide-foam;
Some in the reeds
  Of the black mountain lake,
With frogs for their watch-dogs,
  All night awake.

High on the hill-top
  The old King sits;
He is now so old and gray
  He's nigh lost his wits.
With a bridge of white mist
  Columbkill he crosses,
On his stately journeys
  From Slieveleague to Rosses;

Or going up with music
  On cold starry nights
To sup with the Queen
  Of the gay Northern Lights.

They stole little Bridget
  For seven years long;
When she came down again
  Her friends were all gone.
They took her lightly back,
  Between the night and morrow,
They thought that she was fast asleep,
  But she was dead with sorrow.
They have kept her ever since
  Deep within the lake,
On a bed of flag-leaves,
  Watching till she wake.

By the craggy hill-side,
  Through the mosses bare,
They have planted thorn-trees
  For pleasure here and there.
Is any man so daring
  As dig them up in spite,
He shall find their sharpest thorns
  In his bed at night.

Up the airy mountain,
  Down the rushy glen,
We daren't go a-hunting
  For fear of little men;
Wee folk, good folk,
  Trooping all together;
Green jacket, red cap,
  And white owl's feather!

---

*Legends of wee folk persist everywhere, a survival or atavism that predates most of the modern religions.*

# GEORGE MEREDITH 1828–1909

Meredith stands higher among the novelists than among the poets, and most readers who know of him will think of him as the author of such novels as *The Ordeal of Richard Feverel* and *The Egoist*. But Meredith's poetry deserves as much respect: it is varied, animated, witty, humane, and consistently dramatic.

## *Lucifer in Starlight*

❦❦❦

On a starred night Prince Lucifer uprose.
  Tired of his dark dominion, swung the fiend
  Above the rolling ball in cloud part screened,
Where sinners hugged their specter of repose.
Poor prey to his hot fit of pride were those.
  And now upon his western wing he leaned,
  Now his huge bulk o'er Afric's sands careened,
Now the black planet shadowed Arctic snows.
Soaring through wider zones that pricked his scars
  With memory of the old revolt from Awe,
He reached a middle height, and at the stars,
Which are the brain of heaven, he looked, and sank.
Around the ancient track marched, rank on rank,
  The army of unalterable law.

---

*Meredith excelled in prose and poetry, in some moods looking forward to modernist realism and skepticism. In this powerful sonnet he assumes, however, the grand manner of a Victorian Milton — soon to be mocked by T. S. Eliot, whose "Cousin Nancy," written at about the time of Meredith's death, ends:*

> *Upon the glazen shelves kept watch*
> *Matthew and Waldo, guardians of the faith,*
> *The army of unalterable law.*

# *Thus Piteously Love Closed What He Begat*

>>>>>>>

Thus piteously Love closed what he begat:
The union of this ever-diverse pair!
These two were rapid falcons in a snare,
Condemned to do the flitting of the bat.
Lovers beneath the singing sky of May,
They wandered once, clear as the dew on flowers:
But they fed not on the advancing hours:
Their hearts held cravings for the buried day.
Then each applied to each that fatal knife,
Deep questioning, which probes to endless dole.
Ah, what a dusty answer gets the soul
When hot for certainties in this our life! —
In tragic hints here see what evermore
Moves dark as yonder midnight ocean's force,
Thundering like ramping hosts of warrior horse,
To throw that faint thin line upon the shore!

from Modern Love

---

*Meredith's forward-looking "Modern Love," in sixteen-line variations on the son-
net, tells the sternly honest story of the all-too-familiar failure of his own
miserable first marriage to the widowed daughter of Thomas Love Peacock.*

A painter as well as a poet, Dante Gabriel Rossetti was one of the founders of the Pre-Raphaelite Brotherhood, a movement that had broad influence on English literature, criticism, painting, architecture, and design. Dante Gabriel Rossetti was the older brother of Christina Georgina Rossetti. He is the only poet in this anthology whose sister is also here.

## The Blessed Damozel

The blessed damozel leaned out
  From the gold bar of Heaven;
Her eyes were deeper than the depth
  Of waters stilled at even;
She had three lilies in her hand,
  And the stars in her hair were seven.

Her robe, ungirt from clasp to hem,
  No wrought flowers did adorn,
But a white rose of Mary's gift,
  For service meetly worn;
Her hair that lay along her back
  Was yellow like ripe corn.

Herseemed she scarce had been a day
  One of God's choristers;
The wonder was not yet quite gone
  From that still look of hers;
Albeit, to them she left, her day
  Had counted as ten years.

(To one, it is ten years of years.
  . . . Yet now, and in this place,
Surely she leaned o'er me—her hair
  Fell all about my face . . .
Nothing: the autumn fall of leaves.
  The whole year sets apace.)

It was the rampart of God's house
  That she was standing on;
By God built over the sheer depth
  The which is Space begun;
So high, that looking downward thence
  She scarce could see the sun.

It lies in Heaven, across the flood
  Of ether, as a bridge.
Beneath, the tides of day and night
  With flame and darkness ridge
The void, as low as where this earth
  Spins like a fretful midge.

Around her, lovers, newly met
  'Mid deathless love's acclaims,
Spoke evermore among themselves
  Their heart remembered names;
And the souls mounting up to God
  Went by her like thin flames.

And still she bowed herself and stooped
  Out of the circling charm;
Until her bosom must have made
  The bar she leaned on warm,
And the lilies lay as if asleep
  Along her bended arm.

From the fixed place of Heaven she saw
   Time like a pulse shake fierce
Through all the worlds. Her gaze still strove
   Within the gulf to pierce
Its path; and now she spoke as when
   The stars sang in their spheres.

The sun was gone now; the curled moon
   Was like a little feather
Fluttering far down the gulf; and now
   She spoke through the still weather.
Her voice was like the voice the stars
   Had when they sang together.

(Ah sweet! Even now, in that bird's song,
   Strove not her accents there,
Fain to be hearkened? When those bells
   Possessed the mid-day air,
Strove not her steps to reach my side
   Down all the echoing stair?)

"I wish that he were come to me,
   For he will come," she said.
"Have I not prayed in Heaven? —on earth,
   Lord, Lord, has he not prayed?
Are not two prayers a perfect strength?
   And shall I feel afraid?

"When round his head the aureole clings,
   And he is clothed in white,
I'll take his hand and go with him
   To the deep wells of light;
As unto a stream we will step down
   And bathe there in God's sight.

"We two will stand beside that shrine,
　　Occult, withheld, untrod,
Whose lamps are stirred continually
　　With prayer sent up to God;
And see our old prayers, granted, melt
　　Each like a little cloud.

"We two will lie i' the shadow of
　　That living mystic tree
Within whose secret growth the Dove
　　Is sometimes felt to be,
While every leaf that His plumes touch
　　Saith His Name audibly.

"And I myself will teach to him,
　　I myself, lying so,
The songs I sing here; which his voice
　　Shall pause in, hushed and slow,
And find some knowledge at each pause,
　　Or some new thing to know."

(Alas! We two, we two, thou sayst!
　　Yea, one wast thou with me
That once of old. But shall God lift
　　To endless unity
The soul whose likeness with thy soul
　　Was but its love for thee?)

"We two," she said, "will seek the groves
　　Where the lady Mary is,
With her five handmaidens, whose names
　　Are five sweet symphonies,
Cecily, Gertrude, Magdalen,
　　Margaret and Rosalys.

"Circlewise sit they, with bound locks
　And foreheads garlanded;
Into the fine cloth white like flame
　Weaving the golden thread,
To fashion the birth-robes for them
　Who are just born, being dead.

"He shall fear, haply, and be dumb:
　Then will I lay my cheek
To his, and tell about our love,
　Not once abashed or weak:
And the dear Mother will approve
　My pride, and let me speak.

"Herself shall bring us, hand in hand,
　To Him round whom all souls
Kneel, the clear-ranged unnumbered heads
　Bowed with their aureoles:
And angels meeting us shall sing
　To their citherns and citoles.

"There will I ask of Christ the Lord
　Thus much for him and me:—
Only to live as once on earth
　With Love,—only to be,
As then awhile, for ever now
　Together, I and he."

She gazed and listened and then said,
　Less sad of speech than mild,—
"All this is when he comes." She ceased.
　The light thrilled towards her, filled
With angels in strong level flight.
　Her eyes prayed, and she smiled.

(I saw her smile.) But soon their path
   Was vague in distant spheres:
And then she cast her arms along
   The golden barriers,
And laid her face between her hands,
   And wept. (I heard her tears.)

---

*Of "The Raven" (p. 625), Rossetti supposedly said, "I saw that Poe had done the utmost it was possible to do with grief of the lover on earth, and I determined to reverse the conditions." This poem, along with some of Blake's, has the uncommon distinction of possessing a companion-painting by the same artist.*

# The Woodspurge

The wind flapped loose, the wind was still,
Shaken out dead from tree and hill:
I had walked on at the wind's will, —
I sat now, for the wind was still.

Between my knees my forehead was, —
My lips, drawn in, said not Alas!
My hair was over in the grass,
My naked ears heard the day pass.

My eyes, wide open, had the run
Of some ten weeds to fix upon;
Among those few, out of the sun,
The woodspurge flowered, three cups in one.

From perfect grief there need not be
Wisdom or even memory:
One thing then learnt remains to me, —
The woodspurge has a cup of three.

---

*Byron, who remarked tartly that Keats could not look at an oak tree without seeing a dryad, might have admired Rossetti's lucidity in looking at a woodspurge and seeing—a woodspurge. (Cups and threes can mean much to pagan and Christian interpreters alike, and spurge is, by definition, an instrument of purgation; but Rossetti is above all that—or below it.)*

# EMILY DICKINSON 1830–1886

Dickinson spent most of her strange life in Amherst, Massachusetts, where she had been born. Her father was a lawyer who served in the United States House of Representatives. She seems to have been gregarious when young but became reclusive as time passed. Of her many poems—upwards of 1,800—only eight or so were published in her lifetime. Since she was such a great and eloquent poet, people have naturally been curious about her, but biographical speculations have encountered many barriers, and the poetry itself continues to present inconsistencies, enigmas, anomalies, and opacities. Whatever the truth about her life, she remains a poet of unmatched strength and vitality. The primitive simplicity of some of her stanzas is balanced by the audacious complexity of syntax and rhythm, along with eccentric rhymes.

## "Because I could not stop for Death"

Because I could not stop for Death—
He kindly stopped for me—
The Carriage held but just Ourselves—
And Immortality.

We slowly drove—He knew no haste
And I had put away
My labor and my leisure too,
For His Civility—

We passed the School, where Children strove
At Recess—in the Ring—
We passed the Fields of Gazing Grain—
We passed the Setting Sun—

Or rather—He passed Us—
The Dews drew quivering and chill—
For only Gossamer, my Gown—
My Tippet—only Tulle—

We paused before a House that seemed
A Swelling of the Ground—
The Roof was scarcely visible—
The Cornice—in the Ground—

Since then—'tis Centuries—and yet
Feels shorter than the Day
I first surmised the Horses' Heads
Were toward Eternity—

---

*Dickinson, a generation younger than Poe, came along just in time to witness a mass-movement in obituary poetry so widespread and so bathetically lugubrious that it became a joke. Mark Twain and others repeatedly made fun of the death poems of Julia A. Moore, who appears as Emmeline Grangerford in* Huckleberry Finn. *"Because I could not stop for Death" personifies Death as a civil gentleman, not so different from Whitman's "lovely and soothing death" ("When Lilacs Last in the Dooryard Bloomed," p. 694) or even Keats's "easeful death" ("Ode to a Nightingale," p. 542).*

# "I heard a Fly buzz—when I died"

~~~~~~

I heard a Fly buzz—when I died—
The Stillness in the Room
Was like the Stillness in the Air—
Between the Heaves of Storm—

The Eyes around—had wrung them dry—
And Breaths were gathering firm
For that last Onset—when the King
Be witnessed—in the Room—

I willed my Keepsakes—Signed away
What portion of me be
Assignable—and then it was
There interposed a Fly—

With Blue—uncertain stumbling Buzz—
Between the light—and me—
And then the Windows failed—and then
I could not see to see—

---

*In Dickinson's time, improvements in public health favored large families, but illness and death were all around. Dickinson, born in 1830, probably had more firsthand experience of death than most people born in 1930. Dickinson's fly has more tangible, terrifying reality than Melville's whale or Poe's raven. It is rendered in its full fly-hood of things seen and heard, as well as with "Blue—uncertain stumbling Buzz."*

# "A narrow Fellow in the Grass"

A narrow Fellow in the Grass
Occasionally rides—
You may have met Him—did you not
His notice sudden is—

The Grass divides as with a Comb—
A spotted shaft is seen—
And then it closes at your feet
And opens further on—

He likes a Boggy Acre
A Floor to cool for Corn—
Yet when a Boy, and Barefoot—
I more than once at Noon
Have passed, I thought, a Whip lash
Unbraiding in the Sun
When stooping to secure it
It wrinkled, and was gone—

Several of Nature's People
I know, and they know me—
I feel for them a transport
Of cordiality—

But never met this Fellow
Attended, or alone
Without a tighter breathing
And Zero at the Bone—

---

*Charms and riddles are among the oldest poems, and they are also, in a sense, the "oldest" or earliest poems for many readers. The point is to describe something without naming it. There are riddles in the Bible, in Homer, in Old English literature, and in any schoolyard or workplace.*

# "There's a certain Slant of light"

There's a certain Slant of light,
Winter Afternoons—
That oppresses, like the Heft
Of Cathedral Tunes—

Heavenly Hurt, it gives us—
We can find no scar,
But internal difference,
Where the Meanings, are—

None may teach it—Any—
'Tis the Seal Despair—
An imperial affliction
Sent us of the Air—

When it comes, the Landscape listens—
Shadows—hold their breath—
When it goes, 'tis like the Distance
On the look of Death—

---

*Dickinson was a generation ahead of Ferdinand de Saussure and a century ahead of Jacques Derrida in recognizing that "internal difference" is "Where the Meanings, are." Neither dot nor dash means anything; it is the difference between that makes the Morse code possible.*

# "A Bird came down the Walk"

❖❖❖❖

A Bird came down the Walk—
He did not know I saw—
He bit an Angleworm in halves
And ate the fellow, raw,

And then he drank a Dew
From a convenient Grass—
And then hopped sidewise to the Wall
To let a Beetle pass—

He glanced with rapid eyes
That hurried all around—
They looked like frightened Beads, I thought—
He stirred his Velvet Head

Like one in danger, Cautious,
I offered him a Crumb
And he unrolled his feathers
And rowed him softer home—

Than Oars divide the Ocean,—
Too silver for a seam—
Or Butterflies, off Banks of Noon
Leap, plashless as they swim.

---

*Dickinson's life was reduced to a few essentials (Thoreau, in comparison, was a boulevardier and globetrotter). She had the leisure to compose hundreds of poems and the patience to devote herself to detailed observation of the minute particulars of the world.*

# "The Soul selects her own Society"

❦❦❦

The Soul selects her own Society—
Then—shuts the Door—
To her divine Majority—
Present no more—

Unmoved—she notes the Chariots—pausing—
At her low Gate—
Unmoved—an Emperor be kneeling
Upon her Mat—

I've known her—from an ample nation—
Choose One—
Then—close the Valves of her attention—
Like Stone—

---

*As in so many of her lyrics, Dickinson here adapts an idiom peculiar to American politics, which stresses the Majority and rejects any Emperor, to the requirements of a wholly personal poem.*

# "I like to see it lap the Miles"

>>>>>>>

I like to see it lap the Miles—
And lick the Valleys up—
And stop to feed itself at Tanks—
And then—prodigious step

Around a Pile of Mountains—
And supercilious peer
In Shanties—by the sides of Roads—
And then a Quarry pare

To fit its Ribs
And crawl between
Complaining all the while
In horrid—hooting stanza—
Then chase itself down Hill—

And neigh like Boanerges—
Then—punctual as a Star
Stop—docile and omnipotent
At its own stable door—

---

*Many poets recoiled in horror and anxiety from the new machinery of the nineteenth century, but the locomotive found adherents in Whitman (who wrote a poem called "To a Locomotive in Winter") and Dickinson, who needed the figurative arsenal of the New Testament to reinforce the metaphor of the Iron Horse.*

# "My life closed twice before its close"

My life closed twice before its close—
It yet remains to see
If Immortality unveil
A third event to me

So huge, so hopeless to conceive
As these that twice befell.
Parting is all we know of heaven,
And all we need of hell.

---

*Closure, partition, separation—all are kinds of death. After the final death, the departure is all we know of those headed for heaven; parting itself is so painful that no other news of hell is needed to make it hellish.*

# "Success is counted sweetest"

Success is counted sweetest
By those who ne'er succeed.
To comprehend a nectar
Requires sorest need.

Not one of all the purple Host
Who took the Flag today
Can tell the definition
So clear of Victory

As he defeated—dying—
On whose forbidden ear
The distant strains of triumph
Burst agonized and clear!

---

*One wise moment in J. D. Salinger's* Catcher in the Rye *comes with the suggestion (made by Holden Caulfield's older brother) that Emily Dickinson was a great war poet, even though she did not fight in a war.*

# "I taste a liquor never brewed"

I taste a liquor never brewed—
From Tankards scooped in Pearl—
Not all the Vats upon the Rhine
Yield such an Alcohol!

Inebriate of Air—am I—
And Debauchee of Dew—
Reeling—thro endless summer days—
From inns of Molten Blue—

When "Landlords" turn the drunken Bee
Out of the Foxglove's door—
When Butterflies—renounce their "drams"—
I shall but drink the more!

Till Seraphs swing their snowy Hats—
And Saints—to windows run—
To see the little Tippler
Leaning against the—Sun—

---

*The highest annual per capita consumption of alcoholic beverages in the United States was in 1830, the year of Dickinson's birth. Drinking was only casually disciplined by law, and quality control was so quixotic that the drinker might feel either nothing or a 200-proof belt. The environment favored the immemorial metaphors of intoxication.*

# "After great pain, a formal feeling comes"

〰〰〰〰〰

After great pain, a formal feeling comes—
The Nerves sit ceremonious, like Tombs—
The stiff Heart questions was it He, that bore,
And Yesterday, or Centuries before?

The Feet, mechanical, go round—
Of Ground, or Air, or Ought—
A Wooden way
Regardless grown,
A Quartz contentment, like a stone—

This is the Hour of Lead—
Remembered, if outlived,
As Freezing persons, recollect the Snow—
First—Chill—then Stupor—then the letting go—

---

*Like Poe before her, Dickinson could imagine death from the inside and from the far side. Her subject was that of the oldest scriptures, but her idiom included such state-of-the-art locutions as "Nerves" and "mechanical."*

# "I felt a Funeral, in my Brain"

()◄━►()

I felt a Funeral, in my Brain,
And Mourners to and fro
Kept treading—treading—till it seemed
That Sense was breaking through—

And when they all were seated,
A Service, like a Drum—
Kept beating—beating—till I thought
My Mind was going numb—

And then I heard them lift a Box
And creak across my Soul
With those same Boots of Lead, again,
Then Space—began to toll,

As all the Heavens were a Bell,
And Being, but an Ear,
And I, and Silence, some strange Race
Wrecked, solitary, here—

And then a Plank in Reason, broke,
And I dropped down, and down—
And hit a World, at every plunge,
And Finished knowing—then—

---

*One hallmark of Dickinson's genius is her skill in capturing extremes of extraordinary vision and horror by means of the simplest verbal traps: "And then . . . And . . . And . . . And . . . ."*

# "I never saw a Moor"

I never saw a Moor—
I never saw the Sea—
Yet know I how the Heather looks
And what a Billow be.

I never spoke with God
Nor visited in Heaven—
Yet certain am I of the spot
As if the Checks were given—

---

*One hears about a cult of hands-on experience in America, but Dickinson shows
again and again that the imagination can function magnificently in a person
who seldom leaves the house.*

# "Much Madness is divinest Sense"

❖❖❖❖

Much madness is divinest sense
To a discerning eye;
Much sense the starkest madness.
'T is the majority
In this, as all, prevails.
Assent, and you are sane;
Demur,—you're straightway dangerous,
And handled with a chain.

---

*Dickinson could sound like an American Blake, insisting on individual liberty so emphatically that collective standards ("manacles," according to Blake; "a Chain," according to Dickinson) counted for nothing.*

# CHRISTINA GEORGINA ROSSETTI 1830–1894

Christina Rossetti is the only woman represented in this anthology who also has a brother (Dante Gabriel Rossetti) represented. (Another brother, William Michael Rossetti, was also important as a writer.) Although the Rossettis shared an Italian heritage, Christina Rossetti was a devout Anglican; and much of her poetry is religious. In some more personal lyrics, she shows a persistent melancholy but an equally persistent stoicism. Two men proposed marriage to her, but she remained single.

# When I Am Dead

When I am dead, my dearest,
    Sing no sad songs for me;
Plant thou no roses at my head,
    Nor shady cypress tree:
Be the green grass above me
    With showers and dewdrops wet;
And if thou wilt, remember,
    And if thou wilt, forget.

I shall not see the shadows,
    I shall not feel the rain;
I shall not hear the nightingale
    Sing on, as if in pain:
And dreaming through the twilight
    That doth not rise nor set,
Haply I may remember,
    And haply may forget.

---

*These tough verses gain in power when compared with Rupert Brooke's "Soldier" (p. 951). Christina Rossetti's sentiment will probably strike the modern reader as the more genuine of the two.*

# Up-Hill

>>>>>>>

Does the road wind uphill all the way?
   Yes, to the very end.
Will the day's journey take the whole long day?
   From morn to night, my friend.

But is there for the night a resting-place?
   A roof for when the slow, dark hours begin,
May not the darkness hide it from my face?
   You cannot miss that inn.

Shall I meet other wayfarers at night?
   Those who have gone before.
Then must I knock, or call when just in sight?
   They will not keep you waiting at that door.

Shall I find comfort, travel-sore and weak?
   Of labour you shall find the sum.
Will there be beds for me and all who seek?
   Yea, beds for all who come.

---

*Reminiscent in some ways of old ballads and in some ways of seventeenth-century religious lyrics, "Up-Hill" also seems to be a prelude to A. E. Housman's meditative poems a generation later.*

# A Birthday

My heart is like a singing bird
   Whose nest is in a watered shoot;
My heart is like an apple-tree
   Whose boughs are bent with thickset fruit;
My heart is like a rainbow shell
   That paddles in a halcyon sea;
My heart is gladder than all these
   Because my love is come to me.

Raise me a dais of silk and down;
   Hang it with vair and purple dyes;
Carve it in doves and pomegranates,
   And peacocks with a hundred eyes;
Work it in gold and silver grapes,
   In leaves and silver fleurs-de-lys;
Because the birthday of my life
   Is come, my love is come to me.

---

*The poet's brother William Michael Rossetti was unable to account for the happiness of this birthday poem, at least on the basis of any happiness in the author's actual life.*

# Remember

Remember me when I am gone away,
　　Gone far away into the silent land;
　　When you can no more hold me by the hand,
Nor I half turn to go yet turning stay.
Remember me when no more day by day
　　You tell me of our future that you planned:
　　Only remember me; you understand
It will be late to counsel then or pray.
Yet if you should forget me for a while
　　And afterwards remember, do not grieve:
　　For if the darkness and corruption leave
A vestige of the thoughts that once I had,
Better by far you should forget and smile
　　Than that you should remember and be sad.

---

*The sentiments here expressed are said to be associated with the Pre-Raphaelite painter James Collinson, to whom Christina Rossetti was briefly engaged.*

# "Lewis Carroll" (Charles Lutwidge Dodgson) 1832–1898

"Lewis Carroll" was an ordained minister, a talented amateur photographer, and an accomplished mathematician and classicist. A deeper, and perhaps darker, self communicated with children, mostly little girls. To amuse Alice Liddell, he wrote something first called "Alice's Adventures Underground," eventually published as *Alice's Adventures in Wonderland* (1865), followed by *Through the Looking-Glass and What Alice Found There* (1871).

# Jabberwocky

'Twas brillig, and the slithy toves
  Did gyre and gimble in the wabe;
All mimsy were the borogoves,
  And the mome raths out grabe.

"Beware the Jabberwock, my son!
  The jaws that bite, the claws that catch!
Beware the Jubjub bird, and shun
  The frumious Bandersnatch!"

He took his vorpal sword in hand:
  Long time the manxome foe he sought—
So rested he by the Tumtum tree,
  And stood awhile in thought.

And as in uffish thought he stood,
  The Jabberwock, with eyes of flame,
Came whiffling through the tulgey wood,
  And burbled as it came!

One, two! One, two! And through and through
   The vorpal blade went snicker-snack!
He left it dead, and with its head
   He went galumphing back.

"And hast thou slain the Jabberwock!
   Come to my arms, my beamish boy!
O frabjous day! Callooh! Callay!"
   He chortled in his joy.

'Twas brillig, and the slithy toves
   Did gyre and gimble in the wabe;
All mimsy were the borogoves,
   And the mome raths outgrabe.

from Through the Looking-Glass

---

*This poem—a version of which was published earlier as a joke "Stanza of Anglo-Saxon Poetry"—is in* Through the Looking-Glass, *where it is read by Alice and explicated by Humpty Dumpty. Formation of words by the blend or "portmanteau" device has become common, as in "motel," "smog," "palimony," and "modem." "Chortle," coined here by Carroll, is now a part of the language.*

# The Walrus and the Carpenter

>>>><<<<

The sun was shining on the sea,
  Shining with all his might:
He did his very best to make
  The billows smooth and bright—
And this was odd, because it was
  The middle of the night.

The moon was shining sulkily,
  Because she thought the sun
Had got no business to be there
  After the day was done—
"It's very rude of him," she said,
  "To come and spoil the fun!"

The sea was wet as wet could be,
  The sands were dry as dry.
You could not see a cloud, because
  No cloud was in the sky:
No birds were flying overhead—
  There were no birds to fly.

The Walrus and the Carpenter
  Were walking close at hand:
They wept like anything to see
  Such quantities of sand:
"If this were only cleared away,"
  They said, "it would be grand!"

"If seven maids with seven mops
  Swept it for half a year,
Do you suppose," the Walrus said,
  "That they could get it clear?"
"I doubt it," said the Carpenter,
  And shed a bitter tear.

"O Oysters, come and walk with us!"
  The Walrus did beseech.
"A pleasant walk, a pleasant talk,
  Along the briny beach:
We cannot do with more than four,
  To give a hand to each."

The eldest Oyster looked at him,
  But never a word he said:
The eldest Oyster winked his eye,
  And shook his heavy head—
Meaning to say he did not choose
  To leave the oyster-bed.

But four young Oysters hurried up,
  All eager for the treat:
Their coats were brushed, their faces washed,
  Their shoes were clean and neat—
And this was odd, because, you know,
  They hadn't any feet.

Four other Oysters followed them,
  And yet another four;
And thick and fast they came at last,
  And more, and more, and more—
All hopping through the frothy waves,
  And scrambling to the shore.

The Walrus and the Carpenter
  Walked on a mile or so,
And then they rested on a rock
  Conveniently low:
And all the little Oysters stood
  And waited in a row.

"The time has come," the Walrus said,
    "To talk of many things:
Of shoes—and ships—and sealing wax—
    Of cabbages—and kings—
And why the sea is boiling hot—
    And whether pigs have wings."

"But wait a bit," the Oysters cried,
    "Before we have our chat;
For some of us are out of breath,
    And all of us are fat!"
"No hurry!" said the Carpenter.
    They thanked him much for that.

"A loaf of bread," the Walrus said,
    "Is what we chiefly need:
Pepper and vinegar besides
    Are very good indeed—
Now, if you're ready, Oysters dear,
    We can begin to feed."

"But not on us!" the Oysters cried,
    Turning a little blue.
"After such kindness, that would be
    A dismal thing to do!"
"The night is fine," the Walrus said.
    "Do you admire the view?

"It was so kind of you to come!
    And you are very nice!"
The Carpenter said nothing but
    "Cut us another slice.
I wish you were not quite so deaf—
    I've had to ask you twice!"

"It seems a shame," the Walrus said,
  "To play them such a trick,
After we've brought them out so far,
  And made them trot so quick!"
The Carpenter said nothing but
  "The butter's spread too thick!"

"I weep for you," the Walrus said:
  "I deeply sympathize."
With sobs and tears he sorted out
  Those of the largest size,
Holding his pocket-handkerchief
  Before his streaming eyes.

"O Oysters," said the Carpenter,
  "You've had a pleasant run!
Shall we be trotting home again?"
  But answer came there none—
And this was scarcely odd, because
  They'd eaten every one.

from Through the Looking-Glass

---

*Tweedledee recites this lighthearted horror story in an augmented ballad stanza that had been used earlier by Coleridge (intermittently in "The Rime of the Ancient Mariner," p. 433) and by Thomas Hood; the form would be used later by Oscar Wilde in "The Ballad of Reading Gaol" (p. 810). The measure seems rather simple, but danger of some sort lurks just under the surface.*

# Father William

() ◄██► ()

"You are old, Father William," the young man said,
  "And your hair has become very white;
And yet you incessantly stand on your head—
  Do you think, at your age, it is right?"

"In my youth," Father William replied to his son,
  "I feared it might injure the brain;
But now that I'm perfectly sure I have none,
  Why, I do it again and again."

"You are old," said the youth, "as I mentioned before,
  And have grown most uncommonly fat;
Yet you turned a back somersault in at the door—
  Pray, what is the reason of that?"

"In my youth," said the sage, as he shook his gray locks,
  "I kept all my limbs very supple
By the use of this ointment—one shilling the box—
  Allow me to sell you a couple."

"You are old," said the youth, "and your jaws are too weak
  For anything tougher than suet;
Yet you finished the goose, with the bones and the beak—
  Pray, how did you manage to do it?"

"In my youth,"said his father, "I took to the law,
  And argued each case with my wife;
And the muscular strength, which it gave to my jaw,
  Has lasted the rest of my life."

"You are old," said the youth, "one would hardly suppose
  That your eye was as steady as ever;
Yet you balanced an eel on the end of your nose—
  What made you so awfully clever?"

"I have answered three questions, and that is enough,"
  Said his father; "don't give yourself airs!
Do you think I can listen all day to such stuff?
  Be off, or I'll kick you downstairs!"

from Alice's Adventures in Wonderland

---

*Only two or three of the 500 poems in this anthology qualify as proper parodies, aimed immediately at another poem. "Father William" parodies Robert Southey's "Old Man's Comforts" and follows its pattern of a dialogue in quatrains between "the young man" and Father William. Oddly for a parody, "Father William" is two stanzas longer than Southey's original.*

# I'll Tell Thee Everything I Can

"I'll tell thee everything I can;
  There's little to relate.
I saw an aged aged man,
  A-sitting on a gate.
'Who are you, aged man?' I said,
  'And how is it you live?'
And his answer trickled through my head
  Like water through a sieve.

He said, 'I look for butterflies
  That sleep among the wheat:
I make them into mutton-pies
  And sell them in the street.
I sell them unto men,' he said,
  'Who sail on stormy seas;
And that's the way I get my bread—
  A trifle, if you please.'

But I was thinking of a plan
  To dye one's whiskers green,
And always use so large a fan
  That they could not be seen.
So, having no reply to give
  To what the old man said,
I cried, 'Come, tell me how you live!'
  And thumped him on the head.

His accents mild took up the tale:
  He said, 'I go my ways,
And when I find a mountain rill,
  I set it in a blaze:
And thence they make a stuff they call
  Rowland's Macassar-Oil—
Yet twopence-halfpenny is all
  They give me for my toil.'

But I was thinking of a way
  To feed oneself on batter,
And so go on from day to day
  Getting a little fatter.
I shook him well from side to side,
  Until his face was blue:
'Come, tell me how you live,' I cried,
  'And what it is you do!'

He said, 'I hunt for haddocks' eyes
  Among the heather bright,
And work them into waistcoat buttons
  In the silent night.
And these I do not sell for gold
  Or coin of silvery shine,
But for a copper halfpenny,
  And that will purchase nine.

I sometimes dig for buttered rolls.
  Or set limed twigs for crabs;
I sometimes search the grassy knolls
  For wheels of hansom-cabs.
And that's the way' (he gave a wink)
  'By which I get my wealth—
And very gladly will I drink
  Your Honor's noble health.'

I heard him then, for I had just
   Completed my design
To keep the Menai bridge from rust
   By boiling it in wine.
I thanked him much for telling me
   The way he got his wealth,
But chiefly for his wish that he
   Might drink my noble health.

And now, if e'er by chance I put
   My fingers into glue,
Or madly squeeze a right-hand foot
   Into a left-hand shoe,
Or if I drop upon my toe
   A very heavy weight,
I weep, for it reminds me so
Of that old man I used to know—
Whose look was mild, whose speech was slow,
Whose hair was whiter than the snow,
Whose face was very like a crow,
With eyes, like cinders, all aglow,
Who seemed distracted with his woe,
Who rocked his body to and fro,
And muttered mumblingly and low,
As if his mouth were full of dough,
Who snorted like a buffalo—
That summer evening long ago
   A-sitting on a gate."

            from Through the Looking-Glass

---

*An early version of this travesty of Wordsworth's "Resolution and Independence" (p. 421) was published anonymously in a magazine before the* Alice *books.*

# How Doth the Little Crocodile

⟡⟡⟡⟡

How doth the little crocodile
　　Improve his shining tail,
And pour the waters of the Nile
　　On every golden scale!

How cheerfully he seems to grin,
　　How neatly spreads his claws,
And welcomes little fishes in
　　With gently smiling jaws!

from Alice's Adventures in Wonderland

---

*For many readers, this expert parody has so eclipsed the original (Isaac Watts's "Against Idleness and Mischief") that they may need to be reminded of it—at least of its first two stanzas:*

*How doth the little busy bee*
*　　Improve each shining hour,*
*And gather honey all the day*
*　　From every opening flower?*

*How skillfully she builds her cell!*
*　　How neat she spreads the wax!*
*And labours hard to store it well*
*　　With the sweet food she makes.*

# SIR WILLIAM SCHWENCK GILBERT 1836–1911

Gilbert's early career was as a writer and illustrator of comic verse (such as the ballad in this anthology), and he also wrote verse dramas. He is, however, much better known as the collaborator with Sir Arthur Sullivan on more than a dozen sparkling operettas.

# The Yarn of the Nancy Bell

'Twas on the shores that round our coast
   From Deal to Ramsgate span,
That I found alone on a piece of stone
   An elderly naval man.

His hair was weedy, his beard was long,
   And weedy and long was he,
And I heard this wight on the shore recite
   In a singular minor key:

"Oh, I am a cook and a captain bold,
   And the mate of the *Nancy* brig,
And a bo'sun tight, and a midshipmite,
   And the crew of the captain's gig."

And he shook his fists, and he tore his hair,
   Till I really felt afraid,
For I couldn't help thinking the man had been drinking,
   And so I simply said:

"Oh elderly man, it's little I know
   Of the duties of men of the sea,
And I'll eat my hand if I understand
   However you can be

At once a cook, and a captain bold,
　And the mate of the *Nancy* brig,
And a bo'sun tight, and a midshipmite,
　And the crew of the captain's gig."

Then he gave a hitch to his trousers, which
　Is a trick all seamen larn,
And having got rid of a thumping quid,
　He spun this painful yarn:

" 'Twas in the good ship *Nancy Bell*
　That we sailed to the Indian Sea,
And there on a reef we came to grief,
　Which has often occurred to me.

And pretty nigh all the crew was drowned
　(There was seventy-seven o'soul),
And only ten of the *Nancy's* men
　Said "Here!" to the muster-roll.

There was me and the cook and the captain bold,
　And the mate of the *Nancy* brig,
And the bo'sun tight, and a midshipmite,
　And the crew of the captain's gig.

For a month we'd neither wittles nor drink,
　Till a-hungry we did feel,
So we drawed a lot, and, accordin' shot
　The captain for our meal.

The next lot fell to the *Nancy's* mate,
　And a delicate dish he made;
Then our appetite with the midshipmite
　We seven survivors stayed.

And then we murdered the bo'sun tight,
  And he much resembled the pig;
Then we wittled free, did the cook and me,
  On the crew of the captain's gig.

Then only the cook and me was left,
  And the delicate question, "Which
Of us two goes to the kettle?" arose,
  And we argued it out as sich.

For I loved that cook as a brother, I did,
  And the cook he worshiped me;
But we'd both be blowed if we'd either be stowed
  In the other chap's hold, you see.

"I'll be eat if you dines off me," says Tom;
  "Yes, that" says I "you'll be—"
"I'm boiled if I die, my friend," quoth I;
  And "Exactly so," quoth he.

Says he, "Dear James, to murder me
  Were a foolish thing to do,
For don't you see that you can't cook *me*,
  While I can—and will—cook *you!*"

So he boils the water, and takes the salt
  And the pepper in portions true
(Which he never forgot) and some chopped shallot,
  And some sage and parsley too.

"Come here," says he, with a proper pride
  Which his smiling features tell,
" 'Twill soothing be if I let you see
  How extremely nice you'll smell."

And he stirred it round and round and round,
   And he sniffed at the foaming froth;
When I ups with his heels, and smothers his squeals
   In the scum of the boiling broth.

And I eat that cook in a week or less,
   And—as I eating be
The last of his chops, why, I almost drops,
   For a wessel in sight I see!
. . . . . . . . . . . . . . . . . . . . . . . . . . .

And I never larf, and I never smile,
   And I never lark nor play,
But sit and croak, a single joke
   I have—which is to say:

"Oh, I am a cook and a captain bold,
   And the mate of the *Nancy* brig,
And a bos'sun tight, and a midshipmite,
   And the crew of the captain's gig!"

---

*Gilbert said that this Victorian demonstration that you are indeed what you eat was the first of his "Bab" Ballads. It was offered to* Punch, *whose editor declined it "on the ground that it was 'too cannibalistic for his readers' tastes.' " Note how the "elderly naval man" resembles an "ancient mariner" (p. 433).*

# ALGERNON CHARLES
## SWINBURNE 1837–1909

Although he was associated with D. G. Rossetti and others of the Pre-Raphaelite group, Swinburne stood alone with his gift for gorgeous music and trenchant caricature (which includes a brilliant parody of his own poetry). He was a controversial figure in the last third of the nineteenth century, causing ripples of disapproval with his anti-Christian attitude, political idealism, devotion to masochism, and fondness for strong drink. But he was a fine critic (as his work on Chapman and Marlowe testifies), and he was a loyal supporter of worthy fellow-artists (as the tribute of Thomas Hardy eloquently demonstrates).


# *When the Hounds of Spring Are on Winter's Traces*

## ≫≫≫≫≫

When the hounds of spring are on winter's traces,
   The mother of months in meadow or plain
Fills the shadows and windy places
   With lisp of leaves and ripple of rain;
And the brown bright nightingale amorous
Is half assuaged for Itylus,
For the Thracian ships and the foreign faces,
   The tongueless vigil, and all the pain.

Come with bows bent and with emptying of quivers,
   Maiden most perfect, lady of light,
With a noise of winds and many rivers,
   With a clamour of waters, and with might;
Bind on thy sandals, O thou most fleet,
Over the splendour and speed of thy feet;
For the faint east quickens, the wan west shivers,
   Round the feet of the day and the feet of the night.

Where shall we find her, how shall we sing to her,
    Fold our hands round her knees, and cling?
O that man's heart were as fire and could spring to her,
    Fire, or the strength of the streams that spring!
For the stars and the winds are unto her
As raiment, as songs of the harp-player;
For the risen stars and the fallen cling to her,
    And the southwest-wind and the west-wind sing.

For winter's rains and ruins are over,
    And all the season of snows and sins;
The days dividing lover and lover,
    The light that loses, the night that wins;
And time remembered is grief forgotten,
And frosts are slain and flowers begotten,
And in green underwood and cover
    Blossom by blossom the spring begins.

The full streams feed on flower of rushes,
    Ripe grasses trammel a travelling foot,
The faint fresh flame of the young year flushes
    From leaf to flower and flower to fruit;
And fruit and leaf are as gold and fire,
And the oat is heard above the lyre,
And the hoofèd heel of a satyr crushes
    The chestnut-husk at the chestnut-root.

And Pan by noon and Bacchus by night,
    Fleeter of foot than the fleet-foot kid,
Follows with dancing and fills with delight
    The Mænad and the Bassarid;
And soft as lips that laugh and hide
The laughing leaves of the trees divide,
And screen from seeing and leave in sight
    The god pursuing, the maiden hid.

The ivy falls with the Bacchanal's hair
  Over her eyebrows hiding her eyes;
The wild vine slipping down leaves bare
  Her bright breast shortening into sighs;
The wild vine slips with the weight of its leaves,
But the berried ivy catches and cleaves
To the limbs that glitter, the feet that scare
  The wolf that follows, the fawn that flies.

from Atalanta in Calydon

---

*This is the first of several choruses in* Atalanta in Calydon, *Swinburne's early attempt at Greek-style verse-tragedy. The chorus uses both vigorous rhythm and vivid image to catch the spirit of pagan spring. The percussive alliteration, more like Old English than Greek, is one of Swinburne's most characteristic flourishes (a device that he was to mock in his self-caricaturing "Nephelidia": "From the depth of the dreamy decline of the dawn through a notable nimbus of nebulous noonshine . . .").*

# The Garden of Proserpine

Here, where the world is quiet;
Here, where all trouble seems
Dead winds' and spent waves' riot
In doubtful dreams of dreams;
I watch the green field growing
For reaping folk and sowing
For harvest-time and mowing,
A sleepy world of streams.

I am tired of tears and laughter,
And men that laugh and weep;
Of what may come hereafter
For men that sow to reap:
I am weary of days and hours,
Blown buds of barren flowers,
Desires and dreams and powers
And everything but sleep.

Here life has death for neighbour,
    And far from eye or ear
Wan waves and wet winds labour,
    Weak ships and spirits steer;
They drive adrift, and whither
They wot not who make thither;
But no such winds blow hither,
    And no such things grow here.

No growth of moor or coppice,
No heather-flower or vine,
But bloomless buds of poppies,
Green grapes of Proserpine,
Pale beds of blowing rushes
Where no leaf blooms or blushes
Save this whereout she crushes
For dead men deadly wine.

Pale, without name or number,
In fruitless fields of corn,
They bow themselves and slumber
All night till light is born;
And like a soul belated,
In hell and heaven unmated,
By cloud and mist abated
Comes out of darkness morn.

Though one were strong as seven,
He too with death shall dwell,
Nor wake with wings in heaven,
Nor weep for pains in hell;
Though one were fair as roses,
His beauty clouds and closes;
And well though love reposes,
In the end it is not well.

Pale, beyond porch and portal,
Crowned with calm leaves, she stands
Who gathers all things mortal
With cold immortal hands;
Her languid lips are sweeter
Than love's who fears to greet her
To men that mix and meet her
From many times and lands.

She waits for each and other,
　She waits for all men born;
Forgets the earth her mother,
　The life of fruits and corn;
And spring and seed and swallow
Take wing for her and follow
Where summer song rings hollow
　And flowers are put to scorn.

There go the loves that wither,
　The old loves with wearier wings;
And all dead years draw thither,
　And all disastrous things;
Dead dreams of days forsaken,
Blind buds that snows have shaken,
Wild leaves that winds have taken,
　Red strays of ruined springs.

We are not sure of sorrow,
　And joy was never sure;
To-day will die to-morrow;
　Time stoops to no man's lure;
And love, grown faint and fretful,
With lips but half regretful
Sighs, and with eyes forgetful
Weeps that no loves endure.

From too much love of living,
From hope and fear set free,
We thank with brief thanksgiving
Whatever gods may be
That no life lives for ever;
That dead men rise up never;
That even the weariest river
Winds somewhere safe to sea.

Then star nor sun shall waken,
Nor any change of light:
Nor sound of waters shaken,
Nor any sound or sight;
Nor wintry leaves nor vernal,
Nor days nor things diurnal;
Only the sleep eternal
In an eternal night.

---

*Swinburne's passion and learning were equally remarkable, and he was inspired in this poem by a still-potent nature myth that was attractive to the great adherents of classical stoicism, a myth associated with the cyclical recurrence of life. Proserpine—also called Proserpina, Persephone, and Kore—was the daughter of the earth goddess Demeter (Ceres). She spent part of her year aboveground and part in the underworld, where she was queen of the dead land. Her garden was in the world beyond. The key rhyme between "ever" and "river" is also found in Shelley's "Hellas."*

# THOMAS HARDY \text{1840–1928}

After some years as an architectural apprentice, Hardy began writing fiction and, over a thirty-year period, produced fourteen novels and several stories. Then, from 1898, in another thirty-year career, he produced eight volumes of poetry as well as the epic drama *The Dynasts*. Hardy is among the very few English-speaking writers who have any serious claim to superlative distinction in both fiction and poetry.

## *The Darkling Thrush*

I leant upon a coppice gate
  When Frost was specter-gray,
And Winter's dregs made desolate
  The weakening eye of day.
The tangled bine-stems scored the sky
  Like strings of broken lyres,
And all mankind that haunted nigh
  Had sought their household fires.

The land's sharp features seemed to be
  The Century's corpse outleant,
His crypt the cloudy canopy,
  The wind his death-lament.
The ancient pulse of germ and birth
  Was shrunken hard and dry,
And every spirit upon earth
  Seemed fervorless as I.

At once a voice arose among
  The bleak twigs overhead
In a full-hearted evensong
  Of joy illimited;
An aged thrush, frail, gaunt, and small,
  In blast-beruffled plume,
Had chosen thus to fling his soul
  Upon the growing gloom.

So little cause for carolings
  Of such ecstatic sound
Was written on terrestrial things
  Afar or nigh around,
That I could think there trembled through
  His happy good-night air
Some blessed Hope, whereof he knew
  And I was unaware.

---

*"The Darkling Thrush" is dated "31st December 1900": it is set on the last day of the nineteenth century (actually, it was published in a magazine a few days before that date). It is the evening of the end of the month, year, century; the author is sixty. The poem is also poised on a liminal gate, and it mentions two acts of* leaning.

# The Oxen

Christmas Eve, and twelve of the clock.
   "Now they are all on their knees,"
An elder said as we sat in a flock
   By the embers in hearthside ease.

We pictured the meek and mild creatures where
   They dwelt in their strawy pen,
Nor did it occur to one of us there
   To doubt they were kneeling then.

So fair a fancy few would weave
   In these years! Yet, I feel,
If someone said on Christmas Eve,
   "Come; see the oxen kneel,

"In the lonely barton by yonder coomb
   Our childhood used to know,"
I should go with him in the gloom,
   Hoping it might be so.

---

*As with "The Darkling Thrush" (p. 770), we see here a poem set on a holiday and ending on a conditional note of hope somehow stimulated by the behavior of animals.*

# In Time of "The Breaking of Nations"

Only a man harrowing clods
    In a slow silent walk
With an old horse that stumbles and nods
    Half asleep as they stalk.

Only thin smoke without flame
    From the heaps of couch-grass;
Yet this will go onward the same
    Though Dynasties pass.

Yonder a maid and her wight
    Come whispering by:
War's annals will cloud into night
    Ere their story die.

---

*The title comes from the account in Jeremiah in the Bible of God's judgment against Babylon. The immediate occasion of the poem is the First World War, but Hardy claimed to have planned the poem as early as 1870, the time of the Franco-Prussian War. The lovely stanza, graced by the long third line, recalls that in Tennyson's "Crossing the Bar" (p. 644).*

# Channel Firing

That night your great guns, unawares,
Shook all our coffins as we lay,
And broke the chancel window-squares,
We thought it was the Judgment-day

And sat upright. While drearisome
Arose the howl of wakened hounds:
The mouse let fall the altar-crumb,
The worms drew back into the mounds,

The glebe cow drooled. Till God called, "No;
It's gunnery practice out at sea
Just as before you went below;
The world is as it used to be:

"All nations striving strong to make
Red war yet redder. Mad as hatters
They do no more for Christés sake
Than you who are helpless in such matters.

"That this is not the judgment-hour
For some of them's a blessed thing,
For if it were they'd have to scour
Hell's floor for so much threatening. . . .

"Ha, ha. It will be warmer when
I blow the trumpet (if indeed
I ever do; for you are men,
And rest eternal sorely need)."

So down we lay again. "I wonder,
Will the world ever saner be,"
Said one, "than when He sent us under
In our indifferent century!"

And many a skeleton shook his head.
"Instead of preaching forty year,"
My neighbor Parson Thirdly said,
"I wish I had stuck to pipes and beer."

Again the guns disturbed the hour,
Roaring their readiness to avenge,
As far inland as Stourton Tower,
And Camelot, and starlit Stonehenge.

---

*A flat expression — "Loud enough to wake the dead" — is given new life and depth here in a poem that eccentrically but convincingly mixes humor and pathos. The reader of Hardy's greatest novel,* Tess of the d'Urbervilles, *will remember how that book, set about thirty years before this poem, places the capture of Tess at Stonehenge, on Salisbury Plain in Hardy's native Wessex. Even in 1914, it was technically possible for the sound of naval gunfire in the Channel to be heard many miles inland.*

# Afterwards

When the Present has latched its postern behind my tremulous
stay,
   And the May month flaps its glad green leaves like wings,
Delicate-filmed as new-spun silk, will the neighbors say,
   "He was a man who used to notice such things"?

If it be in the dusk when, like an eyelid's soundless blink,
   The dewfall-hawk comes crossing the shades to alight
Upon the wind-warped upland thorn, a gazer may think,
   "To him this must have been a familiar sight."

If I pass during some nocturnal blackness, mothy and warm,
   When the hedgehog travels furtively over the lawn,
One may say, "He strove that such innocent creatures should
     come to no harm,
   But he could do little for them; and now he is gone."

If, when hearing that I have been stilled at last, they stand at the
door,
   Watching the full-starred heavens that winter sees,
Will this thought rise on those who will meet my face no more,
   "He was one who had an eye for such mysteries"?

And will any say when my bell of quittance is heard in the
gloom,
   And a crossing breeze cuts a pause in its outrollings,
Till they rise again, as they were a new bell's bloom,
   "He hears it not now, but used to notice such things"?

---

*As the fourteen novels, eight volumes of poetry, and several other works over-whelmingly testify, Hardy did notice things and did devote his genius to setting down the truth about innocent creatures.*

# The Convergence of the Twain

◆◆◆◆◆

(Lines on the loss of the *Titanic*)

1

In a solitude of the sea
Deep from human vanity,
And the Pride of Life that planned her, stilly couches she.

2

Steel chambers, late the pyres
Of her salamandrine fires,
Cold currents thrid, and turn to rhythmic tidal lyres.

3

Over the mirrors meant
To glass the opulent
The sea-worm crawls—grotesque, slimed, dumb, indifferent.

4

Jewels in joy designed
To ravish the sensuous mind
Lie lightless, all their sparkles bleared and black and blind.

5

Dim moon-eyed fishes near
Gaze at the gilded gear
And query: "What does this vaingloriousness down here?" . . .

6

Well: while was fashioning
This creature of cleaving wing,
The Immanent Will that stirs and urges everything

7

Prepared a sinister mate
For her—so gaily great—
A Shape of Ice, for the time far and dissociate.

8

And as the smart ship grew
In stature, grace, and hue,
In shadowy silent distance grew the Iceberg too.

9

Alien they seemed to be:
No mortal eye could see
The intimate welding of their later history,

10

Or sign that they were bent
By paths coincident
On being anon twin halves of one august event,

11

Till the Spinner of the Years
Said "Now!" And each one hears,
And consummation comes, and jars two hemispheres.

---

*Whitman's "When Lilacs Last in the Dooryard Bloomed" (p. 694), Yeats's "Easter 1916" (p. 864), and Eliot's "Waste Land" (p. 968), like this poem from Hardy's* Satires of Circumstance, *could all be classified as "April elegies." The irony is right on the surface: the ship had a divine name, was advertised as unsinkable, and sank on her maiden voyage. The stanza (meter and rhyme) seems to be adapted from that in Robert Browning's "Rabbi ben Ezra."*

# The Man He Killed

"Had he and I but met
By some old ancient inn,
We should have sat us down to wet
Right many a nipperkin!

"But ranged as infantry,
And staring face to face,
I shot at him as he at me,
And killed him in his place.

"I shot him dead because—
Because he was my foe,
Just so: my foe of course he was;
That's clear enough; although

"He thought he'd 'list, perhaps,
Off-hand—just as I—
Was out of work—had sold his traps—
No other reason why.

"Yes; quaint and curious war is!
You shoot a fellow down
You'd treat if met where any bar is,
Or help to half-a-crown."

---

*The date 1902 attaches the poem to the Boer War, about which Hardy wrote several poems. The stanza (meter and rhyme) is what hymnals call Short Measure; it was used by few poets except Hardy and Dickinson, who was ten years his senior. (See "There's a certain Slant of light," p. 732, "A Bird Came down the Walk," p. 733, and "I never saw a Moor," p. 741). The stanza seems best adapted for use in elementary situations like war and peace, life and death.*

# Neutral Tones

>>>>>>>

We stood by a pond that winter day,
And the sun was white, as though chidden of God,
And a few leaves lay on the starving sod;
   —They had fallen from an ash, and were gray.

Your eyes on me were as eyes that rove
Over tedious riddles of years ago;
And some words played between us to and fro
   On which lost the more by our love.

The smile on your mouth was the deadest thing
Alive enough to have strength to die;
And a grin of bitterness swept thereby
   Like an ominous bird a-wing. . . .

Since then, keen lessons that love deceives,
And wrings with wrong, have shaped to me
Your face, and the God-curst sun, and a tree,
   And a pond edged with grayish leaves.

---

*A sonnet called "Hap" (dated 1866) and this poem (dated 1867) are both recalled in "He Never Expected Much," written about sixty years later. The World tells the aged speaker:*

    *"I do not promise overmuch,*
       *Child, overmuch;*
    *Just neutral-tinted haps and such."*

# The Ruined Maid

"O 'Melia, my dear, this does everything crown!
Who could have supposed I should meet you in Town?
And whence such fair garments, such prosperi-ty?"— "O didn't
you know I'd been ruined?" said she.

—"You left us in tatters, without shoes or socks,
Tired of digging potatoes, and spudding up docks;
And now you've gay bracelets and bright feathers three!"
"Yes: that's how we dress when we we're ruined," said she.

—"At home in the barton you said 'thee' and 'thou,'
And 'thik oon,' and 'theas oon,' and 't'other'; but now
Your talking quite fits 'ee for high compa-ny!"—
"Some polish is gained with one's ruin," said she.

—"Your hands were like paws then, your face blue and bleak
But now I'm bewitched by your delicate cheek,
And your little gloves fit as on any la-dy!"—
"We never do work when we're ruined," said she.

—"You used to call home-life a hag-ridden dream,
And you'd sigh, and you'd sock; but at present you seem
To know not of megrims or melancho-ly!"—
"True. One's pretty lively when ruined," said she.

—"I wish I had feathers, a fine sweeping gown,
And a delicate face, and could strut about Town!"— "My
dear—a raw country girl, such as you be,
Cannot quite expect that. You ain't ruined," said she.

*Hardy had a humorous side and could produce a mock-ballad in which a whole story (not so different from that of Tess Durbeyfield, after all) is told purely by a dialogue between two speakers who repeat the same rhyme-word, like a refrain. Hardy's "blue and bleak" here and Hopkins's "blue-bleak" in "The Windhover" (p. 790) seem to have been written independently.*

# The Voice

Woman much missed, how you call to me, call to me,
Saying that now you are not as you were
When you had changed from the one who was all to me,
But as at first, when our day was fair.

Can it be you that I hear? Let me view you, then,
Standing as when I drew near to the town
Where you would wait for me: yes, as I knew you then,
Even to the original air-blue gown!

Or is it only the breeze, in its listlessness
Travelling across the wet mead to me here,
You being ever dissolved to wan wistlessness,
Heard no more again far or near?

Thus I; faltering forward,
Leaves around me falling,
Wind oozing thin through the thorn from norward,
And the woman calling.

---

*As Catherine Frank notes, the twenty-one works that make up* Poems of 1912–13 *are all in different forms. "The Voice" complements "The Haunter," which is spoken by the woman addressed here. Hardy and his first wife, Emma, seemed to be living a bitterly strained existence for many years, at least for the last twenty years of their marriage, but, when she died in November 1912, he let all the bitterness go and returned most touchingly to their earliest days together, more than forty years before.*

# During Wind and Rain

They sing their dearest songs—
He, she, all of them—yea,
Treble and tenor and bass,
    And one to play;
With the candles mooning each face. . . .
    Ah, no; the years O!
How the sick leaves reel down in throngs!

They clear the creeping moss—
Elders and juniors—aye,
Making the pathways neat
    And the garden gay;
And they build a shady seat. . . .
    Ah, no; the years, the years;
See, the white storm-birds wing across!

They are blithely breakfasting all—
Men and maidens—yea,
Under the summer tree,
    With a glimpse of the bay,
While pet fowl come to the knee. . . .
    Ah, no; the years O!
And the rotten rose is ript from the wall.

They change to a high new house,
He, she, all of them—aye,
Clocks and carpets and chairs
    On the lawn all day,
And brightest things that are theirs. . . .
    Ah, no; the years, the years;
Down their carved names the rain-drop ploughs.

*The weather here, as well as the songs, may come from Shakespeare's "When That I Was and a Little Tiny Boy" (p. 103). Robert Frost's late poem called "The Wind and the Rain" owes a debt to Shakespeare and to Hardy and to many other bards who were weather-wise.*

# ROBERT BRIDGES 1844-1930

Trained in medicine, Bridges was an admirable versifier and an influential student of prosody (particularly Milton's). He was the first editor of the poems of Gerard Manley Hopkins, who had been a good friend and robust correspondent. Bridges's long tenure as Poet Laureate covered an important period of the twentieth century (1913–1930).

## London Snow

><><><><

When men were all asleep the snow came flying,
In large white flakes falling on the city brown,
Stealthily and perpetually settling and loosely lying,
   Hushing the latest traffic of the drowsy town;
Deadening, muffling, stifling its murmurs failing;
Lazily and incessantly floating down and down:
   Silently sifting and veiling road, roof and railing;
Hiding difference, making unevenness even,
Into angles and crevices softly drifting and sailing.
   All night it fell, and when full inches seven
It lay in the depth of its uncompacted lightness,
The clouds blew off from a high and frosty heaven;
   And all woke earlier for the unaccustomed brightness
Of the winter dawning, the strange unheavenly glare:
The eye marvelled—marvelled at the dazzling whiteness;
   The ear hearkened to the stillness of the solemn air;
No sound of wheel rumbling nor of foot falling,
And the busy morning cries came thin and spare.
   Then boys I heard, as they went to school, calling,
They gathered up the crystal manna to freeze
Their tongues with tasting, their hands with snowballing;
   Or rioted in a drift, plunging up to the knees;
Or peering up from under the white-mossed wonder,

"O look at the trees!" they cried, "O look at the trees!"
With lessened load a few carts creak and blunder,
Following along the white deserted way,
A country company long dispersed asunder:
When now already the sun, in pale display
Standing by Paul's high dome, spread forth below
His sparkling beams, and awoke the stir of the day.
For now doors open, and war is waged with the snow;
And trains of sombre men, past tale of number,
Tread long brown paths, as toward their toil they go:
But even for them awhile no cares encumber
Their minds diverted; the daily word is unspoken,
The daily thoughts of labour and sorrow slumber
At the sight of the beauty that greets them, for the charm they
    have broken.

---

*Bridges, a bold experimenter if not an avant-garde iconoclast, here seems to be testing how much ongoing activity a poem can register with words ending in -ing. (See also Emerson's "Snow-Storm," p. 574, and Whittier's "Snow-Bound," p. 593, for American versions of the same sort of picture.)*

# Nightingales

Beautiful must be the mountains whence ye come,
And bright in the fruitful valleys the streams, wherefrom
Ye learn your song:
Where are those starry woods? O might I wander there,
Among the flowers, which in that heavenly air
Bloom the year long!

Nay, barren are those mountains and spent the streams:
Our song is the voice of desire, that haunts our dreams,
A throe of the heart,
Whose pining visions dim, forbidden hopes profound,
No dying cadence nor long sigh can sound,
For all our art.

Alone, aloud in the raptured ear of men
We pour our dark nocturnal secret; and then,
As night is withdrawn
From these sweet-springing meads and bursting boughs of May,
Dream, while the innumerable choir of day
Welcome the dawn.

---

*The human speaker says only the first stanza. By imagining that nightingales can respond to our speculative addresses, Bridges gives a new interpretation to the "selfsame song" that Keats heard in an earlier May (p. 542).*

Hopkins converted to Catholicism while an Oxford undergraduate and became a Jesuit priest in 1877. He wrote little, and none of his poetry was published in his lifetime. Idiosyncrasies of diction and prosody set his poems apart from those of his contemporaries and delayed the appreciation of his genius for many decades. Even now we are still learning to appreciate his innovations, which are testimony to the authenticity of Hopkins's enormous feeling—ecstasy in many cases, desperation in a few.

# Pied Beauty

Glory be to God for dappled things—
    For skies of couple-colour as a brinded cow;
       For rose-moles all in stipple upon trout that swim;
Fresh-firecoal chestnut-falls; finches' wings;
    Landscape plotted and pieced—fold, fallow, and plough;
       And áll trádes, their gear and tackle and trim.
All things counter, original, spare, strange;
    Whatever is fickle, freckled (who knows how?)
       With swift, slow; sweet, sour; adazzle, dim;
He fathers-forth whose beauty is past change:
       Praise him.

---

*The first words of this poem echo the motto of the Society of Jesus:* Ad maiorem Dei gloriam, *"To the greater glory of God." Just as "The Windhover" (p. 790) puts a dangerous predator in the place of the meek Dove of conventional Christian symbolism, "Pied Beauty" puts changeable nature, freckled and fickle, in the place of the immutable spotlessness of a remote Platonic ideal.*

# The Windhover

## To Christ Our Lord

≪≪≪

I caught this morning morning's minion, king-
    dom of daylight's dauphin, dapple-dawn-drawn
        Falcon, in his riding
Of the rolling level underneath him steady
    air, and striding
High there, how he rung upon the rein of a wimpling
    wing
In his ecstasy! then, off, off forth on swing,
    As a skate's heel sweeps smooth on a bow-bend:
        the hurl and gliding
    Rebuffed the big wind. My heart in hiding
Stirred for a bird,—the achieve of, the mastery of the
    thing!

Brute beauty and valour and act, oh, air, pride,
    plume, here
    Buckle! AND the fire that breaks from thee then, a
        billion
Times told lovelier, more dangerous, O my chevalier!

    No wonder of it: shéer plód makes plough down
        sillion
Shine, and blue-bleak embers, ah my dear,
    Fall, gall themselves, and gash gold-vermilion.

*After the fantastic description of the bird in the first nine lines, Hopkins turns to the poem's divine addressee and asserts that His glory is a billion times greater (a British billion: 1,000,000,000,000). The comparison of Christ to a million-million predators is breathtaking enough, to be sure, but the final three lines are even more spectacular. In imagery drawn from accounts of the Crucifixion ("gall" and "gash") and the Eucharist (gold-vermilion parallel to bread-wine, in turn parallel to flesh-blood), the ember sends out brilliant light. (Note that: "sillion" is "ridge between furrows.")*

# God's Grandeur

>>>>>>>

The world is charged with the grandeur of God.
　　It will flame out, like shining from shook foil;
　　It gathers to a greatness, like the ooze of oil
Crushed. Why do men then now not reck his rod?
Generations have trod, have trod, have trod;
　　And all is seared with trade; bleared, smeared with toil;
　　And wears man's smudge and shares man's smell: the soil
Is bare now, nor can foot feel, being shod.

And for all this, nature is never spent;
　　There lives the dearest freshness deep down things;
And though the last lights off the black West went
　　Oh, morning, at the brown brink eastward, springs—
Because the Holy Ghost over the bent
　　World broods with warm breast and with ah! bright wings.

---

*As we see with "Pied Beauty" (p. 789), a good deal of Hopkins's practice as a poet was devoted to living up to the motto of the Jesuit order to which he belonged: "To the greater glory of God."*

# Spring and Fall

•✐•

Márgarét, áre you grieving
Over Goldengrove unleaving?
Leáves, líke the things of man, you
With your fresh thoughts care for, can you?
Ah! ás the heart grows older
It will come to such sights colder
By and by, nor spare a sigh
Though worlds of wanwood leafmeal lie;
And yet you *will* weep and know why.
Now no matter, child, the name:
Sórrow's spríngs áre the same.
Nor mouth had, no nor mind, expressed
What heart heard of, ghost guessed:
It ís the blight man was born for,
It is Margaret you mourn for.

---

*All but three of the words in this poem are of Germanic extraction, and Hopkins uses the Germanic "sprung" rhythm that counts only stressed syllables. He also makes up words like "wanwood" and "leafmeal" on a Germanic basis—all with the effect of primal strangeness but also of undeniable originality and sincerity.*

# *Felix Randal*

Felix Randal the farrier, O he is dead then? my duty all ended,
Who have watched his mold of man, big-boned and hardy-
    handsome
Pining, pining, till time when reason rambled in it and some
Fatal four disorders, fleshed there, all contended?

Sickness broke him. Impatient he cursed at first, but mended
Being anointed and all; though a heavenlier heart began some
Months earlier, since I had our sweet reprieve and ransom
Tendered to him. Ah, well, God rest him all road ever he
    offended!

This seeing the sick endears them to us, us too it endears.
My tongue had taught the comfort, touch had quenched thy
    tears,
Thy tears that touched my heart, child, Felix, poor Felix
    Randal;

How far from then forethought of, all thy more boisterous
    years,
When thou at the random grim forge, powerful amidst peers,
Didst fettle for the great gray drayhorse his bright and
    battering sandal!

---

*The Latin for "iron," ferrum, gives us "farrier," which means "blacksmith."
Here Hopkins uses language with great physical force to represent a man and a
job of great physical force. A fifteenth-century poem called "The Smiths" begins,
"Swarte-smeked smethes, smatered with smoke" ("Swart-smocked smiths,
smirched with smoke"). Nowadays, a century after Hopkins's death, few people
have ever seen a smith at work.*

# No Worst, There Is None

No worst, there is none. Pitched past pitch of grief,
More pangs will, schooled at forepangs, wilder wring.
Comforter, where, where is your comforting?
Mary, mother of us, where is your relief?
My cries heave, herds-long; huddle in a main, a chief-
woe, world-sorrow; on an age-old anvil wince and sing—
Then lull, then leave off. Fury had shrieked "No ling-
ering! Let me be fell: force I must be brief."
O the mind, mind has mountains; cliffs of fall
Frightful, sheer, no-man-fathomed. Hold them cheap
May who ne'er hung there. Nor does long our small
Durance deal with that steep or deep. Here! creep,
Wretch, under a comfort serves in a whirlwind: all
Life death does end and each day dies with sleep.

---

*This poem, the next poem, and "Carrion Comfort" (p. 802) belong to the group called "Terrible Sonnets" that Hopkins wrote towards the end of his life. The diction of these poems is somewhat more restrained and chastened than that in Hopkins's earlier poems.*

# Thou Art Indeed Just, Lord

Justus quidem tu es, Domine, si disputem tecum;
verumtamen justa loquar ad te: Quare via impiorum
prosperatur? &c.

Thou art indeed just, Lord, if I contend
With thee; but, sir, so what I plead is just.
Why do sinners' ways prosper? and why must
Disappointment all I endeavour end?

Wert thou my enemy, O thou my friend,
How wouldst thou worse, I wonder, than thou dost
Defeat, thwart me? Oh, the sots and thralls of lust
Do in spare hours more thrive than I that spend,

Sir, life upon thy cause. See, banks and brakes
Now, leavèd how thick! lacèd they are again
With fretty chervil, look, and fresh wind shakes

Them; birds build—but not I build; no, but strain,
Time's eunuch, and not breed one work that wakes.
Mine, O thou lord of life, send my roots rain.

---

*Manuscripts of this spare sonnet are dated March 17, 1889, and Hopkins died less than three months later, on June 8, seven weeks short of his forty-fifth birthday. Much of the poem translates and extends the twelfth chapter of Jeremiah.*

# Spring

()◄███►()

Nothing is so beautiful as Spring—
　　When weeds, in wheels, shoot long and lovely and lush;
　　Thrush's eggs look little low heavens, and thrush
Through the echoing timber does so rinse and wring
The ear, it strikes like lightnings to hear him sing;
　　The glassy peartree leaves and blooms, they brush
　　The descending blue; that blue is all in a rush
With richness; the racing lambs too have fair their fling.

What is all this juice and all this joy?
　　A strain of the earth's sweet being in the beginning
In Eden garden.—Have, get, before it cloy,

　　Before it cloud, Christ, lord, and sour with sinning,
Innocent mind and Mayday in girl and boy,
　　Most, O maid's child, thy choice and worthy the winning.

---

*Manuscripts of this poem are dated "May 1877." Hopkins says in "The May Magnificat" that "May is Mary's month." "Spring" recalls the association of Mary's month with that of Maia, a Roman earth goddess. Also present, possibly, is the tradition that the Creation, the Fall, and the Crucifixion all happened in the spring (usually in April).*

# Heaven-Haven

I have desired to go
  Where springs not fail,
To fields where flies no sharp and sided hail
  And a few lilies blow.

And I have asked to be
  Where no storms come,
Where the green swell is in the havens dumb,
  And out of the swing of the sea.

---

*The consonance of "heaven" and "haven," though audible to any speaker of English, is traceable to a poem by George Herbert called "The Size." The quatrain with a gracefully prolonged third line is also used in Tennyson's "Crossing the Bar" (p. 644) and Hardy's "In Time of 'The Breaking of Nations' " (p. 773).*

# Inversnaid

◆◆◆◆◆

This darksome burn, horseback brown,
His rollrock highroad roaring down,
In coop and in comb the fleece of his foam
Flutes and low to the lake falls home.

A windpuff-bonnet of fáwn-fróth
Turns and twindles over the broth
Of a pool so pitchblack, féll frówning,
It rounds and rounds Despair to drowning.

Degged with dew, dappled with dew
Are the groins of the braes that the brook treads through,
Wiry heathpacks, flitches of fern,
And the beadbonny ash that sits over the burn.

What would the world be, once bereft
Of wet and of wildness? Let them be left,
O let them be left, wildness and wet;
Long live the weeds and the wilderness yet.

---

*Here is Hopkins at his wittiest. Unlike the grandeur and beauty celebrated in many of his more popular poems, "Inversnaid" — even the name is unattractive — could be called "Pied Ugliness." The landscape and history of Scotland are fearsome: "one fell swoop" comes from Macbeth; but this pitchblack pool is so absurdly "fell-frowning" that it cheers one up. No one claims that Hopkins invented Rock n' Roll, but in his coinage "rollrock" the two key terms are combined for the first time.*

# The Habit of Perfection

Elected Silence, sing to me
And beat upon my whorlèd ear,
Pipe me to pastures still and be
The music that I care to hear.

Shape nothing, lips; be lovely-dumb:
It is the shut, the curfew sent
From there where all surrenders come
Which only makes you eloquent.

Be shellèd, eyes, with double dark
And find the uncreated light:
This ruck and reel which you remark
Coils, keeps, and teases simple sight.

Palate, the hutch of tasty lust,
Desire not to be rinsed with wine:
The can must be so sweet, the crust
So fresh that come in fasts divine!

Nostrils, your careless breath that spend
Upon the stir and keep of pride,
What relish shall the censers send
Along the sanctuary side!

O feel-of-primrose hands, O feet
That want the yield of plushy sward,
But you shall walk the golden street
And you unhouse and house the Lord.

And, Poverty, be thou the bride
And now the marriage feast begun,
And lily-coloured clothes provide
Your spouse not laboured-at nor spun.

---

*Readers are accustomed to erotic poems that systematically itemize the beloved's physical charms: Shakespeare's Sonnet CXXX (p. 99), Campion's "There Is a Garden in Her Face" (p. 116), and Herrick's "Delight in Disorder" (p. 174) are distinguished examples. Here, however, the austere Jesuit Hopkins converts the erotic conventions to a catalogue of asceticism, which, in its way, can be as rewarding.*

# Carrion Comfort

≫≫≫≫≫

Not, I'll not, carrion comfort, Despair, not feast on thee:
Not untwist—slack they may be—these last strands of man
In me ór, most weary, cry *I can no more*. I can;
Can something, hope, wish day come, not choose not to be.

But ah, but O thou terrible, why wouldst thou rude on me
Thy wring-world right foot rock? lay a lionlimb against me? scan
With darksome devouring eyes my bruisèd bones? and fan,
O in turns of tempest, me heaped there; me frantic to avoid thee
    and flee?

Why? That my chaff might fly; my grain lie, sheer and clear.
Nay in all that toil, that coil, since (seems) I kissed the rod,
Hand rather, my heart lo! lapped strength, stole joy, would
    laugh, chéer.
Cheer whom though? The hero whose heaven-handling flung me,
    fóot tród
Me? or me that fought him? O which one? is it each one? That
    night, that year
Of now done darkness I wretch lay wrestling with (my God!)
    my God.

---

*This poem, untitled by Hopkins, is grouped with six or seven others called
Terrible Sonnets, Dark Sonnets, or Sonnets of Desolation (see also "No Worst,
There Is None," p. 795). The rejection of Despair resembles the drowning of
Despair in "Inversnaid" (p. 799). Significantly, the earlier parts of the poem
echo the Old Testament, while the later echo the New Testament.*

# E UGENE  F IELD  1850–1895

For more than a quarter of his short life, Field was a Chicago newspaper columnist in the old style, writing anecdotes and verses, some in the so-called dialect that was immensely popular at the time. Some of his poems for the juvenile market gained added popularity by being set to music.

## *Wynken, Blynken, and Nod*

Wynken, Blynken, and Nod one night
Sailed off in a wooden shoe—
Sailed on a river of crystal light,
Into a sea of dew.
"Where are you going, and what do you wish?"
The old moon asked the three.
"We have come to fish for the herring fish
That live in this beautiful sea;
Nets of silver and gold have we!"
Said Wynken,
Blynken,
And Nod.

The old moon laughed and sang a song,
As they rocked in the wooden shoe,
And the wind that sped them all night long
Ruffled the waves of dew.
The little stars were the herring fish
That lived in that beautiful sea— — —
"Now cast your nets wherever you wish— — —
Never afeard are we";
So cried the stars to the fishermen three:
Wynken,
Blynken,
And Nod.

All night long their nets they threw
    To the stars in the twinkling foam— — —
Then down from the skies came the wooden shoe,
    Bringing the fishermen home;
'T was all so pretty a sail it seemed
    As if it could not be,
And some folks thought 'twas a dream they'd dreamed
    Of sailing that beautiful sea— — —
    But I shall name you the fishermen three:
Wynken,
Blynken,
And Nod.

Wynken and Blynken are two little eyes,
    And Nod is a little head,
And the wooden shoe that sailed the skies
    Is a wee one's trundle-bed.
So shut your eyes while your mother sings
    Of wonderful sights that be,
And you shall see the beautiful things
    As you rock in the misty sea,
    Where the old shoe rocked the fishermen three:
Wynken,
Blynken,
And Nod.

---

*People charged with the care of small children will recognize the functional tendency of children's stories to be sleep-inducing. Field cleverly added the Knickerbocker-Dutch element (and "Wynken" is close to a real Dutch name) and the anatomical allegory of winkin', blinkin', and nod.*

# The Duel

The gingham dog and the calico cat
Side by side on the table sat;
'Twas half-past twelve, and (what do you think!)
Nor one nor t' other had slept a wink!
　The old Dutch clock and the Chinese plate
　Appeared to know as sure as fate
There was going to be a terrible spat.

　　*(I wasn't there; I simply state*
　　*What was told to me by the Chinese plate!)*

The gingham dog went "bow-wow-wow!"
And the calico cat replied "mee-ow!"
The air was littered, an hour or so,
With bits of gingham and calico,
　While the old Dutch clock in the chimney-place
　Up with its hands before its face,
For it always dreaded a family row!

　　*(Now mind: I'm only telling you*
　　*What the old Dutch clock declares is true!)*

The Chinese plate looked very blue,
And wailed, "Oh, dear! what shall we do!"
But the gingham dog and the calico cat
Wallowed this way and tumbled that,
　Employing every tooth and claw
　In the awfullest way you ever saw—
And, oh! how the gingham and calico flew!

*(Don't fancy I exaggerate —*
*I got my news from the Chinese plate!)*

Next morning, where the two had sat
They found no trace of dog or cat;
And some folks think unto this day
That burglars stole that pair away!
   But the truth about the cat and pup
   Is this: they ate each other up!
Now what do you really think of that!

*(The old Dutch clock it told me so,*
*And that is how I came to know.)*

---

*Folklore contains innumerable tales of a vicious fight between mutually destructive adversaries. Children still get a kick out of re-staging the great bout.*

Stevenson belongs in the company of Scott, Poe, and Wilde, whose works in prose and verse have appealed to a mass audience and continue to do so via movies, radio, television, and the vernacular. Thanks to Stevenson, we can talk about "Jekyll-Hyde" personalities, and recent congressional hearings touched on a vulgar variant of "Long John Silver." In addition to his poetry and fiction, Stevenson wrote many essays and travel books.

# Requiem

Under the wide and starry sky,
Dig the grave and let me lie.
Glad did I live and gladly die,
    And I laid me down with a will.

This be the verse you grave for me:
*Here he lies where he longed to be;*
*Home is the sailor, home from the sea,*
    *And the hunter home from the hill.*

---

*T. S. Eliot recollected one part of Stevenson's little poem in the third part of "The Waste Land" (p. 968). Philip Larkin borrowed another part for the title of the late poem "This Be the Verse."*

# EDWIN MARKHAM 1852–1940

Markham was born in Oregon and lived more than half
of his life in California, where he was a schoolteacher.
His poetry, which was extremely popular, recorded
genuine sentiments of pity and patriotism.

## The Man with the Hoe

✖✖✖✖✖✖

God made man in His own image,
in the image of God he made him.

Genesis

Bowed by the weight of centuries he leans
Upon his hoe and gazes on the ground,
The emptiness of ages in his face,
And on his back the burden of the world.
Who made him dead to rapture and despair,
A thing that grieves not and that never hopes,
Stolid and stunned, a brother to the ox?
Who loosened and let down this brutal jaw?
Whose was the hand that slanted back this brow?
Whose breath blew out the light within this brain?

Is this the Thing the Lord God made and gave
To have dominion over sea and land?
To trace the stars and search the heavens for power;
To feel the passion of Eternity?
Is this the dream He dreamed who shaped the suns
And marked their ways upon the ancient deep?
Down all the caverns of Hell to their last gulf
There is no shape more terrible than this —
More tongued with censure of the world's blind greed —
More filled with signs and portents for the soul —
More packt with danger to the universe.

[808]

What gulfs between him and the seraphim!
Slave of the wheel of labor, what to him
Are Plato and the swing of Pleiades?
What the long reaches of the peaks of song,
The rift of dawn, the reddening of the rose?
Through this dread shape the suffering ages look;
Time's tragedy is in that aching stoop;
Through this dread shape humanity betrayed,
Plundered, profaned and disinherited,
Cries protest to the Powers that made the world,
A protest that is also prophecy.

O masters, lords and rulers in all lands,
Is this the handiwork you give to God,
This monstrous thing distorted and soul-quencht?
How will you ever straighten up this shape;
Touch it again with immortality;
Give back the upward looking and the light;
Rebuild in it the music and the dream;
Make right the immemorial infamies,
Perfidious wrongs, immedicable woes?

O masters, lords and rulers in all lands,
How will the future reckon with this Man?
How answer his brute question in that hour
When whirlwinds of rebellion shake all shores?
How will it be with kingdoms and with kings—
With those who shaped him to the thing he is—
When this dumb Terror shall rise to judge the world,
After the silence of the centuries?

---

*For at least a quarter of a century after its first appearance in 1899, Markham's poem enjoyed a good deal of respect and celebrity. It can still appeal to instincts of Art History and Aesthetic Moralizing. The fame of Markham's poem reflected back on Millet's painting that inspired it. (Gertrude Stein reports that her no-nonsense brother Michael looked at a reproduction of the painting and said, "A hell of a hoe"; later, seeing the painting with another brother, Leo, Gertrude agreed that it was a hell of a hoe.)*

# OSCAR WILDE 1854–1900

Wilde's genius illuminated every sort of literature: comedy, farce, lyric tragedy, symbolic fiction, poetry, critical essays and dialogues, and some of the greatest letters in the language. He was both audacious and humane, and he seems never to have been at a loss for a witty and true thing to say. There is no doubt that his two years in prison (1895–1897) for indecent conduct brought about his early death, right at the end of the nineteenth century. He passed on a marvelous legacy to many modern Irish writers, including James Joyce and Brendan Behan, and his plays are still being performed all over the world.

## The Ballad of Reading Gaol

I

He did not wear his scarlet coat,
  For blood and wine are red,
And blood and wine were on his hands
  When they found him with the dead,
The poor dead woman whom he loved,
  And murdered in her bed.

He walked amongst the Trial Men
  In a suit of shady grey;
A cricket cap was on his head,
  And his step seemed light and gay;
But I never saw a man who looked
  So wistfully at the day.

I never saw a man who looked
  With such a wistful eye
Upon that little tent of blue
  Which prisoners call the sky,
And at every drifting cloud that went
  With sails of silver by.

I walked, with other souls in pain,
  Within another ring,
And was wondering if the man had done
  A great or little thing,
When a voice behind me whispered low,
  *"That fellow's got to swing."*

Dear Christ! the very prison walls
  Suddenly seemed to reel,
And the sky above my head became
  Like a casque of scorching steel;
And, though I was a soul in pain,
  My pain I could not feel.

I only knew what hunted thought
  Quickened his step, and why
He looked upon the garish day
  With such a wistful eye;
The man had killed the thing he loved,
  And so he had to die.

. . . . . . . . . . . . . .

Yet each man kills the thing he loves,
  By each let this be heard,
Some do it with a bitter look,
  Some with a flattering word,
The coward does it with a kiss,
  The brave man with a sword!

Some kill their love when they are young,
    And some when they are old;
Some strangle with the hands of Lust,
    Some with the hands of Gold:
The kindest use a knife, because
    The dead so soon grow cold.

Some love too little, some too long,
    Some sell, and others buy;
Some do the deed with many tears,
    And some without a sigh:
For each man kills the thing he loves,
    Yet each man does not die.

He does not die a death of shame
    On a day of dark disgrace,
Nor have a noose about his neck,
    Nor a cloth upon his face,
Nor drop feet foremost through the floor
    Into an empty space.

He does not sit with silent men
    Who watch him night and day;
Who watch him when he tries to weep,
    And when he tries to pray;
Who watch him lest himself should rob
    The prison of its prey.

He does not wake at dawn to see
    Dread figures throng his room,
The shivering Chaplain robed in white,
    The Sheriff stern with gloom,
And the Governor all in shiny black,
    With the yellow face of Doom.

He does not rise in piteous haste
  To put on convict-clothes,
While some coarse-mouthed Doctor gloats, and notes
  Each new and nerve-twitched pose,
Fingering a watch whose little ticks
  Are like horrible hammer-blows.

He does not know that sickening thirst
  That sands one's throat, before
The hangman with his gardener's gloves
  Slips through the padded door,
And binds one with three leathern thongs,
  That the throat may thirst no more.

He does not bend his head to hear
  The Burial Office read,
Nor, while the terror of his soul
  Tells him he is not dead,
Cross his own coffin, as he moves
  Into the hideous shed.

He does not stare upon the air
  Through a little roof of glass:
He does not pray with lips of clay
  For his agony to pass;
Nor feel upon his shuddering cheek
  The kiss of Caiaphas.

II

Six weeks our guardsman walked the yard,
  In the suit of shabby grey:
His cricket cap was on his head,
  And his step seemed light and gay,
But I never saw a man who looked
  So wistfully at the day.

I never saw a man who looked
  With such a wistful eye
Upon that little tent of blue
  Which prisoners call the sky,
And at every wandering cloud that trailed
  Its ravelled fleeces by.

He did not wring his hands, as do
  Those witless men who dare
To try to rear the changeling Hope
  In the cave of black Despair:
He only looked upon the sun,
  And drank the morning air.

He did not wring his hands nor weep,
  Nor did he peek or pine,
But he drank the air as though it held
  Some healthful anodyne;
With open mouth he drank the sun
  As though it had been wine!

And I and all the souls in pain,
  Who tramped the other ring,
Forgot if we ourselves had done
  A great or little thing,
And watched with gaze of dull amaze
  The man who had to swing.

And strange it was to see him pass
  With a step so light and gay,
And strange it was to see him look
  So wistfully at the day,
And strange it was to think that he
  Had such a debt to pay.

For oak and elm have pleasant leaves
    That in the spring-time shoot:
But grim to see is the gallows-tree,
    With its adder-bitten root,
And, green or dry, a man must die
    Before it bears its fruit!

The loftiest place is that seat of grace
    For which all worldlings try:
But who would stand in hempen band
    Upon a scaffold high,
And through a murderer's collar take
    His last look at the sky?

It is sweet to dance to violins
    When Love and Life are fair:
To dance to flutes, to dance to lutes
    Is delicate and rare:
But it is not sweet with nimble feet
    To dance upon the air!

So with curious eyes and sick surmise
    We watched him day by day,
And wondered if each one of us
    Would end the self-same way,
For none can tell to what red Hell
    His sightless soul may stray.

At last the dead man walked no more
    Amongst the Trial Men,
And I knew that he was standing up
    In the black dock's dreadful pen,
And that never would I see his face
    In God's sweet world again.

Like two doomed ships that pass in storm
    We had crossed each other's way:
But we made no sign, we said no word,
    We had no word to say;
For we did not meet in the holy night,
    But in the shameful day.

A prison wall was round us both,
    Two outcast men we were:
The world had thrust us from its heart,
    And God from out His care:
And the iron gin that waits for Sin
    Had caught us in its snare.

### III

In Debtors' Yard the stones are hard,
    And the dripping wall is high,
So it was there he took the air
    Beneath the leaden sky,
And by each side a Warder walked,
    For fear the man might die.

Or else he sat with those who watched
    His anguish night and day;
Who watched him when he rose to weep,
    And when he crouched to pray;
Who watched him lest himself should rob
    Their scaffold of its prey.

The Governor was strong upon
    The Regulations Act:
The Doctor said that Death was but
    A scientific fact:
And twice a day the Chaplain called,
    And left a little tract.

And twice a day he smoked his pipe,
  And drank his quart of beer:
His soul was resolute, and held
  No hiding-place for fear;
He often said that he was glad
  The hangman's hands were near.

But why he said so strange a thing
  No Warder dared to ask:
For he to whom a watcher's doom
  Is given as his task,
Must set a lock upon his lips,
  And make his face a mask.

Or else he might be moved, and try
  To comfort or console:
And what should Human Pity do
  Pent up in Murderers' Hole?
What word of grace in such a place
  Could help a brother's soul?

        . . . . . . . . . . . . . . .

With slouch and swing around the ring
  We trod the Fool's Parade!
We did not care: we knew we were
  The Devil's Own Brigade;
And shaven head and feet of lead
  Make a merry masquerade.

We tore the tarry rope to shreds
  With blunt and bleeding nails;
We rubbed the doors, and scrubbed the floors,
  And cleaned the shining rails:
And, rank by rank, we soaped the plank,
  And clattered with the pails.

We sewed the sacks, we broke the stones,
   We turned the dusty drill:
We banged the tins, and bawled the hymns,
   And sweated on the mill:
But in the heart of every man
   Terror was lying still.

So still it lay that every day
   Crawled like a weed-clogged wave:
And we forgot the bitter lot
   That waits for fool and knave,
Till once, as we tramped in from work,
   We passed an open grave.

With yawning mouth the yellow hole
   Gaped for a living thing;
The very mud cried out for blood
   To the thirsty asphalt ring:
And we knew that ere one dawn grew fair
   Some prisoner had to swing.

Right in we went, with soul intent
   On Death and Dread and Doom:
The hangman, with his little bag,
   Went shuffling through the gloom:
And each man trembled as he crept
   Into his numbered tomb.

      . . . . . . . . . . . . . .

That night the empty corridors
   Were full of forms of Fear,
And up and down the iron town
   Stole feet we could not hear,
And through the bars that hide the stars
   White faces seemed to peer.

He lay as one who lies and dreams
   In a pleasant meadow-land,
The watchers watched him as he slept,
   And could not understand
How one could sleep so sweet a sleep
   With a hangman close at hand.

But there is no sleep when men must weep
   Who never yet have wept:
So we—the fool, the fraud, the knave—
   That endless vigil kept,
And through each brain on hands of pain
   Another's terror crept.

Alas! it is a fearful thing
   To feel another's guilt!
For, right within, the sword of Sin
   Pierced to its poisoned hilt,
And as molten lead were the tears we shed
   For the blood we had not spilt.

The Warders with their shoes of felt
   Crept by each padlocked door,
And peeped and saw, with eyes of awe,
   Grey figures on the floor,
And wondered why men knelt to pray
   Who never prayed before.

All through the night we knelt and prayed,
   Mad mourners of a corse!
The troubled plumes of midnight were
   The plumes upon a hearse:
And bitter wine upon a sponge
   Was the savour of Remorse.

      . . . . . . . . . . . . . . .

The grey cock crew, the red cock crew,
  But never came the day:
And crooked shapes of Terror crouched,
  In the corners where we lay:
And each evil sprite that walks by night
  Before us seemed to play.

They glided past, they glided fast,
  Like travellers through a mist:
They mocked the moon in a rigadoon
  Of delicate turn and twist,
And with formal pace and loathsome grace
  The phantoms kept their tryst.

With mop and mow, we saw them go,
  Slim shadows hand in hand:
About, about, in ghostly rout
  They trod a saraband:
And the damned grotesques made arabesques,
  Like the wind upon the sand!

With the pirouettes of marionettes,
  They tripped on pointed tread:
But with flutes of Fear they filled the ear,
  As their grisly masque they led,
And loud they sang, and long they sang,
  For they sang to wake the dead.

*"Oho!"* they cried, *"The world is wide,*
  *But fettered limbs go lame!*
*And once, or twice, to throw the dice*
  *Is a gentlemanly game,*
*But he does not win who plays with Sin*
  *In the secret House of Shame."*

No things of air these antics were,
  That frolicked with such glee:
To men whose lives were held in gyves,
  And whose feet might not go free,
Ah! wounds of Christ! they were living things,
  Most terrible to see.

Around, around, they waltzed and wound;
  Some wheeled in smirking pairs;
With the mincing step of a demirep
  Some sidled up the stairs:
And with subtle sneer, and fawning leer,
  Each helped us at our prayers.

The morning wind began to moan,
  But still the night went on:
Through its giant loom the web of gloom
  Crept till each thread was spun:
And, as we prayed, we grew afraid
  Of the Justice of the Sun.

The moaning wind went wandering round
  The weeping prison-wall:
Till like a wheel of turning steel
  We felt the minutes crawl:
O moaning wind! what had we done
  To have such a seneschal?

At last I saw the shadowed bars,
  Like a lattice wrought in lead,
Move right across the whitewashed wall
  That faced my three-plank bed,
And I knew that somewhere in the world
  God's dreadful dawn was red.

At six o'clock we cleaned our cells,
    At seven all was still,
But the sough and swing of a mighty wing
    The prison seemed to fill,
For the Lord of Death with icy breath
    Had entered in to kill.

He did not pass in purple pomp,
    Nor ride a moon-white steed.
Three yards of cord and a sliding board
    Are all the gallows' need:
So with rope of shame the Herald came
    To do the secret deed.

We were as men who through a fen
    Of filthy darkness grope:
We did not dare to breathe a prayer,
    Or to give our anguish scope:
Something was dead in each of us,
    And what was dead was Hope.

For Man's grim Justice goes its way,
    And will not swerve aside:
It slays the weak, it slays the strong,
    It has a deadly stride:
With iron heel it slays the strong,
    The monstrous parricide!

We waited for the stroke of eight:
    Each tongue was thick with thirst:
For the stroke of eight is the stroke of Fate
    That makes a man accursed,
And Fate will use a running noose
    For the best man and the worst.

We had no other thing to do,
　　Save to wait for the sign to come:
So, like things of stone in a valley lone,
　　Quiet we sat and dumb:
But each man's heart beat thick and quick,
　　Like a madman on a drum!

With sudden shock the prison-clock
　　Smote on the shivering air,
And from all the gaol rose up a wail
　　Of impotent despair,
Like the sound that frightened marshes hear
　　From some leper in his lair.

And as one sees most fearful things
　　In the crystal of a dream,
We saw the greasy hempen rope
　　Hooked to the blackened beam,
And heard the prayer the hangman's snare
　　Strangled into a scream.

And all the woe that moved him so
　　That he gave that bitter cry,
And the wild regrets, and the bloody sweats,
　　None knew so well as I:
For he who lives more lives than one
　　More deaths than one must die.

IV

There is no chapel on the day
　　On which they hang a man:
The Chaplain's heart is far too sick,
　　Or his face is far too wan,
Or there is that written in his eyes
　　Which none should look upon.

So they kept us close till nigh on noon,
  And then they rang the bell,
And the Warders with their jingling keys
  Opened each listening cell,
And down the iron stair we tramped,
  Each from his separate Hell.

Out into God's sweet air we went,
  But not in wonted way,
For this man's face was white with fear,
  And that man's face was grey,
And I never saw sad men who looked
  So wistfully at the day.

I never saw sad men who looked
  With such a wistful eye
Upon that little tent of blue
  We prisoners called the sky,
And at every careless cloud that passed
  In happy freedom by.

But there were those amongst us all
  Who walked with downcast head,
And knew that, had each got his due,
  They should have died instead:
He had but killed a thing that lived,
  Whilst they had killed the dead.

For he who sins a second time
  Wakes a dead soul to pain,
And draws it from its spotted shroud,
  And makes it bleed again,
And makes it bleed great gouts of blood,
  And makes it bleed in vain!

Like ape or clown, in monstrous garb
  With crooked arrows starred,
Silently we went round and round,
  The slippery asphalt yard;
Silently we went round and round
  And no man spoke a word.

Silently we went round and round,
  And through each hollow mind
The Memory of dreadful things
  Rushed like a dreadful wind,
And Horror stalked before each man,
  And Terror crept behind.

The Warders strutted up and down,
  And kept their herd of brutes,
Their uniforms were spick and span,
  And they wore their Sunday suits,
But we knew the work they had been at,
  By the quicklime on their boots.

For where a grave had opened wide,
  There was no grave at all:
Only a stretch of mud and sand
  By the hideous prison-wall,
And a little heap of burning lime,
  That the man should have his pall.

For he has a pall, this wretched man,
  Such as few men can claim:
Deep down below a prison-yard,
  Naked for greater shame,
He lies, with fetters on each foot,
  Wrapt in a sheet of flame!

And all the while the burning lime
  Eats flesh and bone away,
It eats the brittle bone by night,
  And the soft flesh by day,
It eats the flesh and bone by turns,
  But it eats the heart alway.

For three long years they will not sow
  Or root or seedling there:
For three long years the unblessed spot
  Will sterile be and bare,
And look upon the wondering sky
  With unreproachful stare.

They think a murderer's heart would taint
  Each simple seed they sow.
It is not true! God's kindly earth
  Is kindlier than men know,
And the red rose would but blow more red,
  The white rose whiter blow.

Out of his mouth a red, red rose!
  Out of his heart a white!
For who can say by what strange way,
  Christ brings His will to light,
Since the barren staff the pilgrim bore
  Bloomed in the great Pope's sight?

But neither milk-white rose nor red
  May bloom in prison air;
The shard, the pebble, and the flint,
  Are what they give us there:
For flowers have been known to heal
  A common man's despair.

So never will wine-red rose or white,
  Petal by petal, fall
On that stretch of mud and sand that lies
  By the hideous prison-wall,
To tell the men who tramp the yard
  That God's Son died for all.

Yet though the hideous prison-wall
  Still hems him round and round,
And a spirit may not walk by night
  That is with fetters bound,
And a spirit may but weep that lies
  In such unholy ground,

He is at peace—this wretched man—
  At peace, or will be soon:
There is no thing to make him mad,
  Nor does Terror walk at noon,
For the lampless Earth in which he lies
  Has neither Sun nor Moon.

They hanged him as a beast is hanged:
  They did not even toll
A requiem that might have brought
  Rest to his startled soul,
But hurriedly they took him out,
  And hid him in a hole.

They stripped him of his canvas clothes,
  And gave him to the flies:
They mocked the swollen purple throat,
  And the stark and staring eyes:
And with laughter loud they heaped the shroud
  In which their convict lies.

The Chaplain would not kneel to pray
  By his dishonoured grave:
Nor mark it with that blessed Cross
  That Christ for sinners gave,
Because the man was one of those
  Whom Christ came down to save.

Yet all is well; he has but passed
  To Life's appointed bourne:
And alien tears will fill for him
  Pity's long-broken urn,
For his mourners will be outcast men,
  And outcasts always mourn.

V

I know not whether Laws be right,
  Or whether Laws be wrong;
All that we know who lie in gaol
  Is that the wall is strong;
And that each day is like a year,
  A year whose days are ong.

But this I know, that every Law
  That men have made for Man,
Since first Man took his brother's life,
  And the sad world began,
But straws the wheat and saves the chaff
  With a most evil fan.

This too I know—and wise it were
  If each could know the same—
That every prison that men build
  Is built with bricks of shame,
And bound with bars lest Christ should see
  How men their brothers maim.

With bars they blur the gracious moon,
  And blind the goodly sun:
And they do well to hide their Hell,
  For in it things are done
That Son of God nor son of Man
  Ever should look upon!

The vilest deeds like poison weeds,
  Bloom well in prison-air;
It is only what is good in Man
  That wastes and withers there:
Pale Anguish keeps the heavy gate,
  And the Warder is Despair.

For they starve the little frightened child
  Till it weeps both night and day:
And they scourge the weak, and flog the fool,
  And gibe the old and grey,
And some grow mad, and all grow bad,
  And none a word may say.

Each narrow cell in which we dwell
  Is a foul and dark latrine,
And the fetid breath of living Death
  Chokes up each grated screen,
And all, but Lust, is turned to dust
  In Humanity's machine.

The brackish water that we drink
  Creeps with a loathsome slime,
And the bitter bread they weigh in scales
  Is full of chalk and lime,
And Sleep will not lie down, but walks
  Wild-eyed, and cries to Time.

But though lean Hunger and green Thirst
   Like asp with adder fight,
We have little care of prison fare,
   For what chills and kills outright
Is that every stone one lifts by day
   Becomes one's heart by night.

With midnight always in one's heart,
   And twilight in one's cell,
We turn the crank, or tear the rope,
   Each in his separate Hell,
And the silence is more awful far
   Than the sound of a brazen bell.

And never a human voice comes near
   To speak a gentle word:
And the eye that watches through the door
   Is pitiless and hard:
And by all forgot, we rot and rot,
   With soul and body marred.

And thus we rust Life's iron chain
   Degraded and alone:
And some men curse, and some men weep,
   And some men make no moan:
But God's eternal Laws are kind
   And break the heart of stone:

And every human heart that breaks,
   In prison-cell or yard,
Is as that broken box that gave
   Its treasure to the Lord,
And filled the unclean leper's house
   With the scent of costliest nard.

Ah! happy they whose hearts can break
   And peace of pardon win!
How else may man make straight his plan
   And cleanse his soul from Sin?
How else but through a broken heart
   May Lord Christ enter in?

And he of the swollen purple throat,
   And the stark and staring eyes,
Waits for the holy hands that took
   The Thief to Paradise;
And a broken and a contrite heart
   The Lord will not despise.

The man in red who reads the Law
   Gave him three weeks of life,
Three little weeks in which to heal
   His soul of his soul's strife,
And cleanse from every blot of blood
   The hand that held the knife.

And with tears of blood he cleansed the hand,
   The hand that held the steel:
For only blood can wipe out blood,
   And only tears can heal:
And the crimson stain that was of Cain
   Became Christ's snow-white seal.

## VI

In Reading gaol by Reading town
   There is a pit of shame,
   And in it lies a wretched man
   Eaten by teeth of flame,
In a burning winding-sheet he lies,
   And his grave has got no name.

And there, till Christ call forth the dead,
  In silence let him lie:
No need to waste the foolish tear,
  Or heave the windy sigh:
The man had killed the thing he loved,
  And so he had to die.

And all men kill the thing they love,
  By all let this be heard,
Some do it with a bitter look,
  Some with a flattering word,
The coward does it with a kiss,
  The brave man with a sword!

---

*In 1895, by a grotesque tissue of ironies, Wilde was found guilty of having done something that had not been a crime ten years earlier and subjected to two years of imprisonment of a kind (accompanied by genuinely hard labor) that would be much softened by prison reforms just ten years later. Wilde's prison experience led to his two final works, which could hardly differ more from each other: the unique letter called* De Profundis *that is one of the great personal documents in the language; and this Ballad, which uses a haunting stanza found here and there in Coleridge's "Rime of the Ancient Mariner" (p. 433) and also in some verses by Thomas Hood. Wilde, always the wit and always the self-conscious critic, said, "I am out-Henleying Kipling!"—referring to Kipling's "Danny Deever" (p. 851), also about a soldier hanged for murder, which was first published in a magazine that W. E. Henley edited. At the Paris Exposition of 1900, not long before his death at forty-six, Wilde made a recording of his own reading of some stanzas from the Ballad.*

# ALFRED EDWARD HOUSMAN 1859–1936

Although the book for which he is most famous is called *A Shropshire Lad*, A. E. Housman did not come from Shropshire and was hardly a lad when the book was published in 1896. He was born in Worcestershire, near Shropshire, and spent a melancholy and undistinguished time at Oxford before taking a clerical job in 1882. In time, however, he joined the faculty of University College, London, as a teacher of Latin and later went on to Cambridge. He was a distinguished and acerbic editor of classical texts. Housman was old-fashioned, patriotic, conservative, and conventional in literature; but he was also adventuresome enough to be one of the first people to fly commercially!

# *Loveliest of Trees*

Loveliest of trees, the cherry now
Is hung with bloom along the bough,
And stands about the woodland ride
Wearing white for Eastertide.

Now, of my threescore years and ten,
Twenty will not come again,
And take from seventy springs a score,
It only leaves me fifty more.

And since to look at things in bloom
Fifty springs are little room,
About the woodlands I will go
To see the cherry hung with snow.

from A Shropshire Lad

---

*Housman used a persona called Terence Hearsay to express many of the Romantic sentiments of the late nineteenth century, as though in conscious continuation of Byron's "So, We'll Go No More a-Roving" (p. 479), although Housman adds a tender stoicism not explicit in Byron.*

# To an Athlete Dying Young

The time you won your town the race
We chaired you through the market-place;
Man and boy stood cheering by,
And home we brought you shoulder-high.

To-day, the road all runners come,
Shoulder-high we bring you home,
And set you at your threshold down,
Townsman of a stiller town.

Smart lad, to slip betimes away
From fields where glory does not stay
And early though the laurel grows
It withers quicker than the rose.

Eyes the shady night has shut
Cannot see the record cut,
And silence sounds no worse than cheers
After earth has stopped the ears:

Now you will not swell the rout
Of lads that wore their honours out,
Runners whom renown outran
And the name died before the man.

So set, before its echoes fade,
The fleet foot on the sill of shade,
And hold to the low lintel up
The still-defended challenge-cup.

And round that early-laurelled head
Will flock to gaze the strengthless dead,
And find unwithered on its curls
The garland briefer than a girl's.

---

*Housman could approach a modern subject with the humble simplicity of folk art but, at the same time, with matchless sophistication and learning. This elegy was published in 1896, but, with a change of language, it could have been written in 1896 B.C.*

# With Rue My Heart Is Laden

With rue my heart is laden
  For golden friends I had,
For many a rose-lipt maiden
  And many a lightfoot lad.

By brooks too broad for leaping
  The lightfoot boys are laid;
The rose-lipt girls are sleeping
  In fields where roses fade.

from A Shropshire Lad

---

*Housman seems to have challenged himself to try the discipline of making do with minimal materials — here, just a handful of related sounds: "laden . . . lad . . . laid . . ." and the story is told.*

# *When I Was One-and-Twenty*

>>>>>>>

When I was one-and-twenty
 I heard a wise man say,
"Give crowns and pounds and guineas
 But not your heart away;
Give pearls away and rubies
 But keep your fancy free."
But I was one-and-twenty,
 No use to talk to me.

When I was one-and-twenty
 I heard him say again,
"The heart out of the bosom
 Was never given in vain;
'Tis paid with sighs a plenty
 And sold for endless rue."
And I am two-and-twenty,
 And oh, 'tis true, 'tis true.

from A Shropshire Lad

---

*What remains, after a hundred years, so surprising about this delightful and moving poem is the disclosure, right at the end, that our perspective on life at twenty-one has come from a philosopher of twenty-two.*

# Terence, This Is Stupid Stuff

"Terence, this is stupid stuff:
You eat your victuals fast enough;
There can't be much amiss, 'tis clear,
To see the rate you drink your beer.
But oh, good Lord, the verse you make,
It gives a chap the belly-ache.
The cow, the old cow, she is dead;
It sleeps well, the hornèd head:
We poor lads, 'tis our turn now
To hear such tunes as killed the cow.
Pretty friendship 'tis to rhyme
Your friends to death before their time
Moping melancholy mad:
Come, pipe a tune to dance to, lad."

Why, if 'tis dancing you would be,
There's brisker pipes than poetry.
Say, for what were hop-yards meant,
Or why was Burton built on Trent?
Oh many a peer of England brews
Livelier liquor than the Muse,
And malt does more than Milton can
To justify God's ways to man.
Ale, man, ale's the stuff to drink
For fellows whom it hurts to think:
Look into the pewter pot
To see the world as the world's not.
And faith, 'tis pleasant till 'tis past:
The mischief is that 'twill not last.
Oh I have been to Ludlow fair
And left my necktie God knows where,
And carried half-way home, or near,
Pints and quarts of Ludlow beer:

Then the world seemed none so bad,
And I myself a sterling lad;
And down in lovely muck I've lain,
Happy till I woke again.
Then I saw the morning sky:
Heigho, the tale was all a lie;
The world, it was the old world yet,
I was I, my things were wet,
And nothing now remained to do
But begin the game anew.

Therefore, since the world has still
Much good, but much less good than ill,
And while the sun and moon endure
Luck's a chance, but trouble's sure,
I'd face it as a wise man would,
And train for ill and not for good.
'Tis true, the stuff I bring for sale
Is not so brisk a brew as ale:
Out of a stem that scored the hand
I wrung it in a weary land.
But take it: if the smack is sour,
The better for the embittered hour;
It should do good to heart and head
When your soul is in my soul's stead;
And I will friend you, if I may,
In the dark and cloudy day.

There was a king reigned in the East:
There, when kings will sit to feast,
They get their fill before they think
With poisoned meat and poisoned drink.
He gathered all that springs to birth
From the many-venomed earth;
First a little, thence to more,
He sampled all her killing store;
An easy, smiling, seasoned sound,
Sate the king when healths went round.

They put arsenic in his meat
And stared aghast to watch him eat;
They poured strychnine in his cup
And shook to see him drink it up:
They shook, they stared as white's their shirt:
Them it was their poison hurt.
—I tell the tale that I heard told.
Mithridates, he died old.

from A Shropshire Lad

---

*Housman had planned to call his first volume* The Poems of Terence Hearsay *but settled finally on* A Shropshire Lad. *The Terence in this poem is a good-enough representation of certain sides of Housman's complex character: the classical learning, the stoicism, the wit.*

# Into My Heart an Air That Kills

Into my heart an air that kills
From yon far country blows:
What are those blue remembered hills,
What spires, what farms are those?

That is the land of lost content,
I see it shining plain,
The happy highways where I went
And cannot come again.

from A Shropshire Lad

---

*From Housman's native Worcestershire (now Hereford and Worcester), Shropshire was a "far country" with hills and spires visible to westward. Like Hardy, whose work he admired, Housman made a local landscape an abstract symbol as well as a concrete setting. For mysterious reasons, it is much more effective to say "blue remembered hills," with the words seemingly out of order, than the expected "remembered blue hills."*

# On Wenlock Edge

On Wenlock Edge the wood's in trouble;
   His forest fleece the Wrekin heaves;
The gale, it plies the saplings double,
   And thick on Severn snow the leaves.

'Twould blow like this through holt and hanger
   When Uricon the city stood:
'Tis the old wind in the old anger,
   But then it threshed another wood.

Then, 'twas before my time, the Roman
   At yonder heaving hill would stare:
The blood that warms an English yeoman,
   The thoughts that hurt him, they were there.

There, like the wind through woods in riot,
   Through him the gale of life blew high;
The tree of man was never quiet:
   Then 'twas the Roman, now 'tis I.

The gale, it plies the saplings double,
   It blows so hard, 'twill soon be gone:
To-day the Roman and his trouble
   Are ashes under Uricon.

from A Shropshire Lad

---

*With Housman, as with Hardy, Kipling, Chesterton, and some other late Victorians, one is aware of eons of history underfoot almost anywhere in Britain: a Catholic Christianity under the Protestant surface, Roman and Druid layers of paganism under the Christian layers, millions of centuries of prehistory under any human time. Roman Uricon (Uriconium or Viroconium) is the modern Wroxeter.*

Poverty, failure, illness, and drug addiction almost destroyed Thompson until, in about 1888, he was rescued
by Wilfred and Alice Meynell, who took care of him
and gave him some literary connections. He published
three volumes of verse during the 1890s, along with a
good deal of literary journalism.

# The Hound of Heaven

I fled Him, down the nights and down the days;
I fled Him, down the arches of the years;
I fled Him, down the labyrinthine ways
Of my own mind; and in the midst of tears
I hid from Him, and under running laughter.
     Up vistaed hopes I sped;
     And shot, precipitated,
Adown Titanic glooms of chasmèd fears,
  From those strong Feet that followed, followed after.
     But with unhurrying chase,
     And unperturbèd pace,
  Deliberate speed, majestic instancy,
    They beat—and a Voice beat
    More instant than the Feet—
"All things betray thee, who betrayest Me."

     I pleaded, outlaw-wise,
By many a hearted casement, curtained red,
  Trellised with intertwining charities;
(For, though I knew His love Who followèd,
    Yet was I sore adread
Lest, having Him, I must have naught beside);
But, if one little casement parted wide,
  The gust of His approach would clash it to.
  Fear wist not to evade, as Love wist to pursue.

Across the margent of the world I fled,
   And troubled the gold gateways of the stars,
   Smiting for shelter on their clangèd bars;
      Fretted to dulcet jars
And silvern chatter the pale ports o' the moon.
I said to Dawn: Be sudden—to Eve: Be soon;
   With thy young skiey blossoms heap me over
      From this tremendous Lover!
Float thy vague veil about me, lest He see!
   I tempted all His servitors, but to find
My own betrayal in their constancy,
In faith to Him their fickleness to me,
   Their traitorous trueness, and their loyal deceit.
To all swift things for swiftness did I sue;
   Clung to the whistling mane of every wind.
      But whether they swept, smoothly fleet,
      The long savannahs of the blue;
         Or whether, Thunder-driven,
      They clanged his chariot 'thwart a heaven
Plashy with flying lightnings round the spurn o' their feet: —
   Fear wist not to evade as Love wist to pursue.
         Still with unhurrying chase,
         And unperturbèd pace,
      Deliberate speed, majestic instancy,
         Came on the following Feet,
         And a Voice above their beat—
      " Naught shelters thee, who wilt not shelter Me."

I sought no more that after which I strayed
         In face of man or maid;
But still within the little children's eyes
         Seems something, something that replies,
*They* at least are for me, surely for me!
I turned me to them very wistfully;
But just as their young eyes grew sudden fair
         With dawning answers there,
Their angel plucked them from me by the hair.
"Come then, ye other children, Nature's—share

With me" (said I) "your delicate fellowship;
    Let me greet you lip to lip,
    Let me twine with you caresses,
      Wantoning
    With our Lady-Mother's vagrant tresses,
      Banqueting
    With her in her wind-walled palace,
    Underneath her azured daïs,
    Quaffing, as your taintless way is,
      From a chalice
Lucent-weeping out of the dayspring."
      So it was done:
*I* in their delicate fellowship was one —
Drew the bolt of Nature's secrecies.
    *I* knew all the swift importings
    On the willful face of skies;
    I knew how the clouds arise
    Spumèd of the wild sea-snortings;
      All that's born or dies
    Rose and drooped with; made the shapers
Of mine own moods, or wailful or divine;
    With them joyed and was bereaven.
    I was heavy with the even,
    When she lit her glimmering tapers
    Round the day's dead sanctities.
    I laughed in the morning's eyes.
I triumphed and I saddened with all weather,
    Heaven and I wept together,
And its sweet tears were salt with mortal mine.
Against the red throb of its sunset-heart
    I laid my own to beat,
    And share commingling heat;
But not by that, by that, was eased my human smart.
In vain my tears were wet on Heaven's grey cheek.
For ah! we know not what each other says,
    These things and I; in sound *I* speak —

*Their* sound is but their stir, they speak by silences.
Nature, poor stepdame, cannot slake my drouth;
  Let her, if she would owe me,
Drop yon blue bosom-veil of sky, and show me
  The breasts o' her tenderness:
Never did any milk of hers once bless
   My thirsting mouth.
   Nigh and nigh draws the chase,
   With unperturbèd pace,
  Deliberate speed, majestic instancy;
   And past those noisèd Feet
   A Voice comes yet more fleet—
"Lo! naught contents thee, who content'st not Me."


Naked I wait Thy love's uplifted stroke!
My harness piece by piece Thou hast hewn from me,
   And smitten me to my knee;
  I am defenceless utterly.
  I slept, methinks, and woke,
And, slowly gazing, find me stripped in sleep.
In the rash lustihead of my young powers,
  I shook the pillaring hours
And pulled my life upon me; grimed with smears,
I stand amid the dust o' the mounded years—
My mangled youth lies dead beneath the heap,
My days have crackled and gone up in smoke,
Have puffed and burst as sun-starts on a stream.
  Yea, faileth now even dream
The dreamer, and the lute the lutanist;
Even the linked fantasies, in whose blossomy twist
I swung the earth a trinket at my wrist,
Are yielding; cords of all too weak account
For earth with heavy griefs so overplussed.
  Ah! is Thy love indeed
A weed, albeit an amaranthine weed,
Suffering no flowers except its own to mount?
  Ah! must—
  Designer infinite!—

Ah! must Thou char the wood ere Thou canst limn with it?
My freshness spent its wavering shower i' the dust;
And now my heart is as a broken fount,
Wherein tear-drippings stagnate, spilt down ever
  From the dank thoughts that shiver
Upon the sighful branches of my mind.
  Such is; what is to be?
The pulp so bitter, how shall taste the rind?
I dimly guess what Time in mists confounds;
Yet ever and anon a trumpet sounds
From the hid battlements of Eternity;
Those shaken mists a space unsettle, then
Round the half-glimpsèd turrets slowly wash again.
  But not ere him who summoneth
  I first have seen, enwound
With glooming robes purpureal, cypress-crowned;
His name I know, and what his trumpet saith.
Whether man's heart or life it be which yields
  Thee harvest, must Thy harvest-fields
  Be dunged with rotten death?
   Now of that long pursuit
   Comes at hand the bruit;
  That Voice is round me like a bursting sea:
   "And is thy earth so marred,
   Shattered in shard on shard?
  Lo, all things fly thee, for thou fliest Me!
  Strange, piteous, futile thing!
Wherefore should any set thee love apart?
Seeing none but I make much of naught" (He said),
"And human love needs human meriting:
  How hast thou merited—
Of all man's clotted clay the dingiest clot?
  Alack, thou knowest not
How little worthy of any love thou art!
Whom wilt thou find to love ignoble thee
  Save Me, save only Me?
All which I took from thee I did but take,
  Not for thy harms,

But just that thou might'st seek it in My arms.
 All which thy child's mistake
Fancies as lost, I have stored for thee at home:
 Rise, clasp My hand, and come!"
Halts by me that footfall:

 Is my gloom, after all,
Shade of His hand, outstretched caressingly?
 "Ah, fondest, blindest, weakest,
 I am He Whom thou seekest!
Thou dravest love from thee, who dravest Me."

---

*Thompson's tormented verse takes the characteristically emotional idiom of the 1890s back to the agonies and ecstasies of certain religious poets of the seventeenth century, including George Herbert (pp. 186–195) and Henry Vaughan (pp. 247–254), along with Abraham Cowley and Richard Crashaw. Thompson's canine pursuer shocked some Victorian readers who were more accustomed to Cecil Frances Alexander's holy "Child so dear and gentle" who "leads his children on / To the place where he is gone."*

It may surprise some former Cub Scouts to learn that much of the lore and law of their movement is drawn from *The Jungle Book* by Kipling (who also suspected Edgar Rice Burroughs of felonious plagarism, since Tarzan is so much like Mowgli). Kipling's stories, novels, and poems remain unforgettable for many readers, especially those who were exposed to his influence as children—if not through Cub Scouts then maybe in the form of stirring musical settings and movie adaptations. Before he died, Kipling seemed awfully right-wing, particularly to left-wing critics of his day; but efforts of redemption on the parts of T. S. Eliot and W. H. Auden did much to restore the luster to Kipling's reputation, which had never faded for many younger readers.

# Recessional

()◀▬▶()

1897

God of our fathers, known of old,
   Lord of our far-flung battle-line,
Beneath whose awful Hand we hold
   Dominion over palm and pine—
Lord God of Hosts, be with us yet,
Lest we forget—lest we forget!

The tumult and the shouting dies;
   The Captains and the Kings depart:
Still stands Thine ancient sacrifice,
   An humble and a contrite heart.
Lord God of Hosts, be with us yet,
Lest we forget—lest we forget!

Far-called, our navies melt away;
　On dune and headland sinks the fire:
Lo, all our pomp of yesterday
　Is one with Nineveh and Tyre!
Judge of the Nations, spare us yet,
Lest we forget—lest we forget!

If, drunk with sight of power, we loose
　Wild tongues that have not Thee in awe,
Such boastings as the Gentiles use,
　Or lesser breeds without the Law—
Lord God of Hosts, be with us yet,
Lest we forget—lest we forget!

For heathen heart that puts her trust
　In reeking tube and iron shard,
All valiant dust that builds on dust,
　And guarding, calls not Thee to guard,
For frantic boast and foolish word—
Thy mercy on Thy People, Lord!

*Victoria became Queen in 1837 and ruled until she died in 1901. During the Jubilee of 1897 that celebrated her first sixty years on the throne, Kipling wrote a touchingly cautionary hymn of receding: recessionals come at the end of a service or ceremony, when people are leaving.*

# Danny Deever

"What are the bugles blowin' for?" said Files-on-Parade.
"To turn you out, to turn you out," the Color-Sergeant said.
"What makes you look so white, so white?" said Files-on-
  Parade.
"I'm dreadin' what I've got to watch," the Color-Sergeant said.
  For they're hangin' Danny Deever, you can hear the Dead
    March play,
  The Regiment's in 'ollow square—they're hangin' him
    today;
  They've taken of his buttons off an' cut his stripes away,
An' they're hangin' Danny Deever in the mornin'.

"What makes the rear-rank breathe so 'ard?" said Files-on-
  Parade.
"It's bitter cold, it's bitter cold," the Color-Sergeant said.
"What makes that front-rank man fall down?" said Files-on-
  Parade.
"A touch o' sun, a touch o' sun," the Color-Sergeant said.
  They are hangin' Danny Deever, they are marchin' of 'im
    round.
  They 'ave 'alted Danny Deever by 'is coffin on the
    ground;
  And 'e'll swing in 'arf a minute for a sneakin' shootin'
    hound—
  O they're hangin' Danny Deever in the mornin'!

" 'Is cot was right-'and cot to mine," said Files-on-Parade.
" 'E's sleepin' out an' far tonight," the Color-Sergeant said.
"I've drunk 'is beer a score o' times," said Files-on-Parade.
" 'E's drinkin' bitter beer alone," the Color-Sergeant said.
 They are hangin' Danny Deever, you must mark 'im to 'is
  place,
 For 'e shot a comrade sleepin'—you must look 'im in the
  face;
 Nine 'undred of 'is county an' the Regiment's disgrace,
 While they're hangin' Danny Deever in the mornin'.

"What's that so black agin the sun?" said Files-on-Parade.
"It's Danny fightin' 'ard for life," the Color-Sergeant said.
"What's that that whimpers over'ead?" said Files-on-Parade.
"It's Danny's soul that's passin' now," the Color-Sergeant said.
 For they're done with Danny Deever, you can 'ear the
  quickstep play,
 The Regiment's in column, an' they're marchin' us away;
 Ho! the young recruits are shakin', an' they'll want their
  beer today,
After hangin' Danny Deever in the mornin'!

---

*Writing of "The Ballad of Reading Gaol" (p. 810), Oscar Wilde said in a letter, "I am out-Henleying Kipling!" He was most probably thinking of "Danny Deever," which also concerns the public hanging of an enlisted soldier convicted of murder. (Kipling's poem first appeared, only a few years before Wilde's, in a magazine edited by W. E. Henley.)*

# WILLIAM BUTLER YEATS 1865–1939

William Butler Yeats first studied art (his father was a
celebrated painter), but he soon turned to literature and
produced a succession of lovely works in many modes:
romantic lyric, political satire, mythic metamorphosis
(transforming one of his great loves, Maud Gonne, into
a Helen), verse drama, aesthetic criticism, visionary history, and some of the deepest and most entertaining
autobiographical writing of the modern age. He remained single until his fifties, when he married the
young Georgie Hyde Lees, with whom he had a son
and a daughter, for both of whom he wrote engaging
prayers. Many readers consider Yeats the greatest
English-speaking poet of the twentieth century.

# The Second Coming

Turning and turning in the widening gyre
The falcon cannot hear the falconer;
Things fall apart; the center cannot hold;
Mere anarchy is loosed upon the world,
The blood-dimmed tide is loosed, and everywhere
The ceremony of innocence is drowned;
The best lack all conviction, while the worst
Are full of passionate intensity.

Surely some revelation is at hand;
Surely the Second Coming is at hand.
The Second Coming! Hardly are those words out
When a vast image out of *Spiritus Mundi*
Troubles my sight: somewhere in the sands of the desert
A shape with lion body and the head of a man,
A gaze blank and pitiless as the sun,
Is moving its slow thighs, while all about it
Reel shadows of the indignant desert birds.

The darkness drops again; but now I know
That twenty centuries of stony sleep
Were vexed to nightmare by a rocking cradle,
And what rough beast, its hour come round at last,
Slouches towards Bethlehem to be born?

---

*"The Second Coming" feints in the direction of mumbo jumbo in its reference to* Spiritus Mundi, *but, against this farfetched realm of sphinxes and poppycock, there is a picture of Yeats struggling with the greatest problem of the modern world: war. The irony is that this second coming is hardly the peace-bringing Second Coming of Christ but rather the reappearance of a terrible beast.*

# Sailing to Byzantium

### I

That is no country for old men. The young
In one another's arms, birds in the trees
— Those dying generations — at their song,
The salmon-falls, the mackerel-crowded seas,
Fish, flesh, or fowl, commend all summer long
Whatever is begotten, born, and dies.
Caught in that sensual music all neglect
Monuments of unageing intellect.

### II

An aged man is but a paltry thing,
A tattered coat upon a stick, unless
Soul clap its hands and sing, and louder sing
For every tatter in its mortal dress,
Nor is there singing school but studying
Monuments of its own magnificence;
And therefore I have sailed the seas and come
To the holy city of Byzantium.

### III

O sages standing in God's holy fire
As in the gold mosaic of a wall,
Come from the holy fire, perne in a gyre,
And be the singing-masters of my soul.
Consume my heart away; sick with desire
And fastened to a dying animal
It knows not what it is; and gather me
Into the artifice of eternity.

IV

Once out of nature I shall never take
My bodily form from any natural thing,
But such a form as Grecian goldsmiths make
Of hammered gold and gold enamelling
To keep a drowsy Emperor awake;
Or set upon a golden bough to sing
To lords and ladies of Byzantium
Of what is past, or passing, or to come.

---

*What is sought is not the rural peace of a small island in a beautiful lake* (see
*"The Lake Isle of Innisfree," p. 858) but the concentrated unity of life in an ideal
city, medieval Byzantium (which was the name of the place until* A.D. *330, when
it became Constantinople, changed in 1930 to Istanbul—but a note by Yeats
suggests that he has in mind the city as it might have been in the sixth century).
(Note that: "perne" is "spin.")*

# Leda and the Swan

>>>>>>>

A sudden blow: the great wings beating still
Above the staggering girl, her thighs caressed
By the dark webs, her nape caught in his bill,
He holds her helpless breast upon his breast.

How can those terrified vague fingers push
The feathered glory from her loosening thighs?
And how can body, laid in that white rush,
But feel the strange heart beating where it lies?

A shudder in the loins engenders there
The broken wall, the burning roof and tower
And Agamemnon dead.
                    Being so caught up,
So mastered by the brute blood of the air,
Did she put on his knowledge with his power
Before the indifferent beak could let her drop?

---

*Hopkins's "Windhover" (p. 790) was first published in 1918. It included "mastery of the thing" and "Brute beauty and valour and act, oh, air . . .," and Yeats writes here, in another poem about a terrifying bird, almost the same words in the same order: "So mastered by the brute blood of the air."*

# The Lake Isle of Innisfree

•⌇•

I will arise and go now, and go to Innisfree,
And a small cabin build there, of clay and wattles made:
Nine bean-rows will I have there, a hive for the honey-bee,
And live alone in the bee-loud glade.

And I shall have some peace there, for peace comes dropping
    slow,
Dropping from the veils of the morning to where the cricket
    sings;
There midnight's all a glimmer, and noon a purple glow,
And evening full of the linnet's wings.

And I will arise and go now, for always night and day
I hear the lake water lapping with low sounds by the shore;
While I stand on the roadway, or on the pavements gray,
I hear it in the deep heart's core.

---

*Yeats's celebrated poem of nostalgia was apparently inspired—not by a genuine desire to lead a simple agricultural life—but by falling asleep over Thoreau's* Walden. *The poem is parodied in Ezra Pound's "Mauberley."*

# When You Are Old

When you are old and gray and full of sleep,
And nodding by the fire, take down this book,
And slowly read, and dream of the soft look
Your eyes had once, and of their shadows deep;

How many loved your moments of glad grace,
And loved your beauty with love false or true,
But one man loved the pilgrim soul in you,
And loved the sorrows of your changing face;

And bending down beside the glowing bars,
Murmur, a little sadly, how love fled
And paced upon the mountains overhead
And hid his face amid a crowd of stars.

---

*Yeats wrote few translations, and in fact there are not many translations or adaptations in this book. "When You Are Old," represents a reworking by the young Yeats (in 1892) of a poem by the sixteenth-century French poet Pierre Ronsard, "Quand vous serez bien vielle, au soir à la chandelle."*

# Among School Children

### I

I walk through the long schoolroom questioning;
A kind old nun in a white hood replies;
The children learn to cipher and to sing,
To study reading-books and history,
To cut and sew, be neat in everything
In the best modern way—the children's eyes
In momentary wonder stare upon
A sixty-year-old smiling public man.

### II

I dream of a Ledaean body, bent
Above a sinking fire, a tale that she
Told of a harsh reproof, or trivial event
That changed some childish day to tragedy—
Told, and it seemed that our two natures blent
Into a sphere from youthful sympathy,
Or else, to alter Plato's parable,
Into the yolk and white of the one shell.

### III

And thinking of that fit of grief or rage
I look upon one child or t'other there
And wonder if she stood so at that age—
For even daughters of the swan can share
Something of every paddler's heritage—
And had that colour upon cheek or hair,
And thereupon my heart is driven wild:
She stands before me as a living child.

IV

Her present image floats into the mind—
Did Quattrocento finger fashion it
Hollow of cheek as though it drank the wind
And took a mess of shadows for its meat?
And I though never of Ledaean kind
Had pretty plumage once—enough of that,
Better to smile on all that smile, and show
There is a comfortable kind of old scarecrow.

V

What youthful mother, a shape upon her lap
Honey of generation had betrayed,
And that must sleep, shriek, struggle to escape
As recollection or the drug decide,
Would think her son, did she but see that shape
With sixty or more winters on its head,
A compensation for the pang of his birth,
Or the uncertainty of his setting forth?

VI

Plato thought nature but a spume that plays
Upon a ghostly paradigm of things;
Solider Aristotle played the taws
Upon the bottom of a king of kings;
World-famous golden-thighed Pythagoras
Fingered upon a fiddle-stick or strings
What a star sang and careless Muses heard:
Old clothes upon old sticks to scare a bird.

VII

Both nuns and mothers worship images,
But those the candles light are not as those
That animate a mother's reveries,
But keep a marble or a bronze repose.
And yet they too break hearts—O Presences
That passion, piety or affection knows,
And that all heavenly glory symbolise—
O self-born mockers of man's enterprise;

VIII

Labour is blossoming or dancing where
The body is not bruised to pleasure soul,
Nor beauty born out of its own despair,
Nor blear-eyed wisdom out of midnight oil.
O chestnut tree, great rooted blossomer,
Are you the leaf, the blossom or the bole?
O body swayed to music, O brightening glance,
How can we know the dancer from the dance?

*In eight eight-line stanzas, the poet moves from a literally pedestrian statement about bureaucratic walking to a literally ecstatic question about charismatic dancing. Within this orbit, there is room for personal considerations and for the grandest philosophical and theological speculation.*

# An Irish Airman Foresees His Death

I know that I shall meet my fate
Somewhere among the clouds above;
Those that I fight I do not hate,
Those that I guard I do not love;
My country is Kiltartan Cross,
My countrymen Kiltartan's poor,
No likely end could bring them loss
Or leave them happier than before.
Nor law, nor duty bade me fight,
Nor public men, nor cheering crowds,
A lonely impulse of delight
Drove to this tumult in the clouds;
I balanced all, brought all to mind,
The years to come seemed waste of breath,
A waste of breath the years behind
In balance with this life, this death.

*Major Robert Gregory was the son of Lady Augusta Gregory, Yeats's friend and co-founder of the Abbey Theatre. He was killed in early 1918.*

# Easter, 1916

()◄███► ()

I have met them at close of day
Coming with vivid faces
From counter or desk among grey
Eighteenth-century houses.
I have passed with a nod of the head
Or polite meaningless words,
Or have lingered awhile and said
Polite meaningless words,
And thought before I had done
Of a mocking tale or a gibe
To please a companion
Around the fire at the club,
Being certain that they and I
But lived where motley is worn:
All changed, changed utterly:
A terrible beauty is born.

That woman's days were spent
In ignorant good-will,
Her nights in argument
Until her voice grew shrill.
What voice more sweet than hers
When, young and beautiful,
She rode to harriers?
This man had kept a school
And rode our wingèd horse;
This other his helper and friend
Was coming into his force;
He might have won fame in the end,
So sensitive his nature seemed,
So daring and sweet his thought.
This other man I had dreamed
A drunken, vainglorious lout.
He had done most bitter wrong

To some who are near my heart,
Yet I number him in the song;
He, too, has resigned his part
In the casual comedy;
He, too, has been changed in his turn,
Transformed utterly:
A terrible beauty is born.
Hearts with one purpose alone
Through summer and winter seem
Enchanted to a stone
To trouble the living stream.
The horse that comes from the road,
The rider, the birds that range
From cloud to tumbling cloud,
Minute by minute they change;
A shadow of cloud on the stream
Changes minute by minute;
A horse-hoof slides on the brim,
And a horse plashes within it;
The long-legged moor-hens dive,
And hens to moor-cocks call;
Minute by minute they live:
The stone's in the midst of all.

Too long a sacrifice
Can make a stone of the heart.
O when may it suffice?
That is Heaven's part, our part
To murmur name upon name,
As a mother names her child
When sleep at last has come
On limbs that had run wild.
What is it but nightfall?
No, no, not night but death;
Was it needless death after all?
For England may keep faith
For all that is done and said.
We know their dream; enough

To know they dreamed and are dead;
And what if excess of love
Bewildered them till they died?
I write it out in a verse —
MacDonagh and MacBride
And Connolly and Pearse
Now and in time to be,
Wherever green is worn,
Are changed, changed utterly:
A terrible beauty is born.

---

*In "September 1913" Yeats had announced the death of Romantic Ireland. After the failure of the Easter Rebellion and the execution of sixteen of the Irish leaders in late April and early May of 1916, the Irish-American Joyce Kilmer wrote a lament that began by mocking Yeats's earlier "Romantic Ireland's dead and gone." In September 1916, as though in answer to Kilmer, from whom he borrowed some verbiage and rhetoric, Yeats produced one of the great political elegies of all time.*

# The Wild Swans at Coole

The trees are in their autumn beauty,
The woodland paths are dry,
Under the October twilight the water
Mirrors a still sky;
Upon the brimming water among the stones
Are nine-and-fifty swans.

The nineteenth autumn has come upon me
Since I first made my count;
I saw, before I had well finished,
All suddenly mount
And scatter wheeling in great broken rings
Upon their clamorous wings.

I have looked upon those brilliant creatures,
And now my heart is sore.
All's changed since I, hearing at twilight,
The first time on this shore,
The bell-beat of their wings above my head,
Trod with a lighter tread.

Unwearied still, lover by lover,
They paddle in the cold
Companionable streams or climb the air;
Their hearts have not grown old;
Passion or conquest, wander where they will,
Attend upon them still.

But now they drift on the still water,
Mysterious, beautiful;
Among what rushes will they build,
By what lake's edge or pool
Delight men's eyes when I awake some day
To find they have flown away?

---

*Yeats seems to have produced a touchstone poem for certain lower slopes of the postmodern mentality. Clive James has ironically entitled a book* Brilliant Creatures; *the teacher in the movie* Educating Rita *cites "stones"/"swans" as an instance of consonance (which Rita explains as "The rhyme's not right"). Like many of Yeats's poems, this one ends with a question.*

# The Circus Animals' Desertion

### I

I sought a theme and sought for it in vain,
I sought it daily for six weeks or so.
Maybe at last, being but a broken man,
I must be satisfied with my heart, although
Winter and summer till old age began
My circus animals were all on show,
Those stilted boys, that burnished chariot,
Lion and woman and the Lord knows what.

### II

What can I but enumerate old themes?
First that sea-rider Oisin led by the nose
Through three enchanted islands, allegorical dreams,
Vain gaiety, vain battle, vain repose,
Themes of the embittered heart, or so it seems,
That might adorn old songs or courtly shows;
But what cared I that set him on to ride,
I, starved for the bosom of his faery bride?
And then a counter-truth filled out its play,
*The Countess Cathleen* was the name I gave it;
She, pity-crazed, had given her soul away,
But masterful Heaven had intervened to save it.
I thought my dear must her own soul destroy,
So did fanaticism and hate enslave it,
And this brought forth a dream and soon enough
This dream itself had all my thought and love.

And when the Fool and Blind Man stole the bread
Cuchulain fought the ungovernable sea;
Heart-mysteries there, and yet when all is said
It was the dream itself enchanted me:
Character isolated by a deed
To engross the present and dominate memory.
Players and painted stage took all my love,
And not those things that they were emblems of.

### III

Those masterful images because complete
Grew in pure mind, but out of what began?
A mound of refuse or the sweepings of a street,
Old kettles, old bottles, and a broken can,
Old iron, old bones, old rags, that raving slut
Who keeps the till. Now that my ladder's gone,
I must lie down where all the ladders start,
In the foul rag-and-bone shop of the heart.

---

*In this late poem, Yeats looks back on his earliest works, some of them fifty and more years in the past. The references are to a long allegorical poem (The Wanderings of Oisin) and two plays (The Countess Cathleen and On Baile's Strand) as well as to his long-standing vexatious relationship with Maud Gonne, the most important personage in Yeats's work from beginning to end.*

# A Prayer for My Daughter

Once more the storm is howling, and half hid
Under this cradle-hood and coverlid
My child sleeps on. There is no obstacle
But Gregory's wood and one bare hill
Whereby the haystack- and roof-levelling wind,
Bred on the Atlantic, can be stayed;
And for an hour I have walked and prayed
Because of the great gloom that is in my mind.

I have walked and prayed for this young child an hour
And heard the sea-wind scream upon the tower,
And under the arches of the bridge, and scream
In the elms above the flooded stream;
Imagining in excited reverie
That the future years had come,
Dancing to a frenzied drum,
Out of the murderous innocence of the sea.

May she be granted beauty and yet not
Beauty to make a stranger's eye distraught,
Or hers before a looking-glass, for such,
Being made beautiful overmuch,
Consider beauty a sufficient end,
Lose natural kindness and maybe
The heart-revealing intimacy
That chooses right, and never find a friend.

Helen being chosen found life flat and dull
And later had much trouble from a fool,
While that great Queen, that rose out of the spray,
Being fatherless could have her way
Yet chose a bandy-leggèd smith for man.
It's certain that fine women eat
A crazy salad with their meat
Whereby the Horn of Plenty is undone.

In courtesy I'd have her chiefly learned;
Hearts are not had as a gift but hearts are earned
By those that are not entirely beautiful;
Yet many, that have played the fool
For beauty's very self, has charm made wise,
And many a poor man that has roved,
Loved and thought himself beloved,
From a glad kindness cannot take his eyes.

May she become a flourishing hidden tree
That all her thoughts may like the linnet be,
And have no business but dispensing round
Their magnanimities of sound,
Nor but in merriment begin a chase,
Nor but in merriment a quarrel.
O may she live like some green laurel
Rooted in one dear perpetual place.

My mind, because the minds that I have loved,
The sort of beauty that I have approved,
Prosper but little, has dried up of late,
Yet knows that to be choked with hate
May well be of all evil chances chief.
If there's no hatred in a mind
Assault and battery of the wind
Can never tear the linnet from the leaf.

An intellectual hatred is the worst,
So let her think opinions are accursed.
Have I not seen the loveliest woman born
Out of the mouth of Plenty's horn,
Because of her opinionated mind
Barter that horn and every good
By quiet natures understood
For an old bellows full of angry wind?

Considering that, all hatred driven hence,
The soul recovers radical innocence
And learns at last that it is self-delighting,
Self-appeasing, self-affrighting,
And that its own sweet will is Heaven's will;
She can, though every face should scowl
And every windy quarter howl
Or every bellows burst, be happy still.

And may her bridegroom bring her to a house
Where all's accustomed, ceremonious;
For arrogance and hatred are the wares
Peddled in the thoroughfares.
How but in custom and in ceremony
Are innocence and beauty born?
Ceremony's a name for the rich horn,
And custom for the spreading laurel tree.

---

*Some readers, including some feminists, find it strange and even objectionable that Yeats should seemingly ask so little in a prayer for his only daughter. But Yeats bases his prayer for courtesy and modesty on experience (he was already fifty-three when she was born); he had seen the terrible damage that too much beauty can wreak.*

# *Lapis Lazuli*

For Harry Clifton

I have heard that hysterical women say
They are sick of the palette and fiddle-bow,
Of poets that are always gay,
For everybody knows or else should know
That if nothing drastic is done
Aeroplane and Zeppelin will come out,
Pitch like King Billy bomb-balls in
Until the town lie beaten flat.

All perform their tragic play,
There struts Hamlet, there is Lear,
That's Ophelia, that Cordelia;
Yet they, should the last scene be there,
The great stage curtain about to drop,
If worthy their prominent part in the play,
Do not break up their lines to weep.
They know that Hamlet and Lear are gay;
Gaiety transfiguring all that dread.
All men have aimed at, found and lost;
Black out; Heaven blazing into the head:
Tragedy wrought to its uttermost.
Though Hamlet rambles and Lear rages,
And all the drop-scenes drop at once
Upon a hundred thousand stages,
It cannot grow by an inch or an ounce.

On their own feet they came, or on shipboard,
Camelback, horseback, ass-back, mule-back,
Old civilizations put to the sword.
Then they and their wisdom went to rack:
No handiwork of Callimachus,
Who handled marble as if it were bronze,

Made draperies that seemed to rise
When sea-wind swept the corner, stands;
His long lamp-chimney shaped like the stem
Of a slender palm, stood but a day;
All things fall and are built again,
And those that build them again are gay.

Two Chinamen, behind them a third,
Are carved in lapis lazuli,
Over them flies a long-legged bird,
A symbol of longevity;
The third, doubtless a serving-man,
Carries a musical instrument.

Every discoloration of the stone,
Every accidental crack or dent,
Seems a water-course or an avalanche,
Or lofty slope where it still snows
Though doubtless plum or cherry-branch
Sweetens the little half-way house
Those Chinamen climb towards, and I
Delight to imagine them seated there;
There, on the mountain and the sky,
On all the tragic scene they stare.
One asks for mournful melodies;
Accomplished fingers begin to play.
Their eyes mid many wrinkles, their eyes,
Their ancient, glittering eyes, are gay.

---

*Such a theatrical poem about tragedy and gaiety deserves the full theatrical treatment. Kingsley Amis, among others, reports that Dylan Thomas would read "Lapis Lazuli" with all the tricks at his command, including a ten-second pause before the last two words. Amis may mean to disparage or ridicule both Thomas's performance and Yeats's poem, but for some readers Amis's account just raises both to an even grander level.*

# The Song of Wandering Aengus

I went out to the hazel wood,
Because a fire was in my head,
And cut and peeled a hazel wand,
And hooked a berry to a thread;
And when white moths were on the wing,
And moth-like stars were flickering out,
I dropped the berry in a stream
And caught a little silver trout.

When I had laid it on the floor
I went to blow the fire aflame,
But something rustled on the floor,
And some one called me by my name:
It had become a glimmering girl
With apple blossoms in her hair
Who called me by my name and ran
And faded through the brightening air.

Though I am old with wandering
Through hollow lands and hilly lands,
I will find out where she has gone,
And kiss her lips and take her hands;
And walk among long dappled grass,
And pluck till time and times are done
The silver apples of the moon,
The golden apples of the sun.

---

*Yeats was inspired by an ancient story of Aengus (or Óengus, also called the Macc Óc, "great son") who "was asleep one night when he saw something like a young girl . . . and she was the most beautiful woman in Ériu" (Gantz,* Early Irish Myths and Sagas*). He wandered for years in search of her.*

# No Second Troy

Why should I blame her that she filled my days
With misery, or that she would of late
Have taught to ignorant men most violent ways,
Or hurled the little streets upon the great,
Had they but courage equal to desire?
What could have made her peaceful with a mind
That nobleness made simple as a fire,
With beauty like a tightened bow, a kind
That is not natural in an age like this,
Being high and solitary and most stern?
Why, what could she have done, being what she is?
Was there another Troy for her to burn?

---

*In a poem made exclusively of rhetorical questions, Yeats likens Maud Gonne to
Helen: a superlatively beautiful and charismatic woman who also causes terrible
trouble. The likeness turns up in many other poems by Yeats, including "A
Prayer for My Daughter" (p. 871) and "Among School Children" (p. 860).*

Burgess is a lot like Ernest Lawrence Thayer (1863–1940), the author of "Casey at the Bat": born in the East, associated with California in its first heyday in the late nineteenth century, and remembered almost exclusively for a single piece of light verse.

## The Purple Cow

I never saw a Purple Cow,
I never hope to see one;
But I can tell you, anyhow,
I'd rather see than be one.

---

*Some poets live to regret having written wildly successful poems. Five years (presumably) after writing "The Purple Cow," Burgess offered "Cinq Ans Après":*

Ah, yes! I wrote the "Purple Cow"—
I'm Sorry, now, I Wrote it!
But I can Tell you, Anyhow,
I'll Kill you if you Quote it!

# ERNEST DOWSON 1867–1900

Although Dowson was born in Kent and schooled at
Oxford, he spent much of his short life in France, the
incarnation of dissipation and decadence. He was con-
sumptive and made his condition worse by drinking.
While living in the slums of London's East End, he met
his "Cynara," a café-owner's daughter who was to
marry a waiter.

## Non Sum Qualis Eram
## Bonae sub Regno Cynarae

Last night, ah, yesternight, betwixt her lips and mine
There fell thy shadow, Cynara! thy breath was shed
Upon my soul between the kisses and the wine;
And I was desolate and sick of an old passion,
   Yea, I was desolate and bowed my head:
I have been faithful to thee, Cynara! in my fashion.

All night upon mine heart I felt her warm heart beat,
Night-long within mine arms in love and sleep she lay;
Surely the kisses of her bought red mouth were sweet;
But I was desolate and sick of an old passion,
   When I awoke and found the dawn was gray:
I have been faithful to thee, Cynara! in my fashion.

I have forgot much, Cynara! gone with the wind,
Flung roses, roses riotously with the throng,
Dancing, to put thy pale, lost lilies out of mind;
But I was desolate and sick of an old passion,
   Yea, all the time, because the dance was long:
I have been faithful to thee, Cynara! in my fashion.

I cried for madder music and for stronger wine,
But when the feast is finished and the lamps expire,
Then falls thy shadow, Cynara! the night is thine;
And I am desolate and sick of an old passion,
   Yea, hungry for the lips of my desire:
I have been faithful to thee, Cynara! in my fashion.

---

*"I am not what I was under the rule of the kind Cynara" (Horace, Odes, I.iv). This modest poem provides the model for a memorable Cole Porter song and the phrase "Gone with the wind" that turns up in Joyce's Ulysses and elsewhere.*

## Vitae Summa Brevis
## Spem Nos Vetat Incohare Longam

They are not long, the weeping and the laughter,
   Love and desire and hate:
I think they have no portion in us after
   We pass the gate.

They are not long, the days of wine and roses:
   Out of a misty dream
Our path emerges for a while, then closes
   Within a dream.

---

*The title comes from Horace: "The brief sum of life forbids us the hope of enduring long." Dowson's poem furnished the title of a movie about alcoholics,* Days of Wine and Roses.

# EDGAR LEE MASTERS 1868-1950

Although Masters wrote history, biography, fiction, and
poetry of many sorts in many styles, he is remembered
only for one volume, *The Spoon River Anthology*, in which
free-verse epitaphs are spoken by the miscellaneous
dead (a few of whom had been real people) of a typical
midwestern village. The themes are those of Midwestern populism, but the form is in some ways classical,
based on the *Greek Anthology*, much of which is epitaphs
spoken by the dead themselves.

# Anne Rutledge

Out of me unworthy and unknown
The vibrations of deathless music;
"With malice toward none, with charity for all."
Out of me the forgiveness of millions toward millions,
And the beneficent face of a nation
Shining with justice and truth.
I am Anne Rutledge who sleep beneath these weeds,
Beloved in life of Abraham Lincoln,
Wedded to him, not through union,
But through separation.
Bloom forever, O Republic,
From the dust of my bosom!

from Spoon River Anthology

*Masters's* Spoon River Anthology, *consists of epitaphs, also spoken by the
dead. In most cases, Masters's characters are fictional and typical; Anne
Rutledge, however, is real, with plangent meaning for Americans and especially
for Midwesterners like Masters.*

Robinson's early books were not successful, but for the last twenty years of his life he was among the most honored American poets, receiving three Pulitzer Prizes. In addition to the quick, incisive sketches of the blighted lives of those doomed to a small-town existence—such as the poems of Robinson's that have made it into this anthology—he also wrote ambitious philosophical poems and, in his final years, Arthurian narratives, including *Merlin, Lancelot,* and *Tristram.*

# Mr. Flood's Party

Old Eben Flood, climbing alone one night
Over the hill between the town below
And the forsaken upland hermitage
That held as much as he should ever know
On earth again of home, paused warily.
The road was his with not a native near;
And Eben, having leisure, said aloud,
For no man else in Tilbury Town to hear:

"Well, Mr. Flood, we have the harvest moon
Again, and we may not have many more;
The bird is on the wing, the poet says,
And you and I have said it here before.
Drink to the bird." He raised up to the light
The jug that he had gone so far to fill,
And answered huskily: "Well, Mr. Flood,
Since you propose it, I believe I will."

Alone, as if enduring to the end
A valiant armor of scarred hopes outworn,
He stood there in the middle of the road
Like Roland's ghost winding a silent horn.
Below him, in the town among the trees,
Where friends of other days had honored him,
A phantom salutation of the dead
Rang thinly till old Eben's eyes were dim.

Then, as a mother lays her sleeping child
Down tenderly, fearing it may awake,
He set the jug down slowly at his feet
With trembling care, knowing that most things break;
And only when assured that on firm earth
It stood, as the uncertain lives of men
Assuredly did not, he paced away,
And with his hand extended paused again:

"Well, Mr. Flood, we have not met like this
In a long time; and many a change has come
To both of us, I fear, since last it was
We had a drop together. Welcome home!"
Convivially returning with himself,
Again he raised the jug up to the light;
And with an acquiescent quaver said:
"Well, Mr. Flood, if you insist, I might.

"Only a very little, Mr. Flood—
For auld lang syne. No more, sir; that will do."
So, for the time, apparently it did,
And Eben evidently thought so too;
For soon amid the silver loneliness
Of night he lifted up his voice and sang,
Secure, with only two moons listening,
Until the whole harmonious landscape rang—

"For auld lang syne." The weary throat gave out,
The last word wavered; and the song being done,
He raised again the jug regretfully
And shook his head, and was again alone.
There was not much that was ahead of him,
And there was nothing in the town below—
Where strangers would have shut the many doors
That many friends had opened long ago.

---

*By simply asserting the presence of two moons (instead of belaboring the point that drunkenness caused Mr. Flood to see double), the poem enters into the character's consciousness. The comparisons to a mother and to the heroic knight Roland also add sympathy.*

# Miniver Cheevy

Miniver Cheevy, child of scorn,
  Grew lean while he assailed the seasons;
He wept that he was ever born,
  And he had reasons.

Miniver loved the days of old
  When swords were bright and steeds were prancing;
The vision of a warrior bold
  Would set him dancing.

Miniver sighed for what was not,
  And dreamed, and rested from his labors;
He dreamed of Thebes and Camelot,
  And Priam's neighbors.

Miniver mourned the ripe renown
  That made so many a name so fragrant;
He mourned Romance, now on the town,
  And Art, a vagrant.

Miniver loved the Medici,
  Albeit he had never seen one;
He would have sinned incessantly
  Could he have been one.

Miniver cursed the commonplace
  And eyed a khaki suit with loathing;
He missed the medieval grace
  Of iron clothing.

Miniver scorned the gold he sought,
  But sore annoyed was he without it;
Miniver thought, and thought, and thought,
  And thought about it.

Miniver Cheevy, born too late,
  Scratched his head and kept on thinking;
Miniver coughed, and called it fate,
  And kept on drinking.

---

*"Miniver Cheevy" is partly a lucid, ironic caricature of a common village type ridiculously in love with Middle Ages that never existed, but it is partly a self-portrait as well: Robinson himself certainly "kept on drinking" and came to write some notoriously inert poems on Arthurian subjects.*

# Richard Cory

Whenever Richard Cory went down town,
We people on the pavement looked at him:
He was a gentleman from sole to crown,
Clean favored, and imperially slim.

And he was always quietly arrayed,
And he was always human when he talked;
But still he fluttered pulses when he said,
"Good-morning," and he glittered when he walked.

And he was rich—yes, richer than a king—
And admirably schooled in every grace:
In fine, we thought that he was everything
To make us wish that we were in his place.

So on we worked, and waited for the light,
And went without the meat, and cursed the bread;
And Richard Cory, one calm summer night,
Went home and put a bullet through his head.

---

*Robinson takes over the heroic quatrain of Gray's "Elegy Written in a Country Churchyard" (p. 327) to fashion a modern ironic epitaph. You can probably read an obituary for a Richard Cory in a local newspaper within the next twelve-month.*

# Eros Turannos

She fears him, and will always ask
  What fated her to choose him;
She meets in his engaging mask
  All reasons to refuse him;
But what she meets and what she fears
Are less than are the downward years,
Drawn slowly to the foamless weirs
  Of age, were she to lose him.

Between a blurred sagacity
  That once had power to sound him,
And Love, that will not let him be
  The Judas that she found him,
Her pride assuages her almost,
As if it were alone the cost.—
He sees that he will not be lost,
  And waits and looks around him.

A sense of ocean and old trees
  Envelopes and allures him;
Tradition, touching all he sees,
  Beguiles and reassures him;
And all her doubts of what he says
Are dimmed with what she knows of days—
Till even prejudice delays
  And fades, and she secures him.

The falling leaf inaugurates
The reign of her confusion;
The pounding wave reverberates
The dirge of her illusion;
And home, where passion lived and died,
Becomes a place where she can hide,
While all the town and harbor side
Vibrate with her seclusion.

We tell you, tapping on our brows,
The story as it should be,
As if the story of a house
Were told, or ever could be;
We'll have no kindly veil between
Her visions and those we have seen,
As if we guessed what hers have been,
Or what they are or would be.

Meanwhile we do no harm; for they
That with a god have striven,
Not hearing much of what we say,
Take what the god has given;
Though like waves breaking it may be,
Or like a changed familiar tree,
Or like a stairway to the sea
Where down the blind are driven.

---

*In a stanza form that seems to owe something to Swinburne's "Garden of Proserpine" (p. 766), Robinson locates the outline of a sad but familiar domestic story in a setting of pagan realism and irony, underscored by the Greek title ("Love the King" or "Love the Tyrant").*

# For a Dead Lady

No more with overflowing light
Shall fill the eyes that now are faded,
Nor shall another's fringe with night
Their woman-hidden world as they did.
No more shall quiver down the days
The flowing wonder of her ways,
Whereof no language may requite
The shifting and the many-shaded.

The grace, divine, definitive,
Clings only as a faint forestalling;
The laugh that love could not forgive
Is hushed, and answers to no calling;
The forehead and the little ears
Have gone where Saturn keeps the years;
The breast where roses could not live
Has done with rising and with falling.

The beauty, shattered by the laws
That have creation in their keeping,
No longer trembles at applause,
Or over children that are sleeping;
And we who delve in beauty's lore
Know all that we have known before
Of what inexorable cause
Makes Time so vicious in his reaping.

---

*It is typical of Robinson's iron discipline that he says that we "Know all that we have known before" but leaves the reader to figure out that all we know is nothing. It is typical of his fine craft that the fifth line of each stanza contains a word with an "-ore" sound, as though a mournful note were being softly repeated.*

# Luke Havergal

Go to the western gate, Luke Havergal,
There where the vines cling crimson on the wall,
And in the twilight wait for what will come.
The leaves will whisper there of her, and some,
Like flying words, will strike you as they fall;
But go, and if you listen she will call.
Go to the western gate, Luke Havergal—
Luke Havergal.

No, there is not a dawn in eastern skies
To rift the fiery night that's in your eyes;
But there, where western glooms are gathering,
The dark will end the dark, if anything:
God slays Himself with every leaf that flies,
And hell is more than half of paradise.
No, there is not a dawn in eastern skies—
In eastern skies.

Out of a grave I come to tell you this,
Out of a grave I come to quench the kiss
That flames upon your forehead with a glow
That blinds you to the way that you must go.
Yes, there is yet one way to where she is,
Bitter, but one that faith may never miss.
Out of a grave I come to tell you this—
To tell you this.

There is the western gate, Luke Havergal,
There are the crimson leaves upon the wall.
Go, for the winds are tearing them away,—
Nor think to riddle the dead words they say,
Nor any more to feel them as they fall;
But go, and if you trust her she will call.
There is the western gate, Luke Havergal—
Luke Havergal.

---

*The unobtrusive general imagery, powerful feeling, and subtle repetitions of words and rhythms all locate Robinson somewhere between Poe and Hardy.*

# WILLIAM HENRY DAVIES 1871–1940

The title of W. H. Davies's autobiography tells more of
his story than the titles of most such books: *The Autobiography of a Super-Tramp* (1908). Of his years as a
wanderer, several were spent in America.

## *Leisure*

What is this life if, full of care,
We have no time to stand and stare.

No time to stand beneath the boughs
And stare as long as sheep or cows.

No time to see, when woods we pass,
Where squirrels hide their nuts in grass.

No time to see, in broad daylight,
Streams full of stars like skies at night.

No time to turn at Beauty's glance,
And watch her feet, how they can dance.

No time to wait till her mouth can
Enrich that smile her eyes began.

A poor life this if, full of care,
We have no time to stand and stare.

---

*Davies gives us some idea of what Joyce Kilmer might have done had he been a
somewhat better writer.*

Walter de la Mare, born in Kent, was too poor to go to school beyond adolescence and worked for many years as a bookkeeper for a petroleum conglomerate. It was not until middle age that he could spend all his time as a writer. He is best known for his fanciful poetry (praised by Hardy, Eliot, and Auden), but he also wrote fiction, including the celebrated *Memoirs of a Midget* (1931).

## The Listeners

"Is there anybody there?" said the Traveler,
  Knocking on the moonlit door;
And his horse in the silence champed the grasses
  Of the forest's ferny floor:
And a bird flew up out of the turret,
  Above the Traveler's head:
And he smote upon the door again a second time;
  "Is there anybody there?" he said.
But no one descended to the Traveler;
  No head from the leaf-fringed sill
Leaned over and looked into his gray eyes,
  Where he stood perplexed and still.
But only a host of phantom listeners
  That dwelt in the lone house then
Stood listening in the quiet of the moonlight
  To that voice from the world of men:
Stood thronging the faint moonbeams on the dark stair,
  That goes down to the empty hall,
Hearkening in an air stirred and shaken
  By the lonely Traveler's call.
And he felt in his heart their strangeness,
  Their stillness answering his cry,
While his horse moved, cropping the dark turf,
  'Neath the starred and leafy sky;

For he suddenly smote on the door, even
   Louder, and lifted his head: —
"Tell them I came, and no one answered,
   That I kept my word," he said.
Never the least stir made the listeners,
   Though every word he spake
Fell echoing through the shadowiness of the still house
   From the one man left awake:
Ay, they heard his foot upon the stirrup,
   And the sound of iron on stone,
And how the silence surged softly backward,
   When the plunging hoofs were gone.

---

*Thomas Hardy, according to his widow's account of his last days, at the end "could no longer listen to the reading of prose, though a short poem now and again interested him." In the middle of one night he asked his wife to read "The Listeners" aloud to him.*

# ROBERT FROST 1874–1963

Although Frost was born in California and named for the Confederate general Robert E. Lee, he was associated for most of his long life with New England, where he was raised. Frost lived mostly in New Hampshire and Vermont but also spent significant periods in Michigan and Florida. He was unique in his power to combine a modernist sensibility and learning with a knack for the genuinely popular.

## Stopping by Woods on a Snowy Evening

Whose woods these are I think I know.
His house is in the village, though;
He will not see me stopping here
To watch his woods fill up with snow.

My little horse must think it queer
To stop without a farmhouse near
Between the woods and frozen lake
The darkest evening of the year.

He gives his harness bells a shake
To ask if there is some mistake.
The only other sound's the sweep
Of easy wind and downy flake.

The woods are lovely, dark and deep,
But I have promises to keep,
And miles to go before I sleep,
And miles to go before I sleep.

---

*The arrangement of the adjectives in the thirteenth line may be puzzling: the woods are lovely and dark and deep, or they are lovely because they are dark and deep. The second reading lends a measure of subtlety not evident in the simpler sequence.*

# Mending Wall

❖❖❖❖

Something there is that doesn't love a wall,
That sends the frozen-ground-swell under it
And spills the upper boulders in the sun,
And makes gaps even two can pass abreast.
The work of hunters is another thing:
I have come after them and made repair
Where they have left not one stone on a stone,
But they would have the rabbit out of hiding,
To please the yelping dogs. The gaps I mean,
No one has seen them made or heard them made,
But at spring mending-time we find them there.
I let my neighbor know beyond the hill;
And on a day we meet to walk the line
And set the wall between us once again.
We keep the wall between us as we go.
To each the boulders that have fallen to each.
And some are loaves and some so nearly balls
We have to use a spell to make them balance:
"Stay where you are until our backs are turned!"
We wear our fingers rough with handling them.
Oh, just another kind of outdoor game,
One on a side. It comes to little more:
There where it is we do not need the wall:
He is all pine and I am apple orchard.
My apple trees will never get across
And eat the cones under his pines, I tell him.
He only says, "Good fences make good neighbors."
Spring is the mischief in me, and I wonder
If I could put a notion in his head:
"*Why* do they make good neighbors? Isn't it
Where there are cows? But here there are no cows.
Before I built a wall I'd ask to know
What I was walling in or walling out,
And to whom I was like to give offense.

Something there is that doesn't love a wall,
That wants it down." I could say "Elves" to him,
But it's not elves exactly, and I'd rather
He said it for himself. I see him there,
Bringing a stone grasped firmly by the top
In each hand, like an old-stone savage armed.
He moves in darkness as it seems to me,
Not of woods only and the shade of trees.
He will not go behind his father's saying,
And he likes having thought of it so well
He says again, "Good fences make good neighbors."

---

*The sentiment can be traced back to* Poor Richard's Almanac, *but the wording is Frost's own, so that he is alone among modern poets distinguished by having composed a genuine proverb. One can read the poem as a justification for verse form, which itself is a fence, wall, or net for containing the unruly fears and desires that motivate us.*

# Fire and Ice

Some say the world will end in fire,
Some say in ice.
From what I've tasted of desire
I hold with those who favor fire.
But if it had to perish twice,
I think I know enough of hate
To say that for destruction ice
Is also great
And would suffice.

---

*Frost's treatment of elementary emblems matches the grace if not the depth of Eliot's "Little Gidding" (p. 987).*

# The Road Not Taken

>>>>>>>

Two roads diverged in a yellow wood,
And sorry I could not travel both
And be one traveler, long I stood
And looked down one as far as I could
To where it bent in the undergrowth;

Then took the other, as just as fair,
And having perhaps the better claim,
Because it was grassy and wanted wear;
Though as for that the passing there
Had worn them really about the same,

And both that morning equally lay
In leaves no step had trodden black.
Oh, I kept the first for another day!
Yet knowing how way leads on to way,
I doubted if I should ever come back.

I shall be telling this with a sigh
Somewhere ages and ages hence:
Two roads diverged in a wood, and I—
I took the one less traveled by,
And that has made all the difference.

---

*This was the opening poem in Frost's third book,* Mountain Interval *(1916).
It is said that Frost was thinking mainly of his friend and fellow-poet Edward
Thomas (see p. 917).*

# Birches

When I see birches bend to left and right
Across the line of straighter darker trees,
I like to think some boy's been swinging them.
But swinging doesn't bend them down to stay.
Ice-storms do that. Often you must have seen them
Loaded with ice a sunny winter morning
After a rain. They click upon themselves
As the breeze rises, and turn many-colored
As the stir cracks and crazes their enamel.
Soon the sun's warmth makes them shed crystal shells
Shattering and avalanching on the snow-crust—
Such heaps of broken glass to sweep away
You'd think the inner dome of heaven had fallen.
They are dragged to the withered bracken by the load,
And they seem not to break; though once they are bowed
So low for long, they never right themselves:
You may see their trunks arching in the woods
Years afterwards, trailing their leaves on the ground
Like girls on hands and knees that throw their hair
Before them over their heads to dry in the sun.
But I was going to say when Truth broke in
With all her matter-of-fact about the ice-storm
I should prefer to have some boy bend them
As he went out and in to fetch the cows—
Some boy too far from town to learn baseball,
Whose only play was what he found himself,
Summer or winter, and could play alone.
One by one he subdued his father's trees
By riding them down over and over again
Until he took the stiffness out of them,
And not one but hung limp, not one was left
For him to conquer. He learned all there was
To learn about not launching out too soon
And so not carrying the tree away

Clear to the ground. He always kept his poise
To the top branches, climbing carefully
With the same pains you use to fill a cup
Up to the brim, and even above the brim.
Then he flung outward, feet first, with a swish,
Kicking his way down through the air to the ground.

So was I once myself a swinger of birches;
And so I dream of going back to be.
It's when I'm weary of considerations,
And life is too much like a pathless wood
Where your face burns and tickles with the cobwebs
Broken across it, and one eye is weeping
From a twig's having lashed across it open.
I'd like to get away from earth awhile
And then come back to it and begin over.
May no fate willfully misunderstand me
And half grant what I wish and snatch me away
Not to return. Earth's the right place for love:
I don't know where it's likely to go better.
I'd like to go by climbing a birch tree,
And climb black branches up a snow-white trunk
*Toward* heaven, till the tree could bear no more,
But dipped its top and set me down again.
That would be good both going and coming back.
One could do worse than be a swinger of birches.

---

*"Birches" came out in 1915, a year after Joyce Kilmer's extraordinarily popular "Trees" appeared in* Poetry (Chicago). *It is as though Frost were saying, "If you want to write a real poem about trees, start with a specific tree, then report some personal experience, then . . . ."*

# After Apple-Picking

❖❖❖❖❖

My long two-pointed ladder's sticking through a tree
Toward heaven still,
And there's a barrel that I didn't fill
Beside it, and there may be two or three
Apples I didn't pick upon some bough.
But I am done with apple-picking now.
Essence of winter sleep is on the night,
The scent of apples: I am drowsing off.
I cannot rub the strangeness from my sight
I got from looking through a pane of glass
I skimmed this morning from the drinking trough
And held against the world of hoary grass.
It melted, and I let it fall and break.
But I was well
Upon my way to sleep before it fell,
And I could tell
What form my dreaming was about to take.
Magnified apples appear and disappear,
Stem end and blossom end,
And every fleck of russet showing clear.
My instep arch not only keeps the ache,
It keeps the pressure of a ladder-round.
I feel the ladder sway as the boughs bend.
And I keep hearing from the cellar bin
The rumbling sound
Of load on load of apples coming in.
For I have had too much
Of apple-picking: I am overtired
Of the great harvest I myself desired.
There were ten thousand thousand fruit to touch,
Cherish in hand, lift down, and not let fall.
For all
That struck the earth,
No matter if not bruised or spiked with stubble,

Went surely to the cider-apple heap
As of no worth.
One can see what will trouble
This sleep of mine, whatever sleep it is.
Were he not gone,
The woodchuck could say whether it's like his
Long sleep, as I describe its coming on,
Or just some human sleep.

---

*Frost gives enough anecdotal detail about actual apple-picking to invite the reader along on a symbolic interpretation, especially when the poem mentions heaven and earth outright and talks about the damnation of the fallen, even if blameless. (Such apples are still called "drops.") But there's no heavy lesson.*

# Acquainted with the Night

I have been one acquainted with the night. *
I have walked out in rain—and back in rain.
I have outwalked the furthest city light.

I have looked down the saddest city lane.
I have passed by the watchman on his beat
And dropped my eyes, unwilling to explain.

I have stood still and stopped the sound of feet
When far away an interrupted cry
Came over houses from another street,

But not to call me back or say good-by;
And further still at an unearthly height
One luminary clock against the sky

Proclaimed the time was neither wrong nor right.
I have been one acquainted with the night.

---

*Frost here shows his virtuosity in one of the rarest of verse forms, the "terza rima sonnet" that is also used in Shelley's "Ode to the West Wind" (p. 497).*

# Provide, Provide

The witch that came (the withered hag)
To wash the steps with pail and rag,
Was once the beauty Abishag,

The picture pride of Hollywood.
Too many fall from great and good
For you to doubt the likelihood.

Die early and avoid the fate.
Or if predestined to die late,
Make up your mind to die in state.

Make the whole stock exchange your own!
If need be occupy a throne,
Where nobody can call *you* crone.

Some have relied on what they knew;
Others on being simply true.
What worked for them might work for you.

No memory of having starred
Atones for later disregard,
Or keeps the end from being hard.

Better to go down dignified
With boughten friendship at your side
Than none at all. Provide, provide!

---

*The sad end of Rita Hayworth's life reminded some of this poem; such falls from greatness happen all the time, as the weekly tabloids are all-too-eager to document. One may object that the dialectical word "boughten" hints that Frost is not sincerely urging the reader to try to buy friendship, but the poem certainly sounds earnest. In public readings, Frost changed "Atones" to "Makes up," an earthier wording that adds to the credibility of the poem.*

# The Gift Outright

()◀━━▶()

The land was ours before we were the land's.
She was our land more than a hundred years
Before we were her people. She was ours
In Massachusetts, in Virginia,
But we were England's, still colonials,
Possessing what we still were unpossessed by,
Possessed by what we now no more possessed.
Something we were withholding made us weak
Until we found it was ourselves
We were withholding from our land of living,
And forthwith found salvation in surrender.
Such as we were we gave ourselves outright
(The deed of gift was many deeds of war)
To the land vaguely realizing westward,
But still unstoried, artless, unenhanced,
Such as she was, such as she would become.

---

*At the request of John F. Kennedy, Frost read this poem at the Inauguration of the President in 1961. Kennedy requested that the "would" in the last line be changed to "will," and Frost went along with the President, although the printed text was unchanged.*

# Directive

Back out of all this now too much for us,
Back in a time made simple by the loss
Of detail, burned, dissolved, and broken off
Like graveyard marble sculpture in the weather,
There is a house that is no more a house
Upon a farm that is no more a farm
And in a town that is no more a town.
The road there, if you'll let a guide direct you
Who only has at heart your getting lost,
May seem as if it should have been a quarry—
Great monolithic knees the former town
Long since gave up pretense of keeping covered.
And there's a story in a book about it:
Besides the wear of iron wagon wheels
The ledges show lines ruled southeast northwest,
The chisel work of an enormous Glacier
That braced his feet against the Arctic Pole.
You must not mind a certain coolness from him
Still said to haunt this side of Panther Mountain.
Nor need you mind the serial ordeal
Of being watched from forty cellar holes
As if by eye pairs out of forty firkins.
As for the woods' excitement over you
That sends light rustle rushes to their leaves,
Charge that to upstart inexperience.
Where were they all not twenty years ago?
They think too much of having shaded out
A few old pecker-fretted apple trees.
Make yourself up a cheering song of how
Someone's road home from work this once was,
Who may be just ahead of you on foot
Or creaking with a buggy load of grain.
The height of the adventure is the height
Of country where two village cultures faded

Into each other. Both of them are lost.
And if you're lost enough to find yourself
By now, pull in your ladder road behind you
And put a sign up CLOSED to all but me.
Then make yourself at home. The only field
Now left's no bigger than a harness gall.
First there's the children's house of make believe,
Some shattered dishes underneath a pine,
The playthings in the playhouse of the children.
Weep for what little things could make them glad.
Then for the house that is no more a house,
But only a belilaced cellar hole,
Now slowly closing like a dent in dough.
This was no playhouse but a house in earnest.
Your destination and your destiny's
A brook that was the water of the house,
Cold as a spring as yet so near its source,
Too lofty and original to rage.
(We know the valley streams that when aroused
Will leave their tatters hung on barb and thorn.)
I have kept hidden in the instep arch
Of an old cedar at the waterside
A broken drinking goblet like the Grail
Under a spell so the wrong ones can't find it,
So can't get saved, as Saint Mark says they mustn't.
(I stole the goblet from the children's playhouse.)
Here are your waters and your watering place.
Drink and be whole again beyond confusion.

---

*As with Williams's "Spring and All" (p. 937), Frost's "Directive" can be read as an answer to Eliot's "Waste Land" (p. 968). Or one could say that Frost joins Eliot in writing modern extensions of Oliver Goldsmith's "Deserted Village" (p. 341). As with "The Waste Land," "Directive" includes lilacs, a rock-water contrast, and reference to the legend of the Grail.*

# Design

·❖·❖·❖·❖·

I found a dimpled spider, fat and white,
On a white heal-all, holding up a moth
Like a white piece of rigid satin cloth—
Assorted characters of death and blight
Mixed ready to begin the morning right,
Like the ingredients of a witches' broth—
A snow-drop spider, a flower like a froth,
And dead wings carried like a paper kite.

What had that flower to do with being white,
The wayside blue and innocent heal-all?
What brought the kindred spider to that height,
Then steered the white moth thither in the night?
What but design of darkness to appall?—
If design govern in a thing so small.

---

*Stevens's "Thirteen Ways of Looking at a Blackbird" (p. 932) furnishes several new meanings of blackness, and Frost's "Design" makes whiteness—the outcome of the process of appalling, after all—a sign of (anticlimactic) death and blight.*

# JOHN MASEFIELD 1878–1967

Like W. H. Davies and Vachel Lindsay (who were also born in the 1870s), Masefield spent some of his early years in what is politely known as vagrancy. In time, Masefield turned to journalism and the steady production of poetry, more than fifty volumes all told. From 1930 until his death, Masefield was Poet Laureate, an honor that recognized his excellence in recording so much of British life, including the nautical experience and the country life.

## Cargoes

Quinquireme of Nineveh from distant Ophir
Rowing home to haven in sunny Palestine,
With a cargo of ivory,
And apes and peacocks,
Sandalwood, cedarwood, and sweet white wine.

Stately Spanish galleon coming from the Isthmus,
Dipping through the Tropics by the palm-green shores,
With a cargo of diamonds,
Emeralds, amethysts,
Topazes, and cinnamon, and gold moidores.

Dirty British coaster with a salt-caked smoke stack
Butting through the Channel in the mad March days,
With a cargo of Tyne coal,
Road-rail, pig-lead,
Firewood, iron-ware, and cheap tin trays.

---

*Masefield was one of the finest English poets of the sea, in a noble tradition going back to the Middle Ages. As Joseph Conrad demonstrates in the opening of* Heart of Darkness, *following the sea gives one a sense of a continuous maritime effort from prehistory to the present.*

# CARL SANDBURG 1878–1967

Sandburg was first recognized as a substantial poet
with the publication of *Chicago Poems* in 1916. He continued to produce short, free-verse poems, later writing
also a much longer evocation of America called *The
People, Yes* and a six-volume biography of Abraham
Lincoln.

# *Chicago*

Hog Butcher for the World,
Tool Maker, Stacker of Wheat,
Player with Railroads and the Nation's Freight Handler;
Stormy, husky, brawling,
City of the Big Shoulders:

They tell me you are wicked and I believe them, for I have seen
    your painted women under the gas lamps luring the farm
    boys.
And they tell me you are crooked and I answer: Yes, it is true I
    have seen the gunman kill and go free to kill again.
And they tell me you are brutal and my reply is: On the faces
    of women and children I have seen the marks of wanton
    hunger.
And having answered so I turn once more to those who sneer at
    this my city, and I give them back the sneer and say to
    them:
Come and show me another city with lifted head singing so
    proud to be alive and coarse and strong and cunning.
Flinging magnetic curses amid the toil of piling job on job, here
    is a tall bold slugger set vivid against the little soft cities;
Fierce as a dog with tongue lapping for action, cunning as a
    savage pitted against the wilderness,
    Bareheaded,
    Shoveling,

Wrecking,
Planning,
Building, breaking, rebuilding,
Under the smoke, dust all over his mouth, laughing with white
teeth,
Under the terrible burden of destiny laughing as a young man
laughs,
Laughing even as an ignorant fighter laughs who has never lost
a battle,
Bragging and laughing that under his wrist is the pulse, and
under his ribs the heart of the people,
     Laughing!
Laughing the stormy, husky, brawling laughter of Youth, half-
naked, sweating, proud to be Hog Butcher, Tool Maker,
Stacker of Wheat, Player with Railroads and Freight
Handler to the Nation.

---

*Chicago was long known as the second city (after New York). It was and is a tough town, especially in the winter, and the stockyards are still there. But, early in Sandburg's lifetime, energetic Chicago was also the home of some of America's most distinguished architecture, its most advanced poetry magazine, and one of its greatest universities.*

# Fog

The fog comes
on little cat feet.

It sits looking
over harbor and city
on silent haunches
and then, moves on.

---

*Sandburg is content to let a single metaphoric equation carry a whole poem; the same fog-cat image appears in Eliot's "Love Song of J. Alfred Prufrock" (p. 961).*

# Cool Tombs

When Abraham Lincoln was shoveled into the tombs he forgot
the copperheads and the assassin . . . in the dust, in the
cool tombs.

And Ulysses Grant lost all thought of con men and Wall Street,
cash and collateral turned ashes . . . in the dust, in the cool
tombs.

Pocahontas' body, lovely as a poplar, sweet as a red haw in
November or a pawpaw in May, did she wonder? does she
remember? . . . in the dust, in the cool tombs?

Take any streetful of people buying clothes and groceries,
cheering a hero or throwing confetti and blowing tin
horns . . . tell me if the lovers are losers . . . tell me if any
get more than the lovers . . . in the dust . . . in the cool
tombs.

---

*Like Edgar Lee Masters (see p. 882) and Vachel Lindsay (see pp. 918–919),
Sandburg was a Midwestern modernist taking advantage of the surge of energy
radiating from Chicago after 1890. For such poets, Lincoln and Grant were local
heroes of historic resonances, capable of being given a place among the other great
figures (Pocahontas . . . Cleopatra . . .) in a catalogue of oblivion.*

# Grass

Pile the bodies high at Austerlitz and Waterloo.
Shovel them under and let me work—
     I am the grass; I cover all.

And pile them high at Gettysburg
And pile them high at Ypres and Verdun.
Shovel them under and let me work.
Two years, ten years, and passengers ask the conductor:
     What place is this?
     Where are we now?

     I am the grass.
     Let me work.

---

*The original 1918 version of "Grass" catalogued battles from the Napoleonic Wars, the American Civil War, and the First World War. Later, in phonograph recordings made in the 1940s, Sandburg would add "Stalingrad" after "Verdun."*

# EDWARD THOMAS 1878–1917

In his early maturity, up to about the age of thirty-two,
Thomas was content to write prose, including a biography of the fascinating Victorian naturalist Richard
Jefferies. At the urging of his American friend Robert
Frost, however, Thomas turned to poetry, for which he
had a genuine calling. He belonged in the age-old, English rural-pastoral tradition, which has survived any
number of revolutions and vicissitudes since the Middle
Ages. Thomas enlisted in the army in 1915 and was
killed in Flanders.

# The Owl

Downhill I came, hungry, and yet not starved;
Cold, yet had heat within me that was proof
Against the North wind; tired, yet so that rest
Had seemed the sweetest thing under a roof.

Then at the inn I had food, fire, and rest,
Knowing how hungry, cold, and tired was I.
All of the night was quite barred out except
An owl's cry, a most melancholy cry

Shaken out long and clear upon the hill,
No merry note, nor cause of merriment,
But one telling me plain what I escaped
And others could not, that night, as in I went.

And slated was my food, and my repose,
Salted and sobered, too, by the bird's voice
Speaking for all who lay under the stars,
Soldiers and poor, unable to rejoice.

*As Robert Frost recognized, Edward Thomas belonged to an English tradition of
bucolic realists with heightened sensitivity but without heightened rhetoric.*

Externally, Lindsay's life resembles that of his contemporary, W. H. Davies; both men were poets who also spent time as tramps. Lindsay has forebears in a number of American traditions, including vaudeville, Whitman, revival meetings, and political oratory. He seemed always to be trying to live up to his heritage as a child of Springfield, Illinois, where Abraham Lincoln had lived and where he practiced law.

## Abraham Lincoln Walks at Midnight

In Springfield, Illinois

It is portentous, and a thing of state
That here at midnight, in our little town
A mourning figure walks, and will not rest,
Near the old court-house pacing up and down,
Or by his homestead, or in shadowed yards
He lingers where his children used to play,
Or through the market, on the well-worn stones
He stalks until the dawn-stars burn away.

A bronzed, lank man! His suit of ancient black,
A famous high top-hat and plain worn shawl
Make him the quaint great figure that men love,
The prairie-lawyer, master of us all.

He cannot sleep upon his hillside now.
He is among us:—as in times before!
And we who toss and lie awake for long
Breathe deep, and start, to see him pass the door.

His head is bowed. He thinks on men and kings.
Yea, when the sick world cries, how can he sleep?
Too many peasants fight, they know not why,
Too many homesteads in black terror weep.

The sins of all the war-lords burn his heart.
He sees the dreadnaughts scouring every main.
He carries on his shawl-wrapped shoulders now
The bitterness, the folly and the pain.

He cannot rest until a spirit-dawn
Shall come; — the shining hope of Europe free:
The league of sober folk, the Workers' Earth,
Bringing long peace to Cornland, Alp and Sea.

It breaks his heart that kings must murder still,
That all his hours of travail here for men
Seem yet in vain. And who will bring white peace
That he may sleep upon his hill again?

---

*Lindsay came from Springfield, Illinois, where Lincoln had practiced law before being elected to the Presidency in 1860. As with Masters's "Anne Rutledge" (p. 881), this is a poem by a Midwesterner about a Midwestern hero. From the perspective of the twentieth century's end, the ideal of "the Worker's Earth" may indeed sound quaint.*

# WALLACE STEVENS 1879–1955

Stevens, a lawyer, worked most of his adult life as an officer of a major insurance company (now called The Hartford). He did not publish his first book, *Harmonium*, until 1923, when he was in his middle forties. Thereafter at irregular intervals he published a succession of volumes of increasing solemnity and profundity. He was relegated to the margins of dandyism during most of his writing career but, since his death, has been recognized as uniquely central and important.

## Sunday Morning

### I

Complacencies of the peignoir, and late
Coffee and oranges in a sunny chair,
And the green freedom of a cockatoo
Upon a rug mingle to dissipate
The holy hush of ancient sacrifice.
She dreams a little, and she feels the dark
Encroachment of that old catastrophe,
As a calm darkens among water-lights.
The pungent oranges and bright, green wings
Seem things in some procession of the dead,
Winding across wide water, without sound.
The day is like wide water, without sound,
Stilled for the passing of her dreaming feet
Over the seas, to silent Palestine,
Dominion of the blood and sepulchre.

II

Why should she give her bounty to the dead?
What is divinity if it can come
Only in silent shadows and in dreams?
Shall she not find in comforts of the sun,
In pungent fruit and bright, green wings, or else
In any balm or beauty of the earth,
Things to be cherished like the thought of heaven,
Divinity must live within herself:
Passions of rain, or moods in falling snow;
Grievings in loneliness, or unsubdued
Elations when the forest blooms; gusty
Emotions on wet roads on autumn nights;
All pleasures and all pains, remembering
The bough of summer and the winter branch.
These are the measures destined for her soul.

III

Jove in the clouds had his inhuman birth.
No mother suckled him, no sweet land gave
Large-mannered motions to his mythy mind.
He moved among us, as a muttering king,
Magnificent, would move among his hinds,
Until our blood, commingling, virginal,
With heaven, brought such requital to desire
The very hinds discerned it, in a star.
Shall our blood fail? Or shall it come to be
The blood of paradise? And shall the earth
Seem all of paradise that we shall know?
The sky will be much friendlier then than now,
A part of labor and a part of pain,
And next in glory to enduring love,
Not this dividing and indifferent blue.

IV

She says, "I am content when wakened birds,
Before they fly, test the reality
Of misty fields, by their sweet questionings;
But when the birds are gone, and their warm field
Return no more, where, then, is paradise?"
There is not any haunt of prophecy,
Nor any old chimera of the grave,
Neither the golden underground, nor isle
Melodious, where spirits gat them home,
Nor visionary south, nor cloudy palm
Remote on heaven's hill, that has endured
As April's green endures; or will endure
Like her remembrance of awakened birds,
Or her desire for June and evening, tipped
By the consummation of the swallow's wings.


V

She says, "But in contentment I still feel
The need of some imperishable bliss."
Death is the mother of beauty; hence from her,
Alone, shall come fulfilment to our dreams
And our desires. Although she strews the leaves
Of sure obliteration on our paths,
The path sick sorrow took, the many paths
Where triumph rang its brassy phrase, or love
Whispered a little out of tenderness,
She makes the willow shiver in the sun
For maidens who were wont to sit and gaze
Upon the grass, relinquished to their feet.
She causes boys to pile new plums and pears
On disregarded plate. The maidens taste
And stray impassioned in the littering leaves.

VI

Is there no change of death in paradise?
Does ripe fruit never fall? Or do the boughs
Hang always heavy in that perfect sky,
Unchanging, yet so like our perishing earth,
With rivers like our own that seek for seas
They never find, the same receding shores
That never touch with inarticulate pang?
Why set the pear upon those river-banks
Or spice the shores with odors of the plum?
Alas, that they should wear our colors there,
The silken weavings of our afternoons,
And pick the strings of our insipid lutes!
Death is the mother of beauty, mystical,
Within whose burning bosom we devise
Our earthly mothers waiting, sleeplessly.


VII

Supple and turbulent, a ring of men
Shall chant in orgy on a summer morn
Their boisterous devotion to the sun,
Not as a god, but as a god might be,
Naked among them, like a savage source.
Their chant shall be a chant of paradise,
Out of their blood, returning to the sky;
And in their chant shall enter, voice by voice,
The windy lake wherein their lord delights,
The trees, like serafin, and echoing hills,
That choir among themselves long afterward.
They shall know well the heavenly fellowship
Of men that perish and of summer morn.
And whence they came and whither they shall go
The dew upon their feet shall manifest.

VIII

She hears, upon that water without sound,
A voice that cries, "The tomb in Palestine
Is not the porch of spirits lingering.
It is the grave of Jesus, where he lay."
We live in an old chaos of the sun,
Or old dependency of day and night,
Or island solitude, unsponsored, free,
Of that wide water, inescapable.
Deer walk upon our mountains, and the quail
Whistle about us their spontaneous cries;
Sweet berries ripen in the wilderness;
And, in the isolation of the sky,
At evening, casual flocks of pigeons make
Ambiguous undulations as they sink,
Downward to darkness, on extended wings.

---

*In some ways the most secular of poets, Stevens could write great poems of the earth by transforming the dignified idiom of the great poems of heaven and hell. Stevens emerged, by the time of his centennial in 1979, a central visionary of depth and substance, although, for him, as for Oscar Wilde, the aesthetic surface is the profoundest substance that we know.*

# Anecdote of the Jar

❖❖❖❖

I placed a jar in Tennessee,
And round it was, upon a hill.
It made the slovenly wilderness
Surround that hill.

The wilderness rose up to it,
And sprawled around, no longer wild.
The jar was round upon the ground
And tall and of a port in air.

It took dominion everywhere.
The jar was gray and bare.
It did not give of bird or bush,
Like nothing else in Tennessee.

---

*We seem to have here not only Stevens's but the whole twentieth century's version of Keats's "Ode on a Grecian Urn" (p. 546) — a poem that is about the power of a symmetrical and useful artifact to tame a wilderness.*

# The Emperor of Ice-Cream

Call the roller of big cigars,
The muscular one, and bid him whip
In kitchen cups concupiscent curds.
Let the wenches dawdle in such dress
As they are used to wear, and let the boys
Bring flowers in last month's newspapers.
Let be be finale of seem.
The only emperor is the emperor of ice-cream.

Take from the dresser of deal,
Lacking the three glass knobs, that sheet
On which she embroidered fantails once
And spread it so as to cover her face.
If her horny feet protrude, they come
To show how cold she is, and dumb.
Let the lamp affix its beam.
The only emperor is the emperor of ice-cream.

---

*Stevens enlarges on a joke in* Hamlet: *"Your worm is your only emperor for diet." Romance and ritual gloss over certain facts that an honest obituary needs to face. As palpably physical objects inviting attention to their own visible and audible reality, all poems remind us of our own mortality, which has an up-side as well as a down. The cold splendor of ice-cream is a function of our limitations, and, as Stevens says in "Sunday Morning" (p. 920), "Death is the mother of beauty."*

# The Idea of Order at Key West

>>>>>>>

She sang beyond the genius of the sea.
The water never formed to mind or voice,
Like a body wholly body, fluttering
Its empty sleeves; and yet its mimic motion
Made constant cry, caused constantly a cry,
That was not ours although we understood,
Inhuman, of the veritable ocean.

The sea was not a mask. No more was she.
The song and water were not medleyed sound
Even if what she sang was what she heard,
Since what she sang was uttered word by word.
It may be that in all her phrases stirred
The grinding water and the gasping wind;
But it was she and not the sea we heard.

For she was the maker of the song she sang.
The ever-hooded, tragic-gestured sea
Was merely a place by which she walked to sing.
Whose spirit is this? we said, because we knew
It was the spirit that we sought and knew
That we should ask this often as she sang.

If it was only the dark voice of the sea
That rose, or even colored by many waves;
If it was only the outer voice of sky
And cloud, of the sunken coral water-walled,
However clear, it would have been deep air,
The heaving speech of air, a summer sound
Repeated in a summer without end
And sound alone. But it was more than that,
More even than her voice, and ours, among
The meaningless plungings of water and the wind,
Theatrical distances, bronze shadows heaped

On high horizons, mountainous atmospheres
Of sky and sea.
                    It was her voice that made
The sky acutest at its vanishing.
She measured to the hour its solitude.
She was the single artificer of the world
In which she sang. And when she sang, the sea,
Whatever self it had, became the self
That was her song, for she was the maker. Then we,
As we beheld her striding there alone,
Knew that there never was a world for her
Except the one she sang and, singing, made.

Ramon Fernandez, tell me, if you know,
Why, when the singing ended and we turned
Toward the town, tell why the glassy lights,
The lights in the fishing boats at anchor there,
As the night descended, tilting in the air,
Mastered the night and portioned out the sea,
Fixing emblazoned zones and fiery poles,
Arranging, deepening, enchanting night.

Oh! Blessed rage for order, pale Ramon,
The maker's rage to order words of the sea,
Words of the fragrant portals, dimly-starred,
And of ourselves and of our origins,
In ghostlier demarcations, keener sounds.

---

*If "Anecdote of the Jar" (p. 925) is the counterpart of Keats's "Ode on a Grecian Urn" (p. 546), then "The Idea of Order at Key West" is one of many modern avatars of Matthew Arnold's "Dover Beach" (p. 706).*

# Peter Quince at the Clavier

### 1

Just as my fingers on these keys
Make music, so the selfsame sounds
On my spirit make a music, too.

Music is feeling, then, not sound;
And thus it is that what I feel,
Here in this room, desiring you,

Thinking of your blue-shadowed silk,
Is music. It is like the strain
Waked in the elders by Susanna.

Of a green evening, clear and warm,
She bathed in her still garden, while
The red-eyed elders watching, felt

The basses of their beings throb
In witching chords, and their thin blood
Pulse pizzicati of Hosanna.

### 2

In the green water, clear and warm,
Susanna lay.
She searched
The touch of springs,
And found
Concealed imaginings.
She sighed,
For so much melody.

Upon the bank, she stood
In the cool
Of spent emotions.
She felt, among the leaves,
The dew
Of old devotions.

She walked upon the grass,
Still quavering.
The winds were like her maids,
On timid feet,
Fetching her woven scarves,
Yet wavering.

A breath upon her hand
Muted the night.
She turned—
A cymbal crashed,
And roaring horns.

### 3

Soon, with a noise like tambourines,
Came her attendant Byzantines.
They wondered why Susanna cried
Against the elders by her side;

And as they whispered, the refrain
Was like a willow swept by rain.

Anon, their lamps' uplifted flame
Revealed Susanna and her shame.

And then, the simpering Byzantines
Fled, with a noise like tambourines.

4

Beauty is momentary in the mind—
The fitful tracing of a portal;
But in the flesh it is immortal.

The body dies; the body's beauty lives.
So evenings die, in their green going,
A wave, interminably flowing.
So gardens die, their meek breath scenting
The cowl of winter, done repenting.
So maidens die, to the auroral
Celebration of a maiden's choral.
Susanna's music touched the bawdy strings
Of those white elders; but, escaping,
Left only Death's ironic scraping.
Now, in its immortality, it plays
On the clear viol of her memory,
And makes a constant sacrament of praise.

---

A Midsummer Night's Dream, *in which Peter Quince is a clownish carpenter, contains four levels of romantic love: proletarian, aristocratic, heroic, and supernatural. The four parts of this poem can be matched up with that quartet of loves, along with autoerotism and religious devotion such as that in the Apocryphal Book of Susannah. As a formal encomium, Stevens's poem ends with "praise," as does Auden's "In Memory of W. B. Yeats" (p. 1028).*

# Thirteen Ways
## of Looking at a Blackbird

### I

Among twenty snowy mountains
The only moving thing
Was the eye of the blackbird.

### II

I was of three minds,
Like a tree
In which there are three blackbirds.

### III

The blackbird whirled in the autumn winds.
It was a small part of the pantomime.

### IV

A man and a woman
Are one.
A man and a woman and a blackbird
Are one.

### V

I do not know which to prefer,
The beauty of inflexions
Or the beauty of innuendos,
The blackbird whistling
Or just after.

VI

Icicles filled the long window
With barbaric glass.
The shadow of the blackbird
Crossed it, to and fro.
The mood
Traced in the shadow
An indecipherable cause.

VII

O thin men of Haddam,
Why do you imagine golden birds?
Do you not see how the blackbird
Walks around the feet
Of the women about you?

VIII

I know noble accents
And lucid, inescapable rhythms;
But I know, too,
That the blackbird is involved
In what I know.

IX

When the blackbird flew out of sight,
It marked the edge
Of one of many circles.

X

At the sight of blackbirds
Flying in a green light
Even the bawds of euphony
Would cry out sharply.

### XI

He road over Connecticut
In a glass coach.
Once, a fear pierced him,
In that he mistook
The shadow of his equipage
For blackbirds.

### XII

The river is moving.
The blackbird must be flying.

### XIII

It was evening all afternoon.
It was snowing
And it was going to snow.
The blackbird sat
In the cedar limbs.

---

*Poe's "Raven" (p. 625) seems to have laid down a reverberating challenge: the world distilled into the negative message of a single black bird at midnight. Stevens multiplies the single to thirteen—another loaded symbol—but suggests that neither thirteen nor black necessarily mean anything negative.*

# WILLIAM CARLOS WILLIAMS 1883–1963

Williams went straight from high school to medical school and then spent the bulk of his long life as a physician in Rutherford, New Jersey, not far from New York City. In his youth he knew both Ezra Pound and Hilda Doolittle, and his poetry grew and developed in much the same way theirs did: from mannered derivative romanticism to a tougher poetry of colloquial language and homely image.

## *The Red Wheelbarrow*

so much depends
upon

a red wheel
barrow

glazed with rain
water

beside the white
chickens

---

See *Stevens's* "*Thirteen Ways of Looking at a Blackbird*" *(p. 932). Williams takes up Poe's challenge and metamorphoses the Raven into many white domestic birds by daylight; and, as with Stevens, the meaning is obscure but affirmative.*

# The Dance

〰〰〰〰

In Breughel's great picture, The Kermess,
the dancers go round, they go round and
around, the squeal and the blare and the
tweedle of bagpipes, a bugle and fiddles
tipping their bellies (round as the thick-
sided glasses whose wash they impound)
their hips and their bellies off balance
to turn them. Kicking and rolling about
the Fair Grounds, swinging their butts, those
shanks must be sound to bear up under such
rollicking measures, prance as they dance
in Breughel's great picture, The Kermess.

---

*Williams must have loved Brueghel's paintings. In addition to this poem (one of few by Williams that take advantage of the powers of rhyme and regular rhythm), he wrote a dozen others about them, collected in a volume called* Pictures from Brueghel.

# Spring and All

()◀━▶()

By the road to the contagious hospital
under the surge of the blue
mottled clouds driven from the
northeast—a cold wind. Beyond, the
waste of broad, muddy fields
brown with dried weeds, standing and fallen

patches of standing water
the scattering of tall trees

All along the road the reddish
purplish, forked, upstanding, twiggy
stuff of bushes and small trees
with dead, brown leaves under them
leafless vines—

Lifeless in appearance, sluggish
dazed spring approaches—

They enter the new world naked,
cold, uncertain of all
save that they enter. All about them
the cold, familiar wind—

Now the grass, tomorrow
the stiff curl of wildcarrot leaf
One by one objects are defined—
It quickens: clarity, outline of leaf

But now the stark dignity of
entrance—Still, the profound change
has come upon them: rooted, they
grip down and begin to awaken

---

*"The Waste Land" (p. 968) challenged others to defend the idea of the good place (as Frost did in his* New Hampshire *in 1923) and the idea of the good season, as Williams did with* Spring and All, *also in 1923. The very word "waste" strengthens the similarity with Eliot's poem. Originally, this poem was untitled.*

# The Yachts

contend in a sea which the land partly encloses
shielding them from the too-heavy blows
of an ungoverned ocean which when it chooses

tortures the biggest hulls, the best man knows
to pit against its beatings, and sinks them pitilessly.
Mothlike in mists, scintillant in the minute

brilliance of cloudless days, with broad bellying sails
they glide to the wind tossing green water
from their sharp prows while over them the crew crawls

ant-like, solicitously grooming them, releasing,
making fast as they turn, lean far over and having
caught the wind again, side by side, head for the mark.

In a well guarded arena of open water surrounded by
lesser and greater craft which, sycophant, lumbering
and flittering follow them, they appear youthful, rare

as the light of a happy eye, live with the grace
of all that in the mind is feckless, free and
naturally to be desired. Now the sea which holds them

is moody, lapping their glossy sides, as if feeling
for some slightest flaw but fails completely.
Today no race. Then the wind comes again. The yachts

move, jockeying for a start, the signal is set and they
are off. Now the waves strike at them but they are too
well made, they slip through, though they take in canvas.

Arms with hands grasping seek to clutch at the prows.
Bodies thrown recklessly in the way are cut aside.
It is a sea of faces about them in agony, in despair

until the horror of the race dawns staggering the mind,
the whole sea become an entanglement of watery bodies
lost to the world bearing what they cannot hold. Broken,

beaten, desolate, reaching from the dead to be taken up
they cry out, failing, failing! their cries rising
in waves still as the skillful yachts pass over.

---

*Still a mysterious poem and, for Williams, an obscure one, beginning like Manet and ending like Dante. Yachts are superlative works of engineering, shaped with beautiful economy to engage the forces of wind and water. Racing yachts contend, among themselves and also with nature—perhaps the "horror of the race" means that of the human "race," for whom life is a supremely dangerous contest.*

# DAVID HERBERT LAWRENCE 1885–1930

It seems improbable that D. H. Lawrence will ever be more respected for his poetry than for his fiction, but stranger vicissitudes have befallen literary reputations. Lawrence came from a working-class Nottinghamshire family and worked briefly as a clerk and a schoolmaster. He eloped spectacularly with the wife of one of his Nottingham professors (she was six years older than he and had three young children) and set off on a life of wandering around the world, producing stories and novels that passionately explore the meaning of life and love. It was only after his death that the world had a chance to realize what an accomplished poet he had been, never more so than towards the end of his life when he produced a succession of powerful and moving elegies.

## Piano

◆◆◆◆

Softly, in the dusk, a woman is singing to me;
Taking me back down the vista of years, till I see
A child sitting under the piano, in the boom of the tingling
    strings
And pressing the small, poised feet of a mother who smiles as she
    sings.

In spite of myself, the insidious mastery of song
Betrays me back, till the heart of me weeps to belong
To the old Sunday evenings at home, with winter outside
And hymns in the cozy parlor, the tinkling piano our guide.

So now it is vain for the singer to burst into clamor
With the great black piano appassionato. The glamour
Of childish days is upon me, my manhood is cast
Down in the flood of remembrance, I weep like a child for the
    past.

---

*Lawrence sounds like a combination of Walt Whitman and Marcel Proust. The "glamour" here is the magic revived by Sir Walter Scott, not the later cosmetic debasement.*

[941]

# Snake

《《‹《《‹《《‹

A snake came to my water-trough
On a hot, hot day, and I in pajamas for the heat,
To drink there.
In the deep, strange-scented shade of the great dark carob tree
I came down the steps with my pitcher
And must wait, must stand and wait, for there he was at the
 trough before me.

He reached down from a fissure in the earth-wall in the gloom
And trailed his yellow-brown slackness soft-bellied down, over
 the edge of the stone trough
And rested his throat upon the stone bottom,
And where the water had dripped from the tap, in a small
 clearness,
He sipped with his straight mouth,
Softly drank through his straight gums, into his slack long
 body,
Silently.

Someone was before me at my water-trough,
And I, like a second comer, waiting.

He lifted his head from his drinking, as cattle do,
And looked at me vaguely, as drinking cattle do,
And flickered his two-forked tongue from his lips, and mused a
 moment,
And stooped and drank a little more,
Being earth-brown, earth-golden from the burning bowels of the
 earth
On the day of Sicilian July, with Etna smoking.

The voice of my education said to me
He must be killed,
For in Sicily the black, black snakes are innocent, the gold are
    venomous.

And voices in me said, If you were a man
You would take a stick and break him now, and finish him off.

But must I confess how I liked him,
How glad I was he had come like a guest in quiet, to drink at
    my water-trough
And depart peaceful, pacified, and thankless,
Into the burning bowels of this earth?

Was it cowardice, that I dared not kill him?
Was it perversity, that I longed to talk to him?
Was it humility, to feel so honored?
I felt so honored.

And yet those voices:
*If you were not afraid, you would kill him!*

And truly I was afraid, I was most afraid,
But even so, honored still more
That he should seek my hospitality
From out the dark door of the secret earth.

He drank enough
And lifted his head, dreamily, as one who has drunken,
And flickered his tongue like a forked night on the air, so
    black,
Seeming to lick his lips,
And looked around like a god, unseeing, into the air,
And slowly turned his head,
And slowly, very slowly, as if thrice adream,
Proceeded to draw his slow length curving round
And climb again the broken bank of my wall-face.

And as he put his head into that dreadful hole,
And as he slowly drew up, snake-easing his shoulders, and
    entered farther,
A sort of horror, a sort of protest against his withdrawing into
    that horrid black hole,
Deliberately going into the blackness, and slowly drawing
    himself after,
Overcame me now his back was turned.

I looked round, I put down my pitcher,
I picked up a clumsy log
And threw it at the water-trough with a clatter.

I think it did not hit him,
But suddenly that part of him that was left behind convulsed in
    undignified haste,
Writhed like lightning, and was gone
Into the black hole, the earth-lipped fissure in the wall-front,
At which, in the intense still noon, I stared with fascination.

And immediately I regretted it.
I thought how paltry, how vulgar, what a mean act!
I despised myself and the voices of my accursed human
    education.

And I thought of the albatross,
And I wished he would come back, my snake.

For he seemed to me again like a king,
Like a king in exile, uncrowned in the underworld,
Now due to be crowned again.

And so, I missed my chance with one of the lords
Of life.
And I have something to expiate;
A pettiness.

Not "A Snake" or "The Snake," "Snake" has to do with an archetypal snake at once real and symbolic. The biblical serpent remains an object of fear and evil. Some serpents can, however, be symbols of health (as on the caduceus) and good luck (as with certain dragons).

# Bavarian Gentians

>>>>>>>

Not every man has gentians in his house
in soft September, at slow, sad Michaelmas.

Bavarian gentians, big and dark, only dark
darkening the daytime, torch-like with the smoking blueness of
    Pluto's gloom,
ribbed and torch-like, with their blaze of darkness spread blue
down flattening into points, flattened under the sweep of white
    day
torch-flower of the blue-smoking darkness, Pluto's dark-blue
    daze,
black lamps from the halls of Dis, burning dark blue,
giving off darkness, blue darkness, as Demeter's pale lamps give
    off light,
lead me then, lead the way.

Reach me a gentian, give me a torch!
let me guide myself with the blue, forked torch of this flower
down the darker and darker stairs, where blue is darkened on
    blueness
even where Persephone goes, just now, from the frosted
    September
to the sightless realm where darkness is awake upon the dark
and Persephone herself is but a voice
or a darkness invisible enfolded in the deeper dark
of the arms Plutonic, and pierced with the passion of dense
    gloom,
among the splendor of torches of darkness, shedding darkness on
the lost bride and her groom.

*Looking at blue autumn flowers made Lawrence think of the year's death in late September, when Persephone must return to the underworld ruled by Pluto (Dis). Lawrence probably thought also of William Cullen Bryant's well-known poem "To the Fringed Gentian," which emphasizes the blueness of the flower and the frostiness of its season; and, as Lawrence would also be, Bryant was put in mind of his own "hour of death."*

# EZRA POUND 1885–1972

Pound was born in Idaho, educated in Pennsylvania
and New York, employed briefly in Indiana, and was
an expatriate for many years in England, France, and
Italy. During World War II he made scores of radio
broadcasts from Rome defending the Fascist powers
and attacking the Allies, including the United States.
He was indicted for treason but adjudged insane and
unfit for trial. He was held in the prison wing of a
federal mental hospital for more than a dozen years but
was finally released, too old any longer to threaten anyone. He returned to Italy in 1959 and lived on for thirteen more years, lapsing toward the end into humility
and silence after a long life of obstreperous racket,
much of it silly, some of it insane, but some of it of
matchless brilliance.

## The River-Merchant's Wife: A Letter

While my hair was still cut straight across my forehead
I played about the front gate, pulling flowers.
You came by on bamboo stilts, playing horse,
You walked about my seat, playing with blue plums.
And we went on living in the village of Chokan:
Two small people, without dislike or suspicion.

At fourteen I married My Lord you.
I never laughed, being bashful.
Lowering my head, I looked at the wall.
Called to, a thousand times, I never looked back.

At fifteen I stopped scowling,
I desired my dust to be mingled with yours
Forever and forever and forever.
Why should I climb the look out?

At sixteen you departed,
You went into far Ku-to-yen, by the river of swirling eddies,
And you have been gone five months.
The monkeys make sorrowful noise overhead.
You dragged your feet when you went out.
By the gate now, the moss is grown, the different mosses,
Too deep to clear them away!
The leaves fall early this autumn, in wind.
The paired butterflies are already yellow with August
Over the grass in the West garden;
They hurt me. I grow older.
If you are coming down through the narrows of the river Kiang,
Please let me know beforehand,
And I will come out to meet you
        As far as Cho-fu-Sa.

---

*Maybe because of his amateur standing as a sinologist (abetted by genius), Pound simplified the subtle style of Li Po's verse to a flat and rather commercial prose (the addressee is a merchant, after all) concentrating on visual images of objects with primary colors, like a woodblock print.*

# In a Station of the Metro

The apparition of these faces in the crowd;
Petals on a wet, black bough.

---

*The quintessential distillation of the principle of the Image. For poets of the Imagist school, which flourished between 1910 and 1920, the ideal of poetry is a clear presentation of the visual.*

# RUPERT BROOKE 1887–1915

Brooke, one of the most talented and attractive members of his generation, has been anthologized mostly as a war poet, but he is also recognized as a playwright and as the author of some very fine light verse.

## The Soldier

If I should die, think only this of me;
 That there's some corner of a foreign field
That is for ever England. There shall be
 In that rich earth a richer dust concealed;
A dust whom England bore, shaped, and made aware,
 Gave, once, her flowers to love, her ways to roam
A body of England's, breathing English air,
 Washed by the rivers, blest by the aura of home.

And think, this heart, all evil shed away,
 A pulse in the eternal mind, no less
  Gives somewhere back the thoughts by England given;
Her sights and sounds; dreams happy as her day;
 And laughter, learnt of friends; and gentleness,
  In hearts at peace, under an English heaven.

---

*Three poets in this anthology were killed in action in the First World War: Edward Thomas, Isaac Rosenberg, and Wilfred Owen. Brooke died of blood poisoning while en route to the Dardanelles but had earlier been involved in military operations and would certainly have seen action later if he had lived. "The Soldier," one of five war sonnets that Brooke wrote in 1914, cannot be interpreted as strictly autobiographical, since Brooke was not a soldier but a sailor. In any event, he is buried in a foreign field, on the Greek island of Scyros.*

Rather theatrically, Jeffers situated himself and his poetry in a stark landscape with inhospitable rocks, con-
temptuous hawks, and as few people as possible. He
was not always capable of living up to his stoical atti-
tudes, but he was consistent and stubborn, and once in
a while his language works like a harpoon. He is still
honored by such younger poets as William Everson,
James Tate, and Alan Williamson.

# Hurt Hawks

I

The broken pillar of the wing jags from the clotted shoulder,
The wing trails like a banner in defeat,
No more to use the sky forever but live with famine
And pain a few days: cat nor coyote
Will shorten the week of waiting for death, there is game
    without talons.
He stands under the oak-bush and waits
The lame feet of salvation; at night he remembers freedom
And flies in a dream, the dawns ruin it.
He is strong and pain is worse to the strong, incapacity is
    worse.
The curs of the day come and torment him
At distance, no one but death the redeemer will humble that
    head,
The intrepid readiness, the terrible eyes.
The wild God of the world is sometimes merciful to those
That ask mercy, not often to the arrogant.
You do not know him, you communal people, or you have
    forgotten him;
Intemperate and savage, the hawk remembers him;
Beautiful and wild, the hawks, and men that are dying,
    remember him.

II

I'd sooner, except the penalties, kill a man than a hawk; but the
      great redtail
Had nothing left but unable misery
From the bone too shattered for mending, the wing that trailed
      under his talons when he moved.
We had fed him six weeks, I gave him freedom,
He wandered over the foreland hill and returned in the evening,
      asking for death,
Not like a beggar, still eyed with the old
Implacable arrogance. I gave him the lead gift in the twilight.
      What fell was relaxed,
Owl-downy, soft feminine feathers; but what
Soared: the fierce rush: the night-herons by the flooded river
      cried fear at its rising
Before it was quite unsheathed from reality.

---

*Some readers may find Jeffers somewhat too melodramatic, too willing to identify
himself with an arrogant individualist bird, but, for many, he remains a powerfully eloquent champion of life away from "communal people." William Everson's "Poet Is Dead," which is a memorial for Jeffers, includes a reference to a
structure called Hawk Tower that Jeffers himself built: "On the top of the tower
/ The hawk will not perch tomorrow."*

# Shine, Perishing Republic

()◀━▶()

While this America settles in the mould of its vulgarity, heavily
thickening to empire,
And protest, only a bubble in the molten mass, pops and sighs
out, and the mass hardens,

I sadly smiling remember that the flower fades to make fruit, the
fruit rots to make earth.
Out of the mother; and through the spring exultances, ripeness
and decadence; and home to the mother.

You making haste haste on decay: not blameworthy; life is
good, be it stubbornly long or suddenly
A mortal splendor: meteors are not needed less than mountains:
shine, perishing republic.

But for my children, I would have them keep their distance
from the thickening center; corruption
Never has been compulsory, when the cities lie at the monster's
feet there are left the mountains.

And boys, be in nothing so moderate as in love of man, a clever
servant, insufferable master.
There is the trap that catches noblest spirits, that caught—they
say—God, when he walked on earth.

---

*One of Robert Frost's last poems is called "Our Doom to Bloom," and its
epigraph is "Shine, perishing republic." Frost's poem is much lighter-hearted
than Jeffers's.*

# MARIANNE MOORE 1887–1972

Marianne Moore was born in St. Louis, Missouri, the
year before T. S. Eliot was born in the same city. After
graduation from Bryn Mawr, she lived most of her long
life in New York City, much of the time in Brooklyn.
She was an editor of *The Dial* during the 1920s. In 1921,
she began publication of a succession of distinguished
books of poetry marked by scrupulous observation of
nature, a plucky spirit, and technical wizardry.

## Poetry

I, too, dislike it: there are things that are important beyond all
   this fiddle.
Reading it, however, with a perfect contempt for it, one
   discovers in
it after all, a place for the genuine.
   Hands that can grasp, eyes
   that can dilate, hair that can rise
      if it must, these things are important not because a

high-sounding interpretation can be put upon them but because
   they are
useful. When they become so derivative as to become
   unintelligible,
the same thing may be said for all of us, that we
   do not admire what
   we cannot understand: the bat
      holding on upside down or in quest of something to

eat, elephants pushing, a wild horse taking a roll, a tireless wolf under
    a tree, the immovable critic twitching his skin like a horse that feels a
        flea, the base-
        ball fan, the statistician—
    nor is it valid
        to discriminate against 'business documents and

school-books'; all these phenomena are important. One must make a distinction
    however: when dragged into prominence by half poets, the result is not poetry,
    nor till the poets among us can be
        'literalists of
        the imagination'—above
        insolence and triviality and can present

for inspection, 'imaginary gardens with real toads in them', shall we have
    it. In the meantime, if you demand on the one hand,
    the raw material of poetry in
        all its rawness and
        that which is on the other hand
        genuine, you are interested in poetry.

---

*A fastidious reviser, Marianne Moore produced several different versions of this poem, the last with just a few lines, ending with "genuine." Since the longer versions were the works represented in anthologies, however, the 1921 version that appeared in* Poetry *is given here.*

# A Grave

❖❖❖❖

Man looking into the sea,
taking the view from those who have as much right to it as you
   have to it yourself,
it is human nature to stand in the middle of a thing,
but you cannot stand in the middle of this;
the sea has nothing to give but a well excavated grave.
The firs stand in a procession, each with an emerald turkey foot
   at the top,
reserved as their contours, saying nothing;
repression, however, is not the most obvious characteristic of
   the sea;
the sea is a collector, quick to return a rapacious look.
There are others besides you who have worn that look—
whose expression is no longer a protest; the fish no longer
   investigate them
for their bones have not lasted:
men lower nets, unconscious of the fact that they are
   desecrating a grave,
and row quickly away—the blades of the oars
moving together like the feet of water spiders as if there were
   no such thing as death.
The wrinkles progress among themselves in a phalanx—beautiful
   under networks of foam,
and fade breathlessly while the sea rustles in and out of the
   seaweed;
the birds swim through the air at top speed, emitting catcalls as
   heretofore—
the tortoise shell scourges about the feet of the cliffs, in motion
   beneath them;
and the ocean, under the pulsation of lighthouses and noise of
   bell buoys,
advances as usual, looking as if it were not that ocean in which
   dropped things are bound to sink—

in which if they turn and twist, it is neither with volition nor consciousness.

---

*Marianne Moore here gave up her syllabic stanzas for an elegantly undulating look at much the same ocean as that addressed in Byron's* Childe Harold's Pilgrimage *(p. 486). Both pieces end with a sinking motion.*

# DAME EDITH SITWELL 1887–1964

The Sitwells have been a twentieth-century literary family, much as the Rossettis were a nineteenth-century literary family. For the purposes of this book, however, neither of Dame Edith's writing brothers (Sacheverell and Sir Osbert) are qualified for inclusion. At the time of World War I, Dame Edith edited a magazine called *Wheels*, in which Wilfred Owen's poems were first published. Her own earlier poems were gaudy and experimental, bristling with outlandish images and hyperkinetic syncopations, but, by the time of World War II, her tone had deepened into a most moving solemnity, achieving scriptural eloquence in many lines.

## Still Falls the Rain

(The Raids, 1940. Night and Dawn)

Still falls the Rain—
Dark as the world of man, black as our loss—
Blind as the nineteen hundred and forty nails
Upon the Cross.

Still falls the Rain
With a sound like the pulse of the heart that is changed to the
    hammerbeat
In the Potters' Field, and the sound of the impious feet
On the Tomb:
      Still falls the Rain
In the Field of Blood where the small hopes breed and the
    human brain
Nurtures its greed, that worm with the brow of Cain.

Still falls the Rain
At the feet of the Starved Man hung upon the Cross.
Christ that each day, each night, nails there, have mercy on us—
On Dives and on Lazarus:
Under the Rain the sore and the gold are as one.

Still falls the Rain—
Still falls the Blood from the Starved Man's wounded Side
He bears in his Heart all wounds,—those of the light that died,
The last faint spark
In the self-murdered heart, the wounds of the sad
    uncomprehending dark,
The wounds of the baited bear,—
The blind and weeping bear whom the keepers beat
On his helpless flesh . . . the tears of the hunted hare.

Still falls the Rain—
Then—O Ile leape up to my God: who pulles me doune—
See, see where Christ's blood streames in the firmament:
It flows from the Brow we nailed upon the tree
Deep to the dying, to the thirsting heart
That holds the fires of the world,—dark-smirched with pain
As Caesar's laurel crown.

Then sounds the voice of One who like the heart of man
Was once a child who among beasts has lain—
'Still do I love, still shed my innocent light, my Blood, for thee.'

---

*Her earlier poetry, published in the 1920s, was jazzy, and playful, but, with the coming of age Sitwell changed her style completely and achieved a level of dignity reminiscent of the great poets of the sixteenth and seventeenth centuries.*

Eliot emigrated to England in 1914 and became a British subject in 1927, but he retained an attachment to his native Saint Louis, Missouri, on the banks of the Mississippi, and to coastal Massachusetts, where his family had a summer home near Gloucester. His education was more in philosophy than in literature, and he all-but-finished the work for a Harvard doctorate. He worked for a time as an officer of a bank and then became a valued member of the directorate of Faber and Faber, publishers. In the 1920s he established a potent reputation as a poet and critic, and for many years he edited the influential magazine *The Criterion.* Like Thomas Hardy, he was given the Order of Merit; like W. B. Yeats, he was awarded the Nobel Prize for Literature.

# The Love Song of J. Alfred Prufrock

≫≫≫≫≫

*S'io credessi che mia risposta fosse*
*a persona che mai tornasse al mondo,*
*questa fiamma staria senza più scosse.*
*Ma per ciò che giammai di questo fondo*
*non tornò vivo alcun, s'i' odo il vero,*
*senza tema d'infamia ti rispondo.*

Dante Alighieri
*Inferno*

Let us go then, you and I,
When the evening is spread out against the sky
Like a patient etherised upon a table;
Let us go, through certain half-deserted streets,
The muttering retreats
Of restless nights in one-night cheap hotels
And sawdust restaurants with oyster-shells:
Streets that follow like a tedious argument
Of insidious intent
To lead you to an overwhelming question . . .
Oh, do not ask, "What is it?"
Let us go and make our visit.

In the room the women come and go
Talking of Michelangelo.

The yellow fog that rubs its back upon the window-panes,
The yellow smoke that rubs its muzzle on the window-panes,
Licked its tongue into the corners of the evening,
Lingered upon the pools that stand in drains,
Let fall upon its back the soot that falls from chimneys,
Slipped by the terrace, made a sudden leap,
And seeing that it was a soft October night,
Curled once about the house, and fell asleep.

And indeed there will be time
For the yellow smoke that slides along the street
Rubbing its back upon the window-panes;
There will be time, there will be time
To prepare a face to meet the faces that you meet;
There will be time to murder and create,
And time for all the works and days of hands
That lift and drop a question on your plate;
Time for you and time for me,
And time yet for a hundred indecisions,
And for a hundred visions and revisions,
Before the taking of a toast and tea.

In the room the women come and go
Talking of Michelangelo.

And indeed there will be time
To wonder, "Do I dare?" and, "Do I dare?"
Time to turn back and descend the stair,
With a bald spot in the middle of my hair—
(They will say: "How his hair is growing thin!")
My morning coat, my collar mounting firmly to the chin,
My necktie rich and modest, but asserted by a simple pin—
(They will say: "But how his arms and legs are thin!")
Do I dare
Disturb the universe?

In a minute there is time
For decisions and revisions which a minute will reverse.

For I have known them all already, known them all—
Have known the evenings, mornings, afternoons,
I have measured out my life with coffee spoons;
I know the voices dying with a dying fall
Beneath the music from a farther room.
    So how should I presume?

And I have known the eyes already, known them all—
The eyes that fix you in a formulated phrase,
And when I am formulated, sprawling on a pin,
When I am pinned and wriggling on the wall,
Then how should I begin
To spit out all the butt-ends of my days and ways?
    And how should I presume?

And I have known the arms already, known them all—
Arms that are braceleted and white and bare
(But in the lamplight, downed with light brown hair!)
Is it perfume from a dress
That makes me so digress?
Arms that lie along a table, or wrap about a shawl.
    And should I then presume?
    And how should I begin?

            . . . . . . . . . . . . . .

Shall I say, I have gone at dusk through narrow streets
And watched the smoke that rises from the pipes
Of lonely men in shirt-sleeves, leaning out of windows? . . .

I should have been a pair of ragged claws
Scuttling across the floors of silent seas.

            . . . . . . . . . . . . . .

And the afternoon, the evening, sleeps so peacefully!
Smoothed by long fingers,
Asleep . . . tired . . . or it malingers,
Stretched on the floor, here beside you and me.
Should I, after tea and cakes and ices,
Have the strength to force the moment to its crisis?
But though I have wept and fasted, wept and prayed,
Though I have seen my head (grown slightly bald) brought in
    upon a platter,
I am no prophet—and here's no great matter;
I have seen the moment of my greatness flicker,
And I have seen the eternal Footman hold my coat, and
    snicker,
And in short, I was afraid.

And would it have been worth it, after all,
After the cups, the marmalade, the tea,
Among the porcelain, among some talk of you and me,
Would it have been worth while,
To have bitten off the matter with a smile,
To have squeezed the universe into a ball
To roll it towards some overwhelming question,
To say: "I am Lazarus, come from the dead,
Come back to tell you all, I shall tell you all"—
If one, settling a pillow by her head,
    Should say: "That is not what I meant at all.
    That is not it, at all."

And would it have been worth it, after all,
Would it have been worth while,
After the sunsets and the dooryards and the sprinkled streets,
After the novels, after the teacups, after the skirts that trail
    along the floor—
And this, and so much more?—
It is impossible to say just what I mean!
But as if a magic lantern threw the nerves in patterns on a
    screen:
Would it have been worth while

If one, settling a pillow or throwing off a shawl,
And turning toward the window, should say:
  "That is not it, at all,
  That is not what I meant, at all."

. . . . . . . . . . . . . . .

No! I am not Prince Hamlet, nor was meant to be;
Am an attendant lord, one that will do
To swell a progress, start a scene or two,
Advise the prince; no doubt, an easy tool,
Deferential, glad to be of use,
Politic, cautious, and meticulous;
Full of high sentence, but a bit obtuse;
At times, indeed, almost ridiculous—
Almost, at times, the Fool.

I grow old . . . I grow old . . .
I shall wear the bottoms of my trousers rolled.

Shall I part my hair behind? Do I dare to eat a peach?
I shall wear white flannel trousers, and walk upon the beach.
I have heard the mermaids singing, each to each.

I do not think that they will sing to me.

I have seen them riding seaward on the waves
Combing the white hair of the waves blown back
When the wind blows the water white and black.

We have lingered in the chambers of the sea
By sea-girls wreathed with seaweed red and brown
Till human voices wake us, and we drown.

---

*Although it remains the last word in tired modernist irony and sophistication,*
*"The Love Song of J. Alfred Prufrock" was written by an uncommonly robust*
*twenty-year-old. The title is off-target, since this is a non-song about unlove, an*
*affair of inversions and subversions.*

# *Journey of the Magi*

"A cold coming we had of it,
Just the worst time of the year
For a journey, and such a long journey:
The ways deep and the weather sharp,
The very dead of winter."
And the camels galled, sore-footed, refractory,
Lying down in the melting snow.
There were times we regretted
The summer palaces on slopes, the terraces,
And the silken girls bringing sherbet.
Then the camel men cursing and grumbling
And running away, and wanting their liquor and women,
And the night-fires going out, and the lack of shelters,
And the cities hostile and the towns unfriendly
And the villages dirty and charging high prices:
A hard time we had of it.
At the end we preferred to travel all night,
Sleeping in snatches,
With the voices singing in our ears, saying
That this was all folly.

Then at dawn we came down to a temperate valley,
Wet, below the snow line, smelling of vegetation,
With a running stream and a water-mill beating the darkness,
And three trees on the low sky.
And an old white horse galloped away in the meadow.
Then we came to a tavern with vine-leaves over the lintel,
Six hands at an open door dicing for pieces of silver,
And feet kicking the empty wine-skins.
But there was no information, and so we continued
And arrived at evening, not a moment too soon
Finding the place; it was (you may say) satisfactory.

All this was a long time ago, I remember.
And I would do it again, but set down
This set down
This: were we led all that way for
Birth or Death? There was a Birth, certainly,
We had evidence and no doubt. I had seen birth and death,
But had thought they were different; this Birth was
Hard and bitter agony for us, like Death, our death.
We returned to our places, these Kingdoms,
But no longer at ease here, in the old dispensation,
With an alien people clutching their gods.
I should be glad of another death.

---

*This is the first of the five "Ariel Poems" that Eliot wrote after becoming an Anglo-Catholic in 1927. It is spoken by one of the Wise Men. The first five lines are quoted from a Jacobean sermon by Lancelot Andrewes (1555–1626), a preacher much admired by Eliot.*

# The Waste Land

Nam Sibyllam quidem Cumis ego ipse oculis meis vidi in ampulla
pendere, et cum illi pueri dicerent: Σίβυλλα τί θέλεις; respondebat
illa: ἀποθανεῖν θέλω.

Petronius
*Satyricon*

For Ezra Pound
*il miglior fabbro.*

## I. THE BURIAL OF THE DEAD

April is the cruellest month, breeding
Lilacs out of the dead land, mixing
Memory and desire, stirring
Dull roots with spring rain.
Winter kept us warm, covering
Earth in forgetful snow, feeding
A little life with dried tubers.
Summer surprised us, coming over the Starnbergersee
With a shower of rain; we stopped in the colonnade,
And went on in sunlight, into the Hofgarten,
And drank coffee, and talked for an hour.
Bin gar keine Russin, stamm' aus Litauen, echt deutsch.
And when we were children, staying at the arch-duke's,
My cousin's, he took me out on a sled,
And I was frightened. He said, Marie,
Marie, hold on tight. And down we went.
In the mountains, there you feel free.
I read, much of the night, and go south in the winter.

What are the roots that clutch, what branches grow
Out of this stony rubbish? Son of man,
You cannot say, or guess, for you know only
A heap of broken images, where the sun beats,
And the dead tree gives no shelter, the cricket no relief,
And the dry stone no sound of water. Only
There is shadow under this red rock,

(Come in under the shadow of this red rock),
And I will show you something different from either
Your shadow at morning striding behind you
Or your shadow at evening rising to meet you;
I will show you fear in a handful of dust.
>     *Frisch weht der Wind*
>     *Der Heimat zu*
>     *Mein Irisch Kind,*
>     *Wo weilest du?*
"You gave me hyacinths first a year ago;
"They called me the hyacinth girl."
—Yet when we came back, late, from the hyacinth garden,
Your arms full, and your hair wet, I could not
Speak, and my eyes failed, I was neither
Living nor dead, and I knew nothing,
Looking into the heart of light, the silence.
*Oed' und leer das Meer.*


Madame Sosostris, famous clairvoyante,
Had a bad cold, nevertheless
Is known to be the wisest woman in Europe,
With a wicked pack of cards. Here, said she,
Is your card, the drowned Phoenician Sailor,
(Those are pearls that were his eyes. Look!)
Here is Belladonna, the Lady of the Rocks,
The lady of situations.
Here is the man with three staves, and here the Wheel,
And here is the one-eyed merchant, and this card,
Which is blank, is something he carries on his back,
Which I am forbidden to see. I do not find
The Hanged Man. Fear death by water.
I see crowds of people, walking round in a ring.
Thank you. If you see dear Mrs. Equitone,
Tell her I bring the horoscope myself:
One must be so careful these days.

Unreal city,
Under the brown fog of a winter dawn,
A crowd flowed over London Bridge, so many,
I had not thought death had undone so many.
Sighs, short and infrequent, were exhaled,
And each man fixed his eyes before his feet.
Flowed up the hill and down King William Street,
To where Saint Mary Woolnoth kept the hours
With a dead sound on the final stroke of nine.
There I saw one I knew, and stopped him, crying: "Stetson!
"You who were with me in the ships at Mylae!
"That corpse you planted last year in your garden,
"Has it begun to sprout? Will it bloom this year?
"Or has the sudden frost disturbed its bed?
"O keep the Dog far hence, that's friend to men,
"Or with his nails he'll dig it up again!
"You! hypocrite lecteur! —mon semblable, —mon frère!"

## II. A GAME OF CHESS

The Chair she sat in, like a burnished throne,
Glowed on the marble, where the glass
Held up by standards wrought with fruited vines
From which a golden Cupidon peeped out
(Another hid his eyes behind his wing)
Doubled the flames of sevenbranched candelabra
Reflecting light upon the table as
The glitter of her jewels rose to meet it,
From satin cases poured in rich profusion.
In vials of ivory and coloured glass
Unstoppered, lurked her strange synthetic perfumes,
Unguent, powdered, or liquid—troubled, confused
And drowned the sense in odours; stirred by the air
That freshened from the window, these ascended
In fattening the prolonged candle-flames,
Flung their smoke into the laquearia,
Stirring the pattern on the coffered ceiling.
Huge sea-wood fed with copper
Burned green and orange, framed by the coloured stone,

In which sad light a carvèd dolphin swam.
Above the antique mantel was displayed
As though a window gave upon the sylvan scene
The change of Philomel, by the barbarous king
So rudely forced; yet there the nightingale
Filled all the desert with inviolable voice
And still she cried, and still the world pursues,
"Jug Jug" to dirty ears.
And other withered stumps of time
Were told upon the walls; staring forms
Leaned out, leaning, hushing the room enclosed.
Footsteps shuffled on the stair.
Under the firelight, under the brush, her hair
Spread out in fiery points
Glowed into words, then would be savagely still.

"My nerves are bad to-night. Yes, bad. Stay with me.
"Speak to me. Why do you never speak. Speak.
   "What are you thinking of? What thinking? What?
"I never know what you are thinking. Think."

I think we are in rats' alley
Where the dead men lost their bones.
"What is that noise?"
                    The wind under the door.
"What is that noise now? What is the wind doing?"
                    Nothing again nothing.
                                   "Do
"You know nothing? Do you see nothing? Do you remember
"Nothing?"

   I remember
Those are pearls that were his eyes.
"Are you alive, or not? Is there nothing in your head?"

But

O O O O that Shakespeherian Rag—
It's so elegant
So intelligent
"What shall I do now? What shall I do?
"I shall rush out as I am, and walk the street
"With my hair down, so. What shall we do tomorrow?
What shall we ever do?"
                     The hot water at ten.
And if it rains, a closed car at four.
And we shall play a game of chess,
Pressing lidless eyes and waiting for a knock upon the door.

When Lil's husband got demobbed, I said—
I didn't mince my words, I said to her myself,
HURRY UP PLEASE ITS TIME
Now Albert's coming back, make yourself a bit smart.
He'll want to know what you done with that money he gave
    you
To get yourself some teeth. He did, I was there.
You have them all out, Lil, and get a nice set,
He said, I swear, I can't bear to look at you.
And no more can't I, I said, and think of poor Albert,
He's been in the army four years, he wants a good time,
And if you don't give it him, there's others will, I said.
Oh is there, she said. Something o' that, I said.
Then I'll know who to thank, she said, and give me a straight
    look.
HURRY UP PLEASE ITS TIME
If you don't like it you can get on with it, I said.
Others can pick and choose if you can't.
But if Albert makes off, it won't be for lack of telling.
You ought to be ashamed, I said, to look so antique.
(And her only thirty-one.)
I can't help it, she said, pulling a long face,

It's them pills I took, to bring it off, she said.
(She's had five already, and nearly died of young George.)
The chemist said it would be all right, but I've never been the
    same.
You *are* a proper fool, I said.
Well, if Albert won't leave you alone, there it is, I said,
What you get married for if you don't want children?
HURRY UP PLEASE ITS TIME
Well, that Sunday Albert was home, they had a hot gammon,
And they asked me in to dinner, to get the beauty of it hot —
HURRY UP PLEASE ITS TIME
HURRY UP PLEASE ITS TIME
Goonight Bill. Goonight Lou. Goonight May. Goonight.
Ta ta. Goonight. Goonight.
Good night, ladies, good night, sweet ladies, good night, good
night.

### III. THE FIRE SERMON

The river's tent is broken; the last fingers of leaf
Clutch and sink into the wet bank. The wind
Crosses the brown land, unheard. The nymphs are departed.
Sweet Thames, run softly, till I end my song.
The river bears no empty bottles, sandwich papers,
Silk handkerchiefs, cardboard boxes, cigarette ends
Or other testimony of summer nights. The nymphs are
    departed.
And their friends, the loitering heirs of City directors;
Departed, have left no addresses.
By the waters of Leman I sat down and wept . . .
Sweet Thames, run softly, till I end my song,
Sweet Thames, run softly, for I speak not loud or long.
But at my back in a cold blast I hear
The rattle of the bones, and chuckle spread from ear to ear.

A rat crept softly through the vegetation
Dragging its slimy belly on the bank
While I was fishing in the dull canal
On a winter evening round behind the gashouse

Musing upon the king my brother's wreck
And on the king my father's death before him.
White bodies naked on the low damp ground
And bones cast in a little low dry garret,
Rattled by the rat's foot only, year to year.
But at my back from time to time I hear
The sound of horns and motors, which shall bring
Sweeney to Mrs. Porter in the spring.
O the moon shone bright on Mrs. Porter
And on her daughter
They wash their feet in soda water
*Et O ces voix d'enfants, chantant dans la coupole!*

Twit twit twit
Jug jug jug jug jug jug
So rudely forc'd.
Tereu

Unreal City
Under the brown fog of a winter noon
Mr. Eugenides, the Smyrna merchant
Unshaven, with a pocket full of currants
C.i.f. London: documents at sight,
Asked me in demotic French
To luncheon at the Cannon Street Hotel
Followed by a weekend at the Metropole.

At the violet hour, when the eyes and back
Turn upward from the desk, when the human engine waits
Like a taxi throbbing waiting,
I Tiresias, though blind, throbbing between two lives,
Old man with wrinkled female breasts, can see
At the violet hour, the evening hour that strives
Homeward, and brings the sailor home from sea,
The typist home at teatime, clears her breakfast, lights
Her stove, and lays out food in tins.
Out of the window perilously spread
Her drying combinations touched by the sun's last rays,

On the divan are piled (at night her bed)
Stockings, slippers, camisoles, and stays.
I Tiresias, old man with wrinkled dugs
Perceived the scene, and foretold the rest—
I too awaited the expected guest.
He, the young man carbuncular, arrives,
A small house agent's clerk, with one bold stare,
One of the low on whom assurance sits
As a silk hat on a Bradford millionaire.
The time is now propitious, as he guesses,
The meal is ended, she is bored and tired,
Endeavours to engage her in caresses
Which still are unreproved, if undesired..
Flushed and decided, he assaults at once;
Exploring hands encounter no defence;
His vanity requires no response,
And makes a welcome of indifference.
(And I Tiresias have foresuffered all
Enacted on this same divan or bed;
I who have sat by Thebes below the wall
And walked among the lowest of the dead.)
Bestows one final patronising kiss,
And gropes his way, finding the stairs unlit . . .

She turns and looks a moment in the glass,
Hardly aware of her departed lover;
Her brain allows one half-formed thought to pass:
"Well now that's done: and I'm glad it's over."
When lovely woman stoops to folly and
Paces about her room again, alone,
She smoothes her hair with automatic hand,
And puts a record on the gramophone.
"This music crept by me upon the waters"
And along the Strand, up Queen Victoria Street.
O City city, I can sometimes hear
Beside a public bar in Lower Thames Street,
The pleasant whining of a mandoline
And a clatter and a chatter from within

Where fishmen lounge at noon: where the walls
Of Magnus Martyr hold
Inexplicable splendour of Ionian white and gold.

The river sweats
Oil and tar
The barges drift
With the turning tide
Red sails
Wide
To leeward, swing on the heavy spar.
The barges wash
Drifting logs
Down Greenwich reach
Past the Isle of Dogs.
　　Weialala leia
　　Wallala leialala

Elizabeth and Leicester
Beating oars
The stern was formed
A gilded shell
Red and gold
The brisk swell
Rippled both shores
Southwest wind
Carried down stream
The peal of bells
White towers
　　Weialala leia
　　Wallala leialala

"Trams and dusty trees.
Highbury bore me. Richmond and Kew
Undid me. By Richmond I raised my knees
Supine on the floor of a narrow canoe."

"My feet are at Moorgate, and my heart
Under my feet. After the event
He wept. He promised 'a new start.'
I made no comment. What should I resent?"
"On Margate Sands.
I can connect
Nothing with nothing.
The broken fingernails of dirty hands.
My people humble people who expect
Nothing."
        la la

To Carthage then I came

Burning burning burning burning
O Lord Thou pluckest me out
O Lord Thou pluckest

burning

### IV. DEATH BY WATER

Phlebas the Phoenician, a fortnight dead,
Forgot the cry of gulls, and the deep sea swell
And the profit and loss.
                A current under sea
Picked his bones in whispers. As he rose and fell
He passed the stages of his age and youth
Entering the whirlpool.
                Gentile or Jew
O you who turn the wheel and look to windward,
Consider Phlebas, who was once handsome and tall as you.

### V. WHAT THE THUNDER SAID

After the torchlight red on sweaty faces
After the frosty silence in the gardens
After the agony in stony places
The shouting and the crying

Prison and palace and reverberation
Of thunder of spring over distant mountains
He who was living is now dead
We who were living are now dying
With a little patience

Here is no water but only rock
Rock and no water and the sandy road
The road winding above among the mountains
Which are mountains of rock without water
If there were water we should stop and drink
Amongst the rock one cannot stop or think
Sweat is dry and feet are in the sand
If there were only water amongst the rock
Dead mountain mouth of carious teeth that cannot spit
Here one can neither stand nor lie nor sit
There is not even silence in the mountains
But dry sterile thunder without rain
There is not even solitude in the mountains
But red sullen faces sneer and snarl
From doors of mudcracked houses
                    If there were water
    And no rock
    If there were rock
    And also water
    And water
    A spring
    A pool among the rock
    If there were the sound of water only
    Not the cicada
    And dry grass singing
    But sound of water over a rock
    Where the hermit-thrush sings in the pine trees
    Drip drop drip drop drop drop drop
    But there is no water

Who is the third who walks always beside you?
When I count, there are only you and I together
But when I look ahead up the white road
There is always another one walking beside you
Gliding wrapt in a brown mantle, hooded
I do not know whether a man or a woman
— But who is that on the other side of you?
What is that sound high in the air
Murmur of maternal lamentation
Who are those hooded hordes swarming
Over endless plains, stumbling in cracked earth
Ringed by the flat horizon only
What is the city over the mountains
Cracks and reforms and bursts in the violet air
Falling towers
Jerusalem Athens Alexandria
Vienna London
Unreal

A woman drew her long black hair out tight
And fiddled whisper music on those strings
And bats with baby faces in the violet light
Whistled, and beat their wings
And crawled head downward down a blackened wall
And upside down in air were towers
Tolling reminiscent bells, that kept the hours
And voices singing out of empty cisterns and exhausted wells

In this decayed hole among the mountains
In the faint moonlight, the grass is singing
Over the tumbled graves, about the chapel
There is the empty chapel, only the wind's home.
It has no windows, and the door swings,
Dry bones can harm no one.

Only a cock stood on the rooftree
Co co rico co co rico
In a flash of lightning. Then a damp gust
Bringing rain

Ganga was sunken, and the limp leaves
Waited for rain, while the black clouds
Gathered far distant, over Himavant.
The jungle crouched, humped in silence.
Then spoke the thunder
DA
*Datta:* what have we given?
My friend, blood shaking my heart
The awful daring of a moment's surrender
Which an age of prudence can never retract
By this, and this only, we have existed
Which is not to be found in our obituaries
Or in memories draped by the beneficent spider
Or under seals broken by the lean solicitor
In our empty rooms
DA
*Dayadhvam:* I have heard the key
Turn in the door once and turn once only
We think of the key, each in his prison
Thinking of the key, each confirms a prison
Only at nightfall, aethereal rumours
Revive for a moment a broken Coriolanus
DA
*Damyata:* The boat responded
Gaily, to the hand expert with sail and oar
The sea was calm, your heart would have responded
Gaily, when invited, beating obedient
To controlling hands

I sat upon the shore
Fishing, with the arid plain behind me
Shall I at least set my lands in order?
London Bridge is falling down falling down falling down
*Poi s'ascose nel foco che gli affina*
*Quando fiam uti chelidon*—O swallow swallow
*Le Prince d'Aquitaine à la tour abolie*
These fragments I have shored against my ruins
Why then Ile fit you. Hieronymo's mad againe.
Datta. Dayadhvam. Damyata.
　　　　Shantih　　　shantih　　　shantih

---

*After seventy years, "The Waste Land" remains the most influential poem of the twentieth century. Although obscure in many places and even opaque in some, it appeals to a great audience by the force of its images, rhythms, and overall design, which owes something to the five-act structure of Senecan and Elizabethan plays.*

# Sweeney among the Nightingales

ὤμοι, πέπληγμαι καιρίαν πληγὴν ἔσω.
Aeschylus
*Agamemnon*

Apeneck Sweeney spreads his knees
Letting his arms hang down to laugh,
The zebra stripes along his jaw
Swelling to maculate giraffe.

The circles of the stormy moon
Slide westward toward the River Plate,
Death and the Raven drift above
And Sweeney guards the hornèd gate.

Gloomy Orion and the Dog
Are veiled; and hushed the shrunken seas;
The person in the Spanish cape
Tries to sit on Sweeney's knees

Slips and pulls the table cloth
Overturns a coffee-cup,
Reorganized upon the floor
She yawns and draws a stocking up;

The silent man in mocha brown
Sprawls at the window-sill and gapes;
The waiter brings in oranges
Bananas figs and hothouse grapes;

The silent vertebrate in brown
Contracts and concentrates, withdraws;
Rachel *née* Rabinovitch
Tears at the grapes with murderous paws;

She and the lady in the cape
Are suspect, thought to be in league;
Therefore the man with heavy eyes
Declines the gambit, shows fatigue,

Leaves the room and reappears
Outside the window, leaning in,
Branches of wistaria
Circumscribe a golden grin;

The host with someone indistinct
Converses at the door apart,
The nightingales are singing near
The Convent of the Sacred Heart,

And sang within the bloody wood
When Agamemnon cried aloud,
And let their liquid siftings fall
To stain the stiff dishonoured shroud.

---

*Eliot, a reader of Thackeray, here adapts the two charades acted out in* Vanity
Fair: *Agamemnon and Nightingale. As with Thackeray's, Eliot's handling of the
myths brings out their depth and brutality.*

# Gerontion

Thou hast nor youth nor age
But as it were an after dinner sleep
Dreaming of both.

Here I am, an old man in a dry month,
Being read to by a boy, waiting for rain.
I was neither at the hot gates
Nor fought in the warm rain
Nor knee deep in the salt marsh, heaving a cutlass,
Bitten by flies, fought.
My house is a decayed house,
And the jew squats on the window sill, the owner,
Spawned in some estaminet of Antwerp,
Blistered in Brussels, patched and peeled in London.
The goat coughs at night in the field overhead;
Rocks, moss, stonecrop, iron, merds.
The woman keeps the kitchen, makes tea,
Sneezes at evening, poking the peevish gutter.
                    I an old man,
A dull head among windy spaces.

Signs are taken for wonders. "We would see a sign!"
The word within a word, unable to speak a word,
Swaddled with darkness. In the juvescence of the year
Came Christ the tiger
In depraved May, dogwood and chestnut, flowering judas,
To be eaten, to be divided, to be drunk
Among whispers; by Mr. Silvero
With caressing hands, at Limoges
Who walked all night in the next room;

By Hakagawa, bowing among the Titians;
By Madame de Tornquist, in the dark room
Shifting the candles; Fräulein von Kulp
Who turned in the hall, one hand on the door. Vacant shuttles
Weave the wind. I have no ghosts,
An old man in a draughty house
Under a windy knob.


After such knowledge, what forgiveness? Think now
History has many cunning passages, contrived corridors
And issues, deceives with whispering ambitions,
Guides us by vanities. Think now
She gives when our attention is distracted
And what she gives, gives with such supple confusions
That the giving famishes the craving. Gives too late
What's not believed in, or if still believed,
In memory only, reconsidered passion. Gives too soon
Into weak hands, what's thought can be dispensed with
Till the refusal propagates a fear. Think
Neither fear nor courage saves us. Unnatural vices
Are fathered by our heroism. Virtues
Are forced upon us by our impudent crimes.
These tears are shaken from the wrath-bearing tree.


The tiger springs in the new year. Us he devours. Think at last
We have not reached conclusions, when I
Stiffen in a rented house. Think at last
I have not made this show purposelessly
And it is not by any concitation
Of the backward devils.
I would meet you upon this honestly.
I that was near your heart was removed therefrom
To lose beauty in terror, terror in inquisition.
I have lost my passion: why should I need to keep it
Since what is kept must be adulterated?
I have lost my sight, smell, hearing, taste and touch:
How should I use them for your closer contact?

These with a thousand small deliberations
Protract the profit of their chilled delirium,
Excite the membrane, when the sense has cooled,
With pungent sauces, multiply variety
In a wilderness of mirrors. What will the spider do,
Suspend its operations, will the weevil
Delay? De Bailhache, Fresca, Mrs. Cammel, whirled
Beyond the circuit of the shuddering Bear
In fractured atoms. Gull against the wind, in the windy straits
Of Belle Isle, or running on the Horn,
White feathers in the snow, the Gulf claims,
And an old man driven by the Trades
To a sleepy corner.
                    Tenants of the house,
Thoughts of a dry brain in a dry season.

---

*Planned at one time to serve as the prologue to "The Waste Land," "Gerontion"
seems to be a cross-section or core-sample of the Western mind since the Persian
Wars. This "little old man" in a "dry month" was created by a thirty-year-old
poet in May and June of 1919, when there was a record drought in England.*

# Little Gidding

()◀━━▶()

I

Midwinter spring is its own season
Sempiternal though sodden towards sundown,
Suspended in time, between pole and tropic.
When the short day is brightest, with frost and fire,
The brief sun flames the ice, on pond and ditches,
In windless cold that is the heart's heat,
Reflecting in a watery mirror
A glare that is blindness in the early afternoon.
And glow more intense than blaze of branch, or brazier,
Stirs the dumb spirit: no wind, but pentecostal fire
In the dark time of the year. Between melting and freezing
The soul's sap quivers. There is no earth smell
Or smell of living thing. This is the spring time
But not in time's covenant. Now the hedgerow
Is blanched for an hour with transitory blossom
Of snow, a bloom more sudden
Than that of summer, neither budding nor fading,
Not in the scheme of generation.
Where is the summer, the unimaginable
Zero summer?

If you came this way,
Taking the route you would be likely to take
From the place you would be likely to come from,
If you came this way in may time, you would find the hedges
White again, in May, with voluptuary sweetness.
It would be the same at the end of the journey,
If you came at night like a broken king,
If you came by day not knowing what you came for,
It would be the same, when you leave the rough road
And turn behind the pig-sty to the dull façade
And the tombstone. And what you thought you came for
Is only a shell, a husk of meaning

From which the purpose breaks only when it is fulfilled
If at all. Either you had no purpose
Or the purpose is beyond the end you figured
And is altered in fulfillment. There are other places
Which also are the world's end, some at the sea jaws,
Or over a dark lake, in a desert or a city—
But this is the nearest, in place and time,
Now and in England.

If you came this way,
Taking any route, starting from anywhere,
At any time or at any season,
It would always be the same: you would have to put off
Sense and notion. You are not here to verify,
Instruct yourself, or inform curiosity
Or carry report. You are here to kneel
Where prayer has been valid. And prayer is more
Than an order of words, the conscious occupation
Of the praying mind, or the sound of the voice praying.
And what the dead had no speech for, when living,
They can tell you, being dead: the communication
Of the dead is tongued with fire beyond the language of the
living.
Here, the intersection of the timeless moment
Is England and nowhere. Never and always.

II

Ash on an old man's sleeve
Is all the ash the burnt roses leave.
Dust in the air suspended
Marks the place where a story ended.
Dust inbreathed was a house—
The wall, the wainscot and the mouse.
The death of hope and despair,
    This is the death of air.

There are flood and drouth
Over the eyes and in the mouth,

Dead water and dead sand
Contending for the upper hand.
The parched eviscerate soil
Gapes at the vanity of toil,
Laughs without mirth.
    This is the death of earth.

Water and fire succeed
The town, the pasture and the weed.
Water and fire deride
The sacrifice that we denied.
Water and fire shall rot
The marred foundations we forgot,
Of sanctuary and choir.
    This is the death of water and fire.

In the uncertain hour before the morning
    Near the ending of interminable night
    At the recurrent end of the unending
After the dark dove with the flickering tongue
    Had passed below the horizon of his homing
    While the dead leaves still rattled on like tin
Over the asphalt where no other sound was
    Between three districts whence the smoke arose
    I met one walking, loitering and hurried
As if blown towards me like the metal leaves
    Before the urban dawn wind unresisting.
    And as I fixed upon the down-turned face
That pointed scrutiny with which we challenge
    The first-met stranger in the waning dusk
    I caught the sudden look of some dead master
Whom I had known, forgotten, half recalled
    Both one and many; in the brown baked features
    The eyes of a familiar compound ghost
Both intimate and unidentifiable.
    So I assumed a double part, and cried
    And heard another's voice cry: "What! are *you* here?"
Although we were not. I was still the same,

Knowing myself yet being someone other—
And he a face still forming; yet the words sufficed
To compel the recognition they preceded.
And so, compliant to the common wind,
Too strange to each other for misunderstanding,
In concord at this intersection time
Of meeting nowhere, no before and after,
We trod the pavement in a dead patrol.
I said: "The wonder that I feel is easy,
Yet ease is cause of wonder. Therefore speak:
I may not comprehend, may not remember."
And he: "I am not eager to rehearse
My thought and theory which you have forgotten.
These things have served their purpose: let them be.
So with your own, and pray they be forgiven
By others, as I pray you to forgive
Both bad and good. Last season's fruit is eaten
And the fullfed beast shall kick the empty pail.
For last year's words belong to last year's language
And next year's words await another voice.
But, as the passage now presents no hindrance
To the spirit unappeased and peregrine
Between two worlds become much like each other,
So I find words I never thought to speak
In streets I never thought I should revisit
When I left my body on a distant shore.
Since our concern was speech, and speech impelled us
To purify the dialect of the tribe
And urge the mind to aftersight and foresight,
Let me disclose the gifts reserved for age
To set a crown upon your lifetime's effort.
First, the cold friction of expiring sense
Without enchantment, offering no promise
But bitter tastelessness of shadow fruit
As body and soul begin to fall asunder.
Second, the conscious impotence of rage
At human folly, and the laceration
Of laughter at what ceases to amuse.

And last, the rending pain of re-enactment
Of all that you have done, and been; the shame
Of motives late revealed, and the awareness
Of things ill done and done to others' harm
Which once you took for exercise of virtue.
Then fools' approval stings, and honour stains.
From wrong to wrong the exasperated spirit
Proceeds, unless restored by that refining fire
Where you must move in measure, like a dancer."
The day was breaking. In the disfigured street
He left me, with a kind of valediction,
And faded on the blowing of the horn.

III

There are three conditions which often look alike
Yet differ completely, flourish in the same hedgerow:
Attachment to self and to things and to persons, detachment
From self and from things and from persons; and, growing
    between them, indifference
Which resembles the others as death resembles life,
Being between two lives—unflowering, between
The live and the dead nettle. This is the use of memory:
For liberation—not less of love but expanding
Of love beyond desire, and so liberation
From the future as well as the past. Thus, love of a country
Begins as attachment to our own field of action
And comes to find that action of little importance
Though never indifferent. History may be servitude,
History may be freedom. See, now they vanish,
The faces and places, with the self which, as it could, loved
    them,
To become renewed, transfigured, in another pattern.
Sin is Behovely, but
All shall be well, and
All manner of thing shall be well.
If I think, again, of this place,
And of people, not wholly commendable,
Of no immediate kin or kindness,

But some of peculiar genius,
All touched by a common genius,
United in the strife which divided them;
If I think of a king at nightfall,
Of three men, and more, on the scaffold
And a few who died forgotten
In other places, here and abroad,
And of one who died blind and quiet,
Why should we celebrate
These dead men more than the dying?
It is not to ring the bell backward
Nor is it an incantation
To summon the spectre of a Rose.
We cannot revive old factions
We cannot restore old policies
Or follow an antique drum.
These men, and those who opposed them
And those whom they opposed
Accept the constitution of silence
And are folded in a single party.
Whatever we inherit from the fortunate
We have taken from the defeated
What they had to leave us—a symbol:
A symbol perfected in death.
And all shall be well and
All manner of thing shall be well
By the purification of the motive
In the ground of our beseeching.

IV

The dove descending breaks the air
With flame of incandescent terror
Of which the tongues declare
The one discharge from sin and error.
The only hope, or else despair
    Lies in the choice of pyre or pyre—
    To be redeemed from fire by fire.

Who then devised the torment? Love.
Love is the unfamiliar Name
Behind the hands that wove
The intolerable shirt of flame
Which human power cannot remove.
   We only live, only suspire
   Consumed by either fire or fire.

                    V
What we call the beginning is often the end
And to make an end is to make a beginning.
The end is where we start from. And every phrase
And sentence that is right (where every word is at home,
Taking its place to support the others,
The word neither diffident nor ostentatious,
An easy commerce of the old and the new,
The common word exact without vulgarity,
The formal word precise but not pedantic,
The complete consort dancing together)
Every phrase and every sentence is an end and a beginning,
Every poem an epitaph. And any action
Is a step to the block, to the fire, down the sea's throat
Or to an illegible stone: and that is where we start.
We die with the dying:
See, they depart, and we go with them.
We are born with the dead:
See, they return, and bring us with them.
The moment of the rose and the moment of the yew-tree
Are of equal duration. A people without history
Is not redeemed from time, for history is a pattern
Of timeless moments. So, while the light fails
On a winter's afternoon, in a secluded chapel
History is now and England.

With the drawing of this Love and the voice of this Calling

We shall not cease from exploration
And the end of all our exploring

Will be to arrive where we started
And know the place for the first time.
Through the unknown, remembered gate
When the last of earth left to discover
Is that which was the beginning;
At the source of the longest river
The voice of the hidden waterfall
And the children in the apple-tree
Not known, because not looked for
But heard, half-heard, in the stillness
Between two waves of the sea.
Quick now, here, now, always—
A condition of complete simplicity
(Costing not less than everything)
And all shall be well and
All manner of thing shall be well
When the tongues of flame are in-folded
Into the crowned knot of fire
And the fire and the rose are one.

---

*"Little Gidding" is the fourth of* Four Quartets. *It summarizes not only the earlier quartets but also much else of Eliot's work as well as that of his friends ("See, they return" comes from a poem by Ezra Pound). The scope of the whole poem, from title page to last word, goes from "Four" to "one"—from multiplicity and perplexity to unity and repose.*

# JOHN CROWE RANSOM 1888–1974

Ransom, a Tennessean educated at Vanderbilt and Oxford, was closely associated with the Agrarians (editing *The Fugitive*) and later the New Critics (editing *The Kenyon Review*), but his tastes were catholic and his interests not bound by regional or ideological prejudices. As a poet, Ransom is honored almost exclusively for poems issued in three small volumes between 1919 and 1927.

# *Bells for John Whiteside's Daughter*

There was such speed in her little body,
And such lightness in her footfall,
It is no wonder her brown study
Astonishes us all.

Her wars were bruited in our high window.
We looked among orchard trees and beyond
Where she took arms against her shadow,
Or harried unto the pond

The lazy geese, like a snow cloud
Dripping their snow on the green grass,
Tricking and stopping, sleepy and proud,
Who cried in goose, Alas,

For the tireless heart within the little
Lady with rod that made them rise
From their noon apple-dreams and scuttle
Goose-fashion under the skies!

But now go the bells, and we are ready,
In one house we are sternly stopped
To say we are vexed at her brown study,
Lying so primly propped.

---

*Ransom undermines the sentiment and the stanza (meter and rhyme) of Gray's "Elegy Written in a Country Churchyard" (p. 327) for a nicely mannered, modern ironic study of the immemorial challenge: how to write about a dead child (Ransom also wrote a poem called "Dead Boy"). See Jonson's "On My First Son" (p. 158) and Thomas's "A Refusal to Mourn the Death, by Fire, of a Child in London" (p. 1054).*

# Piazza Piece

—I am a gentleman in a dustcoat trying
To make you hear. Your ears are soft and small
And listen to an old man not at all,
They want the young men's whispering and sighing.
But see the roses on your trellis dying
And hear the spectral singing of the moon;
For I must have my lovely lady soon,
I am a gentleman in a dustcoat trying.

—I am a lady young in beauty waiting
Until my truelove comes, and then we kiss.
But what grey man among the vines is this
Whose words are dry and faint as in a dream?
Back from my trellis, Sir, before I scream!
I am a lady young in beauty waiting.

---

*Some say this poem is an exchange between Death and the Maiden. December and May seem to be likelier participants, or even a gentleman and a lady, going through the age-old rituals of courtship. The verse form is a unique adaptation of the Italian sonnet.*

# CLAUDE McKAY 1890–1948

McKay was born in Jamaica and came to the United States in 1912, publishing his first volume, *Songs of Jamaica*, the same year; *Harlem Shadows* followed in 1922. McKay also wrote hard-hitting novels about the Black experience in Europe, the Caribbean, and the United States. He also wrote the respected sociological study *Harlem: Negro Metropolis* (1940).

# If We Must Die

If we must die, let it not be like hogs
Hunted and penned in an inglorious spot,
While round us bark the mad and hungry dogs,
Making their mock at our accursèd lot.
If we must die, O let us nobly die,
So that our precious blood may not be shed
In vain; then even the monsters we defy
Shall be constrained to honor us though dead!
O kinsmen! we must meet the common foe!
Though far outnumbered let us show us brave,
And for their thousand blows deal one deathblow!
What though before us lies the open grave?
Like men we'll face the murderous, cowardly pack,
Pressed to the wall, dying, but fighting back!

---

*Although he is chiefly remembered for his prose writings, McKay could work just as effectively in verse. In technique, this sonnet ignores all modernist innovations and goes back to Shakespeare and Milton ("what though" comes straight from* Paradise Lost*). This poem so successfully transcends its origins (in a Harlem race riot of 1919) that it became a rallying cry for the British as well as the Americans in the Second World War.*

# ISAAC ROSENBERG 1890–1918

A poor urban Jew, Rosenberg attended the Slade School of Art and published two volumes of strong verse in 1912 and 1915, before going off to the war in which he was killed.

## Break of Day in the Trenches

≫≫≫≫≫

The darkness crumbles away—
It is the same old druid Time as ever.
Only a live thing leaps my hand—
A queer sardonic rat—
As I pull the parapet's poppy
To stick behind my ear.
Droll rat, they would shoot you if they knew
Your cosmopolitan sympathies.
Now you have touched this English hand
You will do the same to a German—
Soon, no doubt, if it be your pleasure
To cross the sleeping green between.
It seems you inwardly grin as you pass
Strong eyes, fine limbs, haughty athletes
Less chanced than you for life,
Bonds to the whims of murder,
Sprawled in the bowels of the earth,
The torn fields of France.
What do you see in our eyes
At the shrieking iron and flame
Hurled through still heavens?
What quaver—what heart aghast?
Poppies whose roots are in man's veins
Drop, and are ever dropping;
But mine in my ear is safe,
Just a little white with the dust.

*Through the end of the first World War, it is probable that most war literature was produced by officers. Rosenberg, however, was a common enlisted footsoldier. Much of the worst fighting of the war was in the trenches. It was there that Rosenberg spent eighteen months, and there that he died.*

MacLeish spent his early career in the company of
modernist expatriates and bohemians but repatriated
himself during the Depression and turned his attention
to problems of history and politics. His powerful *Con-
quistador* used the conquest of Mexico as material for an
epic. He held higher appointive positions in government
than any other modern American poet in this anthology,
serving as Librarian of Congress for five years and
briefly as Assistant Secretary of State from 1944 to
1945.

# *You, Andrew Marvell*

•⟋•

And here face down beneath the sun
And here upon earth's noonward height
To feel the always coming on
The always rising of the night

To feel creep up the curving east
The earthy chill of dusk and slow
Upon those under lands the vast
And ever-climbing shadow grow

And strange at Ecbatan the trees
Take leaf by leaf the evening strange
The flooding dark about their knees
The mountains over Persia change

And now at Kermanshah the gate
Dark empty and the withered grass
And through the twilight now the late
Few travelers in the westward pass

And Baghdad darken and the bridge
Across the silent river gone
And through Arabia the edge
Of evening widen and steal on

And deepen on Palmyra's street
The wheel rut in the ruined stone
And Lebanon fade out and Crete
High through the clouds and overblown

And over Sicily the air
Still flashing with the landward gulls
And loom and slowly disappear
The sails above the shadowy hulls

And Spain go under and the shore
Of Africa the gilded sand
And evening vanish and no more
The low pale light across that land

Nor now the long light on the sea—
And here face downward in the sun
To feel how swift how secretly
The shadow of the night comes on . . .

---

*MacLeish furnishes a commentary, much indebted to a globe or atlas, on the lines "But at my back I always hear / Time's wingèd chariot hurrying near," from Marvell's "To His Coy Mistress" (p. 229).*

# Ars Poetica

A poem should be palpable and mute
As a globed fruit,

Dumb
As old medallions to the thumb,

Silent as the sleeve-worn stone
Of casement ledges where the moss has grown—

A poem should be wordless
As the flight of birds.

A poem should be motionless in time
As the moon climbs,

Leaving, as the moon releases
Twig by twig the night-entangled trees,

Leaving, as the moon behind the winter leaves,
Memory by memory the mind—

A poem should be motionless in time
As the moon climbs.

A poem should be equal to:
Not true.

For all the history of grief
An empty doorway and a maple leaf.

For love
The leaning grasses and two lights above the sea—

A poem should not mean
But be.

---

*Horace's verse epistle on the art of poetry is sometimes given the title* Ars
Poetica *or* De Arte Poetica. *MacLeish appropriates the title for a critical poem
that is not very Horatian or even Roman but more in the style of what is called
the New Criticism—a study of literary works on their own terms, not so much
something you say as something you make.*

# The End of the World

Quite unexpectedly as Vasserot
The armless ambidextrian was lighting
A match between his great and second toe,
And Ralph the lion was engaged in biting
The neck of Madame Sossman while the drum
Pointed, and Teeny was about to cough
In waltz-time swinging Jocko by the thumb—
Quite unexpectedly the top blew off:

And there, there overhead, there, there hung over
Those thousands of white faces, those dazed eyes,
There in the starless dark the poise, the hover,
There with vast wings across the canceled skies,
There in the sudden blackness the black pall
Of nothing, nothing, nothing—nothing at all.

*Strangely, MacLeish combines light verse, apocalypse, and the familiar format of the sonnet.*

# WILFRED OWEN 1893–1918

Owen was killed right at the end of the First World War. He was only twenty-five, but he had had time to produce an impressive variety of poems, most of them dealing with war. He was also a notable technical innovator, especially in rhyming. He was born in Shropshire and educated at London University.

## Anthem for Doomed Youth

⟩⟨⟩⟨⟩⟨

What passing-bells for these who die as cattle?
  —Only the monstrous anger of the guns.
  Only the stuttering rifles' rapid rattle
Can patter out their hasty orisons.
No mockeries now for them; no prayers nor bells,
  Nor any voice of mourning save the choirs,—
The shrill, demented choirs of wailing shells;
  And bugles calling for them from sad shires.

What candles may be held to speed them all?
  Not in the hands of boys but in their eyes
Shall shine the holy glimmers of goodbyes.
  The pallor of girls' brows shall be their pall;
Their flowers the tenderness of patient minds,
And each slow dusk a drawing-down of blinds.

---

*Paul Fussell's* The Great War and Modern Memory *shows that the First World War came as a distinct and horrible shock to a Europe that had been relatively at peace for a hundred years. The new technology produced weapons of unexampled ferocity and efficiency, and the utter horror of warfare could no longer be ignored or camouflaged as patriotic glory.*

# Dulce et Decorum Est

()◀━▶()

Bent double, like old beggars under sacks,
Knock-kneed, coughing like hags, we cursed through sludge,
Till on the haunting flares we turned our backs
And towards our distant rest began to trudge.
Men marched asleep. Many had lost their boots
But limped on, blood-shod. All went lame; all blind;
Drunk with fatigue; deaf even to the hoots
Of tired, outstripped Five-Nines that dropped behind.

Gas! Gas! Quick, boys! — An ecstasy of fumbling,
Fitting the clumsy helmets just in time;
But someone still was yelling out and stumbling
And flound'ring like a man in fire or lime . . .
Dim, through the misty panes and thick green light,
As under a green sea, I saw him drowning.
In all my dreams, before my helpless sight,
He plunges at me, guttering, choking, drowning.

If in some smothering dreams you too could pace
Behind the wagon that we flung him in,
And watch the white eyes writhing in his face,
His hanging face, like a devil's sick of sin;
If you could hear, at every jolt, the blood
Come gargling from the froth-corrupted lungs,
Obscene as cancer, bitter as the cud
Of vile, incurable sores on innocent tongues, —
My friend, you would not tell with such high zest
To children ardent for some desperate glory,
The old Lie: Dulce et decorum est
Pro patria mori.

---

*As with his "Greater Love" (p. 1010), Owen gives the lie to a conviction from a
scriptural or, as here, classical source (Horace's Ode III.2). Ezra Pound, writing
at about the same time as Owen, mocked the same Horatian text in "Hugh
Selwyn Mauberley."*

# Strange Meeting

It seemed that out of battle I escaped
Down some profound dull tunnel, long since scooped
Through granites which titanic wars had groined.
Yet also there encumbered sleepers groaned,
Too fast in thought or death to be bestirred.
Then, as I probed them, one sprang up, and stared
With piteous recognition in fixed eyes,
Lifting distressful hands as if to bless.
And by his smile, I knew that sullen hall,
By his dead smile I knew we stood in Hell.
With a thousand pains that vision's face was grained;
Yet no blood reached there from the upper ground,
And no guns thumped, or down the flues made moan.
"Strange friend," I said, "here is no cause to mourn."
"None," said that other, "save the undone years,
The hopelessness. Whatever hope is yours,
Was my life also; I went hunting wild
After the wildest beauty in the world,
Which lies not calm in eyes, or braided hair,
But mocks the steady running of the hour,
And if it grieves, grieves richlier than here.
For of my glee might many men have laughed,
And of my weeping something had been left,
Which must die now. I mean the truth untold,
The pity of war, the pity war distilled.
Now men will go content with what we spoiled,
Or, discontent, boil bloody, and be spilled.
They will be swift with swiftness of the tigress.
None will break ranks, though nations trek from progress.
Courage was mine, and I had mystery,
Wisdom was mine, and I had mastery:
To miss the march of this retreating world
Into vain citadels that are not walled.
Then, when much blood had clogged their chariot-wheels,

I would go up and wash them from sweet wells,
Even with truths that lie too deep for taint.
I would have poured my spirit without stint
But not through wounds; not on the cess of war.
Foreheads of men have bled where no wounds were.
I am the enemy you killed, my friend.
I knew you in this dark: for so you frowned
Yesterday through me as you jabbed and killed.
I parried; but my hands were loath and cold.
Let us sleep now. . . ."

---

*The strangeness of this nightmare poem is made even stranger by a most peculiar technical device: line endings linked not by conventional rhyme but mostly by syllables that both begin and end with the same consonants but embrace different vowels (as in "hall" and "Hell"), creating a weird dissonance.*

# Greater Love

Red lips are not so red
  As the stained stones kissed by the English dead.
Kindness of wooed and wooer
Seems shame to their love pure.
O Love, your eyes lose lure
  When I behold eyes blinded in my stead!

Your slender attitude
  Trembles not exquisite like limbs knife-skewed,
Rolling and rolling there
Where God seems not to care;
Till the fierce love they bear
  Cramps them in death's extreme decrepitude.

Your voice sings not so soft, —
  Though even as wind murmuring through raftered loft, —
Your dear voice is not dear,
Gentle, and evening clear,
As theirs whom none now hear,
  Now earth has stopped their piteous mouths that coughed.

Heart, you were never hot
  Nor large, nor full like hearts made great with shot;
And though your hand be pale,
Paler are all which trail
Your cross through flame and hail:
  Weep, you may weep, for you may touch them not.

---

*Jesus said, "Greater love hath no man than this, that a man lay down his life
for his friends" (John XV:13). The anatomical inventory is somewhat like the
catalogue in Hopkins's "Habit of Perfection" (p. 800) but with bitter ironies.*

The son of a clergyman, E. E. Cummings received two
degrees from Harvard before going off to serve as an
ambulance driver in the First World War. He wrote
plays and nonfiction prose, and he was a notable
graphic artist as well, but he will be remembered most
fondly as a versatile and original poet rather in the style
of Donne or Byron—capable, that is, of passionate love
poems and caustic satires.

# anyone lived in a pretty how town

anyone lived in a pretty how town
(with up so floating many bells down)
spring summer autumn winter
he sang his didn't he danced his did.

Women and men (both little and small)
cared for anyone not at all
they sowed their isn't they reaped their same
sun moon stars rain

children guessed(but only a few
and down they forgot as up they grew
autumn winter spring summer)
that noone loved him more by more

when by now and tree by leaf
she laughed his joy she cried his grief
bird by snow and stir by still
anyone's any was all to her

someones married their everyones
laughed their cryings and did their dance
(sleep wake hope and then)they
said their nevers they slept their dream

stars rain sun moon
(and only the snow can begin to explain
how children are apt to forget to remember
with up so floating many bells down)

one day anyone died i guess
(and noone stooped to kiss his face)
busy folk buried them side by side
little by little and was by was

all by all and deep by deep
and more by more they dream their sleep
noone and anyone earth by april
wish by spirit and if by yes.

Women and men(both dong and ding)
summer autumn winter spring
reaped their sowing and went their came
sun moon stars rain

---

*Cummings takes traditional themes of Everyman and Utopia ("Noplace"), traditional tetrameter couplets such as those used by Marvell and Blake, and a modernist freedom of language, converting indefinite pronouns into three-dimensional human characters.*

# next to of course god america i

>>>>>>

"next to of course god america i
love you land of the pilgrims' and so forth oh
say can you see by the dawn's early my
country 'tis of centuries come and go
and are no more what of it we should worry
in every language even deafanddumb
thy sons acclaim your glorious name by gorry
by jingo by gee by gosh by gum
why talk of beauty what could be more beautiful than these heroic happy dead
who rushed like lions to the roaring slaughter
they did not stop to think they died instead
then shall the voice of liberty be mute?"

He spoke. And drank rapidly a glass of water

---

*In this tour de force, Cummings welds political rhetoric and the structural music of the sonnet. Cummings was one of the great poets of satire, mockery, and caricature, and at the same time—and often in the same poem, as here—one of the great sonneteers.*

# HART CRANE 1899–1932

In a tragically short and sad life, Hart Crane became one of America's most ambitious and most eloquent poets, amalgamating traditions from Marlowe, Shelley, Baudelaire, Poe, Whitman, and Dickinson. Crane's father was a candy manufacturer (responsible for the original Life Savers, among other products) whose marriage to a complex and somewhat cultivated woman was turbulent and finally dissolved. Crane was tormented most of his life by difficulties with alcohol, with both parents, with friends, with lovers—male and female—and with his own craft. Through all the troubles, however, Crane sought to perfect his great gifts of vision and expression. It was on a return journey from Mexico that he jumped from a ship, probably a suicide.

## To Brooklyn Bridge

How many dawns, chill from his rippling rest
The seagull's wings shall dip and pivot him,
Shedding white rings of tumult, building high
Over the chained bay waters Liberty—

Then, with inviolate curve, forsake our eyes
As apparitional as sails that cross
Some page of figures to be filed away;
—Till elevators drop us from our day . . .

I think of cinemas, panoramic sleights
With multitudes bent toward some flashing scene
Never disclosed, but hastened to again,
Foretold to other eyes on the same screen;

And Thee, across the harbor, silver-paced
As though the sun took step of thee, yet left
Some motion ever unspent in thy stride,—
Implicitly thy freedom staying thee!

Out of some subway scuttle, cell or loft
A bedlamite speeds to thy parapets,
Tilting there momently, shrill shirt ballooning,
A jest falls from the speechless caravan.

Down Wall, from girder into street noon leaks,
A rip-tooth of the sky's acetylene;
All afternoon the cloud-flown derricks turn . . .
Thy cables breathe the North Atlantic still.

And obscure as that heaven of the Jews,
Thy guerdon . . . Accolade thou dost bestow
Of anonymity time cannot raise:
Vibrant reprieve and pardon thou dost show.

O harp and altar, of the fury fused,
(How could mere toil align thy choiring strings!)
Terrific threshold of the prophet's pledge,
Prayer of pariah, and the lover's cry, —

Again the traffic lights that skim thy swift
Unfractioned idiom, immaculate sigh of stars,
Beading thy path — condense eternity:
And we have seen night lifted in thine arms.

Under thy shadow by the piers I waited;
Only in darkness is thy shadow clear.
The City's fiery parcels all undone,
Already snow submerges an iron year . . .

O Sleepless as the river under thee,
Vaulting the sea, the prairies' dreaming sod,
Unto us lowliest sometime sweep, descend
And of the curveship lend a myth to God.

from The Bridge

*T. S. Eliot's "Waste Land" (p. 968), when it was published in 1922, provoked a number of responses, none stronger than Crane's prodigiously eloquent "The Bridge" (1930), which countered the myth of Waste with its own myth: the Bridge. Crane never quite achieved his impossible ambition in his own terrific voice, but it is to his everlasting credit that he conceived that ambition in the first place. (Note that: "guerdon" is "reward.")*

# ALLEN TATE 1899–1979

Like John Crowe Ransom, Allen Tate was a Tennessean associated with Vanderbilt University and the magazine called *The Fugitive*. He wrote studies of Confederate leaders "Stonewall" Jackson and Jefferson Davis, and he established a solid reputation as a discerning critic, intuitive but passionate. He was uncommonly sensitive to the genius of Poe and Dickinson, and he was personally close to Ransom, Hart Crane, and Robert Lowell.

# Ode to the Confederate Dead

Row after row with strict impunity
The headstones yield their names to the element,
The wind whirrs without recollection;
In the riven troughs the splayed leaves
Pile up, of nature the casual sacrament
To the seasonal eternity of death;
Then driven by the fierce scrutiny
Of heaven to their election in the vast breath,
They sough the rumor of mortality.

Autumn is desolation in the plot
Of a thousand acres where these memories grow
From the inexhaustible bodies that are not
Dead, but feed the grass row after rich row.
Think of the autumns that have come and gone! —
Ambitious November with the humors of the year,
With a particular zeal for every slab,
Staining the uncomfortable angels that rot
On the slabs, a wing chipped here, an arm there:
The brute curiosity of an angel's stare
Turns you, like them, to stone,
Transforms the heaving air
Till plunged to a heavier world below

You shift your sea-space blindly
Heaving, turning like the blind crab.

   Dazed by the wind, only the wind
   The leaves flying, plunge

You know who have waited by the wall
The twilight certainty of an animal,
Those midnight restitutions of the blood
You know—the immitigable pines, the smoky frieze
Of the sky, the sudden call: you know the rage,
The cold pool left by the mounting flood,
Of muted Zeno and Parmenides.
You who have waited for the angry resolution
Of those desires that should be yours tomorrow,
You know the unimportant shrift of death
And praise the vision
And praise the arrogant circumstance
Of those who fall
Rank upon rank, hurried beyond decision—
Here by the sagging gate, stopped by the wall.

   Seeing, seeing only the leaves
   Flying, plunge and expire

Turn your eyes to the immoderate past,
Turn to the inscrutable infantry rising
Demons out of the earth—they will not last.
Stonewall, Stonewall, and the sunken fields of hemp,
Shiloh, Antietam, Malvern Hill, Bull Run.
Lost in that orient of the thick-and-fast
You will curse the setting sun.

   Cursing only the leaves crying
   Like an old man in a storm

You hear the shout, the crazy hemlocks point
With troubled fingers to the silence which
Smothers you, a mummy, in time.

> The hound bitch
Toothless and dying, in a musty cellar
Hears the wind only.

> Now that the salt of their blood
Stiffens the saltier oblivion of the sea,
Seals the malignant purity of the flood,
What shall we who count our days and bow
Our heads with a commemorial woe
In the ribboned coats of grim felicity,
What shall we say of the bones, unclean,
Whose verdurous anonymity will grow?
The ragged arms, the ragged heads and eyes
Lost in these acres of the insane green?
The gray lean spiders come, they come and go;
In a tangle of willows without light
The singular screech-owl's tight
Invisible lyric seeds the mind
With the furious murmur of their chivalry.

We shall say only the leaves
Flying, plunge and expire
We shall say only the leaves whispering
In the improbable mist of nightfall
That flies on multiple wing;
Night is the beginning and the end
And in between the ends of distraction
Waits mute speculation, the patient curse
That stones the eyes, or like the jaguar leaps
For his own image in a jungle pool, his victim.

What shall we say who have knowledge
Carried to the heart? Shall we take the act
To the grave? Shall we, more hopeful, set up the grave
In the house? The ravenous grave?

                    Leave now
The shut gate and the decomposing wall:
The gentle serpent, green in the mulberry bush,
Riots with his tongue through the hush—
Sentinel of the grave who counts us all!

---

*For people from the southern United States, at least, the Civil War remains the great defining event. In some ways, as Mark Twain suggested, the war called chivalry's bluff (not entirely in jest, Mark Twain blamed the war on Sir Walter Scott). Southern writers still feel called on to address the Confederate dead, and courthouse lawns across eleven states have monuments to those who died between 1861 and 1865.*

# LANGSTON HUGHES 1902–1967

Hughes, one of the greatest and most versatile of African-American writers, was born in Missouri and wandered over much of the United States and Europe. He wrote many plays and novels but remains best known for more than a dozen volumes of poetry published in the forty years before his death in 1967. Hughes was a leader of the Harlem Renaissance in the 1920s.

## The Negro Speaks of Rivers

I've known rivers:
I've known rivers ancient as the world and older than the flow
of human blood in human veins.

My soul has grown deep like the rivers.

I bathed in the Euphrates when dawns were young.
I built my hut near the Congo and it lulled me to sleep.

I looked upon the Nile and raised the pyramids above it.
I heard the singing of the Mississippi when Abe Lincoln went
down to New Orleans, and I've seen its muddy bosom turn
all golden in the sunset.

I've known rivers:
Ancient, dusky rivers.

My soul has grown deep like the rivers.

---

*Hughes's poem appeared in 1926; fifteen years later, T. S. Eliot's "Dry Salvages" (the third of* Four Quartets*) was to make much the same claim about rivers.*

# STEVIE SMITH 1902–1971

Glenda Jackson has given a memorable portrayal of the poet in a movie called *Stevie*. (The poet was formally named Florence Margaret Smith but preferred to use her family nickname.) She could write fiction and draw pictures, but she will be remembered as a poet of prodigious personal character, wisdom, and humor.

## *Not Waving But Drowning*

✖✖✖✖✖

Nobody heard him, the dead man,
But still he lay moaning:
I was much further out than you thought
And not waving but drowning.

Poor chap, he always loved larking
And now he's dead
It must have been too cold for him his heart gave way,
They said.

Oh, no no no, it was too cold always
(Still the dead one lay moaning)
I was much too far out all my life
And not waving but drowning.

---

*Stevie Smith based her poem on the report of an actual episode. This prismatic poem has become an emblem of the ironies and absurdities of postmodern life, when appearance and reality have grown grotesquely far apart.*

# RICHARD EBERHART b.1904

A native Minnesotan, Eberhart was educated at Dartmouth and Cambridge. He began publishing poetry in 1930 and kept up a steady output afterwards. In 1956 he returned to Dartmouth.

# The Fury of Aerial Bombardment

()◄►()

You would think the fury of aerial bombardment
Would rouse God to relent; the infinite spaces
Are still silent. He looks on shock-pried faces.
History, even, does not know what is meant.

You would feel that after so many centuries
God would give man to repent; yet he can kill
As Cain could, but with multitudinous will,
No farther advanced than in his ancient furies.

Was man made stupid to see his own stupidity?
Is God by definition indifferent, beyond us all?
Is the eternal truth man's fighting soul
Wherein the Beast ravens in its own avidity?

Of Van Wettering I speak, and Averill,
Names on a list, whose faces I do not recall
But they are gone to early death, who late in school
Distinguished the belt feed lever from the belt holding pawl.

---

*The airplane, a peculiarly twentieth-century development, was adapted to warfare within ten years of its invention. The combination of modern machinery and ancient myth (particularly that of Icarus) has been compelling, as is shown by Yeats's "Irish Airman Foresees His Death" (p. 863) and Jarrell's "Death of the Ball Turret Gunner" (p. 1047). The new vocabulary exploited by Eberhart also appears in Reed's "Naming of Parts" (p. 1048).*

# The Groundhog

In June, amid the golden fields,
I saw a groundhog lying dead.
Dead lay he; my senses shook,
And mind outshot our naked frailty.
There lowly in the vigorous summer
His form began its senseless change,
And made my senses waver dim
Seeing nature ferocious in him.
Inspecting close his maggot's might
And seething cauldron of his being,
Half with loathing, half with a strange love,
I poked him with an angry stick.
The fever arose, became a frame
And Vigor circumscribed the skies,
Immense energy in the sun,
And through my frame a sunless trembling.
My stick had done nor good nor harm.
Then stood I silent in the day
Watching the object, as before;
And kept my reverence for knowledge
Trying for control, to be still,
To quell the passion of the blood;
Until I had bent down on my knees
Praying for joy in the sight of decay.
And so I left; and I returned
In Autumn strict of eye, to see
The sap gone out of the groundhog,
But the bony sodden hulk remained.
But the year had lost its meaning,
And in intellectual chains
I lost both love and loathing,
Mured up in the wall of wisdom.
Another summer took the fields again
Massive and burning, full of life,

But when I chanced upon the spot
There was only a little hair left,
And bones bleaching in the sunlight
Beautiful as architecture;
I watched them like a geometer,
And cut a walking stick from a birch.
It has been three years, now.
There is no sign of the groundhog.
I stood there in the whirling summer,
My hand capped a withered heart,
And thought of China and of Greece,
Of Alexander in his tent;
Of Montaigne in his tower,
Of Saint Theresa in her wild lament.

---

*Twentieth-century poets have specialized in making capacious symbols out of humble creatures (see "The Fish," by Elizabeth Bishop, p. 1043, and Robert Lowell's "Skunk Hour," p. 1058). The real mortal fate of the physical body of an unlovely actual creature permits both a close observation of nature and a well-buttressed ascent into the grandeur of conquerors, thinkers, and saints.*

# W Y S T A N  H U G H  A U D E N  1907–1973

Although W. H. Auden was born in England and died there, he spent about thirty of his productive years in the United States, from 1939 onwards. A chameleon of styles and tones, he probably commanded a greater range of forms than any other twentieth-century poet.

## Musée des Beaux Arts

•❖•❖•❖•❖•

About suffering they were never wrong,
The Old Masters: how well they understood
Its human position; how it takes place
While someone else is eating or opening a window or just
    walking dully along;
How, when the aged are reverently, passionately waiting
For the miraculous birth, there always must be
Children who did not specially want it to happen, skating
On a pond at the edge of the wood:
They never forgot
That even the dreadful martyrdom must run its course
Anyhow in a corner, some untidy spot
Where the dogs go on with their doggy life and the torturer's
    horse
Scratches its innocent behind on a tree.

In Brueghel's *Icarus*, for instance: how everything turns away
Quite leisurely from the disaster; the plowman may
Have heard the splash, the forsaken cry,
But for him it was not an important failure; the sun shone
As it had to on the white legs disappearing into the green
Water; and the expensive delicate ship that must have seen
Something amazing, a boy falling out of the sky,
Had somewhere to get to and sailed calmly on.

*Someone suffering, perhaps from a painful experience, seeks consolation in a foreign art museum and discovers a highly conditional truth about suffering. Brueghel's* Landscape with the Fall of Icarus *is also the subject of a poem by William Carlos Williams.*

# In Memory of W. B. Yeats

### I

He disappeared in the dead of winter
The brooks were frozen, the airports almost deserted,
And snow disfigured the public statues;
The mercury sank in the month of the dying day.
What instruments we have agree
The day of his death was a dark cold day.

Far from his illness
The wolves ran on through the evergreen forests,
The peasant river was untempted by the fashionable quays;
By mourning tongues
The death of the poet was kept from his poems.

But for him it was his last afternoon as himself,
An afternoon of nurses and rumours;
The provinces of his body revolted,
The squares of his mind were empty,
Silence invaded the suburbs,
The current of his feeling failed; he became his admirers.

Now he is scattered among a hundred cities
And wholly given over to unfamiliar affections,
To find his happiness in another kind of wood
And be punished under a foreign code of conscience.
The words of a dead man
Are modified in the guts of the living.

But in the importance of noise of to-morrow
When the brokers are roaring like beasts on the floor of the
  Bourse,
And the poor have the sufferings to which they are fairly
  accustomed,
And each in the cell of himself is almost convinced of his
  freedom,
A few thousand will think of this day
As one thinks of a day when one did something slightly unusual.
What instruments we have agree
The day of his death was a dark cold day.

II

You were silly like us; your gift survived it all:
The parish of rich women, physical decay,
Yourself. Mad Ireland hurt you into poetry.
Now Ireland has her madness and her weather still,
For poetry makes nothing happen: it survives
In the valley of its making where executives
Would never want to tamper, flows on south
From ranches of isolation and the busy griefs,
Raw towns that we believe and die in; it survives,
A way of happening, a mouth.

III

Earth, receive an honoured guest:
William Yeats is laid to rest.
Let the Irish vessel lie
Emptied of its poetry.

In the nightmare of the dark
All the dogs of Europe bark,
And the living nations wait,
Each sequestered in its hate;

Intellectual disgrace
Stares from every human face,
And the seas of pity lie
Locked and frozen in each eye.

Follow, poet, follow right
To the bottom of the night,
With your unconstraining voice
Still persuade us to rejoice;

With the farming of a verse
Make a vineyard of the curse,
Sing of human unsuccess
In a rapture of distress;

In the deserts of the heart
Let the healing fountain start,
In the prison of his days
Teach the free man how to praise.

---

*Auden brings the pastoral elegy up to date. In Milton's "Lycidas" (p. 203) and Shelley's "Adonais" (p. 509), one poet mourns another by putting on the garb of a Greek shepherd, inherited from Theocritus, Bion, and Moschus. Auden puts airports in the place of sheepfolds, but he keeps one feature of some pastoral elegies: the honoring of the style of the dead. Just as "Adonais" is a Keatsian poem, using the rich Spenserian stanzas of Keats's "Eve of St. Agnes" (p. 551), Auden produces a Yeatsian poem, particularly in the third section here, which is modeled on Yeats's "Under Ben Bulben."*

# *Lullaby*

Lay your sleeping head, my love,
Human on my faithless arm;
Time and fevers burn away
Individual beauty from
Thoughtful children, and the grave
Proves the child ephemeral:
But in my arms till break of day
Let the living creature lie,
Mortal, guilty, but to me
The entirely beautiful.

Soul and body have no bounds:
To lovers as they lie upon
Her tolerant enchanted slope
In their ordinary swoon,
Grave the vision Venus sends
Of supernatural sympathy,
Universal love and hope;
While an abstract insight wakes
Among the glaciers and the rocks
The hermit's carnal ecstasy.

Certainty, fidelity
On the stroke of midnight pass
Like vibrations of a bell,
And fashionable madmen raise
Their pedantic boring cry:
Every farthing of the cost,
All the dreaded cards foretell,
Shall be paid, but from this night
Not a whisper, not a thought,
Not a kiss nor look be lost.

Beauty, midnight, vision dies:
Let the winds of dawn that blow
Softly round your dreaming head
Such a day of sweetness show
Eye and knocking heart may bless,
Find the mortal world enough;
Noons of dryness see you fed
By the involuntary powers,
Nights of insult let you pass
Watched by every human love.

---

*Compared with the early seventeenth and early nineteenth centuries, the modern age seems deficient in the production of love poems, unless you want to count popular songs. Auden's "Lullaby" is a magnificent exception.*

# LOUIS MACNEICE 1907–1963

MacNeice, an Ulsterman, was educated at Merton College, Oxford. His poetry is experimental, passionate, varied, and nostalgic for a lost past. Like Archibald MacLeish, he was an accomplished writer for radio at a time (c.1935–1955) when that medium flourished.

## Bagpipe Music

It's no go the merry-go-round, it's no go the rickshaw,
All we want is a limousine and a ticket for the peepshow.
Their knickers are made of crêpe-de-chine, their shoes are
    made of python.
Their halls are lined with tiger rugs and their walls with
    heads of bison.

John MacDonald found a corpse, put it under the sofa,
Waited till it came to life and hit it with a poker,
Sold its eyes for souvenirs, sold its blood for whiskey,
Kept its bones for dumb-bells to use when he was fifty.

It's no go the Yogi-Man, it's no go Blavatsky,
All we want is a bank balance and a bit of skirt in a taxi.

Annie MacDougall went to milk, caught her foot in the
    heather,
Woke to hear a dance record playing of Old Vienna.
It's no go your maidenheads, it's no go your culture,
All we want is a Dunlop tyre and the devil mend the
    puncture.
The laird o'Phelps spent Hogmannay declaring he was sober;
Counted his feet to prove the fact and found he had one foot
    over.
Mrs. Carmichael had her fifth, looked at the job with
    repulsion,

Said to the midwife "Take it away; I'm through with
  overproduction."
It's no go the gossip column, it's no go the Ceilidh,
All we want is a mother's help and a sugar-stick for the baby.

Willie Murray cut his thumb, couldn't count the damage,
Took the hide of an Ayrshire cow and used it for a bandage.
His brother caught three hundred cran when the seas were
  lavish,
Threw the bleeders back in the sea and went upon the parish.

It's no go the Herring Board, it's no go the Bible,
All we want is a packet of fags when our hands are idle.

It's no go the picture palace, it's no go the stadium,
It's no go the country cot with a pot of pink geraniums.
It's no go the Government grants, it's no go the elections,
Sit on your arse for fifty years and hang your hat on pension.

It's no go my honey love, it's no go my poppet;
Work your hands from day to day, the winds will blow the
  profit.
The glass is falling hour by hour, the glass will fall forever,
But if you break the bloody glass you won't hold up the
  weather.

---

*MacNeice seems to be foreseeing the humor of "The Goon Show" and Monty Python. Since MacNeice was born in Belfast, it may help to keep in mind that the bagpipe is associated with Ireland as well as with Scotland. (Note that: "knickers" is "underpants"; "Hogmanay" is "New Year's Eve"; "Ceilidh"— rhymes with "gaily"—is an evening celebration with singing and drinking; "cran" is a measure of herring; "upon the parish" is "on the dole"; "cot" is "cottage.")*

# THEODORE ROETHKE 1908–1963

Roethke was born in Michigan and spent much of his mature life in the Northwest, teaching at the University of
Washington. In much of his poetry, it is difficult to avoid
the vegetable kingdom, from weeds to roses, from germi-
nation to fermentation; he came from a long line of foresters
and nurserymen. Roethke may have taken fewer chances
than his immediate forebears—fewer, even, that the more
remote Hardy and Yeats—but he was a vigorous, witty,
and faithful inheritor and conservator of a great tradition.

## My Papa's Waltz

The whiskey on your breath
Could make a small boy dizzy;
But I hung on like death:
Such waltzing was not easy.

We romped until the pans
Slid from the kitchen shelf;
My mother's countenance
Could not unfrown itself.

The hand that held my wrist
Was battered on one knuckle;
At every step you missed
My right ear scraped a buckle.

You beat time on my head
With a palm caked hard by dirt,
Then waltzed me off to bed
Still clinging to your shirt.

---

*Roethke, Kenneth Rexroth, and others growing up during Prohibition had a love-hate
relationship with alcoholism—parental and personal. John Frederick Nims points
out that the waltz (in three-quarter time) is rendered here in lines of three stresses.*

# I Knew a Woman

I knew a woman, lovely in her bones,
When small birds sighed, she would sigh back at them;
Ah, when she moved, she moved more ways than one:
The shapes a bright container can contain!
Of her choice virtues only gods should speak,
Or English poets who grew up on Greek
(I'd have them sing in chorus, cheek to cheek).

How well her wishes went! She stroked my chin,
She taught me Turn, and Counter-turn, and Stand;
She taught me Touch, that undulant white skin;
I nibbled meekly from her proffered hand;
She was the sickle; I, poor I, the rake,
Coming behind her for her pretty sake
(But what prodigious mowing we did make).

Love likes a gander, and adores a goose:
Her full lips pursed, the errant note to seize;
She played it quick, she played it light and loose;
My eyes, they dazzled at her flowing knees;
Her several parts could keep a pure repose,
Or one hip quiver with a mobile nose
(She moved in circles, and those circles moved).

Let seed be grass, and grass turn into hay:
I'm martyr to a motion not my own;
What's freedom for? To know eternity.
I swear she cast a shadow white as stone.
But who would count eternity in days?
These old bones live to learn her wanton ways:
(I measure time by how a body sways).

*It is possible that Roethke, unconsciously or deliberately, is preserving Louise Bogan's initials in the phrase "lovely in her bones." At any rate, he and she were lovers. She, about ten years his senior, could have taught him a thing or two about poetry: "Turn, and Counter-turn, and Stand" are at once erotic and poetic (translating Strophe, and Antistrophe, and Epode).*

# The Waking

I wake to sleep, and take my waking slow.
I feel my fate in what I cannot fear.
I learn by going where I have to go.

We think by feeling. What is there to know?
I hear my being dance from ear to ear.
I wake to sleep, and take my waking slow.

Of those so close beside me, which are you?
God bless the Ground! I shall walk softly there,
And learn by going where I have to go.

Light takes the Tree; but who can tell us how?
The lowly worm climbs up a winding stair;
I wake to sleep, and take my waking slow.

Great Nature has another thing to do
To you and me; so take the lively air,
And, lovely, learn by going where to go.

This shaking keeps me steady. I should know.
What falls away is always. And is near.
I wake to sleep, and take my waking slow.
I learn by going where I have to go.

*The complex villanelle form was used infrequently during the nineteenth century, but it was not until William Empson set a contemporary example during the 1930s that poets learned how to adapt the form to peculiarly modern needs. Here, as in Dylan Thomas's "Do Not Go Gentle into That Good Night" (p. 1050), the poet exploits the elementary energy of the patterned recurrence.*

# Elegy for Jane

()◄━━►()

(My student, thrown by a horse)

I remember the neckcurls, limp and damp as tendrils;
And her quick look, a sidelong pickerel smile;
And how, once startled into talk, the light syllables leaped for
    her.
And she balanced in the delight of her thought,
A wren, happy, tail into the wind,
Her song trembling the twigs and small branches.
The shade sang with her;
The leaves, their whispers turned to kissing,
And the mould sang in the bleached valleys under the rose.

Oh, when she was sad, she cast herself down into such a pure
    depth,
Even a father could not find her:
Scraping her cheek against straw,
Stirring the clearest water.
My sparrow, you are not here,
Waiting like a fern, making a spiney shadow.
The sides of wet stones cannot console me,
Nor the moss, wound with the last light.

If only I could nudge you from this sleep,
My maimed darling, my skittery pigeon.
Over this damp grave I speak the words of my love:
I, with no rights in this matter,
Neither father nor lover.

---

*Roethke's generation of poets was the first to be routinely employed in university teaching. Roethke, Randall Jarrell, Howard Nemerov, and others developed a novel academic idiom to deal with new relationships, such as that between teacher and student. It can be a kind of love but not parental, collegial, religious, or erotic.*

# In a Dark Time

In a dark time, the eye begins to see,
I meet my shadow in the deepening shade;
I hear my echo in the echoing wood—
A lord of nature weeping to a tree.
I live between the heron and the wren,
Beasts of the hill and serpents of the den.

What's madness but nobility of soul
At odds with circumstance? The day's on fire!
I know the purity of pure despair,
My shadow pinned against a sweating wall.
That place among the rocks—is it a cave,
Or winding path? The edge is what I have.

---

*Although he was a thoroughly postmodern American, Roethke would have been at home with almost any of the lyric poets of the sixteenth and seventeenth centuries.*

# SIR STEPHEN SPENDER b.1909

Spender has turned out to be among the most durable
of the group of Oxford poets that emerged during the
1930s; the group included Spender's friends W. H.
Auden and Louis MacNeice. Spender's poetry, like
theirs, shows a concern for social issues and demonstrates technical experimentation.

## I Think Continually of Those Who Were Truly Great

❖❖❖❖

I think continually of those who were truly great.
Who, from the womb, remembered the soul's history
Through corridors of light where the hours are suns,
Endless and singing. Whose lovely ambition
Was that their lips, still touched with fire,
Should tell of the spirit clothed from head to foot in song.
And who hoarded from the spring branches
The desires falling across their bodies like blossoms.

What is precious is never to forget
The delight of the blood drawn from ageless springs
Breaking through rocks in worlds before our earth;
Never to deny its pleasure in the simple morning light,
Nor its grave evening demand for love;
Never to allow gradually the traffic to smother
With noise and fog the flowering of the spirit.

Near the snow, near the sun, in the highest fields
See how those names are fêted by the wavering grass,
And by the streamers of white cloud,
And whispers of wind in the listening sky;
The names of those who in their lives fought for life,
Who wore at their hearts the fire's centre.
Born of the sun they traveled a short while towards the sun,
And left the vivid air signed with their honour.

---

*If you have a diamond-point pencil, you can have a poet inscribe a poem on an appropriate pane of glass. Edmund Wilson had Spender copy this poem on a pane for a high window, showing the air, sky, and sun (see Wilson's* Upstate*).*

# ELIZABETH BISHOP 1911–1979

## The Fish

I caught a tremendous fish
and held him beside the boat
half out of water, with my hook
fast in a corner of his mouth.
He didn't fight.
He hadn't fought at all.
He hung a grunting weight,
battered and venerable
and homely. Here and there
his brown skin hung in strips
like ancient wallpaper,
and its pattern of darker brown
was like wallpaper:
shapes like full-blown roses
stained and lost through age.
He was speckled with barnacles,
fine rosettes of lime,
and infested
with tiny white sea-lice,
and underneath two or three
rags of green weed hung down.
While his gills were breathing in
the terrible oxygen
—the frightening gills,
fresh and crisp with blood,
that can cut so badly—
I thought of the coarse white flesh

packed in like feathers,
the big bones and the little bones,
the dramatic reds and blacks
of his shiny entrails,
and the pink swim-bladder
like a big peony.
I looked into his eyes
which were far larger than mine
but shallower, and yellowed,
the irises backed and packed
with tarnished tinfoil
seen through the lenses
of old scratched isinglass.
They shifted a little, but not
to return my stare.
—It was more like the tipping
of an object toward the light.
I admired his sullen face,
the mechanism of his jaw,
and then I saw
that from his lower lip
—if you could call it a lip—
grim, wet, and weaponlike,
hung five old pieces of fish-line,
or four and a wire leader
with the swivel still attached,
with all their five big hooks
grown firmly in his mouth.
A green line, frayed at the end
where he broke it, two heavier lines,
and a fine black thread
still crimped from the strain and snap
when it broke and he got away.
Like medals with their ribbons
frayed and wavering,
a five-haired beard of wisdom
trailing from his aching jaw.
I stared and stared

and victory filled up
the little rented boat,
from the pool of bilge
where oil had spread a rainbow
around the rusted engine
to the bailer rusted orange,
the sun-cracked thwarts,
the oarlocks on their strings,
the gunnels—until everything
was rainbow, rainbow, rainbow!
And I let the fish go.

---

*We are still telling fish stories, a venerable tradition that goes from Jonah through Melville to Hemingway, James Dickey, and an episode of "The Simpsons" in which Homer catches a fabled fish called "General Sherman." Bishop, however, with characteristic profundity, goes beyond the folklore and symbolism to look closely at the far side of the actual experience.*

# ROBERT HAYDEN 1913–1980

Hayden received his education at Detroit City College
(now Wayne State University) and at the University of
Michigan, where W. H. Auden was one of his teachers.
Hayden himself was a university teacher, at Fisk University for about twenty years and then back at Michigan.

## Those Winter Sundays

>>>>>>>

Sundays too my father got up early
and put his clothes on in the blueblack cold,
then with cracked hands that ached
from labor in the weekday weather made
banked fires blaze. No one ever thanked him.

I'd wake and hear the cold splintering, breaking.
When the rooms were warm, he'd call,
and slowly I would rise and dress,
fearing the chronic angers of that house,

Speaking indifferently to him,
who had driven out the cold
and polished my good shoes as well.
What did I know, what did I know
of love's austere and lonely offices?

---

*As Hayden incandescently demonstrates, a good way to avoid ponderous sentimentality is to avoid outright declaration. Consider how puny this poem would be if it ended, "Love's offices are lonely and austere."*

# RANDALL JARRELL 1914–1965

Jarrell was born in Tennessee and died in North Carolina, but significant parts of his life were spent outside
the South—childhood in California, the Second World
War in the Army Air Corps, some teaching time at
Kenyon College and elsewhere. Sometimes included as
a younger member of the Fugitive-Agrarian group and
the New Critics, Jarrell wrote some fiction and criticism as well as poetry. His poetry is marked by strong
but indefinite feeling and accurate observation of the
technology of the modern world.

# The Death of the Ball Turret Gunner

From my mother's sleep I fell into the State
And I hunched in its belly till my wet fur froze.
Six miles from earth, loosed from its dream of life,
I woke to black flak and the nightmare fighters.
When I died they washed me out of the turret with a hose.

---

*Bombers like the B-17 and B-24 had a plexiglass turret on their undersides for
protection against fighters attacking from below. As Jarrell noted, these fighters
were "armed with cannon firing explosive shells." He added, "The hose was a
steam hose."*

# HENRY REED 1914–1986

Reed's single poem in this anthology comes from his 1946 volume, *A Map of Verona*. In addition to war poems, Reed wrote significant radio dramas and some marvelous parodies, including "Chard Whitlow," the best takeoff of Eliot's *Four Quartets*.

## *Naming of Parts*

◆◇◆◇◆

Today we have naming of parts. Yesterday,
We had daily cleaning. And tomorrow morning,
We shall have what to do after firing. But today,
Today we have naming of parts. Japonica
Glistens like coral in all of the neighbouring gardens,
   And today we have naming of parts.

This is the lower sling swivel. And this
Is the upper sling swivel, whose use you will see,
When you are given your slings. And this is the piling swivel,
Which in your case you have not got. The branches
Hold in the gardens their silent, eloquent gestures,
   Which in our case we have not got.

This is the safety-catch, which is always released
With an easy flick of the thumb. And please do not let me
See anyone using his finger. You can do it quite easy
If you have any strength in your thumb. The blossoms
Are fragile and motionless, never letting anyone see
   Any of them using their finger.

And this you can see is the bolt. The purpose of this
Is to open the breech, as you see. We can slide it
Rapidly backwards and forwards: we call this
Easing the spring. And rapidly backwards and forwards
The early bees are assaulting and fumbling the flowers:
    They call it easing the Spring.

They call it easing the Spring: it is perfectly easy
If you have any strength in your thumb: like the bolt,
And the breech, and the cocking-piece, and the point of balance,
Which in our case we have not got; and the almond-blossom
Silent in all of the gardens and the bees going backwards and
    forwards,
    For today we have naming of parts.

---

*Invasion is one of the unavoidable figures of war: here, as in Richard Eberhart's
"Fury of Aerial Bombardment" (p. 1023), the usual language of poetry is bar-
barically invaded by the nomenclature of mechanical contraptions. Thanks to the
many meanings of "spring" (all from a common source), the poem can glide
easily from weapon to season to elementary water. Any army is pathetic, one
without even enough equipment for training is doubly so.*

# DYLAN THOMAS 1914–1953

Dylan Thomas was a fully mature poet while still an adolescent and published his first book before his twenty-first birthday. The son of a schoolteacher, he was born in Swansea, Wales. Skipping college, he worked as a writer from the age of twenty until his death, not yet forty years old, in New York. He was by far one of the greatest performers among the poets. He was in some ways alien to the austerities of the modernists before him and the postmodernists after, but one would have to be deaf and ice-cold not to respond to Thomas's magnificent voice. As his four grand poems in this anthology attest, Thomas belonged in a great tradition that includes Blake, Keats, Hardy, Hopkins, and Yeats—poets who sang ecstatically and wisely of birth, love, death, and glory.

## Do Not Go Gentle into That Good Night

Do not go gentle into that good night,
Old age should burn and rave at close of day;
Rage, rage against the dying of the light.

Though wise men at their end know dark is right,
Because their words had forked no lightning they
Do not go gentle into that good night.

Good men, the last wave by, crying how bright
Their frail deeds might have danced in a green bay,
Rage, rage against the dying of the light.

Wild men who caught and sang the sun in flight,
And learn, too late, they grieved it on its way,
Do not go gentle into that good night.

Grave men, near death, who see with blinding sight
Blind eyes could blaze like meteors and be gay,
Rage, rage against the dying of the light.

And you, my father, there on the sad height,
Curse, bless, me now with your fierce tears, I pray,
Do not go gentle into that good night.
Rage, rage against the dying of the light.

---

*This poem originated as an address to the poet's dying father. It is surely the finest villanelle ever written as well as one of the finest poems of the twentieth century in any form.*

# Fern Hill

Now as I was young and easy under the apple boughs
About the lilting house and happy as the grass was green,
   The night above the dingle starry,
     Time let me hail and climb
    Golden in the heydays of his eyes,
And honored among wagons I was prince of the apple towns
And once below a time I lordly had the trees and leaves
    Trail with daisies and barley
   Down the rivers of the windfall light.

And as I was green and carefree, famous among the barns
About the happy yard and singing as the farm was home,
   In the sun that is young once only,
     Time let me play and be
    Golden in the mercy of his means,
And green and golden I was huntsman and herdsman, the calves
Sang to my horn, the foxes on the hills barked clear and cold,
    And the sabbath rang slowly
   In the pebbles of the holy streams.

All the sun long it was running, it was lovely, the hay
Fields high as the house, the tunes from the chimneys, it was air
   And playing, lovely and watery
    And fire green as grass.
    And nightly under the simple stars
As I rode to sleep the owls were bearing the farm away,
All the moon long I heard, blessed among stables, the nightjars
   Flying with the ricks, and the horses
    Flashing into the dark.

And then to awake, and the farm, like a wanderer white
With the dew, come back, the cock on his shoulder: it was all
　　Shining, it was Adam and maiden,
　　　　The sky gathered again
　　And the sun grew round that very day.
So it must have been after the birth of the simple light
In the first, spinning place, the spellbound horses walking warm
　　Out of the whinnying green stable
　　　　On to the fields of praise.

And honored among foxes and pheasants by the gay house
Under the new made clouds and happy as the heart was long,
　　In the sun born over and over,
　　　　I ran my heedless ways,
　　My wishes raced through the house high hay
And nothing I cared, at my sky blue trades, that time allows
In all his tuneful turning so few and such morning songs
　　Before the children green and golden
　　　　Follow him out of grace,

Nothing I cared, in the lamb white days, that time would take
　　me
Up to the swallow thronged loft by the shadow of my hand,
　　In the moon that is always rising,
　　　　Nor that riding to sleep
　　I should hear him fly with the high fields
And wake to the farm forever fled from the childless land.
Oh as I was young and easy in the mercy of his means,
　　　　Time held me green and dying
　　　　Though I sang in my chains like the sea.

---

*Thomas was in some ways a primitive and in some ways a sophisticate, but in "Fern Hill" he produced a great ode in a complex stanza that could have been devised by Donne or Keats. The title refers to the name of Thomas's aunt's country house, where he spent some time as a boy.*

# A Refusal to Mourn the Death, by Fire, of a Child in London

Never until the mankind making
Bird beast and flower
Fathering and all humbling darkness
Tells with silence the last light breaking
And the still hour
Is come of the sea tumbling in harness

And I must enter again the round
Zion of the water bead
And the synagogue of the ear of corn
Shall I let pray the shadow of a sound
Or sow my salt seed
In the least valley of sackcloth to mourn

The majesty and burning of the child's death.
I shall not murder
The mankind of her going with a grave truth
Nor blaspheme down the stations of the breath
With any further
Elegy of innocence and youth.

Deep with the first dead lies London's daughter,
Robed in the long friends,
The grains beyond age, the dark veins of her mother,
Secret by the unmourning water
Of the riding Thames.
After the first death, there is no other.

*The first thirteen lines here—more than half the poem—are a single breath-takingly apocalyptic sentence. Thomas, recalling the Welsh Henry Vaughan (see pp.*

*247–254)* *and other devotional poets of the seventeenth century, prodigiously sends the mind back to the beginning of life ("the first dead") and forward to the end of time.*

# The Force That through the Green Fuse Drives the Flower

The force that through the green fuse drives the flower
Drives my green age; that blasts the roots of trees
Is my destroyer.
And I am dumb to tell the crooked rose
My youth is bent by the same wintry fever.

The force that drives the water through the rocks
Drives my red blood; that dries the mouthing streams
Turns mine to wax.
And I am dumb to mouth unto my veins
How at the mountain spring the same mouth sucks.

The hand that whirls the water in the pool
Stirs the quicksand; that ropes the blowing wind
Hauls my shroud sail.
And I am dumb to tell the hanging man
How of my clay is made the hangman's lime.

The lips of time leech to the fountain head;
Love drips and gathers, but the fallen blood
Shall calm her sores.
And I am dumb to tell a weather's wind
How time has ticked a heaven round the stars.

And I am dumb to tell the lover's tomb
How at my sheet goes the same crooked worm.

---

*Although he is one of the youngest poets in this anthology, Thomas returns to the oldest themes and techniques. It is reassuring that atavistic alliteration can be used to express the unity and economy of forces—principles accepted by modern physics and psychology alike; atoms do resemble solar systems.*

Brooks's verse narrative *Annie Allen* won her a Pulitzer Prize. Most of Brooks's varied work in prose and verse is set in Chicago, where she grew up.

# We Real Cool

❖❖❖❖

The Pool Players.
Seven at the Golden Shovel.

We real cool. We
Left school. We

Lurk late. We
Strike straight. We

Sing sin. We
Thin gin. We

Jazz June. We
Die soon.

---

*Brooks's Chicago, even though a couple of generations newer, is at least as tough as Sandburg's (p. 912); hers, moreover, is more percussively registered in three-word sentences spoken by recognizable people.*

# ROBERT LOWELL 1917–1977

Robert Lowell, who belonged to the same large New
England family as James Russell Lowell and Amy
Lowell, was a student of John Crowe Ransom and
Allen Tate. Lowell's earlier poetry shows the technical
finesse and the concern with large philosophical issues
that were favored by the so-called New Critics. Later,
moved by the example of William Carlos Williams,
Lowell loosened his style somewhat and concentrated
more on the details of his own life. He taught on and off
at Boston University and Harvard.

## Skunk Hour

Nautilus Island's hermit
heiress still lives through winter in her Spartan cottage;
her sheep still graze above the sea.
Her son's a bishop. Her farmer
is first selectman in our village;
she's in her dotage.

Thirsting for
the hierarchic privacy
of Queen Victoria's century,
she buys up all
the eyesores facing her shore,
and lets them fall.

The season's ill—
we've lost our summer millionaire,
who seemed to leap from an L. L. Bean
catalogue. His nine-knot yawl
was auctioned off to lobstermen.
A red fox stain covers Blue Hill.

And now our fairy
decorator brightens his shop for fall;
his fishnet's filled with orange cork,
orange, his cobbler's bench and awl;
there is no money in his work,
he'd rather marry.

One dark night,
my Tudor Ford climbed the hill's skull;
I watched for love-cars. Lights turned down,
they lay together, hull to hull,
where the graveyard shelves on the town. . . .
My mind's not right.

A car radio bleats,
"Love, O careless Love. . . ." I hear
my ill-spirit sob in each blood cell,
as if my hand were at its throat. . . .
I myself am hell;
nobody's here—

only skunks, that search
in the moonlight for a bite to eat.
They march on their soles up Main Street:
white stripes, moonstruck eyes' red fire
under the chalk-dry and spar spire
of the Trinitarian Church.

I stand on top
of our back steps and breathe the rich air—
a mother skunk with her column of kittens swills the garbage
        pail.
She jabs her wedge-head in a cup
of sour cream, drops her ostrich tail,
and will not scare.

The poem is dedicated to Elizabeth Bishop (see pp. 1043–1045), and Lowell said that he modelled "Skunk Hour" on Bishop's "Armadillo," which happens to be dedicated to Lowell.

# For the Union Dead

>>>>>>>

*"Relinquunt Omnia Servare Rem Publicam."*

The old South Boston Aquarium stands
in a Sahara of snow now. Its broken windows are boarded:
The bronze weathervane cod has lost half its scales.
The airy tanks are dry.

Once my nose crawled like a snail on the glass;
my hand tingled
to burst the bubbles
drifting from the noses of the cowed, compliant fish.

My hand draws back. I often sigh still
for the dark downward and vegetating kingdom
of the fish and reptile. On a morning last March,
I pressed against the new barbed and galvanized

fence on the Boston Common. Behind their cage,
yellow dinosaur steamshovels were grunting
as they cropped up tons of mush and grass
to gouge their underworld garage.

Parking spaces luxuriate like civic
sandpiles in the heart of Boston.
A girdle of orange, Puritan-pumpkin colored girders
braces the tingling Statehouse,

shaking over the excavations, as it faces Colonel Shaw
and his bell-cheeked Negro infantry
on St. Gaudens shaking Civil War relief,
propped by a plank splint against the garage's earthquake.

Two months after marching through Boston,
half the regiment was dead;
at the dedication,
William James could almost hear the bronze Negroes breathe.

Their monument sticks like a fishbone
in the city's throat.
Its Colonel is as lean
as a compass-needle.

He has an angry wrenlike vigilance,
a greyhound's gentle tautness;
he seems to wince at pleasure,
and suffocate for privacy.

He is out of bounds now. He rejoices in man's lovely,
peculiar power to choose life and die—
when he leads his black soldiers to death,
he cannot bend his back.

On a thousand small town New England greens,
the old white churches hold their air
of sparse, sincere rebellion; frayed flags
quilt the graveyards of the Grand Army of the Republic.

The stone statues of the abstract Union Soldier
grow slimmer and younger each year—
wasp-waisted, they doze over muskets
and muse through their sideburns . . .

Shaw's father wanted no monument
except the ditch,
where his son's body was thrown
and lost with his "niggers."

The ditch is nearer.
There are no statues for the last war here;
on Boylston Street, a commercial photograph
shows Hiroshima boiling

over a Mosler Safe, the "Rock of Ages"
that survived the blast. Space is nearer.
When I crouch to my television set,
the drained faces of Negro school-children rise like balloons.

Colonel Shaw
is riding on his bubble,
he waits
for the blesséd break.

The Aquarium is gone. Everywhere,
giant finned cars nose forward like fish;
a savage servility
slides by on grease.

---

*Since Lowell was a close friend of Allen Tate, it is certain that he meant to produce a response to "Ode to the Confederate Dead" (p. 1017). Colonel Shaw has been the subject of sculpture, music (by Charles Ives and others), and a recent movie (Glory). (Note that: "Relinquunt Omnia Servare Rem Publican" is "they give up everything to preserve the Republic"—adapted from the motto of the Society of the Cincinnati.)*

# Mr. Edwards and the Spider

I saw the spiders marching through the air,
Swimming from tree to tree that mildewed day
  In late August when the hay
  Came creaking to the barn. But where
    The wind is westerly,
Where gnarled November makes the spiders fly
Into the apparitions of the sky,
  They purpose nothing but their ease and die
Urgently beating east to sunrise and the sea;

What are we in the hands of the great God?
It was in vain you set up thorn and briar
  In battle array against the fire
  And treason crackling in your blood;
    For the wild thorns grow tame
And will do nothing to oppose the flame;
Your lacerations tell the losing game
  You play against a sickness past your cure.
How will the hands be strong? How will the heart endure?

A very little thing, a little worm,
Or hourglass-blazoned spider, it is said,
  Can kill a tiger. Will the dead
  Hold up his mirror and affirm
    To the four winds the smell
And flash of his authority? It's well
If God who holds you to the pit of hell,
  Much as one holds a spider, will destroy,
Baffle and dissipate your soul. As a small boy

On Windsor Marsh, I saw the spider die
When thrown into the bowels of fierce fire:
    There's no long struggle, no desire
    To get up on its feet and fly—
        It stretches out its feet
And dies. This is the sinner's last retreat;
Yes, and no strength exerted on the heat
    Then sinews the abolished will, when sick
And full of burning, it will whistle on a brick.

But who can plumb the sinking of that soul?
Josiah Hawley, picture yourself cast
    Into a brick-kiln where the blast
    Fans your quick vitals to a coal—
        If measured by a glass,
How long would it seem burning! Let there pass
A minute, ten, ten trillion; but the blaze
    Is infinite, eternal: this is death,
To die and know it. This is the Black Widow, death.

---

*Lowell combines two texts by the eighteenth-century American preacher Jonathan Edwards: "The Flying Spider" and "Sinners in the Hands of an Angry God," the latter a hellfire-and-brimstone sermon of a sort that can still be heard.*

# RICHARD WILBUR b.1921

Educated at Amherst and Harvard, Richard Wilbur
spent most of his long and distinguished teaching career
at Wesleyan University in Middletown, Connecticut.
He was the second holder of the annual title of Poet
Laureate of the United States. He is also a distinguished translator, mostly from the French.

# Love Calls Us
# to the Things of This World

◆◆◆◆◆

The eyes open to a cry of pulleys,
And spirited from sleep, the astounded soul
Hangs for a moment bodiless and simple
As false dawn.
        Outside the open window
The morning air is all awash with angels.

Some are in bed-sheets, some are in blouses,
Some are in smocks: but truly there they are.
Now they are rising together in calm swells
Of halcyon feeling, filling whatever they wear
With the deep joy of their impersonal breathing;

Now they are flying in place, conveying
The terrible speed of their omnipresence, moving
And staying like white water; and now of a sudden
They swoon down into so rapt a quiet
That nobody seems to be there.
        The soul shrinks

From all that it is about to remember,
From the punctual rape of every blesséd day,
And cries,
        "Oh, let there be nothing on earth but laundry,
Nothing but rosy hands in the rising steam
And clear dances done in the sight of heaven."

    Yet, as the sun acknowledges
With a warm look the world's hunks and colors,
The soul descends once more in bitter love
To accept the waking body, saying now
In a changed voice as the man yawns and rises,

    "Bring them down from their ruddy gallows;
Let there be clean linen for the backs of thieves;
Let lovers go fresh and sweet to be undone,
And the heaviest nuns walk in a pure floating
Of dark habits,
        keeping their difficult balance."

*The pulleys seem to come, in equal parts, from George Herbert (see p. 191) and from the obsolescent, current urban practice of stringing mobile clotheslines between apartment buildings.*

# PHILIP LARKIN 1922–1985

Larkin chose to preserve little of his poetry, so that his reputation rests largely on three slim volumes published at approximately ten-year intervals (1955, 1964, 1974). But what a reputation he has had! It now seems probable that between the death of Dylan Thomas in 1953 and his own death in 1985, Larkin was the best practicing poet in Britain. He was a master of two rare arts: his poetry could use language that seems totally genuine and conversational, and at the same time he could craft a stanza—fully outfitted with rhyme, rhythm, and meter—quite as polished as any turned out in the seventeenth century. Larkin also wrote novels, some scattered essays and reviews, and regular jazz columns. For most of his adult life he was employed as a university librarian.

## *Church Going*

Once I am sure there's nothing going on
I step inside, letting the door thud shut.
Another church: matting, seats, and stone,
And little books; sprawlings of flowers, cut
For Sunday, brownish now; some brass and stuff
Up at the holy end; the small neat organ;
And a tense, musty, unignorable silence,
Brewed God knows how long. Hatless, I take off
My cycle-clips in awkward reverence,

Move forward, run my hand around the font.
From where I stand, the roof looks almost new—
Cleaned, or restored? Someone would know: I don't.
Mounting the lectern, I peruse a few
Hectoring large-scale verses, and pronounce
"Here endeth" much more loudly than I'd meant.
The echoes snigger briefly. Back at the door
I sign the book, donate an Irish sixpence,
Reflect the place was not worth stopping for.

Yet stop I did: in fact I often do,
And always end much at a loss like this,
Wondering what to look for; wondering, too,
When churches fall completely out of use
What we shall turn them into, if we shall keep
A few cathedrals chronically on show,
Their parchment, plate and pyx in locked cases,
And let the rest rent-free to rain and sheep.
Shall we avoid them as unlucky places?

Or, after dark, will dubious women come
To make their children touch a particular stone;
Pick simples for a cancer; or on some
Advised night see walking a dead one?
Power of some sort or other will go on
In games, in riddles, seemingly at random;
But superstition, like belief, must die,
And what remains when disbelief has gone?
Grass, weedy pavement, brambles, buttress, sky,

A shape less recognisable each week,
A purpose more obscure. I wonder who
Will be the last, the very last, to seek
This place for what it was; one of the crew
That tap and jot and know what rood-lofts were?
Some ruin-bibber, randy for antique,
Or Christmas-addict, counting on a whiff
Of gown-and-bands and organ-pipes and myrrh?
Or will he be my representative,

Bored, uninformed, knowing the ghostly silt
Dispersed, yet tending to this cross of ground
Through suburb scrub because it held unspilt
So long and equably what since is found
Only in separation—marriage, and birth,
And death, and thoughts of these—for whom was built
This special shell? For, though I've no idea
What this accoutred frowsty barn is worth,
It pleases me to stand in silence here;

A series house on serious earth it is,
In whose blent air all our compulsions meet,
Are recognised, and robed as destinies,
And that much never can be obsolete,
Since someone will forever be surprising
A hunger in himself to be more serious,
And gravitating with it to this ground,
Which, he once heard, was proper to grow wise in,
If only that so many dead lie round.

---

*Larkin consciously continues—with some sophistication and irony—an English tradition going back to George Herbert (see pp. 186–195), Gray's "Elegy" (p. 327), Wordsworth's "Tintern Abbey" (p. 407), and Eliot's "Little Gidding" (p. 987). The poet, situated in a sacred place, reflects on the meaning of it all. Larkin adds the modern note by giving his poem an ambiguous title, wherein "Churchgoing" dissolves into "Church Going." Larkin also wrote poems called "Going" and "Going, Going." (Note that: "pyx" is a box in which Communion wafers are kept.)*

# ALLEN GINSBERG b.1926

Ginsberg, the son of the poet Louis Ginsberg, was born
in New Jersey and educated at Columbia University.
He has been one of the most famous poets in the world
since the publication of his sensational first volume,
*Howl and Other Poems*, in 1956.

# A Supermarket in California

❧❧❧❧❧

What thoughts I have of you tonight, Walt Whitman, for I
walked down the sidestreets under the trees with a headache
self-conscious looking at the full moon.

In my hungry fatigue, and shopping for images, I went into
the neon fruit supermarket, dreaming of your enumerations!

What peaches and what penumbras! Whole families
shopping at night! Aisles full of husbands! Wives in the
avocados, babies in the tomatoes! — and you, Garcia Lorca, what
were you doing down by the watermelons?

I saw you, Walt Whitman, childless, lonely old grubber,
poking among the meats in the refrigerator and eyeing the
grocery boys.

I heard you asking questions of each: Who killed the pork
chops? What price bananas? Are you my Angel?

I wandered in and out of the brilliant stacks of cans
following you, and followed in my imagination by the store
detective.

We strode down the open corridors together in our solitary
fancy tasting artichokes, possessing every frozen delicacy, and
never passing the cashier.

Where are we going, Walt Whitman? The doors close in an hour. Which way does your beard point tonight?

(I touch your book and dream of our odyssey in the supermarket and feel absurd.)

Will we walk all night through solitary streets? The trees add shade to shade, lights out in the houses, we'll both be lonely.

Will we stroll dreaming of the lost America of love past blue automobiles in driveways, home to our silent cottage?

Ah, dear father, graybeard, lonely old courage-teacher, what America did you have when Charon quit poling his ferry and you got out on a smoking bank and stood watching the boat disappear on the black waters of Lethe?

---

*In subject, style, and tone, Ginsberg's poem takes Whitman at his word, especially in his anti-bardic plea that the muse be "installed amid the kitchenware." That, literally, is what Ginsberg does, adding the spice of humor that Whitman usually lacks.*

Despite an early life seemingly full of advantage and privilege, Plath recorded little but painful suffering in her intense and eloquent poems. She married the British poet Ted Hughes (later Poet Laureate) and was living in England at the time of her suicide.

# *Daddy*

()◄━━► ()

You do not do, you do not do
Any more, black shoe
In which I have lived like a foot
For thirty years, poor and white,
Barely daring to breathe or Achoo.

Daddy, I have had to kill you.
You died before I had time—
Marble-heavy, a bag full of God,
Ghastly statue with one gray toe
Big as a Frisco seal

And a head in the freakish Atlantic
Where it pours bean green over blue
In the waters off beautiful Nauset.
I used to pray to recover you.
Ach, du.

In the German tongue, in the Polish town
Scraped flat by the roller
Of wars, wars, wars.
But the name of the town is common.
My Polack friend

Says there are a dozen or two.
So I never could tell where you
Put your foot, your root,
I never could talk to you.
The tongue stuck in my jaw.

It stuck in a barb wire snare.
Ich, ich, ich, ich,
I could hardly speak.
I thought every German was you.
And the language obscene

An engine, an engine
Chuffing me off like a Jew.
A Jew to Dachau, Auschwitz, Belsen.
I began to talk like a Jew.
I think I may well be a Jew.

The snows of the Tyrol, the clear beer of Vienna
Are not very pure or true.
With my gipsy ancestress and my weird luck
And my Taroc pack and my Taroc pack
I may be a bit of a Jew.

I have always been scared of *you,*
With your Luftwaffe, your gobbledygoo.
And your neat mustache
And your Aryan eye, bright blue.
Panzer-man, panzer-man, O You — —

Not God but a swastika
So black no sky could squeak through.
Every woman adores a Fascist,
The boot in the face, the brute
Brute heart of a brute like you.

You stand at the blackboard, daddy,
In the picture I have of you,
A cleft in your chin instead of your foot
But no less a devil for that, no not
Any less the black man who

Bit my pretty red heart in two.
I was ten when they buried you.
At twenty I tried to die
And get back, back, back to you.
I thought even the bones would do.

But they pulled me out of the sack,
And they stuck me together with glue.
And then I knew what to do.
I made a model of you,
A man in black with a Meinkampf look

And a love of the rack and the screw.
And I said I do, I do.
So daddy, I'm finally through.
The black telephone's off at the root,
The voices just can't worm through.

If I've killed one man, I've killed two— —
The vampire who said he was you
And drank my blood for a year,
Seven years, if you want to know.
Daddy, you can lie back now.

There's a stake in your fat black heart
And the villagers never liked you.
They are dancing and stamping on you.
They always *knew* it was you.
Daddy, daddy, you bastard, I'm through.

These short lines hit the reader so hard that many think the poem has to reflect the poet's feelings for her own father. All of the available evidence suggests, however, that "Daddy" really has much more to do with the feelings of any child—female or male—for any father.

# THE POEMS IN ORDER OF POPULARITY

*Here is a list of the top 500 poems in English, starting with the most popular (that is, the most often anthologized), William Blake's "The Tiger."*

1. *The Tiger.* Blake
2. *Sir Patrick Spens.* Anonymous
3. *To Autumn.* Keats
4. *That Time of Year Thou Mayst in Me Behold.* Shakespeare
5. *Pied Beauty.* Hopkins
6. *Stopping by Woods on a Snowy Evening.* Frost
7. *Kubla Khan.* Coleridge
8. *Dover Beach.* Arnold
9. *La Belle Dame sans Merci.* Keats
10. *To the Virgins, to Make Much of Time.* Herrick
11. *To His Coy Mistress.* Marvell
12. *The Passionate Shepherd to His Love.* Marlowe
13. *Death, Be Not Proud.* Donne
14. *Upon Julia's Clothes.* Herrick
15. *To Lucasta, Going to the Wars.* Lovelace
16. *The World Is Too Much with Us.* Wordsworth
17. *On First Looking into Chapman's Homer.* Keats
18. *Jabberwocky.* "Carroll"
19. *The Second Coming.* Yeats
20. *Elegy Written in a Country Churchyard.* Gray
21. *Ozymandias.* Shelley
22. *Sailing to Byzantium.* Yeats
23. *Shall I Compare Thee to a Summer's Day?* Shakespeare

24. *Let Me Not to the Marriage of True Minds.*   Shakespeare
25. *Fear No More the Heat o' the Sun.*   Shakespeare
26. *Ode to a Nightingale.*   Keats
27. *The Love Song of J. Alfred Prufrock.*   Eliot
28. *To Helen.*   Poe
29. *"Because I could not stop for Death."*   Dickinson
30. *The Windhover.*   Hopkins
31. *Anthem for Doomed Youth.*   Owen
32. *When Icicles Hang by the Wall.*   Shakespeare
33. *Batter My Heart, Three-Person'd God.*   Donne
34. *Love Bade Me Welcome.*   Herbert
35. *Ode to the West Wind.*   Shelley
36. *God's Grandeur.*   Hopkins
37. *Do Not Go Gentle into That Good Night.*   Thomas
38. *Western Wind.*   Anonymous
39. *They Flee from Me That Sometimes Did Me Seek.*   Wyatt
40. *The Good Morrow.*   Donne
41. *Delight in Disorder.*   Herrick
42. *I Wandered Lonely as a Cloud.*   Wordsworth
43. *My Last Duchess.*   R. Browning
44. *Spring and Fall.*   Hopkins
45. *Leda and the Swan.*   Yeats
46. *The River-Merchant's Wife: A Letter.*   Pound
47. *Go, Lovely Rose.*   Waller
48. *The Retreat.*   Vaughan
49. *Ode on a Grecian Urn.*   Keats
50. *London.*   Blake
51. *And Did Those Feet in Ancient Times.*   Blake
52. *Composed upon Westminster Bridge, September 3, 1802.*   Wordsworth
53. *The Splendor Falls.*   Tennyson
54. *The Darkling Thrush.*   Hardy
55. *Loveliest of Trees.*   Housman

56. *Mending Wall.* Frost
57. *Fern Hill.* Thomas
58. *Adieu, Farewell, Earth's Bliss.* Nashe
59. *Drink to Me Only with Thine Eyes.* Jonson
60. *The Collar.* Herbert
61. *Why So Pale and Wan, Fond Lover?* Suckling
62. *The Garden.* Marvell
63. *The Solitary Reaper.* Wordsworth
64. *Break, Break, Break.* Tennyson
65. *Crossing the Bar.* Tennyson
66. *Mr. Flood's Party.* Robinson
67. *Musée des Beaux Arts.* Auden
68. *The Death of the Ball Turret Gunner.* Jarrell
69. *Full Fathom Five Thy Father Lies.* Shakespeare
70. *When to the Sessions of Sweet Silent Thought.* Shakespeare
71. *Piping down the Valleys Wide.* Blake
72. *So We'll Go No More a-Roving.* Byron
73. *"I heard a Fly buzz—when I died."* Dickinson
74. *Miniver Cheevy.* Robinson
75. *To Brooklyn Bridge.* Crane
76. *Edward, Edward.* Anonymous
77. *Since There's No Help, Come Let Us Kiss and Part.* Drayton
78. *O Mistress Mine.* Shakespeare
79. *At the Round Earth's Imagined Corners.* Donne
80. *On My First Son.* Jonson
81. *Virtue.* Herbert
82. *Ask Me No More Where Jove Bestows.* Carew.
83. *Ode on the Death of a Favorite Cat, Drowned in a Tub of Gold Fishes.* Gray
84. *The Rime of the Ancient Mariner.* Coleridge
85. *Concord Hymn.* Emerson
86. *The Lake Isle of Innisfree.* Yeats
87. *Non Sum Qualis Eram Bonae sub Regno Cynarae.* Dowson

88. *My Papa's Waltz.* Roethke
89. *The Nymph's Reply to the Shepherd.* Ralegh
90. *Go and Catch a Falling Star.* Donne
91. *The Sun Rising.* Donne
92. *Lycidas.* Milton
93. *To Althea, from Prison.* Lovelace
94. *The Sick Rose.* Blake
95. *Ulysses.* Tennyson
96. *The Eagle.* Tennyson
97. *Home Thoughts from Abroad.* R. Browning
98. *"A narrow Fellow in the Grass."* Dickinson
99. *When You Are Old.* Yeats
100. *The Listeners.* De la Mare
101. *Bells for John Whiteside's Daughter.* Ransom
102. *Dulce et Decorum Est.* Owen
103. *Shunk Hour.* Lowell
104. *With How Sad Steps, O Moon, Thou Climb'st the Skies!* Sidney
105. *The Expense of Spirit in a Waste of Shame.* Shakespeare
106. *A Valediction: Forbidding Mourning.* Donne
107. *Hymn to Diana.* Jonson
108. *The Pulley.* Herbert
109. *The Lamb.* Blake
110. *Ode: Intimations of Immortality from Recollections of Early Childhood.* Wordsworth
111. *She Walks in Beauty.* Byron
112. *The Raven.* Poe
113. *Tears, Idle Tears.* Tennyson
114. *When I Am Dead.* C. Rossetti
115. *When the Hounds of Spring Are on Winter's Traces.* Swinburne
116. *Sunday Morning.* Stevens
117. *The Red Wheelbarrow.* Williams

118. *A Refusal to Mourn the Death, by Fire, of a Child in London.* Thomas

119. *The Burning Babe.* Southwell

120. *When in Disgrace with Fortune and Men's Eyes.* Shakespeare

121. *To Daffodils.* Herrick

122. *A Red, Red Rose.* Burns

123. *To a Waterfall.* Bryant

124. *Annabel Lee.* Poe

125. *Felix Randal.* Hopkins

126. *No Worst, There Is None.* Hopkins

127. *To an Athlete Dying Young.* Housman

128. *Among School Children.* Yeats

129. *Fire and Ice.* Frost

130. *I Knew a Woman.* Roethke

131. *The Waking.* Roethke

132. *The Force That through the Green Fuse Drives the Flower.* Thomas

133. *When Daisies Pied.* Shakespeare

134. *A Hymn to God the Father.* Donne

135. *The Ecstasy.* Donne

136. *The Canonization.* Donne

137. *On His Deceased Wife.* Milton

138. *The World.* Vaughan

139. *Lines Composed a Few Miles above Tintern Abbey.* Wordsworth

140. *To a Skylark.* Shelley

141. *When I Have Fears.* Keats

142. *Meeting at Night.* R. Browning

143. *Remembrance.* Brontë

144. *"There's a certain Slant of light."* Dickinson

145. *Up-Hill.* C. Rossetti

146. *London Snow.* Bridges

147. *An Irish Airman Foresees His Death.* Yeats

148. *Richard Cory.* Robinson

149. *The Road Not Taken.* Frost
150. *Anecdote of the Jar.* Stevens
151. *Piano.* Lawrence
152. *Journey of the Magi.* Eliot
153. *You, Andrew Marvell.* MacLeish
154. *Strange Meeting.* Owen
155. *Thomas the Rhymer.* Anonymous
156. *The Wife of Usher's Well.* Anonymous
157. *The Flea.* Donne
158. *Still to Be Neat.* Jonson
159. *The Triumph of Charis.* Jonson
160. *The Argument of His Book.* Herrick
161. *The Definition of Love.* Marvell
162. *Ah! Sun-Flower.* Blake
163. *Lucy.* Wordsworth
164. *Rose Aylmer.* Landor
165. *The Destruction of Sennacherib.* Byron
166. *How Do I Love Thee? Let Me Count the Ways.* E. Browning
167. *Now Sleeps the Crimson Petal.* Tennyson
168. *The Battle Hymn of the Republic.* Howe
169. *A Noiseless Patient Spider.* Whitman
170. *A Bird came down the Walk.* Dickinson
171. *Recessional.* Kipling
172. *Easter, 1916.* Yeats
173. *The Emperor of Ice-Cream.* Stevens
174. *Poetry.* M. Moore
175. *Ars Poetica.* MacLeish
176. *In Memory of W. B. Yeats.* Auden
177. *The Fish.* Bishop
178. *Daddy.* Plath
179. *The Lie.* Ralegh
180. *It Was a Lover and His Lass.* Shakespeare
181. *Redemption.* Herbert

182. *On His Blindness.* Milton
183. *To My Dear and Loving Husband.* Bradstreet
184. *Bermudas.* Marvell
185. *They Are All Gone into the World of Light.* Vaughan
186. *Ode to Evening.* Collins
187. *It Is a Beauteous Evening.* Wordsworth
188. *London, 1802.* Wordsworth
189. *Ode on Melancholy.* Keats
190. *The Oxen.* Hardy
191. *Thou Art Indeed Just, Lord.* Hopkins
192. *Danny Deever.* Kipling
193. *Snake.* Lawrence
194. *Bavarian Gentians.* Lawrence.
195. *The Waste Land.* Eliot
196. *For the Union Dead.* Lowell
197. *My Mistress' Eyes Are Nothing like the Sun.* Shakespeare
198. *Poor Soul, the Center of My Sinful Earth.* Shakespeare
199. *My Sweetest Lesbia.* Campion
200. *Corinna's Going a-Maying.* Herrick
201. *On the Late Massacre in Piedmont.* Milton
202. *Peace.* Vaughan
203. *To a Mouse on Turning Her Up in Her Nest with the Plough, November, 1785.* Burns
204. *A Visit from St. Nicholas.* C. Moore
205. *The Snow-Storm.* Emerson
206. *The Owl and the Pussy-Cat.* Lear
207. *Not to Say the Struggle Nought Availeth.* Clough
208. *O Captain! My Captain!* Whitman
209. *Lucifer in Starlight.* Meredeth
210. *"The Soul selects her own Society."* Dickinson
211. *In Time of "The Breaking of Nations."* Hardy
212. *Channel Firing.* Hardy
213. *The Idea of Order at Key West.* Stevens

214. *The Dance.*   Williams
215. *The Negro Speaks of Rivers.*   Hughes
216. *The Fury of Aerial Bombardment.*   Eberhart
217. *As You Came from the Holy Land of Walsingham.*   Anonymous
218. *Cuckoo Song.*   Anonymous
219. *To Mistress Margaret Hussey.*   Skelton
220. *Tichborne's Elegy.*   Tichborne
221. *Call for the Robin Redbreast and the Wren.*   Webster
222. *Easter Wings.*   Herbert
223. *L'Allegro.*   Milton
224. *Light Shining out of Darkness.*   Cowper
225. *Proud Maisie.*   Scott
226. *Thanatopsis.*   Bryant
227. *My Lost Youth.*   Longfellow
228. *The Latest Decalogue.*   Clough
229. *"I like to see it lap the Miles."*   Dickinson
230. *The Walrus and the Carpenter.*   "Carroll"
231. *Father William.*   "Carroll"
232. *The Hymn to Proserpine.*   Swinburne
233. *Afterwards.*   Hardy
234. *With Rue My Heart Is Laden.*   Housman
235. *The Wild Swans at Coole.*   Yeats
236. *Birches.*   Frost
237. *Chicago.*   Sandburg
238. *The Soldier.*   Brooke
239. *Sweeney among the Nightingales.*   Eliot
240. *anyone lived in a pretty how town.*   Cummings
241. *Corpus Christi Carol.*   Anonymous
242. *The Three Ravens.*   Anonymous
243. *Even Such Is Time.*   Ralegh
244. *Hark! Hark! the Lark.*   Shakespeare
245. *Hymn to God My God, in My Sickness.*   Donne
246. *Sweetest Love, I Do Not Go.*   Donne

247. *Epitath on S. P.*   Jonson
248. *Exequy on His Wife.*   King
249. *Hear the Voice of the Bard.*   Blake
250. *My Heart Leaps Up.*   Wordsworth
251. *Dirce.*   Landor
252. *I Am.*   Clare
253. *The Eve of St. Agnes.*   Keats
254. *Bright Star.*   Keats
255. *The Rhodora.*   Emerson
256. *The Year's at the Spring.*   R. Browning
257. *When Lilacs Last in the Dooryard Bloomed.*   Whitman
258. *I'll Tell Thee Everything I Can.*   "Carroll"
259. *The Convergence of the Twain.*   Hardy
260. *Spring.*   Hopkins
261. *Requiem.*   Stevenson
262. *After Apple-Picking.*   Frost
263. *Acquainted with the Night.*   Frost
264. *The Owl.*   Thomas
265. *In a Station of the Metro.*   Pound
266. *Those Winter Sundays.*   Hayden
267. *A Supermarket in California.*   Ginsberg
268. *Tom o' Bedlam's Song.*   Anonymous
269. *Adam Lay I-bounden.*   Anonymous
270. *Lord Randal.*   Anonymous
271. *The Lover Complaineth the Unkindness of His Love.*   Wyatt
272. *One Day I Wrote Her Name upon the Strand.*   Spenser
273. *O Love, Which Reachest But to Dust.*   Sidney
274. *Take, O Take Those Lips Away.*   Shakespeare
275. *On His Mistress, the Queen of Bohemia.*   Wotton
276. *The Night-Piece to Julia.*   Herrick
277. *Il Penseroso.*   Milton
278. *An Horatian Ode upon Cromwell's Return from Ireland.*   Marvell
279. *John Anderson, My Jo.*   Burns

280. *I Strove with None, for None Was Worth My Strife.*   Landor
281. *Music, When Soft Voices Die.*   Shelley
282. *Barbara Frietchie.*   Whittier
283. *The Deacon's Masterpiece; or, The Wonderful "One-Hoss Shay."*   Holmes
284. *The Charge of the Light Brigade.*   Tennyson
285. *"My life closed twice before its close."*   Dickinson
286. *Heaven-Haven.*   Hopkins
287. *The Circus Animals' Desertion.*   Yeats
288. *Eros Turranos.*   Robinson
289. *Leisure.*   Davies
290. *Hurt Hawks.*   Jeffers
291. *Ode to the Confederate Dead.*   Tate
292. *The Cherry-Tree Carol.*   Anonymous
293. *The Lord Is My Shepherd.*   Anonymous
294. *The Passionate Man's Pilgrimage.*   Ralegh
295. *My True Love Hath My Heart.*   Sidney
296. *Farewell! Thou Art Too Dear for My Possessing.*   Shakespeare
297. *Where the Bee Sucks, There Suck I.*   Shakespeare
298. *Rose-cheeked Laura.*   Campion
299. *A Nocturnal upon St. Lucy's Day, Being the Shortest Day.*   Donne
300. *Grace for a Child.*   Herrick
301. *Jordan.*   Herbert
302. *On a Girdle.*   Waller
303. *To the Memory Mr. Oldham.*   Dryden
304. *How Sleep the Brave.*   Collins
305. *When Lovely Woman Stoops to Folly.*   Goldsmith
306. *Auguries of Innocence.*   Blake
307. *The Banks o' Doon.*   Burns
308. *Past Ruined Ilion Helen Lives.*   Landor
309. *Jenny Kissed Me.*   Hunt
310. *Abou Ben Adhem.*   Hunt

311. *The Burial of Sir John Moore after Corunna.*  Wolfe
312. *To Night.*  Shelley
313. *Paul Revere's Ride.*  Longfellow
314. *The Jumblies.*  Lear
315. *I Hear America Singing.*  Whitman
316. *The Scholar-Gipsy.*  Arnold
317. *The Fairies.*  Allingham
318. *"Success is counted sweetest."*  Dickinson
319. *"I taste a liquor never brewed."*  Dickinson
320. *A Birthday.*  C. Rossetti
321. *Inversnaid.*  Hopkins
322. *When I Was One-and-Twenty.*  Wilde
323. *A Prayer for My Daughter.*  Yeats
324. *Lapis Lazuli.*  Yeats
325. *Vitae Summa Brevis Spem Nos Vetat Incohare Longam.*  Dowson
326. *Provide, Provide.*  Frost
327. *The Gift Outright.*  Frost
328. *Directive.*  Frost
329. *Abraham Lincoln Walks at Midnight.*  Lindsay
330. *Peter Quince at the Clavier.*  Stevens
331. *Gerontion.*  Eliot
332. *Piazza Piece.*  Ransom
333. *Break of Day in the Trenches.*  Rosenberg
334. *Not Waving But Drowning.*  Smith
335. *We Real Cool.*  Brooks
336. *Love Calls Us to the Things of This World.*  Wilbur
337. *Church Going.*  Larkin
338. *I Sing of a Maiden.*  Anonymous
339. *Loving in Truth, and Fain in Verse My Love to Show.*  Sidney
340. *When That I Was and a Little Tiny Boy.*  Shakespeare
341. *Full Many a Glorious Morning Have I Seen.*  Shakespeare
342. *No Longer Mourn for Me When I Am Dead.*  Shakespeare

343. *Tired with All These, for Restful Death I Cry.* Shakespeare
344. *Like as the Waves Make toward the Pebbled Shore.* Shakespeare
345. *There Is a Garden in Her Face.* Campion
346. *The Funeral.* Donne
347. *The Apparition.* Donne
348. *The Relic.* Donne
349. *On the Countess Dowager of Pembroke.* Browne
350. *Prayer the Church's Banquet.* Herbert
351. *Mac Flecknoe.* Dryden
352. *A Song for St. Cecilia's Day, 1687.* Dryden
353. *How Sweet I Roam'd from Field to Field.* Blake
354. *The Little Black Boy.* Blake
355. *A Poison Tree.* Blake
356. *The Chimney Sweeper.* Blake
357. *To the Evening Star.* Blake
358. *Surprised by Joy.* Wordsworth
359. *She Was a Phantom of Delight.* Wordsworth
360. *Resolution and Independence.* Wordsworth
361. *Hohenlinden.* Campbell
362. *England in 1819.* Shelley
363. *To — — —.* Shelley
364. *Old Adam, the Carrion Crow.* Beddoes
365. *Brahma.* Emerson
366. *The Chambered Nautilus.* Holmes
367. *Mariana.* Tennyson
368. *The Blessed Damozel.* D. Rossetti
369. *"After great pain, a formal feeling comes."* Dickinson
370. *How Doth the Little Crocodile.* "Carroll"
371. *The Man He Killed.* Hardy
372. *Neutral Tones.* Hardy
373. *The Ruined Maid.* Hardy
374. *Wynken, Blynken, and Nod.* Field

375. *The Purple Cow.* Burgess
376. *For a Dead Lady.* Robinson
377. *Design.* Frost
378. *Cargoes.* Masefield
379. *Fog.* Sandburg
380. *Cool Tombs.* Sandburg
381. *Grass.* Sandburg
382. *Thirteen Ways of Looking at a Blackbird.* Stevens
383. *Spring and All.* Williams
384. *The End of the World.* MacLeish
385. *Little Gidding.* Eliot
386. *Shine, Perishing Republic.* Jeffers
387. *Lullaby.* Auden
388. *Bagpipe Music.* MacNeice
389. *Elegy for Jane.* Roethke
390. *I Think Continually of Those Who Were Truly Great.* Spender
391. *Naming of Parts.* Reed
392. *A Lyke-Wake Dirge.* Anonymous
393. *My Love in Her Attire.* Anonymous
394. *The Demon Lover.* Anonymous
395. *Care-Charmer Sleep, Son of the Sable Night.* Daniel
396. *When Daffodils Begin to Peer.* Shakespeare
397. *How Like a Winter Hath My Absence Been.* Shakespeare
398. *Since Brass, nor Stone, nor Earth, nor Boundless Sea.* Shakespeare
399. *Spring, the Sweet Spring.* Nashe
400. *Good Friday, 1613. Riding Westward.* Donne
401. *Slow, Slow, Fresh Fount, Keep Time with My Salt Tears.* Jonson
402. *The Lark Now Leaves His Watery Nest.* Davenant
403. *The Picture of Little T. C. in a Prospect of Flowers.* Marvell
404. *The Mower to the Glow-Worms.* Marvell
405. *A Dialogue between the Soul and Body.* Marvell

406. *The Night.* Vaughan

407. *An Elegy on the Death of a Mad Dog.* Goldsmith

408. *The Garden of Love.* Blake

409. *The Clod and the Pebble.* Blake

410. *For A' That and A' That.* Burns

411. *Breathes There the Man with Soul so Dead.* Scott

412. *Lochinvar.* Scott

413. *Dejection: An Ode.* Coleridge

414. *Frost at Midnight.* Coleridge

415. *When We Two Parted.* Byron

416. *The Ocean.* Byron

417. *Fable.* Emerson

418. *Days.* Emerson

419. *Old Ironsides.* Holmes

420. *The City in the Sea.* Poe

421. *The Lady of Shalott.* Tennyson

422. *The Bishop Orders His Tomb at St. Praxed's Church.*
R. Browning

423. *Parting at Morning.* R. Browning

424. *Two in the Campagna.* R. Browning

425. *Cavalry Crossing a Ford.* Whitman

426. *Thus Piteously Love Closed What He Begat.* Meredith

427. *"I felt a Funeral, in my Brain."* Dickinson

428. *The Voice.* Hardy

429. *Terence, This Is Stupid Stuff.* Housman

430. *Anne Rutledge.* Masters

431. *The Yachts.* Williams

432. *A Grave.* M. Moore

433. *Still Falls the Rain.* Sitwell

434. *If We Must Die.* McKay

435. *Greater Love.* Owen

436. *"next to of course god america i."* Cummings

437. *The Groundhog.* Eberhart

438. *In a Dark Time.*  Roethke

439. *Mr. Edwards and the Spider.*  Lowell

440. *General Prologue to* The Canterbury Tales.  Chaucer

441. *Weep You No More, Sad Fountains.*  Anonymous

442. *The Unquiet Grave.*  Anonymous

443. *Waly, Waly.*  Anonymous

444. *Whoso List to Hunt.*  Wyatt

445. *Prothalamion.*  Spenser

446. *Come Sleep! O Sleep, the Certain Knot of Peace.*  Sidney

447. *His Golden Locks Time Hath to Silver Turned.*  Peele

448. *Whenas the Rye Reach the Chin.*  Peele

449. *Come Away, Come Away, Death.*  Shakespeare

450. *Come unto These Yellow Sands.*  Shakespeare

451. *Tell Me Where Is Fancy Bred.*  Shakespeare

452. *Thrice Toss These Oaken Ashes in the Air.*  Campion

453. *The Anniversary.*  Donne

454. *Come, My Celia, Let Us Prove.*  Jonson

455. *To Penshurst.*  Jonson

456. *To My Inconstant Mistress.*  Carew

457. *The Grasshopper.*  Lovelace

458. *Alexander's Feast; or, The Power of Music.*  Dryden

459. *Huswifery.*  Taylor

460. *A Description of the Morning.*  Swift

461. *Know Then Thyself.*  Pope

462. *Epistle to Dr. Arbuthnot.*  Pope

463. *An Essay on Criticism.*  Pope

464. *A Short Song of Congratulation.*  Johnson

465. *On the Death of Mr. Robert Levet, a Practiser in Physic.*  Johnson

466. *The Vanity of Human Wishes: The Tenth Satire of Juvenal Imitated.*  Johnson

467. *The Deserted Village.*  Goldsmith

468. *The Poplar Field.*  Cowper

469. *The Indian Burying Ground.*   Freneau
470. *Holy Thursday.*   Blake
471. *Mock On, Mock On, Voltaire, Rousseau.*   Blake
472. *Holy Willie's Prayer.*   Burns
473. *The Battle of Blenheim.*   Southey
474. *There Was a Sound of Revelry by Night.*   Byron
475. *Adonais.*   Shelley
476. *Ode to Psyche.*   Keats
477. *I Remember, I Remember.*   Hood
478. *Chaucer.*   Longfellow
479. *Snow-Bound; A Winter Idyl.*   Whittier
480. *The Bells.*   Poe
481. *The Haunted Palace.*   Poe
482. *Flower in the Crannied Wall.*   Tennyson
483. *The Woodspurge.*   D. Rossetti
484. *"I never saw a Moor."*   Dickinson
485. *"Much Madness is divinest Sense."*   Dickinson
486. *Remember.*   C. Rossetti
487. *The Yarn of the* Nancy Bell.   Gilbert
488. *During Wind and Rain.*   Hardy
489. *Nightingales.*   Bridges
490. *The Habit of Perfection.*   Hopkins
491. *Carrion Comfort.*   Hopkins
492. *The Duel.*   Field
493. *The Man with the Hoe.*   Markham
494. *The Ballad of Reading Gaol.*   Wilde
495. *Into My Heart an Air That Kills.*   Housman
496. *On Wenlock Edge.*   Housman
497. *The Hound of Heaven.*   Thompson
498. *The Song of Wandering Aengus.*   Yeats
499. *No Second Troy.*   Yeats
500. *Luke Havergal.*   Robinson

# ACKNOWLEDGMENTS

W. H. Auden: "In Memory of W. B. Yeats," "Lullaby," "Musée des Beaux Arts" from *W. H. Auden: Collected Poems*, edited by E. Mendelson. Copyright 1940 and renewed 1968 by W. H. Auden. Reprinted by permission of Random House, Inc. Also from *Collected Shorter Poems* by W. H. Auden. Reprinted by permission of Faber and Faber Ltd.

Elizabeth Bishop: "The Fish" from *The Complete Poems 1927–1979*, by Elizabeth Bishop. Copyright © 1979, 1983 by Alice Helen Methfessel. Reprinted by permission of Farrar, Straus & Giroux, Inc.

Gwendolyn Brooks: "We Real Cool" from *Blacks*, issued by Third World Press, Chicago. Copyright 1987 and 1991 by Gwendolyn Brooks. Reprinted by permission of the author.

Hart Crane: "To Brooklyn Bridge" from *The Complete Poems and Selected Letters and Prose of Hart Crane*, edited by Brom Weber. Copyright 1933, © 1958, 1966 by Liveright Publishing Corporation. Reprinted by permission of Liveright Publishing Corporation.

E. E. Cummings: "anyone lived in a pretty how town," "next to of course god america i," from *Complete Poems, 1913–1962*, by E. E. Cummings. Copyright © 1923, 1925, 1931, 1935, 1938, 1939, 1940, 1944, 1945, 1946, 1947, 1948, 1949, 1950, 1951, 1952, 1953, 1954, 1955, 1956, 1957, 1958, 1959, 1960, 1961, 1962 by the Trustees for the E. E. Cummings Trust. Copyright © 1961, 1963, 1968 by Marion Morehouse Cummings and © MacGibbon & Kee, an imprint of HarperCollins Publishers Ltd. Reprinted by permission of Liveright Publishing Corporation and HarperCollins Publishers Ltd.

W. H. Davies: "Leisure" from *The Complete Poems of W. H. Davies*. Copyright 1963 by Jonathan Cape Ltd. Reprinted by permission of Wesleyan University Press.

Walter de la Mare: "The Listeners." Reprinted by permission of The Literary Trustees of Walter de la Mare and The Society of Authors as their representative.

Emily Dickinson: "After great pain a formal feeling comes," from *The Complete Poems of Emily Dickinson*, edited by Thomas H. Johnson. Copyright 1929 by Martha Dickinson Bianche, renewed 1957 by Mary L. Hampson. Reprinted by permission of Little, Brown and Company. All other poems from *The Poems of Emily Dickinson*, edited by Thomas H. Johnson (Cambridge, Mass: The Belknap Press of Harvard University Press). Copyright 1951, © 1955, 1979, 1983 by the President and Fellows of Harvard College. Reprinted by permission of the publishers and the Trustees of Amherst College.

Richard Eberhart: "The Fury of Aerial Bombardment" and "The Groundhog" from *Collected Poems 1930–1986*, by Richard Eberhart. Copyright © 1960, 1976, 1988 by Richard Eberhart. Reprinted by permission of Oxford University Press, Inc.

T. S. Eliot: "The Love Song of J. Alfred Prufrock," "Journey of the Magi," "The Waste Land," "Sweeney among the Nightingales," "Gerontion" from *Collected Poems 1909–1962*, by T. S. Eliot. Copyright 1936 by Harcourt Brace Jovanovich, Inc., and © 1964, 1963 by T. S. Eliot. Reprinted by permission of the publisher and Faber and Faber Ltd. "Little Gidding" from *Collected Poems 1909–1962*, by T. S. Eliot, reprinted by permission of Faber and Faber Ltd., and from *Four Quartets*, copyright 1943 by T. S. Eliot, renewed 1971 by Esme Valerie Eliot, reprinted by permission of Harcourt Brace Jovanovich, Inc.

Robert Frost: All poems from *The Poetry of Robert Frost*, edited by Edward Connery Lathem. Copyright 1923, 1928, 1947, © 1969 by Holt, Rinehart and Winston. Copyright 1936, 1942, 1951, © 1956 by Robert Frost. Copyright © 1964, 1970, 1975 by Lesley Frost Ballantine. Reprinted by permission of Henry Holt and Company, Inc., and Jonathan Cape Ltd.

Allen Ginsberg: "A Supermarket in California" from *Collected Poems 1947–1980*, by Allen Ginsberg. Copyright © 1955 by Allen Ginsberg and © for Viking, 1985 edition by Allen Ginsberg, 1985. Reprinted by permission of HarperCollins Publishers Ltd. and Penguin Books Ltd.

Thomas Hardy: All poems from *The Complete Poems of Thomas Hardy*, edited by James Gibson (New York: Macmillan, 1978).
Robert Hayden: "Those Winter Sundays" from *Angle of Ascent, New and Selected Poems*, by Robert Hayden. Copyright © 1966, 1970, 1972, 1975 by Robert Hayden. Reprinted by permission of Liveright Publishing Corporation.
A. E. Housman: All poems from "A Shropshire Lad"—Authorized Edition—from *The Collected Poems of A. E. Housman*. Copyright 1939, 1940, © 1965 by Holt, Rinehart and Winston and © 1967, 1968 by Robert E. Symons. Reprinted by permission of Henry Holt and Company, Inc.
Langston Hughes: "The Negro Speaks of Rivers" from *Selected Poems*, by Langston Hughes. Copyright © 1959 by Langston Hughes. Reprinted by permission of Alfred A. Knopf, Inc., and Harold Ober Associates, Inc.
Randall Jarrell: "Death of the Ball Turret Gunner" from *The Complete Poems*, by Randall Jarrell. Copyright © 1945, renewed 1972 by Mrs. Randall Jarrell. Reprinted by permission of Farrar, Straus & Giroux, Inc., and by Faber and Faber Ltd.
Robinson Jeffers: "Hurt Hawks" and "Shine, Perishing Republic" from *The Selected Poetry of Robinson Jeffers*, by Robinson Jeffers. Copyright 1925, 1928, renewed 1953, 1956 by Robinson Jeffers. Reprinted by permission of Random House, Inc.
Philip Larkin: "Church Going" from *The Less Deceived*. Reprinted by permission of The Marvell Press, England.
D. H. Lawrence: All poems from *The Complete Poems of D. H. Lawrence*, by D. H. Lawrence. Copyright © 1964, 1971 by Angelo Ragli and C. M. Weekley, Executors of the Estate of Frieda Lawrence Ravagli. Reprinted with the acknowledgment of Laurence Pollinger Ltd. and by permission of Viking Penguin, a division of Penguin Books USA, Inc.
Vachel Lindsay: "Abraham Lincoln Walks at Midnight" from *Collected Poems of Vachel Lindsay* (New York: Macmillan, 1925).
Robert Lowell: "For the Union Dead" from *For the Union Dead*, by Robert Lowell. Copyright © 1964 by Robert Lowell. "Skunk Hour" from *Life Studies*, by Robert Lowell. Copyright © 1956, 1959 by Robert Lowell, renewed 1987 by Harriet W. Lowell. Reprinted by permission of Farrar, Straus & Giroux, Inc. "Mr. Edwards and the Spider" from *Lord Weary's Castle*. Copyright 1946, renewed 1974 by Robert Lowell. Reprinted by permission of Harcourt Brace Jovanovich, Inc.

Edwin Arlington Robinson: "Miniver Cheevy" and "For a Dead Lady" from *The Town Down the River*, by Edwin Arlington Robinson. "Richard Cory" and "Luke Havergal" from *The Children of the Night*, by Edwin Arlington Robinson (Charles Scribner's Sons, publisher).

Theodore Roethke: All poems from *The Collected Poems of Theodore Roethke*, by Theodore Roethke. "I Knew a Woman" copyright 1954 by Theodore Roethke. "Waking" copyright 1948 by Theodore Roethke. "Elegy for Jane" copyright 1950 by Theodore Roethke. "My Papa's Waltz" copyright 1942 by Hearst Magazines, Inc. "In a Dark Time" copyright © 1960 by Beatrice Roethke, Administratrix of The Estate of Theodore Roethke. Reprinted by permission of Bantam Doubleday Dell Publishing Group, Inc., and Faber and Faber Ltd.

Isaac Rosenberg: "Break of Day in the Trenches" from *Collected Poems*, by Isaac Rosenberg. Chatto & Windus, Ltd., publisher.

Carl Sandburg: "Cool Tombs" and "Grass" from *Cornhuskers*, by Carl Sandburg. Copyright 1918 by Holt, Rinehart and Winston, Inc., renewed 1946 by Carl Sandburg. "Chicago" and "Fog" from *Chicago Poems*, by Carl Sandburg. Copyright 1916 by Holt, Rinehart and Winston, Inc., renewed 1944 by Carl Sandburg. All poems reprinted by permission of Harcourt Brace Jovanovich, Inc.

Edith Sitwell: "Still Falls the Rain" from *The Collected Poems of Edith Sitwell*. Reprinted by permission of David Higham Associates.

Stevie Smith: "Not Waving But Drowning" from *The Collected Poems of Stevie Smith*. Copyright © 1972 by Stevie Smith. Reprinted by permission of New Directions Publishing Corporation and James MacGibbon as Executor of The Estate of Stevie Smith.

Stephen Spender: "I Think Continually of Those Who Were Truly Great" from *Collected Poems 1928–1953*, by Stephen Spender. Copyright 1934, renewed 1962 by Stephen Spender. Reprinted by permission of Random House, Inc. Also from *Collected Poems 1928–1985*, by Stephen Spender, reprinted by permission of Faber and Faber Ltd.

Wallace Stevens: All poems from *Collected Poems*, by Wallace Stevens. Copyright 1923, renewed 1951 by Wallace Stevens. Reprinted by permission of Alfred A. Knopf, Inc., and Faber and Faber Ltd.

Allen Tate: "Ode to the Confederate Dead" from *Collected Poems 1919–1976*, by Allen Tate. Copyright © by Allen Tate. Reprinted by permission of Farrar, Straus & Giroux, Inc., and Faber and Faber, Ltd.

Dylan Thomas: All poems printed from *Poems of Dylan Thomas*. Copyright 1945 by the Trustees for the Copyrights of Dylan Thomas, and 1952 by Dylan Thomas. Reprinted by permission of New Directions Publishing Corporation and David Higham Associates.

Richard Wilbur: "Love Calls Us to the Things of This World" from *Things of This World*. Copyright © 1956, renewed 1984 by Richard Wilbur. Reprinted by permission of Harcourt Brace Jovanovich, Inc.

William Carlos Williams: All poems printed from *The Collected Poems of William Carlos Williams, 1919–1939, vol. 1*. Copyright 1938 by New Directions Publishing Corporation. Reprinted by permission of New Directions Publishing Corporation and Carcanet Press Ltd.

William Butler Yeats: All poems reprinted from *The Poems of W. B. Yeats: A New Edition*, edited by Richard J. Finneran. "The Circus Animals' Desertion" and "Lapis Lazuli" copyright 1940 by Georgie Yeats, renewed 1968 by Bertha Georgie Yeats. "Sailing to Byzantium," "Leda and the Swan," "Among School Children" copyright 1928 by Macmillan Publishing Company, renewed 1956 by Georgie Yeats. "The Second Coming," "Easter 1916," "A Prayer for My Daughter" copyright 1924 by Macmillan Publishing Company, renewed 1952 by Bertha Georgie Yeats. "The Wild Swans at Coole," "An Irish Airman Foresees His Death" copyright 1919 by Macmillan Publishing Company, renewed 1947 by Bertha Georgie Yeats. All poems reprinted by permission of Macmillan Publishing Company.

# INDEX OF POETS

# INDEX OF TITLES AND FIRST LINES

*Titles of poems are in italics, first lines in roman type. If title and first line are identical, or virtually so, only the title is given.*